inis Literary
and Criticism

A Norton Reader

Feminist Literary Theory and Criticism

A Norton Reader

Sandra M. Gilbert
UNIVERSITY OF CALIFORNIA, DAVIS

Susan Gubar
INDIANA UNIVERSITY

W • W • NORTON & COMPANY • *New York* • *London*

W. W. Norton & Company has been independent since its founding in 1923, when William Warder Norton and Mary D. Herter Norton first published lectures delivered at the People's Institute, the adult education division of New York City's Cooper Union. The Nortons soon expanded their program beyond the Institute, publishing books by celebrated academics from America and abroad. By mid-century, the two major pillars of Norton's publishing program—trade books and college texts—were firmly established. In the 1950s, the Norton family transferred control of the company to its employees, and today—with a staff of four hundred and a comparable number of trade, college, and professional titles published each year—W. W. Norton & Company stands as the largest and oldest publishing house owned wholly by its employees.

Composition by Binghamton Valley Composition.
Manufacturing by R. R. Donnelley—Crawfordsville.
Book design by Antonina Krass.
Production manager: Benjamin Reynolds.

Library of Congress Cataloging-in-Publication Data

Feminist literary theory and criticism : a Norton reader / [introduction by] Sandra M. Gilbert, Susan Gubar. — 1st ed.
    p. cm.
A collection of women's meditations on literary creativity, beginning with medieval and early modern women of letters and concluding with contemporary scholars, with emphasis on writings by English-language poets and novelists, whose thinking is represented in a range of genres, including letters, tracts, prefaces, introductions, essays, and lectures, etc.
    Includes bibliographical references and index.

ISBN 978-0-393-92790-0 (pbk.)

1. English literature—Women authors. 2. American literature—Women authors. 3. Literature—Women authors. 4. Feminist literary criticism—Literary collections. 5. Feminist—Literary collections. 6. Feminist literary criticism—History. 7. Feminism and literature—History. 8. Women and literature—History. I. Gilbert, Sandra M. II. Gubar, Susan, 1944–
    PR1110.W6F46 2007
    820.8'09287—dc22

                                        2007020372

W. W. Norton & Company, Inc., 500 Fifth Avenue, New York, N.Y. 10110
www.wwnorton.com

W. W. Norton & Company Ltd., Castle House, 75/76 Wells Street, London W1T 3QT

1 2 3 4 5 6 7 8 9 0

Contents

Part 2. Theory: On Gender and Culture   291

Part 3. Practice:
Representative Readings and Analyses   835

Preface

This collection is the first to bring together the long history of women's sometimes lyrical, sometimes comic, sometimes radical meditations on literary creativity. Beginning with medieval and early modern women of letters considering their experiences as both readers and authors, concluding with contemporary scholars analyzing the interactions between gender and a host of sociocultural factors, *Feminist Literary Theory and Criticism: A Norton Reader* traces a centuries-long conversation among women writers and scholars that is of vital interest both inside and outside college classrooms.

The past quarter century has seen extraordinary changes in the American academy, and few have been as striking as the rise of multidisciplinary gender research. Propelled by the "second wave" of feminism and now the "third," programs in women's studies and gender studies thrive on many campuses worldwide. Similarly, in response to strong student demand, equally strong faculty interest, and widespread public curiosity, English and comparative literature departments, along with a range of area studies programs, have expanded their curricula to offer undergraduate and graduate courses on women writers, on representations of women in literature, and on feminist theory.

As these courses have proliferated in recent decades, so have anthologies of feminist scholarship. Yet no anthology focuses exclusively on the complex and varied ways in which women have theorized literature and literary culture from their first ventures into criticism up to the present day. In fact, the collections of readings now available tend to be limited chronologically to a few decades of criticism, or geographically to the literary production in a single country, or else to be focused on themes and topics—sexuality, visual cultures, epistemologies, interdisciplinarity, global politics, or technologies—rather than on the history of women's literary thought. While such specialized collections are undoubtedly useful, they do not offer the scope that distinguishes *Feminist Literary Theory and Criticism: A Norton Reader,* which was designed as a flexible sourcebook for the many people studying or teaching women's literature and the historical evolution of what we now define as feminist criticism.

Rooted as it is in literary history, this collection reflects a twin commitment: it documents creative women's responses to their situations as writers and readers through six centuries, and it explores contemporary scholarly debates about both aesthetic and societal issues concerning literary productivity. While the introductions to Part 1 (written by Sandra M. Gilbert) and Part 2 (written by Susan Gubar) make clear our view that there is no hard-and-fast division between creative and critical formulations of feminism—many creative women produced critical essays, and many feminist intellectuals have crafted creative works—as an aid for students we have produced an organizational scheme with, as it were, permeable borders. More, to encourage border crossings, we have provided alternate tables of contents with readings grouped by historical period, genre, and topic.

Thus we begin our table of contents with chronologically organized documents about female literary creativity. Then we turn to contemporary theoretical writings on literary topics: changing images and myths of femininity, the psychosexual dynamics of female creativity, the relationships between gender and genre, the role of women artists as critics, and the periodization of male and female literary traditions. Finally, we represent recent feminist works shaped by such multidisciplinary perspectives as those of postcolonial studies, race and ethnicity studies, and queer theory.

Starting with Christine de Pizan's fifteenth-century meditation on the "many wicked insults" to women promulgated by men of letters, Part 1, "Women Writers: On Writing," explores women's responses to the challenges presented by aspirations to female authorship in cultures that denied or derided female authority. Our selections include often neglected or marginalized literary criticism by such early modern authors as Jane Anger and Margaret Cavendish as well as texts by contemporary artists—for instance, Lyn Hejinian and June Jordan—who are not usually taught in the context of feminist theory. But of course Part 1 also includes widely read documents by such major figures as Mary Wollstonecraft, Charlotte Brontë, Emily Dickinson, Zora Neale Hurston, Tillie Olsen, and Adrienne Rich. While works by a few influential thinkers—for example, our extract from Christine de Pizan's *City of Ladies*—appear in translation, our emphasis has been on writings by English-language poets and novelists, whose thinking we represent in a range of genres, including letters, tracts, prefaces, introductions, essays, and lectures. And we have necessarily paid special attention to the flowering of feminist thinking in the modernist period, with important meditations not only by that key precursor Virginia Woolf, but also by H. D., Dorothy Richardson, Rebecca West, Sylvia Townsend Warner, and others. Similarly, we have offered a rich selection of writings by such crucial contemporaries as Audre Lorde, Joanna Russ, Margaret Atwood, Alice Walker, and Gloria Anzaldúa. Taken together, these selections illuminate the problems posed by misogyny, inadequate education, and a male-dominated literary marketplace, together with the strategies that early and later women writers developed to overcome such obstacles.

Part 2 of the *Reader*, "Theory: On Gender and Culture," turns to post–World War II intellectuals, many within the academy, whose thinking shaped and was shaped by feminist insights into the lives of literary women as well as by literary representations of those lives. Analyses of mythology—broached by Simone de Beauvoir, Mary Ellmann, and Kate Millett—enabled subsequent feminist theorists to examine such prototypical figures of the "feminine" as the Sphinx, Eve, Mary, and other key images through the lens of what Elaine Showalter has called "feminist critique." Again following the lead of Beauvoir, but also influenced by the cultural anthropology of Sherry Ortner, such feminist thinkers as Margaret Homans, Donna Haraway, and Susan Bordo considered how and why the female body has been represented as more closely related to nature and natural forces than the male body. Similarly, the work of Gayle Rubin and Nancy Chodorow began to highlight the impact of family and kinship networks as well as reproductive biology on definitions of femininity and masculinity. Finally, in African American, Native American, Asian American, Chicana, and sexuality studies, such theorists as Hortense Spillers, Paula Gunn Allen, Shirley Geok-lin Lim, Paula M. L. Moya, and Bonnie Zimmerman illuminate the relationships between, on the one hand, gender, and, on the other hand, race, ethnicity, and sexual orientation. Throughout this section, however, as if heeding Barbara Christian's advice to focus on creative literature, many of these thinkers pursue their inquiries through analyses of specific texts—novels, poems, plays—produced by authors situated in specific national contexts.

Designed especially for use in theory-oriented courses, Part 2, "Theory: On Gender and Culture," also features influential writings that demonstrate the strategies through which a French feminist mode of deconstruction and psychoanalysis has explored the historical subjugation of women. Luce Irigaray, Julia Kristeva, and Hélène Cixous approach the devaluation of women and of nature in different ways, but each deploys poststructuralist methodologies to examine gender inequities. In addition, this section represents various positions in ongoing debates between "essentialist" and "social constructionist" definitions of womanhood. Among the "social constructionists" represented here, Judith Butler, Eve Kosofsky Sedgwick, and Gayatri Chakravorty Spivak extend gender analysis into sexuality studies and postcolonial studies. Of course "essentialism" is rarely a term avowed as a positive identification by theorists; however, such different thinkers as Jane P. Tompkins and Carol Gilligan, Carolyn Heilbrun and Elizabeth Abel examine the representational consequences of women's embodiment. Taken together, the self-identified feminist thinkers in this section of the *Reader* often elaborate on the ideas presented by the authors in Part 1; in doing so, they extend a self-reflexive and evolving tradition.

Part 3 of our reader—"Practice: Representative Readings and Analysis"— focuses specifically on six major examples of critical cruxes, assembling mini "casebooks" on notable authors, works, and movements that have generated lively theoretical and historical debate. These clusters of discussion—on medieval women, on Aphra Behn, on Charlotte Brontë's *Jane Eyre,* on Emily Dickinson, on the Harlem Renaissance, and on Sylvia Plath—can provide only a small sampling of the excellent analyses devoted to the selected topics; however, they typify the significant and often strikingly divergent approaches to aesthetic and cultural issues that mark feminist literary-critical conversations today.

Our own conversations about the construction of this book have been enhanced by many colleagues and friends who have shared syllabi with us, discussed their teaching practices, and made suggestions about possible inclusions. Especially helpful were Elizabeth Abel, Elyse Blankley, Alison Booth, Purnima Bose, Eva Cherniavsky, Margo Crawford, Joanne Feit Diehl, Mary Favret, Susan Fraiman, Linda Gardiner, George Hutchinson, Patricia Ingham, Karma Lochrie, Tricia Lootens, Deidre Lynch, Ruth Perry, Laura Runge, Janet Sorensen, Elisa Sparks, Martha Vicinus, Yung-Hsing Wu, and Sandra Zagarell. The research assistance of Jamie Horrocks, Francisco Reinking, Augustus Rose, and Julie Wise was exemplary. At Norton, Julia Reidhead and Marian Johnson exhibited great patience and forbearance in keeping us on course, as did Alice Falk, with her scrupulous manuscript editing.

We have aspired to offer the best of what has been thought and said by and about women composing English-language poems, novels, autobiographies, plays, stories, polemics, so we are confident that the texts we include here are eminently readable. We hope that *Feminist Literary Theory and Criticism: A Norton Reader* will be a useful teaching text—indeed an essential one—in undergraduate literature classes and graduate seminars alike. In addition, as the academy continues to evolve in the twenty-first century, we hope that this collection will be a valuable sourcebook not only for feminist teachers and scholars in a range of fields but also for the audience Virginia Woolf so resonantly defined as the "common reader"—an audience to whom so many feminist writers, like Woolf herself, have sought to speak.

Feminist Literary Theory and Criticism

A Norton Reader

Part 1
Women Writers: On Writing

Introduction

Until the past few decades, what some students now experience as a nearly unbridgeable gap between those who produce what we call "theory" and those who practice what we consider "creative writing" simply didn't exist. For centuries, poets speculated on the nature of their art, and novelists sought to define the parameters of their genre. From Sir Phillip Sidney to Percy Bysshe Shelley, from William Wordsworth to Matthew Arnold and, later, T. S. Eliot, poets were the central critics and philosophers of verse. Similarly, key theoreticians of the novel included such major practitioners as Henry Fielding and Henry James, D. H. Lawrence and E. M. Forster. And while men of letters consistently produced powerfully influential treatises on the art and craft of writing, women of letters were equally concerned to theorize their own work—in particular the relationship in the female literary career between gender and genre but also, more generally, the phenomenon of (literary) creativity. Thus, from the medieval French moralist and visionary Christine de Pizan to the contemporary Irish poet Eavan Boland, from the Elizabethan polemicist Jane Anger to the American poet-critic Adrienne Rich, literary women have constructed notable theories of art and commentaries on writing that we have collected here in an effort to suggest the scope of female, and often feminist, thinking about the contours and canons of literature.

One of the first feminists, Christine de Pizan was also one of the first feminist *critics.* Passionate in the Renaissance debate about the social position of woman that was called in French the *querelle des femmes,* she took the side of women from the start of her career and earned a good living in the process. Indeed, a widow at twenty-five, she supported her family with (among her other writings) polemics denouncing the misogyny of Jean de Meun, whose continuation of Guillaume de Loris's *Roman de la rose* aggressively revised Guillaume's mystical idealization of the flower of femininity with scurrilous attacks on woman as vile, vulgar, corrosively shrewish.

How to combat such vituperation while also arguing against idealization that transported woman to the stars, denying her full humanity? To dramatize her case for women's abilities, Christine sought to build a *Cité des dames*—a City of Ladies—as the spirit of "Reason" whom she met in a vision commanded her to do, declaiming "Get up, daughter! Without waiting any longer, let us go to the Field of Letters. There the City of Ladies will be founded on a flat and fertile plain, where all fruits and freshwater rivers are found and where the earth abounds in all good things." And as Christine "began to excavate and dig," following the marks of Reason "with the pick of cross-examination," she decided that "the more women have been wrongfully attacked, the greater waxes the merit of their glory." Thus, like many other feminists who were to come after her, she amassed a dream army of women "worthies," with whom she planned to populate her utopian city-state. And, like most of her other writings, the pages on which she transcribed her carefully justified plans for this state were widely read for more than a century, until they sank into obscurity, perhaps weighted down by later decades of such misogynistic critiques as those of the magisterial Gustave Lanson, who omitted her from his classic *Histoire de la littérature française* (1895) with the explanation that

> We will not stop to consider the excellent Christine de Pisan, a good girl, good wife, good mother, and moreover a veritable bluestocking, the first of that insufferable lineage of women authors . . . who have no concern but to multiply the proof of their tireless facility, equal to their universal mediocrity.

To be sure, women seeking precursors did locate Christine as if through some sort of feminist radar, even in the oblivion to which such scholars as Lanson had consigned her. "The [early Renaissance] revival of learning had its influence upon woman," noted the American suffragist Matilda Joslyn Gage in the nineteenth century, adding that "we find in the early part of the fourteenth century a decided tendency toward a recognition of [female] equality. Christine of Pisa, the most eminent woman of this period, supported a family of six persons by her pen, taking high ground on the conservation of morals." Yet for some five hundred years after Christine's death, the visionary work in which she outlined her scheme for illuminating the history of "women worthies" was out of print. In fact, the reevaluation that restored her to a canon of women's literature did not begin until 1975, when Maureen Cheney Curnow, a graduate student at Vanderbilt University, offered a critical edition of the Old French version of *The Book of the City of Ladies* as her Ph.D. dissertation.

More recently, the nature of Christine's feminism has been much debated; indeed, a few historians doubt that she was in any significant sense what we would now consider a "feminist." Some advocates for women, for instance, wonder whether she overemphasized the more suffocating qualities of female "virtue" and suggest that her notions of the proper education for women were stiflingly dutiful. But as the Renaissance scholar Maureen Quilligan has perhaps most definitively shown, Christine was surely as proto-feminist in her search for literary authority as in her yearning to wield that authority in defining a company of women that could properly populate her dream city. And the very dream of such a city is undoubtedly a feminist one, even if some of the qualities Christine attributed to its citizens occasionally seem problematic from a contemporary perspective.

In fact, it's arguable that one of the special characteristics of any female literary canon is precisely a sometimes conflicted consciousness of its own specialness. For better or worse, in other words, almost all the women writers who make up what we would consider a canon of literature by women are aware that they inhabit a canon (or "city") of literary *women*, a corporate body about which they always have *feelings*—which may be positive or negative. In contrast, the supposedly mainstream canon of male-authored "masterpieces" is not as a rule marked by such self-consciousness. True, as Harold Bloom has claimed in *The Anxiety of Influence* (1973), male writers may understand themselves to be agonistically engaged in struggles with a community of strong paternal precursors; but it's hard to imagine, say, a masculine contemporary of Christine's seeking to found a City of *Men* in order to justify the propriety of male education to a readership of judgmental *women*.

Yet ambivalent justifications of the very idea of a literary canon authored by educated women have certainly long characterized the canon of literary women writing in English, and have in fact given this body of work its distinct contours *as* a canon. The canon of women's literature is thus a self-reflexive canon that continually attempts to *theorize itself,* a canon formed by a consciousness of its own vexed and often vexing canonicity. For this reason, Christine, a speaker of Old French, can be said to function for English-language women writers and for her French descendants as a paradigmatic theorist of "our" canon. For what we ourselves have called an "anxiety of authorship" that continually puts the whole female literary project in question has historically indicated the self-reflexive need of this special canon to keep theorizing itself and its own specialness.

How does this self-theorizing manifest itself in the writings of such major authors as Jane Austen, Charlotte Brontë, George Eliot, Emily Dickinson, and their successors? Although most of these writers didn't produce what we'd now consider sophisticated literary theory of the sort that, forming a canon of its own, has been collected recently in *The Norton Anthology of Theory and Criticism,* all at one time or another sought to define their own identity as *women* writers. Most notably, perhaps, many were engaged in a search *for* rather than a struggle *against* precursors. Indeed, even before there was a significant women's movement, women of letters were attempting to uncover and justify a history of their own through meditations on both genre and tradition.

Early in the nineteenth century, for instance, Jane Austen exuberantly defended the largely female-authored novel in a self-reflexive scene in *Northanger Abbey* (1817), denouncing a hypothetical young lady who comments "with affected indifference or momentary shame" that she is "only" reading a novel:

> "It is only Cecilia or Camilla or Belinda"; or, in short, only some work in which the greatest powers of the mind are displayed, in which the most thorough knowledge of human nature, the happiest delineation of its varieties, the liveliest effusions of wit and humour, are conveyed to the world in the best-chosen language.

More wistfully, in the mid–nineteenth century Elizabeth Barrett Browning acknowledged her hunger for the words of poetic precursors, declaring "England has had many learned ladies but where are the poetesses? I look everywhere for grandmothers and find none." A few decades later, Emily Dickinson defined Barrett Browning herself as such an empowering ancestress, confessing that "I think I was enchanted / When first a sombre girl / I read that Foreign Lady." And of course in the twentieth century Virginia Woolf was to theorize such yearnings as these in her famous observation in *A Room of One's Own* (1929) that "we think back through our [literary] mothers, if we are women."

Like Christine's search for women worthies with whom to populate her city, these efforts at self-validation through the construction of a sufficient literary community were clearly attempts at canon formation: some oblique (for example, the comments of Austen and Dickinson), some more straightforward (for instance, the remarks of Barrett Browning and Woolf). Yet they were often shadowed by rather different and surprisingly negative visions of a female literary tradition that were equally significant as efforts to comprehend and comment on a canon of literature by women that was sometimes more troubling than it was triumphant. A number of nineteenth-century authors—even writers such as Austen and Dickinson who had recorded their fascination with a community of precursors—were sometimes remarkably self-deprecating in their often brief and hesitant statements of their own aesthetic aspirations.

Best known, perhaps, are comments from Austen and Charlotte Brontë, both of whom on occasion diplomatically downplayed their literary ambitions. Austen referred to her own work as "a little bit (two Inches wide) of Ivory, on which I work with so fine a brush as to produce little effect after much labour"; satirized the novels of Mrs. Radcliffe and other Gothic romancers in *Northanger Abbey;* and cast her high-spirited Emma as a self-deluding weaver of flighty, self-indulgent fantasies. In response to Robert Southey's infamous assertion that "Literature cannot be the business of a woman's life; and it ought not to be," Charlotte Brontë assured him "I have endeavored . . . to observe all the duties a woman ought to fulfill," although, she added, "In the evenings, I confess, I do think, but I never trouble any one else with my thoughts." And even in her own journals she was uneasy about her imaginative compulsions, noting in her Roe Head Diary that she longed to "quit for a while" the "burning clime" of what she elsewhere called the "infernal world"— the imaginary kingdom of Angria—where she had "sojourned too long." By implication, both these writers were recording their sense that the female-authored canon was, on the one hand, comically Gothic or infernally desirous and, on the other hand, modest, miniature, self-effacing.

Similarly self-deprecating apologies for authorship, sometimes coupled with efforts at affiliation with *masculinity* rather than *femininity,* marked aesthetic statements by such other major writers as Mary Shelley, George Eliot, Emily Dickinson, and Christina Rossetti. Shelley introduced an edition of *Frankenstein* by nervously attempting to explain " 'How I, then a young girl, came to think of, and to dilate upon, so very hideous an idea?' " Writing to her brother, the poet Dante Gabriel Rossetti, Christina Rossetti conceded that "the world you and yours frequent" is "delightful, noble, memorable," but insisted that she herself was "well content in my shady crevice—which crevice enjoys the unique advantage of being to my certain knowledge the place assigned me." Dickinson, of course, claimed that " 'Publication' " was as "foreign" to her "as Firmament to Fin," implicitly defining herself as a creature of subaqueous shadows rather than soaring ambition, while also expressing scorn for "Publication" as an "Auction / Of the Mind." To her earliest intellectual mentor, Dr. R. H. Brabant, Mary Anne Evans (who was eventually to become George Eliot) humbly defined herself as "Deutera" (which, she explained, "*means* second and *sounds* a little like daughter").

Among seventeenth- and eighteenth-century writers, aesthetic self-definitions were customarily even more excessive in their modesty. Anne Bradstreet, though defined by her publisher as *The Tenth Muse, Lately Sprung Up in America,* anxiously assured her readers that she asked only for a domestically savory "thyme or parsley wreath" rather than manly "bays," arguing (with perhaps ironic humility) that "this mean and unrefinéd ore of mine / Will make [men's] glistering gold but more to shine." Mary Astell, in a poem titled "Ambition," urged "Let me obscured be, and never known," seeking only to be "great in humility." The aristocratic Anne Finch, countess of Winchilsea, while protesting the "mistaken rules" that had cast women poets in a subordinate role, nevertheless apologized for her "cramped numbers" and resolved that she would "with contracted wing, / To some few friends and to [her] sorrows sing." Another aristocrat, Margaret Cavendish, duchess of Newcastle, noted that "It cannot be expected" that she "should write so wisely or wittily as men, being of the effeminate sex, whose brains nature has mixed with the coldest and softest elements." Similarly, though Aphra Behn's plays were the toast of Restoration England, she complained that "poor woman" has been "Debarred from sense and sacred poetry."

But even in the twentieth century, such descriptions of a female literary canon as modestly subordinate persisted. Virginia Woolf—arguably the first major modern feminist critic—decided that "a woman's sentence" had yet to be written, while also noting that among women writers poetry "is still denied outlet." Three decades later, the brilliant and ambitious poet Sylvia Plath deployed a similar rhetoric of modesty, insisting in a letter to her mother that she was "glad" her poet-husband, Ted Hughes, was "always first." Taken together as a kind of corporate self-definition, these guarded statements subtly say: Yes, we want to write, we *do* write, but don't worry: because we're women we don't want to write *that* much, and we certainly can't write that *well*. Just as woman is a secondary creature, created from Adam's rib, ours is a secondary canon, always as aware of its own inferiority as of its own potential impropriety.

Explicit definitions of the canon were equally problematic. Where early feminist polemicists had followed Christine in urging women to educate themselves by reading texts that would educate them in morality (as opposed to sentimental romances, most of which were presumably penned by women), a number of women writers defined a female literary canon by attacking it. Most famously, perhaps, George Eliot mounted a scathing assault on "silly novels by lady novelists." Here, much as Austen had done in *Northanger Abbey* and in an even earlier, parodic "Plan of a Novel," the author of such ambitious works as *The Mill on the Floss* (1860) and *Middlemarch* (1871–72) comically demolished what she called "the mind-and-millinery school" of romance in which "the lover has a manly breast; . . . hearts are hollow . . . friends are consigned to the tomb; . . . the sun is a luminary that goes to his western couch; . . . life is a melancholy boon." Even more strikingly, however, this deeply philosophical writer commented with special acrimony on "the *oracular* species" of novel, a genre produced by women who consider themselves equipped to address "the knottiest moral and speculative questions":

> Apparently, their recipe for solving all such difficulties is something like this:—Take a woman's head, stuff it with a smattering of philosophy and literature chopped small, and with false notions of society baked hard, let it hang over a desk a few hours every day, and serve up hot in feeble English. . . . You will rarely meet with a lady novelist of the oracular class who is diffident of her ability to decide on theological questions, . . . and pity philosophers in general that they have not had the opportunity of consulting her.

A century later, in the same mode, Plath, who claimed that she wanted to be "the Poetess of America," insisted that her verse wouldn't be "quailing and whining like Teasdale or simple lyrics like Millay." Rather, she wished to be "drunker than Dylan, harder than Hopkins, younger than Yeats in my saying" (even while she was supposedly rejoicing that her husband was "always first").

Again, implicit in these assertions is a definition of female literary production as secondary and even—here—polluted or contaminated by an inescapable, and inescapably *feminine,* weakness. For both these women, the only resolution of this dilemma is a flight into masculinity. In Eliot's case (as in the case of George Sand; Currer, Ellis, and Acton Bell; and countless other women writers), that flight was literalized in the adoption of a male pseudonym, while Plath fantasized such a flight in the rhetoric of her aspiration to be "harder than Hopkins, younger than Yeats," and so on. But regardless of the method chosen, these writers, like so many other women of letters, were defining themselves as secretly male, assuming that the masculine *is* the "human" while the feminine is somehow, as Dorothy Sayers once sardonically put it, "the human less than human." All joined Aphra Behn in longing for a space in which to express the creativity of what Behn called "my masculine part the Poet in me." In this mode, Emily Dickinson, too, frequently postulated a fictive but powerful male self, at one point calling herself "Uncle Emily" and at another remembering a childhood when "Ourself" was "a boy." Indeed, in her celebrated theory of imaginative androgyny, even Virginia Woolf suggested that she too felt the "masculine part" somehow necessary to the "poet" in any woman; significantly, her radiant *Orlando* (1928) incarnates English literary history in a figure who is male from the originary age of Shakespeare to the eighteenth century, even though "he" becomes a "she" in the era of Pope. The primordial artist, Woolf's narrative implies, is masculine.

To be sure, quite a few women writers, especially in the twentieth century, have firmly insisted on the genderlessness of the artist's mind. Despite Elizabeth Bishop's celebrations in prose and verse of Marianne Moore as a precursor who resembled a kind of magical fairy godmother, she resolutely declared in a letter to a friend that although "undoubtedly gender does play an important part in the making of any art, . . . art is art and to separate writings, paintings, musical compositions, etc., into two sexes is to emphasize values in them that are *not* art." More recently, the poet Laura Riding Jackson insisted that an anthology of women's literature was "a type of compilation" that she found "demeaning," explaining:

> I regard the treatment of literary work as falling into a special category of women's writing as an offence against literature as of a human generalness, and an offence against the human identity of women. I refuse every request made of me to contribute to, participate in, such a trivializing of the issues of literature, and oppose this categorization in public commentary, as I can.

We need hardly note that these expressions of anxiety about being associated with the authors of masterpieces whose works are customarily considered staples of the English-language literary canon suggest once again the singularity of a *female*-authored canon whose contours are shaped by apologies and protests. (One can hardly imagine a male author protesting the inclusion of his work in an anthology consisting solely of male-authored texts.)

So far, we've pointed to few moves by English-speaking women critics and writers that could be considered, like Christine's establishment of a *cité des dames,* conscious attempts at canon formation. But as we focus more closely on the theoretical works of Christine's literary descendants, we can discern four crucial strategies through which women of letters have historically attempted to define, study, and expand the canon of literature by women. And, interestingly, all are tactics Christine employed in her proto-feminist polemics.

First, women of letters have long struggled to strengthen their own literary canon by proposing not just the education but the *reeducation* of women. Basic education—fundamental literacy—is of course a right for which feminists since Christine have fought. But reeducation not just in basic letters but in rational thought has been equally significant to a long line of feminist thinkers. Christine herself urged that all women should have access to learning, arguing that "moral education amends and ennobles" those fortunate enough to be graced with it. In addition, the very construction of a *city* or community of women worthies was a radically ambitious pedagogical project designed to inculcate in both women and men the merits of a luminous female history.

From the seventeenth century to the twentieth, Christine's English-speaking descendants outlined similar projects. In 1694 the learned essayist Mary Astell presented in *A Serious Proposal to the Ladies* a plan for "a religious retirement"—really a sort of women's college—where, though men may "resent . . . to have their enclosure broke down," women would be "invited to taste of that tree of knowledge [men] have so long unjustly monopolized." Similarly, in 1792 the polemicist, journalist, and novelist Mary Wollstonecraft contended that women's "faculties" should "have room to unfold," deploring the "folly which the ignorance of women generates." In a somewhat different vein, the African American writer and educator Anna Julia Cooper argued in the late nineteenth century for "the higher education of women" as an antidote to the "greed and cruelty" of a male-dominated Western culture.

Perhaps most prominently, in 1929 Virginia Woolf devoted much of her classic *A Room of One's Own* to a meditation on female education, famously comparing the poverty and austerity of an Oxbridge women's college to the wealth, ease, and smugness of its brother institution for men. In an earlier work, too—the wistfully utopian essay "A Woman's College from Outside" (1926)—Woolf recorded an ecstatic vision of the "miraculous tree [of knowledge] with the golden fruit at its summit" (the same tree toward which Astell was also drawn) that would offer itself to women in a "good world," a "new world." And if we translate this range of sometimes combative, sometimes nearly mystical feminist visions of female education into the recent history of feminism, we can see that the interdisciplinary academic project known as women's studies constitutes a comparable effort to teach women (and men too) to understand not only their own dilemmas but also their own potentialities, on the assumption that such instruction is urgently needed to correct a skewed social order.

But Christine's selection of women worthies for inclusion in her canonical city of ladies also pioneered a second (and perhaps even more obvious) strategy through which feminists past and present sought to define a canon of their own: by specifically recovering and reevaluating individual women of letters. Again, such recovery of individual "grandmothers" and "mothers" was an enterprise in which, as it turns out, women from the Middle Ages onward were engaged in one way or another, with Margery Kempe recording a life-

changing visit to the aging Julian of Norwich, Anne Finch expressing a mixture of admiration and envy toward her precursor Katherine Philips ("the
Matchless Orinda"), and Jane Austen celebrating the works of Fanny Burney
and Maria Edgeworth; even the sometimes antifeminist George Eliot
affirmed the intellectual contributions of Margaret Fuller and Mary Wollstonecraft, while Elizabeth Bishop paid homage to her muse and patroness
Marianne Moore.

Once more, though, Woolf's ambitions most vividly reiterate Christine's
aspirations. Not only in *A Room* but also throughout *The Common Reader*
(1925) this exemplary twentieth-century feminist critic excavated and analyzed countless works by women, among them not just canonical novels by
Eliot and the Brontës but also such writings as the plays of Aphra Behn and
Anne Finch's ode on the neurotic melancholy defined in the eighteenth century as "the Spleen"—writings that had largely fallen into obscurity by the
time of Woolf's (re)evaluations. In offering such readings (not all celebratory
but all seriously attentive), she pioneered another significant strategy that has
been persistently deployed by contemporary feminists who have sought to
reconstitute a canon of literature by women through painstaking research,
including the scholarly recovery of forgotten texts and the scrupulous rehabilitation of reputations. Among the most recent writers whose works are
represented in this section, Alice Walker and June Jordan have dramatically
reimagined the accomplishments of major precursors—Zora Neale Hurston
and Phillis Wheatley; but Christine herself, as already noted, was a beneficiary of precisely such recovery and rehabilitation.

Yet even while feminists have long struggled to define a female literary
canon by rehabilitating women as readers and writers of their own destinies, their efforts have necessarily involved them in a third strategy for
canon (re)formation: reeducating readers in general, but especially (it
should go without saying) misogynistic male readers. Arguably, almost all
the writings we've included in part 1 of this collection have been in some
sense addressed to men, with the overt or covert goal of—as the Quaker
admonition puts it—speaking truth to power. Like the simultaneously
apologetic and defiant assertions of such poets as Anne Bradstreet and
Anne Finch, a number of these addresses to what female authors fear is an
unsympathetic audience tend to be plaintive, even frankly melancholy.
Bradstreet, for example, cynically noted that "If what I do prove well, it
won't advance, / *They'll* say it's stolen, or else it was by chance" (emphasis
added), even as she ingratiatingly suggested to male rivals that her "mean
and unrefinéd ore" would make their "glistering gold but more to shine." In
the same mode, Finch argued that women may be misread because "mistaken rules" label them "fallen" so that feminine art is inevitably and
unhappily considered "insipid, empty, uncorrect."

More recently, however, feminist thinkers have begun to characterize the
censorious male reader as himself somehow "fallen"—even as something of
a fool. Virginia Woolf's infamous "Professor von X.," the red-faced and angry
villain of *A Room of One's Own* who is investigating "the mental, moral and
physical inferiority of the female sex," is perhaps the paradigmatic image of
the male reader-as-buffoon; but long before Woolf caricatured this especially
obnoxious whipping boy, her precursors had parodied the misogyny of some
male reviewers with comparably bitter verve. The nineteenth-century Amer-

ican humorist Fanny Fern (Sarah Willis Parton) was especially adept at such salutary send-ups. Her "Male Criticism on Ladies' Books," together with her mock self-review " 'Fresh Leaves, by Fanny Fern,' " comically demolished what she called the "shallow, unfair, wholesale, sneering criticism" produced by "*male* spleen." But contemporary women writers, too, have continued to defy the protean forms of literary misogyny that linger in our culture. In their various ways, Cynthia Ozick's "We Are the Crazy Lady," Joanna Russ's "What Can a Heroine Do? or Why Women Can't Write," and Margaret Atwood's "Paradoxes and Dilemmas: The Woman as Writer" deride or denounce the arrogance with which Professor von X. represses female creativity.

To recognize the need for reeducating male readers, however, is to understand that the apparently *main*stream *male* canon has long been dialectically engaged with a shadowy (because not clearly outlined) *female* canon. In other words, just as the female canon is defined by its own uncertainties and ambiguities, so too it is defined by "male spleen." That spleen (which evoked, of course, the answering "Spleen" from which Anne Finch and other women poets suffered) goes back at least as far as Jean de Meun's misogyny and, more specifically, Alexander Pope's splenetic assertion that the "wayward Queen" of spleen rules women "to fifty from fifteen," a comment followed by countless other masculine denunciations of what Nathaniel Hawthorne called the "damn'd mob of scribbling women."

But to perceive that this dialogue between a foregrounded male canon and a backgrounded female canon has such a long history is to understand, suddenly, how in some sense everyone has always realized, secretly or not so secretly, that the lost continent of the women's literary canon was already *there*: not just in the collective unconscious of our civilization, not just in our civilization's discontents, but also in the more conscious contents of the minds with which both sexes theorize the repository of intellectual achievements that some critics now call "cultural capital." Thus, a fourth major strategy through which women critics—especially recent ones—have sought to define their own literary canon has been an excavation and reexamination not just of individual women writers, not just of a female tradition, but of an intricate female and male history reimagined to factor in an overlooked yet powerfully influential female-male dialectic. In such revisionary historicizing, the "mainstream"/male stream canon appears no less new and different than the formerly subaqueous female canon. And just as Christine's retorts to her antagonists in the *querelle des femmes* suggest the complexity of the conversation in which she was engaged, so quite a few second wave feminist writers have long since dramatized their understanding of the ways in which the engendering of our literature is shaped by at least two interlocking canons.

"Diving into the Wreck" (1973), a major early work by the American feminist poet-theorist Adrienne Rich, can stand here for a range of writings—from Woolf's *A Room of One's Own* (1929) to Toni Morrison's "Unspeakable Things Unspoken" (1989) and Eavan Boland's "Letter to a Young Woman Poet" (1997)—that seek to explore such a drowned history. In this brilliant quest poem, the speaker describes her descent into a sunken world where, carrying "a book of myths / in which / our names do not appear," she explores "the wreck" peopled by the lost dead bodies of her ancestry ("the mermaid whose dark hair / streams black, the merman in his armored body") and understands that her history—and, that of her culture—is constituted out of the dialectic between the two. Noting the necessity of definitional words ("The words are purposes. / The words are maps"), she concedes that "I am she: I am he," yet seeks to surface the mysterious cargo that must still be exhumed.

Such efforts at self-analysis constitute perhaps the single most enduring thread that knits together the texts we've included in this section of our *Reader.* For in one way or another, almost all the writers represented here have sought to reflect upon their own authorial practice, commenting in letters and prefaces, poems and polemics, essays and reviews not only on the impediments to women's ambition but also on the hard-earned achievements of the female imagination. With Audre Lorde, each would assert that poetry—as *poiesis,* the Greek word for "making"—is "not a luxury," even while most would also second the famous claim central to Rich's crucial essay "When We Dead Awaken" (1972): "Re-vision—the act of looking back, of seeing with fresh eyes, . . . is for women more than a chapter in cultural history: it is an act of survival." For as Lorde, Rich, and all the other writers included here would no doubt warmly agree, the intellectual activities we name "criticism" and "theory" are integrally related to the imaginative energy we call "creativity."

SANDRA M. GILBERT

CHRISTINE DE PIZAN
ca. 1365–1429

Although Christine de Pizan was the first woman in Europe to write professionally as well as prolifically, and although her landmark *Book of the City of Ladies* (1405) is a major early instance of feminist theory, to this date there is no complete edition of her writings in either English or French. Indeed, it wasn't until 1975 that a critical edition of *Le livre de la cité des dames* in the original Old French was prepared; before that time, the book was available only in a few rare early copies held in specialized libraries. Yet as our selection here reveals, *The Book of the City of Ladies* offers not only a dream vision of a feminist utopia but also a sophisticated critique of the medieval misogyny it is designed to counter. Before composing it, Christine had entered vigorously into a debate over the popular *Romance of the Rose* (ca. 1230–35, 1275–80), deploring its problematic representations of women in a "Quarrel of the Rose" that led her to dispute a range of prominent fifteenth-century French intellectuals, including the chancellor of the University of Paris and the provost of Lille. Influenced by, and engaging with, Boccaccio's *Concerning Famous Women* (1360–74), her celebrations of significant women in *The City of Ladies* made her a key participant in the ongoing *querelle des femmes* (debate over the nature of women) that engaged many thinkers in her period.

The daughter of an astrologer-physician, Christine was born in Venice but came to Paris as a child when her father was offered a post at the court of Charles V. At fifteen—in her own words, "the age when young girls are customarily assigned husbands"—she was married to Etienne de Castel, with whom she had three children. But in 1389, when she was just twenty-five, both her father and her husband died, leaving her with many debts and little money. Because she had been comparatively well educated for a woman of her day, she began writing professionally in order to support her family; and in the course of her career she produced more than twenty volumes of prose and verse, work that was remunerated (albeit uncertainly) by patronage from the French court. Although, as some recent commentators have noted, her "social vision of women's proper sphere is ultimately quite conservative," her lively participation in the debates of her era and in particular her ambitious entry into the *querelle des femmes* make her a proto-feminist figure of extraordinary power and significance. Our selection here is drawn from Earl Jeffrey Richards's translation of *The Book of the City of Ladies* (1982).

From The Book of the City of Ladies[1]

From Part One

1. HERE BEGINS THE BOOK OF THE CITY OF LADIES, WHOSE FIRST CHAPTER TELLS WHY AND FOR WHAT PURPOSE THIS BOOK WAS WRITTEN.

[1.1.1] One day as I was sitting alone in my study surrounded by books on all kinds of subjects, devoting myself to literary studies, my usual habit, my mind dwelt at length on the weighty opinions of various authors whom I had studied for a long time. I looked up from my book, having decided to leave such subtle questions in peace and to relax by reading some light poetry. With this in mind, I searched for some small book. By chance a strange volume came

---

1. Translated by Earl Jeffrey Richards.

into my hands, not one of my own, but one which had been given to me along with some others. When I held it open and saw from its title page that it was by Mathéolus,[2] I smiled, for though I had never seen it before, I had often heard that like other books it discussed respect for women. I thought I would browse through it to amuse myself. I had not been reading for very long when my good mother called me to refresh myself with some supper, for it was evening. Intending to look at it the next day, I put it down. The next morning, again seated in my study as was my habit, I remembered wanting to examine this book by Mathéolus. I started to read it and went on for a little while. Because the subject seemed to me not very pleasant for people who do not enjoy lies, and of no use in developing virtue or manners, given its lack of integrity in diction and theme, and after browsing here and there and reading the end, I put it down in order to turn my attention to more elevated and useful study. But just the sight of this book, even though it was of no authority, made me wonder how it happened that so many different men—and learned men among them—have been and are so inclined to express both in speaking and in their treatises and writings so many wicked insults about women and their behavior. Not only one or two and not even just this Mathéolus (for this book had a bad name anyway and was intended as a satire) but, more generally, judging from the treaties of all philosophers and poets and from all the orators—it would take too long to mention their names—it seems that they all speak from one and the same mouth. They all concur in one conclusion: that the behavior of women is inclined to and full of every vice. Thinking deeply about these matters, I began to examine my character and conduct as a natural woman and, similarly, I considered other women whose company I frequently kept, princesses, great ladies, women of the middle and lower classes, who had graciously told me of their most private and intimate thoughts, hoping that I could judge impartially and in good conscience whether the testimony of so many notable men could be true. To the best of my knowledge, no matter how long I confronted or dissected the problem, I could not see or realize how their claims could be true when compared to the natural behavior and character of women. Yet I still argued vehemently against women, saying that it would be impossible that so many famous men—such solemn scholars, possessed of such deep and great understanding, so clear-sighted in all things, as it seemed—could have spoken falsely on so many occasions that I could hardly find a book on morals where, even before I had read it in its entirety, I did not find several chapters or certain sections attacking women, no matter who the author was. This reason alone, in short, made me conclude that, although my intellect did not perceive my own great faults and, likewise, those of other women because of its simpleness and ignorance, it was however truly fitting that such was the case. And so I relied more on the judgment of others than on what I myself felt and knew. I was so transfixed in this line of thinking for such a long time that it seemed as if I were in a stupor. Like a gushing fountain, a series of authorities, whom I recalled one after another, came to mind, along with their opinions on this topic. And I finally decided that God formed a vile creature when He made woman, and

2. The *Liber Lamentationum Matheoluli* (*The Book of the Lamentations of Mathéolus*), composed around 1300.

I wondered how such a worthy artisan could have deigned to make such an abominable work which, from what they say, is the vessel as well as the refuge and abode of every evil and vice. As I was thinking this, a great unhappiness and sadness welled up in my heart, for I detested myself and the entire feminine sex, as though we were monstrosities in nature. And in my lament I spoke these words:

[1.1.2] "Oh, God, how can this be? For unless I stray from my faith, I must never doubt that Your infinite wisdom and most perfect goodness ever created anything which was not good. Did you yourself not create woman in a very special way and since that time did You not give her all those inclinations which it pleased You for her to have? And how could it be that You could go wrong in anything? Yet look at all these accusations which have been judged, decided, and concluded against women. I do not know how to understand this repugnance. If it is so, fair Lord God, that in fact so many abominations abound in the female sex, for You Yourself say that the testimony of two or three witnesses lends credence, why shall I not doubt that this is true? Alas, God, why did You not let me be born in the world as a man, so that all my inclinations would be to serve You better, and so that I would not stray in anything and would be as perfect as a man is said to be? But since Your kindness has not been extended to me, then forgive my negligence in Your service, most fair Lord God, and may it not displease You, for the servant who receives fewer gifts from his lord is less obliged in his service." I spoke these words to God in my lament and a great deal more for a very long time in sad reflection, and in my folly I considered myself most unfortunate because God had made me inhabit a female body in this world.[3]

4. HERE THE LADY EXPLAINS TO CHRISTINE THE CITY WHICH SHE HAS BEEN COMMISSIONED TO BUILD AND HOW SHE WAS CHARGED TO HELP CHRISTINE BUILD THE WALL AND ENCLOSURE, AND THEN GIVES HER NAME.

[1.4.1] "Thus, fair daughter, the prerogative among women has been bestowed on you to establish and build the City of Ladies. For the foundation and completion of this City you will draw fresh waters from us as from clear fountains, and we will bring you sufficient building stone, stronger and more durable than any marble with cement could be. Thus your City will be extremely beautiful, without equal, and of perpetual duration in the world.

[1.4.2] "Have you not read that King Tros founded the great city of Troy with the aid of Apollo, Minerva, and Neptune, whom the people of that time considered gods, and also how Cadmus founded the city of Thebes with the admonition of the gods? And yet over time these cities fell and have fallen into ruin. But I prophesy to you, as a true sybil, that this City, which you will found with our help, will never be destroyed, nor will it ever fall, but will remain prosperous forever, regardless of all its jealous enemies. Although it will be stormed by numerous assaults, it will never be taken or conquered.

[1.4.3] "Long ago the Amazon kingdom was begun through the arrangement and enterprise of several ladies of great courage who despised servitude, just as history books have testified. For a long time afterward they maintained it under

---

3. While she is engaged in this lamentation, three ladies appear to Christine, comforting her. The first speaks to her, telling her that with their help she will build a city of ladies, which would house "all ladies of fame and women worthy of praise."

the rule of several queens, very noble ladies whom they elected themselves, who governed them well and maintained their dominion with great strength. Yet, although they were strong and powerful and had conquered a large part of the entire Orient in the course of their rule and terrified all the neighboring lands (even the Greeks, who were then the flower of all countries in the world, feared them), nevertheless, after a time, the power of this kingdom declined, so that as with all earthly kingdoms, nothing but its name has survived to the present. But the edifice erected by you in this City which you must construct will be far stronger, and for its founding I was commissioned, in the course of our common deliberation, to supply you with durable and pure mortar to lay the sturdy foundations and to raise the lofty walls all around, high and thick, with mighty towers and strong bastions, surrounded by moats with firm blockhouses, just as is fitting for a city with a strong and lasting defense. Following our plan, you will set the foundations deep to last all the longer, and then you will raise the walls so high that they will not fear anyone. Daughter, now that I have told you the reason for our coming and so that you will more certainly believe my words, I want you to learn my name, by whose sound alone you will be able to learn and know that, if you wish to follow my commands, you have in me an administrator so that you may do your work flawlessly. I am called Lady Reason; you see that you are in good hands. For the time being then, I will say no more."[4]

8. HERE CHRISTINE TELLS HOW, UNDER REASON'S COMMAND AND ASSISTANCE, SHE BEGAN TO EXCAVATE THE EARTH AND LAY THE FOUNDATION.

[1.8.1] Then Lady Reason responded and said, "Get up, daughter! Without waiting any longer, let us go to the Field of Letters. There the City of Ladies will be founded on a flat and fertile plain, where all fruits and freshwater rivers are found and where the earth abounds in all good things. Take the pick of your understanding and dig and clear out a great ditch wherever you see the marks of my ruler, and I will help you carry away the earth on my own shoulders."

[1.8.2] I immediately stood up to obey her commands and, thanks to these three ladies, I felt stronger and lighter than before. She went ahead, and I followed behind, and after we had arrived at this field I began to excavate and dig, following her marks with the pick of cross-examination. And this was my first work:

[1.8.3] "Lady, I remember well what you told me before, dealing with the subject of how so many men have attacked and continue to attack the behavior of women, that gold becomes more refined the longer it stays in the furnace, which means the more women have been wrongfully attacked, the greater waxes the merit of their glory. But please tell me why and for what reason different authors have spoken against women in their books, since I already know from you that this is wrong; tell me if Nature makes man so inclined or whether they do it out of hatred and where does this behavior come from?"

Then she replied, "Daughter, to give you a way of entering into the question more deeply, I will carry away this first basketful of dirt. This behavior most certainly does not come from Nature, but rather is contrary to Nature, for no connection in the world is as great or as strong as the great love which, through the will of God, Nature places between a man and a woman. The

---

4. The second and third ladies introduce themselves as Rectitude and Justice. Christine thanks the ladies for their comfort and promises to obey them in all things.

causes which have moved and which still move men to attack women, even those authors in those books, are diverse and varied, just as you have discovered. For some have attacked women with good intentions, that is, in order to draw men who have gone astray away from the company of vicious and dissolute women, with whom they might be infatuated, or in order to keep these men from going mad on account of such women, and also so that every man might avoid an obscene and lustful life. They have attacked all women in general because they believe that women are made up of every abomination."

"My lady," I said then, "excuse me for interrupting you here, but have such authors acted well, since they were prompted by a laudable intention? For intention, the saying goes, judges the man."

"That is a misleading position, my good daughter," she said, "for such sweeping ignorance never provides an excuse. If someone killed you with good intention but out of foolishness, would this then be justified? Rather, those who did this, whoever they might be, would have invoked the wrong law; causing any damage or harm to one party in order to help another party is not justice, and likewise attacking all feminine conduct is contrary to the truth, just as I will show you with a hypothetical case. Let us suppose they did this intending to draw fools away from foolishness. It would be as if I attacked fire—a very good and necessary element nevertheless—because some people burnt themselves, or water because someone drowned. The same can be said of all good things which can be used well or used badly. But one must not attack them if fools abuse them, and you have yourself touched on this point quite well elsewhere in your writings. But those who have spoken like this so abundantly—whatever their intentions might be—have formulated their arguments rather loosely only to make their point. Just like someone who has a long and wide robe cut from a very large piece of cloth when the material costs him nothing and when no one opposes him, they exploit the rights of others. But just as you have said elsewhere, if these writers had only looked for the ways in which men can be led away from foolishness and could have been kept from tiring themselves in attacking the life and behavior of immoral and dissolute women—for to tell the straight truth, there is nothing which should be avoided more than an evil, dissolute, and perverted woman, who is like a monster in nature, a counterfeit estranged from her natural condition, which must be simple, tranquil, and upright—then I would grant you that they would have built a supremely excellent work. But I can assure you that these attacks on all women—when in fact there are so many excellent women—have never originated with me, Reason, and that all who subscribe to them have failed totally and will continue to fail. So now throw aside these black, dirty, and uneven stones from your work, for they will never be fitted into the fair edifice of your City.

[1.8.4] "Other men have attacked women for other reasons: such reproach has occurred to some men because of their own vices and others have been moved by the defects of their own bodies, others through pure jealousy, still others by the pleasure they derive in their own personalities from slander. Others, in order to show they have read many authors, base their own writings on what they have found in books and repeat what other writers have said and cite different authors."

✳   ✳   ✳

From Part Two

36. AGAINST THOSE MEN WHO CLAIM IT IS NOT GOOD FOR WOMEN TO BE EDUCATED.

[2.36.1] Following these remarks,[5] I, Christine, spoke, "My lady, I realize that women have accomplished many good things and that even if evil women have done evil, it seems to me, nevertheless, that the benefits accrued and still accruing because of good women—particularly the wise and literary ones and those educated in the natural sciences whom I mentioned above—outweigh the evil. Therefore, I am amazed by the opinion of some men who claim that they do not want their daughters, wives, or kinswomen to be educated because their mores would be ruined as a result."

She responded, "Here you can clearly see that not all opinions of men are based on reason and that these men are wrong. For it must not be presumed that mores necessarily grow worse from knowing the moral sciences, which teach the virtues, indeed, there is not the slightest doubt that moral education amends and ennobles them. How could anyone think or believe that whoever follows good teaching or doctrine is the worse for it? Such an opinion cannot be expressed or maintained. I do not mean that it would be good for a man or a woman to study the art of divination or those fields of learning which are forbidden—for the holy Church did not remove them from common use without good reason—but it should not be believed that women are the worse for knowing what is good.

[2.36.2] "Quintus Hortensius, a great rhetorician and consummately skilled orator in Rome, did not share this opinion. He had a daughter, named Hortensia, whom he greatly loved for the subtlety of her wit. He had her learn letters and study the science of rhetoric, which she mastered so thoroughly that she resembled her father Hortensius not only in wit and lively memory but also in her excellent delivery and order of speech—in fact, he surpassed her in nothing. As for the subject discussed above, concerning the good which comes about through women, the benefits realized by this woman and her learning were, among others, exceptionally remarkable. That is, during the time when Rome was governed by three men,[6] this Hortensia began to support the cause of women and to undertake what no man dared to undertake. There was a question whether certain taxes should be levied on women and on their jewelry during a needy period in Rome. This woman's eloquence was so compelling that she was listened to, no less readily than her father would have been, and she won her case.

[2.36.3] "Similarly, to speak of more recent times, without searching for examples in ancient history, Giovanni Andrea, a solemn law professor in Bologna not quite sixty years ago, was not of the opinion that it was bad for women to be educated. He had a fair and good daughter, named Novella, who was educated in the law to such an advanced degree that when he was occupied by some task and not at leisure to present his lectures to his students, he would send Novella, his daughter, in his place to lecture to the students from his chair. And to prevent her beauty from distracting the concentration

---

5. By Christine's second guide, Rectitude.
6. Republican Rome was usually governed by two

men (consuls elected for two-year terms); the third here is the dictator.

of her audience, she had a little curtain drawn in front of her. In this manner she could on occasion supplement and lighten her father's occupation. He loved her so much that, to commemorate her name, he wrote a book of remarkable lectures on the law which he entitled *Novella super Decretalium,*[7] after his daughter's name.

[2.36.4] "Thus, not all men (and especially the wisest) share the opinion that it is bad for women to be educated. But it is very true that many foolish men have claimed this because it displeased them that women knew more than they did. Your father, who was a great scientist and philosopher, did not believe that women were worth less by knowing science; rather, as you know, he took great pleasure from seeing your inclination to learning. The feminine opinion of your mother, however, who wished to keep you busy with spinning and silly girlishness, following the common custom of women, was the major obstacle to your being more involved in the sciences. But just as the proverb already mentioned above says, 'No one can take away what Nature has given,' your mother could not hinder in you the feeling for the sciences which you, through natural inclination, had nevertheless gathered together in little droplets. I am sure that, on account of these things, you do not think you are worth less but rather that you consider it a great treasure for yourself; and you doubtless have reason to."

And I, Christine, replied to all of this, "Indeed, my lady, what you say is as true as the Lord's Prayer."

1405

---

7. Literally, "new things about the decrees" (Latin).

JANE ANGER
fl. 1589

Little is known of the woman who called herself "Jane Anger" except that she was the first major feminist polemicist to write in English. Signing herself "JA: A. Gent.," Anger published a passionate rebuttal to the misogynistic attacks that were part of an ongoing debate about the differences between the sexes known as the *querelle des femmes,* or what we would now call the "woman question." Addressing "all Women in genenerall, and gentle Reader whatsoever," this early advocate for gender justice denounced what she considered masculinist representations of her sex, vigorously declaring "Fie on the falshoode of men, whose minds goe oft a madding," and wondering "Was there ever any so abused, so slaundered, so railed upon, or so wickedly handeled undeservedly, as are we women?" Although her true identity remains unclear, her name—whether real or pseudonymous—has allegorical force.

Studies of Anger's place in the history of feminist polemic and reprintings of her work have now appeared in several volumes, including Katherine Usher Henderson and Barbara F. McManus's *Half-Humankind: Contexts and Texts of the Controversy about Women in England, 1540–1640* (1985) and Moira Ferguson's *First Feminists: British Women Writers, 1578–1799* (1985). Our selection focuses particularly on the pernicious images of women that Anger thought were distressingly prevalent in much writing produced by men.

From Jane Anger: Her Protection for Women

To all Women in genenerall, and gentle Reader whatsoever.

Fie on the falshoode of men, whose minds goe oft a madding, & whose tongues can not so soone bee wagging, but straight they fal a railing. Was there ever any so abused, so slaundered, so railed upon, or so wickedly handeled undeservedly, as are we women? Will the Gods permit it, the Goddesses stay there punishing judgments, and we ourselves not pursue their undoinges for such develish practices. O *Paules steeple* and *Charing Crosse*.[1] A halter hold al such persons. Let the streames of the channels in *London* streates run so swiftly, as they may be able alone to carrie them from that sanctuarie. Let the stones be as Ice, the soales of their shooes as Glasse, the waies steep like AEtna, & every blast a Whyrl-wind puffed out of Boreas[2] his long throat, that these may hasten their passage to the Devils haven. Shal surfeiters raile on our kindnes, you stand stil & say nought, and shall not *Anger* stretch the vaines of her braines, the stringes of her fingers, and the listes[3] of her modestie, to answere their Surfeitings? Yes truely, And herein I conjure all you to aide assist me in defence of my willingnes, which shall make me rest at your commaundes. Fare you well.

Your friend,
Ja. A.

A Protection for Women, &c.

The desire that every man hath to shewe his true vaine[4] in writing is unspeakable, and their mindes are so caried away with the manner, as no care at all is had of the matter: they run so into Rethorick,[5] as often times they overrun the boundes of their own wits, and goe they knowe not whether. If they have stretched their invention so hard on a last, as it is at a stand, there remaines but one help, which is, to write of us women. If they may once encroach so far into our presence, as they may but see the lyning of our outermost garment, they straight think that Apollo honours them, in yeelding so good a supply to refresh their sore overburdened heads, through studying for matters to indite off. And therfore that the God may see how thankfully they receive his liberality, (their wits whetted, and their braines almost broken with botching his bountie) they fall straight to dispraising & slaundering our silly[6] sex. But judge what the cause should be, of this their so great malice towards simple women. Doubtles the weaknesse of our wits, and our honest bashfulnesse, by reason whereof they suppose that there is not one amongst us who can, or dare reproove their slanders and false reproches: their slaunderous tongues are so short, and the time wherein they have lavished out their wordes fully, hath bene so long, that they know we cannot catch hold of them to pull them out, and they think we wil not write to reproove their lying lips: which conceites have already made them cockes & wolde (should they not be cravened) make themselves among themselves bee thought to be of the game.

---

1. Sites in London.
2. The north wind.
3. Limits.
4. I.e., vein: inclination, disposition.
5. I.e., rhetoric.
6. Defenseless; simple, innocent.

They have bene so daintely fed with our good natures, that like jades[7] (their stomaches are grown so quesie) they surfeit of our kindnes. If we wil not suffer them to smell on our smockes, they will snatch at our peticotes: but if our honest natures cannot away with that uncivil kinde of jesting then we are coy: yet if we beare with their rudenes, and be som what modestly familiar with them, they will straight make matter of nothing, blazing abroad that they have surfeited with love, and then their wits must be showen in telling the maner how.

Among the innumerable number of bookes to that purpose, of late (unlooked for) the newe surfeit of an olde Lover (sent abroad to warn those which are of his own kind, from catching the like disease) came by chance to my handes: which, because as well women as men are desirous of novelties, I willinglie read over: neither did the ending there of lesse please me then[8] the beginning, for I was so carried away with the conceit of the Gent. as that I was quite out of the booke before I thought I had bene in the middest thereof: So pithie were his sentences, so pure his wordes, and so pleasing his stile. The chiefe matters therein contained were of two sortes: the one in the dispraise of mans follie, and the other, invective against our sex, their folly proceeding of their own flatterie joined with fancie, & our faultes are through our follie, with which is some faith.

*　　*　　*

ca. 1589

7. Those jaded by continual indulgence. 8. Please me less than.

MARGARET CAVENDISH,
DUCHESS OF NEWCASTLE
1623–1673

"Women live like bats or owls, labour like beasts, and die like worms," Margaret Cavendish once observed. An ambitious poet, playwright, and philosopher, she herself aspired to become, as she puts it in our selection here, "Authoress of a whole World," and in her speculative *The Description of a New World, called the Blazing-World* (1668)—a proto–science fiction narrative—she attempted just such a project. Born to an aristocratic family, Cavendish served as a maid of honor to Queen Henrietta Maria before marrying William Cavendish, duke of Newcastle, a Royalist soldier with whom she remained in exile on the Continent during Cromwell's reign. But after the Restoration she returned with him to an English estate where the couple lived in comparative isolation while she wrote so assiduously and voluminously that Virginia Woolf believed the duchess's "philosophical fancies" evoked "a vision of loneliness and riot," even though the "vast bulk" of her writings are "leavened by a vein of authentic fire."

As one scholar has recently noted, Cavendish was the first woman in England to write mainly for publication. Our selections from the prefaces and epilogues in which she comments on her own work capture some of the "authentic fire" that animated her art as well as her thought about art's purposes.

From Preface to *Observations upon Experimental Philosophy*

It is probable, some will say, that my much writing is a disease; but what disease they will judg it to be, I cannot tell; I do verily believe they will take it to be a disease of the Brain, but surely they cannot call it an Apoplexical or Lethargical disease: Perhaps they will say, it is an extravagant, or at least a Fantastical disease; but I hope they will rather call it a disease of wit.[1] But, let them give it what name they please, yet of this I am sure, that if much writing be a disease, then the best philosophers, both Moral and Natural, as also the best Divines, Lawyers, Physitians, Poets, Historians, Orators, Mathematicians, Chymists, and many more have been grievously sick, and Seneca, Plinius, Aristotle, Cicero, Tacitus, Plutarch, Euclid, Homer, Virgil, Ovid, St. Augustin, St. Ambrose, Scotus, Hippocrates, Galen, Paracelsus,[2] and hundreds more, have been at deaths door with the disease of writing; but to be infected with the same disease, which the devoutest, wisest, wittiest, subtilest, most learned and eloquent men have been troubled withal, is no disgrace, but the greatest honour, even to the most ambitious person in the world: and next to the honour of being thus infected, it is also a great delight and pleasure to me, as being the onely Pastime which imploys my idle hours; in so much, that, were I sure no body did read my Works, yet I would not quit my pastime for all this; for although they should not delight others, yet they delight me; and if all Women that have no imployment in worldly affairs, should but spend their time as harmlessly as I do, they would not commit such faults as many are accused of. . . .

1666

From The Description of a New World, called the Blazing-World

From *To the Reader*

. . . And this is the reason, why I added this Piece of Fancy to my Philosophical Observations,[1] and joined them as two Worlds at the ends of their Poles; both for my own sake, to divert my studious thoughts, which I Imployed in the Contemplation thereof, and to delight the Reader with variety, which is always pleasing. But lest my Fancy should stray too much, I chose such a Fiction as would be agreeable to the subject I treated of in the former parts; it is a Description of a New World, not such as Lucian's, or the French-man's World in the Moon;[2] but a World of my own Creating, which I

---

1. Intelligence.
2. Roman and Greek philosophers, historians, poets, and scientists, as well as early Christian writers.
1. I.e., her *Observations upon Experimental Philosophy* (1666).
2. Cyrano de Bergerac's *Histoire comique, par M.*

Cyrano de Bergerac, contenant les états et les empires de la lune (1657), translated in 1659 as *Selenarchia; or, The Government of the World in the Moon*. The Greek writer Lucian (b. ca. 120 C.E.) was a rhetorician and satirist whose most famous work, *The True History*, is a fantastic travel tale.

call the Blazing-World: The first part whereof is Romancical, the second Philosophical, and the third is meerly Fancy, or (as I may call it) Fantastical; which if it add any satisfaction to you, I shall account my Self a Happy Creatoress; If not, I must be content to live a melancholy Life in my own World. I cannot call it a poor World, if poverty be onely want of Gold, Silver, and Jewels; for there is more Gold in it then all the Chymists ever did, and (as I verily believe) will ever be able to make. As for the Rocks of Diamonds, I wish with all my soul they might be shared amongst my noble Female Friends, and upon that condition, I would willingly quit my part; and of the Gold I should onely desire so much as might suffice to repair my Noble Lord and Husbands Losses:[3] For I am not Covetous, but as Ambitious as ever any of my Sex was, is, or can be; which makes, that though I cannot be Henry the Fifth, or Charles the Second, yet I endeavour to be Margaret the First. And although I have neither power, time nor occasion to Conquer the World as Alexander and Caesar did; yet rather then not to be Mistress of one, since Fortune and the Fates would give me none, I have made a World of my own: for which no body, I hope, will blame me, since it is in every ones power to do the like.

The Epilogue to the Reader

By this Poetical Description, you may perceive, that my ambition is not onely to be Empress, but Authoress of a whole World; and that the Worlds I have made, both the Blazing-and the other Philosophical World, mentioned in the first part of this Description, are framed and composed of the most pure, that is, the Rational parts of Matter, which are the parts of my Mind; which Creation was more easily and suddenly effected, than the Conquests of the two famous Monarchs of the World, Alexander and Caesar. Neither have I made such disturbances, and caused so many dissolutions of particulars, otherwise named deaths, as they did; for I have destroyed but some few men in a little Boat, which dyed through the extremity of cold, and that by the hand of Justice, which was necessitated to punish their crime of stealing away a young and beauteous Lady. And in the formation of those Worlds, I take more delight and glory, than ever Alexander or Caesar did in conquering this terrestrial world; and though I have made my Blazing-world a Peaceable World allowing it but one Religion, one Language, and one Government; yet could I make another World, as full of Factions, Divisions, and Warrs, as this is of Peace and Tranquility; and the Rational figures of my Mind might express as much courage to fight, as Hector and Achilles had; and be as wise as Nestor, as Eloquent as Ulysses, and as beautiful as Hellen. But I esteeming Peace before Warr, Wit before Policy, Honesty before Beauty; instead of the figures of Alexander, Cesar, Hector, Achilles, Nestor, Ulysses, Hellen, &c. chose rather the figure of Honest Margaret Newcastle, which now I would not change for all this Terrestrial World; and if any should like the World I have made, and be willing to be my Subjects, they may imagine themselves such, and they are such, I mean in their Minds, Fancies or Imaginations; but if they cannot endure to be Subjects, they may create Worlds of their own, and Govern themselves as they please: But yet let them have a care, not to prove unjust Usurpers, and to rob me of mine: for, concerning the Philosophical World,

---

3. Because her husband was a Royalist, he lost his property and was forced into exile after the English civil war.

I am Empress of it my self; and as for the Blazing-world, it having an Empress already, who rules it with great Wisdom and Conduct, which Empress is my dear Platonick Friend; I shall never prove so unjust, treacherous and unworthy to her, as to disturb her Government, much less to depose her from her Imperial Throne, for the sake of any other, but rather chuse to create another World for another Friend.

1668

APHRA BEHN
1640–1689

Poet and playwright, actress and spy, novelist and wit, Aphra Behn was the first Englishwoman to become an openly commercial writer. When she burst upon the London literary scene as a middle-class widow of uncertain parentage, she was as insouciant about her adventures, sexual and otherwise, as she was independent in thought and art. In the course of her successful literary career, she authored eighteen plays and a number of innovative prose fictions, most notably the antislavery novel *Oroonoko, or the Royal Slave* (1688), while also composing a number of exuberantly witty and daringly frank verses. As a critic and theorist of her own writing, she also drafted incisive prefaces and dedicatory letters for her high-spirited comedies, including an "epistle to the reader" that prefaced *The Dutch Lover* (1673) and a preface to *The Lucky Chance* (1687), our selection here. In both these texts, Behn analyzed her situation as a woman writer who had been denied a university education and whose works were often seen as both aesthetically and morally transgressive. Rejecting "Academick frippery" in her *Dutch Lover* piece, she also pleaded, in her preface to *The Lucky Chance,* for freedom to express "my Masculine Part the Poet in me."

Reviewing Behn's career some centuries after her death, Virginia Woolf declared that "All women together ought to let flowers fall upon the tomb of Aphra Behn[,] . . . for it was she who earned them the right to speak their minds." But in her own time this pioneering and rebellious author was considered rather a "shady lady." The epitaph that appears on her tomb has been attributed to a former lover, John Hoyle, and instead of celebrating her eternal genius it comments bleakly on the fate of her satiric intelligence: "Here lies proof that wit can never be / Defence enough against mortality."

Preface to *The Lucky Chance*

The little Obligation I have to some of the witty Sparks[1] and Poets of the Town, has put me on a Vindication of this Comedy from those Censures that Malice, and ill Nature have thrown upon it, tho in vain: The Poets, I heartily excuse, since there is a sort of Self-Interest in their Malice, which I shou'd rather call a witty Way they have in this Age, of Railing at every thing they find

1. Fops.

with pain successful, and never to shew good Nature and speak well of any thing; but when they are sure 'tis damn'd, then they afford it that worse Scandal, their Pity. And nothing makes them so thorough-stitcht an Enemy as a full Third Day,[2] that's Crime enough to load it with all manner of infamy; and when they can no other way prevail with the Town, they charge it with the old never failing Scandal—That 'tis not fit for the Ladys: As if (if it were as they falsly give it out) the Ladys were oblig'd to hear Indecencys only from their Pens and Plays, and some of them have ventur'd to treat 'em as Coursely as 'twas possible, without the least Reproach from them; and in some of their most Celebrated Plays have entertained 'em with things, that if I should here strip from their Wit and Occasion that conducts 'em in and makes them proper, their fair Cheeks would perhaps wear a natural Colour at the reading them: yet are never taken Notice of because a Man writ them, and they may hear that from them, they blush at from a Woman—But I make a Challenge to any Person of common Sense and Reason—that is not wilfully bent on ill Nature, and will in spight of Sense wrest a double Entendre from every thing, lying upon the Catch for a Jest or a Quibble, like a Rook for a Cully;[3] but any inprejudic'd Person that knows not the Author, to read any of my Comedys and compare 'em with others of this Age, and if they find one Word that can offend the chastest Ear, I will submit to all their peevish Cavills; but Right or Wrong they must be Criminal because a Woman's; condemning them without having the Christian Charity, to examine whether it be guilty or not, with reading, comparing, or thinking; the Ladies taking up any Scandal on Trust from some conceited Sparks, who will in spight of Nature be Wits and Beaus; then scatter it for Authentick all over the Town and Court, poysoning of others Judgments with their false Notions, condemning it to worse than Death, Loss of Fame. And to fortifie their Detraction, charge me with all the Plays that have ever been offensive; though I wish with all their Faults I had been the Author of some of those they have honour'd me with.

For the farther Justification of this Play; it being a Comedy of Intrigue, Dr. Davenought[4] out of Respect to the Commands he had from Court, to take great Care that no Indecency should be in Plays, sent for it and nicely look't it over, putting out any thing he but imagin'd the Criticks would play with. After that, Sir Roger L'Estrange[5] read it and licens'd it, and found no such Faults as 'tis charg'd with: Then Mr. Killigrew,[6] who more severe than any, from the strict Order he had, perus'd it with great Circumspection; and lastly the Master Players, who you will I hope in some Measure esteem Judges of Decency and their own interest, having been so many Years Prentice to the Trade of Judging.

I say, after all these Supervisors the Ladys may be convinc'd, they left nothing that cou'd offend, and the Men of their unjust Reflections on so many Judges of Wit and Decencys. When it happens that I challenge any one, to point me out the least Expression of what some have made their Discourse, they cry, That Mr. Leigh[7] opens his Night Gown, when he comes into the Bride-chamber; if he do, which is a jest of his own making, and which I never saw, I hope he has his Cloaths on underneath? And if so, where is the Inde-

2. I.e., a full house on a play's third night, the profits of which went to the playwright.
3. A swindler for a dupe. "Quibble": a pun.
4. I.e., Devanant, co-manager of the United Company, whose Theatre Royal staged *The Lucky Chance*.
5. The English surveyor of printing presses and licenser of published works (1663–88).
6. Charles Killigrew, co-manager of the United Company.
7. Anthony Leigh, a leading actor of Restoration theater.

cency? I have seen in that admirable Play of Oedipus,[8] the Gown open'd wide, and the Man shown in his Drawers and Waistcoat, and never thought it an Offence before. Another crys, Why we know not what they mean, when the Man takes a Woman off the Stage, and another is thereby cuckolded; is that any more than you see in the most Celebrated of your Plays? as the City Politicks, the Lady Mayoress, and the Old Lawyers Wife,[9] who goes with a Man she never saw before, and comes out again the joyfull'st Women alive, for having made her Husband a Cuckold with such Dexterity, and yet I see nothing unnatural nor obscene: 'tis proper for the Characters. So in that lucky Play of the London Cuckolds,[1] not to recite Particulars. And in that good Comedy of Sir Courtly Nice,[2] the Taylor to the young Lady—in the fam'd Sir Fopling Dorimont and Bellinda, see the very Words—in Valentianian,[3] see the Scene between the Court Bawds. And Valentianian all loose and ruffl'd a Moment after the Rape, and all this you see without scandal, and a thousand others. The Moor of Venice in many places. The Maids Tragedy[4]—see the Scene of undressing the Bride, and between the King and Amintor, and after between the King and Evadne—All these I Name as some of the best Plays I know; If I should repeat the Words exprest in these Scenes I mention, I might justly be charg'd with course ill Manners, and very little Modesty, and yet they so naturally fall into the places they are designed for, and so are proper for the Business, that there is not the least Fault to be found with them; though I say those things in any of mine wou'd damn the whole Peice, and alarm the Town. Had I a Day or two's time, as I have scarce so many Hours to write this in (the Play, being all printed off and the Press waiting,) I would sum up all your Beloved Plays, and all the things in them that are past with such Silence by; because written by Men: such Masculine Strokes in me, must not be allow'd. I must conclude those Women (if there be any such) greater Criticks in that sort of Conversation than my self, who find any of that sort in mine, or any thing that can justly be reproach't. But 'tis in vain by dint of Reason or Comparison to consider the Obstinate Criticks, whose Business is to find Fault, if not by a loose and gross Imagination to create them, for they must either find the Jest, or make it; and those of this sort fall to my share, they find Faults of another kind for the Men Writers. And this one thing I will venture to say, though against my Nature, because it has a Vanity in it; That had the Plays I have writ come forth under any Mans Name, and never known to have been mine; I appeal to all unbyast Judges of Sense, if they had not said that Person had made as many good Comedies, as any one Man that has writ in our Age; but a Devil on't the Woman damns the Poet.

Ladies, for its further Justification to you, be pleas'd to know, that the first Copy of this Play was read by several Ladys of very great Quality, and unquestioned Fame, and received their most favorable Opinion, not one charging it

---

8. *Oedipus* (1678), a play by John Dryden and Nathaniel Lee.
9. Characters in John Crowne's *City Politiques* (1683).
1. Edward Ravenscroft's *The London Cuckolds* (1681).
2. John Crowne's *Sir Courtly Nice, or It Cannot Be* (1685).
3. Francis Beaumont and John Fletcher's *Valentinian* (ca. 1612), in which Lucina is raped by the Roman emperor Valentinian. Sir Fopling, Dorimant, and Belinda are characters in Sir George Etherege's *The Man of Mode; or, Sir Fopling Flutter* (1676).
4. Beaumont and Fletcher's *The Maid's Tragedy* (ca. 1611), whose protagonist, Amintor, is ordered by the king to marry Evadne on his wedding night that Evadne is the king's mistress and refuses to consummate the marriage. "The Moor of Venice": i.e., Shakespeare's *Othello*.

with the Crime, that some have been pleas'd to find in the Acting. Other Ladys who saw it more than once, whose Quality and Vertue can sufficiently justifie any thing they design to favour, were pleas'd to say, they found an Entertainment in it very far from scandalous; and for the Generality of the Town; I found by my Receipts it was not thought so Criminal. However, that shall not be an Incouragement to me to trouble the Criticks with new Occasion of affronting me, for endeavouring at least to divert; and at this rate, both the few Poets that are left, and the Players who toil in vain, will be weary of their Trade.

I cannot omit to tell you, that a Wit of the Town, a Friend of mine at Wills Coffee House, the first Night of the Play, cry'd it down as much as in him lay, who before had read it and assured me he never saw a prettier Comedy. So complaisant one pestilent Wit will be to another, and in the full Cry make his Noise too; but since 'tis to the witty Few I speak, I hope the better Judges will take no Offence, to whom I am oblig'd for better Judgments; and those I hope will be so kind to me, knowing my Conversation not at all addicted to the Indecencys alledged, that I would much less practice it in a Play, that must stand the Test of the censuring World. And I must want common Sense, and all the Degrees of good Manners, renouncing my Fame, all Modesty and Interest for a silly Sawcy fruitless Jest, to make Fools laugh, and Women blush, and wise Men asham'd; My self all the while, if I had been guilty of this Crime charg'd to me, remaining the only stupid, insensible. Is this likely, is this reasonable to be believ'd by any body, but the wilfully blind? All I ask is the Priviledge for my Masculine Part the Poet in me, (if any such you will allow me) to tread in those successful Paths my Predecessors have so long thriv'd in, to take those Measures that both the Ancient and Modern Writers have set me, and by which they have pleas'd the World so well. If I must not, because of my Sex, have this Freedom, but that you will usurp all to your selves; I lay down my Quill, and you shall hear no more of me, no not so much as to make Comparisons, because I will be kinder to my Brothers of the Pen, than they have been to a defenceless Woman; for I am not content to write for a Third day only. I value Fame as much as if I had been born a Hero; and if you rob me of that, I can retire from the ungrateful World, and scorn its fickle Favours.

1687

MARY ASTELL
1666–1731

One of the first feminists in England to gain success as what we would today call a "public intellectual," Mary Astell was born to a prosperous middle-class coal merchant family in Newcastle and may have been educated privately by a clergyman uncle. Orphaned at eighteen, she journeyed to London, possibly in the hope of earning her living by her pen, although (except for the scandalous example of Aphra Behn) there was little precedent for a woman to have a productive literary career. Once settled in the capital, Astell gained the patronage of well-placed churchmen and aristocrats, among them William Sancroft, archbishop of Canterbury, and the learned Lady Mary Wortley Montague. Perhaps because of such support, her first major publication, *A Serious Proposal to the Ladies* (1694), was a striking success, going through four editions by 1701 and gaining her an admiring readership.

Astell's "proposal"—a vision of "a religious retirement" or female "monastery" in which women could "expel that cloud of ignorance which custom has involved us in [and] furnish our minds with a stock of solid and useful knowledge"—summarized the idealistic projects to which she dedicated her life and work. Since "God has given women as well as men intelligent souls, why should they be forbidden to improve them?" she wondered. She pursued the implications of this question in such other writings as her letters to the Cambridge Platonist John Norris, eventually published as *Letters Concerning the Love of God* (1795), and, more radically, her *Reflections on Marriage* (1700). Our selection from *A Serious Proposal* illustrates the long-standing proto-feminist effort to strengthen women through education; our selection from an explanatory preface that she eventually added to *Reflections* demonstrates the brilliance and rigor with which she argued for a distinction between the decrees of "custom" and the "right" behaviors discernible by "reason."

From A Serious Proposal to the Ladies

[A RELIGIOUS RETIREMENT]

Now as to the proposal, it is to erect a monastery, or if you will (to avoid giving offence to the scrupulous and injudicious, by names which though innocent in themselves, have been abused by superstitious practices), we will call it a religious retirement, and such as shall have a double aspect, being not only a retreat from the world for those who desire that advantage, but likewise, an institution and previous discipline, to fit us to do the greatest good in it; such an institution as this (if I do not mightily deceive my self) would be the most probable method to amend the present, and improve the future age. * * *

You are therefore ladies, invited into a place, where you shall suffer no other confinement, but to be kept out of the road of sin: * * * Happy retreat! which will be the introducing you into such a paradise as your mother Eve forfeited, where you shall feast on pleasures, that do not, like those of the world, disappoint your expectations, pall your appetites, and by the disgust they give you put you on the fruitless search after new delights, which when obtained are as empty as the former; but such as will make you truly happy now, and prepare you to be perfectly so hereafter. Here are no serpents to deceive you, whilst you entertain your selves in these delicious gardens. No provocations will be given in this amicable society, but to love and to good works, which will afford such an entertaining employment, that you'll have as little inclination as leisure to pursue those follies, which in the time of your ignorance passed with you under the name of love, although there is not in nature two more different things, than true love and that brutish passion, which pretends to ape it. Here will be no rivalling but for the love of God, no ambition but to procure his favour, to which nothing will more effectually recommend you, than a great and dear affection to each other. * * *

One great end of this institution shall be, to expel that cloud of ignorance which custom has involved us in, to furnish our minds with a stock of solid and useful knowledge, that the souls of women may no longer be the only unadorned and neglected things. It is not intended that our religious should waste their time, and trouble their heads about such unconcerning matters, as the vogue of the world has turned up for learning, the impertinency of which has been excellently exposed by an ingenious pen,[1] but busy themselves in a serious inquiry after necessary and perfective truths, something which it concerns them to know, and which tends to their real interest and perfection, and what that is the excellent author just now mentioned will sufficiently inform them. Such a course of study will neither be too troublesome nor out of the reach of a female virtuoso;[2] for it is not intended she should spend her hours in learning words but things, and therefore no more languages than are necessary to acquaint her with useful authors. Nor need she trouble her self in turning over a great number of books, but take care to understand and digest a few well chosen and good ones. Let her but obtain right ideas, and be truly acquainted with the nature of those objects that present themselves to her mind, and then no matter whether or no she be able to tell what fanciful people have said about them: And thoroughly to understand Christianity as professed by the Church of England, will be sufficient to confirm her in the truth, though she have not a catalogue of those particular errors which oppose it. Indeed a learned education of the women will appear so unfashionable, that I began to startle at the singularity of the proposition, but was extremely pleased when I found a late ingenious author (whose book I met with since the writing of this) agree with me in my opinion.[3] For speaking of the repute that learning was in about 150 years ago, "It was so very modish," says he "that the fair sex seemed to believe that Greek and Latin added to their charms: and Plato and Aristotle untranslated, were frequent ornaments of their closets.[4] One would think by the effects, that it was a proper way of educating them, since there are no accounts in history of so many great women in any one age, as are to be found between the years 15 and 1600."

For since God has given women as well as men intelligent souls, why should they be forbidden to improve them? Since he has not denied us the faculty of thinking, why should we not (at least in gratitude to him) employ our thoughts on himself their noblest object, and not unworthily bestow them on trifles and gaieties and secular affairs? Being the soul was created for the contemplation of truth as well as for the fruition of good, is it not as cruel and unjust to exclude women from the knowledge of the one as from the enjoyment of the other? Especially since the will is blind, and cannot choose but by the direction of the understanding; or to speak more properly, since the soul always wills according as she understands, so that if she understands amiss, she wills amiss. And as exercise enlarges and exalts any faculty, so through want of using it becomes cramp and lessened; if therefore we make little or no use of our understandings, we shall shortly have none to use; and the more contracted and unemployed the deliberating and directive power is, the more liable is the elective to unworthy and mischievous choices. What is it but the want of an ingenious education, that renders the generality of

1. Astell's note cites John Norris's *Reflections upon the Conduct of Human Life with Reference to the Study of Learning and Knowledge* (1690).
2. I.e., one interested in the pursuit of knowledge.
3. Astell's note cites William Wotton's *Reflections upon Ancient and Modern Learning* (1691).
4. Private chambers, studies.

feminine conversations so insipid and foolish and their solitude so insupportable? Learning is therefore necessary to render them more agreeable and useful in company, and to furnish them with becoming entertainments when alone, that so they may not be driven to those miserable shifts,[5] which too many make use of to put off their time, that precious talent that never lies on the hands of a judicious person. And since our happiness in the next world, depends so far on those dispositions which we carry along with us out of this, that without a right habitude and temper of mind we are not capable of felicity; and seeing our beatitude consists in the contemplation of the divine truth and beauty, as well as in the fruition of his goodness, can ignorance be a fit preparative for Heaven? Is't likely that she whose understanding has been busied about nothing but froth and trifles, should be capable of delighting her self in noble and sublime truths? Let such therefore as deny us the improvement of our intellectuals, either take up his[6] Paradox, who said that women have no souls, which at a time when the most contend to have them allowed to brutes, would be as unphilosophical as it is unmannerly, or else let them permit us to cultivate and improve them. There is a sort of learning indeed which is worse than the greatest ignorance: A woman may study plays and romances all her days, and be a great deal more knowing but never a jot the wiser. Such a knowledge as this serves only to instruct and put her forward in the practice of the greatest follies, yet how can they justly blame her who forbid, or at least won't afford opportunity of better? A rational mind will be employed, it will never be satisfied in doing nothing, and if you neglect to furnish it with good materials, 'tis like to take up with such as come to hand.

We pretend not that women should teach in the church, or usurp authority where it is not allowed them; permit us only to understand our own duty, and not be forced to take it upon trust from others; to be at least so far learned, as to be able to form in our minds a true idea of Christianity, it being so very necessary to fence us against the danger of these last and perilous days, in which deceivers a part of whose character is to lead captive silly women, need not creep into houses since they have authority to proclaim their errors on the housetop. And let us also acquire a true practical knowledge, such as will convince us of the absolute necessity of holy living as well as of right believing, and that no heresy is more dangerous than that of an ungodly and wicked life. And since the French tongue is understood by most ladies, methinks they may much better improve it by the study of philosophy (as I hear the French ladies do) Descartes, Malebranche and others, than by reading idle novels and romances. 'Tis strange we shou'd be so forward to imitate their fashions and fopperies, and have no regard to what really deserves our imitation. And why shall it not be thought as genteel to understand French philosophy, as to be accoutred in a French mode? Let therefore the famous Madam D'acier, Scudery, &c, and our own incomparable Orinda,[7] excite the emulation of the English ladies.

The ladies, I'm sure, have no reason to dislike this proposal, but I know not how the men will resent it to have their enclosure broke down, and women

---

5. Expedients.
6. Perhaps the Prophet Muhammed, who was commonly thought to have claimed in the Qur'an that women lack souls.
7. Katherine Philips (1631–1664), English poet

known as "the Matchless Orinda." Anne Lefebvre Dacier and Madeleine de Scudéry were French contemporaries, a classicist and a poet and novelist, respectively.

invited to taste of that tree of knowledge they have so long unjustly monopolized. But they must excuse me, if I be as partial to my own sex as they are to theirs, and think women as capable of learning as men are, and that it becomes them as well. For I cannot imagine wherein the hurt lies, if instead of doing mischief to one another, by an uncharitable and vain conversation, women be enabled to inform and instruct those of their own sex at least; the holy ghost having left it on record, that Priscilla as well as her husband, catechized the eloquent Apollos[8] and the great Apostle found no fault with her. It will therefore be very proper for our ladies to spend part of their time in this retirement, in adorning their minds with useful knowledge.

1694

From Preface to *Some Reflections upon Marriage*

These Reflections being made in the Country, where the Book that occasion'd them came but late to Hand, the *Reader* is desir'd to excuse their Unseasonableness as well as other Faults; and to believe that they have no other Design than to Correct some Abuses, which are not the less because Power and Prescription seem to Authorize them. If any are so needlessly curious as to enquire from what Hand they come, they may please to know, that it is not good Manners to ask, since the Title-Page does not tell them: We are all of us sufficiently Vain, and without doubt the Celebrated Name of *Author*, which most are so fond of, had not been avoided but for very good Reasons: To name but one; *Who will care to pull upon themselves an Hornet's Nest?* 'Tis a very great Fault to regard rather who it is that Speaks, than what is Spoken; and either to submit to Authority, when we should only yield to Reason; or if Reason press too hard, to think to ward it off by Personal Objections and Reflections. Bold Truths may pass while the Speaker is Incognito, but are not endur'd when he is known; few Minds being strong enough to bear what Contradicts their Principles and Practices without Recriminating when they can. And tho' to tell the Truth be the most Friendly Office,[1] yet whosoever is so hardy as to venture at it, shall be counted an Enemy for so doing.

Thus far the old Advertisement, when the Reflections first appear'd, A.D. 1700.[2]

But the *Reflector*, who hopes *Reflector* is not bad English, now Governor is happily of the feminine Gender,[3] had as good or better have said nothing; For People by being forbid, are only excited to a more curious Enquiry. A certain Ingenuous Gentleman (as she is inform'd) had the Good-Nature to own these Reflections, so far as to affirm that he had the Original M.S. in his Closet, a Proof she is not able to produce; and so to make himself responsible for all their Faults, for which she returns him all due Acknowledgment. However, the Generality being of Opinion, that a Man would have had more Prudence and Manners than to have Publish'd such unseasonable Truths, or to have betray'd the *Arcana Imperii*[4] of his Sex, she humbly confesses, that

---

8. See Acts 18.24–26.
1. Duty.
2. Astell did not add this preface until the 3rd edition (1706).

3. In Latin, the ending *-or* is masculine in grammatical gender.
4. Secrets of supreme command or authority (Latin).

the Contrivance and Execution of this Design, which is unfortunately accus'd of being so destructive to the Government, of the Men I mean, is entirely her own. She neither advis'd with Friends, nor turn'd over Antient or Modern Authors, nor prudently submitted to the Correction of such as are, or such as *think* they are good Judges, but with an *English* Spirit and Genius, set out upon the Forlorn Hope, meaning no hurt to any body, nor designing any thing but the Publick Good, and to retrieve, if possible, the Native Liberty, the Rights and Privileges of the Subject.

Far be it from her to stir up Sedition of any sort, none can abhor it more; and she heartily wishes that our Masters wou'd pay their Civil and Ecclesiastical Governors the same Submission, which they themselves extract from their Domestic Subjects. Nor can she imagine how she any way undermines the Masculine Empire, or blows the Trumpet of Rebellion to the Moiety of Mankind. Is it by exhorting Women, not to expect to have their own Will in any thing, but to be entirely Submissive, when once they have made choice of a Lord and Master, tho' he happen not to be so Wise, so Kind, or even so Just a Governor as was expected? She did not indeed advise them to think his Folly Wisdom, nor his Brutality that Love and Worship he promised in his Matrimonial Oath, for this required a Flight of Wit and Sense much above her poor Ability, and proper only to Masculine Understandings. However she did not in any manner prompt them to Resist, or to Abdicate the Perjur'd Spouse, tho' the Laws of GOD and the Land make special Provision for it, in a case wherein, as is to be fear'd, few Men can truly plead Not Guilty.

Tis true, thro' Want of Learning, and of that Superior Genius which Men as Men lay claim to, she was ignorant of the *Natural Inferiority* of our Sex, which our Masters lay down as a Self-Evident and Fundamental Truth. She saw nothing in the Reason of Things, to make this either a Principle or a Conclusion, but much to the contrary; it being Sedition at least, if not Treason to assert it in this Reign. For if by the Natural Superiority of their Sex, they mean that every Man is by Nature superior to every Woman, which is the obvious meaning, and that which must be stuck to if they would speak Sense, it wou'd be a Sin in *any* Woman to have Dominion over *any* Man, and the greatest Queen ought not to command but to obey her Footman, because no Municipal Laws can supersede or change the Law of Nature; so that if the Dominion of the Men be such, the *Salique Law*,[5] as unjust as *English Men* have ever thought it, ought to take place over all the Earth, and the most glorious Reigns in the *English, Danish, Castilian,* and other Annals, were wicked Violations of the Law of Nature!

If they mean that *some* Men are superior to *some* Women, this is no great Discovery; had they turn'd the Tables they might have seen that *some* Women are Superior to *some* Men. Or had they been pleased to remember their Oaths of Allegiance and Supremacy, they might have known that *One* Woman[6] is superior to *All* the Men in these Nations, or else they have sworn to very little purpose. And it must not be suppos'd, that their Reason and Religion wou'd suffer them to take Oaths, contrary to the Law of Nature and Reason of things.

By all which it appears, that our Reflector's Ignorance is very pitiable, it may be her Misfortune but not her Crime, especially since she is willing to

---

5. The code forbidding female succession to titles or offices (now spelled "Salic").

6. Queen Anne (1665–1714), who assumed the throne in Great Britain in 1702.

be better inform'd, and hopes she shall never be so obstinate as to shut her Eyes against the Light of Truth, which is not to be charg'd with Novelty, how late soever we may be bless'd with the Discovery. Nor can Error, be it as Antient as it may, ever plead Prescription against Truth. And since the only way to remove all Doubts, to answer all Objections, and to give the Mind entire Satisfaction, is not by *Affirming*, but by *Proving*, so that every one may see with their *own* Eyes, and Judge according to the best of their *own* Understandings, She hopes it is no Presumption to insist on this Natural Right of Judging for her self, and the rather, because by quitting it, we give up all the Means of Rational Conviction. Allow us then as many Glasses as you please to help our Sight, and as many good Arguments as you can afford to Convince our Understandings: But don't exact of us we beseech you, to affirm that we see such things as are only the Discovery of Men who have quicker Senses; or that we understand and Know what we have by Hearsay only, for to be so excessively Complaisant, is neither to see nor to understand.

That the Custom of the World has put Women, generally speaking, into a State of Subjection, is not deny'd; but the Right can no more be prov'd from the Fact, than the Predominancy of Vice can justifie it. A certain great Man has endeavour'd to prove by Reasons not contemptible, that in the Original State of things the Woman was the Superior, and that her Subjection to the Man is an Effect of the Fall, and the Punishment of her Sin. And that Ingenious Theorist Mr *Whiston*[7] asserts, That before the Fall there was a greater equality between the two Sexes. However this be 'tis certainly no Arrogance in a Woman to conclude, that she was made for the Service of GOD, and that this is her End. Because GOD made all Things for Himself, and a Rational Mind is too noble a Being to be Made for the Sake and Service of any Creature.

*   *   *

1700, 1706

7. William Whiston (1667–1752), English theologian and mathematician.

ANNE FINCH, COUNTESS OF WINCHILSEA
1661–1720

When the former Anne Kingsmill, once a lady-in-waiting to Mary Modena, duchess of York, took the radical step of publishing a volume of her verse, she prefaced the book with a poem that offered a notably melancholy prophecy about the critical reception she expected: "Alas! a woman that attempts the pen / Such an intruder on the rights of men, / Such a presumptuous creature is esteemed, / The fault can by no virtue be redeemed." Yet although, as the scholar Cora Kaplan has noted, Finch had indeed become "a prime butt for anti-'bluestocking' jokes on the stage and in verse," she had also earned a considerable share of the approbation her talent deserved. During her years at court she met and married the aristocratic Heneage Finch, a "gentleman of the bedchamber," and he warmly supported her work throughout her lifetime. After her death he carefully transcribed and preserved her unpublished manuscripts, affirming in an obituary that she was "a fine Writer and an excellent Poet." In addition, when Heneage had inherited the earldom of Winchilsea upon the death of a distant relative, the couple had become the center of a literary circle in which Anne's poems were circulated and admired.

Nonetheless, this ambitious poet had clearly been traumatized by "jokes" that some men of letters made at her expense. Even her supposed friend Alexander Pope had, after all, caricatured her (in a play he coauthored with John Gay and John Arbuthnot) as a mad poetess named "Phoebe Clinket," so when she took the radical step of putting her poetry into print she was justifiably wary. Our selection here is a prose apologia with which she prefaced the group of poems that she gathered in 1702 and eventually published in 1713. In it she anxiously explains that she experiences verse writing as a kind of troublesome compulsion ("I have writt, and expos'd my uncorrect Rimes, and immediatly repented; and yett have writt again"), though she was "not so far abandon'd by my prudence . . . to lett any attempts of mine in Poetry, shew themselves whilst I liv'd in such a publick place as the Court, where every one wou'd have made their remarks upon a Versifying Maid of Honour." Nevertheless, comparing herself to Katherine Philips, a poet who gained fame a generation earlier as the "Matchless Orinda," Finch makes her literary aspirations quite plain even while she defines poetry itself as merely a pastime or "play."

The Preface

Beaumont in the beginni[n]g of a Coppy of Verses to his freind Fletcher (upon the ill successe of his Faithfull Shepheardesse[1]) tells him,

> I know too well! that no more, then the man
> That travells throo' the burning Deserts, can
> When he is beaten with the raging Sun,
> Half smother'd in the dust, have power to run
> From a cool River, which himself doth find,
> E're he be slack'd; no more can he, whose mind
>   Joys in the Muses, hold from that delight,
>   When Nature, and his full thoughts, bid him write.

And this indeed, I not only find true by my own experience, but have also too many wittnesses of itt against me, under my own hand in the following Poems; which tho' never meritting more then to be once read, and then carlessly scatter'd or consum'd; are grown by the partiality of some of my freinds, to the formidable appearance of a Volume; tho' but in Manuscript, and have been solicited to a more daring manefestation, which I shall ever resist, both from the knowledge of their incapassity, of bearing a publick tryal; and also, upon recalling to my memory, some of the first lines I ever writt, which were part of an invocation of Apollo, whose wise and limitted answer to me, I did there suppose to be

> I grant thee no pretence to Bays,
>   Nor in bold print do thou appear.
> Nor shalt thou reatch Orinda's[2] prayse,
>   Tho' all thy aim, be fixt on Her.

---

1. John Fletcher's pastoral tragicomedy (ca. 1608); after its unsuccessful staging, it appeared in print, prefaced by laudatory verses by other playwrights, including Fletcher's sometime coauthor Francis Beaumont.

2. Katherine Philips (1632–1664), known to her contemporaries as "the Matchless Orinda," from the neoclassical pseudonym she used in her poems. "Bays": i.e., the laurel crown awarded to the victor in contests of poetry.

And tho' I have still avoided the confident producing anything of mine in thatt manner, yett have I come too neer itt, and been like those imperfect penitents, who are ever relenting, and yett ever returning to the same offences. For I have writt, and expos'd my uncorrect Rimes, and immediatly repented; and yett have writt again, and again suffer'd them to be seen; tho' att the expence of more uneasy reflections, till at last (like them) wearied with uncertainty, and irresolution, I rather chuse to be harden'd in an errour, then to be still att the trouble of endeavering to over come itt: and now, neither deny myself the pleasure of writing, or any longer make a mistery of that to my friends and acquaintance, which does so little deserve itt; tho' itt is still a great satisfaction to me, that I was not so far abandon'd by my prudence, as out of a mistaken vanity, to lett any attempts of mine in Poetry, shew themselves whilst I liv'd in such a publick place as the Court, where every one wou'd have made their remarks upon a Versifying Maid of Honour; and far the greater number with prejudice, if not contempt. And indeed, the apprehension of this, had so much wean'd me from the practice and inclination to itt; that had nott an utter change in my Condition, and Circumstances, remov'd me into the solitude, & security of the Country, and the generous kindnesse of one that possest the most delightfull seat in itt;[3] envited him, from whom I was inseparable, to partake of the pleasures of itt, I think I might have stopp'd ere it was too late, and suffer'd those few compositions I had then by me, to have sunk into that oblivion, which I ought to wish might be the lott of all that have succeeded them. But when I came to Eastwell, and cou'd fix my eyes only upon objects naturally inspiring soft and Poeticall immaginations, and found the Owner of itt, so indulgent to that Art, so knowing in all the rules of itt, and att his pleasure, so capable of putting them in practice; and also most obligingly favorable to some lines of mine, that had fall'n under his Lordship's perusal, I cou'd no longer keep within the limmitts I had prescrib'd myself, nor be wisely reserv'd, in spite of inclination, and such powerfull temptations to the contrary. Again I engage my self in the service of the Muses, as eagerly as if

> From their new Worlds, I know not where,
> Their golden Indies in the air—[4]

they cou'd have supply'd the material losses, which I had lately sustain'd in this. And now, whenever I contemplate all the several beautys of this Park, allow'd to be (if not of the Universal yett) of our British World infinitely the finest,

> A pleasing wonder throo' my fancy moves,
> Smooth as her lawnes, and lofty as her Groves.
> Boundlesse my Genius seems, when my free sight,
> Finds only distant skys to stop her flight.
> Like mighty Denhams, then, methinks my hand,
> Might bid the Landskip, in strong numbers stand,
> Fix all itts charms, with a Poetick skill,
> And raise itts Fame, above his Cooper's hill.[5]

---

3. The nephew of Finch's husband invited them to live on the family estate at Eastwell, in Kent.
4. Slightly misquoted from Abraham Cowley's "The Complaint" (1663).
5. This fragment by Finch appears to be an imitation of John Denham's Coopers Hill (1642).

This, I confesse, is whatt in itts self itt deserves, but the unhappy difference is, that he by being a real Poet, cou'd make that place (as he sais) a Parnassus to him; whilst I, that behold a real Parnassus here, in that lovely Hill, which in this Park bears that name, find in my self, so little of the Poet, that I am still restrain'd from attempting a description of itt in verse, tho' the agreeablenesse of the subject, has often prompted me most strongly to itt.

But now, having pleaded an irresistable impulse, as my excuse for writing, which was the cheif design of this Preface, I must also expresse my hopes of excaping all suspition of vanity, or affectation of applause from itt; since I have in my introduction, deliver'd my sincere opinion that when a Woman meddles with things of this nature,

> So strong, th' opposing faction still appears,
> The hopes to thrive, can ne're outweigh the fears.[6]

And, I am besides sensible, that Poetry has been of late so explain'd, the laws of itt being putt into familiar languages, that even those of my sex, (if they will be so presumptuous as to write) are very accountable for their transgressions against them. For what rule of Aristotle, or Horace is there, that has not been given us by Rapin, Despreaux, D'acier, my Lord Roscomon, etc.? What has Mr. Dryden omitted,[7] that may lay open the very misteries of this Art? and can there any where be found a more delightsome, or more usefull piece of Poetry, then that,

> correct Essay,
> Which so repairs, our old Horatian way.[8]

If then, after the perusal of these, we fail, we cannott plead any want, but that of capacity, or care, in both of which I own myself so very defective, y^t whenever any things of mine, escape a censure, I allways attribute itt, to the good nature or civility of the Reader; and not to any meritt in the Poems, which I am satisfy'd are so very imperfect, and uncorrect, that I shall not attempt their justifycation.

For the subjects, I hope they are att least innofensive; tho' sometimes of Love; for keeping within those limmitts which I have observ'd, I know not why itt shou'd be more faulty, to treat of that passion, then of any other violent excursion, or transport of the mind. Tho' I must confesse, the great reservednesse of Mrs. Philips in this particular, and the prayses I have heard given her upon that account, together with my desire not to give scandal to the most severe, has often discourag'd me from making use of itt, and given me some regrett for what I had writt of that kind, and wholy prevented me from putting the Aminta of Tasso[9] into English verse, from the verbal translation that I procured out of the Italian, after I had finish'd

---

6. Finch's "The Introduction" (1713), ll. 57–58.
7. In *An Essay of Dramatic Poesy* (1668; rev. 1684). René Rapin wrote reflections on Aristotle's *Poetics* (1674), Nicholas Boileau Despréaux wrote one of the definitive treatises on classical French verse (1674), and Andre Dacier and Wentworth Dillon, 4th earl of Roscommon, translated Aristotle's

treatise and Horace's *Art of Poetry*.
8. Slightly misquoted from Roscommon, *An Essay on Translated Verse* (1684).
9. The pastoral drama *Aminta* (1573), by the Italian poet Torquato Tasso. Finch's 1713 volume includes "Five Pieces out of the Aminta of Tasso."

the first act extreamly to my satisfaction; and was convinc'd, that in the original, itt must be as soft and full of beautys, as ever anything of that nature was; but there being nothing mixt with itt, of a serious morality, or usefullnesse, I sacrafis'd the pleasure I took in itt, to the more sollid reasonings of my own mind; and hope by so doing to have made an attonement, to my gravest readers, for the two short pieces of that Pastoral, taken from the French, the Songs, and other few lighter things, which yett remain in the following sheetts.

As to Lampoons, and all sorts of abusive verses, I ever so much detested, both the underhand dealing and uncharitablenesse which accompanys them, that I never suffer'd my small talent, to be that way employ'd; tho' the facility of doing itt, is too well known to many, who can but make two words rime; and there wants not some provocation often, either from one's own resentments, or those of others, to put such upon itt, as are any way capable of that mean sort of revenge. The only coppy of mine that tends towards this, is the letter to Ephelia, in answer to an invitation to the Town;[1] but, as that appears to have been long written, by the mention made of my Lord Roscommon, under the name of Piso, given to him first, in a Panegerick, of Mr. Wallers, before his Art of Poetry;[2] so I do declare, that att the time of composing itt, there was no particular person meant by any of the disadvantageous Caracters; and the whole intention of itt, was in general to expose the Censorious humour, foppishnesse and coquetterie that then prevail'd. And I am so far from thinking there is any ill in this, that I wish itt oftener done, by such hands as might sufficiently ridicule, and wean us from those mistakes in our manners, and conversation.

Plays, were translated by our most vertuous Orinda; and mine, tho' originals, I hope are not lesse reserv'd. The Queen of Cyprus, I once thought to have call'd the Triumphs of Love and Innocence; and doubted not but the latter part of the Title, wou'd have been as aptly apply'd as the former. Aristomenes is wholy Tragicall, and, if itt answer my intention, moral and inciting to Vertue.[3] What they are as to the performance, I leave to the judgment of those who shall read them; and if any one can find more faults then I think to be in y^m; I am much mistaken. I will only add, that when they were compos'd, itt was far from my intention ever to own them, the first was for my own private satisfaction, only an Essay wheither I cou'd go throo' with such a peice of Poetry. The other, I was led to, by the strong impressions, which some wonderfull circumstances in the life of Aristomenes, made upon my fancy; and cheifly the sweetnesse of his temper, observable in itt, wrought upon me; for which reason tho' itt may be I did not so Poetically, I chose rather to represent him Good, then Great; and pitch'd upon such parts of the relation, and introduc'd such additional circumstances of my own, as might most illustrate that, and shew him to be (as declared by the Oracle) the best of Men. I know not what effect they will have upon others, but I must acknowledge, that the giving some interruption to those melancholy thoughts, which posesst me,

1. "Ardelia's Answer to Ephelia."
2. I.e., Roscommon's translation of *The Art of Poetry* (1684). In praise of it, Edmund Waller wrote "Upon the Earl of Roscommon's Translation of Horace" (1684).
3. *Aristomenes* is included in the 1713 collection; *The Queen of Cyprus* is not.

not only for my own, but much more for the misfortunes of those to whom I owe all immaginable duty, and gratitude, was so great a benefitt; that I have reason to be satisfy'd with the undertaking, be the performance never so inconsiderable. And indeed, an absolute solitude (which often was my lott) under such dejection of mind, cou'd not have been supported, had I indulg'd myself (as was too natural to me) only in the contemplation of present and real afflictions, which I hope will plead my excuse, for turning them for relief, upon such as were immaginary, & relating to Persons no more in being. I had my end in the writing, and if they please not those who will take the pains to peruse them, itt will be a just accusation to my weaknesse, for letting them escape out of their concealment; but if attended with a better successe, the satisfaction any freind of mine, may take in them, will make me think my time past, not so unprofitably bestowed, as otherwise I might; and which I shall now endeavour to redeem, by applying myself to better employments, and when I do write to chuse, my subjects generally out of Devinity, or from moral and serious occasions; which made me place them last, as capable of addi-tion; For when we have run throo' all the amusements of life, itt will be found, that there is but one thing necessary; and they only Wise, who chuse the bet-ter part. But since there must be also, some relaxation, some entertaining of the spiritts,

> Whilst Life by Fate is lent to me,
> Whilst here below, I stay,
> Religion, my sole businesse be,
> And Poetry, my play.

ca. 1702   1713

FRANCES BURNEY
1752–1840

The popular novelist Frances (Fanny) Burney is widely credited with having helped establish a new genre, the novel of manners, in which such successors as Jane Austen and Maria Edgeworth would achieve so many triumphs. Burney's first book, the epis-tolary fiction *Evelina; or, The History of a Young Lady's Entrance into the World* (1778), published anonymously when she was twenty-six, was itself a triumph, gaining her such friends and admirers as Samuel Johnson, Sir Joshua Reynolds, Richard Sheri-dan, and Edmund Burke. The daughter of Dr. Charles Burney, a prominent musicol-ogist, Burney had little formal education but had been raised in a cultivated and worldly household where her talent was fostered not only by her father but by his friend Samuel Crisp, who became a second "daddy" to her. As one commentator puts it, her "father's drawing-room, where she met many of the chief musicians, actors and authors of the day, was Frances' only school, but he had a huge library." After the strik-ing success of *Evelina*, Burney was to publish several more novels—most notably *Cecilia; or, Memoirs of an Heiress* (1782) and *Camilla; or, A Picture of Youth* (1796)—

which also offered high-spirited analyses of manners, morals, and the problems of women. In 1793 she married a French exile, General Alexandre D'Arblay, to whom she bore a son in 1794.

Throughout her career, Burney kept a lively diary in which she recorded social scenes and settings with the same verve that marked her fiction. Her gift for observation of the quotidian served her in all her writings, and it was a gift whose nature she understood. Keenly aware of the novel's "inferior rank" in the "republic of letters," in the preface to *Evelina* she defends her chosen genre by noting that her book would not transport readers "to the fantastic regions of Romance" but rather offer a portrait "of Nature in her simplest attire."

Preface to *Evelina*

In the republic of letters, there is no member of such inferior rank, or who is so much disdained by his brethren of the quill, as the humble Novelist: nor is his fate less hard in the world at large, since, among the whole class of writers, perhaps not one can be named of which the votaries are more numerous but less respectable.

Yet, while in the annals of those few of our predecessors, to whom this species of writing is indebted for being saved from contempt, and rescued from depravity, we can trace such names as Rousseau, Johnson,[1] Marivaux, Fielding, Richardson, and Smollet, no man need blush at starting from the same post, though many, nay, most men, may sigh at finding themselves distanced.

The following letters are presented to the public—for such, by novel writers, novel readers will be called,—with a very singular mixture of timidity and confidence, resulting from the peculiar situation of the editor; who, though trembling for their success from a consciousness of their imperfections, yet fears not being involved in their disgrace, while happily wrapped up in a mantle of impenetrable obscurity.

To draw characters from nature, though not from life, and to mark the manners of the times, is the attempted plan of the following letters. For this purpose, a young female, educated in the most secluded retirement, makes, at the age of seventeen, her first appearance upon the great and busy stage of life; with a virtuous mind, a cultivated understanding, and a feeling heart, her ignorance of the forms, and inexperience in the manners, of the world, occasion all the little incidents which these volumes record, and which form the natural progression of the life of a young woman of obscure birth, but conspicuous beauty, for the first six months after her *Entrance* into the world.

Perhaps were it possible to effect the total extirpation of novels, our young ladies in general, and boarding-school damsels in particular, might profit from their annihilation: but since the distemper they have spread seems incurable, since their contagion bids defiance to the medicine of advice or reprehension, and since they are found to baffle all the mental art of physic, save what is prescribed by the slow regimen of Time, and bitter diet of Expe-

1. However superior the capacities in which these great writers deserve to be considered, they must pardon me that, for the dignity of my subject, I here rank the authors of Rasselas and Eloise as Novelists [Burney's note]. Jean-Jacques Rousseau, author of *La nouvelle Héloise, ou Julie* (1761), is better known as social theorist; Samuel Johnson, author of *The History of Rasselas, Prince of Abyssinia* (1759), as an essayist and lexicographer. All the men named here are 17th-century writers.

rience, surely all attempts to contribute to the number of those which may be read, if not with advantage, at least without injury, ought rather to be encouraged than contemned.

Let me, therefore, prepare for disappointment those who, in the perusal of these sheets, entertain the gentle expectation of being transported to the fantastic regions of Romance, where Fiction is coloured by all the gay tints of luxurious Imagination, where Reason is an outcast, and where the sublimity of the *Marvellous*, rejects all aid from sober Probability. The heroine of these memoirs, young, artless, and inexperienced, is

No faultless Monster that the world ne'er saw,[2]

but the offspring of Nature, and of Nature in her simplest attire.

In all the Arts, the value of copies can only be proportioned to the scarceness of originals: among sculptors and painters, a fine statue, or a beautiful picture, of some great master, may deservedly employ the imitative talents of younger and inferior artists, that their appropriation to one spot, may not wholly prevent the more general expansion of their excellence; but, among authors, the reverse is the case, since the noblest productions of literature are almost equally attainable with the meanest. In books, therefore, imitation cannot be shunned too sedulously; for the very perfection of a model which is frequently seen, serves but more forcibly to mark the inferiority of a copy.

To avoid what is common, without adopting what is unnatural, must limit the ambition of the vulgar herd of authors: however zealous, therefore, my veneration of the great writers I have mentioned, however I may feel myself enlightened by the knowledge of Johnson, charmed with the eloquence of Rousseau, softened by the pathetic powers of Richardson, and exhilarated by the wit of Fielding, and humour of Smollet, I yet presume not to attempt pursuing the same ground which they have tracked; whence, though they may have cleared the weeds, they have also culled the flowers, and though they have rendered the path plain, they have left it barren.

The candour of my readers, I have not the impertinence to doubt, and to their indulgence I am sensible I have no claim: I have, therefore, only to entreat, that my own words may not pronounce my condemnation, and that what I have here ventured to say in regard to imitation, may be understood, as it is meant, in a general sense, and not be imputed to an opinion of my own originality, which I have not the vanity, the folly, or the blindness, to entertain.

Whatever may be the fate of these letters, the editor is satisfied they will meet with justice; and commits them to the press, though hopeless of fame, yet not regardless of censure.

1778

---

2. In *An Essay on Poetry* (1682), John Sheffield, duke of Buckingham, calls a perfect character "A faultless monster which the world ne'er saw."

MARY WOLLSTONECRAFT
1759–1797

A "hyena in petticoats" and a "philosophical wanton"—these are only two of the splenetic epithets with which the impassioned, influential, and energetic feminist Mary Wollstonecraft was attacked after her death at thirty-six from childbed fever. Most famous as the author of the powerful polemic titled *A Vindication of the Rights of Woman* (1792), Wollstonecraft also produced a number of other political and historical works, including *A Vindication of the Rights of Men* (1790), *A Historical and Moral View of the Origin and Progress of the French Revolution* (1794), and *Letters Written during a Short Residence in Sweden, Norway, and Denmark* (1796), as well as the novels *Mary, a Fiction* (1788) and the unfinished, posthumously published *Maria; or, The Wrongs of Woman* (1798). Raised in an unhappy and impoverished household—her alcoholic father regularly abused her passive, submissive mother—Wollstonecraft had broken away from her family at nineteen, seeking to earn her living as a lady's companion or a governess. In 1787, however, she began supporting herself as an essayist and translator, and by the end of the decade she had become a professional writer. All the books she subsequently published were infused with the revolutionary fervor of the age that shaped her short but fiery career.

Wollstonecraft's circle of associates included the poet William Blake, the political theorist Tom Paine, the painter Henry Fuseli, the American adventurer Gilbert Imlay, and—eventually most important—the philosopher and novelist William Godwin, whom she married in 1797, not long before she died. The child who was born of the union between these two major intellectuals, Mary Wollstonecraft Godwin Shelley, would go on to write one of the most riveting novels of the nineteenth century: *Frankenstein* (1818). And it was Godwin's grief-stricken *Memoirs of the Author of A Vindication of the Rights of Woman* (1798) that elicited such opprobrium from a public scandalized by the sexual freedom that had marked her life as well as by the rebellious feminism of her thought.

While Wollstonecraft's famous *Vindication of the Rights of Woman* meditates at length on the social and cultural damage caused by the miseducation of young girls, by their addiction to the reading of sentimental romances, and by the misogynistic images of women perpetuated in, for instance, Milton's *Paradise Lost,* our other selections here also reveal her procedures as a working novelist-critic, appraising a book by a female contemporary (Charlotte Lennox) and explaining her own feminist projects in *Mary* and *Maria.*

Advertisement to *Mary, a Fiction*

In delineating the Heroine of this Fiction, the Author attempts to develop a character different from those generally portrayed. This woman is neither a Clarissa, a Lady G—, nor a Sophie.[1]—It would be vain to mention the various modifications of these models, as it would to remark, how widely artists wander from nature, when they copy the originals of great masters. They

---

1. The much-enduring virtuous heroine of Samuel Richardson's *Clarissa* (1847–48), the witty and aggressive sister of the hero of Richardson's *Sir* *Charles Grandison* (1753–54), and the hero's helpmate in Jean-Jacques Rousseau's *Émile* (1762).

catch the gross parts; but the subtile spirit evaporates; and not having the just ties, affectation disgusts, when grace was expected to charm.

Those compositions only have power to delight, and carry us willing captives, where the soul of the author is exhibited, and animates the hidden springs. Lost in a pleasing enthusiasm, they live in the scenes they represent; and do not measure their steps in a beaten track, solicitous to gather expected flowers, and bind them in a wreath, according to the prescribed rules of art.

These chosen few, wish to speak for themselves, and not to be an echo—even of the sweetest sounds—or the reflector of the most sublime beams. The[2] paradise they ramble in, must be of their own creating—or the prospect soon grows insipid, and not varied by a vivifying principle, fades and dies.

In an artless tale, without episodes, the mind of a woman, who has thinking powers is displayed. The female organs have been thought too weak for this arduous employment; and experience seems to justify the assertion. Without arguing physically about *possibilities*—in a fiction, such a being may be allowed to exist; whose grandeur is derived from the operations of its own faculties, not subjugated to opinion; but drawn by the individual from the original source.

1788

From Review of *Euphemia*[1]

ART.XLIII. *Euphemia.* By Mrs. Charlotte Lennox. In Four Volumes 12mo. 957 p. Pr. 12s. sewed. Cadell. 1790.

As a great number of pernicious and frivolous novels are daily published, which only serve to heat and corrupt the minds of young women, and plunge them (by co-operating with their amusements) into that continual dissipation of thought which renders all serious employment irksome, we open a novel with a certain degree of pleasure, when a respectable name appears in the title-page. This was the case with the present work; but as we advanced, so many cold romantic flights struck us in the main story, and still more in the episodes, that we could not avoid ranking it with those novels, which, perhaps, tend to lead the female mind further astray from nature and common sense, than even the tales of chivalry to which Mrs. L. has allowed no quarter.[2] Her notions of female delicacy and reserve are carried as far as any sentimental French writer ever pushed them; and though this prudery might arise from a different cause, yet it may be equally baneful in its effects, and banish true frankness and delicacy of mind, to make room for that false enervating refinement, which eradicates not only simplicity, but all dignity of character. We will appeal to any of our readers whether they would not think that woman very affected, or *ridiculously* squeamish, who could promise to give her hand to her lover one moment, and the next scruple to admit him to a tête-à-tête breakfast. But if the ladies are to be cold and *indisposed to the marriage state*, the gentlemen are sufficiently ardent; weep, kneel and faint

---

2. I here give the Reviewers an opportunity of being very witty about the Paradise of Fools, &c. [Wollstonecraft's note].

1. Published in *The Analytical Review* (1790).

2. In an earlier work, *The Female Quixote; or, The Adventures of Arabella* (1752), Lennox had mocked the ideas of chivalry as presented in literature.

in the most impassioned manner. With respect to Mr. Harley, who is termed a hero for acting as any man would have done, that had the least spark of honour in his soul, to say nothing of religion, we think no knight of ancient days ever cherished a more *refined* passion, or more accidentally gained his bride. If the ladies, for such artificial beings must not be familiarly called women, are something like the cherubim under the organ-loft, soft, simple, and good, the gentlemen, and more particularly the poor husbands, are painted in stronger colours, and several of them appear to be drawn from the life by a faithful feminine pencil: the maternal affection and solicitude, which takes place of every other, is much of the same cast, blind and weak; but the virtue of Mrs. Freeman towers above her sex—Lucretia[3] was a washerwoman to her!

In speaking thus of Mrs. L.'s production, which we were sorry to find so much on a par with the general run of novels, we do not mean to insinuate that it has not sufficient merit to come forward in the second class; nay, we wish to add, that the information it contains respecting America is both curious and entertaining.

* * *

1790

From A Vindication of the Rights of Woman

From Chapter II

THE PREVAILING OPINION OF A SEXUAL CHARACTER DISCUSSED

To account for, and excuse the tyranny of man, many ingenious arguments have been brought forward to prove, that the two sexes, in the acquirement of virtue, ought to aim at attaining a very different character: or, to speak explicitly, women are not allowed to have sufficient strength of mind to acquire what really deserves the name of virtue. Yet it should seem, allowing them to have souls, that there is but one way appointed by Providence to lead *mankind* to either virtue or happiness.

If then women are not a swarm of ephemeron[1] triflers, why should they be kept in ignorance under the specious name of innocence? Men complain, and with reason, of the follies and caprices of our sex, when they do not keenly satirize our headstrong passions and groveling vices.—Behold, I should answer, the natural effect of ignorance! The mind will ever be unstable that has only prejudices to rest on, and the current will run with destructive fury when there are no barriers to break its force. Women are told from their infancy, and taught by the example of their mothers, that a little knowledge of human weakness, justly termed cunning, softness of temper, *outward* obedience, and a scrupulous attention to a puerile kind of propriety, will obtain for them the protection of man; and should they be beautiful, everything else is needless, for, at least, twenty years of their lives.

---

3. Legendary woman who was the Roman ideal of female virtue. After she was raped by the son of the king of Rome, she told her husband what had happened, demanded vengeance, and stabbed herself to death; the revolt that followed ended the Roman monarchy.
1. Short-lived.

Thus Milton describes our first frail mother; though when he tells us that women are formed for softness and sweet attractive grace.[2] I cannot comprehend his meaning, unless, in the true Mahometan strain,[3] he meant to deprive us of souls and insinuate that we were beings only designed by sweet attractive grace, and docile blind obedience, to gratify the senses of man when he can no longer soar on the wing of contemplation.

How grossly do they insult us who thus advise us only to render ourselves gentle, domestic brutes! For instance, the winning softness so warmly, and frequently, recommended, that governs by obeying. What childish expressions, and how insignificant is the being—can it be an immortal one? who will condescend to govern by such sinister methods! "Certainly," says Lord Bacon, "man is of kin to the beasts by his body; and if he be not of kin to God by his spirit, he is a base and ignoble creature!"[4] Men, indeed, appear to me to act in a very unphilosophical manner when they try to secure the good conduct of women by attempting to keep them always in a state of childhood. Rousseau was more consistent when he wished to stop the progress of reason in both sexes,[5] for if men eat of the tree of knowledge, women will come in for a taste but, from the imperfect cultivation which their understandings now receive, they only attain a knowledge of evil.

Children, I grant, should be innocent; but when the epithet is applied to men, or women, it is but a civil term for weakness. For if it be allowed that women were destined by Providence to acquire human virtues, and by the exercise of their understandings, that stability of character which is the firmest ground to rest our future hopes upon, they must be permitted to turn to the fountain of light, and not forced to shape their course by the twinkling of a mere satellite. Milton, I grant, was of a very different opinion; for he only bends to the indefeasible right of beauty, though it would be difficult to render two passages which I now mean to contrast, consistent. But into similar inconsistencies are great men often led by their senses.

> To whom thus Eve with *perfect beauty* adorned.
> My Author and Disposer, what thou bidst
> *Unargued* I obey; So God ordains;
> God is thy *law, thou mine:*—to know no more
> Is Woman's *happiest* knowledge and her *praise*.[6]

These are exactly the arguments that I have used to children; but I have added, your reason is now gaining strength, and, till it arrives at some degree of maturity, you must look up to me for advice—then you ought to *think*, and only rely on God.

Yet in the following lines Milton seems to coincide with me; when he makes Adam thus expostulate with his Maker.

> Hast thou not made me here thy substitute,
> And these inferior far beneath me set?

---

2. See John Milton's *Paradise Lost* (1667, 1674), 4.297–99.
3. The Prophet Muhammed was commonly thought to have claimed in the Qur'an that women lack souls.
4. From Francis Bacon's *Of Atheism* (1597).

5. For Jean-Jacques Rousseau on education, see *Émile* (1762); on the education of women, see chapter 5, "Sophie; or, the Woman."
6. *Paradise Lost* 4.634–38 (Wollstonecraft's italics).

Among *unequals* what society
Can sort, what harmony or true delight?
Which must be mutual, in proportion due
Giv'n and *received*; but in *disparity*
The one intense, the other still remiss
Cannot well suit with either, but soon prove
Tedious alike: of *fellowship* I speak
Such as I seek, fit to participate
All rational delight—[7]

In treating, therefore, of the manners of women, let us, disregarding sensual arguments, trace what we should endeavor to make them in order to cooperate, if the expression be not too bold, with the supreme Being.

By individual education, I mean, for the sense of the word is not precisely defined, such an attention to a child as will slowly sharpen the senses, form the temper,[8] regulate the passions as they begin to ferment, and set the understanding to work before the body arrives at maturity; so that the man may only have to proceed, not to begin, the important task of learning to think and reason.

To prevent any misconstruction, I must add, that I do not believe that a private education can work the wonders which some sanguine writers have attributed to it. Men and women must be educated, in a great degree, by the opinions and manners of the society they live in. In every age there has been a stream of popular opinion that has carried all before it, and given a family character, as it were, to the century. It may then fairly be inferred, that, till society be differently constituted, much cannot be expected from education. It is, however, sufficient for my present purpose to assert, that, whatever effect circumstances have on the abilities, every being may become virtuous by the exercise of its own reason; for if but one being was created with vicious inclinations, that is positively bad, what can save us from atheism? or if we worship a god, is not that god a devil?

Consequently, the most perfect education, in my opinion, is such an exercise of the understanding as is best calculated to strengthen the body and form the heart. Or, in other words, to enable the individual to attain such habits of virtue as will render it independent. In fact, it is a farce to call any being virtuous whose virtues do not result from the exercise of its own reason. This was Rousseau's opinion respecting men: I extend it to women, and confidently assert that they have been drawn out of their sphere by false refinement, and not by an endeavor to acquire masculine qualities. Still the regal homage which they receive is so intoxicating, that till the manners of the times are changed, and formed on more reasonable principles, it may be impossible to convince them that the illegitimate power, which they obtain, by degrading themselves, is a curse, and that they must return to nature and equality, if they wish to secure the placid satisfaction that unsophisticated affections impart. But for this epoch we must wait—wait, perhaps, till kings and nobles, enlightened by reason, and, preferring the real dignity of man to

---

7. *Paradise Lost* 8.381–91 (Wollstonecraft's italics).   8. Character.

childish state throw off their gaudy hereditary trappings: and if then women do not resign the arbitrary power of beauty—they will prove that they have *less* mind than man.

I may be accused of arrogance; still I must declare what I firmly believe, that all the writers who have written on the subject of female education and manners from Rousseau to Dr. Gregory,[9] have contributed to render women more artificial, weak characters, than they would otherwise have been, and, consequently, more useless members of society. I might have expressed this conviction in a lower key; but I am afraid it would have been the whine of affectation, and not the faithful expression of my feelings, of the clear result, which experience and reflection have led me to draw. When I come to that division of the subject, I shall advert to the passages that I more particularly disapprove of, in the works of the authors I have just alluded to; but it is first necessary to observe, that my objection extends to the whole purport of those books, which tend, in my opinion, to degrade one half of the human species, and render women pleasing at the expense of every solid virtue.

Though, to reason on Rousseau's ground, if man did attain a degree of perfection of mind when his body arrived at maturity, it might be proper, in order to make a man and his wife *one*, that she should rely entirely on his understanding: and the graceful ivy, clasping the oak that supported it, would form a whole in which strength and beauty would be equally conspicuous. But, alas! husbands, as well as their helpmates, are often only overgrown children: nay, thanks to early debauchery, scarcely men in their outward form—and if the blind lead the blind, one need not come from heaven to tell us the consequence.

Many are the causes that, in the present corrupt state of society, contribute to enslave women by cramping their understandings and sharpening their senses. One, perhaps, that silently does more mischief than all the rest, is their disregard of order.

To do everything in an orderly manner, is a most important precept, which women, who, generally speaking, receive only a disorderly kind of education, seldom attend to with that degree of exactness that men, who from their infancy are broken into method, observe. This negligent kind of guess-work, for what other epithet can be used to point out the random exertions of a sort of instinctive common sense, never brought to the test of reason? prevents their generalizing matters of fact—so they do today, what they did yesterday, merely because they did it yesterday.

This contempt of the understanding in early life has more baneful consequences than is commonly supposed; for the little knowledge which women of strong minds attain, is, from various circumstances, of a more desultory kind than the knowledge of men, and it is acquired more by sheer observations on real life, than from comparing what has been individually observed with the results of experience generalized by speculation. Led by their dependent situation and domestic employments more into society, what they learn is rather by snatches; and as learning is with them, in general, only a secondary thing, they do not pursue any one branch with that persevering

9. John Gregory, author of *A Father's Legacy to His Daughters* (1774).

ardor necessary to give vigor to the faculties, and clearness to the judgment. In the present state of society, a little learning is required to support the character of a gentleman; and boys are obliged to submit to a few years of discipline. But in the education of women, the cultivation of the understanding is always subordinate to the acquirement of some corporeal accomplishment: even while enervated by confinement and false notions of modesty, the body is prevented from attaining that grace and beauty which relaxed half-formed limbs never exhibit. Besides, in youth their faculties are not brought forward by emulation; and having no serious scientific study, if they have natural sagacity it is turned too soon on life and manners. They dwell on effects, and modifications, without tracing them back to causes; and complicated rules to adjust behavior are a weak substitute for simple principles.

As a proof that education gives this appearance of weakness to females, we may instance the example of military men, who are, like them, sent into the world before their minds have been stored with knowledge or fortified by principles. The consequences are similar; soldiers acquire a little superficial knowledge, snatched from the muddy current of conversation, and, from continually mixing with society, they gain, what is termed a knowledge of the world; and this acquaintance with manners and customs has frequently been confounded with a knowledge of the human heart. But can the crude fruit of casual observation, never brought to the test of judgment, formed by comparing speculation and experience, deserve such a distinction? Soldiers, as well as women, practice the minor virtues with punctilious politeness. Where is then the sexual difference, when the education has been the same? All the difference that I can discern, arises from the superior advantage of liberty, which enables the former to see more of life.

* * *

1792

Preface to *The Wrongs of Woman; or, Maria*

The Wrongs of Woman, like the wrongs of the oppressed part of mankind, may be deemed necessary by their oppressors: but surely there are a few, who will dare to advance before the improvement of the age, and grant that my sketches are not the abortion of a distempered fancy, or the strong delineations of a wounded heart.

In writing this novel, I have rather endeavoured to pourtray passions than manners.

In many instances I could have made the incidents more dramatic, would I have sacrificed my main object, the desire of exhibiting the misery and oppression, peculiar to women, that arise out of the partial laws and customs of society.

In the invention of the story, this view restrained my fancy; and the history ought rather to be considered, as of woman, than of an individual.

The sentiments I have embodied.

In many works of this species, the hero is allowed to be mortal, and to become wise and virtuous as well as happy, by a train of events and circumstances. The heroines, on the contrary, are to be born immaculate; and to act like goddesses of wisdom, just come forth highly finished Minervas from the head of Jove.

ca. 1797   1798

MARIA EDGEWORTH
1768–1849

The second of twenty-one children born to Richard Lovell Edgeworth, an Anglo-Irish inventor and eccentric, Maria Edgeworth grew exceptionally close to her domineering father after the death of her mother, his first wife. Although she was schooled for a time in Derby and London, as a teenager she accompanied him to Edgeworthstown, his Irish estate, where he completed her education himself and introduced her to the local culture. Her subsequent writings were deeply influenced both by his pedagogical theories and by the painful realities she encountered in a country struggling under British rule.

In significant ways, *Letters for Literary Ladies* (1795), Edgeworth's first major publication, summarizes a debate over the proper procedures for educating women and the propriety of female intellectual ambition in which her liberally inclined father and his more conservative friend Thomas Day had been engaged. Her *Letters* offers exceptionally incisive formulations of their positions in our two excerpts, one attacking "literary ladies" on the grounds that they would neglect household duties while also exposing themselves to scandal, and the other arguing that women—freed from the "melancholy apparatus of learning" inflicted on men by the traditional upper-class male education in the classics—are more likely than men to read with interest and write with clarity.

After the appearance of this work, Edgeworth went on to produce the novels for which she is best known today: *Castle Rackrent* (1800), *Belinda* (1801), *The Absentee* (1812), and *Ormond* (1817). All these books are enlivened by precisely the clarity of observation and creative energy that she claimed for women in her *Letters*. In *Belinda* and *Ormond*, she elaborated the genre Frances Burney had established in her novels of manners, while in *Castle Rackrent* and *The Absentee* she pioneered a regionalist realism that was to influence, among others, Sir Walter Scott, who once said that he hoped to portray his native land, Scotland, with "the rich humor, pathetic tenderness and admirable taste" Edgeworth had "so fortunately achieved for Ireland."

Edgeworth never married, rejecting a proposal from a Swedish admirer because it would have meant living away from her beloved Ireland. Instead, she devoted herself to Irish causes, critiquing exploitative English landlords and, in her seventies, attempting to relieve the suffering caused by the famine of 1847. Ironically, much of her writing was done at a desk on which her father inscribed his opinion that in works "which were chiefly written to please me," she had "improved and amused her own mind, and gratified her heart, which I do believe is better than her head."

From Letters to Literary Ladies[1]

[AN ATTACK ON LITERARY LADIES]

Women of literature are much more numerous of late than they were a few years ago. They make a class in society, they fill the public eye, and have acquired a degree of consequence and an appropriate character. The esteem of private friends, and the admiration of the public for their talents, are circumstances highly flattering to their vanity, and as such I will allow[2] them to be substantial pleasures. I am also ready to acknowledge that a taste for literature adds much to the happiness of life, and that women may enjoy to a certain degree this happiness as well as men. But with literary women this silent happiness seems at best but a subordinate consideration; it is not by the treasures they possess, but by those which they have an opportunity of displaying, that they estimate their wealth. To obtain public applause, they are betrayed too often into a miserable ostentation of their learning. Coxe[3] tells us, that certain Russian ladies split their pearls, in order to make a greater display of finery.

The pleasure of being admired for wit[4] or erudition I cannot exactly measure in a female mind; but state it to be as delightful as you can imagine it to be, there are evils attendant upon it, which, in the estimation of a prudent father, may overbalance the good. The intoxicating effect of wit upon the brain has been well remarked by a poet, who was a friend to the fair sex, and too many ridiculous, and too many disgusting, examples confirm the truth of the observation. The deference that is paid to genius sometimes makes the fair sex forget, that genius will be respected only when united with discretion. Those who have acquired fame, fancy that they can afford to sacrifice reputation. I will suppose, however, that their heads shall be strong enough to bear inebriating admiration; and that their conduct shall be essentially irreproachable, yet they will show in their manners and conversation that contempt of inferior minds, and that neglect of common forms and customs, which will provoke the indignation of fools, and which cannot escape the censure of the wise. Even whilst we are secure of their innocence, we dislike that daring spirit in the female sex, which delights to oppose the common opinions of society, and from apparent trifles we draw unfavourable omens, which experience too often confirms. * * *

Men of literature, if we may trust to the bitter expressions of anguish in their writings, and in their private letters, feel acutely all the stings of envy. Women, who have more susceptibility of temper, and less strength of mind, and who, from the delicate nature of their reputation, are more exposed to attack, are also less able to endure it. Malignant critics, when they cannot attack an author's peace in his writings, frequently scrutinize his private life; and every personal anecdote is published without regard to truth or propriety. How will the delicacy of the female character endure this treatment? how will her friends bear to see her pursued even in domestic retirement, if she should be wise enough to make that retirement her choice? how will they like

1. The first selection is written from the point of view of Thomas Day, a family friend, while the second is supposedly Edgeworth's father's perspective.
2. Admit.

3. The Reverend William Coxe (1747–1828), an English historian and travel writer.
4. Intelligence.

to see premature memoirs and spurious collections of familiar letters published by needy booksellers or designing enemies? Yet to all these things men of letters are subject; and such must literary ladies expect, if they attain to any degree of eminence.—Judging, then, from the experience of our sex, I may pronounce envy to be one of the evils which women of uncommon genius have to dread. "Censure," says a celebrated writer, "is a tax which every man must pay to the public, who seeks to be eminent."[5] Women must expect to pay it doubly.

Your daughter, perhaps, shall be above scandal. She shall despise the idle whisper, and the common tattle of her sex; her soul shall be raised above the ignorant and the frivolous; she shall have a relish for higher conversation, and a taste for higher society. But where is she to find, or how is she to obtain this society? You make her incapable of friendship with her own sex. Where is she to look for friends, for companions, for equals? Amongst men? Amongst what class of men? Not amongst men of business, or men of gallantry, but amongst men of literature.

Learned men have usually chosen for their wives, or for their companions, women who were rather below than above the standard of mediocrity: this seems to me natural and reasonable. Such men, probably, feel their own incapacity for the daily business of life, their ignorance of the world, their slovenly habits, and neglect of domestic affairs. They do not want wives who have precisely their own defects; they rather desire to find such as shall, by the opposite habits and virtues, supply their deficiencies. I do not see why two books should marry, any more than two estates. Some few exceptions might be quoted against Stuart's[6] observations. I have just seen, under the article "A Literary Wife," in D'Israeli's Curiosities of Literature, an account of Francis Phidelphus, a great scholar in the fifteenth century, who was so desirous of acquiring the Greek language in perfection, that he travelled to Constantinople in search of a *Grecian wife*: the lady proved a scold. "But to do justice to the name of Theodora," as this author adds, "she has been honourably mentioned in the French Academy of Sciences." I hope this proved an adequate compensation to her husband for his domestic broils.

Happy Madame Dacier! you found a husband suited to your taste! You and Monsieur Dacier, if D'Alembert[7] tells the story rightly, once cooked a dish in concert, by a receipt, which you found in Apicius,[8] and you both sat down and ate of your learned ragout till you were both like to die.

Were I sure, my dear friend, that every literary lady would be equally fortunate in finding in a husband a man who would sympathise in her tastes, I should diminish my formidable catalogue of evils. But alas! Monsieur Dacier is no more! "and we shall never live to see his fellow." Literary ladies will, I am afraid, be losers in love as well as in friendship, by their superiority.— Cupid is a timid, playful child, and is frightened at the helmet of Minerva. It has been observed, that gentlemen are not apt to admire a prodigious quantity of learning and masculine acquirements in the fair sex—we usually con-

---

5. Slightly misquoted from Jonathan Swift's *Miscellanies in Prose and Verse* (1711).
6. Probably the Scottish philosopher Dugald Stewart (1753–1828).
7. Jean Le Rond Alembert (1717–1783), French

scientist and philosopher; Anne Dacier (1647–1720) and her husband, André (1651–1722), were both French classical scholars.
8. Roman epicure. "Receipt": recipe.

sider a certain degree of weakness, both of mind and body, as friendly to female grace. I am not absolutely of this opinion, yet I do not see the advantage of supernatural force, either of body or mind, to female excellence. Hercules-Spinster[9] found his strength rather an incumbrance than an advantage.

Superiority of mind must be united with great temper and generosity, to be tolerated by those who are forced to submit to its influence. I have seen witty and learned ladies, who did not seem to think it at all incumbent upon them to sacrifice any thing to the sense of propriety. On the contrary, they seemed to take both pride and pleasure in showing the utmost stretch of their strength, regardless of the consequences, panting only for victory. Upon such occasions, when the adversary has been a husband or a father, I must acknowledge that I have felt sensations, which few ladies can easily believe they excite. Airs and graces I can bear as well as another—but airs without graces, no man thinks himself bound to bear—and learned airs least of all. Ladies of high rank, in the Court of Parnassus,[1] are apt, sometimes, to claim precedency out of their own dominions, which creates much confusion, and generally ends in their being affronted. That knowledge of the world, which keeps people in their proper places, they will never learn from the Muses.

Molière has pointed out with all the force of comic ridicule, in the Femmes Savantes,[2] that a lady who aspires to the sublime delights of philosophy and poetry, must forego the simple pleasures, and will despise the duties of domestic life. I should not expect that my house affairs would be with haste dispatched by a Desdemona,[3] weeping over some unvarnished tale, or petrified with some history of horrors, at the very time when she should be ordering dinner, or paying the butcher's bill—I should have the less hope of rousing her attention to my culinary concerns and domestic grievances, because I should probably incur her contempt for hinting at these sublunary matters, and her indignation for supposing that she ought to be employed in such degrading occupations. I have heard that if these sublime geniuses are wakened from their reveries by the *appulse*[4] of external circumstances, they start and exhibit all the perturbation and amazement of *cataleptic* patients.

[A DEFENSE OF LITERARY LADIES]

* * * I acknowledge with regret that women who have been but half instructed, who have seen only superficially the relations of moral and political ideas, who have obtained but an imperfect knowledge of the human heart, and who have conducted themselves so as to disgrace their talents and their sex: these are conspicuous and melancholy examples, which are cited oftener with malice than with pity. But I appeal to examples amongst our contemporaries, to which every man of literature will immediately advert to prove, that where the female understanding has been properly cultivated, women have not only

---

9. I.e., Hercules when forced to dress in women's clothes and do women's work.
1. A Greek mountain sacred to the god Apollo and the Muses.
2. *The Learned Women* (1672), a farce.

3. A character in Shakespeare's tragedy *Othello* who reacts with great sympathy to stories of suffering and hardship.
4. Energetic approach.

obtained admiration by their useful abilities, but respect by their exemplary conduct.

I apprehend that many of the errors into which women of literature have fallen, may have arisen from an improper choice of books: those who read chiefly works of imagination, receive from them false ideas of life and of the human heart. Many of these productions I shall keep as I would deadly poison from my child; I should rather endeavour to turn her attention to science than to romance,[5] and to give her early that taste for truth and utility, which when once implanted can scarcely be eradicated. There is a wide difference between innocence and ignorance; ignorant women may have minds the most debased and perverted, whilst the most cultivated understanding may be united with the most perfect innocence and simplicity.

Even if literature were of no other use to the fair sex than to supply them with employment, I should think the time dedicated to the cultivation of their minds well bestowed: they are surely better occupied when they are reading or writing than when coquetting or gaming, losing their fortunes or their characters. You despise the writings of women—you think that they might have made a better use of the pen than to write plays, and poetry, and romances. Considering that the pen was to women a new instrument, I think they have made at least as good a use of it as learned men did of the needle some centuries ago, when they set themselves to determine how many spirits could stand upon its point, and were ready to tear one another to pieces in the discussion of this sublime question. Let the sexes mutually forgive each other their follies, or what is much better, let them combine their talents for their general advantage.—You say that the experiments we have made do not encourage us to proceed, that the increased care and pains which have been of late years bestowed upon female education, have produced no adequate returns; but you in the same breath allow that amongst your contemporaries whom you prudently forbear to mention, there are some instances of great talents applied to useful purposes. Did you expect that the fruits of good cultivation should appear before the seed was sown?—You triumphantly enumerate the disadvantages to which women, from the laws and customs of society, are liable—they cannot converse freely with men of wit, science, and learning, nor even with the artist, or artificers;[6] they are excluded from academies, public libraries, &c. Even our politeness prevents us, you say, from ever speaking plain truth and sense to the fair sex—every assistance that foreign or domestic ingenuity can invent to encourage literary studies, is, as you boast, almost exclusively ours: and after pointing out all these causes for the inferiority of women in knowledge, you ask for a list of the inventions and discoveries of those who, by your own statement of the question, have not been allowed opportunities for observation. With the insulting injustice of an Egyptian task-master, you demand the work, and deny the necessary materials.[7]

I admit, that with respect to the opportunities of acquiring knowledge, institution and manners, are, as you have stated, much in favour of our sex;

5. I.e., imaginative fiction.
6. Craftsmen.
7. See Exodus 5.7.

but your argument concerning *time* appears to me to be unfounded.— Women who do not love dissipation must have more time for the cultivation of their understandings than men can have, if you compute the whole of life—whilst the knowledge of the learned languages continues to form an indispensable part of a gentleman's education, many years of childhood and youth must be devoted to their attainment.—During these studies, the general cultivation of the understanding is in some degree retarded. All the intellectual powers are cramped, except the memory, which is sufficiently exercised, but which is overloaded with words, and with words that are not always understood.—The genius of living and of dead languages differs so much, that the pains which are taken to write elegant Latin frequently spoil the English style.—Girls usually write much better than boys; they think and express their thoughts clearly at an age when young men can scarcely write an easy letter upon any common occasion. Women do not read the good authors of antiquity as school-books, but they can have excellent translations of most of them when they are capable of tasting the beauties of composition.—I know that it is supposed we cannot judge of the classics by translations, and I am sensible that much of the merit of the originals may be lost; but I think the difference in pleasure is more than overbalanced to women by the *time* that is saved, and by the labour and misapplication of abilities which is spared. If they do not acquire a classical taste, neither do they imbibe classic prejudices, nor are they early disgusted with literature by pedagogues, lexicons, grammars, and all the melancholy apparatus of learning.—Women begin to taste the pleasures of reading, and the best authors in the English language are their amusement just at the age when young men disgusted by their studies begin to be ashamed of alluding to literature amongst their companions. Travelling, lounging, field sports, gaming, and what is called pleasure in various shapes, usually fill the interval between quitting the university and settling for life.—When this period is past, business, the necessity of pursuing a profession, the ambition to shine in parliament, or to rise in public life, occupy a large portion of their lives.—In many professions the understanding is but partially cultivated; and general literature must be neglected by those who are occupied in earning bread or amassing riches for their family:—men of genius are often heard to complain, that in the pursuit of a profession they are obliged to contract their inquiries and concentrate their powers.—Statesmen lament that they must often pursue the *expedient* even when they discern that it is not *the right*; and men of letters who earn their bread by their writings, inveigh bitterly against the tyranny of booksellers who degrade them to the state of "literary artisans."—"Literary artisans" is the comprehensive term under which a celebrated philosopher[8] classes all those who cultivate only particular talents or powers of the mind, and who suffer[9] their other faculties to lose all strength and vigour for want of exercise. The other sex have no such constraint upon their understandings; neither the necessity of earning their bread, nor the ambition to shine in public affairs, hurry or prejudice their minds; in domestic life they have leisure to be wise.

---

8. Professor Dugald Stewart—*Elements of the Philosophy of the Human Mind* [1792] [Edgeworth's note].

9. Allow.

Far from being ashamed that so little has been done by female abilities in science and useful literature, I am surprised that so much has been affected.[1] On natural history, on criticism, on moral philosophy, on education, they have written with elegance, eloquence, precision, and ingenuity. Your complaint that women do not turn their attention to useful literature, is surely ill timed: if they merely increased the number of books in circulation, you might declaim against them with success; but when they add to the general fund of useful and entertaining knowledge, you cannot with any show of justice prohibit their labours: there can be no danger that the market should ever be overstocked with produce of intrinsic worth.

1795

1. I.e., effected, accomplished.

GERMAINE NECKER DE STAËL
1766–1817

A great heiress and a brilliant intellectual, the redoubtable Mme de Staël was perhaps the most dazzling of European *salonnières,* hosting gatherings of major thinkers at her magnificent Château de Coppet in Switzerland. Born Germaine Necker but married in a match of convenience to the Swedish Baron de Staël-Holstein, the man among her suitors whom "she least disliked," she had many lovers, both in Paris and in Switzerland, including the statesman Charles-Maurice de Talleyrand, the novelist Benjamin Constant, and another Swedish nobleman, Adolphe Ribbing, who successfully plotted to assassinate the same Swedish king who had facilitated her marriage to de Staël-Holstein. In addition to her lovers, among members of the so-called Groupe de Coppet who gathered regularly in her drawing rooms were such eminent thinkers and writers as Johann Wolfgang von Goethe, Lord Byron, Julie Récamier, August Wilhelm von Schlegel, and Wilhelm von Humboldt. At her chateau, it is said, lunch was served at 5 P.M. and dinner at 11 P.M., with countless musicales, playlets, and debates ongoing throughout the day and lasting well into the night.

Yet in the midst of all this activity, de Staël not only conversed but read and wrote vigorously and indefatigably. Her first novel, *Delphine* (1802), was in part a roman à clef about which Talleyrand sardonically remarked: "Mme de Staël has disguised both herself and me as women in her novel." Her second, *Corinne, or Italy* (1807), was a compelling portrait of the dilemmas confronted by a renowned woman of genius not unlike herself. Among her theoretical and political writings the most crucial were *On Literature in Its Relationship to Social Institutions* (1800), which ambitiously contextualizes art with history seen as, in the words of one commentator, "an ongoing process that . . . ultimately heads toward human progress and perfectability," and *On Germany* (1810–13), which introduced the central tenets of German Romanticism to Napoleonic France. In our selection, drawn from *On Literature,* de Staël examines (as she did in *Corinne*) the various social conditions that affect "the destinies of women who set their minds upon literary celebrity."

From On Literature Considered in Its Relationship to Social Institutions[1]

On Women Writers (2.4)

> Unhappiness is like the black mountain of Bember, at the edge of the blazing kingdom of Lahor. As long as you are climbing it, you see nothing ahead of you but sterile rocks; but once you are at the peak, heaven is at your head, and at your feet the kingdom of Cashmere.
> —*The Indian Hut,*[2] by Bernadin de Saint-Pierre

The existence of women in society is still uncertain in many ways. A desire to please excites their minds; reason recommends obscurity; and their triumphs and failures are equally and completely arbitrary.

I believe a day will come when philosophical legislators will give serious attention to the education of women, to the laws protecting them, to the duties which should be imposed on them, to the happiness which can be guaranteed them. At present, however, most women belong neither to the natural nor to the social order. What succeeds for some women is the ruin of others; their good points may do them harm, their faults may prove useful. One minute they are everything, the next nothing. Their destiny resembles that of freedmen under the emperors: if they try to gain any influence, this unofficial power is called criminal, while if they remain slaves their destiny is crushed.

It would no doubt be generally preferable for women to devote themselves entirely to the domestic virtues, but the peculiar thing about men's judgments of women is that they are much likelier to forgive women for neglecting these duties than for attracting attention by unusual talent. Men are quite willing to tolerate women's degradation of the heart, so long as it is accompanied by mediocrity of mind. The best behavior in the world can scarcely obtain forgiveness for real superiority.

I am now going to discuss the various causes of this peculiar phenomenon, beginning with the condition of women writers in monarchies, then in republics. I am interested in the differences these political situations make in the destinies of women who set their minds upon literary celebrity; I will then consider more generally the sort of happiness fame can promise these women.

In monarchies, women have ridicule to fear; in republics, hatred.

In a monarchy, the sense of the right and proper is so acute that any unusual act or impulse to change one's situation looks ridiculous right away. Anything your rank or position forces you to do finds a thousand admirers; everything you invent spontaneously, with no obligation, is judged severely and in advance. The jealousy natural to all men calms down only if you can apologize for success under cover of some obligation. Unless you cover fame itself with the excuse of your situation and practical interests, if people think your only motive is a need to distinguish yourself, you will annoy those whom ambition is leading in the same direction as yourself.

Men can always hide their vanity or their craving for applause under the appearance or reality of stronger, nobler passions; but women who write are

---

1. Translated by Vivian Folkenfilk.
2. A novel published in 1791. "Lahor" and "Cash-mere" are the regions now known as Lahore and Kashmir.

generally assumed to be primarily inspired by a wish to show off their wit. As a result, the public is very reluctant to grant its approval, and the public's sense that women cannot do without this approval is precisely what tempts it to deny it. In every walk of life, as soon as a man sees your obvious need of him, his feelings for you almost always cool down. A woman publishing a book makes herself so dependent on public opinion that those who mete it out make her harshly aware of their power.

These general causes, acting more or less uniformly in all countries, are reinforced by various circumstances peculiar to the French monarchy. The spirit of chivalry, still lingering on in France, was opposed in some respects to the overeager cultivation of letters even by men; it must have aroused all the more dislike for women concentrating on literary studies and turning their thoughts away from their primary concern, the sentiments of the heart. The niceties of the code of honor might well make men averse from submitting themselves to the motley criticism attracted by publicity. How much more must they have disliked seeing the creatures entrusted to their protection—their wives, sisters, daughters—running the gauntlet of public criticism, or even giving the public the right to make a habit of talking about them!

Great talent could triumph over all these considerations, but it was still hard for women to bear reputations as authors nobly, simultaneously combining them with the independence of high rank and keeping up the dignity, grace, ease, and unself-consciousness that were supposed to distinguish their habitual style and manners.

Women were certainly allowed to sacrifice household occupations to a love of society and its pleasures; serious study, however, was condemned as pedantic. If from the very first moment one did not rise above the teasing which went on from all sides, this teasing would end by discouraging talent and poisoning the well of confidence and exaltation.

Some of these disadvantages are not found in republics, especially if one of the goals of the republic is the encouragement of enlightenment. It might perhaps be natural for literature to become women's portion in such a state, and for men to devote themselves entirely to higher philosophy.

The education of women has always followed the spirit of the constitutions established in free countries. In Sparta, women were accustomed to the exercises of war; in Rome, they were expected to have austere and patriotic virtues. If we want the moving principle of the French Republic to be the emulation of enlightenment and philosophy, it is only reasonable to encourage women to cultivate their minds, so that men can talk with them about ideas that would hold their interest.

Nevertheless, ever since the Revolution men have deemed it politically and morally useful to reduce women to a state of the most absurd mediocrity. They have addressed women only in a wretched language with no more delicacy than wit. Women have no longer any motive to develop their minds. This has been no improvement in manners or morality. By limiting the scope of ideas we have not succeeded in bringing back the simplicity of primitive life: the only result of less wit has been less delicacy, less respect for public opinion, fewer ways to endure solitude. And this applies to everything else in the current intellectual climate too: people invariably think that enlightenment is the cause of whatever is going wrong, and they want to make up for it by making reason go backward. Either morality is a false concept, or the more enlightened we are the more attached to morality we become.

If Frenchmen could give their wives all the virtues of Englishwomen, including retiring habits and a taste for solitude, they would do very well to prefer such virtues to the gifts of brilliant wit. All the French will manage to do this way, however, is to make their women read nothing, know nothing, and become incapable of carrying on a conversation with an interesting idea, or an apt expression, or eloquent language. Far from being kept at home by this happy ignorance, Frenchwomen unable to direct their children's education would become less fond of them. Society would become more necessary to these women—and also more dangerous, because no one could talk to them of anything but love, and this love would not even have the delicacy that can stand in for morality.

If such an attempt to make women completely insipid and frivolous ever succeeded, there would be several important losses to national morality and happiness. Women would have fewer ways to calm men's furious passions. They would no longer have any useful influence over opinion—and women are the ones at the heart of everything relating to humanity, generosity, delicacy. Women are the only human being outside the realm of political interest and the career of ambition, able to pour scorn on base actions, point out ingratitude, and honor even disgrace if that disgrace is caused by noble sentiments. The opinion of society would no longer have any power over men's actions at all if there were no women left in France enlightened enough to make their judgments count, and imposing enough to inspire genuine respect.

I firmly believe that under the ancien régime, when opinion exerted such wholesome authority, this authority was the work of women distinguished by character and wit. Their eloquence was often quoted when they were inspired by some generous scheme or defending the unfortunate; if the expression of some sentiment demanded courage because it would offend those in power.

These are the same women who gave the strongest possible proofs of devotion and energy during the course of the Revolution.

Men in France will never be republican enough to manage without the independence and pride that comes naturally to women. Women may indeed have had too much influence on public affairs under the ancien régime; but they are no less dangerous when bereft of enlightenment, and therefore of reason. Their influence then turns to an inordinate craving for luxury, undiscerning choices, indelicate recommendations. Such women debase the men they love, instead of exalting them. And is the state the better off for it? Should the very limited risk of meeting a woman whose superiority is out of line with the destiny of her sex deprive the republic of France's reputation for the art of pleasing and living in society? Without any women, society can be neither agreeable nor amusing; with women bereft of wit, or the kind of conversational grace which requires the best education, society is spoiled rather than embellished. Such women introduce a kind of idiotic chatter and cliquish gossip into the conversation, alienating all the superior men and reducing brilliant Parisian gatherings to young men with nothing to do and young women with nothing to say.

We can find disadvantages to everything in life. There are probably disadvantages to women's superiority—and to men's; to the vanity of clever people; to the ambition of heroes; to the imprudence of kind hearts, the irritability of independent minds, the recklessness of courage, and so forth. But does that mean we should use all our energy to fight natural gifts, and direct our social institutions toward humbling our abilities? It is hardly as if there were some guarantee that such degradation would promote familial or governmental authority. Women without the wit for conversation or writing are usually just that much more skillful at escaping their duties. Unenlightened countries may not understand how to be free, but they are able to change their masters with some frequency.

Enlightening, teaching, and perfecting women together with men on the national and individual level: this must be the secret for the achievement of every reasonable goal, as well as the establishment of any permanent social or political relationships.

The only reason to fear women's wit would be some sort of scrupulous anxiety about their happiness. And indeed, by developing their rational minds one might well be enlightening them as to the misfortunes often connected with their fate; but that same reasoning would apply to the effect of enlightenment on the happiness of the human race in general, a question which seems to me to have been decided once and for all.

If the situation of women in civil society is so imperfect, what we must work toward is the improvement of their lot, not the degradation of their minds. For women to pay attention to the development of mind and reason would promote both enlightenment and the happiness of society in general. The cultivated education they deserve could have only one really unfortunate result: if some few of them were to acquire abilities distinguished enough to make them hungry for glory. Even this risk, however, would do society no harm, and would only be unfortunate for the very limited number of women whom nature might dedicate to the torture of useless superiority.

And if there were to be some woman seduced by intellectual celebrity and insistent on achieving it! How easy it would be to divert her, if she were caught in time! She could be shown the dreadful destiny to which she was on the verge of committing herself. Examine the social order, she would be told; you will soon see it up in arms against any woman trying to raise herself to the height of masculine reputation.

As soon as any woman is pointed out as a person of distinction, the general public is prejudiced against her. The common people judge according to a few common rules which can be followed without taking any risks. Whatever goes beyond the habitual immediately offends people who consider daily routine the safeguard of mediocrity. A superior man is enough to startle them; a superior woman, straying even farther from the beaten track, must surprise and annoy them even more. A distinguished man almost always has some important career as his field of action, so his talents may turn out to be useful to the interests of even those who least value the delights of the mind. The man of genius may become a man of power, so envious and silly people humor him. But a clever woman is only called upon to offer them new ideas and lofty sentiments, about which they could not care less; her celebrity seems to them much ado about nothing.

Even glory can be a source of reproach to a woman, because it contrasts with her natural destiny. Strict virtue condemns the celebrity even of something which is good in itself, because it damages the perfection of modesty.

Men of wit are so astounded by the existence of women rivals that they cannot judge them with either an adversary's generosity or a protector's indulgence. This is a new kind of combat, in which men follow the laws of neither kindness nor honor.

Suppose, as a crowning misfortune, a woman were to acquire celebrity in a time of political dissension. People would think her influence unbounded, even if she had no influence at all; accuse her of all her friends' actions; and hate her for everything she loved. It is far preferable to attack a defenseless target than a dangerous one.

Nothing lends itself more quickly to vague assumptions than the dubious life of a woman with a famous name and an obscure career. An empty-witted man may inspire ridicule, a man of bad character may drop under the weight of contempt, a mediocre man may be cast aside—but everyone would much rather attack the unknown power they call a woman. When the plans of the ancients did not work out, they used to convince themselves that fate had thwarted them. Our modern vanity also prefers to attribute its failures to secret causes instead of to itself; in time of need, what stands in for fatality is the supposed power of famous women.

Women have no way to show the truth, no way to throw light on their lives. The public hears the lie; only their intimate friends can judge the truth. What real way is there for a woman to disprove slanderous accusations? A man who had been slandered lets his actions answer the universe, saying, "My life is a witness: it too must be heard."[3] But where can a woman find any such witness? A few private virtues, hidden favors, feelings locked into the narrow circle of her situation, writings which may make her known in places where she does not live, in times when she will no longer exist.

A man can refute calumny in his work itself, but self-defense is an additional handicap for women. For a woman to justify herself is a new topic for gossip. Women feel there is something pure and delicate in their nature, quickly withered by the very gaze of the public. Wit, talent, passion in the soul may make them emerge from this mist which should always be surrounding them, but they will always yearn for it as their true refuge.

However distinguished women may be, the sight of ill will makes them tremble. Courageous in misfortune, they are cowards against dislike; thought uplifts them, but their character is still weak and sensitive. Most women whose superior abilities make them want renown are like Erminia dressed in armor.[4] Warriors see the helmet, the lance, the bright plume of feathers, and think they are up against strength, so they attack with violence; with the very first blows, they have struck at the heart.

Such injustices can not only spoil a woman's happiness and peace of mind, but also alienate even the most important objects of her affection. Who can be sure that a libelous portrayal will not strike at the truth of memory? Who knows whether or not slanderers, having wreaked havoc with life, will rob death itself of the tender, regretful feelings that should be associated with the memory of a beloved woman?

So far I have portrayed only the unfairness of men: but what about the threat of injustice from other women? Do not women secretly arouse the

---

3. A line of poetry (source unidentified).
4. In Tasso's *Jerusalem Delivered* (1581), the princess Erminia wears borrowed armor to seek her love Tancred in the Christian camp [translator's note].

malevolence of men? Do women ever form an alliance with a famous woman, sustaining her, defending her, supporting her faltering steps?

And that is still not all. Public opinion seems to release men from every duty toward a recognizably superior woman. Men can be ungrateful to her, unfaithful, even wicked, without making public opinion responsible for avenging her. "Is she not an extraordinary woman?" That says it all; she is abandoned to her own strength, and left to struggle with misery. She lacks both the sympathy inspired by a woman and the power protecting a man. Like the pariahs of India,[5] such a woman parades her peculiar existence among classes she cannot belong to, which consider her as destined to exist on her own, the object of curiosity and perhaps a little envy: what she deserves, in fact, is pity.

1800

5. Individuals at the bottom of or outside India's caste system (the speaker of this section's epigraph is a pariah).

STÉPHANIE-FÉLICITÉ DUCREST, COMTESSE DE GENLIS
1746–1830

"She was ill-natured, and in her *Memoirs* inaccurate, as well as prejudiced," pronounced a contributor to the *Nuttall Encyclopedia* in 1907, three-quarters of a century after the death of Stéphanie-Felicité Ducrest, comtesse de Genlis, a talented aristocrat whose voluminous writings were widely read in her own day, both in French and in the English into which they were immediately translated. In England, indeed, Madame de Genlis's many admirers included such different figures as the Gothic romancer Anne Radcliffe and the novelist of manners Jane Austen. Yet just as de Genlis herself was after her death caricatured as "ill-natured" and "prejudiced," her works were dismissively characterized (in the famous eleventh edition of the *Encyclopaedia Britannica*) as owing "much of their success to adventitious causes which have long ceased to operate," though "useful . . . as furnishing material for history."

The talented and phenomenally energetic woman whose reputation had gone into so radical an eclipse by the early twentieth century was born into a noble Burgundian family in straitened circumstances and educated at home at Champcery, near Autun. By the time she was in her teens, however, she had been introduced into Parisian society, where her skill as a harpist, her intelligence, her charm, and her beauty attracted considerable attention. Married young to Charles Brillart de Genlis, a colonel of grenadiers and later marquis de Sillery, in 1870 she obtained a position as lady-in-waiting to the duchess of Chartres, the wife of the heir to the French throne. She soon became so successful and diligent a governess to the royal daughters that by 1781 the duke of Chartres himself (with whom she was rumored to have had an affair) took the unusual step of appointing her *gouverneur* (or tutor) to the royal sons as well. Thus she became the principal teacher of Louis-Phillipe (king of the French, 1830–48), in whom she is said to have "instilled a fondness for liberal thought."

Among her many carefully argued treatises on education, the best known are a series of plays for young people (*Théâtre d'éducation*, 1779–80) and a novel, *Adèle and Théodore* (1782), in which she implicitly revises Jean-Jacques Rousseau's prescription of an education in docility for women. Where in *Émile* (1762) Rousseau had preached that his character Sophie—a representative young girl, destined to be the bride of his eponymous Émile—"should early be accustomed to restraint," de Genlis argued that, as Judith Clark Schaneman has recently put it, "the education of daughters [should extend] beyond Sophie's limited formation to assume significance equal to that accorded to . . . sons."

Madame de Genlis's later years were vexed and hectic. A supporter of the French Revolution, she was nevertheless forced to flee to Switzerland along with one of her royal pupils, and in 1793, her husband—from whom she had been separated for some time—was guillotined. Returning to France in 1799, she received a small pension from Louis-Philippe but supported herself mostly by writing numerous volumes, including a controversial attack on the *philosophes* who had reigned over French intellectual life in the eighteenth century. Our selection here, drawn from her study titled *The Influence of Women on French Literature* (1811), underlines her belief—analogous to that of Mary Wollstonecraft, Anne Finch, and others—that only the lack of education has "in all ages cut off women from a literary vocation."

From Preliminary Reflections to *The Influence of Women on French Literature*[1]

Men of letters have over women authors a superiority of achievement that, assuredly, one cannot fail to recognize or contest. All of the works of women taken together are not worth a few choice pages from Bossuet or Pascal, or a few scenes from Corneille, Racine, or Molière. But it is not necessary to infer from this that women's natural ability is inferior to that of men. Genius composes itself out of all those qualities which we know that women possess, often to the highest degree: imagination, sensibility, and elevation of spirit. Lack of study and education having in all ages cut off women from a literary vocation, they have displayed their grandeur of spirit not through tracing historic deeds, nor in presenting ingenious fictions, but rather through genuine, material actions. They have done more than write: they have often, by their conduct, furnished models of sublime heroism. It may be true that not one woman has, in her writing, painted the great spirit of Cornelia, but what does this matter, seeing that Cornelia herself is not an imaginary being?[2] And have we not seen, in our days, during the revolutionary tempests, some women equal the male heroes by the vigor of their courage and grandeur of their spirit? "Great thoughts come from the heart,"[3] and similar effects should spring (when nothing is there to obstruct them) from the same source.

In order to establish woman's inferiority, men repeat that not one woman has penned good tragedy or epic poetry. An innumerable multitude of men of letters have written tragedies, yet when we count only four great French tragic poems, it is thought a great number, considering that no other nation can count as many. On the other hand, we have just one French epic poem, and we must admit that it is extremely inferior to *Paradise Lost* or *Jerusalem Delivered*.[4] Only five women among us have tried their hand at tragedy. Not

---

1. Translated by Matthew Bray and Amy Simowitz.
2. Cornelia (fl. 2nd century B.C.E.) was an exemplar of Roman feminine virtue, famous for devoting herself to the education of her two sons, the notable statemen and social reformers Tiberius and Caius Gracchus.
3. Vauvenargues [de Genlis's note]. From *Reflec-*

tions and Maxims (1746) by the soldier and moralist Luc de Clapiers, marquis de Vauvenargues.
4. I.e., epics written in English and Italian by Milton and Tasso, respectively. The French epic more or less contemporary with these to which she alludes is probably Pierre de Ronsard's *Franciade* (1572), an unfinished failure.

only were none of these women exposed, as some authors are, to the vexation of shameful failure, but all of their tragedies experienced great success on opening night.[5]

Young men at college, nourished by reading Greek and Latin, are almost all poets. If they have a little talent, they form the ambitious desire of working for the theatre. We ought to acknowledge that this idea does not naturally occur to a convent student or a young woman who has just entered the world. Can we say that none of our kings, great captains, or men of state have possessed genius, merely because not one of them has written a tragedy, even though several have been poets? Can we say of the Swiss, the Danes, the Russians, the Poles, and the Dutch—people so lively and so civilized—that their mental capacity is inferior to that of the French, the English, the Italians, the Spanish, and the Germans just because they have not produced great dramatic poetry? We can only excel in a particular art when that art is generally cultivated in our nation, and by the class into which we are born. The Romans, the most celebrated people in history, did not have good tragic poets. Millions of street porters, thousands of nuns or mothers—any of these people could have, with a different education and in different circumstances, composed excellent tragedies. The ability to feel and admire that which is good and which is beautiful, and the power to love, are the same for men and women. Therefore, they are morally equal.

But if too few women (for want of study and sheer audacity) have written tragedies in order to prove that they could equal men in this regard, they have often surpassed men in another genre. Not a single man has left behind a collection of personal letters which can hold a candle to the letters of Madame de Sévigné or Madame de Maintenon. La Princesse de Clèves, the Lettres Péruviennes,[6] the letters of Madame Riccoboni, and the two most recent novels of Madame Cotin are infinitely superior to the entire output of the male romancers. I am not excepting the works of Marivaux from this evaluation or worse still, the boring and voluminous works of l'Abbé Prevot. And Gilblas[7] is another sort of work; it is a picture of vice, of the ridiculous products of ambition, vanity and cupidity, and not the development of the natural sentiments of the heart—love, friendship, jealousy, filial piety, and so on. The author, spirited and often quite profound in his witticisms, had only studied subaltern intrigues and the absurdities of pride. When he lays down his satiric pencil, he becomes common; all the episodes of Gilblas intended to be interesting and touching are instead poorly written and dull.

Madame Deshoulières had no equal for the genre of poetry in which she left such charming models.[8] The men who assign ranks in literature—dispensing honors and distributing places to authors, always excluding women—often give celebrity to talents which are quite mediocre. For example, if d'Alembert were neither a geometrician, nor a member of the French Academy—despite his relentless hatred of religion and his contempt for France and her king—his writing, so cold, so devoid of substance, grace and

---

5. Arrie et Petus, by Mademoiselle Barbier, was performed sixteen times. Laodamie, by Mademoiselle Bernard, was performed twenty times, and her Brutus received twenty-five showings. Les Amazons, by Madame du Bocage, was also performed many times. Her epic poem, the Colombiade, was a great success and was translated into several languages [de Genlis's note].

6. Lettres d'une péruvienne (1747), a best-selling novel by Mme de Grafigny.

7. The picaresque romance Gil Blas (1715–35), by the novelist and playwright Alain-René Lesage.

8. Pastoral poetry (idyls and eclogues).

naturalness, would be forgotten already. A woman, if she had the unhappiness of having composed the majority of his academic eulogies, would be dismissed by the public as a "*précieuse ridicule.*"[9] And yet the Academy received d'Alembert as a most distinguished writer. The author of *Ariane* and *Comte d'Essex,*[1] brother to the creator of French tragedy and comedy, was elected only after the death of the great Corneille; the marquis of Saint-Aulaire, however, was welcomed for a madrigal. The son of the great Racine,[2] himself author of a beautiful poem, was never admitted! This same Academy issued a most unjust critique of *The Cid,* the first masterpiece to grace the French stage, yet went into mourning for the death of Voiture! . . . If there existed an academy of women, one ventures to guess that it could, without trouble, better conduct itself and judge more sanely.

It is difficult to reconcile the various judgments made of women; they are either contradictory or devoid of sense. Women are said to possess an extreme sensibility, beyond that of men, and a lack of energy. But what is an extreme sensibility without energy? It is a sensibility incapable of making all the sacrifices of a great devotion. And what is energy, or else this strength of spirit, this power of the will which, well or poorly employed, provides unshakable constancy in order to arrive at its mark and braves everything—all obstacles, peril and death—for the object of a dominant passion? Women's tenacity of will for all that they ardently desire has passed into proverb. Therefore, one does not contest that they possess the type of energy which requires an extreme perseverance. Who could not fail to recognize in women the energy which an heroic courage demands? Does she lack it, that unfortunate princess who has just hurled herself into flames to find her daughter? And among so many noble victims of the faith, so many martyrs who persisted in their belief with an energy so sublime, and despite the horror of shocking torments, do you not count as many women as men?

We maintain that women are endowed with a delicacy that men can not possess. This favorable judgment does not appear to me better founded than all of the others which are to the disadvantage of women. Several works by men of letters prove that this quality is by no means an exclusively female trait, but it is true that it is one of the distinctive characteristics of almost all their works.

That must be because education and propriety impose upon them the law of restraint—of concentrating almost all of their feelings, of always softening their expressions by delicate turns of phrase. This delicacy tries to convey what they cannot venture to explain. This is not dissimulation; this art, in general, is not hiding what one feels. Its perfection, to the contrary, is making known without explaining, without using the words that one could cite as a positive confession. Love especially renders this delicacy ingenious. In such a case, it grants women a touching and mysterious language that, because it is made only for the heart and the imagination, has something heavenly in it. Spoken words are nothing; the secret sense is all, and is fully understood only by the lover to whom it is addressed.

Apart from all the principles which render modesty and discretion so indispensable in a woman, what contrasts are provided by timidity on the one hand

---

9. An affected laughingstock (French).
1. Two tragedies (1672, 1678) by Thomas Corneille, the younger brother of "the great" Pierre

Corneille.
2. Louis Racine; his "beautiful poem" was *Religion* (1742).

and audacity and ardor on the other! Grace exists in a young woman when she is that which she must be: all of her is in accord: the delicacy of her traits and of her discourse, the modesty of her bearing, of her long garments, and the sweetness of her voice and character. She does not disguise herself, but she always conceals herself. Her expressions of affection are all the more touching because she does not exaggerate; rather she must understate her feeling. Her sensibility is more profound than that of men because she is more constrained. She discloses herself, but not completely. In order to know and understand her, it is necessary to conjecture about her. She appeals as much by the attraction of piqued curiosity as by genuine charms. What poor taste it is to unveil all of this mystery, to destroy all these graces, by presenting the heroine of a novel or play without modesty, and having her express the most impetuous outbursts of love! Yet this is what we have seen for some years now. In thus transforming women, we believed we were giving them energy, but we deceived ourselves. Not only were we unable to strip them of their natural graces without removing all their dignity, but this vehement and passionate language strips them also of all they might possess of what is truly stirring and moving.

1811

JANE AUSTEN
1775–1817

Lauded by Virginia Woolf as "the most perfect artist among women," the author of such classics as *Pride and Prejudice* (1813), *Emma* (1816), *Northanger Abbey* (1818), and *Persuasion* (1818) led a superficially uneventful life, first in her father's rectory at Steventon and then, after his retirement and death, at Chawton on one of her brother Edward's estates, in a cottage that she shared with her mother, her sister Cassandra, and an unmarried family friend. Yet although Austen had been mostly educated at home and lived in comparative retirement, her thought and art are richly literary. She had read (besides standard masterpieces by Milton and Shakespeare) not only the male-authored English classics of her era—works by Richardson, Fielding, Pope, Goldsmith, Johnson, Scott, and Byron—but also countless works by her female contemporaries in England, among whom Frances Burney and Maria Edgeworth were special favorites. In addition, she had absorbed and appraised the writings of such continental figures as Goethe and Mme de Genlis.

Much of this reading became overtly or covertly central in Austen's fiction from her insouciant juvenilia onward. *Love and Freindship* (composed 1790), for instance, lampoons the sentimental epistolary novel, while *Northanger Abbey* parodies the Gothic yet also offers a spirited defense of the novel as a genre, declaring that novelists

> have afforded more extensive and unaffected pleasure than those of any other literary corporation in the world [but] no species of composition has been so much decried. From pride, ignorance, or fashion, our foes are almost as many as our readers. And while the abilities of the nine-hundredth abridger of the History of England, or of the man who collects and publishes in a volume some dozen lines

of Milton, Pope, and Prior, with a paper from the Spectator, and a chapter from Sterne, are eulogized by a thousand pens—there seems almost a general wish of decrying the capacity and undervaluing the labour of the novelist, and of slighting the performances which have only genius, wit, and taste to recommend them. "I am no novel-reader—I seldom look into novels—Do not imagine that *I* often read novels—It is really very well for a novel." Such is the common cant. "And what are you reading, Miss—?" "Oh! It is only a novel!" replies the young lady, while she lays down her book with affected indifference, or momentary shame. "It is only Cecilia, or Camilla, or Belinda"; or, in short, only some work in which the greatest powers of the mind are displayed, in which the most thorough knowledge of human nature, the happiest delineation of its varieties, the liveliest effusions of wit and humour, are conveyed to the world in the best-chosen language.

More generally, *Persuasion* features a denouement in which the protagonist, Anne Elliot, muses on the very nature of authorship, noting that "Men have had every advantage of us in telling their own story. Education has been theirs in so much higher a degree; the pen has been in their hands. I will not allow books to prove anything."

Our selections here show Austen's skills both as a working novelist and as a parodist of what her literary descendant George Eliot was to call "Silly Novels by Lady Novelists." In passages from two letters to her oldest niece, Anna Austen, who had asked advice about a novel in progress, the author of *Pride and Prejudice* offers the kind of detailed commentary that would not be out of place in a twenty-first-century fiction-writing workshop. At the same time, in a "Plan of a Novel" she wittily dramatizes the foibles of fiction that she herself shrewdly seeks to avoid.

Letters to Anna Austen[1]

[ADVICE ON A NOVEL IN PROGRESS]

9–18 SEPTEMBER 1814

Chawton Sept: 9

My dear Anna

We have been very much amused by your 3 books, but I have a good many criticisms to make—more than you will like. We are not satisfied with Mrs F.'s settling herself as Tenant & near Neighbour to such a Man as Sir T. H. without having some other inducement to go there; she ought to have some friend living thereabouts to tempt her. A woman, going with two girls just growing up, into a Neighbourhood where she knows nobody but one Man, of not very good character, is an awkwardness which so prudent a woman as M^rs F would not be likely to fall into. Remember, she is very prudent;—you must not let her act inconsistently.—Give her a friend, & let that friend be invited to meet her at the Priory, & we shall have no objection to her dining there as she does; but otherwise, a woman in her situation would hardly go there, before she had been visited by other Families.—I like the scene itself, the Miss Lesleys, Lady Anne, & the Music, very much.—Lesley *is* a noble name.—Sir T. H. You always do very well; I have only taken the liberty of expunging one phrase of his, which would not be allowable. "Bless my Heart"—It is too familiar & inelegant. Your G. M.[2] is more disturbed at Mrs F.'s not returning the Egertons

1. Jane Anna Elizabeth Austen, the daughter of Austen's oldest brother, James.

2. I.e., grandmother, Cassandra Austen.

visit sooner, than anything else. They ought to have called at the Parsonage before Sunday.—

You describe a sweet place, but your descriptions are often more minute than will be liked. You give too many particulars of right hand & left.—

Mrs F. is not careful enough of Susan's health;—Susan ought not to be walking out so soon after Heavy rains, taking long walks in the dirt. An anxious Mother would not suffer it.—I like your Susan very much indeed, she is a sweet Creature, her playfulness of fancy is very delightful. I like her as she is *now* exceedingly, but I am not so well satisfied with her behaviour to George R. At first she seemed all over attachment & feeling, & afterwards to have none at all; she is so extremely composed at the Ball, & so well-satisfied apparently with Mr Morgan. She seems to have changed her Character.—You are now collecting your People delightfully, getting them exactly into such a spot as is the delight of my life;—3 or 4 Families in a Country Village is the very thing to work on— & I hope you will write a great deal more, & make full use of them while they are so very favourably arranged. You are but *now* coming to the heart & beauty of your book; till the heroine grows up, the fun must be imperfect—but I expect a great deal of entertainment from the next 3 or 4 books, & I hope you will not resent these remarks by sending me no more.—We like the Egertons very well, we see no Blue Pantaloons, or Cocks & Hens;—there is nothing to *enchant* one certainly in Mr L. L.—but we make no objection to him, & his inclination to like Susan is pleasing.—The Sister is a good contrast—but the name of Rachael is as much as I can bear.—They are not so much like the Papillons as I expected. Your last Chapter is very entertaining—the conversation on Genius &c. Mr St J.- & Susan both talk in character & very well.—In some former parts, Cecilia is perhaps a little too solemn & good, but upon the whole, her disposition is very well opposed to Susan's—her want of Imagination is very natural.—I wish you could make Mrs F. talk more, but she must be difficult to manage & make entertaining, because there is so much good common sence & propriety about her that nothing can be very *broad*. Her Economy & her Ambition must not be staring.[3]—The Papers left by Mrs Fisher is very good.—Of course, one guesses something.—I hope when you have written a great deal more you will be equal to scratching out some of the past.—The scene with Mrs Mellish, I should condemn; it is prosy & nothing to the purpose—& indeed, the more you can find in your heart to curtail between Dawlish & Newton Priors, the better I think it will be.—One does not care for girls till they are grown up.—Your Aunt C.[4] quite enters into the exquisiteness of that name. Newton Priors is really a Nonpareil.—Milton w^d have given his eyes to have thought of it.—Is not the Cottage taken from Tollard Royal?[5]—

Sunday 18th—I am very glad dear Anna, that I wrote as I did before this sad Event[6] occurred. I have now only to add that your G. Mama does not seem the worse now for the Shock.—I shall be very happy to receive more of your work, if more is ready; & you write so fast, that I have great hopes M^r D[igweed] will come freighted back with such a Cargo as not all his Hops or his Sheep could equal the value of.

Your Grandmama desires me to say that she will have finished your Shoes

3. Glaringly conspicuous.
4. Cassandra, Austen's older sister.
5. A small village southwest of Salisbury; it was the home of the sister of Anna's fiancé.

6. The death of Fanny Austen, the wife of Austen's younger brother, Charles, a few weeks after childbirth.

tomorrow & thinks they will look very well;—and that she depends upon seeing you, as you promise, before you quit the Country, & hopes you will give
her more than a day.—Y^{rs} affect:^{ly}

J. Austen

[MORE ADVICE ON A NOVEL IN PROGRESS]

28 SEPTEMBER 1814

Chawton Wednesday Sept: 28

My dear Anna
    I hope you do not depend on having your book back again immediately. I
keep it that your G:Mama may hear it—for it has not been possible yet to have
any public reading. I have read it to your Aunt Cassandra however—in our
own room at night, while we undressed—and with a great deal of pleasure.
We like the first chapter extremely—with only a little doubt whether Ly
Helena is not almost *too* foolish. The matrimonial Dialogue is very good certainly.—I like Susan as well as ever—& begin now not to care at all about
Cecilia—she may stay at Easton Court as long as she likes.—Henry Mellish
I am afraid will be too much in the common Novel style—a handsome, amiable, unexceptionable Young Man (such as do not much abound in real Life)
desperately in Love, & all in vain. But I have no business to judge him so
early.—Jane Egerton is a very natural, comprehendable Girl—& the whole of
her acquaintance with Susan, & Susan's Letter to Cecilia, very pleasing &
quite in character.—But *Miss* Egerton does not entirely satisfy us. She is too
formal & solemn, we think, in her advice to her Brother not to fall in love; &
it is hardly like a sensible Woman; it is putting it into his head.—We should
like a few hints from her better.—We feel really obliged to you for introducing a Lady Kenrick, it will remove the greatest fault in the work, & I give you
credit for considerable forbearance as an Author in adopting so much of our
opinion.—I expect high fun about Mrs Fisher & Sir Thomas.—You have been
perfectly right in telling Ben of your work, & I am very glad to hear how much
he likes it. *His* encouragement & approbation must be quite "beyond everything."—I do not at all wonder at his not expecting to like anybody so well as
Cecilia *at first*, but shall be surprised if he does not become a Susan-ite in
time.—Devereux Forester's being ruined by his Vanity is extremely good; but
I wish you would not let him plunge into a "vortex of Dissipation". I do not
object to the Thing, but I cannot bear the expression;—it is such thorough
novel slang—and so old, that I dare say Adam met with it in the first novel he
opened.—Indeed I did very much like to know Ben's opinion.—I hope he will
continue to be pleased with it, I think he must—but I cannot flatter him with
there being much Incident. We have no great right to wonder at his not val-
ueing the name of Progillian. *That* is a source of delight which he hardly ever
can be quite competent to.—Walter Scott has no business to write novels,
especially good ones.—It is not fair.—He has Fame & Profit enough as a Poet,
and should not be taking the bread out of other people's mouths.—I do not
like him, & do not mean to like Waverley if I can help it—but fear I must.—
I am quite determined however not to be pleased with Mrs West's Alicia de
Lacy,[7] should I ever meet with it, which I hope I may not.—I think I *can* be

7. A novel by Jane West, published in 1814 (as was *Waverley*).

stout against any thing written by M[rs] West.—I have made up my mind to like no Novels really, but Miss Edgeworth's, Yours & my own.—

What can you do with Egerton to increase the interest for him? I wish you c[d] contrive something, some family occurrence to draw out his good qualities more—some distress among Brothers or Sisters to releive by the sale of his Curacy—something to [take] him mysteriously away, & then heard of at York or Edinburgh—in an old great Coat.—I would not seriously recommend anything Improbable, but if you c[d] invent something spirited for him, it w[d] have a good effect.—He might lend all his Money to Capt[n] Morris—but then he w[d] be a great fool if he did. Cannot the Morrises quarrel, & he reconcile them?—Excuse the liberty I take in these suggestions.—

Your Aunt Frank's Housemaid has just given her warning,[8] but whether she is worth your having, or w[d] take your place I know not.—She was M[rs] Webb's maid before she went to the G[t] House. She leaves your Aunt, because she cannot agree with her fellow servants. She is in love with the Man—& her head seems rather turned; he returns her affection, but she fancies every body else is wanting to get him too, & envying her. Her previous service must have fitted her for such a place as yours, & she is very active & cleanly.—She is own Sister to the favourite Beatrice. The Webbs are really gone. When I saw the Waggons at the door, & thought of all the trouble they must have in moving, I began to reproach myself for not having liked them better—but since the Waggons have disappeared, my Conscience has been closed again—& I am excessively glad they are gone.—

I am very fond of Sherlock's Sermons,[9] prefer them to almost any.

Your affec[te] Aunt
J. Austen

If you wish me to speak to the Maid, let me know.—

Plan of a Novel, According to Hints from Various Quarters

Scene to be in the Country, Heroine the Daughter of a Clergyman,[1] one who after having lived much in the World had retired from it, & settled in a Curacy, with a very small fortune of his own.—He, the most excellent Man that can be imagined, perfect in Character, Temper & Manners—without the smallest drawback or peculiarity to prevent his being the most delightful companion to his Daughter from one year's end to the other.—Heroine a faultless Character[2] herself—, perfectly good, with much tenderness & sentiment, & not the least Wit[3]—very highly accomplished,[4] understanding modern Languages & (generally speaking) everything that the most accomplished young Women learn, but particularly excelling in Music—her favourite pursuit—& playing equally well on the Piano Forte & Harp—& singing in the first stile.

---

8. I.e., has given notice.
9. *Sherlock's Sermons: Several Discourses Preached at the Temple Church*, 5 vols. (1754–97; reprint, 1812), by Thomas Sherlock, bishop of London.
1. Mr. Gifford [except as indicated, all notes are Austen's, as she named the friends who supplied the various "hints."]
2. Fanny Knight.
3. Mary Cooke.
4. Fanny Knight.

Her Person, quite beautiful—dark eyes & plump cheeks.[5]—Book to open with the description of Father & Daughter—who are to converse in long speeches, elegant Language—& a tone of high, serious sentiment.—The Father to be induced, at his Daughter's earnest request, to relate to her the past events of his Life. This Narrative will reach through the greatest part of the 1st vol.—as besides all the circumstances of his attachment to her Mother & their Marriage, it will comprehend his going to sea as Chaplain[6] to a distinguished Naval Character about the Court, his going afterwards to Court himself, which introduced him to a great variety of Characters & involved him in many interesting situations, concluding with his opinion of the Benefits to result from Tythes[7] being done away, & his having buried his own Mother (Heroine's lamented Grandmother) in consequence of the High Priest of the Parish in which she died, refusing to pay her Remains the respect due to them. The Father to be of a very literary turn, an Enthusiast in Literature, nobody's Enemy but his own—at the same time most zealous in the discharge of his Pastoral Duties, the model of an exemplary Parish Priest.[8]—The heroine's friendship to be sought after by a young Woman in the same Neighbourhood, of Talents & Shrewdness, with light eyes & a fair skin,[9] but having a considerable degree of Wit, Heroine shall shrink from the acquaintance.—From this outset, the Story will proceed, & contain a striking variety of adventures. Heroine & her Father never above a fortnight together in one place,[1] *he* being driven from his Curacy by the vile arts of some totally unprincipled & heart-less young Man, desperately in love with the Heroine, & pursuing her with unrelenting passion—no sooner settled in one Country of Europe than they are necessitated to quit it & retire to another—always making new acquaintance, & always obliged to leave them.—This will of course exhibit a wide variety of Characters—but there will be no mixture; the scene will be for ever shifting from one Set of People to another—but all the Good will be unexceptionable in every respect[2]—and there will be no foibles or weaknesses but with the Wicked, who will be completely depraved & infamous, hardly a resemblance of Humanity left in them.—Early in her career, in the progress of her first removals, Heroine must meet with the Hero—all perfection of course[3]—& only prevented from paying his addresses to her, by some excess of refinement.—Wherever she goes, somebody falls in love with her, & she receives repeated offers of Marriage—which she always refers wholly to her Father, exceedingly angry that *he*[4] shd not be first applied to.—Often carried away by the anti-hero, but rescued either by her Father or the Hero—often reduced to support herself & her Father by her Talents & work for her Bread;—continually cheated & defrauded of her hire, worn down to a Skeleton, & now & then starved to death.—At last, hunted out of civilized Society, denied the poor Shelter of the humblest Cottage, they are compelled to retreat into Kamschatka where the poor Father, quite worn down, finding his end approaching, throws himself

5. Mary Cooke.
6. Mr. Clarke.
7. Payments (originally in kind, a fixed proportion of the yearly profits of the produce of the land) made to maintain the parish church and its clergy; tithes were finally done away with in 1936 [editor's note].

8. Mr. Sherer.
9. Mary Cooke.
1. Many critics.
2. Mary Cooke.
3. Fanny Knight.
4. Mrs. Pearse of Chilton-Lodge.

on the Ground, & after 4 or 5 hours of tender advice & parental Admonition to his miserable Child, expires in a fine burst of Literary Enthusiasm, intermingled with Invectives against Holder's of Tythes.—Heroine inconsolable for some time—but afterwards crawls back towards her former Country—having at least 20 narrow escapes of falling into the hands of Anti-hero—& at last in the very nick of time, turning a corner to avoid him, runs into the arms of the Hero himself, who having just shaken off the scruples which fetter'd him before, was at the very moment setting off in pursuit of her.—The Tenderest & completest Eclaircissement takes place, & they are happily united.—Throughout the whole work, Heroine to be in the most elegant Society & living in high style.[5] The name of the work *not* to be *Emma*[6]—but of the same sort as S & S. and P & P.[7]

1816

5. Fanny Knight.
6. Mrs. Craven.
7. Mr. H. Sanford. [I.e., *Sense and Sensibility*
(1811) and *Pride and Prejudice* (1813): novels by Austen, as is *Emma* (1815)—editor's note.]

MARY SHELLEY
1797–1851

As a nineteen-year-old newlywed mother of two—one a premature girl who died at two weeks, the other a six-month-old boy—Mary Shelley found herself, as she recounts in our selection here, telling tales of the supernatural in the candlelit salon of a villa on Lake Geneva. Her companions included her husband, the rebellious poet Percy Bysshe Shelley; his good friend George Gordon, Lord Byron—a dashing aristocrat and, like Percy Shelley, a rebellious Romantic poet; and Byron's eccentric Italian physician, William Polidori. "We will each write a ghost story," Byron suddenly declared, or so Mary remembered when she sat down in 1831 to draft an introduction to the novel she wrote in response to the poet's command: the compelling bestseller *Frankenstein* (1818). Setting out to discuss the book's inception, she too seems bemused by the question she tells us readers often pose to her, as if herself wondering "How I, then a young girl, came to think of . . . so very hideous an idea?" As she goes on to disclose, she was at first frustratingly empty of inspiration, but after brooding for a few days, she had a terrifying nightmare about a "pale student of unhallowed arts" who employed a "powerful engine" to awaken "the hideous phantasm of a man." Almost at once she understood that this horrifying dream might be the basis of "my ghost story—my tiresome, unlucky ghost story!" for she longed to "contrive [a tale] which would frighten my reader as I myself had been frightened that night!"

Mary Shelley's world-famous and resonantly shocking tale—featuring a hero who creates a monster from body parts dug up in a cemetery—seems surprising coming from an author who was "then a young girl," but in fact the youthful writer's life had already been marked by a series of shocking events. Her mother, the radical theoretician Mary Wollstonecraft, the author of *A Vindication of the Rights of Woman* (1792), had died shortly after giving birth to her, and her father, the noted philosopher William Godwin, had remarried a woman—described by his friends as "second-rate"—who frankly favored her own children from an earlier marriage. Along with her half-sister Fanny Imlay, Wollstonecraft's daughter from a former liaison, Mary was forlorn and rebellious. When she met Shelley, who was already married at twenty-two and had himself been living a tumultuous life, the two trysted at Mary's mother's grave, then fled to the Continent, where their lives continued to be marked by tragedy: the deaths of all their children except one; the suicides of Fanny Imlay and of Harriet Shelley, the poet's first wife; and finally Percy Shelley's death in a boating accident. "I am now on the eve of completing my five & twentieth year," Mary confided to her journal eight years after her elopement, exclaiming "how drearily young for one so lost as I! [for] what I have suffered . . . will write years on my brow & intrench them in my heart."

Yet Mary was to live some thirty more years after Shelley's death, and in those years she remained remarkably productive, publishing a number of tales, five more novels, and a range of essays, travel sketches, and biographies, along with insightful notes to her husband's poems. Always conscious of her maternal inheritance, she once declared: "If I have never written to vindicate the rights of women, I have ever befriended and supported victims to the social system"—including, one might add, even so bizarre a victim as Victor Frankenstein's notorious monster.

Introduction to *Frankenstein*

The Publishers of the Standard Novels, in selecting "Frankenstein" for one of their series, expressed a wish that I should furnish them with some account of the origin of the story. I am the more willing to comply, because I shall thus give a general answer to the question, so very frequently asked me—"How I, then a young girl, came to think of, and to dilate upon, so very hideous an idea?" It is true that I am very averse to bringing myself forward in print; but as my account will only appear as an appendage to a former production, and as it will be confined to such topics as have connection with my authorship alone, I can scarcely accuse myself of a personal intrusion.

It is not singular that, as the daughter of two persons of distinguished literary celebrity, I should very early in life have thought of writing. As a child I scribbled; and my favorite pastime, during the hours given me for recreation, was to "write stories." Still I had a dearer pleasure than this, which was the formation of castles in the air—the indulging in waking dreams—the following up trains of thought, which had for their subject the formation of a succession of imaginary incidents. My dreams were at once more fantastic and agreeable than my writings. In the latter I was a close imitator—rather doing as others had done, than putting down the suggestions of my own mind. What I wrote was intended at least for one other eye—my childhood's companion and friend; but my dreams were all my own; I accounted for them to nobody; they were my refuge when annoyed—my dearest pleasure when free.

I lived principally in the country as a girl, and passed a considerable time in Scotland. I made occasional visits to the more picturesque parts; but my habitual residence was on the blank and dreary northern shores of the Tay, near Dundee. Blank and dreary on retrospection I call them; they were not so to me then. They were the aerie of freedom, and the pleasant region where unheeded I could commune with the creatures of my fancy. I wrote then— but in a most commonplace style. It was beneath the trees of the grounds belonging to our house, or on the bleak sides of the woodless mountains near, that my true compositions, the airy flights of my imagination, were born and fostered. I did not make myself the heroine of my tales. Life appeared to me too commonplace an affair as regarded myself. I could not figure to myself that romantic woes or wonderful events would ever be my lot; but I was not confined to my own identity, and I could people the hours with creations far more interesting to me at that age, than my own sensations.

After this my life became busier, and reality stood in place of fiction. My husband, however, was from the first, very anxious that I should prove myself worthy of my parentage, and enroll myself on the page of fame. He was forever inciting me to obtain literary reputation, which even on my own part I cared for then, though since I have become infinitely indifferent to it. At this time he desired that I should write, not so much with the idea that I could produce anything worthy of notice, but that he might himself judge how far I possessed the promise of better things hereafter. Still I did nothing. Traveling, and the cares of a family, occupied my time; and study, in the way of reading, or improving my ideas in communication with his far more cultivated mind, was all of literary employment that engaged my attention.

In the summer of 1816, we visited Switzerland, and became the neighbors of Lord Byron. At first we spent our pleasant hours on the lake, or wandering on its shores; and Lord Byron, who was writing the third canto of *Childe Harold*, was the only one among us who put his thoughts upon paper. These, as he brought them successively to us, clothed in all the light and harmony of poetry, seemed to stamp as divine the glories of heaven and earth, whose influences we partook with him.

But it proved a wet, ungenial summer, and incessant rain often confined us for days to the house. Some volumes of ghost stories, translated from the German into French, fell into our hands. There was *The History of the Inconstant Lover*, who, when he thought to clasp the bride to whom he had pledged his vows, found himself in the arms of the pale ghost of her whom he had deserted. There was the tale of the sinful founder of his race, whose miserable doom it was to bestow the kiss of death on all the younger sons of his fated house, just when they reached the age of promise. His gigantic, shadowy form, clothed like the ghost in *Hamlet*, in complete armor, but with the beaver up, was seen at midnight, by the moon's fitful beams, to advance slowly along the gloomy avenue. The shape was lost beneath the shadow of the castle walls; but soon a gate swung back, a step was heard, the door of the chamber opened, and he advanced to the couch of the blooming youths, cradled in healthy sleep. Eternal sorrow sat upon his face as he bent down and kissed the forehead of the boys, who from that hour withered like flowers snapped upon the stalk. I have not seen these stories since then; but their incidents are as fresh in my mind as if I had read them yesterday.

"We will each write a ghost story," said Lord Byron; and his proposition was acceded to. There were four of us. The noble author began a tale, a fragment of which he printed at the end of his poem of *Mazeppa*. Shelley, more apt to embody ideas and sentiments in the radiance of brilliant imagery, and in the music of the most melodious verse that adorns our language, than to invent the machinery of a story, commenced one founded on the experiences of his early life. Poor Polidori[1] had some terrible idea about a skull-headed lady, who was so punished for peeping through a key-hole—what to see I forget—something very shocking and wrong of course; but when she was reduced to a

---

1. John William Polidori, Byron's doctor and friend.

worse condition than the renowned Tom of Coventry,[2] he did not know what to do with her, and was obliged to despatch her to the tomb of the Capulets, the only place for which she was fitted. The illustrious poets also, annoyed by the platitude of prose, speedily relinquished their uncongenial task.

I busied myself *to think of a story,*—a story to rival those which had excited us to this task. One which would speak to the mysterious fears of our nature, and awaken thrilling horror—one to make the reader dread to look round, to curdle the blood, and quicken the beatings of the heart. If I did not accomplish these things, my ghost story would be unworthy of its name. I thought and pondered—vainly. I felt that blank incapability of invention which is the greatest misery of authorship, when dull Nothing replies to our anxious invocations. *Have you thought of a story?* I was asked each morning, and each morning I was forced to reply with a mortifying negative.

Everything must have a beginning, to speak in Sanchean phrase;[3] and that beginning must be linked to something that went before. The Hindus give the world an elephant to support it, but they make the elephant stand upon a tortoise. Invention, it must be humbly admitted, does not consist in creating out of void, but out of chaos; the materials must, in the first place, be afforded: it can give form to dark, shapeless substances, but cannot bring into being the substance itself. In all matters of discovery and invention, even of those that appertain to the imagination, we are continually reminded of the story of Columbus and his egg.[4] Invention consists in the capacity of seizing on the capabilities of a subject, and in the power of molding and fashioning ideas suggested to it.

Many and long were the conversations between Lord Byron and Shelley, to which I was a devout but nearly silent listener. During one of these, various philosophical doctrines were discussed, and among others the nature of the principle of life, and whether there was any probability of its ever being discovered and communicated. They talked of the experiments of Dr. Darwin[5] (I speak not of what the Doctor really did, or said that he did, but, as more to my purpose, of what was then spoken of as having been done by him), who preserved a piece of vermicelli in a glass case, till by some extraordinary means it began to move with voluntary motion. Not thus, after all, would life be given. Perhaps a corpse would be reanimated; galvanism had given token of such things: perhaps the component parts of a creature might be manufactured, brought together, and endued with vital warmth.

Night waned upon this talk, and even the witching hour had gone by, before we retired to rest. When I placed my head on my pillow, I did not sleep, nor could I be said to think. My imagination, unbidden, possessed and guided me, gifting the successive images that arose in my mind with a vividness far beyond the usual bounds of reverie. I saw—with shut eyes, but acute mental vision,—I saw the pale student of unhallowed arts kneeling beside the thing he had put together. I saw the hideous phantasm of a man stretched out, and

2. Peeping Tom; according to legend, his eyes shriveled in his head when he alone looked at Lady Godiva riding naked through Coventry.
3. I.e., befitting the practical Sancho Panza of *Don Quixote* (1615).
4. A story is told that Columbus was dining with men who disparaged his accomplishments; and after they dismissed his challenge to make an egg stand on its end as impossible, he gently cracked the small end and succeeded, explaining that this (like his journey across the ocean) was easy, once someone had shown the way.
5. Erasmus Darwin (1731–1802), physician, poet, and scientist.

then, on the working of some powerful engine, show signs of life, and stir with an uneasy, half vital motion. Frightful must it be; for supremely frightful would be the effect of any human endeavor to mock the stupendous mechanism of the Creator of the world. His success would terrify the artist; he would rush away from his odious handiwork, horror-stricken. He would hope that, left to itself, the slight spark of life which he had communicated would fade; that this thing, which had received such imperfect animation, would subside into dead matter; and he might sleep in the belief that the silence of the grave would quench for ever the transient existence of the hideous corpse which he had looked upon as the cradle of life. He sleeps; but he is awakened; he opens his eyes; behold the horrid thing stands at his bedside, opening his curtains, and looking on him with yellow, watery, but speculative eyes.

I opened mine in terror. The idea so possessed my mind, that a thrill of fear ran through me, and I wished to exchange the ghastly image of my fancy for the realities around. I see them still; the very room, the dark *parquet,* the closed shutters, with the moonlight struggling through, and the sense I had that the glassy lake and white high Alps were beyond. I could not so easily get rid of my hideous phantom; still it haunted me. I must try to think of something else. I recurred to my ghost story,—my tiresome unlucky ghost story! O! if I could only contrive one which would frighten my reader as I myself had been frightened that night!

Swift as light and as cheering was the idea that broke in upon me. "I have found it! What terrified me will terrify others; and I need only describe the specter which had haunted my midnight pillow." On the morrow I announced that I had *thought of a story*. I began that day with the words, *It was on a dreary night of November,* making only a transcript of the grim terrors of my waking dream.

At first I thought but of a few pages—of a short tale; but Shelley urged me to develop the idea at greater length. I certainly did not owe the suggestion of one incident, nor scarcely of one train of feeling, to my husband, and yet but for his incitement, it would never have taken the form in which it was presented to the world. From this declaration I must except the preface. As far as I can recollect, it was entirely written by him.

And now, once again, I bid my hideous progeny go forth and prosper. I have an affection for it, for it was the offspring of happy days, when death and grief were but words, which found no true echo in my heart. Its several pages speak of many a walk, many a drive, and many a conversation, when I was not alone; and my companion was one who, in this world, I shall never see more. But this is for myself; my readers have nothing to do with these associations.

I will add but one word as to the alterations I have made. They are principally those of style. I have changed no portion of the story, nor introduced any new ideas of circumstances. I have mended the language where it was so bald as to interfere with the interest of the narrative; and these changes occur almost exclusively in the beginning of the first volume. Throughout they are entirely confined to such parts as are mere adjuncts to the story, leaving the core and substance of it untouched.

1831

CHARLOTTE BRONTË
1816–1855

Few nineteenth-century English novels had the impact of Charlotte Brontë's most famous work, about which the journalist Margaret Oliphant once mused that "the most alarming revolution of modern times has followed the invasion of *Jane Eyre*"— a book that, in her opinion, radically disrupted "an orthodox system of novel-making." And indeed, simultaneously a Gothic romance and a realistic bildungsroman, *Jane Eyre* (1847) riveted Victorian readers with an impassioned, first-person narrative spoken by a governess who was racked by fiery feelings even while, as she herself admitted, she was not only "poor, obscure, plain, and little" but apparently decorous and retiring.

The creator of this compelling character was herself comparatively poor, obscure, plain, and little, besides being also a woman of smoldering passion and ambition. Raised in a parsonage in the bleak Yorkshire town of Haworth, Charlotte Brontë and her brilliant siblings were brought up by a clergyman father with literary inclinations and by an austere aunt whom he invited to help care for the children after their mother's death. Like Jane Eyre, Charlotte and three of her sisters were sent to a nightmarish boarding school for girls, where the two older sisters—Maria and Elizabeth— died of consumption, just as Jane's friend Helen Burns does. But unlike Jane, Charlotte and Emily returned to a home in which, despite "Aunt Branwell's" sourness and the isolation of their moorland village, they formed a creative community, a kind of proto–writer's colony, with their brother Branwell and sister Anne.

After the deaths of all the Brontës, the juvenilia they collaboratively produced began to be published. Conceived as nighttime tales ("bed-plays") centered on a set of wooden soldiers that the Reverend Brontë had bought for his son, Branwell, these early fictions developed into a series of epic fantasies chronicling the histories of two imaginary kingdoms, "Angria" and "Gondal." In these, the children mimicked the styles and themes of such writers as Walter Scott and Lord Byron, "printing" their tales in miniature books, each the size of a pack of cards. All four were so enthralled by the narratives that they continued transcribing them even when they were well into their twenties. But Charlotte, in particular, became increasingly anxious about what she considered the dangerous draw of such romancing. Unlike Jane Austen, she had no inclination to parody the genre. Rather, she felt herself caught in the "fascinating spell" of what she called the "infernal world" of Angria.

In our selection excerpted from a diary she kept while working as a teacher at the Roe Head School for girls, Brontë struggles against what she experienced as an addiction to her fantasies; and finally, in "Farewell to Angria," she resolves to renounce romance in favor of realism. Yet as readers from Mrs. Oliphant to the present have discovered, in such novels as *Jane Eyre* and *Villette* (1853) she gained extraordinary artistic strength by drawing on both the "burning clime" of Angria and the "cooler region" of nineteenth-century England.

From Roe Head Journal

[ALL THIS DAY I HAVE BEEN IN A DREAM]

Friday August 11th—All this day I have been in a dream, half miserable and half ecstatic: miserable because I could not follow it out uninterruptedly; ecstatic because it shewed almost in the vivid light of reality the ongoings of the infernal world.[1] I had been toiling for nearly an hour with Miss Lister,

---

1. I.e., the imaginary world of Angria.

Miss Marriott and Ellen Cook, striving to teach them the distinction between an article and a substantive. The parsing lesson was completed, and dead silence had succeeded it in the schoolroom, and I sat sinking from irritation and weariness into a kind of lethargy.

The thought came over me: am I to spend all the best part of my life in this wretched bondage, forcibly suppressing my rage at the idleness, the apathy and the hyperbolical and most asinine stupidity of those fatheaded oafs, and on compulsion assuming an air of kindness, patience and assiduity? Must I from day to day sit chained to this chair prisoned within these four bare walls, while these glorious summer suns are burning in heaven and the year is revolving in its richest glow and declaring at the close of every summer day the time I am losing will never come again?

Stung to the heart with this reflection, I started up and mechanically walked to the window. A sweet August morning was smiling without. The dew was not yet dried off the field. The early shadows were stretching cool and dim from the haystack and the roots of the grand old oaks and thorns scattered along the sunk fence. All was still except the murmur of the scrubs about me over their tasks. I flung up the sash. An uncertain sound of inexpressible sweetness came on a dying gale from the south. I looked in that direction. Huddersfield[2] and the hills beyond it were all veiled in blue mist; the woods of Hopton and Heaton Lodge were clouding the water's edge; and the Calder, silent but bright, was shooting among them like a silver arrow. I listened. The sound sailed full and liquid down the descent. It was the bells of Huddersfield parish church. I shut the window and went back to my seat.

Then came on me, rushing impetuously, all the mighty phantasm that this had conjured from nothing to a system strange as some religious creed. I felt as if I could have written gloriously. I longed to write. The spirit of all Verdopolis, of all the mountainous North, of all the woodland West, of all the river-watered East[3] came crowding into my mind. If I had time to indulge it, I felt that the vague sensations of that moment would have settled down into some narrative better at least than anything I ever produced before. But just then a dolt came up with a lesson. I thought I should have vomited.

In the afternoon; Miss Ellen Lister was trigonometrically oecumenical about her French lessons. She nearly killed me between the violence of the irritation her horrid willfulness excited and the labour it took to subdue it to a moderate appearance of calmness. My fingers trembled as if I had had twenty-four hours' toothache, and my spirits felt worn down to a degree of desperate despondence. Miss Wooler tried to make me talk at tea time and was exceedingly kind to me, but I could not have roused if she had offered me worlds. After tea we took a long weary walk. I came back [?abime[4]] to the last degree, for Miss L[ister] and Miss M[arriot]t had been boring me with their vulgar familiar trash all the time we were out. If those girls knew how I loathe their company, they would not seek mine so much as they do.

The sun had set nearly a quarter of an hour before we returned and it was getting dusk. The ladies went into the schoolroom to do their exercises and I crept up to the bedroom to be *alone* for the first time that day. Delicious was the sensation I experienced as I laid down on the spare bed and resigned

2. A town in West Yorkshire.
3. All places in the "infernal world."
4. Perhaps "in the depths" (from the French *abîme*); the manuscript has *abyme*.

myself to the luxury of twilight and solitude. The stream of thought, checked all day, came flowing free and calm along the channel. My ideas were too shattered to form any defined picture, as they would have done in such circumstances at home, but detached thoughts soothingly flitted round me, and unconnected scenes occurred and then vanished, producing an effect certainly strange but, to me, very pleasing.

The toil of the day, succeeded by this moment of divine leisure, had acted on me like opium and was coiling about me a disturbed but fascinating spell, such as I never felt before. What I imagined grew morbidly vivid. I remember I quite seemed to see, with my bodily eyes, a lady standing in the hall of a gentleman's house, as if waiting for someone. It was dusk and there was the dim outline of antlers, with a hat and a rough greatcoat upon them. She had a flat candlestick in her hand and seemed coming from the kitchen or some such place. She was very handsome. It is not often we can form from pure idea faces so individually fine. She had black curls, hanging rather low on her neck, and very blooming skin and dark, anxious-looking eyes. I imagined it the sultry close of a summer's day, and she was dressed in muslin—not at all romantically—a flimsy, printed fabric with large sleeves and a full skirt.

As she waited, I most distinctly heard the front door open and saw the soft moonlight disclosed upon a lawn outside, and beyond the lawn at a distance I saw a town with lights twinkling through the gloaming. Two or three gentlemen entered, one of whom I knew by intuition to be called Dr Charles Brandon and another William Locksley Esqr. The doctor was a tall, handsomely built man, habited in cool, ample-looking white trowsers and a large straw hat, which being set on one side, shewed a great deal of dark hair and a sunburnt but smooth and oval cheek. Locksley and the other went into an inner room, but Brandon stayed a minute in the hall. There was a bason of water on a slab, and he went and washed his hands, while the lady held the light.

'How has Ryder borne the operation?' she asked.

'Very cleverly. He'll be well in three weeks.' was the reply. 'But Lucy won't do for a nurse at the hospital. You must take her for your head servant, to make my cambric fronts and handkerchiefs, and to wash and iron your lace aprons. Little silly thing, she fainted at the very sight of the instruments.'

Whilst Brandon spoke, a dim concatenation of ideas describing a passage in some individual's life, a varied scene in which persons and events, features and incidents, revolved in misty panorama, entered my mind. The mention of the hospital, of Ryder, of Lucy, each called up a certain set of reminiscences or rather fancies. It would be endless to tell all that was at that moment suggested.

Lucy first appeared before me as sitting at the door of a lone cottage on a kind of moorish waste, sorrowful and sickly; a young woman with those mild, regular features that always interest us, however poorly set off by the meanness of surrounding adjuncts. It was a calm afternoon. Her eyes were turned towards a road crossing the heath. A speck appeared on it far, far away. Lucy smiled to herself as it dawned into view, and while she did so there was something about her melancholy brow, her straight nose and faded bloom that reminded me of one who might, for anything I at that instant knew, be dead and buried under the newly plotted sod. It was this likeness and the feeling of its existence that had called Dr Brandon so far from his bodily circle and that made him now, when he stood near his patient, regard her meek face, turned submissively and gratefully to him, with tenderer kindness than he bestowed on employers of aristocratic rank and wealth.

No more. I have not time to work out the vision. A thousand things were connected with it—a whole country, statesmen and kings, a revolution, thrones and princedoms subverted and reinstated.

Meantime, the tall man washing his bloody hands in a bason and the dark beauty standing by with a light remained pictured on my visual eye with irksome and alarming distinctness. I grew frightened at the vivid glow of the candle, at the reality of the lady's erect and symmetrical figure, of her spirited and handsome face, of her anxious eye watching Brandon's and seeking out its meaning, diving for its real expression through the semblance of severity that habit and suffering had given to his stern aspect.

I felt confounded and annoyed. I scarcely knew by what. At last I became aware of a feeling like a heavy weight laid across me. I knew I was wide awake and that it was dark, and that, moreover, the ladies were now come into the room to get their curl-papers. They perceived me lying on the bed and I heard them talking about me. I wanted to speak, to rise. It was impossible. I felt that this was a frightful predicament, that it would not do. The weight pressed me as if some huge animal had flung itself across me. A horrid apprehension quickened every pulse I had. 'I must get up,' I thought, and did so with a start. I have had enough of morbidly vivid realizations. Every advantage has its corresponding disadvantage. Tea's ready. Miss Wooler is impatient.

October 14th 1836

[Farewell to Angria]

I have now written a great many books, and for a long time I have dwelt on the same characters and scenes and subjects. I have shewn my landscapes in every variety of shade and light, which morning, noon and evening—the rising, the meridian and the setting sun—can bestow upon them. Sometimes I have filled the air with the whitened tempest of winter: snow has embossed the dark arms of the beech and oak and filled with drifts the parks of the lowlands or the mountain-pass of wilder districts. Again, the same mansion with its woods, the same moor with its glens, has been softly coloured with the tints of moonlight in summer. And in the warmest June night the trees have clustered their full-plumed heads over glades flushed with flowers.

So it is with persons. My readers have been habituated to one set of features, which they have seen now in profile, now in full-face, now in outline, and again in finished painting, varied but by the change of feeling or temper or age; lit with love; flushed with passion; shaded with grief; kindled with ecstasy; in meditation and mirth, in sorrow and scorn and rapture; with the round outline of childhood; the beauty and fullness of youth; the strength of manhood and the furrow of thoughtful decline. But we must change, for the eye is tired of the picture so oft recurring and now so familiar.

Yet do not urge me too fast reader. It is no easy thing to dismiss from my imagination the images which have filled it so long. They were my friends and my intimate acquaintance, and I could with little labour describe to you the faces, the voices, the actions of those who peopled my thoughts by day and not seldom stole strangely even into my dreams by night. When I depart from these I feel almost as if I stood on the threshold of a home and were bidding farewell to its inmates. When I strive to conjure up new inmates, I feel as if I had got into a distant country where every face was unknown and the character of all the population an enigma which it would take much study to comprehend and much talent to expound. Still, I long to quit for a while that burning clime where we have sojourned too long—its skies flame; the glow of sunset is always upon it. The mind would cease from excitement and turn now to a cooler region, where the dawn breaks grey and sober and the coming day, for a time at least, is subdued in clouds.

ca. 1839

GEORGE ELIOT
1819–1880

The powerful and passionate thinker who produced such major novels as *The Mill on the Floss* (1866), *Middlemarch* (1871–72), and *Daniel Deronda* (1874–76) under the pseudonym George Eliot began her career as a translator, editor, philosopher, and critic. Musing on her "astonishing intellectual vitality," Virginia Woolf noted that there was "a dogged determination in [Eliot's] advance upon the citadel of culture," adding that although her "development was very slow . . . it had the irresistible impetus behind it of a deep-seated and noble ambition." And indeed, George Eliot—born Mary Anne Evans—was raised in the provinces about which she was to write with such nuanced and meditative brilliance in fiction after fiction, and kept house for her father, an estate agent in Warwickshire, until he died when she was thirty. At that point, she had already abandoned the Low Church faith in which she had been brought up for a more skeptical view of Christianity, and in 1846 she had translated David Friedrich Strauss's radically revisionary *Life of Jesus* (1835–36). Journeying first to the Continent and then to London, she began working as a journalist and editor for *The Westminster Review*, where she came to know such major literary and philosophical figures as Charles Dickens, Harriet Martineau, John Stuart Mill, Herbert Spencer, and, most importantly for her creative future, George Henry Lewes, a married writer-editor with whom she was to elope to Germany in 1854.

It was Lewes who facilitated Mary Anne Evans's transformation from an editor and journalist into a fiction writer. He encouraged her to compose and publish the stories that were eventually collected as *Scenes of Clerical Life* (1858) and helped foster her decision to publish under a male pseudonym, believing that "people would have sniffed" at her first novel, *Adam Bede* (1859), "if they had known the writer to be a woman." But even while George Eliot—whose pseudonym offered homage to George Lewes and implied an anagrammatic "To L.—I owe it"—continued producing and publishing major novels, she remained a reviewer of considerable authority. Her "Silly Novels by Lady Novelists" (1856) is perhaps the most famous of her essays on the writings of women of letters; but our other selection here, which offers her considered analyses of a major precursor and a powerful contemporary, demonstrates, as the critic Barbara Hardy puts it, her "generous sympathy with Victorian feminism" even while it dramatizes her way of confronting what Hardy has defined as a central concern in Eliot's novels: "the *ex-officio* disability of being a woman."

Margaret Fuller and Mary Wollstonecraft[1]

The dearth of new books just now gives us time to recur to less recent ones which we have hitherto noticed but slightly; and among these we choose the late edition of Margaret Fuller's *Woman in the Nineteenth Century,* because we think it has been unduly thrust into the background by less comprehensive and candid productions on the same subject. Notwithstanding certain defects of taste and a sort of vague spiritualism and grandiloquence which belong to all but the very best American writers, the book is a valuable one; it has the enthusiasm of a noble and sympathetic nature, with the moderation and breadth and large allowance of a vigorous and cultivated understanding. There is no exaggeration of woman's moral excellence or intellectual capabilities; no injudicious insistence on her fitness for this or that function hitherto engrossed by men; but a calm plea for the removal of unjust laws and artificial restrictions, so that the possibilities of her nature may have room for full development, a wisely stated demand to disencumber her of the

> Parasitic forms
> That seem to keep her up, but drag her down—
> And leave her field to burgeon and to bloom
> From all within her, make herself her own
> To give or keep, to live and learn and be
> All that not harms distinctive womanhood.[2]

It is interesting to compare this essay of Margaret Fuller's published in its earliest form in 1843,[3] with a work on the position of woman, written between sixty and seventy years ago—we mean Mary Wollstonecraft's *Rights of Woman.* The latter work was not continued beyond the first volume; but so far as this carries the subject, the comparison, at least in relation to strong sense and loftiness of moral tone, is not at all disadvantageous to the woman of the last century. There is in some quarters a vague prejudice against the *Rights of Woman* as in some way or other a reprehensible book, but readers who go to it with this impression will be surprised to find it eminently serious, severely moral, and withal rather heavy—the true reason, perhaps, that no edition has been published since 1796, and that it is now rather scarce. There are several points of resemblance, as well as of striking difference, between the two books. A strong understanding is present in both; but Margaret Fuller's mind was like some regions of her own American continent, where you are constantly stepping from the sunny "clearings" into the mysterious twilight of the tangled forest—she often passes in one breath from

---

1. Published in *The Leader* in 1855, this essay is a retrospective book review of two important feminist publications—*A Vindication of the Rights of Woman* (1792) by Mary Wollstonecraft and *Woman in the Nineteenth Century* (1855; published originally as "The Great Lawsuit," 1843), by Margaret Fuller.

2. Tennyson's *The Princess* 7.253–58. As noted by Thomas Plinney, the quotation, slightly inaccurate, is from the unrevised 1847 text of the poem.

3. I.e., the original version published in *The Dial*; revised and expanded in 1855.

forcible reasoning to dreamy vagueness; moreover, her unusually varied culture gives her great command of illustration. Mary Wollstonecraft, on the other hand, is nothing if not rational; she has no erudition, and her grave pages are lit up by no ray of fancy. In both writers we discern, under the brave bearing of a strong and truthful nature, the beating of a loving woman's heart, which teaches them not to undervalue the smallest offices of domestic care or kindliness. But Margaret Fuller, with all her passionate sensibility, is more of the literary woman, who would not have been satisfied without intellectual production; Mary Wollstonecraft, we imagine, wrote not at all for writing's sake, but from the pressure of other motives. So far as the difference of date allows, there is a striking coincidence in their trains of thought; indeed, every important idea in the *Rights of Woman*, except the combination of home education with a common day-school for boys and girls, reappears in Margaret Fuller's essay.

One point on which they both write forcibly is the fact that, while men have a horror of such faculty or culture in the other sex as tends to place it on a level with their own, they are really in a state of subjection to ignorant and feeble-minded women. Margaret Fuller says:

> Wherever man is sufficiently raised above extreme poverty or brutal stupidity, to care for the comforts of the fireside, or the bloom and ornament of life, woman has always power enough, if she chooses to exert it, and is usually disposed to do so, in proportion to her ignorance and childish vanity. Unacquainted with the importance of life and its purposes, trained to a selfish coquetry and love of petty power, she does not look beyond the pleasure of making herself felt at the moment, and governments are shaken and commerce broken up to gratify the pique of a female favorite. The English shopkeeper's wife does not vote, but it is for her interest that the politician canvasses by the coarsest flattery.

Again:

> All wives, bad or good, loved or unloved, inevitably influence their husbands from the power their position not merely gives, but necessitates of coloring evidence and infusing feelings in hours when the—patient, shall I call him?—is off his guard.

Hear now what Mary Wollstonecraft says on the same subject:

> Women have been allowed to remain in ignorance and slavish dependence many, very many years, and still we hear of nothing but their fondness of pleasure and sway, their preference of rakes and soldiers, their childish attachment to toys, and the vanity that makes them value accomplishments more than virtues. History brings forward a fearful catalogue of the crimes which their cunning has produced, when the weak slaves have had sufficient address to overreach their masters. . . . When, therefore, I call women slaves, I mean in a political and civil sense; for indirectly they obtain too much power, and are debased by their exertions to obtain illicit sway. . . . The libertinism, and even the virtues of superior men, will always give women of some description great power over them; and these weak women, under the influence of childish passions and selfish vanity, *will throw a false light over the objects which the very men view with their eyes who ought to enlighten their judgment.* Men of

fancy, and those sanguine characters who mostly hold the helm of human affairs in general, relax in the society of women; and surely I need not cite to the most superficial reader of history the numerous examples of vice and oppression which the private intrigues of female favorites have produced; not to dwell on the mischief that naturally arises from the blundering interposition of well-meaning folly. *For in the transactions of business it is much better to have to deal with a knave than a fool, because a knave adheres to some plan, and any plan of reason may be seen through sooner than a sudden flight of folly.* The power which vile and foolish women have had over wise men who possessed sensibility is notorious.

There is a notion commonly entertained among men that an instructed woman, capable of having opinions, is likely to prove an unpracticable yoke-fellow, always pulling one way when her husband wants to go the other, oracular in tone, and prone to give curtain lectures[4] on metaphysics. But surely, so far as obstinacy is concerned, your unreasoning animal is the most unmanageable of creatures, where you are not allowed to settle the question by a cudgel, a whip and bridle, or even a string to the leg. For our own parts, we see no consistent or commodious medium between the old plan of corporal discipline and that thorough education of women which will make them rational beings in the highest sense of the word. Wherever weakness is not harshly controlled it must *govern,* as you may see when a strong man holds a little child by the hand, how he is pulled hither and thither, and wearied in his walk by his submission to the whims and feeble movements of his companion. A really cultured woman, like a really cultured man, will be ready to yield in trifles. So far as we see, there is no indissoluble connection between infirmity of logic and infirmity of will, and a woman quite innocent of an opinion in philosophy, is as likely as not to have an indomitable opinion about the kitchen. As to airs of superiority, no woman ever had them in consequence of true culture, but only because her culture was shallow or unreal, only as a result of what Mrs. Malaprop well calls "the ineffectual qualities in a woman"[5]—mere acquisitions carried about, and not knowledge thoroughly assimilated so as to enter into the growth of the character.

To return to Margaret Fuller, some of the best things she says are on the folly of absolute definitions of woman's nature and absolute demarcations of woman's mission. "Nature," she says, "seems to delight in varying the arrangements, as if to show that she will be fettered by no rule; and we must admit the same varieties that she admits." Again: "If nature is never bound down, nor the voice of inspiration stifled, that is enough. We are pleased that women should write and speak, if they feel need of it, from having something to tell; but silence for ages would be no misfortune, if that silence be from divine command, and not from man's tradition." And here is a passage, the beginning of which has been often quoted:

> If you ask me what offices they [women] may fill, I reply—any. I do not care what case you put; let them be sea-captains if you will. I do not doubt there are women well fitted for such an office, and, if so, I should

---

4. See Douglas Jerrold's comic sketches of a wife who delivers nightly lectures to her husband from behind their bed curtains, *Mrs. Caudle's Curtain Lectures* (1846).
5. In response to compliments about her "intel-

lectual accomplishments," Mrs. Malaprop exclaims: "Ah! few gentlemen, nowadays, know how to value the ineffectual qualities in a woman!" Richard Brinsley Sheridan, *The Rivals* (1775), 3.2.

be as glad as to welcome the Maid of Saragossa, or the Maid of Misso-longhi, or the Suliote heroine, or Emily Plater.[6] I think women need, especially at this juncture, a much greater range of occupation than they have, to rouse their latent powers. . . . In families that I know, some lit-tle girls like to saw wood, others to use carpenter's tools. Where these tastes are indulged, cheerfulness and good-humor are promoted. Where they are forbidden, because "such things are not proper for girls," they grow sullen and mischievous. Fourier had observed these wants of women, as no one can fail to do who watches the desires of little girls, or knows the *ennui* that haunts grown women, except where they make to themselves a serene little world by art of some kind. He, therefore, in pro-posing a great variety of employments, in manufactures or the care of plants and animals, allows for one-third of women as likely to have a taste for masculine pursuits, one-third of men for feminine.[7] . . . I have no doubt, however, that a large proportion of women would give themselves to the same employments as now, because there are circumstances that must lead them. Mothers will delight to make the nest soft and warm. Nature would take care of that; no need to clip the wings of any bird that wants to soar and sing, or finds in itself the strength of pinion for a migra-tory flight unusual to its kind. The difference would be that *all* need not be constrained to employments for which *some* are unfit.

Apropos of the same subject, we find Mary Wollstonecraft offering a sug-gestion which the women of the United States have already begun to carry out. She says:

> Women, in particular, all want to be ladies, which is simply to have nothing to do, but listlessly to go they scarcely care where, for they can-not tell what. But what have women to do in society? I may be asked, but to loiter with easy grace; surely you would not condemn them all to suckle fools and chronicle small beer.[8] No. *Women might certainly study the art of healing, and be physicians as well as nurses.* . . . Business of var-ious kinds they might likewise pursue, if they were educated in a more orderly manner. . . . Women would not then marry for a support, as men accept of places under government, and neglect the implied duties.

Men pay a heavy price for their reluctance to encourage self-help and independent resources in women. The precious meridian years of many a man of genius have to be spent in the toil of routine, that an "establishment" may be kept up for a woman who can understand none of his secret yearn-ings, who is fit for nothing but to sit in her drawing-room like a doll-Madonna in her shrine. No matter. Anything is more endurable than to change our established formulae about women, or to run the risk of looking up to our wives instead of looking down on them. *Sit divus, dummodo non sit vivus* (let him be a god, provided he be not living), said the Roman magnates of Romu-

---

6. A Polish patriot, who became a captain in com-mand of a company in the insurgent army fighting the Russians in 1831. "Maid of Saragossa": Maria Agustin, who fought against the French at the siege of Saragossa, in Spain, in 1808. "Maid of Missolonghi": an unidentified Greek who fought during the Turkish sieges of that town in 1822 or 1826. "The Suliote heroine": probably Moscha, who led a band of three hundred women to rout the Turks during the siege of Souli, in Albania, in 1803.
7. Charles Fourier (1772–1837), in his utopian treatise *The New Industrial World* (1829–30), develops these theories in his discussion of "the Little Hordes."
8. Iago on the role of women; Shakespeare's *Othello* 2.1.162.

lus;[9] and so men say of women, let them be idols, useless absorbents of previous things, provided we are not obliged to admit them to be strictly fellow-beings, to be treated, one and all, with justice and sober reverence.

On one side we hear that woman's position can never be improved until women themselves are better; and, on the other, that women can never become better until their position is improved—until the laws are made more just, and a wider field opened to feminine activity. But we constantly hear the same difficulty stated about the human race in general. There is a perpetual action and reaction between individuals and institutions; we must try and mend both by little and little—the only way in which human things can be mended. Unfortunately, many over-zealous champions of women assert their actual equality with men—nay, even their moral superiority to men—as a ground for their release from oppressive laws and restrictions. They lose strength immensely by this false position. If it were true, then there would be a case in which slavery and ignorance nourished virtue, and so far we should have an argument for the continuance of bondage. But we want freedom and culture for woman, because subjection and ignorance have debased her, and with her, Man; for—

> If she be small, slight-natured, miserable,
> How shall men grow?[1]

Both Margaret Fuller and Mary Wollstonecraft have too much sagacity to fall into this sentimental exaggeration. Their ardent hopes of what women may become do not prevent them from seeing and painting women as they are. On the relative moral excellence of men and women Mary Wollstonecraft speaks with the most decision:

> Women are supposed to possess more sensibility, and even humanity, than men, and their strong attachments and instantaneous emotions of compassion are given as proofs; but the clinging affection of ignorance has seldom anything noble in it, and may mostly be resolved into self-ishness, as well as the affection of children and brutes. I have known many weak women whose sensibility was entirely engrossed by their husbands; and as for their humanity, it was very faint indeed, or rather it was only a transient emotion of compassion. Humanity does not consist "in a squeamish ear," says an eminent orator.[2] "It belongs to the mind as well as to the nerves." But this kind of exclusive affection, though it degrades the individual, should not be brought forward as a proof of the inferiority of the sex, because it is the natural consequence of confined views; for even women of superior sense, having their attention turned to little employments and private plans, rarely rise to heroism, unless when spurred on by love! and love, as an heroic passion, like genius, appears but once in an age. I therefore agree with the moralist who asserts "that women have seldom so much generosity as men";[3] and that their narrow affections, to which justice and humanity are often sacrificed, render the sex apparently inferior, especially as they are commonly inspired by men;

---

9. Cf. *Historia Augusta* (?ca. 4th c. C.E.), *Geta* 2, in which the same cynical comment is made on a proposal to have a man deified.
1. Tennyson's *The Princess* 7.249–50.

2. The English politician Charles James Fox (1749–1806), in a debate on the slave trade.
3. Quoted from Adam Smith, *The Theory of Moral Sentiments* (1759).

but I contend that the heart would expand as the understanding gained strength, if women were not depressed from their cradles.

We had marked several other passages of Margaret Fuller's for extract, but as we do not aim at an exhaustive treatment of our subject, and are only touching a few of its points, we have, perhaps, already claimed as much of the reader's attention as he will be willing to give to such desultory material.

1855

From Silly Novels by Lady Novelists

Silly Novels by Lady Novelists are a genus with many species, determined by the particular quality of silliness that predominates in them—the frothy, the prosy, the pious, or the pedantic. But it is a mixture of all these—a composite order of feminine fatuity, that produces the largest class of such novels, which we shall distinguish as the *mind-and-millinery* species. The heroine is usually an heiress, probably a peeress in her own right, with perhaps a vicious baronet, an amiable duke, and an irresistible younger son of a marquis as lovers in the foreground, a clergyman and a poet sighing for her in the middle distance, and a crowd of undefined adorers dimly indicated beyond. Her eyes and her wit are both dazzling; her nose and her morals are alike free from any tendency to irregularity; she has a superb *contralto* and a superb intellect; she is perfectly well-dressed and perfectly religious; she dances like a sylph, and reads the Bible in the original tongues. Or it may be that the heroine is not an heiress—that rank and wealth are the only things in which she is deficient; but she infallibly gets into high society, she has the triumph of refusing many matches and securing the best, and she wears some family jewels or other as a sort of crown of righteousness at the end. Rakish men either bite their lips in impotent confusion at her repartees, or are touched to penitence by her reproofs, which, on appropriate occasions, rise to a lofty strain of rhetoric; indeed, there is a general propensity in her to make speeches, and to rhapsodize at some length when she retires to her bedroom. In her recorded conversations she is amazingly eloquent, and in her unrecorded conversations, amazingly witty. She is understood to have a depth of insight that looks through and through the shallow theories of philosophers, and her superior instincts are a sort of dial by which men have only to set their clocks and watches, and all will go well. The men play a very subordinate part by her side. You are consoled now and then by a hint that they have affairs, which keeps you in mind that the working-day business of the world is somehow being carried on, but ostensibly the final cause of their existence is that they may accompany the heroine on her "starring" expedition through life. They see her at a ball, and are dazzled; at a flower-show, and they are fascinated; on a riding excursion, and they are witched by her noble horsemanship; at church, and they are awed by the sweet solemnity of her demeanour. She is the ideal woman in feelings, faculties, and flounces. For all this, she as often as not marries the wrong person to begin with, and she suffers terribly from the plots and intrigues of the vicious baronet; but even death has a soft place in his heart for such a paragon, and remedies all mistakes for her just at the right moment. The vicious baronet is sure to be killed in a duel, and the tedious husband dies in his bed requesting his wife, as a particular favour to him, to marry the man she loves best, and having already dispatched a note to the lover informing him of the comfortable arrangement. Before matters arrive at this desirable issue our feelings are tried by seeing the noble, lovely, and gifted heroine pass through many *mauvais* moments,[1] but we have the satisfaction of knowing that her sorrows are wept into embroidered pocket-handkerchiefs, that her fainting form reclines on the very best upholstery, and that whatever vicissitudes she may undergo, from being dashed out of her carriage to having her head shaved in a fever, she comes out of them all with a complexion more blooming and locks more redundant than ever.

We may remark, by the way, that we have been relieved from a serious scruple by discovering that silly novels by lady novelists rarely introduce us into any other than very lofty and fashionable society. We had imagined that destitute women turned novelists, as they turned governesses, because they had no other "lady-like" means of getting their bread. On this supposition, vacillating syntax and improbable incident had a certain pathos for us, like the extremely supererogatory pincushions and ill-devised nightcaps that are offered for sale by a blind man. We felt the commodity to be a nuisance, but we were glad to think that the money went to relieve the necessitous, and we pictured to ourselves lonely women struggling for a maintenance, or wives and daughters devoting themselves to the production of "copy" out of pure heroism,—perhaps to pay their husband's debts, or to purchase luxuries for a sick father. Under these impressions we shrank from criticising a lady's novel: her English might be faulty, but, we said to ourselves, her motives are irreproachable; her imagination may be uninventive, but her patience is untiring. Empty writing was excused by an empty stomach, and twaddle was consecrated by tears. But no! This theory of ours, like many other pretty theories, has had to give way before observation. Women's silly novels, we are now convinced, are written under totally different circumstances. The fair writers have evidently never talked to a tradesman except from a carriage window; they have no notion of the working-classes except as "dependents;" they think five hundred a-year a miserable pittance; Belgravia[2] and "baronial halls" are their primary truths; and they have no idea of feeling interest in any man who is not at least a great landed proprietor, if not a prime minister. It is clear that they write in elegant boudoirs, with violet-colored ink and a ruby pen; that they must be entirely indifferent to publishers' accounts, and inexperienced in every form of poverty except poverty of brains. It is true that we are constantly struck with the want of verisimilitude in their representations of the high society in which they seem to live; but then they betray no closer acquaintance with any other form of life. If their peers and peeresses are improbable, their literary men, tradespeople, and cottagers are impossible; and their intellect seems to have the peculiar impartiality of reproducing both what they *have* seen and heard, and what they have *not* seen and heard, with equal unfaithfulness.

* * *

1. Bad moments (French).　　　2. A wealthy neighborhood in London.

Writers of the mind-and-millinery school are remarkably unanimous in their choice of diction. In their novels, there is usually a lady or gentleman who is more or less of a upas tree:[3] the lover has a manly breast; minds are redolent of various things; hearts are hollow; events are utilized; friends are consigned to the tomb; infancy is an engaging period; the sun is a luminary that goes to his western couch, or gathers the rain-drops into his refulgent bosom; life is a melancholy boon; Albion and Scotia are conversational epithets. There is a striking resemblance, too, in the character of their moral comments, such, for instance, as that "It is a fact, no less true than melancholy, that all people, more or less, richer or poorer, are swayed by bad example;" that "Books, however trivial, contain some subjects from which useful information may be drawn;" that "Vice can too often borrow the language of virtue;" that "Merit and nobility of nature must exist, to be accepted, for clamour and pretension cannot impose upon those too well read in human nature to be easily deceived;" and that, "In order to forgive, we must have been injured." There is, doubtless, a class of readers to whom these remarks appear peculiarly pointed and pungent; for we often find them doubly and trebly scored with the pencil, and delicate hands giving in their determined adhesion to these hardy novelties by a distinct *très vrai*,[4] emphasized by many notes of exclamation. The colloquial style of these novels is often marked by much ingenious inversion, and a careful avoidance of such cheap phraseology as can be heard every day. Angry young gentlemen exclaim—" 'Tis ever thus, methinks;" and in the half-hour before dinner a young lady informs her next neighbour that the first day she read Shakspeare she "stole away into the park, and beneath the shadow of the greenwood tree, devoured with rapture the inspired page of the great magician." But the most remarkable efforts of the mind-and-millinery writers lie in their philosophic reflections. The authoress of "Laura Gay,"[5] for example, having married her hero and heroine, improves the event by observing that "if those sceptics, whose eyes have so long gazed on matter that they can no longer see aught else in man, could once enter with heart and soul into such bliss as this, they would come to say that the soul of man and the polypus are not of common origin, or of the same texture." Lady novelists, it appears, can see something else besides matter; they are not limited to phenomena, but can relieve their eyesight by occasional glimpses of the *noumenon,* and are, therefore, naturally better able than any one else to confound sceptics, even of that remarkable, but to us unknown school, which maintains that the soul of man is of the same texture as the polypus.

The most pitiable of all silly novels by lady novelists are what we may call the *oracular* species—novels intended to expound the writer's religious, philosophical, or moral theories. There seems to be a notion abroad among women, rather akin to the superstition that the speech and actions of idiots are inspired, and that the human being most entirely exhausted of common sense is the fittest vehicle of revelation. To judge from their writings, there are certain ladies who think that an amazing ignorance, both of science and of life, is the best possible qualification for forming an opinion on the knottiest moral and speculative questions. Apparently, their recipe for solving all

3. I.e., a poisonous influence.
4. Very true (French).

5. An 1856 novel by Laura Gay, which Eliot has satirized in the previous section.

such difficulties is something like this:—Take a woman's head, stuff it with a smattering of philosophy and literature chopped small, and with false notions of society baked hard, let it hang over a desk a few hours every day, and serve up hot in feeble English, when not required. You will rarely meet with a lady novelist of the oracular class who is diffident of her ability to decide on theological questions,—who has any suspicion that she is not capable of discriminating with the nicest accuracy between the good and evil in all church parties,—who does not see precisely how it is that men have gone wrong hitherto,—and pity philosophers in general that they have not had the opportunity of consulting her. Great writers, who have modestly contented themselves with putting their experience into fiction, and have thought it quite a sufficient task to exhibit men and things as they are, she sighs over as deplorably deficient in the application of their powers. "They have solved no great questions"—and she is ready to remedy their omission by setting before you a complete theory of life and manual of divinity, in a love story, where ladies and gentlemen of good family go through genteel vicissitudes, to the utter confusion of Deists, Puseyites, and ultra-Protestants, and to the perfect establishment of that particular view of Christianity which either condenses itself into a sentence of small caps, or explodes into a cluster of stars on the three hundred and thirtieth page. It is true, the ladies and gentlemen will probably seem to you remarkably little like any you have had the fortune or misfortune to meet with, for, as a general rule, the ability of a lady novelist to describe actual life and her fellow-men, is in inverse proportion to her confident eloquence about God and the other world, and the means by which she usually chooses to conduct you to true ideas of the invisible is a totally false picture of the visible.

*   *   *

The epithet "silly" may seem impertinent, applied to a novel which indicates so much reading and intellectual activity as "The Enigma;"[6] but we use this epithet advisedly. If, as the world has long agreed, a very great amount of instruction will not make a wise man, still less will a very mediocre amount of instruction make a wise woman. And the most mischievous form of feminine silliness is the literary form, because it tends to confirm the popular prejudice against the more solid education of women. When men see girls wasting their time in consultations about bonnets and ball dresses, and in giggling or sentimental love-confidences, or middle-aged women mismanaging their children, and solacing themselves with acrid gossip, they can hardly help saying, "For Heaven's sake, let girls be better educated; let them have some better objects of thought—some more solid occupations." But after a few hours' conversation with an oracular literary woman, or a few hours' reading of her books, they are likely enough to say, "After all, when a woman gets some knowledge, see what use she makes of it! Her knowledge remains acquisition, instead of passing into culture; instead of being subdued into modesty and simplicity by a larger acquaintance with thought and fact, she has a feverish consciousness of her attainments; she keeps a sort of mental pocket-mirror, and is continually looking in it at her own " 'intellectuality;' she spoils the taste of one's muffin by questions of metaphysics; 'puts down' men at a dinner table with her superior information; and seizes the opportunity of

6. *The Enigma: A Leaf from the Archives of Wolchorley House* (1856), an anonymously published novel just ridiculed by Eliot.

a *soirée* to catechise us on the vital question of the relation between mind and matter. And then, look at her writings! She mistakes vagueness for depth, bombast for eloquence, and affectation for originality; she struts on one page, rolls her eyes on another, grimaces in a third, and is hysterical in a fourth. She may have read many writings of great men, and a few writings of great women; but she is as unable to discern the difference between her own style and theirs as a Yorkshireman[7] is to discern the difference between his own English and a Londoner's: rhodomontade is the native accent of her intellect. No—the average nature of women is too shallow and feeble a soil to bear much tillage; it is only fit for the very lightest crops."

It is true that the men who come to such a decision on such very superficial and imperfect observation may not be among the wisest in the world; but we have not now to contest their opinion—we are only pointing out how it is unconsciously encouraged by many women who have volunteered themselves as representatives of the feminine intellect. We do not believe that a man was ever strengthened in such an opinion by associating with a woman of true culture, whose mind had absorbed her knowledge instead of being absorbed by it. A really cultured woman, like a really cultured man, is all the simpler and the less obtrusive for her knowledge; it has made her see herself and her opinions in something like just proportions; she does not make it a pedestal from which she flatters herself that she commands a complete view of men and things, but makes it a point of observation from which to form a right estimate of herself. She neither spouts poetry nor quotes Cicero on slight provocation; not because she thinks that a sacrifice must be made to the prejudices of men, but because that mode of exhibiting her memory and Latinity does not present itself to her as edifying or graceful. She does not write books to confound philosophers, perhaps because she is able to write books that delight them. In conversation she is the least formidable of women, because she understands you, without wanting to make you aware that you *can't* understand her. She does not give you information, which is the raw material of culture,—she gives you sympathy, which is its subtlest essence.

A more numerous class of silly novels than the oracular, (which are generally inspired by some form of High Church, or transcendental Christianity,) is what we may call the *white neck-cloth* species, which represent the tone of thought and feeling in the Evangelical party. This species is a kind of genteel tract on a large scale, intended as a sort of medicinal sweetmeat for Low Church young ladies; an Evangelical substitute for the fashionable novel, as the May Meetings[8] are a substitute for the Opera. Even Quaker children, one would think, can hardly have been denied the indulgence of a doll; but it must be a doll dressed in a drab gown and a coal-scuttle bonnet—not a worldly doll, in gauze and spangles. And there are no young ladies, we imagine,—unless they belong to the Church of the United Brethren, in which people are married without any love-making—who can dispense with love stories. Thus, for Evangelical young ladies there are Evangelical love stories, in which the vicissitudes of the tender passion are sanctified by saving views of Regeneration and the Atonement. These novels differ from the oracular ones, as a Low Churchwoman often differs from a High Churchwoman: they are a little less

7. Assumed to speak an unrefined dialect.
8. The annual spring meetings of the Church of England's Missionary Society.

supercilious, and a great deal more ignorant, a little less correct in their syntax, and a great deal more vulgar.

The Orlando[9] of Evangelical literature is the young curate, looked at from the point of view of the middle class, where cambric bands are understood to have as thrilling an effect on the hearts of young ladies as epaulettes have in the classes above and below it. In the ordinary type of these novels, the hero is almost sure to be a young curate, frowned upon, perhaps, by worldly mammas, but carrying captive the hearts of their daughters, who can "never forget *that* sermon;" tender glances are seized from the pulpit stairs instead of the opera-box; *tête-à-têtes* are seasoned with quotations from Scripture, instead of quotations from the poets; and questions as to the state of the heroine's affections are mingled with anxieties as to the state of her soul. The young curate always has a background of well-dressed and wealthy, if not fashionable society;—for Evangelical silliness is as snobbish as any other kind of silliness; and the Evangelical lady novelist, while she explains to you the type of the scapegoat on one page, is ambitious on another to represent the manners and conversation of aristocratic people. Her pictures of fashionable society are often curious studies considered as efforts of the Evangelical imagination; but in one particular the novels of the White Neck-cloth School are meritoriously realistic,—their favourite hero, the Evangelical young curate is always rather an insipid personage.

*   *   *

But, perhaps, the least readable of silly women's novels, are the *modern-antique* species, which unfold to us the domestic life of Jannes and Jambres, the private love affairs of Sennacherib, or the mental struggles and ultimate conversion of Demetrius the silversmith.[1] From most silly novels we can at least extract a laugh; but those of the modern antique school have a ponderous, a leaden kind of fatuity, under which we groan. What can be more demonstrative of the inability of literary women to measure their own powers, than their frequent assumption of a task which can only be justified by the rarest concurrence of acquirement with genius? The finest effort to reanimate the past is of course only approximative—is always more or less an infusion of the modern spirit into the ancient form,—

> Was ihr den Geist der Zeiten heisst,
> Das ist im Grund der Herren eigner Geist,
> In dem die Zeiten sich bespiegeln.[2]

Admitting that genius which has familiarized itself with all the relics of an ancient period can sometimes, by the force of its sympathetic divination, restore the missing notes in the "music of humanity," and reconstruct the fragments into a whole which will really bring the remote past nearer to us, and interpret it to our duller apprehension,—this form of imaginative power must always be among the very rarest, because it demands as much accurate and minute knowledge as creative vigour. Yet we find ladies constantly choosing to make their mental mediocrity more conspicuous, by clothing it in a masquerade of ancient names; by putting their feeble sentimentality into the

9. I.e., the romantic hero (from the character in Shakespeare's *As You Like It*).
1. All examples of the antique: Egyptian magicians (see 2 Timothy 3.8); a king of Assyria, ruling from 704 to 681 B.C.E.; and an Ephesian craftsman who opposed Paul (Acts 19.24–27).
2. What they call the spirit of the age / Is at the base the gentlemen's own spirit, / In which the ages are reflected (German); Goethe's *Faust*, part I (1808), lines 577–79.

mouths of Roman vestals or Egyptian princesses, and attributing their rhetorical arguments to Jewish high-priests and Greek philosophers. * * *

"Be not a baker if your head be made of butter," says a homely proverb, which, being interpreted, may mean, let no woman rush into print who is not prepared for the consequences. We are aware that our remarks are in a very different tone from that of the reviewers who, with a perennial recurrence of precisely similar emotions, only paralleled, we imagine, in the experience of monthly nurses,[3] tell one lady novelist after another that they "hail" her productions "with delight." We are aware that the ladies at whom our criticism is pointed are accustomed to be told, in the choicest phraseology of puffery, that their pictures of life are brilliant, their characters well drawn, their style fascinating, and their sentiments lofty. But if they are inclined to resent our plainness of speech, we ask them to reflect for a moment on the chary praise, and often captious blame, which their panegyrists give to writers whose works are on the way to become classics. No sooner does a woman show that she has genius or effective talent, than she receives the tribute of being moderately praised and severely criticised. By a peculiar thermometric adjustment, when a woman's talent is at zero, journalistic approbation is at the boiling pitch; when she attains mediocrity, it is already at no more than summer heat; and if ever she reaches excellence, critical enthusiasm drops to the freezing point. Harriet Martineau, Currer Bell,[4] and Mrs. Gaskell have been treated as cavalierly as if they had been men. And every critic who forms a high estimate of the share women may ultimately take in literature, will, on principle, abstain from any exceptional indulgence towards the productions of literary women. For it must be plain to every one who looks impartially and extensively into feminine literature, that its greatest deficiencies are due hardly more to the want of intellectual power than to the want of those moral qualities that contribute to literary excellence—patient diligence, a sense of the responsibility involved in publication, and an appreciation of the sacredness of the writer's art. In the majority of women's books you see that kind of facility which springs from the absence of any high standard; that fertility in imbecile combination or feeble imitation which a little self-criticism would check and reduce to barrenness; just as with a total want of musical ear people will sing out of tune, while a degree more melodic sensibility would suffice to render them silent. The foolish vanity of wishing to appear in print, instead of being counterbalanced by any consciousness of the intellectual or moral derogation implied in futile authorship, seems to be encouraged by the extremely false impression that to write *at all* is a proof of superiority in a woman. On this ground, we believe that the average intellect of women is unfairly represented by the mass of feminine literature, and that while the few women who write well are very far above the ordinary intellectual level of their sex, the many women who write ill are very far below it. So that, after all, the severer critics are fulfilling a chivalrous duty in depriving the mere fact of feminine authorship of any false prestige which may give it a delusive attraction, and in recommending women of mediocre faculties—as at least a negative service they can render their sex—to abstain from writing.

The standing apology for women who become writers without any special qualification is, that society shuts them out from other spheres of occupation. Society is a very culpable entity, and has to answer for the manufacture of

---

3. Women hired to nurse infants.   4. I.e., Charlotte Brontë.

many unwholesome commodities, from bad pickles to bad poetry. But society, like "matter," and Her Majesty's Government, and other lofty abstractions, has its share of excessive blame as well as excessive praise. Where there is one woman who writes from necessity, we believe there are three women who write from vanity; and, besides, there is something so antiseptic in the mere healthy fact of working for one's bread, that the most trashy and rotten kind of feminine literature is not likely to have been produced under such circumstances. "In all labour there is profit;"[5] but ladies' silly novels, we imagine, are less the result of labour than of busy idleness.

Happily, we are not dependent on argument to prove that Fiction is a department of literature in which women can, after their kind, fully equal men. A cluster of great names, both living and dead, rush to our memories in evidence that women can produce novels not only fine, but among the very finest;—novels, too, that have a precious speciality, lying quite apart from masculine aptitudes and experience. No educational restrictions can shut women out from the materials of fiction, and there is no species of art which is so free from rigid requirements. Like crystalline masses, it may take any form, and yet be beautiful; we have only to pour in the right elements—genuine observation, humour, and passion. But it is precisely this absence of rigid requirement which constitutes the fatal seduction of novel-writing to incompetent women. Ladies are not wont to be very grossly deceived as to their power of playing on the piano; here certain positive difficulties of execution have to be conquered, and incompetence inevitably breaks down. Every art which has its absolute *technique* is, to a certain extent, guarded from the intrusions of mere left-handed imbecility. But in novel-writing there are no barriers for incapacity to stumble against, no external criteria to prevent a writer from mistaking foolish facility for mastery. And so we have again and again the old story of La Fontaine's ass, who puts his nose to the flute, and, finding that he elicits some sound, exclaims, "Moi, aussi, je joue de la flute;"[6]—a fable which we commend, at parting, to the consideration of any feminine reader who is in danger of adding to the number of "silly novels by lady novelists."

1856

---

5. Proverbs 14.23.
6. "*I also play the flute*" (French). "The Ass and the Flute" is a fable by the French writer Jean-

Pierre Florian (1755–1794), not his precedessor Jean de La Fontaine (1621–1695).

FANNY FERN (SARAH WILLIS PARTON)
1811–1872

The first woman in the United States to have her own newspaper column, Sarah Payson Willis Eldredge Farrington Parton, who wrote under the pseudonym Fanny Fern, eventually earned an unprecedented $100 per column for each of the pieces that appeared regularly in the New York *Ledger*. But her triumph as a journalist came only after a number of personal tribulations. Born in Maine, Fern had been married twice, widowed, divorced, and was the mother of three by the time she decided to support herself as a professional writer. Once she established herself as a lively commentator on current affairs, however, she produced not only lucrative columns but also best-selling collections of essays based on her newspaper publications—among them *Fern Leaves from Fanny's Port-Folio* (1853)—and two popular novels, *Ruth Hall* (1855) and *Rose Clark* (1856).

In intellectual circles Fern was admired too: Nathaniel Hawthorne praised *Ruth Hall* and Walt Whitman imitated the cover design of *Fern Leaves* in the first edition of *Leaves of Grass*. Happily married for a third time (to James Parton, a journalistic colleague), she maintained an energetic career as a feminist and activist until her death in 1872. Our selections here reveal her clear-eyed analysis of the critical double standard to which women writers were all too often subjected. In the first, she incisively deconstructs the "sneering criticism" frequently promulgated by male reviewers of female-authored texts, and in the second she cleverly spoofs such criticism in a mock review of her own work.

Male Criticism on Ladies' Books

> Courtship and marriage, servants and children, these are the great objects of a woman's thoughts, and they necessarily form the staple topics of their writings and their conversation. We have no right to expect anything else in a woman's book.
> —N.Y. TIMES

Is it in feminine novels *only* that courtship, marriage, servants, and children are the staple? Is not this true of all novels?—of Dickens, of Thackeray, of Bulwer[1] and a host of others? Is it peculiar to feminine pens, most astute and liberal of critics? Would a novel be a novel if it did not treat of courtship and marriage? and if it could be so recognized, would it find readers? When I see such a narrow, snarling criticism as the above, I always say to myself, the writer is some unhappy man, who has come up without the refining influence of mother, or sister, or reputable female friends; who has divided his migratory life between boarding-houses, restaurants, and the outskirts of editorial sanctums; and who knows as much about reviewing a woman's book, as I do about navigating a ship, or engineering an omnibus from the South Ferry, through Broadway, to Union Park. I think I see him writing that paragraph in a fit of spleen—of *male* spleen—in his small boarding-house upper chamber, by the cheerful light of a solitary candle, flickering alternately on cobwebbed walls, dusty wash-stand, begrimed bowl and pitcher, refuse cigar stumps, boot-jacks, old hats, buttonless coats, muddy trousers, and all the wretched accompaniments of solitary, selfish male existence, not to speak of his own puckered, unkissable face; perhaps, in addition, his boots hurt, his cravat-bow persists in slipping under his ear for want of a pin, and a wife to pin it, (poor wretch!) or he has been refused by some pretty girl, as he deserved to be, (narrow-minded old vinegar-cruet!) or snubbed by some lady authoress; or, more trying than all to the male constitution, has had a weak cup of coffee for that morning's breakfast.

But seriously—we have had quite enough of this shallow criticism (?) on lady-books. Whether the book which called forth the remark above quoted, was a good book or a bad one, I know not: I should be inclined to think the *former* from the dispraise of such a pen. Whether ladies can write novels or not, is a question I do not intend to discuss; but that some of them have no difficulty in finding either publishers or readers, is a matter of history; and

---

1. Edward George Bulwer Lytton, another contemporary British novelist.

that gentlemen often write over feminine signatures would seem also to argue that feminine literature is, after all, in good odor with the reading public. Granting that lady-novels are not all that they should be—is such shallow, unfair, wholesale, sneering criticism (?) the way to reform them? Would it not be better and more manly to point out a better way kindly, justly, *and, above all, respectfully?* or—what would be a much harder task for such critics—write a better book!

1857

"Fresh Leaves, by Fanny Fern"

This little volume has just been laid upon our table. The publishers have done all they could for it, with regard to outward adorning. No doubt it will be welcomed by those who admire this lady's style of writing: we confess ourselves not to be of that number. We have never seen Fanny Fern, nor do we desire to do so. We imagine her, from her writings, to be a muscular, black-browed, grenadier-looking female, who would be more at home in a boxing gallery than in a parlor,—a vociferous, demonstrative, strong-minded horror,—a woman only by virtue of her dress. Bah! the very thought sickens us. We have read, or, rather, tried to read, her halloo-there effusions. When we take up a woman's book we expect to find gentleness, timidity, and that lovely reliance on the patronage of our sex which constitutes a woman's greatest charm. We do not wish to be startled by bold expressions, or disgusted with exhibitions of masculine weaknesses. We do not desire to see a woman wielding the scimitar blade of sarcasm. If she be, unfortunately, endowed with a gift so dangerous, let her—as she values the approbation of our sex—fold it in a napkin. Fanny's strong-minded nose would probably turn up at this inducement. Thank heaven! there are still women who *are* women—who know the place Heaven assigned them, and keep it—who do not waste floods of ink and paper, brow-beating men and stirring up silly women;—who do not teach children that a game of romps is of as much importance as Blair's Philosophy;[1]—who have not the presumption to advise clergymen as to their duties, or lecture doctors, and savans;[2]—who live for something else than to astonish a gaping, idiotic crowd. Thank heaven! there are women writers who do not disturb our complacence or serenity; whose books lull one to sleep like a strain of gentle music; who excite no antagonism, or angry feeling. Woman never was intended for an irritant: she should be oil upon the troubled waters of manhood—soft and amalgamating, a necessary but unobtrusive ingredient;—never challenging attention—never throwing the gauntlet of defiance to a beard, but softly purring beside it lest it bristle and scratch.

The very fact that Fanny Fern has, in the language of her admirers, "elbowed her way through unheard of difficulties," shows that she is an antagonistic, pugilistic female. One must needs, forsooth, get out of her way, or be pushed one side, or trampled down. How much more womanly to have allowed herself to be doubled up by adversity, and quietly laid away on the shelf of fate, than to have rolled up her sleeves, and gone to fisticuffs with

---

1. *Moral Philosophy, etc.; On the Duties of the Young* (1798), by the Scottish clergyman Hugh Blair.

2. I.e., savants.

it. Such a woman may conquer, it is true, but her victory will cost her dear; it will neither be forgotten nor forgiven—let her put that in her apron pocket.

As to Fanny Fern's grammar, rhetoric, and punctuation, they are beneath criticism. It is all very well for her to say, those who wish commas, semi-colons and periods, must look for them in the printer's case, or that she who finds ideas must not be expected to find rhetoric or grammar; for our part, we should be gratified if we had even found any ideas!

We regret to be obliged to speak thus of a lady's book: it gives us pleasure, when we can do so conscientiously, to pat lady writers on the head; but we owe a duty to the public which will not permit us to recommend to their favorable notice an aspirant who has been unwomanly enough so boldly to contest every inch of ground in order to reach them—an aspirant at once so high-stepping and so ignorant, so plausible, yet so pernicious. We have a con-servative horror of this pop-gun, torpedo female; we predict for Fanny Fern's "Leaves" only a fleeting autumnal flutter.

1857

EMILY DICKINSON
1830–1886

Outwardly uneventful, the life of the woman who was sometimes known as the "Myth of Amherst" was inwardly tumultuous. Educated at Amherst Academy and, for a year, at the Mount Holyoke Female Seminary, Dickinson was the daughter of one of the leading citizens of her community: the lawyer and (eventually) congressman Edward Dickinson. As a girl, she was spirited and socially active, but for most of the second half of her life she was famously eccentric and reclusive, dressing entirely in white and almost never leaving her father's house. In her twenties, however, she began compos-ing the 1,776 poems for which she has gained enduring fame. Most of them neatly sewed into booklets, called "fascicles," these were found by her sister, Lavinia, after her death and subsequently published—at first in relatively small selected editions but finally, more than half a century after their discovery, in definitive editions produced by the scholars Thomas Johnson (in 1955) and Ralph Franklin (in 1998).

When Dickinson's verse was first presented to the public in book-length collections it struck many professional reviewers as odd, if not downright anti-poetic, with some critics insisting that hers was "bad poetry . . . divorced from meaning, from music, from grammar, from rhyme," or that "her style is clumsy, her language is poor; her technique is appalling." But as her letters and the variants she inscribed in the mar-gins of her manuscripts indicate, Dickinson was herself extraordinarily professional—perhaps so much so that she understood how alien her art might seem to conventional contemporaries. To be sure, in addition to her beloved sister-in-law and neighbor Susan Gilbert Dickinson, with whom she shared many drafts of her work, such fig-ures as the poet-novelist Helen Hunt Jackson and the editor Thomas Wentworth Hig-ginson regarded her as a genius, albeit an iconoclastic one. But even Higginson, who was to assemble the first posthumous volume of her poems in collaboration with an Amherst neighbor, Mabel Loomis Todd, considered that she didn't write what *he* would call "poetry," urging her to relinquish what she defined as "the Bells whose jingling cooled [her] Tramp"—her distinctively inventive meters—in favor of standard prosody. Nor did he ever abandon his notion that Dickinson's poetry was "uncontrolled," while his co-editor, Mrs. Todd, similarly confessed herself "exasperated" by Dickinson's "carelessness of form."

But both Dickinson's poetic aspirations and her critical sophistication are evident in records of her reading; in her verse comments on such writers as George Eliot, Charlotte Brontë, and Elizabeth Barrett Browning; and even in the pictures that she hung on the walls of her bedroom (portraits of such authors as Eliot, Barrett Browning, and Thomas Carlyle). Our selections here—three letters that she wrote to Higginson, whom she called her literary "Preceptor" despite their aesthetic differences—reveal the clarity with which she formulated her influences and procedures as an artist as well as her fierce ambition.

Letters to T. W. Higginson

260

[SAY IF MY VERSE IS ALIVE?]

To T. W. Higginson

15 April 1862

Mr Higginson,

Are you too deeply occupied to say if my Verse is alive?

The Mind is so near itself—it cannot see, distinctly—and I have none to ask—

Should you think it breathed—and had you the leisure to tell me, I should feel quick gratitude—

If I make the mistake—that you dared to tell me—would give me sincerer honor—toward you—

I enclose my name—asking you, if you please—Sir—to tell me what is true?

That you will not betray me—it is needless to ask—since Honor is its own pawn—

261

[MY "COMPANIONS"]

To T. W. Higginson

25 April 1862

Mr Higginson,

Your kindness claimed earlier gratitude—but I was ill—and write today, from my pillow.

Thank you for the surgery—it was not so painful as I supposed. I bring you others—as you ask—though they might not differ—

While my thought is undressed—I can make the distinction, but when I put them in the Gown—they look alike, and numb.

You asked how old I was? I made no verse—but one or two—until this winter—Sir—

I had a terror—since September—I could tell to none—and so I sing, as the Boy does by the Burying Ground—because I am afraid—You inquire my

Books—For Poets—I have Keats—and Mr and Mrs Browning. For Prose—
Mr Ruskin—Sir Thomas Browne—and the Revelations. I went to school—
but in your manner of the phrase—had no education. When a little Girl, I had
a friend, who taught me Immortality—but venturing too near, himself—he
never returned—Soon after, my Tutor, died—and for several years, my Lexicon—was my only companion—Then I found one more—but he was not contented I be his scholar—so he left the Land.

You ask of my Companions Hills—Sir—and the Sundown—and a Dog—
large as myself, that my Father bought me—They are better than Beings—
because they know—but do not tell—and the noise in the Pool, at
Noon—excels my Piano. I have a Brother and Sister—My Mother does not
care for thought—and Father, too busy with his Briefs—to notice what we
do—He buys me many Books—but begs me not to read them—because he
fears they joggle the Mind. They are religious—except me—and address an
Eclipse, every morning—whom they call their "Father." But I fear my story
fatigues you—I would like to learn—Could you tell me how to grow—or is it
unconveyed—like Melody—or Witchcraft?

You speak of Mr Whitman[1]—I never read his Book—but was told that he
was disgraceful—

I read Miss Prescott's[2] "Circumstance," but it followed me, in the Dark—
so I avoided her—

Two Editors of Journals came to my Father's House, this winter—and asked
me for my Mind—and when I asked them "Why," they said I was penurious—
and they, would use it for the World—

I could not weigh myself—Myself—

My size felt small—to me—I read your Chapters in the Atlantic—and experienced honor for you—I was sure you would not reject a confiding question—

Is this—Sir—what you asked me to tell you?

Your friend,
E—Dickinson.

265

[FAME]

To T. W. HIGGINSON

7 JUNE 1862

Dear friend.

Your letter gave no Drunkenness, because I tasted Rum before—Domingo[3]
comes but once—yet I have had few pleasures so deep as your opinion, and
if I tried to thank you, my tears would block my tongue—

My dying Tutor told me that he would like to live till I had been a poet, but
Death was much of Mob as I could master—then—And when far afterward—
a sudden light on Orchards, or a new fashion in the wind troubled my attention—I felt a palsy, here—the Verses just relieve—

Your second letter surprised me, and for a moment, swung—I had not sup-

---

1. Walt Whitman, whose "disgraceful" book was
   Leaves of Grass (1855).
2. Harriet Prescott (1835–1921), popular short

story writer.
3. Santo Domingo, capital of the Dominican
Republic in the West Indies.

posed it. Your first—gave no dishonor, because the True—are not ashamed—I thanked you for your justice—but could not drop the Bells whose jingling cooled my Tramp—Perhaps the Balm, seemed better, because you bled me, first.

I smile when you suggest that I delay "to publish"—that being foreign to my thought, as Firmament to Fin—

If fame belonged to me, I could not escape her—if she did not, the longest day would pass me on the chase—and the approbation of my Dog, would forsake me—then—My Barefoot-Rank is better—

You think my gait "spasmodic"—I am in danger—Sir—

You think me "uncontrolled"—I have no Tribunal.

Would you have time to be the "friend" you should think I need? I have a little shape—it would not crowd your Desk—nor make much Racket as the Mouse, that dents your Galleries—

If I might bring you what I do—not so frequent to trouble you—and ask you if I told it clear—'twould be control, to me—

The Sailor cannot see the North—but knows the Needle[4] can—

The "hand you stretch me in the Dark," I put mine in, and turn away—I have no Saxon,[5] now—

> As if I asked a common Alms,
> And in my wondering hand
> A Stranger pressed a Kingdom,
> And I, bewildered, stand—
> As if I asked the Orient
> Had it for me a Morn—
> And it should lift it's purple Dikes,
> And shatter me with Dawn!

But, will you be my Preceptor, Mr Higginson?

Your friend
E Dickinson—

---

4. The compass needle.   5. I.e., language.

HARRIET BEECHER STOWE
1811–1896

Reportedly described by Abraham Lincoln as "the little woman who started this big war," the author of the best-selling and extraordinarily influential *Uncle Tom's Cabin; or, Life among the Lowly* (1851–52) was "little" neither in intellect nor in ambition. One of thirteen children fathered by the prominent Congregational minister Lyman Beecher, Stowe was brought up with a commitment to public service and with the belief, inculcated by her aunt, Catherine Beecher—an educator and moralist—that women have a special obligation to promote social welfare. In 1836 she married Calvin Ellis Stowe, an unworldly professor of biblical literature; the couple had seven children whom she helped support by writing and publishing regional sketches.

A passionate abolitionist, Stowe claimed that after the death of one of her babies she could vividly imagine "what a poor slave mother may feel when her child is torn from her." In *Uncle Tom's Cabin* she dramatized her horror at such domestic catastrophes and at the injustice of the Fugitive Slave Act as well as, more generally, the evils of American slavery. As Jane Tompkins has observed in an essay we include here (see pp. 514–26), the work can be seen as a characteristic "American jeremiad," inveighing against a blight on the body politic, even while it was also a compellingly readable sentimental fiction. Selling 350,000 copies in the United States in the year after it appeared and more than a million pirated copies in England, this sensational jeremiad may indeed have helped start "this big [civil] war" even while it won Stowe the friendship of such major figures as Charles Dickens and George Eliot. But although Eliot and Stowe were brought together by common political sympathies, the letters from Stowe to Eliot that we include here show their author focusing on practical criticism in a way that reveals the conscious skill with which she herself shaped *Uncle Tom's Cabin* and other popular fictions. We are grateful to Jennifer Cognard-Black and Elizabeth MacLeod Walls for making these hitherto unpublished letters available to us.

Letters to George Eliot

[ON *MIDDLEMARCH*, AND MARRIAGE]

To MARY ANN EVANS
HARTFORD, CONNECTICUT

23 SEPTEMBER 1872

My Darling Friend

For once, I am going to write a letter for no other reason but *just because I feel like it* I have just had a letter from my Rabbi[1] & he has just had he says such a lovely letter from you as quite sets him up into the seventh heaven—

Then again dear, I have been following you brokenly and by snatches thro "Middlemarch" for I have been travelling all summer & could only see the paper that had it in, at intervals.[2] Just the other day I came across a saying of Dorothea to young Ladislaw or whatever his name is to the effect that whatever is honestly & purely attempted for good becomes part of the great force that is moving for good thro the universe[3]—Well—I thought—good—I will cut out that sentence as one article of my creed—I have not the paper by me now & cannot reproduce it.

My darling I confess to being very much amused & sympathetic with Dorothea's trials with a literary husband.[4] Of course I see that he was a stick & all that but the wifely feeling of Dorothea is exactly what you & I and all of us who make real marriages marry with & then these husbands!—Now, dont show this to Mr Lewes[5] but I know by my own experience with my Rabbi that

1. Harriet Beecher Stowe's husband, Calvin Stowe, a professor of Greek and of biblical literature.
2. *Middlemarch* (1871–72) was serialized in the United States in *Harper's Weekly* between 1871 and 1873.
3. See *Middlemarch*, chap. 39: "[B]y desiring what is perfectly good, even when we don't quite know what it is and cannot do what we would, we are part of the divine power against evil—widening the skirts of light and making the struggle with darkness narrower."
4. Dorothea has married the Reverend Edward Casaubon, an elderly scholar who labors fruitlessly on his "Key to All Mythologies."
5. George Henry Lewes, the English philosopher and critic who lived with George Eliot from 1854 until his death in 1878 (because he had earlier tolerated the adultery of his wife, he was unable to obtain a divorce).

you learned how to write some of those things by *experience*. Dont these men go on forever getting ready to begin—absorbing learning like sponges—planning sublime literary enterprises which never have a *now* to them?—Years ago my husband made all the researches for writing a life of Martin Luther He imported tons of books—he read he lectured he fired me into a flame of eagerness he prepared & prepared & prepared but his ideal grew & he *never* came to the time of completion—& now alas—never will. Still he goes on reading studying investigating subject after subject apparently for no object but to entertain me & when I try to make him write the books he ought to he is *never* ready—& I believe I sometimes make myself a sort of trouble some outside conscience to him by trying to push him up to do what he has been so long getting ready to do—So you see I sympathise with poor Dorothea but then her husband is too much of a stick!—How could she marry him!—Yet I understand too that girls often make a false marriage & plight their faith to an unreal shadow who they suppose inhabits a certain body—I am intensely curious to know what is to become of her.

You write too well my darling—altogether too well to be pitched into Harpers Weekly along with Edmond Yates & Miss Braddon[6] & the sensation mongers of the day—Your story is for the thoughtful—for the artist for the few—when it is all out I shall try and interpret it to the many. Generally you live & speak in a surge of thought above the average of society. Dickens was intelligible—I saw a beautiful & very true article by Mr Lewes about him lately[7]—

Your forte is the morale—& you are as Dorothea said part of the great current for good in our times I would have hope of a young girl or young man that I could get to read Romola but I cannot often do it I did see its effect once on a young officer who having traveled in Florence could understand the scenery so he was powerfully affected shaken with the terrible moral of Tito[8]—The same idea runs in Adam Bede the 'facilis descensus &c'[9]—it is terrible!—

But what shall we say of the children of this generation sitting in the marketplace[1] eager only for sensation & with no time to think?—What shall people so solemnly impressed with real living as you do with them? —

As to the spirits—I only wanted to show you & Mr Lewes that there is an immense field of *facts* there, unexplored unclassified—undeveloped & to me it is intensely a practical question. For in a certain way I am a pastor & confessor of hundreds who know me only thro the spirit—& the sorrows of life lie open to me—Even this summer I have been the confidant of many who have had the central nerve of life cut in the tearing from them a friend without whom life seems not worth having—Then they ask me the question—Is there a way of communication Would you seek relief this way? —

Now if I had not patiently & sympathetically explored if I had scornfully denounced or declared all such things imposture I should have no power. But

6. Mary Elizabeth Braddon, many of whose popular sensation novels were serialized. Edmund Yates, Scottish journalist and novelist.
7. Lewes, "Dickens in Relation to Criticism," *Fortnightly Review*, February 1, 1872.
8. The husband of the eponymous heroine of *Romola* (1862–63); his selfish self-aggrandizement and amoral pursuit of political ambition lead to his

destruction.
9. Easy [is the] descent (Latin), from Virgil's *Aeneid* 6.126 (for the full thought, see 126–28: descending to the underworld is easy—the labor is in returning). In *Adam Bede* (1859), the "descent" of indulging one's selfish desires ends in blighted lives and a baby's death.
1. See Luke 7.32.

now I say as I lately said to a heartbroken mother who asked me Are there such facts—I answer Yes—there are—I have seen I have examined patiently I have listened & no spiritualist could tell more extraordinary facts than have passed under my own observation—Trust me then, when I tell you that this field is a dangerous one for you with your weakened nerves & suffering heart to explore. It is a *real* force but an *unknown—unregulated* one, & one which in the present state of knowledge would be unsafe for you to trust yourself to —

There is where I differ from Mr Owen[2] But much must be pardoned to a man whose only hope of immortality & consolation in the future have come thro this channel Owen is a charming man & for a while pursued the inquiry in a truly philosophic manner & spirit. But he is a Scotchman & of course has an itching after theology & cannot resist the temptation to make up one —

There we part—I say the facts are facts—so far as I can see they are honestly investigated & presented but these are not yet enough to build any system on & to form any religious conclusions from them would be dangerous. To resort to it as consolation for mourners is dangerous—There my friend & I differ—Yet you too be charmed with Owen did you know him —

I wonder what will be the fate of our poor Undine Katy Fox[3]—poor child what a life hers has been Let us believe in an infinite Love & Pity that cares for all & will bring the blind by a way they know not.

Good bye my darling—

Ever your true love

H B Stowe

I send this to you thro Lowe & co because being away from my papers I have not your address

[ON CASAUBON]

To Mary Ann Evans
Boston, Massachusetts

26 September 1872

My Dear Friend.

I think when you see my name again so soon you will think it rains, hails, & snows notes from this quarter.

Just now however I am in this lovely little nest in Boston where dear Mrs. Field like a dove sits "brooding on the charmed wave"[4] & we are both, so much wishing we had you here with us—& she has not received any answer from you as yet in reply to the invitation you spoke of in your last letter to me. It seems as if you must have written & the letter somehow gone astray, because I know of course, you would write

Yesterday we were both out of our senses with mingled pity & indignation at that dreadful stick of a Casaubon – & think of poor Dorothea dashing like a warm sunny wave against so cold & repulsive a rock

---

2. Robert Dale Owen, a Scottish-born American political and diplomat who became an advocate of the spiritualist movement.
3. As children in upstate New York, Katie Fox and her sister claimed in 1848 to have heard rappings from spirits; Fox later became famous as a medium.
4. From John Milton's "On the Morning of Christ's Nativity" (1645). Annie Fields, an author and a central figure in Boston's literary world; she was married to the publisher James T. Fields.

He is a little too dreadful for any thing—there does not seem to be a drop of warm blood in him—& so as it is his misfortune & not his fault to be a cold blooded, one must not get angry with him It is the scene in the garden after the interview with the Doctor that rests on our mind at this present.[5] There was such a man as he over in Boston high in literary circles but I fancy *his* wife wasn't like Dorothea & a vastly proper time they had of it treating each other with mutual reverence like two Chinese Mandarins

My love: what I miss in this story is just what we would have if you would come to our tumble down, jolly, improper, but joyous country—namely "jolitude"—(You write & live on so high a plane it is all self abnegation—we want to get you over here, & into this house where with closed doors we sometimes make the rafters ring with fun—& say any thing & every thing no matter what & wont be any properer than we's a mind to be [)]—I am wishing every day you could see *our America*—travel as I have been doing from one bright thriving pretty flowery town after another & see so much wealth, ease progress, culture & all sorts of nice things

This dove cote where I now am is the sweetest little nest—fronting on a city street with back windows opening on a sea view—with still quiet rooms filled with books pictures & all sorts of things such as you & Mr. Lewes would enjoy Dont be afraid of the ocean now Ive crossed it six times & assure you it is an over rated item Froude is coming here[6]—why not you?—Besides we have the fountain of Eternal Youth here—that is in Florida where I live & if you should come you would both of you take a new lease on life & what glorious poems and philosophies & what not we should have My Rabbi writes in the seventh heaven on account of your note to him—to think of his setting off on his own account are when I was away!—

Come now, since your answer to dear Mrs. Fields is yet to come let it be a glad yes & we will clasp you to our heart of hearts—

Your ever loving
HBS

[ON *DANIEL DERONDA*]

TO MARY ANN EVANS
HARTFORD, CONNECTICUT

25 SEPTEMBER 1876

My dear Friend.

Well—Daniel Deronda is at last achieved!—We, my husband & I, have strictly confined ourselves to the *serial* form,[7] taking it in our monthly instalments & meditating there on—as if it were a passage of scripture. Great talks have we had together as it proceeded, great searchings of heart as to what was to be done with the various characters.

The story divides itself as a parson might say, into two heads—English life & Jewish life. Here let me give you a little anecdote in point A lady met at one of our fashionable watering places, a Jewish lady of the name of Cohen—She said to her that she was lost in admiration of George Elliot in *daring* to make

---

5. *Middlemarch,* chap. 42; after Casaubon is told he may die suddenly from heart disease, Dorothea joins him in the garden and is repulsed by his "unresponsive hardness."
6. The English historian Fames Anthony Froude,

who undertook a lecture tour of the United States in 1872.
7. *Daniel Deronda* was originally published serially in *Blackwood's Magazine* (and in America in *Harper's*) between February and September 1876.

her hero and heroine Jewish!—I think myself, that tho Scott, Miss Edgeworth & Disraeli have all done the same,[8] it was somewhat *venturesome*.

Of course the "children sitting in the market place," find the rhapsodies of Mordecai,[9] tomes—& one lively friend of mine describes that part of her reading as "wading through a Jewish morass." to reach the firm land of English character & life—In return, my husband a most enthusiastic old Rabbi who boasts the possession of both the Babylonian & Jerusalem Talmud in his library—who rejoices in the only copies in America of Schudt Mer[c]kwürdigkeiten des Juden & Eisenmenger's Entdecktes Judenthum.[1]— he is most specially devoted to the "Jewish Morass" & therein meditates day & night He has for many years cultivated a personal intimacy with the leading Rabbi, & is a frequent attendant at the synagogue—I, myself share this interest, from some of his spare learning having rubbed off onto me, by mere accident of contact, so that I was prepared to understand & care for that part.

But after all I confess that my hearts blood vibrates more toward Gwendolin than Mirah[2] & that I feel a more *living* interest in her feelings, struggles & sorrows than those of Mirah—the two characters of Gwendolin & Grandcourt are I think the artistic genius. Grandcourt as doing the work of the villain in the play without any of the burnt cork of a stage villain—I cant imagine any character more utterly worthless & disagreeable, yet invested throughout with such an air of worldly respectability and *probability*. There is great reticence in his wickedness. Not a monster by any means. Making suitable & even generous provision for the woman he is tired of—. & treating the woman he marries with every external form of consideration & only occasionally swearing at her in the strictest privacy. The point in the courtship where he ejaculates "damn her!" under his breath[3] is a comment on such marriages worth pages of disquisition & the beauty of it is—that you have no moral reflection The grim distinctness with which you set forth "marriage a la mode" with the rector pointing out to the young girl the duty of securing a brilliant match & comforting himself with the reflection that she cannot know any thing about previous irregularities[4]—is a stroke of satire on English good society which I suppose they hardly appreciate—but I do —

Your clergymen of the English church for the most part give me a cold chill, those in your books. When I think that no man enters that church without solemnly declaring that he is inwardly moved by the Holy Ghost & called according to the will of Christ to take that office—& then see that gentlemenly men take it avowedly for no other purpose than as a genteel livelihood for men of good family—I lose all faith in the power of vows to bind—or threats to terrify—& I cease to wonder at scepticism where the church is so represented. The baptismal service, the ordination vows—marriage vows & burial service of that church are aweful enough to make an angel tremble but seem to be taken lightly enough by good English society

8. Major Jewish characters are sympathetically portrayed in Sir Walter Scott's *Ivanhoe* (1819), Maria Edgeworth's *Harrington* (1817), and Benjamin Disraeli's *Coningsby* (1844).
9. Mordecai Cohen, a Zionist visionary who become in effect Daniel's guide to Judaism.
1. Johann Schudt's *Judische Merckwürdigkeiten* (Jewish curiosities, 1714), a study of Jewish magic and superstition, and Johann Eisenmenger's *Entdecktes Judentum* (Judaism uncovered, 1700), a compendium of Christian prejudice against Jews.

2. I.e., she is more drawn to the "Christian half" of the novel, centered on Gwendolen Harleth and her unhappy marriage to Grandcourt, than to the story of the Jewish Mirah Cohen.
3. See *Daniel Deronda,* chap. 13; he believes Gwendolen may simply be playing the coquette with him.
4. Also in chap. 13. Grandcourt has a mistress who has borne him four children and who confronts Gwendolen shortly after this conversation with the rector, Gwendolen's uncle.

So that if your young Jew Daniel Deronda is educated a member in good standing of the English church[5] I can easily perceive that there is no barrier which should prevent his going back to his people except the barrier of good society. The Jews are 'mauvais ton'[6]—that is all. Christ is nothing to the average young Briton—& it does not appear that any feelings about *Him* stand in Derondas way when Mordicai asks him if he accepts the religion of his people—Christ is not much more to Mr Gasgoine[7] than to Mordicai—in fact, if unselfishness, & self surrender & sacrifice for a noble cause are Christ like Mordicai has the more Christ like spirit of the two. If Deronda had been *a christian*, after the manner of Paul or John—that scene would have been widely different—Although England wants in *such* christians as that, & we should not hear so much about modern scepticism.

But infinitely the most interesting character to me is Gwendolin—Of the artistic *vitality* of the character I need no other proof than that I have been called at various tea tables to defend her as earnestly as if she had been an actual neighbor giving parties round the corner To my mind, so far from being an exceptionally selfish or worldly woman—she stands in the midst of a heartlessly selfish & utterly worldly state of society a creature of higher impulses sensitive to the very first suggestion of moral right

She is like a young eagle who has been brought up among barn yard chickens with clipped wings—full of uneasy instructs that point to soaring among the clouds of heaven. A frivolous or hard, or worldly selfish woman would have worn the diamonds with a self satisfied grin & taken the good the Gods provided without too many reflections on how or at whose expense she came by them.[8] Now is there any thing in the world to me more painfully pathetic, than the blind struggles of such a soul for its native air—its ideal completeness—and it is mournful to see how utterly Godless are all who undertake to guide her Had Deronda been educated a Jew he might have told her out of his old testament scripture that there was a teacher & Guide who dwells in the soul of those who aspire after good—that the High & Lofty One who inhabiteth the eternity dwells in the stricken spirit of the humble "to revive the heart of the contrite one["]—he might have told her of One who "to those of no might increaseth strength"—of One who says "I will bring the blind by a way that they knew not, & I will make darkness light before them & crooked things strait—these things will I do to them & *not forsake them*!["][9] And it appears that the well educated serious minded young English gentleman of our time knows neither the God of the old testament nor the Jesus of the new—the Jesus who came to save his people from their sins—& has nothing to give to this imploring anguish & vague aspiration of a soul longing for purity—literally nothing

If this is the last result of modern culture—if it is only to tutor helpless humanity—do your best & dont hope for comfort or help then what a mockery is our existence! But I *know* in whom I believe—& you when you wrote Dinahs prayer with poor Hetty—& Mr Fryans counsels to Janet[1]—knew full

---

5. Deronda learns of his Jewish heritage only as an adult.
6. Bad form (French).
7. Mr. Gascoigne, the rector.
8. The diamonds were originally given to Grandcourt's mistress, who sends them to Gwendolen on his orders and whose son is disinherited by their marriage.

9. See Isaiah 57.15, 40.29, 42.16.
1. In chap. 18 of "Janet's Repentence" (1857), one of the long stories in *Scenes of Clerical Life* (1858), Mr. Tryan is an evangelical clergyman. In *Adam Bede,* chap. 17, the prayers of the Methodist preacher Dinah Morris brings the imprisoned Hetty Sorrel to repentence.

well what a power there is in the living Christ to say to the impotent "Rise up & walk."[2] It is not instruction *about* goodness people need—They need an almighty inseperable Friend of their souls ever present, pure yet sympathetic wise yet strong—to protect them from themselves & bear them above themselves—& alas—if I am to read your picture of English life as you see it there is no such Friend there. For me, it is now fifty years since that Friend because a living presence to me & ever since He has been the Inspirer—consoler & strength of my life,—& to read of those who struggle for goodness without knowing *him* is painful to me as to read of those who die of hunger when there is bread enough & to spare. Christ is my Life—all I ever have been able to do or suffer—all my hope for the poor & oppressed has been my feeling sense of his living presence & that He is ruling all things —

He shall not *fail* nor be discouraged till he have set judgment in the Earth. —

Your book dear friend is a splendid success artistically—& I am happy to learn, financially. Even genius must have the pounds & shillings & I know what they are worth & I hope you have what will purchase you a season of leisure & rest.

As to the criticisms of our American papers—or any free comments on your personality which may have found their way into them—I can only speak for the *great* ones—the large dailys of N York & Boston are all warm in admiration—& incapable I am quite sure of printing any thing about you or your affairs which might be painful. I am so interested in all that concerns you that if any such thing had appeared in well known papers I should have heard of it. I send you to day the notice of the Christian Union. The religious papers are generally I think approbative—or admiring

My only living son is now at Bonn university—a theological student. He is to be a minister. Perhaps he may see you sometime in your continental wanderings or in London—he will visit England next summer—Since *he* is there the Rabbi & I often look longingly at Germany & discuss the question whether we could not go over & stay with him awhile. If Mr Stowe were only ten years younger how he would enjoy it.—It is not quite improbable & in that case we should see you. I hope you will have a nice easy time now helping your husband with his work thro the press[3]—Charley (my son) reads his works—I have not (head enough left)—I believe he (your husband) knows how fortunate above mortals he is to have *you*—Well dear sister friend—may the All Loving bless you—& may he *rest* you as only He can. I know all about the head aches & weariness of over driven nerves—but there is a rest in God that heals all—Your own true friend[,]

HBS

I have tried in vain to get the Rabbi to say *to* you some of the handsome things he is all the while saying of you—but alas—he is lazy—& the labor of forming those arabic quail tracks in which he expresses himself is too great for him. He loses himself in a perfect swamp of reading—& he *would* write isnt he too bad?

I send you my little, *only* grandson the cherub grown to six years—Your description of the little Deronda reminded me of Him

---

2. Luke 5.23.
3. In 1876, Lewes would have been working on

The Physical Basis of Mind: Being the Second Series of Problems of Life and Mind (1877).

HARRIET MARTINEAU
1802–1876

Activist, feminist, journalist, educator, and editor, the versatile Harriet Martineau was a major Victorian public intellectual, following in the footsteps of such eminent thinkers as Mary Astell and Mary Wollstonecraft. The daughter of a Norwich textile manufacturer, she was one of six children—three brothers and three sisters—who received similarly good educations until it was time for the boys to go to university while the girls were supposed to stay at home. Rebelling against this inequity, the young Harriet drafted and published an anonymous article "On Female Education," which appeared in a Unitarian journal, the *Monthly Repository*. As she discloses in the excerpt from her *Autobiography* that we have included here, one of her brothers admired the piece, and when he discovered her authorship he urged her to devote herself to writing.

Eventually, when her father died leaving his wife and daughters almost penniless, Martineau did decide, with considerable relief, to earn her living by her pen, producing volumes on a range of subjects, from religion (*Devotional Exercises for the Use of Young Persons,* 1823) to politics (*Illustrations of Political Economy,* 1832–34). Now financially independent, she traveled in the United States, reporting in *Society in America* (1837) on what she acidly called "the political non-existence of women" in what was supposed to be a democracy. Later, she published novels, tales for children, and skeptical appraisals of traditional religious beliefs while also writing for the *Daily News* and advocating passionately for women's suffrage and more generally for the rights of women. In our selection she recounts some memories of the origin of her extraordinary career, revealing the impediments to reading, writing, and scholarship that continued to encumber ambitious girls in the nineteenth century.

From Autobiography

When I was young, it was not thought proper for young ladies to study very conspicuously; and especially with pen in hand. Young ladies (at least in provincial towns) were expected to sit down in the parlour to sew,—during which reading aloud was permitted,—or to practice their music; but so as to be fit to receive callers, without any signs of bluestockingism which could be reported abroad. Jane Austen herself, the Queen of novelists, the immortal creator of Anne Elliott, Mr. Knightley, and a score or two more of unrivalled intimate friends of the whole public, was compelled by the feelings of her family to cover up her manuscripts with a large piece of muslin work, kept on the table for the purpose, whenever any genteel people came in. So it was with other young ladies, for some time after Jane Austen was in her grave; and thus my first studies in philosophy were carried on with great care and reserve. I was at the work table regularly after breakfast,—making my own clothes, or the shirts of the household, or about some fancy work: I went out walking with the rest,—before dinner in winter, and after tea in summer: and if ever I shut myself into my own room for an hour of solitude, I knew it was at the risk of being sent for to join the sewing-circle, or to read aloud,—I being the reader, on account of my growing deafness. But I won time for what my heart was set upon, nevertheless,—either in the early morning, or late at night. I had a strange passion for translating, in those days; and a good preparation it proved for the subsequent work of my life. Now, it was meeting James at seven in the morning to read Lowth's Prelections[1] in the Latin, after having been busy since five about something else, in my own room. Now it was translating Tacitus, in order to try what was the utmost compression of style that I could attain.—About this I may mention an incident while it occurs. We had all grown up with a great reverence for Mrs. Barbauld[2] (which she fully deserved from much wiser people than ourselves) and, reflectively, for Dr. Aikin, her brother,—also able in his way, and far more industrious, but without her genius. Among a multitude of other labours, Dr. Aikin had translated the Agricola[3] of Tacitus. I went into such an enthusiasm over the original, and especially over the celebrated concluding passage, that I thought I would translate it, and correct it by Dr. Aikin's, which I could procure from our public library. I did it, and found my own translation unquestionably the best of the two. I had spent an infinity of pains over it,—word by word; and I am confident I was not wrong in my judgment. I stood pained and mortified before my desk, I remember, thinking how strange and small a matter was human achievement, if Dr. Aikin's fame was to be taken as a testimony of literary desert. I had beaten him whom I had taken for my master. I need not point out that, in the first place, Dr. Aikin's fame did not hang on this particular work; nor that, in the second place, I had exaggerated his fame by our sectarian estimate of him. I give the incident as a curious little piece of personal experience, and one which helped to make me like literary labour more for its own sake, and less for its rewards, than I might otherwise have done.— Well: to return to my translating propensities. Our cousin J. M. L., then studying for his profession in Norwich, used to read Italian with Rachel[4] and me,—also before breakfast. We made some considerable progress, through the usual course of prose authors and poets; and out of this grew a fit which Rachel and I at one time took, in concert with our companions and neighbours, the C.'s, to translate Petrarch. Nothing could be better as an exercise in composition than translating Petrarch's sonnets into English of the same limits. It was putting ourselves under compulsion to do with the Italian what I had set myself voluntarily to do with the Latin author. I believe we really succeeded pretty well; and I am sure that all these exercises were a singularly apt preparation for my after work. At the same time, I went on studying Blair's Rhetoric[5] (for want of a better guide) and inclining mightily to every kind of book or process which could improve my literary skill,—really as if I had foreseen how I was to spend my life.

*　　*　　*

At this time,—(I think it must have been in 1821,) was my first appearance in print. * * * My brother James, then my idolized companion, discovered how wretched I was when he left me for his college, after the vacation; and he told me that I must not permit myself to be so miserable. He advised me to take refuge, on each occasion, in a new pursuit; and on that particu-

---

1. *Praelectiones de Sacra Poesi Herbraeorum* (*Lectures on Hebrew Poetry,* 1753–70), by Robert Lowth, an English bishop and scholar. "James": Martineau's younger brother.
2. Anna Laetitia Barbauld (1743–1825), poet and writer of prose for children.
3. A biography of Julius Agricola (40–93), Taci-

tus's father-in-law and a Roman senator and general.
4. Martineau's sister.
5. *Lectures on Rhetoric and Belles Lettres* (1784) by Hugh Blair, a Scottish divine and professor of rhetoric, which expressed 18th-century ideals of prose style.

lar occasion, in an attempt at authorship. I said, as usual, that I would if he would: to which he answered that it would never do for him, a young student, to rush into print before the eyes of his tutors; but he desired me to write something that was in my head, and try my chance with it in the "Monthly Repository,"—the poor little Unitarian periodical in which I have mentioned that Talfourd[6] tried his young powers. What James desired, I always did, as of course; and after he had left me to my widowhood soon after six o'clock, one bright September morning, I was at my desk before seven, beginning a letter to the Editor of the "Monthly Repository,"—that editor being the formidable prime minister of his sect,—Rev. Robert Aspland. I suppose I must tell what that first paper was, though I had much rather not; for I am so heartily ashamed of the whole business as never to have looked at the article since the first flutter of it went off. It was on Female Writers on Practical Divinity. I wrote away, in my abominable scrawl of those days, on foolscap paper, feeling mightily like a fool all the time. I told no one, and carried my expensive packet to the post-office myself, to pay the postage. I took the letter V for my signature,—I cannot at all remember why. The time was very near the end of the month: I had no definite expectation that I should ever hear any thing of my paper; and certainly did not suppose it could be in the forthcoming number. That number was sent in before service-time on a Sunday morning. My heart may have been beating when I laid hands on it; but it thumped prodigiously when I saw my article there, and, in the Notices to Correspondents, a request to hear more from V. of Norwich. There is certainly something entirely peculiar in the sensation of seeing oneself in print for the first time:—the lines burn themselves in upon the brain in a way of which black ink is incapable, in any other mode. So I felt that day, when I went about with my secret.—I have said what my eldest brother was to us,—in what reverence we held him. He was just married, and he and his bride asked me to return from chapel with them to tea. After tea he said, "Come now, we have had plenty of talk; I will read you something;" and he held out his hand for the new "Repository." After glancing at it, he exclaimed, "They have got a new hand here. Listen." After a paragraph, he repeated, "Ah! this is a new hand; they have had nothing so good as this for a long while." (It would be impossible to convey to any who do not know the "Monthly Repository" of that day, how very small a compliment this was.) I was silent, of course. At the end of the first column, he exclaimed about the style, looking at me in some wonder at my being as still as a mouse. Next (and well I remember his tone, and thrill to it still) his words were—"What a fine sentence that is! Why, do you not think so?" I mumbled out, sillily enough, that it did not seem any thing particular. "Then," said he, "you were not listening. I will read it again. There now!" As he still got nothing out of me, he turned round upon me, as we sat side by side on the sofa, with "Harriet, what is the matter with you? I never knew you so slow to praise any thing before." I replied, in utter confusion,—"I never could baffle any body. The truth is, that paper is mine." He made no reply; read on in silence, and spoke no more till I was on my feet to come away. He then laid his hand on my shoulder, and said gravely (calling me 'dear' for the first time) "Now, dear, leave it to other women to make shirts and darn stockings; and do you devote yourself to this." I went home in a sort

6. Sir Thomas Noon Talfourd (1795–1854), English lawyer and author.

of dream, so that the squares of the pavement seemed to float before my eyes. That evening made me an authoress.

*   *   *

While I was at Newcastle [1829], a change, which turned out a very happy one, was made in our domestic arrangements. * * * I call it a misfortune, because in common parlance it would be so treated; but I believe that my mother and all her other daughters would have joined heartily, if asked, in my conviction that it was one of the best things that ever happened to us. My mother and her daughters lost, at a stroke, nearly all they had in the world by the failure of the house,—the old manufactory,—in which their money was placed. We never recovered more than the merest pittance; and at the time, I, for one, was left destitute;—that is to say, with precisely one shilling in my purse. The effect upon me of this new "calamity," as people called it, was like that of a blister upon a dull, weary pain, or series of pains. I rather enjoyed it, even at the time; for there was scope for action; whereas, in the long, dreary series of preceding trials, there was nothing possible but endurance. In a very short time, my two sisters at home and I began to feel the blessing of a wholly new freedom. I, who had been obliged to write before breakfast, or in some private way, had henceforth liberty to do my own work in my own way; for we had lost our gentility. Many and many a time since have we said that, but for that loss of money, we might have lived on in the ordinary provincial method of ladies with small means, sewing, and economizing, and growing narrower every year; whereas, by being thrown, while it was yet time, on our own resources, we have worked hard and usefully, won friends, reputation and independence, seen the world abundantly, abroad and at home, and, in short, have truly lived instead of vegetated.

1855   1877

HELEN HUNT JACKSON
1830–1885

Characterized by the historian Carl Degler as "the most brilliant, impetuous, and thoroughly individual woman of her time," Helen Hunt Jackson was born Helen Maria Fiske, the daughter of a Congregational minister who was professor of classics at Amherst College and a literarily inclined mother. A school friend of Emily Dickinson, Jackson was married twice—first to Edward Bissell Hunt, an army officer who died in a military accident, and some years later to William Sharpless Jackson, a wealthy banker and railroad magnate whom she met in Colorado where she went to seek a cure for tuberculosis. By then, she had also journeyed to California and become engaged in advocacy for Indian rights, a cause that was to occupy her for the rest of her life and inspire two of her most famous works: the fiery polemic *A Century of Dishonor* (1881), a scathing attack on the government's Indian policy, and the best-selling, often-reprinted and dramatized protest novel *Ramona* (1884), sometimes called "the *Uncle Tom's Cabin* of California."

Like Dickinson, Jackson became a protégée of Thomas Wentworth Higginson, the powerful editor of *The Atlantic,* toward the start of her literary career. With his encouragement, she began to write children's stories, poems, novels, and essays, at first under such pseudonyms as "H.H." and "Saxe Holm" but eventually, as she became increasingly engaged in public affairs, under her own name. Praised by Ralph Waldo Emerson as "the greatest woman poet" in America, she produced more than thirty books and countless articles while maintaining close ties with Stowe, Dickinson, and other writers. The protagonist of her novel *Mercy Philbrick's Choice* (1876) is thought to have been modeled in part on Emily Dickinson, while *Ramona* was based on a notorious 1883 episode in southern California in which Juan Diego, a Cahuilla Indian, was murdered by one Sam Temple for allegedly stealing a horse. Our selections here reveal the intensity and energy with which, as she conceived and composed *Ramona,* Jackson struggled to "do one hundredth part for the Indians that Mrs. Stowe did for the Negro."

Letters

[A STORY FOR THE "INDIAN CAUSE"]

To William Hayes Ward[1]

[January 1, 1884]

Dear Mr. Ward,

Thanks for the cheque — & the papers. — Can you send me the "Justifiable Homicide in S. Cal."[2] I have no copy of that. —

A happy New Year to you & many of them.

I hope you will find time to come up & see me. —

I take lunch always at half past one — and would be delighted to have you lunch with me, any day: — Let me know the day before hand. —

I am sure you will be interested to know that I am at work on a story — which I hope will do something for the Indian cause: it is laid in So. California — and there is so much Mexican life in it, that I hope to get people so interested in it, before they suspect anything Indian, that they will keep on. — If I can do one hundredth part for the Indians that Mrs. Stowe did for the Negro,[3] I will be thankful. — I have been considering it, and planning it for two years nearly — so there now remains little but the writing out: — and I hope to have it done next month. — I would like to consult you about the title. — *"In the Name of the Law"* — It is so good a title that I feel as if it must have been used before — but the literary friends I have consulted say, not. Have you ever heard of a story by that title?

Yours ever truly
Helen Jackson

[ON WRITING *RAMONA*]

To an Intimate Friend[4]

The Berkeley, *February* 5, 1884

. . . I am glad you say you are rejoiced that I am writing a story. But about the not hurrying it — I want to tell you something. You know I have for three

---

1. An editor of the *New York Independent*.
2. An article by Jackson, published in the *New York Independent* (September 27, 1883), that described the "barbaric" murder of a Cahuilla Indian; a justice of the peace ruled that no trial was
necessary.
3. I.e., in *Uncle Tom's Cabin* (1851–52).
4. Thomas Wentworth Higginson; he published the letter in *The Atlantic,* in November 1900, as "How Ramona Was Written."

or four years longed to write a story that should "tell" on the Indian question. But I knew I could not do it; knew I had no background, — no local color for it.

Last spring, in Southern California, I began to feel that I had; that the scene laid there — and the old Mexican life mixed in with just enough Indian to enable me to tell what had happened to them — would be the very perfection of coloring. You know that I had lived six months in Southern California.

Still I did not see my way clear; got no plot; till one morning late last October, before I was wide awake, the whole plot flashed into my mind, — not a vague one — the whole story just as it stands to-day, — in less than five minutes, as if some one spoke it. I sprang up, went to my husband's room, and told him; I was half frightened. From that time, till I came here, it haunted me, becoming more and more vivid. I was impatient to get at it. I wrote the first word of it December 1. As soon as I began, it seemed impossible to write fast enough. In spite of myself, I write faster than I would write a letter. I write two thousand to three thousand words in a morning, and I *cannot* help it. It racks me like a struggle with an outside power. I cannot help being superstitious about it. I have never done *half* the amount of work in the same time. Ordinarily it would be a simple impossibility. Twice, since beginning it, I have broken down utterly for a week — with a cold ostensibly, but with great nervous prostration added. What I have to endure in holding myself away from it, afternoons, on the days I am compelled to be in the house, no words can tell.

It is like keeping away from a lover, whose hand I can reach.

Now you will ask what sort of English it is I write at this lightning speed. So far as I can tell, the best I ever wrote! I have read it aloud as I have gone on, to one friend, of keen literary perceptions and judgment, the most purely intellectual woman I know — Mrs. Trimble.[5] She says it is smooth — strong — clear. "Tremendous" is her frequent epithet.

. . . The success of it — if it succeeds — will be that I do not even suggest any Indian history, — till the interest is so aroused in the heroine — and hero — that people will not lay the book down. There is but one Indian in the story.

Every now and then I force myself to stop, and write a short story or a bit of verse; I can't bear the strain; but the instant I open the pages of the other, I write as I am writing now — as fast as I could copy! What do you think? Am I possessed of a demon? Is it a freak of mental disturbance? or what.

I have the feeling that if I could only read it to you, you would know. — If it is as good as Mrs. Trimble, Mr. Jackson, and Miss Woolsey[6] think, I shall be indeed rewarded, for it will "tell." But I can't believe it is. I am uneasy about it; but try as I may — all I can — I cannot write slowly for more than a few moments. I sit down at 9.30 or ten, and it is one before I know it. In good weather I then go out, after lunching, and keep out, religiously, till five, — but there have not been more than three out of eight good days all winter, — and the days when I am shut up in my room from two till five alone — with my Ramona and Alessandro[7] — and cannot go along with them on their journey are maddening.

5. Mary Trimble, a Quaker woman from New York whom Jackson met in San Francisco in 1882.
6. Sarah Woolsey, one of Jackson's closest friends; she wrote magazine articles, poetry, and children's books under the pseudonym Susan Coolidge.

William Sharpless Jackson was Jackson's second husband.
7. The two lovers who are the main characters of *Ramona*.

Fifty-two last October — and I'm not a bit steadier-headed, you see, than ever?

I don't know whether to send this or burn it up. Don't laugh at me whatever you do.

Yours always,
H.J.

ANNA JULIA COOPER
1858?–1964

The daughter of a black slave and her white master, Anna Julia Cooper survived an enslaved childhood whose details she claimed not to remember and forged an extraordinary career as an educator, writer, civil rights activist, and feminist. One of the first African Americans to earn a Ph.D., she was educated at St. Augustine's Normal School, a teacher's training institution whose faculty she eventually joined, and then at Oberlin College, where she earned a master's degree in mathematics. During her tenure at St. Augustine's she married a colleague, George Cooper, an instructor of Greek, but was widowed early and remained single thereafter. In later years she also studied at Columbia University and eventually at the University of Paris, where she was awarded a Ph.D. in French in 1925. While pursuing these studies, she worked as a teacher of science and mathematics in Washington, D.C., becoming principal of the Washington Colored High School in 1902, and later president of Frelinghuysen University in the same city. In addition, she helped organize the Colored Woman's League of Washington, D.C., and in 1893 was one of only a few African American women who addressed the Women's Congress that was convened during the Columbian Exposition in Chicago.

Cooper's busy professional and public life did not deter her literary activities. In the 1890s she helped edit the journal *The Southland* and in the same years she produced a major collection of essays, *A Voice from the South: By a Black Woman of the South* (1892). Our selection, drawn from this volume, stresses the significance of higher education for women as a "means of setting free and invigorating [a] long desired feminine force in the world." In particular, Cooper pressed here for her "special cause"— "THE HIGHER EDUCATION OF COLORED WOMEN." Arguing elsewhere that, as one commentator put it, "the education and elevation of black women are crucial to racial uplift," she brought her feminist concerns together with her passion to improve the status of her people, focusing on literacy in the broadest sense as a key to social and cultural transformation.

From The Higher Education of Women

In the very first year of our century, the year 1801, there appeared in Paris a book by Silvain Marechal, entitled *Shall Woman Learn the Alphabet*. The book proposes a law prohibiting the alphabet to women, and quotes authorities weighty and various, to prove that the woman who knows the alphabet has already lost part of her womanliness. The author declares that women can use the alphabet only as Molière predicted they would, in spelling out the verb *amo;* that they have no occasion to peruse Ovid's *Ars Amoris*,[1] since that is already the ground and limit of their intuitive furnishing; that Madame Guion[2] would have been far more adorable had she remained a beautiful ignoramus as nature made her; that Ruth, Naomi, and Spartan woman, the Amazons, Penelope, Andromache, Lucretia, Joan of Arc, Petrarch's Laura, the daughters of Charlemagne, could not spell their names; while Sappho, Aspasia, Madame de Maintenon, and Madame de Staël[3] could read altogether too well for their good; finally, that if women were once permitted to read Sophocles and work with logarithms, or to nibble at any side of the apple of knowledge, there would be an end forever to their sewing on buttons and embroidering slippers.

Please remember this book was published at the *beginning* of the Nineteenth Century. At the end of its first third, (in the year 1833) one solitary college in America decided to admit women within its sacred precincts, and organized what was called a "Ladies' Course" as well as the regular B.A. or Gentlemen's course.

It was felt to be an experiment—a rather dangerous experiment—and was adopted with fear and trembling by the good fathers, who looked as if they had been caught secretly mixing explosive compounds and were guiltily expecting every moment to see the foundations under them shaken and rent and their fair superstructure shattered into fragments.

But the girls came, and there was no upheaval. They performed their tasks modestly and intelligently. Once in a while one or two were found choosing the gentlemen's course. Still no collapse; and the dear, careful, scrupulous, frightened old professors were just getting their hearts out of their throats and preparing to draw one good free breath, when they found they would have to change the names of those courses; for there were as many ladies in the gentlemen's course as in the ladies', and a distinctively Ladies's Course, inferior in scope and aim to the regular classical course, did not and could not exist.

Other colleges gradually fell into line, and to-day there are one hundred and ninety-eight colleges for women, and two hundred and seven coeducational colleges and universities in the United States alone offering the degree of B.A. to women, and sending out yearly into the arteries of this nation a warm, rich flood of strong, brave, active, energetic, well-equipped, thoughtful women—women quick to see and eager to help the needs of this needy world—women who can think as well as feel, and who feel none the less because they think—women who are none the less tender and true for the parchment scroll they bear in their hands—women who have given a deeper, richer, nobler and grander meaning to the word "womanly" than any one-sided masculine definition could ever have suggested or inspired—women whom the world has long waited for in pain and anguish till there should be at last added to its forces and allowed to permeate its thought the complement of that masculine influence which has dominated it for fourteen centuries.

※　　※　　※

1. Cooper probably means the *Ars Amatoria* (*Art of Love*), a didactic poem in three books (two addressed to men, one to women). "*Amo*": I love (Latin).
2. French autobiographer, poet, and mystic (1648–1717).
3. A mix of biblical, historical, and legendary figures (the last four are all historical, and all were criticized for supposed sexual immorality).

Nay,[4] put your ear now close to the pulse of the time. What is the key-note of the literature of these days? What is the banner cry of all the activities of the last half decade? What is the dominant seventh which is to add richness and tone to the final cadences of this century and lead by a grand modulation into the triumphant harmonies of the next? It is not compassion for the poor and unfortunate, and, as Bellamy has expressed it, "indignant outcry against the failure of the social machinery as it is, to ameliorate the miseries of men!"[5] Even Christianity is being brought to the bar of humanity and tried by the standard of its ability to alleviate the world's suffering and lighten and brighten its woe. What else can be the meaning of Matthew Arnold's saddening protest, "We cannot do without Christianity," cried he, "and we cannot endure it as it is."[6]

When went there by an age, when so much time and thought, so much money and labor were given to God's poor and God's invalids, the lowly and unlovely, the sinning as well as the suffering—homes for inebriates and homes for lunatics, shelter for the aged and shelter for babes, hospitals for the sick, props and braces for the falling, reformatory prisons and prison reformatories, all show that a "mothering" influence from some source is leavening the nation.

Now please understand me. I do not ask you to admit that these benefactions and virtues are the exclusive possession of women, or even that women are their chief and only advocates. It may be a man who formulates and makes them vocal. It may be, and often is, a man who weeps over the wrongs and struggles for the amelioration: but that man has imbibed those impulses from a mother rather than from a father and is simply materializing and giving back to the world in tangible form the ideal love and tenderness, devotion and care that have cherished and nourished the helpless period of his own existence.

All I claim is that there is a feminine as well as a masculine side to truth; that these are related not as inferior and superior, not as better and worse, not as weaker and stronger, but as complements—complements in one necessary and symmetric whole. That as the man is more noble in reason, so the woman is more quick in sympathy. That as he is indefatigable in pursuit of abstract truth, so is she in caring for the interests by the way—striving tenderly and lovingly that not one of the least of these "little ones" should perish.[7] That while we not unfrequently see women who reason, we say, with the coolness and precision of a man, and men as considerate of helplessness as a woman, still there is a general consensus of mankind that the one trait is essentially masculine and the other is peculiarly feminine. That both are needed to be worked into the training of children, in order that our boys may supplement their virility by tenderness and sensibility, and our girls may round out their gentleness by strength and self-reliance. That, as both are alike necessary in giving symmetry to the individual, so a nation or a race will degenerate into mere emotionalism on the one hand, or bullyism on the other, if dominated by either exclusively; lastly, and most emphatically, that the feminine factor can have its proper effect only through women's devel-

4. Cooper has just predicted how the influence of educated women will benefit religion, science, and economics.

5. From Edward Bellamy's novel *Looking Back-*ward (1888), chap. 26.

6. Paraphrased from Arnold's preface to *God and the Bible* (1875).

7. See Matthew 18.14.

opment and education so that she may fitly and intelligently stamp her force on the forces of her day, and add her modicum to the riches of the world's thought.

> For woman's cause is man's: they rise or sink
> Together, dwarfed or godlike, bond or free:
> For she that out of Lethe scales with man
> The shining steps of nature, shares with man
> His nights, his days, moves with him to one goal.
> If she be small, slight-natured, miserable,
> How shall men grow?
> * * * Let her make herself her own
> To give or keep, to live and learn and be
> All that not harms distinctive womanhood.
> For woman is not undeveloped man
> But diverse: could we make her as the man
> Sweet love were slain; his dearest bond is this,
> Not like to like, but like in difference.
> Yet in the long years liker must they grow;
> The man be more of woman, she of man;
> He gain in sweetness and in moral height,
> Nor lose the wrestling thews that throw the world;
> She mental breadth, nor fail in childward care,
> Nor lose the childlike in the larger mind;
> Till at the last she set herself to man,
> Like perfect music unto noble words.[8]

Now you will argue, perhaps, and rightly, that higher education for women is not a modern idea, and that, if that is the means of setting free and invigorating the long desired feminine force in the world, it has already had a trial and should, in the past, have produced some of these glowing effects. Sappho, the bright, sweet singer of Lesbos, "the violet-crowned, pure, sweetly smiling Sappho" as Alcaeus calls her, chanted her lyrics and poured forth her soul nearly six centuries before Christ, in notes as full and free, as passionate and eloquent as did ever Archilochus or Anacreon.[9]

*   *   *

In soul-culture woman at last dares to contend with men, and we may cite Grant Allen (who certainly cannot be suspected of advocating the unsexing of woman) as an example of the broadening effect of this contest on the ideas at least of the men of the day. He says in his *Plain Words on the Woman Question*, recently published:

> The position of women was not [in the past a] position which could bear the test of nineteenth-century scrutiny. Their education was inadequate, their social status was humiliating, their political power was nil, their practical and personal grievances were innumerable; above all, their relations to the family—to their husbands, their children, their friends, their property—were simply insupportable.

And again:

8. Tennyson's *The Princess* (1847), 7.243–70.
9. All lyric poets of classical Greece, respectively contemporary with, earlier than, and later than Sappho.

As a body we "Advanced men" are, I think, prepared to reconsider, and to reconsider fundamentally, without prejudice or misconception, the entire question of the relation between the sexes. We are ready to make any modifications in those relations which will satisfy the woman's just aspiration for personal independence, for intellectual and moral development, for physical culture, for political activity, and for a voice in the arrangement of her own affairs, both domestic and national.

Now this is magnanimous enough, surely; and quite a step from eighteenth century preaching, is it not? The higher education of Woman has certainly developed the men;—let us see what it has done for the women.

Matthew Arnold during his last visit to America in [18]82 or [18]83, lectured before a certain co-educational college in the West. After the lecture he remarked, with some surprise, to a lady professor, that the young women in his audience, he noticed, "paid as close attention as the men, *all the way through.*" This led, of course, to a spirited discussion of the higher education for women, during which he said to his enthusiastic interlocutor, eyeing her philosophically through his English eyeglass: "But—eh—don't you think it—eh—spoils their *chawnces,* you know!"

Now, as to the result to women, this is the most serious argument ever used against the higher education. If it interferes with marriage, classical training has a grave objection to weigh and answer.

For I agree with Mr. Allen at least on this one point, that there must be marrying and giving in marriage[1] even till the end of time.

I grant you that intellectual development, with the self-reliance and capacity for earning a livelihood which it gives, renders woman less dependent on the marriage relation for physical support (which, by the way, does not always accompany it). Neither is she compelled to look to sexual love as the one sensation capable of giving tone and relish, movement and vim to the life she leads. Her horizon is extended. Her sympathies are broadened and deepened and multiplied. She is in closer touch with nature. Not a bud that opens, not a dew drop, not a ray of light, not a cloud-burst or a thunderbolt, but adds to the expansiveness and zest of her soul. And if the sun of an absorbing passion be gone down, still 'tis night that brings the stars. She has remaining the mellow, less obtrusive, but none the less enchanting and inspiring light of friendship, and into its charmed circle she may gather the best the world has known. She can commune with Socrates about the *daimon* he knew[2] and to which she too can bear witness; she can revel in the majesty of Dante, the sweetness of Virgil, the simplicity of Homer, and strength of Milton. She can listen to the pulsing heart throbs of passionate Sappho's encaged soul, as she beats her bruised wings against her prison bars and struggles to flutter out into Heaven's aether, and the fires of her own soul cry back as she listens. "Yes; Sappho, I know it all; I know it all." Here, at last, can be communion without suspicion; friendship without misunderstanding; love without jealousy.

We must admit then that Byron's picture, whether a thing of beauty or not, has faded from the canvas of to-day. "Man's love," he wrote,

> is of man's life a thing apart,
> 'Tis woman's whole existence.

---

1. Matthew 24.38. 2. I.e., his divine guide (see Plato, *Apology* 31D).

Man may range the court, camp, church, the vessel and the mart,
Sword, gown, gain, glory offer in exchange.
Pride, fame, ambition, to fill up his heart—
And few there are whom these cannot estrange.
Men have all these resources, we *but one*—
To love again and be again undone.[3]

This may have been true when written. *It is not true to-day.* The old, subjective, stagnant, indolent and wretched life for woman has gone. She has as many resources as men, as many activities beckon her on. As large possibilities swell and inspire her heart.

Now, then, does it destroy or diminish her capacity for loving?

Her standards have undoubtedly gone up. The necessity of speculating in "chawnces" has probably shifted. The question is not now with the woman "How shall I so cramp, stunt, simplify and nullify myself as to make me eligible to the honor of being swallowed up into some little man?" but the problem, I trow, now rests with the man as to how he can so develop his God-given powers as to reach the ideal of a generation of women who demand the noblest, grandest and best achievements of which he is capable; and this surely is the only fair and natural adjustment of the chances. Nature never meant that the ideals and standards of the world should be dwarfing and minimizing ones, and the men should thank us for requiring of them the richest fruits which they can grow. If it makes them work, all the better for them.

As to the adaptability of the educated woman to the marriage relation, I shall simply quote from that excellent symposium of learned women that appeared recently under Mrs. Armstrong's signature in answer to the *Plain Words* of Mr. Allen, already referred to.

> Admitting no longer any question as to their intellectual equality with the men whom they meet, with the simplicity of conscious strength, they take their place beside the men who challenge them, and fearlessly face the result of their actions. They deny that their education in any way unfits them for the duty of wifehood and maternity or primarily renders these conditions any less attractive to them than to the domestic type of woman. On the contrary, they hold that their knowledge of physiology makes them better mothers and housekeepers; their knowledge of chemistry makes them better cooks; while from their training in other natural sciences and in mathematics, they obtain an accuracy and fair-mindedness which is of great value to them in dealing with their children or employees.

So much for their willingness. Now the apple may be good for food and pleasant to the eyes, and a fruit to be desired to make one wise. Nay, it may even assure you that it has no aversion whatever to being tasted. Still, if you do not like the flavor all these recommendations are nothing. Is the intellectual woman *desirable* in the matrimonial market?

This I cannot answer I confess my ignorance. I am no judge of such things. I have been told that strong-minded women could be, when they thought it worth their while, quite endurable, and, judging from the number of female names I find in college catalogues among the alumnae with double patronymics, I surmise that quite a number of men are willing to put up with them.

---

3. Byron's *Don Juan*, canto 1 (1817), stanza 194 (Cooper's emphasis).

Now I would that my task ended here. Having shown that a great want of the world in the past has been a feminine force; that that force can have its full effect only through the untrammelled development of woman; that such development, while it gives her to the world and to civilization, does not necessarily remove her from the home and fireside; finally, that while past centuries have witnessed sporadic instances of this higher growth, still it was reserved for the latter half of the nineteenth century to render it common and general enough to be effective; I might close with a glowing prediction of what the twentieth century may expect from this heritage of twin forces—the masculine battered and toil-worn as a grim veteran after centuries of warfare, but still strong, active, and vigorous, ready to help with his hard-won experience the young recruit rejoicing in her newly found freedom, who so confidently places her hand in his with mutual pledges to redeem the ages.

> And so the twain upon the skirts of Time,
> Sit side by side, full-summed in all their powers,
> Dispensing harvest, sowing the To-be,
> Self-reverent each and reverencing each.[4]

Fain would I follow them, but duty is nearer home. The high ground of generalities is alluring but my pen is devoted to a special cause: and with a view to further enlightenment on the achievements of the century for THE HIGHER EDUCATION OF COLORED WOMEN, I wrote a few days ago to the colleges which admit women and asked how many colored women had completed the B.A. course in each during its entire history. These are the figures returned: Fisk leads the way with twelve; Oberlin next with five; Wilberforcè, four; Ann Arbor and Wellesley three each, Livingstone two, Atlanta one, Howard, as yet, none.

*   *   *

1890–91   1892

4. Tennyson, *The Princess* 7.271–74.

CHARLOTTE PERKINS GILMAN
1860–1935

The author of "The Yellow Wallpaper," a work once anthologized as a horror story but now widely celebrated as a feminist classic, explains in our selection here why she produced her groundbreaking story of postpartum depression and foiled creativity. Raised by an emotionally withholding mother after her father had deserted the family, Charlotte Perkins married the artist Charles Walter Stetson when she was twenty-four. Following the birth of their daughter Katherine a few years later, she felt herself enveloped in a "dark fog" of despair. She was famously (or, perhaps more accurately, infamously) treated for this condition by a prominent physician, S. Weir Mitchell, who prescribed a rest cure involving not only confinement to bed but a diet rich in milk and cream along with a renunciation of all intellectual aspirations. Such a cure, strangely enough, was to work wonders for Gilman's contemporary, Edith Wharton, a decade later; but on Gilman its effects were grim, as her renowned story reveals. Nevertheless, she recovered from her breakdown, divorced Stetson, and made the controversial decision to send her daughter to live with him and his new wife, her friend

Grace Ellery Channing. Although newspaper commentaries excoriated her as hard-hearted, she went on to a brilliant career as a feminist lecturer, activist, editor, and author. Married to a supportive husband, George Houghton Gilman, she produced such major works of feminist thought as *The Home* (1903), *The Man-Made World* (1911), and *His Religion and Hers* (1923), as well as her utopian fantasy *Herland* (1915), which celebrates a matriarchal culture of parthenogenetic women.

Why I Wrote "The Yellow Wall-paper"?

Many and many a reader has asked that. When the story first came out, in the *New England Magazine* about 1891, a Boston physician made protest in *The Transcript*. Such a story ought not to be written, he said; it was enough to drive anyone mad to read it.

Another physician, in Kansas I think, wrote to say that it was the best description of incipient insanity he had ever seen, and—begging my pardon—had I been there?

Now the story of the story is this:

For many years I suffered from a severe and continuous nervous break-down tending to melancholia—and beyond. During about the third year of this trouble I went, in devout faith and some faint stir of hope, to a noted specialist in nervous diseases,[1] the best known in the country. This wise man put me to bed and applied the rest cure, to which a still good physique responded so promptly that he concluded there was nothing much the matter with me, and sent me home with solemn advice to "live as domestic a life as far as possible," to "have but two hours' intellectual life a day," and "never to touch pen, brush or pencil again as long as I lived." This was in 1887.

I went home and obeyed those directions for some three months, and came so near the border line of utter mental ruin that I could see over.

Then, using the remnants of intelligence that remained, and helped by a wise friend,[2] I cast the noted specialist's advice to the winds and went to work again—work, the normal life of every human being; work, in which is joy and growth and service, without which one is a pauper and a parasite; ultimately recovering some measure of power.

Being naturally moved to rejoicing by this narrow escape, I wrote "The Yellow Wall-paper," with its embellishments and additions to carry out the ideal (I never had hallucinations or objections to my mural decorations) and sent a copy to the physician who so nearly drove me mad. He never acknowledged it.

The little book is valued by alienists[3] and as a good specimen of one kind of literature. It has to my knowledge saved one woman from a similar fate—so terrifying her family that they let her out into normal activity and she recovered.

But the best result is this. Many years later I was told that the great specialist had admitted to friends of his that he had altered his treatment of neurasthenia since reading "The Yellow Wall-paper."

It was not intended to drive people crazy, but to save people from being driven crazy, and it worked.

1913

---

1. Silas Weir Mitchell, a Philadelphia Physician.   3. Psychologists.
2. Almost certainly the writer Grace Channing.

H. D. (HILDA DOOLITTLE)
1886–1961

A major poet and writer of innovative, experimental prose, H. D. was relegated to comparative obscurity until the 1970s, when such critics as Norman Holmes Pearson, Susan Stanford Friedman, and Louis Martz undertook to return her to the central canon of modernism, after asking—as Friedman put it in a pioneering essay—"Who Buried H.D.?" But this poet's eclipse had in any case been difficult to understand, given her unflagging creative energy, her centrality to the early-twentieth-century movement that Ezra Pound called Imagism, and the poetic ambition that energized her composition of such major modernist epics as *Trilogy* (1944–46) and *Helen in Egypt* (1961).

Born Hilda Doolittle in Bethlehem, Pennsylvania, where her father was a professor of astronomy at Lehigh University, H. D. moved with her family to Philadelphia when her father became the director of the Flower Observatory at the University of Pennsylvania. There she attended Bryn Mawr, was briefly engaged to the young Ezra Pound, and was also much admired by Pound's friend William Carlos Williams. When she traveled to London in 1911, Pound introduced her to his extended literary circle, which included such luminaries as D. H. Lawrence, W. B. Yeats, May Sinclair, and Richard Aldington (to whom she was married for a time). More important, dubbing her "H. D., Imagiste," Pound launched her on a literary career in the course of which she would write a number of novels (for instance, *Bid Me To Live*, 1960) and memoirs (*Tribute to Freud*, 1956) along with some dozen volumes of verse.

In our selection here, drawn from *Notes on Thought and Vision*—material transcribed during a visit to the Scilly Islands in 1919—H. D. meditates on the special states of consciousness that she associated with aesthetic creativity not only in her own life but in the lives of other artists, positing what she called an intensified "jellyfish consciousness" that facilitates artistic vision and is located either in the brain or the "love-region." "Should we be able to think with the womb and feel with the brain?" she wondered, anticipating a metaphor for female creativity that would also be proposed by the diarist and novelist Anaïs Nin.

From Notes on Thought and Vision

Three states or manifestations of life: body, mind, over-mind.

Aim of men and women of highest development is equilibrium, balance, growth of the three at once; brain without physical strength is a manifestation of weakness, a disease comparable to cancerous growth or tumor; body without reasonable amount of intellect is an empty fibrous bundle of glands as ugly and little to be desired as body of a victim of some form of elephantiasis or fatty-degeneracy; over-mind without the balance of the other two is madness and a person so developed should have as much respect as a reasonable maniac and no more.

○

All reasoning, normal, sane and balanced men and women need and seek at certain times of their lives, certain definite physical relationships. Men and women of temperament, musicians, scientists, artists especially, need these relationships to develop and draw forth their talents. Not to desire and make every effort to develop along these natural physical lines, cripples and dwarfs the being. To shun, deny and belittle such experiences is to bury one's talent carefully in a napkin.

○

When a creative scientist, artist or philosopher has been for some hours or days intent on his work, his mind often takes on an almost physical character. That is, his mind becomes his real body. His over-mind becomes his brain.

When Leonardo da Vinci worked, his brain was Leonardo, the personality, Leonardo da Vinci. He saw the faces of many of his youths and babies and young women definitely with his over-mind. The *Madonna of the Rocks* is not a picture. It is a window. We look through a window into the world of pure over-mind.

○

If I could visualise or describe that over-mind in my own case, I should say this: it seems to me that a cap is over my head, a cap of consciousness over my head, my forehead, affecting a little my eyes. Sometimes when I am in that state of consciousness, things about me appear slightly blurred as if seen under water.

Ordinary things never become quite unreal nor disproportionate. It is only an effort to readjust, to focus, seemingly a slight physical effort.

○

That over-mind seems a cap, like water, transparent, fluid yet with definite body, contained in a definite space. It is like a closed sea-plant, jelly-fish or anemone.

Into that over-mind, thoughts pass and are visible like fish swimming under clear water.

○

The swing from normal consciousness to abnormal consciousness is accompanied by grinding discomfort of mental agony.

○

I should say—to continue this jelly-fish metaphor—that long feelers reached down and through the body, that these stood in the same relation to the nervous system as the over-mind to the brain or intellect.

There is, then, a set of super-feelings. These feelings extend out and about us; as the long, floating tentacles of the jelly-fish reach out and about him. They are not of different material, extraneous, as the physical arms and legs are extraneous to the gray matter of the directing brain. The super-feelers are part of the super-mind, as the jelly-fish feelers are the jelly-fish itself, elongated in fine threads.

I first realised this state of consciousness in my head. I visualise it just as well, now, centered in the love-region of the body or placed like a foetus in the body.

The centre of consciousness is either the brain or the love-region of the body.

○

Is it easier for a woman to attain this state of consciousness than for a man?

For me, it was before the birth of my child that the jelly-fish conciousness seemed to come definitely into the field or realm of the intellect or brain.

○

Are these jelly-fish states of consciousness interchangeable? Should we be able to think with the womb and feel with the brain?

May this consciousness be centered entirely in the brain or entirely in the womb or corresponding love-region of a man's body?

○

Vision is of two kinds—vision of the womb and vision of the brain. In vision of the brain, the region of consciousness is above and about the head; when the centre of consciousness shifts and the jelly-fish is in the body, (I visualise it in my case lying on the left side with the streamers or feelers floating up toward the brain) we have vision of the womb or love-vision.

○

The majority of dream and of ordinary vision is vision of the womb.

The brain and the womb are both centres of consciousness, equally important.

○

Most of the so-called artists of today have lost the use of their brain. There is no way of arriving at the over-mind, except through the intellect. To arrive at the world of over-mind vision any other way, is to be the thief that climbs into the sheep-fold.

I believe there are artists coming in the next generation, some of whom will have the secret of using their over-minds.

○

Over-mind artists usually come in a group. There were the great Italians: Verrochio, Angelo, Ghiberti, the lot that preceded and followed da Vinci, including statesmen, explorers, and men and women of curious and sensitive development.

There was the great Athenian group: the dramatists, Socrates, the craftsmen and the men and women, their followers and lovers.

○

There is no great art period without great lovers.

○

Socrates' whole doctrine of vision was a doctrine of love.

We must be "in love" before we can understand the mysteries of vision.

A lover must choose one of the same type of mind as himself, a musician, a musician, a scientist, a scientist, a general, a young man also interested in the theory and practice of arms and armies.

We begin with sympathy of thought.

The minds of the two lovers merge, interact in sympathy of thought.

The brain, inflamed and excited by this interchange of ideas, takes on its character of over-mind, becomes (as I have visualised in my own case) a jelly-fish, placed over and about the brain.

The love-region is excited by the appearance or beauty of the loved one, its energy not dissipated in physical relation, takes on its character of mind, becomes this womb-brain or love-brain that I have visualised as a jelly-fish *in* the body.

The love-brain and over-brain are both capable of thought. This thought is vision.

○

All men have possibilities of developing this vision.

The over-mind is like a lens of an opera-glass. When we are able to use this over-mind lens, the whole world of vision is open to us.

I have said that the over-mind is a lens. I should say more exactly that the love-mind and the over-mind are two lenses. When these lenses are properly adjusted, focused, they bring the world of vision into consciousness. The two work separately, perceive separately, yet make one picture.

○

The mystic, the philosopher is content to contemplate, to examine these pictures. The Attic dramatist reproduced them for men of lesser or other gifts. He realised, the whole time, that they were not his ideas. They were eternal, changeless ideas that he had grown aware of, dramas already conceived that he had watched; memory is the mother, begetter of all drama, idea, music, science or song.

○

We may enter the world of over-mind consciousness directly, through the use of our over-mind brain. We may enter it indirectly, in various ways. Every person must work out his own way.

*　　*　　*

1919   1981

VIRGINIA WOOLF
1882–1941

Although, as our table of contents for this reader reveals, feminist literary thought has a long history, contemporary "feminist criticism" as we currently understand the phrase arguably originated with Virginia Woolf's dazzling meditation on "women and fiction" titled *A Room of One's Own* (1929). Here this daughter of "well-to-do parents, born into a very communicative, literate, letter writing, visiting, articulate, late-nineteenth-century world" examined the cultural constraints against which even privileged women like herself had to struggle in order to forge literary careers, noting not only the inadequacy of female education but also the negative images of women, the domestic obligations, and the problematic material conditions that had historically impeded female creativity.

Born Virginia Stephen, subject to recurrent emotional breakdowns, but happily married to the "penniless Jew" Leonard Woolf, with whom she had founded the Hogarth Press, Woolf could speak with some authority about such issues because by the time she wrote *A Room* she had herself confronted and overcome many of the obstacles she defined in that book and had triumphantly produced numerous literary essays and six major novels: *The Voyage Out* (1915), *Night and Day* (1919), *Jacob's Room* (1922), *Mrs. Dalloway* (1925), *To the Lighthouse* (1927), and *Orlando* (1928). In these works, she gradually developed an innovative way of representing consciousness—she called it her "tunneling process"—through which she excavated the complexities of past and present with which each character is continually engaged.

In the first of our selections here, Woolf deploys a kind of critical analysis very similar to such a "tunneling process" in order to compare and contrast the literary achievements of Charlotte and Emily Brontë. In the second of our selections, from *A Room* itself, she composes a lyrical fantasy "review" of a work by a hypothetical novelist of the future, "Mary Carmichael," whose novel begins, she posits, with the unexpected sentence "Chloe liked Olivia. They worked in a laboratory together." Whether, as in *"Jane Eyre* and *Wuthering Heights,"* illuminating the accomplishments of women's aesthetic past or, as in her fantasy about "Mary Carmichael," dreaming of a different literary future, Woolf consistently focused her own cultural consciousness on the many ways in which the intricate relationships between gender and genre are continually shaped and re-shaped in the crucible of history.

Jane Eyre and *Wuthering Heights*

Of the hundred years that have passed since Charlotte Brontë was born, she, the centre now of so much legend, devotion, and literature, lived but thirty-nine. It is strange to reflect how different those legends might have been had her life reached the ordinary human span. She might have become, like some of her famous contemporaries, a figure familiarly met with in London and elsewhere, the subject of pictures and anecdotes innumerable, the writer of many novels, of memoirs possibly, removed from us well within the memory of the middle-aged in all the splendour of established fame. She might have been wealthy, she might have been prosperous. But it is not so. When we think of her we have to imagine some one who had no lot in our modern world; we have to cast our minds back to the 'fifties of the last century, to a remote parsonage upon the wild Yorkshire moors. In that parsonage, and on those moors, unhappy and lonely, in her poverty and her exaltation, she remains for ever.

These circumstances, as they affected her character, may have left their traces on her work. A novelist, we reflect, is bound to build up his structure with much very perishable material which begins by lending it reality and ends by cumbering it with rubbish. As we open *Jane Eyre* once more we cannot stifle the suspicion that we shall find her world of imagination as antiquated, mid-Victorian, and out of date as the parsonage on the moor, a place only to be visited by the curious, only preserved by the pious. So we open *Jane Eyre;* and in two pages every doubt is swept clean from our minds.

Folds of scarlet drapery shut in my view to the right hand; to the left were the clear panes of glass, protecting, but not separating me from the drear November day. At intervals, while turning over the leaves of my book, I studied the aspect of that winter afternoon. Afar, it offered a pale blank of mist and cloud; near, a scene of wet lawn and storm-beat shrub, with ceaseless rain sweeping away wildly before a long and lamentable blast.

There is nothing there more perishable than the moor itself, or more subject to the sway of fashion than the "long and lamentable blast." Nor is this exhilaration short-lived. It rushes us through the entire volume, without giving us time to think, without letting us lift our eyes from the page. So intense is our absorption that if some one moves in the room the movement seems to take place not there but up in Yorkshire. The writer has us by the hand, forces us along her road, makes us see what she sees, never leaves us for a moment or allows us to forget her.[1] At the end we are steeped through and through with the genius, the vehemence, the indignation of Charlotte Brontë. Remarkable faces, figures of strong outline and gnarled feature have flashed upon us in passing; but it is through her eyes that we have seen them. Once she is gone, we seek for them in vain. Think of Rochester[2] and we have to think of Jane Eyre. Think of the moor, and again, there is Jane Eyre. Think of the drawing-room, even, those "white carpets on which seemed laid brilliant garlands of flowers," that "pale Parian mantelpiece" with its Bohemia glass of "ruby red" and the "general blending of snow and fire"—what is all that except Jane Eyre?

The drawbacks of being Jane Eyre are not far to seek. Always to be a governess and always to be in love is a serious limitation in a world which is full, after all, of people who are neither one nor the other. The characters of a Jane Austen or of a Tolstoi have a million facets compared with these. They live and are complex by means of their effect upon many different people who serve to mirror them in the round. They move hither and thither whether their creators watch them or not, and the world in which they live seems to us an independent world which we can visit, now that they have created it, by ourselves. Thomas Hardy is more akin to Charlotte Brontë in the power of his personality and the narrowness of his vision. But the differences are vast. As we read *Jude the Obscure* we are not rushed to a finish; we brood and ponder and drift away from the text in plethoric trains of thought which build up round the characters an atmosphere of question and suggestion of which they are themselves, as often as not, unconscious. Simple peasants as they are, we are forced to confront them with destinies and questionings of the hugest import, so that often it seems as if the most important characters in a Hardy novel are those which have no names. Of this power, of this speculative curiosity, Charlotte Brontë has

1. Charlotte and Emily Brontë had much the same sense of colour. ". . . we saw—ah! it was beautiful— a splendid place carpeted with crimson, and crimson-covered chairs and tables, and a pure white ceiling bordered by gold, a shower of glass drops hanging in silver chains from the centre, and shimmering with little soft tapers" (*Wuthering Heights*). Yet it was merely a very pretty drawing-room, and within it a boudoir, both spread with white carpets, on which seemed laid brilliant garlands of flowers; both ceiled with snowy mouldings of white grapes and vine leaves, beneath which glowed in rich contrast crimson couches and ottomans; while the ornaments on the pale Parian mantelpiece were of sparkling Bohemia glass, ruby red; and between the windows large mirrors repeated the general blending of snow and fire [Woolf 's note].
2. Jane Eyre's employer, with whom she falls in love.

no trace. She does not attempt to solve the problems of human life; she is even unaware that such problems exist; all her force, and it is the more tremendous for being constricted, goes into the assertion, "I love," "I hate," "I suffer."

For the self-centred and self-limited writers have a power denied the more catholic and broad-minded. Their impressions are close packed and strongly stamped between their narrow walls. Nothing issues from their minds which has not been marked with their own impress. They learn little from other writers, and what they adopt they cannot assimilate. Both Hardy and Charlotte Brontë appear to have founded their styles upon a stiff and decorous journalism. The staple of their prose is awkward and unyielding. But both with labour and the most obstinate integrity by thinking every thought until it has subdued words to itself, have forged for themselves a prose which takes the mould of their minds entire; which has, into the bargain, a beauty, a power, a swiftness of its own. Charlotte Brontë, at least, owed nothing to the reading of many books. She never learnt the smoothness of the professional writer, or acquired his ability to stuff and sway his language as he chooses. "I could never rest in communication with strong, discreet, and refined minds, whether male or female," she writes, as any leader-writer[3] in a provincial journal might have written; but gathering fire and speed goes on in her own authentic voice "till I had passed the outworks of conventional reserve and crossed the threshold of confidence, and won a place by their hearts' very hearthstone." It is there that she takes her seat; it is the red and fitful glow of the heart's fire which illumines her page. In other words, we read Charlotte Brontë not for exquisite observation of character—her characters are vigorous and elementary; not for comedy—hers is grim and crude; not for a philosophic view of life—hers is that of a country parson's daughter; but for her poetry. Probably that is so with all writers who have, as she has, an overpowering personality, who, as we should say in real life, have only to open the door to make themselves felt. There is in them some untamed ferocity perpetually at war with the accepted order of things which makes them desire to create instantly rather than to observe patiently. This very ardour, rejecting half shades and other minor impediments, wings its way past the daily conduct of ordinary people and allies itself with their more inarticulate passions. It makes them poets, or, if they choose to write in prose, intolerant of its restrictions. Hence it is that both Emily and Charlotte are always invoking the help of nature. They both feel the need of some more powerful symbol of the vast and slumbering passions in human nature than words or actions can convey. It is with a description of a storm that Charlotte ends her finest novel *Villette*. "The skies hang full and dark—a wrack sails from the west; the clouds cast themselves into strange forms." So she calls in nature to describe a state of mind which could not otherwise be expressed. But neither of the sisters observed nature accurately as Dorothy Wordsworth observed it, or painted it minutely as Tennyson painted it. They seized those aspects of the earth which were most akin to what they themselves felt or imputed to their characters, and so their storms, their moors, their lovely spaces of summer weather are

3. Editorial writer.

not ornaments applied to decorate a dull page or display the writer's powers of observation—they carry on the emotion and light up the meaning of the book.

The meaning of a book, which lies so often apart from what happens and what is said and consists rather in some connection which things in themselves different have had for the writer, is necessarily hard to grasp. Especially this is so when, like the Brontës, the writer is poetic, and his meaning inseparable from his language, and itself rather a mood than a particular observation. *Wuthering Heights* is a more difficult book to understand than *Jane Eyre,* because Emily was a greater poet than Charlotte. When Charlotte wrote she said with eloquence and splendour and passion "I love," "I hate," "I suffer." Her experience, though more intense, is on a level with our own. But there is no "I" in *Wuthering Heights*. There are no governesses. There are no employers. There is love, but it is not the love of men and women. Emily was inspired by some more general conception. The impulse which urged her to create was not her own suffering or her own injuries. She looked out upon a world cleft into gigantic disorder and felt within her the power to unite it in a book. That gigantic ambition is to be felt throughout the novel—a struggle, half thwarted but of superb conviction, to say something through the mouths of her characters which is not merely "I love" or "I hate," but "we, the whole human race" and "you, the eternal powers . . ." the sentence remains unfinished. It is not strange that it should be so; rather it is astonishing that she can make us feel what she had it in her to say at all. It surges up in the half-articulate words of Catherine Earnshaw,[4] "If all else perished and *he* remained, I should still continue to be; and if all else remained and he were annihilated, the universe would turn to a mighty stranger; I should not seem part of it." It breaks out again in the presence of the dead. "I see a repose that neither earth nor hell can break, and I feel an assurance of the endless and shadowless hereafter—the eternity they have entered—where life is boundless in its duration, and love in its sympathy and joy in its fulness." It is this suggestion of power underlying the apparitions of human nature, and lifting them up into the presence of greatness that gives the book its huge stature among other novels. But it was not enough for Emily Brontë to write a few lyrics, to utter a cry, to express a creed. In her poems she did this once and for all, and her poems will perhaps outlast her novel. But she was novelist as well as poet. She must take upon herself a more laborious and a more ungrateful task. She must face the fact of other existences, grapple with the mechanism of external things, build up, in recognisable shape, farms and houses and report the speeches of men and women who existed independently of herself. And so we reach these summits of emotion not by rant or rhapsody but by hearing a girl sing old songs to herself as she rocks in the branches of a tree; by watching the moor sheep crop the turf; by listening to the soft wind breathing through the grass. The life at the farm with all its absurdities and its improbability is laid open to us. We are given every opportunity of comparing *Wuthering Heights* with a real farm and Heathcliff with a real man. How, we are allowed to ask, can there be truth or insight or the

---

4. The novel's main female character, whose daughter is also named Catherine; the "he" she mentions is Heathcliff, the central male character, whom she loves.

finer shades of emotion in men and women who so little resemble what we have seen ourselves? But even as we ask it we see in Heathcliff the brother that a sister of genius might have seen; he is impossible, we say, but nevertheless no boy in literature has so vivid an existence as his. So it is with the two Catherines; never could women feel as they do or act in their manner, we say. All the same, they are the most lovable women in English fiction. It is as if she could tear up all that we know human beings by, and fill these unrecognisable transparences with such a gust of life that they transcend reality. Hers, then, is the rarest of all powers. She could free life from its dependence on facts; with a few touches indicate the spirit of a face so that it needs no body; by speaking of the moor make the wind blow and the thunder roar.

1916   1925

From A Room of One's Own

Chapter Five

I had come at last, in the course of this rambling, to the shelves which hold books by the living, by women and by men; for there are almost as many books written by women now as by men. Or if that is not yet quite true, if the male is still the voluble sex, it is certainly true that women no longer write novels solely. There are Jane Harrison's books on Greek archaeology; Vernon Lee's books on aesthetics; Gertrude Bell's books on Persia. There are books on all sorts of subjects which a generation ago no woman could have touched. There are poems and plays and criticism; there are histories and biographies, books of travel and books of scholarship and research; there are even a few philosophies and books about science and economics. And though novels predominate, novels themselves may very well have changed from association with books of a different feather. The natural simplicity, the epic age of women's writing, may have gone. Reading and criticism may have given her a wider range, a greater subtlety. The impulse towards autobiography may be spent. She may be beginning to use writing as an art, not as a method of self-expression. Among these new novels one might find an answer to several such questions.

I took down one of them at random. It stood at the very end of the shelf, was called *Life's Adventure,* or some such title, by Mary Carmichael, and was published in this very month of October. It seems to be her first book, I said to myself, but one must read it as if it were the last volume in a fairly long series, continuing all those other books that I have been glancing at—Lady Winchilsea's poems and Aphra Behn's plays and the novels of the four great novelists.[1] For books continue each other, in spite of our habit of judging them separately. And I must also consider her—this unknown woman—as the descendant of all those other women whose circumstances I have been glancing at and see what she inherits of their characteristics and restrictions.

---

1. In the previous chapter, Woolf discussed novels by Jane Austen, Charlotte and Emily Brontë, and George Eliot, as well as 17th- and early-18th-century writings by Behn and Lady Winchilsea.

So, with a sigh, because novels so often provide an anodyne and not an anti-dote, glide one into torpid slumbers instead of rousing one with a burning brand, I settled down with a notebook and a pencil to make what I could of Mary Carmichael's first novel, *Life's Adventure*.

To begin with, I ran my eye up and down the page. I am going to get the hang of her sentences first, I said, before I load my memory with blue eyes and brown and the relationship that there may be between Chloe and Roger. There will be time for that when I have decided whether she has a pen in her hand or a pickaxe. So I tried a sentence or two on my tongue. Soon it was obvious that something was not quite in order. The smooth gliding of sentence after sentence was interrupted. Something tore, something scratched; a single word here and there flashed its torch in my eyes. She was "unhand-ing" herself as they say in the old plays. She is like a person striking a match that will not light, I thought. But why, I asked her as if she were present, are Jane Austen's sentences not of the right shape for you? Must they all be scrapped because Emma and Mr. Woodhouse are dead? Alas, I sighed, that it should be so. For while Jane Austen breaks from melody to melody as Mozart from song to song, to read this writing was like being out at sea in an open boat. Up one went, down one sank. This terseness, this short-windedness, might mean that she was afraid of something; afraid of being called "sentimental" perhaps; or she remembers that women's writing has been called flowery and so provides a superfluity of thorns; but until I have read a scene with some care, I cannot be sure whether she is being herself or some one else. At any rate, she does not lower one's vitality, I thought, read-ing more carefully. But she is heaping up too many facts. She will not be able to use half of them in a book of this size. (It was about half the length of *Jane Eyre*.) However, by some means or other she succeeded in getting us all—Roger, Chloe, Olivia, Tony and Mr. Bigham—in a canoe up the river. Wait a moment, I said, leaning back in my chair, I must consider the whole thing more carefully before I go any further.

I am almost sure, I said to myself, that Mary Carmichael is playing a trick on us. For I feel as one feels on a switchback railway when the car, instead of sinking, as one has been led to expect, swerves up again. Mary is tampering with the expected sequence. First she broke the sentence; now she has bro-ken the sequence. Very well, she has every right to do both these things if she does them not for the sake of breaking, but for the sake of creating. Which of the two it is I cannot be sure until she has faced herself with a situation. I will give her every liberty, I said, to choose what that situation shall be; she shall make it of tin cans and old kettles if she likes; but she must convince me that she believes it to be a situation; and then when she has made it she must face it. She must jump. And, determined to do my duty by her as reader if she would do her duty by me as writer, I turned the page and read . . . I am sorry to break off so abruptly. Are there no men present? Do you promise me that behind that red curtain over there the figure of Sir Chartres Biron[2] is not concealed? We are all women, you assure me? Then I may tell you that the very next words I read were these—"Chloe liked Olivia . . ." Do not start. Do

2. The presiding magistrate in the obscenity trial involving *The Well of Loneliness* (1828), Radcliffe Hall's novel with a lesbian protagonist.

not blush. Let us admit in the privacy of our own society that these things sometimes happen. Sometimes women do like women.

"Chloe liked Olivia," I read. And then it struck me how immense a change was there. Chloe liked Olivia perhaps for the first time in literature. Cleopatra did not like Octavia. And how completely *Antony and Cleopatra* would have been altered had she done so! As it is, I thought, letting my mind, I am afraid, wander a little from *Life's Adventure*, the whole thing is simplified, conventionalised, if one dared say it, absurdly. Cleopatra's only feeling about Octavia is one of jealousy. Is she taller than I am? How does she do her hair? The play, perhaps, required no more. But how interesting it would have been if the relationship between the two women had been more complicated. All these relationships between women, I thought, rapidly recalling the splendid gallery of fictitious women, are too simple. So much has been left out, unattempted. And I tried to remember any case in the course of my reading where two women are represented as friends. There is an attempt at it in *Diana of the Crossways*.[3] They are confidantes, of course, in Racine and the Greek tragedies. They are now and then mothers and daughters. But almost without exception they are shown in their relation to men. It was strange to think that all the great women of fiction were, until Jane Austen's day, not only seen by the other sex, but seen only in relation to the other sex. And how small a part of a woman's life is that; and how little can a man know even of that when he observes it through the black or rosy spectacles which sex puts upon his nose. Hence, perhaps, the peculiar nature of woman in fiction; the astonishing extremes of her beauty and horror; her alternations between heavenly goodness and hellish depravity—for so a lover would see her as his love rose or sank, was prosperous or unhappy. This is not so true of the nineteenth-century novelists, of course. Woman becomes much more various and complicated there. Indeed it was the desire to write about women perhaps that led men by degrees to abandon the poetic drama which, with its violence, could make so little use of them, and to devise the novel as a more fitting receptacle. Even so it remains obvious, even in the writing of Proust, that a man is terribly hampered and partial in his knowledge of women, as a woman in her knowledge of men.

Also, I continued, looking down at the page again, it is becoming evident that women, like men, have other interests besides the perennial interests of domesticity. "Chloe liked Olivia. They shared a laboratory together. . . ." I read on and discovered that these two young women were engaged in mincing liver, which is, it seems, a cure for pernicious anaemia: although one of them was married and had—I think I am right in stating—two small children. Now all that, of course, has had to be left out, and thus the splendid portrait of the fictitious woman is much too simple and much too monotonous. Suppose, for instance, that men were only represented in literature as the lovers of women, and were never the friends of men, soldiers, thinkers, dreamers; how few parts in the plays of Shakespeare could be allotted to them; how literature would suffer! We might perhaps have most of Othello; and a good deal of Antony; but no Caesar, no Brutus, no Hamlet, no Lear, no Jaques—literature would be incredibly impoverished, as indeed literature is impoverished

---

3. Novel by George Meredith (1885).

beyond our counting by the doors that have been shut upon women. Married against their will, kept in one room, and to one occupation, how could a dramatist give a full or interesting or truthful account of them? Love was the only possible interpreter. The poet was forced to be passionate or bitter, unless indeed he chose to "hate women," which meant more often than not that he was unattractive to them.

Now if Chloe likes Olivia and they share a laboratory, which of itself will make their friendship more varied and lasting because it will be less personal; if Mary Carmichael knows how to write, and I was beginning to enjoy some quality in her style; if she has a room to herself, of which I am not quite sure; if she has five hundred a year of her own—but that remains to be proved—then I think that something of great importance has happened.

For if Chloe likes Olivia and Mary Carmichael knows how to express it she will light a torch in that vast chamber where nobody has yet been. It is all half lights and profound shadows like those serpentine caves where one goes with a candle peering up and down, not knowing where one is stepping. And I began to read the book again, and read how Chloe watched Olivia put a jar on a shelf and say how it was time to go home to her children. That is a sight that has never been seen since the world began, I exclaimed. And I watched too, very curiously. For I wanted to see how Mary Carmichael set to work to catch those unrecorded gestures, those unsaid or half-said words, which form themselves, no more palpably than the shadows of moths on the ceiling, when women are alone, unlit by the capricious and coloured light of the other sex. She will need to hold her breath, I said, reading on, if she is to do it; for women are so suspicious of any interest that has not some obvious motive behind it, so terribly accustomed to concealment and suppression, that they are off at the flicker of an eye turned observingly in their direction. The only way for you to do it, I thought, addressing Mary Carmichael as if she were there, would be to talk of something else, looking steadily out of the window, and thus note, not with a pencil in a notebook, but in the shortest of short-hand, in words that are hardly syllabled yet, what happens when Olivia—this organism that has been under the shadow of the rock these million years—feels the light fall on it, and sees coming her way a piece of strange food—knowledge, adventure, art. And she reaches out for it, I thought, again raising my eyes from the page, and has to devise some entirely new combination of her resources, so highly developed for other purposes, so as to absorb the new into the old without disturbing the infinitely intricate and elaborate balance of the whole.

But, alas, I had done what I had determined not to do; I had slipped unthinkingly into praise of my own sex. "Highly developed"—"infinitely intricate"—such are undeniably terms of praise, and to praise one's own sex is always suspect, often silly; moreover, in this case, how could one justify it? One could not go to the map and say Columbus discovered America and Columbus was a woman; or take an apple and remark, Newton discovered the laws of gravitation and Newton was a woman; or look into the sky and say aeroplanes are flying overhead and aeroplanes were invented by women. There is no mark on the wall to measure the precise height of women. There are no yard measures, neatly divided into the fractions of an inch, that one can lay against the qualities of a good mother or the devotion of a daughter, or the fidelity of a sister, or the capacity of a housekeeper. Few women even now have been graded at the universities; the great trials of the professions, army and navy, trade, politics and diplomacy have hardly tested them. They remain even at this moment almost unclassified. But if I want to know all that a human being can tell me about Sir Hawley Butts, for instance, I have only to open Burke or Debrett[4] and I shall find that he took such and such a degree; owns a hall; has an heir; was Secretary to a Board; represented Great Britain in Canada; and has received a certain number of degrees, offices, medals and other distinctions by which his merits are stamped upon him indelibly. Only Providence can know more about Sir Hawley Butts than that.

When, therefore, I say "highly developed," "infinitely intricate," of women, I am unable to verify my words either in Whitaker, Debrett or the University Calendar. In this predicament what can I do? And I looked at the bookcase again. There were the biographies: Johnson and Goethe and Carlyle and Sterne and Cowper and Shelley and Voltaire and Browning and many others. And I began thinking of all those great men who have for one reason or another admired, sought out, lived with, confided in, made love to, written of, trusted in, and shown what can only be described as some need of and dependence upon certain persons of the opposite sex. That all these relationships were absolutely Plantonic I would not affirm, and Sir William Joynson Hicks[5] would probably deny. But we should wrong these illustrious men very greatly if we insisted that they got nothing from these alliances but comfort, flattery and the pleasures of the body. What they got, it is obvious, was something that their own sex was unable to supply; and it would not be rash, perhaps, to define it further, without quoting the doubtless rhapsodical words of the poets, as some stimulus, some renewal of creative power which is in the gift only of the opposite sex to bestow. He would open the door of drawing-room or nursery, I thought, and find her among her children perhaps, or with a piece of embroidery on her knee— at any rate, the centre of some different order and system of life, and the contrast between this world and his own, which might be the law courts or the House of Commons, would at once refresh and invigorate; and there would follow, even in the simplest talk, such a natural difference of opinion that the dried ideas in him would be fertilised anew; and the sight of her creating in a different medium from his own would so quicken his creative power that insensibly his sterile mind would begin to plot again, and he would find the phrase or the scene which was lacking when he put on his hat to visit her. Every Johnson has his Thrale, and holds fast to her for some such reasons as these, and when the Thrale marries her Italian music master Johnson goes half mad with rage and disgust,[6] not merely that he will miss his pleasant evenings at Streatham, but that the light of his life will be "as if gone out."

4. Directories of the titled families in Great Britain (as is Whitaker, in the next paragraph).
5. An English Conservative politician who, as home secretary in the 1920s, was an authoritarian and socially reactionary figure.
6. For sixteen years, Samuel Johnson spent more time living with the Thrale family (in their country estate in Streatham and in London, in Southwark) than at his own home. Henry Thrale died in 1781, and in 1784 Hester Lynch Thrale married Gabriel Piozzi, her daughters' music teacher.

And without being Dr. Johnson or Goethe or Carlyle or Voltaire, one may feel, though very differently from these great men, the nature of this intricacy and the power of this highly developed creative faculty among women. One goes into the room—but the resources of the English language would be much put to the stretch, and whole flights of words would need to wing their way illegitimately into existence before a woman could say what happens when she goes into a room. The rooms differ so completely; they are calm or thunderous; open on to the sea, or, on the contrary, give on to a prison yard; are hung with washing; or alive with opals and silks; are hard as horsehair or soft as feathers—one has only to go into any room in any street for the whole of that extremely complex force of femininity to fly in one's face. How should it be otherwise? For women have sat indoors all these millions of years, so that by this time the very walls are permeated by their creative force, which has, indeed, so overcharged the capacity of bricks and mortar that it must needs harness itself to pens and brushes and business and politics. But this creative power differs greatly from the creative power of men. And one must conclude that it would be a thousand pities if it were hindered or wasted, for it was won by centuries of the most drastic discipline, and there is nothing to take its place. It would be a thousand pities if woman wrote like men, or lived like men, or looked like men, for if two sexes are quite inadequate, considering the vastness and variety of the world, how should we manage with one only? Ought not education to bring out and fortify the differences rather than the similarities? For we have too much likeness as it is, and if an explorer should come back and bring word of other sexes looking through the branches of other trees at other skies, nothing would be of greater service to humanity; and we should have the immense pleasure into the bargain of watching Professor X[7] rush for his measuring-rods to prove himself "superior,"

Mary Carmichael, I thought, still hovering at a little distance above the page, will have her work cut out for her merely as an observer. I am afraid indeed that she will be tempted to become, what I think the less interesting branch of the species—the naturalist-novelist, and not the contemplative. There are so many new facts for her to observe. She will not need to limit herself any longer to the respectable houses of the upper middle classes, She will go without kindness or condescension, but in the spirit of fellowship into those small, scented rooms where sit the courtesan, the harlot and the lady with the pug dog. There they still sit in the rough and ready-made clothes that the male writer has had perforce to clap upon their shoulders. But Mary Carmichael will have out her scissors and fit them close to every hollow and angle. It will be a curious sight, when it comes, to see these women as they are, but we must wait a little, for Mary Carmichael will still be encumbered with that self-consciousness in the presence of "sin" which is the legacy of our sexual barbarity. She will still wear the shoddy old fetters of class on her feet.

However, the majority of women are neither harlots nor courtesans; nor do they sit clasping pug dogs to dusty velvet all through the summer afternoon.

7. A character introduced in chapter 2, Woolf's neighbor in the reading room of the British Museum: he is "engag[ed] in writing his monu-mental work entitled *The Mental, Moral, and Physical Inferiority of the Female Sex*"—fueled, she suspects, by his need to prove his own superiority.

But what do they do then? and there came to my mind's eye one of those long streets somewhere south of the river whose infinite rows are innumerably populated. With the eye of the imagination I saw a very ancient lady crossing the street on the arm of a middle-aged woman, her daughter, perhaps, both so respectably booted and furred that their dressing in the afternoon must be a ritual, and the clothes themselves put away in cupboards with camphor, year after year, throughout the summer months. They cross the road when the lamps are being lit (for the dusk is their favourite hour), as they must have done year after year. The elder is close on eighty; but if one asked her what her life has meant to her, she would say that she remembered the streets lit for the battle of Balaclava, or had heard the guns fire in Hyde Park for the birth of King Edward the Seventh.[8] And if one asked her, longing to pin down the moment with date and season, but what were you doing on the fifth of April 1868, or the second of November 1875, she would look vague and say that she could remember nothing. For all the dinners are cooked; the plates and cups washed; the children sent to school and gone out into the world. Nothing remains of it all. All has vanished. No biography or history has a word to say about it. And the novels, without meaning to, inevitably lie.

All these infinitely obscure lives remain to be recorded, I said, addressing Mary Carmichael as if she were present; and went on in thought through the streets of London feeling in imagination the pressure of dumbness, the accumulation of unrecorded life, whether from the women at the street corners with their arms akimbo, and the rings embedded in their fat swollen fingers, talking with a gesticulation like the swing of Shakespeare's words; or from the violet-sellers and match-sellers and old crones stationed under doorways; or from drifting girls whose faces, like waves in sun and cloud, signal the coming of men and women and the flickering lights of shop windows. All that you will have to explore, I said to Mary Carmichael, holding your torch firm in your hand. Above all, you must illumine your own soul with its profundities and its shallows, and its vanities and its generosities, and say what your beauty means to you or your plainness, and what is your relation to the everchanging and turning world of gloves and shoes and stuffs swaying up and down among the faint scents that come through chemists' bottles down arcades of dress material over a floor of pseudo-marble. For in imagination I had gone into a shop; it was laid with black and white paving; it was hung, astonishingly beautifully, with coloured ribbons. Mary Carmichael might well have a look at that in passing, I thought, for it is a sight that would lend itself to the pen as fittingly as any snowy peak or rocky gorge in the Andes. And there is the girl behind the counter too—I would as soon have her true history as the hundred and fiftieth life of Napoleon or seventieth study of Keats and his use of Miltonic inversion which old Professor Z and his like are now inditing. And then I went on very warily, on the very tips of my toes (so cowardly am I, so afraid of the lash that was once almost laid on my own shoulders), to murmur that she should also learn to laugh, without bitterness, at the vanities—say rather at the peculiarities, for it is a less offensive word—of the other sex.

8. Events of 1854 and 1841, respectively.

For there is a spot the size of a shilling at the back of the head which one can never see for oneself. It is one of the good offices that sex can discharge for sex—to describe that spot the size of a shilling at the back of the head. Think how much women have profited by the comments of Juvenal; by the criticism of Strindberg.[9] Think with what humanity and brilliancy men, from the earliest ages, have pointed out to women that dark place at the back of the head! And if Mary were very brave and very honest, she would go behind the other sex and tell us what she found there. A true picture of man as a whole can never be painted until a woman has described that spot the size of a shilling. Mr. Woodhouse and Mr. Casaubon[1] are spots of that size and nature. Not of course that any one in their senses would counsel her to hold up to scorn and ridicule of set purpose—literature shows the futility of what is written in that spirit. Be truthful, one would say, and the result is bound to be amazingly interesting. Comedy is bound to be enriched. New facts are bound to be discovered.

However, it was high time to lower my eyes to the page again. It would be better, instead of speculating what Mary Carmichael might write and should write, to see what in fact Mary Carmichael did write. So I began to read again. I remembered that I had certain grievances against her. She had broken up Jane Austen's sentence, and thus given me no chance of pluming myself upon my impeccable taste, my fastidious ear. For it was useless to say, "Yes, yes, this is very nice; but Jane Austen wrote much better than you do," when I had to admit that there was no point of likeness between them. Then she had gone further and broken the sequence—the expected order. Perhaps she had done this unconsciously, merely giving things their natural order, as a woman would, if she wrote like a woman. But the effect was somehow baffling; one could not see a wave heaping itself, a crisis coming round the next corner. Therefore I could not plume myself either upon the depths of my feelings and my profound knowledge of the human heart. For whenever I was about to feel the usual things in the usual places, about love, about death, the annoying creature twitched me away, as if the important point were just a little further on. And thus she made it impossible for me to roll out my sonorous phrases about "elemental feelings," the "common stuff of humanity," "depths of the human heart," and all those other phrases which support us in our belief that, however clever we may be on top, we are very serious, very profound and very humane underneath. She made me feel, on the contrary, that instead of being serious and profound and humane, one might be—and the thought was far less seductive—merely lazy minded and conventional into the bargain.

But I read on, and noted certain other facts. She was no "genius"—that was evident. She had nothing like the love of Nature, the fiery imagination, the wild poetry, the brilliant wit, the brooding wisdom of her great predecessors, Lady Winchilsea, Charlotte Brontë, Emily Brontë, Jane Austen and George Eliot; she could not write with the melody and the dignity of Dorothy Osborne[2]—indeed

---

9. The Roman poet Juvenal (ca. 55-ca. 140 C.E.) wrote scathing satires, and many works of the Swedish playwright August Strindberg (1849–1912) are viewed as misogynist.
1. Characters in Jane Austen's *Emma* (1815) and

George Eliot's *Middlemarch* (1871–72).
2. A 17th-century woman (discussed by Woolf in chapter 4) whose letters to her future husband were published in 1888.

she was no more than a clever girl whose books will no doubt be pulped by the publishers in ten years' time. But, nevertheless, she had certain advantages which women of far greater gift lacked even half a century ago. Men were no longer to her "the opposing faction"; she need not waste her time railing against them; she need not climb on to the roof and ruin her peace of mind longing for travel, experience and a knowledge of the world and character that were denied her. Fear and hatred were almost gone, or traces of them showed only in a slight exaggeration of the joy of freedom, a tendency to the caustic and satirical, rather than to the romantic, in her treatment of the other sex. Then there could be no doubt that as a novelist she enjoyed some natural advantages of a high order. She had a sensibility that was very wide, eager and free. It responded to an almost imperceptible touch on it. It feasted like a plant newly stood in the air on every sight and sound that came its way. It ranged, too, very subtly and curiously, among almost unknown or unrecorded things; it lighted on small things and showed that perhaps they were not small after all. It brought buried things to light and made one wonder what need there had been to bury them. Awkward though she was and without the unconscious bearing of long descent which makes the least turn of the pen of a Thackeray or a Lamb[3] delightful to the ear, she had—I began to think—mastered the first great lesson; she wrote as a woman, but as a woman who has forgotten that she is a woman, so that her pages were full of that curious sexual quality which comes only when sex is unconscious of itself.

All this was to the good. But no abundance of sensation or fineness of perception would avail unless she could build up out of the fleeting and the personal the lasting edifice which remains unthrown. I had said that I would wait until she faced herself with "a situation." And I meant by that until she proved by summoning, beckoning and getting together that she was not a skimmer of surfaces merely, but had looked beneath into the depths. Now is the time, she would say to herself at a certain moment, when without doing anything violent I can show the meaning of all this. And she would begin—how unmistakable that quickening is!—beckoning and summoning, and there would rise up in memory, half forgotten, perhaps quite trivial things in other chapters dropped by the way. And she would make their presence felt while some one sewed or smoked a pipe as naturally as possible, and one would feel, as she went on writing, as if one had gone to the top of the world and seen it laid out, very majestically, beneath.

At any rate, she was making the attempt. And as I watched her lengthening out for the test, I saw, but hoped that she did not see, the bishops and the deans, the doctors and the professors, the patriarchs and the pedagogues all at her shouting warning and advice. You can't do this and you shan't do that! Fellows and scholars only allowed on the grass! Ladies not admitted without a letter of introduction![4] Aspiring and graceful female novelists this way! So they kept at her like the crowd at a fence on the race-course, and it was her trial to take her fence without looking to right or left. If you stop to curse you

---

3. The Romantic essayist Charles Lamb.
4. In the first chapter, Woolf is scolded by an Oxbridge beadle for walking on the college turf, and then prevented from entering a college library.

are lost, I said to her; equally, if you stop to laugh. Hesitate or fumble and you are done for. Think only of the jump, I implored her, as if I had put the whole of my money on her back; and she went over it like a bird. But there was a fence beyond that and a fence beyond that. Whether she had the staying power I was doubtful, for the clapping and the crying were fraying to the nerves. But she did her best. Considering that Mary Carmichael was no genius, but an unknown girl writing her first novel in a bedsitting-room, without enough of those desirable things, time, money and idleness, she did not do so badly, I thought.

Give her another hundred years, I concluded, reading the last chapter— people's noses and bare shoulders showed naked against a starry sky, for some one had twitched the curtain in the drawing-room—give her a room of her own and five hundred a year, let her speak her mind and leave out half that she now puts in, and she will write a better book one of these days. She will be a poet, I said, putting *Life's Adventure,* by Mary Carmichael, at the end of the shelf, in another hundred years' time.

1929

REBECCA WEST
1892–1983

It would be hard to say why women have refused to become great writers," mused the young journalist who wrote under the pseudonym Rebecca West in an early book review. Born Cicely Fairfield, she had renamed herself in honor of a feminist charac- ter in Henrik Ibsen's play *Rosmersholm,* and she was not only an energetic feminist- activist but also an accomplished essayist, reporter, novelist, and literary commentator. Indeed, although she sardonically declared, "Women are capable of all things yet, inconveniently, they will not be geniuses," West's own extraordinary talent led George Bernard Shaw to quip in 1915, when she was still in her early twenties, that "Rebecca can handle a pen as brilliantly as ever I could, and much more savagely."

A great beauty, West became the mistress of H. G. Wells when she was nineteen, and bore his son, Anthony West, in 1914, although mother and son were later bitterly estranged. After her affair with Wells ended, she had an assortment of other lovers, including Charlie Chaplin and the newspaper mogul Lord Max Beaverbrook. But her tumultuous romantic life never impeded her productive—and lucrative—writing career. A fierce socialist in her youth (Wells called her "Panther" and she called him "Jaguar"), she became increasingly conservative after her marriage in 1930 to Henry Andrews, a wealthy banker, but at least one commentator suggested that the waning of her revolutionary fervor was inevitable, noting that "Rebecca West is a Socialist by habit of mind and a conservative by cell structure."

In addition to such novels as *The Return of the Soldier* (1918), *The Judge* (1922), and *Harriet Hume* (1929), West produced a classic study of what was then Yugoslavia, *Black Lamb and Grey Falcon* (1941), along with a study of Henry James (1916), a biog- raphy of St. Augustine (1933), and, among numerous other volumes, two collections of literary criticism, *Strange Necessity* (1928) and *Ending in Earnest* (1931). In these, beginning with the assumption that literature functions as a "collective external brain," she offered, respectively, a controversial appraisal of James Joyce and a sympathetic study of D. H. Lawrence. The critic Samuel Hynes once declared that her book on James, which reproached that author for his problematic representations of women, was "the first book that could be called feminist criticism." And our selection here, a brilliant appreciation of Charlotte Brontë as a "supreme artist," shows how deftly she could explore the trials and triumphs of women's literary history.

Charlotte Brontë

This generation knows that Charlotte Brontë's own generation gave her too high a place in the artistic hierarchy when it exalted her above her sister Emily, but is itself tempted to place her too low because of the too easily recognizable *naïveté* of her material.

It is true that the subject-matter of all her work is, under one disguise or another, the Cinderella theme which is the stand-by of the sub-artist in fiction and the theatre, all the world over and in any age. She treats it in the form it takes in the hands of those who have moved just one degree away from complete *naïveté*: instead of it being supposed that Cinderella has the advantage of physical beauty over the Ugly Sisters, it is supposed (as an absolute and more magical compensation to the sense of inferiority which weaves and needs the story) that it is they who are beautiful, and she who is ugly, though possessed of an invisible talisman of spiritual quality which wholly annuls that disadvantage. This is the theme of *Jane Eyre* and *Villette*, and, with certain elaborations and feints, of *Shirley* also; and it cannot be denied that we have grave reason to associate it with work which is not artistic at all, which sets out not to explore reality, but to nourish the neurotic fantasies with which feebler brains defend themselves from reality.

Charlotte Brontë also uses material which many people denounce as naïve with, I think, less foundation. She records oppressions practised by the dowered on the dowerless, and by adults on children, and seems to many of her readers absurd and unpleasant when she does so; but that is perhaps not because such incidents never happen, but because we dislike admitting that they happen. There is hardly a more curious example of the gap we leave between life and literature than the surprise and incredulity recorded by successive generations of Brontëan commentators at the passages in the sisters' works which suggest that the well-to-do are sometimes uncivil to their employees. In actual fact, all of us, even today, if we were connected with a young girl who was going out into the world as a governess, would feel an anxiety that she should be with "nice people," which would imply a lively fear of what nasty people are capable of doing to governesses; but these commentators write as if Charlotte and Anne[1] must have been the victims of hysterical morbidity when they implied that governesses were sometimes treated rudely, although the idea then prevalent, that one was divinely appointed to one's social station, cannot have improved the manners of employers. It has been the opinion of all moral teachers from the days of the Psalmist that riches

---

1. The title character of Anne Brontë's novel *Agnes Grey* (1847) was a governess.

lead to haughtiness and froward bearing; yet when Miss Blanche Ingram tells the footman, "Cease that chatter, blockhead," the commentators shake their heads and smile, without reflecting that she was supposed to have made that remark in the year preceding Queen Victoria's accession to the throne, when much of the eighteenth-century coarseness of manners still lingered, and that even today women can be found who have the tiresome habit of being rude to waiters and menservants.

We may suspect, then, that the common objection to this material is not that it has no correspondence with reality, but that it is intensely embarrassing for us to contemplate. The feeling of inferiority, under which we all labour, may find a gratifying opportunity for self-pity in the accounts of the suffering which superiors can unjustly inflict on their inferiors, but only if they are not too vivid; for if they are, then we feel terror at the quality of the universe. And if that be so when the accounts refer to the relatively remote symbolism of social matters, which we all of us can discount by reference to some other system of values which we have devised to suit our special case, how much more will it be so when they refer to the actual and agonizing experiences of our childhood! In these days one is weaker than nearly all the world. However kindly one is treated, one is frustrated and humiliated, one's natural habits are corrected, and one's free speech censored; and if one is not kindly treated, one can take no revenge, one is without means of protecting one's dignity. There must be something shameful in such a phase to an organism as much in love with the idea of its own free will as the human being. Thus the descriptions of Jane Eyre's ill-treatment at the hands of the Reeds,[2] and the sufferings of the pupils at Lowood, revive a whole series of associations in the readers' minds which the more imaginative and intellectually developed among them will hate to recall. They will turn from Charlotte Brontë's work with the accusation that it is infantile; but what they mean is that she exposes her own and their infantilism. She lifts a curtain, and reveals what the world usually keeps hidden. In her pictures of these oppressions she demonstrates the workings of our universal sense that we are worms; as in her use of the Cinderella theme she demonstrates our universal hope that, though we are but worms, a miracle will happen, and we shall be made kings of the world. It may be objected that any hack writer of penny dreadfuls does as much; but that is untrue. The hack writer spins the consoling fantasy, and so does Charlotte Brontë; but she also depicts the hunger that goads the spinner to the task. Her work, considered as a whole, is as powerful an analysis of the working of the sense of inferiority and its part in creating romanticism as the mind of man has ever made.

But colour is lent to the suspicion that Charlotte Brontë is not an artist but a sub-artist, that she does not analyse experience, but weaves fantasies to hang between man and his painful experience, by her frequent use of the sub-artist's chosen weapon, sentimental writing. This also is a feature of her work which is specially repugnant to the present generation's hyper-sensitiveness to the superficial decorum of literature; and it remains an indefensible defect. But it adds to Charlotte Brontë's power over our attentions, because in so far as she discloses it with her unequalled ardour and honesty, she gives us a picture of the eternal artist experiencing an eternally recurrent misadventure.

---

2. Jane's aunt and cousins, with whom she lived before being sent to the Lowood school.

For Charlotte Brontë's tendency to sentimental writing was not due to an innate inaptitude for the artistic process, but to the pressure of external circumstance. In one important respect her life was unfavourable to the practice of art. This was not loneliness and privation: Emily Brontë, suffering the same portion of these ills, was the complete artist. It was not the misconduct of her brother Branwell, though that was a contributing factor to it. It was her specially acute need to make, by separate and violent acts of the will, the place in the world for herself and her two younger sisters which should have been made for them by their elders. Her realization of this need must have been panic-stricken and desperate, for the whole of her life was ravaged by a series of progressively bitter disappointments in the protection which children expect from adults and which women expect from men.

Mrs Brontë died of cancer when Charlotte was five years old, and for some time before her death the progress of her malady and her regular confinements prevented her from giving her children much attention. Mr Brontë was an eccentric recluse whose capacity for parenthood seems to have been purely physical. Even before he had taken to the bottle, he took no trouble to provide his children with either his own sympathy or proper companionship, or any but the barest preparation for adult life. Mrs Brontë's sister, who came North from Cornwall to take charge of the orphaned children, disliked Yorkshire, retired to her bedroom, and cared for none of them except Branwell. From the terrible matter-of-factness with which Emily and Charlotte Brontë draw (in Nelly Deans and in Bessie) the servant whose unimaginative cruelty changes to a not very reliable kindness, one sees that there was no steady comfort for the children in the kitchen. It was in her sister Maria, the oldest of the family, that Charlotte found a substitute for her mother: we know that from the portrait of Helen Burns in *Jane Eyre*. But Maria died at the age of twelve, when Charlotte was eight; and her only other older sister, Elizabeth, died two months later.

About the time of Charlotte's ninth birthday, then, the negligence and death of her elders left her with her own way to make in the world. But that is an understatement, for it supposes her burdenless. It would be more accurate to say that she became the head of the family, with one brother and two sisters, all deeply loved, dependent on her for everything above the bare physical necessities of life. The records of the Brontës' childhood show her eagerly answering the call to leadership; but she was not then altogether to be pitied. She was still supported by her penultimate hope. Whatever the defections of Mr Brontë, they would not be without a man to look after them as soon as their brother grew up. It is confessed honestly and radiantly in Charlotte Brontë's books how she craved for the support that the child-bearing faculty of woman logically entitles her to expect from man, and there was a special factor in her environment to give intensity to that craving.

Victorian England was a man's country. She might well have hoped that with Branwell Brontë's fine natural endowment he would easily find a place in it, and that she would see herself and her sisters decently maintained or helped to decent employment. But she was still a girl when it became apparent that Branwell, in spite of all his brilliant promise, was growing up, not into a man, but into a pathetic nuisance, who would not even decently maintain himself. For the sixth time natural supports had failed her. She knew the terrible fear felt by the young who begin to suspect that they are going to be cheated out of the fullness of life; and she was not fearful for herself alone, but also for Anne and Emily, in whose gifts she had faith, and for whose health she had every reason to fear. She had seen her two elder sisters die, and she had probably forebodings that she was to see the other two die also. It is known that she had such forebodings about Anne.

During the years when it was becoming plain that Branwell was going to be of no help to them, but "a drain on every source," Charlotte became more and more desperate. By this time, it is interesting to note, she was half-blind. But if no one would give her and her sisters their fair share of life, she herself would see that they got what she could snatch; and she snatched far more than one would think possible. The astounding thing about the Brontës' life is not its emptiness but—considering the bareness of Haworth Parsonage—its full-ness. There were several friends; there was a good deal of employment, includ-ing the Brussels expedition;[3] there was the literary adventure. And it was Charlotte who made the friends, Charlotte who found the teaching posts, Charlotte who wrote the letters to the publishers. Now, it is easy to sneer at these achievements, on the ground that the greatest of the three sisters, Emily, found them purely vexatious, since she was shy of strangers, loathed leaving the moors of Haworth, and would rather have kept her poems to herself. Nev-ertheless, Charlotte's actions followed the natural direction of sanity. Like all living things, she strove for the survival of herself and her belongings with the balance of her impulses. It was hardly to be expected that reverence of Emily's genius should oust the desire to keep her alive, and any change which removed her from the rigours of the Parsonage must have at first seemed favourable to that end. There is nothing to be said against Charlotte's frenzied efforts to counter the nihilism of her surroundings, unless one is among those who would find amusement in the sight of the starving fighting for food.

In the sphere of life they were unquestionably noble; but it unfortunately happened—and here lies the disconcerting value of Charlotte as a revelation of the artist-type—that in the sphere of art they had a disintegrating effect. They committed her to a habit of activism which was the very antithesis of the quietism demanded from the artist. In her desire to make a place in the world for herself and her family against time, she could let nothing establish itself by slow growth, she had to force the pace of every intimacy and every action, which means that she had constantly to work upon people with the aim of immediately provoking them to certain emotions. Sprightly or touch-ing letters had to be written to the friends to keep them near in spite of distance; Miss Branwell had to be induced to finance the Brussels expedition, and Mrs Wooler had to have her interest in the new school kept warm; Southey, Wordsworth, Tennyson, Lockhart, and de Quincey had to be addressed in the vain attempt to rouse their interest in Currer, Ellis, and Acton Bell.[4] In fact, she was forced to a passionate participation in a business of working on people's feelings exclusive of the true business of art, and the root of the evil that we call sentimentality.

This, therefore, was Charlotte's special temptation: she was so used to manipulating people's feelings in life that she could not lose the habit in her

3. In 1842 and 1843, Charlotte Brontë studied in Brussels at a finishing school run by Zoë and Con-stantin Héger (Emily accompanied her in 1842). "New school": the three sisters planned to open their own school, and attending the Pensionnat Héger was a step toward that end; but when Char-lotte advertised for pupils in 1844, none replied.
4. The pseudonyms used by Charlotte, Emily, and Anne Brontë, beginning with their jointly pub-lished *Poems* (1846).

art, and was apt to fall into sentimentality. All her novels are defaced to varying degrees by passages which have nothing to do with the organic growth of
the story, and are inspired simply by guess-work as to the state of the reader's
feelings. An extreme example of this is the scene where the Yorkes call on
Miss Moore and find Caroline Helstone in her parlour, in the twenty-third
chapter of *Shirley*. The same error is committed in an earlier scene of the
book, but it is here more noteworthy and disastrous, because here there is
promise of high poetic value. Caroline is sick with love for Robert Moore, and
faint with despair. Mrs Yorke looms over her like a personification of the cruelty that must govern the world if it is true that she is not to have her love;
the Yorke children have the fantastic, unclassical quality that all objects not
the beloved assume under the lover's eye. When Caroline's veins are flushed
with quicksilver rage against that cruelty, the scene should end, and she
should be left still waiting for Robert at the jessamined window. But Miss
Brontë's habit of bustling was too strong for her then. She could not trust her
slow magic to make the reader's interest slowly mount. She felt she must put
them under a swiftly growing debt to her for entertainment. She remembered
how Martha Taylor, who was the original of little Jessy Yorke, had often entertained her with her precocious tirades; so she reproduced one there and then.
She also remembered what a poignant effect had been made by this child's
early death; so she inserted a description of her funeral. The continuity of the
scene is broken, the author's and the reader's contacts with Caroline are lost,
and whatever emotion is felt is diverted from the real theme.

It would be easy to point to many other pages in Charlotte Brontë's novels
where sentimental writing has been allowed to destroy the structure of the
work; and there is one case where sentimentality has been allowed to plan such
a structure faultily. The melodramatic plot of *Jane Eyre* is not a symbol honestly
conceived by extreme *naïveté*, but was invented, in her own admission, to suit
a supposed popular demand for sensationalism. That was a pity, for there are
pages in the book, such as the scene where the lovers walk in the orchard under
the rising moon, which deserve the best of settings. But great as is the harm
done to the valuable content of Charlotte Brontë's work by her choice of certain episodes and series of episodes simply for their immediate effect on her
readers, still greater is the harm done by the diffusion of sentimentality through
her style. It is crammed with direct appeals to the emotions, which make it
tediously repetitive, explosive, and irrelevant to the deeper themes discussed.

That this defect was not inborn in Charlotte, but was the product of her
circumstances, can be proved by a reference to a letter quoted by Mrs Gaskell
from *The Little Magazine*, which the Brontës composed in their childhood.
It begins: "Sir,—It is well known that the Genii have declared that unless
they perform certain arduous duties every year, of a mysterious nature, all the
worlds in the firmament will be burnt up and gathered together in one mighty
globe," and no style could be more decorous and more sincere. But she wrote
it at the age of thirteen, before she had become a panic-stricken adept in the
art of negotiation. She was never to write such prose again until her passion
for M. Héger made her forget all her schemes and anxieties, and changed her
to the insanely honest instrument of one intention and one need.

The obviousness with which what was a virtue in Charlotte Brontë's life
became a vice in her art makes her one of the most disconcerting among great
writers to contemplate. She is suspended between the two spheres of art and

life, and not in a state of rest. She is torn between them. But where this generation will probably err is in supposing that her plight is unique. There is sentimentality in every age, even in our own; and we swallow it whole if its subject-matter is not of a sort that arouses suspicion. That was where Charlotte Brontë erred. All of us not actually illiterate or imbecile feel that something is wrong when a writer attempts to compel his readers' feelings by the exploitation of early deaths, handsome sinners with lunatic wives, and ecstatic dithyrambs. The march of culture has forced such knowledge on the least of us.

But let us examine the current attitude to the great Russians. A great many readers, and some of these drawn from the professionally fastidious, place Tolstoy above Turgenev and Dostoevski. Yet Turgenev was, as Mr George Moore has said in that incomparable book of criticism, *Avowals,* "a sort of Jesus of Nazareth in art," who gave himself to the artistic process with so little reservation for his personal ends, that there is no conflict in his work, only serenity; and though it is true, as Mr Moore says in the same book, that, before we can admire Dostoevski's novels, "modern life must wring all the Greek out of us," he also, albeit with constant cries of protest at the pain it cost him, forced himself to the honest analysis of experience. But Tolstoy is fully as sentimental a writer as Charlotte Brontë. In *War and Peace, Anna Karenina,* and *Resurrection,* he pushes his characters about with the greatest conceivable brusqueness in order to prove his thesis, and exhorts his readers to accept his interpretations of their movements. He even admits in *What Is Art?* that he thinks this the proper way for the artist to behave. Nevertheless, Tolstoy arouses no repugnance in this generation, although this use of art to prove what man already knows is a shameful betrayal of the mission of art to tell man more than he knows. This is only because the subject-matter of his sentimentality is unfamiliar. He attempts to influence his readers in favour of a thesis dependent on the primitive sense of guilt, and the need for expiation by the endurance and infliction of suffering, which had been forbidden expression above a certain cultural level in the rationalist nineteenth century. We are not on our guard against it as we are against Charlotte Brontë's Cinderella theme; and we succumb to what must be an eternally recurrent temptation.

Yet if Charlotte Brontë represents an eternally recurrent defeat of the artist, she also represents his eternally recurrent triumph. She told the truth even about matters concerning which the whole civilization round her had conspired to create a fiction; and her telling of it is not an argument, but an affirmation, that comes and is, like the light of the sun and the moon. It is not only true that, as Swinburne said, again and again she shows the

> power to make us feel in every nerve, at every step forward which our imagination is compelled to take under the guidance of another's, that thus and not otherwise, but in all things altogether even as we are told and shown, it was, and must have been, with the human figures set before us in their action and their suffering; that thus, and not otherwise, they absolutely must and would have felt and thought and spoken under the proposed conditions.[5]

It is not only true that she abounds in touches of that kind of strange beauty which, dealing solely with the visible world, nevertheless persuades us

5. Algernon Charles Swinburne, *A Note on Charlotte Brontë* (1877).

that the visible world is going to swing open as if it were a gate and disclose a further view: like the description of the stable-yard in Thornfield[6] at dawn, with the blinds still drawn in the windows, and the birds twittering in the blossom-laden orchard, when the mysterious stranger drives away with the surgeon after his mysterious wounding. She does more than that, she makes a deeper revelation of the soul.

In an age which set itself to multiply the material wants of mankind (with what results we see today) and to whittle down its spiritual wants to an ethical anxiety that was often mean, Charlotte Brontë serenely lifted up her voice, and testified to the existence of the desires which are the buds of all human thoughts and actions. Her candid and clairvoyant vision of such things is displayed again and again throughout her works, but never more notably than in the two instances which make *Villette* one of the most interesting of English novels. The first is the description of the innocent but passionate love of the little girl Polly for the schoolboy John. The second is the description of how Lucy Snowe's love passed without a break from John Bretton to Paul Emanuel; never before has there been such a frank admission of the subtle truth that the romantic temperament writes a lover's part, and then casts an actor to play it, and that nevertheless there is more there than make-believe. To realize how rare a spirit it required to make and record such observations at the time one must turn to Miss Harriet Martineau's comments on the book as given in Mrs Gaskell's *Life*;[7] though one should remember that Miss Martineau was herself to suffer from the age's affectation of wantlessness. For when, as an elderly lady, she received a present of money from her admirers, the subscribers were greatly incensed when she proposed to spend an undue proportion of it on a silver tea equipage; yet surely any earlier age would have understood this belated desire for a little handsomeness.

But Charlotte Brontë did more than unconsciously correct the error of her age; she saw as deeply as poets do. There are surely two scenes which have the dignity and significance of great poetry. One is the scene in *Villette*, where the fevered girl wanders by night out of the silent school, with the intention of seeking a certain stone basin that she remembers to have seen, brimming with cool water, in a glade of the park; and finds the city ablaze with light, thronged with a tide of happy people, which bears up to the park that is now fantastic with coloured lights and pasteboard palaces, a phantasmagoria in which she walks and sees her friends, her foes, her beloved, but is not seen. There has never before been found a more vivid symbolic representation of the state of passion in which the whole universe, lacking the condition of union with the beloved, seems a highly coloured but insubstantial illusion, objective counterpart to delirium. Yet even finer is the scene in *Shirley* called "A Summer Night," when Shirley and Caroline creep across the moonlit fields to warn Moore of the approach of rioters, and are too late. There, when the two girls stand "alone with the friendly night, the mute stars, and these whispering trees," listening to the shouts and watching the fires of masculine dissension (which is their opposite and what they live by), and while what is male in woman speaks with the voice of Shirley, and what is female speaks

---

6. The country house where Jane Eyre serves as a governess.
7. I.e., Elizabeth Gaskell's *Life of Charlotte Brontë*

(1857), which reports that Martineau criticized *Villette* for a lack of womanly propriety both in an article and in a letter to Charlotte.

with the voice of Caroline, one perceives that a statement is being found for that which the intellect has not yet stated in direct terms.

Charlotte Brontë was a supreme artist; and yet she was very nearly not an artist at all. That will make her an unsympathetic figure to many in these days, when a school of criticism, determined to exert authority but without the intellectual power to evolve an authoritative doctrine, has imported into this country its own puerile version of the debate between romanticism and classicism which has cut up the French world of letters into sterile sectionalism, and trots about frivolously inventing categories on insufficient bases, rejecting works of art that do not fit into them, and attaching certificates to those that do. But she will inspire and console those who realize that art is a spiritual process committed to imperfection by the flesh, which is its medium; that though there are artists who seem to transcend the limitations of that medium, like Bach and Mozart and Emily Brontë, they are rare as the saints, and like them, sublime but not final in their achievements; and that the complete knowledge and mastery of experience which would be attained in a perfect world of art is like the *summum bonum*[8] of the theologians, the vision of God which is to reward the pure in heart, and cannot be realized until time is changed to eternity.

1932

JESSIE REDMON FAUSET
1884–1961

Often described as a "midwife" to the Harlem Renaissance and as particularly crucial in fostering a "New Negro literature," Jessie Fauset was a brilliant editor of the *Crisis,* working with the influential intellectual W. E. B. Du Bois on that major African American journal and on the development of the important children's monthly *The Brownie's Book.* At the same time, she was a productive novelist and poet. The daughter of a clergyman, Fauset was educated in Philadelphia, then went on to study classics and modern languages at Cornell University, where she became the first black woman in America to be elected to Phi Beta Kappa. As an undergraduate she began corresponding with Du Bois, who was then teaching at Atlanta University, and in 1918, after teaching high school in Washington, D.C., for some years and earning a master's in French from the University of Pennsylvania, she joined him as literary editor of the *Crisis,* where she persuaded him that "the arts, and creative writing in particular could be a force in racial uplift."

In 1924 Fauset published her first novel, *There Is Confusion,* following it with three others—most importantly *Plum Bun* (1929), an examination of racial "passing" that is generally considered her finest book. Married in 1929 to Herbert E. Harris, she left the *Crisis* in 1927 and returned to teaching, working at New York City's De Witt Clinton High School for the remainder of her career. As a fiction writer, she focused on the dilemmas of middle-class black families, noting that the "Colored American who is not being pressed too hard by the Furies of Prejudice, Ignorance and Economic Injustice is not so very different from any other American, just distinctive." Our selection, a letter to the influential editor of *The New Negro* anthology, illuminates tensions and disagreements among the vanguard intellectuals in the Harlem Renaissance.

Letter to Alain Locke

[ON A REVIEW OF THE "NEGRO LITERATURE"]

9 January [1934]

Dear Alain:

I have always disliked your attitude toward my work dating from the time years ago when you went out of your way to tell my brother that the dinner given at the civic club for "There Is Confusion" wasn't for me.[1] Incidentally I may tell you now that that idea originated with Regina Anderson and Gwendolyn Bennett, both members of a little library club with which I was then associated. How you and one or two others sought to distort the idea and veil its original graciousness I in common with one or two others have known for years. And I still remember the consummate cleverness with which you that night as toastmaster strove to keep speech and comment away from the person for whom the occasion was meant.

It has always both amused and annoyed me to read your writings. Amused because as in the case of your multiple articles in the New Negro[2] they are stuffed with a pedantry which fails to conceal their poverty of thought. Annoyed because your criticisms such as the one I've just read in Opportunity point most effectively to the adage that a critic is a self-acknowledged failure as a writer. It has always seemed to me that you who cannot write have had the utmost arrogance to presume to criticize those who are at all possessed of the creative art or even of the art of marshalling facts and recording them. Nor am I alone, Alain, in this thought.

But today's article[3] is positively the worst because in it you have shown yourself so clearly as a subscriber to that purely Negroid school whose motto is "whatever is white is right."

For instance, very slightly, very haltingly you have pointed to certain faults in Mrs. Peterkin and Mr. Bradford.[4] But all this you have quickly glossed over with hearty praise and approbation on other lives.

Also since Mr. Johnson[5] has been approved by the grand white folks you have graciously approved of him too without one word as to his style—what is it mid-Victorian, or purest Locksien or modernistic—with those page paragraphs and parentheses? You've said not a word about the grouping of his facts—all of his acts are equally important aren't they?

But in the case of Mr. McKay and myself[6]—our virtues are barely outlined, our faults greatly stressed and in my own case I am left without a leg to stand on, characterization, style, sentiment, treatment are all wrong. My art is "slowly maturing"; my "championship of upper and middle class Negro life" is not even "singlehanded"; it is "*almost* singlehanded." And what does such an expression as this mean: "Her characterization is too close to type?"—Just

1. The gathering on March 21, 1924, was originally intended to honor the publication of Fauset's novel.
2. The 1925 anthology edited by Locke, who included four of his own essays.
3. Locke's "The Saving Grace of Realism," *Opportunity* (January 1934), a review essay of the "Negro literature" published in 1933.
4. Locke reviewed *Roll, Jordan, Roll,* a collection of essays and sketches by Julia Peterkin, and *Kingdom Coming,* a novel by Roark Bradford.
5. James Weldon Johnson, who published his autobiography, *Along This Way,* in 1933.
6. Locke reviewed the novels *Banana Bottom,* by Claude McKay, and *Comedy, American Style,* by Fauset.

nothing! I was telling the story of a real family—how could it be a story of types?

One last point—the one that made me most furious—I wasn't telling the story of "one dark child in a family" etc. If I had been even poor mid-Victorian, sentimental, persevering Miss Fauset would have told the story from a different angle. I was telling the story of a woman who was obsessed with the desire for whiteness.

I am hoping that you will never review another book of mine. I am going to ask Mr. Carter to send you no more of my work. (Later: I've changed my mind about this; now that I've let you know how I feel I don't care how many books you review.)

No dear Alain, your malice, your lack of true discrimination and above all your tendency to play safe with the grand white folks renders you anything but a reliable critic. Better stick to your own field and let us writers alone. At least I can tell a story convincingly.

Very sincerely,
Jessie F. Harris[7]

Your total failure to understand my work goads me to more words. For instance what on earth are you talking about when you speak of my having missed "the deep potential tragedy of the situation and its biting satire"? Who but *you* could succeed in missing both & then just because you wanted to?

---

7. In 1929, Fauset married Herbert Harris, an insurance broker.

ANAÏS NIN
1903–1977

Anaïs Nin was as famous for her extended, introspective diary—a journal she kept throughout her life—as for a series of lyrical stories titled *Cities of the Interior* (1959), in which she offered nuanced examinations of the fluctuations of female consciousness. But she was noted, too, for the depth of her long friendship with the radical American novelist Henry Miller, whose circle she joined when he was writing his sexually explicit *Tropic of Cancer* (1934), and for her relationships with Miller's wife June, the French poet Antonin Artaud, the novelist Lawrence Durrell, and the psychiatrist Otto Rank.

Born in Paris to a French-Danish singer and a Spanish pianist-composer, Nin was raised in New York City and did not return to the city of her birth until the 1930s, after she had married a banker, Hugh Guiler. Her first book was a tribute to the poet-novelist D. H. Lawrence, whose work she admired not only for its erotic energy but also for its sensitive representations of women. As the excerpt from her diary included here indicates, she herself sought to explore a network of intimate connections between sexuality and creativity, positing, as the poet H. D. also did, that—in Nin's words—"The art of woman must be born in the womb-cells of the mind."

From The Diary

August 1937

[GENDER AND CREATIVITY]

As to all that nonsense Henry and Larry[1] talked about, the necessity of "I am God" in order to create (I suppose they mean "I am God, I am not a woman"). Woman never had direct communication with God anyway, but only through man, the priest. She never created directly except through man, was never able to create as a woman. But what neither Larry nor Henry understands is that woman's creation far from being like man's must be exactly like her creation of children, that is it must come out of her own blood, englobed by her womb, nourished with her own milk. It must be a human creation, of flesh, it must be different from man's abstractions. As to this "I am God," which makes creation an act of solitude and pride, this image of God alone making sky, earth, sea, it is this image which has confused woman. (Man too, because he thinks God did it all alone, and he thinks he did it all alone. And behind every achievement of man lies a woman, and I am sure God was helped too but never acknowledged it.)

Woman does not forget she needs the fecundator, she does not forget that everything that is born of her is planted in her. If she forgets this she is lost. What will be marvelous to contemplate will not be her solitude but this image of woman being visited at night by man and the marvelous things she will give birth to in the morning. God alone, creating, may be a beautiful spectacle. I don't know. Man's objectivity may be an imitation of this God so detached from us and human emotion. But a woman alone creating is not a beautiful spectacle. The woman was born mother, mistress, wife, sister, she was born to represent union, communion, communication, she was born to give birth to life, and not to insanity. It is man's separateness, his so-called objectivity, which has made him lose contact, and then his reason. Woman was born to *be* the connecting link between man and his human self. Between abstract ideas and the personal pattern which creates them. Man, to create, must become man.

Woman has this life-role, but the woman artist has to fuse creation and life in her own way, or in her own womb if you prefer. She has to create something different from man. Man created a world cut off from nature. Woman has to create within the mystery, storms, terrors, the infernos of sex, the battle against abstractions and art. She has to sever herself from the myth man creates, from being created by him, she has to struggle with her own cycles, storms, terrors which man does not understand. Woman wants to destroy aloneness, recover the original paradise. The art of woman must be born in the womb-cells of the mind. She must be the link between the synthetic products of man's mind and the elements.

I do not delude myself as man does, that I create in proud isolation. I say we are bound, interdependent. Woman is not deluded. She must create without these proud delusions of man, without megalomania, without schizophrenia,

---

1. The novelists Henry Miller and Lawrence Durrell.

without madness. She must create that unity which man first destroyed by his proud consciousness.

Henry and Larry tried to lure me out of the womb. They call it objectivity. No woman died the kind of death Rimbaud died. I have never seen in a woman a skeleton like Fraenkel,[2] killed by the dissections of analysis, the leprosy of egotism, the black pest of the brain cells.

Man today is like a tree that is withering at the roots. And most women painted and wrote nothing but imitations of phalluses. The world was filled with phalluses, like totem poles, and no womb anywhere. I must go the opposite way from Proust who found eternal moments in creation. I must find them in life. My work must be the closest to the life flow. I must install myself inside of the seed, growth, mysteries. I must prove the possibility of instantaneous, immediate, spontaneous art. My art must be like a miracle. Before it goes through the conduits of the brain and becomes an abstraction, a fiction, a lie. It must be for woman, more like a personified ancient ritual, where every spiritual thought was made visible, enacted, represented.

A sense of the infinite in the present, as the child has.

Woman's role in creation should be paralled to her role in life. I don't mean the good earth. I mean the bad earth too, the demon, the instincts, the storms of nature. Tragedies, conflicts, mysteries are personal. Man fabricated a detachment which became fatal. Woman must not fabricate. She must descend into the real womb and expose its secrets and its labyrinths. She must describe it as the city of Fez,[3] with its Arabian Nights gentleness, tranquility and mystery. She must describe the voracious moods, the desires, the worlds contained in each cell of it. For the womb has dreams. It is not as simple as the good earth. I believe at times that man created art out of fear of exploring woman. I believe woman stuttered about herself out of fear of what she had to say. She covered herself with taboos and veils. Man invented a woman to suit his needs. He disposed of her by identifying her with nature and then paraded his contemptuous domination of nature. But woman is not nature only.

She is the mermaid with her fish-tail dipped in the unconscious. Her creation will be to make articulate this obscure world which dominates man, which he denies being dominated by, but which asserts its domination in destructive proofs of its presence, madness.

1937   1967

---

2. Ludwig Frankl (1810–1893), Austrian Jewish poet. Arthur Rimbaud (1854–1891), French Symbolist poet; he ended his life in a self-imposed exile from France.

3. A city in north-central Morocco, the country's religious center.

DOROTHY RICHARDSON
1873–1957

The innovative novelist Dorothy Richardson lived and wrote in comparative obscurity, supporting herself for eight years with a job as a dental assistant and then eking out a thin livelihood publishing sketches and reviews as well as articles about dentistry in various journals. But her chef d'oeuvre was the experimental thirteen-volume sequence titled *Pilgrimage* (1915–67), in which she recounted the experiences of Miriam Henderson, a protagonist who shared many details of her own background. It won her considerable praise from such eminent contemporaries as Virginia Woolf and John Cowper Powys. "She has invented a sentence that we might call the psychological sentence of the feminine gender," Woolf declared admiringly, and Powys asserted that she was "the greatest woman genius of our time."

Richardson was born in Abingdon, Berkshire, to a wealthy family, but her father lost most of his money in the 1890s and her emotionally disturbed mother committed suicide in 1895, an event that the novelist recorded with hallucinatory vividness in the third book of *Pilgrimage*. After her mother's death, Richardson moved to London, where she had an extended affair with the novelist H. G. Wells, while embarking on her own literary career. In 1917, she married the artist Allan Odle, with whom she lived until his death in 1948. She herself died in 1957 in a London nursing home, where she had been living for five years, and where, when she explained to the staff that she was a writer, the nurses "believed at first that she had delusions." But Richardson's clear-eyed commitment to her art, and her success in realizing her aspirations, were in no way delusory. As she indicates in her foreword to an omnibus edition of *Pilgrimage*—our selection here—she had planned her project carefully, seeking "to produce a feminine equivalent of the current masculine realism" and believing (for better or worse) that "[f]eminine prose . . . should properly be unpunctuated, moving from point to point without formal obstructions."

Foreword to *Pilgrimage*

Although the translation of the impulse behind his youthful plan for a tremendous essay on *Les Forces humaines*[1] makes for the population of his great cluster of novels with types rather than with individuals, the power of a sympathetic imagination, uniting him with each character in turn, gives to every portrait the quality of a faithful self-portrait, and his treatment of backgrounds, contemplated with an equally passionate interest and themselves, indeed, individual and unique, would alone qualify Balzac to be called the father of realism.

Less deeply concerned with the interplay of human forces, his first English follower portrays with complete fidelity the lives and adventures of inconspicuous people, and for a while, when in the English literary world it began its career as a useful label, realism was synonymous with Arnold Bennett.

But whereas both Balzac and Bennett, while representing, the one in regard to a relatively concrete and coherent social system, the other in regard

---

1. The human strength (French), the subject of an "essay" described by Balzac in a letter as part of his grand conception into which almost all his fiction would fit (which he would later name "The Human Comedy").

to a society already showing signs of disintegration, the turning of the human spirit upon itself, may be called realists by nature and unawares, their immediate successors possess an articulate creed. They believe themselves to be substituting, for the telescopes of the writers of romance whose lenses they condemn as both rose-coloured and distorting, mirrors of plain glass.

By 1911, though not yet quite a direct supply of documentary material for the dossiers of the *cause célèbre*, Man versus conditions impeached as the authors of his discontent, realist novels are largely explicit satire and protest, and every form of conventionalized human association is being arraigned by biographical and autobiographical novelists.

Since all these novelists happened to be men, the present writer, proposing at this moment to write a novel and looking round for a contemporary pattern, was faced with the choice between following one of her regiments and attempting to produce a feminine equivalent of the current masculine realism. Choosing the latter alternative, she presently set aside, at the bidding of a dissatisfaction that revealed its nature without supplying any suggestion as to the removal of its cause, a considerable mass of manuscript. Aware, as she wrote, of the gradual falling away of the preoccupations that for a while had dictated the briskly moving script, and of the substitution, for these inspiring preoccupations, of a stranger in the form of contemplated reality having for the first time in her experience its own say, and apparently justifying those who acclaim writing as the surest means of discovering the truth about one's own thoughts and beliefs, she had been at the same time increasingly tormented, not only by the failure, of this now so independently assertive reality, adequately to appear within the text, but by its revelation, whencesoever focused, of a hundred faces, any one of which, the moment it was entrapped within the close mesh of direct statement, summoned its fellows to disqualify it.

In 1913, the opening pages of the attempted chronicle became the first chapter of 'Pilgrimage,' written to the accompaniment of a sense of being upon a fresh pathway, an adventure so searching and, sometimes, so joyous as to produce a longing for participation; not quite the same as a longing for publication, whose possibility, indeed, as the book grew, receded to vanishing point.

To a publisher, nevertheless, at the bidding of Mr. J. D. Beresford,[2] the book was ultimately sent. By the time it returned, the second chapter was partly written and the condemned volume, put away and forgotten, would have remained in seclusion but for the persistence of the same kind friend, who acquired and sent it to Edward Garnett, then reading for Messrs Duckworth. In 1915, the covering title being at the moment in use elsewhere, it was published as 'Pointed Roofs.'

The lonely track, meanwhile, had turned out to be a populous highway. Amongst those who had simultaneously entered it, two figures stood out. One a woman mounted upon a magnificently caparisoned charger, the other a man walking, with eyes devoutly closed, weaving as he went a rich garment of new words wherewith to clothe the antique dark material of his engrossment.

---

2. British writer of fiction and essays, a friend of Richardson; they met around 1911.

News came from France of one Marcel Proust, said to be producing an unprecedentedly profound and opulent reconstruction of experience focused from within the mind of a single individual, and, since Proust's first volume had been published and several others written by 1913, the France of Balzac now appeared to have produced the earliest adventurer.

Finally, however, the role of pathfinder was declared to have been played by a venerable gentleman, a charmed and charming high priest of nearly all the orthodoxies, inhabiting a softly lit enclosure he mistook, until 1914, for the universe, and celebrated by evolving, for the accommodation of his vast tracts of urbane commentary, a prose style demanding, upon the first reading, a perfection of sustained concentration akin to that which brought it forth, and bestowing, again upon the first reading, the recreative delights peculiar to this form of spiritual exercise.

And while, indeed, it is possible to claim for Henry James, keeping the reader incessantly watching the conflict of human forces through the eye of a single observer, rather than taking him, before the drama begins, upon a tour amongst the properties, or breaking in with descriptive introductions of the players as one by one they enter his enclosed resounding chamber where no plant grows and no mystery pours in from the unheeded stars, a far from inconsiderable technical influence, it was nevertheless not without a sense of relief that the present writer recently discovered, in 'Wilhelm Meister,'[3] the following manifesto:

> In the novel, reflections and incidents should be featured; in drama, character and action. The novel must proceed slowly, and the thought-processes of the principal figure must, by one device or another, hold up the development of the whole. . . . The hero of the novel must be acted upon, or, at any rate, not himself the principal operator. . . . Grandison, Clarissa, Pamela, the Vicar of Wakefield, and Tom Jones himself,[4] even where they are not acted upon, are still retarding personalities and all the incidents are, in a certain measure, modelled according to their thoughts.

Phrases began to appear, formulae devised to meet the exigencies of literary criticism. 'The Stream of Consciousness' lyrically led the way, to be gladly welcomed by all who could persuade themselves of the possibility of comparing consciousness to a stream. Its transatlantic successors, 'Interior Monologue' and 'Slow-motion Photography,' may each be granted a certain technical applicability leaving them, to this extent, unhampered by the defects of their qualities.

Lives in plenty have been devoted to the critic's exacting art and a lifetime might be spent in engrossed contemplation of the movements of its continuous ballet. When the dancers tread living boards, the boards will sometimes be heard to groan. The present writer groans, gently and resignedly, beneath the reiterated tap-tap accusing her of feminism, of failure to perceive the value of the distinctively masculine intelligence, of pre-War sentimentality, of post-War Freudianity. But when her work is danced upon for being

---

3. A novel by Goethe (1795–96).   4. All title characters of 18th-century British novels.

unpunctuated and therefore unreadable, she is moved to cry aloud. For here is truth.

Feminine prose, as Charles Dickens and James Joyce have delightfully shown themselves to be aware, should properly be unpunctuated, moving from point to point without formal obstructions. And the author of 'Pilgrimage' must confess to an early habit of ignoring, while writing, the lesser of the stereotyped system of signs, and, further, when finally sprinkling in what appeared to be necessary, to a small unconscious departure from current usage. While meeting approval, first from the friend who discovered and pointed it out to her, then from an editor who welcomed the article she wrote to elucidate and justify it, and, recently, by the inclusion of this article in a text-book for students of journalism and its translation into French, the small innovation, in further complicating the already otherwise sufficiently complicated task of the official reader, helped to produce the chaos for which she is justly reproached.

For the opportunity, afforded by the present publishers, of eliminating this source of a reputation for creating avoidable difficulties, and of assembling the scattered chapters of 'Pilgrimage' in their proper relationship, the author desires here to express her gratitude and, further, to offer to all those readers who have persisted in spite of every obstacle, a heart-felt apology.

D.M.R.

TREVONE, 1938.   1938

SYLVIA TOWNSEND WARNER
1893–1978

The author of seven novels, most notably the best-selling *Lolly Willowes* (1926), Sylvia Townsend Warner was also a musicologist, a poet, a committed feminist, and, for a time, a member of the Communist Party. In *Lolly Willowes* she related the story of a middle-aged spinster who flees London respectability and finds freedom in what one commentator describes as the "pagan pleasures" of the rural countryside, where she becomes a witch and engages in "a light-hearted dialogue with the devil" on, among other subjects, "the wrongs of women." Townsend Warner herself found comparable freedom in the countryside, where she lived for many years with her life partner, the poet Valentine Ackland. It was with Ackland that she joined the Communist Party, and with Ackland she went to Spain during the civil war, where both women worked as medical auxiliaries. Together, too, the women published *Whether a Dove or a Seagull* (1933), a collection of 109 poems, 54 by Townsend Warner. In addition to this project and her novels, Townsend Warner also produced a study of Jane Austen (1951) and a biography of T. H. White (1967) as well as a series of sophisticated stories, *Kingdoms of Elfin* (1977).

Our selection, "Women as Writers," originated as a lecture that Townsend Warner delivered to the Royal Society of Arts in 1959. Meditating on the female literary tradition with the same wit and verve that animates her fantasy-tinged fiction, she asks, "Supposing I had been a man, a gentleman novelist, would I have been asked to lecture on Men as Writers?" and speculates incisively on the way "women have entered literature—breathless, unequipped, and with nothing but their wits to trust to."

Women as Writers

The Peter Le Neve Foster Lecture by
SYLVIA TOWNSEND WARNER,
delivered to the Society on Wednesday, 11th
February, 1959, with Leonard Woolf in the Chair

THE CHAIRMAN: It is a great honour to have been asked to take the Chair for Sylvia Townsend Warner to-day. One of the few famous statesmen who seem to me to be worthy of some admiration was Pericles, but he is reputed to have said, on one occasion, 'As far as women are concerned I have only one thing to say; and that is, the less we hear of them, whether for good or for evil, the better'.[1] That may appear an extraordinarily tactless thing to recall when we are gathered together to hear a poet and a novelist of the very highest quality who happens also to be a woman. But I quoted that saying because I feel quite certain that if Pericles happened to be here to-day he would have agreed that he was quite wrong and that his words applied really not to women, but to Chairmen.

The following lecture was then delivered.

The Lecture

When I received this invitation to lecture to the Royal Society of Arts on 'Women as Writers' (and here let me express my thanks to the responsible Committee, and to the shade of Peter Le Neve Foster, whose family founded the lectureship, and to my Chairman)—when I received this invitation, it was the invitation that surprised me. The choice of subject did not. I am a woman writer myself, and it never surprises me. Even when people tell me I am a lady novelist, it is the wording of the allegation I take exception to, not the allegation itself. One doubt, it is true, crossed my mind. It was inevitable that I should remember a book called *A Room of One's Own*, by Virginia Woolf. What had I to add to that? But *A Room of One's Own*, I thought, is not so much about how women write as about how astonishing it is that they should have managed to write at all. As they have managed to, there might still be something I could add. But then I reread my invitation, and became the prey of uneasiness. Women as Writers. *Women* as Writers. Supposing I had been a man, a gentleman novelist, would I have been asked to lecture on Men as Writers? I thought it improbable.

Here was an implication I might or might not resent. Here, at any rate, was an obligation I couldn't dodge.

1. Paraphrased from the Funeral Oration (430 B.C.E.), as rendered by Thucydides in *The Peloponnesian War* 2.45.

It would appear that when a woman writes a book, the action sets up an extraneous vibration. Something happens that must be accounted for. It is the action that does it, not the product. It is only in very rare, and rather non-literary instances, that the product—*Uncle Tom's Cabin*, say, or the *Memoirs of Harriet Wilson*[2]—is the jarring note. It would also appear that this extraneous vibration may be differently received and differently resounded. Some surfaces mute it. Off others, it is violently resonated. It is also subject to the influence of climate, the climate of popular opinion. In a fine dry climate the dissonance caused by a woman writing a book has much less intensity than in a damp foggy one. Overriding these variations due to surface and climate is the fact that the volume increases with the mass—as summarized in Macheath's Law:

> One wife is too much for most husbands to hear
> But two at a time sure no mortal can bear.[3]

Finally, it would appear that the vibration is not set up until a woman seizes a pen. She may invent, but she may not write down.

Macheath's Law explains why the early women writers caused so little alarm. They only went off one at a time. If a great lady such as Marie de France chose to give her leisure to letters instead of embroidery, this was merely a demonstration that society could afford such luxuries—an example of what Veblen defined as Conspicuous Waste.[4] No one went unfed or unclothed for it. Nor could she be held guilty of setting a bad example to other women, since so few women were in a position to follow it. So things went on, with now and then a literate woman making a little squeak with her pen, while the other women added a few more lines to Mother Goose (about that authorship, I think there can be no dispute). It was not till the retreat from the Renaissance that the extraneous vibration was heard as so very jarring. By then, many women had learned to read and write, so a literate woman was no longer an ornament to society. Kept in bounds, she had her uses. She could keep the account books and transcribe recipes for puddings and horse pills. But she must be kept within bounds; she must subserve. When Teresa of Avila wrote her autobiography, she said in a preface that it had been written with leave, and 'in accordance with my confessor's command'. True she immediately added, 'The Lord himself, I know, has long wished it to be written'—a sentiment felt by most creative writers, I believe; but the woman and the Lord had to wait for permission.

The French have always allowed a place to Conspicuous Waste, it is one of the things they excel at; and Mme. de La Fayette rewarded this tolerance by giving France the first psychological novel, *La Princesse de Clèves*. But Molière was probably a surer mouthpiece of public opinion when he made game of literary ladies. It is more damning to be shown as absurd than to be denounced as scandalous. It is more damning still to be thought old-fashioned.

---

2. Harriette Wilson was a famous Regency-era courtesan; she published her memoirs in 1825.
3. Lines spoken by Macheath in John Gay's *The Beggar's Opera* (1728), 3.4.

4. I.e., part of Thorstein Veblen's idea of conspicuous consumption, as laid out in *The Theory of the Leisure Class* (1902). Marie de France wrote in the late 12th century.

Margaret Countess of Newcastle was derided not only as a figure of fun but as a figure out of the lumber-room. (Much the same condemnation fell on Lady Murasaki, a most eminent woman writer, whose nickname in the Japanese court of the early eleventh century was Dame Annals.) In eighteenth-century England, a woman of fashion wrote at her peril (I doubt if Pope would have laid so much stress on Lady Mary Wortley Montagu being dirty if she had not been inky). A woman who wrote for publication—by then, a fair number did—sank in the social scale. If she wrote fiction, she was a demirep. If she wrote as a scholar, she was a dowdy. However, as men of letters had also gone down in the world, writing women gained more than they lost. They gained companionship, they approached a possibility of being judged on their merits by writers of the opposite sex.

Too much has been made of Dr. Johnson's opinion of women preachers,[5] not enough of the fact that Mrs. Chapone and Elizabeth Carter contributed to *The Rambler*, nor of his goodwill towards Mrs. Lennox, and the hot apple pie he stuck with bay leaves in her honour. In the case of Fanny Burney, Johnson showed more than goodwill. He showed courage. Fanny Burney was his friend's daughter, and a virgin. And Fanny Burney had written a novel. Not even a romance. A novel.

The speed with which women possess themselves of an advantage is something astonishing. Such quantities of virtuous women turned to novel writing that Jane Austen was able to pick and choose among them, to laugh at Ann Radcliffe and Mary Brunton, to admire Miss Edgeworth. It was an Indian summer, the last glow of the Age of Reason. Jane Austen could inscribe her title-page with that majestic, *By a Lady*. The Brontë sisters, not so. They were born too late. The barometer had fallen, the skies had darkened. They grew up in an age which had decided that women had an innate moral superiority. As almost everything was a menace to this innate moral superiority, it was necessary that women should be protected, protected from men, protected from life, protected from being talked about, protected from Euclid—Mary Somerville the mathematician has recorded how hard put to it she was to expose herself to Euclid—protected above all from those dangerous articles, themselves. You couldn't have women dashing their pens into inkpots and writing as if they knew about life and had something to say about it. Determined to write and to be judged on the merit of their writing, women put on men's names: Aurore Dudevant became George Sand, and Mary Ann Evans, George Eliot, and Emily Brontë consented to the ambiguity of Ellis Bell.

I think I can now venture a positive assertion about women as writers. It is a distinguishing assertion; if I were talking about Men as Writers I could not make it. Women as writers are obstinate and sly.

I deliberately make this assertion in the present tense. Though a woman writing to-day is not hampered by an attribution of innate moral superiority she has to reckon with an attribution of innate physical superiority; and this, too, can be cumbersome. There is, for instance, bi-location. It is well known that a woman can be in two places at once; at her desk and at her washing

5. "Sir, a woman's preaching is like a dog's walking on his hinder legs. It is not done well; but you are surprized to find it done at all" (quoted in James Boswell's *Life of Johnson*, 1791). Johnson himself wrote almost all the articles in *The Rambler* (1750–52).

machine. She can practise a mental bi-location also, pinning down some slippery adverb while saying aloud, 'No, not Hobbs, Nokes. And the address is 17 Dalmeny Crescent'. Her mind is so extensive that it can simultaneously follow an intricate train of thought, remember what it was she had to tell the electrician, answer the telephone, keep an eye on the time, and not forget about the potatoes. Obstinacy and slyness still have their uses, although they are not literary qualities.

But I have sometimes wondered if women are literary at all. It is not a thing which is strenuously required of them, and perhaps, finding something not required of them, they thank God and do no more about it. They write. They dive into writing like ducks into water. One would almost think it came naturally to them—at any rate as naturally as plain sewing.

Here is a non-literary woman writing in the nineteenth century. She wrote under her own name, for her sex was already notorious.

> There were three separate registers kept at Scutari. First, the Adjutant's daily Head-Roll of soldiers' burials, on which it may be presumed that no one was entered who was not buried, although it is possible that some may have been buried who were not entered.
>
> Second, the Medical Officer's Return, in regard to which it is quite certain that hundreds of men were buried who never appeared upon it.
>
> Third, the return made in the Orderly Room, which is only remarkable as giving a totally different account of the deaths from either of the others.

I should like to think that Florence Nightingale's work is not yet done. If it could be set as a model before those who write official reports, the publications of Her Majesty's Stationery Office might grow much leaner, much time and money might be saved. But this is by the way.

Here is another, writing in the seventeenth century:

> Take a pint of cream, three spoonfuls of rice flour, the whites of three eggs well beaten, and four spoonfuls of fine sugar. Stir these well into your cream cold; then take a few blanched almonds and beat them in a mortar with two spoonfuls of water, then strain them into your cream and boil it till it comes from the skillet. Then take it up and put in two spoonfuls of sack,[6] and wet your cups with sack and put in your custard, and let it stand till it is cold.

From a cookery book, as you will have realized—but a piece of tight, clear, consecutive writing.

Here is a woman writing from Norwich in July, 1453:

> And as for tidings, Philip Berney is passed to God on Monday last past with the greatest pain that ever I saw man; and on Tuesday Sir John Heveningham went to his church and heard three masses and came home never merrier; and said to his wife that he would go say a little devotion in his garden and then dine; and forthwith he felt a fainting in his leg and slid down. This was at nine of the clock and he was dead ere noon.[7]

---

6. A white wine.
7. A letter from Agnes Paston to her son, John Paston.

Here is another Norfolk woman, writing, or possibly dictating, towards the close of the previous century:

> And after this I saw God in a Point—that is to say, in my understanding; by which I saw he is in all things. I beheld and considered, seeing and knowing in sight, with a soft dread, and thought: What is sin?[8]

I really have not cheated over these examples. The two notable women, the two women of no note, I chose them almost at random, and went to their writings to see what I would find. I found them alike in making themselves clear.

As far as I know, there is only one certain method of making oneself clear, and that is, to have plainly in mind what one wishes to say. When the unequivocal statement matches itself to the predetermined thought and the creative impulse sets fire to them, the quality we call immediacy results. Immediacy has borne other names, it has even been called inspiration—though I think that is too large a term for it. But immediacy has this in common with inspiration, that where it is present, the author becomes absent. The writing is no longer propelled by the author's anxious hand, the reader is no longer conscious of the author's chaperoning presence. Here is an example; it is a poem by Frances Cornford:

> The Cypriot woman, as she closed her dress,
> Smiled at the baby on her broad-lapped knee,
> Beautiful in a calm voluptuousness
> Like a slow sea.[9]

One does not feel that the woman has been written about. She is there.

Women as writers seem to be remarkably adept at vanishing out of their writing so that the quality of immediacy replaces them. Immediacy is the word in *La Princesse de Clèves*, that masterpiece of emotion laced up in the tight embroidered bodice of court dress. Madame de Clèves' heart is laid open before us, and we hang over it; not even pity is allowed to intervene between us and the demonstration. Immediacy is the word when Jane Austen keeps a bookful of rather undistinguished characters not only all alive at once but all aware of each other's existence. In *Wuthering Heights* immediacy makes a bookful of almost incredible characters fastened into a maddeningly entangled plot seem natural and inevitable, as if it were something familiar to us because of a dream. When the goblins fasten on Lizzie and press the fruit against her clenched teeth; when Orlando finds the man in Mrs. Stewkley's room,[1] the man who turned his pen in his fingers, this way and that; and gazed and mused; and then, very quickly, wrote half a dozen lines—and no more need be said, with our own eyes we have looked on William Shakespeare; when Murasaki's Genji takes Yūgao to the deserted house where the ghost steals her away from him; when, at the close of Colette's *La Chatte*, the girl looks back from the turn of the avenue and sees the cat keeping a mistrustful eye on her departure and the young man playing

---

8. From *A Book of Showings* (1390), by the mystic Julian of Norwich.
9. "Behind a Greek Restaurant," reproduced by permission of The Cresset Press Ltd. [Townsend Warner's note]. Cornford (1886–1960), English poet and translator.
1. In the first chapter of Virginia Woolf's *Orlando* (1928). "The goblins": see Christina Rossetti's *Goblin Market* (1862).

deftly as a cat, with the first-fallen chestnuts, it is not the writer one is conscious of. One is conscious of a happening, of something taking place under one's very nose. As for Sappho, I cannot speak. She rises in my mind like a beautiful distant island, but I cannot set foot on her because I haven't learned Greek. But I have been assured that immediacy is the word for Sappho.

While all these splendid examples were rushing into my mind, I realized that a great many examples which could not be called splendid were accompanying them: that when the gust of wind flutters the hangings and extinguishes the solitary taper and Mrs. Radcliffe's heroine is left in darkness, it is a darkness that can be felt; that in George Sand's writing, for all its exploitation and rhetoric. George Sand may suddenly be replaced by the first frost prowling under cover of night through an autumn garden; that the short stories of Mary Wilkins a New England writer of the last century whose characters appear to be made of lettuce, can remain in one's mind and call one back to a re-reading because one remembers a queer brilliant verisimilitude, the lighting of immediacy.

There is, of course, George Eliot. She makes herself admirably clear and her mind, such a fine capacious mind, too, is stored with things she wishes to say but in her case, immediacy does not result. We remember scenes and characters but do they ever haunt us? She dissects a heart, but something intervenes between us and the demonstration—the lecturer's little wand. There is a class of women writers, praiseworthily combining fiction with edification, and among them is Mrs. Sherwood of *The Fairchild Family*, Mrs. Gatty of *Parables from Nature*, Mrs. Trimmer[2] . . . it seems to me that George Eliot insisted upon being a superlative Mrs. Trimmer.

Still, George Eliot apart—a considerable apart—I think one might claim that this quality of immediacy, though common to either sex, is proportionately of more frequent occurrence in the work of women writers. And though it is impossible in judging the finished product to pronounce on which pages were achieved with effort, which came easily, the fact that even quite mediocre women writers will sometimes wear this precious jewel in their heads seems to indicate that it is easier for a woman to make herself air and vanish off her pages than it is for a man, with his heavier equipment of learning and self-consciousness. Perhaps this is really so, and for a reason. Suppose, for instance, there was a palace, which you could only know from outside. Sometimes you heard music playing within, and the corks popping, and sometimes splendid figures came to an open window and spoke a few words in a solemn chanting voice; and from time to time you met someone who had actually been inside, and was carrying away under his arm—it was always a man—a lute or a casket or the leg of a turkey. And then one day you discovered that you could climb into this palace by the pantry window. In the excitement of the moment you wouldn't wait; you wouldn't go home to smooth your hair or borrow your grandmother's garnets or consult the Book of Etiquette. Even at the risk of being turned out by the butler, rebuked by the chaplain, laughed at by the rightful guests, you'd climb in.

2. Sarah Trimmer (1741–1810), a prolific writer of religious and didactic works for children, as was Mary Martha Sherwood (1775–1851). Mrs. Alfred Gatty published little beyond the multiple editions of *Parables from Nature* (1864–65).

In something of the same way, women have entered literature—breathless, unequipped, and with nothing but their wits to trust to. A few minutes ago, or a few centuries ago, they were writing a letter about an apoplexy, or a recipe for custard. Now they are inside the palace, writing with great clearness what they have in mind to say—for that is all they know about it, no one has groomed them for a literary career—writing on the kitchen table, like Emily Brontë, or on the washstand, like Christina Rossetti, writing in the attic, like George Sand, or in the family parlour, protected by a squeaking door from being discovered at it, like Jane Austen, writing away for all they are worth, and seldom blotting a line.

Do you see what we are coming to?—I have put in several quotations to prepare you for it. We are coming to those other writers who have got into literature by the pantry window, and who have left the most illustrious footprints on the windowsill. It is a dizzying conclusion, but it must be faced. Women, entering literature, entered it on the same footing as William Shakespeare.

So if women writers have what might appear an unfairly large share of the quality of immediacy which is sometimes called inspiration—and in the case of Shakespeare we all agree to call it so—it is not, after all, original in them—like sin. It derives from their circumstances, not from their sex. It is interesting to see what other qualities, also deriving from circumstance, the circumstance of entering literature by the pantry window, they share with Shakespeare. I can think of several. One is their conviction that women have legs of their own, and can move about of their own volition, and give as good as they get. Lady Macbeth, and Beatrice, and Helena in *All's Well*, could almost be taken for women writers' heroines, they are so free and uninhibited, and ready to jump over stiles and appear in the drawing-room with muddy stockings, like Lizzie Bennet.[3]

Another pantry window trait is the kind of workaday democracy, an ease and appreciativeness in low company. It is extremely rare to find the conventional comic servant or comic countryman in books by women. A convention is a *pis-aller*, a stopgap where experience is lacking. A woman has to be most exceptionally secluded if she never goes to her own back door, or is not on visiting terms with people poorer than herself. I have said before—but as the remark has only appeared in Russian I can decently repeat myself—Emily Brontë was fortunate in being the daughter of a clergyman, because the daughter of a clergyman, with her duty of parish visiting, has wonderful opportunities to become acquainted with human passions and what they can lead to. Another trait in common is a willing ear for the native tongue, for turns of phrase used by carpenters, gardeners, sailors, milliners, tinkers, old nurses, and that oldest nurse of all, ballad and folklore. Just as Mme. de Sévigné was always improving her French by picking up words and idioms from her tenants at Les Rochers, Colette listened to every trade, every walk in life, and kept dictionaries of professional terms beside her desk—while Edith Sitwell's poetry reaches back through centuries of English poetical idiom to *Nuts in May*[4] and Mother Goose.

---

3. The heroine of Jane Austen's *Pride and Prejudice* (1813), who appears with muddy stockings in vol. 1, chap. 7. Beatrice is the heroine of *Much Ado About Nothing*.
4. I.e., the nursery rhyme.

These traits, as you will have noticed, are technical assets. They affect presentation, not content. Their absence may be deadening, but their presence does not make their possessor any more eligible to be compared with Shakespeare. The resemblance is in the circumstances. Women writers have shared his advantage of starting with no literary advantages. No butlers were waiting just inside the front door to receive their invitation cards and show them in. Perhaps the advantage is not wholly advantageous; but circumstances do alter cases. It was not very surprising that young Mr. Shelley should turn to writing; it was surprising that young Mr. Keats did, and his poetry reflects his surprise, his elation. It is the poetry of a young man surprised by joy. So is the poetry of John Clare.[5] But though the male entrants by the pantry window possess the quality of immediacy just as women writers do, are at ease in low company and in the byways of their native language, they do not employ these advantages with the same fluency—I hesitate to use the word *exploit*; I will say, they are not so much obliged to them. I see a possible explanation for this, which I will come to presently.

But first I must come to the present day, when women, one might think, have so well established themselves as writers that the extraneous vibration must be hushed, and the pantry window supplanted as an entrance to literature by the Tradesman's Door. No woman writer should despise the Tradesman's Door. It is a very respectable entrance, the path to it was first trodden by Mrs. Aphra Behn, and many women have trodden it since, creditably and contentedly too. I should be failing my title if I did not remind you that we now have women newspaper reporters working in such vexed places as Cyprus—a signal advance. Yet, when we use the term *hack-writer*, we still feel that it must apply to a man; that a woman writer is once and for always an amateur. In the same spirit, if she happens to make a great deal of money by a book, well and good, it is one of those lucky accidents that happen from time to time, no one is the worse for it, and she is unexpectedly the better. But if she earns her living by her pen, we are not so ready to accept the idea. If we are polite enough to dissemble our feelings we say that it is a pity that with so much talent she should be reduced to this kind of thing. If we are candid and pure-souled, we say it's outrageous and that she ought to become a hospital nurse. If she marries—again it's a pity—a polite pity that she will have to give up her writing. So much pity is ominous.

And in fact, the vibration may start up at any moment. Macheath's Law still holds; not for numbers, perhaps, but for area. It is admitted that women may write very nearly what they please, just as, within limits, they may do what they please: though I suppose it will be a long time before they can enter the priesthood or report football matches on the B.B.C. But this liberty is zoned. It applies to women belonging to the middle classes. You know those shiny papers one reads in waiting-rooms, and how, every week, they show a photograph of a woman of the upper classes, with a little notice underneath. One has just come out.[6] One has recently married. One wins prizes with her Shetland ponies, another has a charming pair of twins,

---

5. Of these three early-19th-century poets, only Shelley had an aristocratic background; Clare was the uneducated son of a field laborer, and Keats was apprenticed at 15 to an apothecary-surgeon. 6. Made formal entrance into society as a young woman (especially by being presented at court).

another is an M.F.H. But despite Edith Sitwell and Dorothy Wellesley,[7] one does not expect to read below the photograph that the lady is a poet. Take it a step higher. Suppose that a royal princess would not tear herself from the third act of her tragedy in order to open a play-centre. People would be gravely put out, especially the men who had been building the play-centre, men who have taught their wives to know their place, and who expect princesses to be equally dutiful.

A working-class woman may be as gifted as all the women writers I have spoken of to-day, all rolled into one; but it is no part of her duty to write a masterpiece. Her brain may be teeming, but it is not the fertility of her brain she must attend to, perishable citizens is what her country expects of her, not imperishable Falstaffs and Don Quixotes. The Lord himself may long have wished for her books to be written; but leave has yet to be granted. Apart from one or two grandees like Mme. de La Fayette, women writers have come from the middle class, and their writing carries a heritage of middle-class virtues; good taste, prudence, acceptance of limitations, compliance with standards, and that typically middle-class merit of making the most of what one's got—in other words, that too-conscious employment of advantages which I mentioned a few minutes ago, and which one does not observe in Clare, or Burns, or Bunyan. So when we consider women as writers, we must bear in mind that we have not very much to go on, and that it is too early to assess what they may be capable of. It may well be that the half has not been told us: that unbridled masterpieces, daring innovations, epics, tragedies, works of genial impropriety—all the things that so far women have signally failed to produce—have been socially, not sexually, debarred; that at this moment a Joan Milton or a Françoise Rabelais may have left the washing unironed and the stew uncared for because she can't wait to begin.

THE CHAIRMAN: I have never believed in the truth of any generalization—more especially generalizations about women and about men. But the generalizations which Miss Townsend Warner has given us this afternoon seem to have been both true and brilliant; and I believe that if Pericles had been here to-day he would have agreed that his original saying was nonsense.

A vote of thanks to the Lecturer was carried with acclamation and, another having been accorded to the Chairman upon the proposal of Dr. R. W. Holland, the meeting then ended.

1959

---

7. Sitwell was the daughter of a baronet (and granddaughter of an earl), and Wellesley's husband was a duke. "M.F.H.": Mistress of the Foxhounds.

MARIANNE MOORE
1887–1972

One of the most innovative, famous—and famously eccentric—American poets of the mid–twentieth century, Marianne Moore was celebrated by such diverse literary figures as William Carlos Williams and T. S. Eliot. A schoolmate of the poet H. D., who helped arrange for the publication of her first volume of verse, Moore was raised in Carlisle, Pennsylvania, where her mother taught at the Metzger Institute, then studied biology at Bryn Mawr before embarking on a brief career as a teacher of shorthand, typing, and commercial law at the U.S. Industrial Indian School in Carlisle. In 1915, however, her verse began appearing in such distinguished literary periodicals as *The Egoist* in London and *Poetry* in Chicago, and she soon won a reputation as a rarefied "poet's poet."

When Moore's brother, a Presbyterian minister, moved east, she and her mother, to whom she remained exceptionally close all her life, followed him, sharing apartments in Greenwich Village and later in Brooklyn. In New York, the poet at first supported herself with part-time jobs as a secretary and librarian, but she quickly joined a group of avant-garde painters and writers connected with the little magazine *Others,* and eventually became editor of the influential literary journal *The Dial.* In this position, which she held between 1925 and 1929, Moore exercised considerable authority, accepting or rejecting, praising or critiquing works by such major artists as Ezra Pound, Hart Crane, and James Joyce. In 1935, her *Selected Poems* was published with a laudatory introduction by T. S. Eliot, and in the same year she befriended the twenty-four-year-old Elizabeth Bishop, a promising young woman writer who was eventually to become as prominent as Moore herself.

In a famous memoir, Bishop remembered Moore as "not very tall and not in the least intimidating," although, as she admitted, she was often "foolishly bemused" by some of the older woman's crotchets. To most readers, however, Moore frequently appeared extraordinarily "intimidating"—or at least her verse did, since, as the editor Louis Untermeyer once put it, her erudite allusions seemed "to erect a barrier of jagged clauses [and] barbed quotations . . . between herself and her audience." Yet Moore herself explained that "I was just trying to be honorable and not to steal things" while self-deprecatingly (and notoriously) writing about poetry that "I, too, dislike it," because "There are things that are important beyond all this fiddle." In addition to accuracy of quotation and integrity in citation, among the things Moore considered "important" were zoos, clothes, and baseball players. At their first meeting, she and Bishop visited the zoo together, and in her later years she notoriously attired herself in an old-fashioned three-cornered hat and cape, in which, on one occasion, she threw out the first ball of the season at a Brooklyn Dodgers game.

We have included here Moore's own foreword to the richly varied *Marianne Moore Reader* because it captures much of this extraordinary woman's lively literary personality. Explaining her "inordinate interest in animals and athletes," she remarks that "Pangolins, hornbills, pitchers, catchers, do not pry or prey—or prolong the conversation" and "look their best when caring least"; and of her own often formidably learned and complex art she declares, perhaps disingenuously, that "I like straight writing, end-stopped lines, an effect of flowing continuity." At the same time, the terse assurance with which she lists her criteria for inclusion in her anthology of her own work ("How would it seem to me if someone else had written it? Does it hold the attention? 'Has it human value?' ") reflects the steely authority with which she had for four years ruled *The Dial* and with which throughout her long and brilliant career she governed her own tasks as poet, editor, translator, and critic.

Foreword to
A *Marianne Moore Reader*

Published: it is enough. The magazine was discontinued. The edition was small. One paragraph needs restating. Newspaper cuts on the fold or disintegrates. When was it published, and where? "The title was 'Words and . . .' something else. Could you say what it was?" I have forgotten. Happened upon years later, it seems to have been "Words and Modes of Expression." What became of "Tedium and Integrity," the unfinished manuscript of which there was no duplicate? A housekeeper is needed to assort the untidiness. For whom? A curioso or just for the author? In that case "as safe at the publisher's as if chained to the shelves of Bodley," Lamb[1] said, smiling.

Verse: prose: a specimen or so of translation for those on whom completeness would weigh as a leg-iron. How would it seem to me if someone else had written it? Does it hold the attention? "Has it human value?" Or seem as if one had ever heard of "lucidity, force, and ease" or had any help from past thinkers? Is it subservient singsong or has it "muscles"?

La Fontaine's Fables. Professor Brower—if I am not inventing it—says a translator must have "depth of experience." The rhythm of a translation as motion, I think, should suggest the rhythm of the original, and the words be very nearly an equivalent of the author's meaning. After endless last choices, digressions, irrelevances, defiances, and futile imprudences, I am repaid for attempting to translate "The Grasshopper and the Ant" by hitting upon a substitute for an error, the most offensive and meaningless of a long list: "an't you please."

> "—I sang for those who might pass by chance—
> Night and day, an't you please"

for which I am substituting "Night and day. Please do not be repelled," with the ant's reply, "Sang? A delight when someone has excelled." In harmonizing notes or words, there is more room for originality than in moralizing, and "the point," prefixed or appended to a tale irresistibly told, seems redundant. Although La Fontaine's primary concern was the poetry; even so, for him and for us, indifference to being educated has been conquered, and certain lessons in these fables contrive to be indelible: *Greed:* The owner of the hen that laid the golden eggs, "cut the magic chain and she'd never lay again. / Think this when covetous!" *Ingratitude:* The reanimated adder lunged at the farmer, "Its foster father who had been its rescuer. / . . . Two strokes made three snakes of the coil— / A body, a tail, and a head. / The pestilent thirds writhed together to rear / But of course could no longer adhere." "Ingrates," La Fontaine says, "will always die in agony." *Be content with your lot:* A shepherd "was lured to part with his one and only flock / And invest all he'd earned, in a ship; but ah, the shock— / Wrecked in return for all he'd paid."

Prose: mine will always be "essays" and verse of mine, observations. Of "Tedium and Integrity" the first few pages are missing—summarized sufficiently

---

1. The Romantic essayist Charles Lamb. "Bodley": Oxford's Bodleian Library (early books were so valuable that they were chained to library shelves).

by: manner for matter; shadow for substance; ego for rapture. As antonym, integrity was suggested to me by a blossoming peach branch—a drawing by Hsieh Ho—reproduced above a *New York Times Book Review* notice of *The Mustard Seed Garden Manual of Painting* formulated about 500 A.D.—translated and edited by Miss Mai-mai Sze, published by the Bollingen Foundation in 1956 and as a Modern Library paperback in 1959. The plum branch led me to *The Tao of Painting*, of which "The Mustard Seed Garden" is a part, the (not "a") Tao being a way of life, a "oneness" that is tireless; whereas egotism, synonymous with ignorance in Buddhist thinking, is tedious. And the Tao led me to the dragon in the classification of primary symbols, "symbol of the power of heaven"—changing at will to the size of a silkworm; or swelling to the totality of heaven and earth;[2] at will invisible, made personal by a friend at a party—an authority on gems, finance, painting, and music—who exclaimed obligingly, as I concluded a digression on cranes, peaches, bats, and butterflies as symbols of long life and happiness, "O to be a dragon!" (The exclamation, lost sight of for a time, was appropriated as a title later.)

Verse: "Why the many quotation marks?" I am asked. Pardon my saying more than once, When a thing has been said so well that it could not be said better, why paraphrase it? Hence my writing is, if not a cabinet of fossils, a kind of collection of flies in amber.

More than once after a reading, I have been asked with circumspectly hesitant delicacy, "Your . . . poem, 'Marriage'; would you care to . . . make a statement about it?" Gladly. The thing (I would hardly call it a poem) is no philosophic precipitate; nor does it veil anything personal in the way of triumphs, entrapments, or dangerous colloquies. It is a little anthology of statements that took my fancy—phrasings that I liked.

Rhythm: The clue to it all (for me originally)—something built-in as in music.

No man may him hyde
From Deth holow-eyed.[3]

I dislike the reversed order of words; don't like to be impeded by an unnecessary capital at the beginning of every line; I don't like, here, the meaning; the cadence coming close to being the sole reason for all that follows, the accent on "holow" rather than on "eyed," so firmly placed that the most willful reader cannot misplace it. "A fig for thee, O Death!"[4]—meaning the opposite—has for me the same fascination. Appoggiaturas—a charmed subject. A study of trills can be absorbing to the exclusion of everything else—"the open, over-lapping, regular. . . ." A London *Times Literary Supplement* reviewer (perforce anonymous), reviewing *The Interpretation of Bach's Keyboard Works* by Erwin Bodky (Oxford University Press) on April 7, 1961, says, "phrasing is rarely marked by Bach . . . except as a warning that something abnormal is intended"—a remark which has a bearing, for prose and verse, on the matter of "ease" alluded to earlier. I like straight writing, end-stopped lines, an effect

---

2. The dragon as lord of space makes relevant Miss Mai-mai Sze's emphasis on "space as China's chief contribution to painting; the essential part of the wheel being the inner space between its spokes; the space in a room, its usefulness" in keeping with the Manual: "a crowded ill-arranged composition is one of the Twelve Faults of Paint-

ing"; as a man "if he had eyes all over his body, would be a monstrosity" [Moore's note].

3. From John Skelton's "Upon a Dead Man's Head" (1557).

4. A poem by Edward Taylor (written ca. 1700; published 1960).

of flowing continuity, and after 1929—perhaps earlier—wrote no verse that did not (in my opinion) rhyme. *However,* when a friendly, businesslike, shrewd, valiant government official in a broadcast summarizes me in handsome style—a man who feels that in writing as in conduct I distinguish between liberty and license, agrees with me that punctuation and syntax have a bearing on meaning, and looks at human weakness to determine the possibilities of strength—when he says in conclusion, "She writes in free verse," I am not irascible.

Why an inordinate interest in animals and athletes? They are subjects for art and exemplars of it, are they not? minding their own business. Pangolins, hornbills, pitchers, catchers, do not pry or prey—or prolong the conversation; do not make us selfconscious; look their best when caring least; although in a Frank Buck documentary I saw a leopard insult a crocodile (basking on a river bank—head only visible on the bank)—bat the animal on the nose and continue on its way without so much as a look back. Perhaps I really don't know. I do know that I don't know how to account for a person who could be indifferent to miracles of dexterity, a certain feat by Don Zimmer—a Dodger at the time—making a backhand catch, of a ball coming hard from behind on the left, fast enough to take his hand off. "The fabric of existence weaves itself whole," as Charles Ives said (*Time,* August 22, 1960). "You cannot set art off in a corner and hope for it to have vitality, reality, and substance. My work in music helped my business [insurance] and my work in business helped my music."

I am deplored "for extolling President Eisenhower for the very reasons for which I should reprehend him." Attacked for vetoing the Farm Bill—April 1956—he said, "To produce more crops when we need less, squandering resources on what we cannot eat or sell . . . would it solve the problem? Is it in the best interests of all?" Anything reprehensible in that? While visiting Mr. Macmillan[5]—London, May 6, 1959—he said, "Our strength is in dedication to freedom; . . . if we are sufficiently dedicated, we will discipline ourselves to make the sacrifices to do what needs to be done." He was not speaking to political aesthetes but to those who do not wish to join theorists in Suzanne Labin's *The Anthill:*[6] those who farmed and were starved; the worker who was "overworked and underpaid"; thinkers who were "forced to lie"—a confederation in which "all were terrified" (*New York Herald Tribune,* December 25, 1960). "I think I might call you a moralist," the inquirer began, "or do you object?" "No," I said, "I think perhaps I am. I do not thrust promises or deeds of mercy right and left to write a lyric—if what I write ever is one"—a qualification received with smiles by a specialist (or proseur turned poseur)—(leopard and crocodile). "Poetry must not be drawn by the ears,"[7] Sidney says; in either the writing or the reading. T. S. Eliot is convinced that the work of contemporary poets should be read by students for enjoyment, not for credits; not taught formally but out of enthusiasm—with the classics as criterion (*New York Times,* December 30, 1960—printed a year earlier in Chicago). He is right about it, I think.

5. Harold Macmillan, then prime minister of Great Britain.
6. Labin's *The Anthill: The Human Condition in* *Communist China* (1960).
7. From Philip Sidney's *The Defense of Poesy* (1595).

Prosody is a tool; poetry is "a maze, a trap, a web"—Professor Richards' epitome—and the quarry is captured in his own lines, "Not No" (in *Goodbye Earth*).[8]

> *Not mine this life that must be lived in me.*
>
> Inside as out Another's: let it be.
> Ha, Skater on the Brink!
>   Come whence,
>   Where go?
>
> Anywhere
>   Elsewhere
>   Where I would not know
> *Not mine, not mine, all this lived through in me.*
>
> Who asks? Who answers? What ventriloquy!

My favorite poem? asked not too aggressively—perhaps recalling that Henry James could not name his "favorite letter of the alphabet or wave of the sea." The Book of Job, I have sometimes thought—for the verity of its agony and a fidelity that contrives glory for ashes. I do not deplore it that Sir Francis Bacon was often scathing, since he said, "By far the greatest obstacle . . . to advancement of anything is despair."[9] Prizing Henry James, I take his worries for the most part with detachment; those of William James to myself when he says, "man's chief difference from the brutes lies in the exuberant excess of his subjective propensities. Prune his extravagance, sober him, and you undo him."[1]

1961

---

8. Published in 1958. I. A. Richards was a prominent literary theorist.
9. From Bacon's *The New Organon* (1620).

1. From William James's "Reflex Action and Theism" (1897).

SYLVIA PLATH
1932–1963

Since her suicide in 1963, the tumultuous story of Sylvia Plath's life has become the stuff of myth and movie. In particular, biographers, critics, novelists, and filmmakers have focused on the vicissitudes of her marriage to the darkly handsome Ted Hughes—who was eventually to become England's poet laureate—together with the marital breakup that seemingly led to the icy February night when Plath put her head in the oven of the London flat where she was living alone with her one-year-old son and three-year-old daughter. This troubled young woman had in her late poems become, thought her former teacher Robert Lowell, "one of those super-real, hypnotic, great classical heroines." Yet she was not only a highly ambitious professional writer but also an accomplished scholar and a sophisticated thinker. Keenly conscious of the magnitude of her achievement in the work she was to leave behind, she wrote to her mother that "I am a writer. . . . I am a genius of a writer. . . . I am writing the best poems of my life; they will make my name." And indeed her self-assessment was correct: the manuscript that eventually became the posthumously published *Ariel* (1963) did ensure her place as a major twentieth-century artist.

Born and raised in Massachusetts, Plath was the daughter of highly educated German immigrants. Her father, Otto Plath, was a Boston University entomologist who specialized in bees and her mother, Aurelia, was a teacher of shorthand and typing at the same institution. But Otto's death from a gangrenous leg when Sylvia was only eight marked and marred her childhood, becoming a central event that she herself mythologized in "The Colossus," "Daddy," and other poems, while her ambivalent relationship with her widowed mother also inspired a number of key verses, among them "Medusa" and "The Disquieting Muses."

Such self-mythologizings were shaped not only by a keen self-awareness but also by a highly developed literary sensibility. A *summa cum laude* graduate of Smith, Plath worked as a guest editor of *Mademoiselle*—an experience she fictionalized in her novel *The Bell Jar* (1963)—and she later spent two years on a Fulbright Fellowship at Cambridge University, where she met and married Hughes. At Smith she had produced a senior thesis on the double in the novels of Dostoyevsky, and after receiving her degree from Cambridge she and her husband returned to the States, where she taught English for a year at her alma mater and later enrolled in verse-writing workshops with Robert Lowell at Boston University.

Although Plath admitted that "my poems immediately come out of the sensuous and emotional experiences I have," she once noted to an interviewer that "I cannot sympathize with these cries from the heart that are informed by nothing except a needle or a knife, or whatever it is," adding, in statements that reflect her conscious mastery of her craft: "I believe that one should be able to manipulate these experiences with an informed and intelligent mind" and that such experiences should be "relevant" to "bigger things," such as "Hiroshima and Dachau." "Context," which consists of Plath's responses to a questionnaire that the *London Magazine* sent to a number of poets in the winter of 1962, similarly demonstrates her awareness of the skill required to dramatize large political and metaphysical issues by focusing on apparently "smaller" domestic observations. At the same time, this set of brief comments also reveals her powerful and empowering commitment to her art, as she confesses that "Certain poems and lines of poetry seem as solid and miraculous to me as church altars or the coronation of queens must seem to people who revere quite different images."

Context

The issues of our time which preoccupy me at the moment are the incalculable genetic effects of fallout and a documentary article on the terrifying, mad, omnipotent marriage of big business and the military in America—"Juggernaut, The Warfare State," by Fred J. Cook in a recent *Nation*. Does this influence the kind of poetry I write? Yes, but in a sidelong fashion. I am not gifted with the tongue of Jeremiah, though I may be sleepless enough before my vision of the apocalypse. My poems do not turn out to be about Hiroshima, but about a child forming itself finger by finger in the dark. They are not about the terrors of mass extinction, but about the bleakness of the moon over a yew tree in a neighboring graveyard. Not about the testaments of tortured Algerians, but about the night thoughts of a tired surgeon.

In a sense, these poems are deflections. I do not think they are an escape. For me, the real issues of our time are the issues of every time—the hurt and wonder of loving; making in all its forms—children, loaves of bread, paint-ings, buildings; and the conservation of life of all people in all places, the jeopardizing of which no abstract doubletalk of "peace" or "implacable foes" can excuse.

I do not think a "headline poetry" would interest more people any more profoundly than the headlines. And unless the up-to-the-minute poem grows out of something closer to the bone than a general, shifting philanthropy and is, indeed, that unicorn-thing—a real poem—it is in danger of being screwed up as rapidly as the news sheet itself.

The poets I delight in are possessed by their poems as by the rhythms of their own breathing. Their finest poems seem born all-of-a-piece, not put together by hand; certain poems in Robert Lowell's *Life Studies*, for instance; Theodore Roethke's greenhouse poems; some of Elizabeth Bishop and a very great deal of Stevie Smith ("Art is wild as a cat and quite separate from civi-lization").

Surely the great use of poetry is its pleasure—not its influence as reli-gious or political propaganda. Certain poems and lines of poetry seem as solid and miraculous to me as church altars or the coronation of queens must seem to people who revere quite different images. I am not worried that poems reach relatively few people. As it is, they go surprisingly far—among strangers, around the world, even. Farther than the words of a class-room teacher or the prescriptions of a doctor; if they are very lucky, farther than a lifetime.

1962

TILLIE OLSEN
1913–2007

"We [women] who write are survivors, 'only's,' "declared Tillie Olsen in her influen-tial essay "One out of Twelve: Women Who Are Writers in Our Century" (1972), a piece that we reprint here in its entirety. Like Adrienne Rich, Olsen was one of the key figures in the 1970s revival of feminism known as the "second wave"; and while she incisively theorized the dilemmas faced by all ambitious literary women, she spoke with special eloquence about the cultural marginalization and dispossession confronted by working-class women with creative aspirations. She herself, she explained, had faced such obstacles. As she noted in "Silences" (1962), another of her classic essays, "In the twenty years I bore and reared my children, usually had to work on a paid job as well, the simplest circumstances for creation did not exist"; thus, she felt repeatedly driven to explore the "relationship of circumstances—including class, color, sex"—to "the unnatural thwarting of what struggles to come into being."

Born in Nebraska, Olsen dropped out of high school to enter the world of every-day jobs but also began early to work for political causes and to write fiction, includ-ing a novel, *Yonnondio,* that wasn't completed and published until she produced a "rewoven" version of it in 1974. Married in 1943 to Jack Olsen, a printer and labor movement activist, she bore and raised four children, whose care and support—as she explains in "Silences"—consumed so much of her time that she wasn't able to resume her literary career until the 1950s. Then she produced the four stories that were collected in her brilliant volume *Tell Me a Riddle* (1961).

But the years of silence had taken their toll, and although Olsen continued to read, write, and meditate, she devoted herself in later life primarily to critical writing and to an ongoing effort to "re-dedicate and encourage" other women in their struggles against the "unnatural thwarting" of the creative impulse. Her distinguished critical volume *Silences* (1978) includes not only her groundbreaking essays but scrupulous documentations of her reading on the subjects they address.

One Out of Twelve: Writers Who Are Women in Our Century

> An unwritten talk, spoken from notes in 1971 at the Modern Language Association Forum on Women Writers in the Twentieth Century. In this reconstituted, edited form, it appeared in the "Women Writing, Women Teaching" issue of *College English*, October 1972.
>
> Happily, some of what follows is by now, in varying degrees, familiar. It was only beginning to be so in 1971. The tone, markedly different from that of "Silences," is distinctly of that year of cumulative discovery.
>
> The content was conditioned somewhat by its being addressed to college teachers of literature. A few quotations from "Silences,"[1] then unavoidable, herein repetitious, are kept intact.

It is the women's movement, part of the other movements of our time for a fully human life, that has brought this forum into being; kindling a renewed, in most instances a first-time, interest in the writings and writers of our sex.

Linked with the old, resurrected classics on women, this movement in three years has accumulated a vast new mass of testimony, of new comprehensions as to what it is to be female. Inequities, restrictions, penalties, denials, leechings have been painstakingly and painfully documented; damaging differences in circumstances and treatment from that of males attested to; and limitations, harms, a sense of wrong, voiced.

It is in the light and dark of this testimony that I examine my subject today: the lives and work of writers, women, in our century (though I speak primarily of those writing in the English language—and in prose).[2]

Compared to the countless centuries of the silence of women, compared to the century preceding ours—the first in which women wrote in any noticeable numbers—ours has been a favorable one.

The road was cut many years ago, as Virginia Woolf reminds us:

> by Fanny Burney, by Aphra Behn, by Harriet Martineau, by Jane Austen, by George Eliot, many famous women and many more unknown and forgotten. . . . Thus, when I came to write . . . writing was a reputable and harmless occupation.[3]

Predecessors, ancestors, a body of literature, an acceptance of the right to write: each in themselves an advantage.

In this second century we have access to areas of work and of life experience previously denied; higher education; longer, stronger lives; for the first

---

1. The text used here is from Olsen's 1978 collection, *Silences* [except as indicated, all subsequent notes are Olsen's].

2. This is the poorer for such limitation.
3. Woolf, "Professions for Women" (1942) [editor's note].

time in human history, freedom from compulsory childbearing; freer bodies and attitudes toward sexuality; a beginning of technological easing of household tasks; and—of the greatest importance to those like myself who come from generations of illiterate women—increasing literacy, and higher degrees of it. *Each one of these a vast gain.*[4]

And the results?

Productivity: books of all manner and kind. My own crude sampling, having to be made without benefit of research assistants, secretary, studies (nobody's made them), or computer (to feed the entire *Books in Print* and *Contemporary Authors* into, for instance) indicates that at present four to five books are published by men to every one by a woman.[5]

Comparative earnings: no authoritative figures available.

Achievement: as gauged by what supposedly designates it: appearance in twentieth-century literature courses, required reading lists, textbooks, quality anthologies, the year's best, the decade's best, the fifty years' best, consideration by critics or in current reviews—*one woman writer for every twelve men* (8 percent women, 92 percent men). For a week or two, make your own survey whenever you pick up an anthology, course bibliography, quality magazine or quarterly, book review section, book of criticism.

What weights my figures so heavily toward the one-out-of-twelve ratio are twentieth-century literature course offerings, and writers decreed worthy of critical attention in books and articles. Otherwise my percentage figures would have come closer to one out of seven.

But it would not matter if the ratio had been one out of six or five. Any figure but one to one would insist on query: Why? What, not true for men but only for women, makes this enormous difference? (Thus, class—economic circumstance—and color, those other traditional silencers of humanity, can be relevant only in the special ways that they affect the half of their numbers who are women.)

Why are so many more women silenced than men? Why, when women do write (one out of four or five works published) is so little of their writing known, taught, accorded recognition? What is the nature of the critical judgments made throughout that (along with the factors different in women's lives) steadily reduce the ratio from one out of three in anthologies of student work, to one out of seventeen in course offerings.

This talk, originally intended to center on the writing, the achievement of women writers in our century, became instead these queryings. Yet—in a way sadder, angrier, prouder—it still centers on the writing, the achievement.[6]

One woman writer of achievement for every twelve men writers so ranked. Is this proof again—and in this so much more favorable century—of women's innately inferior capacity for creative achievement?

Only a few months ago (June 1971), during a Radcliffe sponsored panel on "Women's Liberation, Myth or Reality," Diana Trilling, asking why it is that women

4. These are measured phrases, enormously compressed. Each asks an entire book or books, to indicate its enabling relationship to literature written by women in this century—including the very numbers of women enabled to write.
5. Richard Altick in his "Sociology of Authorship" [1962] found the proportion of women writers to men writers in Britain a fairly constant one for the years 1800 to 1935: 20 percent. This was based on books published, not on recognized achievement.
6. Added to text, 1976.

have not made even a fraction of the intellectual, scientific or artistic-cultural contributions which men have made

came again to the traditional conclusion that

> it is not enough to blame women's place in culture or culture itself, because that leaves certain fundamental questions unanswered . . . necessarily raises the question of the biological aspects of the problem.

Biology: that difference.[7] Evidently unknown to or dismissed by her and the others who share her conclusion, are the centuries of prehistory during which biology did not deny equal contribution; and *the other determining difference—not* biology—between male and female in the centuries after; the *differing past of women*—that should be part of every human consciousness, certainly every woman's consciousness (in the way that the 400 years of bondage, colonialism, the slave passage, are to black humans).

Work first:

> Within our bodies we bore the race. Through us it was shaped, fed and clothed. . . . Labour more toilsome and unending than that of man was ours. . . . No work was too hard, no labour too strenuous to exclude us.[8]

True for most women in most of the world still.

Unclean; taboo. The Devil's Gateway. The three steps behind; the girl babies drowned in the river; the baby strapped to the back. Buried alive with the lord, burned alive on the funeral pyre, burned as witch at the stake. Stoned to death for adultery. Beaten, raped. Bartered. Bought and sold. Concubinage, prostitution, white slavery. The hunt, the sexual prey, "I am a lost creature, O the poor Clarissa." Purdah, the veil of Islam, domestic confinement. Illiterate. Denied vision. Excluded, excluded, excluded from council, ritual, activity, learning, language, when there was neither biological nor economic reason to be excluded.

Religion, when all believed. In sorrow shalt thou bring forth children. May thy wife's womb never cease from bearing. Neither was the man created for the woman but the woman for the man. Let the woman learn in silence and in all subjection. Contrary to biological birth fact: Adam's rib. The Jewish male morning prayer: thank God I was not born a woman. Silence in holy places, seated apart, or not permitted entrance at all; castration of boys because women too profane to sing in church.

And for the comparative handful of women born into the privileged class; being, not doing; man does, woman is; to you the world says work, to us it says seem. God is thy law, thou mine. Isolated. Cabin'd, cribb'd, confin'd; the private sphere. Bound feet: corseted, cosseted, bedecked; denied one's body. Powerlessness. Fear of rape, male strength. Fear of aging. Subject to. Fear of expressing capacities. Soft attractive graces; the mirror to magnify man. Marriage as property arrangement. The vices of slaves:[9] dissembling, flattering, manipulating, appeasing.

Bolstering. Vicarious living, infantilization, trivialization. Parasitism, indi-

---

7. Biologically, too, the change for women now is enormous: life expectancy (USA) seventy-eight years—as contrasted with forty-eight years in 1900. Near forty-eight years of life before and after one is "a woman," that is: "capable of conceiving and bearing young." (And childbearing more and more voluntary.)

8. Olive Schreiner, *Women and Labour* [1911].
9. Elizabeth Barrett Browning's phrase; other phrases throughout from the Bible, John Milton, Richardson's *Clarissa*, Matthew Arnold, Elizabeth Cady Stanton, Virginia Woolf, Viola Klein, Mountain Wolf Woman.

vidualism, madness. Shut up, you're only a girl. O Elizabeth, why couldn't you have been born a boy? For twentieth-century woman: roles, discontinuities, part-self, part-time; conflict; imposed "guilt"; "a man can give full energy to his profession, a woman cannot."

How is it that women have not made a fraction of the intellectual, scientific, or artistic-cultural contributions that men have made?

Only in the context of this punitive difference in circumstance, in history, between the sexes; this past, hidden or evident, that (though objectively obsolete—yes, even the toil and the compulsory childbearing obsolete) *continues so terribly, so determiningly to live on, only in this context can the question be answered or my subject here today—the women writer in our century: one out of twelve—be understood.*

How much it takes to become a writer. Bent (far more common than we assume), circumstances, time, development of craft—but beyond that: how much conviction as to the importance of what one has to say, one's right to say it. And the will, the measureless store of belief in oneself to be able to come to, cleave to, find the form for one's own life comprehensions. Difficult for any male not born into a class that breeds such confidence. Almost impossible for a girl, a woman.

The leeching of belief, of will, the damaging of capacity begin so early. Sparse indeed is the literature on the way of denial to small girl children of the development of their endowment as born human: active, vigorous bodies; exercise of the power to do, to make, to investigate, to invent, to conquer obstacles, to resist violations of the self; to think, create, choose; to attain community, confidence in self. Little has been written on the harms of instilling constant concern with appearance; the need to please, to support; the training in acceptance, deferring. Little has been added in our century to George Eliot's *The Mill on the Floss* on the effect of the differing treatment— "climate of expectation"—for boys and for girls.

But it is there if one knows how to read for it, and indelibly there in the resulting damage. One—out of twelve.

In the vulnerable girl years, unlike their sisters in the previous century, women writers go to college.[1] The kind of experience it may be for them is stunningly documented in Elaine Showalter's pioneering "Women and the Literary Curriculum."[2] Freshman texts in which women have little place, if at all; language itself, all achievement, anything to do with the human in male terms—*Man in Crises, The Individual and His World.* Three hundred thirteen male writers taught; seventeen women writers: That classic of adolescent rebellion, *A Portrait of the Artist as a Young Man;* and sagas (male) of the quest for identity (but then Erikson, the father of the concept, propounds that identity concerns girls only insofar as making themselves into attractive beings for the right kind of man).[3]

1. True almost without exception among the writers who are women in *Twentieth Century Authors* and *Contemporary Authors.*

2. *College English,* May 1971. A year later (October 1972), *College English* published an extensive report, "Freshman Textbooks," by Jean Mullens. In the 112 most used texts, she found 92.47 percent (5,795) of the selections were by men; 7.53 percent (472) by women (One Out of Twelve). Mullens deepened Showalter's insights as to the subtly undermining effect on freshman students of the texts' contents and language, as well as the minuscule proportion of women writers.

3. In keeping with his 1950s–60s thesis of a distinctly female "biological, evolutionary need to fulfil self through serving others."

Most, *not all*, of the predominantly male literature studied, written by men whose understandings are not universal, but restrictively male (as Mary Ellmann, Kate Millett, and Dolores Schmidt have pointed out); in our time more and more surface, hostile, one-dimensional in portraying women.

In a writer's young years, susceptibility to the vision and style of the great is extreme. Add the aspiration-denying implication, consciously felt or not (although reinforced daily by one's professors and reading) that (as Virginia Woolf noted years ago) women writers, women's experience, and literature written by women are by definition minor. (Mailer will not grant even the minor: "the one thing a writer has to have is balls.") No wonder that Showalter observes:

> Women [students] are estranged from their own experience and unable to perceive its shape and authenticity, in part because they do not see it mirrored and given resonance in literature. . . . They are expected to identify with masculine experience, which is presented as the human one, and have no faith in the validity of their own perceptions and experiences, rarely seeing them confirmed in literature, or accepted in criticism . . . [They] notoriously lack the happy confidence, the exuberant sense of the value of their individual observations which enables young men to risk making fools of themselves for the sake of an idea.

Harms difficult to work through. Nevertheless, some young women (others are already lost) maintain their ardent intention to write—fed indeed by the very glories of some of this literature that puts them down.

But other invisible worms are finding out the bed of crimson joy.[4] Self-doubt; seriousness, also questioned by the hours agonizing over appearance; concentration shredded into attracting, being attractive; the absorbing real need and love for working with words felt as hypocritical self-delusion ("I'm not truly dedicated"), for what seems (and is) esteemed is being attractive to men. High aim, and accomplishment toward it, discounted by the prevalent attitude that, as girls will probably marry (attitudes not applied to boys who will probably marry), writing is no more than an attainment of a dowry to be spent later according the needs and circumstances within the true vocation: husband and family. The growing acceptance that going on will threaten other needs, to love and be loved; ("a woman has to sacrifice all claims to femininity and family to be a writer").[5]

And the agony—peculiarly mid-century, escaped by their sisters of pre-Freudian, pre-Jungian times—that "creation and femininity are incompatible."[6] Anaïs Nin's words.

> The aggressive act of creation; the guilt for creating. I did not want to rival man; to steal man's creation, his thunder. I must protect them, not outshine them.[7]

The acceptance—against one's experienced reality—of the sexist notion that the act of creation is not as inherently natural to a woman as to a man, but rooted instead in unnatural aggression, rivalry, envy, or thwarted sexuality.

---

4. O Rose thou art sick./The invisible worm,
   That flies in the night/In the howling storm:

   Has found out thy bed/Of crimson joy:
   And his dark secret love/Does thy life destroy.

   —William Blake

5. Plath. A letter when a graduate student.
6. *The Diary of Anaïs Nin*, Vol. III, 1939–1944.
7. A statement that would have baffled Austen, the Brontës, Mrs. Gaskell, Eliot, Stowe, Alcott, etc. The strictures were felt by them in other ways.

And in all the usual college teaching—the English, history, psychology, sociology courses—little to help that young woman understand the source or nature of this inexplicable draining self-doubt, loss of aspiration, of confidence.

It is all there in the extreme in Plath's *Bell Jar*—that (inadequate)[8] portrait of the artist as young woman (significantly, one of the few that we have)— from the precarious sense of vocation to the paralyzing conviction that (in a sense different from what she wrote years later)

> Perfection is terrible. It cannot have children.
> It tamps the womb.[9]

And indeed, in our century as in the last, until very recently almost all distinguished achievement has come from childless women: Willa Cather, Ellen Glasgow, Gertrude Stein, Edith Wharton, Virginia Woolf, Elizabeth Bowen, Katherine Mansfield, Isak Dinesen, Katherine Anne Porter, Dorothy Richardson, Henry Handel Richardson, Susan Glaspell, Dorothy Parker, Lillian Hellman, Eudora Welty, Djuna Barnes, Anaïs Nin, Ivy Compton-Burnett, Zora Neale Hurston, Elizabeth Madox Roberts, Christina Stead, Carson McCullers, Flannery O'Connor, Jean Stafford, May Sarton, Josephine Herbst, Jessamyn West, Janet Frame, Lillian Smith, Iris Murdoch, Joyce Carol Oates, Hannah Green, Lorraine Hansberry.

Most never questioned, or at least accepted (a few sanctified) this different condition for achievement, not imposed on men writers. Few asked the fundamental human equality question regarding it that Elizabeth Mann Borghese, Thomas Mann's daughter, asked when she was eighteen and sent to a psychiatrist for help in getting over an unhappy love affair (revealing also a working ambition to become a great musician although "women cannot be great musicians"). "You must choose between your art and fulfillment as a woman," the analyst told her, "between music and family life." "Why?" she asked. "Why must I choose? No one said to Toscanini or to Bach or my father that they must choose between their art and personal, family life; fulfillment as a man. . . . Injustice everywhere." Not where it is free choice. But where it is forced because of the circumstances for the sex into which one is born— a choice men of the same class do not have to make in order to do their work—that is not choice, that is a coercive working of sexist oppression.[1]

What possible difference, you may ask, does it make to literature whether or not a woman writer remains childless—free choice or not—especially in view of the marvels these childless women have created.

Might there not have been other marvels as well, or other dimensions to these marvels? Might there not have been present profound aspects and understandings of human life as yet largely absent in literature?

More and more women writers in our century, primarily in the last two decades, are assuming as their right fullness of work *and* family life.[2] Their

8. Inadequate, for the writer-being ("muteness is sickness for me") is not portrayed. By contrast, how present she is in Plath's own *Letters Home*.

9. Plath, "The Munich Mannequins" (1965) [editor's note].

1. "Them lady poets must not marry, pal," is how John Berryman, poet (himself oft married) expressed it. The old patriarchal injunction: "Woman, this is man's realm. If you insist on invading it, unsex yourself—and expect the road to be made difficult." Furthermore, this very unmarriedness and childlessness has been used to discredit women as unfulfilled, inadequate, somehow abnormal.

2. Among those with children: Harriette Arnow, Mary Lavin, Mary McCarthy, Tess Slesinger, Eleanor Clark, Nancy Hale, Storm Jameson, Janet Lewis, Jean Rhys, Kay Boyle, Ann Petry, Dawn Powell, Meridel LeSueur, Evelyn Eaton, Dorothy Canfield Fisher, Pearl Buck, Josephine Johnson,

emergence is evidence of changing circumstances making possible for them what (with rarest exception) was not possible in the generations of women before. I hope and I fear for what will result. I hope (and believe) that complex new richness will come into literature; I fear because almost certainly their work will be impeded, lessened, partial. For the fundamental situation remains unchanged. Unlike men writers who marry, most will not have the societal equivalent of a wife—nor (in a society hostile to growing life) anyone but themselves to mother their children. Even those who can afford help, good schools, summer camps, may *(may)* suffer what seventy years ago W. E. B. Du Bois called "The Damnation of Women": "that only at the sacrifice of the chance to do their best work can women bear and rear children."[3]

> Substantial creative achievement demands time . . . and with rare exceptions only full-time workers have created it.[4]

I am quoting myself from "Silences," a talk nine years ago. In motherhood, as it is structured,

> circumstances for sustained creation are almost impossible. Not because the capacities to create no longer exist, or the need (though for a while as in any fullness of life the need may be obscured), but . . . the need cannot be first. It can have at best only part self, part time . . . Motherhood means being instantly interruptible, responsive, responsible. Children need one *now* (and remember, in our society, the family must often try to be the center for love and health the outside world is not). The very fact that these are needs of love, not duty, that one feels them as one's self; *that there is no one else to be responsible for these needs,* gives them primacy. It is distraction, not meditation, that becomes habitual; interruption, not continuity; spasmodic, not constant, toil. Work interrupted, deferred, postponed makes blockage—at best, lesser accomplishment. Unused capacities atrophy, cease to be.

There are other vulnerabilities to loss, diminishment. Most women writers (being women) have had bred into them the "infinite capacity"; what Virginia Woolf named (after the heroine of a famous Victorian poem) *The Angel in the House*, who "must charm . . . sympathize . . . flatter . . . conciliate . . . be extremely sensitive to the needs and moods and wishes of others before her own . . . excel in the difficult arts of family life . . ."

Caroline Gordon, Shirley Jackson; and a sampling in the unparalleled last two decades: Doris Lessing, Nadine Gordimer, Margaret Laurence, Grace Paley, Hortense Calisher, Edna O'Brien, Sylvia Ashton-Warner, Pauli Murray, Françoise Mallet-Joris, Cynthia Ozick, Joanne Greenberg, Joan Didion, Penelope Mortimer, Alison Lurie, Hope Hale Davis, Doris Betts, Muriel Spark, Adele Wiseman, Lael Wertenbaker, Shirley Ann Grau, Maxine Kumin, Margaret Walker, Gina Barriault, Mary Gray Hughes, Maureen Howard, Norma Rosen, Lore Segal, Alice Walker, Nancy Willard, Charlotte Painter, Sallie Bingham. (I would now add Clarice Lispector, Ruth Prawer Jhabvala, June Arnold, Ursula Le Guin, Diane Johnson, Alice Munro, Helen Yglesias, Susan Cahill, Rosellen Brown, Alta, and Susan Griffin.) Some wrote before children, some only in the middle or later years. Not many have directly used the material open to them

out of motherhood as central source for their work.
3. *Darkwater: Voices from Within the Veil* [1920].
4. This does not mean that these full-time writers were hermetic or denied themselves social or personal life (think of James, Turgenev, Tolstoy, Balzac, Joyce, Gide, Colette, Yeats, Woolf, etc. etc.); nor did they, except perhaps at the flood, put in as many hours daily as those doing more usual kinds of work. Three to six hours daily have been the norm ("the quiet, patient, generous mornings will bring it"). Zola and Trollope are famous last-century examples of the four hours; the *Paris Review* interviews disclose many contemporary ones.

Full-timeness consists not in the actual number of hours at one's desk, but in that writing is one's major profession, practiced habitually, in freed, protected, undistracted time as needed, when it is needed.

It was she who used to come between me and my paper . . . who bothered me and wasted my time and so tormented me that at last I killed her . . . or she would have plucked out my heart as a writer.[5]

There is another angel, so lowly as to be invisible, although without her no art, or any human endeavor, could be carried on for even one day—the essential angel, with whom Virginia Woolf (and most women writers, still in the privileged class) did not have to contend—the angel who must assume the physical responsibilities for daily living, for the maintenance of life.

Almost always in one form or another (usually in the wife, two-angel form) she has dwelt in the house of men. She it was who made it possible for Joseph Conrad to "wrestle with the Lord for his creation":

Mind and will and conscience engaged to the full, hour after hour, day after day . . . never aware of the even flow of daily life made easy and noiseless for me by a silent, watchful, tireless affection.[6]

The angel who was "essential" to Rilke's "great task":

like a sister who would run the house like a friendly climate, there or not there as one wished . . . and would ask for nothing except just to be there working and warding at the frontiers of the invisible.

Men (even part-time writers who must carry on work other than writing[7]) have had and have this inestimable advantage toward productivity. I cannot help but notice how curiously absent both of these angels, these watchers and warders at the frontiers of the invisible, are from the actual contents of most men's books, except perhaps on the dedication page:

To my wife, without whom . . .

I digress, and yet I do not; the disregard for the essential angel, the large absence of any sense of her in literature or elsewhere, has not only cost literature great contributions from those so occupied or partially occupied, but by failing to help create an arousing awareness (as literature has done in other realms) has contributed to the agonizingly slow elimination of this technologically and socially obsolete, human-wasting drudgery: Virginia Woolf's dream of a long since possible "economical, powerful and efficient future when houses will be cleaned by a puff of hot wind."[8]

Sometimes the essential angel is present in women's books,[9] though still most "heroines are in white dresses that never need washing" (Rebecca Harding Davis's phrase of a hundred years ago). Some poets admit her as occasional domestic image; a few preen her as femininity; Sylvia Plath could escape her only by suicide:

. . . flying . . .
Over the engine that killed her—
The mausoleum, the wax house.[1]

For the first time in literary history, a woman poet of stature, accustomed through years to the habits of creation, began to live the life of most of her

---

5. *Professions for Women.*
6. Conrad, *Some Reminiscences* (1912) [editor's note].
7. As must many women writers.
8. Woolf, "Evening over Sussex: Reflections in a Motor Car" (1942) [editor's note].
9. Among them: Harriette Arnow, Willa Cather, Dorothy Canfield Fisher, H. H. Richardson (of *Ultima Thule*), Ruth Suckow, Elizabeth Madox Roberts, Sarah Wright, Agnes Smedley; Emily Dickinson, pre-eminently; Sylvia Plath, sometimes Christina Stead, Doris Lessing. (I would now add Edith Summers Kelley (*Weeds* and *The Devil's Hand*), the Marge Piercy of *Small Changes*, and my own fiction.)
1. Plath, "Stings" (1965) [editor's note].

sex: the honey drudgers: the winged unmiraculous two-angel, whirled mother-maintenance life, that most women, not privileged, know. A situation without help or husband and with twenty-four hours' responsibility for two small human lives whom she adored and at their most fascinating and demanding. The world was blood-hot and personal. Creation's needs at its height. She had to get up at

> four in the morning, that still blue almost eternal hour before the baby's cry

to write at all.[2] After the long expending day, tending, caring, cleaning, enjoying, laundering, feeding, marketing, delighting, outing; being

> a very efficient tool or weapon, used and in demand from moment to moment. . . . Nights [were] no good [for writing]. I'm so flat by then that all I can cope with is music and brandy and water.

The smog of cooking, the smog of hell floated in her head. The smile of the icebox annihilated. There was a stink of fat and baby crap; viciousness in the kitchen! And the blood jet poetry (for which there was never time and self except in that still blue hour before the baby's cry) there was no stopping it:[3]

> It is not a question in these last weeks of the conflict in a woman's life between the claims of the feminine and the agonized work of art

Elizabeth Hardwick, a woman, can say of Sylvia Plath's suicide,

> Every artist is either a man or woman, and the struggle is pretty much the same for both.[4]

A comment as insensible of the two-angel realities ("so lowly as to be invisible") as are the oblivious masculine assumptions, either that the suicide was because of Daddy's death twenty-three years before, revived and compounded by her husband's desertion; or else a real-life *Story of O* (that elegant pornography) sacramental culmination of being used up by ecstasy (poetry in place of sex this time):

> the pride of an utter and ultimate surrender, like the pride of O, naked and chained in he owl mask as she asks Sir Stephen for death. . . .[5]

If in such an examined extremity, the profound realities of woman's situation are ignored, how much less likely are they—particularly the subtler ones—to be seen, comprehended, taken into account, as they affect lesser-known women writers in more usual circumstances.

In younger years, confidence and vision leeched, aspiration reduced. In adult years, sporadic effort and unfinished work; women made "mediocre caretakers of their talent": that is, writing is not first. The angel in the house situation; probably also the essential angel, maintenance-of-life necessity; increasingly in our century, work on a paid job as well; and for more and more women writers, the whirled expending motherhood years. Is it so difficult to

---

2. In the long tradition of early rising, an hour here and there, or late-night mother-writers from Mrs. Trollope to Harriette Arnow to this very twenty-four hours—necessarily fitting in writing time in accordance with maintenance of life, and children's, needs.

3. Phrases, lines, throughout from Plath's *Ariel*, letters, BBC broadcasts.
4. Hardwick, "On Sylvia Plath," *New York Review of Books*, August 12, 1971 [editor's note].
5. Richard Howard, in *The Art of Sylvia Plath*, edited by Charles Newman.

account for the many occasional-fine-story or one-book writers; the distinguished but limited production of others (Janet Lewis, Ann Petry, for example); the years and years in getting one book done (thirty years for Margaret Walker's *Jubilee*, twenty for Marguerite Young's *Miss Macintosh My Darling*); the slowly increasing numbers of women who not until their forties, fifties, sixties, publish for the first time (Dorothy Richardson, Hortense Calisher, Theodora Kroeber, Linda Hoyer—John Updike's mother); the women who start with children's, girls' books (Maxine Kumin), some like Cid Ricketts Sumner (*Tammy*) seldom or never getting to adult fiction that would encompass their wisdom for adults; and most of all, the unsatisfactory quality of book after book that evidence the marks of part-time, part-self authorship, and to whose authors Sarah Orne Jewett's words to the part-time, part-self young Willa Cather still apply, seventy years after:

> If you don't keep and mature your force and above all have time and quiet to perfect your work, you will be writing things not much better than you did five years ago. . . . Otherwise, what might be strength is only crudeness, and what might be insight is only observation. You will write about life, but never life itself.[6]

Yes, the loss in quality, the minor work, the hidden silences, are there in woman after woman writer in our century.[7] We will never have the body of work that we were capable of producing. Blight, said Blake, never does good to a tree:

> And if a blight kill not a tree but it still bear fruit, let none say that the fruit was in consequence of the blight.[8]

As for myself, who did not publish a book until I was fifty, who raised children without household help or the help of the "technological sublime" (the atom bomb was in manufacture before the first automatic washing machine); who worked outside the house on everyday jobs as well (as nearly half of all women do now, though a woman with a paid job, except as a maid or prostitute, is still rarest of any in literature); who could not kill the essential angel (there was no one else to do her work); would not—if I could—have killed the caring part of the Woolf angel, as distant from the world of literature most of my life as literature is distant (in content too) from my world:

The years when I should have been writing, my hands and being were at other (inescapable) tasks. Now, lightened as they are, when I must do those tasks into which most of my life went, like the old mother, grandmother in my *Tell Me a Riddle* who could not make herself touch a baby, I pay a psychic cost: "the sweat beads, the long shudder begins." The habits of a lifetime when everything else had to come before writing are not easily broken, even when circumstances now often make it possible for writing to be first; habits of years—response to others, distractibility, responsibility for daily matters—stay with you, mark you, become you. The cost of "discontinuity" (that pattern still imposed on women) is such a weight of things unsaid, an

6. *Letters of Sarah Orne Jewett,* edited by Annie Fields.
7. Compared to men writers of like distinction and years of life, few women writers have had lives of unbroken productivity, or leave behind a "body of work." Early beginnings, then silence; or clogged late ones (foreground silences); long periods between books (hidden silences); characterize most of us. A Colette, Wharton, Glasgow, Millay, Lessing, Oates, are the exceptions.
8. Letter from William Blake to William Hayley (1803) [editor's note].

accumulation of material so great, that everything starts up something else in me; what should take weeks, takes me sometimes months to write; what should take months, takes years.

I speak of myself to bring here the sense of those others to whom this is in the process of happening (unnecessarily happening, for it need not, must not continue to be) and to remind us of those (I so nearly was one) who never come to writing at all.

We must not speak of women writers in our century (as we cannot speak of women in any area of recognized human achievement) without speaking also of the invisible, the as-innately-capable: the born to the wrong circumstances—diminished, excluded, foundered, silenced.

We who write are survivors, *"only's."*[9] *One-out-of-twelve.*

I must go very fast now, telescope and omit (there has already been so much telescoping and omitting), move to work, professional circumstances.

Devaluation: Still in our century, women's books of great worth suffer the death of being unknown, or at best a peculiar eclipsing, far outnumbering the similar fate of the few such books by men. I think of the writers Kate Chopin, Mary Austin, Dorothy Richardson, Henry Handel Richardson (*Ultima Thule*), Susan Glaspell (*Jury of Her Peers*), Elizabeth Madox Roberts (*Time of Man*), Janet Lewis, Ann Petry, Harriette Arnow (*The Dollmaker*), Agnes Smedley (*Daughter of Earth*), Christina Stead, Kay Boyle, Jean Rhys—every one of them absorbing, and some with the stamp of enduring.[1] Considering their acknowledged stature, how comparatively unread, untaught, are Edith Wharton, Ellen Glasgow, Elizabeth Bowen, Dorothy Parker, Gertrude Stein, Katherine Mansfield—even Virginia Woolf, Willa Cather, and Katherine Anne Porter.[2]

Critical attitudes: Two centuries later, still what Cynthia Ozick calls "the *perpetual* dancing dog phenomena,"[3] the injurious reacting to a book, not for its quality or content, but on the basis of its having been written by a woman—with consequent misreading, mistreatment.[4]

One addition to the "she writes like a man" "with masculine power" kind of "praise." Power is seldom recognized as the power it is at all, if the subject

---

9. For myself, "survivor" contains its other meaning: one who must bear witness for those who foundered; try to tell how and why it was that they, also worthy of life, did *not* survive. And pass on ways of surviving; and tell our chancy luck, our special circumstances.

"*Only's*" is an expression out of the 1950s Civil Rights time: the young Ralph Abernathy reporting to his Birmingham Church congregation on his trip up north for support:

> I go to Seattle and they tell me, "Brother, you got to meet so and so, why he's the only Negro Federal Circuit Judge in the Northwest"; I go to Chicago and they tell me, "Brother, you've got to meet so and so, why he's the only full black professor of Sociology there is"; I go to Albany and they tell me, "Brother, you *got* to meet so and so, why he's the only black senator in the state legislature . . ." [long dramatic pause] . . . WE DON'T WANT NO ONLY'S.

Only's are used to rebuke ("to be models"); to imply the unrealistic, "see, it can be done, all you

need is capacity and will." Accepting a situation of "only's" means: "let inequality of circumstance continue to prevail."

1. 1976: At least some of these writers are now coming out of eclipse. But Glaspell, Mary Austin, Roberts, and H. H. Richardson are still out of print. So is most of Christina Stead.

2. Eclipsing, devaluation, neglect, are the result of critical judgments, a predominantly male domain. The most damaging, and still prevalent, critical attitude remains "that women's experience, and literature written by women are, by definition, minor." Indeed, for a sizable percentage of male writers, critics, academics, writer-women are eliminated from consideration (consciousness) altogether. (See the one-out-of-twelve compilations beginning on page 186 [in *Silences*].)

3. "Women and Creativity," *Motive*, April 1969. ["The dancing dog": i.e., marveling that it is done at all, however badly—editor's note.]

4. Savor Mary Ellmann's inimitable *Thinking About Women*.

matter is considered woman's: it is minor, moving, evocative, instinctive, delicate. "As delicate as a surgeon's scalpel," says Katherine Anne Porter of such a falsifying description for Katherine Mansfield's art. Instinctive?

> I judge her work to have been to a great degree a matter of intelligent use of her faculties, a conscious practice of a hard won craftsmanship, a triumph of discipline. . . . [5]

Climate in literary circles for those who move in them:[6] Writers know the importance of being taken seriously, with respect for one's vision and integrity; of comradeship with other writers; of being dealt with as a writer on the basis of one's work and not for other reasons; and how chancy is recognition and getting published. There is no time to speak of this today; but nearly all writers who are women are at a disadvantage here.

Restriction: For all our freer life in this century, our significantly greater access to work, education, travel, varied experience, there is still limitation of circumstances for scope, subject, social context, the kind of comprehensions which come only in situations beyond the private. (What Charlotte Brontë felt so keenly 125 years ago as a denial of "facilities for observation . . . a knowledge of the world" which gives other writers "Thackeray, Dickens . . . an importance, variety, depth greatly beyond what I can offer.")[7] "Trespass vision" cannot substitute.

Constriction: not always recognized as constriction. The age-old coercion of women toward one dimension continues to be "terribly, determiningly" present. Women writers are still suspect as unnatural if they concern themselves with aspects of their experience, interests, being, beyond the traditionally defined women's sphere. Hortense Calisher is troubled that women writers

> straining toward a world sensibility, or one equivalent to the roaming consciences of the men . . . or dispens[ing] with whatever was clearly female in their sensibility or experience . . . flee from the image society projects on [them].[8]

But conscience and world sensibility are as natural to women as to men; men have been freer to develop and exercise them, that is all. Indeed, one of the most characteristic strains in literature written by women (however dropped out of sight, or derided) *is* conscience, concern with wrongs to human beings in their time—from the first novel in our language by a woman, Aphra Behn's *Oroonoko,* that first by anyone against slavery, through Harriet Martineau, Elizabeth Gaskell, George Sand, Harriet Beecher Stowe, Elizabeth Barrett Browning, Rebecca Harding Davis, Helen Hunt Jackson, Olive Schreiner, Ethel Voynich, Charlotte Perkins Gilman—to our own century's Gabriela Mistral, Virginia Woolf (the essays), Nelly Sachs, Anna Seghers, Rachel Carson, Lillian Hellman, Lorraine Hansberry, Theodora Kroeber (*Ishi*), Agnes Smedley, Harriette Arnow, Doris Lessing, Nadine Gordimer, Sylvia Ashton-Warner.

5. "The Art of Katherine Mansfield," *The Collected Essays of Katherine Anne Porter.*
6. See Carolyn Kizer's "Pro Femina" in her *Knock Upon Silence.*
7. Letter to her publisher, W. S. Williams, 1849.
8. "No Important Woman Writer . . . ," *Mademoiselle,* February 1970. These excerpts and my exceptions to them are not wholly fair to this superb essay, which I read originally and quoted from in a copy with an important page (unnoticed) missing. My abashed apologies to Calisher.

In contradiction to the compass of her own distinguished fiction, Calisher defines the "basic female experience from puberty on through childbed" as women's natural subject:

> For myself the feminism that comes straight from the belly, from the bed, and from childbed. A sensibility trusting itself for what it is, as the *other* half of basic life.

Constriction to the stereotypic biological-woman (breeder, sex-partner) sphere. Not only leaving out (what men writers usually leave out), ongoing motherhood, the maintenance-of-life, and other angel in the house so deter-miningly the experience of most women once they get out of bed and up from childbed, but other common female realities as well.[9]

And it leaves out the rest of women's biological endowment as born human (including the creative capacity out of which women and men write). *It was the denial of this endowment to live the whole of human life,* the confinement of woman to a sphere, that brought the Women's Rights movement into being in the last century—feminism born of humanism (and that prevented our Calishers from writing throughout centuries).

The acceptance of these age-old constrictive definitions of woman at a time when they are less true than ever to the realities of most women's lives—and need not be true at all—remains a complex problem for women writing in our time. (Mary Wollstonecraft defined it as "the consciousness of being always female which degrades our sex.")[1]

So Anaïs Nin: accepting the constriction to a "feminine sensibility that would not threaten man." Dwelling in the private, the inner; endless vibra-tions of mood; writing what was muted, exquisite, sensuous, subterranean. That is, in her fiction. In her *Diaries* (along with the narcissistic), the public, the social; power of characterization, penetrating observation, hard intellect, range of experience and relationship; different beauties. Qualities and com-plexities not present in her fiction—to its impoverishment.

The Bold New Women, to use another example (this from the title of a recent anthology), are the old stereotypic women, depicting themselves within the confines of the sexual-creature, biological-woman literary ghetto; mistaking themselves as new because the sex is explicit as in current male genre; the style and conception of female sexuality, out of Lawrence or Miller. "Whole areas of me are made by the kind of experience women haven't had before," reminds Doris Lessing. "Liberty is the right not to lie," says Camus.

These pressures toward censorship, self-censorship; toward accepting, abiding by entrenched attitudes, thus falsifying one's own reality, range, vision, truth, voice, are extreme for women writers (indeed have much to do with the fear, the sense of powerlessness that pervades certain of our books, the "above all, amuse" tone of others). Not to be able to come to one's truth or not to use it in one's writing, even in telling the truth having to "tell it

---

9. Among them: ways in which innate human drives and capacities (intellect; art; organization; invention; sense of justice; love of beauty, life; courage; resilience, resistance; need for commu-nity) denied development and scope, nevertheless struggle to express themselves and function; what goes on in jobs; penalties for aging; the profound experience of children—and the agonizing having to raise them in a world not yet fit for human life; what it is to live as a single woman; having to raise children alone; going on; causes besides the accepted psychiatric ones, of breakdown in women. The list goes on and on.

1. See Wollstonecraft, *A Vindication of the Rights of Woman* (1792), chap. 5: "This desire of being always woman, is the very consciousness that degrades the sex" [editor's note].

slant,"[2] robs one of drive, of conviction; limits potential stature; results in loss to literature and the comprehensions we seek in it.[3]

My time is up.

You who teach, read writers who are women. There is a whole literature to be re-estimated, revalued. Some works will prove to be, like the lives of their human authors, mortal—speaking only to their time. Others now forgotten, obscured, ignored, will live again for us.

Read, listen to, living women writers; our new as well as our established, often neglected ones. Not to have audience is a kind of death.

Read the compass of women writers in our infinite variety. Not only those who tell us of ourselves as "the other half," but also those who write of the other human dimensions, realms.

Teach women's lives through the lives of the women who wrote the books, as well as through the books themselves; and through autobiography, biography, journals, letters. Because most literature concerns itself with the lives of the few, know and teach the few books closer to the lives of the many. It should not be that Harriette Arnow's *The Dollmaker*, Elizabeth Madox Robert's *Time of Man*, Grace Paley's *Little Disturbances*, are out of paperback print; that a Zora Neale Hurston is reprinted for the first time; that Agnes Smedley's classic *Daughter of Earth*,[4] has been out of print, unread, unknown, for forty years—a book of the greatest meaning, too, for those many students who are the first generation of their families to come into college.

Be critical. Women have the right to say: this is surface, this falsifies reality, this degrades.

Help create writers, perhaps among them yourselves. There is so much unwritten that needs to be written. There are others besides the silenced eleven-out-of-twelve who could bring into literature what is not there now. That first generation of their families to come into college, who come from my world which (in Camus's words) gives "emotion without measure," are a special hope. It does not matter if in its beginning what emerges is not great, or even (as ordinarily defined) "good" writing.

> Whether that is literature, or whether that is not literature, I will not presume to say,

wrote Virginia Woolf in her preface to *Life As We Have Known It, Memoirs of the Working Women's Guild,*

> but that it explains much and tells much, that is certain.

The greatness of literature is not only in the great writers, the good writers; it is also in that which explains much and tells much[5] (the soil, too, of great literature).

---

2. Emily Dickinson, "Tell all the truth but tell it slant—" (written ca. 1868).
3. Compounding the difficulty is that experiences and comprehensions not previously admitted into literature—especially when at variance with the canon—are exceedingly hard to come to, validate, establish as legitimate material for literature—let alone, shape into art.
4. In 1976 these books are all back in print.
5. Lessing's description of the novel (in her afterword to Schreiner's *Story of an African Farm*) pertains to this writing which "explains much and tells

much": "com[ing] out of a part of the human consciousness which is trying to understand itself, to come into the light. Not on the level where poetry works, or music, or mathematics, the high arts; no, but on the rawest and most workaday level, like earthworms making new soil where things can grow." But there are other forms of expression which can do this, and more: the journal, letters, memoirs, personal utterances—for they come more natural for most, closer to possibility of use, of shaping—and, *in one's own words*, become source, add to the authentic store of human life,

Soil or blossom, the hope and intention is that before the end of our second writing century, we will begin to have writers who are women in numbers equal to our innate capacity—at least twelve, for every one writer-woman of recognized achievement now.[6]

1971   1972, 1978

human experience. The inestimable value of this, its emergence as a form of literature, is only beginning to be acknowledged. As yet, there is no place in literature analogous to the honored one accorded "folk" and "primitive" expression in art and in music.

6. And for every twelve enabled to come to recognized achievement, remember: there would still remain countless others still lessened or silenced—as long as the other age-old silencers of humanity, class and/or color, prevail.

CYNTHIA OZICK
b. 1928

A virtuoso short story writer, acclaimed novelist, and accomplished critic, Cynthia Ozick has meditated on a range of literary subjects in essays on Virginia Woolf, Edith Wharton, Henry James, and T. S. Eliot as well as more general topics. Born and raised in the Bronx by a pharmacist father who was also a scholar of Yiddish and a mother who was related to the Hebrew poet Abraham Regelson, Ozick graduated from NYU in 1949 and went on to earn a master's in English literature at Ohio State. There she wrote a thesis titled "Parable in the Later Novels of Henry James" and, as she later confessed in her witty "The Lesson of the Master," was so influenced by the "Master's" style that her early fiction offered, she comically declared, "an Extreme and Hideous Example of Premature Exposure to Henry James."

In 1952, Ozick married Bernard Hallote, a lawyer, with whom she settled in suburban Westchester, New York, raising a daughter and producing *Trust* (1966), the first of her many novels (and the only Jamesian one). Her experiences as a mid-twentieth-century "homemaker" who was also a serious professional writer clearly underlie her scathing "We Are the Crazy Lady and Other Feisty Feminist Fables," a comic yet deeply rebellious investigation into the dilemmas confronted by women writers in the subtly oppressive years of the "man in the gray flannel suit," his "little woman," and what Betty Friedan was to call the "problem that has no name" generated by "the feminine mystique." "Ambition," our selection here, summarizes one such dilemma with irony and verve, supporting the critic Robert Kiely's shrewd comment that "As an essayist, Cynthia Ozick is a very good storyteller."

From We Are the Crazy Lady and Other Feisty Feminist Fables

VI: Ambition

After thirteen years, I at last finished a novel. The first seven years were spent in a kind of apprenticeship—the book that came out of that time was abandoned without much regret. A second one was finished in six weeks and buried. It took six years to write the third novel, and this one was finally published.

How I lived through those years is impossible to recount in a short space. I was a recluse, a priest of Art. I read seas of books. I believed in the idea of masterpieces. I was scornful of the world of journalism, jobs, everydayness.

I did not live like any woman I knew. I lived like some men I had read about—Flaubert, or Proust, or James—the subjects of those literary biographies I endlessly drank in. I did not think of them as men, but as writers. I read the diaries of Virginia Woolf, and biographies of George Eliot, but I did not think of them as women. I thought of them as writers. I thought of myself as a writer.

It goes without saying that all this time my relatives regarded me as abnormal. I accepted this. It seemed to me, from what I had read, that most writers were abnormal. Yet on the surface, I could easily have passed for normal. The husband goes to work, the wife stays home—that is what is normal. Well, I was married. My husband went to his job every day. His job paid the rent and bought the groceries. I stayed home, reading and writing, and felt myself to be an economic parasite. To cover guilt, I joked that I had been given a grant from a very private, very poor, foundation—my husband.

But my relatives never thought of me as a parasite. The very thing I was doubtful about—my economic dependence—they considered my due as a woman. They saw me not as a failed writer without an income, but as a childless housewife, a failed woman. They did not think me abnormal because I was a writer, but because I was not properly living my life as a woman. In one respect we were in agreement utterly—my life was failing terribly, terribly. For me it was because, already deep into my thirties, I had not yet published a book. For them, it was because I had not yet borne a child.

I was a pariah, not only because I was a deviant, but because I was not recognized as the kind of deviant I meant to be. A failed woman is not the same as a failed writer. Even as a pariah I was the wrong kind of pariah.

Still, relations are only relations. What I aspired to, what I was in thrall to, was Art, was Literature, not familial contentment. I knew how to distinguish the trivial from the sublime. In Literature and in Art, I saw, my notions were not pariah notions. There, I inhabited the mainstream. So I went on reading and writing. I went on believing in Art, and my intention was to write a masterpiece. Not a saucer of well-polished craft (the sort of thing "women writers" are always accused of being accomplished at), but something huge, contemplative, Tolstoyan. My ambition was a craw.

I called the book *Trust*. I began it in the summer of 1957 and finished it in November of 1963, on the day President John Kennedy was assassinated. In manuscript, it was 801 pages divided into four parts: "America," "Europe," "Birth," and "Death." The title was meant to be ironic. In reality, it was about distrust. It seemed to me I had touched on distrust in every order or form of civilization. It seemed to me I had left nothing out. It was (though I did not know this then) a very hating book. What it hated above all was the whole—the whole—of Western Civilization. It told how America had withered into another Europe. It dreamed dark and murderous pagan dreams, and hated what it dreamed.

In style, the book was what has come to be called "mandarin": a difficult, aristocratic, unrelenting virtuoso prose. It was, in short, unreadable. I think I knew this. I was sardonic enough to say, echoing Joyce about *Finnegan's Wake*, "I expect you to spend your life at this." In any case, I had spent a decade-and-a-half of my own life at it. Though I did not imagine the world would fall asunder at its appearance, I thought—at the very least—the ambition, the all-swallowingness, the wild insatiability of the writer would be plain to everyone who read it. I had, after all, taken History for my subject: not merely History as an aggregate of events, but History as a judgment on events. No one could say my theme was flighty. Of all the novelists I read (and in those days I read them all, broiling in the envy of the unpublished, which is like no envy on earth), who else had dared so vastly?

During that period, Françoise Sagan's first novel was published.[1] I held the thin little thing and laughed. Women's pulp!

My own novel, I believed, contained everything—the whole world.

But there was one element I had consciously left out. Though on principle I did not like to characterize it or think about it much, the truth is I was thinking about it all the time. It was only a fiction-technicality, but I was considerably afraid of it. It was the question of the narrator's "sensibility." The narrator, as it happened, was a young woman; I had chosen her to be the eye—and the "I"—of the novel because all the other characters in some way focused on her. She was the one most useful to my scheme. Nevertheless, I wanted her not to live. Everything I was reading in reviews of other people's books made me fearful: I would have to be very cautious; I would have to drain my narrator of emotive value of any kind, because I was afraid to be pegged as having written a "woman's" novel. Nothing was more certain to lead to that than a point-of-view seemingly lodged in a woman, and no one takes a woman's novel seriously. I was in terror, above all, of sentiment and feelings, those telltale taints. I kept the fury and the passion for other, safer, characters.

So what I left out of my narrator entirely, sweepingly, with exquisite consciousness of what exactly I *was* leaving out, was any shred of "sensibility." I stripped her of everything, even a name. I crafted and carpentered her. She was for me a bloodless device, fulcrum or pivot, a recording voice, a language-machine. She confronted moment or event, took it in, gave it out. And what to me was all the more wonderful about this nameless fiction-machine I had invented was that the machine itself, though never alive, was a character in the story, without ever influencing the story. My machine-narrator was there for efficiency only, for flexibility, for craftiness, for subtlety, but never, never, as a "woman." I wiped the "woman" out of her. And I did it out of fear, out of vicarious vindictive critical imagination, out of the terror of my ambition, out of, maybe, paranoia. I meant my novel to be taken for what it really was. I meant to make it impossible for it to be mistaken for something else.

Publication. Review in *The New York Times* Sunday Book Review.

Review is accompanied by a picture of a naked woman seen from the back. Her bottom is covered by some sort of drapery.

Title of review: "Daughter's Reprieve."

Excerpts from review: "These events, interesting in themselves, exist to reveal the sensibility of the narrator." "She longs to play some easy feminine role." "She has been unable to define herself as a woman." "The main body of the novel, then, is a revelation of the narrator's inner, turbulent, psychic drama."

O rabid rotten Western Civilization, where are you? O judging History, O foul Trust and fouler Distrust, where?

O Soap Opera, where did you come from?

(Meanwhile the review in *Time* was calling me a "housewife.")

---

1. *Bonjour tristesse* (1954), published before Sagan was 20; not only was it an enormous commercial success, but it won the prestigious Prix des Critiques.

Pause.

All right, let us take up the rebuttals.

Q. Maybe you *did* write a soap opera without knowing it. Maybe you only *thought* you were writing about Western Civilization when you were really only rewriting Stella Dallas.[2]

A. A writer may be unsure of everything—trust the tale not the teller is a good rule—but not of his obsessions; of these he is certain. If I were rewriting Stella Dallas, I would turn her into the Second Crusade and demobilize her.

Q. Maybe you're like the blind Jew who wants to be a pilot, and when they won't give him the job he says they're anti-Semitic. Look, the book was lousy, you deserved a lousy review.

A. You mistake me, I never said it was a bad review. It was in fact an extremely favorable review, full of gratifying adjectives.

Q. Then what's eating you?

A. I don't know. Maybe the question of language. By language I mean literacy. See the next section, please.

Q. No Moral for *this* section?

A. Of course. If you look for it, there will always be a decent solution for female ambition. For instance, it is still not too late to enroll in a good secretarial school.

Q. Bitter, bitter! You mean your novel failed?

A. Perished, is dead and buried. I sometimes see it exhumed on the shelf in the public library. It's always there. No one ever borrows it.

Q. Dummy! You should've written a soap opera. Women are good at that.

A. Thank you. You almost remind me of a Second Moral: In conceptual life, junk prevails. Even if you do not produce junk, it will be taken for junk.

Q. What does that have to do with women?

A. The products of women are frequently taken for junk.

Q. And if a woman *does* produce junk . . . ?

A. Glory—they will treat her almost like a man who produces junk. They will say her name on television. Do please go on to the next section. Thank you.

1972

---

2. A novel by Olive Higgins Prouty (1923); the 1937 film adaptation was a popular tearjerker.

ADRIENNE RICH
b. 1929

A major poet as well as a political activist and a feminist theorist, Adrienne Rich was arguably one of the shapers of the so-called second wave of the women's movement that transformed American sexual politics in the 1970s. In the words of the critic David Kalstone, her career "is a jagged present, always pitched toward the future and change." The author of more than a dozen books of poetry, among them the influential *Diving into the Wreck* (1973) and the equally resonant *The Dream of a Common*

Language (1978), she has also published a number of works of literary and cultural theory. The first of these to achieve wide circulation was "When We Dead Awaken: Writing as Re-Vision" (1972, 1976, 1978), which we reprint here and which functioned, along with Virginia Woolf's *A Room of One's Own* (1929), as an aesthetic and political manifesto for contemporary feminist critics, poets, and fiction writers. Other significant texts include *Of Woman Born: Motherhood as Experience and Institution* (1976), "Compulsory Heterosexuality and Lesbian Existence" (1980), and "Notes toward a Politics of Location" (1985), the last of which we also reprint in this *Reader* (pp. 228–39).

Born and raised in Baltimore, Rich was a "Southern Jew" who experienced herself as "split at the root" and "raised in a castle of air" by—in the words of her longtime editor and close friend John Benedict—a "taskmaster father" and a mother "who gave over her life to her husband and children." Educated at Radcliffe, the young writer published her first book of verse, *A Change of World* (1951), in the prestigious Yale Younger Poets series; it was introduced by W. H. Auden, who noted somewhat patronizingly that the poems were "neatly and modestly dressed, . . . respect their elders but are not cowed by them, and do not tell lies." After her 1954 marriage to the economist Alfred Conrad, the birth of three sons, the couple's divorce and Conrad's suicide, however, Rich's poems became decidedly less neat and modest—nor did they continue to "respect their elders" as they had in the fifties.

"The moment of change is the only poem," Rich wrote, as she embarked on a new life as a lesbian feminist activist, arguing in another essay, "It Is the Lesbian in Us" (1976), that "it is the lesbian in every woman who is compelled by female energy, who gravitates toward strong women, who seeks a literature that will express that energy and strength." For decades now Rich herself has produced writings that give what she defines as "energy and strength" to many readers while also working as a teacher at the City College of New York, Douglass College, and Stanford University, among other institutions. When in 1997 she was chosen by the Clinton administration to be one of twelve recipients of the National Medal for the Arts, she refused the award, explaining that the "radical disparities of wealth and power in America are widening at a devastating rate. A president cannot meaningfully honor certain token artists while the people at large are so dishonored." "Why I Refused the Medal for the Arts," an essay in which she elaborates on this point, appears in the prose collection *Arts of the Possible: Essays and Conversations* (2001). Other recent works include *The School among the Ruins: Poems, 2000–2004* (2004) and *What Is Found There: Notebooks on Poetry and Politics*, first published in 1993 but revised and expanded in 2003 to include a new preface and the post-9/11 "Six Meditations in Place of a Lecture."

When We Dead Awaken: Writing as Re-Vision (1971)[1]

The Modern Language Association is both marketplace and funeral parlor for the professional study of Western literature in North America. Like all gatherings of the professions, it has been and remains a "procession of the sons of educated men" (Virginia Woolf):[2] a congeries of old-boys' networks, academicians rehearsing their numb canons in sessions dedicated to the literature of white males, junior scholars under the lash of "publish or perish" delivering papers in the bizarrely lit drawing-rooms of immense hotels: a ritual competition veering between cynicism and desperation.

1. As Rich explains, this essay—written in 1971—was first published in 1972 and then included in her volume *On Lies, Secrets, and Silence* (1978). At that time she added the introductory note reprinted here, as well as some notes beginning "A.R., 1978."
2. The phrase is a quote from Woolf's *Three Guineas* (1938).

However, in the interstices of these gentlemanly rites (or, in Mary Daly's words, on the boundaries of this patriarchal space),[3] some feminist scholars, teachers, and graduate students, joined by feminist writers, editors, and publishers, have for a decade been creating more subversive occasions, challenging the sacredness of the gentlemanly canon, sharing the rediscovery of buried works by women, asking women's questions, bringing literary history and criticism back to life in both senses. The Commission on the Status of Women in the Profession was formed in 1969, and held its first public event in 1970. In 1971 the Commission asked Ellen Peck Killoh, Tillie Olsen, Elaine Reuben, and myself, with Elaine Hedges as moderator, to talk on "The Woman Writer in the Twentieth Century." The essay that follows was written for that forum, and later published, along with the other papers from the forum and workshops, in an issue of College English *edited by Elaine Hedges ("Women Writing and Teaching," vol. 34, no. 1, October 1972). With a few revisions, mainly updating, it was reprinted in* American Poets in 1976, *edited by William Heyen (New York: Bobbs-Merrill, 1976). That later text is the one published here.*

The challenge flung by feminists at the accepted literary canon, at the methods of teaching it, and at the biased and astigmatic view of male "literary scholarship," has not diminished in the decade since the first Women's Forum; it has become broadened and intensified more recently by the challenges of black and lesbian feminists pointing out that feminist literary criticism itself has overlooked or held back from examining the work of black women and lesbians. The dynamic between a political vision and the demand for a fresh vision of literature is clear: without a growing feminist movement, the first inroads of feminist scholarship could not have been made; without the sharpening of a black feminist consciousness, black women's writing would have been left in limbo between misogynist black male critics and white feminists still struggling to unearth a white women's tradition: without an articulate lesbian/feminist movement, lesbian writing would still be lying in that closet where many of us used to sit reading forbidden books "in a bad light."

Much, much more is yet to be done; and university curricula have of course changed very little as a result of all this. What *is* changing is the availability of knowledge, of vital texts, the visible effects on women's lives of seeing, hearing our wordless or negated experience affirmed and pursued further in language.

Ibsen's *When We Dead Awaken* is a play about the use that the male artist and thinker—in the process of creating culture as we know it—has made of women, in his life and in his work; and about a woman's slow struggling awakening to the use to which her life has been put. Bernard Shaw wrote in 1900 of this play:

> [Ibsen] shows us that no degradation ever devized or permitted is as disastrous as this degradation; that through it women can die into luxuries for men and yet can kill them; that men and women are becoming conscious of this; and that what remains to be seen as perhaps the most interesting of all imminent social developments is what will happen "when we dead awaken."[4]

---

3. Mary Daly, *Beyond God the Father* (Boston: Beacon, 1971), pp. 40–41 [Rich's note].

4. G. B. Shaw, *The Quintessence of Ibsenism* (New York: Hill & Wang, 1922), p. 139 [Rich's note].

It's exhilarating to be alive in a time of awakening consciousness; it can also be confusing, disorienting, and plainful. This awakening of dead or sleeping consciousness has already affected the lives of millions of women, even those who don't know it yet. It is also affecting the lives of men, even those who deny its claims upon them. The argument will go on whether an oppressive economic class system is responsible for the oppressive nature of male/female relations, or whether, in fact, patriarchy—the domination of males—is the original model of oppression on which all others are based. But in the last few years the women's movement has drawn inescapable and illuminating connections between our sexual lives and our political institutions. The sleep-walkers are coming awake, and for the first time this awakening has a collective reality; it is no longer such a lonely thing to open one's eyes.

Re-vision—the act of looking back, of seeing with fresh eyes, of entering an old text from a new critical direction—is for women more than a chapter in cultural history: it is an act of survival. Until we can understand the assumptions in which we are drenched we cannot know ourselves. And this drive to self-knowledge, for women, is more than a search for identity: it is part of our refusal of the self-destructiveness of male-dominated society. A radical critique of literature, feminist in its impulse, would take the work first of all as a clue to how we live, how we have been living, how we have been led to imagine ourselves, how our language has trapped as well as liberated us, how the very act of naming has been till now a male prerogative, and how we can begin to see and name—and therefore live—afresh. A change in the concept of sexual identity is essential if we are not going to see the old political order reassert itself in every new revolution. We need to know the writing of the past, and know it differently than we have ever known it; not to pass on a tradition but to break its hold over us.

For writers, and at this moment for women writers in particular, there is the challenge and promise of a whole new psychic geography to be explored. But there is also a difficult and dangerous walking on the ice, as we try to find language and images for a consciousness we are just coming into, and with little in the past to support us. I want to talk about some aspect of this difficulty and this danger.

Jane Harrison, the great classical anthropologist, wrote in 1914 in a letter to her friend Gilbert Murray:

> By the by, about "Women," it has bothered me often—why do women never want to write poetry about Man as a sex—why is Woman a dream and a terror to man and not the other way around? . . . Is it mere convention and propriety, or something deeper?[5]

I think Jane Harrison's question cuts deep into the myth-making tradition, the romantic tradition; deep into what women and men have been to each other; and deep into the psyche of the woman writer. Thinking about that question, I began thinking of the work of two twentieth-century women poets, Sylvia Plath and Diane Wakoski. It strikes me that in the work of both Man appears as, if not a dream, a fascination and a terror; and that the source of the fascination and the terror is, simply, Man's power—to dominate, tyrannize, choose, or reject the woman. The charisma of Man seems to come purely from his power over her and his control of the world by force, not from

---

5. J. G. Stewart, *Jane Ellen Harrison: A Portrait from Letters* (London: Merlin, 1959), p. 140 [Rich's note].

anything fertile or life-giving in him. And, in the work of both these poets, it is finally the woman's sense of *herself*—embattled, possessed—that gives the poetry its dynamic charge, its rhythms of struggle, need, will, and female energy. Until recently this female anger and this furious awareness of the Man's power over her were not available materials to the female poet, who tended to write of Love as the source of her suffering, and to view that victimization by Love as an almost inevitable fate. Or, like Marianne Moore and Elizabeth Bishop, she kept sexuality at a measured and chiseled distance in her poems.

One answer to Jane Harrison's question has to be that historically men and women have played very different parts in each others' lives. Where woman has been a luxury for man, and has served as the painter's model and the poet's muse, but also as comforter, nurse, cook, bearer of his seed, secretarial assistant, and copyist of manuscripts, man has played a quite different role for the female artist. Henry James repeats an incident which the writer Prosper Mérimée described, of how, while he was living with George Sand,

> he once opened his eyes, in the raw winter dawn, to see his companion, in a dressing-gown, on her knees before the domestic hearth, a candlestick beside her and a red *madras* round her head, making bravely, with her own hands the fire that was to enable her to sit down betimes to urgent pen and paper. The story represents him as having felt that the spectacle chilled his ardor and tried his taste; her appearance was unfortunate, her occupation an inconsequence, and her industry a reproof—the result of all which was a lively irritation and an early rupture.[6]

The specter of this kind of male judgment, along with the misnaming and thwarting of her needs by a culture controlled by males, has created problems for the woman writer: problems of contact with herself, problems of language and style, problems of energy and survival.

In rereading Virginia Woolf's *A Room of One's Own* (1929) for the first time in some years, I was astonished at the sense of effort, of pains taken, of dogged tentativeness, in the tone of that essay. And I recognized that tone. I had heard it often enough, in myself and in other women. It is the tone of a woman almost in touch with her anger, who is determined not to appear angry, who is *willing* herself to be calm, detached, and even charming in a roomful of men where things have been said which are attacks on her very integrity. Virginia Woolf is addressing an audience of women, but she is acutely conscious—as she always was—of being overheard by men: by Morgan and Lytton and Maynard Keynes[7] and for that matter by her father, Leslie Stephen.[8] She drew the language out into an exacerbated thread in her determination to have her own sensibility yet protect it from those masculine presences. Only at rare moments in that essay do you hear the passion in her voice; she was trying to sound as cool as Jane Austen, as Olympian as Shake-

---

6. Henry James, "Notes on Novelists," in *Selected Literary Criticism of Henry James*, Morris Shapira, ed. (London: Heinemann, 1963), pp. 157–58 [Rich's note].
7. I.e., E. M. Forster, Lytton Strachey, and John Maynard Keynes, all members of Woolf's Bloomsbury circle.
8. A. R., 1978: This intuition of mine was corroborated when, early in 1978, I read the correspondence between Woolf and Dame Ethel Smyth (Henry W. and Albert A. Berg Collection, The New York Public Library, Astor, Lenox and Tilden Foundations): in a letter dated June 8, 1933, Woolf speaks of having kept her own personality out of *A Room of One's Own* lest she not be taken seriously: ". . . how personal, so will they say, rubbing their hands with glee, women always are; *I even hear them as I write.*" (Italics mine.) [Rich's note.]

speare, because that is the way the men of the culture thought a writer should sound.

No male writer has written primarily or even largely for women, or with the sense of women's criticism as a consideration when he chooses his materials, his theme, his language. But to a lesser or greater extent, every woman writer has written for men even when, like Virginia Woolf, she was supposed to be addressing women. If we have come to the point when this balance might begin to change, when women can stop being haunted, not only by "convention and propriety" but by internalized fears of being and saying themselves, then it is an extraordinary moment for the woman writer—and reader.

I have hesitated to do what I am going to do now, which is to use myself as an illustration. For one thing, it's a lot easier and less dangerous to talk about other women writers. But there is something else. Like Virginia Woolf, I am aware of the women who are not with us here because they are washing the dishes and looking after the children. Nearly fifty years after she spoke, that fact remains largely unchanged. And I am thinking also of women whom she left out of the picture altogether—women who are washing other people's dishes and caring for other people's children, not to mention women who went on the streets last night in order to feed their children. We seem to be special women here, we have liked to think of ourselves as special, and we have known that men would tolerate, even romanticize us as special, as long as our words and actions didn't threaten their privilege of tolerating or rejecting us and our work according to *their* ideas of what a special woman ought to be. An important insight of the radical women's movement has been how divisive and how ultimately destructive is this myth of the special woman, who is also the token woman. Every one of us here in this room has had great luck—we are teachers, writers, academicians; our own gifts could not have been enough, for we all know women whose gifts are buried or aborted. Our struggles can have meaning and our privileges—however precarious under patriarchy—can be justified only if they can help to change the lives of women whose gifts—and whose very being—continue to be thwarted and silenced.

My own luck was being born white and middle-class into a house full of books, with a father who encouraged me to read and write. So for about twenty years I wrote for a particular man, who criticized and praised me and made me feel I was indeed "special." The obverse side of this, of course, was that I tried for a long time to please him, or rather, not to displease him. And then of course there were other men—writers, teachers—the Man, who was not a terror or a dream but a literary master and a master in other ways less easy to acknowledge. And there were all those poems about women, written by men: it seemed to be a given that men wrote poems and women frequently inhabited them. These women were almost always beautiful, but threatened with the loss of beauty, the loss of youth—the fate worse than death. Or, they were beautiful and died young, like Lucy and Lenore. Or, the woman was like Maud Gonne,[9] cruel and disastrously mistaken, and the poem reproached her because she had refused to become a luxury for the poet.

A lot is being said today about the influence that the myths and images of women have on all of us who are products of culture. I think it has been a

9. Irish revolutionary activist (1865–1953), beautiful beloved of William Butler Yeats, and subject of many of his poems. "Lucy and Lenore": in poems written by William Wordsworth and Edgar Allan Poe.

peculiar confusion to the girl or woman who tries to write because she is peculiarly susceptible to language. She goes to poetry or fiction looking for *her* way of being in the world, since she too has been putting words and images together; she is looking eagerly for guides, maps, possibilities; and over and over in the "words' masculine persuasive force" of literature she comes up against something that negates everything she is about: she meets the image of Woman in books written by men. She finds a terror and a dream, she finds a beautiful pale face, she finds La Belle Dame Sans Merci, she finds Juliet or Tess or Salomé,[1] but precisely what she does not find is that absorbed, drudging, puzzled, sometimes inspired creature, herself, who sits at a desk trying to put words together.

So what does she do? What did I do? I read the older women poets with their peculiar keenness and ambivalence: Sappho, Christina Rossetti, Emily Dickinson, Elinor Wylie, Edna Millay, H. D. I discovered that the woman poet most admired at the time (by men) was Marianne Moore, who was maidenly, elegant, intellectual, discreet. But even in reading these women I was looking in them for the same things I had found in the poetry of men, because I wanted women poets to be the equals of men, and to be equal was still confused with sounding the same.

I know that my style was formed first by male poets: by the men I was reading as an undergraduate—Frost, Dylan Thomas, Donne, Auden, MacNeice, Stevens, Yeats. What I chiefly learned from them was craft.[2] But poems are like dreams: in them you put what you don't know you know. Looking back at poems I wrote before I was twenty-one, I'm startled because beneath the conscious craft are glimpses of the split I even then experienced between the girl who wrote poems, who defined herself in writing poems, and the girl who was to define herself by her relationships with men. "Aunt Jennifer's Tigers" (1951), written while I was a student, looks with deliberate detachment at this split. In writing this poem, composed and apparently cool as it is, I thought I was creating a portrait of an imaginary woman. But this woman suffers from the opposition of her imagination, worked out in tapestry, and her life-style, "ringed with ordeals she was mastered by." It was important to me that Aunt Jennifer was a person as distinct from myself as possible—distanced by the formalism of the poem, by its objective, observant tone—even by putting the woman in a different generation.

In those years formalism was part of the strategy—like asbestos gloves, it allowed me to handle materials I couldn't pick up bare-handed. A later strategy was to use the persona of a man, as I did in "The Loser" (1958):

> *A man thinks of the woman he once loved: first, after her*
> *wedding, and then nearly a decade later.*
>
> I
> I kissed you, bride and lost, and went
> home from that bourgeois sacrament,
> your cheek still tasting cold upon
> my lips that gave you benison

---

1. All title characters—terrifying in John Keats's poem, tragic in Shakespeare's play and Thomas Hardy's novel, and murderous in Oscar Wilde's play.
2. A. R. 1978: Yet I spent months, at sixteen, memorizing and writing imitations of Millay's sonnets; and in notebooks of that period I find what are obviously attempts to imitate Dickinson's metrics and verbal compression. I knew H. D. only through anthologized lyrics; her epic poetry was not then available to me [Rich's note].

with all the swagger that they knew—
as losers somehow learn to do.

Your wedding made my eyes ache; soon
the world would be worse off for one
more golden apple dropped to ground
without the least protesting sound,
and you would windfall lie, and we
forget your shimmer on the tree.

Beauty is always wasted: if
not Mignon's song[3] sung to the deaf,
at all events to the unmoved.
A face like yours cannot be loved
long or seriously enough.
Almost, we seem to hold it off.

II
Well, you are tougher than I thought.
Now when the wash with ice hangs taut
this morning of St. Valentine,
I see you strip the squeaking line,
your body weighed against the load,
and all my groans can do no good.

Because you are still beautiful,
though squared and stiffened by the pull
of what nine windy years have done.
You have three daughters, lost a son.
I see all your intelligence
flung into that unwearied stance.

My envy is of no avail.
I turn my head and wish him well
who chafed your beauty into use
and lives forever in a house
lit by the friction of your mind.
You stagger in against the wind.

I finished college, published my first book by a fluke, as it seemed to me,
and broke off a love affair. I took a job, lived alone, went on writing, fell in
love. I was young, full of energy, and the book seemed to mean that others
agreed I was a poet. Because I was also determined to prove that as a woman
poet I could also have what was then defined as a "full" woman's life, I
plunged in my early twenties into marriage and had three children before I
was thirty. There was nothing overt in the environment to warn me: these
were the fifties, and in reaction to the earlier wave of feminism, middle-class
women were making careers of domestic perfection, working to send their
husbands through professional schools, then retiring to raise large families.
People were moving out to the suburbs, technology was going to be the
answer to everything, even sex; the family was in its glory. Life was extremely
private; women were isolated from each other by the loyalties of marriage. I
have a sense that women didn't talk to each other much in the fifties—not

3. From Ambroise Thomas's *Mignon* (1866), an opera based on Goethe's *Wilhelm Meister's Apprenticeship*
(1795–96).

about their secret emptinesses, their frustrations. I went on trying to write; my second book and first child appeared in the same month. But by the time that book came out I was already dissatisfied with those poems, which seemed to me mere exercises for poems I hadn't written. The book was praised, however, for its "gracefulness"; I had a marriage and a child. If there were doubts, if there were periods of null depression or active despairing, these could only mean that I was ungrateful, insatiable, perhaps a monster.

About the time my third child was born, I felt that I had either to consider myself a failed woman and a failed poet, or to try to find some synthesis by which to understand what was happening to me. What frightened me most was the sense of drift, of being pulled along on a current which called itself my destiny, but in which I seemed to be losing touch with whoever I had been, with the girl who had experienced her own will and energy almost ecstatically at times, walking around a city or riding a train at night or typing in a student room. In a poem about my grandmother I wrote (of myself): "A young girl, thought sleeping, is certified dead" ("Halfway"). I was writing very little, partly from fatigue, that female fatigue of suppressed anger and loss of contact with my own being; partly from the discontinuity of female life with its attention to small chores, errands, work that others constantly undo, small children's constant needs. What I did write was unconvincing to me; my anger and frustration were hard to acknowledge in or out of poems because in fact I cared a great deal about my husband and my children. Trying to look back and understand that time I have tried to analyze the real nature of the conflict. Most, if not all, human lives are full of fantasy—passive day-dreaming which need not be acted on. But to write poetry or fiction, or even to think well, is not to fantasize, or to put fantasies on paper. For a poem to coalesce, for a character or an action to take shape, there has to be an imaginative transformation of reality which is no way passive. And a certain freedom of the mind is needed—freedom to press on, to enter the currents of your thought like a glider pilot, knowing that your motion can be sustained, that the buoyancy of your attention will not be suddenly snatched away. Moreover, if the imagination is to transcend and transform experience it has to question, to challenge, to conceive of alternatives, perhaps to the very life you are living at that moment. You have to be free to play around with the notion that day might be night, love might be hate; nothing can be too sacred for the imagination to turn into its opposite or to call experimentally by another name. For writing is re-naming. Now, to be maternally with small children all day in the old way, to be with a man in the old way of marriage, requires a holding-back, a putting-aside of that imaginative activity, and demands instead a kind of conservatism. I want to make it clear that I am *not* saying that in order to write well, or think well, it is necessary to become unavailable to others, or to become a devouring ego. This has been the myth of the masculine artist and thinker; and I do not accept it. But to be a female human being trying to fulfill traditional female functions in a traditional way *is* in direct conflict with the subversive function of the imagination. The word traditional is important here. There must be ways, and we will be finding out more and more about them, in which the energy of creation and the energy of relation can be united. But in those years I always felt the conflict as a failure of love in myself. I had thought I was choosing a full life: the life available to most men, in which sexuality, work, and parenthood could coexist. But I felt, at twenty-nine, guilt toward the people closest to me, and guilty toward my own being.

I wanted, then, more than anything, the one thing of which there was never enough: time to think, time to write. The fifties and early sixties were years of rapid revelations: the sit-ins and marches in the South, the Bay of Pigs, the early antiwar movement, raised large questions—questions for which the masculine world of the academy around me seemed to have expert and fluent answers. But I needed to think for myself—about pacifism and dissent and violence, about poetry and society, and about my own relationship to all these things. For about ten years I was reading in fierce snatches, scribbling in notebooks, writing poetry in fragments; I was looking desperately for clues, because if there were no clues then I thought I might be insane. I wrote in a notebook about this time:

> Paralyzed by the sense that there exists a mesh of relationships—e.g., between my anger at the children, my sensual life, pacifism, sex (I mean sex in its broadest significance, not merely sexual desire)—an interconnectedness which, if I could see it, make it valid, would give me back myself, make it possible to function lucidly and passionately. Yet I grope in and out among these dark webs.

I think I began at this point to feel that politics was not something "out there" but something "in here" and of the essence of my condition.

In the late fifties I was able to write, for the first time, directly about experiencing myself as a woman. The poem was jotted in fragments during children's naps, brief hours in a library, or at 3:00 A.M. after rising with a wakeful child. I despaired of doing any continuous work at this time. Yet I began to feel that my fragments and scraps had a common consciousness and a common theme, one which I would have been very unwilling to put on paper at an earlier time because I had been taught that poetry should be "universal," which meant, of course, nonfemale. Until then I had tried very much *not* to identify myself as a female poet. Over two years I wrote a ten-part poem called "Snapshots of a Daughter-in-Law" (1958–1960), in a longer looser mode than I'd ever trusted myself with before. It was an extraordinary relief to write that poem. It strikes me now as too literary, too dependent on allusion; I hadn't found the courage yet to do without authorities, or even to use the pronoun "I"—the woman in the poem is always "she." One section of it, No. 2, concerns a woman who thinks she is going mad; she is haunted by voices telling her to resist and rebel, voices which she can hear but not obey.

> 2.
> Banging the coffee-pot into the sink
> she hears the angels chiding, and looks out
> past the raked gardens to the sloppy sky.
> Only a week since They said: *Have no patience.*
>
> The next time it was: *Be insatiable.*
> Then: *Save yourself; others you cannot save.*
> Sometimes she's let the tapstream scald her arm,
> a match burn to her thumbnail,
>
> or held her hand above the kettle's snout
> right in the woolly steam. They are probably angels,
> since nothing hurts her anymore, except
> each morning's grit blowing into her eyes.

The poem "Orion," written five years later, is a poem of reconnection with a part of myself I had felt I was losing—the active principle, the energetic imagination, the "half-brother" whom I projected, as I had for many years, into the constellation Orion. It's no accident that the words "cold and egotistical" appear in this poem, and are applied to myself.

> Far back when I went zig-zagging
> through tamarack pastures
> you were my genius, you
> my cast-iron Viking, my helmed
> lion-heart king in prison.
> Years later now you're young
>
> my fierce half-brother, staring
> down from that simplified west
> your breast open, your belt dragged down
> by an oldfashioned thing, a sword
> the last bravado you won't give over
> though it weighs you down as you stride
>
> and the stars in it are dim
> and maybe have stopped burning.
> But you burn, and I know it;
> as I throw back my head to take you in
> an old transfusion happens again:
> divine astronomy is nothing to it.
>
> Indoors I bruise and blunder,
> break faith, leave ill enough
> alone, a dead child born in the dark.
> Night cracks up over the chimney,
> pieces of time, frozen geodes
> come showering down in the grate.
>
> A man reaches behind my eyes
> and finds them empty
> a woman's head turns away
> from my head in the mirror
> children are dying my death
> and eating crumbs of my life.
>
> Pity is not your forte.
> Calmly you ache up there
> pinned aloft in your crow's nest,
> my speechless pirate!
> You take it all for granted
> and when I look you back
>
> it's with a starlike eye
> shooting its cold and egotistical spear
> where it can do least damage.
> Breathe deep! No hurt, no pardon
> out here in the cold with you
> you with your back to the wall.

The choice still seemed to be between "love"—womanly, maternal love, altruistic love—a love defined and ruled by the weight of an entire culture; and egotism—a force directed by men into creation, achievement, ambition, often at the expense of others, but justifiably so. For weren't they men, and wasn't that their destiny as womanly, selfless love was ours? We know now that the alternatives are false ones—that the word "love" is itself in need of revision.

There is a companion poem to "Orion," written three years later, in which at last the woman in the poem and the woman writing the poem become the same person. It is called "Planetarium," and it was written after a visit to a real planetarium, where I read an account of the work of Caroline Herschel, the astronomer, who worked with her brother William, but whose name remained obscure, as his did not.

A woman in the shape of a monster
a monster in the shape of a woman
the skies are full of them

a woman   'in the snow
among the Clocks and instruments
or measuring the ground with poles'

in her 98 years to discover
8 comets

she whom the moon ruled
like us
levitating into the night sky
riding the polished lenses

Galaxies of women, there
doing penance for impetuousness
ribs chilled
in those spaces   of the mind

An eye,

'virile, precise and absolutely certain'
from the mad webs of Uranusborg

encountering the NOVA

every impulse of light exploding
from the core
as life flies out of us

Tycho whispering at last
'Let me not seem to have lived in vain'

What we see, we see
and seeing is changing

the light that shrivels a mountain
and leaves a man alive

Heartbeat of the pulsar
heart sweating through my body

The radio impulse
pouring in from Taurus

I am bombarded yet   I stand
I have been standing all my life in the
direct path of a battery of signals
the most accurately transmitted most
untranslatable language in the universe
I am a galactic cloud so deep   so invo-
luted that a light wave could take 15
years to travel through me   And has
taken   I am an instrument in the shape
of a woman trying to translate pulsations
into images   for the relief of the body
and the reconstruction of the mind.

In closing I want to tell you about a dream I had last summer. I dreamed I was asked to read my poetry at a mass women's meeting, but when I began to read, what came out were the lyrics of a blues song. I share this dream with you because it seemed to me to say something about the problems and the future of the woman writer, and probably of women in general. The awakening of consciousness is not like the crossing of a frontier—one step and you are in another country. Much of woman's poetry has been of the nature of the blues song: a cry of pain, of victimization, or a lyric of seduction.[4] And today, much poetry by women—and prose for that matter—is charged with anger. I think we need to go through that anger, and we will betray our own reality if we try, as Virginia Woolf was trying, for an objectivity, a detachment, that would make us sound more like Jane Austen or Shakespeare. We know more than Jane Austen or Shakespeare knew: more than Jane Austen because our lives are more complex, more than Shakespeare because we know more about the lives of women—Jane Austen and Virginia Woolf included.

Both the victimization and the anger experienced by women are real, and have real sources, everywhere in the environment, built into society, language, the structures of thought. They will go on being tapped and explored by poets, among others. We can neither deny them, nor will we rest there. A new generation of women poets is already working out of the psychic energy released when women begin to move out towards what the feminist philosopher Mary Daly has described as the "new space" on the boundaries of patriarchy.[5] Women are speaking to and of women in these poems, out of a newly released courage to name, to love each other, to share risk and grief and celebration.

To the eye of a feminist, the work of Western male poets now writing reveals a deep, fatalistic pessimism as to the possibilities of change, whether societal or personal, along with a familiar and threadbare use of women (and nature) as redemptive on the one hand, threatening on the other; and a new tide of phallocentric sadism and overt woman-hating which matches the sexual brutality of recent films. "Political" poetry by men remains stranded amid the struggles for power among male groups; in condemning U.S. imperialism or the Chilean junta the poet can claim to speak for the oppressed while remaining, as male, part of a system of sexual oppression. The enemy is

4. A. R. 1978: When I dreamed that dream, was I wholly ignorant of the tradition of Bessie Smith and other women's blues lyrics which transcended victimization to sing of resistance and independence? [Rich's note].
5. Mary Daly, *Beyond God the Father: Towards a Philosophy of Women's Liberation* (Boston: Beacon, 1973) [Rich's note].

always outside the self, the struggle somewhere else. The mood of isolation, self-pity, and self-imitation that pervades "nonpolitical" poetry suggests that a profound change in masculine consciousness will have to precede any new male poetic—or other—inspiration. The creative energy of patriarchy is fast running out; what remains is its self-generating energy for destruction. As women, we have our work cut out for us.

1972, 1976, 1978

JOANNA RUSS
b. 1937

Best known as a writer of science fiction and fantasy, Joanna Russ has also been a playwright and remains an incisive literary critic. Born and raised in New York City, she turned early to feminist theory, explaining that because female concerns had been culturally marginalized, she "became aware [in college] of my 'wrong' experience" and consequently "chose fantasy. Convinced that I had no real experience of life, since my own obviously wasn't part of Great Literature, I decided consciously that I'd write of things nobody knew anything about, dammit. So I wrote realism disguised as fantasy, that is, science fiction." Drawn from Russ's witty and passionate collection *To Write Like a Woman* (1995), "What Can a Heroine Do? or Why Women Can't Write," which we include here in its entirety, insists that "Our literature is not about women. It is not about women and men equally. It is by and about men."

As if to demonstrate what "our literature" *could* be if it really were "about women," in some of her major novels and short stories—among them "When It Changed" (1972), its book-length successor *The Female Man* (1975), and *The Two of Them* (1978)—Russ dramatized her visions of the adventurous energy women might wield in an alternative reality where empowering myths and plots would be as available to heroines as to heroes. Further developing her feminist cultural and literary critique, her theoretical and critical works include *How to Suppress Women's Writing* (1983), *What Are We Fighting For? Sex, Race, Class, and the Future of Feminism* (1998), and most recently, *The Country You Have Never Seen: Essays and Reviews* (2005).

What Can a Heroine Do? or Why Women Can't Write

The following essay was written in 1971 and published in 1972 in Susan Koppelman's Images of Women in Fiction: Feminist Perspectives, *one of the earliest pioneering anthologies in a field that was later to blossom as the rose. Although the jargon common today in so much feminist literary criticism and even in queer literary criticism did not exist then (cheers! say I), we were aware of the same issues, and we wrote about them. I do not think that now I would conclude a manifesto like this one with praise of science fiction (it can be just as good or bad as anything and just as timid, clichéd, and dull), but at the time I was, I think, getting ready to write my own science fiction and was—without being explicitly aware of it—looking for a way out of the cultural deprivation described in the essay. That so many women like myself could actually read and enjoy (or watch and enjoy) the kind of white boy's fiction (Susan Koppelman's phrase) that all of us had spent our life reading, explicating, analyzing, and assuming to be Fiction itself is, I think, a tribute to the unselfishness and empathy of the human imagination. But how much more fun it is (not to mention enlightening) to see through the assumption . . . and change it. The essay was written in the years immediately following a three-day symposium on women, hosted by the (then) School of Home Economics during the 1969–1970 intersession. No other college in Cornell University would touch the subject. The result was a ferment of talk (reflected in the attributions listed in the notes) that lasted for years. I went home feeling that the sky had fallen. One of the most immediate results was my understanding that "English literature" had been badly rigged, and out of that insight came this essay.*

1. Two strong women battle for supremacy in the early West.

2. A young girl in Minnesota finds her womanhood by killing a bear.

3. An English noblewoman, vacationing in Arcadia, falls in love with a beautiful, modest young shepherd. But duty calls, she must return to the court of Elizabeth I to wage war on Spain. Just in time the shepherd lad is revealed as the long-lost son of the Queen of a neighboring country; the lovers are united and our heroine carries off her husband-to-be lad-in-waiting to the King of England.

4. A phosphorescently doomed poetess sponges off her husband and drinks herself to death, thus alienating the community of Philistines and businesswomen who would have continued to give her lecture dates.

5. A handsome young man, quite virginal, is seduced by an older woman who has made a pact with the Devil to give her back her youth. When the woman becomes pregnant, she proudly announces the paternity of her child; this revelation so shames the young man that he goes quite insane, steals into the house where the baby is kept, murders it, and is taken to prison where—repentant and surrounded by angel voices—he dies.

6. Alexandra the Great.

7. A young man who unwisely puts success in business before his personal fulfillment loses his masculinity and ends up as a neurotic, lonely eunuch.

8. A beautiful, seductive boy whose narcissism and instinctive cunning hide the fact that he has no mind (and in fact, hardly any sentient consciousness) drives a succession of successful actresses, movie produceresses, cowgirls, and film directresses wild with desire. They rape him.

Authors do not make their plots up out of thin air, nor are the above pure inventions; every one of them is a story familiar to all of us.[1] What makes them look so odd—and so funny—is that in each case the sex of the protagonist has been changed (and, correspondingly, the sex of the other characters). The result is that these very familiar plots simply will not work. They are tales for heroes, not heroines, and one of the things that handicaps women writers in our—and every other—culture is that there are so very few stories in which women can figure as protagonists.

Culture is male.[2] This does not mean that every man in Western (or Eastern) society can do exactly as he pleases, or that every man creates the culture *solus*,[3] or that every man is luckier or more privileged than every woman.

---

1. Number three is a version of *The Winter's Tale*; number four, the life of Dylan Thomas, as popularly believed; number five, the story of Faust and Marguerite; and number eight, a lightly modified version of part of *The Day of the Locust*. The others need no explanation [Russ's note].

2. I am indebted to Linda Finlay of the Philosophy Department of Ithaca College for this formulation and the short discussion that follows it [Russ's note].

3. Alone (Latin).

What it does mean (among other things) is that the society we live in is a patriarchy. And patriarchies imagine or picture themselves from the male point of view. There is a female culture, but it is an underground, unofficial, minor culture, occupying a small corner of what we think of officially as possible human experience. Both men *and women* in our culture conceive the culture from a single point of view—the male.

Now, writers, as I have said, do not make up their stories out of whole cloth; they are pretty much restricted to the attitudes, the beliefs, the expectations, and, above all, the plots that are "in the air"—"plot" being what Aristotle called *mythos;* and in fact it is probably most accurate to call these plot-patterns *myths.* They are dramatic embodiments of what a culture believes to be true—or what it would like to be true—or what it is mortally afraid may be true. Novels, especially, depend upon what central action can be imagined as being performed by the protagonist (or protagonists)—i.e., what can a central character *do* in a book? An examination of English literature or Western literature reveals that of all the possible actions people can do in this fiction, very few can be done by women.

Our literature is not about women. It is not about women and men equally. It is by and about men.

But (you might object) aren't our books and our movies full of women? Isn't there a "love interest" or at least a sexual interest in every movie? What about Cleopatra? What about Juliet? What about Sophia Western, Clarissa Harlowe, Faye Greener, Greta Garbo, Pip's Estella,[4] and the succession of love goddesses without whom film history would hardly exist? Our literature is full of women: bad women, good women, motherly women, bitchy women, faithful women, promiscuous women, beautiful women? Plain women?

Women who have no relations with men (as so many male characters in American literature have no relations with women)?

Oddly enough, no. If you look at the plots summarized at the beginning of this article, and turn them back to their original forms, you will find not women but images of women: modest maidens, wicked temptresses, pretty schoolmarms, beautiful bitches, faithful wives, and so on. They exist only in relation to the protagonist (who is male). Moreover, look at them carefully and you will see that they do not really exist at all—at their best they are depictions of the social roles women are supposed to play and often do play, but they are the public roles and not the private women;[5] at their worst they are gorgeous, Cloud-cuckooland fantasies about what men want, or hate, or fear.

How can women writers possibly use such myths?

In twentieth-century American literature there is a particularly fine example of these impossible "women," a figure who is beautiful, irresistible, ruthless but fascinating, fascinating because she is somehow cheap or contemptible, who (in her more passive form) destroys men by her indiffer-

---

4. These are, respectively, the heroine of Henry Fielding's *Tom Jones* (1749), the title character of Samuel Richardson's *Clarissa* (1747–48), the seductive woman who drives the plot of Nathanael West's *The Day of the Locust* (1939), the beautiful Swedish-born actress whose characters were invariably the object of male desire, and the hero's beloved in Charles Dickens's *Great Expectations*

(1860–61).

5. I am indebted to Mary Uhl for the observation that Dickens's women are accurately portrayed as long as they are in public (where Dickens himself had many opportunities to observe real women) but entirely unconvincing when they are alone or with other women only [Russ's note].

ence and who (when the male author is more afraid of her) destroys men actively, sometimes by shooting them. She is Jean Harlow, Daisy Faye, Faye Greener, Mrs. Macomber, and Deborah Rojack.[6] She is the Bitch Goddess.

Now it is just as useless to ask why the Bitch Goddess is so bitchy as it is to ask why the Noble Savage is so noble. Neither "person" really exists. In existential terms they are both The Other and The Other does not have the kind of inner life or consciousness that you and I have. In fact, The Other has no mind at all. No man in his senses ever says to himself to *himself*: I acted nobly because I am a Noble Savage. His reasons are far more prosaic: I did what I did because I was afraid, or because I was ambitious, or because I wanted to provoke my father, or because I felt lonely, or because I needed money, and so on. Look for reasons like that to explain the conduct of the Bitch Goddess and you will not find them; there is no explanation in terms of human motivation or the woman's own inner life; she simply behaves the way she does because she is a bitch. Q.E.D. No Other ever has the motives that you and I have; the Other contains a mysterious *essence,* which causes it to behave as it does; in fact "it" is not a person at all, but a projected wish or fear.

The Bitch Goddess is not a person.

Virgin-victim Gretchen (see number five, above) is not a person. The faithful wife, the beautiful temptress, the seductive destroyer, the devouring momma, the healing Madonna—none of these are persons in the sense that a novel's protagonist must be a person, and none is of the slightest use as myth to the woman writer who wishes to write about a female protagonist.

Try, for example, to change the Bitch Goddess/Male Victim story into a woman's story—are we to simply change the sex of the characters and write about a male "bitch" and a female victim? The myth still works in male homosexual terms—Man and Cruel Youth—but the female equivalent is something quite different. Changing the sex of the protagonist completely alters the meaning of the tale. The story of Woman/Cruel Lover is the story of so many English ballads—you have the "false true lover" and the pregnant girl left either to mourn or to die, but you do not have—to indicate only some elements of the story—the Cruel Lover as the materially sumptuous but spiritually bankrupt spirit of our civilization, the essence of sex, the "soul" of our corrupt culture, a dramatization of the split between the degrading necessities of the flesh and the transcendence of world-cleaving Will. What you have instead, if the story is told about or by the woman, is a cautionary tale warning you not to break social rules—in short, a much more realistic story of social error or transgression leading to ostracism, poverty, or death. Moral: Get Married First.

No career woman, at least in literature, keeps in the back of her mind the glamorous figure of Daisy Faye, the beautiful, rich, indifferent boy she loved back in Cleveland when she was fighting for a career as a bootlegger. Reversing sexual roles in fiction may make good burlesque or good fantasy, but it is ludicrous in terms of serious literature. Culture is male. Our literary myths are for heroes, not heroines.

---

6. Harlow was American film's top sex symbol of the 1930s, often playing the vamp; the others named are characters in, respectively, F. Scott Fitzgerald's *The Great Gatsby* (1925), *The Day of the Locust*, Ernest Hemingway's "The Short, Happy Life of Francis Macomber" (1936), and Norman Mailer's *An American Dream* (1965).

What can a heroine do?

What myths, what plots, what actions are available to a female protagonist? Very few.

For example, it is impossible to write a conventional success story with a heroine, for success in male terms is failure for a woman, a "fact" movies, books, and television plays have been earnestly proving to us for decades. Nor is the hard-drinking, hard-fighting hero imagined as female, except as an amusing fluke—e.g., Bob Hope and Jane Russell in *The Paleface*. Nor can our heroine be the Romantic Poet Glamorously Doomed, nor the Oversensitive Artist Who Cannot Fulfill His Worldly Responsibilities (Emily Dickinson seems to fit the latter pattern pretty well, but she is always treated as The Spinster, an exclusively female—*and sexual*—role). Nor can a heroine be the Intellectual Born into a Philistine Small Town Who Escapes to the Big City—a female intellectual cannot escape her problems by fleeing to the big city; she is still a woman and Woman as Intellectual is not one of our success myths.

With one or two exceptions (which I will deal with later) all sub-literary genres are closed to the heroine; she cannot be a Mickey Spillane private eye, for example, nor can she be one of H. Rider Haggard's adventure-story Englishmen who discovers a Lost Princess in some imaginary corner of Africa. (She can be the Lost Princess, but a story written with the Princess herself as protagonist would resemble the chronicle of any other monarch and would hardly fit the female figure of Haggard's romances, who is—again—the Other.) The hero whose success in business alienates him from his family is not at all in the position of the heroine who "loses her femininity" by competing with men—*he* is not desexed, but *she* is. The Crass Businessman genre (minor, anyway) is predicated on the assumption that success is masculine and a good thing as long as you don't spend all your time at it; one needs to spend the smaller part of one's life recognizing the claims of personal relations and relaxation. For the heroine the conflict between success and sexuality is itself the issue, and the duality is absolute. The woman who becomes hard and unfeminine, who competes with men, finally becomes—have we seen this figure before?—a Bitch. Again.

Women in twentieth-century American literature seem pretty much limited to either Devourer/Bitches or Maiden/Victims. Perhaps male authors have bad consciences.

So we come at last to the question of utmost importance to novelists—What will my protagonist(s) do? What central action can be the core of the novel? I know of only one plot or myth that is genderless, and in which heroines can figure equally with heroes; this is the Abused Child story (I mean of the Dickensian variety) and indeed many heroines do begin life as Sensitive, Mistreated Waifs. But such a pattern can be used only while the heroine is still a child (as in the first part of *Jane Eyre*). Patient Griselda,[7] who also suffered and endured, was not a Mistreated Child but the adult heroine of a peculiar kind of love story. And here, of course, we come to the one occupation of a female protagonist in literature, the one thing she can do, and by God she does it and does it and does it, over and over and over again.

---

7. The lowborn heroine of Chaucer's *The Clerk's Tale* (borrowed from *The Decameron*), whose noble husband repeatedly and cruelly tests her fidelity.

She is the protagonist of a Love Story.

The tone may range from grave to gay, from the tragedy of *Anna Karenina* to the comedy of *Emma,* but the myth is always the same: innumerable variants on Falling In Love, on courtship, on marriage, on the failure of courtship and marriage. How She Got Married. How She Did Not Get Married (always tragic). How She Fell In Love and Committed Adultery. How She Saved Her Marriage But Just Barely. How She Loved a Vile Seducer And Eloped. How She Loved a Vile Seducer, Eloped, And Died In Childbirth. As far as literature is concerned, heroines are still restricted to one vice, one virtue, and one occupation. In novels of Doris Lessing, an authoress concerned with a great many other things besides love, the heroines still spend most of their energy and time maintaining relations with their lovers (or marrying, or divorcing, or failing to achieve orgasm, or achieving it, or worrying about their sexuality, their men, their loves, and their love lives).

For female protagonists the Love Story includes not only personal relations as such, but *bildungsroman,* worldly success or worldly failure, career, the exposition of character, crucial learning experiences, the transition to adulthood, rebellion (usually adultery) and everything else. Only in the work of a few iconoclasts like George Bernard Shaw do you find protagonists like Vivie Warren,[8] whose work means more to her than marriage, or Saint Joan, who has no "love life" at all. It is interesting that Martha Graham's dance version of Saint Joan's life turns the tale back into a Love Story, with Saint Michael (at one point, in the version I saw) inspiring Joan by walking astride her from head to foot, dragging his robe over her several times as she lies on her back on the stage floor.

How she lost him, how she got him, how she kept him, how she died for/with him. What else is there? A new pattern seems to have been developing in the last few years: authoresses who do not wish to write Love Stories may instead write about heroines whose main action is to go mad—but How She Went Crazy will also lose its charm in time. One cannot write *The Bell Jar,* or *Jane Eyre,* good as it is, forever.

A woman writer may, if she wishes, abandon female protagonists altogether and stick to male myths with male protagonists, but in so doing she falsifies herself and much of her own experience. Part of life is obviously common to both sexes—we all eat, we all get stomachaches, and we all grow old and die—but a great deal of life is not shared by men and women. A woman who refuses to write about women ignores the whole experience of the female culture (a very different one from the official, male culture), all her specifically erotic experiences, and a good deal of her own history. She falsifies her position both artistically and humanly: she is an artist creating a world in which persons of her kind cannot be artists, a consciousness central to itself creating a world in which women have no consciousness, a successful person creating a world in which persons like herself cannot be successes. She is a Self trying to pretend that she is a different Self, one for whom her own self is Other.

If a female writer does not use the two, possibly three, myths available to a she-writer, she must drop the culture's myths altogether. Is this in itself a

8. The daughter of the title character in *Mrs Warren's Profession* (1898).

bad thing? Perhaps what we need here is a digression on the artistic advantages of working with myths, i.e., material that has passed through other hands, that is not raw-brand-new.

The insistence that authors make up their own plots is a recent development in literature; Milton certainly did not do it. Even today, with novelty at such a premium in all the arts, very little is written that is not—at bottom— common property. It's a commonplace that bad writers imitate and great writers steal. Even an iconoclast like Shaw "stole" his plots wholesale, sometimes from melodrama, sometimes from history, sometimes from his friends.[9] Ibsen owes a debt to Scribe, Dickens to theatre melodrama, James to other fiction of his own time—nothing flowers without a history. Something that has been worked on by others in the same culture, something that is "in the air" provides a writer with material that has been distilled, dramatized, stylized, and above all, clarified. A developed myth has its own form, its own structure, its own expectations and values, its own cues-to-nudge-the-reader. When so much of the basic work has already been done, the artist may either give the myth its final realization or stand it on its head, but in any case what he or she does will be neither tentative nor crude and it will not take forever; it can simply be done well. For example, the very pattern of dramatic construction that we take as natural, the idea that a story ought to have a beginning, a middle, and an end, that one ought to be led to something called a "climax" by something called "suspense" or "dramatic tension," is in itself an Occidental myth—Western artists, therefore, do not have to invent this pattern for themselves.

Hemingway, whom we call a realist, spent his whole working life capitalizing on the dramatic lucidity possible to an artist who works with developed myths. The Bitch Goddess did not appear full-blown in "The Short and Happy Life of Francis Macomber"—one can find her in Fitzgerald—or Hawthorne, to name an earlier writer—or Max Beerbohm, whose *Zuleika Dobson* is certainly a Bitch Goddess, though a less serious one than her American cousins. "Macomber" is the ultimate fictional refinement out of the mess and bother of real life. Beyond it lies only nightmare (Faye Greener in West's *Day of the Locust*) or the half-mad, satiric fantastications Mailer uses to get a little more mileage out of an almost exhausted pattern.

"Macomber" is perfectly clear, as is most of Hemingway's work. Nobody can fail to understand that Mrs. Macomber is a Bitch, that the White Hunter is a Real Man, and that Macomber is a Failed Man. The dramatic conflict is extremely clear, very vehement, and completely expectable. The characters are simple, emotionally charged, and larger-than-life. *Therefore* the fine details of the story can be polished to that point of high gloss where everything—weather, gestures, laconic conversation, terrain, equipment, clothing—is all of meaning. (Compare "Macomber" with *Robinson Crusoe,* for example; Defoe is much less sure from moment to moment of what he wants to say or what it means.) One cannot stop to ask why Mrs. Macomber is so bitchy—she's just a Bitch, that's all—or why killing a large animal will restore

---

9. An overstatement. The plot of *Widowers' Houses* was a gift [Russ's note]. In writing his first play, on slumlords and capitalism, Shaw drew on his own experience as a clerk in a Dublin real estate office.

Macomber's manhood—everybody knows it will—or why the Bitch cannot tolerate a Real Man—these things are already explained by the myth.

But this kind of larger-than-life simplicity and clarity is not accessible to the woman writer unless she remains within the limits of the Love Story. Again: what can a heroine do?

There seem to me to be two alternatives open to the woman author who no longer cares about How She Fell in Love or How She Went Mad. These are (1) lyricism, and (2) life.

By "lyricism" I do not mean purple passages or baroque raptures; I mean a particular principle of structure.

If *the narrative mode* (what Aristotle called "epic") concerns itself with *events* connected by the *chronological order* in which they occur, and *the dramatic mode* with *voluntary human actions* which are connected both by *chronology and causation,* then the principle of construction I wish to call *lyric* consists of *the organization of discrete elements* (images, events, scenes, passages, words, what-have-you) *around an unspoken thematic or emotional center.* The lyric mode exists without chronology or causation; its principle of connection is *associative.* Of course, no piece of writing can exist purely in any one mode, but we can certainly talk of the predominance of one element, perhaps two.) In this sense of "lyric" Virginia Woolf is a lyric novelist—in fact she has been criticized in just those terms, i.e., "nothing happens" in her books. A writer who employs the lyric structure is setting various images, events, scenes, or memories to circling round an unspoken, invisible center. The invisible center is what the novel or poem is about; it is also unsayable in available dramatic or narrative terms. That is, there is no action possible to the central character and no series of events that will embody in clear, unequivocal, immediately graspable terms what the artist means. Or perhaps there is no action or series of events that will embody this "center" at all. Unable to use the myths of male culture (and apparently unwilling to spend her life writing love stories), Woolf uses a structure that is basically non-narrative. Hence the lack of "plot," the repetitiousness, the gathering-up of the novels into moments of epiphany, the denseness of the writing, the indirection. There is nothing the female characters can *do*—except exist, except think, except feel. And critics (mostly male) employ the usual vocabulary of denigration: these novels lack important events; they are hermetically sealed; they are too full of sensibility; they are trivial; they lack action; they are feminine.[1]

Not every female author is equipped with the kind of command of language that allows (or insists upon) lyric construction; nor does every woman writer want to employ this mode. The alternative is to take as one's model (and structural principle) not male myth but the structure of one's own experience. So we have George Eliot's (or Doris Lessing's) "lack of structure," the obviously tacked-on ending of *Mill on the Floss;* we have Brontë's spasmodic, jerky world of *Villette,* with a structure modeled on the heroine's (and probably author's) real situation. How to write a novel about a person to whom nothing happens? A person to whom nothing but a love story is *supposed* to hap-

---

1. Mary Ellmann, *Thinking about Women* (New York: Harcourt, Brace & World, 1968). See the chapter on "Phallic Criticism" [Russ's note].

pen? A person inhabiting a world in which the only reality is frustration or endurance—or these plus an unbearably mystifying confusion? The movement of *Villette* is not the perfect curve of *Jane Eyre* (a classic version of the female Love Story)—it is a blocked jabbing, a constant thwarting; it is the protagonist's constantly frustrated will to action, and her alternately losing and regaining her perception of her own situation.[2] There are vestiges of Gothic mystery and there is a Love Story, but the Gothic mysteries turn out to be fakery, and the Love Story (which occupies only the last quarter of the book) vanishes strangely and abruptly on the last page but one. In cases like these the usual epithet is "formless," sometimes qualified by "inexperienced"—obviously life is not like *that*, life is not messy and indecisive; we know what life (and novels) are from Aristotle—who wrote about plays—and male novelists who employ male myths created by a culture that imagines itself from the male point of view. The task of art—we know—is to give form to life, i.e., the very forms that women writers cannot use. So it's clear that women can't write, that they swing wildly from lyricism to messiness once they abandon the cozy realms of the Love Story. And successes within the Love Story (which is itself imagined out of genuine female experience) are not important because the Love Story is not important. It is a commonplace of criticism that only the male myths are valid or interesting; a book as fine (and well-structured) as *Jane Eyre* fails *even to be seen* by many critics because it grows out of experiences—events, fantasies, wishes, fears, daydreams, images of self—entirely foreign to their own. As critics are usually unwilling to believe their lack of understanding to be their own fault, it becomes the fault of the book. Of the author. Of all women writers.

Western European (and North American) culture is not only male in its point of view; it is also Western European. For example, it is not Russian. Nineteenth-century Russian fiction can be criticized in much the same terms as women's fiction: "pointless" or "plotless" narratives stuffed with strange minutiae, and not obeying the accepted laws of dramatic development, lyrical in the wrong places, condensed in the wrong places, overly emotional, obsessed with things we do not understand, perhaps even grotesque. Here we have other outsiders who are trying, in less than a century, to assimilate European myths, producing strange Russian hybrids (*A King Lear of the Steppe, Lady Macbeth of Mtensk*), trying to work with literary patterns that do not suit their experiences and were not developed with them in mind. What do we get? Oddly digressive Pushkin. "Formless" Dostoevsky. (Colin Wilson has called Dostoevsky's novels "sofa pillows stuffed with lumps of concrete.") Sprawling, glacial, all-inclusive Tolstoy. And of course "lyrical" Chekhov, whose magnificent plays are called plotless to this very day.

There is an even more vivid—and tragic—example: what is an American Black writer to make of our accepted myths? For example, what is she or he to make of the still-current myth (so prominent in *King Lear*) that Suffering Brings Wisdom? This is an old, still-used plot. Does suffering bring wisdom to *The Invisible Man*? When critics do not find what they expect, they can-

---

2. Kate Millett, *Sexual Politics* (New York: Doubleday and Company, 1970), pp. 140–47 [Russ's note].

not imagine that the fault may lie in their expectations. I know of a case in which the critics (white and female) decided after long, nervous discussion that Baldwin was "not really a novelist" but that Orwell was.

Critical bias aside, all artists are going to be in the soup pretty soon, if they aren't already. As a culture, we are coasting on the tag-ends of our assumptions about a lot of things (including the difference between fiction and "propaganda"). As novelists we are working with myths that have been so repeated, so triply-distilled, that they are almost exhausted. Outside of commercial genres—which can remain petrified and profitable indefinitely—how many more incarnations of the Bitch Goddess can anybody stand? How many more shoot-'em-ups on Main Street? How many more young men with identity problems?

The lack of workable myths in literature, of acceptable dramatizations of what our experience means, harms much more than art itself. We do not only choose or reject works of art on the basis of these myths; we interpret our own experience in terms of them. Worse still, we actually perceive what happens to us in the mythic terms our culture provides.

The problem of "outsider" artists is the whole problem of what to do with unlabeled, disallowed, disavowed, not-even-consciously-perceived experience, experience which cannot be spoken about because it has no embodiment in existing art. Is one to create new forms wholesale—which is practically impossible? Or turn to old ones, like Blake's Elizabethan lyrics and Yeats's Noh plays? Or "trivial," trashy genres, like Austen's ladies' fiction?

Make something unspeakable and you make it unthinkable.

Hence the lyric structure, which can deal with the unspeakable and unembodiable as its thematic center, or the realistic piling up of detail which may (if you are lucky) eventually *add up to* the unspeakable, undramatizable, unembodiable action-one-cannot-name.

Outsiders' writing is always in critical jeopardy. Insiders know perfectly well that art ought to match their ideas of it. Thus insiders notice instantly that the material of *Jane Eyre* is trivial and the emotionality untenable, even though the structure is perfect. George Eliot, whose point of view is neither peccable nor ridiculously romantic, does not know what fate to award her heroines and thus falsifies her endings.[3] Genet, whose lyrical mode of construction goes unnoticed, is meaningless and disgusting. Kafka, who can "translate" (in his short stories only) certain common myths into fantastic or extreme versions of themselves, does not have Tolstoy's wide grasp of life. (That Tolstoy lacks Kafka's understanding of alienation is sometimes commented upon, but that does not count, of course.) Ellison is passionate but shapeless and crude. Austen, whose sense of form cannot be impugned, is not passionate enough. Blake is inexplicable. Baldwin lacks Shakespeare's gift of reconciliation. And so on and so on.

But outsiders' problems are real enough, and we will all be facing them quite soon, as the nature of human experience on this planet changes radically—unless, of course, we all end up in the Second Paleolithic, in which case we will have to set about re-creating the myths of the First Paleolithic.

---

3. In comparison with the organic integrity of Dickens's, I suppose [Russ's ironic note].

Perhaps one place to look for myths that escape from the equation Culture = Male is in those genres that already employ plots not limited to one sex—i.e., myths that have nothing to do with our accepted gender roles. There seem to me to be three places one can look:

(1) Detective stories, as long as these are limited to genuine intellectual puzzles ("crime fiction" is a different genre). Women write these; women read them; women even figure in them as protagonists. The slang name, "whodunit," neatly describes the myth: Finding Out Who Did It (whatever "It" is).

(2) Supernatural fiction, often written by women (Englishwomen, at least) during the nineteenth and the first part of the twentieth centuries. These are about the intrusion of something strange, dangerous, *and not natural* into one's familiar world. What to do? In the face of the supernatural, knowledge and character become crucial; the accepted gender roles are often irrelevant. After all, potting a twelve-foot-tall batrachian with a kerosene lamp is an act that can be accomplished by either sex, and both heroes and heroines can be expected to feel sufficient horror to make the story interesting. (My example is from a short story by H. P. Lovecraft and August Derleth.[4]) However, much of this genre is as severely limited as the detective story—they both seem to have reached the point of decadence where writers are restricted to the re-enactment of ritual gestures. Moreover, supernatural fiction often relies on very threadbare social/sexual roles, e.g., aristocratic Hungarian counts drinking the blood of beautiful, innocent Englishwomen. (Vampire stories use the myths of an old-fashioned eroticism; other tales trade on the fear of certain animals like snakes or spiders, disgust at "mold" or "slime," human aggression taking the form of literal bestiality (lycanthropy), guilt without intention, the *lex talionis*,[5] severe retribution for venial faults, supernatural "contamination"—in short, what a psychoanalyst would call the "archaic" contents of the mind.)

(3) Science fiction, which seems to me to provide a broad pattern for human myths, even if the specifically futuristic or fantastic elements are subtracted. (I except the kind of male adventure story called Space Opera, which may be part of science fiction as a genre, but is not innate in science fiction as a mode.) The myths of science fiction run along the lines of exploring a new world conceptually (not necessarily physically), creating needed physical or social machinery, assessing the consequences of technological or other changes, and so on. These are not stories about men *qua* Man and women *qua* Woman; they are myths of human intelligence and human adaptability. They not only ignore gender roles but—at least theoretically—are not culture-bound. Some of the most fascinating characters in science fiction are not human. True, the attempt to break through culture-binding may mean only that we transform old myths like Black Is Bad/White Is Good (or the Heart of Darkness myth) into new asininities like Giant Ants Are Bad/People Are Good. At least the latter can be subscribed to by all human races and sexes. (Giant ants might feel differently.)

Darko Suvin of the University of Montreal has suggested that science fiction patterns often resemble those of medieval literature.[6] I think the resem-

---

4. Derleth, "The Shuttered Room" (1959), published as a "collaboration" with Lovecraft.
5. Law of retaliation in kind (Latin).

6. In conversation and in a paper unpublished as of this writing [Russ's note].

blance lies in that medieval literature so often dramatizes not people's social roles but the life of the soul; hence we find the following patterns in both science fiction and medieval tales:

I find myself in a new world, not knowing who I am or where I came from. I must find these out, and also find out the rules of the world I inhabit. (the journey of the soul from birth to death)

Society needs something. I/we must find it. (the quest)

We are miserable because our way of life is out of whack. We must find out what is wrong and change it. (the drama of sin and salvation)

Science fiction, political fiction, parable, allegory, exemplum—all carry a heavier intellectual freight (and self-consciously so) than we are used to. All are didactic. All imply that human problems are collective, as well as individual, and take these problems to be spiritual, social, perceptive, or cognitive—not the fictionally sex-linked problems of success, competition, "castration," education, love, or even personal identity, with which we are all so very familiar. I would go even farther and say that science fiction, political fiction (when successful), and the modes (if not the content) of much medieval fiction all provide myths for dealing with the kinds of experiences we are actually having now, instead of the literary myths we have inherited, which only tell us about the kinds of experiences we think we ought to be having.

This may sound like the old cliché about the Soviet plot of Girl Meets Boy Meets Tractor. And why not? Our current fictional myths leave vast areas of human experience unexplored: work for one, genuine religious experience for another, and above all the lives of the traditionally voiceless, the majority of whom are women. (When I speak of the "traditionally voiceless" I am not pleading for descriptions of their lives—we have had plenty of that by very vocal writers—what I am talking about are fictional myths *growing out of their lives* and told by themselves for themselves.)

Forty years ago those Americans who read books at all read a good deal of fiction. Nowadays such persons read popularized anthropology, psychology, history, and philosophy. Perhaps current fictional myths no longer tell the truth about any of us.

When things are changing, those who know least about them—in the usual terms—may make the best job of them. There is so much to be written about, and here we are with nothing but the rags and tatters of what used to mean something. One thing I think we must know—that our traditional gender roles will not be part of the future, as long as the future is not a second Stone Age. Our traditions, our books, our morals, our manners, our films, our speech, our economic organization, everything we have inherited, tell us that to be a Man one must bend Nature to one's will—or other men. This means ecological catastrophe in the first instance and war in the second. To be a Woman, one must be first and foremost a mother and after that a server of Men; this means overpopulation and the perpetuation of the first two disasters. The roles are deadly. The myths that serve them are fatal.

Women cannot write—using the old myths.

But using new ones—?

1971   1972, 1995

ALICE WALKER
b. 1944

"How was the creativity of the black woman kept alive, year after year and century after century, when for most of the years black people have been in America, it was a punishable crime for a black person to read or write?" So, famously, asked Alice Walker, in "In Search of Our Mothers' Gardens" (1974), one of the most admired and widely read essays produced in the course of the "second wave" of the feminist movement that began to crest in the 1970s. Here, elaborating on Virginia Woolf's well-known claim that "any woman born with a great gift in the sixteenth century would certainly have gone crazed, shot herself or ended her days in some lonely cottage outside the village," she examines the history of the eighteenth-century African American poet Phillis Wheatley, "who, had she been white, would have been easily considered the intellectual superior of all the women and most of the men in the society of her day," dramatizing the sorrowful ambiguities surrounding the life and work of this "sickly little black girl, snatched from [her] home and country and made a slave" who nevertheless "kept alive, in so many of our ancestors, *the notion of song.*"

In numerous volumes of verse, novels, and collections of essays, Walker herself has also kept alive "the notion of song" in its largest sense: song as overflowing, inspired creativity that will find an outlet in countless different channels, including quilts and gardens as well as literary compositions. She herself was born and raised in rural poverty, in the town of Eatonton, Georgia, a heritage whose hardships she examines and whose triumphs she celebrates in the famous piece we reprint here. But she later attended Spelman College and Sarah Lawrence College on scholarship, returning to the South first as a civil rights activist and then to teach at Jackson State College in Mississippi before devoting herself exclusively to writing.

Walker's major works of fiction include *In Love & Trouble* (1973), *Meridian* (1976), *The Color Purple* (1982), and *The Temple of My Familiar* (1989), while her most influential works of cultural and literary criticism are *In Search of Our Mothers' Gardens* (1983) and *Warrior Marks: Female Genital Mutilation and the Sexual Blinding of Women* (1993), coauthored with Pratibha Parmar. Among the individual writers whose works she has attentively analyzed the most notable are Zora Neale Hurston, in "Looking for Zora" (1975), and Flannery O'Connor, in "Beyond the Peacock" (1975).

In Search of Our Mothers' Gardens

> I described her own nature and temperament. Told how they needed a larger life for their expression. . . . I pointed out that in lieu of proper channels, her emotions had overflowed into paths that dissipated them. I talked, beautifully I thought, about an art that would be born, an art that would open the way for women the likes of her. I asked her to hope, and build up an inner life against the coming of that day. . . . I sang, with a strange quiver in my voice, a promise song.
>
> —Jean Toomer, "Avey,"
> *Cane*

The poet speaking to a prostitute who falls asleep while he's talking—

When the poet Jean Toomer walked through the South in the early twenties, he discovered a curious thing: black women whose spirituality was so intense, so deep, so *unconscious,* that they were themselves unaware of the richness they held. They stumbled blindly through their lives: creatures so abused and mutilated in body, so dimmed and confused by pain, that they considered themselves unworthy even of hope. In the selfless abstractions their bodies became to the men who used them, they became more than "sexual objects," more even than mere women: they became "Saints." Instead of being perceived as whole persons, their bodies became shrines: what was thought to be their minds became temples suitable for worship. These crazy Saints stared out at the world, wildly, like lunatics—or quietly, like suicides; and the "God" that was in their gaze was as mute as a great stone.

Who were these Saints? These crazy, loony, pitiful women?

Some of them, without a doubt, were our mothers and grandmothers.

In the still heat of the post-Reconstruction South, this is how they seemed to Jean Toomer: exquisite butterflies trapped in an evil honey, toiling away their lives in an era, a century, that did not acknowledge them, except as "the *mule* of the world."[1] They dreamed dreams that no one knew—not even themselves, in any coherent fashion—and saw visions no one could understand. They wandered or sat about the countryside crooning lullabies to ghosts, and drawing the mother of Christ in charcoal on courthouse walls.

They forced their minds to desert their bodies and their striving spirits sought to rise, like frail whirlwinds from the hard red clay. And when those frail whirlwinds fell, in scattered particles, upon the ground, no one mourned. Instead, men lit candles to celebrate the emptiness that remained, as people do who enter a beautiful but vacant space to resurrect a God.

Our mothers and grandmothers, some of them: moving to music not yet written. And they waited.

They waited for a day when the unknown thing that was in them would be made known; but guessed, somehow in their darkness, that on the day of their revelation they would be long dead. Therefore to Toomer they walked, and even ran, in slow motion. For they were going nowhere immediate, and the future was not yet within their grasp. And men took our mothers and grandmothers, "but got no pleasure from it." So complex was their passion and their calm.

To Toomer, they lay vacant and fallow as autumn fields, with harvest time never in sight: and he saw them enter loveless marriages, without joy; and become prostitutes, without resistance; and become mothers of children, without fulfillment.

For these grandmothers and mothers of ours were not Saints, but Artists; driven to a numb and bleeding madness by the springs of creativity in them for which there was no release. They were Creators, who lived lives of spiritual waste, because they were so rich in spirituality—which is the basis of Art—that the strain of enduring their unused and unwanted talent drove them insane. Throwing away this spirituality was their pathetic attempt to lighten the soul to a weight their work-worn, sexually abused bodies could bear.

What did it mean for a black woman to be an artist in our grandmothers' time? In our great-grandmothers' day? It is a question with an answer cruel enough to stop the blood.

---

1. An echo of a passage in Zora Neale Hurston's *Their Eyes Were Watching God* (1937).

Did you have a genius of a great-great-grandmother who died under some ignorant and depraved white overseer's lash? Or was she required to bake biscuits for a lazy backwater tramp, when she cried out in her soul to paint watercolors of sunsets, or the rain falling on the green and peaceful pasturelands? Or was her body broken and forced to bear children (who were more often than not sold away from her)—eight, ten, fifteen, twenty children—when her one joy was the thought of modeling heroic figures of rebellion, in stone or clay?

How was the creativity of the black woman kept alive, year after year and century after century, when for most of the years black people have been in America, it was a punishable crime for a black person to read or write? And the freedom to paint, to sculpt, to expand the mind with action did not exist. Consider, if you can bear to imagine it, what might have been the result if singing, too, had been forbidden by law. Listen to the voices of Bessie Smith, Billie Holiday, Nina Simone, Roberta Flack, and Aretha Franklin, among others, and imagine those voices muzzled for life. Then you may begin to comprehend the lives of our "crazy," "Sainted" mothers and grandmothers. The agony of the lives of women who might have been Poets, Novelists, Essayists, and Short-Story Writers (over a period of centuries), who died with their real gifts stifled within them.

And, if this were the end of the story, we would have cause to cry out in my paraphrase of Okot p'Bitek's great poem:

> O, my clanswomen
> Let us all cry together!
> Come,
> Let us mourn the death of our mother,
> The death of a Queen
> The ash that was produced
> By a great fire!
> O, this homestead is utterly dead
> Close the gates
> With *lacari* thorns,
> For our mother
> The creator of the Stool is lost!
> And all the young women
> Have perished in the wilderness![2]

But this is not the end of the story, for all the young women—our mothers and grandmothers, *ourselves*—have not perished in the wilderness. And if we ask ourselves why, and search for and find the answer, we will know beyond all efforts to erase it from our minds, just exactly who, and of what, we black American women are.

One example, perhaps the most pathetic, most misunderstood one, can provide a backdrop for our mothers' work: Phillis Wheatley, a slave in the 1700s.

Virginia Woolf, in her book *A Room of One's Own*, wrote that in order for a woman to write fiction she must have two things, certainly: a room of her own (with key and lock) and enough money to support herself.

---

2. The African poet's "Song of Lawino" (1966), with masculine nouns of the original changed to their feminine equivalents.

What then are we to make of Phillis Wheatley, a slave, who owned not even herself? This sickly, frail black girl who required a servant of her own at times—her health was so precarious—and who, had she been white, would have been easily considered the intellectual superior of all the women and most of the men in the society of her day.

Virginia Woolf wrote further, speaking of course not of our Phillis, that "any woman born with a great gift in the sixteenth century [insert "eighteenth century," insert "black woman," insert "born or made a slave"] would certainly have gone crazed, shot herself, or ended her days in some lonely cottage outside the village, half witch, half wizard [insert "Saint"], feared and mocked at. For it needs little skill and psychology to be sure that a highly gifted girl who had tried to use her gift for poetry would have been so thwarted and hindered by contrary instincts [add "chains, guns, the lash, the ownership of one's body by someone else, submission to an alien religion"], that she must have lost her health and sanity to a certainty."

The key words, as they relate to Phillis, are "contrary instincts." For when we read the poetry of Phillis Wheatley—as when we read the novels of Nella Larsen or the oddly false-sounding autobiography of that freest of all black women writers, Zora Hurston—evidence of "contrary instincts" is everywhere. Her loyalties were completely divided, as was, without question, her mind.

But how could this be otherwise? Captured at seven, a slave of wealthy, doting whites who instilled in her the "savagery" of the Africa they "rescued" her from . . . one wonders if she was even able to remember her homeland as she had known it, or as it really was.

Yet, because she did try to use her gift for poetry in a world that made her a slave, she was "so thwarted and hindered by . . . contrary instincts, that she . . . lost her health. . . ." In the last years of her brief life, burdened not only with the need to express her gift but also with a penniless, friendless "freedom" and several small children for whom she was forced to do strenuous work to feed, she lost her health, certainly. Suffering from malnutrition and neglect and who knows what mental agonies, Phillis Wheatley died.

So torn by "contrary instincts" was black, kidnapped, enslaved Phillis that her description of "the Goddess"—as she poetically called the Liberty she did not have—is ironically, cruelly humorous. And, in fact, has held Phillis up to ridicule for more than a century. It is usually read prior to hanging Phillis's memory as that of a fool. She wrote:

> The Goddess comes, she moves divinely fair,
> Olive and laurel binds her *golden* hair.
> Wherever shines this native of the skies,
> Unnumber'd charms and recent graces rise.[3] [My italics]

It is obvious that Phillis, the slave, combed the "Goddess's" hair every morning; prior, perhaps, to bringing in the milk, or fixing her mistress's lunch. She took her imagery from the one thing she saw elevated above all others.

With the benefit of hindsight we ask, "How could she?"

But at last, Phillis, we understand. No more snickering when your stiff, struggling, ambivalent lines are forced on us. We know now that you were not an idiot or a traitor; only a sickly little black girl, snatched from your home

---

3. From Wheatley's "To His Excellency General Washington" (1775).

and country and made a slave; a woman who still struggled to sing the song that was your gift, although in a land of barbarians who praised you for your bewildered tongue. It is not so much what you sang, as that you kept alive, in so many of our ancestors, *the notion of song.*

Black women are called, in the folklore that so aptly identifies one's status in society, "the *mule* of the world," because we have been handed the burdens that everyone else—*everyone* else—refused to carry. We have also been called "Matriarchs," "Superwomen," and "Mean and Evil Bitches." Not to mention "Castraters" and "Sapphire's[4] Mama." When we have pleaded for understanding, our character has been distorted; when we have asked for simple caring, we have been handed empty inspirational appellations, then stuck in the farthest corner. When we have asked for love, we have been given children. In short, even our plainer gifts, our labors of fidelity and love, have been knocked down our throats. To be an artist and a black woman, even today, lowers our status in many respects, rather than raises it: and yet, artists we will be.

Therefore we must fearlessly pull out of ourselves and look at and identify with our lives the living creativity some of our great-grandmothers were not allowed to know. I stress *some* of them because it is well known that the majority of our great-grandmothers knew, even without "knowing" it, the reality of their spirituality, even if they didn't recognize it beyond what happened in the singing at church—and they never had any intention of giving it up.

How they did it—those millions of black women who were not Phillis Wheatley, or Lucy Terry or Frances Harper or Zora Hurston or Nella Larsen or Bessie Smith; or Elizabeth Catlett, or Katherine Dunham,[5] either—brings me to the title of this essay, "In Search of Our Mothers' Gardens," which is a personal account that is yet shared, in its theme and its meaning, by all of us. I found, while thinking about the far-reaching world of the creative black woman, that often the truest answer to a question that really matters can be found very close.

In the late 1920s my mother ran away from home to marry my father. Marriage, if not running away, was expected of seventeen-year-old girls. By the time she was twenty, she had two children and was pregnant with a third. Five children later, I was born. And this is how I came to know my mother: she seemed a large, soft, loving-eyed woman who was rarely impatient in our home. Her quick, violent temper was on view only a few times a year, when she battled with the white landlord who had the misfortune to suggest to her that her children did not need to go to school.

She made all the clothes we wore, even my brothers' overalls. She made all the towels and sheets we used. She spent the summers canning vegetables and fruits. She spent the winter evenings making quilts enough to cover all our beds.

During the "working" day, she labored beside—not behind—my father in the fields. Her day began before sunup, and did not end until late at night. There was never a moment for her to sit down, undisturbed, to unravel her

4. Wife of the Kingfish on *Amos and Andy,* a popular early radio and television show featuring stereotyped black characters.
5. A roughly chronological list—Terry wrote poetry and fiction in the 18th century, Harper wrote poetry in the 19th, and in the 20th century Catlett created sculptures and lithographs while Dunham was a dancer and choreographer.

own private thoughts; never a time free from interruption—by work or the noisy inquiries of her many children. And yet, it is to my mother—and all our mothers who were not famous—that I went in search of the secret of what has fed that muzzled and often mutilated, but vibrant, creative spirit that the black woman has inherited, and that pops out in wild and unlikely places to this day.

But when, you will ask, did my overworked mother have time to know or care about feeding the creative spirit?

The answer is so simple that many of us have spent years discovering it. We have constantly looked high, when we should have looked high—and low.

For example: in the Smithsonian Institution in Washington, D.C., there hangs a quilt unlike any other in the world. In fanciful, inspired, and yet simple and identifiable figures, it portrays the story of the Crucifixion. It is considered rare, beyond price. Though it follows no known pattern of quilt-making, and though it is made of bits and pieces of worthless rags, it is obviously the work of a person of powerful imagination and deep spiritual feeling. Below this quilt I saw a note that says it was made by "an anonymous Black woman in Alabama, a hundred years ago."

If we could locate this "anonymous" black woman from Alabama, she would turn out to be one of our grandmothers—an artist who left her mark in the only materials she could afford, and in the only medium her position in society allowed her to use.

As Virginia Woolf wrote further, in *A Room of One's Own*:

> Yet genius of a sort must have existed among women as it must have existed among the working class. [Change this to "slaves" and "the wives and daughters of sharecroppers."] Now and again an Emily Brontë or a Robert Burns [change this to "a Zora Hurston or a Richard Wright"] blazes out and proves its presence. But certainly it never got itself on to paper. When, however, one reads of a witch being ducked, of a woman possessed by devils [or "Sainthood"], of a wise woman selling herbs [our root workers], or even a very remarkable man who had a mother, then I think we are on the track of a lost novelist, a suppressed poet, of some mute and inglorious Jane Austen. . . . Indeed, I would venture to guess that Anon, who wrote so many poems without signing them, was often a woman. . . .

And so our mothers and grandmothers have, more often than not anonymously, handed on the creative spark, the seed of the flower they themselves never hoped to see: or like a sealed letter they could not plainly read.

And so it is, certainly, with my own mother. Unlike "Ma" Rainey's songs, which retained their creator's name even while blasting forth from Bessie Smith's mouth, no song or poem will bear my mother's name. Yet so many of the stories that I write, that we all write, are my mother's stories. Only recently did I fully realize this: that through years of listening to my mother's stories of her life, I have absorbed not only the stories themselves, but something of the manner in which she spoke, something of the urgency that involves the knowledge that her stories—like her life—must be recorded. It is probably for this reason that so much of what I have written is about characters whose counterparts in real life are so much older than I am.

But the telling of these stories, which came from my mother's lips as naturally as breathing, was not the only way my mother showed herself as an artist. For stories, too, were subject to being distracted, to dying without conclusion. Dinners must be started, and cotton must be gathered before the big rains. The artist that was and is my mother showed itself to me only after many years. This is what I finally noticed:

Like Mem, a character in *The Third Life of Grange Copeland*,[6] my mother adorned with flowers whatever shabby house we were forced to live in. And not just your typical straggly country stand of zinnias, either. She planted ambitious gardens—and still does—with over fifty different varieties of plants that bloom profusely from early March until late November. Before she left home for the fields, she watered her flowers, chopped up the grass, and laid out new beds. When she returned from the fields she might divide clumps of bulbs, dig a cold pit, uproot and replant roses, or prune branches from her taller bushes or trees—until night came and it was too dark to see.

Whatever she planted grew as if by magic, and her fame as a grower of flowers spread over three counties. Because of her creativity with her flowers, even my memories of poverty are seen through a screen of blooms—sunflowers, petunias, roses, dahlias, forsythia, spirea, delphiniums, verbena . . . and on and on.

And I remember people coming to my mother's yard to be given cuttings from her flowers; I hear again the praise showered on her because whatever rocky soil she landed on, she turned into a garden. A garden so brilliant with colors, so original in its design, so magnificent with life and creativity, that to this day people drive by our house in Georgia—perfect strangers and imperfect strangers—and ask to stand or walk among my mother's art.

I notice that it is only when my mother is working in her flowers that she is radiant, almost to the point of being invisible—except as Creator: hand and eye. She is involved in work her soul must have. Ordering the universe in the image of her personal conception of Beauty.

Her face, as she prepares the Art that is her gift, is a legacy of respect she leaves to me, for all that illuminates and cherishes life. She has handed down respect for the possibilities—and the will to grasp them.

For her, so hindered and intruded upon in so many ways, being an artist has still been a daily part of her life. This ability to hold on, even in very simple ways, is work black women have done for a very long time.

This poem is not enough, but it is something, for the woman who literally covered the holes in our walls with sunflowers:

> They were women then
> My mama's generation
> Husky of voice—Stout of
> Step
> With fists as well as
> Hands
> How they battered down
> Doors
> And ironed

6. Walker's first novel (1970).

Starched white
Shirts
How they led
Armies
Headragged Generals
Across mined
Fields
Booby-trapped
Kitchens
To discover books
Desks
A place for us
How they knew what we
Must know
Without knowing a page
Of it
Themselves.

Guided by my heritage of a love of beauty and a respect for strength—in search of my mother's garden, I found my own.

And perhaps in Africa over two hundred years ago, there was just such a mother; perhaps she painted vivid and daring decorations in oranges and yellows and greens on the walls of her hut; perhaps she sang—in a voice like Roberta Flack's—*sweetly* over the compounds of her village; perhaps she wove the most stunning mats or told the most ingenious stories of all the village storytellers. Perhaps she was herself a poet—though only her daughter's name is signed to the poems that we know.

Perhaps Phillis Wheatley's mother was also an artist.

Perhaps in more than Phillis Wheatley's biological life is her mother's signature made clear.

1974, 1983

MARGARET ATWOOD
b. 1934

One of contemporary Canada's foremost literary figures, Margaret Atwood is a prolific novelist, poet, and literary critic who has long been concerned with politics of all kinds: sexual politics, literary politics, and international politics, including what she sees as the cultural colonization of Canada by its American neighbor to the south. Born and raised in Ottawa, she studied at the University of Toronto and then at Radcliffe College, where she took a master's degree. Over the years she has taught at several Canadian universities while also working as an editor at the House of Anansi Press, producing in *Survival* (1972) what she called "a map" for the uncharted terrain of Canadian literature, and compiling the *Oxford Book of Canadian Verse* (1982). Although her contributions to literary history and criticism are significant, Atwood is best known for her fiction and poetry, in particular for (among many others) such powerful novels as *The Edible Woman* (1969), *Surfacing* (1972), *Lady Oracle* (1976), and more recently *The Handmaid's Tale* (1987) and *The Robber Bride* (1993), all of which focus in one way or another on feminist concerns, including women's cultural subordination.

Married to the novelist Graeme Gibson, Atwood is the mother of a daughter, and in such poems as "Spelling" (1981) and "Marsh Languages" (1995) she meditates on the "either/or" choices that meant "many women / denied themselves daughters, / closed themselves in rooms, / drew the curtains / so they could mainline words" and yearns for a revival of the "dark soft languages" of the "Mothertongue." But in the relatively early (1976) essay we present here, she explores the "paradoxes and dilemmas" confronted by women writers whose critics insist on inappropriately sexualizing their works, offering a brisk, businesslike analysis of the often prejudicial reviewing practices that have marginalized so many female-authored texts.

From Paradoxes and Dilemmas: The Woman as Writer

Reviewing and the Absence of an Adequate Critical Vocabulary

Cynthia Ozick, in the American magazine *Ms.*, says, "For many years, I had noticed that no book of poetry by a woman was ever reviewed without reference to the poet's sex. The curious thing was that, in the two decades of my scrutiny, there were *no* exceptions whatever. It did not matter whether the reviewer was a man or a woman; in every case, the question of the 'feminine sensibility' of the poet was at the centre of the reviewer's response. The maleness of male poets, on the other hand, hardly ever seemed to matter."

Things aren't this bad in Canada, possibly because we were never thoroughly indoctrinated with the Holy Gospel according to the distorters of Freud. Many reviewers manage to get through a review without displaying the kind of bias Ozick is talking about. But that it does occur was demonstrated to me by a project I was involved with at York University in 1971–72.

One of my student groups was attempting to study what we called "sexual bias in reviewing", by which we meant not unfavourable reviews, but points being added or subtracted by the reviewer on the basis of the author's sex and supposedly associated characteristics rather than on the basis of the work itself. Our study fell into two parts: i) a survey of writers, half male, half female, conducted by letter: had they ever experienced sexual bias directed against them in a review?; ii) the reading of a large number of reviews from a wide range of periodicals and newspapers.

The results of the writers' survey were perhaps predictable. Of the men, none answered Yes, a quarter Maybe, and three-quarters No. Of women, half were Yeses, a quarter Maybes and a quarter Nos. The women replying Yes often wrote long, detailed letters, giving instances and discussing their own attitudes. All the men's letters were short.

This proved only that women were more likely to *feel* they had been discriminated against on the basis of sex. When we got round to the reviews, we discovered they were sometimes justified. Here are the kinds of things we found.

ASSIGNMENT OF REVIEWS

Several of our letter-writers discussed the mechanics of review assignment. Some felt books by women tended to be passed over by book-page editors assigning books for review; others that books by women tended to get assigned to women reviewers. When we started toting up reviews we found that most books in this society are written by men, and so are most reviews. Disproportionately often, books by women were assigned to women reviewers, indicating that books by women fell in the minds of those dishing out the reviews into a special "female" category. Likewise, woman reviewers tended to be reviewing books by women rather than books by men (though because of the preponderance of male reviewers, there were quite a few male-written reviews of books by women).

THE QUILLER-COUCH SYNDROME

This phrase refers to the turn-of-the-century essay by Quiller-Couch, defining "masculine" and "feminine" styles in writing. The "masculine" style is, of course, bold, forceful, clear, vigorous, etc.; the "feminine" style is vague, weak, tremulous, pastel, etc. In the list of pairs you can include "objective" and "subjective", "universal" or "accurate depiction of society" versus "confessional", "personal", or even "narcissistic" and "neurotic". It's roughly seventy years since Quiller-Couch's essay, but the "masculine" group of adjectives is still much more likely to be applied to the work of male writers; female writers are much more likely to get hit with some version of "the feminine style" or "feminine sensibility", whether their work merits it or not.

THE LADY PAINTER SYNDROME, OR SHE WRITES LIKE A MAN

This is a pattern in which good equals male, bad equals female. I call it the Lady Painter Syndrome because of a conversation I had about female painters with a male painter in 1960. "When she's good," he said, "we call her a painter; when she's bad, we call her a lady painter." "She writes like a man" is part of the same pattern; it's usually used by a male reviewer who is impressed by a female writer. It's meant as a compliment. See also "She thinks like a man," which means the author thinks, unlike most women, who are held to be incapable of objective thought (their province is "feeling"). Adjectives which often have similar connotations are ones such as "strong", "gutsy", "hard", "mean", etc. A hard-hitting piece of writing by a man is liable to be thought of as merely realistic; an equivalent piece by a woman is much more likely to be labelled "cruel" or "tough". The assumption is that women are by nature soft, weak and not very talented, and that if a woman writer happens to be a good writer, she should be deprived of her identity as a female and provided with higher (male) status. Thus the woman writer has, in the minds of such reviewers, two choices. She can be bad but female, a carrier of the "feminine sensibility" virus; or she can be "good" in male-adjective terms, but sexless. Badness seems to be ascribed then to a surplus of female hormones, whereas badness in a male writer is usually ascribed to nothing but badness (though a "bad" male writer is sometimes held, by adjectives implying sterility or impotence, to be deficient in maleness). "Maleness" is exemplified by the "good" male writer; "femaleness", since it is seen by such reviewers as a handicap or deficiency, is held to be transcended or discarded by the "good" female one. In other words, there is no critical vocabulary for expressing the concept "good/female". Work by a male writer is often spoken of by critics admiring it as having "balls"; have you ever heard anyone speak admiringly of work by a woman as having "tits"?

Possible antidotes: Development of a "good/female" vocabulary ("wow, has that ever got womb . . ."); or, preferably, the development of a vocabulary that can treat structures made of words as though they are exactly that, not biological entities possessed of sexual organs.

DOMESTICITY

One of our writers noted a (usually male) habit of concentrating on domestic themes in the work of a female writer, ignoring any other topic she might have dealt with, then patronizing her for an excessive interest in domestic themes. We found several instances of reviewers identifying an author as a "housewife" and consequently dismissing anything she has produced (since, in our society, a "housewife" is viewed as a relatively brainless and talentless creature). We even found one instance in which the author was called a "housewife" and put down for writing like one when in fact she was no such thing.

For such reviewers, when a man writes about things like doing the dishes, it's realism; when a woman does, it's an unfortunate feminine genetic limitation.

SEXUAL COMPLIMENT/PUT-DOWN

This syndrome can be summed up as follows:

> *She:* "How do you like my (design for an airplane/mathematical formula/medical miracle)?"
> *He:* "You sure have a nice ass."

In reviewing it usually takes the form of commenting on the cute picture of the (female) author on the cover, coupled with dismissal of her as a writer.

1976

AUDRE LORDE
1934–1992

"The white fathers told us: I think, therefore I am. The Black mother within each of us—the poet—whispers our dreams: I feel, therefore I can be free. Poetry coins the language to express and charter this revolutionary demand, the implementation of that freedom." So declared Audre Lorde in "Poetry Is Not a Luxury" (1977), a brief but stirring political and aesthetic manifesto that we include here in its entirety. One of the most compelling voices of her generation, Lorde was, in her own words, a "black lesbian feminist warrior poet." Born to West Indian parents living in Harlem, she was raised in New York City, where she earned a B.A. from Hunter College and an M.L.S. from Columbia University. The divorced mother of two, she taught for years at Tougaloo College in Mississippi and at John Jay College and Hunter College in New York, while publishing numerous collections of verse, among the most crucial *Cables to Rage* (1970), *Coal* (1976), *The Black Unicorn* (1978), and *Undersong: Chosen Poems, Old and New* (1992).

Even while writing poetry, however, Lorde produced an impressive body of autobiographical, theoretical, and polemical prose. In *The Cancer Journals* (1980) and *A Burst of Light* (1988) she recorded her long, courageous struggle with the cancer to which she finally succumbed in 1992, including her pioneering (and influential) decision to refuse a prosthesis following a mastectomy. In *Zami: A New Spelling of My Name* (1982) she composed a fictionalized memoir of her artistic and personal development that she called a "biomythography." And in both "Uses of the Erotic: The Erotic as Power" (1978) and *Sister Outsider* (1984) she formulated impassioned critiques of white patriarchal culture along with feminist calls to "language and action" through the shattering of silences between women of different races and sexual orientations.

Poetry Is Not a Luxury

The quality of light by which we scrutinize our lives has direct bearing upon the product which we live, and upon the changes which we hope to bring about through those lives. It is within this light that we form those ideas by which we pursue our magic and make it realized. This is poetry as illumination, for it is through poetry that we give name to those ideas which are—until the poem—nameless and formless, about to be birthed, but already felt. That distillation of experience from which true poetry springs births thought as dream births concept, as feeling births idea, as knowledge births (precedes) understanding.

As we learn to bear the intimacy of scrutiny and to flourish within it, as we learn to use the products of that scrutiny for power within our living, those fears which rule our lives and form our silences begin to lose their control over us.

For each of us as women, there is a dark place within, where hidden and growing our true spirit rises, "beautiful/and tough as chestnut/stanchions against (y)our nightmare of weakness/"[1] and of impotence.

These places of possibility within ourselves are dark because they are ancient and hidden; they have survived and grown strong through that darkness. Within these deep places, each one of us holds an incredible reserve of creativity and power, of unexamined and unrecorded emotion and feeling. The woman's place of power within each of us is neither white nor surface; it is dark, it is ancient, and it is deep.

When we view living in the european mode only as a problem to be solved, we rely solely upon our ideas to make us free, for these were what the white fathers told us were precious.

But as we come more into touch with our own ancient, non-european consciousness of living as a situation to be experienced and interacted with, we learn more and more to cherish our feelings, and to respect those hidden sources of our power from where true knowledge and, therefore, lasting action comes.

At this point in time, I believe that women carry within ourselves the possibility for fusion of these two approaches so necessary for survival, and we come closest to this combination in our poetry. I speak here of poetry as a rev-

---

1. From Lorde's "Black Mother Woman" (1973).

elatory distillation of experience, not the sterile word play that, too often, the white fathers distorted the word *poetry* to mean—in order to cover a desperate wish for imagination without insight.

For women, then, poetry is not a luxury. It is a vital necessity of our existence. It forms the quality of the light within which we predicate our hopes and dreams toward survival and change, first made into language, then into idea, then into more tangible action. Poetry is the way we help give name to the nameless so it can be thought. The farthest horizons of our hopes and fears are cobbled by our poems, carved from the rock experiences of our daily lives.

As they become known to and accepted by us, our feelings and the honest exploration of them become sanctuaries and spawning grounds for the most radical and daring of ideas. They become a safe-house for that difference so necessary to change and the conceptualization of any meaningful action. Right now, I could name at least ten ideas I would have found intolerable or incomprehensible and frightening, except as they came after dreams and poems. This is not idle fantasy, but a disciplined attention to the true meaning of "it feels right to me." We can train ourselves to respect our feelings and to transpose them into a language so they can be shared. And where that language does not yet exist, it is our poetry which helps to fashion it. Poetry is not only dream and vision; it is the skeleton architecture of our lives. It lays the foundations for a future of change, a bridge across our fears of what has never been before.

Possibility is neither forever nor instant. It is not easy to sustain belief in its efficacy. We can sometimes work long and hard to establish one beachhead of real resistance to the deaths we are expected to live, only to have that beachhead assaulted or threatened by those canards we have been socialized to fear, or by the withdrawal of those approvals that we have been warned to seek for safety. Women see ourselves diminished or softened by the falsely benign accusations of childishness, of nonuniversality, of changeability, of sensuality. And who asks the question: Am I altering your aura, your ideas, your dreams, or am I merely moving you to temporary and reactive action? And even though the latter is no mean task, it is one that must be seen within the context of a need for true alteration of the very foundations of our lives.

The white fathers told us: I think, therefore I am. The Black mother within each of us—the poet—whispers in our dreams: I feel, therefore I can be free. Poetry coins the language to express and charter this revolutionary demand, the implementation of that freedom.

However, experience has taught us that action in the now is also necessary, always. Our children cannot dream unless they live, they cannot live unless they are nourished, and who else will feed them the real food without which their dreams will be no different from ours? "If you want us to change the world someday, we at least have to live long enough to grow up!" shouts the child.

Sometimes we drug ourselves with dreams of new ideas. The head will save us. The brain alone will set us free. But there are no new ideas still waiting in the wings to save us as women, as human. There are only old and forgotten ones, new combinations, extrapolations and recognitions from within ourselves—along with the renewed courage to try them out. And we must constantly encourage ourselves and each other to attempt the heretical actions that our dreams imply, and so many of our old ideas disparage. In the forefront of our move toward change, there is only poetry to hint at possibility made real. Our poems formulate the implications of ourselves, what we feel within and dare make real (or bring action into accordance with), our fears, our hopes, our most cherished terrors.

For within living structures defined by profit, by linear power, by institutional dehumanization, our feelings were not meant to survive. Kept around as unavoidable adjuncts or pleasant pastimes, feelings were expected to kneel to thought as women were expected to kneel to men. But women have survived. As poets. And there are no new pains. We have felt them all already. We have hidden that fact in the same place where we have hidden our power. They surface in our dreams, and it is our dreams that point the way to freedom. Those dreams are made realizable through our poems that give us the strength and courage to see, to feel, to speak, and to dare.

If what we need to dream, to move our spirits most deeply and directly toward and through promise, is discounted as a luxury, then we give up the core—the fountain—of our power, our womanness; we give up the future of our worlds.

For there are no new ideas. There are only new ways of making them felt—of examining what those ideas feel like being lived on Sunday morning at 7 A.M., after brunch, during wild love, making war, giving birth, mourning our dead—while we suffer the old longings, battle the old warnings and fears of being silent and impotent and alone, while we taste new possibilities and strengths.

1977

The Transformation of Silence into Language and Action

I have come to believe over and over again that what is most important to me must be spoken, made verbal and shared, even at the risk of having it bruised or misunderstood. That the speaking profits me, beyond any other effect. I am standing here as a Black lesbian poet, and the meaning of all that waits upon the fact that I am still alive, and might not have been. Less than two months ago I was told by two doctors, one female and one male, that I would have to have breast surgery, and that there was a 60 to 80 percent chance that the tumor was malignant. Between that telling and the actual surgery, there was a three-week period of the agony of an involuntary reorganization of my entire life. The surgery was completed, and the growth was benign.

But within those three weeks, I was forced to look upon myself and my living with a harsh and urgent clarity that has left me still shaken but much stronger. This is a situation faced by many women, by some of you here today. Some of what I experienced during that time has helped elucidate for me much of what I feel concerning the transformation of silence into language and action.

In becoming forcibly and essentially aware of my mortality, and of what I wished and wanted for my life, however short it might be, priorities and omissions became strongly etched in a merciless light, and what I most regretted were my silences. Of what had I *ever* been afraid? To question or to speak as

I believed could have meant pain, or death. But we all hurt in so many different ways, all the time, and pain will either change or end. Death, on the other hand, is the final silence. And that might be coming quickly, now, without regard for whether I had ever spoken what needed to be said, or had only betrayed myself into small silences, while I planned someday to speak, or waited for someone else's words. And I began to recognize a source of power within myself that comes from the knowledge that while it is most desirable not to be afraid, learning to put fear into a perspective gave me great strength.

I was going to die, if not sooner then later, whether or not I had ever spoken myself. My silences had not protected me. Your silence will not protect you. But for every real word spoken, for every attempt I had ever made to speak those truths for which I am still seeking, I had made contact with other women while we examined the words to fit a world in which we all believed, bridging our differences. And it was the concern and caring of all those women which gave me strength and enabled me to scrutinize the essentials of my living.

The women who sustained me through that period were Black and white, old and young, lesbian, bisexual, and heterosexual, and we all shared a war against the tyrannies of silence. They all gave me a strength and concern without which I could not have survived intact. Within those weeks of acute fear came the knowledge—within the war we are all waging with the forces of death, subtle and otherwise, conscious or not—I am not only a casualty, I am also a warrior.

What are the words you do not yet have? What do you need to say? What are the tyrannies you swallow day by day and attempt to make your own, until you will sicken and die of them, still in silence? Perhaps for some of you here today, I am the face of one of your fears. Because I am woman, because I am Black, because I am lesbian, because I am myself—a Black woman warrior poet doing my work—come to ask you, are you doing yours?

And of course I am afraid, because the transformation of silence into language and action is an act of self-revelation, and that always seems fraught with danger. But my daughter, when I told her of our topic and my difficulty with it, said, "Tell them about how you're never really a whole person if you remain silent, because there's always that one little piece inside you that wants to be spoken out, and if you keep ignoring it, it gets madder and madder and hotter and hotter, and if you don't speak it out one day it will just up and punch you in the mouth from the inside."

In the cause of silence, each of us draws the face of her own fear—fear of contempt, of censure, or some judgment, or recognition, of challenge, of annihilation. But most of all, I think, we fear the visibility without which we cannot truly live. Within this country where racial difference creates a constant, if unspoken, distortion of vision, Black women have on one hand always been highly visible, and so, on the other hand, have been rendered invisible through the depersonalization of racism. Even within the women's movement, we have had to fight, and still do, for that very visibility which also renders us most vulnerable, our Blackness. For to survive in the mouth of this dragon we call america, we have had to learn this first and most vital lesson— that we were never meant to survive. Not as human beings. And neither were most of you here today, Black or not. And that visibility which makes us most vulnerable is that which also is the source of our greatest strength. Because the machine will try to grind you into dust anyway, whether or not we speak.

We can sit in our corners mute forever while our sisters and our selves are wasted, while our children are distorted and destroyed, while our earth is poisoned; we can sit in our safe corners mute as bottles, and we will still be no less afraid.

In my house this year we are celebrating the feast of Kwanza, the Africanamerican festival of harvest which begins the day after Christmas and lasts for seven days. There are seven principles of Kwanza, one for each day. The first principle is Umoja, which means unity, the decision to strive for and maintain unity in self and community. The principle for yesterday, the second day, was Kujichagulia—self-determination—the decision to define ourselves, name ourselves, and speak for ourselves, instead of being defined and spoken for by others. Today is the third day of Kwanza, and the principle for today is Ujima—collective work and responsibility—the decision to build and maintain ourselves and our communities together and to recognize and solve our problems together.

Each of us is here now because in one way or another we share a commitment to language and to the power of language, and to the reclaiming of that language which has been made to work against us. In the transformation of silence into language and action, it is vitally necessary for each one of us to establish or examine her function in that transformation and to recognize her role as vital within that transformation.

For those of us who write, it is necessary to scrutinize not only the truth of what we speak, but the truth of that language by which we speak it. For others, it is to share and spread also those words that are meaningful to us. But primarily for us all, it is necessary to teach by living and speaking those truths which we believe and know beyond understanding. Because in this way alone we can survive, by taking part in a process of life that is creative and continuing, that is growth.

And it is never without fear—of visibility, of the harsh light of scrutiny and perhaps judgment, of pain, of death. But we have lived through all of those already, in silence, except death. And I remind myself all the time now that if I were to have been born mute, or had maintained an oath of silence my whole life long for safety, I would still have suffered, and I would still die. It is very good for establishing perspective.

And where the words of women are crying to be heard, we must each of us recognize our responsibility to seek those words out, to read them and share them and examine them in their pertinence to our lives. That we not hide behind the mockeries of separations that have been imposed upon us and which so often we accept as our own. For instance, "I can't possibly teach Black women's writing—their experience is so different from mine." Yet how many years have you spent teaching Plato and Shakespeare and Proust? Or another, "She's a white woman and what could she possibly have to say to me?" Or, "She's a lesbian, what would my husband say, or my chairman?" Or again, "This woman writes of her sons and I have no children." And all the other endless ways in which we rob ourselves of ourselves and each other.

We can learn to work and speak when we are afraid in the same way we have learned to work and speak when we are tried. For we have been socialized to respect fear more than our own needs for language and definition, and while we wait in silence for that final luxury of fearlessness, the weight of that silence will choke us.

The fact that we are here and that I speak these words is an attempt to break that silence and bridge some of those differences between us, for it is not difference which immobilizes us, but silence. And there are so many silences to be broken.

1977   1978, 1980

ADRIENNE RICH
b. 1929

Repudiating the notion that "white feminism can know for 'all women,' that only when a white mind formulates is the formulation to be taken seriously," Adrienne Rich's powerful, lucid, and deeply reasoned "Notes toward a Politics of Location" was first offered as a talk at a feminist conference in Utrecht, Holland, in June 1984, but it has become a touchstone for many scholars and teachers of women's studies around the world. Here, investigating—and celebrating—the diversity of women, one of our major contemporary poet-critics repudiates what she sees as a dated, misleading notion of "the common oppression of women" that she traces back, in her own thought, to the 1970s, in favor of a "politics of location" shaped by divergences of race and ethnicity as well as gender. Biographical notes on Rich, along with her key essay "When We Dead Awaken: Writing as Re-Vision" (1972, 1976, 1978), appear on pp. 187–200 of this reader.

Notes toward a Politics of Location

I am to speak these words in Europe, but I have been searching for them in the United States of America. A few years ago I would have spoken of the common oppression of women, the gathering movement of women around the globe, the hidden history of women's resistance and bonding, the failure of all previous politics to recognize the universal shadow of patriarchy, the belief that women, now, in a time of rising consciousness and global emergency may join across all national and cultural boundaries to create a society free of domination, in which "sexuality, politics, . . . work . . . intimacy . . . thinking itself will be transformed." (Rich 1976: 286)

I would have spoken these words as a feminist who "happened" to be a white United States citizen, conscious of my government's proven capacity for violence and arrogance of power, but as self-separated from that government, quoting without second thoughts Virginia Woolf's statement in *Three Guineas* that "As a woman I have no country. As a woman I want no country. As a woman my country is the whole world."

This is not what I come here to say in 1984. I come here with notes, but without absolute conclusions. This is not a sign of loss of faith or hope. These notes are the marks of a struggle to keep moving, a struggle for accountability.

———

Beginning to write, then getting up. Stopped by the movements of a huge early bumble bee which has somehow gotten inside this house and is reeling, bumping, stunning itself against windowpanes and sills. I open the front door and speak to it, trying to attract it outside. It is looking for what it needs, just as I am, and like me, it has gotten trapped in a place where it cannot fulfill its own life. I could open the jar of honey on the kitchen counter and perhaps it would take honey from that jar; but its life-process, its work, its mode of being, cannot be fulfilled inside this house.

And I, too, have been bumping my way against glassy panes, falling half-stunned, gathering myself up and crawling, then again taking-off, searching.

I don't hear the bumblebee any more, and I leave the front door. I sit down and pick up a second-hand, faintly-annotated student copy of Marx's *The German Ideology*, which "happens" to be lying on the table.

———

I will speak these words in Europe but I am having to search for them in the United States of North America. When I was ten or eleven, early in World War II, a girl-friend and I used to write each other letters which we addressed like this:

> Adrienne Rich
> 14 Edgevale Road
> Baltimore, Maryland
> The United States of America
> The Continent of North America
> The Western Hemisphere
> The Earth
> The Solar System
> The Universe

You could see your own house as a tiny fleck on an ever-widening land-scape; or as the center of it all, from which the circles expanded into the infinite unknown.

It is that question of feeling at the center that gnaws at me now—at the center of what?

———

As a woman I have a country; as a woman I cannot divest myself of that country merely by condemning its government, or by saying three times, "As a woman my country is the whole world." Tribal loyalties aside, and even if nation-states are now just pretexts used by multinational conglomerates to serve their interest, I need to understand how a place on the map is also a place in history, within which as a woman, a Jew, a lesbian, a feminist, I am created and trying to create.

Begin, though, not with a continent or a country or a house, but with the geography closest-in. The body. Here at least I know I exist, that living human individual whom the young Marx called "the first premise of all human history".[1] But it was not as a Marxist that I turned to this place, back from philosophy and literature and science and theology in which I had looked for myself in vain. It was as a radical feminist.

The politics of pregnability and motherhood. The politics of orgasm. The politics of rape and incest, of abortion, birth control, forcible sterilization. Of prostitution and marital sex. Of what had been named sexual liberation. Of prescriptive heterosexuality. Of lesbian existence.

---

1. From Marx and Engels's *The German Ideology* (written 1845–46).

And Marxist feminists were often pioneers in this work. But for many women I knew, the need to begin with the female body—our own—was understood not as applying a Marxist principle *to* women but as locating the grounds from which to speak with authority *as* women. Not to transcend this body but to reclaim it. To re-connect our thinking and speaking with the body of this particular living human individual, a woman. Begin, we said, with the material, with matter, mma, madre, mutter, moeder, modder, etc. etc.

————

Begin with the material. Pick up again the long struggle against lofty and privileged abstraction. Perhaps this is the core of revolutionary process, whether it calls itself Marxist or Third World or feminist or all three. Long before the 19th century, the empirical witch of the European Middle Ages trusting her senses, practising her tried remedies against the anti-material, anti-sensuous, anti-empirical dogmas of the Church. Dying for that, by the millions. "A female-led peasant rebellion"? in any event, a rebellion against the idolatry of pure ideas, the belief that ideas have a life of their own and float along above the heads of ordinary people—women, the poor, the uninitiated (Ehrenreich & English, 1973).

Abstractions severed from the doings of living people, fed back to people as slogans.

Theory—the seeing of patterns, showing the forest as well as the trees— theory can be a dew that rises from the earth and collects in the raincloud and returns to earth, over and over. But if it doesn't smell of the earth, it isn't good for the earth.

————

I wrote a sentence just now and x'd it out. In it I said that women have always understood the struggle against free-floating abstraction even when we were intimidated by abstract ideas. I don't want to write that kind of sentence now, the sentence that begins, "Women have always. . . ." We started by rejecting the sentences that began, "Women have always had an instinct for mothering" or, "Women have always been in subjugation to men." If we have learned anything, in these years of late twentieth century feminism, it's that that "always" blots out what we really need to know: when, where and under what conditions has the statement been true?

————

The absolute necessity to raise these questions in the world: where, when, and under what conditions have women acted and been acted-on, as women? Wherever people are struggling against subjection, the specific subjection of women, through our location in a female body, from now on has to be addressed. The necessity to go on speaking of it, refusing to let the discussion go on as before, speaking where silence has been advised and enforced, not just about our subjection but about our active presence and practise as women. We believed (I go on believing) that the liberation of women is a wedge driven into all other radical thought, can open out the structures of resistance, unbind the imagination, connect what's been dangerously disconnected. Let us pay attention now, we said, to women: let men and women make a conscious act of attention when women speak, let us insist on kinds of process which allow more women to speak, let us get back to earth. Not as paradigm for "woman", but as place of location.

———

Perhaps we need a moratorium on saying "the body". For it's also possible to abstract the body. When I write "the body" I see nothing in particular. To write "my body" plunges me into lived experience, particularity: I see scars, disfigurements, discolorations, damages, losses, as well as what pleases me. White skin, marked and scarred by three pregnancies, a sterilization, progressive arthritis, four joint operations, calcium deposits, no rapes, no abortions, much time at the typewriter, and so forth. To say "the body" lifts me away from what has given me a primary perspective. To say "my body" reduces the temptation to grandiose assertions.

———

This body. White, female; or, female, white. The first obvious, lifelong facts. But I was born in the white section of a hospital which separated Black and white women in labor and Black and white babies in the nursery, just as it separated Black and white bodies in its morgue. I was defined as white before I was defined as female.

The politics of location. Even to begin with my body I have to say that from the outset that body had more than one identity. When I was carried out of the hospital into the world, I was viewed and treated as female, but also viewed and treated as white—by both Black and white people. I was located by color and sex as surely as a Black child was located by color and sex—though the implications of white identity were mystified by the presumption that white people are the center of the universe.

To locate myself in my body means more than understanding what it has meant to me to have a vulva and clitoris and uterus and breasts. It means recognizing this white skin, the places it has taken me, the places it has not let me go.

———

Trying as women to see from the center. "A politics", I wrote once, "of asking women's questions." (Rich 1979). We are not "the woman question" asked by somebody else, we are the women who ask the questions.

Trying to see so much, aware of so much to be seen, brought into the light, changed. Breaking down again and again the false male universal. Piling piece by piece of concrete experience side by side, comparing, beginning to discern patterns. Anger, frustration with Marxist or Leftist dismissals of these questions, this struggle. Easy now to call this disillusionment facile, but the anger was deep, the frustration real, both in personal relationships and political organizations. I wrote in 1975: *Much of what is narrowly termed "politics" seems to rest on a longing for certainty even at the cost of honesty, for an analysis which, once given, need not be re-examined. Such is the dead-endedness—for women—of Marxism in our time.* (Rich 1979: 193)

And it has felt like a dead-end wherever politics has been externalized, cut off from the on-going lives of women or of men, rarefied into an élite jargon, defined by little sects who feed off each others' errors.

But even as we shrugged away Marx along with the academic Marxists and the sectarian Left, some of us, calling ourselves radical feminist, never meant anything less by women's liberation than the creation of a society without domination; we never meant less than the making-new of all relationships. The problem was that we did not know who we meant when we said "we".

———

The literature of the West (I read) is the white man's reflection of himself. So should it be supplemented by the white woman's reflection of herself? And nothing more?

This from the East German novelist Christa Wolf, in her recent book, *Cassandra*. (Wolf 1984: 220)

———

. . . the power men everywhere wield over women, power which has become a model for every other form of exploitation and illegitimate control. (Rich 1981) I wrote these words in 1977 at the end of an essay called "Compulsory Heterosexuality and Lesbian Existence". Patriarchy as the "model" for other forms of domination—this idea was not original with me, it has been put forward insistently by white Western feminists, and in 1972 I had quoted from Lévi-Strauss: *I would go so far as to say that even before slavery or class domination existed, men built an approach to women that would serve one day to introduce differences among us all.*[2] (Rich 1979: 84)

Living for fifty-some years, having watched even minor bits of history unfold, I am less quick than I once was to search for single "causes" or origins in the dealings among human beings. But suppose that we could trace back and establish that patriarchy has been everywhere the model—to what choices of action does that lead us in the present? Patriarchy exists nowhere in a pure state; we are the latest to set foot in a tangle of oppressions grown up and around each other for centuries. This isn't the old children's game where you choose one strand of color in the web and follow it back to find your prize, ignoring the others as mere distractions. The prize is life itself, and most women in the world must fight for our lives on many fronts at once.

———

We . . . often find it difficult to separate race from class from sex oppression because in our lives they are most often experienced simultaneously. We know that there is such a thing as racial-sexual oppression which is neither solely racial nor solely sexual. . . . We need to articulate the real class situation of persons who are not merely raceless, sexless workers but for whom racial and sexual oppression are significant determinants in their working/economic lives.

This from the 1977 Combahee River Collective Statement, a major document of the U.S. women's movement, which gives a clear and uncompromising Black feminist naming to the experience of *simultaneity of oppressions*.[3] (Smith, ed. 1984)

Even in the struggle against free-floating abstraction, we have abstracted. Marxists and radical feminists have both done this, why not admit it, get it said, so we can get on to the work to be done, back down to earth again? The faceless, sexless, raceless proletariat. The faceless, raceless, classless category of "all women". Both creations of white western self-centeredness.

———

To come to terms with the circumscribing nature of (our) whiteness. (Joseph 1981) Marginalized though we have been as women, as white and western

2. From Claude Lévi-Strauss, *The Elementary Structures of Kinship* (1949).
3. For a description of simultaneity of African Women's oppression under apartheid see also

Hilda Bernstein, *For Their Triumphs and For Their Tears: Women in Apartheid South Africa*. International Defence and Aid Fund, London 1978 [Rich's note].

makers of theory, we also marginalize others. Because our lived experience is thoughtlessly white, because even our "women's cultures" are rooted in some western tradition. Recognizing our location, having to name the ground we're coming from, the conditions we have taken for granted—there is a confusion between our claims to the white and western eye and the woman-seeing eye, (Frye 1983: 171) fear of losing the centrality of the one even as we claim the other.

———

How does the white western feminist define theory? Is it something made only by white women, and only by women acknowledged as writers? How does the white western feminist define "an idea"? Who are the "women of ideas"? How do we actively work to build a white western feminist consciousness that is not simply centered on itself, that resists white circumscribing?

———

It was in the writings but also the actions and speeches and sermons of Black United States citizens that I began to experience the meaning of my whiteness as a point of location for which I needed to take responsibility. It was in reading poems by contemporary Cuban women that I began to experience the meaning of North America as a location which had also shaped my ways of seeing and my ideas of who and what was important, a location for which I was also responsible. I travelled then to Nicaragua, where, in a tiny, richly green yet impoverished country, in a four-year-old society dedicated to eradicating poverty, under the hills of the Nicaragua-Honduras border, I could physically feel the weight of the United States of North America, its military forces, its vast appropriations of money, its mass media, at my back; I could feel what it means, dissident or not, to be part of that raised boot of power, the cold shadow we cast everywhere to the south.

———

I come from a country stuck fast for forty years in the deepfreeze of history. Any United States citizen alive today has been saturated with Cold War rhetoric, the horrors of communism, the betrayals of socialism, the warning that any collective restructuring of society spells the end of personal freedom. And yes, there have been horrors and betrayals, deserving open discussion. But we are not invited to consider the butcheries of Stalinism alongside the butcheries of white supremacism and Manifest Destiny. We are not urged to help create a more liveable society in response to the one we are taught to dread. Discourse itself is frozen at this level. Tonight as I turned a switch searching for "the news", that shinily animated silicone mask was on television again, telling the citizens of my country we are menaced by Communism from El Salvador, that Communism—Soviet-variety, obviously—is on the move in Central America, that freedom is imperilled, that the suffering peasants of Latin America must be stopped just as Hitler had to be stopped.

The discourse has never really changed; it is wearyingly abstract. (Lillian Smith, white anti-racist writer and activist, spoke of the "deadly sameness" of abstraction.) It allows no differences among places, times, cultures, conditions, movements. Words which should possess a depth and breadth of allusions, words like socialism, communism, democracy, collectivism—are stripped of their historical roots. The many faces of the struggles for social justice and independence, reduced to an ambition to dominate the world.

Is there a connection between this state of mind—the Cold War mentality, the attribution of all our problems to an external enemy—and a form of feminism so focussed on male evil and female victimization that it, too, allows for no differences among women, men, places, times, cultures, conditions, movements? Living in the climate of an enormous either/or, we absorb some of it, unless we actively take heed.

———

In the United States large numbers of people have been cut off from their own process and movement. We have been hearing for forty years that we are the guardians of freedom, while "behind the Iron Curtain" all is duplicity and manipulation, if not sheer terror. Yet the legacy of fear lingering after the witch-hunts of the fifties hangs on like the after-smell of a burning. The sense of obliquity, mystery, paranoia, surrounding the American Communist Party after the Krushchev Report of 1956: the Party lost 30,000 members within weeks, and few who remained were talking about it. To be a Jew, a homosexual, any kind of marginal person, was to be liable for suspicion of being "Communist". A blanketing snow had begun to drift over the radical history of the United States.

And—though parts of the North American feminist movement actually sprang from the Black movements of the Sixties and the student anti-war movement—feminists have suffered not only from the burying and distortion of women's experience, but from the overall burying and distortion of the great movements for social change. (Bulkin 1984)

———

The first American woman astronaut is interviewed by the liberal-feminist editor of a mass-circulation women's magazine.[4] She is a splendid creature, healthy, young, thick dark head of hair, scientific doctorates from an elite university, an athletic self-confidence. She is also white. She speaks of the future of space, the potential uses of spaces colonies by private industry, especially for producing materials which can be advantageously processed under conditions of weightlessness. Pharmaceuticals, for example. By extension one thinks of chemicals. Neither of these two spirited women speak of the alliances between the the military and the "private" sector of the North American economy. nor do they speak of Depo-Provera, Valium, Librium, napalm, dioxin. *When big companies decide that it's now to their advantage to put a lot of their money into production of materials in space. . . . we'll really get the funding that we need*, says the astronaut. No mention of who "we" are, and what "we" need funding for; no questions about the poisoning and impoverishment of women here on earth, or of the earth itself. Women too may leave the earth behind. (*MS* January 1984: 86)

The astronaut is young, feels her own power, works hard for her exhilaration. She has swung out over the earth and come back, one more time passed all the tests. It's not that I expect her to come back to earth as Cassandra.[5] But this experience of hers has nothing to do with the liberation of women. A female proletariat—uneducated, ill-nourished, unorganized, and largely from the Third World—will create the profits which will stimulate the "big companies" to invest in space.

---

4. Sally Ride, interviewed by Gloria Steinem. 5. I.e., a prophetess of doom.

On a split screen in my brain I see two versions of her story: the backward gaze through streaming weightlessness to the familiar globe, pale blue and green and white, the strict and sober presence of it, the true intuition of relativity battering the heart; and the swiftly calculated move to a further suburb, the male technocrats and the women they have picked and tested, leaving the familiar globe behind: the toxic rivers, the cancerous wells, the strangled valleys, the closed-down urban hospitals, the shattered schools, the atomic desert blooming, the lilac suckers run wild, the blue grape-hyacinths spreading, the ailanthus and kudzu doing their final desperate part: the beauty that won't travel, that can't be stolen away.

A movement for change lives in feelings, actions, and words. Whatever circumscribes or mutilates our feelings makes it more difficult to act: abstract thinking, tribal loyalties, every kind of self-righteousness, the arrogance of believing ourselves at the center. It's hard to look back on the limits of my understanding a year, five years ago—how did I look without seeing, hear without listening? It's difficult to be generous to earlier selves, and keeping faith with the continuity of our journeys is especially hard in the United States, where identities and loyalties have been shed and replaced without a tremor, all in the name of becoming "American". Yet how, except through ourselves, do we discover what moves other people to change? Our old fears and denials—what helps us let go of them? What makes us decide we have to re-educate ourselves, even those of us with "good" educations? A politicized life ought to sharpen both the senses and the memory.

——

The difficulty of saying I—another phrase from Christa Wolf. (Wolf 1970: 174) But once having said it, as we realize the necessity to go further, isn't there a difficulty of saying "we"? *You cannot speak for me. I cannot speak for us.* Two thoughts: there is no liberation that only knows how to say "I". There is no collective movement that speaks for each of us all the way through.

And so even ordinary pronouns become a political problem. (Reagon 1983: 356–368 & Bulkin 1984: 103, 190–193)

——

Sixty-four cruise missiles in Greenham Common and Molesworth.
One hundred and twelve at Comiso.[6]
Ninety-six Pershing II Missiles in West Germany.
Ninety-six for Belgium and the Netherlands.
That is the projection for the next few years.[7]
Thousands of women, in Europe and the United States, saying *no* to this and to the militarization of the world.

. . . *An approach which traces militarism back to patriarchy and patriarchy back to the fundamental quality of maleness can be demoralizing and even paralyzing. . . . Perhaps it is possible to be less fixed on the discovery of "original causes". It might be more useful to ask, How do these values and behaviors get repeated generation after generation?* (Enloe 1983: Ch. 8)

The valorization of manliness and masculinity. The armed forces as the extreme embodiment of the patriarchal family. The archaic idea of women as a "home front" even as the missiles are deployed in the backyards of Wyoming

6. Site of a U.S. Air Force base in Sicily; Greenham Common and Molesworth are bases in England.

7. Information as of May 1984 thanks to the War Resisters League [Rich's note].

and Mutlangen. The growing urgency that an anti-nuclear, anti-militarist movement must be a feminist movement, must be a socialist movement, must be an anti-racist, anti-imperialist movement. That it's not enough to fear for the people we know, our own kind, ourselves. Nor is it empowering to give ourselves up to abstract terrors of pure annihilation. The anti-nuclear, anti-military movement cannot sweep away the missiles as a movement to save white civilization in the West. The movement for change is a changing movement, changing itself, de-masculinizing itself, de-westernizing itself, becoming a critical mass that is saying in so many different voices, languages, gestures, actions: *It must change. We ourselves can change it.*

We—who are not the same. We who are many and do not want to be the same.

———

Trying to watch myself in the process of writing this, I keep coming back to something Sheila Rowbotham, the British socialist-feminist, wrote in *Beyond the Fragments:*

> . . . *there are enormous and serious difficulties in the relationship between groups of people who have been subordinated and theory. A movement helps you to overcome some of the oppressive distancing of theory and this has been a . . . continuing creative endeavour of women's liberation. But some paths are not mapped and our footholds vanish. . . . I see what I'm writing as part of a wider claiming which is beginning. I am part of the difficulty myself. The difficulty is not out there.* (Rowbotham, Segal & Wainwright 1981: 55–56)

My difficulties too are not out there—except in the social conditions that make all this necessary. I do not any longer *believe,* my feelings do not allow me to believe, that the white eye sees from the center. Yet I often find myself thinking as if I still believed that were true. Or rather, my thinking stands still. I feel in a state of arrest, as if my brain and heart were refusing to speak to each other. My brain, a woman's brain, has exulted in breaking the taboo against women thinking, has taken off on the wind, saying, *I am the woman who asks the questions.* My heart has been learning in a much more humble and laborious way, learning that feelings are useless without facts, that all privilege is ignorant at the core.

———

The United States has never been a white country, though it has long served what white men defined as their interests. The Mediterranean was never white. England, Northern Europe, if ever absolutely white, are so no longer. In a Leftist bookstore in Manchester, a Third World poster: WE ARE HERE BECAUSE YOU WERE THERE. In Europe there have always been the Jews, the original ghetto dwellers, identified as a racial type, who suffered under pass laws and special entry taxes, enforced relocations, massacres: the scapegoats, the aliens, never seen as truly European but as part of that darker world that must be controlled, eventually exterminated. Today the cities of Europe have new scapegoats as well: the diaspora from the old colonial empires. Is anti-Semitism the model for racism? Or racism for anti-Semitism? Once more, where does the question lead us? Don't we have to start here, where we are, forty years after the Holocaust, in the churn of Middle Eastern violence, on the edge of decisive ferment in South Africa?—not in some debate over origins and precedents but in the recognition of simultaneous oppressions.

———

I've been thinking a lot about this obsession with origins. It seems a way of stopping time in its tracks. The Neolithic sacred triangles, the Minoan vases with staring eyes and breasts, the female figurines of Anatolia—weren't they concrete evidence of a kind, like Sappho's fragments, for earlier woman-affirming cultures, cultures that enjoyed centuries of peace? But haven't they also served as arresting images, which have kept women attached and immobilized? Human activity didn't stop in Crete or Çatal Hüyuk. We can't build a society free from domination by fixing our sights backward on some long-ago tribe or city.

The continuing spiritual power of an image lives in the interplay between what it reminds us of—what it *brings to mind*—and our own continuing actions in the present. When the labrys[8] becomes a badge for a cult of Minoan goddesses, when the wearer of the labrys has ceased to ask herself what she is doing on this earth, where her love of women is taking her, it too becomes abstraction—lifted away from the heat and friction of human activity. The Jewish star on my neck must serve me both as reminder and as a goad to continuing, and changing, responsibility.

———

When I learn that in 1913 mass women's marches were held in South Africa which caused the rescinding of entry permit laws; that in 1956 20,000 women assembled in Pretoria to protest pass laws for women, that resistance to these laws was carried out in remote country villages and punished by shootings, beatings, and burnings; that in 1959 two thousand women demonstrated in Durban against laws which provided beerhalls for African men and criminalized women's traditional home brewing; that at one and the same time African women have played a major role alongside men in resisting apartheid, I have to ask myself why it took me so long to learn these chapters of women's history, why the leadership and strategies of African women have been so unrecognized as theory in action, by white western feminist thought. (And in a book by two men, entitled *South African Politics* and published in 1982, there is one entry under "Women" (franchise) and no reference anywhere to women's political leadership and mass actions.)[9]

When I read that a major strand in the conflicts of the past decade in Lebanon has been political organizing by women of women, across class and tribal and religious lines, women working and teaching together within refugee camps and armed communities, and of the violent undermining of their efforts through the Civil War and the Israeli invasion, I am forced to think. (Wheatley 1984) Iman Khalife, the young teacher who tried to organize a silent peace march on the Christian-Moslem border of Beirut—a protest which was quelled by the threat of a massacre of the participants—Iman Khalife and women like her do not come out of nowhere. But we, Western feminists, living under other kinds of conditions, are not encouraged, to know this background.

———

8. A double-headed axe, commonly represented in Neolithic and Minoan art and now sometimes used as a symbol of matriarchy or lesbianism.
9. *Women Under Apartheid*, International Defence and Aid Fund for Southern Africa, in cooperation with United Nations Centre against Apartheid. London, 1981, pp. 87–99; and Leonard Thompson and Andrew Prior, *South African Politics*, Yale University Press 1982 [Rich's note].

And I turn to Etel Adnan's brief extraordinary novel *Sitt Marie Rose*, about a middle-class Christian Lebanese woman tortured for joining the Palestinian Resistance; and read:

> She was also subject to another great delusion believing that women are protected from repression, and that the leaders considered political fights to be strictly between males. In fact, with women's greater access to certain powers, they began to watch them more closely, and perhaps with even greater hostility. Every feminine act, even charitable and seemingly unpolitical ones, were regarded as a rebellion in this world where women had always played servile roles. Marie Rose inspired scorn and hate long before the fateful day of her arrest. (Adnan 1982: 101)

———

In almost everything I read these days there are women getting up before dawn, in the blackness before the point of light, in the twilight before sunrise, there are women rising earlier than men and children, to break the ice, to start the stove, to put up the pap, the coffee, the rice, to iron the pants, to braid the hair, to pull the day's water up from the well, to boil water for tea, to wash the children for school, to pull the vegetables and start the walk to market, to run to catch the bus for the work that is paid. I don't know when most women sleep. In big cities at dawn women are travelling home after cleaning offices all night, or waxing the halls of hospitals, or sitting up with the old and sick and frightened, at the hour when death is supposed to do its work.

In Peru: "Women invest hours in cleaning tiny stones and chaff out of beans, wheat and rice; they shell peas and clean fish and grind spices in small mortars. They buy bones or tripe at the market and cook cheap, nutritious soups. They repair clothes until they will not sustain another patch. They . . . search . . . out the cheapest school uniforms, payable in the greatest number of installments. They trade old magazines for plastic washbasins and buy second-hand toys and shoes. They walk long distances to find a spool of thread at a slightly lower price." (Figueroa & Anderson 1981)

The unpaid female labor which means the survival of the poor.

In minimal light I see her, over and over, her inner clock pushing her out of bed with her heavy and maybe painful limbs, her breath breathing life into her stove, her house, her family, taking the last cold swatch of night on her body, meeting the sudden leap of the rising sun.

In my white North American world they have tried to tell me that this woman—politicized by intersecting forces—doesn't think and reflect on her life. That her ideas are not real ideas like those of Karl Marx and Simone de Beauvoir. That her calculations, her spiritual philosophy, her gifts for law and ethics, her daily emergency political decisions, are merely instinctual or conditioned reactions. That only certain kinds of people can make theory, that white minds are capable of formulating everything, that white feminism can know for "all women", that only when a white mind formulates is the formulation to be taken seriously.

It seems to me that these opinions can only isolate those who hold them, from the great movements for bread and justice within and against which women define ourselves.

Once again: who is *we*?

This is the end of these notes but it is not an ending.

REFERENCES

Adnan, Etel. 1982. *Sitt Marie Rose.* Translated from the French by Georgina Kleege. Sausalito, Cal.: Post Apollo Press.

Bulkin, Elly. 1984. "Hard Ground: Jewish Identity, Racism and Anti-Semitism." In Bulkin, E., M. B. Pratt & B. Smith, *Yours in Struggle: Three Perspectives on Anti-Semitism and Racism.* Brooklyn, N.Y.: Long Haul Press.

Ehrenreich, Barbara, and Deirdre English. 1973. *Witches, Midwives and Nurses: A History of Women Healers.* Old Westbury, N.Y.: Feminist Press.

Enloe, Cynthia. 1983. *Does Khaki Become You? The Militarisation of Women's Lives.* London: Pluto Press.

Figueroa, Blanca, and Jeanine Anderson. 1981. "Women in Peru." International Reports: Women and Society.

Frye, Marilyn. 1983. *The Politics of Reality.* Trumansburg, N.Y.: Crossing Press.

Joseph, Gloria I. 1981. "The Incompatible Ménage à Trois: Marxism, Feminism and Racism." Lydia Sargent (ed.), *Women and Revolution.* Boston: South End Press.

Lorde, Audre. 1984. *Sister Outsider: Essays and Speeches.* Trumansburg, N.Y.: Crossing Press.

Reagon, Bernice. 1983. "Coalition Politics: Turning the Century." In Smith 1983.

Rich, Adrienne. 1976. *Of Woman Born.* New York: W. W. Norton.

———. 1979. *On Lies, Secrets, and Silence.* New York: W. W. Norton.

———. 1981. "Compulsory Heterosexuality and Lesbian Existence." Published in Dutch ("Gedwongen Heterosexualiteit en Lesbisch Bestaan"), translated by Patty Pattynama. Amsterdam: Lust & Gratie.

Smith, Barbara (ed.). 1983. *Home Girls: A Black Feminist Anthology.* New York: Kitchen Table Women of Color Press.

Rowbotham, Sheila, Lynne Segal, and Hilary Wainwright. 1981. *Beyond the Fragments: Feminism and the Making of Socialism.* Boston: Alyson Publications.

Wheatley, Helen. 1984. "Palestinian Women in Lebanon: Targets of Repression." *TWANAS*, Third World Student Newspaper, University of California, Santa Cruz.

Wolf, Christa. 1970. *The Quest for Christa T.* Translated from the German by Christopher Middleton. New York: Farrar, Straus and Giroux.

———. 1984. *Cassandra: A Novel and Four Essays.* Translated from the German by Jan van Heurck. New York: Farrar, Straus and Giroux.

1984   1985

JUNE JORDAN
1936–2002

"I too am a descendant of Walt Whitman," the poet June Jordan once wrote; yet as she notes in "The Difficult Miracle of Black Poetry in America or Something Like a Sonnet for Phillis Wheatley," it is through the stubbornly brilliant yet ambiguous example of a young woman whom she names "Phillis Miracle" that "Black poetry in America" and its dedicated practitioners "persist, published or not, and loved or unloved: we persist." Echoing Alice Walker's homage to Wheatley in "In Search of Our Mothers' Gardens," Jordan's essay explores the story of young Phillis's education in whiteness along with her ultimate consignment to obscurity as a paradigm for the plots and impediments against which so many African American poets—including Walker and Jordan herself—have had to struggle. Born of Jamaican immigrants and raised in Harlem, Jordan studied at Barnard College, explaining that (like Wheatley) "I diligently followed orthodox directions" in literature until the Black Arts movement and the second wave of the women's movement turned her toward a poetry of her own.

While teaching at several schools, including Sarah Lawrence; the State University of New York, Stony Brook; and the University of California, Berkeley, Jordan published verse, fiction, plays, essays, and books for children. Her most notable works include *Things That I Do in the Dark: Selected Poetry* (1977, 1981), *Kissing God Goodbye: Poems, 1991–1997* (1997), and *Affirmative Acts: Political Essays* (1998). She died in 2002, after a long battle against breast cancer, but the difficult miracle of her art and thought endures.

From The Difficult Miracle of Black Poetry in America or Something Like a Sonnet for Phillis Wheatley

It was not natural. And she was the first. Come from a country of many tongues tortured by rupture, by theft, by travel like mismatched clothing packed down into the cargo hold of evil ships sailing, irreversibly, into slavery; come to a country where, to be docile and dumb, to be big and breeding, easily, to be turkey/horse/cow to be cook/carpenter/plow to be 5'6" 140 lbs. in good condition and answering to the name of Tom or Mary; to be bed bait; to be legally spread legs for rape by the master/the master's son/the master's overseer/the master's visiting nephew; to be nothing human nothing family nothing from nowhere nothing that screams nothing that weeps nothing that dreams nothing that keeps anything/anyone deep in your heart; to live forcibly illiterate forcibly itinerant; to live eyes lowered head bowed; to be worked without rest to be worked without pay to be worked without thanks to be worked day up to nightfall; to be 3/5ths of a human being at best: to be this valuable, this hated thing among strangers who purchased your life and then cursed it unceasingly: to be a slave: to be a slave: come to this country a slave and how should you sing? After the flogging the lynch rope the general terror and weariness what should you know of a lyrical life? How could you, belonging to no one, but property to those despising the smiles of your soul, how could you dare to create yourself: A poet?

A poet can read. A poet can write.

A poet is African in Africa, or Irish in Ireland, or French on the Left Bank of Paris, or white in Wisconsin. A Poet writes in her own language. A poet writes of her own people, her own history, her own vision, her own room, her own house where she sits at her own table quietly placing one word after another word until she builds a line and a movement and an image and a meaning that somersaults all of these into the singing, the absolutely individual voice of the poet: At liberty. A poet is somebody free. A poet is someone at home.

How should there be Black poets in America?

It was not natural. And she was the first. In 1761, so far back before the revolution that produced these United States, so far back before the concept of freedom disturbed the insolent crimes of this continent, in 1761, when seven year old Phillis stood, as she must, when she stood nearly naked, as small as a seven year old, by herself, standing on land at last, at last, after the long, annihilating horrors of the middle Passage. Phillis, standing on the auctioneer's rude platform: Phillis For Sale:

Was it a nice day?

Does it matter? Should she muse on the sky or remember the sea? Until then Phillis had been somebody's child. Now she was about to become somebody's slave.

Suzannah and John Wheatley finished their breakfast and ordered the carriage brought 'round. They would ride to the auction. This would be an important outing. They planned to buy yet another human being to help with the happiness of their comfortable life in Boston. You don't buy a human being, you don't purchase a slave, without thinking ahead. So they had planned this excursion. They were dressed for the occasion, and excited, probably. And experienced, certainly. The Wheatleys already owned several slaves. They had done this before; the transaction would not startle or confound or embarrass or appall either one of them.

Was it a nice day?

When the Wheatleys arrived at the auction they greeted their neighbors, they enjoyed this business of mingling with other townsfolk politely shifting about the platform, politely adjusting positions for gain of a better view of the bodies for sale. The Wheatleys were good people. They were kind people. They were openminded and thoughtful. They looked at the bodies for sale. They looked and they looked. This one could be useful for that. That one might be useful for this. But then they looked at that child, that black child standing nearly naked, by herself. Seven or eight years old, at the most, and frail. Now that was a different proposal! Not a strong body, not a grown set of shoulders, not a promising wide set of hips, but a little body, a delicate body, a young, surely terrified face! John Wheatley agreed to the whim of his wife, Suzannah. He put in his bid. He put down his cash. He called out the numbers. He competed successfully. He had a good time. He got what he wanted. He purchased yet another slave. He bought that Black girl standing on the platform, nearly naked. He gave this new slave to his wife and Suzannah Wheatley was delighted. She and her husband went home. They rode there by carriage. They took that new slave with them. An old slave commanded the horses that pulled the carriage that carried the Wheatleys home, along with the new slave, that little girl they named Phillis.

Why did they give her that name?

Was it a nice day?

Does it matter?

It was not natural. And she was the first: Phillis Miracle: Phillis Miracle Wheatley: The first Black human being to be published in America. She was the second female to be published in America.

And the miracle begins in Africa. It was there that a bitterly anonymous man and a woman conjoined to create this genius, this lost child of such prodigious aptitude and such beguiling attributes that she very soon interposed the reality of her particular, dear life between the Wheatley's notions about slaves and the predictable outcome of such usual blasphemies against Black human beings.

Seven-year-old Phillis changed the slaveholding Wheatleys. She altered their minds. She entered their hearts. She made them see her and when they truly saw her, Phillis, darkly amazing them with the sweetness of her spirit and the alacrity of her forbidden, strange intelligence, they, in their own way, loved her as a prodigy, as a girl mysterious but godly.

Sixteen months after her entry into the Wheatley household Phillis was talking the language of her owners. Phillis was fluently reading The Scriptures. At eight and a half years of age, this Black child, or "Afric's Muse," as she would later describe herself, was fully literate in the language of this slaveholding land. She was competent and eargerly asking for more: more books, more and more information. And Suzannah Wheatley loved this child of her whimsical good luck. It pleased her to teach and to train and to tutor this Black girl, this Black darling of God. And so Phillis delved into kitchen studies commensurate, finally, to a classical education available to young white men at Harvard.

She was nine years old.

What did she read? What did she memorize? What did the Wheatleys give to this African child? Of course, it was white, all of it: White. It was English, most of it, from England. It was written, all of it, by white men taking their pleasure, their walks, their pipes, their pens and their paper, rather seriously, while somebody else cleaned the house, washed the clothes, cooked the food, watched the children: Probably not slaves, but possibly a servant, or, commonly, a wife: It was written, this white man's literature of England, while somebody else did the other things that have to be done. And that was the literature absorbed by the slave, Phillis Wheatley. That was the writing, the thoughts, the nostalgia, the lust, the conceits, the ambitions, the mannerisms, the games, the illusions, the discoveries, the filth and the flowers that filled up the mind of the African child.

At fourteen, Phillis published her first poem, "To the University of Cambridge": Not a brief limerick or desultory, teenager's verse, but 32 lines of blank verse telling those fellows what for and whereas, according to their own strict Christian codes of behavior. It is in that poem that Phillis describes the miracle of her own Black poetry in America:

> While an intrinsic ardor bids me write
> the muse doth promise to assist my pen

She says that her poetry results from "an intrinsic ardor," not to dismiss the extraordinary kindness of the Wheatleys, and not to diminish the wealth of white men's literature with which she found herself quite saturated, but it was none of these extrinsic factors that compelled the labors of her poetry. It was she who created herself a poet, notwithstanding and in despite of everything around her.

Two years later, Phillis Wheatley, at the age of sixteen, had composed three additional, noteworthy poems. This is one of them, "On Being Brought from Africa to America":

> Twas mercy brought me from my Pagan land,
> Taught my benighted soul to understand
> That there's a God, that there's a Savior too:
> Once I redemption neither sought nor knew
> Some view our sable race with scornful eye,
> "Their color is a diabolic die."
> Remember, *Christians*, Negroes, black as Cain,
> May be refin'd, and join the angelic train.

Where did Phillis get these ideas?

It's simple enough to track the nonsense about herself "benighted": *benighted* means surrounded and preyed upon by darkness. That clearly reverses what had happened to that African child, surrounded by and captured by the greed of white men. Nor should we find puzzling her depiction of Africa as "Pagan" versus somewhere "refined." Even her bizarre interpretation of slavery's theft of Black life as a merciful rescue should not bewilder anyone. These are regular kinds of iniquitous nonsense found in white literature, the literature that Phillis Wheatley assimilated, with no choice in the matter.

But here, in this surprising poem, this first Black poet presents us with something wholly her own, something entirely new: It is her matter-of-fact assertion that "once I redemption neither sought nor knew," as in: Once I existed beyond and without these terms under consideration. *Once I existed on other than your terms.* And, she says, *but* since we are talking with your talk about good and evil/redemption and damnation, let me tell you something you had better understand. I am Black as Cain *and* I may very well be an angel of the Lord: Take care not to offend the Lord!

Where did that thought come to Phillis Wheatley?

Was it a nice day?

Does it matter?

Following her "intrinsic ardor," and attuned to the core of her own person, this girl, the first Black poet in America, had dared to redefine herself from house slave to, possibly, an angel of the Almighty.

And she was making herself at home.

And, depending on whether you estimated that nearly naked Black girl on the auction block to be seven or eight years old, in 1761, by the time she was eighteen or nineteen, she had published her first book of poetry, *Poems on Various Subjects Religious and Moral.* It was published in London, in 1773, and the American edition appeared, years later, in 1786.

*　　*　　*

Repeatedly singing for liberty, singing against the tyrannical, repeatedly avid in her trusting support of the American Revolution (how could men want freedom enough to die for it but then want slavery enough to die for that), repeatedly lifting witness to the righteous and the kindly factors of her days, she was no ordinary teenage poet, male or female, Black or white. Indeed, the insistently concrete content of her tribute to the revolutionaries who would forge America, an independent nation state, indeed the specific daily substance of her poetry establishes Phillis Wheatley as the first decidedly American poet on this continent, Black or white, male or female.

Nor did she only love the ones who purchased her, a slave, those ones who loved her, yes, but with astonishment. Her lifelong friend was a young Black woman, Obour Tanner, who lived in Newport, Rhode Island, and one of her few poems dedicated to a living person, but neither morbid nor ethereal, was written to the young Black visual artist, Sapio Moorhead, himself a slave. It is he who crafted the portrait of Phillis that serves as her frontispiece profile in her book of poems. Here are the opening lines from her poem, "To S. M., A Young African Painter, On Seeing His Works":

> To show the lab'ring bosom's deep intent,
> And thought in living characters to paint.
> When first thy pencil did those beauties give,
> And breathing figures learnt from thee to live,
> How did those prospects give my soul delight,
> A new creation rushing on my sight?
> Still, wondrous youth! each noble path pursue,
> On deathless glories fix thine ardent view:
> Still may the painter's and the poet's fire
> To aid thy pencil, and thy verse conspire!
> And many the charms of each seraphic theme
> Conduct thy footsteps to immortal fame!

Remember that the poet so generously addressing the "wondrous youth" is certainly no older than eighteen, herself! And this, years before the American Revolution, and how many many years before the 1960's! This is the first Black poet of America addressing her Brother Artist not as so-and-so's Boy, but as "Sapio Moorhead, A Young African Painter."

Where did Phillis Miracle acquire this consciousness?

Was it a nice day?

It was not natural. And she was the first.

But did she, we may persevere, critical from the ease of the 1980's, did she love, did she Need, freedom?

In a poem typically titled at such length and in such deferential rectitude as to discourage most readers from scanning the poem that follows, in the poem titled, "To the Right Honorable William, Earl of Dartmouth, His Majesty's Principal Secretary of State for North America, etc.", Phillis Miracle has written these irresistible, authentic, felt lines:

> No more America in mournful strain
> Of wrongs, and grievance unredress'd complain,
> No longer shalt Thou dread the iron chain,
> Which wanton tyranny with lawless head
> Had made, and with it meant t' enslave the land
> Should you, my Lord, while you peruse my song,
> Wonder from whence my love of Freedom sprung,
> Whence flow these wishes for the common food,
> By feeling hearts alone best understood,
> I, young in life, by seeming cruel of fate
> Was snatch'd from Afric's fancy'd happy seat.
> What pangs excruciating most molest
> What sorrows labour in my parent's breast?
> Steel'd was that soul and by no misery mov'd
> That from a father seized his babe belov'd
> Such, such my case. And can I then but pray
> Others may never feel tyrannic sway?

So did the darling girl of God compose her thoughts, prior to 1772.

And then.

And then her poetry, these poems, were published in London.

And then, during her twenty-first year, Suzannah Wheatley, the white woman slaveholder who had been changed into the white mother, the white mentor, the white protectorate of Phillis, died.

Without that white indulgence, that white love, without that white sponsorship, what happened to the young African daughter, the young African poet?

No one knows for sure.

With the death of Mrs. Wheatley, Phillis came of age, a Black slave in America.

Where did she live?

How did she eat?

No one knows for sure.

But four years later she met and married a Black man, John Peters. Mr. Peters apparently thought well of himself, and of his people. He comported himself with dignity, studied law, argued for the liberation of Black people, and earned the everyday dislike of whitefolks. His wife bore him three children; all of them died.

His wife contined to be Phillis Miracle.

His wife continued to obey the "intrinsic ardor" of her calling and she never ceased the practise of her poetry.

She hoped, in fact, to publish a second volume of her verse.

This would be the poetry of Phillis the lover of John, Phillis the woman, Phillis the wife of a Black man pragmatically premature in his defiant self-respect, Phillis giving birth to three children, Phillis the mother, who must bury the three children she delivered into American life.

None of these poems was ever published.

This would have been the poetry of someone who has chosen herself, free, and brave to be free in a land of slavery.

When she was thirty-one years old, in 1784, Phillis Wheatley, the first Black poet in America, she died.

Her husband, John Peters, advertised and begged that the manuscript of her poems she had given to someone, please be returned.

But no one returned them.

And I believe we would not have seen them, anyway. I believe no one would have published the poetry of Black Phillis Wheatley, that grown woman who stayed with her chosen Black man. I believe that the death of Suzannah Wheatley, coincident with the African poet's twenty-first birthday, signalled, decisively, the end of her status as a child, as a dependent. From there we would hear from an independent Black woman poet in America.

Can you imagine that, in 1775?

Can you imagine that, today?

America has long been tolerant of Black children, compared to its reception of independent Black men and Black women.

She died in 1784.

Was it a nice day?

It was not natural. And she was the first.

Last week, as the final judge for this year's Loft McKnight Awards in creative writing, Awards distributed in Minneapolis, Minnesota, I read through sixteen manuscripts of rather fine poetry.

These are the terms, the lexical items, that I encountered there:

> Rock, moon, star, roses, chimney, Prague, elms,
> lilac, railroad tracks, lake, lilies, snow geese,
> crow, mountain, arrow feathers, ear of corn, marsh
> sandstone, rabbitbush, gulley, pumpkins, eagle,
> tundra, dwarf willow dipper-bird, brown creek,
> lizards, sycamores, glacier, canteen, skate eggs,
> birch, spruce, pumphandle

Is there anything about that listing odd? I didn't suppose so. These are the terms, the lexical items accurate to the specific white Minnesota daily life of those white poets.

And so I did not reject these poems, I did not despise them saying, "How is this possible: Sixteen different manuscripts of poetry written in 1985 and not one of them uses the terms of my own Black life! Not one of them writes about the police murder of Eleanor Bumpurs or the Bernard Goetz shooting of four Black boys[1] or apartheid in South Africa, or unemployment, or famine in

---

1. Bumpurs, a woman in her late 60s with a history of mental illness, was killed by police trying to evict her from her apartment in the Bronx in Octo- ber 1986; in December 1984, Goetz shot four young men he thought were about to rob him in a Manhattan subway car.

Ethiopia, or rape, or fire escapes, or cruise missiles in the New York harbor, or medicare, or alleyways, or napalm, or $4 an hour, and no time off for lunch.

I did not and I would not presume to impose my urgencies upon white poets writing in America. But the miracle of Black poetry in America, the *difficult* miracle of Black poetry in America, is that we have been rejected and we are frequently dismissed as "political" or "topical" or "sloganeering" and "crude" and "insignificant" because, like Phillis Wheatley, we have persisted for freedom. We will write against South Africa and we will seldom pen a poem about wild geese flying over Prague, or grizzlies at the rain barrel under the dwarf willow trees. We will write, published or not, however we may, like Phillis Wheatley, of the terror and the hungering and the quandries of our African lives on this North American soil. And as long as we study white literature, as long as we assimilate the English language and its implicit, English values, as long as we allude and defer to gods we "neither sought nor knew," as long as we, Black poets in America, remain the children of slavery, as long as we do not come of age and attempt, then, to speak the truth of our difficult maturity in an alien place, then we will be beloved, and sheltered, and published, and praised.

But not otherwise. And yet we persist.

And it was not natural. And she was the first.

This is the difficult miracle of Black poetry in America: that we persist, published or not, and loved or unloved: we persist.

And this is: "Something like A Sonnet for Phillis Miracle Wheatley":

> Girl from the realm of birds florid and fleet
> flying full feather in far or near weather
> Who fell to a dollar lust coffled like meat
> Captured by avarice and hate spit together
> Trembling asthmatic alone on the slave bloc
> built by a savagery travelling by carriage
> Viewed like a species of flaw in the livestock
> A child without safety of mother or marriage
>
> Chosen by whimsy but born to surprise
> They taught you to read but you learned how to write
> Begging the universe into your eyes:
> They dressed you in light but you dreamed
> with the night.
>
> From Africa singing of justice and grace,
> Your early verse sweetens the fame of our Race,

And because we Black people in North America persist in an irony profound, Black poetry persists in this way:

> Like the trees of winter and
> like the snow which has no power
> makes very little sound
> but comes and collects itself
> edible light on the black trees
> The tall black trees of winter
> lifting up a poetry of snow
> so that we may be astounded

by the poems of black
trees inside a cold environment.

1986

GLORIA ANZALDÚA
1942–2004

Describing herself as a "border woman" who "grew up between two cultures, the Mexican (with a heavy Indian influence) and the Anglo (as a member of a colonized people in our own territory)," the Chicana writer Gloria Anzaldúa was a major theorist of what she called the "borderlands" between and among ethnic and racial identities as well as the ways in which the ambiguities of those zones help to shape the politics of lesbianism and feminism. Combining historical scholarship with poetry, linguistics with mythology, her work is therefore as focused on "sexual borderlands, and spiritual borderlands" as it is on geographical lines of demarcation. "Borderlands are physically present wherever two or more cultures edge each other," she once commented, and in "The New Mestiza," which we have reprinted here, she dreams, along with the Mexican philosopher José Vasconcelos, of a new mixed race, "*la primera raza síntesis del globo*" that would be, as Vasconcelos put it, "a cosmic race[,] . . . a fifth race embracing the four major races of the world."

Born into a seventh-generation Mexican American family in south Texas, Anzaldúa worked for a time as a farm laborer before going on to college, becoming the first member of her family to gain an education beyond high school. She graduated from Pan American University in 1969, earned an M.A. from the University of Texas at Austin in 1972, and later studied for a doctorate at the University of California, Santa Cruz, while teaching both there and at San Francisco State. Eventually, Anzaldúa devoted herself primarily to writing; in addition to the influential multicultural anthology *This Bridge Called My Back* (1981), which she co-edited with Cherríe Moraga, and her powerful *Borderlands/La Frontera* (1987), from which our selection is drawn, she produced a number of other projects demonstrating the *mestiza* consciousness with which she sought to replace "the policy of racial purity that white America practices." These included another anthology, *Making Face, Making Soul/Haciendo Caras: Creative and Critical Perspectives by Feminists of Color* (1990), and three bilingual children's books. Anzaldúa died from complications of diabetes when she was only weeks away from finally receiving the doctorate for which she had long been studying at UC Santa Cruz.

From Borderlands/*La Frontera*: The New Mestiza

Chapter 7. La conciencia de la mestiza:[1]
Towards a New Consciousness

> Por la mujer de mi raza
> hablará el espíritu.

José Vasconcelos, Mexican philosopher, envisaged *una raza mestiza, una mezcla de razas afines, una raza de color—la primera raza síntesis del globo*. He

---

1. At Anzaldúa's request, Spanish words are not translated in the notes (all subsequent notes are hers, except as indicated).

called it a cosmic race, *la raza cósmica*, a fifth race embracing the four major races of the world.[2] Opposite to the theory of the pure Aryan, and to the policy of racial purity that white America practices, his theory is one of inclusivity. At the confluence of two or more genetic streams, with chromosomes constantly "crossing over," this mixture of races, rather than resulting in an inferior being, provides hybrid progeny, a mutable, more malleable species with a rich gene pool. From this racial, ideological, cultural and biological cross-pollinization, an "alien" consciousness is presently in the making—a new *mestiza* consciousness, *una conciencia de mujer*. It is a consciousness of the Borderlands.

UNA LUCHA DE FRONTERAS/A STRUGGLE OF BORDERS

> Because I, a *mestiza*,
> continually walk out of one culture
> and into another,
> because I am in all cultures at the same time,
> *alma entre dos mundos, tres, cuatro,*
> *me zumba la cabeza con lo contradictorio.*
> *Estoy norteada por todas las voces que me hablan*
> *simultáneamente.*

The ambivalence from the clash of voices results in mental and emotional states of perplexity. Internal strife results in insecurity and indecisiveness. The *mestiza*'s dual or multiple personality is plagued by psychic restlessness.

In a constant state of mental nepantilism, an Aztec word meaning torn between ways, *la mestiza* is a product of the transfer of the cultural and spiritual values of one group to another. Being tricultural, monolingual, bilingual, or multilingual, speaking a patois, and in a state of perpetual transition, the *mestiza* faces the dilemma of the mixed breed: which collectivity does the daughter of a darkskinned mother listen to?

El choque de un alma atrapado entre el mundo del espíritu y el mundo de la técnica a veces la deja entullada. Cradled in one culture, sandwiched between two cultures, straddling all three cultures and their value systems, *la mestiza* undergoes a struggle of flesh, a struggle of borders, an inner war. Like all people, we perceive the version of reality that our culture communicates. Like others having or living in more than one culture, we get multiple, often opposing messages. The coming together of two self-consistent but habitually incomparable frames of reference[3] causes *un choque*, a cultural collision.

Within us and within *la cultura chicana*, commonly held beliefs of the white culture attack commonly held beliefs of the Mexican culture, and both attack commonly held beliefs of the indigenous culture. Subconsciously, we see an attack on ourselves and our beliefs as a threat and we attempt to block with a counterstance.

But it is not enough to stand on the opposite river bank, shouting questions, challenging patriarchal, white conventions. A counterstance locks one into a duel of oppressor and oppressed; locked in mortal combat, like the cop and the

2. This is my own "take off" on José Vasconcelos' idea. José Vasconcelos, *La Raza Cósmica: Misión de la Raza Ibero-Americana* (Mexico City: Aguilar S.A. de Ediciones, 1961).

3. Arthur Koestler termed this "bisociation." Albert Rothenberg, *The Creative Process in Art, Science, and Other Fields* (Chicago: University of Chicago Press, 1979), 12.

criminal, both are reduced to a common denominator of violence. The counterstance refutes the dominant culture's views and beliefs, and, for this, it is proudly defiant. All reaction is limited by, and dependent on, what it is reacting against. Because the counterstance stems from a problem with authority—outer as well as inner—it's a step towards liberation from cultural domination. But it is not a way of life. At some point, on our way to a new consciousness, we will have to leave the opposite bank, the split between the two mortal combatants somehow healed so that we are on both shores at once and, at once, see through serpent and eagle eyes. Or perhaps we will decide to disengage from the dominant culture, write it off altogether as a lost cause, and cross the border into a wholly new and separate territory. Or we might go another route. The possibilities are numerous once we decide to act and not react.

A TOLERANCE FOR AMBIGUITY

These numerous possibilities leave *la mestiza* floundering in uncharted seas. In perceiving conflicting information and points of view, she is subjected to a swamping of her psychological borders. She has discovered that she can't hold concepts or ideas in rigid boundaries. The borders and walls that are supposed to keep the undesirable ideas out are entrenched habits and patterns of behavior; these habits and patterns are the enemy within. Rigidity means death. Only by remaining flexible is she able to stretch the psyche horizontally and vertically. *La mestiza* constantly has to shift out of habitual formations; from convergent thinking, analytical reasoning that tends to use rationality to move toward a single goal (a Western mode), to divergent thinking,[4] characterized by movement away from set patterns and goals and toward a more whole perspective, one that includes rather than excludes.

The new *mestiza* copes by developing a tolerance for contradictions, a tolerance for ambiguity. She learns to be an Indian in Mexican culture, to be Mexican from an Anglo point of view. She learns to juggle cultures. She has a plural personality, she operates in a pluralistic mode—nothing is thrust out, the good the bad and the ugly, nothing rejected, nothing abandoned. Not only does she sustain contradictions, she turns the ambivalence into something else.

She can be jarred out of ambivalence by an intense, and often painful, emotional event which inverts or resolves the ambivalence. I'm not sure exactly how. The work takes place underground—subconsciously. It is work that the soul performs. That focal point or fulcrum, that juncture where the *mestiza* stands, is where phenomena tend to collide. It is where the possibility of uniting all that is separate occurs. This assembly is not one where severed or separated pieces merely come together. Nor is it a balancing of opposing powers. In attempting to work out a synthesis, the self has added a third element which is greater than the sum of its severed parts. That third element is a new consciousness—a *mestiza* consciousness—and though it is a source of intense pain, its energy comes from continual creative motion that keeps breaking down the unitary aspect of each new paradigm.

En unas pocas centurias, the future will belong to the *mestiza*. Because the future depends on the breaking down of paradigms, it depends on the strad-

---

4. In part, I derive my definitions for "convergent" and "divergent" thinking from Rothenberg, 12–13.

dling of two or more cultures. By creating a new mythos—that is, a change in the way we perceive reality, the way we see ourselves, and the ways we behave—*la mestiza* creates a new consciousness.

The work of *mestiza* consciousness is to break down the subject-object duality that keeps her a prisoner and to show in the flesh and through the images in her work how duality is transcended. The answer to the problem between the white race and the colored, between males and females, lies in healing the split that originates in the very foundation of our lives, our culture, our languages, our thoughts. A massive uprooting of dualistic thinking in the individual and collective consciousness is the beginning of a long struggle, but one that could, in our best hopes, bring us to the end of rape, of violence, of war.

LA ENCRUCIJADA/THE CROSSROADS

A chicken is being sacrificed
    at a crossroads, a simple mound of earth
a mud shrine for *Eshu*,
    Yoruba[5] god of indeterminacy,
who blesses her choice of path.
    She begins her journey.

Su cuerpo es una bocacalle. La mestiza has gone from being the sacrificial goat to becoming the officiating priestess at the crossroads.

As a *mestiza* I have no country, my homeland cast me out; yet all countries are mine because I am every woman's sister or potential lover. (As a lesbian I have no race, my own people disclaim me; but I am all races because there is the queer of me in all races.) I am cultureless because, as a feminist, I challenge the collective cultural/religious male-derived beliefs of Indo-Hispanics and Anglos; yet I am cultured because I am participating in the creation of yet another culture, a new story to explain the world and our participation in it, a new value system with images and symbols that connect us to each other and to the planet. *Soy un amasamiento*, I am an act of kneading, of uniting and joining that not only has produced both a creature of darkness and a creature of light, but also a creature that questions the definitions of light and dark and gives them new meanings.

We are the people who leap in the dark, we are the people on the knees of the gods. In our very flesh, (r)evolution works out the clash of cultures. It makes us crazy constantly, but if the center holds, we've made some kind of evolutionary step forward. *Nuestra alma el trabajo*, the opus, the great alchemical work; spiritual *mestizaje*, a "morphogenesis,"[6] an inevitable unfolding. We have become the quickening serpent movement.

Indigenous like corn, like corn, the *mestiza* is a product of crossbreeding, designed for preservation under a variety of conditions. Like an ear of corn—a female seed-bearing organ—the *mestiza* is tenacious, tightly wrapped in the husks of her culture. Like kernels she clings to the cob; with thick stalks and strong brace roots, she holds tight to the earth—she will survive the crossroads.

Lavando y remojando el maíz en agua de cal, despojando el pellejo.

---

5. One of the two largest ethnic groups in Nigeria.
6. To borrow chemist Ilya Prigogine's theory of "dissipative structures." Prigogine discovered that substances interact not in predictable ways as it was taught in science, but in different and fluctu-ating ways to produce new and more complex structures, a kind of birth he called "morphogenesis," which created unpredictable innovation. Harold Gilliam, "Searching for a New World View," *This World*, January 1981, 23.

Moliendo, mixteando, amasando, haciendo tortillas de masa.[7] She steeps the corn in lime, it swells, softens. With stone roller on *metate* she grinds the corn, then grinds again. She kneads and moulds the dough, pats the round balls into *tortillas*.

> We are the porous rock in the stone *metate*
> squatting on the ground
> We are the rolling pin, *el maíz y agua,*
> *la masa harina. Somos el amasijo.*
> *Somos lo molido en el metate.*
> We are the *comal* sizzling hot,
> the hot *tortilla*, the hungry mouth.
> We are the coarse rock.
> We are the grinding motion,
> the mixed potion, *somos el molcajete.*
> We are the pestle, the *comino, ajo, pimienta,*
> We are the *chile colorado,*
> the green shoot that cracks the rock.
> We will abide.

EL CAMINO DE LA MESTIZA/THE MESTIZA WAY

Caught between the sudden contraction, the breath sucked in and the endless space, the brown woman stands still, looks at the sky. She decides to go down, digging her way along the roots of trees. Sifting through the bones, she shakes them to see if there is any marrow in them. Then, touching the dirt to her forehead, to her tongue, she takes a few bones, leaves the rest in their burial place.

She goes through her backpack, keeps her journal and address book, throws away the muni-bart metromaps.[8] The coins are heavy and they go next, then the greenbacks flutter through the air. She keeps her knife, can opener and eyebrow pencil. She puts bones, pieces of bark, *hierbas*, eagle feather, snakeskin, tape recorder, the rattle and drum in her pack and she sets out to become the complete *tolteca*.[9]

Her first step is to take inventory. *Despojando, desgranando, quitando paja.* Just what did she inherit from her ancestors? This weight on her back—which is the baggage from the Indian mother, which the baggage from the Spanish father, which the baggage from the Anglo?

Pero es difícil differentiating between *lo heredado, lo adquirido, lo impuesto.* She puts history through a sieve, winnows out the lies, looks at the forces that we as a race, as women, have been a part of. *Luego bota lo que no vale, los desmientos, los desencuentos, el embrutecimiento. Aguarda el juicio, hondo y enraízado, de la gente antigua.* This step is a conscious rupture with all oppressive traditions of all cultures and religions. She communicates that rupture, documents the struggle. She reinterprets history and, using new symbols, she shapes new myths. She adopts new perspectives toward the darkskinned, women and queers. She strengthens her tolerance (and intolerance) for ambiguity. She is willing to share, to make herself vulnerable to foreign ways of seeing and thinking. She surrenders all notions of safety, of

---

7. *Tortillas de masa harina:* corn tortillas are of two types, the smooth uniform ones made in a tortilla press and usually bought at a tortilla factory or supermarket, and *gorditas*, made by mixing *masa* with lard or shortening or butter (my mother some-

times puts in bits of bacon or *chicarrones*).
8. Maps of San Francisco's bus and subway routes [editor's note].
9. Gina Valdés, *Puentes y Fronteras: Coplas Chicanas* (Los Angeles Castle Lithograph, 1982), 2.

the familiar. Deconstruct, construct. She becomes a *nahual*,[1] able to transform herself into a tree, a coyote, into another person. She learns to transform the small "I" into the total Self. *Se hace moldeadora de su alma. Según la concepción que tiene de sí misma, así será.*

> "*Tú no sirves pa' nada*—
> you're good for nothing.
> *Eres pura vieja.*"

"You're nothing but a woman" means you are defective. Its opposite is to be *un macho*. The modern meaning of the word "machismo," as well as the concept, is actually an Anglo invention. For men like my father, being "macho" meant being strong enough to protect and support my mother and us, yet being able to show love. Today's macho has doubts about his ability to feed and protect his family. His "machismo" is an adaptation to oppression and poverty and low self-esteem. It is the result of hierarchical male dominance. The Anglo, feeling inadequate and inferior and powerless, displaces or transfers these feelings to the Chicano by shaming him. In the Gringo world, the Chicano suffers from excessive humility and self-effacement, shame of self and self-depreciation. Around Latinos he suffers from a sense of language inadequacy and its accompanying discomfort; with Native Americans he suffers from a racial amnesia which ignores our common blood, and from guilt because the Spanish part of him took their land and oppressed them. He has an excessive compensatory hubris when around Mexicans from the other side. It overlays a deep sense of racial shame.

The loss of a sense of dignity and respect in the macho breeds a false machismo which leads him to put down women and even to brutalize them. Coexisting with his sexist behavior is a love for the mother which takes precedence over that of all others. Devoted son, macho pig. To wash down the shame of his acts, of his very being, and to handle the brute in the mirror, he takes to the bottle, the snort, the needle, and the fist.

Though we "understand" the root causes of male hatred and fear, and the subsequent wounding of women, we do not excuse, we do not condone, and we will no longer put up with it. From the men of our race, we demand the admission/acknowledgment/disclosure/testimony that they wound us, violate us, are afraid of us and of our power. We need them to say they will begin to eliminate their hurtful put-down ways. But more than the words, we demand acts. We say to them: We will develop equal power with you and those who have shamed us.

It is imperative that *mestizas* support each other in changing the sexist elements in the Mexican-Indian culture. As long as woman is put down, the Indian and the Black in all of us is put down. The struggle of the *mestiza* is above all a feminist one. As long as *los hombres* think they have to *chingar mujeres* and each other to be men, as long as men are taught that they are superior and therefore culturally favored over *la mujer*, as long as to be a *vieja* is a thing of derision, there can be no real healing of our psyches. We're halfway there—we have such love of the Mother, the good mother. The first

1. In some Native American legends of Mexico and Central America, a shape changer.

step is to unlearn the *puta/virgen* dichotomy and to see *Coatlapopeuh-Coatlicue* in the Mother, *Guadalupe*.[2]

Tenderness, a sign of vulnerability, is so feared that it is showered on women with verbal abuse and blows. Men, even more than women, are fettered to gender roles. Women at least have had the guts to break out of bondage. Only gay men have had the courage to expose themselves to the woman inside them and to challenge the current masculinity. I've encountered a few scattered and isolated gentle straight men, the beginnings of a new breed, but they are confused, and entangled with sexist behaviors that they have not been able to eradicate. We need a new masculinity and the new man needs a movement.

Lumping the males who deviate from the general norm with man, the oppressor, is a gross injustice. *Asombra pensar que nos hemos quedado en ese pozo oscuro donde el mundo encierra a las lesbianas. Asombra pensar que hemos, como femenistas y lesbianas, cerrado nuestros corazónes a los hombres, a nuestros hermanos los jotos, desheredados y marginales como nosotros.* Being the supreme crossers of cultures, homosexuals have strong bonds with the queer white, Black, Asian, Native American, Latino, and with the queer in Italy, Australia and the rest of the planet. We come from all colors, all classes, all races, all time periods. Our role is to link people with each other—the Blacks with Jews with Indians with Asians with whites with extraterrestrials. It is to transfer ideas and information from one culture to another. Colored homosexuals have more knowledge of other cultures; have always been at the forefront (although sometimes in the closet) of all liberation struggles in this country; have suffered more injustices and have survived them despite all odds. Chicanos need to acknowledge the political and artistic contributions of their queer. People, listen to what your *jotería* is saying.

The *mestizo* and the queer exist at this time and point on the evolutionary continuum for a purpose. We are a blending that proves that all blood is intricately woven together, and that we are spawned out of similar souls.

SOMOS UNA GENTE

Hay tantísimas fronteras
que dividen a la gente,
pero por cada frontera
existe también un puente.

—Gina Valdés[3]

Divided Loyalties. Many women and men of color do not want to have any dealings with white people. It takes too much time and energy to explain to the downwardly mobile, white middle-class women that it's okay for us to want to own "possessions," never having had any nice furniture on our dirt floors or "luxuries" like washing machines. Many feel that whites should help their own people rid themselves of race hatred and fear first. I, for one, choose to use some of my energy to serve as mediator. I think we need to allow whites to be our allies. Through our literature, art, *corridos*, and folktales we

2. Our Lady of Guadalupe, the Virgin Mary (who is said to have appeared to a Native American in that Mexican city in 1531). *Coatlapopeuh-* *Coatlicue*: Aztec earth goddess who is the mother of the gods [editor's note].

3. Valdés, *Puentes y Fronteras*, 2.

must share our history with them so when they set up committees to help Big Mountain Navajos or the Chicano farmworkers or *los Nicaragüenses*[4] they won't turn people away because of their racial fears and ignorances. They will come to see that they are not helping us but following our lead.

Individually, but also as a racial entity, we need to voice our needs. We need to say to white society: We need you to accept the fact that Chicanos are different, to acknowledge your rejection and negation of us. We need you to own the fact that you looked upon us as less than human, that you stole our lands, our personhood, our self-respect. We need you to make public restitution: to say that, to compensate for your own sense of defectiveness, you strive for power over us, you erase our history and our experience because it makes you feel guilty—you'd rather forget your brutish acts. To say you've split yourself from minority groups, that you disown us, that your dual consciousness splits off parts of yourself, transferring the "negative" parts onto us. (Where there is persecution of minorities, there is shadow projection. Where there is violence and war, there is repression of shadow.) To say that you are afraid of us, that to put distance between us, you wear the mask of contempt. Admit that Mexico is your double, that she exists in the shadow of this country, that we are irrevocably tied to her. Gringo, accept the doppelganger in your psyche. By taking back your collective shadow the intracultural split will heal. And finally, tell us what you need from us.

BY YOUR TRUE FACES WE WILL KNOW YOU

I am visible—see this Indian face—yet I am invisible. I both blind them with my beak nose and aim their blind spot. But I exist, we exist. They'd like to think I have melted in the pot. But I haven't, we haven't.

The dominant white culture is killing us slowly with its ignorance. By taking away our self-determination, it has made us weak and empty. As a people we have resisted and we have taken expedient positions, but we have never been allowed to develop unencumbered—we have never been allowed to be fully ourselves. The whites in power want us people of color to barricade ourselves behind our separate tribal walls so they can pick us off one at a time with their hidden weapons; so they can whitewash and distort history. Ignorance splits people, creates prejudices. A misinformed people is a subjugated people.

Before the Chicano and the undocumented worker and the Mexican from the other side can come together, before the Chicano can have unity with Native Americans and other groups, we need to know the history of their struggle and they need to know ours. Our mothers, our sisters and brothers, the guys who hang out on street corners, the children in the playgrounds, each of us must know our Indian lineage, our afro-*mestisaje*, our history of resistance.

To the immigrant *mexicano* and the recent arrivals we must teach our history. The 80 million *mexicanos* and the Latinos from Central and South America must know of our struggles. Each one of us must know basic facts about Nicaragua, Chile and the rest of Latin America.[5] The Latinoist movement (Chicanos, Puerto Ricans, Cubans and other Spanish-speaking people

---

4. In the 1980s the U.S. government funded soldiers fighting against the Sandinista government of Nicaragua [editor's note].
5. This history includes U.S. government interventions in various Latin and Central American countries from 1950 to 1990, undermining governments thought to be too leftist and supporting right-wing governments [editor's note].

working together to combat racial discrimination in the market place) is good but it is not enough. Other than a common culture we will have nothing to hold us together. We need to meet on a broader communal ground.

The struggle is inner: Chicano, *indio*, American Indian, *mojado, mexicano*, immigrant Latino, Anglo in power, working class Anglo, Black, Asian—our psyches resemble the bordertowns and are populated by the same people. The struggle has always been inner, and is played out in the outer terrains. Awareness of our situation must come before inner changes, which in turn come before changes in society. Nothing happens in the "real" world unless it first happens in the images in our heads.

EL DÍA DE LA CHICANA

I will not be shamed again
Nor will I shame myself.

I am possessed by a vision that we Chicanas and Chicanos have taken back or uncovered our true faces, our dignity and self-respect. It's a validation vision.

Seeing the Chicana anew in light of her history. I seek an exoneration, a seeing through the fictions of white supremacy, a seeing of ourselves in our true guises and not as the false racial personality that has been given to us and that we have given to ourselves. I seek our woman's face, our true features, the positive and the negative seen clearly, free of the tainted biases of male dominance. I seek new images of identity, new beliefs about ourselves, our humanity and worth no longer in question.

Estamos viviendo en la noche de la Raza, un tiempo cuando el trabajo se hace a lo quieto, en el oscuro. El día cuando aceptamos tal y como somos y para en donde vamos y porque—ese día será de la Raza. Yo tengo el conpromiso de expresar mi visión, mi sensibilidad, mi percepión de la revalidación de la gente mexicana, su mérito estimación, honra, aprecio, y validez.

On December 2nd when my sun goes into my first house, I celebrate *el día de la Chicana y el Chicano*. On that day I clean my altars, light my *Coatlalopeuh* candle, burn sage and copal, take *el baño para espantar basura*, sweep my house. On that day I bare my soul, make myself vulnerable to friends and family by expressing my feelings. On that day I affirm who we are.

On that day I look inside our conflicts and our basic introverted racial temperament. I identify our needs, voice them. I acknowledge that the self and the race have been wounded. I recognize the need to take care of our personhood, of our racial self. On that day I gather the splintered and disowned parts of *la gente mexicana* and hold them in my arms. *Todas las partes de nosotros valen.*

On that day I say, "Yes, all you people wound us when you reject us. Rejection strips us of self-worth; our vulnerability exposes us to shame. It is our innate identity you find wanting. We are ashamed that we need your good opinion, that we need your acceptance. We can no longer camouflage our needs, can no longer let defenses and fences sprout around us. We can no longer withdraw. To rage and look upon you with contempt is to rage and be contemptuous of ourselves. We can no longer blame you, nor disown the white parts, the male parts, the pathological parts, the queer parts, the vulnerable parts. Here we are weaponless with open arms, with only our magic. Let's try it our way, the *mestiza* way, the Chicana way, the woman way.

On that day, I search for our essential dignity as a people, a people with a sense of purpose—to belong and contribute to something greater than our *pueblo*. On that day I seek to recover and reshape my spiritual identity. *¡Aní-mate! Raza, a celebrar el día de la Chicana.*

EL RETORNO

All movements are accomplished in six stages,
and the seventh brings return.
—I Ching[6]

Tanto tiempo sin verte casa mía,
mi cuna, mi hondo nido de la huerta.
—"Soledad"[7]

I stand at the river, watch the curving, twisting serpent, a serpent nailed to the fence where the mouth of the Rio Grande empties into the Gulf.

I have come back. *Tanto dolor me costó el alejamiento.* I shade my eyes and look up. The bone beak of a hawk slowly circling over me, checking me out as potential carrion. In its wake a little bird flickering its wings, swimming sporadically like a fish. In the distance the expressway and the slough of traffic like an irritated sow. The sudden pull in my gut, *la tierra, los aguaceros.* My land, *el viento soplando la arena, el lagartijo debajo de un nopalito. Me acuerdo como era antes. Una región desértica de vasta llanuras, costeras de baja altura, de escasa lluvia, de chaparrales formados por mesquites y huizaches.* If I look real hard I can almost see the Spanish fathers who were called "the cavalry of Christ" enter this valley riding their burros, see the clash of cultures commence.

Tierra natal. This is home, the small towns in the Valley, *los pueblitos* with chicken pens and goats picketed to mesquite shrubs. *En las colonias* on the other side of the tracks, junk cars line the front yards of hot pink and lavender-trimmed houses—Chicano architecture we call it, self-consciously. I have missed the TV shows where hosts speak in half and half, and where awards are given in the category of Tex-Mex music. I have missed the Mexican cemeteries blooming with artificial flowers, the fields of aloe vera and red pepper, rows of sugar cane, of corn hanging on the stalks, the cloud of *polvareda* in the dirt roads behind a speeding pickup truck, *el sabor de tamales de rez y venado.* I have missed *la yegua colorada* gnawing the wooden gate of her stall, the smell of horse flesh from Carito's corrals. *He hecho menos las noches calientes sin aire, noches de linternas y lechuzas* making holes in the night.

I still feel the old despair when I look at the unpainted, dilapidated, scrap lumber houses consisting mostly of corrugated aluminum. Some of the poorest people in the U.S. live in the Lower Rio Grande Valley, an arid and semi-arid land of irrigated farming, intense sunlight and heat, citrus groves next to chaparral and cactus. I walk through the elementary school I attended so long ago, that remained segregated until recently. I remember how the white teachers used to punish us for being Mexican.

---

6. Richard Wilhelm, *The I Ching or Book of Changes*, trans. Cary F. Baynes (Princeton: Princeton University Press, 1950), 98.

7. "Soledad" is sung by the group Haciendo Punto and Otto Son.

How I love this tragic valley of South Texas, as Ricardo Sánchez[8] calls it; this borderland between the Nueces and the Rio Grande. This land has survived possession and ill-use by five countries: Spain, Mexico, the Republic of Texas, the U.S., the Confederacy, and the U.S. again. It has survived Anglo-Mexican blood feuds, lynchings, burnings, rapes, pillage.

Today I see the Valley still struggling to survive. Whether it does or not, it will never be as I remember it. The borderlands depression that was set off by the 1982 peso devaluation in Mexico resulted in the closure of hundreds of Valley businesses. Many people lost their homes, cars, land. Prior to 1982, U.S. store owners thrived on retail sales to Mexicans who came across the border for groceries and clothes and appliances. While goods on the U.S. side have become 10, 100, 1000 times more expensive for Mexican buyers, goods on the Mexican side have become 10, 100, 1000 times cheaper for Americans. Because the Valley is heavily dependent on agriculture and Mexican retail trade, it has the highest unemployment rates along the entire border region; it is the Valley that has been hardest hit.[9]

"It's been a bad year for corn," my brother, Nune, says. As he talks, I remember my father scanning the sky for a rain that would end the drought, looking up into the sky, day after day, while the corn withered on its stalk. My father has been dead for 29 years, having worked himself to death. The life span of a Mexican farm laborer is 56—he lived to be 38. It shocks me that I am older than he. I, too, search the sky for rain. Like the ancients, I worship the rain god and the maize goddess, but unlike my father I have recovered their names. Now for rain (irrigation) one offers not a sacrifice of blood, but of money.

"Farming is in a bad way," my brother says. "Two to three thousand small and big farmers went bankrupt in this country last year. Six years ago the price of corn was $8.00 per hundred pounds," he goes on. "This year it is $3.90 per hundred pounds." And, I think to myself, after taking inflation into account, not planting anything puts you ahead.

I walk out to the back yard, stare at *los rosales de mamá*. She wants me to help her prune the rose bushes, dig out the carpet grass that is choking them. *Mamagrande Ramona también tenía rosales*. Here every Mexican grows flowers. If they don't have a piece of dirt, they use car tires, jars, cans, shoe boxes. Roses are the Mexican's favorite flower. I think, how symbolic—thorns and all.

Yes, the Chicano and Chicana have always taken care of growing things and the land. Again I see the four of us kids getting off the school bus, changing into our work clothes, walking into the field with Papí and Mamí, all six of us bending to the ground. Below our feet, under the earth lie the watermelon seeds. We cover them with paper plates, putting *terremotes* on top of the plates to keep them from being blown away by the wind. The paper plates keep the freeze away. Next day or the next, we remove the plates, bare the tiny green shoots to the elements. They survive and grow, give fruit hundreds of times the size of the seed. We water them and hoe them. We harvest them.

8. American poet and critic (1941–1995) [editor's note].
9. Out of the 22 border counties in the four border states, Hidalgo County (named for Father Hidalgo who was shot in 1810 after instigating Mexico's revolt against Spain under the banner of *la Virgen de Guadalupe*) is the most poverty-stricken county in the nation as well as the largest home base (along with Imperial in California) for migrant farm-workers. It was here that I was born and raised. I am amazed that both it and I have survived.

The vines dry, rot, are plowed under. Growth, death, decay, birth. The soil prepared again and again, impregnated, worked on. A constant changing of forms, *renacimientos de latierra madre.*

> This land was Mexican once
> was Indian always
> and is.
> And will be again.

1987

URSULA K. LE GUIN
b. 1929

Ursula K. Le Guin is among the major writers of science fiction, fantasy, and what she herself calls "speculative fiction" at work today. The daughter of the distinguished anthropologist Alfred L. Kroeber and the psychologist and biographer Theodora Kroeber (author of the best-selling *Ishi in Two Worlds*, 1961), Le Guin has frequently defined herself as a kind of ethnologist, noting that "Science fiction allows a fiction writer to make up cultures, to *invent*—not only a new world, but a new *culture*," and adding that although "my father preferred to go find [other civilizations,] I prefer to invent them." Born and raised in Berkeley, California, she attended Radcliffe College and Columbia University, and is married to the historian Charles A. Le Guin, with whom she has long lived in Portland, Oregon. From the start, Le Guin has explained, her writing always had "what you'd have to call a fantasy element. . . . It took place in an imaginary country or something like that"; but it was not until she "got back to reading science fiction in [her] late twenties" that she realized "I could *call* my stuff science fiction."

Among the fascinating cultures Le Guin has invented, perhaps the most famous is the fluidly gendered Gethenian society on which she focuses in her pioneering novel *The Left Hand of Darkness* (1969), a work that ranks with Virginia Woolf's *Orlando* (1928) as a triumphant fantasy of transsexuality. "Is Gender Necessary? Redux" (1987), which we reprint here, recounts Le Guin's own story of the genesis of this important text, explaining why and how she wrote it in the mid-1960s while also recording, through "a running commentary in bracketed italics," the ways in which over the years she has changed her views of the novel. "It is rather in the feminist mode to let one's changes of mind, and the process of change, stand as evidence," Le Guin remarks in a prefatory statement, adding that it's worthwhile "to remind people that minds that don't change are like clams that don't open."

As the arguments dramatized both in "Is Gender Necessary? Redux" and in *The Left Hand of Darkness* suggest, Le Guin has long been a passionate feminist, and many of her writings functioned as icons for the second wave of the women's movement that crested in the 1970s and 1980s. In "Sur" (1982), one of her most brilliant short stories, she imagined what would have happened if a group of female explorers, rather than a group of men, had been the first expedition to reach the South Pole, while in "She Unnames Them" (1985) she considers the linguistic differences that might have arisen if Eve, rather than Adam, had controlled the primordial processes of naming. Her other works include more than twenty novels, among them *The Dispossessed* (1974) and most recently *The Telling* (2000), *The Other Wind* (2001), and *Gifts* (2004), as well as numerous short story collections and (along with other books for young people) three popular fantasies for children—*A Wizard of Earthsea* (1968), *The Tombs of Atuan* (1971), and *The Farthest Shore* (1972)—that make up the prize-winning *Earthsea* trilogy. But Le Guin has also been a poet as well as an incisive critic and essayist. Her major critical and theoretical texts include *Dancing at the Edge of the World: Thoughts on Words, Women, Places* (1989)—in which "Is Gender Necessary? Redux" appears—and *The Language of the Night: Essays on Fantasy and Science Fiction* (1992).

Is Gender Necessary? Redux

(1976/1987)

"Is Gender Necessary?" first appeared in Aurora, *that splendid first anthology of science fiction written by women, edited by Susan Anderson and Vonda N. McIntyre. It was later included in* The Language of the Night. *Even then I was getting uncomfortable with some of the statements I made in it, and the discomfort soon became plain disagreement. But those were just the bits that people kept quoting with cries of joy.*

It doesn't seem right or wise to revise an old text severely, as if trying to obliterate it, hiding the evidence that one had to go there to get here. It is rather in the feminist mode to let one's changes of mind, and the processes of change, stand as evidence—and perhaps to remind people that minds that don't change are like clams that don't open. So I here reprint the original essay entire, with a running commentary in bracketed italics. I request and entreat anyone who wishes to quote from this piece henceforth to use or at least include these reconsiderations. And I do very much hope that I don't have to print re-reconsiderations in 1997, since I'm a bit tired of chastising myself.

In the mid-1960s the women's movement was just beginning to move again, after a fifty-year halt. There was a groundswell gathering. I felt it, but I didn't know it was a groundswell; I just thought it was something wrong with me. I considered myself a feminist; I didn't see how you could be a thinking woman and not be a feminist; but I had never taken a step beyond the ground gained for us by Emmeline Pankhurst and Virginia Woolf.

[Feminism has enlarged its ground and strengthened its theory and practice immensely, and enduringly, in these past twenty years; but has anyone actually taken a step "beyond" Virginia Woolf? The image, implying an ideal of "progress," is not one I would use now.]

Along about 1967, I began to feel a certain unease, a need to step on a little farther, perhaps, on my own. I began to want to define and understand the meaning of sexuality and the meaning of gender, in my life and in our society. Much had gathered in the unconscious—both personal and collective—which must either be brought up into consciousness or else turn destructive. It was that same need, I think, that had led Beauvoir to write *The Second Sex*, and Friedan to write *The Feminine Mystique*, and that was, at the same time, leading Kate Millett and others to write their books, and to create the new feminism. But I was not a theoretician, a political thinker or activist, or a sociologist. I was and am a fiction writer. The way I did my thinking was to write a novel. That novel, *The Left Hand of Darkness*, is the record of my consciousness, the process of my thinking.

Perhaps, now that we have all *[well, quite a lot of us, anyhow]* moved on to a plane of heightened consciousness about these matters, it might be of some interest to look back on the book, to see what it did, what it tried to do, and what it might have done, insofar as it is a "feminist" [*strike the quotation marks, please*] book. (Let me repeat that last qualification, once. The fact is that the real subject of the book is not feminism or sex or gender or anything of the sort; as far as I can see, it is a book about betrayal and fidelity. That is why one of its two dominant sets of symbols is an extended metaphor of winter, of ice, snow, cold: the winter journey. The rest of this discussion will concern only half, the lesser half, of the book.)

[*This parenthesis is overstated; I was feeling defensive, and resentful that critics of the book insisted upon talking only about its "gender problems," as if it were an essay not a novel. "The fact is that the real subject of the book is . . ." This is bluster. I had opened a can of worms and was trying hard to shut it. "The fact is," however, that there are other aspects to the book, which are involved with its sex/gender aspects quite inextricably.*]

It takes place on a planet called Gethen, whose human inhabitants differ from us in their sexual physiology. Instead of our continuous sexuality, the Gethenians have an oestrus period, called *kemmer*. When they are not in kemmer, they are sexually inactive and impotent; they are also androgynous. An observer in the book describes the cycle:

> In the first phase of kemmer [the individual] remains completely androgynous. Gender, and potency, are not attained in isolation. . . . Yet the sexual impulse is tremendously strong in this phase, controlling the entire personality. . . . When the individual finds a partner in kemmer, hormonal secretion is further stimulated (most importantly by touch—secretion? scent?) until in one partner either a male or female hormonal dominance is established. The genitals engorge or shrink accordingly, foreplay intensifies, and the partner, triggered by the change, takes on the other sexual role (apparently without exception). . . . Normal individuals have no predisposition to either sexual role in kemmer; they do not know whether they will be the male or the female, and have no choice in the matter. . . . The culminant phase of kemmer lasts from two to five days, during which sexual drive and capacity are at maximum. It ends fairly abruptly, and if conception has not taken place, the individual returns to the latent phase and the cycle begins anew. If the individual was in the female role and was impregnated, hormonal activity of course continues, and for the gestation and lactation periods this individual remains female. . . . With the cessation of lactation the female becomes once more a perfect androgyne. No physiological habit is established, and the mother of several children may be the father of several more.

Why did I invent these peculiar people? Not just so that the book could contain, halfway through it, the sentence "The king was pregnant"—though I admit that I am fond of that sentence. Not, certainly not, to propose Gethen as a model for humanity. I am not in favor of genetic alteration of the human organism—not at our present level of understanding. I was not recommending the Gethenian sexual setup: I was using it. It was a heuristic device, a thought-experiment. Physicists often do thought-experiments. Einstein shoots a light ray through a moving elevator; Schrödinger puts a cat in a box. There is no elevator, no cat, no box. The experiment is performed, the question is asked, in the mind. Einstein's elevator, Schrödinger's cat, my Gethenians, are simply a way of thinking. They are questions, not answers; process, not stasis. One of the essential functions of science fiction, I think, is precisely this kind of question-asking: reversals of a habitual way of thinking, metaphors for what our language has no words for as yet, experiments in imagination.

The subject of my experiment, then, was something like this: Because of our lifelong social conditioning, it is hard for us to see clearly what, besides purely physiological form and function, truly differentiates men and women. Are there real differences in temperament, capacity, talent, psychic processes, etc.? If so, what are they? Only comparative ethnology offers, so far, any solid evidence on the matter, and the evidence is incomplete and often contradictory. The only going social experiments that are truly relevant are the kibbutzim and the Chinese communes, and they too are inconclusive—and hard to get unbiased information about. How to find out? Well, one can always put a cat in a box. One can send an imaginary, but conventional, indeed rather stuffy, young man from Earth into an imaginary culture which is totally free of sex roles because there is no, absolutely no, physiological sex distinction. I eliminated gender, to find out what was left. Whatever was left would be, presumably, simply human. It would define the area that is shared by men and women alike.

I still think that this was a rather neat idea. But as an experiment, it was messy. All results were uncertain; a repetition of the experiment by someone else, or by myself seven years later, would probably give quite different results. [*Strike the word "probably" and replace it with "certainly."*] Scientifically, this is most disreputable. That's all right; I am not a scientist. I play the game where the rules keep changing.

Among these dubious and uncertain results, achieved as I thought, and wrote, and wrote, and thought, about my imaginary people, three appear rather interesting to me.

First: the absence of war. In the thirteen thousand years of recorded history on Gethen, there has not been a war. The people seem to be as quarrelsome, competitive, and aggressive as we are; they have fights, murders, assassinations, feuds, forays, and so on. But there have been no great invasions by peoples on the move, like the Mongols in Asia or the Whites in the New World: partly because Gethenian populations seem to remain stable in size, they do not move in large masses, or rapidly. Their migrations have been slow, no one generation going very far. They have no nomadic peoples, and no societies that live by expansion and aggression against other societies. Nor have they formed large, hierarchically governed nation-states, the mobilizable entity that is the essential factor in modern war. The basic social unit all over the planet is a group of two hundred to eight hundred people, called a *hearth,* a structure founded less on economic convenience than on sexual necessity (there must be others in kemmer at the same time), and therefore more tribal than urban in nature, though overlaid and interwoven with a later urban pattern. The hearth tends to be communal, independent and somewhat introverted. Rivalries between hearths, as between individuals, are channeled into a socially approved form of aggression called *shifgrethor,* a conflict without physical violence, involving one-upsmanship, the saving and losing of face—conflict ritualized, stylized, controlled. When shifgrethor breaks down there may be physical violence, but it does not become mass violence, remaining limited, personal. The active group remains small. The dispersive trend is as strong as the cohesive. Historically, when hearths gathered into a nation for economic reasons, the cellular pattern still dominated the centralized one. There might be a king and a parliament, but authority was not enforced so much by might as by the use of shifgrethor and intrigue, and was accepted as custom, without appeal to patriarchal ideals of divine right, patriotic duty, etc. Ritual and parade were far more effective agents of order than armies or police. Class structure was flexible and open; the value of the social hierarchy was less economic than aesthetic, and there was no great gap between rich and poor. There was no slavery or servitude. Nobody owned anybody. There were no chattels. Economic organization was rather communistic or syndicalistic than capitalistic, and was seldom highly centralized.

During the time span of the novel, however, all this is changing. One of the two large nations of the planet is becoming a genuine nation-state, complete with patriotism and bureaucracy. It has achieved state capitalism and the centralization of power, authoritarian government, and a secret police; and it is on the verge of achieving the world's first war.

Why did I present the first picture, and show it in the process of changing to a different one? I am not sure. I think it is because I was trying to show a balance—and the delicacy of a balance. To me the "female principle" is, or at least historically has been, basically anarchic. It values order without constraint, rule by custom not by force. It has been the male who enforces order, who constructs power structures, who makes, enforces, and breaks laws. On Gethen, these two principles are in balance: the decentralizing against the centralizing, the flexible against the rigid, the circular against the linear. But balance is a precarious state, and at the moment of the novel the balance, which had leaned toward the "feminine," is tipping the other way.

[At the very inception of the whole book, I was interested in writing a novel about people in a society that had never had a war. That came first. The androgyny came second. (Cause and effect? Effect and cause?)

I would now write this paragraph this way: . . . The "female principle" has historically been anarchic; that is, anarchy has historically been identified as female. The domain allotted to women—"the family," for example—is the area of order without coercion, rule by custom not by force. Men have reserved the structures of social power to themselves (and those few women whom they admit to it on male terms, such as queens, prime ministers); men make the wars and peaces, men make, enforce, and break the laws. On Gethen, the two polarities we perceive through our cultural conditioning as male and female are neither, and are in balance: consensus with authority, decentralizing with centralizing, flexible with rigid, circular with linear, hierarchy with network. But it is not a motionless balance, there being no such thing in life, and at the moment of the novel, it is wobbling perilously.]

Second: the absence of exploitation. The Gethenians do not rape their world. They have developed a high technology, heavy industry, automobiles, radios, explosives, etc., but they have done so very slowly, absorbing their technology rather than letting it overwhelm them. They have no myth of Progress at all. Their calendar calls the current year always the Year One, and they count backward and forward from that.

In this, it seems that what I was after again was a balance: the driving linearity of the "male," the pushing forward to the limit, the logicality that admits no boundary—and the circularity of the "female," the valuing of patience, ripeness, practicality, livableness. A model for this balance, of course, exists on Earth: Chinese civilization over the past six millennia. (I did not know when I wrote the book that the parallel extends even to the calendar; the Chinese historically never had a linear dating system such as the one that starts with the birth of Christ.)

[A better model might be some of the pre-Conquest cultures of the Americas, though not those hierarchical and imperialistic ones approvingly termed, by our hierarchical and imperialistic standards, "high." The trouble with the Chinese model is that their civilization instituted and practiced male domination as thoroughly as the other "high" civilizations. I was thinking of a Taoist ideal, not of such practices as bride-selling and foot-binding, which we are trained to consider unimportant, nor of the deep misogyny of Chinese culture, which we are trained to consider normal.]

Third: the absence of sexuality as a continuous social factor. For four-fifths of the month, a Gethenian's sexuality plays no part at all in his social life (unless he's pregnant); for the other one-fifth, it dominates him absolutely. In kemmer, one must have a partner, it is imperative. (Have you ever lived in a small apartment with a tabby-cat in heat?) Gethenian society fully accepts this imperative. When a Gethenian has to make love, he does make love, and everybody expects him to, and approves of it.

[I would now write this paragraph this way: . . . For four-fifths of the month, sexuality plays no part at all in a Gethenian's social behavior; for the other one-fifth, it controls behavior absolutely. In kemmer, one must have a partner, it is imperative. (Have you ever lived in a small apartment with a tabby-cat in heat?) Gethenian society fully accepts this imperative. When Gethenians have to make love, they do make love, and everybody else expects it and approves of it.]

But still, human beings are human beings, not cats. Despite our continuous sexuality and our intense self-domestication (domesticated animals tend to be promiscuous, wild animals pair-bonding, familial, or tribal in their mating), we are very seldom truly promiscuous. We do have rape, to be sure—no other animal has equaled us there. We have mass rape, when an army (male, of course) invades; we have prostitution, promiscuity controlled by economics; and sometimes ritual abreactive promiscuity controlled by religion; but in general we seem to avoid genuine license. At most we award it as a prize to the Alpha Male, in certain situations; it is scarcely ever permitted to the female without social penalty. It would seem, perhaps, that the mature human being, male or female, is not satisfied by sexual gratification without psychic involvement, and in fact may be *afraid of it,* to judge by the tremendous variety of social, legal, and religious controls and sanctions exerted over it in all human societies. Sex is a great mana, and therefore the immature society, or psyche, sets great taboos about it. The maturer culture, or psyche, can integrate these taboos or laws into an internal ethical code, which, while allowing great freedom, does not permit the treatment of another person as an object. But, however irrational or rational, there is always a code.

Because the Gethenians cannot have sexual intercourse unless both partners are willing, because they cannot rape or be raped, I figured that they would have less fear and guilt about sex than we tend to have; but still it is a problem for them, in some ways more than for us, because of the extreme, explosive, imperative quality of the oestrous phase. Their society would have to control it, though it might move more easily than we from the taboo stage to the ethical stage. So the basic arrangement, I found, in every Gethenian community, is that of the kemmerhouse, which is open to anyone in kemmer, native or stranger, so that he can find a partner [read: so that they can find sexual partners]. Then there are various customary (not legal) institutions, such as the kemmering group, a group who choose to come together during kemmer as a regular thing; this is like the primate tribe, or group marriage. Or there is the possibility of vowing kemmering, which is marriage, pair-bonding for life, a personal commitment without legal sanction. Such commitments have intense moral and psychic significance, but they are not controlled by Church or State. Finally, there are two forbidden acts, which might be taboo or illegal or simply considered contemptible, depending on which of the regions of Gethen you are in: first, you don't pair off with a relative of a different generation (one who might be your own parent or child); second, you may mate, but not vow kemmering, with your own sibling. These are the old incest prohibitions. They are so general among us—and with good cause, I think, not so much genetic as psychological—that they seemed likely to be equally valid on Gethen.

These three "results," then, of my experiment, I feel were fairly clearly and successfully worked out, though there is nothing definitive about them.

In other areas where I might have pressed for at least such plausible results, I see now a failure to think things through, or to express them clearly. For example, I think I took the easy way in using such familiar governmental structures as a feudal monarchy and a modern-style bureaucracy for the two Gethenian countries that are the scene of the novel. I doubt that Gethenian governments, rising out of the cellular hearth, would resemble any of our own so closely. They might be better, they might be worse, but they would certainly be different.

I regret even more certain timidities or ineptnesses I showed in following up the psychic implications of Gethenian physiology. Just for example, I wish I had known Jung's work when I wrote the book: so that I could have decided whether a Gethenian had *no* animus or anima, or *both*, or an animum. . . . [*For another example (and Jung wouldn't have helped with this, more likely hindered) I quite unnecessarily locked the Gethenians into heterosexuality. It is a naively pragmatic view of sex that insists that sexual partners must be of opposite sex! In any kemmer-house homosexual practice would, of course, be possible and acceptable and welcomed—but I never thought to explore this option; and the omission, alas, implies that sexuality is heterosexuality. I regret this very much.*] But the central failure in this area comes up in the frequent criticism I receive, that the Gethenians seem like *men*, instead of menwomen.

This rises in part from the choice of pronoun. I call Gethenians "he" because I utterly refuse to mangle English by inventing a pronoun for "he/she." [*This "utter refusal" of 1968 restated in 1976 collapsed, utterly, within a couple of years more. I still dislike invented pronouns, but I now dislike them less than the so-called generic pronoun he/him/his, which does in fact exclude women from discourse; and which was an invention of male grammarians, for until the sixteenth century the English generic singular pronoun was they/them/their, as it still is in English and American colloquial speech. It should be restored to the written language, and let the pedants and pundits squeak and gibber in the streets. In a screenplay of* The Left Hand of Darkness *written in 1985, I referred to Gethenians not pregnant or in kemmer by the invented pronouns a/un/a's, modeled on a British dialect. These would drive the reader mad in print, I suppose; but I have read parts of the book aloud using them, and the audience was perfectly happy, except that they pointed out that the subject pronoun, "a" pronounced "uh" [ə], sounds too much like "I" said with a Southern accent.]* "He" is the generic pronoun, damn it, in English. (I envy the Japanese, who, I am told, do have a he/she pronoun.) But I do not consider this really very important. *[I now consider it very important.]* The pronouns wouldn't matter at all if I had been cleverer at *showing* the "female" component of the Gethenian characters in *action. [If I had realized how the pronouns I used shaped, directed, controlled my own thinking, I might have been "cleverer."]* Unfortunately, the plot and structure that arose as I worked the book out cast the Gethenian protagonist, Estraven, almost exclusively in roles that we are culturally conditioned to perceive as "male"—a prime minister (it takes more than even Golda Meir and Indira Gandhi to break a stereotype), a political schemer, a fugitive, a prison-breaker, a sledge-hauler. . . . I think I did this because I was privately delighted at watching, not a man, but a manwoman, do all these things, and do them with considerable skill and flair. But, for the reader, I left out too much. One does not see Estraven as a mother, with his children *[strike "his"]*, in any role that we automatically perceive as "female": and therefore, we tend to see him as a man *[place "him" in quotation marks, please]*. This is a real flaw in the book, and I can only be very grateful to those readers, men and women, whose willingness to participate in the experiment led them to fill in that omission with the work of their own imagination, and to see Estraven as I saw him *[read: as I did]*, as man and woman, familiar and different, alien and utterly human.

It seems to be men, more often than women, who thus complete my work for me: I think because men are often more willing to identify as they read with poor, confused, defensive Genly, the Earthman, and therefore to participate in his painful and gradual discovery of love.

[I now see it thus: Men were inclined to be satisfied with the book, which allowed them a safe trip into androgyny and back, from a conventionally male viewpoint. But many women wanted it to go further, to dare more, to explore androgyny from a woman's point of view as well as a man's. In fact, it does so, in that it was written by a woman. But this is admitted directly only in the chapter "The Question of Sex," the only voice of a woman in the book. I think women were justified in asking more courage of me and a more rigorous thinking-through of implications.]

Finally, the question arises, Is the book a Utopia? It seems to me that it is quite clearly not; it poses no *practicable* alternative to contemporary society, since it is based on an imaginary, radical change in human anatomy. All it tries to do is open up an alternative viewpoint, to widen the imagination, without making any very definite suggestions as to what might be seen from that new viewpoint. The most it says is, I think, something like this: If we were socially ambisexual, if men and women were completely and genuinely equal in their social roles, equal legally and economically, equal in freedom, in responsibility, and in self-esteem, then society would be a very different thing. What our problems might be, God knows; I only know we would have them. But it seems likely that our central problem would not be the one it is now: the problem of exploitation—exploitation of the woman, of the weak, of the earth. Our curse is alienation, the separation of yang from yin [*and the moralization of yang as good, of yin as bad*]. Instead of a search for balance and integration, there is a struggle for dominance. Divisions are insisted upon, interdependence is denied. The dualism of value that destroys us, the dualism of superior/inferior, ruler/ruled, owner/owned, user/used, might give way to what seems to me, from here, a much healthier, sounder, more promising modality of integration and integrity.

1976, 1987

TONI MORRISON
b. 1931

It "is to my great relief that such terms as 'white' and 'race' can enter serious discussion of literature," notes the Nobel Prize–winner Toni Morrison early in her ground-breaking "Unspeakable Things Unspoken: The Afro-American Presence in American Literature," with which we have represented her here. First delivered as the Tanner Lecture on Human Values at the University of Michigan in 1988, the piece has become a classic not only because Morrison opens her discussion with a powerful analysis of the ways in which "the presence of Afro-American literature and the awareness of its culture" inflected both white society and white-authored literature produced by writers from Herman Melville to Ernest Hemingway but also because of the frankness with which she goes on to reflect upon her own creative practice. The first two sections of the essay became the foundation of *Playing in the Dark: Whiteness and the Literary Imagination* (1992), an important critical volume elaborating the thesis that it is "a more than fruitful project" to investigate "instances where early American literature identifies itself, risks itself, to asserts its antithesis to blackness." The final third of the essay, which we excerpt here, offers a rare glimpse into the mental workshop of one of the major novelists of our time.

Born Chloe Anthony Wofford, Morrison was the second of four children raised by working-class parents in a small Ohio steel-manufacturing town which she herself has described as "neither plantation nor ghetto" and on which she has drawn for the settings of such compelling novels as *The Bluest Eye* (1970), *Sula* (1973), and *Beloved* (1987). After graduating from Howard University, Wofford—who had begun calling herself "Toni" as an undergraduate—went on to do graduate work at Cornell University, where she produced a master's thesis on representations of suicide in the writings of Virginia Woolf and William Faulkner. Later, while teaching at Howard University, she married Harold Morrison, a Jamaican architect, and gave birth to two sons, Harold Ford and Kevin Slade; but after divorcing Morrison she left academia for editorial jobs in New York. As a senior editor at Random House, she edited books by such major African American writers as Toni Cade Bambara, Lucille Clifton, and Gloria Naylor while publishing her own novels.

More recently, Morrison has taught at a number of universities, including the State University of New York, Albany, and Princeton University, where she is currently Robert F. Goheen Professor in Humanities. In addition to her novels and her influential *Playing in the Dark,* she has published several edited or co-edited collections, including *Race-ing Justice, En-gendering Power: Essays on Anita Hill, Clarence Thomas, and the Construction of Social Reality* (1992) and *Birth of a Nation'hood: Gaze, Script, and Spectacle in the O. J. Simpson Trial* (1997). As she notes in our selection here, she "practice[s] language" as "a search for and deliberate posture of vulnerability to those aspects of Afro-American culture that can inform and position my work." Yet in exploring vulnerability both as critic and artist, she has significantly empowered herself and the complex culture for which and of which she so eloquently speaks.

From Unspeakable Things Unspoken: The Afro-American Presence in American Literature

I

*　　*　　*

Canon building is Empire building. Canon defense is national defense. Canon debate, whatever the terrain, nature and range (of criticism, of history, of the history of knowledge, of the definition of language, the universality of aesthetic principles, the sociology of art, the humanistic imagination), is the clash of cultures. And *all* of the interests are vested.

In such a melee as this one—a provocative, healthy, explosive melee— extraordinarily profound work is being done. Some of the controversy, however, has degenerated into *ad hominem* and unwarranted speculation on the personal habits of artists, specious and silly arguments about politics (the destabilizing forces are dismissed as merely political; the status quo sees itself as not—as though the term "*a*political" were only its prefix and not the most obviously political stance imaginable since one of the functions of political ideology is to pass itself off as immutable, natural and "innocent"), and covert expressions of critical inquiry designed to neutralize and disguise the political interests of the discourse. Yet much of the research and analysis has rendered speakable what was formerly unspoken and has made humanistic studies once again the place where one has to go to find out what's going on. Cultures whether silenced or monologistic, whether repressed or repressing, seek meaning in the language and images available to them.

Silences are being broken, lost things have been found and at least two generations of scholars are disentangling received knowledge from the apparatus of control, most notably those who are engaged in investigations of French and British Colonialist Literature, American slave narratives, and the delineation of the Afro-American literary tradition.

Now that Afro-American artistic presence has been "discovered" actually to exist, now that serious scholarship has moved from silencing the witnesses and erasing their meaningful place in and contribution to American culture, it is no longer acceptable merely to imagine us and imagine for us. We have always been imagining ourselves. We are not Isak Dinesen's "aspects of nature," nor Conrad's unspeaking.[1] We are the subjects of our own narrative, witnesses to and participants in our own experience, and, in no way coinci-

---

1. Important works of both these European writers focused on Africa.

dentally, in the experience of those with whom we have come in contact. We are not, in fact, "other." We are choices. And to read imaginative literature by and about us is to choose to examine centers of the self and to have the opportunity to compare these centers with the "raceless" one with which we are, all of us, most familiar.

III

It is on this area, the impact of Afro-American culture on contemporary. American literature, that I now wish to comment. I have already said that works by Afro-Americans can respond to this presence (just as non-black works do) in a number of ways. The question of what constitutes the art of a black writer, for whom that modifier is more search than fact, has some urgency. In other words, other than melanin and subject matter, what, in fact, may make me a black writer? Other than my own ethnicity—what is going on in my work that makes me believe it is demonstrably inseparable from a cultural specificity that is Afro-American?

Please forgive the use of my own work in these observations. I use it not because it provides the best example, but because I know it best, know what I did and why, and know how central these queries are to me. Writing is, *after* all, an act of language, its practice. But *first* of all it is an effort of the will to discover.

Let me suggest some of the ways in which I activate language and ways in which that language activates me. I will limit this perusal by calling attention only to the first sentences of the books I've written, and hope that in exploring the choices I made, prior points are illuminated.

The Bluest Eye begins "Quiet as it's kept, there were no marigolds in the fall of 1941." That sentence, like the ones that open each succeeding book, is simple, uncomplicated. Of all the sentences that begin all the books, only two of them have dependent clauses; the other three are simple sentences and two are stripped down to virtually subject, verb, modifier. Nothing fancy here. No words need looking up; they are ordinary, everyday words. Yet I hoped the simplicity was not simpleminded, but devious, even loaded. And that the process of selecting each word, for itself and its relationship to the others in the sentence, along with the rejection of others for their echoes, for what is determined and what is not determined, what is almost there and what must be gleaned, would not theatricalize itself, would not erect a proscenium—at least not a noticeable one. So important to me was this unstaging, that in this first novel I summarized the whole of the book on the first page. (In the first edition, it was printed in its entirety on the jacket.)

The opening phrase of this sentence, "Quiet as it's kept," had several attractions for me. First, it was a familiar phrase familiar to me as a child listening to adults; to black women conversing with one another; telling a story, an anecdote, gossip about someone or event within the circle, the family, the neighborhood. The words are conspiratorial. "Shh, don't tell anyone else," and "No one is allowed to know this." It is a secret between us and a secret that is being kept from us. The conspiracy is both held and withheld, exposed and sustained. In some sense it was precisely what the act of writing the book was: the public exposure of a private confidence. In order fully to comprehend the duality of that position, one needs to think of the immediate political climate in which the writing took place, 1965–1969, during great social upheaval in the life of black people. The publication (as opposed to the writing) involved the exposure; the writing was the disclosure of secrets, secrets "we" shared and those withheld from us by ourselves and by the world outside the community.

"Quiet as it's kept," is also a figure of speech that is written, in this instance, but clearly chosen for how speakerly it is, how it speaks and bespeaks a particular world and its ambience. Further, in addition to its "back fence" connotation, its suggestion of illicit gossip, of thrilling revelation, there is also, in the "whisper," the assumption (on the part of the reader) that the teller is on the inside, knows something others do not, and is going to be generous with this privileged information. The intimacy I was aiming for, the intimacy between the reader and the page, could start up immediately because the secret is being shared, at best, and eavesdropped upon, at the least. Sudden familiarity or instant intimacy seemed crucial to me then, writing my first novel. I did not want the reader to have time to wonder "What do I have to do, to give up, in order to read this? What defense do I need, what distance maintain?" Because I know (and the reader does not—he or she has to wait for the second sentence) that this is a terrible story about things one would rather not know anything about.

What, then, is the Big Secret about to be shared? The thing we (reader and I) are "in" on? A botanical aberration. Pollution, perhaps. A skip, perhaps, in the natural order of things: a September, an autumn, a fall without marigolds. Bright common, strong and sturdy marigolds. When? In 1941, and since that is a momentous year (the beginning of World War II for the United States), the "fall" of 1941, just before the declaration of war, has a "closet" innuendo. In the temperate zone where there is a season known as "fall" during which one expects marigolds to be at their peak, in the months before the beginning of U.S. participation in World War II, something grim is about to be divulged. The next sentence will make it clear that the sayer, the one who knows, is a child speaking, mimicking the adult black women on the porch or in the back yard. The opening phrase is an effort to be grown-up about this shocking information. The point of view of a child alters the priority an adult would assign the information. "We thought it was because Pecola was having her father's baby that the marigolds did not grow" foregrounds the flowers, backgrounds illicit, traumatic, incomprehensible sex coming to its dreamed fruition. This foregrounding of "trivial" information and backgrounding of shocking knowledge secures the point of view but gives the reader pause about whether the voice of children can be trusted at all or is more trustworthy than an adult's. The reader is thereby protected from a confrontation too soon with the painful details, while simultaneously provoked into a desire to know them. The novelty, I thought, would be in having this story of female violation revealed from the vantage point of the victims or could-be victims of rape—the persons no one inquired of (certainly not in 1965)—the girls themselves. And since the victim does not have the vocabulary to understand the violence or its context, gullible, vulnerable girl friends, looking back as the knowing adults they pretended to be in the beginning, would have to do that for her, and would have to fill those silences with their own reflective lives. Thus, the opening provides the stroke that announces something more than a secret shared, but a silence broken, a void filled, an unspeakable thing spoken at last. And they draw the connection between a minor destabilization in seasonal flora with the insignificant destruction of a black girl. Of course "minor" and "insignificant" represent the outside world's view—for the girls both phenomena are earthshaking depositories of information they spend that whole year of childhood (and afterwards) trying to fathom, and cannot. If they have any success, it will be in transferring the problem of fathoming to the presumably adult reader, to the inner circle of listeners. At the least they have distributed the weight of these problematical questions to a larger constituency, and justified the public exposure of a privacy. If the conspiracy that the opening words announce is entered into by the reader, then the book can be seen to open with its close: a speculation on the disruption of "nature," as being a social disruption with tragic individual consequences in which the reader, as part of the population of the text, is implicated.

However a problem, unsolved, lies in the central chamber of the novel. The shattered world I built (to complement what is happening to Pecola), its pieces held together by seasons in childtime and commenting at every turn on the incompatible and barren white-family primer,[2] does not in its present form handle effectively the silence at its center. The void that is Pecola's "unbeing." It should have had a shape—like the emptiness left by a boom or a cry. It required a sophistication unavailable to me, and some deft manipulation of the voices around her. She is not *seen* by herself until she hallucinates a self. And the fact of her hallucination becomes a point of outside-the-book conversation, but does not work in the reading process.

Also, although I was pressing for a female expressiveness (a challenge that re-surfaced in *Sula*), it eluded me for the most part, and I had to content myself with female personae because I was not able to secure throughout the work the feminine subtext that is present in the opening sentence (the women gossiping, eager and aghast in "Quiet as it's kept"). The shambles this struggle became is most evident in the section on Pauline Breedlove where I resorted to two voices, hers and the urging narrator's, both of which are extremely unsatisfactory to me. It is interesting to me now that where I thought I would have the most difficulty subverting the language to a feminine mode, I had the least: connecting Cholly's "rape" by the whitemen to his own of his daughter. This most masculine act of aggression becomes feminized in my language, "passive," and, I think, more accurately repellent when deprived of the male "glamor of shame" rape is (or once was) routinely given.

The points I have tried to illustrate are that my choices of language (speakerly, aural, colloquial), my reliance for full comprehension on codes embedded in black culture, my effort to effect immediate co-conspiracy and intimacy (without any distancing, explanatory fabric), as well as my (failed) attempt to shape a silence while breaking it are attempts (many unsatisfactory) to transfigure the complexity and wealth of Afro-American culture into a language worthy of the culture.

In *Sula*, it's necessary to concentrate on the *two* first sentences because what survives in print is not the one I had intended to be the first. Originally the book opened with "Except for World War II nothing ever interfered with National

---

2. Serving as the epigraph of *The Bluest Eye* is a parodic paragraph describing a family; it is written in the style of the Dick and Jane readers (published by Scott, Foresman) that dominated U.S. elementary education from the 1940s to the 1960s.

Suicide Day." With some encouragement, I recognized that it was a false beginning. "*In medias res*"[3] with a vengeance, because there was no *res* to be in the middle of—no implied world in which to locate the specificity and the resonances in the sentence. More to the point, I knew I was writing a second novel, and that it too would be about people in a black community not just foregrounded but totally dominant; and that it was about black women—also foregrounded and dominant. In 1988, certainly, I would not need (or feel the need for) the sentence—the short section—that now opens *Sula*. The threshold between the reader and the black-topic text need not be the safe, welcoming lobby I persuaded myself it needed at that time. My preference was the demolition of the lobby altogether. As can be seen from *The Bluest Eye*, and in every other book I have written, only *Sula* has this "entrance." The others refuse the "presentation"; refuse the seductive safe harbor; the line of demarcation between the sacred and the obscene, public and private, them and us. Refuse, in effect, to cater to the diminished expectations of the reader, or his or her alarm heightened by the emotional luggage one carries into the black-topic text. (I should remind you that *Sula* was begun in 1969, while my first book was in proof, in a period of extraordinary political activity.)

Since I had become convinced that the effectiveness of the original beginning was only in my head, the job at hand became how to construct an alternate beginning that would not force the work to genuflect and would complement the outlaw quality in it. The problem presented itself this way: to fashion a door. Instead of having the text open wide the moment the cover is opened (or, as in *The Bluest Eye*, to have the book stand exposed before the cover is even touched, much less opened, by placing the complete "plot" on the first page—and finally on the cover of the first edition), here I was to posit a door, turn its knob and beckon for some four or five pages. I had determined not to mention any characters in those pages, there would be no people in the lobby—but I did, rather heavy-handedly in my view, end the welcome aboard with the mention of Shadrack and Sula. It was a craven (to me, still) surrender to a worn-out technique of novel writing: the overt announcement to the reader whom to pay attention to. Yet the bulk of the opening I finally wrote is about the community, a view of it, and the view is not from within (this is a door, after all) but from the point of view of a stranger—the "valley man" who might happen to be there on some errand, but who obviously does not live there and to and for whom all this is mightily strange, even exotic. You can see why I despise much of this beginning. Yet I tried to place in the opening sentence the signature terms of loss: "There used to be a neighborhood here; not any more." That may not be the world's worst sentence, but it doesn't "play," as they say in the theater.

My new first sentence became "In that place, where they tore the nightshade and blackberry patches from their roots to make room for the Medallion City Golf Course, there was once a neighborhood." Instead of my original plan, here I am introducing an outside-the-circle reader into the circle. I am translating the anonymous into the specific, a "place" into a "neighborhood," and letting a stranger in through whose eyes it can be viewed. In between "place" and "neighborhood" I now have to squeeze the specificity and the *difference*; the nostalgia, the history, and the nostalgia for the history;

---

3. In the middle of things (Latin); *res* means "thing" or "things."

the violence done to it and the consequences of that violence. (It took three months, those four pages, a whole summer of nights.) The nostalgia is sounded by "once"; the history and a longing for it is implied in the connotation of "neighborhood." The violence lurks in having something torn out by its roots—it will not, cannot grow again. Its consequences are that what has been destroyed is considered weeds, refuse necessarily removed in urban "development" by the unspecified but no less known "they" who do not, cannot, afford to differentiate what is displaced, and would not care that this is "refuse" of a certain kind. Both plants have darkness in them: "black" and "night." One is unusual (nightshade) and has two darkness words: "night" and "shade." The other (blackberry) is common. A familiar plant and an exotic one. A harmless one and a dangerous one. One produces a nourishing berry; one delivers toxic ones. But they both thrived there together, *in that place when it was a neighborhood*. Both are gone now, and the description that follows is of the other specific things, in this black community, destroyed in the wake of the golf course. Golf conveys what it is not, in this context: not houses, or factories, or even a public park, and certainly not residents. It is a manicured place where the likelihood of the former residents showing up is almost nil.

I want to get back to those berries for a moment (to explain, perhaps, the length of time it took for the language of that section to arrive). I always thought of Sula as quintessentially black, metaphysically black, if you will, which is not melanin and certainly not unquestioning fidelity to the tribe. She is new world black and new world woman extracting choice from choicelessness, responding inventively to found things. Improvisational. Daring, disruptive, imaginative, modern, out-of-the-house, outlawed, unpolicing, uncontained and uncontainable. And dangerously female. In her final conversation with Nel she refers to herself as a special kind of black person woman, one with choices. Like a redwood, she says. (With all due respect to the dream landscape of Freud, trees have always seemed feminine to me.) In any case, my perception of Sula's double-dose of *chosen* blackness and *biological* blackness is in the presence of those two words of darkness in "nightshade" as well as in the uncommon quality of the vine itself. One variety is called "enchanter," and the other "bittersweet" because the berries taste bitter at first and then sweet. Also nightshade was thought to counteract witchcraft. All of this seemed a wonderful constellation of signs for Sula. And "blackberry patch" seemed equally appropriate for Nel: nourishing, never needing to be tended or cultivated, once rooted and bearing. Reliably sweet but thorn-bound. Her process of becoming, heralded by the explosive dissolving of her fragilely-held-together ball of string and fur (when the thorns of her self-protection are removed by Eva), puts her back in touch with the complex, contradictory, evasive, independent, liquid modernity Sula insisted upon. A modernity which overturns pre-war definitions, ushers in the Jazz Age (an age *defined* by Afro-American art and culture), and requires new kinds of intelligences to define oneself.

The stage-setting of the first four pages is embarrassing to me now, but the pains I have taken to explain it may be helpful in identifying the strategies one can be forced to resort to in trying to accommodate the mere fact of writing about, for and out of black culture while accommodating and responding to mainstream "white" culture. The "valley man's" guidance into the territory was my compromise. Perhaps it "worked," but it was not the work I wanted to do.

Had I begun with Shadrack, I would have ignored the smiling welcome and put the reader into immediate confrontation with his wound and his scar. The difference my preferred (original) beginning would have made would be calling greater attention to the traumatic displacement this most wasteful capitalist war had on black people in particular, and throwing into relief the creative, if outlawed, determination to survive it whole. Sula as (feminine) solubility and Shadrack's (male) fixative are two extreme ways of dealing with displacement—a prevalent theme in the narrative of black people. In the final opening I replicated the demiurge of discriminatory, prosecutorial racial oppression in the loss to commercial "progress" of the village, but the references to the community's stability and creativeness (music, dancing, craft, religion, irony, wit all referred to in the "valley man's" presence) refract and subsume their pain while they are in the thick of it. It is a softer embrace than Shadrack's organized, public madness—his disruptive remembering presence which helps (for a while) to cement the community, until Sula challenges them.

"The North Carolina Mutual Life Insurance agent promised to fly from Mercy to the other side of Lake Superior at 3:00."

This declarative sentence is designed to mock a journalistic style; with a minor alteration it could be the opening of an item in a small-town newspaper. It has the tone of an everyday event of minimal local interest. Yet I wanted it to contain (as does the scene that takes place when the agent fulfills his promise) the information that *Song of Solomon* both centers on and radiates from.

The name of the insurance company is real, a well-known black-owned company dependent on black clients, and in its corporate name are "life" and "mutual;" *agent* being the necessary ingredient of what enables the relationship between them. The sentence also moves from North Carolina to Lake Superior—geographical locations, but with a sly implication that the move from North Carolina (the south) to Lake Superior (the north) might not actually involve progress to some "superior state"—which, of course it does not. The two other significant words are "fly," upon which the novel centers and "Mercy," the name of the place from which he is to fly. Both constitute the heartbeat of the narrative. Where is the insurance man flying to? The other side of Lake Superior is Canada, of course, the historic terminus of the escape route for black people looking for asylum. "Mercy," the other significant term, is the grace note; the earnest though, with one exception, unspoken wish of the narrative's population. Some grant it; some never find it; one, at least, makes it the text and cry of her extemporaneous sermon upon the death of her granddaughter. It touches, turns and returns to Guitar at the end of the book—he who is least deserving of it—and moves him to make it his own final gift. It is what one wishes for Hagar; what is unavailable to and unsought by Macon Dead, senior; what his wife learns to demand from him, and what can never come from the white world as is signified by the inversion of the name of the hospital from Mercy to "no-Mercy." It is only available from within. The center of the narrative is flight; the springboard is mercy.

But the sentence turns, as all sentences do, on the verb: promised. The insurance agent does not declare, announce, or threaten his act. He promises, as though a contract is being executed—faithfully—between himself and others. Promises broken, or kept; the difficulty of ferreting out loyalties and ties that bind or bruise wend their way throughout the action and the shifting relationships. So the agent's flight, like that of the Solomon in the title, although toward asylum (Canada, or freedom, or home, or the company of the welcoming dead), and although it carries the possibility of failure and the certainty of danger, is toward change, an alternative way, a cessation of things-as-they-are. It should not be understood as a simple desperate act, the end of a fruitless life, a life without gesture, without examination, but as obedience to a deeper contract with his people. It is his commitment to them, regardless of whether, in all its details, they understand it. There is, however, in their response to his action, a tenderness, some contrition, and mounting respect ("They didn't know he had it in him.") and an awareness that the gesture enclosed rather than repudiated themselves. The note he leaves asks for forgiveness. It is tacked on his door as a mild invitation to whomever might pass by, but it is not an advertisement. It is an almost Christian declaration of love as well as humility of one who was not to do more.

There are several other flights in the work and they are motivationally different. Solomon's the most magical, the most theatrical and, for Milkman, the most satisfying. It is also the most problematic—to those left behind. Milkman's flight binds these two elements of loyalty (Mr. Smith's) and abandon and self-interest (Solomon's) into a third thing: a merging of fealty and risk that suggests the "agency" for "mutual" "life," which he offers at the end and which is echoed in the hills behind him, and is the marriage of surrender and domination, acceptance and rule, commitment to a group *through* ultimate isolation. Guitar recognizes this marriage and recalls enough of how lost he himself is to put his weapon down.

The journalistic style at the beginning, its rhythm of a familiar, hand-me-down dignity is pulled along by an accretion of detail displayed in a meandering unremarkableness. Simple words, uncomplex sentence structures, persistent understatement, highly aural syntax—but the ordinariness of the language, its colloquial vernacular, humorous and, upon occasion, parabolic quality sabotage expectations and mask judgments when it can no longer defer them. The composition of red, white and blue in the opening scene provides the national canvas/flag upon which the narrative works and against which the lives of these black people must be seen, but which must not overwhelm the enterprise the novel is engaged in. It is a composition of color that heralds Milkman's birth, protects his youth, hides its purpose and though which he must burst (through blue Buicks, red tulips in his waking dream, and his sisters' white stockings, ribbons and gloves) before discovering that the gold of his search is really Pilate's yellow orange and the glittering metal of the box in her ear.

These spaces, which I am filling in, and can fill in because they were planned, can conceivably be filled in with other significances. That is planned as well. The point is that into these spaces should fall the ruminations of the reader and his or her invented or recollected or misunderstood knowingness. The reader as narrator asks the questions the community asks, and both reader and "voice" stand among the crowd, within it, with privileged intimacy and contact, but without any more privileged information than the crowd has. That egalitarianism which places us all (reader, the novel's population, the narrator's voice) on the same footing reflected for me the force of flight and mercy, and the precious, imaginative yet realistic gaze of black people who (at one time, anyway) did not mythologize what or whom it mythologized. The "song" itself contains this unblinking evaluation of the miraculous and heroic flight of the legendary Solomon, an unblinking gaze which is lurking in the tender but amused choral-community response to the agent's flight. Sotto[4] (but not completely) is my own giggle (in Afro-American terms) of the proto-myth of the journey to manhood. Whenever characters are cloaked in Western fable, they are in deep trouble, but the African myth is also contaminated. Unprogressive, unreconstructed, self-born Pilate is unimpressed by Solomon's flight and knocks Milkman down when, made new by his appropriation of his own family's fable, he returns to educate her with it. Upon hearing all he has to say, her only interest is filial. "Papa? . . . I've been carryin' Papa?" And her longing to hear the song, finally, is a longing for balm to die by, not a submissive obedience to history—anybody's.

The opening sentence of *Tar Baby*, "He believed he was safe," is the second version of itself. The first, "He thought he was safe," was discarded because "thought" did not contain the doubt I wanted to plant in the reader's mind about whether or not he really was—safe. "Thought" came to me at once because it was the verb my parents and grandparents used when describing what they had dreamed the night before. Not "I dreamt," or "It seemed" or even "I saw or did" this or that—but "I thought." It gave the dream narrative distance (a dream is not "real") and power (the control implied in *thinking* rather than *dreaming*). But to use "thought" seemed to undercut the faith of the character and the distrust I wanted to suggest to the reader. "Believe" was chosen to do the work properly. And the person who does the believing is, in a way, about to enter a dream world, and convinces himself, eventually, that he is in control of it. He believed; was convinced. And although the word suggests his conviction, it does not reassure the reader. If I had wanted the reader to trust this person's point of view I would have written "He was safe." Or, "Finally, he was safe." The unease about this view of safety is important because safety itself is the desire of each person in the novel. Locating it, creating it, losing it.

You may recall that I was interested in working out the mystery of a piece of lore, a folk tale, which is also about safety and danger and the skills needed to secure the one and recognize and avoid the other. I was not, of course, interested in re-telling the tale; I suppose that is an idea to pursue, but it is certainly not interesting enough to engage me for four years. I have said, elsewhere, that the exploration of the Tar Baby tale[5] was like stroking a pet to see what the anatomy was like but not to disturb or distort its mystery. Folk lore may have begun as allegory for natural or social phenomena; it may have been employed as a retreat from contemporary issues in art, but folk lore can also contain myths that re-activate themselves endlessly through providers—the people who repeat, reshape, reconstitute and reinterpret them. The Tar Baby tale seemed to me to be about masks. Not masks as covering what is to be hidden,

---

4. I.e., sotto voce, in an undertone (literally, "under the voice"; Italian).
5. "The Wonderful Tar-Baby Story" is the best-

known of the folktales retold in dialect by Joel Chandler Harris in *Uncle Remus: His Songs and His Sayings* (1880).

but how masks come to life, take life over, exercise the tensions between itself and what it covers. For Son, the most effective mask is none. For the others the construction is careful and delicately borne, but the masks they make have a life of their own and collide with those they come in contact with. The texture of the novel seemed to want leanness, architecture that was worn and ancient like a piece of mask sculpture: exaggerated, breathing, just athwart the representational life it displaced. Thus, the first and last sentences had to match, as the exterior planes match the interior, concave ones inside the mask. Therefore "He believed he was safe" would be the twin of "Lickety split, lickety split, lickety lickety split." This close is 1) the last sentence of the folk tale. 2) the action of the character. 3) the indeterminate ending that follows from the untrustworthy beginning. 4) the complimentary meter of its twin sister [u u / u u / with u u u / u u u /] and 5) the wide and marvelous space between the contradiction of those two images: from a dream of safety to the sound of running feet. The whole mediated world in between. This masked and unmasked; enchanted, disenchanted; wounded and wounding world is played out on and by the varieties of interpretation (Western and Afro-American) the Tar Baby myth has been (and continues to be) subjected to. Winging one's way through the vise and expulsion of history becomes possible in creative encounters with that history. Nothing, in those encounters, is safe, or should be. Safety is the foetus of power as well as protection from it, as the uses to which masks and myths are put in Afro-American culture remind us.

"124 was spiteful. Full of a baby's venom."

Beginning *Beloved* with numerals rather than spelled out numbers, it was my intention to give the house an identity separate from the street or even the city; to name it the way "Sweet Home" was named; the way plantations were named, but not with nouns or "proper" names—with numbers instead because numbers have no adjectives, no posture of coziness or grandeur or the haughty yearning of arrivistes and estate builders for the parallel beautifications of the nation they left behind, laying claim to instant history and legend. Numbers here constitute an address, a thrilling enough prospect for slaves who had owned nothing, least of all an address. And although the numbers, unlike words, can have no modifiers, I give these an adjective—spiteful (There are three others). The address is therefore personalized, but personalized by its own activity, not the pasted on desire for personality.

Also there is something about numerals that makes them spoken, heard, in this context, because one expects words to read in a book, not numbers to say, or hear. And the sound of the novel, sometimes cacophonous, sometimes harmonious, must be an inner ear sound or a sound just beyond hearing, infusing the text with a musical emphasis that words can do sometimes even better than music can. Thus the second sentence is not one: it is a phrase that properly, grammatically, belongs as a dependent clause with the first. Had I done that, however (124 was spiteful, comma, full of a baby's venom, or 124 was full of a baby's venom) I could not have had the accent on *full* [/ u u / u / u pause / u u u u / u].

Whatever the risks of confronting the reader with what must be immediately incomprehensible in that simple, declarative authoritative sentence, the risk of unsettling him or her, I determined to take. Because the *in medias res* opening that I am so committed to is here excessively demanding. It is abrupt, and should appear so. No native informant here. The reader is snatched, yanked, thrown into an environment completely foreign, and I want it as the first stroke of the shared experience that might be possible between the reader and the novel's population. Snatched just as the slaves were from one place to another, from any place to another, without preparation and without defense. No lobby, no door, no entrance—a gangplank, perhaps (but a very short one). And the house into which this snatching—this kidnapping—propels one, changes from spiteful to loud to quiet, as the sounds in the body of the ship itself may have changed. A few words have to be read before it is clear that 124 refers to a house (in most of the early drafts "The women *in the house* knew it" was simply "The women knew it." "House" was not mentioned for seventeen lines), and a few more have to be read to discover why it is spiteful, or rather the source of the spite. By then it is clear, if not at once, that something is beyond control, but is not beyond understanding since it is not beyond accommodation by both the "women" and the "children." The fully realized presence of the haunting is both a major incumbent of the narrative and sleight of hand. One of its purposes is to keep the reader preoccupied with the nature of the incredible spirit world while being supplied a controlled diet of the incredible political world.

The subliminal, the underground life of a novel is the area most likely to link arms with the reader and facilitate making it one's own. Because one must, to get from the first sentence to the next, and the next and the next. The friendly observation post I was content to build and man in *Sula* (with the stranger in the midst), or the down-home journalism of *Song of Solomon* or the calculated mistrust of the point of view in *Tar Baby* would not serve here. Here I wanted the compelling confusion of being there as they (the characters) are; suddenly, without comfort or succor from the "author," with only imagination, intelligence, and necessity available for the journey. The painterly language of *Song of Solomon* was not useful to me in *Beloved*. There is practically no color whatsoever in its pages, and when there is, it is so stark and remarked upon, it is virtually raw. Color seen for the first time, without its history. No built architecture as in *Tar Baby*, no play with Western chronology as in *Sula*; no exchange between book life and "real" life discourse—with printed text units rubbing up against seasonal black childtime units as in *The Bluest Eye*. No compound of houses, no neighborhood, no sculpture, no paint, no time, especially no time because memory, pre-historic memory, has no time. There is just a little music, each other and the urgency of what is at stake. Which is all they had. For that work, the work of language is to get out of the way.

I hope you understand that in this explication of how I practice language is a search for and deliberate posture of vulnerability to those aspects of Afro-American culture that can inform and position my work. I sometimes know when the work works, when *nommo*[6] has effectively summoned, by reading and listening to those who have entered the text. I learn nothing from those who resist it, except, of course, the sometimes fascinating display of their struggle. My expectations of and my gratitude to those critics who enter, are great. To those who talk about how as well as what; who identify the workings as well as the work; for whom the study of Afro-American literature is

---

6. In West African tribal cultures, the generative and creative power of the word.

neither a crash course in neighborliness and tolerance, nor an infant to be carried, instructed or chastised or even whipped like a child, but the serious study of art forms that have much work to do, but are already legitimatized by their own cultural sources and predecessors—in or out of the canon—I owe much.

For an author, regarding canons, it is very simple: in fifty, a hundred or more years his or her work may be relished for its beauty or its insight or its power; or it may be condemned for its vacuousness and pretension—and junked. Or in fifty or a hundred years the critic (as canon builder) may be applauded for his or her intelligent scholarship and powers of critical inquiry. Or laughed at for ignorance and shabbily disguised assertions of power—and junked. It's possible that the reputations of both will thrive, or that both will decay. In any case, as far as the future is concerned, when one writes, as critic or as author, all necks are on the line.

1988   1989

EAVAN BOLAND
b. 1944

Musing on her formative years as a poet in the fictive "Letter to a Young Woman Poet" that is our selection here, the Irish writer Eavan Boland recalls in eloquent detail a time when it "was harder than I thought proper to record the life I lived in the poems I wrote." Even Rainer Maria Rilke, to whose *Letters to a Young Poet* (1929) her title alludes, would not, Boland implies, have quite grasped the nature of the past whose weight she seeks to lighten, though she notes that his "name should be raised whenever one poet writes to another." For, she argues, the tradition that she had inherited from a century shaped by the magisterial pronouncements of such poet-critics as Matthew Arnold and T. S. Eliot "had determined the relation between the ordinary object and the achieved poem," effectively excluding from aesthetic significance the quotidian domesticity experienced by so many women. "When I was young in Ireland," Boland has also commented, emphasizing this problem, "I felt there was almost a magnetic distance between the word 'woman' and the word 'poet,' "—although, she adds, "I don't feel that now," given the transformations feminism has brought to the world of letters.

In her own verse Boland has explored the "domestic interiors" that shape women's (and men's) dailiness with such verve that she has herself become part of a revisionary poetic tradition in which, like such a precursor as Adrienne Rich, the common language of feminine dailiness is essential, rather than antithetical, to literary art. Born in Dublin, she studied at Trinity College as well as, later, the Iowa Writers' Workshop, and she is married to the novelist Kevin Casey, with whom she has two daughters. In the past three decades she has published collections of verse that include *Night Feed* (1982), *Outside History* (1990), and *Against Love Poetry* (2001). An incisive critic and feminist thinker, Boland teaches at Stanford University and has authored a collection of essays, *Object Lessons: The Life of the Woman and the Poet in Our Time* (1995); she has also co-edited, with the American poet Mark Strand, *The Making of a Poem: A Norton Anthology of Poetic Forms* (2000).

Letter to a Young Woman Poet

I wish I knew you. I wish I could stand for a moment in that corridor of craft and doubt where you will spend so much of your time. But I don't and I can't. And given the fact, in poetic terms, that you are the future and I am the past, I never will. Then why write this? It is not, after all, a real letter. It doesn't have an address. I can't put a name at the top of it. So what reason can I have for writing in a form without a basis to a person without a name?

I could answer that the hopes and silences of my first years as a poet are still fresh to me. But that in itself is not an explanation. I could tell you that I am a woman in my early fifties, writing this on a close summer night in Ireland. But what would that mean to you? If I tell you, however, that my first habitat as a poet is part of your history as a poet: is that nineteenth century full of the dangerous indecision about who the poet really is. If I say I saw that century survive into the small, quarrelsome city where I began as a poet. That I studied its version of the poet and took its oppressions to heart. If I say my present is your past, that my past is already fixed as part of your tradition. And that until we resolve our relation to both past and tradition, we are still hostages to that danger, that indecision. And, finally, that there is something I want to say to you about the present and past of poetry—something that feels as if it needs to be said urgently—then maybe I can justify this letter.

And if some awkwardness remains, rather than trying to disguise it, I want to propose an odd and opposite fiction. If most real letters are conversation by other means, think of this as a different version. Imagine a room at dusk, with daylight almost gone. I can do this because I associate that light, that hour, with ease and conversation. I was born at dusk. Right in the centre of Dublin in fact, in a nursing home beside Stephen's Green. Big, cracking heaps of sycamore and birch leaves are burned there in Autumn and I like to think of the way bitter smoke must have come the few hundred yards or so towards the room where I was born.

And so I have no difficulty imagining us sitting there and talking in that diminishing light. Maybe the sights of late summer were visible through the window only moments ago. Fuchsia and green leaves, perhaps. But now everything is retreating into skeletal branches and charcoal leaves. My face is in shadow. You cannot see it, although your presence shapes what I am saying. And so in the last light, at the end of the day, what matters is language. Is the unspoken at the edge of the spoken. And so I have made a fiction to sustain what is already a fiction: this talking across time and absence.

But about what? What name will I give it? In the widest sense, I want to talk about the past. The past, that is, of poetry: the place where so much of the truth and power of poetry is stored. 'Poetry is the past which breaks out in our hearts' said Rilke—whose name should be raised whenever one poet writes to another. But the past I want to talk about is more charged and less lyrical than that for women poets. It is, after all, the place where authorship of the poem eluded us. Where poetry itself was defined by and in our absence. There has been a debate since I was a young poet, about whether women poets should engage with that past at all. 'For writers, and at this moment for women writers in particular' Adrienne Rich wrote eloquently in *When We Dead Awaken* 'there is the challenge and promise of a whole new psychic geography to be explored. But there is also a difficult and dangerous walking on ice, as we try to find language and images for a consciousness we are just coming into and with little in the past to support us.'

Then why go there? Why visit the site of our exclusion? We need to go to that past: not to learn from it, but to change it. If we do not change that past, it will change us. And I, for one, do not want to become a grateful daughter in a darkened house.

But in order to change the past of poetry, we have to know what happened there. We have to be able to speak about it as poets, and even that can be difficult. Ever since I began as a poet I have heard people say that fixed positions—on gender, on politics of any kind—distort and cloud the question of poetry. In those terms, this letter can seem to be a clouding, a distortion. But poetry is not a pure stream. It will never be sullied by partisan argument. The only danger to poetry is the reticence and silence of poets. This piece is about the past and our right as women poets to avail of it. It is about the art and against the silence. Even so, I still need to find a language with which to approach that past. The only way of doing that, within the terms of this fiction, is to go back to the space you now occupy: in other words, to the beginning.

When I was young I had only a present. I began in a small, literary city. Such a voluble, self-confident place, in fact, that at times it was even possible to believe the city itself would confer a sort of magical, unearned poetic identity. At night the streets were made of wet lights and awkward angles. Occasionally fog came in from the coast, a dense space filled with street-grit and salt and the sound of foghorns. By day things were plainer: a city appeared, trapped by hills and defined by rivers. Its centre was a squashed clutter of streets and corners. There were pubs and green buses. Statues of orators. Above all, the cool, solid air of the Irish sea at every turn.

The National Library was a cold, domed and friendly building. The staircase was made of marble and formed an imposing ascent to a much less elaborate interior. Old books, shelves and newspapers crowded a huge room. The tables were scarred oak and small lamps were attached to the edge of them and could be lit by individual readers. As twilight pressed on the glass roof where pigeons slipped and fluttered, the pools of light fell on pages and haloed the faces above them.

I read poetry there. I also read in my flat late at night. But the library was in the centre of town. Often it was easier just to stay in and go there and take a bus home later. There was something about the earnest, homeless feel of a big library that comforted me.

I read all kinds of poetry here. I also read about poets. I was eighteen. Then nineteen. Then twenty and twenty-one. I read about Eliot in Paris, and Yeats in Coole, I read Pound and Housman and Auden. It was the reading of my time and my place: Too many men. Not enough women. Too much acceptance. Too few questions.

I memorized the poems. I learned the poetics—although I had no use for that word. But I had a real, practical hunger nevertheless for instruction and access in the form. And so I learned something about cadence and rhythm there. And something about the weather and circumstance of tradition as well. If I had known what to look for I would have had plenty of evidence of the tensions of a tradition as I read about the big, moonlit coldness of Ullswater and the intimacy of Wordsworth's hand-to-hand struggle with the eighteenth century. About the vowel changes in the fifteenth century. About the letters between John Clare and Lord Radstock.[1] *Tell Clare if he still has a recollection of what I have done, and am still doing for him, he must give me unquestionable proofs of being that man I would have him be—he must expunge!*

When I came out of the library, I got on the bus and watched for ten or so minutes as the rainy city went by. During the journey I thought about what I had read. I was not just reading poems at this time, I was beginning to write them. I was looking for that solid land-bridge between writing poems and being a poet. I was taking in information, therefore, at two levels. One was simple enough. I was seeing at first hand the outcome of a hundred years of intense excitement and change in an art form: how the line had altered, how the lyric had opened out. I was also absorbing something that was less easy to define: the idea of the poet. The very thing which should have helped me transit from writing to being. But just as the line and the lyric had opened out and become volatile, the idea of the poet had drawn in, and distanced itself from the very energies the poems were proposing.

This made no sense at all. When I read poems in the library I felt as though a human face was turned towards me, alive with feeling, speaking urgently to me about love and time. But when I came across the idea of the poet I felt as if someone had displaced that speaker with a small, cold sculpture: a face from which the tears and intensity were gone, on which only the pride and self-consciousness of the Poet remained. I had no words for this. And yet I began to wonder if the makers of the poem and the makers of the idea of the poet could be one and the same. It was an amateurish, shot-in-the-dark thought. And yet all I could do was ask questions. What other way had I of dealing with a poetic past whose history I didn't know, and a tradition composed of the seeming assurance that only those it confirmed and recognized would ever be part of it? Besides I felt my questions would bring me, if not to the front, at least to the back entrance of this formidable past. But if these were the gates, who were the gatekeepers?

Stay with the fiction. Imagine the light is less. That we can no longer see the water drops and wasps under the fuchsia. That the talk continues, but in a more mysterious space. I know when I was young I could barely imagine challenging the poetic past. It seemed infinitely remote and untouchable: fixed in place by giant hands.

And yet what a strange argument I am about to make to you. *That the past needs us.* That very past in poetry which simplified us as women and excluded us as poets now needs us to change it. To bring to it our warm and fractious present: our recent decades of intense debate and excited composition. And we need to do it. After all, stored in that past is a template of poetic identity which still affects us as women. When we are young poets it has the power to make us feel subtly less official, less welcome in the tradition than our male contemporaries. *If we are not careful it is that template we will aspire to, alter ourselves for, warp our self-esteem as poets to fit.*

Therefore we need to change the past. Not by intellectualizing it. But by

---

1. In the 19th century.

eroticizing it. The concept that a template of poetic authority can actually be changed, altered, radicalized by those very aspects of humanity which are excluded from it is at the heart of what I am saying. And yet these ideas are so difficult, so abstract that I sense them dissolving almost at the point of articulation. If you were not in a make-believe twilight in an unreal room in a fictive letter you might ask a question there. How can you eroticize a past? My hope is that this story—this strange story—will make it clearer.

When I was seventeen years of age I found myself, as many teenagers do, with time to spare between graduating from school and getting ready for college. Three months in fact of a wet, cool Irish summer. I lived in Dublin. In those times it wasn't hard to get summer jobs. So I got a job in a hotel just over the river on the north side of the city. I worked at house-keeping in the hotel. I carried keys and straightened out the rooms. The job was not difficult and the hours were not long.

The hotel was placed above the river Liffey and it was right at the end of one of the showpiece streets of Ireland. O'Connell Street. Its bridge, the widest in Europe, had once been a claim to fame when Dublin was a garrison city. On this street a group of Irish patriots in 1916 had taken their stand against British rule in Ireland. They had established themselves at the Post Office just above the river. The British troops had shelled the building. The position had fallen after a week of struggle and bloodshed. The patriots in the Post Office had been arrested and several of the leaders had been shot.

It was not hard when I was young to get off the bus on a summer morning beside a sluggish river that ran into the Irish sea, and walk straight into Irish history. There was the Post Office. Inside it was the bronze statue of Cuchulain[2] with a raven on his shoulder. Here was the stone building and the remembered action. And all up the street, placed only fifty yards or so apart was statue after statue of Irish patriots and orators. Burke. Grattan. O'Connell. Parnell. Made of stone and bronze and marble and granite. With plaques and wreaths and speeches at their feet. I got off the bus between the river and the hotel. And I walked past them, a seventeen-year-old girl—past their hands, their gestures, their quoted eloquence, all the way to work.

There was a manager in the hotel. He was a quietly spoken middle-aged man. He looked after all the inventory in the hotel and he sat in an old-fashioned office with a ledger and a telephone. One day one of the other girls there, a bit older than I was, told me something strange about him. She told me he had a wound which had never properly healed. Every day, she said, he went up to his room and dressed it and bandaged it. And I was fascinated in a horrified sort of way, by the contrast between this almost demure man, with his dark suit and pin-striped trousers, wearing the formal clothes of small daily ceremonies, hiding his damaged secret.

But what I remember now is not exactly what I'm describing here. And that wounded man is only one part of the story. And the whole of the story is maybe not something I will be able to tell, not because I knew that man. Because I didn't. I spoke to him once or twice. Not more. Once I waited with the voyeuristic curiosity of youth, of which I still feel ashamed, at the top of

2. Legendary Irish hero of Ulster; in Celtic lore, the raven is associated with deities of war, and it is said that Cuchulain's enemies were persuaded that he was dead only after the battle goddess Morrigu, in the form of a raven, landed on his shoulder.

the stairs to see him climb up to his room to dress that wound, but I never knew him. And never really spoke to him.

The story is something different. It has something to do with realizing that I could change the past. With going in every day to work in that hotel. With having my imagination seized, in a fragmented and distracted way, by a man whose body had not healed. And then, when the drizzling summer day was coming to an end, it had something to do with going out into the long, spacious street and walking down it to the river. Which also meant walking past the statues which had not moved or changed in the day. Which still stood on their columns, above their grandiose claims. It meant leaving the hotel with one idea of a manhood which had been made frail in a mysterious way and walking down a long well-lit street where no such concession could ever be made. Where manhood was made of bronze and granite and marble. Where no one's thigh or side had ever been wounded or ever could be. But where— so intense was my sense of contrast—I could almost imagine that the iron moved and the granite flinched. And where by accident and chance I had walked not only into history, but into the erotics of history.

The erotics of history. In a certain sense I discovered my country by eroticizing it: by plotting those correlatives between maleness and strength, between imagination and power which allowed me not only to enter the story, but to change it. And yet at seventeen my own sexuality was so rudimentary, so unformed that neither I nor anyone else would have thought it could have been an accurate guide to the history I inherited. In fact, it served. I walked down that street of statues, a girl who had come back late to her own country. Who lacked its language. Who was ignorant of its battles. Who knew only a little about its heroes. And yet my skin, my flesh, my sex—without learning any of this—stood as a subversive historian, ready to edit the text.

If you and I were really there in that room with the air darkening around us, this would be a good place to stop. To be quiet for a moment. And then to start again. This time with another question. Is it possible to eroticize a poetic tradition in the way in which I eroticized my own history? Maybe the real answer to this is the most obvious one. The only way of entering the poetic tradition, of confronting its formidable past, is through a living present. And yet it hardly seems possible that the painful, complex, single present of any one poet could offer a contest to a tradition. Despite that, what I am about to tell you, is how I discovered it. Just how tentatively I put together my sense of being a poet with my sense of a past that did not offer me an easy definition for it. And how, in a house on a summer night, with sleeping children, when I wondered how to do it, I would think back to those summer mornings, that long street with its iron orators. Of looking up, made subversive by alternative senses of power and weakness. Of how I asked myself: Would I ever be able to eroticize this tradition, this formidable past, stretching back and reaching above, so that I could look up confidently. Could I make the iron breathe and the granite move?

When did I discover the past? Perhaps the answer should be, which past? My sense of it as a problematic poetic terrain came late. All through my first years as a poet it was just the place where poems I loved had been written, where patterns had been made which invited an automatic reverence I could not give. And so I continued to turn to that past to read those poems, but never to be part of the tradition they belonged to.

But when I married and had small children, when at last I lived at a distance from any poetic centre, things changed. I started to have an intense engagement with every aspect of writing a poem. So much so, that the boundaries between the edges of the poem and the limits of the world began at times to dissolve. I was fascinated by the page in the notebook on the table, with a child's cry at its perimeter and the bitterness of peat smoke at its further edge. I loved the illusion, the conviction, the desire—whatever you want to call it—that the words were agents rather than extensions of reality. That they made my life happen, rather than just recorded it happening.

But what life? My life day to day was lived through ordinary actions and powerful emotions. But the more ordinary, actual, the more intense the day I lived. The more I lifted a child, conscious of nothing but the sweetness of a child's skin, or the light behind an apple tree, or rain on slates, the more language and poetry came to my assistance. The words that had felt stilted, dutiful and decorative when I was a young and anxious poet, now sang and flew. Finally, I had joined together my life as a woman and a poet. On the best days I lived as a poet, the language at the end of my day—when the children were asleep and the curtains drawn—was the language all through my day: it had waited for me.

What this meant was crucial to me. For the first time as a poet, I could believe in my life as the source of the language I used, and not the other way around. At last I had the means to challenge what I believed had distorted the idea of the poet: the belief that poetry had the power to dignify and select a life, instead of the reverse. That a life, in other words, became important only because it was the subject matter for a poem.

I knew from everything that I had read that the poets who changed the tradition first had to feel they owned the tradition. Instead, I had come slowly and painfully to a number of hard-won positions which did not feel at all like the privileges of ownership. First and foremost, I had wanted to feel that those things I had lived as a woman I could write as a poet. Once I did that, I felt there was a fusion, a not-to-be-denied indebtedness between those identities: the woman providing the experience, the poet the expression. This fusion in turn created a third entity: the past, who not only engaged in these actions, but began to develop a critique about them.

This critique may have had its origin in the life of a woman, may have begun in the slanted light of a nursery or a kitchen, but its outcome was about something entirely different. The interior of the poem itself: about tone, distance from the subject, management of the stanza. It was about the compromised and complex act of language. It was about the historic freedom of the poet, granted right down through the tradition—the precious and dignified franchise—to return to the past with the discoveries of the present. *To return triumphant to the present with a changed past.*

I did not have that sense of entitlement. The interior sense that I could change poetry, rather than my own poems, was never exactly there. But if the tradition would no admit me, could I change its rules of admission? Either I would have to establish an equal relation with it, or I would have to adopt a submissive posture: admiring its achievements and accepting its exclusions. Yet what tools had I to change the resistances I felt around me and within me? Certainly neither intellectual or theoretical ones. Gradually I began to believe that the only way to change a tradition was to go to the sources which had made it in the first place: But what were they? Intuitively I felt that the way to touch them was by reaching back into my own imagination, attempting to become not just the author of the poem but the author of myself. The author, that is, of myself as a poet. This in turn meant uncovering and challenging that elusive source of authoring within the tradition which had made not only the poem, but also the identity of the poet.

Who makes a poetic tradition? Who makes the idea of the maker? 'We are accustomed to think of the poet,' wrote Randall Jarrell ironically, 'when we think of him at all as someone Apart.'[3] But customs have to be made. They have to be stored deep in the culture and layered into habits of thought in order to change from custom into customary. Wherever the custom had started, I was certain it was a damaging, limiting one.

Of course it's arguable that I felt this because I was not an author in that past: neither named nor present. But I don't think so. The truth was that in my reading—scattered and inexpert as it was—I had picked up a fault line: something strange and contradictory which I began to follow with fascination and unease. Obviously the language I use now is not the outcome of the perception I had then. I was young, badly read, just beginning. Nevertheless I know now that the fault line stretched from the end of the Romantic movement to the end of modernism. That it marked and weakened a strange, confused terrain of technical widening and ethical narrowing: just as the line and the lyric began to grow plastic, open, volatile, the idea of the poet contracted, became defensive, shrugged off links with the community.

Here for instance is T. S. Eliot.

> We can only say that it appears likely that poets in our civilization, as it exists at present, must be difficult. Our civilization comprehends great variety and complexity, and this variety and complexity, playing upon a refined sensibility, must produce various and complex results. The poet must become more and more comprehensive, more allusive, more indirect, in order to force, to dislocate if necessary, language into his meaning.[4]

Our civilization. The poet must. This exclusivity was too pure for the warm, untidy enterprise of imagination as I understood it. What exactly was our civilization? Why should a poet try to reflect it in a dislocated language, instead of trying to find a plain and luminous one for standing outside that civilization?

Further back again. Here is Mathew Arnold, seeming to claim for an art the devotions of a sect.

> We should conceive of poetry worthily, and more highly than it has been the custom to conceive of it. We should conceive of it as capable of higher uses, and called to higher destinies, than those which in general men have assigned to it hitherto. More and more mankind will discover that we have to turn to poetry to interpret life for us, to console us, to sustain us. Without poetry our science will appear incomplete, and most of what now passes for religion and philosophy will be replaced by poetry.[5]

What higher destinies? What civilization? I repeat these questions only because it seems to me they have something to do with the fault line I spoke

---

3. From Jarrell, *Poetry and the Age* (1953).
4. From Eliot, "The Metaphysical Poets" (1921).
5. From Arnold, "The Study of Poetry" (1880).

about. Reading through nineteenth-century poetry, even haphazardly, was to become an eyewitness to the gradual dissolving of the beautiful, maverick radicalism of the Romantic movement—where individualism was an adventure which freed the poet to experiment with the self—into a cautious and rigid hubris. Perhaps a sociologist or a historian could explain how the concept of the poet became mixed with ideas of power which had too little to do with art and too much to do with a concept of culture shadowed by empire-building and conservative ideology. And how in the process men like Arnold and Eliot accepted the task of making the poet an outcome of a civilization rather than a subversive within it.

Whatever the causes, the effect was clear. Poetry in the last century had hit into a massive inconsistency which was not resolved in my century. One of the most vociferous movements in twentieth-century poetry—modernism—had been openly anti-authoritarian. 'It was not a revolt against form,' said Eliot, 'but against dead form.'[6] But this apparent anti-authoritarianism had been built on the increasingly authoritarian idea of the poet as part of *our civilization* as called to *higher destinies*. The fault line lay here: the poets of the first part of the century had dismantled a style: they had not dismantled a self. Without the second, the first was incomplete.

Darkness. No trees. Not even outlines. Just the shadow of a profile and the sense of someone speaking. Let me remind you of who I am: a woman on a summer night writing a fictive letter from a real place. Suppose I were now to turn a harsh and scornful light on my own propositions, and say why should a great tradition—an historic tradition of poetry with all its composure and assurance—be held accountable to the criticisms of a woman in a suburb?

The truth is simple: However wrong-headed my criticisms, I—no less than any poet who lifts a pen and looks at a page—was an inheritor of that tradition. The difference was that as a young woman I undertook that act in circumstances which were relatively new for a poet. Not in the London of coffee houses. Or in Greenwich Village. Or even in the city that was only four miles from me. But in a house with tiny children, with a washing machine in the background, with a child's antibiotic on a shelf and a spoon beside it.

And the fact was and is, that the words, decisions, insistences of poets and canon-makers—but more canon-makers than poets—had determined the status of my machines, my medicine bottles, my child's hand reaching up into mine. They had determined the relation between the ordinary object and the achieved poem. They had winnowed and picked, and sifted and refined. They had made the authority of the poet conditional upon a view of reality, which then became a certainty about subject matter, and a prescription about language. They had debated and divided, subtracted and reduced the relation of the ordinary life to the achieved poem, so that it was harder than seemed right or proper to include the angle of light falling across copper, or returning to the kitchen from the gap between the poplar trees, into the poems I planned. It was harder than I thought proper to record the life I lived in the poems I wrote.

Gradually, it became apparent to me that the identity of the poet—on which was predicated the mysterious idea of the authority of the poet—had something to do with the permission granted or withheld, not simply to subject matter, but to the claim that could be made for it. Gradually I came to

6. See Eliot's "The Music of Poetry" (1942).

believe that in that nineteenth century, where Matthew Arnold proposed his higher destinies, the barriers between religion and poetry had shimmered and dissolved. Out of that had come a view I needed to challenge: which argued that the poem made the experience important; that the experience was not important until the poem had laid hands upon it.

Somewhere in that century, it seemed to me, if I could find it, would be a recognizable turning point, where the poet failed to distinguish between the hubris and the history, between the expression and the experience. And to which I as a poet—and I believed other poets like me from new and challenging constituencies—needed to return: to revise and argue and engage.

No light at all. Stars somewhere. And if this was a summer darkness in Ireland the morning would already be stored in the midnight: visible in an odd brightness to the east. I have finished talking. I have to finish also with the fiction of your company, and I am surprised at how real my regret is. Nevertheless this letter is still full of irony and hope. The hope is that you will read in my absence, what was so thoroughly shaped by the irony of your non-presence. And despite the fact that this room, with its darkening window and its summer shadows, has only been made of words, I will miss it.

Occasionally I see myself, or the ghost of myself, in the places where I first became a poet. On the pavement just around Stephen's Green for instance, with its wet trees and sharp railings. What I see is not an actual figure, but a sort of remembered loneliness. The poets I knew were not women: the women I knew were not poets. The conversations I had, or wanted to have, were never complete.

Sometimes I think of how time might become magical: How I might get out of the car even now and cross the road and stop that young woman and surprise her with the complete conversation she hardly knew she missed. How I might stand there with her in the dusk, the way neighbours stand on their front steps before they go in to their respective houses for the night: half-talking and half-leaving. She and I would argue about the past. Would surely disagree about the present.

Time is not magical. The conversation will not happen. Even writing this letter to you has been flawed by similar absences and inventions. And yet there is something poignant and helpful to me in having done it. If women go to the poetic past as I believe they should, if they engage responsibly with it and struggle to change it—seeking no exemption in the process—then they will have the right to influence what is handed on in poetry, as well as the way it is handed on. Then the conversation we have had, the letter I am just finished with, will no longer have to be fictions.

What is more, the strengths that exist in the communal life of women will then be able to refresh and renew the practise and concept of the poetic tradition. Thanks to the women poets in the generation before mine—poets such as Adrienne Rich and Denise Levertov—many of those strengths were already there when I started out. But I believe word such as *canon* and *tradition* and *inheritance* will change even more. And with all that, women poets, from generation to generation, will be able to befriend one another. And that, in the end, is the best reason for writing this letter.

1997

LYN HEJINIAN
b. 1941

Language, Lyn Hejinian has written, "is nothing but meanings, and meanings are nothing but a flow of contexts. Such contexts rarely coalesce into images, rarely come to terms. They are transitions, transmutations, the endless radiating of denotation into relation." One of the foremost practitioners of what is called L*A*N*G*U*A*G*E poetry, Hejinian was born in California and educated at Harvard. In 1976 she founded Tuumba Press, a notable publishing house for innovative writing, and she has also co-edited *Poetics Journal* with fellow poet-theorist Barrett Watten. Now a professor of English at the University of California, Berkeley, she has also taught at the New College of California and the University of Iowa. Her semi-autobiographical prose poem *My Life* (1980, 1987) implements her guiding principles of openness and defamiliarization, as do her numerous other works of prose and verse, including *Oxota: A Short Russian Novel* (1991), *Happily* (2000), and *A Border Comedy* (2001).

"The Rejection of Closure," which we excerpt here, first appeared in Hejinian's influential critical and poetic text *The Language of Inquiry* (2000), but it was originally written and delivered as a talk in 1983. Contextualizing the piece, the author explains that she and Watten were planning an issue of *Poetics Journal* focused on "Women & Language," and that she herself was responding in particular to Carla Harryman's "signal work, *The Middle*[,] . . . an organizationally radiant critique (one might even say trashing) of conventional patriarchal power structures," in which the imperative of closure appears "coercive . . . with its smug pretension to universality and its tendency to cast the poet as guardian to Truth." The "open text," Hejinian adds, "is one which both acknowledges the vastness of the world and is formally differentiating. It is form that provides an opening."

From The Language of Inquiry

From *The Rejection of Closure*

> Two dangers never cease threatening
> the world: order and disorder.
>
> Paul Valéry, *Analects*

Writing's initial situation, its point of origin, is often characterized and always complicated by opposing impulses in the writer and by a seeming dilemma that language creates and then cannot resolve. The writer experiences a conflict between a desire to satisfy a demand for boundedness, for containment and coherence, and a simultaneous desire for free, unhampered access to the world prompting a correspondingly open response to it. Curiously, the term *inclusivity* is applicable to both, though the connotative emphasis is different for each. The impulse to boundedness demands circumscription and that in turn requires that a distinction be made between inside and outside, between the relevant and the (for the particular writing at hand) confusing and irrelevant—the meaningless. The desire for unhampered access and response to the world (an encyclopedic impulse), on the other hand, hates to leave anything out. The essential question here concerns the writer's subject position.

The impasse, meanwhile, that is both language's creative condition and its problem can be described as the disjuncture between words and meaning, but at a particularly material level, one at which the writer is faced with the necessity of making formal decisions—devising an appropriate structure for the work, anticipating the constraints it will put into play, etc.—in the context of the ever-regenerating plenitude of language's resources, in their infinite combinations. Writing's forms are not merely shapes but forces; formal questions are about dynamics—they ask how, where, and why the writing moves, what are the types, directions, number, and velocities of a work's motion. The material aporia objectifies the poem in the context of ideas and of language itself.

These areas of conflict are not neatly parallel. Form does not necessarily achieve closure, nor does raw materiality provide openness. Indeed, the conjunction of *form* with radical *openness* may be what can offer a version of the "paradise" for which writing often yearns—a flowering focus on a distinct infinity.

For the sake of clarity, I will offer a tentative characterization of the terms *open* and *closed*. We can say that a "closed text" is one in which all the elements of the work are directed toward a single reading of it. Each element confirms that reading and delivers the text from any lurking ambiguity. In the "open text," meanwhile, all the elements of the work are maximally excited; here it is because ideas and things exceed (without deserting) argument that they have taken into the dimension of the work.

Though they may be different in different texts, depending on other elements in the work and by all means on the intention of the writer, it is not hard to discover devices—structural devices—that may serve to "open" a poetic text. One set of such devices has to do with arrangement and, particularly, with rearrangement within a work. The "open text," by definition, is open to the world and particularly to the reader. It invites participation, rejects the authority of the writer over the reader and thus, by analogy, the authority implicit in other (social, economic, cultural) hierarchies. It speaks for writing that is generative rather than directive. The writer relinquishes total control and challenges authority as a principle and control as a motive. The "open text" often emphasizes or foregrounds process, either the process of the original composition or of subsequent compositions by readers, and thus resists the cultural tendencies that seek to identify and fix material and turn it into a product; that is, it resists reduction and commodification. As Luce Irigaray says, positing this tendency within a feminine sphere of discourse, "It is really a question of another economy which diverts the linearity of a project, undermines the target-object of a desire, explodes the polarization of desire on only one pleasure, and disconcerts fidelity to only one discourse."[1]

"Field work," where words and lines are distributed irregularly on the page, such as Robert Grenier's poster/map entitled *Cambridge M'ass* and Bruce Andrews's "Love Song 41" (also originally published as a poster), are obvious examples of works in which the order of the reading is not imposed in

---

1. Luce Irigaray, "This Sex Which Is Not One," trans. Claudia Reeder, in *New French Feminisms: An Anthology*, ed. Elaine Marks and Isabelle de Courtivron (Amherst: University of Massachusetts Press, 1980), p. 104 [all notes are Hejinian's].

advance.[2] Any reading of these works is an improvisation; one moves through the work not in straight lines but in curves, swirls, and across intersections, to words that catch the eye or attract attention repeatedly.

Repetition, conventionally used to unify a text or harmonize its parts, as if returning melody to the tonic, instead, in these works, and somewhat differently in a work like my *My Life,* challenges our inclination to isolate, identify, and limit the burden of meaning given to an event (the sentence or line). Here, where certain phrases recur in the work, recontextualized and with new emphasis, repetition disrupts the initial apparent meaning scheme. The initial reading is adjusted; meaning is set in motion, emended and extended, and the rewriting that repetition becomes postpones completion of the thought indefinitely.

But there are more complex forms of juxtaposition. My intention (I don't mean to suggest that I succeeded) in a subsequent work, "Resistance," was to write a lyric poem in a long form—that is, to achieve maximum vertical intensity (the single moment into which the idea rushes) and maximum horizontal extensivity (ideas cross the landscape and become the horizon and weather).[3] To myself I proposed the paragraph as a unit representing a single moment of time, a single moment in the mind, its content all the thoughts, thought particles, impressions, impulses—all the diverse, particular, and contradictory elements—that are included in an active and emotional mind at any given instant. For the moment, for the writer, the poem *is* a mind.

✶   ✶   ✶

1983, 2000

2. Robert Grenier, *Cambridge M'ass* (Berkeley: Tuumba Press, 1979); Bruce Andrews, *Love Songs* (Baltimore: Pod Books, 1982).
3. At the time this essay was written, "Resistance" existed only in manuscript form. A large portion of it was eventually incorporated into "The Green" and published in *The Cold of Poetry* (Los Angeles: Sun & Moon Press, 1994).

Part 2
Theory: On Gender and Culture

Introduction

How can we possibly divide or segregate the women writers meditating on writing in part 1 of this reader from the theorists analyzing gender and culture in part 2? Anyone scrutinizing the authors included in part 1 would have to concede that many creative writers—Adrienne Rich and Gloria Anzaldúa, for instance—composed essays that are major theoretical contributions to our understanding of how gender arrangements influence culture. And a number of theorists in part 2—Simone de Beauvoir, Hélène Cixous, and Shirley Geok-lin Lim, for example—published imaginative novels, stories, and memoirs exploring a range of topics, including their own writing. In other words, it is impossible to isolate "creative" or "literary" approaches from "theoretical" or "analytic" methodologies, because the best writing often melds creative literary strategies with theoretical insights. During the past several decades, *theory* as a term has itself become theorized, contested, and inflected by many sorts of discourses as writers deal with the various subjects related to gender and culture that are addressed throughout this volume.

However, works by the thinkers clustered in the second section of the *Reader* often form the core of courses dedicated to feminist intellectual history during the so-called second wave of the women's movement: that is, from the post–World War II period to the end of the twentieth century. One of the first feminist theorists, Simone de Beauvoir, is paradigmatic of this group of intellectuals in her connections with contemporary male thinkers and her training. Beauvoir reputedly phoned the psychoanalyst Jacques Lacan a year before she completed her monumental *The Second Sex* to ask his advice; when Lacan explained they would need half a year of conversation, she proposed four meetings and finally completed the book without any consultation with him. That she had already established her reputation, while he had not, demonstrates that she had embarked on a pioneering career—a career that typifies the unusual circumstances of the women in this part of the *Reader*. For, as her biographer Toril Moi has explained, Beauvoir "belonged to the first generation of European women to be educated on a par with men." Women from a variety of intellectual disciplines followed her model, competing with men in previously all-male institutions of higher education and later in their professional lives as they began to tackle basic questions pertaining to women's secondary status in Western culture. Starting with *The Second Sex,* which appeared a few years after the end of World War II, and throughout the 1980s and '90s, feminist academics engaged Beauvoir's central insight that "One is not born, but rather becomes, a woman."

How does one "become" a woman? Why are women subordinated to men in most known cultures? How prevalent has women's oppression been? What forms does it take and what are its societal or cultural consequences? What can be done about it? Answers to these questions encouraged feminists to enter into conversations with major male thinkers in a variety of fields and with a variety of methodologies. Psychoanalysis and anthropology were especially useful to feminists seeking to deploy the insights of Sigmund Freud and Claude Lévi-Strauss without recycling the masculine biases evident in their original formulations. Scholars particularly concerned with literary and cultural history revised aesthetic theories promulgated by such thinkers as Harold Bloom, Geoffrey Hartman, Stanley Fish, Henry Louis Gates Jr., Edward Said, and Stuart Hall. With the incursion of French feminist approaches, the Continental philosophical tradition pioneered by Jacques Lacan, Michel Foucault, and Jacques Derrida began shaping poststructuralist insights into social gender roles, anatomical sex, and sexual orientation. While both female and male feminists in gay studies analyzed the history of homosexuality as well as homophobia, female and male feminists in African American, ethnicity, and postcolonial studies studied the gender dynamics of institutionalized and non-institutionalized forms of racism in the United States and of social injustice throughout the world.

In other words, feminist intellectual history cannot be isolated from the trajectory of male-authored criticism and theory during the last three decades of the twentieth century. Yet what feminists did with criticism and theory produced by men or about men can be scrutinized in terms of their conversations not only with their male contemporaries but also with each other. Most foundationally, Simone de Beauvoir utilized the insights of the existentialist Jean-Paul Sartre to posit a cultural connection between masculinity and transcendence (what arises beyond material experience) and a concomitant link between femininity and immanence (what remains within material experience). Such a formation helped Beauvoir and many of her successors explain what she called the alterity of women: because women's status is less than or more than human, they occupy the position of the Other in societies where the default position for personhood is implicitly male. Two decades later, Kate Millett uncovered the dynamics of female Othering by laying bare the political power struggles underlying what had been taken to be erotic or sexual scenarios, most dramatically in representative and often pornographic scenes in American fiction by such writers as Henry Miller and Norman Mailer.

Although this section begins with such writers as Beauvoir and Millett, who considered themselves public intellectuals, it quickly turns to the work of an unprecedented number of women who began entering the professoriate during the 1970s. It thereby makes manifest how feminism itself became an academic enterprise in women's studies and gender studies programs or departments and also how feminist inquiry reshaped traditional disciplines in the humanities and social sciences—particularly English, history, anthropology, sociology, and psychology—as well as in newer programs such as American studies, African American studies, and ethnic studies. By the 1970s, many feminist academics in these various venues were dedicating themselves to analyzing the distinction between gender and sex.

A focus on the sex/gender system enabled feminists to comprehend how biology (sex) is transformed into cultural patterns and social practices (gender). In the influential works of Nancy Chodorow, Juliet Mitchell, Sherry Ortner, and Gayle Rubin, gender signifies not male and female bodies but masculine and feminine social roles that shift dramatically throughout history and across geographical settings. Gender is therefore associated with nurture and with a demonstrable malleability over time and place. Antithetically, sex signifies the physiological facts of embodiment: women's and men's distinctive biological natures—their different genitalia, chromosomes, and life cycles—are assumed to be more fixed or stable. The concept of the so-called sex/gender system did more than provide such thinkers as Chodorow, Mitchell, Ortner, and Rubin with the tools to contrast what they judged to be the universal subordination of women with the multiple cultural arrangements they explored in divergent societies: it also motivated them to raise a number of crucial questions. What are the psychological repercussions of the fact that women provide so much early child care? How does male anatomy come to symbolize primacy? Do menstruation, childbearing, and lactation make women seem closer to nature? and if so, what are the social consequences of such an association? If kinship systems historically depended on the exchange of women by men, what have been their effects on the relationship between the sexes?

Responses to such queries often hinged on an awareness of powerful ideologies that created sexual divisions of labor. In particular, the French feminists Hélène Cixous and Luce Irigaray criticized the male monopoly over the public sphere of economic, political, intellectual, and artistic productivity, juxtaposing that realm with the private sphere of reproduction and domesticity to which women were traditionally relegated. Many of these thinkers also saw the mind/body dualism characteristic of Western culture as tending to assign men to the mental sphere, women to the physical and (presumed to be) lower sphere.

The institutionalization of feminism within academia led to many new course offerings in the humanities, as well as new approaches to the syllabi of existing courses and new types of scholarly investigation. The change was especially dramatic in literature departments, where feminist scholars examined images of women in male literature, the aesthetic traditions created by women writers, and issues clustered around the effects of gender on inspiration, the composition process, reading practices, reception history, canon formation, the dynamics of influence, historical periodization, and genre. These inquiries radically altered the teaching of literature on the undergraduate and graduate levels. On the negative side, however, institutionalization caused some thinkers—particularly those within the rapidly developing fields known as critical race, sexuality, and postcolonial studies—to fear that feminist theory had become isolated from the societal problems facing the vast majority of women outside the academy, in the United States and elsewhere. This self-reflexive trajectory, briefly sketched here, plays itself out in the following section of the *Reader*.

At the risk of oversimplifying a complex intellectual evolution, we propose certain stages in the progress of feminist literary criticism and theory, phases that developed chronologically even though they coexist now in the ongoing work of many feminist scholars. Feminist critics began by investigating images of women in literature composed by men and in male-dominated religious and folkloric, psychoanalytic and philosophic, scientific and political contexts. Feminists dedicated to tracing the imprint of male-domination (or masculinism) dealt with various stereotypes of women that contributed to their alterity, their Otherness. Centered on the history and iconography of misogyny, early investigations into such mythic figures as Eve and Mary quickly led Margaret Homans, among others, to examine related female stereotypes at work in British literary history. Homans uncovered the ways in which a Romantic poet like William Wordsworth tended to imagine the sources of his inspiration—incarnated in his female muse or in his ideas about mother nature—as a silent and instrumental basis for his own linguistic virtuosity. In the context of American letters, Judith Fetterley, Nina Baym, Annette Kolodny, and Lillian Robinson studied the sundry literary representations and cultural practices that buttress the ascendancy of literary men.

In various ways, all four point out, the earliest academic specialists in American culture (almost all of them men) made certain assumptions about what constitutes quintessentially American literature, assumptions that tended to marginalize the contributions of American women writers. Later scholars, such as Susan Bordo, examined debilitating images of women in contemporary popular culture—in Bordo's case, to comprehend women's sense of embodiment, and in particular its reflection in the rising rates of eating disorders.

When feminist critics turned their attention to women authors, characters, and readers, as well as to relationships between women authors, characters, and readers, a number of thinkers began mapping female-inflected traditions in women's literature. Several books produced toward the end of the 1970s emphasized women writers' alienation from male-dominated literary marketplaces and conventions, their complex identifications with each other, and their efforts to forge plots, images, symbols, and languages responsive to women's unique cultural situation: Ellen Moers's *Literary Women* (1976), Elaine Showalter's *A Literature of Their Own* (1977), and our own *Madwoman in the Attic* (1979) predated but also set the stage for the publication of *The Norton Anthology of Literature by Women* (1985), which was originally subtitled *The Tradition in English*. Quickly a host of feminist scholars began exploring such topics as sisterhood, maternity, female desire, and community so as to remap literary geographies, especially those of the United Kingdom and America.

If women writers produced uniquely female traditions, feminists began to speculate, perhaps their literary history had to be reconceptualized. Beginning with the historian Joan Kelly-Gadol's famous question, "Did women have a Renaissance?" feminist thinkers considered the Romantic and the Victorian period, modernism and postmodernism in order to explore both the interactions between literary men and women and their different sorts of achievements. Each period within literary history had to be reconfigured to account for the sort of work literary women did. By engendering periodization as well as the dynamics of literary influence and by recovering many previously neglected female authors, feminists established a host of new areas of inquiry. Carolyn Heilbrun, for example, studied the relationship between the fictional, autobiographical, and actual lives of women in the twentieth century. Joanne Feit Diehl and Isobel Armstrong analyzed the interconnections between sexual and textual conventions in nineteenth-century verse. Judith Kegan Gardiner, Tania Modleski, Janice Radway, Jane Tompkins, and Patricia Yaeger, among many others, scrutinized genres that were predominantly composed by and for women (the romance, for example) or by and for men (the western, for instance).

Feminist theories multiplied when such thinkers began linking gender-related and sex-related subjects to issues that involved women from various racial backgrounds, with diverse sexual orientations, and from a number of nations. Taken together, this work on race, sexual orientation, and nation explains why, in the second edition of *The Norton Anthology of Literature by Women*, we revised the subtitle to make it plural: *The Traditions in English*. Not after but during the prolific explosion of feminist approaches in the 1970s, such pioneering African American scholars as Mary Helen Washington, Toni Cade Bambara, and Barbara Christian produced anthologies and critical studies that made visible black women's cultural productivity in the United States. Throughout the 1980s and '90s, the recovery of female-authored African American literary traditions generated a number of related critical analyses. Hortense Spillers, for example, examined the effects of slavery on the African American family and on the evolution or devolution of gender roles. Just as Barbara Johnson illuminated the rhetorical strategies deployed by Zora Neale Hurston, such scholars as Hazel Carby, Cheryl Wall, and Valerie Smith studied the relationships between black men of letters and their female contemporaries during the period in which Hurston wrote. While Elizabeth Abel drew on Toni Morrison's critical ideas about the centrality of race in American literature to analyze friendships between white and black female characters, bell hooks elaborated on the historical tensions between white and black feminists.

In sexuality studies, scholars committed to excavating a lesbian cultural past drew on the groundbreaking essays of Adrienne Rich, Monique Wittig, and Bonnie Zimmerman in order to excavate lesbian aesthetic history, to consider the historically asymmetrical legal and social positions of lesbians and gay men, to understand the dynamics of homophobia, and to clarify the invisible privileges of heterosexuality. In two major books, *Between Men* (1985) and *Epistemology of the Closet* (1990), Eve Kosofsky Sedgwick demonstrated how problematic and destructive it has been to categorize sexuality through a polarized hetero-/homosexual binary. Along with such important thinkers as Terry Castle, Martha Vicinus, Marjorie Garber, Biddy Martin, Esther Newton, Judith Halberstam, and Carolyn Dever, a host of scholars in lesbian studies began to explore the significance of bisexuality as well as of the intersexed and the transsexed, and to examine the tensions as well as the coalitions between activists in the feminist and gay liberation movements. As in African American studies, much of the foundational work in queer theory was pioneered by self-identified feminists concentrating on the lives and writing of women, although in the case of Sedgwick the focus was often on male homosexuals and their communities.

With respect to nation, also, feminists were at the forefront of ethnic, postcolonial, and transnational studies, where they explored differences among women from various geopolitical and class backgrounds, the sexual consequences of diverse religious fundamentalisms, the economic impact of colonialism on third world women, and the possibility of building global feminist networks between and among first and third world women. The project of the Asian American scholar Shirley Geok-Lin Lim cannot be conflated with the work of the Chicana scholar Paula Moya. However, both sought to understand how ethnic ties shape the work of transnational women writers negotiating between two languages and two cultures. Similarly, Paula Gunn Allen's analyses of Native American feminism cannot be equated with Chandra Mohanty's approach to third world women. Yet just as Allen attempted to comprehend the creolized or hybrid identifications formed by Native American women engaging in feminist projects, so Mohanty stressed the priorities and perspectives that third world women brought to feminism. Especially in African American and postcolonial scholarship, the limitations of feminist theory began to come under scrutiny. In sundry ways, Barbara Christian, Chandra Talpade Mohanty, and Gayatri Chakravorty Spivak critiqued the role of white and first world feminist intellectuals by suggesting that consciously or unconsciously, they either marginalized or caricatured women of color or third world women.

As in the first section of this reader, we have ordered selections in the second part not by the author's date of birth but by the date of her text's publication. This organization highlights the multiple debates that evolved. One of the most important disputes surfaced around the end of the 1980s, when feminist scholars studying race, sexuality, and nation started to question earlier assumptions about sex and gender—about the possibility or problematic of detaching nature from nurture or of isolating either from a host of other (religious or racial, economic or political) considerations. Often abstract, such discussions, which clustered around what is called the essentialism-social constructionism debate, were shaped by the influential work of Judith Butler. Especially in *Gender Trouble* (1990), Butler addressed problems relating to the sex/gender system that were surfacing in African American and postcolonial studies. Although earlier feminists had stressed sex as a category in order to argue for a collective term, *women*, that would politically unify various constituencies, such a view was contested by those who stressed gender as a category in order to emphasize how using a term like *women* could generate an illusory or homogenized totality: many poststructuralists worried that the category *women* obfuscated both the multiple and diverse roles that various women are compelled to perform and also the complex, fluid, and contradictory identifications they adopt. Following Butler, poststructuralist feminists emphasized differences (of beliefs, identifications, affiliations) within any given woman as well as differences between and among women from different backgrounds and with different values.

While the so-called essentialists stressed the impact of biological nature, such social constructionists as Butler and Donna Haraway clarified the cultural lenses through which we necessarily interpret nature. According to Butler, then, "gender is a performance that *produces* the illusion of an inner sex or essence or psychic gender core; it *produces* on the skin, through the gesture, the move, the gait (that array of corporeal theatrics understood as gender presentation), the illusion of an inner depth" (emphases hers). If the essentialists, who tended to be historically empirical in their approach, accentuated physical embodiment, the social constructionists, propelled by poststructuralist theory, underscored what they called performativity: gender roles, they stressed, constitute a masquerade or impersonation, albeit one often enforced by families, schools, churches, law courts, and other regulatory agencies in society. Influential as this debate was, the bifurcation of criticism and theory cannot be conflated with the dichotomy between so-called essentialists and so-called constructionists, because both groups produced empirical analyses of literary and historical texts and contexts as well as abstract descriptions of the mechanisms governing such texts and contexts.

Over the turn of the century, many scholars, including Diana Fuss, questioned the efficacy of polarizing feminism along these oppositional lines. Other differences also emerge in these pages. Some academics use the methodologies of traditional disciplines as well as their languages, whereas others deploy personal, autobiographical approaches to their subject matter. A number are interested in literary issues, but still others are engaged in societal and legal problems related to, for example, violence against women, the effects of bioengineering, lesbian parenting, the intersexed and transsexed, modern warfare, the media, or the history of feminism itself. In such publications as *Listen Up: Voices from the Next Feminist Generation* (1995; rev. ed., 2001), edited by Barbara Findlen, and *Manifesta: Young Women, Feminism, and the Future* (2000), edited by Jennifer Baumgardner and Amy Richards, younger authors also embarked—in works that they associated with the third wave of feminism—on exploring a host of social and psychological issues facing feminists raised by feminist parents.

Regardless of their chosen perspective, the essays collected here constitute touchstone texts. Space constraints forced us to omit works by many outstanding scholars; however, we have included texts that represent the most significant and the most influential work in the field of feminism, especially essays that have redefined the study of imaginative literature. Thus we have had to exclude much important research in such areas as film studies, the institutionalization of women's studies, men's studies, and science (including biotechnology) so as to make room for arguments more central to feminist *literary* criticism and theory. Taken together, these essays show how feminists' engagement with literature transformed traditional critical approaches to literary study. Formalism, psychoanalysis, Marxism, reader-response theory, structuralism, black studies, poststructuralism, deconstruction, New Historicism, cultural studies, postcolonialism, ethnic studies: all inform the following pages and all were, in turn, shaped by the following pages. Just as important, the originality of the theorists included here transfigured our understanding and appreciation of women as producers and interpreters of culture.

SUSAN GUBAR

SIMONE DE BEAUVOIR
1908–1986

An existentialist, Simone de Beauvoir published *The Second Sex* in 1949, before the so-called second wave of feminism, yet it exerted immediate influence and continues to shape feminist elaborations upon her famous sentence that "One is not born, but rather becomes, a woman." The older of two daughters, Beauvoir grew up in Paris, where she studied at the Sorbonne and began her long relationship with the philosopher Jean-Paul Sartre. After cofounding *Les Temps Modernes,* a journal about politics and culture, she published six novels, four books of philosophy, and many volumes of essays and autobiography, including several addressing the later life cycles of women. Toril Moi, in *Simone de Beauvoir: The Making of an Intellectual Woman* (1994) and *What Is a Woman? And Other Essays* (1999), has provided extensive interpretations of the biographical and intellectual frameworks that helped Beauvoir create a touchstone work upon which contemporary feminists continue to draw. Our selection from *The Second Sex* constitutes the beginning of part 3, "Myths," which follows part 1, "Destiny," and part 2, "History." In it, Beauvoir explains why and how women "still dream through the dreams of men."

From The Second Sex[1]

From *Part III. Myths*

FROM CHAPTER I. DREAMS, FEARS, IDOLS

History has shown us that men have always kept in their hands all concrete powers; since the earliest days of the patriarchate they have thought best to keep woman in a state of dependence; their codes of law have been set up against her; and thus she has been definitely established as the Other. This arrangement suited the economic interests of the males; but it conformed also to their ontological and moral pretensions. Once the subject seeks to assert himself, the Other, who limits and denies him, is none the less a necessity to him: he attains himself only through that reality which he is not, which is something other than himself. That is why man's life is never abundance and quietude; it is dearth and activity, it is struggle. Before him, man encounters Nature; he has some hold upon her, he endeavours to mould her to his desire. But she cannot fill his needs. Either she appears simply as a purely impersonal opposition, she is an obstacle and remains a stranger; or she submits passively to man's will and permits assimilation, so that he takes possession of her only through consuming her—that is, through destroying her. In both cases he remains alone; he is alone when he touches a stone, alone when he devours a fruit. There can be no presence of an other unless the other is also present in and for himself: which is to say that true alterity—otherness—is that of a consciousness separate from mine and substantially identical with mine.

It is the existence of other men that tears each man out of his immanence and enables him to fulfil the truth of his being, to complete himself through transcendence, through escape towards some objective, through enterprise. But this liberty not my own, while assuring mine, also conflicts with it: there is the tragedy of the unfortunate human consciousness; each separate conscious being aspires to set himself up alone as sovereign subject. Each tries to fulfil himself by reducing the other to slavery. But the slave, though he works and fears, senses himself somehow as the essential; and, by a dialectical inversion, it is the master who seems to be the inessential. It is possible to rise above this conflict if each individual freely recognizes the other, each regarding himself and the other simultaneously as object and as subject in a reciprocal manner. But friendship and generosity, which alone permit in actuality this recognition of free beings, are not facile virtues; they are assuredly man's highest achievement, and through that achievement he is to be found in his true nature. But this true nature is that of a struggle unceasingly begun, unceasingly abolished; it requires man to outdo himself at every moment. We might put it in other words and say that man attains an authentically moral attitude when he renounces *mere being* to assume his position as an existent; through this transformation also he renounces all possession, for possession is one way of seeking mere being; but the transformation through which he attains true wisdom is never done, it is necessary to make it without ceasing, it demands a constant tension. And so, quite unable to fulfil himself in soli-

---

1. Translated by H. M. Parshley.

tude, man is incessantly in danger in his relations with his fellows: his life is a difficult enterprise with success never assured.

But he does not like difficulty; he is afraid of danger. He aspires in contradictory fashion both to life and to repose, to existence and to merely being; he knows full well that 'trouble of spirit' is the price of development, that his distance from the object is the price of his nearness to himself; but he dreams of quiet in disquiet and of an opaque plenitude that nevertheless would be endowed with consciousness. This dream incarnated is precisely woman; she is the wished-for intermediary between nature, the stranger to man, and the fellow being who is too closely identical.[2] She opposes him with neither the hostile silence of nature nor the hard requirement of a reciprocal relation; through a unique privilege she is a conscious being and yet it seems possible to possess her in the flesh. Thanks to her, there is a means for escaping that implacable dialectic of master and slave[3] which has its source in the reciprocity that exists between free beings.

We have seen that there were not at first free women whom the males had enslaved nor were there even castes based on sex. To regard woman simply as a slave is a mistake; there were women among the slaves, to be sure, but there have always been free women—that is, women of religious and social dignity. They accepted man's sovereignty and he did not feel menaced by a revolt that could make of him in turn the object. Woman thus seems to be the inessential who never goes back to being the essential, to be the absolute Other, without reciprocity. This conviction is dear to the male, and every creation myth has expressed it, among others the legend of Genesis, which, through Christianity, has been kept alive in Western civilization. Eve was not fashioned at the same time as the man; she was not fabricated from a different substance, nor of the same clay as was used to model Adam: she was taken from the flank of the first male. Not even her birth was independent; God did not spontaneously choose to create her as an end in herself and in order to be worshipped directly by her in return for it. She was destined by Him for man; it was to rescue Adam from loneliness that He gave her to him, in her mate was her origin and her purpose; she was his complement in the order of the inessential. Thus she appeared in the guise of privileged prey. She was nature elevated to transparency of consciousness; she was a conscious being, but naturally submissive. And therein lies the wondrous hope that man has often put in woman: he hopes to fulfil himself as a being by carnally possessing a being, but at the same time confirming his sense of freedom through the docility of a free person. No man would consent to be a woman, but every man wants women to exist. 'Thank God for having created woman.' 'Nature is good since she has given women to men.' In such expressions man once more asserts with naïve arrogance that his presence in this world is an ineluctable fact and a right, that of woman a mere accident—but a very happy accident. Appearing as the Other, woman appears at the same time as an abundance of being in contrast to that existence the nothingness of which

---

2. ' . . . Woman is not the useless replica of man, but rather the enchanted place where the living alliance between man and nature is brought about. If she should disappear, men would be alone, strangers lacking passports in an icy world. She is the earth itself raised to life's summit, the earth become sensitive and joyous; and without her, for man the earth is mute and dead' writes Michel Carrouges ('Les Pouvoirs de la femme', *Cahiers du Sud*, No. 291) [Beauvoir's note].

3. Posited by G. W. H. Hegel in *Phenomenology of Spirit* (1807); each identifies him- or herself through the eyes of the other.

man senses in himself; the Other, being regarded as the object in the eyes of the subject, is regarded as *en soi*;[4] therefore as a being. In woman is incarnated in positive form the lack that the existent carries in his heart, and it is in seeking to be made whole through her that man hopes to attain self-realization.

She has not represented for him, however, the only incarnation of the Other, and she has not always kept the same importance throughout the course of history. There have been moments when she has been eclipsed by other idols. When the City or the State devours the citizen, it is no longer possible for him to be occupied with his personal destiny. Being dedicated to the State, the Spartan woman's condition was above that of other Greek women. But it is also true that she was transfigured by no masculine dream. The cult of the leader, whether he be Napoleon, Mussolini, or Hitler, excludes all other cults. In military dictatorships, in totalitarian régimes, woman is no longer a privileged object. It is understandable that woman should be deified in a rich country where the citizens are none too certain of the meaning of life: thus it is in America. On the other hand, socialist ideologies, which assert the equality of all human beings, refuse now and for the future to permit any human category to be object or idol: in the authentically democratic society proclaimed by Marx there is no place for the Other. Few men, however, conform exactly to the militant, disciplined figure they have chosen to be; to the degree in which they remain individuals, woman keeps in their eyes a special value. I have seen letters written by German soldiers to French prostitutes in which, in spite of Nazism, the ingrained tradition of virgin purity was naïvely confirmed. Communist writers, like Aragon in France and Vittorini in Italy, give a place of the first rank in their works to woman, whether mistress or mother. Perhaps the myth of woman will some day be extinguished; the more women assert themselves as human beings, the more the marvellous quality of the Other will die out in them. But today it still exists in the heart of every man.

A myth always implies a subject who projects his hopes and his fears towards a sky of transcendence. Women do not set themselves up as Subject and hence have erected no virile myth in which their projects are reflected; they have no religion or poetry of their own: they still dream through the dreams of men. Gods made by males are the gods they worship. Men have shaped for their own exaltation great virile figures: Hercules, Prometheus, Parsifal; woman has only a secondary part to play in the destiny of these heroes. No doubt there are conventional figures of man caught in his relations to woman: the father, the seducer, the husband, the jealous lover, the good son, the wayward son; but they have all been established by men, and they lack the dignity of myth, being hardly more than clichés. Whereas woman is defined exclusively in her relation to man. The asymmetry of the categories—male and female—is made manifest in the unilateral form of sexual myths. We sometimes say 'the sex' to designate woman; she is the flesh, its delights and dangers. The truth that for woman man is sex and carnality has never been proclaimed because there is no one to proclaim it. Representation of the world, like the world itself, is the work of men; they describe it from their own point of view, which they confuse with absolute truth.

---

4. In itself (French), as opposed to for itself—i.e., an object rather than a consciousness.

It is always difficult to describe a myth; it cannot be grasped or encompassed; it haunts the human consciousness without ever appearing before it in fixed form. The myth is so various, so contradictory, that at first its unity is not discerned: Delilah and Judith, Aspasia and Lucretia, Pandora and Athena—woman is at once Eve and the Virgin Mary. She is an idol, a servant, the source of life, a power of darkness; she is the elemental silence of truth, she is artifice, gossip, and falsehood; she is healing presence and sorceress; she is man's prey, his downfall, she is everything that he is not and that he longs for, his negation and his *raison d'être*.

'To be a woman,' says Kierkegaard in *Stages on the Road of Life*, 'is something so strange, so confused, so complicated, that no one predicate comes near expressing it and that the multiple predicates that one would like to use are so contradictory that only a woman could put up with it.' This comes from not regarding woman positively, such as she seems to herself to be, but negatively, such as she appears to man. For if woman is not the only *Other*, it remains none the less true that she is always defined as the Other. And her ambiguity is just that of the concept of the Other: it is that of the human situation in so far as it is defined in its relation with the Other. As I have already said, the Other is Evil; but being necessary to the Good, it turns into the Good; through it I attain to the Whole, but it also separates me therefrom; it is the gateway to the infinite and the measure of my finite nature. And here lies the reason why woman incarnates no stable concept; through her is made unceasingly the passage from hope to frustration, from hate to love, from good to evil, from evil to good. Under whatever aspect we may consider her, it is this ambivalence that strikes us first.

Man seeks in woman the Other as Nature and as his fellow being. But we know what ambivalent feelings Nature inspires in man. He exploits her, but she crushes him, he is born of her and dies in her; she is the source of his being and the realm that he subjugates to his will; Nature is a vein of gross material in which the soul is imprisoned, and she is the supreme reality; she is contingence and Idea, the finite and the whole; she is what opposes the Spirit, and the Spirit itself. Now ally, now enemy, she appears as the dark chaos from whence life wells up, as this life itself, and as the over-yonder towards which life tends. Woman sums up nature as Mother, Wife, and Idea; these forms now mingle and now conflict, and each of them wears a double visage.

Man has his roots deep in Nature; he has been engendered like the animals and plants; he well knows that he exists only in so far as he lives. But since the coming of the patriarchate, Life has worn in his eyes a double aspect: it is consciousness, will, transcendence, it is the spirit; and it is matter, passivity, immanence, it is the flesh. Aeschylus, Aristotle, Hippocrates proclaimed that on earth as on Olympus it is the male principle that is truly creative: from it came form, number, movement; grain grows and multiples through Demeter's care, but the origin of the grain and its verity lie in Zeus; woman's fecundity is regarded as only a passive quality. She is the earth, and man the seed; she is Water and he is Fire. Creation has often been imagined as the marriage of fire and water; it is warmth and moisture that give rise to living things; the Sun is the husband of the Sea; the Sun, fire, are male divinities; and the Sea is one of the most nearly universal of maternal symbols. Passively the waters accept the fertilizing action of the flaming radiations. So also the sod, broken by the ploughman's labour, passively receives the seeds within its furrows. But it plays a necessary part: it supports the living germ, protects it and furnishes the substance for its growth. And that is why man continued to worship the goddesses of fecundity, even after the Great Mother was dethroned;[5] he is indebted to Cybele for his crops, his herds, his whole prosperity. He even owes his own life to her. He sings the praises of water no less than fire. 'Glory to the sea! Glory to its waves surrounded with sacred fire! Glory to the wave! Glory to the fire! Glory to the strange adventure,' cries Goethe in the Second Part of *Faust*. Man venerates the Earth: 'The matron Clay', as Blake calls her.[6] A prophet of India advises his disciples not to spade the earth, for 'it is a sin to wound or to cut, to tear the mother of us all in the labours of cultiva-tion . . . Shall I go take a knife and plunge it into my mother's breast? . . . Shall I hack at her flesh to reach her bones? . . . How dare I cut off my mother's hair?' In central India the Baidya also consider it a sin to 'tear their earth mother's breast with the plough'. Inversely, Aeschylus says of Oedipus that he 'dared to seed the sacred furrow wherein he was formed'. Sophocles speaks of 'paternal furrows' and of the 'ploughman, master of a distant field that he visits only once, at the time of sowing'. The loved one of an Egyptian song declares: 'I am the earth!' In Islamic texts woman is called 'field . . . vine-yard'. St Francis of Assisi speaks in one of his hymns of 'our sister, the earth, our mother, keeping and caring for us, producing all kinds of fruits, with many-coloured flowers and with grass'. Michelet, taking the mud baths at Acqui, exclaimed: 'Dear mother of all! We are one. I came from you, to you I return! . . . ' And so it is in periods when there flourishes a vitalist romanti-cism that desires the triumph of Life over Spirit; then the magical fertility of the land, of woman, seems to be more wonderful than the contrived opera-tions of the male: then man dreams of losing himself anew in the maternal shadows that he may find there again the true sources of his being. The mother is the root which, sunk in the depths of the cosmos, can draw up its juices; she is the fountain whence springs forth the living water, water that is also a nourishing milk, a warm spring, a mud made of earth and water, rich in restorative virtues.[7]

But more often man is in revolt against his carnal state; he sees himself as a fallen god: his curse is to be fallen from a bright and ordered heaven into the chaotic shadows of his mother's womb. This fire, this pure and active exhalation in which he likes to recognize himself, is imprisoned by woman in the mud of the earth. He would be inevitable, like a pure Idea, like the One, the All, the absolute Spirit; and he finds himself shut up in a body of limited powers, in a place and time he never chose, where he was not called for, use-less, cumbersome, absurd. The contingency of all flesh is his own to suffer in his abandonment, in his unjustifiable needlessness. She also dooms him to death. This quivering jelly which is elaborated in the womb (the womb, secret and sealed like the tomb) evokes too clearly the soft viscosity of car-rion for him not to turn shuddering away. Wherever life is in the making—

5. 'I sing the earth, firmly founded mother of all, venerable grandmother, supporting on her soil all that lives,' says a Homeric hymn. And Aeschylus also glorifies the land which 'brings forth all beings, supports them, and then receives in turn their fer-tile seed' [Beauvoir's note].

6. In *The Book of Thel* (1789–91).
7. 'Literally, woman is Isis, fecund nature. She is the river and the river-bed, the root and the rose, the earth and the cherry tree, the vine-stock and the grape' (Carrouges) [Beauvoir's note].

germination, fermentation—it arouses disgust because it is made only in being destroyed; the slimy embryo begins the cycle that is completed in the putrefaction of death. Because he is horrified by needlessness and death, man feels horror at having been engendered; he would fain deny his animal ties; through the fact of his birth murderous Nature has a hold upon him.

Among primitive peoples childbirth is surrounded by the most severe taboos; in particular, the placenta must be carefully burned or thrown into the sea, for whoever should get possession of it would hold the fate of the newborn in his hands. That membranous mass by which the foetus grows is the sign of its dependency; when it is destroyed, the individual is enabled to tear himself from the living magma and become an autonomous being. The uncleanness of birth is reflected upon the mother. Leviticus and all the ancient codes impose rites of purification upon one who has given birth; and in many rural districts the ceremony of churching (blessing after childbirth) continues this tradition. We know the spontaneous embarrassment, often disguised under mocking laughter, felt by children, young girls, and men at sight of the pregnant abdomen; the swollen bosom of the woman with child. In museums the curious gaze at waxen embryos and preserved foetuses with the same morbid interest they show in a ravaged tomb. With all the respect thrown around it by society, the function of gestation still inspires a spontaneous feeling of revulsion. And if the little boy remains in early childhood sensually attached to the maternal flesh, when he grows older, becomes socialized, and takes note of his individual existence, this same flesh frightens him; he would ignore it and see in his mother only a moral personage. If he is anxious to believe her pure and chaste, it is less because of amorous jealousy than because of his refusal to see her as a body. The adolescent is embarrassed, he blushes, if while with his companions he happens to meet his mother, his sisters, any of his female relatives: it is because their presence calls him back to those realms of immanence whence he would fly, exposes roots from which he would tear himself loose. The little boy's irritation when his mother kisses and cajoles him has the same significance; he disowns family, mother, maternal bosom. He would like to have sprung into the world, like Athena fully grown, fully armed, invulnerable.[8] To have been conceived and then born an infant is the curse that hangs over his destiny, the impurity that contaminates his being. And, too, it is the announcement of his death. The cult of germination has always been associated with the cult of the dead. The Earth Mother engulfs the bones of her children. They are women—the Parcae, the Moirai[9]—who weave the destiny of mankind; but it is they, also, who cut the threads. In most popular representations Death is a woman, and it is for women to bewail the dead because death is their work.[1]

Thus the Woman-Mother has a face of shadows: she is the chaos whence all have come and whither all must one day return; she is Nothingness. In the Night are confused together the multiple aspects of the world which daylight reveals: night of spirit confined in the generality and opacity of matter, night of sleep and of nothingness. In the deeps of the sea it is night: woman is the

---

8. See below [in chapter 2] the study of Montherlant, who embodies this attitude in exemplary fashion [Beauvoir's note].
9. The Fates.
1. Demeter typifies the *mater dolorosa*. But other goddesses—Ishtar, Artemis—are cruel. Kali holds in her hand a cranium filled with blood. A Hindu poet addresses her: 'The heads of thy newly killed sons hang like a necklace about thy neck . . . Thy form is beautiful like rain clouds, thy feet are soiled with blood' [Beauvoir's note]. "*Mater dolorosa*": grieving mother (Latin).

Mare tenebrarum,[2] dreaded by navigators of old; it is night in the entrails of the earth. Man is frightened of this night, the reverse of fecundity, which threatens to swallow him up. He aspires to the sky, to the light, to the sunny summits, to the pure and crystalline frigidity of the blue sky; and under his feet there is a moist, warm, and darkling gulf ready to draw him down; in many a legend do we see the hero lost for ever as he falls back into the maternal shadows—cave, abyss, hell.

But here again is the play of ambivalence: if germination is always associated with death, so is death with fecundity. Hated death appears as a new birth, and then it becomes blessed. The dead hero is resurrected, like Osiris, each spring, and he is regenerated by a new birth. Man's highest hope, says Jung, in *Metamorphoses of the Libido*, 'is that the dark waters of death become the waters of life, that death and its cold embrace be the motherly bosom, which like the ocean, although engulfing the sun, gives birth to it again within its depths'. A theme common to numerous mythologies is the burial of the sun-god in the bosom of the ocean and his dazzling reappearance. And man at once wants to live but longs for repose and sleep and nothingness. He does not wish he were immortal, and so he can learn to love death. Nietzsche writes: 'Inorganic matter is the maternal bosom. To be freed of life is to become true again, it is to achieve perfection. Whoever should understand that would consider it a joy to return to the unfeeling dust.' Chaucer put this prayer into the mouth of an old man unable to die:

> With my staff, night and day
> I strike on the ground, my mother's doorway,
> And I say: Ah, mother dear, let me in.[3]

Man would fain affirm his individual existence and rest with pride on his 'essential difference', but he wishes also to break through the barriers of the ego, to mingle with the water, the night, with Nothingness, with the Whole. Woman condemns man to finitude, but she also enables him to exceed his own limits; and hence comes the equivocal magic with which she is endued.

In all civilizations and still in our day woman inspires man with horror; it is the horror of his own carnal contingence, which he projects upon her. The little girl, not yet in puberty, carries no menace, she is under no taboo and has no sacred character. In many primitive societies her very sex seems innocent: erotic games are allowed from infancy between boys and girls. But on the day she can reproduce, woman becomes impure; and rigorous taboos surround the menstruating female. Leviticus gives elaborate regulations, and many primitive societies have similar rules regarding isolation and purification. In matriarchal societies the powers attributed to menstruation were ambivalent: the flow could upset social activities and ruin crops; but it was also used in love potions and medicines. Even today certain Indians put in the bow of the boat a mass of fibre soaked in menstrual blood, to combat river demons. But since patriarchal times only evil powers have been attributed to the feminine flow. Pliny said that a menstruating woman ruins crops, destroys gardens, kills bees, and so on; and that if she touches wine, it becomes vinegar; milk is soured, and the like. An ancient English poet put the same notion into rhyme:

---

2. Sea of darkness (Latin).

3. From Chaucer, *The Pardoner's Tale* (ca. 1400).

Oh! Menstruating woman, thou'st a fiend
From whom all nature should be screened!

Such beliefs have survived with considerable power into recent times. In 1878 it was declared in the *British Medical Journal* that 'it is an undoubted fact that meat spoils when touched by menstruating women', and cases were cited from personal observation. And at the beginning of this century a rule forbade women having 'the curse' to enter the refineries of northern France, for that would cause the sugar to blacken. These ideas still persist in rural districts, where every cook knows that a mayonnaise will not be successful if a menstruating woman is about; some rustics believe cider will not ferment, others that bacon cannot be salted and will spoil under these circumstances. A few vaguely factual reports may offer some slight support for such beliefs; but it is obvious from their importance and universality that they must have had a superstitious or mystical origin. Certainly there is more here than reaction to blood in general, sacred as it is. But menstrual blood is peculiar, it represents the essence of femininity. Hence it can supposedly bring harm to the woman herself if misused by others. According to C. Lévi-Strauss, among the Chago the girls are warned not to let anyone see any signs of the flow; clothes must be buried, and so on, to avoid danger. Leviticus likens menstruation to gonorrhea, and Vigny associates the notion of uncleanness with that of illness when he writes: 'Woman, sick child and twelve times impure.'

The periodic haemorrhage of woman is strangely timed with the lunar cycle; and the moon also is thought to have her dangerous caprices.[4] Woman is a part of that fearsome machinery which turns the planets and the sun in their courses, she is the prey of cosmic energies that rule the destiny of the stars and the tides, and of which men must undergo the disturbing radiations. But menstrual blood is supposed to act especially on organic substances, half way between matter and life: souring cream, spoiling meat, causing fermentation, decomposition; and this less because it is blood than because it issues from the genital organs. Without comprehending its exact function, people have realized that it is bound to the reproduction of life: ignorant of the ovary, the ancients even saw in the menses the complement of the sperm. The blood, indeed, does not make woman impure; it is rather a sign of her impurity. It concerns generation, it flows from the parts where the foetus develops. Through menstrual blood is expressed the horror inspired in man by woman's fecundity.

One of the most rigorous taboos forbids all sexual relations with a woman in a state of menstrual impurity. In various cultures offenders have themselves been considered impure for certain periods, or they have been required to undergo severe penance; it has been supposed that masculine energy and vitality would be destroyed because the feminine principle is then at its maximum of force. More vaguely, man finds it repugnant to come upon the dreaded essence of the mother in the woman he possesses; he is determined to dissociate these two aspects of femininity. Hence the universal law pro-

---

4. The moon is a source of fertility; it appears as 'master of women'; it is often believed that in the form of man or serpent it couples with women. The serpent is an epiphany of the moon; it sheds its skin and renews itself, it is immortal, it is an influence promoting fecundity and knowledge. It is the serpent that guards the sacred springs, the tree of life, the fountain of youth. But it is also the serpent that took from man his immortality. Persian and rabbinical traditions maintain that menstruation is to be attributed to the relations of the woman with the serpent [Beauvoir's note].

hibiting incest,[5] expressed in the rule of exogamy or in more modern forms; this is why man tends to keep away from woman at the times when she is especially taken up with her reproductive role: during her menses, when she is pregnant, in lactation. The Oedipus complex—which should be redescribed—does not deny this attitude, but on the contrary implies it. Man is on the defensive against woman in so far as she represents the vague source of the world and obscure organic development.

It is in this guise also, however, that woman enables her group, separated from the cosmos and the gods, to remain in communication with them. Today she still assures the fertility of the fields among the Bedouins and the Iroquois; in ancient Greece she heard the subterranean voices; she caught the language of winds and trees: she was Pythia, sibyl, prophetess; the dead and the gods spoke through her mouth. She keeps today these powers of divination: she is medium, reader of palms and cards, clairvoyant, inspired; she hears voices, sees apparitions. When men feel the need to plunge again into the midst of plant and animal life—as Antaeus[6] touched the earth to renew his strength—they make appeal to woman. All through the rationalist civilizations of Greece and Rome the underworld cults continued to exist. They were ordinarily marginal to the official religious life; they even took on in the end, as at Eleusis, the form of mysteries: their meaning was opposite to that of the solar cults in which man asserted his will to independence and spirituality; but they were complementary to them; man sought to escape from his solitude through ecstasy: that was the end and aim of the mysteries, the orgies, the bacchanals. In a world reconquered by the males, it was a male god, Dionysus, who usurped the wild and magical power of Ishtar, of Astarte; but still they were women who revelled madly around his image: maenads, thyiads, bacchantes summoned the men to holy drunkenness, to sacred frenzy. Religious prostitution played a similar part: it was a matter at once of unloosing and channelling the powers of fecundity. Popular festivals today are still marked by outbursts of eroticism; woman appears here not simply as an object of pleasure, but as a means for attaining to that state of *hybris,* riotousness, in which the individual exceeds the bounds of self. 'What a human being possesses deep within him of the lost, of the tragic, of the "blinding wonder" can be found again nowhere but in bed,' writes G. Bataille.

In the erotic release, man embraces the loved one and seeks to lose himself in the infinite mystery of the flesh. But we have seen that, on the contrary, his normal sexuality tends to dissociate Mother from Wife. He feels repugnance for the mysterious alchemies of life, whereas his own life is nourished and delighted with the savoury fruits of earth; he wishes to take them for his own; he covets Venus newly risen from the wave. Woman is disclosed first as wife in the patriarchate, since the supreme creator is male. Before being the mother of the human race, Eve was Adam's companion; she was given to man so that he might possess her and fertilize her as he owns and fertilizes the soil; and through her he makes all nature his realm. It is not only a subjective and fleeting pleasure that man seeks in the sexual act. He wishes

5. According to the view of a sociologist, G. P. Murdock, in *Social Structure* (Macmillan, 1949), incest prohibition can be fully accounted for only by a complex theory, involving factors contributed by psychoanalysis, sociology, cultural anthropology, and behaviouristic psychology. No simple explanation, like 'instinct', or 'familiar association', or 'fear of inbreeding', is at all satisfactory [translator's note].

6. A giant with whom Heracles wrestled; he drew his strength from his mother, Gaia (Earth).

to conquer, to take, to possess; to have woman is to conquer her; he penetrates into her as the ploughshare into the furrow; he makes her his even as he makes his the land he works; he labours, he plants, he sows: these images are old as writing; from antiquity to our own day a thousand examples could be cited: 'Woman is like the field, and man is like the seed,' says the law of Manu. In a drawing by André Masson there is a man with spade in hand, spading the garden of a woman's vulva.[7] Woman is her husband's prey, his possession.

The male's hesitation between fear and desire, between the fear of being in the power of uncontrollable forces and the wish to win them over, is strikingly reflected in the myth of Virginity. Now feared by the male, now desired or even demanded, the virgin would seem to represent the most consummate form of the feminine mystery; she is therefore its most disturbing and at the same time its most fascinating aspect. According to whether man feels himself overwhelmed by the encircling forces or proudly believes himself capable of taking control of them, he declines or demands to have his wife delivered to him a virgin. In the most primitive societies where woman's power is great it is fear that rules him; it is proper for the woman to be deflorated before the wedding night. Marco Polo states of the Tibetans that 'none of them would want to take to wife a girl that was a virgin'. This refusal has sometimes been explained in a rational way: man would not want a wife who had not already aroused masculine desires. The Arab geographer El Bekri, speaking of the Slavs, reports that 'if a man marries and finds his wife a virgin, he says to her: "If you were any good, men would have made love to you and one would have taken your virginity." Then he drives her out and repudiates her'. It is claimed, even, that some primitives will take in marriage only a woman who has already been a mother, thus giving proof of her fecundity.

But the true motives underlying these widespread customs of defloration are mystical. Certain peoples imagine that there is a serpent in the vagina which would bite the husband just as the hymen is broken; some ascribe frightful powers to virginal blood, related to menstrual blood and likewise capable of ruining the man's vigour. Through such imagery is expressed the idea that the feminine principle has the more strength, is more menacing, when it is intact.[8]

There are cases where the question of defloration is not raised; for example, among the Trobriand Islanders described by Malinowski, the girls are never virgins because sexual play is permitted from infancy. In certain cultures the mother, the older sister, or some matron systematically deflowers the young girl and throughout her childhood enlarges the vaginal orifice. Again, the defloration may be performed at puberty, the women making use of a stick, a bone, or a stone and regarding it merely as a surgical operation. In other tribes the girl is subjected at puberty to a savage initiation: men drag her outside the village and deflower her by violation or by means of objects. A common rite consists in offering the virgins to strangers passing through—whether it is thought that they are not allergic to a mana dangerous only to males of the tribe, or whether it is a matter of indifference what evils are let

---

7. Rabelais calls the male sex organ 'nature's ploughman'. We have noted the religious and historical origin of the associations: phallus-ploughshare and woman-furrow [Beauvoir's note].

8. Thence comes the strength in combat attributed to virgins: for example, the Valkyries and the Maid of Orléans [Beauvoir's note]. The Maid of Orléans is Joan of Arc.

loose on strangers. Still more often it is the priest, or the medicine man, or the cacique, the tribal chieftain, who deflowers the bride during the night before the wedding. On the Malabar Coast the Brahmans are charged with this duty, which they are said to perform without pleasure and for which they lay claim to good pay. It is well known that all sacred objects are dangerous for the profane, but that consecrated individuals can handle them without risk; it is understandable, then, that priests and chiefs can conquer the maleficent forces against which the husband must be protected. In Rome only a symbolic ceremony remained as a vestige of such customs: the fiancée was seated on the phallus of a stone Priapus, which served the double purpose supposedly of increasing her fecundity and absorbing the too powerful—and for that reason evil—fluids with which she was charged. The husband may protect himself in still another way: he deflowers the virgin himself, but in the midst of ceremonies that at the critical moment make him invulnerable; for instance, he may operate with a stick or a bone in the presence of the whole village. In Samoa he uses his finger wrapped in a white cloth, which is torn into bloody bits and these distributed to the persons present. Or the husband may be allowed to deflower his wife in normal fashion, but is not to ejaculate inside her for three days, so that the generative germ may not be contaminated by the hymeneal blood.

Through a transvaluation that is classical in the realm of the sacred, virginal blood becomes in less primitive societies a propitious symbol. There still are villages in France where, on the morning after the wedding, the blood-stained sheets are displayed before relatives and friends. What happened is that in the patriarchal régime man became master of woman; and the very powers that are frightening in wild beasts or in unconquered elements became qualities valuable to the owner able to domesticate them. From the fire of the wild horse, the violence of lightning and cataracts, man has made means to prosperity. And so he wishes to take possession of the woman intact in all her richness. Rational motives play a part, no doubt, in the demand for virtue imposed on the young girl: like the chastity of the wife, the innocence of the fiancée is necessary so that the father may run no risk, later, of leaving his property to a child of another. But virginity is demanded for more immediate reasons when a man regards his wife as his personal property. In the first place, it is always impossible to realize positively the idea of possession; in truth, one never has any thing or any person; one tries then to establish ownership in negative fashion. The surest way of asserting that something is mine is to prevent others from using it. And nothing seems to a man to be more desirable than what has never belonged to any human being: then the conquest seems like a unique and absolute event. Virgin lands have always fascinated explorers; mountain-climbers are killed each year because they wish to violate an untouched peak or even because they have merely tried to open a new trail up its side; and the curious risk their lives to descend underground into the depths of unexplored caverns. An object that men have already used has become an instrument; cut from its natural ties, it loses its most profound properties: there is more promise in the untamed flow of torrents than in the water of public fountains.

A virgin body has the freshness of secret springs, the morning sheen of an unopened flower, the orient lustre of a pearl on which the sun has never shone. Grotto, temple, sanctuary, secret garden—man, like the child, is fas-

cinated by enclosed and shadowy places not yet animated by any consciousness, which wait to be given a soul: what he alone is to take and to penetrate
seems to be in truth created by him. And more, one of the ends sought by all
desire is the using up of the desired object, which implies its destruction. In
breaking the hymen man takes possession of the feminine body more intimately than by a penetration that leaves it intact; in the irreversible act of
defloration he makes of that body unequivocally a passive object, he affirms
his capture of it. This idea is expressed precisely in the legend of the knight
who pushed his way with difficulty through thorny bushes to pick a rose of
hitherto unbreathed fragrance; he not only found it, but broke the stem, and
it was then that he made it his own. The image is so clear that in popular language to 'take her flower' from a woman means to destroy her virginity; and
this expression, of course, has given origin to the word 'defloration'.

But virginity has this erotic attraction only if it is in alliance with youth;
otherwise its mystery again becomes disturbing. Many men of today feel a
sexual repugnance in the presence of maidenhood too prolonged; and it is not
only psychological causes that are supposed to make 'old maids' mean and
embittered females. The curse is in their flesh itself, that flesh which is object
for no subject, which no man's desire has made desirable, which has bloomed
and faded without finding a place in the world of men; turned from its proper
destination, it becomes an oddity, as disturbing as the incommunicable
thought of a madman. Speaking of a woman of forty, still beautiful, but presumably virgin, I have heard a man say coarsely: 'It must be full of spiderwebs
inside.' And, in truth, cellars and attics, no longer entered, of no use, become
full of unseemly mystery; phantoms will likely haunt them; abandoned by
people, houses become the abode of spirits. Unless feminine virginity has
been dedicated to a god, one easily believes that it implies some kind of marriage with the demon. Virgins unsubdued by man, old women who have
escaped his power, are more easily than others regarded as sorceresses; for
the lot of woman being bondage to another, if she escapes the yoke of man
she is ready to accept that of the devil.

*　　*　　*

[The] role of pity and tenderness is one of the most important of all those
which have been assigned to woman. Even when fully integrated in a society,
woman subtly extends its frontiers because she has the insidious generosity
of Life. To be sure, this gap between the planned works of man and the contingence of nature seems disquieting in some cases; but it becomes beneficial when woman, too docile to threaten man's works, limits herself to
enriching them and softening their too rugged lines. Male gods represent
Destiny; in goddesses one finds arbitrary benevolence, capricious favour. The
Christian God is full of the rigours of Justice, the Virgin is full of the gentleness of charity. Here on earth men are defenders of the law, of reason, of
necessity; woman is aware of the original contingency of man himself and of
this necessity in which he believes; hence come both the mysterious irony
that flits across her lips and her pliant generosity. She heals the wounds of
the males, she nurses the newborn, and she lays out the dead; she knows
everything about man that attacks his pride and humiliates his self-will.
While she inclines before him and humbles the flesh to the spirit, she stays
on the fleshly frontiers of the spirit, softening, as I have said, the hard angles

of man's constructions and bestowing upon them unforeseen luxury and grace. Woman's power over men comes from the fact that she gently recalls them to a modest realization of their true condition; it is the secret of her disillusioned, sorrowful, ironical, and loving wisdom. In woman even frivolity, capriciousness, and ignorance are charming virtues because they flourish this side of and beyond the world where man chooses to live but where he does not like to feel himself confined. In contrast to set meanings and tools made for useful purposes, she upholds the mystery of intact things; she wafts the breath of poetry through city streets, over cultivated fields. Poetry is supposed to catch what exists beyond the prose of every day; and woman is an eminently poetic reality since man projects into her all that he does not resolve to be. She incarnates the Dream, which is for man most intimate and most strange: what he does not wish and does not do, towards which he aspires and which cannot be attained; the mysterious Other who is deep immanence and far-off transcendence will lend the dream her traits. Thus it is that Aurélia visits Nerval[9] in a dream and gives him the whole world in the image of the dream: 'She began to enlarge in a bright ray of light in such a way that little by little the garden took on her shape, and the flower beds and the trees became the roses and the festoons of her vestments; while her face and her arms impressed their shape upon the reddened clouds in the sky. I lost sight of her as she was transfigured, for she seemed to vanish as she took on grandeur. "Oh, flee not from me!" I cried; "for nature dies with you." '

Woman being the very substance of man's poetic work, it is understandable that she should appear as his inspiration: the Muses are women. A Muse mediates between the creator and the natural springs whence he must draw. Woman's spirit is profoundly sunk in nature, and it is through her that man will sound the depths of silence and of the fecund night. A Muse creates nothing by herself; she is a calm, wise Sibyl, putting herself with docility at the service of a master. Even in concrete and practical realms her counsel will be useful. Man would fain attain his ends without the often embarrassing aid of other men; but he fancies that woman speaks from a sense of different values, with an instinctive wisdom of her own, in close accord with the real. Man seeks her 'intuitions' as he might interrogate the stars. Such 'intuition' is injected even into business and politics: Aspasia and Mme de Maintenon still have successful careers today.[1]

Another function that man readily entrusts to woman is the weighing of values; she is a privileged judge. Man dreams of an Other not only to possess her but also to be ratified by her; to be ratified by other men, his peers, demands a constant tension; hence he wishes consideration from outside to confer an absolute value upon his life, his enterprises, and himself. The consideration of God is hidden, alien, disquieting; even in times of faith only a few mystics longed for it. This divine role has most often devolved upon woman. Being the Other, she remains exterior to man's world and can view it objectively; and being close to man and dominated by him, she does not establish values foreign to his nature. She it is who in each particular case will report the presence or absence of courage, strength, beauty, while giving

9. In Gérard de Nerval's *Aurélia* (1855).
1. But the truth is, of course, that women display intellectual qualities perfectly identical with those of men [Beauvoir's note]. Both women were believed to wield great influence over powerful men—Aspasia as the mistress of the Greek statesman Pericles, and Mme de Maintenon as the wife of Louis XIV.

outside confirmation of their universal value. Men are too much involved in their co-operative and competitive relations to act as a public for one another. Woman is outside the fray: her whole situation destines her to play this role of concerned spectator. The knight jousts for his lady in the tourney; poets seek the approbation of women. Setting out to conquer Paris, Rastignac[2] plans first to *have* women, not so much to possess them physically as to enjoy the reputation that only they can give a man. Balzac projected in such young heroes the story of his own youth: he began to educate and shape himself in the company of older mistresses; and woman plays this educational role not only in his *Lys dans la vallée*.[3] It is assigned to her in Flaubert's *Education sentimentale,* in Stendhal's novels, and in many other stories of apprenticeship. We have noted before that woman is *physis* and *anti-physis*:[4] that is, she incarnates Nature no more than she does Society; in her is summed up the civilization and culture of an epoch, as we see in the poems of chivalry, in the *Decameron,* in *Astrée*.[5] She launches new fashions, presides in the salons, influences and reflects opinion. Renown and glory are women; and Mallarmé said: 'The crowd is a woman.' In the company of women the young man is initiated into 'society', and into that complex reality called 'life'. Woman is a special prize which the hero, the adventurer, and the rugged individualist are destined to win. In antiquity we see Perseus delivering Andromeda, Orpheus seeking Eurydice in the underworld, and Troy fighting to protect fair Helen. The novels of chivalry are concerned chiefly with such prowess as the deliverance of captive princesses. What would Prince Charming have for occupation if he had not to awaken the Sleeping Beauty? The myth of the king marrying a shepherdess gratifies man as much as woman. The rich man needs to give or his useless wealth remains an abstraction: he must have someone at hand to give to. The Cinderella myth flourishes especially in prosperous countries like America. How should the men there spend their surplus money if not upon a woman? Orson Welles, among others, has embodied in *Citizen Kane* that imperial and false generosity: it is to glorify his own power that Kane chooses to shower his gifts upon an obscure singer and to impose her upon the public as a great queen of song. When the hero of another film, *The Razor's Edge,* returns from India equipped with absolute wisdom, the only thing he finds to do with it is to redeem a prostitute.

It is clear that in dreaming of himself as donor, liberator, redeemer, man still desires the subjection of woman; for in order to awaken the Sleeping Beauty, she must have been put to sleep: ogres and dragons must be if there are to be captive princesses. The more man acquires a taste for difficult enterprises, however, the more it will please him to give woman independence. To conquer is still more fascinating than to give gifts or to release.

Thus the ideal of the average Western man is a woman who freely accepts his domination, who does not accept his ideas without discussion, but who yields to his arguments, who resists him intelligently and ends by being convinced. The greater his pride, the more dangerous he likes his adventures to be: it is much more splendid to conquer Penthesilea than it is to marry a yielding Cinderella. 'The warrior loves danger and sport,' said Nietzsche; 'that is

2. A character in Balzac's *Human Comedy*; he is the protagonist of *Father Goriot* (1835).
3. *The Lily in the Valley* (1836).

4. Nature and anti-nature (Greek).
5. A chivalric pastoral romance (1608–27) by Honoré de Urfé.

why he loves woman, the most dangerous sport of all.'[6] The man who likes danger and sport is not displeased to see woman turn into an amazon if he retains the hope of subjugating her. What he requires in his heart of hearts is that this struggle remain a game for him, while for woman it involves her very destiny. Man's true victory, whether he is liberator or conqueror, lies just in this: that woman freely recognizes him as her destiny.

Thus the expression 'to have a woman' hides a double significance: her functions as object and as arbiter are not distinguished. From the moment when woman is regarded as a person, she cannot be conquered except with her consent; she must be won. It is the Sleeping Beauty's smile that crowns the efforts of Prince Charming; the captive princess's tears of joy and gratitude make the knight's prowess valid. On the other hand, her measuring gaze does not have the aloof severity of a masculine gaze, it is susceptible to charm. Thus heroism and poetry are modes of seduction; but in letting herself be charmed, woman glorifies heroism and poetry. In the view of the individualist, she holds a prerogative yet more essential: she seems to him to be not the measure of values recognized by all, but the revelation of his special merits and of his very being. A man is judged by his fellows according to what he does both objectively and with regard to generally accepted standards. But some of his qualities, and among others his vital qualities, can interest woman only; he is virile, charming, seductive, tender, cruel only in reference to her. If he sets a high value on these more secret virtues, he has an absolute need of her; through her he will experience the miracle of seeming to himself to be another, another who is also his profoundest ego. There is a passage from Malraux which expresses admirably what the individualist expects from his loved woman. Kyo is questioning himself: ' "We hear the voices of others with our ears, our own voices with our throats." Yes. One hears his own life, also, with his throat—and those of others? . . . In the eyes of others, I am what I have done . . . But to May alone he was not what he had done; and to him alone she was something quite other than her biography. The embrace in which love unites two beings against solitude did not provide its relief for man; it was for the madman, for the incomparable monster, dearest of all things, that everyone is to himself and that he cherishes in his heart. Since the death of his mother, May was the only person for whom he was not Kyo Gisors but a most intimate companion . . . Men are not my fellows, they are persons who look upon me and judge me; my fellows are those who love me and do not look upon me, who love me regardless of everything, degradation, baseness, treason, who love me and not what I have done or shall do, who will love me as long as I shall love myself, even to the point of suicide.'[7]

What makes the attitude of Kyo human and moving is that it implies reciprocity and that he asks May to love him as he is, not to send back a fawning reflection. With many men this demand is degraded: instead of an exact revelation, they seek to find in two living eyes their image haloed with admiration and gratitude, deified. Woman has often been compared to water because, among other reasons, she is the mirror in which the male, Narcissus-like, contemplates himself: he bends over her in good or bad faith. But in any case what he really asks of her is to be, outside of him, all that

6. From Nietzsche's "On Little Old and Young Women," in part 1 of *Thus Spake Zarathustra* (1883).

7. *La Condition humaine* (*Man's Fate*) [Beauvoir's note].

which he cannot grasp inside himself, because the inwardness of the existent is only nothingness and because he must project himself into an object in order to reach himself. Woman is the supreme recompense for him since, under a shape foreign to him which he can possess in her flesh, she is his own apotheosis. He embraces this 'incomparable monster', himself, when he presses in his arms the being who sums up the World for him and upon whom he has imposed his values and his laws. Then, in uniting with this other whom he has made his own, he hopes to reach himself. Treasure, prey, sport and danger, nurse, guide, judge, mediatrix, mirror, woman is the Other in whom the subject transcends himself without being limited, who opposes him without denying him; she is the Other who lets herself be taken without ceasing to be the Other, and therein she is so necessary to man's happiness and to his triumph that it can be said that if she did not exist, men would have invented her.

They did invent her.[8] But she exists also apart from their inventiveness. And hence she is not only the incarnation of their dream, but also its frustration. There is no figurative image of woman which does not call up at once its opposite: she is Life and Death, Nature and Artifice, Daylight and Night. Under whatever aspect we consider her, we always find the same shifting back and forth, for the nonessential returns necessarily to the essential. In the figures of the Virgin Mary and Beatrice,[9] Eve and Circe still exist.

'Through woman,' writes Kierkegaard in *In Vino Veritas*, 'ideality enters into life, and what would man be without her? Many a man has become a genius thanks to some young girl . . . but none has ever become a genius thanks to the young girl who gave him her hand in marriage . . . '

'Woman makes a man productive in ideality through a negative relation . . . Negative relations with woman can make us infinite . . . positive relations with woman make a man finite for the most part.' Which is to say that woman is necessary in so far as she remains an Idea into which man projects his own transcendence; but that she is inauspicious as an objective reality existing in and for herself. Kierkegaard holds that by refusing to marry his fiancée he established the only valid relation to woman. And he is right in a sense: namely, that the myth of woman set up as the infinite Other entails also its opposite.

Because she is a false Infinite, an Ideal without truth, she stands exposed as finiteness and mediocrity and, on the same ground, as falsehood. In Laforgue she appears in this light; throughout his works he gives voice to his rancour against a mystification for which he blamed man as much as woman. Ophelia, Salome, are in fact only *petites femmes*.[1] Hamlet seems to think: 'Thus would Ophelia have loved me, as her boon and because I was socially and morally superior to what her girlish friends had. And those small, common remarks that she would make, at lamp-lighting time, on ease and comfort!' Woman makes man dream; yet she thinks of comfort, of stew for supper; one speaks to her of her soul when she is only a body. And while her lover fondly believes he is pursuing the Ideal, he is actually the plaything of nature, who employs all this mystification for the ends of reproduction. Woman in

---

8. 'Man created woman, and with what? With a rib of his god, of his ideal,' says Nietzsche in *The Twilight of the Idols* [Beauvoir's note].

9. Dante's beloved and his guide in *Paradiso* (1321).

1. Little (young, childlike) women (French).

truth represents the everyday aspects of life; she is silliness, prudence, shabbiness, boredom.

Man has succeeded in enslaving woman; but in the same degree he has deprived her of what made her possession desirable. With woman integrated in the family and in society, her magic is dissipated rather than transformed; reduced to the condition of servant, she is no longer that unconquered prey incarnating all the treasures of nature. Since the rise of chivalric love it is a commonplace that marriage kills love. Scorned too much, respected too much, too much an everyday matter, the wife ceases to have erotic attraction. The marriage rites were originally intended to protect man against woman; she becomes his property. But all that we possess possesses us in turn, and marriage is a form of servitude for man also. He is taken in the snare set by nature: because he desired a fresh young girl, he has to support a heavy matron or a desiccated hag for life. The dainty jewel intended to decorate his existence becomes a hateful burden: Xantippe[2] has always been a type of woman most horrifying to man; in ancient Greece and in the Middle Ages she was, as we have seen, the theme of many lamentations. But even when the woman is young there is a hoax in marriage, since, while being supposed to socialize eroticism, it succeeds only in killing it.

The fact is that eroticism implies a claim of the instant against time, of the individual against the group; it affirms separation against communication; it is rebellion against all regulation; it contains a principle hostile to society. Customs are never bent quite to the rigour of institutions and laws; against these love has ever hurled defiance. In its sensual form love in Greece and Rome was turned towards young men or courtesans; chivalric love, at once carnal and platonic, was always destined for another's wife. *Tristan* is the epic of adultery. The period which, about 1900, created anew the myth of woman is that in which adultery became the theme of all literature. Certain writers, like Henry Bernstein,[3] in a supreme effort to defend bourgeois institutions, struggled to reintegrate eroticism and love into marriage; but there was more truth in Porto-Riche's *Amoureuse*,[4] in which the incompatibility of these two orders of values was shown. Adultery can disappear only with marriage itself. For the aim of marriage is in a way to immunize man against *his own* wife: but other women keep—for him—their heady attraction; and to them he will turn. Women make themselves a party to this. For they rebel against an order of things which undertakes to deprive them of all their weapons. In order to separate woman from Nature, to subject her to man through ceremonies and contracts, she has been elevated to the dignity of being a human person, she has been given liberty. But liberty is precisely that which escapes all subjugation; and if it be granted to a being originally possessed of maleficent powers, she becomes dangerous. She becomes the more so in that man stops at half-measures; he accepts woman in the masculine world only in making a servant of her and frustrating her transcendence; the liberty given to her can have none but a negative use; she chooses to reject this liberty. Woman has been free only in becoming a captive; she renounces this human privilege in order to regain her power as a natural object. By day she perfidiously plays her role of docile servant, but at night she changes into cat, or hind; she slips

2. The wife of Socrates; she is a proverbial shrew.   4. The comedy *Sweetheart* (1908).
3. French dramatist.

again into her siren's skin or, riding on a broomstick, she takes off for the devil's dances. Sometimes, to be sure, she works her nocturnal magic upon her own husband; but it is wiser to hide her metamorphoses from her master; she chooses strangers as prey; they have no rights over her, and for them she is still vegetation, wellspring, star, sorceress. She is thus fated for infidelity: it is the sole concrete form her liberty can assume. She is unfaithful beyond even her desires, thoughts, awareness; by virtue of the fact that she is regarded as an object, she is offered to any subjectivity who chooses to take possession of her. Locked away in a harem, hidden behind veils, it is still by no means sure that she will not arouse desire in someone; and to inspire desire in a stranger is already to fail her husband and society. But, further, she is often a willing accomplice in the deed; only through deceit and adultery can she prove that she is nobody's chattel and give the lie to the pretensions of the male. This is the reason why the husband's jealousy is so quick to awaken; we see in legends how a woman can be suspected without reason, condemned on the least suspicion, like Genevieve of Brabant and Desdemona. Even before any suspicion arose, Griselda[5] was subjected to the most severe tests; this tale would be absurd if woman was not suspect in advance; there is no question of demonstrating her misbehaviour: it is for her to prove her innocence.

This is, indeed, why jealousy can be insatiable. We have seen that possession can never be positively realized; even if all others are forbidden to dip therein, one never possesses the spring in which one's thirst is quenched: he who is jealous knows this full well. In essence woman is fickle, as water is fluid; and no human power can contradict a natural truth. Throughout literature, in *The Arabian Nights* as in the *Decameron,* we see the clever ruses of woman triumph over the prudence of man. Moreover, it is not alone through individualistic will that he is the jailer: it is society that makes him—as father, brother, husband—responsible for his woman's conduct. Chastity is enforced upon her for economic and religious reasons, since each citizen ought to be authenticated as the son of his proper father.

But it is also very important to compel woman to adapt herself exactly to the role society has forced upon her. There is a double demand of man which dooms woman to duplicity: he wants the woman to be his and to remain foreign to him; he fancies her as at once servant and enchantress. But in public he admits to only the first of these desires; the other is a sly demand that he hides in the secrecy of his heart and flesh. It is against morality and society; it is wicked like the Other, like rebellious Nature, like the 'bad woman'. Man does not devote himself wholly to the Good which he sets up and claims to put in force; he retains shameful lines of communication with the Bad. But wherever the Bad dares indiscreetly to show its face uncovered, man goes to war against it. In the shadows of night man invites woman to sin. But in full daylight he disowns the sin and the fair sinner. And the women, themselves sinners in the secrecy of the bed, are only the more passionate in the public worship of virtue. Just as among primitive people the male sex is secular while that of the female is charged with religious and magical powers, so the misbehaviour of a man in more modern societies is only a minor folly, often

5. The lowborn heroine of Chaucer's *The Clerk's Tale* (borrowed from *The Decameron*), whose noble husband repeatedly and cruelly tests her fidelity. Genevieve, a heroine of medieval legend, was a wife falsely accused of unchastity.

regarded indulgently; even if he disobeys the laws of the community, man continues to belong to it; he is only an *enfant terrible*, offering no profound menace to the order of society.

If, on the other hand, woman evades the rules of society, she returns to Nature and to the demon, she looses uncontrollable and evil forces in the collective midst. Fear is always mixed with the blame attached to woman's licentious conduct. If the husband does not succeed in keeping his wife in the path of virtue, he shares in her fault; in the eyes of society his misfortune is a blot on his honour; there are civilizations severe enough to require him to kill the wrongdoer in order to dissociate himself from her crime. In others the complaisant husband is punished by such mockeries as parading him naked astride a jackass. And the community undertakes to chastise the guilty one in his place: she has offended not him alone, but the whole collectivity. These customs have existed in a particularly harsh form in superstitious and mystical Spain, a sensual land terrorized by the flesh. Calderón, Lorca, Valle Inclán have used this theme in many dramas. In Lorca's *House of Bernado Alba*, the village gossips would punish the seduced girl by burning her with a live coal 'in the place where she sinned'. In Valle Inclán's *Divine Words* the adulterous woman appears as a sorceress dancing with the demon; her fault once discovered, the village assembles to tear off her clothes and then drown her. According to many traditions, the woman sinner was thus disrobed; then she was stoned, as reported in the Bible, or she was buried alive, drowned, or burned. The meaning of these tortures is that she was in this way given back to Nature after being deprived of her social dignity; by her sin she had let loose natural emanations of evil: the expiation was carried out in a kind of sacred orgy in which the women—demanding, striking, massacring the guilty one—released in their turn fluids of mysterious but beneficial nature, since the avengers were acting in accordance with society's rules.

This savage severity disappears as superstition diminishes and fear is dissipated. But in rural districts godless gipsies are still viewed with suspicion as homeless vagabonds. The woman who makes free use of her attractiveness—adventuress, vamp, *femme fatale*—remains a disquieting type. The image of Circe survives in the bad woman of the Hollywood films. Women have been burnt as witches simply because they were beautiful. And in the prudish umbrage of provincial virtue before women of dissolute life, an ancient fear is kept alive.

It is in truth these very dangers that, for the adventurous man, make woman an enticing game. Disdaining marital rights and refusing the support of the laws of society, he will try to conquer her in single combat. He tries to get possession of the woman even in her resistance; he pursues her in the very liberty through which she escapes him. In vain. One does not play a part when free: the free woman will often act as such against man. Even the Sleeping Beauty may awaken with displeasure, she may not regard her awakener as a Prince Charming at all, she may not smile. The hero's wife listens indifferently to the tale of his exploits; the Muse of whom the poet dreams may yawn when she listens to his stanzas. The amazon can with ennui decline combat; and she may also emerge victorious. The Roman women of the decadence, many women of today, impose their caprices or their rule upon men. Where is Cinderella?

Man wants to give, and here is woman taking for herself. It is becoming a matter of self-defence, no longer a game. From the moment when woman is free, she has no other destiny than what she freely creates for herself. The relation of the two sexes is then a relation of struggle. Now become a fellow being, woman seems as formidable as when she faced man as a part of alien Nature. In place of the myth of the laborious honeybee or the mother hen is substituted the myth of the devouring female insect: the praying mantis, the spider. No longer is the female she who nurses the little ones, but rather she who eats the male; the egg is no longer a storehouse of abundance, but rather a trap of inert matter in which the spermatozoon is castrated and drowned. The womb, that warm, peaceful, and safe retreat, becomes a pulp of humours, a carnivorous plant, a dark, contractile gulf, where dwells a serpent that insatiably swallows up the strength of the male. The same dialectic makes the erotic object into a wielder of black magic, the servant into a traitress, Cinderella into an ogress, and changes all women into enemies: it is the payment man makes for having in bad faith set himself up as the sole essential.

This hostile visage, however, is the definitive face of woman no more than the others. Rather, a Manichaeism is introduced in the heart of womankind. Pythagoras likened the good principle to man and the bad principle to woman. Men have tried to overcome the bad by taking possession of woman; they have succeeded in part. But just as Christianity, by bringing in the idea of redemption and salvation, has given the word *damnation* its full meaning, just so it is in contrast to the sanctified woman that the bad woman stands out in full relief. In the course of that 'quarrel of women' which has lasted from the Middle Ages until now, certain men have wished to recognize only the blessed woman of their dreams, others only the cursed woman who belies their dreams. But in truth, if man can find *everything* in woman, it is because she has both these faces. She represents in a living, carnal way all the values and anti-values that give sense to life. Here, quite clear-cut, are Good and Evil in opposition to each other under the form of the devoted Mother and the perfidious Mistress; in the old English ballad *Lord Randal, My Son*, a young knight, poisoned by his mistress, comes home to die in his mother's arms. Richepin's *La Glu*[6] takes up the same theme with more bathos and bad taste in general. Angelic Michaëla stands in contrast to dark Carmen. Mother, faithful fiancée, patient wife—all stand ready to bind up the wounds dealt to man's heart by 'vamps' and witches. Between these clearly fixed poles can be discerned a multitude of ambiguous figures, pitiable, hateful, sinful, victimized, coquettish, weak, angelic, devilish. Woman thus provides a great variety of behaviour and sentiment to stimulate man and enrich his life.

Man is delighted by this very complexity of woman: a wonderful servant who is capable of dazzling him—and not too expensive. Is she angel or demon? The uncertainty makes her a Sphinx. We may note here that one of the most celebrated brothels of Paris operated under this aegis, the sign of the sphinx. In the grand epoch of femininity, at the time of corsets, Paul Bourget, Henri Bataille, and the French can-can, the theme of the Sphinx was all the rage in plays, poetry, and songs: 'Who are you, whence come you, strange

---

6. *The Trap* (1883), a play by Jean Richepin (*glu* literally means "bird lime"; French).

Sphinx?' And there is still no end to dreaming and debating on the feminine mystery. It is indeed to preserve this mystery that men have long begged women not to give up long skirts, petticoats, veils, long gloves, high-heeled shoes: everything that accentuates difference in the Other makes her more desirable, since what man wants to take possession of is the Other as such. We find Alain-Fournier chiding English women for their frank man-like way of shaking hands: what excites him is the modest reserve of French women. Woman must remain secret, unknown, if she is to be adored as a faraway princess. There is no reason to suppose that Fournier was especially deferential to the women in his life; but he put all the wonder of childhood, of youth, all the nostalgia for lost paradises into a woman of his own creation, a woman whose first virtue was to appear inaccessible. His picture of Yvonne de Galais[7] is traced in white and gold.

But men cherish even woman's defects if they create mystery. 'A woman should have her caprice's, a man said authoritatively to an intelligent woman. The caprice is unpredictable, it lends woman the grace of waves in water; falsehood adorns her with fascinating reflections; coquetry, even perversity, gives her a heady perfume. Deceitful, elusive, unintelligible, double-dealing—thus it is that she best lends herself to the contradictory desires of man; she is Maya in innumerable disguises. It is a commonplace to represent the Sphinx as a young woman: virginity is one of the secrets that men find most exciting—the more so as they are greater libertines; the young girl's purity allows hope for every kind of licence, and no one knows what perversities are concealed in her innocence. Still close to animal and plant, already amenable to social forms, she is neither child nor adult; her timid femininity inspires no fear, but a mild disquiet. We feel that she is one of the privileged exponents of feminine mystery. As 'the true young girl' disappears, however, her cult has come somewhat out of date. On the other hand, the figure of the prostitute, whom Gantillon triumphantly presented on the French stage in *Maya*, has kept much of its prestige. It is one of the most plastic feminine types, giving full scope to the grand play of vices and virtues. For the timorous puritan, the prostitute incarnates evil, shame, disease, damnation; she inspires fear and disgust; she belongs to no man, but yields herself to one and all and lives off such commerce. In this way she regains that formidable independence of the luxurious goddess mothers of old, and she incarnates the Femininity that masculine society has not sanctified and that remains charged with harmful powers. In the sexual act the male cannot possibly imagine that he owns her; he has simply delivered himself over to the demon of the flesh. This is a humiliation, a defilement peculiarly resented by the Anglo-Saxons, who regard the flesh as more or less abominable. On the other hand, a man who is not afraid of the flesh will enjoy its generous and straightforward affirmation by the prostitute; he will sense in her the exaltation of a femininity that no morality has made wishy-washy. He will find again upon her body those magic virtues which formerly made woman sister to the stars and sea; a Henry Miller,[8] going to bed with a prostitute, feels that he sounds the very depths of life, death, and the cosmos; he meets God in the deep, moist shadows of a receptive vagina. Since she is a kind of pariah, living at

---

7. The beautiful young woman who haunts the title character of *Le Grand Meaulnes* (1913) by
Henri-Alban Fournier.
8. *Tropic of Cancer* (1934) [translator's note].

the margin of a hypocritically moral world, we can also regard the *fille per-due*[9] as the invalidator of all the official virtues; her low estate relates her to the authentic saints; for that which has been downtrodden shall be exalted. Mary Magdalene was a favourite of Christ; sin opens heaven's gate more readily than does a hypocritical virtue. Dostoyevsky's Raskolnikov[1] sacrifices at Sonia's feet the arrogant masculine pride that led him to crime; he has aggravated by the murder that will to separation which is in every man: a humble prostitute, resigned, abandoned by all, can best receive the avowal of his abdication. The phrase *fille perdue* awakens disturbing echoes. For many men dream of losing themselves, but it is not so simple, one does not easily succeed in attaining Evil in positive form; and even the demoniac is frightened by excessive crimes. Woman enables one to celebrate without great risk Black Masses where Satan is evoked without being exactly invited; she exists at the margin of the masculine world; acts concerned with her are truly of no consequence; but she is a human being and it is possible therefore to carry out dark revolts through her against human law. From Musset to Georges Bataille, real, hideously fascinating debauch is that carried on in company with whores. The Marquis de Sade and Sacher-Masoch satisfy upon women the desires that haunt them; their disciples, and most men who have 'vices' to satisfy, commonly turn to prostitutes. Of all women they are the most submissive to the male, and yet more able to escape him; this it is that makes them take on so many varied meanings. There is no feminine type, however— virgin, mother, wife, sister, servant, loved one, fiercely virtuous one, smiling odalisque—who is not capable of summing up thus the vagrant yearnings of men.

It is for psychology—especially psychoanalysis—to discover why an individual is drawn more particularly to one or another aspect of the many-faced Myth, and why he incarnates it in some one special female. But this myth is implied in all the complexes, the obsessions, the psychoses. Many neuroses in particular have their source in a madness for the forbidden that can appear only if taboos have been previously established; a social pressure from outside is not sufficient to explain its presence; in fact, social prohibitions are not simply conventions; they have—among other meanings—a developmental significance that each person experiences for himself.

By way of example, it will be of interest to examine the 'Oedipus complex', considered too often as being produced by a struggle between instinctual tendencies and social regulations, whereas it is first of all an inner conflict within the subject himself. The attachment of the infant for the mother's breast is at first an attachment to Life in its immediate form, in its generality and its immanence; the rejection by weaning is the beginning of the rejection by abandonment, to which the individual is condemned once he emerges as a separate being from the Whole. It is from that point, and as he becomes more individualized and separate, that the term *sexual* can be applied to the inclination he retains for the maternal flesh henceforth detached from his. His sensuality is then directed through another person, it has become transcendence towards an object foreign to him. But the quicker and the more decidedly the child realizes himself as subject, the more the fleshly bond, opposing

9. Bad or ruined girl (French).
1. The central character in *Crime and Punishment* (1866).

his autonomy, is going to become harassing to him. Then he shuns his mother's caresses; and her authority, the rights she has over him, sometimes her very presence, all inspire in him a kind of shame. In particular it seems embarrassing and obscene to be aware of her as flesh, and he avoids thinking of her body; in the horrified feeling aroused by his father or stepfather or a lover, there is not so much a pang of jealousy as a sense of scandal. To remind him thus that his mother is a carnal being is to remind him of his own birth, an event that he repudiates with all his strength or at least wants to give the dignity of a grand cosmic phenomenon. He feels that his mother should sum up Nature, which invests all individuals without belonging to any; he hates to have her become some man's prey, not, as is often maintained, because he wants to have her himself, but because he wishes her to be beyond all possession: she should not have the paltry dimensions of wife or mistress. When his sexuality becomes manly at adolescence, however, it may well happen that his mother's body arouses him erotically; but this is because she reminds him of femininity in general; and very often the desire aroused by the sight of a thigh or a breast disappears at the young man's realization that this flesh is his mother's flesh. There are numerous cases of perversion, since, adolescence being a disordered period, it is a time of perversion, when disgust leads to sacrilege, and temptation is born of the forbidden. But it is not to be believed that at first the son quite simply wishes to have intercourse with his mother and that exterior prohibitions interfere and tyrannically prevent him; on the contrary, desire is born just because of that prohibition which is set up in the heart of the individual himself. This prohibition is the most normal general reaction. But here again the interdiction does not come from a social regulation repressing instinctive desires. Rather, respect is the sublimation of an original disgust; the young man refuses to regard his mother as carnal; he transfigures her and assimilates her to one of the pure images of sacred womanhood which society holds up for his admiration. Thus he helps to strengthen the ideal figure of the Mother who will be concerned with the welfare of the next generation. But this figure has so much force only because it is called forth by an inner, individual dialectic. And since every woman is endowed with the general essence of Woman, therefore of the Mother, it is certain that the attitude held towards the Mother will have repercussions in a man's relations with wife and mistresses—but less simply than is often supposed. The adolescent who has felt definite, sensual sex desire for his mother may well have been simply desiring woman in general. In this case the ardour of his temperament will be appeased with no matter what woman, for he is no victim of incestuous nostalgia.[2] Inversely, a young man who has felt a tender but platonic reverence for his mother may wish in every instance for woman to share in the maternal purity.

The importance of sexuality, and therefore ordinarily of woman, in both normal and abnormal behaviour is surely well known. It may happen that other objects are feminized. Since woman is indeed in large part man's invention, he can invent her in the male body: in pederasty some pretence of sexual distinction is kept up. But as a rule it is unquestionably in feminine persons that Woman is sought for. It is through her, through what is in her of the best and the worst, that man, as a young apprentice, learns of felicity

---

2. Stendhal is a striking example [Beauvoir's note].

and suffering, of vice, virtue, lust, renunciation, devotion, and tyranny—that as an apprentice he learns to know himself. Woman is sport and adventure, but also a test. She is the triumph of victory and the more bitter triumph of frustration survived; she is the vertigo of ruin, the fascination of damnation, of death. There is a whole world of significance which exists only through woman; she is the substance of men's acts and sentiments, the incarnation of all the values that call out their free activity. It is understandable that, were he condemned to the most cruel disappointments, man would not be willing to relinquish a dream within which all his dreams are enfolded.

This, then, is the reason why woman has a double and deceptive visage: she is all that man desires and all that he does not attain. She is the good mediatrix between propitious Nature and man; and she is the temptation of unconquered Nature, counter to all goodness. She incarnates all moral values, from good to evil, and their opposites; she is the substance of action and whatever is an obstacle to it, she is man's grasp on the world and his frustration: as such she is the source and origin of all man's reflection on his existence and of whatever expression he is able to give to it; and yet she works to divert him from himself, to make him sink down in silence and in death. She is servant and companion, but he expects her also to be his audience and critic and to confirm him in his sense of being; but she opposes him with her indifference, even with her mockery and laughter. He projects upon her what he desires and what he fears, what he loves and what he hates. And if it is so difficult to say anything specific about her, that is because man seeks the whole of himself in her and because she is All. She is All, that is, on the plane of the inessential; she is all the Other. And, as the other, she is other than herself, other than what is expected of her. Being all, she is never quite *this* which she should be; she is everlasting deception, the very deception of that existence which is never successfully attained nor fully reconciled with the totality of existents.

1949, 1952

MARY ELLMANN
1921–1989

In its witty exposé of the sexual politics governing the creation and reception of literature, the second chapter of *Thinking about Women* (1968) typifies the satiric essays and reviews of Mary Ellmann. The wife of Richard Ellmann, an eminent literary critic and biographer, Mary Ellmann was educated at the University of Massachusetts and at Yale University, where she wrote a Ph.D. dissertation on the Victorian poet Tennyson's ten-year silence. It was during a sabbatical year in London that she took a break from teaching and began to concentrate on freelance journalism. In the year that *Thinking about Women* was published to great acclaim, she suffered a cerebral hemorrhage that left her partially paralyzed. When, in 1970, her husband was appointed the Goldsmiths' Professor of English Literature at Oxford University, she moved to England, where she continued to write journalism despite her deteriorating health. Together with Betty Friedan in *The Feminine Mystique* (1963), Mary Ellmann in *Thinking about Women* set the stage for the emergence of scholarly approaches to the impact of gender on the creation and reception of literary work.

From Thinking about Women

II. Phallic Criticism

> "This Neary that does not love Miss Counihan, nor need his Nee-
> dle, any more, may he soon get over Murphy and find himself free,
> following his drift, to itch for an ape, or a woman writer."
> —Samuel Beckett, *Murphy*

Through practice, begun when they begin to read, women learn to read about women calmly. Perhaps there have been some, but I have not heard of women who killed themselves simply and entirely because they were women.[1] They are evidently sustained by the conviction that I can never be They, by the fact that the self always, at least to itself, eludes identification with others. And, in turn, this radical separateness is fortified in some of us by phlegm, in others by vanity or most of all by ignorance (the uneducated are humiliated by class rather than by sex)—by all the usual defenses against self-loathing. Moreover, both men and women are now particularly accustomed, not so much to the resolution of issues, as to the proliferation of irreconcilable opinions upon them. In this intellectual suspension, it is possible for women, most of the time, to be more interested in what *is* said about them than in what presumably and finally *should* be said about them. In fact, none of them knows what should be said.

Their detachment is perhaps especially useful in reading literary criticism. Here, the opinions of men about men and of women about women are at least possibly esthetic, but elsewhere they are, almost inescapably, sexual as well. Like eruptions of physical desire, this intellectual distraction is no less frequent for being gratuitous as well. With a kind of inverted fidelity, the discussion of women's books by men will arrive punctually at the point of preoccupation, which is the fact of femininity. Books by women are treated as though they themselves were women, and criticism embarks, at its happiest, upon an intellectual measuring of busts and hips. Of course, this preoccupation has its engaging and compensatory sides.[2] Like such minor physical disorders as shingles and mumps, it often seems (whether or not it *feels* to the critic) comical as well as distressing. Then too, whatever intellectual risks this criticism runs, one of them is not abstraction. Any sexual reference, even in

1. Men, however, have been known to kill themselves for this reason. Otto Weininger, the German author of *Sex and Character,* killed himself because of the femininity which he ascribed to the Jews, of whom he was one [except as indicated, all notes are Ellmann's].

2. It has an unnerving side as well, though this appears less often in criticism, I think, than in fiction or poetry. For example, James Dickey's poem "Falling" expresses an extraordinary concern with the underwear of a woman who has fallen out of an airplane. While this woman, a stewardess, was in the airplane, her girdle obscured, to the observation of even the most alert passenger, her mesial groove. The effect was, as the poem recalls, "monobuttocked." As the woman falls, however, she undresses and "passes her palms" over her legs, her breasts, and "deeply between her thighs." Beneath her, "widowed farmers" are soon to wake with futile (and irrelevant?) erections. She lands on her back in a field, naked, and dies. The sensation of the poem is necrophilic: it mourns a vagina rather than a person crashing to the ground.

the most dryasdust context, shares the power which any reference to food has, of provoking fresh and immediate interest. As lunch can be mentioned every day without boring those who are hungry, the critic can always return to heterosexual (and, increasingly, to homosexual) relations and opinions with certainty of being read.

Admittedly, everyone is amused by the skillful wrapping of a book, like a negligee, about an author. Stanley Kauffmann opened a review of Françoise Sagan's *La Chamade* with this simile:

> Poor old Françoise Sagan. Just one more old-fashioned old-timer, bypassed in the rush for the latest literary vogue and for youth. Superficially, her career in America resembles the lifespan of those medieval beauties who flowered at 14, were deflowered at 15, were old at 30 and crones at 40.[3]

A superior instance of the mode—the play, for example, between *flowered* and *deflowered* is neat. And quite probably, of course, women might enjoy discussing men's books in similar terms. Some such emulative project would be diverting for a book season or two, if it were possible to persuade conventional journals to print its equivalent remarks. From a review of a new novel by the popular French novelist, François Sagan:

> Poor old François Sagan. . . . Superficially, his career in America resembles the life-span of those medieval troubadours who masturbated at 14, copulated at 15, were impotent at 30 and prostate cases at 40.

Somehow or other, No. It is not that male sexual histories, in themselves, are not potentially funny—even though they seem to be thought perceptibly less so than female sexual histories. It is rather that the literal fact of masculinity, unlike femininity, does not impose an erogenic form upon all aspects of the person's career.

I do not mean to suggest, however, that this imposition necessarily results in injustice. (Stanley Kauffmann went on to be more than just, *merciful* to Françoise Sagan.) In fact, it sometimes issues in fulsome praise. Excess occurs when the critic, like Dr. Johnson congratulating the dog who walked like a man, is impressed that the woman has—not so much written well, as written at all.[4] But unfortunately, benign as this upright-pooch predisposition can be in the estimate of indifferent work, it can also infect the praise of work which deserves (what has to be called) asexual approval. In this case, enthusiasm issues in an explanation of the ways in which the work is free of what the critic ordinarily dislikes in the work of a woman. He had despaired of ever seeing a birdhouse built by a woman; now *here* is a birdhouse built by a woman. Pleasure may mount even to an admission of male envy of the work examined: an exceptionally sturdy birdhouse at that! In *Commentary*, Warren Coffey has expressed his belief that "a man would give his right arm to have written Flannery O'Connor's 'Good Country People.' "[5] And here, not only the sentiment but the confidence with which the cliché is wielded, is distinctly phallic. It is as though, merely by thinking about Flannery O'Connor

3. Stanley Kauffmann, "Toujours Tristesse," *New Republic*, October 29, 1966, p. 2.
4. Samuel Johnson famously used the analogy of a dog walking on its hind legs to describe a woman preaching (James Boswell's *Life of Johnson*, 1791) [editor's note].
5. Warren Coffey, *Commentary*, November 1965, p. 98.

or Mrs. Gaskell or Harriet Beecher Stowe, the critic experienced acute sensations of his own liberty. The more he considers a feeble, cautious and timid existence, the more devil-may-care he seems to himself. This exhilaration then issues, rather tamely, in a daring to be commonplace.

And curiously, it often issues in expressions of contempt for delicate men as well. In this piece, for example, Flannery O'Connor is praised not only as a woman writer who writes as well as a man might wish to write, but also as a woman writer who succeeds in being less feminine than some men. She is less "girlish" than Truman Capote or Tennessee Williams.[6] In effect, once the critic's attention is trained, like Sweeney's, upon the Female Temperament, he invariably sideswipes at effeminacy in the male as well. The basic distinction becomes nonliterary: it is less between the book under review and other books, than between the critic and other persons who seem to him, regrettably, less masculine than he is. The assumption of the piece is that no higher praise of a woman's work exists than that such a critic should like it or think that other men will like it. The same ploy can also be executed in reverse. Norman Mailer, for example, is pleased to think that Joseph Heller's *Catch-22* is a man's book to read, a book which merely "puzzles" women. Women cannot comprehend male books, men cannot tolerate female books. The working rule is simple, basic: there must always be two literatures like two public toilets, one for Men and one for Women.

Sometimes it seems that no achievement can override this division. When Marianne Moore received the Poetry Society of America's Gold Medal for Poetry, she received as well Robert Lowell's encomium, "She is the best woman poet in English." The late Langston Hughes added, "I consider her the most famous Negro woman poet in America," and others would have enjoyed "the best blue-eyed woman poet."[7] Lowell has also praised Sylvia Plath's last book of poems, *Ariel.* His foreword begins:

> In these poems, written in the last months of her life and often rushed out at the rate of two or three a day, Sylvia Plath becomes herself, becomes something imaginary, newly, wildly and subtly created—hardly a person at all, or a woman, certainly not another "poetess," but one of those super-real, hypnotic, great classical heroines. The character is feminine, rather than female, though almost everything we customarily think of as feminine is turned on its head. The voice is now coolly amused, witty, now sour, now fanciful, girlish, charming, now sinking to the strident rasp of the vampire—a Dido, Phaedra, or Medea,[8] who can laugh at herself as "cow-heavy and floral in my Victorian nightgown."

A little cloudburst, a short heavy rain of sexual references. The word *poetess,* whose gender killed it long ago, is exhumed—to be denied. Equivalently, a

6. Though Tennessee Williams is cited here to enhance Flannery O'Connor's virtues, he is just as easily cited to prove other women's defects. For example, Dr. Karl Stern has resorted to Williams and Edward Albee as witnesses to the modern prevalence of the Castrating Woman. (*Barat Review,* January 1967, p. 46.) Naturally, in this context, both playwrights assume a status of unqualified virility.
7. Miss Moore's femininity leaves her vulnerable even to the imagination of John Berryman:

> *Fancy a lark with Sappho,*
> *a tumble in the bushes with Miss Moore,*

> *a spoon with Emily, while Charlotte glare.*
> *Miss Bishop's too noble-O.*

("Four Dream Songs," *Atlantic,* February 1968, p. 68.)
[The other women writers are Emily and Charlotte Brontë, and Moore's friend Elizabeth Bishop—editor's note.]
8. All heroines of classical literature, variously viewed by tradition as the victim of male betrayal, as a lecherous stepmother, and as a murderer [editor's note].

critic of W. H. Auden would be at pains, first of all, to deny that Auden is a poetaster. But *poetess* is only part of the general pelting away at the single fact that Sylvia Plath belonged to a sex (that inescapable membership) and that her sex was not male—*woman, heroines, feminine, female, girlish, fanciful, charming, Dido, Phaedra, Medea. Vampire,* too. And it would of course be this line, "Cow-heavy and floral in my Victorian nightgown," which seizes attention first and evokes the surprised pleasure of realizing that Sylvia Plath "can laugh at herself." Self-mockery, particularly sexual self-mockery, is not expected in a woman, and it is irresistible in the criticism of women to describe what was expected: the actual seems to exist only in relation to the preconceived.

Lowell's distinction between *feminine* and *female* is difficult, though less difficult than a distinction between *masculine* and *male* would be—say, in an introduction to Blake's *Songs of Innocence.* What helps us with the first is our all knowing, for some time now, that femaleness is a congenital fault, rather like eczema or Original Sin. An indicative denunciation, made in 1889: "They are no ladies. The only word good enough for them is the word of opprobrium—females." But fortunately, some women can be saved. By good manners, they are translated from females into ladies; and by talent, into feminine creatures (or even into "classical heroines"). And we are entirely accustomed to this generic mobility on their part: the individual is assumed into the sex and loses all but typical meaning within it. The emphasis is finally macabre, as though women wrote with breasts instead of pens—in which event it would be remarkable, as Lowell feels that it is, if one of them achieved ironic detachment.

When the subject of the work by a woman is also women (as it often has to be, since everyone has to eat what's in the cupboard), its critical treatment is still more aberrant. Like less specialized men, critics seem to fluctuate between attraction and surfeit. An obsessive concern with femininity shifts, at any moment, into a sense of being confined or suffocated by it. In the second condition, a distaste for books *before they are read* is not uncommon, as in Norman Mailer's unsolicited confession of not having been able to read Virginia Woolf, or in Anthony Burgess's inhibitory "impression of high-waisted dresses and genteel parsonage flirtation"[9] in Jane Austen's novels. More luckily, the work may be patronized by mild minds already persuaded that the human temperament combines traits of both sexes and that even masculine natures may respond, through their subterranean femininity, to the thoroughly feminine book.

A similar indulgence is fostered by any association, however tenuous, which the critic forms between the woman writer and some previous student of his own.[1] Now that almost everyone who writes teaches too, the incidence of this association is fairly high. Robert Lowell remembers that Sylvia Plath once audited a class of his at Boston University:

> She was never a student of mine, but for a couple of months seven years ago, she used to drop in on my poetry seminar at Boston University. I see her dim against the bright sky of a high window, viewless unless one cared to look down on the city outskirts' defeated yellow brick and

9. *New York Times Book Review,* December 4, 1966, p. 1.

1. For the especial amicability of this sexual relationship, see "The Student," p. 119.

square concrete pillbox filling stations. She was willowy, long-waisted, sharp-elbowed, nervous, giggly, gracious—a brilliant tense presence embarrassed by restraint. Her humility and willingness to accept what was admired seemed at times to give her an air of maddening docility that hid her unfashionable patience and boldness.[2]

It is not easy, of course, to write about a person whom one knew only slightly in the past. The strain is felt here, for example, in the gratuitous street scene from the classroom window. And in general, there is a sense of a physical recollection emended by a much later intellectual and poetic impression. The "brilliant tense presence" of the final poetry is affixed, generously enough, to the original figure of a young girl. The "maddening docility" too must have been a sexual enlargement, now reduced to an "air" of docility, since again the poems demonstrate the artistic (rather than "feminine") union of "patience and boldness." (Elsewhere they are, according to Lowell, "modest" poems too, they are uniquely "modest" *and* "bold.") But then the poet Anne Sexton's recollections, which originate in the same poetry seminar, make no reference to elbows or giggles or docility. Miss Sexton seems to have seen even at that time a woman entirely congruous with her later work. After class, the two used to drink together—at the Ritz bar, some distance away from those "concrete pillbox filling stations"—and conduct workmanlike discussions of suicidal techniques:

> *But suicides have a special language.*
> *Like carpenters they want to know* which tools.
> *They never ask* why build.
>
>   ("Wanting to Die")[3]

Lowell seems honestly caught between two ways of comprehending what exists outside the self. And certainly there is nothing of the stag posture about his remarks, no pretense of writing only for other men about women. All critics are of course secretly aware that no literary audience, except perhaps in Yemen, is any longer restricted to men. The man's-man tone is a deliberate archaism, coy and even flirtatious, like wearing spats. No one doubts that some silent misogyny may be dark and deep, but written misogyny is now generally a kind of chaffing, and not frightfully clever, gambit. For the critic in this style, the writer whose work is most easily related to established stereotypes of femininity is, oddly, the most welcome. What-to-say then flows effortlessly from the stereotypes themselves. The word *feminine* alone, like a grimace, expresses a displeasure which is not less certain for its being undefined. In a review of Fawn Brodie's biography of Sir Richard Burton, *The Devil Drives,* Josh Greenfeld remarked on the "feminine biographer's attachment to subject," and suggested that this quality (*or else* a "scholarly objectivity") prevented Mrs. Brodie's conceding Burton's homosexuality.[4] So her book is either too subjective or too objective: we will never know which.

2. Foreword to Sylvia Plath's *Ariel,* p. xi.
3. Anne Sexton, "The barfly ought to sing," *Tri-Quarterly,* Fall 1966, p. 90.
4. *Book Week,* May 28, 1967, p. 2. Mrs. Brodie had still more trouble in the *Times Literary Supplement* (January 11, 1968, p. 32), where her nationality as well as her sex was at fault: "So immense is this gulf, so inalienably remote are the societies that produced biographer and subject, *so difficult is it, even now, for a woman to get beneath a man's skin,* that only some imaginative genius could really have succeeded in the task Mrs. Brodie so boldly undertook." [My italics.]

But the same word can be turned upon men too. John Weightman has remarked that Genet's criminals cannot play male and female effectively because "a convicted criminal, however potent, has been classified as an object, and therefore feminized, by society."[5] An admirably simple social equation: a man in prison amounts to a woman. Similarly, *feminine* functions as an eight-letter word in the notorious Woodrow Wilson biography by Freud and William Bullitt.[6] At one heated point, Clemenceau calls Wilson feminine, Wilson calls Clemenceau feminine, then both Freud and Bullitt call Wilson feminine again. The word means that all four men thoroughly dislike each other. It is also sufficient for Norman Mailer to say that Herbert Gold reminds him "of nothing so much as a woman writer,"[7] and for Richard Gilman to consign Philip Roth to the "ladies' magazine" level.[8] In fact, chapters of *When She Was Good* were first published, and seemed to settle in snugly, at the *haut bourgeois* level of *Harper's* and the *Atlantic*. But, except perhaps in the *Daily Worker*, the consciousness of class is less insistent than that of sex: the phrase "ladies' magazine" is one of those which refuses not to be written once a month.[9]

But at heart most of these "the-ladies-bless-them" comments are as cheerful and offhand as they are predictable. When contempt, like anything else, has an assigned route to follow, and when it is accustomed to its course, it can proceed happily. This is evident, for example, in Norman Mailer's lively, even jocular, essay on the deplorable faults of Mary McCarthy's *The Group*. What accounts for these high spirits, except the fact that Mailer rejoices in what he spanks so loudly? The pleasure lies in Mary McCarthy's having capitulated, as it seems to Mailer, having at last written what he can securely and triumphantly call a female novel.[1] Not that Mailer's treatment of *The Group*, even in these familiar terms, is not still remarkable—even frightening, and that is a rare treat in criticism. One does not expect a disdain for feminine concerns, which is entirely commonplace, to mount to cloacal loathing. Mary McCarthy has soiled an abstraction, a genre, the novel-yet-to-be: "Yes, Mary deposited a load on the premise, and it has to be washed all over again, this little long-lived existential premise".[2]

But few rise to that kind of washing-up with Mailer's alacrity. In most critics, revulsion is an under-developed area. What rouses a much more interesting hostility in many is the work which does not conform to sexual preconception. That is, if feminine concerns can be found, they are conven-

5. *New York Review of Books*, August 24, 1967, p. 8.
6. *Thomas Woodrow Wilson, . . . a Psychological Study* (1967), by Sigmund Freud and William C. Bullitt [editor's note].
7. *Advertisements for Myself*, p. 435.
8. Richard Gilman, "Let's Lynch Lucy," *New Republic*, June 24, 1967, p. 19.
9. The phrase is at least sociologically interesting: it suggests the impossibility of remarking that some bad novel is fit for the "men's magazine." For fiction, there is none. At the same level of intelligence and cultivation, women evidently prefer stories (*McCall's*, *Redbook*, *The Ladies' Home Journal*, etc.) and men prefer facts (or quasi-facts) and photographs (*Time*, *Life*, *Look*, *Dude*, *Gent*, etc.). *Playboy* is exceptional in presupposing an eclectic male

audience (does it exist?) for both photographs *and* fiction.
1. A female novel, Mailer indicates, is one which deals with the superficial details of women's lives instead of their lower depths. Such a book is at once tedious and cowardly. On the other hand, Joseph Heller's *Catch-22* is a book for men (rather than a male novel) which deals with the superficial details of men's lives. It speaks, according to Mailer, to the man who "prefers to become interested in quick proportions and contradictions, in the practical surface of things." Both novels, then, are tedious but the first is a disgrace while the second has "a vast appeal." Obviously, it all depends on which practical surface of things the commentator himself is glued to.
2. *Cannibals and Christians*, p. 138.

tionally rebuked; but their absence is shocking. While all women's writing should presumably strive for a supra-feminine condition, it is profoundly distrusted for achieving it. So for all Anthony Burgess's resistance to Jane Austen, he is still less pleased by George Eliot ("The male impersonation is wholly successful") or by Ivy Compton-Burnet ("A big sexless nemesic force"). Similarly, he cannot leave alone what strikes him as the contradiction between Brigid Brophy's appearance and her writing.[3] His review of her book of essays, Don't Never Forget, opens in this sprightly manner:

> An American professor friend of mine, formerly an admirer of Miss Brophy's work, could no longer think of her as an author once he'd seen her in the flesh. "That girl was made for love," he would growl. Various writers who have smarted from her critical attentions might find it hard to agree.[4]

It is as though Elizabeth Hardwick, asked to review William Manchester's Death of a President, was obliged to refuse, growling, "That man was made for love." The same notion of an irreconcilable difference between the nature of woman and the mind of man prompts the hermaphroditic fallacy according to which one half the person, separating from the other half, produces a book by binary fission. So Mary McCarthy has been complimented, though not by Norman Mailer, on her "masculine mind" while, through the ages, poor Virgil has never been complimented on his "effeminacy." (Western criticism begins with this same tedious distinction—between manly Homer and womanish Virgil.) At the same time, while sentiment is a disadvantage, the alternative of feminine coolness is found still more disagreeable. Mary McCarthy used to be too formidable, Jean Stafford has sometimes been clinical, and others (going down, down) are perverse, petulant, catty, waspish.

The point is that comment upon Violette Leduc, who is not directly assertive, will be slurring; but the slur hardens into resentment of those writers who seem to endorse the same standards of restraint and reason which the critic presumably endorses. If for nothing else, for her tolerance of Sade, Simone de Beauvoir must be referred to (scathingly!) as "the lady," and then even her qualifications of tolerance must be described as a reluctance "to give herself unreservedly" to Sade.[5] Similarly, it is possible that much of the voluble male distaste for Jane Austen is based, not upon her military limitations (her infamous failure to discuss the Napoleonic Wars), but upon her antipathetic detachment. So a determined counteremphasis was first placed by her relatives, and has been continued since by most of her critics, upon her allegiance to domestic ideals—when, in fact, she is read only for her mockery of them.

3. Burgess has also furnished this country, in a "Letter from London" (Hudson Review, Spring 1967), the following couplet:

> People who read Brigid Brophy
> Should contend for the Kraft-Ebing Trophy.

In fact, he seems unfailingly exhilarated by Miss Brophy's faults, thrilled by them as Norman Mailer is by Mary McCarthy's. Burgess's most recent agitation was a review of Fifty Works of English Literature We Could Do Without (by Miss Brophy, Michael Levey and Charles Osborne): "The authors are now rubbing themselves in an ecstacy of the kind granted only to Exclusive Brethren." (Encounter, August 1967, p. 71.) [Richard Krafft-Ebing (1840–1902), a pioneering researcher into sexual psychopathology—editor's note.]

4. Manchester Guardian Weekly, November 24, 1966, p. 11. There is, incidentally, An American professor who exists only in the minds of English journalists. The Times Literary Supplement would be halved without him.

5. Leslie Schaeffer, New Republic, August 19, 1967, p. 28.

What seems to be wanted, insisted upon, is the critic's conception of women expressed in his conception of feminine terms—that is, a confirmation of the one sex's opinions by the imagination of the other, a difficult request which can seldom be gratified. It is perhaps this request which explains Louis Auchincloss's erratic view of Mary McCarthy in his *Pioneers and Caretakers*. Suddenly she is sister to Ellen Glasgow and Sarah Orne Jewett, as one of our feminine "caretakers of the culture," a guise in which few other readers can easily recognize her. But if one's thesis is sexual, the attachment of women to the past and the incapacity of women for "the clean sweep," then Mary McCarthy only seems to hate a few present things and actually loves many past things. One might as well argue that it was Swift's finding babies so sweet that made him think of eating them for dinner.[6]

The vague and ominous critical implications of femininity, with which we generally make do now, were more precisely defined by Walter Pater:

> Manliness in art, what can it be, as distinct from that which in opposition to it must be called the feminine quality there,—what but a full consciousness of what one does, of art itself in the work of art, tenacity of intuition and of consequent purpose, the spirit of construction as opposed to what is literally incoherent or ready to fall to pieces, and, in opposition to what is hysteric or works at random, the maintenance of a standard. Of such art ἦθος rather than πάθος[7] will be the predominant mood. To use Plato's own expression, there will be here no παρα-λειπόμενα, no "negligences," no feminine forgetfulness of one's self, nothing in the work of art unconformed to the leading intention of the artist, who will but increase his power by reserve. An artist of this kind will be apt, of course, to express more than he seems actually to say. He economizes. He will not spoil good things by exaggeration. The rough, promiscuous wealth of nature he reduces to grace and order: reduces, it may be, lax verse to staid and temperate prose. With him, the rhythm, the music, the notes, will be felt to follow, or rather literally accompany as ministers, the sense,—ἀκολουθεῖν τυν λὸγον.[8]

The intellectual consequences of unmanliness are prodigal. The feminine is the not fully conscious, not fully assembled, the intemperate, incoherent, hysterical, extravagant and capricious. In the rush of his contrasts, Pater comes to the verge of dismissing poetry: "verse" is a slut, and "staid, temperate prose" is a don. A limited view of the two forms, but understandable in the light of Pater's own twin employments as lecturer on the Renaissance and prose stylist. "The rough, promiscuous wealth of nature" anticipates (unlikely as any association between the two may seem) such a later fancy as Leslie Fiedler's image of the sculpture as male, and the tree out of which the sculpture is carved, as female. Here too, male art imposes form upon female

6. In his satirical pamphlet *A Modest Proposal* (1729) [editor's note].
7. Character rather than emotion (Greek) [editor's note].
8. Walter Pater, "Plato's Esthetics," *Plato and Platonism* (New York, 1899), pp. 253–54. The only term associated with women which Pater seems to have enjoyed was *pregnancy*, and that only in references to men instead: "Goethe, then in all the pregnancy of his wonderful youth. . . ." (*The Renaissance*, Cleveland and New York, The World Publishing Co., 1961, p. 193.) [The Final Greek phrase means "to follow the argument"—editor's note.]

nature. The homosexual contrast is between two possible partners: *nature*, the coarse, indiscriminate and blowsy woman, and *art*, the ordered, graceful and exquisite boy.

Pater foreshadows our present situation, however, in that his concern for "manliness" in art expends itself as much upon the contraindications to masculinity as upon its intrinsic properties. We are now wholly familiar with this emphasis upon the difficulties, rather than the capacities, of the male artist. The same emphasis has, in fact, mounted now to a sense of armies fighting openly against his accomplishment. Danger is unanimously confirmed, only its nature or origin is less agreed upon. Philip Roth has suggested the increasing difficulty of fiction's competing with actuality. What political novelist, he asks, could *imagine* Eisenhower, who yet seems an effect casually thrown off by society? Reality, then, is inimical to the writer, having itself grown incomparably fantastic. On the other hand, Saul Bellow argues that the writer is impeded by literary intellectuals whose respect for past achievements depresses present efforts. And Norman Mailer finds that it is ubiquitous corruption which prevents art. In architecture, for example:

> There is so much corruption in the building codes, overinflation in the value of land, featherbedding built into union rules, so much graft, so much waste, so much public relations, and so much emptiness that no one tries to do more with the roof than leave it flat.[9]

Mailer is forever Gothic and aspirant, possessed by a vision of renewal and of total accomplishment. But meanwhile hostile forces remain in the ascendancy, suppressing and flattening talent. The threat of these forces steadily diverts the writer—not from writing, but from writing what he would write if he did not feel threatened. In self-defense, he does quasi-military exercises for writing in the future, a kind of shadow-typing until the date is set for a real match. For the time being, communiqués are issued, protesting the present and improper circumstances of art and thereby adding to them—rather as people bang on their ceilings to make the upstairs people stop banging on their floors.

I do not mean to underestimate this conviction on the part of many writers that they live among strangers and aliens. On the contrary, I am alienated in turn by the habitual identification of this complex and all-encompassing enmity with the relatively narrow circumstance of sexuality. It is through this identification that phallic criticism regularly and rapidly shifts from writing by women, which can be dismissed as innocuous, to their vicious influence upon writing by men. It is clear that sexual conflict has become the specific focus, literal as well as metaphoric, of a general and amorphous sense of intellectual conflict. A simple instance is this last novel of Philip Roth's, *When She Was Good*, in which a pimple of a young woman is created only to be squeezed, interminably, to death—a small self-gratification which none of us would deny each other, but still prefer not to witness. And yet this tiny tumor, this Emma Bovary in galoshes, is supposed to define the Morality of the Middle West. Nothing much must stand for everything.

But the metaphoric focus is ordinarily more interesting. The capacity to write, even as it is held more and more precariously, is made synonymous with

9. *Cannibals and Christians*, p. 234.

sexual capacity, whereupon the woman becomes the enemy of both. She appears as the risk that the writer has to take, or the appetite, at once sluggish and gargantuan, which must be roused and then satisfied in order to prove that the writer is capable of giving satisfaction of any kind. So she is all that offers stubborn and brute resistance to achievement even as she is its only route. Her range is limitless, all internal obstacle as well as external impediment, all that within the writer himself may prevent his accomplishing his aim—weakness, dullness, caution, fear, dishonesty, triviality.

At the crudest level of this metaphoric struggle, the writer finds his professional and sexual activities incompatible, on the grounds of the distribution of resources. This anxiety seems distinctly modern. The association of the two faculties, intellectual and sexual, is ancient, but the expressed inability to reconcile them is recent. Blake, for example, celebrated "the lineaments of gratified desire,"[1] and seemed to sense no contradiction between them and artistic gratification. In fact, he considered sexual intercourse, rather like having breakfast or a walk in the garden, an essential prelude to composition. Hemingway, instead, found a young writer to warn against making love during periods of composition: the best ideas would be lost in bed. An intense frugality has set in, a determination not to squander vital spirits. Goods produced or released by the self, like semen and words, become oddly equivalent and interdependent. The Samson law: the consumption or removal of one product, particularly by a woman, must inevitably diminish another. Naturally then, the minds which so balance the books of themselves frequently remark upon the materiality of women. The impression is deflected from their own sense of possessing a warehouse of scarce, conglomerate materials, all subtracting strength from each other, and all consequently in need of vigilant supervision. A loss of all one's buttons will inevitably mean a strain on one's supply of safety pins. A fear of insufficiency develops, a terror of running out. All sexual difficulties have therefore shifted in fiction from women to men from feminine barrenness to masculine impotence or sterility or utter indifference. The women are uniformly and insatiably greedy (again, of course, in fiction) for conception. The men cannot afford to give them, indiscriminately, all the children they demand. The expenditure could only mean their going, as writers, into debtors' prison.

And yet there is an opposite dilemma: the testing of talent is confounded with the testing of sexual resources. Both must engage themselves, even though each engagement risks depletion or failure. In this metaphoric distortion, the actual energy and excess of nature is forgotten or does not convince. The rich, against all reason, describe their poverty, and every spermatozoon stands for an item of talent, infinitesimal and yet precious. It is all like (a literary) India, where men are commonly convinced of the debilitating consequences of intercourse even as the population increases by a million a month. In such a context, Milton's old cause for concern,

> And that one talent which is death to hide
> Lodged with me useless,[2]

---

1. What "men in women do require" and "women do in men require," according to a song by Blake [editor's note].

2. Milton, "When I Consider How My Light Is Spent" (1673) [editor's note].

seems cavalier—at least the talent is eager and impatient. Instead now, the cause of death seems to be the extravagant and unguarded employment of talent. It should be housed and protected and kept ready for a crucial moment in the indefinite future. And this future engagement is envisaged as a quarrel which the fighter-lover-writer will probably lose, or (at best) a prize of which he will probably be cheated. The possibility of failure, either of one's own nerve or of the other's loyalty, is always present. The best preparation is to stockpile animosity. In this connection, Norman Mailer has described one of the prize fighter Harry Greb's "training methods":

> That is, before he had a fight he would go to a brothel, and he would have two prostitutes, not one, taking the two of them into the same bed. And this apparently left him feeling like a wild animal. Don't ask me why. Perhaps he picked the two meanest whores in the joint and so absorbed into his system all the small, nasty, concentrated evils which had accumulated from carloads of men. Greb was known as the dirtiest fighter of his time.[3]

The thin chance held by the fighting talent is intertwined with sexual chance, and the possibilities of subversion or treachery are contained, like mutated ova, in the female. The commonplace sexual fiction must now regularly describe a man—preferably gifted, but a fool will do in a pinch—who cannot get his work done because he is involved with a deficient woman. His abilities are either wasted on her stupidity or poisoned by her malice. No one, again, distrusted women more than Milton, and yet it was possible for him to retain a conception of at least a sombre accord, founded upon an unremitting discipline:

> Therefore God's universal law
> Gave to the man despotic power
> Over his female in due awe,
> Nor from that right to part an hour
> Smile she or lour:
> So shall he least confusion draw
> On his whole life, not swayed
> By female usurpation, nor dismayed.
> (*Samson Agonistes*, ll.1053–60)

Occasionally, Mailer attempts the terms of this past coexistence: "she had fled the domination which was liberty for her" ("The Time of Her Time"), but this is only in bed and besides the mood has collapsed. Allowed domination, or at least imaginative domination, Milton also furnished confident images of fructification. The abyss upon which the Holy Ghost broods (rather like a *hen*) is vast and yet yielding to impregnation. The abyss for Mailer is an enticing image of terror, an irresistible descent into horror. At best, it is like a point on Bunyan's map,[4] a Pit of Responsibility. The writer descends to face truths which will diminish previous self-estimations.

Women are waiting in this pit, like large, pallid insects under stones, and whatever grace—or rather *significance*, there must always be some moral significance—the sexual encounter retains is at once masculine and dour: it is

---

3. *Cannibals and Christians*, p. 217.
4. I.e., in the allegorical landscape of *The Pilgrim's Progress* (1678) [editor's note].

a test of courage, a persistence in the face of disgust. Conception is difficult: either the spermatozoa are wasted (thrown away! squandered! from fortune to farm) on contraceptives or they must be assisted by fury: "Satan, if it takes your pitchfork up my gut, let me blast a child into this bitch."[5] And yet these encounters are more intellectual than physical statements, since the effect upon women is premonitory of the effect upon words, of failure (always the more likely) or success in writing: "Every child is a poem someone conceived in short space."[6] (Conceived? Then a *poetess* is meant?) So the hero of Mailer's story, "The Time of Her Time," Sergius O'Shaughnessy, attaches symbolic meaning to his (hardly unparalleled) effort to bring his partner to orgasm. Achieving that, ". . . it was more likely that I would win the next time I gambled my stake on something more appropriate for my ambition."

The concept of femininity is static and resistant, that of masculinity at once dynamic and striving:

> Masculinity is not something given to you, something you're born with, but something you gain. And you gain it by winning small battles with honor. Because there is very little honor left in American life, there is a certain built-in tendency to destroy masculinity.[7]

That is, it is difficult not only to pass a test but to find a test to pass. Everything conspires to make occasions of courage, in the formal and stylized sense of such occasions in the past, hard to come by. Hemingway was reduced to fighting fish, and the only land test in constant supply is fighting females. So armed intercourse must subsume all other single tournaments. In *An American Dream*, the mythomaniac Rojack combats social evil with his honorable penis, cousin to Sergius O'Shaughnessy's chivalric "avenger." And like O'Shaughnessy, Rojack scores by sodomy, his only way with a German housemaid of rebuking the immense social horror of Nazism.

But the avenger-writer, even as he engages with the enemy, risks deception. If the whore-novel (with her "feminine taste for the mortal wound") is not quite deadly, she is always at least devious:

> Every novelist who has slept with the Bitch (only poets and writers of short stories have a *Muse*) comes away bragging afterward like a G.I. tumbling out of a whorehouse spree—"Man, I made her moan," goes the cry of the young writer. But the Bitch laughs afterward in her empty bed. "He was so sweet in the beginning," she declares, "but by the end he just went, 'Peep, peep, peep.' "[8]

The sympathetic role is shuffled: the writer is the Orpheus now, too vulnerable or too impressionable not to be victimized by the cruelties of inspiration. Or deluded into vanity by false success. And worse, in having to deal with dishonesty, writers may grow dishonest too. The Bitch is full of "swilling crafts" by which they can be contaminated. The vision, then, must be of an achievement beyond craft, something wildly and spontaneously pure, beyond practice or calculation or skill. If a writer is always in training, it is nevertheless in order to accomplish something in the end which is quite alien to training.

5. [Mailer,] *An American Dream*, p. 240.
6. *Cannibals and Christians*, p. 202.
7. *Cannibals and Christians*, p. 201.
8. *Cannibals and Christians*, p. 107. From this it follows, as the belch the gas, that "a good novelist can do without everything but the remnant of his balls." (*Advertisements for Myself*, p. 435.)

It is as though one prepared regularly, through sexual promiscuity, for the future assumption of an absolute virginity.

At the lowest level of writing as sexual act, in pornography, the exercise is frankly masturbatory. But actually, in any persistent association of the two experiences, even a metaphoric association, the impression of onanism (which is perhaps appropriate to writing) is inescapable. Mailer has almost forgiven J. D. Salinger's *Raise High the Roof Beam, Carpenters*, in these terms:

> Now, all of us have written as badly. There are nights when one comes home after a cancerously dull party, full of liquor but not drunk, leaden with boredom, somewhere out of Fitzgerald's long dark night. Writing at such a time is like making love at such a time. It is hopeless, it desecrates one's future, but one does it anyway because at least it is an act.[9]

Here, the "act" of making love is as solitary as the act of defecating or of writing, or, for that matter, of dying. ("Herr Hemingway, can you sum up your feelings about death?" and Herr Hemingway: "Yes—just another whore.")[1] All that seems active outside the impacted consciousness, and therefore all that can pierce it, is time: hence, that familiar anxiety for abstractions like the genre or the "future." The only sensation attributed to concrete forms outside the self is implacability, an obscure inimical urge to resist domination. But some signature must be left upon these surroundings, some exertion made, even hopelessly. Encircled by blank forms, one fills them out, one writes over them. In that sense, composition and copulation are now considered identical twins.

1968

9. *Cannibals and Christians*, pp. 123–24. [See F. Scott Fitzgerald's "The Crack-Up" (1936): "In a real dark night of the soul it is always three o'clock in the morning"—editor's note.]

1. See Hemingway's "Poem to Mary (Second Poem)" (written 1944), which begins "Now sleeps he with that old whore death" [editor's note].

KATE MILLETT
b. 1934

After Kate Millett wrote a critique of the standard curricula in women's colleges, which was published by the National Organization for Women in 1967, she completed the Columbia University Ph.D. dissertation that would become *Sexual Politics* (1970), a foundational text in subsequent critical analyses of the power dynamics and ideological underpinnings of the relationship between men and women. From its opening interpretations of the graphic sexual scenes depicted by Henry Miller, Norman Mailer, and Jean Genet to its historical background on the emergence of the sexual revolution throughout the nineteenth and twentieth centuries, *Sexual Politics* helped establish the term *patriarchy* so as to account for the subjection of women. A sculptor, painter, and photographer as well as a filmmaker, Millett continued to dwell on the abuses of power in the oral narratives of *The Prostitution Papers: A Candid Dialogue* (1971), the investigation into a torture-murder in *The Basement: Meditations on a Human Sacrifice* (1979), and a number of autobiographical texts, including *Flying* (1974), *Sita* (1977), *The Loony-Bin Trip* (1990), and *A.D.: A Memoir* (1995).

From Sexual Politics

From *Chapter Two. Theory of Sexual Politics*

* * *

In introducing the term "sexual politics," one must first answer the inevitable question "Can the relationship between the sexes be viewed in a political light at all?" The answer depends on how one defines politics.[1] This essay does not define the political as that relatively narrow and exclusive world of meetings, chairmen, and parties. The term "politics" shall refer to power-structured relationships, arrangements whereby one group of persons is controlled by another. By way of parenthesis one might add that although an ideal politics might simply be conceived of as the arrangement of human life on agreeable and rational principles from whence the entire notion of power *over* others should be banished, one must confess that this is not what constitutes the political as we know it, and it is to this that we must address ourselves.

The following sketch, which might be described as "notes toward a theory of patriarchy," will attempt to prove that sex is a status category with political implications. Something of a pioneering effort, it must perforce be both tentative and imperfect. Because the intention is to provide an overall description, statements must be generalized, exceptions neglected, and sub-headings overlapping and, to some degree, arbitrary as well.

The word "politics" is enlisted here when speaking of the sexes primarily because such a word is eminently useful in outlining the real nature of their relative status, historically and at the present. It is opportune, perhaps today even mandatory, that we develop a more relevant psychology and philosophy of power relationships beyond the simple conceptual framework provided by our traditional formal politics. Indeed, it may be imperative that we give some attention to defining a theory of politics which treats of power relationships on grounds less conventional than those to which we are accustomed.[2] I have therefore found it pertinent to define them on grounds of personal contact and interaction between members of well-defined and coherent groups: races, castes, classes, and sexes. For it is precisely because certain groups have no representation in a number of recognized political structures that their position tends to be so stable, their oppression so continuous.

In America, recent events have forced us to acknowledge at last that the relationship between the races is indeed a political one which involves the general control of one collectivity, defined by birth, over another collectivity, also defined by birth. Groups who rule by birthright are fast disappearing, yet there remains one ancient and universal scheme for the domination of one birth group by another—the scheme that prevails in the area of sex. The study of racism has convinced us that a truly political state of affairs operates between the races to perpetuate a series of oppressive circumstances. The

1. The *American Heritage Dictionary*'s fourth definition is fairly approximate: "methods or tactics involved in managing a state or government." *American Heritage Dictionary* (New York: American Heritage and Houghton Mifflin, 1969). One might expand this to a set of stratagems designed to maintain a system. If one understands patriarchy to be an institution perpetuated by such techniques of control, one has a working definition of how politics is conceived in this essay. [Except as indicated, all notes are Millett's].

2. I am indebted here to Ronald V. Samson's *The Psychology of Power* (New York: Random House, 1968) for his intelligent investigation of the connection between formal power structures and the family and for his analysis of how power corrupts basic human relationships.

subordinated group has inadequate redress through existing political institutions, and is deterred thereby from organizing into conventional political struggle and opposition.

Quite in the same manner, a disinterested examination of our system of sexual relationship must point out that the situation between the sexes now, and throughout history, is a case of that phenomenon Max Weber defined as *herrschaft*, a relationship of dominance and subordinance.[3] What goes largely unexamined, often even unacknowledged (yet is institutionalized nonetheless) in our social order, is the birthright priority whereby males rule females. Through this system a most ingenious form of "interior colonization" has been achieved. It is one which tends moreover to be sturdier than any form of segregation, and more rigorous than class stratification, more uniform, certainly more enduring. However muted its present appearance may be, sexual dominion obtains nevertheless as perhaps the most pervasive ideology of our culture and provides its most fundamental concept of power.

This is so because our society, like all other historical civilizations, is a patriarchy.[4] The fact is evident at once if one recalls that the military, industry, technology, universities, science, political office, and finance—in short, every avenue of power within the society, including the coercive force of the police, is entirely in male hands. As the essence of politics is power, such realization cannot fail to carry impact. What lingers of supernatural authority, the Deity, "His" ministry, together with the ethics and values, the philosophy and art of our culture—its very civilization—as T. S. Eliot once observed, is of male manufacture.

If one takes patriarchal government to be the institution whereby that half of the populace which is female is controlled by that half which is male, the principles of patriarchy appear to be twofold: male shall dominate female, elder male shall dominate younger. However, just as with any human institution, there is frequently a distance between the real and the ideal; contradictions and exceptions do exist within the system. While patriarchy as an institution is a social constant so deeply entrenched as to run through all other political, social, or economic forms, whether of caste or class, feudality or bureaucracy, just as it pervades all major religions, it also exhibits great variety in history and locale. In democracies,[5] for example, females have often held no office or do so (as now) in such minuscule numbers as to be below even token representation. Aristocracy, on the other hand, with its emphasis upon the magic and dynastic properties of blood, may at times permit women to hold power. The principle of rule by elder males is violated even more fre-

3. "Domination in the quite general sense of power, i.e. the possibility of imposing one's will upon the behavior of other persons, can emerge in the most diverse forms." In this central passage of *Wirtschaft und Gesellschaft* Weber is particularly interested in two such forms: control through social authority ("patriarchal, magisterial, or princely") and control through economic force. In patriarchy as in other forms of domination "that control over economic goods, i.e. economic power, is a frequent, often purposively willed, consequence of domination as well as one of its most important instruments." Quoted from Max Rheinstein's and Edward Shil's translation of portions of *Wirtschaft und Gesellschaft* entitled *Max Weber on Law in Economy and Society* (New York: Simon and Schuster, 1967), pp. 323–24.

4. No matriarchal societies are known to exist at present. Matrilineality, which may be, as some anthropologists have held, a residue or a transitional stage of matriarchy, does not constitute an exception to patriarchal rule, it simply channels the power held by males through female descent—e.g. the Avunculate [stress on the relationship between a mother's brother and a sister's son—editor's note].

5. Radical democracy would, of course, preclude patriarchy. One might find evidence of a general satisfaction with a less than perfect democracy in the fact that women have so rarely held power within modern "democracies."

quently. Bearing in mind the variation and degree in patriarchy—as say between Saudi Arabia and Sweden, Indonesia and Red China—we also recognize our own form in the U.S. and Europe to be much altered and attenuated by the reforms described in the next chapter.

I. IDEOLOGICAL

Hannah Arendt[6] has observed that government is upheld by power supported either through consent or imposed through violence. Conditioning to an ideology amounts to the former. Sexual politics obtains consent through the "socialization" of both sexes to basic patriarchal polities with regard to temperament, role, and status. As to status, a pervasive assent to the prejudice of male superiority guarantees superior status in the male, inferior in the female. The first item, temperament, involves the formation of human personality along stereotyped lines of sex category ("masculine" and "feminine"), based on the needs and values of the dominant group and dictated by what its members cherish in themselves and find convenient in subordinates: aggression, intelligence, force, and efficacy in the male; passivity, ignorance, docility, "virtue," and ineffectuality in the female. This is complemented by a second factor, sex role, which decrees a consonant and highly elaborate code of conduct, gesture and attitude for each sex. In terms of activity, sex role assigns domestic service and attendance upon infants to the female, the rest of human achievement, interest, and ambition to the male. The limited role allotted the female tends to arrest her at the level of biological experience. Therefore, nearly all that can be described as distinctly human rather than animal activity (in their own way animals also give birth and care for their young) is largely reserved for the male. Of course, status again follows from such an assignment. Were one to analyze the three categories one might designate status as the political component, role as the sociological, and temperament as the psychological—yet their interdependence is unquestionable and they form a chain. Those awarded higher status tend to adopt roles of mastery, largely because they are first encouraged to develop temperaments of dominance. That this is true of caste and class as well is self-evident.

II. BIOLOGICAL

Patriarchal religion, popular attitude, and to some degree, science as well[7] assumes these psycho-social distinctions to rest upon biological differences between the sexes, so that where culture is acknowledged as shaping behavior, it is said to do no more than cooperate with nature. Yet the temperamental distinctions created in patriarchy ("masculine" and "feminine" personality traits) do not appear to originate in human nature, those of role and status still less.

The heavier musculature of the male, a secondary sexual characteristic and common among mammals, is biological in origin but is also culturally encouraged through breeding, diet and exercise. Yet it is hardly an adequate category

---

6. Hannah Arendt, "Speculations on Violence," *The New York Review of Books*, Vol. XII No. 4, February 27, 1969, p. 24.
7. The social, rather than the physical sciences are referred to here. Traditionally, medical science had often subscribed to such beliefs. This is no longer the case today, when the best medical research points to the conclusion that sexual stereotypes have no bases in biology.

on which to base political relations *within civilization*.[8] Male supremacy, like other political creeds, does not finally reside in physical strength but in the acceptance of a value system which is not biological. Superior physical strength is not a factor in political relations—vide those of race and class. Civilization has always been able to substitute other methods (technic, weaponry, knowledge) for those of physical strength, and contemporary civilization has no further need of it. At present, as in the past, physical exertion is very generally a class factor, those at the bottom performing the most strenuous tasks, whether they be strong or not.

It is often assumed that patriarchy is endemic in human social life, explicable or even inevitable on the grounds of human physiology. Such a theory grants patriarchy logical as well as historical origin. Yet if as some anthropologists believe, patriarchy is not of primeval origin, but was preceded by some other social form we shall call pre-patriarchal, then the argument of physical strength as a theory of patriarchal *origins* would hardly constitute a sufficient explanation—unless the male's superior physical strength was released in accompaniment with some change in orientation through new values or new knowledge. Conjecture about origins is always frustrated by lack of certain evidence. Speculation about prehistory, which of necessity is what this must be, remains nothing but speculation. Were one to indulge in it, one might argue the likelihood of a hypothetical period preceding patriarchy.[9] What would be crucial to such a premise would be a state of mind in which the primary principle would be regarded as fertility or vitalist processes. In a primitive condition, before it developed civilization or any but the crudest technic, humanity would perhaps find the most impressive evidence of creative force in the visible birth of children, something of a miraculous event and linked analogically with the growth of the earth's vegetation.

It is possible that the circumstance which might drastically redirect such attitudes would be the discovery of paternity. There is some evidence that fertility cults in ancient society at some point took a turn toward patriarchy, displacing and downgrading female function in procreation and attributing the power of life to the phallus alone. Patriarchal religion could consolidate this position by the creation of a male God or gods, demoting, discrediting, or eliminating goddesses and constructing a theology whose basic postulates are male supremacist, and one of whose central functions is to uphold and validate the patriarchal structure.[1]

---

8. "The historians of Roman laws, having very justly remarked that neither birth nor affection was the foundation of the Roman family, have concluded that this foundation must be found in the power of the father or husband. They make a sort of primordial institution of this power; but they do not explain how this power was established, unless it was by the superiority of strength of the husband over the wife, and of the father over the children. Now, we deceive ourselves sadly when we thus place force as the origin of law. We shall see farther on that the authority of the father or husband, far from having been the first cause, was itself an effect; it was derived from religion, and was established by religion. Superior strength, therefore, was not the principle that established the family." Numa Denis Fustel de Coulanges, *The Ancient City* (1864). English translation by Willard Small (1873), Doubleday Anchor reprint, pp. 41–42. Unfortunately Fustel de Coulanges neglects to mention how religion came to uphold patriarchal authority, since patriarchal religion is also an effect, rather than an original cause.

9. One might also include the caveat that such a social order need not imply the domination of one sex which the term "matriarchy" would, by its semantic analogue to patriarchy, infer. Given the simpler scale of life and the fact that female-centered fertility religion might be offset by male physical strength, pre-patriarchy might have been fairly equalitarian.

1. Something like this appears to have taken place as the culture of Neolithic agricultural villages gave way to the culture of civilization and to patriarchy with the rise of cities. See Louis Mumford, *The City in History* (New York: Harcourt, Brace, 1961), Chapter One. A discovery such as paternity, a major acquisition of "scientific" knowledge might, hypothetically, have led to an expansion of population, surplus labor and strong class stratification. There is good reason to suppose that the transformation of hunting into war also played a part.

So much for the evanescent delights afforded by the game of origins. The question of the historical origins of patriarchy—whether patriarchy originated primordially in the male's superior strength, or upon a later mobilization of such strength under certain circumstances—appears at the moment to be unanswerable. It is also probably irrelevant to contemporary patriarchy, where we are left with the realities of sexual politics, still grounded, we are often assured, on nature. Unfortunately, as the psycho-social distinctions made between the two sex groups which are said to justify their present political relationship are not the clear, specific, measurable and neutral ones of the physical sciences, but are instead of an entirely different character— vague, amorphous, often even quasi-religious in phrasing—it must be admitted that many of the generally understood distinctions between the sexes in the more significant areas of role and temperament, not to mention status, have in fact, essentially cultural, rather than biological, bases. Attempts to prove that temperamental dominance is inherent in the male (which for its advocates, would be tantamount to validating, logically as well as historically, the patriarchal situation regarding role and status) have been notably unsuccessful. Sources in the field are in hopeless disagreement about the nature of sexual differences, but the most reasonable among them have despaired of the ambition of any definite equation between temperament and biological nature. It appears that we are not soon to be enlightened as to the existence of any significant inherent differences between male and female beyond the bio-genital ones we already know. Endocrinology and genetics afford no definite evidence of determining mental-emotional differences.[2]

Not only is there insufficient evidence for the thesis that the present social distinctions of patriarchy (status, role, temperament) are physical in origin, but we are hardly in a position to assess the existing differentiations, since distinctions which we know to be culturally induced at present so outweigh them. Whatever the "real" differences between the sexes may be, we are not likely to know them until the sexes are treated differently, that is alike. And this is very far from being the case at present. Important new research not only suggests that the possibilities of innate temperamental differences seem more remote than ever, but even raises questions as to the validity and permanence of psycho-sexual identity. In doing so it gives fairly concrete positive evidence of the overwhelmingly *cultural* character of gender, i.e. personality structure in terms of sexual category.

What Stoller and other experts define as "core gender identity" is now thought to be established in the young by the age of eighteen months. This is how Stoller differentiates between sex and gender:

> Dictionaries stress that the major connotation of *sex* is a biological one, as for example, in the phrases *sexual relations* or *the male sex*. In agreement with this, the word *sex*, in this work will refer to the male or female sex and the component biological parts that determine whether one is a male or a female; the word *sexual* will have connotations of anatomy and physiology. This obviously leaves tremendous areas of behavior, feelings, thoughts and fantasies that are related to the sexes and yet do not have

2. No convincing evidence has so far been advanced in this area. Experimentation regarding the connection between hormones and animal behavior not only yields highly ambivalent results but brings with it the hazards of reasoning by analogy to human behavior. For a summary of the arguments see David C. Glass (editor), *Biology and Behavior* (New York: Rockefeller University and the Russell Sage Foundation, 1968).

primarily biological connotations. It is for some of these psychological phenomena that the term gender will be used: one can speak of the male sex or the female sex, but one can also talk about masculinity and feminity and not necessarily be implying anything about anatomy or physiology. Thus, while *sex* and *gender* seem to common sense inextricably bound together, one purpose of this study will be to confirm the fact that the two realms (sex and gender) are not inevitably bound in anything like a one-to-one relationship, but each may go into quite independent ways.[3]

In cases of genital malformation and consequent erroneous gender assignment at birth, studied at the California Gender Identity Center, the discovery was made that it is easier to change the sex of an adolescent male, whose biological identity turns out to be contrary to his gender assignment and conditioning—through surgery—than to undo the educational consequences of years, which have succeeded in making the subject temperamentally feminine in gesture, sense of self, personality and interests. Studies done in California under Stoller's direction offer proof that gender identity (I am a girl, I am a boy) is the primary identity any human being holds—the first as well as the most permanent and far-reaching. Stoller later makes emphatic the distinction that sex is biological, gender psychological, and therefore cultural: "*Gender* is a term that has psychological or cultural rather than biological connotations. If the proper terms for sex are "male" and "female," the corresponding terms for gender are "masculine" and "feminine"; these latter may be quite independent of (biological) sex."[4] Indeed, so arbitrary is gender, that it may even be contrary to physiology: ". . . although the external genitalia (penis, testes, scrotum) contribute to the sense of maleness, no one of them is essential for it, not even all of them together. In the absence of complete evidence, I agree in general with Money, and the Hampsons who show in their large series of intersexed patients that gender role is determined by postnatal forces, regardless of the anatomy and physiology of the external genitalia."[5]

It is now believed[6] that the human fetus is originally physically female until the operation of androgen at a certain stage of gestation causes those with y chromosomes to develop into males. Psychosexually (e.g., in terms of masculine and feminine, and in contradistinction to male and female) there is no differentiation between the sexes at birth. Psychosexual personality is therefore postnatal and learned.

> . . . the condition existing at birth and for several months thereafter is one of psychosexual undifferentiation. Just as in the embryo, morphologic sexual differentiation passes from a plastic stage to one of fixed immutability, so also does psychosexual differentiation become fixed and immutable—so much so, that mankind has traditionally assumed that so strong and fixed a feeling as personal sexual identity must stem from something innate, instinctive, and not subject to postnatal experience

3. Robert J. Stoller, *Sex and Gender* (New York, Science House, 1968), from the preface, pp. viii–ix.
4. *Ibid.*, p. 9.
5. *Ibid.*, p. 48.
6. See Mary Jane Sherfey, "The Evolution and Nature of Female Sexuality in Relation to Psycho-analytic Theory," *Journal of the American Psychoanalytic Association*, vol. 14, January 1966, no. 1 (New York, International University Press Inc.), and John Money, "Psychosexual Differentiation," in *Sex Research, New Developments* (New York, Holt, 1965).

and learning. The error of this traditional assumption is that the power and permanence of something learned has been underestimated. The experiments of animal ethologists on imprinting have now corrected this misconception.[7]

John Money who is quoted above, believes that "the acquisition of a native language is a human counterpart to imprinting," and gender first established "with the establishment of a native language."[8] This would place the time of establishment at about eighteen months. Jerome Kagin's[9] studies in how children of pre-speech age are handled and touched, tickled and spoken to in terms of their sexual identity ("Is it a boy or a girl?" "Hello, little fellow," "Isn't she pretty," etc.) put the most considerable emphasis on purely tactile learning which would have much to do with the child's sense of self, even before speech is attained.

Because of our social circumstances, male and female are really two cultures and their life experiences are utterly different—and this is crucial. Implicit in all the gender identity development which takes place through childhood is the sum total of the parents', the peers', and the culture's notions of what is appropriate to each gender by way of temperament, character, interests, status, worth, gesture, and expression. Every moment of the child's life is a clue to how he or she must think and behave to attain or satisfy the demands which gender places upon one. In adolescence, the merciless task of conformity grows to crisis proportions, generally cooling and settling in maturity.

Since patriarchy's biological foundations appear to be so very insecure, one has some cause to admire the strength of a "socialization" which can continue a universal condition "on faith alone," as it were, or through an acquired value system exclusively. What does seem decisive in assuring the maintenance of the temperamental differences between the sexes is the conditioning of early childhood. Conditioning runs in a circle of self-perpetuation and self-fulfilling prophecy. To take a simple example: expectations the culture cherishes about his gender identity encourage the young male to develop aggressive impulses, and the female to thwart her own or turn them inward. The result is that the male tends to have aggression reinforced in his behavior, often with significant anti-social possibilities. Thereupon the culture consents to believe the possession of the male indicator, the testes, penis, and scrotum, in itself characterizes the aggressive impulse, and even vulgarly celebrates it in such encomiums as "that guy has balls." The same process of reinforcement is evident in producing the chief "feminine" virtue of passivity.

In contemporary terminology, the basic division of temperamental trait is marshaled along the line of "aggression is male" and "passivity is female." All other temperamental traits are somehow—often with the most dexterous ingenuity—aligned to correspond. If aggressiveness is the trait of the master class, docility must be the corresponding trait of a subject group. The usual hope of such line of reasoning is that "nature," by some impossible outside chance, might still be depended upon to rationalize the patriarchal system.

7. Money, op cit., p. 12.
8. Ibid., p. 13.
9. Jerome Kagin, "The Acquisition and Signifi-
cance of Sex-Typing," in *Review of Child Development Research*, ed. M. Hoffman (New York, Russell Sage Foundation, 1964).

An important consideration to be remembered here is that in patriarchy, the function of norm is unthinkingly delegated to the male—were it not, one might as plausibly speak of "feminine" behavior as active, and "masculine" behavior as hyperactive or hyperaggressive.

Here it might be added, by way of a coda, that data from physical sciences has recently been enlisted again to support sociological arguments, such as those of Lionel Tiger[1] who seeks a genetic justification of patriarchy by proposing a "bonding instinct" in males which assures their political and social control of human society. One sees the implication of such a theory by applying its premise to any ruling group. Tiger's thesis appears to be a misrepresentation of the work of Lorenz and other students of animal behavior. Since his evidence of inherent trait is patriarchal history and organization, his pretensions to physical evidence are both specious and circular. One can only advance genetic evidence when one has genetic (rather than historical) evidence to advance. As many authorities dismiss the possibility of instincts (complex inherent behavioral patterns) in humans altogether, admitting only reflexes and drives (far simpler neural responses),[2] the prospects of a "bonding instinct" appear particularly forlorn.

Should one regard sex in humans as a drive, it is still necessary to point out that the enormous area of our lives, both in early "socialization" and in adult experience, labeled "sexual behavior," is almost entirely the product of learning. So much is this the case that even the act of coitus itself is the product of a long series of learned responses—responses to the patterns and attitudes, even as to the object of sexual choice, which are set up for us by our social environment.

The arbitrary character of patriarchal ascriptions of temperament and role has little effect upon their power over us. Nor do the mutually exclusive, contradictory, and polar qualities of the categories "masculine" and "feminine" imposed upon human personality give rise to sufficiently serious question among us. Under their aegis each personality becomes little more, and often less than half, of its human potential. Politically, the fact that each group exhibits a circumscribed but complementary personality and range of activity is of secondary importance to the fact that each represents a status or power division. In the matter of conformity patriarchy is a governing ideology without peer; it is probable that no other system has ever exercised such a complete control over its subjects.

III. SOCIOLOGICAL

Patriarchy's chief institution is the family. It is both a mirror of and a connection with the larger society; a patriarchal unit within a patriarchal whole. Mediating between the individual and the social structure, the family effects control and conformity where political and other authorities are insufficient.[3] As the fundamental instrument and the foundation unit of patriarchal society the family and its roles are prototypical. Serving as an agent of the larger society, the family not only encourages its own members to adjust and con-

---

1. Lionel Tiger, *Men in Groups* (New York, Random House, 1968).
2. Through instinct subhuman species might undertake the activity of building a complex nest or hive; through reflex or drive a human being might

simply blink, feel hunger, etc.
3. In some of my remarks on the family I am indebted to Goode's short and concise analysis. See William J. Goode, *The Family* (Englewood Cliffs, New Jersey, Prentice-Hall, 1964).

form, but acts as a unit in the government of the patriarchal state which rules its citizens through its family heads. Even in patriarchal societies where they are granted legal citizenship, women tend to be ruled through the family alone and have little or no formal relation to the state.[4]

As co-operation between the family and the larger society is essential, else both would fall apart, the fate of three patriarchal institutions, the family, society, and the state are interrelated. In most forms of patriarchy this has generally led to the granting of religious support in statements such as the Catholic precept that "the father is head of the family," or Judaism's delegation of quasi-priestly authority to the male parent. Secular governments today also confirm this, as in census practices of designating the male as head of household, taxation, passports etc. Female heads of household tend to be regarded as undesirable; the phenomenon is a trait of poverty or misfortune. The Confucian prescription that the relationship between ruler and subject is parallel to that of father and children points to the essentially feudal character of the patriarchal family (and conversely, the familial character of feudalism) even in modern democracies.[5]

Traditionally, patriarchy granted the father nearly total ownership over wife or wives and children, including the powers of physical abuse and often even those of murder and sale. Classically, as head of the family the father is both begetter and owner in a system in which kinship is property.[6] Yet in strict patriarchy, kinship is acknowledged only through association with the male line. Agnation excludes the descendants of the female line from property right and often even from recognition.[7] The first formulation of the patriarchal family was made by Sir Henry Maine, a nineteenth-century historian of ancient jurisprudence. Maine argues that the patriarchal basis of kinship is put in terms of dominion rather than blood; wives, though outsiders, are assimilated into the line, while sisters' sons are excluded. Basing his definition of the family upon the *patria potestes*[8] of Rome, Maine defined it as follows: "The eldest male parent is absolutely supreme in his household. His dominion extends to life and death and is as unqualified over his children and their houses as over his slaves."[9] In the archaic patriarchal family "the group consists of animate and inanimate property, of wife, children, slaves, land and goods, all held together by subjection to the despotic authority of the eldest male."[1]

McLennon's rebuttal[2] to Maine argued that the Roman *patria potestes* was an extreme form of patriarchy and by no means, as Maine had imagined, universal. Evidence of matrilineal societies (preliterate societies in Africa and elsewhere) refute Maine's assumption of the universality of agnation. Cer-

4. Family, society, and state are three separate but connected entities: women have a decreasing importance as one goes from the first to the third category. But as each of the three categories exists within or is influenced by the overall institution of patriarchy, I am concerned here less with differentiation than with pointing out a general similarity.
5. J. K. Folsom makes a convincing argument as to the anomalous character of patriarchal family systems within democratic society. See Joseph K. Folsom, *The Family and Democratic Society* (New York: John Wiley, 1934, 1943).
6. Marital as well as consanguine relation to the head of the family made one his property.
7. Strict patriarchal descent is traced and recog-

nized only through male heirs rather than through sisters' sons etc. In a few generations descendants of female branches lose touch. Only those who "bear the name," who descend from male branches, may be recognized for kinship or inheritance.
8. I.e., *patria potestas*, "paternal power" (Latin) [editor's note].
9. Sir Henry Maine, *Ancient Law* (London, Murray, 1861), p. 122.
1. Sir Henry Maine, *The Early History of Institutions* (London), pp. 310–11.
2. John McLennon, *The Patriarchal Theory* (London, Macmillan, 1885).

tainly Maine's central argument, as to the primeval or state of nature character of patriarchy is but a rather naïf[3] rationalization of an institution Maine tended to exalt. The assumption of patriarchy's primeval character is contradicted by much evidence which points to the conclusion that full patriarchal authority, particularly that of the *patria potestes* is a late development and the total erosion of female status was likely to be gradual as has been its recovery.

In contemporary patriarchies the male's *de jure* priority has recently been modified through the granting of divorce[4] protection, citizenship, and property to women. Their chattel status continues in their loss of name, their obligation to adopt the husband's domicile, and the general legal assumption that marriage involves an exchange of the female's domestic service and (sexual) consortium in return for financial support.[5]

The chief contribution of the family in patriarchy is the socialization of the young (largely through the example and admonition of their parents) into patriarchal ideology's prescribed attitudes toward the categories of role, temperament, and status. Although slight differences of definition depend here upon the parents' grasp of cultural values, the general effect of uniformity is achieved, to be further reinforced through peers, schools, media, and other learning sources, formal and informal. While we may niggle over the balance of authority between the personalities of various households, one must remember that the entire culture supports masculine authority in all areas of life and—outside of the home—permits the female none at all.

To insure that its crucial functions of reproduction and socialization of the young take place only within its confines, the patriarchal family insists upon legitimacy. Bronislaw Malinowski describes this as "the principle of legitimacy" formulating it as an insistence that "no child should be brought into the world without a man—and one man at that—assuming the role of sociological father."[6] By this apparently consistent and universal prohibition (whose penalties vary by class and in accord with the expected operations of the double standard) patriarchy decrees that the status of both child and mother is primarily or ultimately dependent upon the male. And since it is not only his social status, but even his economic power upon which his dependents generally rely, the position of the masculine figure within the family—as without—is materially, as well as ideologically, extremely strong.

Although there is no biological reason why the two central functions of the family (socialization and reproduction) need be inseparable from or even take place within it, revolutionary or utopian efforts to remove these functions

---

3. Maine took the patriarchal family as the cell from which society evolved as gens, phratry, tribe, and nation grew, rather in the simplistic manner of Israel's twelve tribes descending from Jacob. Since Maine also dated the origin of patriarchy from the discovery of paternity, hardly a primeval condition, this too operates against the eternal character of patriarchal society.
4. Many patriarchies granted divorce to males only. It has been accessible to women on any scale only during this century. Goode states that divorce rates were as high in Japan during the 1880s as they are in the U.S. today. Goode, *op. cit.*, p. 3.
5. Divorce is granted to a male for his wife's failure in domestic service and consortium: it is not granted him for his wife's failure to render him

financial support. Divorce is granted to a woman if her husband fails to support her, but not for his failure at domestic service or consortium. But see Karczewski versus Baltimore and Ohio Railroad, 274 F. Supp. 169.175 N.D. Illinois, 1967, where a precedent was set and the common law that decrees a wife might not sue for loss of consortium overturned.
6. Bronislaw Malinowski, *Sex, Culture and Myth* (New York, Harcourt, 1962), p. 63. An earlier statement is even more sweeping: "In all human societies moral tradition and the law decree that the group consisting of a woman and her offspring is not a sociologically complete unit." *Sex and Repression in Savage Society* (London, Humanities, 1927), p. 213.

from the family have been so frustrated, so beset by difficulties, that most experiments so far have involved a gradual return to tradition. This is strong evidence of how basic a form patriarchy is within all societies, and of how pervasive its effects upon family members. It is perhaps also an admonition that change undertaken without a thorough understanding of the sociopolitical institution to be changed is hardly productive. And yet radical social change cannot take place without having an effect upon patriarchy. And not simply because it is the political form which subordinates such a large percentage of the population (women and youth) but because it serves as a citadel of property and traditional interests. Marriages are financial alliances, and each household operates as an economic entity much like a corporation. As one student of the family states it, "the family is the keystone of the stratification system, the social mechanism by which it is maintained."[7]

IV. CLASS

It is in the area of class that the castelike status of the female within patriarchy is most liable to confusion, for sexual status often operates in a superficially confusing way within the variable of class. In a society where status is dependent upon the economic, social, and educational circumstances of class, it is possible for certain females to appear to stand higher than some males. Yet not when one looks more closely at the subject. This is perhaps easier to see by means of analogy: a black doctor or lawyer has higher social status than a poor white sharecropper. But race, itself a caste system which subsumes class, persuades the latter citizen that he belongs to a higher order of life, just as it oppresses the black professional in spirit, whatever his material success may be. In much the same manner, a truck driver or butcher has always his "manhood" to fall back upon. Should this final vanity be offended, he may contemplate more violent methods. The literature of the past thirty years provides a staggering number of incidents in which the caste of virility triumphs over the social status of wealthy or even educated women. In literary contexts one has to deal here with wish-fulfillment. Incidents from life (bullying, obscene, or hostile remarks) are probably another sort of psychological gesture of ascendancy. Both convey more hope than reality, for class divisions are generally quite impervious to the hostility of individuals. And yet while the existence of class division is not seriously threatened by such expressions of enmity, the existence of sexual hierarchy has been re-affirmed and mobilized to "punish" the female quite effectively.

The function of class or ethnic mores in patriarchy is largely a matter of how overtly displayed or how loudly enunciated the general ethic of masculine supremacy allows itself to become. Here one is confronted by what appears to be a paradox: while in the lower social strata, the male is more likely to claim authority on the strength of his sex rank alone, he is actually obliged more often to share power with the women of his class who are economically productive; whereas in the middle and upper classes, there is less tendency to assert a blunt patriarchal dominance, as men who enjoy such status have more power in any case.[8]

It is generally accepted that Western patriarchy has been much softened by the concepts of courtly and romantic love. While this is certainly true,

7. Goode, *op. cit.*, p. 80.   8. Goode, *op. cit.*, p. 74.

such influence has also been vastly overestimated. In comparison with the candor of "machismo" or oriental behavior, one realizes how much of a concession traditional chivalrous behavior represents—a sporting kind of reparation to allow the subordinate female certain means of saving face. While a palliative to the injustice of woman's social position, chivalry is also a technique for disguising it. One must acknowledge that the chivalrous stance is a game the master group plays in elevating its subject to pedestal level. Historians of courtly love stress the fact that the raptures of the poets had no effect upon the legal or economic standing of women, and very little upon their social status.[9] As the sociologist Hugo Beigel has observed, both the courtly and the romantic versions of love are "grants" which the male concedes out of his total powers.[1] Both have had the effect of obscuring the patriarchal character of Western culture and in their general tendency to attribute impossible virtues to women, have ended by confining them in a narrow and often remarkably conscribing sphere of behavior. It was a Victorian habit, for example, to insist the female assume the function of serving as the male's conscience and living the life of goodness he found tedious but felt someone ought to do anyway.

The concept of romantic love affords a means of emotional manipulation which the male is free to exploit, since love is the only circumstance in which the female is (ideologically) pardoned for sexual activity. And convictions of romantic love are convenient to both parties since this is often the only condition in which the female can overcome the far more powerful conditioning she has received toward sexual inhibition. Romantic love also obscures the realities of female status and the burden of economic dependency. As to "chivalry," such gallant gesture as still resides in the middle classes has degenerated to a tired ritualism, which scarcely serves to mask the status situation of the present.

Within patriarchy one must often deal with contradictions which are simply a matter of class style. David Riesman has noted that as the working class has been assimilated into the middle class, so have its sexual mores and attitudes. The fairly blatant male chauvinism which was once a province of the lower class or immigrant male has been absorbed and taken on a certain glamour through a number of contemporary figures, who have made it, and a certain number of other working-class male attitudes, part of a new, and at the moment, fashionable life style. So influential is this working-class ideal of brute virility (or more accurately, a literary and therefore middle-class version of it) become in our time that it may replace more discreet and "gentlemanly" attitudes of the past.[2]

9. This is the gist of Valency's summary of the situation before the troubadours, acknowledging that courtly love is an utter anomaly: "With regard to the social background, all that can be stated with confidence is that we know nothing of the objective relationships of men and women in the Middle Ages which might conceivably motivate the strain of love-poetry which the troubadours developed." Maurice Valency, *In Praise of Love* (Macmillan, New York, 1958), p. 5.
1. Hugo Beigel, "Romantic Love," *The American Sociological Review*, Vol. 16, 1951, p. 331.
2. [Norman] Mailer and [Henry] Miller occur to one in this connection, and [D. H.] Lawrence as well. One might trace Rojack's very existence as a fictional figure to the virility symbol of Jack London's Ernest Everhard and Tennessee Williams's Stanley Kowalski. That Rojack is also literate is nothing more than an elegant finish upon the furniture of his "manhood" solidly based in the hard oaken grain of his mastery over any and every "broad" he can better, bludgeon, or bugger. [For Rojack, Everhard, and Kowalski, see Mailer's *An American Dream* (1965), London's *The Iron Heel* (1908), and Williams's *A Streetcar Named Desire* (1947)—editor's note.]

One of the chief effects of class within patriarchy is to set one woman against another, in the past creating a lively antagonism between whore and matron, and in the present between career woman and housewife. One envies the other her "security" and prestige, while the envied yearns beyond the confines of respectability for what she takes to be the other's freedom, adventure, and contact with the great world. Through the multiple advantages of the double standard, the male participates in both worlds, empowered by his superior social and economic resources to play the estranged women against each other as rivals. One might also recognize subsidiary status categories among women: not only is virtue class, but beauty and age as well.

Perhaps, in the final analysis, it is possible to argue that women tend to transcend the usual class stratifications in patriarchy, for whatever the class of her birth and education, the female has fewer permanent class associations than does the male. Economic dependency renders her affiliations with any class a tangential, vicarious, and temporary matter. Aristotle observed that the only slave to whom a commoner might lay claim was his woman, and the service of an unpaid domestic still provides working-class males with a "cushion" against the buffets of the class system which incidentally provides them with some of the psychic luxuries of the leisure class. Thrown upon their own resources, few women rise above working class in personal prestige and economic power, and women as a group do not enjoy many of the interests and benefits any class may offer its male members. Women have therefore less of an investment in the class system. But it is important to understand that as with any group whose existence is parasitic to its rulers, women are a dependency class who live on surplus. And their marginal life frequently renders them conservative, for like all persons in their situation (slaves are a classic example here) they identify their own survival with the prosperity of those who feed them. The hope of seeking liberating radical solutions of their own seems too remote for the majority to dare contemplate and remains so until consciousness on the subject is raised.

As race is emerging as one of the final variables in sexual politics, it is pertinent, especially in a discussion of modern literature, to devote a few words to it as well. Traditionally, the white male has been accustomed to concede the female of his own race, in her capacity as "his woman," a higher status than that ascribed to the black male.[3] Yet as white racist ideology is exposed and begins to erode, racism's older protective attitudes toward (white) women also begin to give way. And the priorities of maintaining male supremacy might outweigh even those of white supremacy; sexism may be more endemic in our own society than racism. For example, one notes in authors whom we

---

3. It would appear that the "pure flower of white womanhood" has at least at times been something of a disappointment to her lord as a fellow-racist. The historic connection of the Abolitionist and the Woman's Movement is some evidence of this, as well as the incident of white female and black male marriages as compared with those of white male and black female. Figures on miscegenation are very difficult to obtain: Goode (*op. cit.*, p. 37) estimates the proportion of white women marrying black men to be between 3 to 10 times the proportion of white men marrying black women. Robert K. Merton, "Intermarriage and the Social Structure" *Psychiatry*, Vol. 4, August 1941, p. 374, states that "most intercaste sex relations—not marriages—are between white men and Negro women." It is hardly necessary to emphasize that the more extensive sexual contacts between white males and black females have not only been extra-marital, but (on the part of the white male) crassly exploitative. Under slavery it was simply a case of rape.

would now term overtly racist, such as D. H. Lawrence—whose contempt for what he so often designates as inferior breeds is unabashed—instances where the lower-caste male is brought on to master or humiliate the white man's own insubordinate mate. Needless to say, the female of the non-white races does not figure in such tales save as an exemplum of "true" woman-hood's servility, worthy of imitation by other less carefully instructed females. Contemporary white sociology often operates under a similar patriarchal bias when its rhetoric inclines toward the assertion that the "matriarchal" (e.g. matrifocal) aspect of black society and the "castration" of the black male are the most deplorable symptoms of black oppression in white racist society, with the implication that racial inequity is capable of solution by a restora-tion of masculine authority. Whatever the facts of the matter may be, it can also be suggested that analysis of this kind presupposes patriarchal values without questioning them, and tends to obscure both the true character of and the responsibility for racist injustice toward black humanity of both sexes.

*　　*　　*

1970

SHERRY B. ORTNER
b. 1941

Sherry Ortner has taught anthropology at Sarah Lawrence College; the University of Michigan; the University of California, Berkeley; Columbia University; and UCLA. "Is Female to Male as Nature Is to Culture?" (1972), her second publication, grapples with the universal subordination of women by considering the reasons why the female of the species is associated with the realm of nature or with natural processes. Her subsequent books include *Sherpas through Their Rituals* (1978), *Sexual Meanings: The Cultural Construction of Gender and Sexuality* (co-edited with Harriet White-head, 1981), *High Religion: A Cultural and Political History of Sherpa Buddhism* (1989), *Making Gender: The Politics and Erotics of Culture* (1996), and *New Jersey Dreaming: Capital, Culture, and the Class of '58* (2003). As did the work of Dorothy Dinnerstein, Ortner's writing shaped the thinking of scholars grappling with the causes and consequences of misogyny.

Is Female to Male as Nature Is to Culture?[1]

Much of the creativity of anthropology derives from the tension between two sets of demands: that we explain human universals, and that we explain cultural

---

1. The first version of this paper was presented in October 1972 as a lecture in the course "Women: Myth and Reality" at Sarah Lawrence College. I received helpful comments from the students and from my co-teachers in the course: Joan Kelly Gadol, Eva Kollisch, and Gerda Lerner. A short account was delivered at the American Anthropo-logical Association meetings in Toronto, November 1972. Meanwhile, I received excellent critical comments from Karen Blu, Robert Paul, Michelle Rosaldo, David Schneider, and Terence Turner, and the present version of the paper, in which the thrust of the argument has been rather signifi-cantly changed, was written in response to those comments. I, of course, retain responsibility for its final form. The paper is dedicated to Simone de

particulars. By this canon, woman provides us with one of the more challenging problems to be dealt with. The secondary status of woman in society is one of the true universals, a pan-cultural fact. Yet within that universal fact, the specific cultural conceptions and symbolizations of woman are extraordinarily diverse and even mutually contradictory. Further, the actual treatment of women and their relative power and contribution vary enormously from culture to culture, and over different periods in the history of particular cultural traditions. Both of these points—the universal fact and the cultural variation—constitute problems to be explained.

My interest in the problem is of course more than academic: I wish to see genuine change come about, the emergence of a social and cultural order in which as much of the range of human potential is open to women as is open to men. The universality of female subordination, the fact that it exists within every type of social and economic arrangement and in societies of every degree of complexity, indicates to me that we are up against something very profound, very stubborn, something we cannot rout out simply by rearranging a few tasks and roles in the social system, or even by reordering the whole economic structure. In this paper I try to expose the underlying logic of cultural thinking that assumes the inferiority of women; I try to show the highly persuasive nature of the logic, for if it were not so persuasive, people would not keep subscribing to it. But I also try to show the social and cultural sources of that logic, to indicate wherein lies the potential for change.

It is important to sort out the levels of the problem. The confusion can be staggering. For example, depending on which aspect of Chinese culture we look at, we might extrapolate any of several entirely different guesses concerning the status of women in China. In the ideology of Taoism, *yin*, the female principle, and *yang*, the male principle, are given equal weight; "the opposition, alternation, and interaction of these two forces give rise to all phenomena in the universe" (Siu, 1968: 2). Hence we might guess that maleness and femaleness are equally valued in the general ideology of Chinese culture.[2] Looking at the social structure, however, we see the strongly emphasized patrilineal descent principle, the importance of sons, and the absolute authority of the father in the family. Thus we might conclude that China is the archetypal patriarchal society. Next, looking at the actual roles played, power and influence wielded, and material contributions made by women in Chinese society—all of which are, upon observation, quite substantial—we would have to say that women are allotted a great deal of (unspoken) status in the system. Or again, we might focus on the fact that a goddess, Kuan Yin, is the central (most worshiped, most depicted) deity in Chinese Buddhism, and we might be tempted to say, as many have tried to say about goddess-worshiping cultures in prehistoric and early historical societies, that China is actually a sort of matriarchy. In short, we must be absolutely clear about *what* we are trying to explain before explaining it.

Beauvoir, whose book *The Second Sex* (1953), first published in French in 1949, remains in my opinion the best single comprehensive understanding of "the woman problem." [Except as indicated, all notes are Ortner's.]

2. It is true of course that *yin*, the female princi-

ple, has a negative valence. Nonetheless, there is an absolute complementarity of *yin* and *yang* in Taoism, a recognition that the world requires the equal operation and interaction of both principles for its survival.

We may differentiate three levels of the problem:

1. The universal fact of culturally attributed second-class status of woman in every society. Two questions are important here. First, what do we mean by this; what is our evidence that this is a universal fact? And second, how are we to explain this fact, once having established it?

2. Specific ideologies, symbolizations, and socio-structural arrangements pertaining to women that vary widely from culture to culture. The problem at this level is to account for any particular cultural complex in terms of factors specific to that group—the standard level of anthropological analysis.

3. Observable on-the-ground details of women's activities, contributions, powers, influence, etc., often at variance with cultural ideology (although always constrained within the assumption that women may never be officially preeminent in the total system). This is the level of direct observation, often adopted now by feminist-oriented anthropologists.

This paper is primarily concerned with the first of these levels, the problem of the universal devaluation of women. The analysis thus depends not upon specific cultural data but rather upon an analysis of "culture" taken generically as a special sort of process in the world. A discussion of the second level, the problem of cross-cultural variation in conceptions and relative valuations of women, will entail a great deal of cross-cultural research and must be postponed to another time. As for the third level, it will be obvious from my approach that I would consider it a misguided endeavor to focus only upon women's actual though culturally unrecognized and unvalued powers in any given society, without first understanding the overarching ideology and deeper assumptions of the culture that render such powers trivial.

The Universality of Female Subordination

What do I mean when I say that everywhere, in every known culture, women are considered in some degree inferior to men? First of all, I must stress that I am talking about *cultural* evaluations; I am saying that each culture, in its own way and on its own terms, makes this evaluation. But what would constitute evidence that a particular culture considers women inferior?

Three types of data would suffice: (1) elements of cultural ideology and informants' statements that *explicitly* devalue women, according them, their roles, their tasks, their products, and their social milieux less prestige than are accorded men and the male correlates; (2) symbolic devices, such as the attribution of defilement, which may be interpreted as *implicitly* making a statement of inferior valuation; and (3) social-structural arrangements that exclude women from participation in or contact with some realm in which the highest powers of the society are felt to reside.[3] These three types of data may all of course be interrelated in any particular system, though they need not necessarily be. Further, any one of them will usually be sufficient to make the point of female inferiority in a given culture. Certainly, female exclusion from the most sacred rite or the highest political council is sufficient evidence. Certainly, explicit cultural ideology devaluing women (and their tasks, roles,

---

3. Some anthropologists might consider this type of evidence (social-structural arrangements that exclude women, explicitly or de facto, from certain groups, roles, or statuses) to be a subtype of the second type of evidence (symbolic formulations of inferiority). I would not disagree with this view, although most social anthropologists would probably separate the two types.

products, etc.) is sufficient evidence. Symbolic indicators such as defilement are usually sufficient, although in a few cases in which, say, men and women are equally polluting to one another, a further indicator is required—and is, as far as my investigations have ascertained, always available.

On any or all of these counts, then, I would flatly assert that we find women subordinated to men in every known society. The search for a genuinely egalitarian, let alone matriarchal, culture has proved fruitless. An example from one society that has traditionally been on the credit side of this ledger will suffice. Among the matrilineal Crow, as Lowie (1956) points out, "Women . . . had highly honorific offices in the Sun Dance; they could become directors of the Tobacco Ceremony and played, if anything, a more conspicuous part in it than the men; they sometimes played the hostess in the Cooked Meat Festival; they were not debarred from sweating or doctoring or from seeking a vision" (p. 61). Nonetheless, "Women [during menstruation] formerly rode inferior horses and evidently this loomed as a source of contamination, for they were not allowed to approach either a wounded man or men starting on a war party. A taboo still lingers against their coming near sacred objects at these times" (p. 44). Further, just before enumerating women's rights of participation in the various rituals noted above, Lowie mentions one particular Sun Dance Doll bundle that was not supposed to be unwrapped by a woman (p. 60). Pursuing this trail we find: "According to all Lodge Grass informants and most others, the doll owned by Wrinkled-face took precedence not only of other dolls but of all other Crow medicines whatsoever. . . . This particular doll was not supposed to be handled by a woman" (p. 229).[4]

In sum, the Crow are probably a fairly typical case. Yes, women have certain powers and rights, in this case some that place them in fairly high positions. Yet ultimately the line is drawn: menstruation is a threat to warfare, one of the most valued institutions of the tribe, one that is central to their self-definition; and the most sacred object of the tribe is taboo to the direct sight and touch of women.

Similar examples could be multiplied ad infinitum, but I think the onus is no longer upon us to demonstrate that female subordination is a cultural universal; it is up to those who would argue against the point to bring forth counterexamples. I shall take the universal secondary status of women as a given, and proceed from there.

Nature and Culture[5]

How are we to explain the universal devaluation of women? We could of course rest the case on biological determinism. There is something genetically inherent in the male of the species, so the biological determinists would argue, that makes them the naturally dominant sex; that "something" is lacking in females, and as a result women are not only naturally subordinate but in general quite satisfied with their position, since it affords them protection and the opportunity to maximize maternal pleasures, which to them are the

---

4. While we are on the subject of injustices of various kinds, we might note that Lowie secretly bought this doll, the most sacred object in the tribal repertoire, from its custodian, the widow of Wrinkled-face. She asked $400 for it, but this price was "far beyond [Lowie's] means," and he finally got it for $80 (p. 300).

5. With all due respect to Lévi-Strauss (1969a,b, and *passim*).

most satisfying experiences of life. Without going into a detailed refutation of this position, I think it fair to say that it has failed to be established to the satisfaction of almost anyone in academic anthropology. This is to say, not that biological facts are irrelevant, or that men and women are not different, but that these facts and differences only take on significance of superior/inferior within the framework of culturally defined value systems.

If we are unwilling to rest the case on genetic determinism, it seems to me that we have only one way to proceed. We must attempt to interpret female subordination in light of other universals, factors built into the structure of the most generalized situation in which all human beings, in whatever culture, find themselves. For example, every human being has a physical body and a sense of nonphysical mind, is part of a society of other individuals and an inheritor of a cultural tradition, and must engage in some relationship, however mediated, with "nature," or the nonhuman realm, in order to survive. Every human being is born (to a mother) and ultimately dies, all are assumed to have an interest in personal survival, and society/culture has its own interest in (or at least momentum toward) continuity and survival, which transcends the lives and deaths of particular individuals. And so forth. It is in the realm of such universals of the human condition that we must seek an explanation for the universal fact of female devaluation.

I translate the problem, in other words, into the following simple question. What could there be in the generalized structure and conditions of existence, common to every culture, that would lead every culture to place a lower value upon women? Specifically, my thesis is that woman is being identified with— or, if you will, seems to be a symbol of—something that every culture devalues, something that every culture defines as being of a lower order of existence than itself. Now it seems that there is only one thing that would fit that description, and that is "nature" in the most generalized sense. Every culture, or, generically, "culture," is engaged in the process of generating and sustaining systems of meaningful forms (symbols, artifacts, etc.) by means of which humanity transcends the givens of natural existence, bends them to its purposes, controls them in its interest. We may thus broadly equate culture with the notion of human consciousness, or with the products of human consciousness (i.e., systems of thought and technology), by means of which humanity attempts to assert control over nature.

Now the categories of "nature" and "culture" are of course conceptual categories—one can find no boundary out in the actual world between the two states or realms of being. And there is no question that some cultures articulate a much stronger opposition between the two categories than others— it has even been argued that primitive peoples (some or all) do not see or intuit any distinction between the human cultural state and the state of nature at all. Yet I would maintain that the universality of ritual betokens an assertion in all human cultures of the specifically human ability to act upon and regulate, rather than passively move with and be moved by, the givens of natural existence. In ritual, the purposive manipulation of given forms toward regulating and sustaining order, every culture asserts that proper relations between human existence and natural forces depend upon culture's employing its special powers to regulate the overall processes of the world and life.

One realm of cultural thought in which these points are often articulated is that of concepts of purity and pollution. Virtually every culture has some such beliefs, which seem in large part (though not, of course, entirely) to be concerned with the relationship between culture and nature (see Ortner, 1973, n.d.). A well-known aspect of purity/pollution beliefs cross-culturally is that of the natural "contagion" of pollution; left to its own devices, pollution (for these purposes grossly equated with the unregulated operation of natural energies) spreads and overpowers all that it comes in contact with. Thus a puzzle—if pollution is so strong, how can anything be purified? Why is the purifying agent not itself polluted? The answer, in keeping with the present line of argument, is that purification is effected in a ritual context; purification ritual, as a purposive activity that pits self-conscious (symbolic) action against natural energies, is more powerful than those energies.

In any case, my point is simply that every culture implicitly recognizes and asserts a distinction between the operation of nature and the operation of culture (human consciousness and its products); and further, that the distinctiveness of culture rests precisely on the fact that it can under most circumstances transcend natural conditions and turn them to its purposes. Thus culture (i.e. every culture) at some level of awareness asserts itself to be not only distinct from but superior to nature, and that sense of distinctiveness and superiority rests precisely on the ability to transform—to "socialize" and "culturalize"—nature.

Returning now to the issue of women, their pan-cultural second-class status could be accounted for, quite simply, by postulating that women are being identified or symbolically associated with nature, as opposed to men, who are identified with culture. Since it is always culture's project to subsume and transcend nature, if women were considered part of nature, then culture would find it "natural" to subordinate, not to say oppress, them. Yet although this argument can be shown to have considerable force, it seems to oversimplify the case. The formulation I would like to defend and elaborate on in the following section, then, is that women are seen "merely" as being *closer* to nature than men. That is, culture (still equated relatively unambiguously with men) recognizes that women are active participants in its special processes, but at the same time sees them as being more rooted in, or having more direct affinity with, nature.

The revision may seem minor or even trivial, but I think it is a more accurate rendering of cultural assumptions. Further, the argument cast in these terms has several analytic advantages over the simpler formulation; I shall discuss these later. It might simply be stressed here that the revised argument would still account for the pan-cultural devaluation of women, for even if women are not equated with nature, they are nonetheless seen as representing a lower order of being, as being less transcendental of nature than men are. The next task of the paper, then, is to consider why they might be viewed in that way.

Why Is Woman Seen as Closer to Nature?

It all begins of course with the body and the natural procreative functions specific to women alone. We can sort out for discussion three levels at which this absolute physiological fact has significance: (1) woman's *body and its functions*, more involved more of the time with "species life," seem to place her closer to nature, in contrast to man's physiology, which frees him more completely to take up the projects of culture; (2) woman's body and its functions place her in *social roles* that in turn are considered to be at a lower order of the cultural process than man's; and (3) woman's traditional social roles, imposed because of her body and its functions, in turn give her a different *psychic structure*, which, like her physiological nature and her social roles, is seen as being closer to nature. I shall discuss each of these points in turn, showing first how in each instance certain factors strongly tend to align woman with nature, then indicating other factors that demonstrate her full alignment with culture, the combined factors thus placing her in a problematic intermediate position. It will become clear in the course of the discussion why men seem by contrast less intermediate, more purely "cultural" than women. And I reiterate that I am dealing only at the level of cultural and human universals. These arguments are intended to apply to generalized humanity; they grow out of the human condition, as humanity has experienced and confronted it up to the present day.

1. *Woman's physiology seen as closer to nature.* This part of my argument has been anticipated, with subtlety, cogency, and a great deal of hard data, by de Beauvoir (1953). De Beauvoir reviews the physiological structure, development, and functions of the human female and concludes that "the female, to a greater extent than the male, is the prey of the species" (p. 60). She points out that many major areas and processes of the woman's body serve no apparent function for the health and stability of the individual; on the contrary, as they perform their specific organic functions, they are often sources of discomfort, pain, and danger. The breasts are irrelevant to personal health; they may be excised at any time of a woman's life. "Many of the ovarian secretions function for the benefit of the egg, promoting its maturation and adapting the uterus to its requirements; in respect to the organism as a whole, they make for disequilibrium rather than for regulation—the woman is adapted to the needs of the egg rather than to her own requirements" (p. 24). Menstruation is often uncomfortable, sometimes painful; it frequently has negative emotional correlates and in any case involves bothersome tasks of cleansing and waste disposal; and—a point that de Beauvoir does not mention—in many cultures it interrupts a woman's routine, putting her in a stigmatized state involving various restrictions on her activities and social contacts. In pregnancy many of the woman's vitamin and mineral resources are channeled into nourishing the fetus, depleting her own strength and energies. And finally, childbirth itself is painful and dangerous (pp. 24–27 *passim*). In sum, de Beauvoir concludes that the female "is more enslaved to the species than the male, her animality is more manifest" (p. 239).

While de Beauvoir's book is ideological, her survey of woman's physiological situation seems fair and accurate. It is simply a fact that proportionately more of woman's body space, for a greater percentage of her lifetime, and at some—sometimes great—cost to her personal health, strength, and general stability, is taken up with the natural processes surrounding the reproduction of the species.

De Beauvoir goes on to discuss the negative implications of woman's "enslavement to the species" in relation to the projects in which humans engage, projects through which culture is generated and defined. She arrives thus at the crux of her argument (pp. 58–59):

> Here we have the key to the whole mystery. On the biological level a species is maintained only by creating itself anew; but this creation results only in repeating the same Life in more individuals. But man assures the repetition of Life while transcending Life through Existence [i.e. goal-oriented, meaningful action]; by this transcendence he creates values that deprive pure repetition of all value. In the animal, the freedom and variety of male activities are vain because no project is involved. Except for his services to the species, what he does is immaterial. Whereas in serving the species, the human male also remodels the face of the earth, he creates new instruments, he invents, he shapes the future.

In other words, woman's body seems to doom her to mere reproduction of life; the male, in contrast, lacking natural creative functions, must (or has the opportunity to) assert his creativity externally, "artificially," through the medium of technology and symbols. In so doing, he creates relatively lasting, eternal, transcendent objects, while the woman creates only perishables— human beings.

This formulation opens up a number of important insights. It speaks, for example, to the great puzzle of why male activities involving the destruction of life (hunting and warfare) are often given more prestige than the female's ability to give birth, to create life. Within de Beauvoir's framework, we realize it is not the killing that is the relevant and valued aspect of hunting and warfare; rather, it is the transcendental (social, cultural) nature of these activities, as opposed to the naturalness of the process of birth: "For it is not in giving life but in risking life that man is raised above the animal; that is why superiority has been accorded in humanity not to the sex that brings forth but to that which kills" (*ibid.*).

Thus if male is, as I am suggesting, everywhere (unconsciously) associated with culture and female seems closer to nature, the rationale for these associations is not very difficult to grasp, merely from considering the implications of the physiological contrast between male and female. At the same time, however, woman cannot be consigned fully to the category of nature, for it is perfectly obvious that she is a full-fledged human being endowed with human consciousness just as a man is; she is half of the human race, without whose cooperation the whole enterprise would collapse. She may seem more in the possession of nature than man, but having consciousness, she thinks and speaks; she generates, communicates, and manipulates symbols, categories, and values. She participates in human dialogues not only with other women but also with men. As Lévi-Strauss says, "Woman could never become just a sign and nothing more, since even in a man's world she is still a person, and since insofar as she is defined as a sign she must [still] be recognized as a generator of signs" (1969a: 496).

Indeed, the fact of woman's full human consciousness, her full involvement in and commitment to culture's project of transcendence over nature, may ironically explain another of the great puzzles of "the woman problem"—woman's nearly universal unquestioning acceptance of her own devaluation. For it would seem that, as a conscious human and member of culture, she has followed out the logic of culture's arguments and has reached culture's conclusions along with the men. As de Beauvoir puts it (p. 59):

> For she, too, is an existent, she feels the urge to surpass, and her project is not mere repetition but transcendence towards a different future—in her heart of hearts she finds confirmation of the masculine pretensions. She joins the men in the festivals that celebrate the successes and victories of the males. Her misfortune is to have been biologically destined for the repetition of Life, when even in her own view Life does not carry within itself its reasons for being, reasons that are more important than life itself.

In other words, woman's consciousness—her membership, as it were, in culture—is evidenced in part by the very fact that she accepts her own devaluation and takes culture's point of view.

I have tried here to show one part of the logic of that view, the part that grows directly from the physiological differences between men and women. Because of woman's greater bodily involvement with the natural functions surrounding reproduction, she is seen as more a part of nature than man is. Yet in part because of her consciousness and participation in human social dialogue, she is recognized as a participant in culture. Thus she appears as something intermediate between culture and nature, lower on the scale of transcendence than man.

2. *Woman's social role seen as closer to nature.* Woman's physiological functions, I have just argued, may tend in themselves to motivate[6] a view of woman as closer to nature, a view she herself, as an observer of herself and the world, would tend to agree with. Woman creates naturally from within her own being, whereas man is free to, or forced to, create artificially, that is, through cultural means, and in such a way as to sustain culture. In addition, I now wish to show how woman's physiological functions have tended universally to limit her social movement, and to confine her universally to certain social contexts which *in turn* are seen as closer to nature. That is, not only her bodily processes but the social situation in which her bodily processes locate her may carry this significance. And insofar as she is permanently associated (in the eyes of culture) with these social milieux, they add weight (perhaps the decisive part of the burden) to the view of woman as closer to nature. I refer here of course to woman's confinement to the domestic family context, a confinement motivated, no doubt, by her lactation processes.

Woman's body, like that of all female mammals, generates milk during and after pregnancy for the feeding of the newborn baby. The baby cannot survive without breast milk or some similar formula at this stage of life. Since the mother's body goes through its lactation processes in direct relation to a pregnancy with a particular child, the relationship of nursing between mother

---

6. Semantic theory uses the concept of motivation of meaning, which encompasses various ways in which a meaning may be assigned to a symbol because of certain objective properties of that symbol, rather than by arbitrary association. In a sense, this entire paper is an inquiry into the motivation of the meaning of woman as a symbol, asking why woman may be unconsciously assigned the significance of being closer to nature. For a concise statement on the various types of motivation of meaning, see Ullman (1963).

and child is seen as a natural bond, other feeding arrangements being seen in most cases as unnatural and make-shift. Mothers and their children, according to cultural reasoning, belong together. Further, children beyond infancy are not strong enough to engage in major work, yet are mobile and unruly and not capable of understanding various dangers; they thus require supervision and constant care. Mother is the obvious person for this task, as an extension of her natural nursing bond with the children, or because she has a new infant and is already involved with child-oriented activities. Her own activities are thus circumscribed by the limitations and low levels of her children's strengths and skills:[7] she is confined to the domestic family group; "woman's place is in the home."

Woman's association with the domestic circle would contribute to the view of her as closer to nature in several ways. In the first place, the sheer fact of constant association with children plays a role in the issue; one can easily see how infants and children might themselves be considered part of nature. Infants are barely human and utterly unsocialized; like animals they are unable to walk upright, they excrete without control, they do not speak. Even slightly older children are clearly not yet fully under the sway of culture. They do not yet understand social duties, responsibilities, and morals; their vocabulary and their range of learned skills are small. One finds implicit recognition of an association between children and nature in many cultural practices. For example, most cultures have initiation rites for adolescents (primarily for boys; I shall return to this point below), the point of which is to move the child ritually from a less than fully human state into full participation in society and culture; many cultures do not hold funeral rites for children who die at early ages, explicitly because they are not yet fully social beings. Thus children are likely to be categorized with nature, and woman's close association with children may compound her potential for being seen as closer to nature herself. It is ironic that the rationale for boys' initiation rites in many cultures is that the boys must be purged of the defilement accrued from being around mother and other women so much of the time, when in fact much of the woman's defilement may derive from her being around children so much of the time.

The second major problematic implication of women's close association with the domestic context derives from certain structural conflicts between the family and society at large in any social system. The implications of the "domestic/public opposition" in relation to the position of women have been cogently developed by Rosaldo (this volume[8]), and I simply wish to show its relevance to the present argument. The notion that the domestic unit—the biological family charged with reproducing and socializing new members of the society—is opposed to the public entity—the superimposed network of alliances and relationships that *is* the society—is also the basis of Lévi-Strauss's argument in the *Elementary Structures of Kinship* (1969a). Lévi-Strauss argues not only that this opposition is present in every social system, but further that it has the significance of the opposition between nature and culture. The universal incest prohibition[9] and its ally, the rule of exogamy

---

7. A situation that often serves to make her more childlike herself.

8. I.e., *Woman, Culture, and Society*; see Rosaldo, 1974 [editor's note].

9. David M. Schneider (personal communication) is prepared to argue that the incest taboo is not universal, on the basis of material from Oceania. Let us say at this point, then, that it is virtually universal.

(marriage outside the group), ensure that "the risk of seeing a biological family become established as a closed system is definitely eliminated; the biological group can no longer stand apart, and the bond of alliance with another family ensures the dominance of the social over the biological, and of the cultural over the natural" (p. 479). And although not every culture articulates a radical opposition between the domestic and the public as such, it is hardly contestable that the domestic is always subsumed by the public; domestic units are allied with one another through the enactment of rules that are logically at a higher level than the units themselves; this creates an emergent unit—society—that is logically at a higher level than the domestic units of which it is composed.

Now, since women are associated with, and indeed are more or less confined to, the domestic context, they are identified with this lower order of social/cultural organization. What are the implications of this for the way they are viewed? First, if the specifically biological (reproductive) function of the family is stressed, as in Lévi-Strauss's formulation, then the family (and hence woman) is identified with nature pure and simple, as opposed to culture. But this is obviously too simple; the point seems more adequately formulated as follows: the family (and hence woman) represents lower-level, socially fragmenting, particularistic sort of concerns, as opposed to interfamilial relations representing higher-level, integrative, universalistic sorts of concerns. Since men lack a "natural" basis (nursing, generalized to child care) for a familial orientation, their sphere of activity is defined at the level of interfamilial relations. And hence, so the cultural reasoning seems to go, men are the "natural" proprietors of religion, ritual, politics, and other realms of cultural thought and action in which universalistic statements of spiritual and social synthesis are made. Thus men are identified not only with culture, in the sense of all human creativity, as opposed to nature; they are identified in particular with culture in the old-fashioned sense of the finer and higher aspects of human thought—art, religion, law etc.

Here again, the logic of cultural reasoning aligning woman with a lower order of culture than man is clear and, on the surface, quite compelling. At the same time, woman cannot be fully consigned to nature, for there are aspects of her situation, even within the domestic context, that undeniably demonstrate her participation in the cultural process. It goes without saying, of course, that except for nursing newborn infants (and artificial nursing devices can cut even this biological tie), there is no reason why it has to be mother—as opposed to father, or anyone else—who remains identified with child care. But even assuming that other practical and emotional reasons conspire to keep woman in this sphere, it is possible to show that her activities in the domestic context could as logically put her squarely in the category of culture.

In the first place, one must point out that woman not only feeds and cleans up after children in a simple caretaker operation; she in fact is the primary agent of their early socialization. It is she who transforms newborn infants from mere organisms into cultured humans, teaching them manners and the proper ways to behave in order to become full-fledged members of the culture. On the basis of her socializing functions alone, she could not be more a representative of culture. Yet in virtually every society there is a point at which the socialization of boys is transferred to the hands of men. The boys are considered, in one set of terms or another, not yet "really" socialized; their entrée into the realm of fully human (social, cultural) status can be accomplished only by men. We still see this in our own schools, where there is a gradual inversion in the proportion of female to male teachers up through the grades: most kindergarten teachers are female; most university professors are male.[1]

Or again, take cooking. In the overwhelming majority of societies cooking is the woman's work. No doubt this stems from practical considerations—since the woman has to stay home with the baby, it is convenient for her to perform the chores centered in the home. But if it is true, as Lévi-Strauss has argued (1969b), that transforming the raw into the cooked may represent, in many systems of thought, the transition from nature to culture, then here we have woman aligned with this important culturalizing process, which could easily place her in the category of culture, triumphing over nature. Yet it is also interesting to note that when a culture (e.g. France or China) develops a tradition of *haute cuisine*—"real" cooking, as opposed to trivial ordinary domestic cooking—the high chefs are almost always men. Thus the pattern replicates that in the area of socialization—women perform lower-level conversions from nature to culture, but when the culture distinguishes a higher level of the same functions, the higher level is restricted to men.

In short, we see once again some sources of woman's appearing more intermediate than man with respect to the nature/culture dichotomy. Her "natural" association with the domestic context (motivated by her natural lactation functions) tends to compound her potential for being viewed as closer to nature, because of the animal-like nature of children, and because of the infrasocial connotation of the domestic group as against the rest of society. Yet at the same time her socializing and cooking functions within the domestic context show her to be a powerful agent of the cultural process, constantly transforming raw natural resources into cultural products. Belonging to culture, yet appearing to have stronger and more direct connections with nature, she is once again seen as situated between the two realms.

3. *Woman's psyche seen as closer to nature.* The suggestion that woman has not only a different body and a different social locus from man but also a different psychic structure is most controversial. I will argue that she probably *does* have a different psychic structure, but I will draw heavily on Chodorow's paper (this volume)[2] to establish first that her psychic structure need not be assumed to be innate; it can be accounted for, as Chodorow convincingly shows, by the facts of the probably universal female socialization experience. Nonetheless, if we grant the empirical near universality of a "feminine psyche" with certain specific characteristics, these characteristics would add weight to the cultural view of woman as closer to nature.

It is important to specify what we see as the dominant and universal aspects of the feminine psyche. If we postulate emotionality or irrationality, we are confronted with those traditions in various parts of the world in which women functionally are, and are seen as, more practical, pragmatic, and this-worldly than men. One relevant dimension that does seem pan-culturally applicable is that of relative concreteness vs. relative abstractness: the feminine personality tends to be involved with concrete feelings, things, and people, rather than with abstract entities; it tends toward personalism and

---

1. I remember having my first male teacher in the fifth grade, and I remember being excited about that—it was somehow more grown-up.

2. I.e., Chodorow, 1974; see below, pp. 367–88 [editor's note].

particularism. A second, closely related, dimension seems to be that of relative subjectivity vs. relative objectivity: Chodorow cites Carlson's study (1971), which concludes that "males represent experiences of self, others, space, and time in individualistic, objective, and distant ways, while females represent experiences in relatively interpersonal, subjective, immediate ways" (this volume, p. 56, quoting Carlson, p. 270). Although this and other studies were done in Western societies, Chodorow sees their findings on the differences between male and female personality—roughly, that men are more objective and inclined to relate in terms of relatively abstract categories, women more subjective and inclined to relate in terms of relatively concrete phenomena—as "general and nearly universal differences" (p. 43).

But the thrust of Chodorow's elegantly argued paper is that these differences are not innate or genetically programmed; they arise from nearly universal features of family structure, namely that "women, universally, are largely responsible for early child care and for (at least) later female socialization" (p. 43) and that "the structural situation of child rearing, reinforced by female and male role training, produces these differences, which are replicated and reproduced in the sexual sociology of adult life" (p. 44). Chodorow argues that, because mother is the early socializer of both boys and girls, both develop "personal identification" with her, i.e. diffuse identification with her general personality, behavior traits, values, and attitudes (p. 51). A son, however, must ultimately shift to a masculine role identity, which involves building an identification with the father. Since father is almost always more remote than mother (he is rarely involved in child care, and perhaps works away from home much of the day), building an identification with father involves a "positional identification," i.e. identification with father's male role as a collection of abstract elements, rather than a personal identification with father as a real individual (p. 49). Further, as the boy enters the larger social world, he finds it in fact organized around more abstract and universalistic criteria (see Rosaldo, this volume, pp. 28–29; Chodorow, p. 58), as I have indicated in the previous section; thus his earlier socialization prepares him for, and is reinforced by, the type of adult social experience he will have.

For a young girl, in contrast, the personal identification with mother, which was created in early infancy, can persist into the process of learning female role identity. Because mother is immediate and present when the daughter is learning role identity, learning to be a woman involves the continuity and development of a girl's relationship to her mother, and sustains the identification with her as an individual; it does not involve the learning of externally defined role characteristics (Chodorow, p. 51). This pattern prepares the girl for, and is fully reinforced by, her social situation in later life; she will become involved in the world of women, which is characterized by few formal role differences (Rosaldo, p. 29), and which involves again, in motherhood, "personal identification" with *her* children. And so the cycle begins anew.

Chodorow demonstrates to my satisfaction at least that the feminine personality, characterized by personalism and particularism, can be explained as having been generated by social-structural arrangements rather than by innate biological factors. The point need not be belabored further. But insofar as the "feminine personality" has been a nearly universal fact, it can be argued that its characteristics may have contributed further to the view of women as being somehow less cultural than men. That is, women would tend to enter into relationships with the world that culture might see as being more "like nature"—immanent and embedded in things as given—than "like culture"—transcending and transforming things through the superimposition of abstract categories and transpersonal values. Woman's relationships tend to be, like nature, relatively unmediated, more direct, whereas man not only tends to relate in a more mediated way, but in fact ultimately often relates more consistently and strongly to the mediating categories and forms than to the persons or objects themselves.

It is thus not difficult to see how the feminine personality would lend weight to a view of women as being "closer to nature." Yet at the same time, the modes of relating characteristic of women undeniably play a powerful and important role in the cultural process. For just as relatively unmediated relating is in some sense at the lower end of the spectrum of human spiritual functions, embedded and particularizing rather than transcending and synthesizing, yet that mode of relating also stands at the upper end of that spectrum. Consider the mother-child relationship. Mothers tend to be committed to their children as individuals, regardless of sex, age, beauty, clan affiliation, or other categories in which the child might participate. Now any relationship with this quality—not just mother and child but any sort of highly personal, relatively unmediated commitment—may be seen as a challenge to culture and society "from below," insofar as it represents the fragmentary potential of individual loyalties vis-à-vis the solidarity of the group. But it may also be seen as embodying the synthesizing agent for culture and society "from above," in that it represents generalized human values above and beyond loyalties to particular social categories. Every society must have social categories that transcend personal loyalties, but every society must also generate a sense of ultimate moral unity for all its members above and beyond those social categories. Thus that psychic mode seemingly typical of women, which tends to disregard categories and to seek "communion" (Chodorow, p. 55, following Bakan, 1966) directly and personally with others, although it may appear infracultural from one point of view, is at the same time associated with the highest levels of the cultural process.

The Implications of Intermediacy

My primary purpose in this paper has been to attempt to explain the universal secondary status of women. Intellectually and personally, I felt strongly challenged by this problem; I felt compelled to deal with it before undertaking an analysis of woman's position in any particular society. Local variables of economy, ecology, history, political and social structure, values, and world view—these could explain variations within this universal, but they could not explain the universal itself. And if we were not to accept the ideology of biological determinism, then explanation, it seemed to me, could only proceed by reference to other universals of the human cultural situation. Thus the general outlines of the approach—although not of course the particular solution offered—were determined by the problem itself, and not by any predilection on my part for global abstract structural analysis.

I argued that the universal devaluation of women could be explained by postulating that women are seen as closer to nature than men, men being seen as more unequivocally occupying the high ground of culture. The culture/nature distinction is itself a product of culture, culture being minimally defined as the transcendence, by means of systems of thought and technology, of the natural givens of existence. This of course is an analytic definition, but I argued that at some level every culture incorporates this notion in one form or other, if only through the performance of ritual as an assertion of the human ability to manipulate those givens. In any case, the core of the paper was concerned with showing why women might tend to be assumed, over and over, in the most diverse sorts of world views and in cultures of every degree of complexity, to be closer to nature than men. Woman's physiology, more involved more of the time with "species of life"; woman's association with the structurally subordinate domestic context, charged with the crucial function of transforming animal-like infants into cultured beings; "woman's psyche," appropriately molded to mothering functions by her own socialization and tending toward greater personalism and less mediated modes of relating—all these factors make woman appear to be rooted more directly and deeply in nature. At the same time, however, her "membership" and fully necessary participation in culture are recognized by culture and cannot be denied. Thus she is seen to occupy an intermediate position between culture and nature.

This intermediacy has several implications for analysis, depending upon how it is interpreted. First, of course, it answers my primary question of why woman is everywhere seen as lower than man, for even if she is not seen as nature pure and simple, she is still seen as achieving less transcendence of nature than man. Here intermediate simply means "middle status" on a hierarchy of being from culture to nature.

Second, intermediate may have the significance of "mediating," i.e. performing some sort of synthesizing or converting function between nature and culture, here seen (by culture) not as two ends of a continuum but as two radically different sorts of processes in the world. The domestic unit—and hence woman, who in virtually every case appears as its primary representative—is one of culture's crucial agencies for the conversion of nature into culture, especially with reference to the socialization of children. Any culture's continued viability depends upon properly socialized individuals who will see the world in that culture's terms and adhere more or less unquestioningly to its moral precepts. The functions of the domestic unit must be closely controlled in order to ensure this outcome; the stability of the domestic unit as an institution must be placed as far as possible beyond question. (We see some aspects of the protection of the integrity and stability of the domestic group in the powerful taboos against incest, matricide, patricide, and fratricide.[3]) Insofar as woman is universally the primary agent of early socialization and is seen as virtually the embodiment of the functions of the domestic group, she will tend to come under the heavier restrictions and circumscriptions surrounding that unit. Her (culturally defined) intermediate position between nature and culture, here having the significance of her *mediation* (i.e. performing conversion functions) between nature and culture, would thus account not only for her lower status but for the greater restrictions placed upon her activities. In virtually every culture her permissible sexual activities are more closely circumscribed than man's, she is offered a much smaller range of role choices, and she is afforded direct access to a far more limited

---

3. Nobody seems to care much about sororicide—a point that ought to be investigated.

range of its social institutions. Further, she is almost universally socialized to have a narrower and generally more conservative set of attitudes and views than man, and the limited social contexts of her adult life reinforce this situation. This socially engendered conservatism and traditionalism of woman's thinking is another—perhaps the worst, certainly the most insidious—mode of social restriction, and would clearly be related to her traditional function of producing well-socialized members of the group.

Finally, woman's intermediate position may have the implication of greater symbolic ambiguity (see also Rosaldo, this volume). Shifting our image of the culture/nature relationship once again, we may envision culture in this case as a small clearing within the forest of the larger natural system. From this point of view, that which is intermediate between culture and nature is located on the continuous periphery of culture's clearing; and though it may thus appear to stand both above and below (and beside) culture, it is simply outside and around it. We can begin to understand then how a single system of cultural thought can often assign to woman completely polarized and apparently contradictory meanings, since extremes, as we say, meet. That she often represents both life and death is only the simplest example one could mention.

For another perspective on the same point, it will be recalled that the psychic mode associated with women seems to stand at both the bottom and the top of the scale of human modes of relating. The tendency in that mode is to get involved more directly with people as individuals and not as representatives of one social category or another; this mode can be seen as either "ignoring" (and thus subverting) or "transcending" (and thus achieving a higher synthesis of) those social categories, depending upon the cultural view for any given purpose. Thus we can account easily for both the subversive feminine symbols (witches, evil eye, menstrual pollution, castrating mothers) and the feminine symbols of transcendence (mother goddesses, merciful dispensers of salvation, female symbols of justice, and the strong presence of feminine symbolism in the realms of art, religion, ritual, and law). Feminine symbolism, far more often than masculine symbolism, manifests this propensity toward polarized ambiguity—sometimes utterly exalted, sometimes utterly debased, rarely within the normal range of human possibilities.

If woman's (culturally viewed) intermediacy between culture and nature has this implication of generalized ambiguity of meaning characteristic of marginal phenomena, then we are also in a better position to account for those cultural and historical "inversions" in which women are in some way or other symbolically aligned with culture and men with nature. A number of cases come to mind: the Siriono of Brazil, among whom, according to Ingham (1971: 1098), "nature, the raw, and maleness" are opposed to "culture, the cooked, and femaleness";[4] Nazi Germany, in which women were said to be the guardians of culture and morals; European courtly love, in which man considered himself the beast and woman the pristine exalted object—a pattern of thinking that persists, for example, among modern Spanish peasants (see Pitt-Rivers, 1961; Rosaldo, this volume). And there are no doubt other

---

4. Ingham's discussion is rather ambiguous itself, since women are also associated with animals: "The contrasts man/animal and man/woman are evidently similar . . . hunting is the means of acquiring women as well as animals" (p. 1095). A careful reading of the data suggests that both women and animals are mediators between nature and culture in this tradition.

cases of this sort, including some aspects of our own culture's view of women. Each such instance of an alignment of women with culture rather than nature requires detailed analysis of specific historical and ethnographic data. But in indicating how nature in general, and the feminine mode of interpersonal relations in particular, can appear from certain points of view to stand both under and over (but really simply outside of) the sphere of culture's hegemony, we have at least laid the groundwork for such analyses.

In short, the postulate that woman is viewed as closer to nature than man has several implications for further analysis, and can be interpreted in several different ways. If it is viewed simply as a *middle* position on a scale from culture down to nature, then it is still seen as lower than culture and thus accounts for the pan-cultural assumption that woman is lower than man in the order of things. If it is read as a *mediating* element in the culture-nature relationship, then it may account in part for the cultural tendency not merely to devalue woman but to circumscribe and restrict her functions, since culture must maintain control over its (pragmatic and symbolic) mechanisms for the conversion of nature into culture. And if it is read as an *ambiguous* status between culture and nature, it may help account for the fact that, in specific cultural ideologies and symbolizations, woman can occasionally be aligned with culture, and in any event is often assigned polarized and contradictory meanings within a single symbolic system. Middle status, mediating functions, ambiguous meaning—all are different readings, for different contextual purposes, of woman's being seen as intermediate between nature and culture.

Conclusions

Ultimately, it must be stressed again that the whole scheme is a construct of culture rather than a fact of nature. Woman is not "in reality" any closer to (or further from) nature than man—both have consciousness, both are mortal. But there are certainly reasons why she appears that way, which is what I have tried to show in this paper. The result is a (sadly) efficient feedback system: various aspects of woman's situation (physical, social, psychological) contribute to her being seen as closer to nature, while the view of her as closer to nature is in turn embodied in institutional forms that reproduce her situation. The implications for social change are similarly circular: a different cultural view can only grow out of a different social actuality; a different social actuality can only grow out of a different cultural view.

It is clear, then, that the situation must be attacked from both sides. Efforts directed solely at changing the social institutions—through setting quotas on hiring, for example, or through passing equal-pay-for-equal-work laws—cannot have far-reaching effects if cultural language and imagery continue to purvey a relatively devalued view of women. But at the same time efforts directed solely at changing cultural assumptions—through male and female consciousness-raising groups, for example, or through revision of educational materials and mass-media imagery—cannot be successful unless the institutional base of the society is changed to support and reinforce the changed cultural view. Ultimately, both men and women can and must be equally involved in projects of creativity and transcendence. Only then will women be seen as aligned with culture, in culture's ongoing dialectic with nature.

WORKS CITED

Bakan, David. 1966. *The Duality of Human Existence: Isolation and Communion in Western Man.* Boston: Beacon.

Carlson, Rae. 1971. "Sex Differences in Ego Functioning: Exploratory Studies of Agency and Communion." *Journal of Consulting and Clinical Psychology* 37: 267–77.

Chodorow, Nancy. "Family Structure and Feminine Personality." In *Woman, Culture, and Society*, ed. Michelle Z. Rosaldo and Louise Lamphere, 43–66. Stanford: Stanford University Press.

De Beauvoir, Simone. 1953. *The Second Sex.* Trans. H. M. Parshley. New York: Knopf. Originally published in French in 1949.

Ingham, John M. 1971. "Are the Sirionó Raw or Cooked?" *American Anthropologist* 73: 1092–99.

Lévi-Strauss, Claude. 1969a. *The Elementary Structures of Kinship.* Trans. James Harle Bell and John Richard Sturmer; ed. Rodney Needham. Rev. ed. Boston: Beacon.

———. 1969b. *The Raw and the Cooked.* Trans. John and Doreen Weightman. New York: Harper & Row.

Lowie, Robert. 1956. *The Crow Indians.* New York: Holt, Rinehart, and Winston. Originally published in 1935.

Ortner, Sherry B. 1973. "Sherpa Purity." *American Anthropologist* 75: 49–63.

———. n.d. "Purification Beliefs and Practices." In *Encyclopaedia Britannica.* Forthcoming. [Published as "Purification Rites and Customs," 15th ed. (1974)—editor's note.]

Pitt-Rivers, Julian. 1961. *People of the Sierra.* Chicago: University of Chicago Press.

Rosaldo, Michelle Z. 1974. "Woman, Culture, and Society: A Theoretical Overview." In *Woman, Culture, and Society,* ed. Michelle Z. Rosaldo and Louise Lamphere, 7–42. Stanford: Stanford University Press.

Siu, R. G. H. 1968. *The Man of Many Qualities.* Cambridge, Mass.: MIT Press.

Ullman, Stephen. 1963. "Semantic Universals." In *Universals of Language,* ed. Joseph H. Greenberg, 172–207. Cambridge, Mass.: MIT Press.

1972, 1974

NANCY CHODOROW
b. 1944

When girls and boys are brought up by women, they develop different relational capacities and therefore different conceptualizations of self: this idea animates the influential work of Nancy Chodorow, a sociologist and a psychoanalyst. Her *The Reproduction of Mothering: Psychoanalysis and the Sociology of Gender* (1978) had a strong impact on literary critics throughout the 1980s. Its major theoretical speculations were condensed and encapsulated into an article—first presented in a pioneering collection titled *Woman, Culture, and Society* (1974), edited by Michelle Zimbalist

Rosaldo and Louise Lamphere—that constitutes our selection here. Chodorow's three subsequent books continued to elaborate on the psychodynamics of engendering: *Feminism and Psychoanalytic Theory* (1989), *Femininities, Masculinities, Sexualities: Freud and Beyond* (1994), and *The Power of Feelings: Personal Meaning in Psychoanalysis, Gender, and Culture* (1999). Chodorow currently teaches at the University of California, Berkeley.

Family Structure and Feminine Personality

I propose here[1] a model to account for the reproduction within each generation of certain general and nearly universal differences that characterize masculine and feminine personality and roles. My perspective is largely psychoanalytic. Cross-cultural and social-psychological evidence suggests that an argument drawn solely from the universality of biological sex differences is unconvincing.[2] At the same time, explanations based on patterns of deliberate socialization (the most prevalent kind of anthropological, sociological, and social-psychological explanation) are in themselves insufficient to account for the extent to which psychological and value commitments to sex differences are so emotionally laden and tenaciously maintained, for the way gender identity and expectations about sex roles and gender consistency are so deeply central to a person's consistent sense of self.

This paper suggests that a crucial differentiating experience in male and female development arises out of the fact that women, universally, are largely responsible for early child care and for (at least) later female socialization. This points to the central importance of the mother-daughter relationship for women, and to a focus on the conscious and unconscious effects of early involvement with a female for children of both sexes. The fact that males and females experience this social environment differently as they grow up accounts for the development of basic sex differences in personality. In particular, certain features of the mother-daughter relationship are internalized universally as basic elements of feminine ego structure (although not necessarily what we normally mean by "femininity").

Specifically, I shall propose that, in any given society, feminine personality comes to define itself in relation and connection to other people more than masculine personality does. (In psychoanalytic terms, women are less individuated than men; they have more flexible ego boundaries.[3]) Moreover,

1. My understanding of mother-daughter relationships and their effect on feminine psychology grows out of my participation beginning in 1971 in a women's group that discusses mother-daughter relationships in particular and family relationships in general. All the women in this group have contributed to this understanding. An excellent dissertation by Marcia Millman (1972) first suggested to me the importance of boundary issues for women and became a major organizational focus for my subsequent work. Discussions with Nancy Jay, Michelle Rosaldo, Philip Slater, Barrie Thorne, Susan Weisskopf, and Beatrice Whiting have been central to the development of the ideas presented here. I am grateful to George Goethals, Edward Payne, and Mal Slavin for their comments and suggestions about earlier versions of this paper.

[Except as indicated, all notes are Chodorow's.]
2. Margaret Mead provides the most widely read and earliest argument for this viewpoint (cf., e.g., 1935 and 1949); see also Chodorow (1971) for another discussion of the same issue.
3. Unfortunately, the language that describes personality structure is itself embedded with value judgment. The implication in most studies is that it is always better to have firmer ego boundaries, that "ego strength" depends on the degree of individuation. Gutmann, who recognizes the linguistic problem, even suggests that "so-called ego pathology may have adaptive implications for women" (1965: 231). The argument can be made that extremes in either direction are harmful. Complete lack of ego boundaries is clearly pathological, but so also, as critics of contemporary Western

issues of dependency are handled and experienced differently by men and women. For boys and men, both individuation and dependency issues become tied up with the sense of masculinity, or masculine identity. For girls and women, by contrast, issues of femininity, or feminine identity, are not problematic in the same way. The structural situation of child rearing, reinforced by female and male role training, produces these differences, which are replicated and reproduced in the sexual sociology of adult life.

The paper is also a beginning attempt to rectify certain gaps in the social-scientific literature, and a contribution to the reformulation of psychological anthropology. Most traditional accounts of family and socialization tend to emphasize only role training, and not unconscious features of personality. Those few that rely on Freudian theory have abstracted a behaviorist methodology from this theory, concentrating on isolated "significant" behaviors like weaning and toilet training. The paper advocates instead a focus on the ongoing interpersonal relationships in which these various behaviors are given meaning.[4]

More empirically, most social-scientific accounts of socialization, child development, and the mother-child relationship refer implicitly or explicitly only to the development and socialization of boys, and to the mother-son relationship. There is a striking lack of systematic description about the mother-daughter relationship, and a basic theoretical discontinuity between, on the one hand, theories about female development, which tend to stress the development of "feminine" qualities in relation to and comparison with men, and on the other hand, theories about women's ultimate mothering role. This final lack is particularly crucial, because women's motherhood and mothering role seem to be the most important features in accounting for the universal secondary status of women (Chodorow, 1971; Ortner, Rosaldo, this volume[5]). The present paper describes the development of psychological qualities in women that are central to the perpetuation of this role.

In a formulation of this preliminary nature, there is not a great body of consistent evidence to draw upon. Available evidence is presented that illuminates aspects of the theory—for the most part psychoanalytic and social-psychological accounts based almost entirely on highly industrialized Western society. Because aspects of family structure are discussed that are universal, however, I think it is worth considering the theory as a general model. In any case, this is in some sense a programmatic appeal to people doing research. It points to certain issues that might be especially important in investigations of child development and family relationships, and suggests that researchers look explicitly at female vs. male development, and that they consider seriously mother-daughter relationships even if these are not of obvious "structural importance" in a traditional anthropological view of that society.

---

men point out (cf., e.g., Bakan, 1966, and Slater, 1970), is individuation gone wild, what Bakan calls "agency unmitigated by communion," which he takes to characterize, among other things, both capitalism based on the Protestant ethic and aggressive masculinity. With some explicit exceptions that I will specify in context I am using the concepts solely in the descriptive sense.

4. Slater (1968) provides one example of such an investigation. LeVine's recent work on psychoanalytic anthropology (1971a,b) proposes a methodology that will enable social scientists to study personality development in this way.
5. I.e., *Woman, Culture, and Society*; see Ortner, 1974; Rosaldo, 1974 [editor's note].

The Development of Gender Personality

According to psychoanalytic theory,[6] personality is a result of a boy's or girl's social-relational experiences from earliest infancy. Personality development is not the result of conscious parental intention. The nature and quality of the social relationships that the child experiences are appropriated, internalized, and organized by her/him and come to constitute her/his personality. What is internalized from an ongoing relationship continues independent of that original relationship and is generalized and set up as a permanent feature of the personality. The conscious self is usually not aware of many of the features of personality, or of its total structural organization. At the same time, these are important determinants of any person's behavior, both that which is culturally expected and that which is idiosyncratic or unique to the individual. The conscious aspects of personality, like a person's general self-concept and, importantly, her/his gender identity, require and depend upon the consistency and stability of its unconscious organization. In what follows I shall describe how contrasting male and female experiences lead to differences in the way that the developing masculine or feminine psyche resolves certain relational issues.

Separation and individuation (preoedipal development). All children begin life in a state of "infantile dependence" (Fairbairn, 1952) upon an adult or adults, in most cases their mother. This state consists first in the persistence of primary identification with the mother: the child does not differentiate herself/himself from her/his mother but experiences a sense of oneness with her. (It is important to distinguish this from later forms of identification, from "secondary identification," which presuppose at least some degree of experienced separateness by the person who identifies.) Second, it includes an oral-incorporative mode of relationship to the world, leading, because of the infant's total helplessness, to a strong attachment to and dependence upon whoever nurses and carries her/him.

Both aspects of this state are continuous with the child's prenatal experience of being emotionally and physically part of the mother's body and of the exchange of body material through the placenta. That this relationship continues with the natural mother in most societies stems from the fact that women lactate. For convenience, and not because of biological necessity, this has usually meant that mothers, and females in general, tend to take all care of babies. It is probable that the mother's continuing to have major responsibility for the feeding and care of the child (so that the child interacts almost entirely with her) extends and intensifies her/his period of primary identification with her more than if, for instance, someone else were to take major or total care of the child. A child's earliest experience, then, is usually of identity with and attachment to a single mother, and always with women.

For both boys and girls, the first few years are preoccupied with issues of separation and individuation. This includes breaking or attenuating the primary identification with the mother and beginning to develop an individuated sense of self, and mitigating the totally dependent oral attitude and attachment to the mother. I would suggest that, contrary to the traditional psycho-

---

6. Particularly as interpreted by object-relations theorists (e.g., Fairbairn, 1952, and Guntrip, 1961) and, with some similarity, by Parsons (1964) and Parsons and Bales (1955).

analytic model, the preoedipal experience is likely to differ for boys and girls. Specifically, the experience of mothering for a woman involves a double identification (Klein and Rivière, 1937). A woman identifies with her own mother and, through identification with her child, she (re)experiences herself as a cared-for child. The particular nature of this double identification for the individual mother is closely bound up with her relationship to her own mother. As Deutsch expresses it, "In relation to her own child, woman repeats her own mother-child history" (1944: 205). Given that she was a female child, and that identification with her mother and mothering are so bound up with her being a woman, we might expect that a woman's identification with a girl child might be stronger; that a mother, who is, after all, a person who is a woman and not simply the performer of a formally defined role, would tend to treat infants of different sexes in different ways.

There is some suggestive sociological evidence that this is the case. Mothers in a women's group in Cambridge, Massachusetts, say that they identified more with their girl children than with boy children. The perception and treatment of girl vs. boy children in high-caste, extremely patriarchal, patrilocal communities in India are in the same vein. Families express preference for boy children and celebrate when sons are born. At the same time, Rajput mothers in North India are "as likely as not" (Minturn and Hitchcock, 1963) to like girl babies better than boy babies once they are born, and they and Havik Brahmins in South India (Harper, 1969) treat their daughters with greater affection and leniency than their sons. People in both groups say that this is out of sympathy for the future plight of their daughters, who will have to leave their natal family for a strange and usually oppressive postmarital household. From the time of their daughters' birth, then, mothers in these communities identify anticipatorily, by reexperiencing their own past, with the experiences of separation that their daughters will go through. They develop a particular attachment to their daughters because of this and by imposing their own reaction to the issue of separation on this new external situation.

It seems, then, that a mother is more likely to identify with a daughter than with a son, to experience her daughter (or parts of her daughter's life) as herself. Fliess's description (1961) of his neurotic patients who were the children of ambulatory psychotic mothers presents the problem in its psychopathological extreme. The example is interesting, because, although Fliess claims to be writing about people defined only by the fact that their problems were tied to a particular kind of relationship to their mothers, an overwhelmingly large proportion of the cases he presents are women. It seems, then, that this sort of disturbed mother inflicts her pathology predominantly on daughters. The mothers Fliess describes did not allow their daughters to perceive themselves as separate people, but simply acted as if their daughters were narcissistic extensions or doubles of themselves, extensions to whom were attributed the mothers' bodily feelings and who became physical vehicles for their mothers' achievement of autoerotic gratification. The daughters were bound into a mutually dependent "hypersymbiotic" relationship. These mothers, then, perpetuate a mutual relationship with their daughters of both primary identification and infantile dependence.

A son's case is different. Cultural evidence suggests that insofar as a mother treats her son differently, it is usually by emphasizing his masculinity in opposition to herself and by pushing him to assume, or acquiescing in his assumption of, a sexually toned male-role relation to her. Whiting (1959) and Whiting et al. (1958) suggest that mothers in societies with mother-child sleeping arrangements and postpartum sex taboos may be seductive toward infant sons. Slater (1968) describes the socialization of precarious masculinity in Greek males of the classical period through their mothers' alternation of sexual praise and seductive behavior with hostile deflation and ridicule. This kind of behavior contributes to the son's differentiation from his mother and to the formation of ego boundaries (I will later discuss certain problems that result from this).

Neither form of attitude or treatment is what we would call "good mothering." However, evidence of differentiation of a pathological nature in the mother's behavior toward girls and boys does highlight tendencies in "normal" behavior. It seems likely that from their children's earliest childhood, mothers and women tend to identify more with daughters and to help them to differentiate less, and that processes of separation and individuation are made more difficult for girls. On the other hand, a mother tends to identify less with her son, and to push him toward differentiation and the taking on of a male role unsuitable to his age, and undesirable at any age in his relationship to her.

For boys and girls, the quality of the preoedipal relationship to the mother differs. This, as well as differences in development during the oedipal period, accounts for the persisting importance of preoedipal issues in female development and personality that many psychoanalytic writers describe.[7] Even before the establishment of gender identity, gender personality differentiation begins.

Gender identity (oedipal crisis and resolution). There is only a slight suggestion in the psychological and sociological literature that preoedipal development differs for boys and girls. The pattern becomes explicit at the next developmental level. All theoretical and empirical accounts agree that after about age three (the beginning of the "oedipal" period, which focuses on the attainment of a stable gender identity) male and female development becomes radically different. It is at this stage that the father, and men in general, begin to become important in the child's primary object world. It is, of course, particularly difficult to generalize about the attainment of gender identity and sex-role assumption, since there is such wide variety in the sexual sociology of different societies. However, to the extent that in all societies women's life tends to be more private and domestic, and men's more public and social (Rosaldo, this volume), we can make general statements about this kind of development.

In what follows, I shall be talking about the development of gender personality and gender identity in the tradition of psychoanalytic theory. Cognitive psychologists have established that by the age of three, boys and girls have an irreversible conception of what their gender is (cf. Kohlberg, 1966). I do not dispute these findings. It remains true that children (and adults) may know definitely that they are boys (men) or girls (women), and at the same time experience conflicts or uncertainty about "masculinity" or "femininity," about what these identities require in behavioral or emotional terms, etc. I am discussing the development of "gender identity" in this latter sense.

A boy's masculine gender identification must come to replace his early primary identification with his mother. This masculine identification is usually

7. Cf., e.g., Brunswick, 1940; Deutsch, 1932, 1944; Fliess, 1948; Freud, 1931; Jones, 1927; and Lampl-de Groot, 1928.

based on identification with a boy's father or other salient adult males. However, a boy's father is relatively more remote than his mother. He rarely plays a major caretaking role even at this period in his son's life. In most societies, his work and social life take place farther from the home than do those of his wife. He is, then, often relatively inaccessible to his son, and performs his male role activities away from where the son spends most of his life. As a result, a boy's male gender identification often becomes a "positional" identification, with aspects of his father's clearly or not-so-clearly defined male role, rather than a more generalized "personal" identification—a diffuse identification with his father's personality, values, and behavioral traits—that could grow out of a real relationship to his father.[8]

Mitscherlich (1963), in his discussion of Western advanced capitalist society, provides a useful insight into the problem of male development. The father, because his work takes him outside of the home most of the time, and because his active presence in the family has progressively decreased, has become an "invisible father." For the boy, the tie between affective relations and masculine gender identification and role learning (between libidinal and ego development) is relatively attenuated. He identifies with a fantasied masculine role, because the reality constraint that contact with his father would provide is missing. In all societies characterized by some sex segregation (even those in which a son will eventually lead the same sort of life as his father), much of a boy's masculine identification must be of this sort, that is, with aspects of his father's role, or what he fantasies to be a male role, rather than with his father as a person involved in a relationship to him.

There is another important aspect to this situation, which explains the psychological dynamics of the universal social and cultural devaluation and subordination of women.[9] A boy, in his attempt to gain an elusive masculine identification, often comes to define this masculinity largely in negative terms, as that which is not feminine or involved with women. There is an internal and external aspect to this. Internally, the boy tries to reject his mother and deny his attachment to her and the strong dependence upon her that he still feels. He also tries to deny the deep personal identification with her that has developed during his early years. He does this by repressing whatever he takes to be feminine inside himself, and, importantly, by denigrating and devaluing whatever he considers to be feminine in the outside world. As a societal member, he also appropriates to himself and defines as superior particular social activities and cultural (moral, religious, and creative) spheres—possibly, in fact, "society" (Rosaldo, this volume) and "culture" (Ortner, this volume) themselves.[1]

Freud's description of the boy's oedipal crisis speaks to the issues of rejection of the feminine and identification with the father. As his early attachment to his mother takes on phallic-sexual overtones, and his father enters the picture as an obvious rival (who, in the son's fantasy, has apparent power to kill or castrate his son), the boy must radically deny and repress his attachment to his

8. The important distinction between "positional" and "personal" identification comes from Slater, 1961, and Winch, 1962.
9. For more extensive arguments concerning this, cf., e.g., Burton and Whiting (1961), Chodorow (1971), and Slater (1968).
1. The processes by which individual personal experiences and psychological factors contribute to or are translated into social and cultural facts, and, more generally, the circularity of explanations in terms of socialization, are clearly very complicated. A discussion of these issues, however, is not within the scope of this paper.

mother and replace it with an identification with his loved and admired, but also potentially punitive, therefore feared, father. He internalizes a superego.[2]

To summarize, four components of the attainment of masculine gender identity are important. First, masculinity becomes and remains a problematic issue for a boy. Second, it involves denial of attachment or relationship, particularly of what the boy takes to be dependence or need for another, and differentiation of himself from another. Third, it involves the repression and devaluation of femininity on both psychological and cultural levels. Finally, identification with his father does not usually develop in the context of a satisfactory affective relationship, but consists in the attempt to internalize and learn components of a not immediately apprehensible role.

The development of a girl's gender identity contrasts with that of a boy. Most important, femininity and female role activities are immediately apprehensible in the world of her daily life. Her final role identification is with her mother and women, that is, with the person or people with whom she also has her earliest relationship of infantile dependence. The development of her gender identity does not involve a rejection of this early identification, however. Rather, her later identification with her mother is embedded in and influenced by their ongoing relationship of both primary identification and preoedipal attachment. Because her mother is around, and she has had a genuine relationship to her as a person, a girl's gender and gender role identification are mediated by and depend upon real affective relations. Identification with her mother is not positional—the narrow learning of particular role behaviors—but rather a personal identification with her mother's general traits of character and values. Feminine identification is based not on fantasied or externally defined characteristics and negative identification, but on the gradual learning of a way of being familiar in everyday life, and exemplified by the person (or kind of people—women) with whom she has been most involved. It is continuous with her early childhood identifications and attachments.

The major discontinuity in the development of a girl's sense of gender identity, and one that has led Freud and other early psychoanalysts to see female development as exceedingly difficult and tortuous, is that at some point she must transfer her primary sexual object choice from her mother and females to her father and males, if she is to attain her expected heterosexual adulthood. Briefly, Freud considers that all children feel that mothers give some cause for complaint and unhappiness: they give too little milk; they have a second child; they arouse and then forbid their child's sexual gratification in the process of caring for her/him. A girl receives a final blow, however: her discovery that she lacks a penis. She blames this lack on her mother, rejects her mother, and turns to her father in reaction.

Problems in this account have been discussed extensively in the general literature that has grown out of the women's movement, and within the psychoanalytic tradition itself. These concern Freud's misogyny and his obvious

---

2. The question of the universality of the oedipus complex as Freud describes it is beyond the scope of this paper. Bakan (1966, 1968) points out that in the original Oedipus myth, it was the father who first tried to kill his son, and that the theme of paternal infanticide is central to the entire Old Testament. He suggests that for a variety of reasons, fathers probably have hostile and aggressive fantasies and feelings about their children (sons). This more general account, along with a variety of psychological and anthropological data, convinces me that we must take seriously the notion that members of both generations may have conflicts over the inevitable replacement of the elder generation by the younger, and that children probably feel both guilt and (rightly) some helplessness in this situation.

assumption that males possess physiological superiority, and that a woman's personality is inevitably determined by her lack of a penis.[3] The psychoanalytic account is not completely unsatisfactory, however. A more detailed consideration of several theorists[4] reveals important features of female development, especially about the mother-daughter relationship, and at the same time contradicts or mitigates the absoluteness of the more general Freudian outline.

These psychoanalysts emphasize how, in contrast to males, the female oedipal crisis is not resolved in the same absolute way. A girl cannot and does not completely reject her mother in favor of men, but continues her relationship of dependence upon and attachment to her. In addition, the strength and quality of her relationship to her father is completely dependent upon the strength and quality of her relationship to her mother. Deutsch suggests that a girl wavers in a "bisexual triangle" throughout her childhood and into puberty, normally making a very tentative resolution in favor of her father, but in such a way that issues of separation from and attachment to her mother remain important throughout a woman's life (1944: 205):

> It is erroneous to say that the little girl gives up her first mother relation in favor of the father. She only gradually draws him into the alliance, develops from the mother-child exclusiveness toward the triangular parent-child relationship and continues the latter, just as she does the former, although in a weaker and less elemental form, all her life. Only the principal part changes: now the mother, now the father plays it. The ineradicability of affective constellations manifests itself in later repetitions.

We might suggest from this that a girl's internalized and external object-relations become and remain more complex, and at the same time more defining of her, than those of a boy. Psychoanalytic preoccupation with constitutionally based libidinal development, and with a normative male model of development, has obscured this fact. Most women are genitally heterosexual. At the same time, their lives always involve other sorts of equally deep and primary relationships, especially with their children, and, importantly, with other women. In these spheres also, even more than in the area of heterosexual relations, a girl imposes the sort of object-relations she has internalized in her preoedipal and later relationship to her mother.

Men are also for the most part genitally heterosexual. This grows directly out of their early primary attachment to their mother. We know, however, that in many societies their heterosexual relationships are not embedded in close personal relationship but simply in relations of dominance and power. Furthermore, they do not have the extended personal relations women have.

---

3. These views are most extreme and explicit in two papers (Freud, 1925, 1933) and warrant the criticism that has been directed at them. Although the issue of penis envy in women is not central to this paper, it is central to Freud's theory of female development. Therefore I think it worthwhile to mention three accounts that avoid Freud's ideological mistakes while allowing that his clinical observations of penis envy might be correct.

Thompson (1943) suggests that penis envy is a symbolic expression of women's culturally devalued and underprivileged position in our patriarchal society; that possession of a penis symbolizes the possession of power and privilege. Bettelheim (1954) suggests that members of either sex envy the sexual functions of the other, and that women are more likely to express this envy overtly, because, since men are culturally superior, such envy is considered "natural." Balint (1954) does not rely on the fact of men's cultural superiority, but suggests that a little girl develops penis envy when she realizes that her mother loves people with penises, i.e., her father, and thinks that possession of a penis will help her in her rivalry for her mother's attentions.

4. See, e.g., Brunswick, 1940; Deutsch, 1925, 1930, 1932, 1944; Freedman, 1961; Freud, 1931; Jones, 1927.

They are not so connected to children, and their relationships with other men tend to be based not on particularistic connection or affective ties, but rather on abstract, universalistic role expectations.

Building on the psychoanalytic assumption that unique individual experiences contribute to the formation of individual personality, culture and personality theory has held that early experiences common to members of a particular society contribute to the formation of "typical" personalities organized around and preoccupied with certain issues: "Prevailing patterns of child-rearing must result in similar internalized situations in the unconscious of the majority of individuals in a culture, and these will be externalized back into the culture again to perpetuate it from generation to generation" (Guntrip, 1961: 378). In a similar vein, I have tried to show that to the extent males and females, respectively, experience similar interpersonal environments as they grow up, masculine and feminine personality will develop differently.

I have relied on a theory which suggests that features of adult personality and behavior are determined, but which is not biologically determinist. Culturally expected personality and behavior are not simply "taught," however. Rather, certain features of social structure, supported by cultural beliefs, values, and perceptions, are internalized through the family and the child's early social object-relationships. This largely unconscious organization is the context in which role training and purposive socialization take place.

Sex-Role Learning and Its Social Context

Sex-role training and social interaction in childhood build upon and reinforce the largely unconscious development I have described. In most societies (ours is a complicated exception) a girl is usually with her mother and other female relatives in an interpersonal situation that facilitates continuous and early role learning and emphasizes the mother-daughter identification and particularistic, diffuse, affective relationships between women. A boy, to a greater or lesser extent, is also with women for a large part of his childhood, which prevents continuous or easy masculine role identification. His development is characterized by discontinuity.

Ariès (1962: 61), in his discussion of the changing concept of childhood in modern capitalist society, makes a distinction that seems to have more general applicability. Boys, he suggests, became "children" while girls remained "little women." "The idea of childhood profited the boys first of all, while the girls persisted much longer in the traditional way of life which confused them with the adults: we shall have cause to notice more than once this delay on the part of the women in adopting the visible forms of the essentially masculine civilization of modern times." This took place first in the middle classes, as a situation developed in which boys needed special schooling in order to prepare for their future work and could not begin to do this kind of work in childhood. Girls (and working-class boys) could still learn work more directly from their parents, and could begin to participate in the adult economy at an earlier age. Rapid economic change and development have exacerbated the lack of male generational role continuity. Few fathers now have either the opportunity or the ability to pass on a profession or skill to their sons.

Sex-role development of girls in modern society is more complex. On the one hand, they go to school to prepare for life in technologically and socially complex society. On the other, there is a sense in which this schooling is a pseudo-training. It is not meant to interfere with the much more important training to be "feminine" and a wife and mother, which is embedded in the girl's unconscious development and which her mother teaches her in a family context where she is clearly the salient parent.

This dichotomy is not unique to modern industrial society. Even if special, segregated schooling is not necessary for adult male work (and many male initiation rites remain a form of segregated role training), boys still participate in more activities that characterize them as a category apart from adult life. Their activities grow out of the boy's need to fill time until he can begin to take on an adult male role. Boys may withdraw into isolation and self-involved play or join together in a group that remains more or less unconnected with either the adult world of work and activity or the familial world.

Jay (1969) describes this sort of situation in rural Modjokuto, Java. Girls, after the age of five or so, begin gradually to help their mothers in their work and spend time with their mothers. Boys at this early age begin to form bands of age mates who roam and play about the city, relating neither to adult men nor to their mothers and sisters. Boys, then, enter a temporary group based on universalistic membership criteria, while girls continue to participate in particularistic role relations in a group characterized by continuity and relative permanence.

The content of boys' and girls' role training tends in the same direction as the context of this training and its results. Barry, Bacon, and Child, in their well-known study (1957), demonstrate that the socialization of boys tends to be oriented toward achievement and self-reliance and that of girls toward nurturance and responsibility. Girls are thus pressured to be involved with and connected to others, boys to deny this involvement and connection.

Adult Gender Personality and Sex Role

A variety of conceptualizations of female and male personality all focus on distinctions around the same issue, and provide alternative confirmation of the developmental model I have proposed. Bakan (1966: 15) claims that male personality is preoccupied with the "agentic," and female personality with the "communal." His expanded definition of the two concepts is illuminating:

> I have adopted the terms "agency" and "communion" to characterize two fundamental modalities in the existence of living forms, agency for the existence of an organism as an individual and communion for the participation of the individual in some larger organism of which the individual is a part. Agency manifests itself in self-protection, self-assertion, and self-expansion; communion manifests itself in the sense of being at one with other organisms. Agency manifests itself in the formation of separations; communion in the lack of separations. Agency manifests itself in isolation, alienation, and aloneness; communion in contact, openness, and union. Agency manifests itself in the urge to master; communion in noncontractual cooperation. Agency manifests itself in the repression of thought, feeling, and impulse; communion in the lack and removal of repression.

Gutmann (1965) contrasts the socialization of male personalities in "allocentric" milieux (milieux in which the individual is part of a larger social organization and system of social bonds) with that of female personalities in "autocentric" milieux (in which the individual herself/himself is a focus of events and ties).[5] Gutmann suggests that this leads to a number of systematic differences in ego functioning. Female ego qualities, growing out of participation in autocentric milieux, include more flexible ego boundaries (i.e. less insistent self-other distinctions), present orientation rather than future orientation, and relatively greater subjectivity and less detached objectivity.[6]

Carlson (1971) confirms both characterizations. Her tests of Gutmann's claims lead her to conclude that "males represent experiences of self, others, space, and time in individualistic, objective, and distant ways, while females represent experiences in relatively interpersonal, subjective, immediate ways" (p. 270). With reference to Bakan, she claims that men's descriptions of affective experience tend to be in agentic terms and women's in terms of communion, and that an examination of abstracts of a large number of social-psychological articles on sex differences yields an overwhelming confirmation of the agency/communion hypothesis.

Cohen (1969) contrasts the development of "analytic" and "relational" cognitive style, the former characterized by a stimulus-centered, parts-specific orientation to reality, the latter centered on the self and responding to the global characteristics of a stimulus in reference to its total context. Although focusing primarily on class differences in cognitive style, she also points out that girls are more likely to mix the two types of functioning (and also to exhibit internal conflict about this). Especially, they are likely to exhibit at the same time both high field dependence and highly developed analytic skills in other areas. She suggests that boys and girls participate in different sorts of interactional subgroups in their families: boys experience their family more as a formally organized primary group; girls experience theirs as a group characterized by shared and less clearly delineated functions. She concludes (p. 836): "Since embedded responses covered the gamut from abstract categories, through language behaviors, to expressions of embeddedness in their social environments, it is possible that embeddedness may be a distinctive characteristic of female sex-role learning in this society regardless of social class, native ability, ethnic differences, and the cognitive impact of the school."

Preliminary consideration suggests a correspondence between the production of feminine personalities organized around "communal" and "auto-

5. Following Cohen (1969), I would suggest that the external structural features of these settings (in the family or in school, for instance) are often similar or the same for boys and girls. The different kind and amount of adult male and female participation in these settings accounts for their being experienced by children of different sexes as different sorts of milieux.

6. Gutmann points out that all these qualities are supposed to indicate lack of adequate ego strength, and suggests that we ought to evaluate ego strength in terms of the specific demands of different people's (e.g. women's as opposed to men's) daily lives. Bakan goes even further and suggests that modern male ego qualities are a pathological extreme. Neither account *is* completely adequate. Gutmann does not consider the possibility (for which we have good evidence) that the everyday demands of an autocentric milieu are unreasonable: although women's ego qualities may be "functional" for their participation in these milieux, they do not necessarily contribute to the psychological strength of the women themselves. Bakan, in his (legitimate) preoccupation with the lack of connection and compulsive independence that characterizes Western masculine success, fails to recognize the equally clear danger (which, I will suggest, is more likely to affect women) of communion unmitigated by agency—of personality and behavior with no sense of autonomous control or independence at all.

I think this is part of a more general social-scientific mistake, growing out of the tendency to equate social structure and society with male social organization and activities within a society. This is exemplified, for instance, in Erikson's idealistic conception of maternal qualities in women (1965) and, less obviously, in the contrast between Durkheim's extensive treatment of "anomic" suicide (1897) and his relegation of "fatalistic" suicide to a single footnote (p. 276).

centric" issues and characterized by flexible ego boundaries, less detached objectivity, and relational cognitive style, on the one hand, and important aspects of feminine as opposed to masculine social roles, on the other.

Most generally, I would suggest that a quality of embeddedness in social interaction and personal relationships characterizes women's life relative to men's. From childhood, daughters are likely to participate in an intergenerational world with their mother, and often with their aunts and grandmother, whereas boys are on their own or participate in a single-generation world of age mates. In adult life, women's interaction with other women in most societies is kin-based and cuts across generational lines. Their roles tend to be particularistic, and to involve diffuse relationships and responsibilities rather than specific ones. Women in most societies are *defined* relationally (as someone's wife, mother, daughter, daughter-in-law; even a nun becomes the Bride of Christ). Men's association (although it too may be kin-based and intergenerational) is much more likely than women's to cut across kinship units, to be restricted to a single generation, and to be recruited according to universalistic criteria and involve relationships and responsibilities defined by their specificity.

Ego Boundaries and the Mother-Daughter Relationship

The care and socialization of girls by women ensures the production of feminine personalities founded on relation and connection, with flexible rather than rigid ego boundaries, and with a comparatively secure sense of gender identity. This is one explanation for how women's relative embeddedness is reproduced from generation to generation, and why it exists within almost every society. More specific investigation of different social contexts suggests, however, that there are variations in the kind of relationship that can exist between women's role performance and feminine personality.

Various kinds of evidence suggest that separation from the mother, the breaking of dependence, and the establishment and maintenance of a consistently individuated sense of self remain difficult psychological issues for Western middle-class women (i.e. the women who become subjects of psychoanalytic and clinical reports and social-psychological studies). Deutsch (1944, 1945) in particular provides extensive clinical documentation of these difficulties and of the way they affect women's relationships to men and children and, because of their nature, are reproduced in the next generation of women. Mothers and daughters in the women's group mentioned above (p. 47) describe their experiences of boundary confusion or equation of self and other, for example, guilt and self-blame for the other's unhappiness; shame and embarrassment at the other's actions; daughters' "discovery" that they are "really" living out their mothers' lives in their choice of career; mothers' not completely conscious reactions to their daughters' bodies as their own (over-identification and therefore often unnecessary concern with supposed weight or skin problems, which the mother is really worried about in herself); etc.

A kind of guilt that Western women express seems to grow out of and to reflect lack of adequate self/other distinctions and a sense of inescapable embeddedness in relationships to others. Tax describes this well (1970: 2; italics mine):

> Since our awareness of others is considered our duty, the price we pay when things go wrong is guilt and self-hatred. And things always go wrong. We respond with apologies; we continue to apologize long after

the event is forgotten—and *even if it had no causal relation to anything we did to begin with*. If the rain spoils someone's picnic, we apologize. We apologize for taking up space in a room, for living.

As if the woman does not differentiate herself clearly from the rest of the world, she feels a sense of guilt and responsibility for situations that did not come about through her actions and without relation to her actual ability to determine the course of events. This happens, in the most familiar instance, in a sense of diffuse responsibility for everything connected to the welfare of her family and the happiness and success of her children. This loss of self in overwhelming responsibility for and connection to others is described particularly acutely by women writers (in the work, for instance, of Simone de Beauvoir, Kate Chopin, Doris Lessing, Tillie Olsen, Christina Stead, Virginia Woolf).

Slater (1961) points to several studies supporting the contention that Western daughters have particular problems about differentiation from their mother. These studies show that though most forms of personal parental identification correlate with psychological adjustment (i.e. freedom from neurosis or psychosis, *not* social acceptability), personal identification of a daughter with her mother does not. The reason is that the mother-daughter relation is the one form of personal identification that, because it results so easily from the normal situation of child development, is liable to be excessive in the direction of allowing no room for separation or difference between mother and daughter.

The situation reinforces itself in circular fashion. A mother, on the one hand, grows up without establishing adequate ego boundaries or a firm sense of self. She tends to experience boundary confusion with her daughter, and does not provide experiences of differentiating ego development for her daughter or encourage the breaking of her daughter's dependence. The daughter, for her part, makes a rather unsatisfactory and artificial attempt to establish boundaries: she projects what she defines as bad within her onto her mother and tries to take what is good into herself. (This, I think, is the best way to understand the girl's oedipal "rejection" of her mother.) Such an arbitrary mechanism cannot break the underlying psychological unity, however. Projection is never more than a temporary solution to ambivalence or boundary confusion.

The implication is that, contrary to Gutmann's suggestion (see note 3 [on p. 363]), "so-called ego pathology" may not be "adaptive" for women. Women's biosexual experiences (menstruation, coitus, pregnancy, childbirth, lactation) all involve some challenge to the boundaries of her body ego ("me"/"not-me" in relation to her blood or milk, to a man who penetrates her, to a child once part of her body). These are important and fundamental human experiences that are probably intrinsically meaningful and at the same time complicated for women everywhere. However, a Western woman's tenuous sense of individuation and of the firmness of her ego boundaries increases the likelihood that experiences challenging these boundaries will be difficult for her and conflictive.

Nor is it clear that this personality structure is "functional" for society as a whole. The evidence presented in this paper suggests that satisfactory mothering, which does not reproduce particular psychological problems in boys and girls, comes from a person with a firm sense of self and of her own value, whose care is a freely chosen activity rather than a reflection of a conscious and unconscious sense of inescapable connection to and responsibility for her children.

Social Structure and the Mother-Daughter Relationship

Clinical and self-analytic descriptions of women and of the psychological component of mother-daughter relationships are not available from societies and subcultures outside of the Western middle class. However, accounts that are primarily sociological about women in other societies enable us to infer certain aspects of their psychological situation. In what follows, I am not claiming to make any kind of general statement about what constitutes a "healthy society," but only to examine and isolate specific features of social life that seem to contribute to the psychological strength of some members of a society. Consideration of three groups with matrifocal tendencies in their family structure (see Tanner, this volume [1974]) highlights several dimensions of importance in the developmental situation of the girl.

Young and Willmott (1957) describe the daily visiting and mutual aid of working-class mothers and daughters in East London. In a situation where household structure is usually nuclear, like the Western middle class, grown daughters look to their mothers for advice, for aid in childbirth and child care, for friendship and companionship, and for financial help. Their mother's house is the ultimate center of the family world. Husbands are in many ways peripheral to family relationships, possibly because of their failure to provide sufficiently for their families as men are expected to do. This becomes apparent if they demand their wife's disloyalty toward or separation from her mother: "The great triangle of childhood is mother-father-child; in Bethnal Green the great triangle of adult life is Mum-wife-husband" (p. 64).

Geertz (1961)[7] and Jay (1969) describe Javanese nuclear families in which women are often the more powerful spouse and have primary influence upon how kin relations are expressed and to whom (although these families are formally centered upon a highly valued conjugal relationship based on equality of spouses). Financial and decision-making control in the family often rests largely in the hands of its women. Women are potentially independent of men in a way that men are not independent of women. Geertz points to a woman's ability to participate in most occupations, and to own farmland and supervise its cultivation, which contrasts with a man's inability, even if he is financially independent, to do his own household work and cooking.

Women's kin role in Java is important. Their parental role and rights are greater than those of men; children always belong to the woman in case of divorce. When extra members join a nuclear family to constitute an extended family household, they are much more likely to be the wife's relatives than those of the husband. Formal and distant relations between men in a family, and between a man and his children (especially his son), contrast with the informal and close relations between women, and between a woman and her children. Jay and Geertz both emphasize the continuing closeness of the mother-daughter relationship as a daughter is growing up and throughout her married life. Jay suggests that there is a certain amount of ambivalence in the mother-daughter relationship, particularly as a girl grows toward adulthood and before she is married, but points out that at the same time the mother remains a girl's "primary figure of confidence and support" (1969: 103).

---

7. This ethnography, and a reading of it that focuses on strong female kin relations, was brought to my attention by Tanner (1971).

Siegel (1969)[8] describes Atjehnese families in Indonesia in which women stay on the homestead of their parents after marriage and are in total control of the household. Women tolerate men in the household only as long as they provide money, and even then treat them as someone between a child and a guest. Women's stated preference would be to eliminate even this necessary dependence on men: "Women, for instance, envision paradise as the place where they are reunited with their children and their mothers; husbands and fathers are absent, and yet there is an abundance all the same. Quarrels over money reflect the women's idea that men are basically adjuncts who exist only to give their families whatever they can earn" (p. 177). A woman in this society does not get into conflicts in which she has to choose between her mother and her husband, as happens in the Western working class (see above; also Komarovsky, 1962), where the reigning ideology supports the nuclear family.

In these three settings, the mother-daughter tie and other female kin relations remain important from a woman's childhood through her old age. Daughters stay closer to home in both childhood and adulthood, and remain involved in particularistic role relations. Sons and men are more likely to feel uncomfortable at home, and to spend work and play time away from the house. Male activities and spheres emphasize universalistic, distancing qualities: men in Java are the bearers and transmitters of high culture and formal relationships; men in East London spend much of their time in alienated work settings; Atjehnese boys spend their time in school, and their fathers trade in distant places.

Mother-daughter ties in these three societies, described as extremely close, seem to be composed of companionship and mutual cooperation, and to be positively valued by both mother and daughter. The ethnographies do not imply that women are weighed down by the burden of their relationships or by overwhelming guilt and responsibility. On the contrary, they seem to have developed a strong sense of self and self-worth, which continues to grow as they get older and take on their maternal role. The implication is that "ego strength" is not completely dependent on the firmness of the ego's boundaries.

Guntrip's distinction between "immature" and "mature" dependence clarifies the difference between mother-daughter relationships and women's psyche in the Western middle class and in the matrifocal societies described. Women in the Western middle class are caught up to some extent in issues of infantile dependence, while the women in matrifocal societies remain in definite connection with others, but in relationships characterized by mature dependence. As Guntrip describes it (1961: 291): "*Mature dependence* is characterized by full differentiation of ego and object (emergence from primary identification) and therewith a capacity for valuing the object for its own sake and for giving as well as receiving; a condition which should be described not as independence but as mature dependence." This kind of mature dependence is also to be distinguished from the kind of forced independence and denial of need for relationship that I have suggested characterizes masculine personality, and that reflects continuing conflict about infantile dependence (Guntrip, 1961: 293; my italics): "Maturity is not equated with independence though it includes a certain capacity for independence. . . . The independence of the

8. See note 7 [on page 381].

mature person is simply that he does not collapse when he has to stand alone. It is not an independence of needs for other persons with whom to have relationship: *that would not be desired by the mature.*"

Depending on its social setting, women's sense of relation and connection and their embeddedness in social life provide them with a kind of security that men lack. The quality of a mother's relationship to her children and maternal self-esteem, on the one hand, and the nature of a daughter's developing identification with her mother, on the other, make crucial differences in female development.

Women's kin role, and in particular the mother role, is central and positively valued in Atjeh, Java, and East London. Women gain status and prestige as they get older; their major role is not fulfilled in early motherhood. At the same time, women may be important contributors to the family's economic support, as in Java and East London, and in all three societies they have control over real economic resources. All these factors give women a sense of self-esteem independent of their relationship to their children. Finally, strong relationships exist between women in these societies, expressed in mutual cooperation and frequent contact. A mother, then, when her children are young, is likely to spend much of her time in the company of other women, not simply isolated with her children.

These social facts have important positive effects on female psychological development. (It must be emphasized that all the ethnographies indicate that these same social facts make male development difficult and contribute to psychological insecurity and lack of ease in interpersonal relationships in men.) A mother is not invested in keeping her daughter from individuating and becoming less dependent. She has other ongoing contacts and relationships that help fulfill her psychological and social needs. In addition, the people surrounding a mother while a child is growing up become mediators between mother and daughter, by providing a daughter with alternative models for personal identification and objects of attachment, which contribute to her differentiation from her mother. Finally, a daughter's identification with her mother in this kind of setting is with a strong woman with clear control over important spheres of life, whose sense of self-esteem can reflect this. Acceptance of her gender identity involves positive valuation of herself, and not an admission of inferiority. In psychoanalytic terms, we might say it involves identification with a preoedipal, active, caring mother. Bibring points to clinical findings supporting this interpretation: "We find in the analysis of the women who grew up in this 'matriarchal' setting the rejection of the feminine role less frequently than among female patients coming from the patriarchal family culture" (1953: 281).

There is another important aspect of the situation in these societies. The continuing structural and practical importance of the mother-daughter tie not only ensures that a daughter develops a positive personal and role identification with her mother, but also requires that the close psychological tie between mother and daughter become firmly grounded in real role expectations. These provide a certain constraint and limitation upon the relationship, as well as an avenue for its expression through common spheres of interest based in the external social world.

All these societal features contrast with the situation of the Western middle-class woman. Kinship relations in the middle class are less important.

Kin are not likely to live near each other, and, insofar as husbands are able to provide adequate financial support for their families, there is no need for a network of mutual aid among related wives. As the middle-class woman gets older and becomes a grandmother, she cannot look forward to increased status and prestige in her new role.

The Western middle-class housewife does not have an important economic role in her family. The work she does and the responsibilities that go with it (household management, cooking, entertaining, etc.) do not seem to be really necessary to the economic support of her family (they are crucial contributions to the maintenance and reproduction of her family's class position, but this is not generally recognized as important either by the woman herself or by the society's ideology). If she works outside the home, neither she nor the rest of society is apt to consider this work to be important to her self-definition in the way that her housewife role is.

Child care, on the other hand, is considered to be her crucially important responsibility. Our post-Freudian society in fact assigns to parents (and especially to the mother[9]) nearly total responsibility for how children turn out. A middle-class mother's daily life is not centrally involved in relations with other women. She is isolated with her children for most of her workday. It is not surprising, then, that she is likely to invest a lot of anxious energy and guilt in her concern for her children and to look to them for her own self-affirmation, or that her self-esteem, dependent on the lives of others than herself, is shaky. Her life situation leads her to an overinvolvement in her children's lives.

A mother in this situation keeps her daughter from differentiation and from lessening her infantile dependence. (She also perpetuates her son's dependence, but in this case society and his father are more likely to interfere in order to assure that, behaviorally, at least, he doesn't *act* dependent.) And there are not other people around to mediate in the mother-daughter relationship. Insofar as the father is actively involved in a relationship with his daughter and his daughter develops some identification with him, this helps her individuation, but the formation of ego autonomy through identification with and idealization of her father may be at the expense of her positive sense of feminine self. Unlike the situation in matrifocal families, the continuing closeness of the mother-daughter relationship is expressed only on a psychological, interpersonal level. External role expectations do not ground or limit it.

It is difficult, then, for daughters in a Western middle-class family to develop self-esteem. Most psychoanalytic and social theorists[1] claim that the mother inevitably represents to her daughter (and son) regression, passivity, dependence, and lack of orientation to reality, whereas the father represents progression, activity, independence, and reality orientation.[2] Given the value implications of this dichotomy, there are advantages for the son in giving up his mother and identifying with his father. For the daughter, feminine gen-

9. See Slater (1970) for an extended discussion of the implications of this.
1. See, e.g., Deutsch, 1944, *passim*; Erikson, 1964: 162; Klein and Rivière, 1937: 18; Parsons, 1964, *passim*; Parsons and Bales, 1955, *passim*.
2. Their argument derives from the universal fact that a child must outgrow her/his primary identification with and total dependence upon the mother.

The present paper argues that the value implications of this dichotomy grow out of the particular circumstances of our society and its devaluation of relational qualities. Allied to this is the suggestion that it does not need to be, and often is not, relationship to the father that breaks the early maternal relationship.

der identification means identification with a devalued, passive mother, and personal maternal identification is with a mother whose own self-esteem is low. Conscious rejection of her oedipal maternal identification, however, remains an unconscious rejection and devaluation of herself, because of her continuing preoedipal identification and boundary confusion with her mother.

Cultural devaluation is not the central issue, however. Even in patrilineal, patrilocal societies in which women's status is very low, women do not necessarily translate this cultural devaluation into low self-esteem, nor do girls have to develop difficult boundary problems with their mother. In the Moslem Moroccan family, for example,[3] a large amount of sex segregation and sex antagonism gives women a separate (domestic) sphere in which they have a real productive role and control, and also a life situation in which any young mother is in the company of other women. Women do not need to invest all their psychic energy in their children, and their self-esteem is not dependent on their relationship to their children. In this and other patrilineal, patrilocal societies, what resentment women do have at their oppressive situation is more often expressed toward their sons, whereas daughters are seen as allies against oppression. Conversely, a daughter develops relationships of attachment to and identification with other adult women. Loosening her tie to her mother therefore does not entail the rejection of all women. The close tie that remains between mother and daughter is based not simply on mutual overinvolvement but often on mutual understanding of their oppression.

Conclusion

Women's universal mothering role has effects both on the development of masculine and feminine personality and on the relative status of the sexes. This paper has described the development of relational personality in women and of personalities preoccupied with the denial of relation in men. In its comparison of different societies, it has suggested that men, while guaranteeing to themselves sociocultural superiority over women, always remain psychologically defensive and insecure. Women, by contrast, although always of secondary social and cultural status, may in favorable circumstances gain psychological security and a firm sense of worth and importance in spite of this.

Social and psychological oppression, then, is perpetuated in the structure of personality. The paper enables us to suggest what social arrangements contribute (and could contribute) to social equality between men and women and their relative freedom from certain sorts of psychological conflict. Daughters and sons must be able to develop a personal identification with more than one adult, and preferably one embedded in a role relationship that gives it a social context of expression and provides some limitation upon it. Most important, boys need to grow up around men who take a major role in child care, and girls around women who, in addition to their child-care responsibilities, have a valued role and recognized spheres of legitimate control. These arrangements could help to ensure that children of both sexes develop a sufficiently individuated and strong sense of self, as well as a positively valued and secure gen-

---

3. Personal communication from Fatima Mernissi, based on her experience growing up in Morocco and her recent sociological fieldwork there.

der identity, that does not bog down either in ego-boundary confusion, low self-esteem, and overwhelming relatedness to others, or in compulsive denial of any connection to others or dependence upon them.

WORKS CITED

Ariès, Philippe. 1962. *Centuries of Childhood: A Social History of Family Life.* Trans. Robert Baldick. New York: Vintage.

Bakan, David. 1966. *The Duality of Human Existence: Isolation and Communion in Western Man.* Boston: Beacon.

———. 1968. *Disease, Pain, and Sacrifice: Toward a Psychology of Suffering.* Boston: Beacon.

Balint, Alice. 1954. *The Early Years of Life: A Psychoanalytic Study.* New York: Basic Books.

Barry, Herbert, III, Margaret K. Bacon, and Irvin L. Child. 1957. "A Cross-Cultural Survey of Some Sex Differences in Socialization." *Journal of Abnormal and Social Psychology* 55, no. 3: 327–32.

Bettelheim, Bruno. 1954. *Symbolic Wounds: Puberty Rites and the Envious Male.* Rev. ed. New York: Collier Books, 1962.

Bibring, Grete. 1953. "On the 'Passing of the Oedipus Complex' in a Matriarchal Family Setting." In *Drives, Affects, and Behavior: Essays in Honor of Marie Bonaparte,* ed. Rudolph M. Loewenstein, 278–84. New York: International Universities Press.

Brunswick, Ruth Mack. 1940. "The Preoedipal Phase of the Libido Development." In Fliess, 1969: 231–53.

Burton, Roger V., and John W. M. Whiting. 1961. "The Absent Father and Cross-Sex Identity." *Merrill-Palmer Quarterly of Behavior and Development* 7, no. 2: 85–95.

Carlson, Rae. 1971. "Sex Differences in Ego Functioning: Exploratory Studies of Agency and Communion." *Journal of Consulting and Clinical Psychology* 37: 267–77.

Chodorow, Nancy. 1971. "Being and Doing: A Cross-Cultural Examination of the Socialization of Males and Females." In *Women in Sexist Society: Studies in Power and Powerlessness,* ed. Vivian Gornick and Barbara K. Moran, 173–97. New York: Basic Books.

Cohen, Rosalie A. 1969. "Conceptual Styles, Culture Conflict, and Nonverbal Tests of Intelligence." *American Anthropologist* 71: 828–56.

Deutsch, Helene. 1925. "The Psychology of Woman in Relation to the Functions of Reproduction." In Fliess, 1969: 165–79.

———. 1930. "The Significance of Masochism in the Mental Life of Women." In Fliess, 1969: 195–207.

———. 1932. "On Female Homosexuality." In Fliess, 1969: 208–30.

———. 1944 and 1945. *Psychology of Women,* vols. 1 and 2. New York: Grune and Stratton.

Durkheim, Emile. 1897. *Suicide: A Study in Sociology.* Trans. John A. Spaulding and George Simpson. New York: Free Press, 1966.

Erikson, Erik. 1964. *Insight and Responsibility.* New York: Norton.

———. 1965. "Inner and Outer Space: Reflections on Womanhood." In *The Woman in America,* ed. Robert Jay Lifton, 1–26. Boston: Houghton Mifflin.

Fairbairn, W. R. D. 1952. *An Object-Relations Theory of the Personality.* New York: Basic Books.

Fliess, Robert. 1948. "Female and Preoedipal Sexuality: A Historical Survey." In Fliess, 1969: 159–64.

———. 1961 [1970]. *Ego and Body Ego: Contributions to Their Psychoanalytic Psychology.* New York: International Universities Press.

———, ed. 1969. *The Psychoanalytic Reader: An Anthology of Essential Papers with Critical Introductions.* New York: International Universities Press.

Freedman, David. 1961. "On Women Who Hate Their Husbands." In Ruitenbeek, 1966: 221–37.

Freud, Sigmund. 1925. "Some Psychical Consequences of the Anatomical Distinction between the Sexes." In *The Standard Edition of the Complete Psychological Works of Sigmund Freud,* trans. under the general editorship of James Strachey in collaboration with Anna Freud, assisted by Alix Strachey and Alan Tyson, 19: 243–58. London: Hogarth, 1931.

———. 1931. "Female Sexuality." In Ruitenbeek, 1966: 88–105.

———. 1933. "Femininity." In *New Introductory Lectures on Psychoanalysis,* trans. James Strachey, 112–35. New York: Norton, 1961.

Geertz, Hildred. 1961. *The Javanese Family: A Study of Kinship and Socialization.* New York: Free Press of Glencoe.

Guntrip, Harry. 1961. *Personality Structure and Human Interaction: The Developing Synthesis of Psycho-dynamic Theory.* New York: International Universities Press.

Gutmann, David. 1965. "Women and the Conception of Ego Strength." *Merrill-Palmer Quarterly of Behavior and Development* 11: 229–40.

Harper, Edward B. 1969. "Fear and the Status of Women." *Southwestern Journal of Anthropology* 25: 81–95.

Jay, Robert R. 1969. *Javanese Villagers. Social Relations in Rural Modjokuto.* Cambridge, Mass.: MIT Press.

Jones, Ernest. 1927. "The Early Development of Female Sexuality." In Ruitenbeek, 1966: 21–35.

Klein, Melanie, and Joan Rivière. 1937 [1964]. *Love, Hate and Reparation.* New York: Norton.

Kohlberg, Lawrence. 1966. "A Cognitive Developmental Analysis of Sex-Role Concepts and Attitudes." In *The Development of Sex Differences,* ed. Eleanor E. Maccoby, 82–173. Stanford: Stanford University Press.

Komarovsky, Mirra. 1962 [1967]. *Blue-Collar Marriage.* New York: Vintage.

Lampl–de Groot, Jeanne. 1928. "The Evolution of the Oedipus Complex in Women." In Fliess, 1969: 180–94.

LeVine, Robert A. 1971a. "The Psychoanalytic Study of Lives in Natural Social Settings." *Human Development* 14: 100–109.

———. 1971b. "Re-thinking Psychoanalytic Anthropology." Paper presented at the Institute on Psychoanalytic Anthropology, 70th Annual Meeting of the American Anthropological Association, New York.

Mead, Margaret. 1935. *Sex and Temperament in Three Primitive Societies.* New York: William Morrow.

———. 1949. *Male and Female.* New York: Dell.

Millman, Marcia. 1972. "Tragedy and Exchange: Metaphoric Understandings of Interpersonal Relationships." Ph.D. diss., Brandeis University.

Minturn, Leigh, and John T. Hitchcock. 1963. "The Rajputs of Khalapur, India." In *Six Cultures: Studies of Child Rearing,* ed. Beatrice B. Whiting. New York: Wiley.

Mitscherlich, Alexander. 1963 [1970]. *Society without the Father: A Contribution to Social Psychology.* New York: Schocken.

Ortner, Sherry B. 1974. "Is Female to Male as Nature Is to Culture?" In Rosaldo and Lamphere, 1974: 67–87.

Parsons, Talcott. 1964. *Social Structure and Personality.* New York: Free Press.

Parsons, Talcott, and Robert F. Bales. 1955. *Family, Socialization and Interaction Process.* New York: Free Press.

Rosaldo, Michelle Z. 1974. "Woman, Culture, and Society: A Theoretical Overview." In Rosaldo and Lamphere, 1974: 17–42.

Rosaldo, Michelle Z., and Louise Lamphere, eds. 1974. *Woman, Culture, and Society.* Stanford: Stanford University Press.

Ruitenbeek, Hendrik M., ed. 1966. *Psychoanalysis and Female Sexuality.* New Haven: College and University Press Services.

Siegel, James T. 1969. *The Rope of God.* Berkeley: University of California Press.

Slater, Philip E. 1961. "Toward a Dualistic Theory of Identification." *Merrill-Palmer Quarterly of Behavior and Development* 7, no. 2: 113–26.

———. 1968. *The Glory of Hera: Greek Mythology and the Greek Family.* Boston: Beacon.

———. 1970. *The Pursuit of Loneliness.* Boston: Beacon.

Tanner, Nancy. 1971. "Matrifocality in Indonesia and among Black Americans." Paper presented at the 70th Annual Meeting of the American Anthropological Association, New York.

———. 1974. "Matrifocality in Indonesia and Africa and among Black Americans." In Rosaldo and Lamphere, 1974: 129–56.

Tax, Meredith. 1970. *Woman and Her Mind: The Story of Daily Life.* Boston: New England Free Press.

Thompson, Clara. 1943. " 'Penis Envy' in Women." In Ruitenbeek, 1966: 246–51.

Whiting, John W. M. 1959. "Sorcery, Sin and the Superego: A Cross-Cultural Study of Some Mechanisms of Social Control." In *Cross-Cultural Approaches: Readings in Comparative Research,* ed. Clellan S. Ford, 147–68. New Haven: Human Relations Area Files.

Whiting, John W. M., Richard Kluckhorn, and Albert Anthony. 1958. "The Function of Male Initiation Rites at Puberty." In *Readings in Social Psychology,* ed. Eleanor E. Maccoby, T. M. Newcomb, and E. L. Hartley, 359–70. New York: Holt.

Winch, Robert F. 1962. *Identification and Its Familial Determinants.* New York: Bobbs-Merrill.

Young, Michael, and Peter Willmott. 1957 [1966]. *Family and Kinship in East London.* London: Penguin.

1974

JULIET MITCHELL
b. 1940

Juliet Mitchell was born in New Zealand and in 1944 emigrated to England, where she was educated at Oxford University. She has taught at a number of institutions, including the University of Leeds and the University of Reading, but also worked as a freelance writer and a psychotherapist. Currently a member of the faculty of Social and Political Sciences at Cambridge University, Mitchell has recently published *Siblings: Sex and Violence* (2003) and *Mad Men and Medusas: Reclaiming Hysteria* (2000), as well as such essays as "The Vortex beneath the Story" in *Whose Freud?* (2000) and "Did Oedipus Have a Sister?" (2001). This writing built on such earlier landmark contributions as *Women's Estate* (1971) and *Women, the Longest Revolution* (1984). However, she remains best known for *Psychoanalysis and Feminism* (1974), which questioned feminist attacks on Freud's insistence that anatomy is destiny, and did so by interpreting his theories not as prescriptive but as descriptive. Her view that the Oedipus complex inscribes women into a male-dominated social structure helped feminists deploy Freudian psychoanalytic models to understand the social construction of femininity. Our selection comes from the introduction to this classic book.

From Psychoanalysis and Feminism

From *Introduction*

The greater part of the feminist movement has identified Freud as the enemy. It is held that psychoanalysis claims women are inferior and that they can achieve true femininity only as wives and mothers. Psychoanalysis is seen as a justification for the status-quo, bourgeois and patriarchal, and Freud in his own person exemplifies these qualities. I would agree that popularized Freudianism must answer to this description; but the argument of this book is that a rejection of psychoanalysis and of Freud's works is fatal for feminism. However it may have been used, psychoanalysis is not a recommendation *for* a patriarchal society, but an analysis *of* one. If we are interested in understanding and challenging the oppression of women, we cannot afford to neglect it.

Where the majority tendency within feminism has denounced Freud's theories of femininity, so, if less deliberately, it has embraced the alternative radical psychologies developed by Wilhelm Reich's work on sexuality and R. D. Laing's on the family. Femininity, sexuality and the family clearly form an important triptych for seeing the position of women. But it seems to me that we have turned things on their head by accepting Reich's and Laing's analyses and repudiating Freud's. This is not to say that I think that there is little of value in Reich's and Laing's work—on the contrary, Reich's political and Laing's sociological observations provide us with a good deal of important material, but I do not believe that we can use these observations until we have freed them from the dubious theoretical and philosophical frameworks in which they are set. Moreover it is these theories and philosophies that have exercised a powerful influence on the women's liberation movement.

This book has a double and criss-cross purpose. Feminist critics of Freud have not only conflated his theories with those of other, often diverging, analysts and with popularizations, but, with more serious consequences still, have extrapolated his ideas about femininity from their context within the larger theories of psychoanalysis. Yet it is only this context that gives meaning to such notorious concepts as say, 'penis-envy'—without their context such notions certainly become either laughable or ideologically dangerous. In the briefest possible terms, we could say that psychoanalysis is about the material reality of ideas both within, and of, man's history; thus in 'penis-envy' we are talking not about an anatomical organ, but about the ideas of it that people hold and live by within the general culture, the order of human society. It is this last factor that also prescribes the reference point of psychoanalysis. The way we live as 'ideas' the necessary laws of human society is not so much conscious as *unconscious*—the particular task of psychoanalysis is to decipher how we acquire our heritage of the ideas and laws of human society within the unconscious mind, or, to put it another way, the unconscious mind *is* the way in which we acquire these laws. I have tried to outline the general precepts of psychoanalysis in the first instance and then place the particular discussion of femininity within this framework. This doubtless will make for a feeling of frustration, for although I have selected only those general concepts which I think to be essential, it has to be some time before we get into the 'meat' of the matter—the description of femininity.

* * *

Of course, no more than is any man an island unto himself, is an intellectual production created completely *ex nihilo*. Freud's work both took place within, and took off from, a dialogue with his times. But such a dialogue is never simple. Freud's scientific debts are obvious, his interest in archaeology and literature explicit, yet though he claimed to be congenitally incapable of philosophic thought, we can see that the terms of his defence of the status of science for psychoanalysis and the words he chose for many of the concepts he developed within it are part of an ongoing contemporary argument about the philosophy of science during that period. His linguistic terminology for what has since become known as 'the language of the unconscious' likewise must have borne some relationship to the intense preoccupation with language and communication of that place and epoch. These are just random examples. Since this book went to press an interesting study of Wittgenstein's Vienna (which was also Freud's) has been published.[1] In this it is claimed that if we consider his *Tractatus* in its historical context of Vienna instead of that of Cambridge Philosophy[2] (the usual practice) we come up with a very different reading. A similar intellectual history of Freud's work, one that did not for example assume that it grew only out of a medical tradition, would be fascinating. But the stress that I am putting here goes the other way—I am interested not in what Freud did, but in what we can get from him, a political rather than an academic exploration.

Certainly, then, psychoanalysis, as any other system of thought, was formed and developed within a particular time and place; that does not invalidate its claim to universal laws, it only means that these laws have to be extracted from their specific problematic—the particular material conditions of their formation. In this connection we need to know of the historical circumstances of their development mainly in order *not* to limit them thereto. Some important factors have clearly changed—sexual mores *are* different, women *have* gained a degree of emancipation, hysteria is no longer the most prevalent manifestation of neurosis amongst middle-class women—does this or does this not affect the theories? Can the Oedipus complex be kept only as a metaphor for the psychic structure of the bourgeois nuclear family under Viennese capitalism, or is it a law that describes the way in which all culture is acquired by each individual? It is only the general aspects of these questions which I have taken up here. This, of course, gives an unbalanced perspective to the interpretation of the psychological

1. [Allan] Janik and [Stephen] Toulmin, *Wittgenstein's Vienna,* Weidenfeld & Nicolson, London, 1973 [Mitchell's note].

2. The Austrian philosopher studied in Cambridge in 1912–13 and returned to the university between 1930 and 1947.

acquisition of patriarchal laws. Though they seem to be universal, different societies, either contemporary or historical, different classes at the same or different times and situations, will not acquire these laws in an identical manner. The argument here has had to sacrifice diversity to what is held in common. Similarly, this general presentation of the theses of psychoanalysis means that there has been no room or time to pursue the specificities of psychological sexual characteristics of our own society. The material is still inadequate, some of the analytical questions are still unformed, but it seems clear that the psychological behaviour patterns of women, the connection of, say, hysteria and femininity, the different role of romantic love in the lives of the two sexes, women's undue share of 'intuition' and men's of 'rationality', can all find at least a partial explanation within a development of the work of psychoanalysis.

Very recently, there has been growing interest by some feminist groups in Freud's work, but so far there is only one part of the movement that has been trying consistently for some time to turn psychoanalytic theory into political practice—to raise both the general questions of patriarchal ideology and the detailed issues of feminine psychology. The series of groups *Psychanalyse et Politique,* based in Paris, is a Marxist part of the *Mouvement de la Libération des Femmes,*[3] and it explicitly opposes what it sees as bourgeois and idealist tendencies within, largely, American radical feminism. It denounces radical feminism's rejection of psychoanalysis, but this does not imply, any more than does this book, an acceptance of the present patriarchal practice of psychoanalysis, nor of the many patriarchal judgements found within Freud's own work. It is the theory, if it is correct, which is to some extent immune from the ideological uses to which it has been put and which, inevitably, surround it, that is being utilized. Influenced, but critically, by the particular interpretation of Freud offered by Jacques Lacan, *Psychanalyse et Politique* would use psychoanalysis for an understanding of the operations of the unconscious. Their concern is to analyse how men and women live *as men and women* within the material conditions of their existence—both general and specific. They argue that psychoanalysis gives us the concepts with which we can comprehend how ideology functions; closely connected with this, it further offers an analysis of the place and meaning of sexuality and of gender differences within society. So where Marxist theory explains the historical and economic situation, psychoanalysis, in conjunction with the notions of ideology already gained by dialectical materialism, is the way into understanding ideology and sexuality. As an English version of the manifesto of *Psychanalyse et Politique* puts it:

> In the political, ideological and social struggle the only theoretical discourse that exists these days about class struggle, and proletarian and cultural revolutions, is to be found in the texts on historical and dialectical materialism (Marx, Lenin, Mao).
>
> . . . In the ideological and sexual fight, the only discourse that exists today on sexuality and the unconscious—that is the discourse of psychoanalysis (Freud, Lacan) and semiology.

---

3. Movement for the Liberation of Women (French). *"Psychanalyse et Politique"*: Psychoanalysis and Politics.

Reich, among others, made the same suggestion in somewhat different terminology; this neither validates nor invalidates it as a proposition; it is a question of how one uses the concepts to carry out the analysis. And there are two further problems: how adequately does psychoanalysis analyse ideology and sexuality, and if it does so, what is the political practice that follows from this theory? It may be true to assert that the women's struggle is determinately against patriarchal ideology where the class struggle is against bourgeois capitalist economic power, but although both struggles have to take place on the political level, the two situations do not have parity. Marx's analysis of the differing modes of production revealed a history of culminating class struggle, the political practice was part of the theory. It has yet to be seen, by all of us in the women's liberation movement, whether the analysis of ideology is tied as closely to a logic of sexual struggle.

London
July 1973   1974

GAYLE RUBIN
b. 1949

The activism of the feminist anthropologist Gayle Rubin is evident in the role she played in founding Samois, the first S/M organization in the world, and in her essays on the policing of sexuality, on the poetry of the lesbian expatriate Renée Vivien, and on the gay male leather community of San Francisco. Frequently reprinted, "Thinking Sex: Notes for a Radical Theory of the Politics of Sexuality" (1984), "Of Catamites and Kings: Reflections on Butch, Gender, and Boundaries" (1992), and "Misguided, Dangerous, and Wrong: An Analysis of Anti-Pornography Politics" (1993) elaborate upon the political implications of the "sex/gender system" Rubin first explored in the influential essay "The Traffic in Women: Notes on the 'Political Economy' of Sex," which is excerpted here. By juxtaposing Claude Lévi-Strauss's theories of kinship with the Freudian concept of the Oedipus complex, Rubin set the stage for a denaturalizing or de-familiarizing of heterosexuality.

From The Traffic in Women:
Notes on the "Political Economy" of Sex[1]

The literature on women—both feminist and anti-feminist—is a long rumination on the question of the nature and genesis of women's oppression and

1. Acknowledgments are an inadequate expression of how much this paper, like most, is the product of many minds. They are also necessary to free others of the responsibility for what is ultimately a personal vision of a collective conversation. I want to free and thank the following persons: Tom Anderson and Arlene Gorelick, with whom I co-authored the paper from which this one evolved; Rayna Reiter, Larry Shields, Ray Kelly, Peggy White, Norma Diamond, Randy Reiter, Frederick Wyatt, Anne Locksley, Juliet Mitchell, and Susan Harding, for countless conversations and ideas; Marshall Sahlins, for the revelation of anthropology; Lynn Eden, for sardonic editing; the members of Women's Studies 340/004, for my initiation into teaching; Sally Brenner, for heroic typing; Susan Lowes, for incredible patience; and Emma Goldman, for the title. [Except as indicated, all notes are Rubin's.]

social subordination. The question is not a trivial one, since the answers given it determine our visions of the future, and our evaluation of whether or not it is realistic to hope for a sexually egalitarian society. More importantly, the analysis of the causes of women's oppression forms the basis for any assessment of just what would have to be changed in order to achieve a society without gender hierarchy. Thus, if innate male aggression and dominance are at the root of female oppression, then the feminist program would logically require either the extermination of the offending sex, or else a eugenics project to modify its character. If sexism is a by-product of capitalism's relentless appetite for profit, then sexism would wither away in the advent of a successful socialist revolution. If the world historical defeat of women occurred at the hands of an armed patriarchal revolt, then it is time for Amazon guerrillas to start training in the Adirondacks.

It lies outside the scope of this paper to conduct a sustained critique of some of the currently popular explanations of the genesis of sexual inequality—theories such as the popular evolution exemplified by *The Imperial Animal,* the alleged overthrow of prehistoric matriarchies, or the attempt to extract all of the phenomena of social subordination from the first volume of *Capital.* Instead, I want to sketch some elements of an alternate explanation of the problem.

Marx once asked: "What is a Negro slave? A man of the black race. The one explanation is as good as the other. A Negro is a Negro. He only becomes a slave in certain relations. A cotton spinning jenny is a machine for spinning cotton. It becomes *capital* only in certain relations. Torn from these relationships it is no more capital than gold in itself is money or sugar is the price of sugar" (Marx, 1971b:28). One might paraphrase: What is a domesticated woman? A female of the species. The one explanation is as good as the other. A woman is a woman. She only becomes a domestic, a wife, a chattel, a playboy bunny, a prostitute, or a human dicta-phone in certain relations. Torn from these relationships, she is no more the helpmate of man than gold in itself is money . . . etc. What then are these relationships by which a female becomes an oppressed woman? The place to begin to unravel the system of relationships by which women become the prey of men is in the overlapping works of Claude Lévi-Strauss and Sigmund Freud. The domestication of women, under other names, is discussed at length in both of their *oeuvres.* In reading through these works, one begins to have a sense of a systematic social apparatus which takes up females as raw materials and fashions domesticated wosmen as products. Neither Freud nor Lévi-Strauss sees his work in this light, and certainly neither turns a critical glance upon the processes he describes. Their analyses and descriptions must be read, therefore, in something like the way in which Marx read the classical political economists who preceded him (on this, see Althusser and Balibar, 1970:11–69). Freud and Lévi-Strauss are in some sense analogous to Ricardo and Smith[2]: They see neither the implications of what they are saying, nor the implicit critique which their work can generate when subjected to a feminist eye. Nevertheless, they provide conceptual tools with which one can build descriptions of the part of social life which is the locus of the oppression of women, of sexual minorities, and of certain aspects of human personality within individu-

2. I.e., the classical economists David Ricardo and Adam Smith [editor's note].

als. I call that part of social life the "sex/gender system," for lack of a more elegant term. As a preliminary definition, a "sex/gender system" is the set of arrangements by which a society transforms biological sexuality into products of human activity, and in which these transformed sexual needs are satisfied.

The purpose of this essay is to arrive at a more fully developed definition of the sex/gender system, by way of a somewhat idiosyncratic and exegetical reading of Lévi-Strauss and Freud. I use the word "exegetical" deliberately. The dictionary defines "exegesis" as a "critical explanation or analysis; especially, interpretation of the Scriptures." At times, my reading of Lévi-Strauss and Freud is freely interpretive, moving from the explicit content of a text to its presuppositions and implications. My reading of certain psychoanalytic texts is filtered through a lens provided by Jacques Lacan, whose own interpretation of the Freudian scripture has been heavily influenced by Lévi-Strauss.[3]

I will return later to a refinement of the definition of a sex/gender system. First, however, I will try to demonstrate the need for such a concept by discussing the failure of classical Marxism to fully express or conceptualize sex oppression. This failure results from the fact that Marxism, as a theory of social life, is relatively unconcerned with sex. In Marx's map of the social world, human beings are workers, peasants, or capitalists; that they are also men and women is not seen as very significant. By contrast, in the maps of social reality drawn by Freud and Lévi-Strauss, there is a deep recognition of the place of sexuality in society, and of the profound differences between the social experience of men and women.

* * *

From *Engels*

* * *

The realm of human sex, gender, and procreation has been subjected to, and changed by, relentless social activity for millennia. Sex as we know it— gender identity, sexual desire and fantasy, concepts of childhood—is itself a social product. We need to understand the relations of its production, and forget, for awhile, about food, clothing, automobiles, and transistor radios. In most Marxist tradition, and even in Engels' book,[4] the concept of the "second aspect of material life" has tended to fade into the background, or to be incorporated into the usual notions of "material life." Engels' suggestion has never been followed up and subjected to the refinement which it needs. But he does indicate the existence and importance of the domain of social life which I want to call the sex/gender system.

Other names have been proposed for the sex/gender system. The most common alternatives are "mode of reproduction" and "patriarchy." It may be foolish to quibble about terms, but both of these can lead to confusion. All

---

3. Moving between Marxism, structuralism, and psychoanalysis produces a certain clash of epistemologies. In particular, structuralism is a can from which worms crawl out all over the epistemological map. Rather than trying to cope with this problem, I have more or less ignored the fact that Lacan and Lévi-Strauss are among the foremost living ancestors of the contemporary French intellectual revolution (see Foucault, 1970). It would be fun, interesting, and, if this were France, essential, to start my argument from the center of the structuralist maze and work my way out from there, along the lines of a "dialectical theory of signifying practices" (see Hefner, 1974).
4. *The Origin of the Family, Private Property, and the State* (1884) [editor's note].

three proposals have been made in order to introduce a distinction between "economic" systems and "sexual" systems, and to indicate that sexual systems have a certain autonomy and cannot always be explained in terms of economic forces. "Mode of reproduction," for instance, has been proposed in opposition to the more familiar "mode of production." But this terminology links the "economy" to production, and the sexual system to "reproduction." It reduces the richness of either system, since "productions" and "reproductions" take place in both. Every mode of production involves reproduction—of tools, labor, and social relations. We cannot relegate all of the multi-faceted aspects of social reproduction to the sex system. Replacement of machinery is an example of reproduction in the economy. On the other hand, we cannot limit the sex system to "reproduction" in either the social or biological sense of the term. A sex/gender system is not simply the reproductive moment of a "mode of production." The formation of gender identity is an example of production in the realm of the sexual system. And a sex/gender system involves more than the "relations of procreation," reproduction in the biological sense.

The term "patriarchy" was introduced to distinguish the forces maintaining sexism from other social forces, such as capitalism. But the use of "patriarchy" obscures other distinctions. Its use is analogous to using capitalism to refer to all modes of production, whereas the usefulness of the term "capitalism" lies precisely in that it distinguishes between the different systems by which societies are provisioned and organized. Any society will have some system of "political economy." Such a system may be egalitarian or socialist. It may be class stratified, in which case the oppressed class may consist of serfs, peasants, or slaves. The oppressed class may consist of wage laborers, in which case the system is properly labeled "capitalist." The power of the term lies in its implication that, in fact, there are alternatives to capitalism.

Similarly, any society will have some systematic ways to deal with sex, gender, and babies. Such a system may be sexually egalitarian, at least in theory, or it may be "gender stratified," as seems to be the case for most or all of the known examples. But it is important—even in the face of a depressing history—to maintain a distinction between the human capacity and necessity to create a sexual world, and the empirically oppressive ways in which sexual worlds have been organized. Patriarchy subsumes both meanings into the same term. Sex/gender system, on the other hand, is a neutral term which refers to the domain and indicates that oppression is not inevitable in that domain, but is the product of the specific social relations which organize it.

Finally, there are gender-stratified systems which are not adequately described as patriarchal. Many New Guinea societies (Enga, Maring, Bena Bena, Huli, Melpa, Kuma, Gahuku-Gama, Fore, Marind Anim, ad nauseam; see Berndt, 1962; Langness, 1967; Buchbinder and Rappaport, 1976; Read, 1952; Meggitt, 1964; Glasse, 1971; Strathern, 1972; Reay, 1959; Van Baal, 1966; Lindenbaum, 1973) are viciously oppressive to women. But the power of males in these groups is not founded on their roles as fathers or patriarchs, but on their collective adult maleness, embodied in secret cults, men's houses, warfare, exchange networks, ritual knowledge, and various initiation procedures. Patriarchy is a specific form of male dominance, and the use of the term ought to be confined to the Old Testament-type pastoral nomads from whom the term comes, or groups like them. Abraham was a Patriarch—

one old man whose absolute power over wives, children, herds, and dependents was an aspect of the institution of fatherhood, as defined in the social group in which he lived.

Whichever term we use, what is important is to develop concepts to adequately describe the social organization of sexuality and the reproduction of the conventions of sex and gender. We need to pursue the project Engels abandoned when he located the subordination of women in a development within the mode of production.[5] To do this, we can imitate Engels in his method rather than in his results. Engels approached the task of analyzing the "second aspect of material life" by way of an examination of a theory of kinship systems. Kinship systems are and do many things. But they are made up of, and reproduce, concrete forms of socially organized sexuality. Kinship systems are observable and empirical forms of sex/gender systems.

Kinship
(On the part played by sexuality in the transition from ape to "man")

To an anthropologist, a kinship system is not a list of biological relatives. It is a system of categories and statuses which often contradict actual genetic relationships. There are dozens of examples in which socially defined kinship statuses take precedence over biology. The Nuer custom of "woman marriage" is a case in point. The Nuer define the status of fatherhood as belonging to the person in whose name cattle bridewealth is given for the mother. Thus, a woman can be married to another woman, and be husband to the wife and father of her children, despite the fact that she is not the inseminator (Evans-Pritchard, 1951:107–09).

In pre-state societies, kinship is the idiom of social interaction, organizing economic, political, and ceremonial, as well as sexual, activity. One's duties, responsibilities, and privileges vis-à-vis others are defined in terms of mutual kinship or lack thereof. The exchange of goods and services, production and distribution, hostility and solidarity, ritual and ceremony, all take place within the organizational structure of kinship. The ubiquity and adaptive effectiveness of kinship has led many anthropologists to consider its invention, along with the invention of language, to have been the developments which decisively marked the discontinuity between semi-human hominids and human beings (Sahlins, 1960; Livingstone, 1969; Lévi-Strauss, 1969).

While the idea of the importance of kinship enjoys the status of a first principle in anthropology, the internal workings of kinship systems have long been a focus for intense controversy. Kinship systems vary wildly from one culture to the next. They contain all sorts of bewildering rules which govern whom one may or may not marry. Their internal complexity is dazzling. Kinship systems have for decades provoked the anthropological imagination into trying to explain incest taboos, cross-cousin marriage, terms of descent, relationships of avoidance or forced intimacy, clans and sections, taboos on names—

---

5. Engels thought that men acquired wealth in the form of herds and, wanting to pass this wealth to their own children, overthrew "mother right" in favor of patrilineal inheritance. "The overthrow of mother right was the *world historical defeat of the female sex*. The man took command in the home also; the woman was degraded and reduced to servitude; she became the slave of his lust and a mere instrument for the production of children" (Engels, 1972:120–21; italics in original). As has been often pointed out, women do not necessarily have significant social authority in societies practicing matrilineal inheritance (Schneider and Gough, 1961).

the diverse array of items found in descriptions of actual kinship systems. In the nineteenth century, several thinkers attempted to write comprehensive accounts of the nature and history of human sexual systems (see Fee, 1973). One of these was *Ancient Society*, by Lewis Henry Morgan. It was this book which inspired Engels to write *The Origin of the Family, Private Property, and the State*. Engels' theory is based upon Morgan's account of kinship and marriage.

In taking up Engels' project of extracting a theory of sex oppression from the study of kinship, we have the advantage of the maturation of ethnology since the nineteenth century. We also have the advantage of a peculiar and particularly appropriate book, Lévi-Strauss' *The Elementary Structures of Kinship*. This is the boldest twentieth-century version of the nineteenth-century project to understand human marriage. It is a book in which kinship is explicitly conceived of as an imposition of cultural organization upon the facts of biological procreation. It is permeated with an awareness of the importance of sexuality in human society. It is a description of society which does not assume an abstract, genderless human subject. On the contrary, the human subject in Lévi-Strauss's work is always either male or female, and the divergent social destinies of the two sexes can therefore be traced. Since Lévi-Strauss sees the essence of kinship systems to lie in an exchange of women between men, he constructs an implicit theory of sex oppression. Aptly, the book is dedicated to the memory of Lewis Henry Morgan.

> *"Vile and precious merchandise"*
> —Monique Wittig

The Elementary Structures of Kinship is a grand statement on the origin and nature of human society. It is a treatise on the kinship systems of approximately one-third of the ethnographic globe. Most fundamentally, it is an attempt to discern the structural principles of kinship. Lévi-Strauss argues that the application of these principles (summarized in the last chapter of *Elementary Structures*) to kinship data reveals an intelligible logic to the taboos and marriage rules which have perplexed and mystified Western anthropologists. He constructs a chess game of such complexity that it cannot be recapitulated here. But two of his chess pieces are particularly relevant to women—the "gift" and the incest taboo, whose dual articulation adds up to his concept of the exchange of women.

The Elementary Structures is in part a radical gloss on another famous theory of primitive social organization, Mauss' *Essay on the Gift* (See also Sahlins, 1972: Chap. 4). It was Mauss who first theorized as to the significance of one of the most striking features of primitive societies: the extent to which giving, receiving, and reciprocating gifts dominates social intercourse. In such societies, all sorts of things circulate in exchange—food, spells, rituals, words, names, ornaments, tools, and powers.

> Your own mother, your own sister, your own pigs, your own yams that you have piled up, you may not eat. Other people's mothers, other people's sisters, other people's pigs, other people's yams that they have piled up, you may eat. (Arapesh, cited in Lévi-Strauss, 1969:27)

In a typical gift transaction, neither party gains anything. In the Trobriand Islands, each household maintains a garden of yams and each household eats yams. But the yams a household grows and the yams it eats are not the same. At harvest time, a man sends the yams he has cultivated to the household of his sister; the household in which he lives is provisioned by his wife's brother (Malinowski, 1929). Since such a procedure appears to be a useless one from the point of view of accumulation or trade, its logic has been sought elsewhere. Mauss proposed that the significance of gift giving is that it expresses, affirms, or creates a social link between the partners of an exchange. Gift giving confers upon its participants a special relationship of trust, solidarity, and mutual aid. One can solicit a friendly relationship in the offer of a gift; acceptance implies a willingness to return a gift and a confirmation of the relationship. Gift exchange may also be the idiom of competition and rivalry. There are many examples in which one person humiliates another by giving more than can be reciprocated. Some political systems, such as the Big Man systems of highland New Guinea, are based on exchange which is unequal on the material plane. An aspiring Big Man wants to give away more goods than can be reciprocated. He gets his return in political prestige.

Although both Mauss and Lévi-Strauss emphasize the solidary aspects of gift exchange, the other purposes served by gift giving only strengthen the point that it is an ubiquitous means of social commerce. Mauss proposed that gifts were the threads of social discourse, the means by which such societies were held together in the absence of specialized governmental institutions. "The gift is the primitive way of achieving the peace that in civil society is secured by the state. . . . Composing society, the gift was the liberation of culture" (Sahlins, 1972:169, 175).

Lévi-Strauss adds to the theory of primitive reciprocity the idea that marriages are a most basic form of gift exchange, in which it is women who are the most precious of gifts. He argues that the incest taboo should best be understood as a mechanism to insure that such exchanges take place between families and between groups. Since the existence of incest taboos is universal, but the content of their prohibitions variable, they cannot be explained as having the aim of preventing the occurrence of genetically close matings. Rather, the incest taboo imposes the social aim of exogamy and alliance upon the biological events of sex and procreation. The incest taboo divides the universe of sexual choice into categories of permitted and prohibited sexual partners. Specifically, by forbidding unions within a group it enjoins marital exchange between groups.

> The prohibition on the sexual use of a daughter or a sister compels them to be given in marriage to another man, and at the same time it establishes a right to the daughter or sister of this other man. . . . The woman whom one does not take is, for that very reason, offered up. (Lévi-Strauss, 1969:51)

> The prohibition of incest is less a rule prohibiting marriage with the mother, sister, or daughter, than a rule obliging the mother, sister, or daughter to be given to others. It is the supreme rule of the gift. . . . (Ibid.:481)

The result of a gift of women is more profound than the result of other gift transactions, because the relationship thus established is not just one of reciprocity, but one of kinship. The exchange partners have become affines, and their descendants will be related by blood: "Two people may meet in friendship and exchange gifts and yet quarrel and fight in later times, but inter-marriage connects them in a permanent manner" (Best, cited in Lévi-Strauss, 1969:481). As is the case with other gift giving, marriages are not always so simply activities to make peace. Marriages may be highly competitive, and there are plenty of affines who fight each other. Nevertheless, in a general sense the argument is that the taboo on incest results in a wide network of relations, a set of people whose connections with one another are a kinship structure. All other levels, amounts, and directions of exchange—including hostile ones—are ordered by this structure. The marriage ceremonies recorded in the ethnographic literature are moments in a ceaseless and ordered procession in which women, children, shells, words, cattle names, fish, ancestors, whale's teeth, pigs, yams, spells, dances, mats, etc., pass from hand to hand, leaving as their tracks the ties that bind. Kinship is organization, and organization gives power. But who is organized?

If it is women who are being transacted, then it is the men who give and take them who are linked, the woman being a conduit of a relationship rather than a partner to it.[6] The exchange of women does not necessarily imply that women are objectified, in the modern sense, since objects in the primitive world are imbued with highly personal qualities. But it does imply a distinction between gift and giver. If women are the gifts, then it is men who are the exchange partners. And it is the partners, not the presents, upon whom reciprocal exchange confers its quasi-mystical power of social linkage. The relations of such a system are such that women are in no position to realize the benefits of their own circulation. As long as the relations specify that men exchange women, it is men who are the beneficiaries of the product of such exchange—social organization.

> The total relationship of exchange which constitutes marriage is not established between a man and a woman, but between two groups of men, and the woman figures only as one of the objects in the exchange, not as one of the partners. . . . This remains true even when the girl's feelings are taken into consideration, as, moreover, is usually the case. In acquiescing to the proposed union, she precipitates or allows the exchange to take place, she cannot alter its nature. . . . (Lévi-Strauss in ibid.:115)[7]

To enter into a gift exchange as a partner, one must have something to give. If women are for men to dispose of, they are in no position to give themselves away.

> "What woman," mused a young Northern Melpa man, "is ever strong enough to get up and say, 'Let us make *moka*, let us find wives and pigs, let us give our daughters to men, let us wage war, let us kill our enemies!' No indeed not! . . . they are little rubbish things who stay at home simply, don't you see?" (Strathern, 1972:161)

6. "What, would you like to marry your sister? What is the matter with you? Don't you want a brother-in-law? Don't you realize that if you marry another man's sister and another man marries your sister, you will have at least two brothers-in-law, while if you marry your own sister you will have none? With whom will you hunt, with whom will you garden, whom will you go visit?" (Arapesh, cited in Lévi-Strauss, 1969:485).

7. This analysis of society as based on bonds between men by means of women makes the separatist responses of the women's movement thoroughly intelligible. Separatism can be seen as a mutation in social structure, as an attempt to form social groups based on unmediated bonds between women. It can also be seen as a radical denial of men's "rights" in women, and as a claim by women of rights in themselves.

What women indeed! The Melpa women of whom the young man spoke can't get wives, they *are* wives, and what they get are husbands, an entirely different matter. The Melpa women can't give their daughters to men, because they do not have the same rights in their daughters that their male kin have, rights of bestowal (although *not* of ownership).

The "exchange of women" is a seductive and powerful concept. It is attractive in that it places the oppression of women within social systems, rather than in biology. Moreover, it suggests that we look for the ultimate locus of women's oppression within the traffic in women, rather than within the traffic in merchandise. It is certainly not difficult to find ethnographic and historical examples of trafficking in women. Women are given in marriage, taken in battle, exchanged for favors, sent as tribute, traded, bought, and sold. Far from being confined to the "primitive" world, these practices seem only to become more pronounced and commercialized in more "civilized" societies. Men are of course also trafficked—but as slaves, hustlers, athletic stars, serfs, or as some other catastrophic social status, rather than as men. Women are transacted as slaves, serfs, and prostitutes, but also simply as women. And if men have been sexual subjects—exchangers—and women sexual semi-objects—gifts—for much of human history, then many customs, clichés, and personality traits seem to make a great deal of sense (among others, the curious custom by which a father gives away the bride).

The "exchange of women" is also a problematic concept. Since Lévi-Strauss argues that the incest taboo and the results of its application constitute the origin of culture, it can be deduced that the world historical defeat of women occurred with the origin of culture, and is a prerequisite of culture. If his analysis is adopted in its pure form, the feminist program must include a task even more onerous than the extermination of men; it must attempt to get rid of culture and substitute some entirely new phenomena on the face of the earth. However, it would be a dubious proposition at best to argue that if there were no exchange of women there would be no culture, if for no other reason than that culture is, by definition, inventive. It is even debatable that "exchange of women" adequately describes all of the empirical evidence of kinship systems. Some cultures, such as the Lele and the Luma, exchange women explicitly and overtly. In other cultures, the exchange of women can be inferred. In some—particularly those hunters and gatherers excluded from Lévi-Strauss's sample—the efficacy of the concept becomes altogether questionable. What are we to make of a concept which seems so useful and yet so difficult?

The "exchange of women" is neither a definition of culture nor a system in and of itself. The concept is an acute, but condensed, apprehension of certain aspects of the social relations of sex and gender. A kinship system is an imposition of social ends upon a part of the natural world. It is therefore "production" in the most general sense of the term: a molding, a transformation of objects (in this case, people) to and by a subjective purpose (for this sense of production, see Marx, 1971a:80–99). It has its own relations of production, distribution, and exchange, which include certain "property" forms in people. These forms are not exclusive, private property rights, but rather different sorts of rights that various people have in other people. Marriage transactions—the gifts and material which circulate in the ceremonies marking a marriage—are a rich source of data for determining exactly who has which rights in whom. It is not difficult to deduce from such transactions that in most cases women's rights are considerably more residual than those of men.

Kinship systems do not merely exchange women. They exchange sexual access, genealogical statuses, lineage names and ancestors, rights and *people*—men, women, and children—in concrete systems of social relationships. These relationships always include certain rights for men, others for women. "Exchange of women" is a shorthand for expressing that the social relations of a kinship system specify that men have certain rights in their female kin, and that women do not have the same rights either to themselves or to their male kin. In this sense, the exchange of women is a profound perception of a system in which women do not have full rights to themselves. The exchange of women becomes an obfuscation if it is seen as a cultural necessity, and when it is used as the single tool with which an analysis of a particular kinship system is approached.

If Lévi-Strauss is correct in seeing the exchange of women as a fundamental principle of kinship, the subordination of women can be seen as a product of the relationships by which sex and gender are organized and produced. The economic oppression of women is derivative and secondary. But there is an "economics" of sex and gender, and what we need is a political economy of sexual systems. We need to study each society to determine the exact mechanisms by which particular conventions of sexuality are produced and maintained. The "exchange of women" is an initial step toward building an arsenal of concepts with which sexual systems can be described.

From *Deeper into the Labyrinth*

More concepts can be derived from an essay by Lévi-Strauss, "The Family," in which he introduces other considerations into his analysis of kinship. In *The Elementary Structures of Kinship*, he describes rules and systems of sexual combination. In "The Family," he raises the issue of the preconditions necessary for marriage systems to operate. He asks what sort of "people" are required by kinship systems, by way of an analysis of the sexual division of labor.

Although every society has some sort of division of tasks by sex, the assignment of any particular task to one sex or the other varies enormously. In some groups, agriculture is the work of women, in others, the work of men. Women carry the heavy burdens in some societies, men in others. There are even examples of female hunters and warriors, and of men performing child-care tasks. Lévi-Strauss concludes from a survey of the division of labor by sex that it is not a biological specialization, but must have some other purpose. This purpose, he argues, is to insure the union of men and women by making the smallest viable economic unit contain at least one man and one woman.

> The very fact that it [the sexual division of labor] varies endlessly according to the society selected for consideration shows that . . . it is the mere fact of its existence which is mysteriously required, the form under which it comes to exist being utterly irrelevant, at least from the point of view of any natural necessity . . . the sexual division of labor is nothing else than a device to institute a reciprocal state of dependency between the sexes. (Lévi-Strauss, 1971:347–48)

The division of labor by sex can therefore be seen as a "taboo": a taboo against the sameness of men and women, a taboo dividing the sexes into two mutually exclusive categories, a taboo which exacerbates the biological differences between the sexes and thereby *creates* gender. The division of labor can also be seen as a taboo against sexual arrangements other than those containing at least one man and one woman, thereby enjoining heterosexual marriage.

The argument in "The Family" displays a radical questioning of all human sexual arrangements, in which no aspect of sexuality is taken for granted as "natural" (Hertz, 1960, constructs a similar argument for a thoroughly cultural explanation of the denigration of left-handedness). Rather, all manifest forms of sex and gender are seen as being constituted by the imperatives of social systems. From such a perspective, even *The Elementary Structures of Kinship* can be seen to assume certain preconditions. In purely logical terms, a rule forbidding some marriages and commanding others presupposes a rule enjoining marriage. And marriage presupposes individuals who are disposed to marry.

It is of interest to carry this kind of deductive enterprise even further than Lévi-Strauss does, and to explicate the logical structure which underlies his entire analysis of kinship. At the most general level, the social organization of sex rests upon gender, obligatory heterosexuality, and the constraint of female sexuality.

Gender is a socially imposed division of the sexes. It is a product of the social relations of sexuality. Kinship systems rest upon marriage. They therefore transform males and females into "men" and "women," each an incomplete half which can only find wholeness when united with the other. Men and women are, of course, different. But they are not as different as day and night, earth and sky, yin and yang, life and death. In fact, from the standpoint of nature, men and women are closer to each other than either is to anything else—for instance, mountains, kangaroos, or coconut palms. The idea that men and women are more different from one another than either is from anything else must come from somewhere other than nature. Furthermore, although there is an average difference between males and females on a variety of traits, the range of variation of those traits shows considerable overlap. There will always be some women who are taller than some men, for instance, even though men are on the average taller than women. But the idea that men and women are two mutually exclusive categories must arise out of something other than a nonexistent "natural" opposition.[8] Far from being an expression of natural differences, exclusive gender identity is the suppression of natural similarities. It requires repression: in men, of whatever is the local version of "feminine" traits; in women, of the local definition of "masculine" traits. The division of the sexes has the effect of repressing some of the personality characteristics of virtually everyone, men and women. The same social system which oppresses women in its relations of exchange, oppresses everyone in its insistence upon a rigid division of personality.

Furthermore, individuals are engendered in order that marriage be guaranteed. Lévi-Strauss comes dangerously close to saying that heterosexuality is an instituted process. If biological and hormonal imperatives were as over-

---

8. "The woman shall not wear that which pertaineth unto a man, neither shall a man put on a woman's garment: for all that do so *are* abomination unto the LORD thy God" (Deuteronomy, 22:5; emphasis not mine).

whelming as popular mythology would have them, it would hardly be necessary to insure heterosexual unions by means of economic interdependency. Moreover, the incest taboo presupposes a prior, less articulate taboo on homosexuality. A prohibition against *some* heterosexual unions assumes a taboo against *non*-heterosexual unions. Gender is not only an identification with one sex; it also entails that sexual desire be directed toward the other sex. The sexual division of labor is implicated in both aspects of gender—male and female it creates them, and it creates them heterosexual. The suppression of the homosexual component of human sexuality, and by corollary, the oppression of homosexuals, is therefore a product of the same system whose rules and relations oppress women.

*　*　*

From *Psychoanalysis and Its Discontents*

*　*　*

[T]he rejection of Freud by the women's and gay movements has deeper roots in the rejection by psychoanalysis of its own insights. Nowhere are the effects on women of male-dominated social systems better documented than within the clinical literature. According to the Freudian orthodoxy, the attainment of "normal" femininity extracts severe costs from women. The theory of gender acquisition could have been the basis of a critique of sex roles. Instead, the radical implications of Freud's theory have been radically repressed. This tendency is evident even in the original formulations of the theory, but it has been exacerbated over time until the potential for a critical psychoanalytic theory of gender is visible only in the symptomatology of its denial—an intricate rationalization of sex roles as they are. It is not the purpose of this paper to conduct a psychoanalysis of the psychoanalytic unconscious; but I do hope to demonstrate that it exists. Moreover, the salvage of psychoanalysis from its own motivated repression is not for the sake of Freud's good name. Psychoanalysis contains a unique set of concepts for understanding men, women, and sexuality. It is a theory of sexuality in human society. Most importantly, psychoanalysis provides a description of the mechanisms by which the sexes are divided and deformed, of how bisexual, androgynous infants are transformed into boys and girls.[9] Psychoanalysis is a feminist theory *manqué*.

The Oedipus Hex

Until the late 1920s, the psychoanalytic movement did not have a distinctive theory of feminine development. Instead, variants of an "Electra" complex in women had been proposed, in which female experience was thought to be a mirror image of the Oedipal complex described for males. The boy loved his mother, but gave her up out of fear of the father's threat of castra-

---

9. "In studying women we cannot neglect the methods of a science of the mind, a theory that attempts to explain how women become women and men, men. The borderline between the biological and the social which finds expression in the family is the land psychoanalysis sets out to chart, the land where sexual distinction originates." (Mitchell, 1971:167)

"What is the *object* of psychoanalysis? . . . but the *'effects,'* prolonged into the surviving adult, of the extraordinary adventure which from birth the liquidation of the Oedipal phase transforms a small animal conceived by a man and a woman into a small human child . . . the 'effects' still present in the survivors of the forced 'humanization' of the small human animal into a *man* or a *woman*. . . ." (Althusser, 1969:57, 59; italics in original)

tion. The girl, it was thought, loved her father, and gave him up out of fear of maternal vengeance. This formulation assumed that both children were subject to a biological imperative toward heterosexuality. It also assumed that the children were already, before the Oedipal phase, "little" men and women.

Freud had voiced reservations about jumping to conclusions about women on the basis of data gathered from men. But his objections remained general until the discovery of the pre-Oedipal phase in women. The concept of the pre-Oedipal phase enabled both Freud and Jeanne Lampl de Groot to articulate the classic psychoanalytic theory of femininity.[1] The idea of the pre-Oedipal phase in women produced a dislocation of the biologically derived presuppositions which underlay notions of an "Electra" complex. In the pre-Oedipal phase, children of both sexes were psychically indistinguishable, which meant that their differentiation into masculine and feminine children had to be explained, rather than assumed. Pre-Oedipal children were described as bisexual. Both sexes exhibited the full range of libidinal attitudes, active and passive. And for children of both sexes, the mother was the object of desire.

In particular, the characteristics of the pre-Oedipal female challenged the ideas of a primordial heterosexuality and gender identity. Since the girl's libidinal activity was directed toward the mother, her adult heterosexuality had to be explained:

> It would be a solution of ideal simplicity if we could suppose that from a particular age onwards the elementary influence of the mutual attraction between the sexes makes itself felt and impels the small woman towards men. . . . But we are not going to find things so easy; we scarcely know whether we are to believe seriously in the power of which poets talk so much and with such enthusiasm but which cannot be further dissected analytically. (Freud, 1965:119)

Moreover, the girl did not manifest a "feminine" libidinal attitude. Since her desire for the mother was active and aggressive, her ultimate accession to "femininity" had also to be explained:

> In conformity with its peculiar nature, psychoanalysis does not try to describe what a woman is . . . but sets about enquiring how she comes into being, how a woman develops out of a child with a bisexual disposition. (Ibid.:116)

In short, feminine development could no longer be taken for granted as a reflex of biology. Rather, it had become immensely problematic. It is in explaining the acquisition of "femininity" that Freud employs the concepts of

---

1. The psychoanalytic theories of femininity were articulated in the context of a debate which took place largely in the *International Journal of Psychoanalysis* and *The Psychoanalytic Quarterly* in the late 1920s and early 1930s. Articles representing the range of discussion include: Freud, 1961a, 1961b, 1965; Lampl de Groot, 1933, 1948; Deutsch, 1948a, 1948b; Horney, 1973; Jones, 1933. Some of my dates are of reprints; for the original chronology, see Chasseguet-Smirgel (1970: introduction). The debate was complex, and I have simplified it. Freud, Lampl de Groot, and Deutsch argued that femininity developed out of a bisexual, "phallic" girl-child; Horney and Jones argued for an innate femininity. The debate was not without its ironies. Horney defended women against penis envy by postulating that women are born and not made; Deutsch, who considered women to be made and not born, developed a theory of feminine masochism whose best rival is *Story of O*. I have attributed the core of the "Freudian" version of female development equally to Freud and to Lampl de Groot. In reading through the articles, it has seemed to me that the theory is as much (or more) hers as it is his.

penis envy and castration which have infuriated feminists since he first introduced them. The girl turns from the mother and represses the "masculine" elements of her libido as a result of her recognition that she is castrated. She compares her tiny clitoris to the larger penis, and in the face of its evident superior ability to satisfy the mother, falls prey to penis envy and a sense of inferiority. She gives up her struggle for the mother and assumes a passive feminine position vis-à-vis the father. Freud's account can be read as claiming that femininity is a consequence of the anatomical differences between the sexes. He has therefore been accused of biological determinism. Nevertheless, even in his most anatomically stated versions of the female castration complex, the "inferiority" of the woman's genitals is a product of the situational context: the girl feels less "equipped" to possess and satisfy the mother. If the pre-Oedipal lesbian were not confronted by the heterosexuality of the mother, she might draw different conclusions about the relative status of her genitals.

Freud was never as much of a biological determinist as some would have him. He repeatedly stressed that all adult sexuality resulted from psychic, not biologic, development. But his writing is often ambiguous, and his wording leaves plenty of room for the biological interpretations which have been so popular in American psychoanalysis. In France, on the other hand, the trend in psychoanalytic theory has been to de-biologize Freud, and to conceive of psychoanalysis as a theory of information rather than organs. Jacques Lacan, the instigator of this line of thinking, insists that Freud never meant to say anything about anatomy, and that Freud's theory was instead about language and the cultural meanings imposed upon anatomy. The debate over the "real" Freud is extremely interesting, but it is not my purpose here to contribute to it. Rather, I want to rephrase the classic theory of femininity in Lacan's terminology, after introducing some of the pieces of Lacan's conceptual chessboard.

Kinship, Lacan, and the Phallus

Lacan suggests that psychoanalysis is the study of the traces left in the psyches of individuals as a result of their conscription into systems of kinship.

> Isn't it striking that Lévi-Strauss, in suggesting that implication of the structures of language with that part of the social laws which regulate marriage ties and kinship, is already conquering the very terrain in which Freud situates the unconscious? (Lacan, 1968:48)

> For where on earth would one situate the determinations of the unconsciousness if it is not in those nominal cadres in which marriage ties and kinship are always grounded. . . . And how would one apprehend the analytical conflicts and their Oedipean prototype outside the engagements which have fixed, long before the subject came into the world, not only his destiny, but his identity itself? (Ibid.:126)

> This is precisely where the Oedipus complex . . . may be said, in this connection, to mark the limits which our discipline assigns to subjectivity: that is to say, what the subject can know of his unconscious participation in the movement of the complex structures of marriage ties, by verifying the symbolic effects in his individual existence of the tangential movement towards incest. . . . (Ibid.:40)

Kinship is the culturalization of biological sexuality on the societal level; psychoanalysis describes the transformation of the biological sexuality of individuals as they are enculturated.

Kinship terminology contains information about the system. Kin terms demarcate statuses, and indicate some of the attributes of those statuses. For instance, in the Trobriand Islands a man calls the women of his clan by the term for "sister." He calls the women of clans into which he can marry by a term indicating their marriageability. When the young Trobriand male learns these terms, he learns which women he can safely desire. In Lacan's scheme, the Oedipal crisis occurs when a child learns of the sexual rules embedded in the terms for family and relatives. The crisis begins when the child comprehends the system and his or her place in it; the crisis is resolved when the child accepts that place and accedes to it. Even if the child refuses its place, he or she cannot escape knowledge of it. Before the Oedipal phase, the sexuality of the child is labile and relatively unstructured. Each child contains all of the sexual possibilities available to human expression. But in any given society, only some of these possibilities will be expressed, while others will be constrained. When the child leaves the Oedipal phase, its libido and gender identity have been organized in conformity with the rules of the culture which is domesticating it.

The Oedipal complex is an apparatus for the production of sexual personality. It is a truism to say that societies will inculcate in their young the character traits appropriate to carrying on the business of society. For instance, E. P. Thompson (1963) speaks of the transformation of the personality structure of the English working class, as artisans were changed into good industrial workers. Just as the social forms of labor demand certain kinds of personality, the social forms of sex and gender demand certain kinds of people. In the most general terms, the Oedipal complex is a machine which fashions the appropriate forms of sexual individuals (see also the discussion of different forms of "historical individuality" in Althusser and Balibar, 1970:112, 251–53).

In the Lacanian theory of psychoanalysis, it is the kin terms that indicate a structure of relationships which will determine the role of any individual or object within the Oedipal drama. For instance, Lacan makes a distinction between the "function of the father" and a particular father who embodies this function. In the same way, he makes a radical distinction between the penis and the "phallus," between organ and information. The phallus is a set of meanings conferred upon the penis. The differentiation between phallus and penis in contemporary French psychoanalytic terminology emphasizes the idea that the penis could not and does not play the role attributed to it in the classical terminology of the castration complex.[2]

2. I have taken my position on Freud somewhere between the French structuralist interpretations and American biologistic ones, because I think that Freud's wording is similarly somewhere in the middle. He does talk about penises, about the "inferiority" of the clitoris, about the psychic consequences of anatomy. The Lacanians, on the other hand, argue from Freud's text that he is unintelligible if his words are taken literally, and that a thoroughly nonanatomical theory can be deduced as Freud's intention (see Althusser, 1969). I think that they are right; the penis is walking around too much for its role to be taken literally. The detachability of the penis, and its transformation in fantasy (e.g., penis = feces = child = gift), argue strongly for a symbolic interpretation. Nevertheless, I don't think that Freud was as consistent as either I or Lacan would like him to have been, and some gesture must be made to what he said, even as we play with what he must have meant.

In Freud's terminology, the Oedipal complex presents two alternatives to a child: to have a penis or to be castrated. In contrast, the Lacanian theory of the castration complex leaves behind all reference to anatomical reality:

> The theory of the castration complex amounts to having the male organ play a dominant role—this time as a symbol—*to the extent that its absence or presence transforms an anatomical difference into a major classification of humans, and to the extent that, for each subject, this presence or absence is not taken for granted, is not reduced purely and simply to a given, but is the problematical result of an intra- and intersubjective process* (the subject's assumption of his own sex). (Laplanche and Pontalis, in Mehlman, 1972:198–99; my italics)

The alternative presented to the child may be rephrased as an alternative between having, or not having, the phallus. Castration is not having the (symbolic) phallus. Castration is not a real "lack," but a meaning conferred upon the genitals of a woman:

> Castration may derive support from . . . the apprehension in the Real of the absence of the penis in women—but even this supposes a symbolization of the object, since the Real is full, and "lacks" nothing. Insofar as one finds castration in the genesis of neurosis, it is never real but symbolic. . . . (Lacan, 1968:271)

The phallus is, as it were, a distinctive feature differentiating "castrated" and "noncastrated." The presence or absence of the phallus carries the differences between two sexual statuses, "man" and "woman" (see Jakobson and Halle, 1971, on distinctive features). Since these are not equal, the phallus also carries a meaning of the dominance of men over women, and it may be inferred that "penis envy" is a recognition thereof. Moreover, as long as men have rights in women which women do not have in themselves, the phallus also carries the meaning of the difference between "exchanger" and "exchanged," gift and giver. Ultimately, neither the classical Freudian nor the rephrased Lacanian theories of the Oedipal process make sense unless at least this much of the paleolithic relations of sexuality are still with us. We still live in a "phallic" culture.

Lacan also speaks of the phallus as a symbolic object which is exchanged within and between families (see also Wilden, 1968:303–305). It is interesting to think about this observation in terms of primitive marriage transactions and exchange networks. In those transactions, the exchange of women is usually one of many cycles of exchange. Usually, there are other objects circulating as well as women. Women move in one direction, cattle, shells, or mats in the other. In one sense, the Oedipal complex is an expression of the circulation of the phallus in intrafamily exchange, an inversion of the circulation of women in interfamily exchange. In the cycle of exchange manifested by the Oedipal complex, the phallus passes through the medium of women from one man to another—from father to son, from mother's brother to sister's son, and so forth. In this family *Kula* ring, women go one way, the phallus the other. It is where we aren't. In this sense, the phallus is more than a feature which distinguishes the sexes: it is the embodiment of the male status, to which men accede, and in which certain rights inhere—among them, the right to a woman. It is an expression of the transmission of male dominance. It passes through women and settles upon men.[3] The tracks which it leaves include gender identity, the division of the sexes. But it leaves more than this. It leaves "penis envy," which acquires a rich meaning of the disquietude of women in a phallic culture.

Oedipus Revisited

We return now to the two pre-Oedipal androgynes, sitting on the border between biology and culture. Lévi-Strauss places the incest taboo on that border, arguing that its initiation of the exchange of women constitutes the origin of society. In this sense, the incest taboo and the exchange of women are the content of the original social contract (see Sahlins, 1972: Chap. 4). For individuals, the Oedipal crisis occurs at the same divide, when the incest taboo initiates the exchange of the phallus.

The Oedipal crisis is precipitated by certain items of information. The children discover the differences between the sexes, and that each child must become one or the other gender. They also discover the incest taboo, and that some sexuality is prohibited—in this case, the mother is unavailable to either child because she "belongs" to the father. Lastly, they discover that the two genders do not have the same sexual "rights" or futures.

In the normal course of events, the boy renounces his mother for fear that otherwise his father would castrate him (refuse to give him the phallus and make him a girl). But by this act of renunciation, the boy affirms the relationships which have given mother to father and which will give him, if he becomes a man, a woman of his own. In exchange for the boy's affirmation of his father's right to his mother, the father affirms the phallus in his son (does not castrate him). The boy exchanges his mother for the phallus, the symbolic token which can later be exchanged for a woman. The only thing required of him is a little patience. He retains his initial libidinal organization and the sex of his original love object. The social contract to which he has agreed will eventually recognize his own rights and provide him with a woman of his own.

What happens to the girl is more complex. She, like the boy, discovers the taboo against incest and the division of the sexes. She also discovers some unpleasant information about the gender to which she is being assigned. For the boy, the taboo on incest is a taboo on certain women. For the girl, it is a taboo on all women. Since she is in a homosexual position vis-à-vis the mother, the rule of heterosexuality which dominates the scenario makes her

---

3. The pre-Oedipal mother is the "phallic mother," e.g., she is believed to possess the phallus. The Oedipal-inducing information is that the mother does not possess the phallus. In other words, the crisis is precipitated by the "castration" of the mother, by the recognition that the phallus only passes through her, but does not settle on her. The "phallus" must pass through her, since the relationship of a male to every other male is defined through a woman. A man is linked to a son by a mother, to his nephew by virtue of a sister, etc. Every relationship between male kin is defined by the woman between them. If power is a male prerogative, and must be passed on, it must go through the woman-in-between. Marshall Sahlins (personal communication) once suggested that the reason women are so often defined as stupid, polluting, disorderly, silly, profane, or whatever, is that such categorizations define women as "incapable" of possessing the power which must be transferred through them.

position excruciatingly untenable. The mother, and all women by extension, can only be properly beloved by someone "with a penis" (phallus). Since the girl has no "phallus," she has no "right" to love her mother or another woman, since she is herself destined to some man. She does not have the symbolic token which can be exchanged for a woman.

If Freud's wording of this moment of the female Oedipal crisis is ambiguous, Lampl de Groot's formulation makes the context which confers meaning upon the genitals explicit:

> . . . *if the little girl comes to the conclusion that such an organ is really indispensable to the possession of the mother, she experiences* in addition to the narcissistic insults common to both sexes still another blow, namely *a feeling of inferiority about her genitals.* (Lampl de Groot, 1933:497; my italics)

The girl concludes that the "penis" is indispensable for the possession of the mother because only those who possess the phallus have a "right" to a woman, and the token of exchange. She does not come to her conclusion because of the natural superiority of the penis either in and of itself, or as an instrument for making love. The hierarchical arrangement of the male and female genitals is a result of the definitions of the situation—the rule of obligatory heterosexuality and the relegation of women (those without the phallus, castrated) to men (those with the phallus).

The girl then begins to turn away from the mother, and to the father.

> To the girl, it [castration] is an accomplished fact, which is irrevocable, but the recognition of which compels her finally to renounce her first love object and to taste to the full the bitterness of its loss . . . the father is chosen as a love-object, the enemy becomes the beloved. . . . (Lampl de Groot, 1948:213)

This recognition of "castration" forces the girl to redefine her relationship to herself, her mother, and her father.

She turns from the mother because she does not have the phallus to give her. She turns from the mother also in anger and disappointment, because the mother did not give her a "penis" (phallus). But the mother, a woman in a phallic culture, does not have the phallus to give away (having gone through the Oedipal crisis herself a generation earlier). The girl then turns to the father because only he can "give her the phallus," and it is only through him that she can enter into the symbolic exchange system in which the phallus circulates. But the father does not give her the phallus in the same way that he gives it to the boy. The phallus is affirmed in the boy, who then has it to give away. The girl never gets the phallus. It passes through her, and in its passage is transformed into a child. When she "recognizes her castration," she accedes to the place of a woman in a phallic exchange network. She can "get" the phallus—in intercourse, or as a child—but only as a gift from a man. She never gets to give it away.

When she turns to the father, she also represses the "active" portions of her libido:

The turning away from her mother is an extremely important step in the course of a little girl's development. It is more than a mere change of object . . . hand in hand with it there is to be observed a marked lowering of the active sexual impulses and a rise of the passive ones. . . . The transition to the father object is accomplished with the help of the passive trends in so far as they have escaped the catastrophe. The path to the development of femininity now lies open to the girl. (Freud, 1961b:239)

The ascendance of passivity in the girl is due to her recognition of the futility of realizing her active desire, and of the unequal terms of the struggle. Freud locates active desire in the clitoris and passive desire in the vagina, and thus describes the repression of active desire as the repression of clitoral eroticism in favor of passive vaginal eroticism. In this scheme, cultural stereotypes have been mapped onto the genitals. Since the work of Masters and Johnson,[4] it is evident that this genital division is a false one. Any organ—penis, clitoris, vagina—can be the locus of either active or passive eroticism. What is important in Freud's scheme, however, is not the geography of desire, but its self-confidence. It is not an organ which is repressed, but a segment of erotic possibility. Freud notes that "more constraint has been applied to the libido when it is pressed into the service of the feminine function . . ." (Freud, 1965:131). The girl has been robbed.

If the Oedipal phase proceeds normally and the girl "accepts her castration," her libidinal structure and object choice are mow congruent with the female gender role. She has become a little woman—feminine, passive, heterosexual. Actually, Freud suggests that there are three alternate routes out of the Oedipal catastrophe. The girl may simply freak out, repress sexuality altogether, and become asexual. She may protest, cling to her narcissism and desire, and become either "masculine" or homosexual. Or she may accept the situation, sign the social contract, and attain "normality."

Karen Horney is critical of the entire Freud/Lampl de Groot scheme. But in the course of her critique she articulates its implications:

. . . when she [the girl] first turns to a man (the father), it is in the main only by way of the narrow bridge of resentment . . . we should feel it a contradiction if the relation of woman to man did not retain throughout life some tinge of this enforced substitute for that which was really desired. . . . The same character of something remote from instinct, secondary and substitutive, would, even in normal women, adhere to the wish for motherhood. . . . The special point about Freud's viewpoint is rather that it sees the wish for motherhood not as an innate formation, but as something that can be reduced psychologically to its ontogenetic elements and draws its energy originally from homosexual or phallic instinctual elements. . . . It would follow, finally, that women's whole reaction to life would be based on a strong subterranean resentment. (Horney, 1973: 148–49)

---

4. William Masters and Virginia Johnson, pioneering American researchers into the physiology of human sexuality; their major works were *Human* *Sexual Response* (1966) and *Human Sexual Inadequacy* (1970) [editor's note].

Horney considers these implications to be so far-fetched that they challenge the validity of Freud's entire scheme. But it is certainly plausible to argue instead that the creation of "femininity" in women in the course of socialization is an act of psychic brutality, and that it leaves in women an immense resentment of the suppression to which they were subjected. It is also possible to argue that women have few means for realizing and expressing their residual anger. One can read Freud's essays on femininity as descriptions of how a group is prepared psychologically, at a tender age, to live with its oppression.

There is an additional element in the classic discussions of the attainment of womanhood. The girl first turns to the father because she must, because she is "castrated" (a woman, helpless, etc.). She then discovers that "castration" is a prerequisite to the father's love, that she must be a woman for him to love her. She therefore begins to desire "castration," and what had previously been a disaster becomes a wish.

> Analytic experience leaves no room for doubt that the little girl's first libidinal relation to her father is masochistic, and the masochistic wish in its earliest distinctively feminine phase is: "I want to be castrated by my father." (Deutsch, 1948a:228)

Deutsch argues that such masochism may conflict with the ego, causing some women to flee the entire situation in defense of their self-regard. Those women to whom the choice is "between finding bliss in suffering or peace in renunciation" (ibid.:231) will have difficulty in attaining a healthy attitude to intercourse and motherhood. Why Deutsch appears to consider such women to be special cases, rather than the norm, is not clear from her discussion.

The psychoanalytic theory of femininity is one that sees female development based largely on pain and humiliation, and it takes some fancy footwork to explain why anyone ought to enjoy being a woman. At this point in the classic discussions biology makes a triumphant return. The fancy footwork consists in arguing that finding joy in pain is adaptive to the role of women in reproduction, since childbirth and defloration are "painful." Would it not make more sense to question the entire procedure? If women, in finding their place in a sexual system, are robbed of libido and forced into a masochistic eroticism, why did the analysts not argue for novel arrangements, instead of rationalizing the old ones?

Freud's theory of femininity has been subjected to feminist critique since it was first published. To the extent that it is a rationalization of female subordination, this critique has been justified. To the extent that it is a description of a process which subordinates women, this critique is a mistake. As a description of how phallic culture domesticates women, and the effects in women of their domestication, psychoanalytic theory has no parallel (see also Mitchell, 1971 and 1974; Lasch, 1974). And since psychoanalysis is a theory of gender, dismissing it would be suicidal for a political movement dedicated to eradicating gender hierarchy (or gender itself). We cannot dismantle something that we underestimate or do not understand. The oppression of women is deep; equal pay, equal work, and all of the female politicians in the world will not extirpate the roots of sexism. Lévi-Strauss and Freud elucidate what would otherwise be poorly perceived parts of the deep structures of sex oppression. They serve as reminders of the intractability and magnitude of what we fight, and their analyses provide preliminary charts of the social machinery we must rearrange.

*   *   *

WORKS CITED

Althusser, Louis. 1969. "Freud and Lacan." *New Left Review*, no. 55: 48–65.

Althusser, Louis, and Etienne Balibar. 1970. *Reading Capital*. Trans. Ben Brewster. London: New Left Books.

Benston, Margaret. 1969. "The Political Economy of Women's Liberation." *Monthly Review* 21, no. 4: 13–27.

Berndt, Ronald. 1962. *Excess and Restraint: Social Control among a New Guinea Mountain People*. Chicago: University of Chicago Press.

Buchbinder, Georgeda, and Roy Rappaport. 1976. "Fertility and Death among the Maring." In *Man and Woman in the New Guinea Highlands*, ed. Paula Brown and Georgeda Buchbinder. Washington, D.C.: American Anthropological Association.

Chasseguit-Smirgel, Janine. 1970. *Female Sexuality: New Psychoanalytic Views*. Ann Arbor: University of Michigan Press.

Deutsch, Helene. 1948a. "The Significance of Masochism in the Mental Life of Women." In *The Psychoanalytic Reader, an Anthology of Essential Papers, with Critical Introductions*, ed. Robert Fliess. New York: International Universities Press.

———. 1948b. "On Female Homosexuality." In *The Psychoanalytic Reader, an Anthology of Essential Papers, with Critical Introductions*, ed. Robert Fliess. New York: International Universities Press.

Engels, Frederick. 1972. *The Origin of the Family, Private Property, and the State, in the Light of the Researches of Lewis H. Morgan*. Ed. Eleanor Leacock. New York: International Publishers.

Evans-Prichard, E. E. 1951. *Kinship and Marriage among the Nuer*. London: Oxford University Press.

Fee, Elizabeth. 1973. "The Sexual Politics of Victorian Social Anthropology." *Feminist Studies* 1 (Winter/Spring): 23–29.

Foucault, Michel. 1970. *The Order of Things: An Archaeology of the Human Sciences*. New York: Pantheon.

Freud, Sigmund. 1961a. "Some Psychical Consequences of the Anatomical Distinction between the Sexes." in *The Complete Works of Sigmund Freud*, ed. James Strachey, vol. 19. London: Hogarth.

———. 1961b. "Female Sexuality." In *The Complete Works of Sigmund Freud*, ed. James Strachey, vol. 21. London: Hogarth.

———. 1965. "Femininity." In *New Introductory Lectures in Psychoanalysis*, ed. James Strachey, New York: Norton.

Glasse, G. M. 1971. "The Mask of Venery." Paper read at the 70th Annual Meeting of the American Anthropological Association, New York, December.

Hefner, Robert. 1974. "The Tel Quel Ideology: Material Practice upon Material Practice." *Substance* 8: 127–38.

Hertz, Robert. 1960. *Death and the Right Hand*. Trans. Rodney and Claudia Needham. Glencoe, Ill.: Free Press.

Horney, Karen. 1973. "The Denial of the Vagina." In her *Feminine Psychology*. Ed. Harold Kelman. New York: Norton.

Jakobson, Roman, and Morris Halle. 1971. *Fundamentals of Language*. 2nd rev. ed. The Hague: Mouton.

Jones, Ernest. 1933. "The Phallic Phase." *International Journal of Psychoanalysis* 14: 1–33.

Lacan, Jacques. 1968. "The Function of Language in Psychoanalysis." In Wilden 1968.

Lampl de Groot, Jeanne. 1933. "Problems of Femininity." *Psychoanalytic Quarterly* 2: 489–518.

———. 1948. In *The Psychoanalytic Reader, an Anthology of Essential Papers, with Critical Introductions,* ed. Robert Fliess. New York: International Universities Press.

Langness, L. L. 1967. "Sexual Antagonism in the New Guinea Highlands: A Bena Bena Example." *Oceania* 37, no. 3: 161–77.

Lasch, Christopher. 1974. "Freud and Women." *New York Review of Books* 21, no. 15: 12–17.

Lévi-Strauss, Claude. 1969. *The Elementary Structures of Kinship.* Trans. French James Harle Bell, John Richard von Sturmer, and Rodney Needham, ed. Rev. ed. Boston: Beacon Press.

———. 1971. "The Family." In *Man, Culture, and Society,* ed. Harry L. Shapiro. Rev. ed. London: Oxford University Press.

Lindenbaum, Shirley. 1973. "A Wife Is the Hand of Man." Paper read at the 72nd Annual Meeting of the American Anthropological Association. New Orleans, November.

Livingstone, Frank. 1969. "Genetics, Ecology, and the Origins of Incest and Exogamy." *Current Anthropology* 10, no. 1: 45–49.

Malinowski, Bronislaw. 1929. *The Sexual Life of Savages in North-Western Melanesia: An Ethnographic Account of Courtship, Marriage, and Family Life among the Natives of the Trobriand Islands, British New Guinea.* London: G. Routledge and Sons.

Marx, Karl. 1971a. *Pre-Capitalist Economic Formations.* New York: International Publishers.

———. 1971b. *Wage-Labor and Capital.* New York: International Publishers.

———. 1972. *Capital.* Ed. Frederick Engels. [Trans. Samuel Moore and Edward Aveling.] Vol. 1. New York: International Publishers.

Meggitt, M. J. 1964. "Male-Female Relationships in the Highlands of Australian New Guinea." *American Anthropologist* 66, no. 4, part 2: 204–24.

Mehlman, Jeffrey. 1972. *French Freud: Structural Studies in Psychoanalysis.* Yale French Studies 48. New Haven: Yale University.

Mitchell, Juliet. 1971. *Woman's Estate.* New York: Vintage.

———. 1974. *Psychoanalysis and Feminism.* New York: Pantheon.

Morgan, Lewis H. 1963. *Ancient Society; or, Researches in the Lines of Human Progress from Savagery through Barbarism to Civilization.* Ed. Eleanor Leacock. Cleveland: World Publishing.

Read, Kenneth. 1952. "The Nama Cult of the Central Highlands, New Guinea." *Oceania* 23, no. 1: 1–25.

Reay, Marie. 1959. *The Kuma: Freedom and Conformity in the New Guinea Highlands.* Carlton: Melbourne University Press on behalf of the Australian National University; London: Cambridge University Press.

Sahlins, Marshall. 1960. "The Origin of Society." *Scientific American* 203, no. 3: 76–86.

———. 1972. *Stone Age Economics.* Chicago: Aldine-Atherton.

Schneider, David, and Kathleen Gough, eds. 1961. *Matrilineal Kinship.* Berkeley: University of California Press.

Strathern, Marilyn. 1972. *Women in Between; Female Roles in a Male World: Mount Hagen, New Guinea.* New York: Seminar.

Thompson, E. P. 1963. *The Making of the English Working Class.* New York: Vintage.

Van Baal, J. 1966. *Dema: Description and Analysis of Marind-anim Culture (South New Guinea).* The Hague: Nijhoff.

Wilden, Anthony. 1968. *The Language of the Self: The Function of Language in Psychoanalysis.* Baltimore: Johns Hopkins University Press.

1975

HÉLÈNE CIXOUS
b. 1937

The concept of *écriture féminine* (woman's writing) derives in large part from the lyrical essays and fiction of Hélène Cixous, who helped establish the first center for women's studies in France. Born in Algeria, Cixous moved to Paris in 1955, at the beginning of the Algerian War; there she studied English literature and produced a number of prize-winning novels. In 1975, she published *La jeune née* with Catherine Clément, a text that was not translated into *The Newly Born Woman* until 1986. But the dialogues between French and American feminists began a decade earlier, when Cixous' translated essay "The Laugh of the Medusa" appeared in *Signs*. A founder of the experimental Université de Paris VIII at Vincennes, of the experimental review *Poétique,* and of the Centre de Recherches en Études Féminines, Cixous has composed a number of autobiographical works as well as critical studies on or influenced by James Joyce, Sigmund Freud, and Georges Bataille. In her fiction, as in her nonfictional prose, Cixous frequently engages the psychoanalytic ideas of Jacques Lacan and the theory of deconstruction formulated by Jacques Derrida; she does so to affirm the value of the devalued, feminine component in what has historically been subordinated, marginalized or repressed in traditional discourses.

The Laugh of the Medusa[1]

I shall speak about women's writing: about *what it will do.* Woman must write her self: must write about women and bring women to writing, from which they have been driven away as violently as from their bodies—for the same reasons, by the same law, with the same fatal goal. Woman must put herself into the text—as into the world and into history—by her own movement.

The future must no longer be determined by the past. I do not deny that the effects of the past are still with us. But I refuse to strengthen them by repeating them, to confer upon them an irremovability the equivalent of destiny, to confuse the biological and the cultural. Anticipation is imperative.

Since these reflections are taking shape in an area just on the point of being discovered, they necessarily bear the mark of our time—a time during which the new breaks away from the old, and, more precisely, the (feminine) new from the old (*la nouvelle de l'ancien*). Thus, as there are no grounds for establishing a discourse, but rather an arid millennial ground to break, what I say has at least two sides and two aims: to break up, to destroy; and to foresee the unforeseeable, to project.

I write this as a woman, toward women. When I say "woman," I'm speaking of woman in her inevitable struggle against conventional man; and of a universal woman subject who must bring women to their senses and to their meaning in history. But first it must be said that in spite of the enormity of the repression that has kept them in the "dark"—that dark which people have been trying to make them accept as their attribute—there is, at this time, no general woman, no one typical woman. What they have *in common* I will say.

---

1. This is a revised version of "Le Rire de la Méduse," which appeared in *L'Arc* (1975), pp. 39–54. Translated by Keith Cohen and Paula Cohen. [Except as indicated, all notes are by Cixous.]

But what strikes me is the infinite richness of their individual constitutions: you can't talk about *a* female sexuality, uniform, homogeneous, classifiable into codes—any more than you can talk about one unconscious resembling another. Women's imaginary is inexhaustible, like music, painting, writing: their stream of phantasms is incredible.

I have been amazed more than once by a description a woman gave me of a world all her own which she had been secretly haunting since early childhood. A world of searching, the elaboration of a knowledge, on the basis of a systematic experimentation with the bodily functions, a passionate and precise interrogation of her erotogeneity. This practice, extraordinarily rich and inventive, in particular as concerns masturbation, is prolonged or accompanied by a production of forms, a veritable aesthetic activity, each stage of rapture inscribing a resonant vision, a composition, something beautiful. Beauty will no longer be forbidden.

I wished that that woman would write and proclaim this unique empire so that other women, other unacknowledged sovereigns, might exclaim: I, too, overflow; my desires have invented new desires, my body knows unheard-of songs. Time and again I, too, have felt so full of luminous torrents that I could burst—burst with forms much more beautiful than those which are put up in frames and sold for a stinking fortune. And I, too, said nothing, showed nothing; I didn't open my mouth, I didn't repaint my half of the world. I was ashamed. I was afraid, and I swallowed my shame and my fear. I said to myself: You are mad! What's the meaning of these waves, these floods, these outbursts? Where is the ebullient, infinite woman who, immersed as she was in her naiveté, kept in the dark about herself, led into self-disdain by the great arm of parental-conjugal phallocentrism, hasn't been ashamed of her strength? Who, surprised and horrified by the fantastic tumult of her drives (for she was made to believe that a well-adjusted normal woman has a . . . divine composure), hasn't accused herself of being a monster? Who, feeling a funny desire stirring inside her (to sing, to write, to dare to speak, in short, to bring out something new), hasn't thought she was sick? Well, her shameful sickness is that she resists death, that she makes trouble.

And why don't you write? Write! Writing is for you, you are for you; your body is yours, take it. I know why you haven't written. (And why I didn't write before the age of twenty-seven.) Because writing is at once too high, too great for you, it's reserved for the great—that is, for "great men"; and it's "silly." Besides, you've written a little, but in secret. And it wasn't good, because it was in secret, and because you punished yourself for writing, because you didn't go all the way; or because you wrote, irresistibly, as when we would masturbate in secret, not to go further, but to attenuate the tension a bit, just enough to take the edge off. And then as soon as we come, we go and make ourselves feel guilty—so as to be forgiven; or to forget, to bury it until the next time.

Write, let no one hold you back, let nothing stop you: not man; not the imbecilic capitalist machinery, in which publishing houses are the crafty, obsequious relayers of imperatives handed down by an economy that works against us and off our backs; and not *yourself*. Smug-faced readers, managing editors, and big bosses don't like the true texts of women—female-sexed texts. That kind scares them.

I write woman: woman must write woman. And man, man. So only an oblique consideration will be found here of man; it's up to him to say where his masculinity and femininity are at: this will concern us once men have opened their eyes and seen themselves clearly.[2]

Now women return from afar, from always: from "without," from the heath where witches are kept alive; from below, from beyond "culture"; from their childhood which men have been trying desperately to make them forget, condemning it to "eternal rest." The little girls and their "ill-mannered" bodies immured, well-preserved, intact unto themselves, in the mirror. Frigidified. But are they ever seething underneath! What an effort it takes—there's no end to it—for the sex cops to bar their threatening return. Such a display of forces on both sides that the struggle has for centuries been immobilized in the trembling equilibrium of a deadlock.

Here they are, returning, arriving over and again, because the unconscious is impregnable. They have wandered around in circles, confined to the narrow room in which they've been given a deadly brainwashing. You can incarcerate them, slow them down, get away with the old Apartheid routine, but for a time only. As soon as they begin to speak, at the same time as they're taught their name, they can be taught that their territory is black: because you are Africa, you are black. Your continent is dark. Dark is dangerous. You can't see anything in the dark, you're afraid. Don't move, you might fall. Most of all, don't go into the forest. And so we have internalized this horror of the dark.

Men have committed the greatest crime against women. Insidiously, violently, they have led them to hate women, to be their own enemies, to mobilize their immense strength against themselves, to be the executants of their virile needs. They have made for women an antinarcissism! A narcissism which loves itself only to be loved for what women haven't got! They have constructed the infamous logic of antilove.

We the precocious, we the repressed of culture, our lovely mouths gagged with pollen, our wind knocked out of us, we the labyrinths, the ladders, the trampled spaces, the bevies—we are black and we are beautiful.

We're stormy, and that which is ours breaks loose from us without our fearing any debilitation. Our glances, our smiles, are spent; laughs exude from all our mouths; our blood flows and we extend ourselves without ever reaching an end; we never hold back our thoughts, our signs, our writing; and we're not afraid of lacking.

What happiness for us who are omitted, brushed aside at the scene of inheritances; we inspire ourselves and we expire without running out of breath, we are everywhere!

From now on, who, if we say so, can say no to us? We've come back from always.

It is time to liberate the New Woman from the Old by coming to know her—by loving her for getting by, for getting beyond the Old without delay,

---

2. Men still have everything to say about their sexuality, and everything to write. For what they have said so far, for the most part, stems from the opposition activity/passivity, from the power relation between a fantasized obligatory virility meant to invade, to colonize, and the consequential phantasm of woman as a "dark continent" to penetrate and to "pacify." (We know what "pacify" means in terms of scotomizing the other and mis-recognizing the self.) Conquering her, they've made haste to depart from her borders, to get out of sight, out of body. The way man has of getting out of himself and into her whom he takes not for the other but for his own, deprives him, he knows, of his own bodily territory. One can understand how man, confusing himself with his penis and rushing in for the attack, might feel resentment and fear of being "taken" by the woman, of being lost in her, absorbed, or alone.

by going out ahead of what the New Woman will be, as an arrow quits the bow with a movement that gathers and separates the vibrations musically, in order to be more than her self.

I say that we must, for, with a few rare exceptions, there has not yet been any writing that inscribes femininity; exceptions so rare, in fact, that, after plowing through literature across languages, cultures, and ages,[3] one can only be startled at this vain scouting mission. It is well known that the number of women writers (while having increased very slightly from the nineteenth century on) has always been ridiculously small. This is a useless and deceptive fact unless from their species of female writers we do not first deduct the immense majority whose workmanship is in no way different from male writing, and which either obscures women or reproduces the classic representations of women (as sensitive—intuitive—dreamy, etc.).[4]

Let me insert here a parenthetical remark. I mean it when I speak of male writing. I maintain unequivocally that there is such a thing as *marked* writing; that, until now, far more extensively and repressively than is ever suspected or admitted, writing has been run by a libidinal and cultural—hence political, typically masculine—economy; that this is a locus where the repression of women has been perpetuated, over and over, more or less consciously, and in a manner that's frightening since it's often hidden or adorned with the mystifying charms of fiction; that this locus has grossly exaggerated all the signs of sexual opposition (and not sexual difference), where woman has never *her* turn to speak—this being all the more serious and unpardonable in that writing is precisely *the very possibility of change*, the space that can serve as a springboard for subversive thought, the precursory movement of a transformation of social and cultural structures.

Nearly the entire history of writing is confounded with the history of reason, of which it is at once the effect, the support, and one of the privileged alibis. It has been one with the phallocentric tradition. It is indeed that same self-admiring, self-stimulating, self-congratulatory phallocentrism.

With some exceptions, for there have been failures—and if it weren't for them, I wouldn't be writing (I-woman, escapee)—in that enormous machine that has been operating and turning out its "truth" for centuries. There have been poets who would go to any lengths to slip something by at odds with tradition—men capable of loving love and hence capable of loving others and of wanting them, of imagining the woman who would hold out against oppression and constitute herself as a superb, equal, hence "impossible" subject, untenable in a real social framework. Such a woman the poet could desire only by breaking the codes that negate her. Her appearance would necessarily bring on, if not revolution—for the bastion was supposed to be immutable—at least harrowing explosions. At times it is in the fissure caused by an earthquake, through that radical mutation of things brought on by a material upheaval when every structure is for a moment thrown off balance and an ephemeral wildness sweeps order away, that the poet slips something

<hr>

3. I am speaking here only of the place "reserved" for women by the Western world.
4. Which works, then, might be called feminine? I'll just point out some examples: one would have to give them full readings to bring out what is pervasively feminine in their significance. Which I shall do elsewhere. In France (have you noted our infinite poverty in this field?—the Anglo-Saxon countries have shown resources of distinctly greater consequence), leafing through what's come out of the twentieth century—and it's not much—the only inscriptions of femininity that I have seen were by Colette, Marguerite Duras, . . . and Jean Genêt.

by, for a brief span, of woman. Thus did Kleist expend himself in his yearning for the existence of sister-lovers, maternal daughters, mother-sisters, who never hung their heads in shame. Once the palace of magistrates is restored, it's time to pay: immediate bloody death to the uncontrollable elements.

But only the poets—not the novelists, allies of representationalism. Because poetry involves gaining strength through the unconscious and because the unconscious, that other limitless country, is the place where the repressed manage to survive: women, or as Hoffmann would say, fairies.

She must write her self, because this is the invention of a *new insurgent* writing which, when the moment of her liberation has come, will allow her to carry out the indispensable ruptures and transformations in her history, first at two levels that cannot be separated.

a) Individually. By writing her self, woman will return to the body which has been more than confiscated from her, which has been turned into the uncanny stranger on display—the ailing or dead figure, which so often turns out to be the nasty companion, the cause and location of inhibitions. Censor the body and you censor breath and speech at the same time.

Write your self. Your body must be heard. Only then will the immense resources of the unconscious spring forth. Our naphtha will spread, throughout the world, without dollars—black or gold—nonassessed values that will change the rules of the old game.

To write. An act which will not only "realize" the decensored relation of woman to her sexuality, to her womanly being, giving her access to her native strength; it will give her back her goods, her pleasures, her organs, her immense bodily territories which have been kept under seal; it will tear her away from the superegoized structure in which she has always occupied the place reserved for the guilty (guilty of everything, guilty at every turn: for having desires, for not having any; for being frigid, for being "too hot"; for not being both at once; for being too motherly and not enough; for having children and for not having any; for nursing and for not nursing . . .)—tear her away by means of this research, this job of analysis and illumination, this emancipation of the marvelous text of her self that she must urgently learn to speak. A woman without a body, dumb, blind, can't possibly be a good fighter. She is reduced to being the servant of the militant male, his shadow. We must kill the false woman who is preventing the live one from breathing. Inscribe the breath of the whole woman.

b) An act that will also be marked by woman's *seizing* the occasion to *speak,* hence her shattering entry into history, which has always been based *on her suppression*. To write and thus to forge for herself the antilogos weapon. To become *at will* the taker and initiator, for her own right, in every symbolic system, in every political process.

It is time for women to start scoring their feats in written and oral language.

Every woman has known the torment of getting up to speak. Her heart racing, at times entirely lost for words, ground and language slipping away—that's how daring a feat, how great a transgression it is for a woman to speak—even just open her mouth—in public. A double distress, for even if she transgresses, her words fall almost always upon the deaf male ear, which hears in language only that which speaks in the masculine.

It is by writing, from and toward women, and by taking up the challenge of speech which has been governed by the phallus, that women will confirm women in a place other than that which is reserved in and by the symbolic, that is, in a place other than silence. Women should break out of the snare of silence. They shouldn't be conned into accepting a domain which is the margin or the harem.

Listen to a woman speak at a public gathering (if she hasn't painfully lost her wind). She doesn't "speak," she throws her trembling body forward; she lets go of herself, she flies; all of her passes into her voice, and it's with her body that she vitally supports the "logic" of her speech. Her flesh speaks true. She lays herself bare. In fact, she physically materializes what she's thinking; she signifies it with her body. In a certain way she *inscribes* what she's saying, because she doesn't deny her drives the intractable and impassioned part they have in speaking. Her speech, even when "theoretical" or political, is never simple or linear or "objectified," generalized: she draws her story into history.

There is not that scission, that division made by the common man between the logic of oral speech and the logic of the text, bound as he is by his anti-quated relation—servile, calculating—to mastery. From which proceeds the niggardly lip service which engages only the tiniest part of the body, plus the mask.

In women's speech, as in their writing, that element which never stops res-onating, which, once we've been permeated by it, profoundly and impercep-tibly touched by it, retains the power of moving us—that element is the song; first music from the first voice of love which is alive in every woman. Why this privileged relationship with the voice? Because no woman stockpiles as many defenses for countering the drives as does a man. You don't build walls around yourself, you don't forgo pleasure as "wisely" as he. Even if phallic mystification has generally contaminated good relationships, a woman is never far from "mother" (I mean outside her role functions: the "mother" as nonname and as source of goods). There is always within her at least a little of that good mother's milk. She writes in white ink.

Woman for women.—There always remains in woman that force which pro-duces/is produced by the other—in particular, the other woman. *In* her, matrix, cradler; herself giver as her mother and child; she is her own sister-daughter. You might object, "What about she who is the hysterical offspring of a bad mother?" Everything will be changed once woman gives woman to the other woman. There is hidden and always ready in woman the source; the locus for the other. The mother, too, is a metaphor. It is necessary and suffi-cient that the best of herself be given to woman by another woman for her to be able to love herself and return in love the body that was "born" to her. Touch me, caress me, you the living no-name, give me my self as myself. The relation to the "mother," in terms of intense pleasure and violence, is cur-tailed no more than the relation to childhood (the child that she was, that she is, that she makes, remakes, undoes, there at the point where, the same, she others herself). Text: my body—shot through with streams of song; I don't mean the overbearing, clutchy "mother" but, rather, what touches you, the equivoice that affects you, fills your breast with an urge to come to language and launches your force; the rhythm that laughs you; the intimate recipient who makes all metaphors possible and desirable; body (body? bodies?), no more describable than god, the soul, or the Other; that part of you that leaves a space between yourself and urges you to inscribe in language your woman's style. In women there is always more or less of the mother who makes everything all right, who nourishes, and who stands up against separation; a force that will not be cut off but will knock the wind out of the codes. We will rethink womankind beginning with every form and every period of her body. The Americans remind us, "We are all Lesbians";[5] that is, don't denigrate woman, don't make of her what men have made of you.

Because the "economy" of her drives is prodigious, she cannot fail, in seizing the occasion to speak, to transform directly and indirectly *all* systems of exchange based on masculine thrift. Her libido will produce far more radical effects of political and social change than some might like to think.

Because she arrives, vibrant, over and again, we are at the beginning of a new history, or rather of a process of becoming in which several histories intersect with one another. As subject for history, woman always occurs simultaneously in several places. Woman un-thinks[6] the unifying, regulating history that homogenizes and channels forces, herding contradictions into a single battlefield. In woman, personal history blends together with the history of all women, as well as national and world history. As a militant, she is an integral part of all liberations. She must be farsighted, not limited to a blow-by-blow interaction. She foresees that her liberation will do more than modify power relations or toss the ball over to the other camp; she will bring about a mutation in human relations, in thought, in all praxis: hers is not simply a class struggle, which she carries forward into a much vaster movement. Not that in order to be a woman-in-struggle(s) you have to leave the class struggle or repudiate it; but you have to split it open, spread it out, push it forward, fill it with the fundamental struggle so as to prevent the class struggle, or any other struggle for the liberation of a class or people, from operating as a form of repression, pretext for postponing the inevitable, the staggering alteration in power relations and in the production of individualities. This alteration is already upon us—in the United States, for example, where millions of night crawlers are in the process of undermining the family and disintegrating the whole of American sociality.

The new history is coming; it's not a dream, though it does extend beyond men's imagination, and for good reason. It's going to deprive them of their conceptual orthopedics, beginning with the destruction of their enticement machine.

It is impossible to *define* a feminine practice of writing, and this is an impossibility that will remain, for this practice can never be theorized, enclosed, coded—which doesn't mean that it doesn't exist. But it will always surpass the discourse that regulates the phallocentric system; it does and will take place in areas other than those subordinated to philosophico-theoretical domination. It will be conceived of only by subjects who are breakers of automatisms, by peripheral figures that no authority can ever subjugate.

Hence the necessity to affirm the flourishes of this writing, to give form to its movement, its near and distant byways. Bear in mind to begin with that (1) that sexual opposition, which has always worked for man's profit to the point of reducing writing, too, to his laws, is only a historico-cultural limit. There is, there will be more and more rapidly pervasive now, a fiction that produces

---

5. A claim by some radical feminists in the early 1970s (including Adrienne Rich, in 1976); also, the title of a 1973 poetry anthology [editor's note].

6. "*Dé-pense*," a neologism formed on the verb *penser*, hence "unthinks," but also "spends" (from *dépenser*) [translator's note].

irreducible effects of femininity. (2) That it is through ignorance that most readers, critics, and writers of both sexes hesitate to admit or deny outright the possibility or the pertinence of a distinction between feminine and masculine writing. It will usually be said, thus disposing of sexual difference: either that all writing, to the extent that it materializes, is feminine; or, inversely—but it comes to the same thing—that the act of writing is equivalent to masculine masturbation (and so the woman who writes cuts herself out a paper penis); or that writing is bisexual, hence neuter, which again does away with differentiation. To admit that writing is precisely working (in) the in-between, inspecting the process of the same and of the other without which nothing can live, undoing the work of death—to admit this is first to want the two, as well as both, the ensemble of the one and the other, not fixed in sequences of struggle and expulsion or some other form of death but infinitely dynamized by an incessant process of exchange from one subject to another. A process of different subjects knowing one another and beginning one another anew only from the living boundaries of the other: a multiple and inexhaustible course with millions of encounters and transformations of the same into the other and into the in-between, from which woman takes her forms (and man, in his turn; but that's his other history).

In saying "bisexual, hence neuter," I am referring to the classic conception of bisexuality, which, squashed under the emblem of castration fear and along with the fantasy of a "total" being (though composed of two halves), would do away with the difference experienced as an operation incurring loss, as the mark of dreaded sectility.

To this self-effacing, merger-type bisexuality, which would conjure away castration (the writer who puts up his sign: "bisexual written here, come and see," when the odds are good that it's neither one nor the other), I oppose the *other bisexuality* on which every subject not enclosed in the false theater of phallocentric representationalism has founded his/her erotic universe. Bisexuality: that is, each one's location in self (*répérage en soi*) of the presence—variously manifest and insistent according to each person, male or female—of both sexes, nonexclusion either of the difference or of one sex, and, from this "self-permission," multiplication of the effects of the inscription of desire, over all parts of my body and the other body.

Now it happens that at present, for historico-cultural reasons, it is women who are opening up to and benefiting from this vatic bisexuality which doesn't annul differences but stirs them up, pursues them, increases their number. In a certain way, "woman is bisexual"; man—it's a secret to no one—being poised to keep glorious phallic monosexuality in view. By virtue of affirming the primacy of the phallus and of bringing it into play, phallocratic ideology has claimed more than one victim. As a woman, I've been clouded over by the great shadow of the scepter and been told: idolize it, that which you cannot brandish. But at the same time, man has been handed that grotesque and scarcely enviable destiny (just imagine) of being reduced to a single idol with clay balls. And consumed, as Freud and his followers note, by a fear of being a woman! For, if psychoanalysis was constituted from woman, to repress femininity (and not so successful a repression at that—men have made it clear), its account of masculine sexuality is now hardly refutable; as with all the "human" sciences, it reproduces the masculine view, of which it is one of the effects.

Here we encounter the inevitable man-with-rock, standing erect in his old Freudian realm, in the way that, to take the figure back to the point where linguistics is conceptualizing it "anew," Lacan preserves it in the sanctuary of the phallus (ɸ) "sheltered" from *castration's lack*! Their "symbolic" exists, it holds power—we, the sowers of disorder, know it only too well. But we are in no way obliged to deposit our lives in their banks of lack, to consider the constitution of the subject in terms of a drama manglingly restaged, to reinstate again and again the religion of the father. Because we don't want that. We don't fawn around the supreme hole. We have no womanly reason to pledge allegiance to the negative. The feminine (as the poets suspected) affirms: ". . . And yes." says Molly, carrying *Ulysses* off beyond any book and toward the new writing; "I said yes, I will Yes."

The Dark Continent is neither dark nor unexplorable.—It is still unexplored only because we've been made to believe that it was too dark to be explorable. And because they want to make us believe that what interests us is the white continent, with its monuments to Lack. And we believed. They riveted us between two horrifying myths: between the Medusa and the abyss. That would be enough to set half the world laughing, except that it's still going on. For the phallologocentric sublation[7] is with us, and it's militant, regenerating the old patterns, anchored in the dogma of castration. They haven't changed a thing: they've theorized their desire for reality! Let the priests tremble, we're going to show them our sexts!

Too bad for them if they fall apart upon discovering that women aren't men, or that the mother doesn't have one. But isn't this fear convenient for them? Wouldn't the worst be, isn't the worst, in truth, that women aren't castrated, that they have only to stop listening to the Sirens (for the Sirens were men) for history to change its meaning? You only have to look at the Medusa straight on to see her. And she's not deadly. She's beautiful and she's laughing.

Men say that there are two unrepresentable things: death and the feminine sex. That's because they need femininity to be associated with death; it's the jitters that gives them a hard-on! for themselves! They need to be afraid of us. Look at the trembling Perseuses moving backward toward us, clad in apotropes.[8] What lovely backs! Not another minute to lose. Let's get out of here.

Let's hurry: the continent is not impenetrably dark. I've been there often. I was overjoyed one day to run into Jean Genêt. It was in *Pompes funèbres*.[9] He had come there led by his Jean. There are some men (all too few) who aren't afraid of femininity.

Almost everything is yet to be written by women about femininity: about their sexuality, that is, its infinite and mobile complexity, about their eroticization, sudden turn-ons of a certain minuscule-immense area of their bodies; not about destiny, but about the adventure of such and such a drive, about trips, crossings, trudges, abrupt and gradual awakenings, discoveries of a zone at one time timorous and soon to be forthright. A woman's body, with

---

7. Standard English term for the Hegelian *Aufhebung*, the French *la relève*. [*Aufhebung* is a technical term in Hegel's notion of the dialectic: it refers to the process of both overcoming and preserving the original thesis—editor's note.]
8. Elements designed to avert evil (according to

Greek myth, Medusa was killed by Perseus, who viewed her in a mirror, backing toward her, so that the sight of her would not turn him to stone) [editor's note].
9. Jean Genêt, *Pompes funèbres* (Paris, 1948), p. 185.

its thousand and one thresholds of ardor—once, by smashing yokes and censors, she lets it articulate the profusion of meanings that run through it in every direction—will make the old single-grooved mother tongue reverberate with more than one language.

We've been turned away from our bodies, shamefully taught to ignore them, to strike them with that stupid sexual modesty; we've been made victims of the old fool's game: each one will love the other sex. I'll give you your body and you'll give me mine. But who are the men who give women the body that women blindly yield to them? Why so few texts? Because so few women have as yet won back their body. Women must write through their bodies, they must invent the impregnable language that will wreck partitions, classes, and rhetorics, regulations and codes, they must submerge, cut through, get beyond the ultimate reserve-discourse, including the one that laughs at the very idea of pronouncing the word "silence," the one that, aiming for the impossible, stops short before the word "impossible" and writes it as "the end."

Such is the strength of women that, sweeping away syntax, breaking that famous thread (just a tiny little thread, they say) which acts for men as a surrogate umbilical cord, assuring them—otherwise they couldn't come—that the old lady is always right behind them, watching them make phallus, women will go right up to the impossible.

When the "repressed" of their culture and their society returns, it's an explosive, *utterly* destructive, staggering return, with a force never yet unleashed and equal to the most forbidding of suppressions. For when the Phallic period comes to an end, women will have been either annihilated or borne up to the highest and most violent incandescence. Muffled throughout their history, they have lived in dreams, in bodies (though muted), in silences, in aphonic revolts.

And with such force in their fragility; a fragility, a vulnerability, equal to their incomparable intensity. Fortunately, they haven't sublimated; they've saved their skin, their energy. They haven't worked at liquidating the impasse of lives without futures. They have furiously inhabited these sumptuous bodies: admirable hysterics who made Freud succumb to many voluptuous moments impossible to confess, bombarding his Mosaic statue[1] with their carnal and passionate body words, haunting him with their inaudible and thundering denunciations, dazzling, more than naked underneath the seven veils of modesty. Those who, with a single word of the body, have inscribed the vertiginous immensity of a history which is sprung like an arrow from the whole history of men and from biblico-capitalist society, are the women, the supplicants of yesterday, who come as forebears of the new women, after whom no intersubjective relation will ever be the same. You, Dora,[2] you the indomitable, the poetic body, you are the true "mistress" of the Signifier. Before long your efficacity will be seen at work when your speech is no longer suppressed, its point turned in against your breast, but written out over against the other.

1. See Freud's "The Moses of Michelangelo" (1914) [editor's note].
2. The name Freud gave to Ida Bauer, the subject of one of his most important case studies, "Fragment of an Analysis of a Case of Hysteria" (1905) [editor's note].

In body.—More so than men who are coaxed toward social success, toward sublimation, women are body. More body, hence more writing. For a long time it has been in body that women have responded to persecution, to the familial-conjugal enterprise of domestication, to the repeated attempts at castrating them. Those who have turned their tongues 10,000 times seven times before not speaking are either dead from it or more familiar with their tongues and their mouths than anyone else. Now, I-woman am going to blow up the Law: an explosion henceforth possible and ineluctable; let it be done, right now, *in* language.

Let us not be trapped by an analysis still encumbered with the old automatisms. It's not to be feared that language conceals an invincible adversary, because it's the language of men and their grammar. We mustn't leave them a single place that's any more theirs alone than we are.

If woman has always functioned "within" the discourse of man, a signifier that has always referred back to the opposite signifier which annihilates its specific energy and diminishes or stifles its very different sounds, it is time for her to dislocate this "within," to explode it, turn it around, and seize it; to make it hers, containing it, taking it in her own mouth, biting that tongue with her very own teeth to invent for herself a language to get inside of. And you'll see with what ease she will spring forth from that "within"—the "within" where once she so drowsily crouched—to overflow at the lips she will cover the foam.

Nor is the point to appropriate their instruments, their concepts, their places, or to begrudge them their position of mastery. Just because there's a risk of identification doesn't mean that we'll succumb. Let's leave it to the worriers, to masculine anxiety and its obsession with how to dominate the way things work—knowing "how it works" in order to "make it work." For us the point is not to take possession in order to internalize or manipulate, but rather to dash through and to "fly."[3]

Flying is woman's gesture—flying in language and making it fly. We have all learned the art of flying and its numerous techniques; for centuries we've been able to possess anything only by flying; we've lived in flight, stealing away, finding, when desired, narrow passageways, hidden crossovers. It's no accident that *voler* has a double meaning, that it plays on each of them and thus throws off the agents of sense. It's no accident: women take after birds and robbers just as robbers take after women and birds. They (*illes*)[4] go by, fly the coop, take pleasure in jumbling the order of space, in disorienting it, in changing around the furniture, dislocating things and values, breaking them all up, emptying structures, and turning propriety upside down.

What woman hasn't flown/stolen? Who hasn't felt, dreamt, performed the gesture that jams sociality? Who hasn't crumbled, held up to ridicule, the bar of separation? Who hasn't inscribed with her body the differential, punctured the system of couples and opposition? Who, by some act of transgression, hasn't overthrown successiveness, connection, the wall of circumfusion?

A feminine text cannot fail to be more than subversive. It is volcanic; as it is written it brings about an upheaval of the old property crust, carrier of mas-

3. Also, "to steal." Both meanings of the verb *voler* are played on, as the text itself explains in the following paragraph [translator's note].
4. *Illes* is a fusion of the masculine pronoun *ils*, which refers back to birds and robbers, with the feminine pronoun *elles*, which refers to women [translator's note].

culine investments; there's no other way. There's no room for her if she's not a he. If she's a her-she, it's in order to smash everything, to shatter the framework of institutions, to blow up the law, to break up the "truth" with laughter.

For once she blazes *her* trail in the symbolic, she cannot fail to make of it the chaosmos of the "personal"—in her pronouns, her nouns, and her clique of referents. And for good reason. There will have been the long history of gynocide. This is known by the colonized peoples of yesterday, the workers, the nations, the species off whose backs the history of men has made its gold; those who have known the ignominy of persecution derive from it an obstinate future desire for grandeur; those who are locked up know better than their jailers the taste of free air. Thanks to their history, women today know (how to do and want) what men will be able to conceive of only much later. I say woman overturns the "personal," for if, by means of laws, lies, blackmail, and marriage, her right to herself has been extorted at the same time as her name, she has been able, through the very movement of mortal alienation, to see more closely the inanity of "propriety," the reductive stinginess of the masculine-conjugal subjective economy, which she doubly resists. On the one hand she has constituted herself necessarily as that "person" capable of losing a part of herself without losing her integrity. But secretly, silently, deep down inside, she grows and multiplies, for, on the other hand, she knows far more about living and about the relation between the economy of the drives and the management of the ego than any man. Unlike man, who holds so dearly to his title and his titles, his pouches of value, his cap, crown, and everything connected with his head, woman couldn't care less about the fear of decapitation (or castration), adventuring, without the masculine temerity, into anonymity, which she can merge with without annihilating herself: because she's a giver.

I shall have a great deal to say about the whole deceptive problematic of the gift. Woman is obviously not that woman Nietzsche dreamed of who gives only in order to.[5] Who could ever think of the gift as a gift-that-takes? Who else but man, precisely the one who would like to take everything?

If there is a "propriety of woman," it is paradoxically her capacity to depropriate unselfishly: body without end, without appendage, without principal "parts." If she is a whole, it's a whole composed of parts that are wholes, not simple partial objects but a moving, limitlessly changing ensemble, a cosmos tirelessly traversed by Eros, an immense astral space not organized around any one sun that's any more of a star than the others.

This doesn't mean that she's an undifferentiated magma, but that she doesn't lord it over her body or her desire. Though masculine sexuality gravitates around the penis, engendering that centralized body (in political anatomy) under the dictatorship of its parts, woman does not bring about the same regionalization which serves the couple head/genitals and which is inscribed only within boundaries. Her libido is cosmic, just as her unconscious is worldwide. Her writing can only keep going, without ever inscribing

---

5. Reread Derrida's text, "Le Style de la femme," in *Nietzsche aujourd'hui* (Paris: Union Générale d'Editions, Coll. 10/18), where the philosopher can be seen operating an *Aufhebung* of all philosophy in its systematic reducing of woman to the place of seduction: she appears as the one who is taken for; the bait in person, all veils unfurled, the one who doesn't give but who gives only in order to (take).

or discerning contours, daring to make these vertiginous crossings of the other(s) ephemeral and passionate sojourns in him, her, them, whom she inhabits long enough to look at from the point closest to their unconscious from the moment they awaken, to love them at the point closest to their drives; and then further, impregnated through and through with these brief, identificatory embraces, she goes and passes into infinity. She alone dares and wishes to know from within, where she, the outcast, has never ceased to hear the resonance of fore-language. She lets the other language speak—the language of 1,000 tongues which knows neither enclosure nor death. To life she refuses nothing. Her language does not contain, it carries; it does not hold back, it makes possible. When id is ambiguously uttered—the wonder of being several—she doesn't defend herself against these unknown women whom she's surprised at becoming, but derives pleasure from this gift of alterability. I am spacious, singing flesh, on which is grafted no one knows which I, more or less human, but alive because of transformation.

Write! and your self-seeking text will know itself better than flesh and blood, rising, insurrectionary dough kneading itself, with sonorous, perfumed ingredients, a lively combination of flying colors, leaves, and rivers plunging into the sea we feed. "Ah, there's her sea," he will say as he holds out to me a basin full of water from the little phallic mother from whom he's inseparable. But look, our seas are what we make of them, full of fish or not, opaque or transparent, red or black, high or smooth, narrow or bankless; and we are ourselves sea, sand, coral, sea-weed, beaches, tides, swimmers, children, waves. . . . More or less wavily sea, earth, sky—what matter would rebuff us? We know how to speak them all.

Heterogeneous, yes. For her joyous benefit she is erogenous; she is the erotogeneity of the heterogeneous: airborne swimmer, in flight, she does not cling to herself; she is dispersible, prodigious, stunning, desirous and capable of others, of the other woman that she will be, of the other woman she isn't, of him, of you.

Woman be unafraid of any other place, of any same, or any other. My eyes, my tongue, my ears, my nose, my skin, my mouth, my body-for-(the)-other—not that I long for it in order to fill up a hole, to provide against some defect of mine, or because, as fate would have it, I'm spurred on by feminine "jealousy"; not because I've been dragged into the whole chain of substitutions that brings that which is substituted back to its ultimate object. That sort of thing you would expect to come straight out of "Tom Thumb," out of the *Penisneid*[6] whispered to us by old grandmother ogresses, servants to their father-sons. If they believe, in order to muster up some self-importance, if they really need to believe that we're dying of desire, that we are this hole fringed with desire for their penis—that's their immemorial business. Undeniably (we verify it at our own expense—but also to our amusement), it's their business to let us know they're getting a hard-on, so that we'll assure them (we the maternal mistresses of their little pocket signifier) that they still can, that it's still there—that men structure themselves only by being fitted with

6. An epic work on the penis (a name formed by analogy with such classical literature as Statius's *Thebaid* and *Achilleid*) [editor's note].

a feather. In the child it's not the penis that the woman desires, it's not that famous bit of skin around which every man gravitates. Pregnancy cannot be traced back, except within the historical limits of the ancients, to some form of fate, to those mechanical substitutions brought about by the unconscious of some eternal "jealous woman"; not to penis envies; and not to narcissism or to some sort of homosexuality linked to the ever-present mother! Begetting a child doesn't mean that the woman or the man must fall ineluctably into patterns or must recharge the circuit of reproduction. If there's a risk there's not an inevitable trap: may women be spared the pressure, under the guise of consciousness-raising, of a supplement of interdictions. Either you want a kid or you don't—*that's your business*. Let nobody threaten you; in satisfying your desire, let not the fear of becoming the accomplice to a sociality succeed the old-time fear of being "taken." And man, are you still going to bank on everyone's blindness and passivity, afraid lest the child make a father and, consequently, that in having a kid the woman land herself more than one bad deal by engendering all at once child—mother—father—family? No; it's up to you to break the old circuits. It will be up to man and woman to render obsolete the former relationship and all its consequences, to consider the launching of a brand-new subject, alive, with defamilialization. Let us demater-paternalize rather than deny woman, in an effort to avoid the co-optation of procreation, a thrilling era of the body. Let us defetishize. Let's get away from the dialectic which has it that the only good father is a dead one, or that the child is the death of his parents. The child is the other, but the other without violence, bypassing loss, struggle. We're fed up with the reuniting of bonds forever to be severed, with the litany of castration that's handed down and genealogized. We won't advance backward anymore; we're not going to repress something so simple as the desire for life. Oral drive, anal drive, vocal drive—all these drives are our strengths, and among them is the gestation drive—just like the desire to write: a desire to live self from within, a desire for the swollen belly, for language, for blood. We are not going to refuse, if it should happen to strike our fancy, the unsurpassed pleasures of pregnancy which have actually been always exaggerated or conjured away— or cursed—in the classic texts. For if there's one thing that's been repressed here's just the place to find it: in the taboo of the pregnant woman. This says a lot about the power she seems invested with at the time, because it has always been suspected, that, when pregnant, the woman not only doubles her market value, but—what's more important—takes on intrinsic value as a woman in her own eyes and, undeniably, acquires body and sex.

There are thousands of ways of living one's pregnancy; to have or not to have with that still invisible other a relationship of another intensity. And if you don't have that particular yearning, it doesn't mean that you're in any way lacking. Each body distributes in its own special way, without model or norm, the nonfinite and changing totality of its desires. Decide for yourself on your position in the arena of contradictions, where pleasure and reality embrace. Bring the other to life. Women know how to live detachment; giving birth is neither losing nor increasing. It's adding to life an other. Am I dreaming? Am I mis-recognizing? You, the defenders of "theory," the sacrosanct yes-men of Concept, enthroners of the phallus (but not of the penis):

Once more you'll say that all this smacks of "idealism," or what's worse, you'll splutter that I'm a "mystic."

And what about the libido? Haven't I read the "Signification of the phallus"? [7] And what about separation, what about that bit of self for which, to be born, you undergo an ablation—an ablation, so they say, to be forever commemorated by your desire?

Besides, isn't it evident that the penis gets around in my texts, that I give it a place and appeal? Of course I do. I want all. I want all of me with all of him. Why should I deprive myself of a part of us? I want all of us. Woman of course has a desire for a "loving desire" and not a jealous one. But not because she is gelded; not because she's deprived and needs to be filled out, like some wounded person who wants to console herself or seek vengeance: I don't want a penis to decorate my body with. But I do desire the other for the other, whole and entire, male or female; because living means wanting everything that is, everything that lives, and wanting it alive. Castration? Let others toy with it. What's a desire originating from a lack? A pretty meager desire.

The woman who still allows herself to be threatened by the big dick, who's still impressed by the commotion of the phallic stance, who still leads a loyal master to the beat of the drum: that's the woman of yesterday. They still exist, easy and numerous victims of the oldest of farces: either they're cast in the original silent version in which, as titanesses lying under the mountains they make with their quivering, they never see erected that theoretic monument to the golden phallus looming, in the old manner, over their bodies. Or, coming today out of their *infans*[8] period and into the second, "enlightened" version of their virtuous de-basement, they see themselves suddenly assaulted by the builders of the analytic empire and, as soon as they've begun to formulate the new desire, naked, nameless, so happy at making an appearance, they're taken in their bath by the new old men, and then, whoops! Luring them with flashy signifiers, the demon of interpretation—oblique, decked out in modernity—sells them the same old handcuffs, baubles, and chains. Which castration do you prefer? Whose degrading do you like better, the father's or the mother's? Oh, what pwetty eyes, you pwetty little girl. Here, buy my glasses and you'll see the Truth-Me-Myself tell you everything you should know. Put them on your nose and take a fetishist's look (you are me, the other analyst—that's what I'm telling you) at your body and the body of the other. You see? No? Wait, you'll have everything explained to you, and you'll know at last which sort of neurosis you're related to. Hold still, we're going to do your portrait, so that you can begin looking like it right away.

Yes, the naives to the first and second degree are still legion. If the New Women, arriving now, dare to create outside the theoretical they're called in by the cops of the signifier, fingerprinted, remonstrated, and brought into the line of order that they are supposed to know; assigned by force of trickery to a precise place in the chain that's always formed for the benefit of a privileged signifier. We are pieced back to the string which leads back, if not to the Name-of-the-Father,[9] then, for a new twist, to the place of the phallic-mother.

Beware, my friend, of the signifier that would take you back to the authority of a signified! Beware of diagnoses that would reduce your generative powers. "Common" nouns are also proper nouns that disparage your singularity

---

7. A 1958 essay by Jacques Lacan [editor's note].
8. Not speaking (Latin) [editor's note].
9. Lacanian term for the function of the father in the Symbolic, the dimension of law and language [editor's note].

by classifying it into species. Break out of the circles, don't remain within the psychoanalytic closure. Take a look around, then cut through!

And if we are legion, it's because the war of liberation has only made as yet a tiny breakthrough. But women are thronging to it. I've seen them, those who will be neither dupe nor domestic, those who will not fear the risk of being a woman; will not fear any risk, any desire, any space still unexplored in themselves, among themselves and others or anywhere else. They do not fetishize, they do not deny, they do not hate. They observe, they approach, they try to see the other woman, the child, the lover—not to strengthen their own narcissism or verify the solidity or weakness of the master, but to make love better, to invent.

Other love.—In the beginning are our differences. The new love dares for the other, wants the other, makes dizzying, precipitous flights between knowledge and invention. The woman arriving over and over again does not stand still; she's everywhere, she exchanges, she is the desire-that-gives. (Not enclosed in the paradox of the gift that takes nor under the illusion of unitary fusion. We're past that.) She comes in, comes-in-between herself me and you, between the other me where one is always infinitely more than one and more than me, without the fear of ever reaching a limit; she thrills in our becoming. And we'll keep on becoming! She cuts through defensive loves, motherages, and devourations: beyond selfish narcissism, in the moving, open, transitional space, she runs her risks. Beyond the struggle-to-the-death that's been removed to the bed, beyond the love-battle that claims to represent exchange, she scorns at an Eros dynamic that would be fed by hatred. Hatred: a heritage, again, a remainder, a duping subservience to the phallus. To love, to watch-think-seek the other in the other, to de-specularize, to unhoard. Does this seem difficult? It's not impossible, and this is what nourishes life—a love that has no commerce with the apprehensive desire that provides against the lack and stultifies the strange; a love that rejoices in the exchange that multiplies. Wherever history still unfolds as the history of death, she does not tread. Opposition, hierarchizing exchange, the struggle for mastery which can end only in at least one death (one master—one slave, or two nonmasters = two dead)—all that comes from a period in time governed by phallocentric values. The fact that this period extends into the present doesn't prevent woman from starting the history of life somewhere else. Elsewhere, she gives. She doesn't "know" what she's giving, she doesn't measure it; she gives, though, neither a counterfeit impression nor something she hasn't got. She gives more, with no assurance that she'll get back even some unexpected profit from what she puts out. She gives that there may be life, thought, transformation. This is an "economy" that can no longer be put in economic terms. Wherever she loves, all the old concepts of management are left behind. At the end of a more or less conscious computation, she finds not her sum but her differences. I am for you what you want me to be at the moment you look at me in a way you've never seen me before: at every instant. When I write, it's everything that we don't know we can be that is written out of me, without exclusions, without stipulation, and everything we will be calls us to the unflagging, intoxicating, unappeasable search for love. In one another we will never be lacking.

1975, 1976

JOAN KELLY-GADOL
1928–1982

Like Gerda Lerner, Carroll Smith-Rosenberg, Joan Wallach Scott, and Natalie Zemon Davis, Joan Kelly-Gadol helped establish the legitimacy of feminist approaches to history and historiography. Born in Brooklyn, New York, she was educated at St. John's University College and Columbia University, and taught at the City College of the City University of New York until she took a position at Sarah Lawrence College. Kelly-Gadol was active in the Committee of Women Historians of the American Historical Association and assumed a leadership role in Women in the Historical Profession. Her question "Did women have a Renaissance?" opened up discussions about periodization not only in political and social history but in literary history, where the distinctive contributions of men and women of letters continue to fuel inquiries into how, for example, the medieval or Romantic or Victorian age encompassed quite different types of achievements for each sex.

From The Social Relation of the Sexes: Methodological Implications of Women's History

Women's history has a dual goal: to restore women to history and to restore our history to women. In the past few years, it has stimulated a remarkable amount of research as well as a number of conferences and courses on the activities, status, and views of and about women. The interdisciplinary character of our concern with women has also newly enriched this vital historical work. But there is another aspect of women's history that needs to be considered: its theoretical significance, its implications for historical study in general.[1] In seeking to add women to the fund of historical knowledge, women's history has revitalized theory, for it has shaken the conceptual foundations of historical study. It has done this by making problematical three of the basic concerns of historical thought: (1) periodization, (2) the categories of social analysis, and (3) theories of social change.

Since all three issues are presently in ferment, I can at best suggest how they may be fruitfully posed. But in so doing, I should also like to show how the conception of these problems expresses a notion which is basic to feminist consciousness, namely, that the relation between the sexes is a social and not a natural one. This perception forms the core idea that upsets traditional thinking in all three cases.

1. The central theme of this paper emerged from regular group discussions, from which I have benefited so much, with Marilyn Arthur, Blanche Cook, Pamela Farley, Mary Feldblum, Alice Kessler-Harris, Amy Swerdlow, and Carole Turbin. Many of the ideas were sharpened in talks with Gerda Lerner, Renate Bridenthal, Dick Vann, and Marilyn Arthur, with whom I served on several panels on women's history and its theoretical implications. My City College students in Marxism/feminism and in fear of women, witchcraft, and the family have stimulated my interests and enriched my understanding of many of the issues presented here. To Martin Fleisher and Nancy Miller I am indebted for valuable suggestions for improving an earlier version of this paper, which I delivered at the Barnard College Conference on the Scholar and the Feminist II: Toward New Criteria of Relevance, April 12, 1975. [Except as indicated, all notes are Kelly-Gadol's.]

Periodization

Once we look to history for an understanding of woman's situation, we are, of course, already assuming that woman's situation is a social matter. But history, as we first came to it, did not seem to confirm this awareness. Throughout historical time, women have been largely excluded from making war, wealth, laws, governments, art, and science. Men, functioning in their capacity as historians, considered exactly those activities constitutive of civilization: hence, diplomatic history, economic history, constitutional history, and political and cultural history. Women figured chiefly as exceptions, those who were said to be as ruthless as, or wrote like, or had the brains of men. In redressing this neglect, women's history recognized from the start that what we call compensatory history is not enough. This was not to be a history of exceptional women, although they too need to be restored to their rightful places. Nor could it be another subgroup of historical thought, a history of women to place alongside the list of diplomatic history, economic history, and so forth, for all these developments impinged upon the history of women. Hence feminist scholarship in history, as in anthropology, came to focus primarily on the issue of women's status. I use "status" here and throughout in an expanded sense, to refer to woman's place and power—that is, the roles and positions women hold in society by comparison with those of men.

In historical terms, this means to look at ages or movements of great social change in terms of their liberation or repression of woman's potential, their import for the advancement of her humanity as well as "his." The moment this is done—the moment one assumes that women are a part of humanity in the fullest sense—the period or set of events with which we deal takes on a wholly different character or meaning from the normally accepted one. Indeed, what emerges is a fairly regular pattern of relative loss of status for women precisely in those periods of so-called progressive change. Since the dramatic new perspectives that unfold from this shift of vantage point have already been discussed at several conferences, I shall be brief here.[2] Let me merely point out that if we apply Fourier's famous dictum—that the emancipation of women is an index of the general emancipation of an age—our notions of so-called progressive developments, such as classical Athenian civilization, the Renaissance, and the French Revolution, undergo a startling reevaluation. For women, "progress" in Athens meant concubinage and confinement of citizen wives in the gynecaeum. In Renaissance Europe it meant domestication of the bourgeois wife and escalation of witchcraft persecution which crossed class lines. And the Revolution expressly excluded women from its liberty, equality, and "fraternity." Suddenly we see these ages with a new, double vision—and each eye sees a different picture.

2. Conference of New England Association of Women Historians, Yale University (October 1973): Marilyn Arthur, Renate Bridenthal, Joan Kelly-Gadol; Second Berkshire Conference on the History of Women, Radcliffe (October 1974): panel on "The Effects of Women's History upon Traditional Historiography," Renate Bridenthal, Joan Kelly-Gadol, Gerda Lerner, Richard Vann (papers deposited at Schlesinger Library); Sarah Lawrence symposium (March 1975): Marilyn Arthur, Renate Bridenthal, Gerda Lerner, Joan Kelly-Gadol (papers available as *Conceptual* *Frameworks in Women's History* [Bronxville, N.Y.: Sarah Lawrence Publications, 1976]). For some recent comments along some of these same lines, see Carl N. Degler, *Is There a History of Women?* (Oxford: Clarendon Press, 1975). As I edit this paper for printing, the present economic crisis is threatening the advances of feminist scholarship once again by forcing the recently arrived women educators out of their teaching positions and severing thereby the professional connections necessary to research and theory, such as the conferences mentioned above.

Only one of these views has been represented by history up to now. Regardless of how these periods have been assessed, they have been assessed from the vantage point of men. Liberal historiography in particular, which considers all three periods as stages in the progressive realization of an individualistic social and cultural order, expressly maintains—albeit without considering the evidence—that women shared these advances with men. In Renaissance scholarship, for example, almost all historians have been content to situate women exactly where Jacob Burckhardt placed them in 1890: "on a footing of perfect equality with men." For a period that rejected the hierarchy of social class and the hierarchy of religious values in its restoration of a classical, secular culture, there was also, they claim, "no question of 'woman's rights' or female emancipation, simply because the thing itself was a matter of course."[3] Now while it is true that a couple of dozen women can be assimilated to the humanistic standard of culture which the Renaissance imposed upon itself, what is remarkable is that *only* a couple of dozen women can. To pursue this problem is to become aware of the fact that there was no "renaissance" for women—at least not during the Renaissance. There was, on the contrary, a marked restriction of the scope and powers of women. Moreover, this restriction is a consequence of the very developments for which the age is noted.[4]

What feminist historiography has done is to unsettle such accepted evaluations of historical periods. It has disabused us of the notion that the history of women is the same as the history of men, and that significant turning points in history have the same impact for one sex as for the other. Indeed, some historians now go so far as to maintain that, because of woman's particular connection with the function of reproduction, history could, and women's history should, be rewritten and periodized from this point of view, according to major turning points affecting childbirth, sexuality, family structure, and so forth.[5] In this regard, Juliet Mitchell refers to modern contraception as a "world-historic event"—although the logic of her thought, and my own, protests against a periodization that is primarily geared to changes in reproduction. Such criteria threaten to detach psychosexual development and family patterns from changes in the general social order, or to utterly reverse the causal sequence. Hence I see in them a potential isolation of women's history from what has hitherto been considered the mainstream of social change.

To my mind, what is more promising about the way periodization has begun to function in women's history is that it has become *relational*. It relates the

3. *The Civilization of the Renaissance in Italy* (London: Phaidon Press, 1950), p. 241. With the exception of Ruth Kelso, *Doctrine for the Lady of the Renaissance* (Urbana: University of Illinois Press, 1956), this view is shared by every work I know of on Renaissance women except for contemporary feminist historians. Even Simone de Beauvoir, and of course Mary Beard, regard the Renaissance as advancing the condition of women, although Burckhardt himself pointed out that the women of whom he wrote "had no thought of the public; their function was to influence distinguished men, and to moderate male impulse and caprice."
4. See the several contemporary studies recently or soon to be published on Renaissance women:

Susan Bell, "Christine de Pizan," *Feminist Studies* (Winter 1975/76 [vol. 3, pp. 173–84]); Joan Kelly-Gadol, "Notes on Women in the Renaissance and Renaissance Historiography," in *Conceptual Frameworks in Women's History* (n. 2 above); Margaret Leah King, "The Religious Retreat of Isotta Nogarola, 1418–66," *Signs* (in press [3 (1978): 807–22]); an article on women in the Renaissance by Kathleen Casey in *Liberating Women's History,* Berenice Carroll, ed. (Urbana: University of Illinois Press, 1976); Joan Kelly-Gadol, "Did Women Have a Renaissance?" in *Becoming Visible,* ed. R. Bridenthal and C. Koonz (Boston: Houghton Mifflin Co., 1976).
5. Vann (n. 2 above).

history of women to that of men, as Engels did in *The Origin of the Family, Private Property and the State,* by seeing in common social developments institutional reasons for the advance of one sex and oppression of the other. Handled this way, traditional periodizing concepts may well be retained—and ought to be insofar as they refer to major structural changes in society. But in the evaluation of such changes we need to consider their effects upon women as distinct from men. We expect by now that those effects may be so different as to be opposed and that such opposition will be socially explicable. When women are excluded from the benefits of the economic, political, and cultural advances made in certain periods, a situation which gives women a different historical experience from men, it is to those "advances" we must look to find the reasons for that separation of the sexes.

Sex as a Social Category

Two convictions are implicit in this more complete and more complex sense of periodization: one, that women do form a distinctive social group and, second, that the invisibility of this group in traditional history is not to be ascribed to female nature. These notions, which clearly arise out of feminist consciousness, effect another, related change in the conceptual foundation of history by introducing sex as a category of social thought.

Feminism has made it evident that the mere fact of being a woman meant having a particular kind of social and hence historical experience, but the exact meaning of "woman" in this historical or social sense has not been so clear. What accounts for woman's situation as "other," and what perpetuates it historically? The "Redstockings Manifesto" of 1969 maintained that "women are an oppressed class" and suggested that the relations between men and women are class relations, that "sexual politics" are the politics of class domination. The most fruitful consequence of this conception of women as a social class has been the extension of class analysis to women by Marxist feminists such as Margaret Benston and Sheila Rowbotham.[6] They have traced the roots of woman's secondary status in history to economics inasmuch as women as a group have had a distinctive relation to production and property in almost all societies. The personal and psychological consequences of secondary status can be seen to flow from this special relation to work. As Rowbotham and Benston themselves make clear, however, it is one thing to extend the tools of class analysis to women and quite another to maintain that women *are* a class. Women belong to social classes, and the new women's history and histories of feminism have borne this out, demonstrating, for example, how class divisions disrupted and shattered the first wave of the feminist movement in nonsocialist countries, and how feminism has been expressly subordinated to the class struggle in socialist feminism.[7]

6. "Redstockings Manifesto," in *Sisterhood Is Powerful,* ed. Robin Morgan (New York: Random House, 1970), pp. 533–36. Margaret Benston, *The Political Economy of Women's Liberation* (New York: Monthly Review reprint, 1970). Sheila Rowbotham, *Woman's Consciousness, Man's World* (Middlesex: Pelican Books, 1973), with bibliography of the periodical literature. A number of significant articles applying Marxist analysis to the oppression of women have been appearing in issues of *Radical America* and *New Left Review.*

7. Eleanor Flexner, *Century of Struggle* (New York: Atheneum Publishers, 1970); Sheila Rowbotham, *Women, Resistance and Revolution* (New York: Random House, 1974); panel at the Second Berkshire Conference on the History of Women, Radcliffe (n. 2 above), on "Clara Zetkin and Adelheid Popp: The Development of Feminist Awareness in the Socialist Women's Movement—Germany and Austria, 1890–1914," with Karen Honeycutt, Ingrun LaFleur, and Jean Quataert. Karen Honeycutt's paper on Clara Zetkin is in *Feminist Studies*

On the other hand, although women may adopt the interests and ideology of men of their class, women as a group cut through male class systems. Although I would quarrel with the notion that women of all classes, in all cultures, and at all times are accorded secondary status, there is certainly sufficient evidence that this is generally, if not universally, the case. From the advent of civilization, and hence of history proper as distinct from prehistorical societies, the social order has been patriarchal. Does that then make women a caste, a hereditary inferior order? This notion has its uses, too, as does the related one drawn chiefly from American black experience, which regards women as a minority group.[8] The sense of "otherness" which both these ideas convey is essential to our historical awareness of women as an oppressed social group. They help us appreciate the social formation of "femininity" as an internalization of ascribed inferiority which serves, at the same time, to manipulate those who have the authority women lack. As explanatory concepts, however, notions of caste and minority group are not productive when applied to women. *Why* should this majority be a minority? And why is it that the members of this particular caste, unlike all other castes, are not of the same rank throughout society? Clearly the minority psychology of women, like their caste status and quasi-class oppression, has to be traced to the universally distinguishing feature of all women, namely their sex. Any effort to understand women in terms of social categories that obscure this fundamental fact has to fail, only to make more appropriate concepts available. As Gerda Lerner put it, laying all such attempts to rest: "All analogies—class, minority group, caste—approximate the position of women, but fail to define it adequately. Women are a category unto themselves: an adequate analysis of their position in society demands new conceptual tools."[9] In short, women have to be defined as women. We are the social opposite, not of a class, a caste, or of a majority, since we are a majority, but of a sex: men. We are a sex, and categorization by gender no longer implies a mothering role and subordination to men, except as social role and relation recognized as such, as socially constructed and socially imposed.

A good part of the initial excitement in women's studies consisted of this discovery, that what had been taken as "natural" was in fact man-made, both as social order and as description of that order as natural and physically determined. Examples of such ideological reasoning go back to the story of Eve, but the social sciences have been functioning the same way, as myth reinforcing patriarchy. A feminist psychologist argues: "It is scientifically unacceptable to advocate the natural superiority of women as child-rearers and socializers of children when there have been so few studies of the effects of make-infant or father-infant interaction on the subsequent development of the child."[1] An anthropologist finds herself constrained to reject, and suspect, so-called scientific contentions that the monogamous family and male dominance belong to primates in general. In fact, she points out, "these features are *not* universal among non-human primates, including some of those most

(Winter 1975/76 [published in 3 (Spring–Summer 1976): 131–44]).

8. Helen Mayer Hacker did interesting work along these lines in the 1950s, "Women as a Minority Group," *Social Forces* 30 (October 1951–May 1952): 60–69, and subsequently, "Women as a Minority Group: Twenty Years Later" (Pittsburgh: Know, Inc., 1972). Degler has recently taken up

these classifications and also finds he must reject them (see n. 2 above).

9. "The Feminists: A Second Look," *Columbia Forum* 13 (Fall 1970): 24–30.

1. Rochelle Paul Wortis, "The Acceptance of the Concept of Maternal Role by Behavioral Scientists: Its Effects on Women," *American Journal of Orthopsychiatry* 41 (October 1971): 733–46.

closely related to humans." And when male domination and male hierarchies do appear, they "seem to be adaptations to particular environments."[2]

Historians could not lay claim to special knowledge about the "natural" roles and relation of the sexes, but they knew what that order was, or ought to be. History simply tended to confirm it. *Bryan's Dictionary of Painters and Engravers* of 1904 says of the Renaissance artist, Propertia Rossi: "a lady of Bologna, best known as a sculptor and carver, but who also engraved upon copper, and learnt drawing and design from Marc Antonio. She is said to have been remarkable for her beauty, virtues, and talents, and to have died at an early age in 1530, in consequence of unrequited love. Her last work was a bas-relief of Joseph and Potiphar's wife!"[3] An exclamation mark ends the entry like a poke in the ribs, signifying that the "lady" (which is not a class designation here), who was beautiful and unhappy in love, was naturally absorbed by just that. Historians really *knew* why there were no great women artists. That is why it was not a historical problem until the feminist art historian, Linda Nochlin, posed it as such—by inquiring into the institutional factors, rather than the native gifts, that sustain artistic activity.[4]

When the issue of woman's place did appear openly, and male historians such as H. D. Kitto rose to defend "their" society, the Greek in his case, the natural order of things again came to the rescue.[5] If Athenian wives were not permitted to go about at will, weren't they too delicate for the strain that travel imposed in those days? If they played no role in political life—the activity that was the source of human dignity to the Greek—was it not because government covered "matters which, inescapably, only men could judge from their own experience and execute by their own exertions"? If girls were not being schooled, weren't they being instructed by mother in the arts of the female citizen? ("If we say 'housework,' " Kitto admits, "it sounds degrading, but if we say Domestic Science it sounds eminently respectable; and we have seen how varied and responsible it was.") But Kitto's major argument was reserved for the family: its religious and social importance in Athenian society. His reasoning on this point sounds to us like an incomplete sentence. He rightly points out that extinction of a family or dissipation of its property was regarded as a disaster. But for him, this fact is an argument, for his position is that it *is* woman's "natural" place to serve that family and continue it by raising legitimate heirs through whom to pass on its property and its rites. If under the conditions of Greek society that task should require confinement to the household and its rounds, that justifies the legal disabilities of wives. As for the other orders of women Athenian society demanded and regulated by law, concubines are not mentioned and hetaerae are "adventuresses who had said No to the serious business of life. Of course they amused men— 'But, my dear fellow, one doesn't *marry* a woman like that.' "

Kitto wrote his history in 1951.

If our understanding of the Greek contribution to social life and consciousness now demands an adequate representation of the life experience of women, so too the sexual order, as shaped by the institutions of family and

2. Kathleen Gough, "The Origin of the Family," *Journal of Marriage and the Family* 33 (November 1971): 760–71.
3. London: Geo. Bell, 1904, 4:285.
4. "Why Have There Been No Great Women Artists?" *Art News* 69, no. 9 (January 1971): 22–39, 67–71.
5. *The Greeks* (Baltimore: Penguin Books, 1962), pp. 219–36.

state, is a matter we now regard as not merely worthy of historical inquiry but central to it. This, I think, is a second major contribution women's history has made to the theory and practice of history in general. We have made of sex a category as fundamental to our analysis of the social order as other classifications, such as class and race. And we consider the relation of the sexes, as those of class and race, to be socially rather than naturally constituted, to have its own development, varying with changes in social organization. Embedded in and shaped by the social order, the relation of the sexes must be integral to any study of it. Our new sense of periodization reflects an assessment of historical change from the vantage point of women as well as men. Our use of sex as a social category means that our conception of historical change itself, as change in the social order, is broadened to include changes in the relation of the sexes.

I find the idea of the social relation of the sexes, which is at the core of this conceptual development, to be both novel and central in feminist scholarship and in works stimulated by it. An art historian, Carol Duncan, asks with respect to modern erotic art, "what are the male-female relations it implies," and finds those relations of domination and victimization becoming more pronounced precisely as women's claims for equality were winning recognition.[6] Michelle Zimbalist Rosaldo, coeditor of a collection of studies by feminist anthropologists, speaks of the need for anthropology to develop a theoretical context "within which the social relation of the sexes can be investigated and understood."[7] Indeed almost all the essays in this collective work are concerned with the structure of the sexual order—patriarchal, matrifocal, and otherwise—of the societies they treat. In art history, anthropology, sociology, and history, studies of the status of women necessarily tend to strengthen the social and relational character of the idea of sex. The activity, power, and cultural evaluation of women simply cannot be assessed except in relational terms: by comparison and contrast with the activity, power, and cultural evaluation of men, and in relation to the institutions and social developments that shape the sexual order. To conclude this point, let me quote Natalie Zemon Davis's address to the Second Berkshire Conference on the History of Women in October 1975:

> It seems to me that we should be interested in the history of both women and men, that we should not be working only on the subjected sex any more than an historian of class can focus exclusively on peasants. Our goal is to understand the significance of the *sexes*, of gender groups in the historical past. Our goal is to discover the range in sex roles and in sexual symbolism in different societies and periods, to find out what meaning they had and how they functioned to maintain the social order or to promote its change.[8]

*   *   *

1976

6. Unpublished paper on "The Esthetics of Power" to appear in *The New Eros*, ed. Joan Semmel (New York: Hacker Art Books, 1975). See also Carol Duncan, "Virility and Domination in Early 20th Century Vanguard Painting," *Artforum* 12 (December 1973):30–39.

7. *Woman, Culture and Society*, ed. Michelle Zimbalist Rosaldo and Louise Lamphere (Stanford, Calif.: Stanford University Press, 1974), p. 17.
8. To be published in *Feminist Studies* (Winter 1975/76). [" 'Women's History' in Transition: The European Case," vol. 3, pp. 83–103—editor's note.]

LUCE IRIGARAY
b. 1930

After moving from her native Belgium to Paris in the 1960s, Luce Irigaray earned degrees in philosophy and linguistics before training to become a psychoanalyst. In 1974, because of her book *Speculum de l'autre femme,* Irigaray was expelled by the followers of Lacan from the first department of psychoanalysis in France, the École Freudienne de Paris (in the experimental University of Paris VIII, established by Hélène Cixous). While her emphasis on the suppression of women in psychoanalysis earned the wrath of Lacanians, it has made her highly influential in the women's movements of France, Italy, and the United States. Many of her books have appeared in English translation, including *Speculum of the Other Woman* (1985), *Elemental Passions* (1992), *Sexes and Genealogies* (1993), *Je, Tu, Nous: Toward a Culture of Difference* (1993), *An Ethics of Sexual Difference* (1993), *Thinking the Difference: For a Peaceful Revolution* (1994), and *I Love to You: Sketch for a Happiness within History* (1996). Her approach to the psychological oppression of women, her often allusive writing style, and her engagement with the history of philosophy from Aristotle and Plato to Kant, Hegel, and Emmanuel Levinas endow her meditations on the engendering of subjectivity with extraordinary nuance and range.

This Sex Which Is Not One[1]

Female sexuality has always been theorized within masculine parameters. Thus, the opposition "viril" clitoral activity/"feminine" vaginal passivity which Freud—and many others—claims are alternative behaviors or steps in the process of becoming a sexually normal woman, seems prescribed more by the practice of masculine sexuality than by anything else. For the clitoris is thought of as a little penis which is pleasurable to masturbate, as long as the anxiety of castration does not exist (for the little boy), while the vagina derives its value from the "home" it offers the male penis when the now forbidden hand must find a substitute to take its place in giving pleasure.

According to these theorists, woman's erogenous zones are no more than a clitoris-sex, which cannot stand up in comparison with the valued phallic organ; or a hole-envelope, a sheath which surrounds and rubs the penis during coition; a nonsex organ or a masculine sex organ turned inside out in order to caress itself.

Woman and her pleasure are not mentioned in this conception of the sexual relationship. Her fate is one of "lack," "atrophy" (of her genitals), and "penis envy," since the penis is the only recognized sex organ of any worth. Therefore she tries to appropriate it for herself, by all the means at her disposal: by her somewhat servile love of the father-husband capable of giving it to her; by her desire of a penis-child, preferably male; by gaining access to those cultural values which are still "by right" reserved for males alone and are therefore always masculine, etc. Woman lives her desire only as an attempt to possess at long last the equivalent of the male sex organ.

---

1. Translated by Claudia Reeder.

All of that seems rather foreign to her pleasure however, unless she remains within the dominant phallic economy. Thus, for example, woman's autoeroticism is very different from man's. He needs an instrument in order to touch himself: his hand, woman's genitals, language—And this self-stimulation requires a minimum of activity. But a woman touches herself by and within herself directly, without mediation, and before any distinction between activity and passivity is possible. A woman "touches herself" constantly without anyone being able to forbid her to do so, for her sex is composed of two lips which embrace continually. Thus, within herself she is already two—but not divisible into ones—who stimulate each other.

This autoeroticism, which she needs in order not to risk the disappearance of her pleasure in the sex act, is interrupted by a violent intrusion: the brutal spreading of these two lips by a violating penis. If, in order to assure an articulation between autoeroticism and heteroeroticism in coition (the encounter with the absolute other which always signifies death), the vagina must also, but not only, substitute for the little boy's hand, how can woman's autoeroticism possibly be perpetuated in the classic representation of sexuality? Will she not indeed be left the impossible choice between defensive virginity, fiercely turned back upon itself, or a body open for penetration, which no longer recognizes in its "hole" of a sex organ the pleasure of retouching itself? The almost exclusive, and ever so anxious, attention accorded the erection in Occidental sexuality proves to what extent the imaginary that commands it is foreign to everything female. For the most part, one finds in Occidental sexuality nothing more than imperatives dictated by rivalry among males: the "strongest" being the one who "gets it up the most," who has the longest, thickest, hardest penis or indeed the one who "pisses the farthest" (cf. little boys' games). These imperatives can also be dictated by sadomasochist fantasies, which in turn are ordered by the relationship between man and mother: his desire to force open, to penetrate, to appropriate for himself the mystery of the stomach in which he was conceived, the secret of his conception, of his "origin." Desire-need, also, once again, to make blood flow in order to revive a very ancient—intrauterine, undoubtedly, but also prehistoric—relation to the maternal.

Woman, in this sexual imaginary, is only a more or less complacent facilitator for the working out of man's fantasies. It is possible, and even certain, that she experiences vicarious pleasure there, but this pleasure is above all a masochistic prostitution of her body to a desire that is not her own and that leaves her in her well-known state of dependency. Not knowing what she wants, ready for anything, even asking for more, if only he will "take" her as the "object" of *his* pleasure, she will not say what *she* wants. Moreover, she does not know, or no longer knows, what she wants. As Freud admits, the beginnings of the sexual life of the little girl are so "obscure," so "faded by the years," that one would have to dig very deep in order to find, behind the traces of this civilization, this history, the vestiges of a more archaic civilization which could give some indication as to what woman's sexuality is all about.[2] This very ancient civilization undoubtedly would not have the same language, the same alphabet— Woman's desire most likely does not speak the same language as man's desire, and it probably has been covered over by the logic that has dominated the West since the Greeks.

2. See Freud's "Female Sexuality" (1931).

In this logic, the prevalence of the gaze, discrimination of form, and individualization of form is particularly foreign to female eroticism. Woman finds pleasure more in touch than in sight and her entrance into a dominant scopic economy signifies, once again, her relegation to passivity: she will be the beautiful object. Although her body is in this way eroticized and solicited to a double movement between exhibition and pudic[3] retreat in order to excite the instincts of the "subject," her sex organ represents the horror of having nothing to see. In this system of representation and desire, the vagina is a flaw, a hole in the representation's scoptophilic[4] objective. It was admitted already in Greek statuary that this "nothing to be seen" must be excluded, rejected, from such a scene of representation. Woman's sexual organs are simply absent from this scene: they are masked and her "slit" is sewn up.

In addition, this sex organ which offers nothing to the view has no distinctive form of its own. Although woman finds pleasure precisely in this incompleteness of the form of her sex organ, which is why it retouches itself indefinitely, her pleasure is denied by a civilization that privileges phallomorphism. The value accorded to the only definable form excludes the form involved in female autoeroticism. The *one* of form, the individual sex, proper name, literal meaning—supersedes, by spreading apart and dividing, this touching of *at least two* (lips) which keeps woman in contact with herself, although it would be impossible to distinguish exactly what "parts" are touching each other.

Whence the mystery that she represents in a culture that claims to enumerate everything, cipher everything by units, inventory everything by individualities. *She is neither one nor two.* She cannot, strictly speaking, be determined either as one person or as two. She renders any definition inadequate. Moreover she has no "proper" name. And her sex organ, which is not *a* sex organ, is counted as *no* sex organ. It is the negative, the opposite, the reverse, the counterpart, of the only visible and morphologically designatable sex organ (even if it does pose a few problems in its passage from erection to detumescence): the penis.

But woman holds the secret of the "thickness" of this "from," its many-layered volume, its metamorphosis from smaller to larger and vice versa, and even the intervals at which this change takes place. Without even knowing it. When she is asked to maintain, to revive, man's desire, what this means in terms of the value of her own desire is neglected. Moreover, she is not aware of her desire, at least not explicitly. But the force and continuity of her desire are capable of nurturing all the "feminine" masquerades that are expected of her for a long time.

It is true that she still has the child, with whom her appetite for touching, for contact, is given free reign, unless this appetite is already lost, or alienated by the taboo placed upon touching in a largely obsessional civilization. In her relation to the child she finds compensatory pleasure for the frustrations she encounters all too often in sexual relations proper. Thus maternity supplants the deficiencies of repressed female sexuality. Is it possible that man and woman no longer even caress each other except indirectly through the mediation between them represented by the child? Preferably male. Man,

3. Pertaining to the external genitalia.
4. Pertaining to the desire to look at sexually stimulating scenes.

identified with his son, rediscovers the pleasure of maternal coddling; woman retouches herself in fondling that part of her body: her baby-penis-clitoris.

What that entails for the amorous trio has been clearly spelled out. The Oedipal interdict seems, however, a rather artificial and imprecise law—even though it is the very means of perpetuating the authoritarian discourse of fathers—when it is decreed in a culture where sexual relations are impracticable, since the desire of man and the desire of woman are so foreign to each other. Each of them is forced to search for some common meeting ground by indirect means: either an archaic, sensory relation to the mother's body, or a current, active or passive prolongation of the law of the father. Their attempts are characterized by regressive emotional behavior and the exchange of words so far from the realm of the sexual that they are completely exiled from it. "Mother" and "father" dominate the couple's functioning, but only as social roles. The division of labor prevents them from making love. They produce or reproduce. Not knowing too well how to use their leisure. If indeed they have any, if moreover they want to have any leisure. For what can be done with leisure? What substitute for amorous invention can be created?

We could go on and on—but perhaps we should return to the repressed female imaginary? Thus woman does not have a sex. She has at least two of them, but they cannot be identified as ones. Indeed she has many more of them than that. Her sexuality, always at least double, is in fact *plural*. Plural as culture now wishes to be plural? Plural as the manner in which current texts are written, with very little knowledge of the censorship from which they arise? Indeed, woman's pleasure does not have to choose between clitoral activity and vaginal passivity, for example. The pleasure of the vaginal caress does not have to substitute itself for the pleasure of the clitoral caress. Both contribute irreplaceably to woman's pleasure but they are only two caresses among many to do so. Caressing the breasts, touching the vulva, opening the lips gently stroking the posterior wall of the vagina, lightly massaging the cervix, etc., evoke a few of the most specifically female pleasures. They remain rather unfamiliar pleasures in the sexual difference as it is currently imagined, or rather as it is currently ignored: the other sex being only the indispensable complement of the only sex.

But *woman has sex organs just about everywhere*. She experiences pleasure almost everywhere. Even without speaking of the hysterization of her entire body, one can say that the geography of her pleasure is much more diversified, more multiple in its differences, more complex, more subtle, than is imagined—in an imaginary centered a bit too much on one and the same.

"She" is indefinitely other in herself. That is undoubtedly the reason she is called temperamental, incomprehensible, perturbed, capricious—not to mention her language in which "she" goes off in all directions and in which "he" is unable to discern the coherence of any meaning. Contradictory words seem a little crazy to the logic of reason, and inaudible for him who listens with ready-made grids, a code prepared in advance. In her statements—at least when she dares to speak out—woman retouches herself constantly. She just barely separates from herself some chatter, an exclamation, a half-secret, a sentence left in suspense— When she returns to it, it is only to set out again from another point of pleasure or pain. One must listen to her differently in order to hear an *"other meaning" which is constantly in the process of weaving itself, at the same time ceaselessly embracing words and yet casting them off to avoid becoming fixed, immobilized*. For when "she" says something, it is already no longer identical to what she means. Moreover, her statements are never identical to anything. Their distinguishing feature is one of contiguity. They touch (*upon*). And when they wander too far from this nearness, she stops and begins again from "zero": her body-sex organ.

It is therefore useless to trap women into giving an exact definition of what they mean, to make them repeat (themselves) so the meaning will be clear. They are already elsewhere than in this discursive machinery where you claim to take them by surprise. They have turned back within themselves, which does not mean the same thing as "within yourself." They do not experience the same interiority that you do and which perhaps you mistakenly presume they share. "Within themselves" means *in the privacy of this silent, multiple, diffuse tact*. If you ask them insistently what they are thinking about, they can only reply: nothing. Everything.

Thus they desire at the same time nothing and everything. It is always more and other than this *one*—of sex, for example—that you give them, that you attribute to them and which is often interpreted, and feared, as a sort of insatiable hunger, a voracity which will engulf you entirely. While in fact it is really a question of another economy which diverts the linearity of a project, undermines the target-object of a desire, explodes the polarization of desire on only one pleasure, and disconcerts fidelity to only one discourse—

Must the multiple nature of female desire and language be understood as the fragmentary, scattered remains of a raped or denied sexuality? This is not an easy question to answer. The rejection, the exclusion of a female imaginary undoubtedly places woman in a position where she can experience herself only fragmentarily as waste or as excess in the little structured margins of a dominant ideology, this mirror entrusted by the (masculine) "subject" with the task of reflecting and redoubling himself. The role of "femininity" is prescribed moreover by this masculine specula (riza)tion and corresponds only slightly to woman's desire, which is recuperated only secretly, in hiding, and in a disturbing and unpardonable manner.

But if the female imaginary happened to unfold, if it happened to come into play other than as pieces, scraps, deprived of their assemblage, would it present itself for all that as *a* universe? Would it indeed be volume rather than surface? No. Unless female imaginary is taken to mean, once again, the prerogative of the maternal over the female. This maternal would be phallic in nature however, closed in upon the jealous possession of its valuable product, and competing with man in his esteem for surplus. In this race for power, woman loses the uniqueness of her pleasure. By diminishing herself in volume, she renounces the pleasure derived from the nonsuture of her lips: she is a mother certainly, but she is a virgin mother. Mythology long ago assigned this role to her in which she is allowed a certain social power as long as she is reduced, with her own complicity, to sexual impotence.

Thus a woman's (re)discovery of herself can only signify the possibility of not sacrificing any of her pleasures to another, of not identifying with anyone in particular, of never being simply one. It is a sort of universe in expansion for which no limits could be fixed and which, for all that, would not be incoherency. Nor would it be the polymorphic perversion of the infant during which its erogenous zones await their consolidation under the primacy of the phallus.

Woman would always remain multiple, but she would be protected from dispersion because the other is a part of her, and is autoerotically familiar to her. That does not mean that she would appropriate the other for herself, that she would make it her property. Property and propriety are undoubtedly rather foreign to all that is female. At least sexually. *Nearness*, however, is not foreign to woman, a nearness so close that any identification of one or the other, and therefore any form of property, is impossible. Woman enjoys a closeness with the other that is *so near she cannot possess it, any more than she can possess herself*. She constantly trades herself for the other without any possible identification of either one of them. Woman's pleasure, which grows indefinitely from its passage in/through the other, poses a problem for any current economy in that all computations that attempt to account for woman's incalculable pleasure are irremediably destined to fail.

However, in order for woman to arrive at the point where she can enjoy her pleasure as a woman, a long detour by the analysis of the various systems of oppression which affect her is certainly necessary. By claiming to resort to pleasure alone as the solution to her problem, she runs the risk of missing the reconsideration of a social practice upon which *her* pleasure depends.

For woman is traditionally use-value for man, exchange-value among men. Merchandise, then. This makes her the guardian of matter whose price will be determined by "subjects": workers, tradesmen, consumers, according to the standard of their work and their need-desire. Women are marked phallically by their fathers, husbands, procurers. This stamp-(ing) determines their value in sexual commerce. Woman is never anything more than the scene of more or less rival exchange between two men, even when they are competing for the possession of mother-earth.

How can this object of transaction assert a right to pleasure without extricating itself from the established commercial system? How can this merchandise relate to other goods on the market other than with aggressive jealousy? How can raw materials possess themselves without provoking in the consumer fear of the disappearance of his nourishing soil? How can this exchange in nothingness that can be defined in "proper" terms of woman's desire not seem to be pure enticement, folly, all too quickly covered over by a more sensible discourse and an apparently more tangible system of values?

A woman's evolution, however radical it might seek to be, would not suffice then to liberate woman's desire. Neither political theory nor political practice have yet resolved nor sufficiently taken into account this historical problem, although Marxism has announced its importance. But women are not, strictly speaking, a class and their dispersion in several classes makes their political struggle complex and their demands sometimes contradictory.

Their underdeveloped condition stemming from their submission by/to a culture which oppresses them, uses them, cashes in on them still remains. Women reap no advantage from this situation except that of their quasi-monopoly of masochistic pleasure, housework, and reproduction. The power of slaves? It is considerable since the master is not necessarily well served in matters of pleasure. Therefore, the inversion of the relationship, especially in sexual economy, does not seem to be an enviable objective.

But if women are to preserve their auto-eroticism, their homo-sexuality, and let it flourish, would not the renunciation of heterosexual pleasure simply be another form of this amputation of power that is traditionally associated with women? Would this renunciation not be a new incarceration, a new cloister that women would willingly build? Let women tacitly go on strike, avoid men long enough to learn to defend their desire notably by their speech, let them discover the love of other women protected from that imperious choice of men which puts them in a position of rival goods, let them forge a social status which demands recognition, let them earn their living in order to leave behind their condition of prostitute— These are certainly indispensable steps in their effort to escape their proletarization on the trade market. But, if their goal is to reverse the existing order—even if that were possible— history would simply repeat itself and return to phallocratism, where neither women's sex, their imaginary, nor their language can exist.

1977, 1980

JUDITH FETTERLEY
b. 1938

When *The Resisting Reader* (1978) appeared along with a cluster of early critical works and editions published by Ellen Moers, Mary Helen Washington, and Patricia Spacks, the academic approach to women's literature was inaugurated. In the case of Judith Fetterley that approach involved a critique of the images of women in canonical fiction composed by American men of letters. In the section reprinted here, the concept of "immasculation"—the idea that women have been taught to identify against themselves and instead with male characters or narrators—sheds light on the reading process, in particular on the ways in which women readers have historically been trained to approach the touchstones of Western discourse. In her subsequent work, Fetterley, the editor of *Provisions: A Reader from Nineteenth-Century American Women* (1985), joined a formidable group of American studies scholars who excavated the neglected or devalued prose literature composed by such novelists as Elizabeth Stuart Phelps, Fanny Fern (Sara Willis Parton), Rebecca Harding Davis, and Harriet Beecher Stowe. In 1992, with Marjorie Pryse, Judith Fetterley edited *American Women Regionalists, 1850–1910.* A graduate of Swarthmore College and Indiana University, Fetterley currently teaches at the State University of New York at Albany.

From The Resisting Reader

From *Introduction: On the Politics of Literature*

I

Literature is political. It is painful to have to insist on this fact, but the necessity of such insistence indicates the dimensions of the problem. John Keats once objected to poetry "that has a palpable design upon us."[1] The major works of American fiction constitute a series of designs on the female reader, all the more potent in their effect because they are "impalpable." One of the main things that keeps the design of our literature unavailable to the consciousness of the woman reader, and hence impalpable, is the very posture of the apolitical, the pretense that literature speaks universal truths through

---

1. Letter to John Hamilton Reynolds, February 3, 1818.

forms from which all the merely personal, the purely subjective, has been burned away or at least transformed through the medium of art into the representative. When only one reality is encouraged, legitimized, and transmitted and when that limited vision endlessly insists on its comprehensiveness, then we have the conditions necessary for that confusion of consciousness in which impalpability flourishes. It is the purpose of this book to give voice to a different reality and different vision, to bring a different subjectivity to bear on the old "universality." To examine American fictions in light of how attitudes toward women shape their form and content is to make available to consciousness that which has been largely left unconscious and thus to change our understanding of these fictions, our relation to them, and their effect on us. It is to make palpable their designs.

American literature is male. To read the canon of what is currently considered classic American literature is perforce to identify as male. Though exceptions to this generalization can be found here and there—a Dickinson poem, a Wharton novel—these exceptions usually function to obscure the argument and confuse the issue: American literature is male. Our literature neither leaves women alone nor allows them to participate. It insists on its universality at the same time that it defines that universality in specifically male terms. "Rip Van Winkle" is paradigmatic of this phenomenon. While the desire to avoid work, escape authority, and sleep through the major decisions of one's life is obviously applicable to both men and women, in Irving's story this "universal" desire is made specifically male. Work, authority, and decision-making are symbolized by Dame Van Winkle, and the longing for flight is defined against her. She is what one must escape from, and the "one" is necessarily male. In Mailer's *An American Dream*, the fantasy of eliminating all one's ills through the ritual of scapegoating is equally male: the sacrificial scapegoat is the woman/wife and the cleansed survivor is the husband/male. In such fictions the female reader is co-opted into participation in an experience from which she is explicitly excluded; she is asked to identify with a selfhood that defines itself in opposition to her; she is required to identify against herself.

The woman reader's relation to American literature is made even more problematic by the fact that our literature is frequently dedicated to defining what is peculiarly American about experience and identity. Given the pervasive male bias of this literature, it is not surprising that in it the experience of being American is equated with the experience of being male. In Fitzgerald's *The Great Gatsby*, the background for the experience of disillusionment and betrayal revealed in the novel is the discovery of America, and Daisy's failure of Gatsby is symbolic of the failure of America to live up to the expectations in the imagination of the men who "discovered" it. America is female; to be American is male; and the quintessential American experience is betrayal by woman. Henry James certainly defined our literature, if not our culture, when he picked the situation of women as the subject of *The Bostonians*, his very American tale.

Power is the issue in the politics of literature, as it is in the politics of anything else. To be excluded from a literature that claims to define one's identity is to experience a peculiar form of powerlessness—not simply the powerlessness which derives from not seeing one's experience articulated, clarified, and legitimized in art, but more significantly the powerlessness which results from the endless division of self against self, the consequence of the invocation to identify as male while being reminded that to be male—to be universal, to be American—is to be *not female*. Not only does powerlessness characterize woman's experience of reading, it also describes the content of what is read. Each of the works chosen for this study presents a version and an enactment of the drama of men's power over women. The final irony, and indignity, of the woman reader's relation to American literature, then, is that she is required to dissociate herself from the very experience the literature engenders. Powerlessness is the subject and powerlessness the experience, and the design insists that Rip Van Winkle/Frederic Henry/Nick Carraway/Stephen Rojack[2] speak for us all.

The drama of power in our literature is often disguised. In "Rip Van Winkle," Rip poses as powerless, the henpecked husband cowering before his termagant Dame. Yet, when Rip returns from the mountains, armed by the drama of female deposition witnessed there, to discover that his wife is dead and he is free to enjoy what he has always wanted, the "Shucks, M'am, I don't mean no harm" posture dissolves. In Sherwood Anderson's "I Want to Know Why," the issue of power is refracted through the trauma of a young boy's discovery of what it means to be male in a culture that gives white men power over women, horses, and niggers. More sympathetic and honest than "Rip," Anderson's story nevertheless exposes both the imaginative limits of our literature and the reasons for those limits. Storytelling and art can do no more than lament the inevitable—boys must grow up to be men; it can provide no alternative vision of being male. Bathed in nostalgia, "I Want to Know Why" is infused with the perspective it abhors, because finally to disavow that perspective would be to relinquish power. The lament is self-indulgent; it offers the luxury of feeling bad without the responsibility of change. And it is completely male-centered, registering the tragedy of sexism through its cost to men. At the end we cry for the boy and not for the whores he will eventually make use of.

In Hawthorne's "The Birthmark," the subject of power is more explicit. The fact of men's power over women and the full implications of that fact are the crux of the story. Aylmer is free to experiment on Georgiana, to the point of death, because she is both woman and wife. Hawthorne indicates the attractiveness of the power that marriage puts in the hands of men through his description of Aylmer's reluctance to leave his laboratory and through his portrayal of Aylmer's inherent discomfort with women and sex. And why does Aylmer want this power badly enough to overcome his initial reluctance and resistance? Hitherto Aylmer has failed in all his efforts to achieve a power equal to that of "Mother" nature. Georgiana provides an opportunity for him to outdo nature by remaking her creation. And if he fails, he still will have won because he will have destroyed the earthly embodiment and representative of his adversary. Hawthorne intends his character to be seen as duplicitous, and he maneuvers Aylmer through the poses of lover, husband, and

2. Characters in, respectively, Washington Irving's "Rip Van Winkle" (1819), Ernest Hemingway's *A Farewell to Arms* (1929), F. Scott Fitzgerald's *The Great Gatsby* (1925), and Norman Mailer's *An American Dream* (1964).

scientist to show us how Aylmer attempts to gain power and to use that power to salve his sense of inadequacy. But even so, Hawthorne, like Anderson, is unwilling to do more with the sickness than call it sick. He obscures the issue of sexual politics behind a haze of "universals" and clothes the murder of wife by husband in the language of idealism.

Though the grotesque may serve Faulkner as a disguise in the same way that the ideal serves Hawthorne, "A Rose for Emily" goes farther than "The Birthmark" in making the power of men over women an overt subject. Emily's life is shaped by her father's absolute control over her; her murder of Homer Barron is reaction, not action. Though Emily exercises the power the myths of sexism make available to her, that power is minimal; her retaliation is no alternative to the patriarchy which oppresses her. Yet Faulkner, like Anderson and Hawthorne, ultimately protects himself and short-circuits the implications of his analysis, not simply through the use of the grotesque, which makes Emily eccentric rather than central, but also through his choice of her victim. In having Emily murder Homer Barron, a northern day-laborer, rather than Judge Stevens, the southern patriarch, Faulkner indicates how far he is willing to go in imagining even the minimal reversal of power involved in retaliation. The elimination of Homer Barron is no real threat to the system Judge Stevens represents. Indeed, a few day-laborers may have to be sacrificed here and there to keep that system going.

In *A Farewell to Arms*, the issue of power is thoroughly obscured by the mythology, language, and structure of romantic love and by the invocation of an abstract, though spiteful, "they" whose goal it is to break the good, the beautiful, and the brave. Yet the brave who is broken is Catherine; at the end of the novel Catherine is dead, Frederic is alive, and the resemblance to "Rip Van Winkle" and "The Birthmark" is unmistakable. Though the scene in the hospital is reminiscent of Aylmer's last visit to Georgiana in her chambers, Hemingway, unlike Hawthorne, separates his protagonist from the source of his heroine's death, locating the agency of Catherine's demise not simply in "them" but in her biology. Frederic survives several years of war, massive injuries, the dangers of a desperate retreat, and the threat of execution by his own army; Catherine dies in her first pregnancy. Clearly, biology is destiny. Yet, Catherine is as much a scapegoat as Dame Van Winkle, Georgiana, Daisy Fay, and Deborah Rojack. For Frederic to survive, free of the intolerable burdens of marriage, family, and fatherhood, yet with his vision of himself as the heroic victim of cosmic antagonism intact, Catherine must die. Frederic's necessities determine Catherine's fate. He is, indeed, the agent of her death.

In its passionate attraction to the phenomenon of wealth, *The Great Gatsby* reveals its author's consuming interest in the issue of power. In the quintessentially male drama of poor boy's becoming rich boy, ownership of women is invoked as the index of power: he who possesses Daisy Fay is the most powerful boy. But when the rich boy, fearing finally for his territory, repossesses the girl and, by asking "Who is he," strips the poor boy of his presumed power, the resultant animus is directed not against the rich boy but against the girl, whose rejection of him exposes the poor boy's powerlessness. The struggle for power between men is deflected into safer and more certain channels, and the consequence is the familiar demonstration of male power over women. This demonstration, however, is not simply the result of a greater safety in directing anger at women than at men. It derives as well from the fact that even the poorest male gains something from a system in which all women are at some level his subjects. Rather than attack the men who represent and manifest that system, he identifies with them and acquires his sense of power through superiority to women. It is not surprising, therefore, that the drama of *The Great Gatsby* involves an attack on Daisy, whose systematic reduction from the glamorous object of Gatsby's romantic longings to the casual killer of Myrtle Wilson provides an accurate measure of the power available to the most "powerless" male.

By his choice of scene, context, and situation, Henry James in *The Bostonians* directly confronts the hostile nature of the relations between men and women and sees in that war the defining characteristics of American culture. His honesty provides the opportunity for a clarification rather than a confusion of consciousness and offers a welcome relief from the deceptions of other writers. Yet the drama, while correctly labeled, is still the same. *The Bostonians* is an unrelenting demonstration of the extent, and an incisive analysis of the sources, of the power of men as a class over women as a class. Yet, though James laments women's oppression, and laments it because of its effects *on women*, he nevertheless sees it as inevitable. *The Bostonians* represents a kind of end point in the literary exploration of sex/class power; it would be impossible to see more clearly and feel more deeply and still remain convinced that patriarchy is inevitable. Indeed, there is revolution latent in James's novel, and, while he would be the last to endorse it, being far more interested in articulating and romanticizing the tragic elements in women's powerlessness, *The Bostonians* provides the material for that analysis of American social reality which is the beginning of change.

Norman Mailer's *An American Dream* represents another kind of end point. Mailer is thoroughly enthralled by the possibility of power that sexism makes available to men, absolutely convinced that he is in danger of losing it, and completely dedicated to maintaining it, at whatever cost. It is impossible to imagine a more frenzied commitment to the maintenance of male power than Mailer's. In *An American Dream* all content has been reduced to the enactment of men's power over women, and to the development and legitimization of that act Mailer brings every strategy he can muster, not the least of which is an extended elaboration of the mythology of female power. In Mailer's work the effort to obscure the issue, disguise reality, and confuse consciousness is so frantic that the antitheses he provides to protect his thesis become in fact his message and his confusions shed a lurid illumination. If *The Bostonians* induces one to rearrange James's conceptual framework and so to make evitable his inevitable, *An American Dream* induces a desire to eliminate Mailer's conceptual framework altogether and start over. Beyond his frenzy is only utter nausea and weariness of spirit and a profound willingness to give up an exhausted, sick, and sickening struggle. In Mailer, the drama of power comes full circle; at once the most sexist writer, he is also the most freeing, and out of him it may be possible to create anew.

1978

SANDRA M. GILBERT
b. 1936

SUSAN GUBAR
b. 1944

At the start of a collaboration that has lasted more than thirty years, Sandra M. Gilbert and Susan Gubar embarked on *The Madwoman in the Attic: The Woman Writer and the Nineteenth-Century Literary Imagination* (1979), which set out to define the aesthetic consequences of the engendering of creativity in British and American fiction and poetry. As in their co-editing of *Shakespeare's Sisters* (1979) and *The Norton Anthology of Literature by Women* (1985; 2nd ed., 1996; 3rd ed., 2006) and in their co-authoring of a trilogy of books about twentieth-century women's literature, *No Man's Land: The Place of the Woman Writer in the Twentieth Century*, in *The Madwoman* Gilbert and Gubar dedicated themselves to the appreciation of a previously unacknowledged but extraordinarily rich and diverse literary inheritance. Besides editing the Norton anthology and completing *Madwoman's* three sequels in *No Man's Land*—*The War of the Words* (1988), *Sexchanges* (1989), and *Letters from the Front* (1994)—along with a spoof filmscript, *Masterpiece Theatre: An Academic Melodrama* (1995), the two have continued to produce a number of independent projects.

In addition to a critical study of the poetry of D. H. Lawrence, Sandra M. Gilbert has published eight collections of poetry, including, most recently, *Ghost Volcano* (1995), *Kissing the Bread: New and Selected Poems, 1969–1999* (2000), and *Belongings* (2005), as well a memoir, *Wrongful Death: A Medical Tragedy* (1995); an anthology of elegies, *Inventions of Farewell: A Book of Elegies* (2001); and a simultaneously critical, cultural, and autobiographical investigation of mourning, *Death's Door: Modern Dying and the Ways We Grieve* (2006).

In addition to her study of cross-racial impersonation, *Racechanges: White Skin, Black Face in American Culture* (1997), and *Poetry after Auschwitz: Remembering What One Never Knew* (2003), Susan Gubar has published two books on the current state of feminist criticism: *Critical Condition: Feminism at the Turn of the Century* (2000) and *Rooms of Our Own* (2006).

From The Madwoman in the Attic

From *Chapter 2. Infection in the Sentence:*
The Woman Writer and the Anxiety of Authorship

The man who does not know sick women does not know women.
—S. Weir Mitchell

I try to describe this long limitation, hoping that with such power as is now mine, and such use of language as is within that power, this will convince any one who cares about it that this "living" of mine had been done under a heavy handicap. . . .
—Charlotte Perkins Gilman

A Word dropped careless on a Page
May stimulate an eye
When folded in perpetual seam
The Wrinkled Maker lie

Infection in the sentence breeds
We may inhale Despair

At distances of Centuries
From the Malaria—
        —Emily Dickinson

I stand in the ring
in the dead city
and tie on the red shoes
. . . .
They are not mine,
they are my mother's,
her mother's before,
handed down like an heirloom
but hidden like shameful letters.[1]
        —Anne Sexton

What does it mean to be a woman writer in a culture whose fundamental definitions of literary authority are, as we have seen, both overtly and covertly patriarchal? If the vexed and vexing polarities of angel and monster, sweet dumb Snow White and fierce mad Queen, are major images literary tradition offers women, how does such imagery influence the ways in which women attempt the pen? If the Queen's looking glass speaks with the King's voice, how do its perpetual kingly admonitions affect the Queen's own voice? Since his is the chief voice she hears, does the Queen try to sound like the King, imitating his tone, his inflections, his phrasing, his point of view? Or does she "talk back" to him in her own vocabulary, her own timbre, insisting on her own viewpoint? We believe these are basic questions feminist literary criticism—both theoretical and practical—must answer, and consequently they are questions to which we shall turn again and again, not only in this chapter but in all our readings of nineteenth-century literature by women.

That writers assimilate and then consciously or unconsciously affirm or deny the achievements of their predecessors is, of course, a central fact of literary history, a fact whose aesthetic and metaphysical implications have been discussed in detail by theorists as diverse as T. S. Eliot, M. H. Abrams, Erich Auerbach, and Frank Kermode.[2] More recently, some literary theorists have begun to explore what we might call the psychology of literary history—the tensions and anxieties, hostilities and inadequacies writers feel when they confront not only the achievements of their predecessors but the traditions of genre, style, and metaphor that they inherit from such "forefathers." Increasingly, these critics study the ways in which, as J. Hillis Miller has put it, a literary text "is inhabited . . . by a long chain of parasitical presences, echoes, allusions, guests, ghosts of previous texts."[3]

As Miller himself also notes, the first and foremost student of such literary psychohistory has been Harold Bloom. Applying Freudian structures to

---

1. *Epigraphs: Doctor on Patient* (Philadelphia: Lippincott, 1888), quoted in Ilza Veith, *Hysteria: The History of a Disease* (Chicago: University of Chicago Press, 1965), pp. 219–20; *The Living of Charlotte Perkins Gilman* (New York: Harper & Row, 1975; first published 1935), p. 104; J. 1261 in *The Poems of Emily Dickinson*, ed. Thomas Johnson, 3 vols. (Cambridge, Mass.: The Belknap Press of Harvard University Press, 1955: all subsequent references are to this edition); "The Red Shoes," *The Book of Folly* (Boston: Houghton Mifflin, 1972), pp. 28–29. [All notes are Gilbert and Gubar's.]

2. In "Tradition and the Individual Talent," Eliot of course considers these matters; in *Mimesis* Auerbach traces the ways in which the realist includes what has been previously excluded from art; and in *The Sense of an Ending* Frank Kermode shows how poets and novelists lay bare the literariness of their predecessors' forms in order to explore the dissonance between fiction and reality.
3. J. Hillis Miller, "The Limits of Pluralism, III: The Critic as Host," *Critical Inquiry* 3, no.3 (Spring 1977):446.

literary genealogies, Bloom has postulated that the dynamics of literary history arise from the artist's "anxiety of influence," his fear that he is not his own creator and that the works of his predecessors, existing before and beyond him, assume essential priority over his own writings. In fact, as we pointed out in our discussion of the metaphor of literary paternity, Bloom's paradigm of the sequential historical relationship between literary artists is the relationship of father and son, specifically that relationship as it was defined by Freud. Thus Bloom explains that a "strong poet" must engage in heroic warfare with his "precursor," for, involved as he is in a literary Oedipal struggle, a man can only become a poet by somehow invalidating his poetic father.[4]

Bloom's model of literary history is intensely (even exclusively) male, and necessarily patriarchal. For this reason it has seemed, and no doubt will continue to seem, offensively sexist to some feminist critics. Not only, after all, does Bloom describe literary history as the crucial warfare of fathers and sons, he sees Milton's fiercely masculine fallen Satan as *the* type of the poet in our culture, and he metaphorically defines the poetic process as a sexual encounter between a male poet and his female muse. Where, then, does the female poet fit in? Does she want to annihilate a "forefather" or a "foremother"? What if she can find no models, no precursors? Does she have a muse, and what is its sex? Such questions are inevitable in any female consideration of Bloomian poetics. And yet, from a feminist perspective, their inevitability may be just the point; it may, that is, call our attention not to what is wrong about Bloom's conceptualization of the dynamics of Western literary history, but to what is right (or at least suggestive) about his theory.

For Western literary history *is* overwhelmingly male—or, more accurately, patriarchal—and Bloom analyzes and explains this fact, while other theorists have ignored it, precisely, one supposes, because they assumed literature had to be male. Like Freud, whose psychoanalytic postulates permeate Bloom's literary psychoanalyses of the "anxiety of influence," Bloom has defined processes of interaction that his predecessors did not bother to consider because, among other reasons, they were themselves so caught up in such processes. Like Freud, too, Bloom has insisted on bringing to consciousness assumptions readers and writers do not ordinarily examine. In doing so, he has clarified the implications of the psychosexual and sociosexual contexts by which every literary text is surrounded, and thus the meanings of the "guests" and "ghosts" which inhabit texts themselves. Speaking of Freud, the feminist theorist Juliet Mitchell has remarked that "psychoanalysis is not a recommendation *for* a patriarchal society, but an analysis of one."[5] The same sort of statement could be made about Bloom's model of literary history, which is not a recommendation for but an analysis of the patriarchal poetics (and attendant anxieties) which underlie our culture's chief literary movements.

For our purposes here, however, Bloom's historical construct is useful not only because it helps identify and define the patriarchal psychosexual context in which so much Western literature was authored, but also because it can

---

4. For a discussion of the woman writer and her place in Bloomian literary history, see Joanne Feit Diehl, " 'Come Slowly—Eden': An Exploration of Women Poets and Their Muse," Signs 3, no. 3 (Spring 1978): 572–87. See also the responses to Diehl in Signs 4, no. 1 (Autumn 1978): 188–96.

5. Juliet Mitchell, *Psychoanalysis and Feminism* (New York: Vintage, 1975), p. xiii.

help us distinguish the anxieties and achievements of female writers from those of male writers. If we return to the question we asked earlier—where does a woman writer "fit in" to the overwhelmingly and essentially male literary history Bloom describes?—we find we have to answer that a woman writer does *not* "fit in." At first glance, indeed, she seems to be anomalous, indefinable, alienated, a freakish outsider. Just as in Freud's theories of male and female psychosexual development there is no symmetry between a boy's growth and a girl's (with, say, the male "Oedipus complex" balanced by a female "Electra complex") so Bloom's male-oriented theory of the "anxiety of influence" cannot be simply reversed or inverted in order to account for the situation of the woman writer.

Certainly if we acquiesce in the patriarchal Bloomian model, we can be sure that the female poet does not experience the "anxiety of influence" in the same way that her male counterpart would, for the simple reason that she must confront precursors who are almost exclusively male, and therefore significantly different from her. Not only do these precursors incarnate patriarchal authority (as our discussion of the metaphor of literary paternity argued), they attempt to enclose her in definitions of her person and her potential which, by reducing her to extreme stereotypes (angel, monster) drastically conflict with her own sense of her self—that is, of her subjectivity, her autonomy, her creativity. On the one hand, therefore, the woman writer's male precursors symbolize authority; on the other hand, despite their authority, they fail to define the ways in which she experiences her own identity as a writer. More, the masculine authority with which they construct their literary personae, as well as the fierce power struggles in which they engage in their efforts of self-creation, seem to the woman writer directly to contradict the terms of her own gender definition. Thus the "anxiety of influence" that a male poet experiences is felt by a female poet as an even more primary "anxiety of authorship"—a radical fear that she cannot create, that because she can never become a "precursor" the act of writing will isolate or destroy her.

This anxiety is, of course, exacerbated by her fear that not only can she not fight a male precursor on "his" terms and win, she cannot "beget" art upon the (female) body of the muse. As Juliet Mitchell notes, in a concise summary of the implications Freud's theory of psychosexual development has for women, both a boy and a girl, "as they learn to speak and live within society, want to take the father's [in Bloom's terminology the precursor's] place, and *only the boy will one day be allowed to do so.* Furthermore both sexes are born into the desire of the mother, and as, through cultural heritage, what the mother desires is the phallus-turned-baby, *both* children desire to be the phallus for the mother. Again, *only the boy can fully recognize himself in his mother's desire.* Thus *both* sexes repudiate the implications of femininity," but the girl learns (in relation to her father) "that her subjugation to the law of the father entails her becoming the representative of 'nature' and 'sexuality,' a chaos of spontaneous, intuitive creativity."[6]

Unlike her male counterpart, then, the female artist must first struggle against the effects of a socialization which makes conflict with the will of her (male) precursors seem inexpressibly absurd, futile, or even—as in the case of the Queen in "Little Snow White"—self-annihilating. And just as the male

6. Ibid., pp. 404–05.

artist's struggle against his precursor takes the form of what Bloom calls revisionary swerves, flights, misreadings, so the female writer's battle for self-creation involves her in a revisionary process. Her battle, however, is not against her (male) precursor's reading of the world but against his reading of *her*. In order to define herself as an author she must redefine the terms of her socialization. Her revisionary struggle, therefore, often becomes a struggle for what Adrienne Rich has called "Re-vision—the act of looking back, of seeing with fresh eyes, of entering an old text from a new critical direction . . . an act of survival."[7] Frequently, moreover, she can begin such a struggle only by actively seeking a *female* precursor who, far from representing a threatening force to be denied or killed, proves by example that a revolt against patriarchal literary authority is possible.

For this reason, as well as for the sound psychoanalytic reasons Mitchell and others give, it would be foolish to lock the woman artist into an Electra pattern matching the Oedipal structure Bloom proposes for male writers. The woman writer—and we shall see women doing this over and over again—searches for a female model not because she wants dutifully to comply with male definitions of her "femininity" but because she must legitimize her own rebellious endeavors. At the same time, like most women in patriarchal society, the woman writer does experience her gender as a painful obstacle, or even a debilitating inadequacy; like most patriarchally conditioned women, in other words, she is victimized by what Mitchell calls "the inferiorized and 'alternative' (second sex) psychology of women under patriarchy."[8] Thus the loneliness of the female artist, her feelings of alienation from male predecessors coupled with her need for sisterly precursors and successors, her urgent sense of her need for a female audience together with her fear of the antagonism of male readers, her culturally conditioned timidity about self-dramatization, her dread of the patriarchal authority of art, her anxiety about the impropriety of female invention—all these phenomena of "inferiorization" mark the woman writer's struggle for artistic self-definition and differentiate her efforts at self-creation from those of her male counterpart.

As we shall see, such sociosexual differentiation means that, as Elaine Showalter has suggested, women writers participate in a quite different literary subculture from that inhabited by male writers, a subculture which has its own distinctive literary traditions, even—though it defines itself *in relation to* the "main," male-dominated, literary culture—a distinctive history.[9] At best, the separateness of this female subculture has been exhilarating for women. In recent years, for instance, while male writers seem increasingly to have felt exhausted by the need for revisionism which Bloom's theory of the "anxiety of influence" accurately describes, women writers have seen themselves as pioneers in a creativity so intense that their male counterparts have probably not experienced its analog since the Renaissance, or at least since the Romantic era. The son of many fathers, today's male writer feels hopelessly belated; the daughter of too few mothers, today's female writer feels that she is helping to create a viable tradition which is at last definitively emerging.

---

7. Adrienne Rich, "When We Dead Awaken: Writing as Re-Vision," in *Adrienne Rich's Poetry*, ed. Barbara Charlesworth Gelpi and Albert Gelpi (New York: Norton, 1975), p. 90.

8. Mitchell, *Psychoanalysis and Feminism*, p. 402.
9. See Elaine Showalter, *A Literature of Their Own* (Princeton: Princeton University Press, 1977).

There is a darker side of this female literary subculture, however, especially when women's struggles for literary self-creation are seen in the psychosexual context described by Bloom's Freudian theories of patrilineal literary inheritance. As we noted above, for an "anxiety of influence" the woman writer substitutes what we have called an "anxiety of authorship," an anxiety built from complex and often only barely conscious fears of that authority which seems to the female artist to be by definition inappropriate to her sex. Because it is based on the woman's socially determined sense of her own biology, this anxiety of authorship is quite distinct from the anxiety about creativity that could be traced in such male writers as Hawthorne or Dostoevsky. Indeed, to the extent that it forms one of the unique bonds that link women in what we might call the secret sisterhood of their literary subculture, such anxiety in itself constitutes a crucial mark of that subculture.

In comparison to the "male" tradition of strong, father-son combat, however, this female anxiety of authorship is profoundly debilitating. Handed down not from one woman to another but from the stern literary "fathers" of patriarchy to all their "inferiorized" female descendants, it is in many ways the germ of a dis-ease or, at any rate, a disaffection, a disturbance, a distrust, that spreads like a stain throughout the style and structure of much literature by women, especially—as we shall see in this study—throughout literature by women before the twentieth century. For if contemporary women do now attempt the pen with energy and authority, they are able to do so only because their eighteenth- and nineteenth-century foremothers struggled in isolation that felt like illness, alienation that felt like madness, obscurity that felt like paralysis to overcome the anxiety of authorship that was endemic to their literary subculture. Thus, while the recent feminist emphasis on positive role models has undoubtedly helped many women, it should not keep us from realizing the terrible odds against which a creative female subculture was established. Far from reinforcing socially oppressive sexual stereotyping, only a full consideration of such problems can reveal the extraordinary strength of women's literary accomplishments in the eighteenth and nineteenth centuries.

Emily Dickinson's acute observations about "infection in the sentence," quoted in our epigraphs, resonate in a number of different ways, then, for women writers, given the literary woman's special concept of her place in literary psychohistory. To begin with, the words seem to indicate Dickinson's keen consciousness that, in the purest Bloomian or Millerian sense, pernicious "guests" and "ghosts" inhabit all literary texts. For any reader, but especially for a reader who is also a writer, every text can become a "sentence" or weapon in a kind of metaphorical germ warfare. Beyond this, however, the fact that "infection in the sentence *breeds*" suggests Dickinson's recognition that literary texts are coercive, imprisoning, fever-inducing; that, since literature usurps a reader's interiority, it is an invasion of privacy. Moreover, given Dickinson's own gender definition, the sexual ambiguity of her poem's "Wrinkled Maker" is significant. For while, on the one hand, "we" (meaning especially women writers) "may inhale Despair" from all those patriarchal texts which seek to deny female autonomy and authority, on the other hand "we" (meaning especially women writers) "may inhale Despair" from all those "foremothers" who have both overtly and covertly conveyed their traditional authorship anxiety to their bewildered female descendants. Finally, such traditional, metaphorically matrilineal anxiety ensures that even the maker of a text, when she is a woman, may feel imprisoned within texts—folded and "wrinkled" by their pages and thus trapped in their "perpetual seam[s]" which perpetually tell her how she *seems*.

Although contemporary women writers are relatively free of the infection of this "Despair" Dickinson defines (at least in comparison to their nineteenth-century precursors), an anecdote recently related by the American poet and essayist Annie Gottlieb summarizes our point about the ways in which, for all women, "Infection in the sentence breeds":

> When I began to enjoy my powers as a writer, I dreamt that my mother had me sterilized! (Even in dreams we still blame our mothers for the punitive choices our culture forces on us.) I went after the mother-figure in my dream, brandishing a large knife; on its blade was writing. I cried, "Do you know what you are doing? You are destroying my femaleness, my *female power*, which is important to me *because of you!*"[1]

Seeking motherly precursors, says Gottlieb, as if echoing Dickinson, the woman writer may find only infection, debilitation. Yet still she must seek, not seek to subvert, her *"female power*, which is important"* to her because of her lost literary matrilineage. In this connection, Dickinson's own words about mothers are revealing, for she alternately claimed that "I never had a mother," that "I always ran Home to Awe as a child. . . . He was an awful Mother but I liked him better than none," and that "a mother [was] a miracle."[2] Yet, as we shall see, her own anxiety of authorship was a "Despair" inhaled not only from the infections suffered by her own ailing physical mother, and her many tormented literary mothers, but from the literary fathers who spoke to her— even "lied" to her—sometimes near at hand, sometimes "at distances of Centuries," from the censorious looking glasses of literary texts.

It is debilitating to be *any* woman in a society where women are warned that if they do not behave like angels they must be monsters. Recently, in fact, social scientists and social historians like Jessie Bernard, Phyllis Chesler, Naomi Weisstein, and Pauline Bart have begun to study the ways in which patriarchal socialization literally makes women sick, both physically and mentally.[3] Hysteria, the disease with which Freud so famously began his investigations into the dynamic connections between *psyche* and *soma*, is by definition a "female disease," not so much because it takes its name from the Greek word for womb, *hyster* (the organ which was in the nineteenth century supposed to "cause" this emotional disturbance), but because hysteria did occur mainly among women in turn-of-the-century Vienna, and because throughout the nineteenth century this mental illness, like many other nerv-

1. Annie Gottlieb, "Feminists Look at Motherhood," *Mother Jones* (November 1976): 53.
2. *The Letters of Emily Dickinson*, ed. Thomas Johnson, 3 vols. (Cambridge, Mass.: The Belknap Press of Harvard University Press, 1958), 2:475; 2:518.
3. See Jessie Bernard, "The Paradox of the Happy Marriage," Pauline B. Bart, "Depression in Middle-Aged Women," and Naomi Weisstein, "Psychology Constructs the Female," all in Vivian Gornick and Barbara K. Moran, ed., *Woman in Sexist Society* (New York: Basic Books, 1971). See also Phyllis Chesler, *Women and Madness* (New York: Doubleday, 1972), and—for a summary of all these matters—Barbara Ehrenreich and Deirdre English, *Complaints and Disorders: The Sexual Politics of Sickness* (Old Westbury: The Feminist Press, 1973).

ous disorders, was thought to be caused by the female reproductive system, as if to elaborate upon Aristotle's notion that femaleness was in and of itself a deformity.[4] And, indeed, such diseases of maladjustment to the physical and social environment as anorexia and agoraphobia did and do strike a disproportionate number of women. Sufferers from anorexia—loss of appetite, self-starvation—are primarily adolescent girls. Sufferers from agoraphobia—fear of open or "public" places—are usually female, most frequently middle-aged housewives, as are sufferers from crippling rheumatoid arthritis.[5]

Such diseases are caused by patriarchal socialization in several ways. Most obviously, of course, any young girl, but especially a lively or imaginative one, is likely to experience her education in docility, submissiveness, self-lessness as in some sense sickening. To be trained in renunciation is almost necessarily to be trained to ill health, since the human animal's first and strongest urge is to his/her *own* survival, pleasure, assertion. In addition, each of the "subjects" in which a young girl is educated may be sickening in a specific way. Learning to become a beautiful object, the girl learns anxiety about—perhaps even loathing of—her own flesh. Peering obsessively into the real as well as metaphoric looking glasses that surround her, she desires literally to "reduce" her own body. In the nineteenth century, as we noted earlier, this desire to be beautiful and "frail" led to tight-lacing and vinegar-drinking. In our own era it has spawned innumerable diets and "controlled" fasts, as well as the extraordinary phenomenon of teenage anorexia.[6] Similarly, it seems inevitable that women reared for, and conditioned to, lives of privacy, reticence, domesticity, might develop pathological fears of public places and unconfined spaces. Like the comb, stay-laces, and apple which the Queen in "Little Snow White" uses as weapons against her hated stepdaughter, such afflictions as anorexia and agoraphobia simply carry patriarchal definitions of "femininity" to absurd extremes, and thus function as essential or at least inescapable parodies of social prescriptions.

In the nineteenth century, however, the complex of social prescriptions these diseases parody did not merely urge women to act in ways which would cause them to become ill; nineteenth-century culture seems to have actually admonished women to *be* ill. In other words, the "female diseases" from which Victorian women suffered were not always byproducts of their training in femininity; they were the goals of such training. As Barbara Ehrenreich and Deirdre English have shown, throughout much of the nineteenth

4. In *Hints on Insanity* (1861) John Millar wrote that "Mental derangement frequently occurs in young females from Amenorrhoea, especially in those who have any strong hereditary predisposition to insanity," adding that "an occasional warm hip-bath or leeches to the pubis will . . . be followed by complete mental recovery." In 1873, Henry Mauldsey wrote in *Body and Mind* that "the monthly activity of the ovaries . . . has a notable effect upon the mind and body; wherefore it may become an important cause of mental and physical derangement." See especially the medical opinions of John Millar, Henry Maudsley, and Andrew Wynter in *Madness and Morals: Ideas on Insanity in the Nineteenth Century,* ed. Vieda Skultans (London and Boston: Routledge & Kegan Paul, 1975), pp. 230–35.
5. See Marlene Boskind-Lodahl, "Cinderella's Stepsisters: A Feminist Perspective on Anorexia Nervosa and Bulimia," *Signs* 2, no. 2 (Winter

1976): 342–56; Walter Blum, "The Thirteenth Guest," (on agoraphobia), in *California Living, The San Francisco Sunday Examiner and Chronicle* (17 April 1977): 8–12; Joan Arehart-Treichel, "Can Your Personality Kill You?" (on female rheumatoid arthritis, among other diseases), *New York* 10, no. 48 (28 November 1977): 45: "According to studies conducted in recent years, four out of five rheumatoid victims are women, and for good reason: The disease appears to arise in those unhappy with the traditional female-sex role."
6. More recent discussions of the etiology and treatment of anorexia are offered in Hilde Bruch, M. D., *The Golden Cage: The Enigma of Anorexia Nervosa* (Cambridge, Mass.: Harvard University Press, 1978), and in Salvador Minuchin, Bernice L. Rosman, and Lester Baker, *Psychosomatic Families: Anorexia Nervosa in Context* (Cambridge, Mass.: Harvard University Press, 1978).

century "Upper- and upper-middle-class women were [defined as] 'sick' [frail, ill]; working-class women were [defined as] 'sickening' [infectious, diseased]." Speaking of the "lady," they go on to point out that "Society agreed that she was frail and sickly," and consequently a "cult of female invalidism" developed in England and America. For the products of such a cult, it was, as Dr. Mary Putnam Jacobi wrote in 1895, "considered natural and almost laudable to break down under all conceivable varieties of strain—a winter dissipation, a houseful of servants, a quarrel with a female friend, not to speak of more legitimate reasons. . . . Constantly considering their nerves, urged to consider them by well-intentioned but short-sighted advisors, [women] pretty soon become nothing but a bundle of nerves."[7]

Given this socially conditioned epidemic of female illness, it is not surprising to find that the angel in the house of literature frequently suffered not just from fear and trembling but from literal and figurative sicknesses unto death. Although her hyperactive stepmother dances herself into the grave, after all, beautiful Snow White has just barely recovered from a catatonic trance in her glass coffin. And if we return to Goethe's Makarie, the "good" woman of *Wilhelm Meister's Travels* whom Hans Eichner has described as incarnating her author's ideal of "contemplative purity," we find that this "model of selflessness and of purity of heart . . . this embodiment of *das Ewig-Weibliche*, suffers from migraine headaches."[8] Implying ruthless self-suppression, does the "eternal feminine" necessarily imply illness? If so, we may have found yet another meaning for Dickinson's assertion that "Infection in the sentence breeds." The despair we "inhale" even "at distances of centuries" may be the despair of a life like Makarie's, a life that "*has no story*."

At the same time, however, the despair of the monster-woman is also real, undeniable, and infectious. The Queen's mad tarantella is plainly unhealthy and metaphorically the result of too much storytelling. As the Romantic poets feared, too much imagination may be dangerous to anyone, male or female, but for women in particular patriarchal culture has always assumed mental exercises would have dire consequences. In 1645 John Winthrop, the governor of the Massachusetts Bay Colony, noted in his journal that Anne Hopkins "has fallen into a sad infirmity, the loss of her understanding and reason, which had been growing upon her divers years, by occasion of her giving herself wholly to reading and writing, and had written many books," adding that "if she had attended her household affairs, and such things as belong to women . . . she had kept her wits."[9] And as Wendy Martin has noted

> in the nineteenth century this fear of the intellectual woman became so intense that the phenomenon . . . was recorded in medical annals. A thinking woman was considered such a breach of nature that a Harvard doctor reported during his autopsy on a Radcliffe graduate he discovered that her uterus had shrivelled to the size of a pea.[1]

If, then, as Anne Sexton suggests (in a poem parts of which we have also used here as an epigraph), the red shoes passed furtively down from woman

7. Quoted by Ehrenreich and English, *Complaints and Disorders*, p. 19.
8. Eichner, "The Eternal Feminine," Norton Critical Edition of *Faust*, p. 620.
9. John Winthrop, *The History of New England* from 1630 to 1649, ed. James Savage (Boston, 1826), 2:216.
1. Wendy Martin, "Anne Bradstreet's Poetry: A Study of Subversive Piety," *Shakespeare's Sisters*, ed. Gilbert and Gubar, pp. 19–31.

to woman are the shoes of art, the Queen's dancing shoes, it is as sickening to be a Queen who wears them as it is to be an angelic Makarie who repudiates them. Several passages in Sexton's verse express what we have defined as "anxiety of authorship" in the form of a feverish dread of the suicidal tarantella of female creativity:

> All those girls
> who wore red shoes,
> each boarded a train that would not stop.
> . . . .
> They tore off their ears like safety pins.
> Their arms fell off them and became hats.
> Their heads rolled off and sang down the street.
> And their feet—oh God, their feet in the market place—
> . . . the feet went on.
> The feet could not stop.
> . . . .
> They could not listen.
> They could not stop.
> What they did was the death dance.
> What they did would do them in.

Certainly infection breeds in these sentences, and despair: female art, Sexton suggests, has a "hidden" but crucial tradition of uncontrollable madness. Perhaps it was her semi-conscious perception of this tradition that gave Sexton herself "a secret fear" of being "a reincarnation" of Edna Millay, whose reputation seemed based on romance. In a letter to DeWitt Snodgrass she confessed that she had "a fear of writing as a woman writes," adding, "I wish I were a man—I would rather write the way a man writes."[2] After all, dancing the death dance, "all those girls/who wore the red shoes" dismantle their own bodies, like anorexics renouncing the guilty weight of their female flesh. But if their arms, ears, and heads fall off, perhaps their wombs, too, will "shrivel" to "the size of a pea"?

In this connection, a passage from Margaret Atwood's *Lady Oracle* acts almost as a gloss on the conflict between creativity and "femininity" which Sexton's violent imagery embodies (or dis-embodies). Significantly, the protagonist of Atwood's novel is a writer of the sort of fiction that has recently been called "female gothic," and even more significantly she too projects her anxieties of authorship into the fairy-tale metaphor of the red shoes. Stepping in glass, she sees blood on her feet, and suddenly feels that she has discovered

> The real red shoes, the feet punished for dancing. You could dance, or you could have the love of a good man. But you were afraid to dance, because you had this unnatural fear that if you danced they'd cut your feet off so you wouldn't be able to dance. . . . Finally you overcame your fear and danced, and they cut your feet off. The good man went away too, because you wanted to dance.[3]

2. "The Uncensored Poet: Letters of Anne Sexton," *Ms.* 6, no. 5 (November 1977): 53.

3. Margaret Atwood, *Lady Oracle* (New York: Simon and Schuster, 1976), p. 335.

Whether she is a passive angel or an active monster, in other words, the woman writer feels herself to be literally or figuratively crippled by the debilitating alternatives her culture offers her, and the crippling effects of her conditioning sometimes seem to "breed" like sentences of death in the bloody shoes she inherits from her literary foremothers.

Surrounded as she is by images of disease, traditions of disease, and invitations both to disease and to dis-ease, it is no wonder that the woman writer has held many mirrors up to the discomforts of her own nature. As we shall see, the notion that "Infection in the sentence breeds" has been so central a truth for literary women that the great artistic achievements of nineteenth-century novelists and poets from Austen and Shelley to Dickinson and Barrett Browning are often both literally and figuratively concerned with disease, as if to emphasize the effort with which health and wholeness were won from the infectious "vapors" of despair and fragmentation. Rejecting the poisoned apples her culture offers her, the woman writer often becomes in some sense anorexic, resolutely closing her mouth on silence (since—in the words of Jane Austen's Henry Tilney—"a woman's only power is the power of refusal"[4]), even while she complains of starvation. Thus both Charlotte and Emily Brontë depict the travails of starved or starving anorexic heroines, while Emily Dickinson declares in one breath that she "had been hungry, all the Years," and in another opts for "Sumptuous Destitution." Similarly, Christina Rossetti represents her own anxiety of authorship in the split between one heroine who longs to "suck and suck" on goblin fruit and another who locks her lips fiercely together in a gesture of silent and passionate renunciation. In addition, many of these literary women become in one way or another agoraphobic. Trained to reticence, they fear the vertiginous openness of the literary marketplace and rationalize with Emily Dickinson that "Publication—is the Auction / Of the Mind of Man" or, worse, punningly confess that "Creation seemed a mighty Crack—/To make me visible."[5]

As we shall also see, other diseases and dis-eases accompany the two classic symptoms of anorexia and agoraphobia. Claustrophobia, for instance, agoraphobia's parallel and complementary opposite, is a disturbance we shall encounter again and again in women's writing throughout the nineteenth century. Eye "troubles," moreover, seem to abound in the lives and works of literary women, with Dickinson matter-of-factly noting that her eye got "put out," George Eliot describing patriarchal Rome as "a disease of the retina," Jane Eyre and Aurora Leigh marrying blind men, Charlotte Brontë deliberately writing with her eyes closed, and Mary Elizabeth Coleridge writing about "Blindness" that came because "Absolute and bright, / The Sun's rays smote me till they masked the Sun."[6] Finally, aphasia and amnesia—two illnesses which symbolically represent (and parody) the sort of intellectual

---

4. See *Northanger Abbey*, chapter 10: "You will allow, that in both [matrimony and dancing], man has the advantage of choice, woman only the power of refusal."
5. See Dickinson, *Poems*, J. 579 ("I had been hungry, all the Years"), J. 709 ("Publication—is the Auction"), and J. 891 ("To my quick ear the

Leaves—conferred"); see also Christina Rossetti, "Goblin Market."
6. See Dickinson, *Poems*, J. 327 ("Before I got my eye put out"), George Eliot, *Middlemarch*, book 2, chapter 20, and M. E. Coleridge, "Doubt," in *Poems by Mary E. Coleridge* (London: Elkin Mathews, 1908), p. 40.

incapacity patriarchal culture has traditionally required of women—appear and reappear in women's writings in frankly stated or disguised forms. "Foolish" women characters in Jane Austen's novels (Miss Bates in *Emma*, for instance) express Malapropish confusion about language, while Mary Shelley's monster has to learn language from scratch and Emily Dickinson herself childishly questions the meanings of the most basic English words: "Will there really be a 'Morning'? / Is there such a thing as 'Day'?"[7] At the same time, many women writers manage to imply that the reason for such ignorance of language—as well as the reason for their deep sense of alienation and inescapable feeling of anomie—is that they have *forgotten* something. Deprived of the power that even their pens don't seem to confer, these women resemble Doris Lessing's heroines, who have to fight their internalization of patriarchal strictures for even a faint trace memory of what they might have become.

"Where are the songs I used to know, / Where are the notes I used to sing?" writes Christina Rossetti in "The Key-Note," a poem whose title indicates its significance for her. "I have forgotten everything / I used to know so long ago."[8] As if to make the same point, Charlotte Brontë's Lucy Snowe conveniently "forgets" her own history and even, so it seems, the Christian name of one of the central characters in her story, while Brontë's orphaned Jane Eyre seems to have lost (or symbolically "forgotten") her family heritage. Similarly, too, Emily Brontë's Heathcliff "forgets" or is made to forget who and what he was; Mary Shelley's monster is "born" without either a memory or a family history; and Elizabeth Barrett Browning's Aurora Leigh is early separated from—and thus induced to "forget"—her "mother land" of Italy. As this last example suggests, however, what all these characters and their authors really fear they have forgotten is precisely that aspect of their lives which has been kept from them by patriarchal poetics: their matrilineal heritage of literary strength, their "female power" which, as Annie Gottlieb wrote, is important to them *because of* (not in spite of) their mothers. In order, then, not only to understand the ways in which "Infection in the sentence breeds" for women but also to learn how women have won through disease to artistic health we must begin by redefining Bloom's seminal definitions of the revisionary "anxiety of influence." In doing so, we will have to trace the difficult paths by which nineteenth-century women overcame their "anxiety of authorship," repudiated debilitating patriarchal prescriptions, and recovered or remembered the lost foremothers who could help them find their distinctive female power.

* * *

1979

---

7. See Dickinson, *Poems*, J. 101.
8. *The Poetical Works of Christina G. Rossetti*, 2 vols. (Boston: Little, Brown, 1909), 2:11.

JULIA KRISTEVA
b. 1941

After *Revolution in Poetic Language* (1974, trans. 1984) and *About Chinese Women* (1974, trans. 1977) established Julia Kristeva's reputation as a sophisticated theorist of poetic writing and an acute transnational observer, she completed her training in psychoanalysis and produced a series of books about various affects or emotional states: *Powers of Horror: An Essay on Abjection* (1980, trans. 1982), *Tales of Love* (1983, trans. 1987), *Black Sun: Depression and Melancholia* (1987, trans. 1989), and *New Maladies of the Soul* (1993, trans. 1995). In *Strangers to Ourselves*(1988, trans. 1991), her attentiveness to the figure of the foreigner reflects her own experience as a Bulgarian-born professor at the University of Paris VII. Married to Philippe Sollers, himself a theorist and the editor of the journal *Tel Quel*, Kristeva was hailed by a number of feminists as a thinker able to bridge the divide within feminism between Anglo-American empiricists and French poststructuralists. Although frequently anthologized and cited by feminists, "Women's Time" remains critical of any feminism founded on a stark opposition between women and men. Thus, Kristeva has been influential in the critique of so-called universalizing, essentializing, or totalizing definitions of women or womanhood.

From Women's Time[1]

* * *

Which Time?

"Father's time, mother's species," as Joyce put it; and, indeed, when evoking the name and destiny of women, one thinks more of the *space* generating and forming the human species than of *time*, becoming, or history. The modern sciences of subjectivity, of its genealogy and accidents, confirm in their own way this intuition, which is perhaps itself the result of a sociohistorical conjuncture. Freud, listening to the dreams and fantasies of his patients, thought that "hysteria was linked to place."[2] Subsequent studies on the acquisition of the symbolic function by children show that the permanence and quality of maternal love condition the appearance of the first spatial references which induce the child's laugh and then induce the entire range of symbolic manifestations which lead eventually to sign and syntax.[3] Moreover, antipsychiatry and psychoanalysis as applied to the treatment of psychoses, before attributing the capacity for transference and communication to the patient, proceed to the arrangement of new places, gratifying substitutes that repair old deficiencies in the maternal space. I could go on giving examples. But

1. Translated by Alice Jardine and Harry Blake [except as indicated, all subsequent notes are Kristeva's].
2. Sigmund Freud and Carl G. Jung, *Correspondance* (Paris: Gallimard, 1975), 1:87.
3. R. Spitz, *La Première année de la vie de l'enfant* [First year of life: a psychoanalytic study of normal and deviant development of object relations] (Paris: PUF, 1958); D. Winnicott, *Jeu et réalité*

[Playing and reality] (Paris: Gallimard, 1975); Julia Kristeva, "Noms de lieu" in *Polylogue* (Paris: Editions du Seuil, 1977), translated as "Place Names" in Julia Kristeva, *Desire in Language: A Semiotic Approach to Literature and Art*, ed. Leon S. Roudiez, trans. Thomas Gora, Alice Jardine, and Leon Roudiez (New York: Columbia University Press, 1980) (hereafter cited as *Desire in Language*).

they all converge on the problematic of space, which innumerable religions of matriarchal (re)appearance attribute to "woman," and which Plato, recapitulating in his own system the atomists of antiquity, designated by the aporia of the *chora*, matrix space, nourishing, unnameable, anterior to the One, to God and, consequently, defying metaphysics.[4]

As for time, female[5] subjectivity would seem to provide a specific measure that essentially retains *repetition* and *eternity* from among the multiple modalities of time known through the history of civilizations. On the one hand, there are cycles, gestation, the eternal recurrence of a biological rhythm which conforms to that of nature and imposes a temporality whose stereotyping may shock, but whose regularity and unison with what is experienced as extrasubjective time, cosmic time, occasion vertiginous visions and unnameable *jouissance*.[6] On the other hand, and perhaps as a consequence, there is the massive presence of a monumental temporality, without cleavage or escape, which has so little to do with linear time (which passes) that the very word "temporality" hardly fits: All-encompassing and infinite like imaginary space, this temporality reminds one of Kronos in Hesiod's mythology, the incestuous son whose massive presence covered all of Gea in order to separate her from Ouranos, the father.[7] Or one is reminded of the various myths of resurrection which, in all religious beliefs, perpetuate the vestige of an anterior or concomitant maternal cult, right up to its most recent elaboration, Christianity, in which the body of the Virgin Mother does not die but moves from one spatiality to another within the same time via dormition (according to the Orthodox faith) or via assumption (the Catholic faith).[8]

The fact that these two types of temporality (cyclical and monumental) are traditionally linked to female subjectivity insofar as the latter is thought of as necessarily maternal should not make us forget that this repetition and this eternity are found to be the fundamental, if not the sole, conceptions of time in numerous civilizations and experiences, particularly mystical ones.[9] The fact that certain currents of modern feminism recognize themselves here does not render them fundamentally incompatible with "masculine" values.

In return, female subjectivity as it gives itself up to intuition becomes a problem with respect to a certain conception of time: time as project, teleology, linear and prospective unfolding; time as departure, progression, and arrival—in other words, the time of history.[1] It has already been abundantly

---

4. Plato *Timeus* 52: "Indefinitely a place; it cannot be destroyed, but provides a ground for all that can come into being; itself being perceptible, outside of all sensation, by means of a sort of bastard reasoning; barely assuming credibility, it is precisely that which makes us dream when we perceive it, and affirm that all that exists must be somewhere, in a determined place . . ." (author's translation).
5. As most readers of recent French theory in translation know, *le féminin* does not have the same pejorative connotations it has come to have in English. It is a term used to speak about women in general, but, as used most often in this article, it probably comes closest to our "female" as defined by Elaine Showalter in *A Literature of Their Own* (Princeton, N.J.: Princeton University Press, 1977). I have therefore used either "women" or "female" according to the context (cf. also n. 9 in Alice Jardine, "Introduction to Julia Kristeva's

'Women's Time,'" *Signs* 7, no. 1 [1981]: 5–12 [hereafter cited as "Introduction"]). "Subjectivity" here refers to the state of being "a thinking, speaking, acting, doing or writing agent" and never, e.g., as opposed to "objectivity" (see the glossary in *Desire in Language*) [Jardine's note].
6. I have retained *jouissance*—that word for pleasure which defies translation—as it is rapidly becoming a "believable neologism" in English (see the glossary in *Desire in Language*) [Jardine's note].
7. This particular mythology has important implications—equal only to those of the oedipal myth—for current French thought [Jardine's note].
8. See Julia Kristeva, "Hérétique de l'amour," *Tel quel*, no. 74 (1977), pp. 30–49.
9. See H. C. Puech, *La Gnose et la temps* (Paris: Gallimard, 1977).
1. See "Introduction" [Jardine's note].

demonstrated that this kind of temporality is inherent in the logical and onto-logical values of any given civilization, that this temporality renders explicit a rupture, an expectation, or an anguish which other temporalities work to conceal. It might also be added that this linear time is that of language con-sidered as the enunciation of sentences (noun + verb; topic-comment; beginning-ending), and that this time rests on its own stumbling block, which is also the stumbling block of that enunciation—death. A psychoanalyst would call this "obsessional time," recognizing in the mastery of time the true structure of the slave. The hysteric (either male or female) who suffers from reminiscences would, rather, recognize his or her self in the anterior tempo-ral modalities: cyclical or monumental. This antinomy, one perhaps embed-ded in psychic structures, becomes, nonetheless, within a given civilization, an antinomy among social groups and ideologies in which the radical posi-tions of certain feminists would rejoin the discourse of marginal groups of spiritual or mystical inspiration and, strangely enough, rejoin recent scientific preoccupations. Is it not true that the problematic of a time indissociable from space, of a space-time in infinite expansion, or rhythmed by accidents or catastrophes, preoccupies both space science and genetics? And, at another level, is it not true that the contemporary media revolution, which is manifest in the storage and reproduction of information, implies an idea of time as frozen or exploding according to the vagaries of demand, returning to its source but uncontrollable, utterly bypassing its subject and leaving only two preoccupations to those who approve of it: Who is to have power over the origin (the programming) and over the end (the use)?

It is for two precise reasons, within the framework of this article, that I have allowed myself this rapid excursion into a problematic of unheard of complexity. The reader will undoubtedly have been struck by a fluctuation in the term of reference: mother, woman, hysteric. . . . I think that the appar-ent coherence which the term "woman" assumes in contemporary ideology, apart from its "mass" or "shock" effect for activist purposes, essentially has the negative effect of effacing the differences among the diverse functions or structures which operate beneath this word. Indeed, the time has perhaps come to emphasize the multiplicity of female expressions and preoccupations so that from the intersection of these differences there might arise, more pre-cisely, less commercially, and more truthfully, the real *fundamental difference* between the two sexes: a difference that feminism has had the enormous merit of rendering painful, that is, productive of surprises and of symbolic life in a civilization which, outside the stock exchange and wars, is bored to death.

It is obvious, moreover, that one cannot speak of Europe or of "women in Europe" without suggesting the time in which this sociocultural distribution is situated. If it is true that a female sensibility emerged a century ago, the chances are great that by introducing *its own* notion of time, this sensibility is not in agreement with the idea of an "eternal Europe" and perhaps not even with that of a "modern Europe." Rather, through and with the Euro-pean past and present, as through and with the ensemble of "Europe," which is the repository of memory, this sensibility seeks its own trans-European temporality. There are, in any case, three attitudes on the part of European feminist movements toward this conception of linear temporal-ity, which is readily labeled masculine and which is at once both civiliza-tional and obsessional.

Two Generations

In its beginnings, the women's movement, as the struggle of suffragists and of existential feminists, aspired to gain a place in linear time as the time of project and history. In this sense, the movement, while immediately universalist, is also deeply rooted in the sociopolitical life of nations. The political demands of women; the struggles for equal pay for equal work, for taking power in social institutions on an equal footing with men; the rejection, when necessary, of the attributes traditionally considered feminine or maternal insofar as they are deemed incompatible with insertion in that history—all are part of the *logic of identification*[2] with certain values: not with the ideological (these are combatted, and rightly so, as reactionary) but, rather, with the logical and ontological values of a rationality dominant in the nation-state. Here it is unnecessary to enumerate the benefits which this logic of identification and the ensuing struggle have achieved and continue to achieve for women (abortion, contraception, equal pay, professional recognition, etc.); these have already had or will soon have effects even more important than those of the Industrial Revolution. Univeralist in its approach, this current in feminism *globalizes* the problems of women of different milieux, ages, civilizations, or simply of varying psychic structures, under the label "Universal Woman." A consideration of *generations* of women can only be conceived of in this global way as a succession, as progression in the accomplishment of the initial program mapped out by its founders.

In a second phase, linked, on the one hand, to the younger women who came to feminism after May 1968 and, on the other, to women who had an aesthetic or psychoanalytic experience, linear temporality has been almost totally refused, and as a consequence there has arisen an exacerbated distrust of the entire political dimension. If it is true that this more recent current of feminism refers to its predecessors and that the struggle for sociocultural recognition of women is necessarily its main concern, this current seems to think of itself as belonging to another generation—qualitatively different from the first one—in its conception of its own identity and, consequently, of temporality as such. Essentially interested in the specificity of female psychology and its symbolic realizations, these women seek to give a language to the intra-subjective and corporeal experiences left mute by culture in the past. Either as artists or writers, they have undertaken a veritable exploration of the *dynamic of signs*, an exploration which relates this tendency, at least at the level of its aspirations, to all major projects of aesthetic and religious upheaval. Ascribing this experience to a new generation does not only mean that other, more subtle problems have been added to the demands for sociopolitical identification made in the beginning. It also means that, by demanding recognition of an irreducible identity, without equal in the opposite sex and, as such, exploded, plural, fluid, in a certain way nonidentical, this feminism situates itself outside the linear time of identities which com-

---

2. The term "identification" belongs to a wide semantic field ranging from everyday language to philosophy and psychoanalysis. While Kristeva is certainly referring in principle to its elaboration in Freudian and Lacanian psychoanalysis, it can be understood here, as a logic, in its most general sense (see the entry on "identification" in Jean LaPlanche and J. B. Pontalis, *Vocabulaire de la psychanalyse* [The language of psychoanalysis] [Paris: Presses Universitaires de France, 1967; rev. ed., 1976]) [Jardine's note].

municate through projection and revindication. Such a feminism rejoins, on the one hand, the archaic (mythical) memory and, on the other, the cyclical or monumental temporality of marginal movements. It is certainly not by chance that the European and trans-European problematic has been posited as such at the same time as this new phase of feminism.

Finally, it is the mixture of the two attitudes—*insertion* into history and the radical *refusal* of the subjective limitations imposed by this history's time on an experiment carried out in the name of the irreducible difference—that seems to have broken loose over the past few years in European feminist movements, particularly in France and in Italy.

If we accept this meaning of the expression "a new generation of women," two kinds of questions might then be posed. What sociopolitical processes or events have provoked this mutation? What are its problems: its contributions as well as dangers?

Socialism and Freudianism

One could hypothesize that if this new generation of women shows itself to be more diffuse and perhaps less conscious in the United States and more massive in Western Europe, this is because of a veritable split in social relations and mentalities, a split produced by socialism and Freudianism. I mean by *socialism* that egalitarian doctrine which is increasingly broadly disseminated and accepted as based on common sense, as well as that social practice adopted by governments and political parties in democratic regimes which are forced to extend the zone of egalitarianism to include the distribution of goods as well as access to culture. By *Freudianism* I mean that lever, inside this egalitarian and socializing field, which once again poses the question of sexual difference and of the difference among subjects who themselves are not reducible one to the other.

Western socialism, shaken in its very beginnings by the egalitarian or differential demands of its women (e.g., Flora Tristan[3]), quickly got rid of those woman who aspired to recognition of a specificity of the female role in society and culture, only retaining from them, in the egalitarian and universalistic spirit of Enlightenment Humanism, the idea of a necessary identification between the two sexes as the only and unique means for liberating the "second sex." I shall not develop here the fact that this "ideal" is far from being applied in practice by these socialist-inspired movements and parties and that it was in part from the revolt against this situation that the new generation of women in Western Europe was born after May 1968. Let us just say that in theory, and as put into practice in Eastern Europe, socialist ideology, based on a conception of the human being as determined by its place in *production* and the *relations of production,* did not take into consideration this same human being according to its place in *reproduction,* on the one hand, or in the *symbolic order,* on the other. Consequently, the specific character of women could only appear as nonessential or even nonexistent to the totalizing and even totalitarian spirit of this ideology.[4] We begin to see that this same

3. A French radical (1803–1844), who promoted a national workers' union [editor's note].
4. See D. Desanti, "L'Autre Sexe des bolcheviks," *Tel quel,* no. 76 (1978); Julia Kristeva, *Des Chi-* noises (Paris: Editions des femmes, 1975), translated as *On Chinese Women,* trans. Anita Barrows (New York: Urizen Press, 1977).

egalitarian and in fact censuring treatment has been imposed, from Enlightenment Humanism through socialism, on religious specificities and, in particular, on Jews.[5]

What has been achieved by this attitude remains nonetheless of capital importance for women, and I shall take as an example the change in the destiny of women in the socialist countries of Eastern Europe. It could be said, with only slight exaggeration, that the demands of the suffragists and existential feminists have, to a great extent, been met in these countries, since three of the main egalitarian demands of early feminism have been or are now being implemented despite vagaries and blunders: economic, political, and professional equality. (The fourth, sexual equality, which implies permissiveness in sexual relations (including homosexual relations), abortion, and contraception, remains stricken by taboo in Marxian ethics as well as for reasons of state. It is, then, this fourth equality which is the problem and which therefore appears *essential* in the struggle of a new generation. But simultaneously and as a consequence of these socialist accomplishments—which are in fact a total deception—the struggle is no longer concerned with the quest for equality but, rather, with difference and specificity. It is precisely at this point that the new generation encounters what might be called the *symbolic* question.[6] Sexual difference—which is at once biological, physiological, and relative to reproduction—is translated by and translates a difference in the relationship of subjects to the symbolic contract which *is* the social contract: a difference, then, in the relationship to power, language, and meaning. The sharpest and most subtle point of feminist subversion brought about by the new generation will henceforth be situated on the terrain of the inseparable conjunction of the sexual and the symbolic, in order to try to discover, first, the specificity of the female, and then, in the end, that of each individual woman.

A certain saturation of socialist ideology, a certain exhaustion of its potential as a program for a new social contract (it is obvious that the effective realization of this program is far from being accomplished, and I am here treating only its system of thought) makes way for . . . Freudianism. I am, of course, aware that this term and this practice are somewhat shocking to the American intellectual consciousness (which rightly reacts to a muddled and normatizing form of psychoanalysis) and, above all, to the feminist consciousness. To restrict my remarks to the latter: Is it not true that Freud has been seen only as a denigrator or even an exploiter of women? as an irritating phallocrat in a Vienna which was at once Puritan and decadent—a man who fantasized women as sub-men, castrated men?

Castrated and/or Subject to Language

Before going beyond Freud to propose a more just or more modern vision of women, let us try, first, to understand his notion of castration. It is, first of

5. See Arthur Hertzberg, *The French Enlightenment and the Jews* (New York: Columbia University Press, 1968); *Les Juifs et la révolution française*, ed. B. Blumenkranz and A. Seboul (Paris: Edition Privat, 1976).
6. Here, "symbolic" is being more strictly used in terms of that function defined by Kristeva in opposition to the semiotic: "it involves the thetic phase, the identification of subject and its distinction from objects, and the establishment of a sign system" (see the glossary in *Desire in Language,* and Alice Jardine, "Theories of the Feminine: Kristeva," *Enclitic,* in press 4 (1980): 5–15) [Jardine's note].

all, a question of an *anguish* or *fear* of castration, or of correlative penis *envy*; a question, therefore, of *imaginary* formations readily perceivable in the *discourse* of neurotics of both sexes, men and women. But, above all, a careful reading of Freud, going beyond his biologism and his mechanism, both characteristic of his time, brings out two things. First, as presupposition for the "primal scene," the castration fantasy and its correlative (penis envy) are hypotheses, a priori suppositions intrinsic to the theory itself, in the sense that these are not the ideological fantasies of their inventor but, rather, logical necessities to be placed at the "origin" in order to explain what unceasingly functions in neurotic discourse. In other words, neurotic discourse, in man and woman, can only be understood in terms of its own logic when its fundamental causes are admitted as the fantasies of the primal scene and castration, even if (as may be the case) nothing renders them present in reality itself. Stated in still other terms, the reality of castration is no more real than the hypothesis of an explosion which, according to modern astrophysics, is at the origin of the universe: Nothing proves it, in a sense it is an article of faith, the only difference being that numerous phenomena of life in this "big-bang" universe are explicable only through this initial hypothesis. But one is infinitely more jolted when this kind of intellectual method concerns inanimate matter than when it is applied to our own subjectivity and thus, perhaps, to the fundamental mechanism of our epistemophilic thought.

Moreover, certain texts written by Freud (*The Interpretation of Dreams*, but especially those of the second topic, in particular the *Metapsychology*) and their recent extensions (notably by Lacan),[7] imply that castration is, in sum, the imaginary construction of a radical operation which constitutes the symbolic field and all beings inscribed therein. This operation constitutes signs and syntax; that is, language, as a *separation* from a presumed state of nature, of pleasure fused with nature so that the introduction of an articulated network of differences, which refers to objects henceforth and only in this way separated from a subject, may constitute *meaning*. This logical operation of separation (confirmed by all psycholinguistic and child psychology) which preconditions the binding of language which is already syntactical, is therefore the common destiny of the two sexes, men and women. That certain biofamilial conditions and relationships cause women (and notably hysterics) to deny this separation and the language which ensues from it, whereas men (notably obsessionals) magnify both and, terrified, attempt to master them— this is what Freud's discovery has to tell us on this issue.

The analytic situation indeed shows that it is the penis which, becoming the major referent in this operation of separation, gives full meaning to the *lack* or to the *desire* which constitutes the subject during his or her insertion into the order of language. I should only like to indicate here that, in order for this operation constitutive of the symbolic and the social to appear in its full truth and for it to be understood by both sexes, it would be just to emphasize its extension to all that is privation of fullfillment and of totality; exclusion of a pleasing, natural, and sound state: in short, the break indispensable to the advent of the symbolic.

It can now be seen how women, starting with this theoretical apparatus,

---

7. See, in general, Jacques Lacan, *Ecrits* (Paris: Editions du Seuil, 1966) and, in particular, Jacques Lacan, *Le Séminaire XX: Encore* (Paris: Editions du Seuil, 1975) [Jardine's note].

might try to understand their sexual and symbolic difference in the framework of social, cultural, and professional realization, in order to try, by seeing their position therein, either to fulfill their own experience to a maximum or—but always starting from this point—to go further and call into question the very apparatus itself.

Living the Sacrifice

In any case, and for women in Europe today, whether or not they are conscious of the various mutations (socialist and Freudian) which have produced or simply accompanied their coming into their own, the urgent question on our agenda might be formulated as follows: *What can be our place in the symbolic contract?* If the social contract, far from being that of equal men, is based on an essentially sacrificial relationship of separation and articulation of differences which in this way produces communicable meaning, what is our place in this order of sacrifice and/or of language? No longer wishing to be excluded or no longer content with the function which has always been demanded of us (to maintain, arrange, and perpetuate this sociosymbolic contract as mothers, wives, nurses, doctors, teachers . . .), how can we reveal our place, first as it is bequeathed to us by tradition, and then as we want to transform it?

It is difficult to evaluate what in the relationship of women to the symbolic as it reveals itself now arises from a sociohistorical conjuncture (patriarchal ideology, whether Christian, humanist, socialist or so forth), and what arises from a structure. We can speak only about a structure observed in a sociohistorical context, which is that of Christian, Western civilization and its lay ramifications. In this sense of psychosymbolic structure, women, "we" (is it necessary to recall the warnings we issued at the beginning of this article concerning the totalizing use of this plural?) seem to feel that they are the casualties, that they have been left out of the sociosymbolic contract, of language as the fundamental social bond. They find no affect there, no more than they find the fluid and infinitesimal significations of their relationships with the nature of their own bodies, that of the child, another woman, or a man. This frustration, which to a certain extent belongs to men also, is being voiced today principally by women, to the point of becoming the essence of the new feminist ideology. A therefore difficult, if not impossible, identification with the sacrificial logic of separation and syntactical sequence at the foundation of language and the social code leads to the rejection of the symbolic—lived as the rejection of the paternal function and ultimately generating psychoses.

But this limit, rarely reached as such, produces two types of counterinvestment of what we have termed the sociosymbolic contract. On the one hand, there are attempts to take hold of this contract, to possess it in order to enjoy it as such or to subvert it. How? The answer remains difficult to formulate (since, precisely, and formulation is deemed frustrating, mutilating, sacrificial) or else is in fact formulated using stereotypes taken from extremist and often deadly ideologies. On the other hand, another attitude is more lucid from the beginning, more self-analytical which—without refusing or sidestepping this sociosymbolic order—consists in trying to explore the constitution and functioning of this contract, starting less from the knowledge accumulated about it (anthropology, psychoanalysis, linguistics) than from the very personal affect experienced when facing it as subject and as a woman. This leads to the active research,[8] still rare, undoubtedly hesitant but always dissident, being carried out by women in the human sciences; particularly those attempts, in the wake of contemporary art, to break the code, to shatter language, to find a specific discourse closer to the body and emotions, to the unnameable repressed by the social contract. I am not speaking here of a "woman's language," whose (at least syntactical) existence is highly problematical and whose apparent lexical specificity is perhaps more the product of a social marginality than of a sexual-symbolic difference.[9]

Nor am I speaking of the aesthetic quality of productions by women, most of which—with a few exceptions (but has this not always been the case with both sexes?)—are a reiteration of a more or less euphoric or depressed romanticism and always an explosion of an ego lacking narcissistic gratification.[1] What I should like to retain, nonetheless, as a mark of collective aspiration, as an undoubtedly vague and unimplemented intention, but one which is intense and which has been deeply revealing these past few years, is this: The new generation of women is showing that its major social concern has become the sociosymbolic contract as a sacrificial contract. If anthropologists and psychologists, for at least a century, have not stopped insisting on this in their attention to "savage thought," wars, the discourse of dreams, or writers, women are today affirming—and we consequently face a mass phenomenon—that they are forced to experience this sacrificial contract against their will.[2] Based on this, they are attempting a revolt which they see as a resurrection but which society as a whole understands as murder. This attempt can lead us to a not less and sometimes more deadly violence. Or to a cultural innovation. Probably to both at once. But that is precisely where the stakes are, and they are of epochal significance.

*　*　*

Creatures and Creatresses

The desire to be a mother, considered alienating and even reactionary by the preceding generation of feminists, has obviously not become a standard for the present generation. But we have seen in the past few years an increas-

---

8. This work is periodically published in various academic women's journals, one of the most prestigious being *Signs: Journal of Women in Culture and Society*, University of Chicago Press. Also of note are the special issues: "Ecriture, féminité, féminisme," *La Revue des sciences humaines* (Lille III), no. 4 (1977); and "Les Femmes et la philosophie," *Le Doctrinal de sapience* (Editions Solin), no. 3 (1977).

9. See linguistic research on "female language": Robin Lakoff, *Language and Women's Place* (New York: Harper & Row, 1974); Mary R. Key, *Male/Female Language* (Metuchen, N.J.: Scarecrow Press, 1973); A. M. Houdebine, "Les Femmes et la langue," *Tel quel*, no. 74 (1977), pp. 84–95. The contrast between these "empirical" investigations of women's "speech acts" and much of the research in France on the conceptual bases for a "female language" must be emphasized here. It is somewhat helpful, if ultimately inaccurate, to think of the former as an "external" study of language and the latter as an "internal" exploration of the process of signification. For further contrast, see, e.g., "Part II: Contemporary Feminist Thought in France: Translating Difference" in *The Future of Difference*, ed. Hester Eisenstein and Alice Jardine (Boston: G. K. Hall & Co., 1980); the "Introductions" to *New French Feminisms*, ed. Elaine Marks and Isabelle de Courtivron (Amherst: University of Massachusetts Press, 1980); and for a very helpful overview of the problem of "difference and language" in France, see Stephen Heath, "Difference" in *Screen* 19, no. 3 (Autumn 1978): 51–112 [Jardine's note].

1. This is one of the more explicit references to the mass marketing of "écriture féminine" in Paris over the last ten years [Jardine's note].

2. The expression *à leur corps défendant* translates as "against their will," but here the emphasis is on women's bodies: literally, "against their bodies." I have retained the former expression in English, partly because of its obvious intertextuality with Susan Brownmiller's *Against Our Will* (New York: Simon & Schuster, 1975). Women are increasingly describing their experience of the violence of the symbolic contract as a form of rape [Jardine's note].

ing number of women who not only consider their maternity compatible with their professional life or their feminist involvement (certain improvements in the quality of life are also at the origin of this: an increase in the number of day-care centers and nursery schools, more active participation of men in child care and domestic life, etc.) but also find it indispensable to their discovery, not of the plenitude, but of the complexity of the female experience, with all that this complexity comprises in joy and pain. This tendency has its extreme: in the refusal of the paternal function by lesbian and single mothers can be seen one of the most violent forms taken by the rejection of the symbolic outlined above, as well as one of the most fervent divinizations of maternal power—all of which cannot help but trouble an entire legal and moral order without, however, proposing an alternative to it. Let us remember here that Hegel distinguished between female right (familial and religious) and male law (civil and political). If our societies know well the uses and abuses of male law, it must also be recognized that female right is designated, for the moment, by a blank. And if these practices of maternity, among others, were to be generalized, women themselves would be responsible for elaborating the appropriate legislation to check the violence to which, otherwise, both their children and men would be subject. But are they capable of doing so? This is one of the important questions that the new generation of women encounters, especially when the members of this new generation refuse to ask those questions, seized by the same rage with which the dominant order originally victimized them.

Faced with this situation, it seems obvious—and feminist groups become more aware of this when they attempt to broaden their audience—that the refusal of maternity cannot be a mass policy and that the majority of women today see the possibility for fulfillment, if not entirely at least to a large degree, in bringing a child into the world. What does this desire for motherhood correspond to? This is one of the new questions for the new generation, a question the preceding generation had foreclosed. For want of an answer to this question, feminist ideology leaves the door open to the return of religion, whose discourse, tried and proved over thousands of years, provides the necessary ingredients for satisfying the anguish, the suffering, and the hopes of mothers. If Freud's affirmation—that the desire for a child is the desire for a penis and, in this sense, a substitute for phallic and symbolic dominion—can be only partially accepted, what modern women have to say about this experience should nonetheless be listened to attentively. Pregnancy seems to be experienced as the radical ordeal of the splitting of the subject:[3] redoubling up of the body, separation and coexistence of the self and of an other, of nature and consciousness, of physiology and speech. This fundamental challenge to identity is then accompanied by a fantasy of totality—narcissistic completeness—a sort of instituted, socialized, natural psychosis. The arrival of the child, on the other hand, leads the mother into the labyrinths of an experience that, without the child, she would only rarely encounter: love for an other. Not for herself, nor for an identical being, and still less for another person with whom "I" fuse (love or sexual passion). But the slow, difficult,

---

3. The "split subject" (from *Spaltung* as both "splitting" and "cleavage"), as used in Freudian psychoanalysis, here refers directly to Kristeva's "subject in process / in question / on trial" as opposed to the unity of the transcendental ego (see n. 14 in "Introduction") [Jardine's note].

and delightful apprenticeship in attentiveness, gentleness, forgetting oneself. The ability to succeed in this path without masochism and without annihilating one's affective, intellectual, and professional personality—such would seem to be the stakes to be won through guiltless maternity. It then becomes a creation in the strong sense of the term. For this moment, utopian?

On the other hand, it is in the aspiration toward artistic and, in particular, literary creation that woman's desire for affirmation now manifests itself. Why literature?

Is it because, faced with social norms, literature reveals a certain knowledge and sometimes the truth itself about an otherwise repressed, nocturnal, secret, and unconscious universe? Because it thus redoubles the social contract by exposing the unsaid, the uncanny? And because it makes a game, a space of fantasy and pleasure, out of the abstract and frustrating order of social signs, the words of everyday communication? Flaubert said, "Madame Bovary, c'est moi."[4] Today many women imagine, "Flaubert, c'est moi." This identification with the potency of the imaginary is not only an identification, an imaginary potency (a fetish, a belief in the maternal penis maintained at all costs), as a far too normative view of the social and symbolic relationship would have it. This identification also bears witness to women's desire to lift the weight of what is sacrificial in the social contract from their shoulders, to nourish our societies with a more flexible and free discourse, one able to name what has thus far never been an object of circulation in the community: the enigmas of the body, the dreams, secret joys, shames, hatreds of the second sex.

It is understandable from this that women's writing has lately attracted the maximum attention of both "specialists" and the media.[5] The pitfalls encountered along the way, however, are not to be minimized: For example, does one not read there a relentless belittling of male writers whose books, nevertheless, often serve as "models" for countless productions by women? Thanks to the feminist label, does one not sell numerous works whose naive whining or market-place romanticism would otherwise have been rejected as anachronistic? And does one not find the pen of many a female writer being devoted to phantasmic attacks against Language and Sign as the ultimate supports of phallocratic power, in the name of a semi-aphonic corporality whose truth can only be found in that which is "gestural" or "tonal"?

And yet, no matter how dubious the results of these recent productions by women, the symptom is there—women are writing, and the air is heavy with expectation: What will they write that is new?

In the Name of the Father, the Son . . . and the Woman?

These few elements of the manifestations by the new generation of women in Europe seem to me to demonstrate that, beyond the sociopolitical level where it is generally inscribed (or inscribes itself), the women's movement—in its present stage, less aggressive but more artful—is situated within the very framework of the religious crisis of our civilization.

I call "religion" this phantasmic necessity on the part of speaking beings to

---

4. That's me [French]; Madame Bovary, heroine of the 1857 novel of the same name, was the best-known character created by Flaubert [editor's note].

5. Again a reference to *écriture féminine* as generically labeled in France over the past few years and not to women's writing in general [Jardine's note].

provide themselves with a *representation* (animal, female, male, parental, etc.) in place of what constitutes them as such, in other words, symbolization—the double articulation and syntactic sequence of language, as well as its preconditions or substitutes (thoughts, affects, etc.). The elements of the current practice of feminism that we have just brought to light seem precisely to constitute such a representation which makes up for the frustrations imposed on women by the anterior code (Christianity or its lay humanist variant). The fact that this new ideology has affinities, often revindicated by its creators, with so-called matriarchal beliefs (in other words, those beliefs characterizing matrilinear societies) should not overshadow its radical novelty. This ideology seems to me to be part of the broader antisacrificial current which is animating our culture and which, in its protest against the constraints of the sociosymbolic contract, is no less exposed to the risks of violence and terrorism. At this level of radicalism, it is the very principle of sociality which is challenged.

Certain contemporary thinkers consider, as is well known, that modernity is characterized as the first epoch in human history in which human beings attempt to live without religion. In its present form, is not feminism in the process of becoming one?

Or is it, on the contrary and as avant-garde feminists hope, that having started with the idea of difference, feminism will be able to break free of its belief in Woman, Her power, Her writing, so as to channel this demand for difference into each and every element of the female whole, and, finally, to bring out the singularity of each woman, and beyond this, her multiplicities, her plural languages, beyond the horizon, beyond sight, beyond faith itself?

A factor for ultimate mobilization? Or a factor for analysis?

Imaginary support in a technocratic era where all narcissism is frustrated? Or instruments fitted to these times in which the cosmos, atoms, and cells—our true contemporaries—call for the constitution of a fluid and free subjectivity?

The question has been posed. Is to pose it already to answer it?

Another Generation Is Another Space

If the preceding can be *said*—the question whether all this is *true* belongs to a different register—it is undoubtedly because it is now possible to gain some distance on these two preceding generations of women. This implies, of course, that a *third* generation is now forming, at least in Europe. I am not speaking of a new group of young women (though its importance should not be underestimated) or of another "mass feminist movement" taking the torch passed on from the second generation. My usage of the word "generation" implies less a chronology than a *signifying space*, a both corporeal and desiring mental space. So it can be argued that as of now a third attitude is possible, thus a third generation, which does not exclude—quite to the contrary—the *parallel* existence of all three in the same historical time, or even that they be interwoven one with the other.

In this third attitude, which I strongly advocate—which I imagine?—the very dichotomy man/woman as an opposition between two rival entities may be understood as belonging to *metaphysics*. What can "identity," even "sexual identity," mean in a new theoretical and scientific space where the very notion of identity is challenged?[6] I am not simply suggesting a very hypothetical bisexuality which, even if it existed, would only, in fact, be the aspiration toward the totality of one of the sexes and thus an effacing of difference. What I mean is, first of all, the demassification of the problematic of *difference,* which would imply, in a first phase, an apparent de-dramatization of the "fight to the death" between rival groups and thus between the sexes. And this not in the name of some reconciliation—feminism has at least had the merit of showing what is irreducible and even deadly in the social contract—but in order that the struggle, the implacable difference, the violence be conceived in the very place where it operates with the maximum intransigence, in other words, in personal and sexual identity itself, so as to make it disintegrate in its very nucleus.

It necessarily follows that this involves risks not only for what we understand today as "personal equilibrium" but also for social equilibrium itself, made up as it now is of the counterbalancing of aggressive and murderous forces massed in social, national, religious, and political groups. But is it not the insupportable situation of tension and explosive risk that the existing "equilibrium" presupposes which leads some of those who suffer from it to divest it of its economy, to detach themselves from it, and to seek another means of regulating difference?

To restrict myself here to a personal level, as related to the question of women, I see arising, under the cover of a relative indifference toward the militance of the first and second generations, an attitude of retreat from sexism (male as well as female) and, gradually, from any kind of anthropomorphism. The fact that this might quickly become another form of spiritualism turning its back on social problems, or else a form of repression[7] ready to support all status quos, should not hide the radicalness of the process. This process could be summarized as an *interiorization of the founding separation of the sociosymbolic contract,* as an introduction of its cutting edge into the very interior of every identity whether subjective, sexual, ideological, or so forth. This in such a way that the habitual and increasingly explicit attempt to fabricate a scapegoat victim as foundress of a society or a countersociety may be replaced by the analysis of the potentialities of *victim/executioner* which characterize each identity, each subject, each sex.

What discourse, if not that of a religion, would be able to support this adventure which surfaces as a real possibility, after both the achievements and the impasses of the present ideological reworkings, in which feminism has participated? It seems to me that the role of what is usually called "aesthetic practices" must increase not only to counterbalance the storage and uniformity of information by present-day mass media, data-bank systems, and, in particular, modern communications technology, but also to demystify the identity of the symbolic bond itself, to demystify, therefore, the *community* of language as a universal and unifying tool, one which totalizes and equalizes. In order to bring out—along with the *singularity* of each person and, even more, along with the multiplicity of every person's possible identifications (with atoms, e.g., stretching from the family to the stars)—the *relativity of his/her symbolic as well as biological existence,* according to the

6. See Seminar on *Identity* directed by Lévi-Strauss (Paris: Grasset & Fasquelle, 1977).
7. Repression (*le refoulement* or *Verdrangung*) as distinguished from the foreclosure (*la foreclusion* or *Verwerfung*) evoked earlier in the article (see LaPlanche and Pontalis) [Jardine's note].

variation in his/her specific symbolic capacities. And in order to emphasize the *responsibility* which all will immediately face of putting this fluidity into play against the threats of death which are unavoidable whenever an inside and an outside, a self and an other, one group and another, are constituted. At this level of interiorization with its social as well as individual stakes, what I have called "aesthetic practices" are undoubtedly nothing other than the modern reply to the eternal question of morality. At least, this is how we might understand an ethics which, conscious of the fact that its order is sacrificial, reserves part of the burden for each of its adherents, therefore declaring them guilty while immediately affording them the possibility for *jouissance*, for various productions, for a life made up of both challenges and differences.

Spinoza's question can be taken up again here: Are women subject to ethics? If not to that ethics defined by classical philosophy—in relationship to which the ups and downs of feminist generations seem dangerously precarious—are women not already participating in the rapid dismantling that our age is experiencing at various levels (from wars to drugs to artificial insemination) and which poses the *demand* for a new ethics? The answer to Spinoza's question can be affirmative only at the cost of considering feminism as but a *moment* in the thought of that anthropomorphic identity which currently blocks the horizon of the discursive and scientific adventure of our species.

1979, 1981

ANNETTE KOLODNY
b. 1941

When Annette Kolodny was denied tenure by the University of New Hampshire, she won a sexual discrimination suit and donated much of the money to establish the Legal Fund of the National Women's Studies Association's Task Force on Discrimination. An activist inside and outside the academy, Kolodny has published two well-received works of American studies scholarship: *The Lay of the Land: Metaphor as Experience and History in American Life and Letters* (1975) and *The Land Before Her: Fantasy and Experience of the American Frontier, 1630–1860* (1984). Additionally, *Failing the Future: A Dean Looks at Higher Education in the Twenty-first Century* (1998) records her administrative goals as a dean at the University of Arizona. Two of her essays, both published in 1980, were particularly influential on feminist critics: "Dancing through the Minefield: Some Observations on the Theory, Practice and Politics of a Feminist Literary Criticism" and "A Map for Rereading: or, Gender and the Interpretation of Literary Texts." The former, reprinted here, fueled immediate responses, challenges, and critiques, some of which were printed in "An Interchange on Feminist Criticism" in a 1982 issue of *Feminist Studies*. Even today, Kolodny's insistence on the extreme relativism of aesthetic value—the idea that works are deemed "great" not because of any intrinsic merit but because of the criteria of evaluation brought to them by readers—remains controversial; however, it helped many of her colleagues in American studies bring back into print the fiction of neglected or marginalized nineteenth-century American women of letters.

Dancing through the Minefield: Some Observations on the Theory, Practice and Politics of a Feminist Literary Criticism[1]

Had anyone the prescience, ten years ago, to pose the question of defining a "feminist" literary criticism, she might have been told, in the wake of Mary Ellmann's *Thinking About Women*,[2] that it involved exposing the sexual stereotyping of women in both our literature and our literary criticism and, as well, demonstrating the inadequacy of established critical schools and methods to deal fairly or sensitively with works written by women. In broad outline, such a prediction would have stood well the test of time, and, in fact, Ellmann's book continues to be widely read and to point us in useful directions. What could not have been anticipated in 1969, however, was the catalyzing force of an ideology that, for many of us, helped to bridge the gap between the world as we found it and the world as we wanted it to be. For those of us who studied literature, a previously unspoken sense of exclusion from authorship, and a painfully personal distress at discovering whores, bitches, muses, and heroines dead in childbirth where we had once hoped to discover ourselves, could—for the first time—begin to be understood as more than "a set of disconnected, unrealized private emotions."[3] With a renewed courage to make public our otherwise private discontents, what had once been "felt individually as personal insecurity" came at last to be "viewed collectively as structural inconsistency"[4] within the very disciplines we studied. Following unflinchingly the full implications of Ellmann's percipient observations, and emboldened by the liberating energy of feminist ideology—in all its various forms and guises—feminist criticism very quickly moved beyond merely "expos[ing] sexism in one work of literature after another,"[5] and promised, instead, that we might at last "begin to record new choices in a new literary history."[6] So powerful was that impulse that we experienced it, along with Adrienne Rich, as much "more than a chapter in cultural history"; it became, rather, "an act of survival."[7] What was at stake was not so much lit-

---

1. "Dancing Through the Minefield" was the winner of the 1979 Florence Howe Essay Contest, which is sponsored by the Women's Caucus of the Modern Language Association.

Some sections of this essay were composed during the time made available to me by a grant from the Rockefeller Foundation, for which I am most grateful.

This essay deals with white feminist critics only, because it was originally conceived as the first of a two-essay dialogue with myself. The second essay, "SharpShooting from the Outskirts of the Minefield: The Radical Critique by American Black and Third World Feminist Literary Critics," was to argue that black and Third World American feminist literary critics stand as a group apart from the whites, united by their far more probing analyses of the institutions which give rise to current literary tastes and by their angrier indictment of current critical practice and theory. Due to recurrent eye problems, however, and some difficulty in obtaining all the articles I sought, the second essay could not be completed along with the first. Despite the omission of any discussion of the fine work done by

black and Third World feminist critics, I decided to allow the first essay into print—for whatever discussion it may initiate. [Except as indicated, all notes are Kolodny's.]

2. Mary Ellmann, *Thinking About Women* (New York: Harcourt Brace Jovanovich, Harvest, 1968).

3. See Clifford Gertz, "Ideology as a Cultural System," in his *The Interpretation of Cultures: Selected Essays* (New York: Basic Books, 1973), p. 232.

4. Ibid., p. 204.

5. Lillian S. Robinson, "Cultural Criticism and the Horror Vacui," *College English* 33, no. 1 (1972); reprinted as "The Critical Task" in her *Sex, Class, and Culture* (Bloomington: Indiana University Press, 1978), p. 51.

6. Elaine Showalter, *A Literature of Their Own: British Women Novelists from Brontë to Lessing* (Princeton: Princeton University Press, 1977), p. 36.

7. Adrienne Rich, "When We Dead Awaken: Writing as Re-Vision," *College English* 34, no. 1 (October 1972); reprinted in *Adrienne Rich's Poetry*, ed. Barbara Charlesworth Gelpi and Albert Gelpi (New York: W. W. Norton Co., 1975), p. 90.

erature or criticism as such, but the historical, social, and ethical consequences of women's participation in, or exclusion from, either enterprise.

The pace of inquiry these last ten years has been fast and furious—especially after Kate Millett's 1970 analysis of the sexual politics of literature[8]
added a note of urgency to what had earlier been Ellmann's sardonic anger—
while the diversity of that inquiry easily outstripped all efforts to define feminist literary criticism as either a coherent system or a unified set of
methodologies. Under its wide umbrella, everything has been thrown into
question: our established canons, our aesthetic criteria, our interpretative
strategies, our reading habits, and, most of all, ourselves as critics and as
teachers. To delineate its full scope would require nothing less than a book—
a book that would be outdated even as it was being composed. For the sake
of brevity, therefore, let me attempt only a summary outline.

Perhaps the most obvious success of this new scholarship has been the
return to circulation of previously lost or otherwise ignored works by women
writers. Following fast upon the initial success of the Feminist Press in reis-
suing gems such as Rebecca Harding Davis's 1861 novella, *Life in the Iron
Mills*, and Charlotte Perkins Gilman's 1892 *The Yellow Wallpaper*, published
in 1972 and 1973, respectively,[9] commercial trade and reprint houses vied
with one another in the reprinting of anthologies of lost texts and, in some
cases, in the reprinting of whole series. For those of us in American literature
especially, the phenomenon promised a radical reshaping of our concepts of
literary history and, at the very least, a new chapter in understanding the development of women's literary traditions. So commercially successful were these
reprintings, and so attuned were the reprint houses to the political attitudes
of the audiences for which they were offered, that many of us found ourselves
wooed to compose critical introductions, which would find in the pages of
nineteenth-century domestic and sentimental fictions, some signs of either
muted rebellions or overt radicalism, in anticipation of the current wave of
"new feminism." In rereading with our students these previously lost works,
we inevitably raised perplexing questions as to the reasons for their disappearance from the canons of "major works," and we worried over the aesthetic
and critical criteria by which they had been accorded diminished status.

This increased availability of works by women writers led, of course, to an
increased interest in what elements, if any, might comprise some sort of unity
or connection among them. The possibility that women had developed either
a unique, or at least a related tradition of their own, especially intrigued those
of us who specialized in one national literature or another, or in historical
periods. Nina Baym's recent *Woman's Fiction: A Guide to Novels by and about
Women in America, 1820–1870*[1] demonstrates the Americanists' penchant
for examining what were once the "best sellers" of their day, the ranks of the
popular fiction writers, among which women took a dominant place throughout the nineteenth century, while the feminist studies of British literature
emphasized instead the wealth of women writers who have been regarded as

---

8. Kate Millett, *Sexual Politics* (Garden City, N.Y.: Doubleday and Co., 1970).
9. Rebecca Harding Davis, *Life in the Iron Mills*, originally published in *The Atlantic Monthly*, April 1861; reprinted with "A Biographical Interpretation" by Tillie Olsen (New York: Feminist Press, 1972). Charlotte Perkins Gilman, *The Yellow Wall-paper*, originally published in *The New England Magazine*, May 1892; reprinted with an Afterword by Elaine R. Hedges (New York: Feminist Press, 1973).
1. Nina Baym, *Woman's Fiction: A Guide to Novels by and about Women in America, 1820–1870* (Ithaca: Cornell University Press, 1978).

worthy of canonization. Not so much building upon one another's work as clarifying, successively, the parameters of the questions to be posed, Sydney Janet Kaplan, Ellen Moers, Patricia Meyer Spacks, and Elaine Showalter, among many others, concentrated their energies on delineating an internally consistent "body of work" by women that might stand as a female countertradition. For Kaplan, in 1975, this entailed examining women writers' various attempts to portray feminine consciousness and self-consciousness, not as a psychological category, but as a stylistic or rhetorical device.[2] That same year, arguing essentially that literature publicizes the private, Spacks placed her consideration of a "female imagination" within social and historical frames, to conclude that, "for readily discernible historical reasons women have characteristically concerned themselves with matters more or less peripheral to male concerns," and she attributed to this fact an inevitable difference in the literary emphases and subject matters of female and male writers.[3] The next year, Moers's *Literary Women: The Great Writers* focused on the pathways of literary influence that linked the English novel in the hands of women.[4] And, finally, in 1977, Showalter took up the matter of a "female literary tradition in the English novel from the generation of the Brontës to the present day" by arguing that, because women in general constitute a kind of "subculture within the framework of a larger society," the work of women writers, in particular, would thereby demonstrate a unity of "values, conventions, experiences, and behaviors impinging on each individual" as she found her sources of "self-expression relative to a dominant [and, by implication, male] society."[5]

At the same time that women writers were being reconsidered and reread, male writers were similarly subjected to a new feminist scrutiny. The continuing result—to put ten years of difficult analysis into a single sentence—has been nothing less than an acute attentiveness to the ways in which certain power relations—usually those in which males wield various forms of influence over females—are inscribed in the texts (both literary and critical), that we have inherited, not merely as subject matter, but as the unquestioned, often unacknowledged *given* of the culture. Even more important than the new interpretations of individual texts are the probings into the consequences (for women) of the conventions that inform those texts. For example, in surveying selected nineteenth- and early twentieth-century British novels which employ what she calls "the two suitors convention," Jean E. Kennard sought to understand why and how the structural demands of the convention, even in the hands of women writers, inevitably work to imply "the inferiority and necessary subordination of women." Her 1978 study, *Victims of Convention*, points out that the symbolic nature of the marriage which conventionally concludes such novels "indicates the adjustment of the protagonist to society's values, a condition which is equated with her maturity." Kennard's concern, however, is with the fact that the structural demands of the form too often sacrifice precisely those "virtues of independence and indi-

2. In her *Feminine Consciousness in the Modern British Novel* (Urbana: University of Illinois Press, 1975), p. 3, Sydney Janet Kaplan explains that she is using the term "feminine consciousness" "not simply as some general attitude of women toward their own femininity, and not as something synonymous with a particular sensibility among female writers. I am concerned with it as a literary device: a method of characterization of females in fiction."

3. Patricia Meyer Spacks, *The Female Imagination* (New York: Avon Books, 1975), p. 6.

4. Ellen Moers, *Literary Women: The Great Writers* (Garden City, N.Y.: Doubleday and Co., 1976).

5. Showalter, *A Literature of Their Own*, p. 11.

viduality," or, in other words, the very "qualities we have been invited to admire in" the heroines.[6] Kennard appropriately cautions us against drawing from her work any simplistically reductive thesis about the mimetic relations between art and life. Yet her approach nonetheless suggests that what is important about a fiction is not whether it ends in a death or a marriage, but what the symbolic demands of that particular conventional ending imply about the values and beliefs of the world that engendered it.

Her work thus participates in a growing emphasis in feminist literary study on the fact of literature as a social institution, embedded not only within its own literary traditions, but also within the particular physical and mental artifacts of the society from which it comes. Adumbrating Millett's 1970 decision to anchor her "literary reflections" to a preceding analysis of the historical, social, and economic contexts of sexual politics,[7] more recent work—most notably Lillian Robinson's—begins with the premise that the process of artistic creation "consists not of ghostly happenings in the head but of a matching of the states and processes of symbolic models against the states and processes of the wider world."[8] The power relations inscribed in the form of conventions within our literary inheritance, these critics argue, reify the encodings of those same power relations in the culture at large. And the critical examination of rhetorical codes becomes, in their hands, the pursuit of ideological codes, because both embody either value systems or the dialectic of competition between value systems. More often than not, these critics also insist upon examining not only the mirroring of life in art, but also the normative impact of art on life. Addressing herself to the popular art available to working women, for example, Robinson is interested in understanding not only "the forms it uses," but, more importantly, "the myths it creates, the influence it exerts." "The way art helps people to order, interpret, mythologize, or dispose of their own experience," she declares, may be "complex and often ambiguous, but it is not impossible to define."[9]

Whether its focus be upon the material or the imaginative contexts of literary invention; single texts or entire canons; the relations between authors, genres, or historical circumstances; lost authors or well-known names, the variety and diversity of all feminist literary criticism finally coheres in its stance of almost defensive rereading. When Adrienne Rich had earlier called "re-vision," that is, "the act of looking back, of seeing with fresh eyes, of entering an old text from a new critical direction,"[1] took on a more actively self-protective coloration in 1978, when Judith Fetterley called upon the woman reader to learn to "resist" the sexist designs a text might make upon her—asking her to identify against herself, so to speak, by manipulating her sympathies on behalf of male heroes, but against female shrew or bitch characters.[2] Underpinning a great deal of this critical rereading has been the not-unexpected alliance between feminist literary study and feminist studies in linguistics and language-acquisition. Tillie Olsen's commonsense observation of the danger of "perpetuating—by continued usage—entrenched, centuries-old oppressive

6. Jean E. Kennard, *Victims of Convention* (Hamden, Conn.: Archon Books, 1978), pp. 164, 18, 14.
7. See Millett, *Sexual Politics*, pt. 3, "The Literary Reflection," pp. 235–361.
8. The phrase is Geertz's, "Ideology as a Cultural System," p. 214.
9. Lillian Robinson, "Criticism—and Self-Criticism," *College English* 36, no. 4 (1974) and

"Criticism: Who Needs It?" in *The Uses of Criticism*, ed. A. P. Foulkes (Bern and Frankfurt: Lang, 1976); both reprinted in *Sex, Class, and Culture*, pp. 67, 80.
1. Rich, "When We Dead Awaken," p. 90.
2. Judith Fetterley, *The Resisting Reader: A Feminist Approach to American Fiction* (Bloomington: Indiana University Press, 1978).

power realities, early-on incorporated into language,"[3] has been given substantive analysis in the writings of feminists who study "language as a symbolic system closely tied to a patriarchal social structure." Taken together, their work demonstrates "the importance of language in establishing, reflecting, and maintaining an asymmetrical relationship between women and men."[4]

To consider what this implies for the fate of women who essay the craft of language is to ascertain, perhaps for the first time, the real dilemma of the poet who finds her most cherished private experience "hedged by taboos, mined with false-namings."[5] It also examines the dilemma of the male reader who, in opening the pages of a woman's book, finds himself entering a strange and unfamiliar world of symbolic significance. For if, as Nelly Furman insists, neither language use nor language acquisition are "gender-neutral," but are, instead, "imbued with our sex-inflected cultural values;"[6] and if, additionally, reading is a process of "sorting out the structures of signification,"[7] in any text, then male readers who find themselves outside of and unfamiliar with the symbolic systems that constitute female experience in women's writings, will necessarily dismiss those systems as undecipherable, meaningless, or trivial. And male professors will find no reason to include such works in the canons of "major authors." At the same time, women writers, coming into a tradition of literary language and conventional forms already appropriated, for centuries, to the purposes of male expression, will be forced virtually to "wrestle" with that language in an effort "to remake it as a language adequate to our conceptual processes."[8] To all of this, feminists concerned with the politics of language and style have been acutely attentive. "Language conceals an invincible adversary," observes French critic Hélène Cixous, "because it's the language of men and their grammar."[9] But equally insistent, as in the work of Sandra M. Gilbert and Susan Gubar, has been the understanding of the need for *all* readers—male and female alike—to learn to penetrate the otherwise unfamiliar universes of symbolic action that comprise women's writings, past and present.[1]

To have attempted so many difficult questions and to have accomplished so much—even acknowledging the inevitable false starts, overlapping, and repetition—in so short a time, should certainly have secured feminist literary criticism an honored berth on that ongoing intellectual journey which we loosely term in academia, "critical analysis." Instead of being welcomed onto the train, however, we've been forced to negotiate a minefield. The very energy and diversity of our enterprise have rendered us vulnerable to attack

3. Tillie Olsen, *Silences* (New York: Delacorte Press/Seymour Lawrence, 1978), pp. 239–40.
4. See Cheris Kramer, Barrie Thorne, and Nancy Henley, "Perspectives on Language and Communication," Review Essay in *Signs* 3, no. 3 (Summer 1978): 646.
5. See Adrienne Rich's discussion of the difficulty in finding authentic language for her experience as a mother in her *Of Woman Born* (New York: W. W. Norton and Co., 1976), p. 15.
6. Nelly Furman, "The Study of Women and Language: Comment on Vol. 3, no. 3" in *Signs* 4, no. 1 (Autumn 1978): 184.
7. Again, my phrasing comes from Geertz, "Thick Description: Toward an Interpretive Theory of Culture" in his *Interpretation of Cultures: Selected Essays* (New York: Basic Books, 1973), p. 9.

8. Julia Penelope Stanley and Susan W. Robbins, "Toward a Feminist Aesthetic," *Chrysalis*, no. 6 (1977): 63.
9. Hélène Cixous, "The Laugh of the Medusa," trans. Keith Cohen and Paula Cohen, *Signs* 1, no. 4 (Summer 1976): 87.
1. In *The Madwoman in the Attic: The Woman Writer and the Nineteenth-Century Literary Imagination* (New Haven: Yale University Press, 1979), Sandra M. Gilbert and Susan Gubar suggest that women's writings are in some sense "palimpsestic" in that their "surface designs conceal or obscure deeper, less accessible (and less socially acceptable) levels of meaning" (p. 73). It is, in their view, an art designed "both to express and to camouflage" (p. 81).

on the grounds that we lack both definition and coherence; while our particular attentiveness to the ways in which literature encodes and disseminates cultural value systems calls down upon us imprecations echoing those heaped upon the Marxist critics of an earlier generation. If we are scholars dedicated to rediscovering a lost body of writings by women, then our finds are questioned on aesthetic grounds. And if we are critics, determined to practice revisionist readings, it is claimed that our focus is too narrow, and our results are only distortions or, worse still, polemical misreadings.

The very vehemence of the outcry, coupled with our total dismissal in some quarters,[2] suggests not our deficiences, however, but the potential magnitude of our challenge. For what we are asking be scrutinized are nothing less than shared cultural assumptions so deeply rooted and so long ingrained that, for the most part, our critical colleagues have ceased to recognize them as such. In other words, what is really being bewailed in the claims that we distort texts or threaten the disappearance of the great Western literary tradition itself[3] is not so much the disappearance of either text or tradition but, instead, the eclipse of that particular *form* of the text, and that particular *shape* of the canon, which previously reified male readers' sense of power and significance in the world. Analogously, by asking whether, as readers, we ought to be "really satisfied by the marriage of Dorothea Brooke to Will Ladislaw? of Shirley Keeldar to Louis Moore?" or whether, as Kennard suggests, we must reckon with the ways in which "the qualities we have been invited to admire in these heroines [have] been sacrificed to structural neatness,"[4] is to raise difficult and profoundly perplexing questions about the ethical implications of our otherwise unquestioned aesthetic pleasures. It is, after all, an imposition of high order to ask the viewer to attend to Ophelia's sufferings in a scene where, before, he'd always so comfortably kept his eye fixed firmly on Hamlet. To understand all this, then, as the real nature of the challenge we have offered and, in consequence, as the motivation for the often overt hostility we've aroused, should help us learn to negotiate the minefield, if not with grace, then with at least a clearer comprehension of its underlying patterns.

The ways in which objections to our work are usually posed, of course, serve to obscure their deeper motivations. But this may, in part, be due to our own reticence at taking full responsibility for the truly radicalizing premises that lie at the theoretical core of all we have so far accomplished. It may be time, therefore, to redirect discussion, forcing our adversaries to deal with the substantive issues and pushing ourselves into a clearer articulation of what, in fact, we are about. Up until now, I fear, we have only piecemeal dealt with

2. Consider, for example, Paul Boyers's reductive and inaccurate generalization that "what distinguishes ordinary books and articles about women from feminist writing is the feminist insistence on asking the same questions of every work and demanding ideologically satisfactory answers to those questions as a means of evaluating it," in his "A Case Against Feminist Criticism," *Partisan Review* 43, no. 4 (1976): 602. It is partly as a result of such misconceptions that we have the paucity of feminist critics who are granted a place in English departments which otherwise pride themselves on the variety of their critical orientations.
3. Ambivalent though he is about the literary continuity that begins with Homer, Harold Bloom nonetheless somewhat ominously prophesies "that

the first true break . . . will be brought about in generations to come, if the burgeoning religion of Liberated Woman spreads from its clusters of enthusiasts to dominate the West," in his *A Map of Misreading* (New York: Oxford University Press, 1975), p. 33. On p. 36, he acknowledges that while something "as violent [as] a quarrel would ensue if I expressed my judgment" on Robert Lowell and Norman Mailer, "it would lead to something more intense than quarrels if I expressed my judgment upon . . . the 'literature of Women's Liberation.' "
4. Kennard, *Victims of Convention*, p. 14. [The marriages occur in George Eliot's *Middlemarch* (1871–72) and Charlotte Brontë's *Shirley* (1849), respectively—editor's note.]

the difficulties inherent in challenging the authority of established canons and then justifying the excellence of women's traditions, sometimes in accord with standards to which they have no intrinsic relation.

At the very point at which we must perforce enter the discourse—that is, claiming excellence or importance for our "finds"—all discussion has already, we discover, long ago been closed. "If Kate Chopin were *really* worth reading," an Oxford-trained colleague once assured me, "she'd have lasted—like Shakespeare"; and he then proceeded to vote against the English department's crediting a women's studies seminar I was offering in American women writers. The canon, for him, conferred excellence; Chopin's exclusion demonstrated only her lesser worth. As far as he was con-concerned, I could no more justify giving English department credit for the study of Chopin than I could dare publicly to question Shakespeare's genius. Through hindsight, I've now come to view that discussion as not only having posed fruitless oppositions, but also as having entirely evaded the much more profound problem lurking just beneath the surface of our disagreement. That is, that the fact of canonization puts any work beyond questions of establishing its merit and, instead, invites students to offer only increasingly more ingenious readings and interpretations, the purpose of which is to validate the greatness already imputed by canonization.

Had I only understood it for what it was then, into this circular and self-serving set of assumptions I might have interjected some statement of my right to question why *any* text is revered and my need to know what it tells us about "how we live, how we have been living, how we have been led to imagine ourselves, [and] how our language has trapped as well as liberated us."[5] The very fact of our critical training within the strictures imposed by an established canon of major works and authors, however, repeatedly deflects us from such questions. Instead, we find ourselves endlessly responding to the *riposte* that the overwhelmingly male presence among canonical authors was only an accident of history—and never intentionally sexist—coupled with claims to the "obvious" aesthetic merit of those canonized texts. It is, as I say, a fruitless exchange, serving more to obscure than to expose the territory being protected and dragging us, again and again, through the minefield.

It is my contention that current hostilities might be transformed into a true dialogue with our critics if we at last made explicit what appear, to this observer, to constitute the three crucial propositions to which our special interests inevitably give rise. They are, moreover, propositions which, if handled with care and intelligence, could breathe new life into now moribund areas of our profession: (1) Literary history (and with that, the historicity of literature) is a fiction; (2) insofar as we are taught how to read, what we engage are not texts but paradigms; and, finally, (3) that since the grounds upon which we assign aesthetic value to texts are never infallible, unchangeable, or universal, we must reexamine not only our aesthetics but, as well, the inherent biases and assumptions informing the critical methods which (in part) shape our aesthetic responses. For the sake of brevity, I won't attempt to offer the full arguments for each but, rather, only sufficient elaboration to demonstrate what I see as their intrinsic relation to the potential scope of and present challenge implied by feminist literary study.

1. *Literary history (and, with that, the historicity of literature) is a fiction.* To

5. Rich, "When We Dead Awaken," p. 90.

begin with, an established canon functions as a model by which to chart the continuities and discontinuities, as well as the influences upon and the interconnections between works, genres, and authors. That model we tend to forget, however, is of our own making. It will take a very different shape, and explain its inclusions and exclusions in very different ways, if the reigning critical ideology believes that new literary forms result from some kind of ongoing internal dialectic within preexisting styles and traditions or if, by contrast, the ideology declares that literary change is dependent upon societal development and thereby determined by upheavals in the social and economic organization of the culture at large.[6] Indeed, whenever in the previous century of English and American literary scholarship one alternative replaced the other, we saw dramatic alterations in canonical "wisdom."

This suggests, then, that our sense of a "literary history" and, by extension, our confidence in a "historical" canon, is rooted not so much in any definitive understanding of the past but, rather, in our need to call up and utilize the past on behalf of a better understanding of the present. Thus, to paraphrase David Couzens Hoy, it becomes "necessary to point out that the understanding of art and literature is such an essential aspect of the present's self-understanding that this self-understanding conditions what even gets taken" as comprising that artistic and literary past. To quote Hoy fully, "this continual reinterpretation of the past goes hand in hand with the continual reinterpretation by the present of itself."[7] In our own time, uncertain as to which, if any, model truly accounts for our canonical choices or accurately explains literary history, and pressured further by the feminists' call for some justification of the criteria by which women's writings were largely excluded from both that canon and history, we suffer what Harold Bloom has called "a remarkable dimming" of "our mutual sense of canonical standards."[8]

Into this apparent impasse, feminist literary theorists implicitly introduce the observation that our choices and evaluations of current literature have the effect either of solidifying or of reshaping our sense of the past. The authority of any established canon, after all, is reified by our perception that current work seems to grow, almost inevitably, out of it (even in opposition or rebellion), and is called into question when what we read appears to have little or no relation to what we recognize as coming before. So, were the larger critical community to begin seriously to attend to the recent outpouring of fine literature by women, this would surely be accompanied by a concomitant researching of the past, by literary historians, in order to account for the present phenomenon. In that process, literary history would itself be altered: works by seventeenth-, eighteenth-, or nineteenth-century women, to which we had not previously attended, might be given new importance as "precursors" or as prior influences upon present-day authors; while selected male writers might also be granted new prominence as figures whom the women today, or even yesterday, needed to reject. I am arguing, in other words, that the choices we make in the present inevitably alter our sense of the past that led to them.

Related to this is the feminist challenge to that patently mendacious criti-

6. The first is a proposition currently expressed by some structuralists and formalist critics; the best statement of the second probably appears in Georg Lukács, *Writer and Critic* (New York: Grosset and Dunlap, 1970), p. 119.

7. David Couzens Hoy, "Hermeneutic Circularity, Indeterminacy, and Incommensurability," *New Literary History* 10, no. 1 (Autumn 1978): 166–67.
8. Bloom, *Map of Misreading*, p. 36.

cal fallacy that we read the "classics" in order to reconstruct the past "the way it really was," and that we read Shakespeare and Milton in order to apprehend the meanings that they intended. Short of time machines or miraculous resurrections, there is simply no way to know, precisely or surely, what "really was," what Homer intended when he sang, or Milton when he dictated. Critics more acute than I have already pointed out the impossibility of grounding a reading in the imputation of authorial intention because the further removed the author is from us, so too must be her or his systems of knowledge and belief points 'of view, and structures of vision (artistic and otherwise).[9] (I omit here the difficulty of finally either proving or disproving the imputation of intentionality because, inescapably, the only appropriate authority is unavailable: deceased.) What we have really come to mean when we speak of competence in reading historical texts, therefore, is the ability to recognize literary conventions which have survived through time—so as to remain operational in the mind of the reader—and, where these are lacking, the ability to translate (or perhaps transform?) the text's ciphers into more current and recognizable shapes. But we never really reconstruct the past in its own terms. What we gain when we read the "classics," then, is neither Homer's Greece nor George Eliot's England *as they knew it* but, rather, an approximation of an already fictively imputed past made available, through our interpretive strategies, for present concerns. Only by understanding this can we put to rest that recurrent delusion that the "continuing relevance" of the classics serves as "testimony to perennial features of human experience."[1] The only "perennial feature" to which our ability to read and reread texts written in previous centuries testifies is our inventiveness—in the sense that all of literary history is a fiction which we daily recreate as we reread it. What distinguishes feminists in this regard is their desire to alter and extend what we take as historically relevant from out of that vast storehouse of our literary inheritance and, further, feminists' recognition of the storehouse for what it really is: a resource for remodeling our literary history, past, present, and future.

2. *Insofar as we are taught how to read, what we engage are not texts but paradigms.* To pursue the logical consequences of the first proposition leads, however uncomfortably, to the conclusion that we appropriate meaning from a text according to what we need (or desire) or, in other words, according to the critical assumptions or predispositions (conscious or not) that we bring to it. And we appropriate different meanings, or report different gleanings, at different times—even from the same text—according to our changed assumptions, circumstances, and requirements. This, in essence, constitutes the heart of the second proposition. For insofar as literature is itself a social institution, so, too, reading is a highly socialized—or learned—activity. What makes it so exciting, of course, is that it can be constantly relearned and refined, so as to provide either an individual or an entire reading community, over time, with infinite variations of the same text. It *can* provide that, but, I must add, too often it

9. John Dewey offered precisely this argument in 1934 when he insisted that a work of art "is recreated every time it is esthetically experienced. . . . It is absurd to ask what an artist 'really' meant by his product: he himself would find different meanings in it at different days and hours and in different stages of his own development." Further, he explained, "It is simply an impossibility that any one today should experience the Parthenon as the devout Athenian contemporary citizen experienced it, any more than the religious statuary of the twelfth century can mean, esthetically, even to a good Catholic today just what it meant to the worshipers of the old period," in *Art as Experience* (New York: Capricorn Books, 1958), pp. 108–109. 1. Charles Altieri, "The Hermeneutics of Literary Indeterminacy: A Dissent from the New Orthodoxy," *New Literary History* 10, no. 1 (Autumn 1978): 90

does not. Frequently our reading habits become fixed, so that each successive reading experience functions, in effect, normatively, with one particular kind of novel stylizing our expectations of those to follow, the stylistic devices of any favorite author (or group of authors) alerting us to the presence or absence of those devices in the works of others, and so on. "Once one has read his first poem," Murray Krieger has observed, "he turns to his second and to the others that will follow thereafter with an increasing series of preconceptions about the sort of activity in which he is indulging. In matters of literary experience, as in other experiences," Krieger concludes, "one is a virgin but once."[2]

For most readers, this is a fairly unconscious process, and, unsurprisingly, what we are taught to read well and with pleasure, when we are young, predisposes us to certain specific kinds of adult reading tastes. For the professional literary critic, the process may be no different, but it is at least more conscious. Graduate schools, at their best, are training grounds for competing interpretive paradigms or reading techniques: affective stylistics, structuralism, and semiotic analysis, to name only a few of the more recent entries. The delight we learn to take in the mastery of these interpretive strategies is then often mistakenly construed as our delight in reading specific texts, especially in the case of works that would otherwise be unavailable or even offensive to us. In my own graduate career, for example, with superb teachers to guide me, I learned to take great pleasure in *Paradise Lost*, even though as both a Jew and a feminist, I can subscribe neither to its theology nor to its hierarchy of sexual valuation. If, within its own terms (as I have been taught to understand them), the text manipulates my sensibilities and moves me to pleasure—as I will affirm it does—then, at least in part, that must be because, in spite of my real-world alienation from many of its basic tenets, I have been able to enter that text through interpretive strategies which allow me to displace less comfortable observations with others to which I have been taught pleasurably to attend. Though some of my teachers may have called this process "learning to read the text properly," I have now come to see it as learning to effectively manipulate the critical strategies which they taught me so well. Knowing, for example, the poem's debt to epic conventions, I am able to discover in it echoes and reworkings of both lines and situations from Virgil and Homer; placing it within the ongoing Christian debate between Good and Evil, I comprehend both the philosophic and the stylistic significance of Satan's ornate rhetoric as compared to God's majestic simplicity in Book III. But, in each case, an interpretative model, already assumed, had guided my discovery of the evidence for it.[3]

When we consider the implications of these observations for the processes of canon formation and for the assignment of aesthetic value, we find ourselves locked in a chicken-and-egg dilemma, unable easily to distinguish as primary the importance of *what* we read as opposed to *how* we have learned to read it. For, simply put, we read well, and with pleasure, what we already know how to read; and what we know how to read is to a large extent dependent upon what we have already read (works from which we've developed our expectations and learned our interpretive strategies). What we then choose to read—and, by extension, teach and thereby "canonize"—usually follows

2. Murray Krieger, *Theory of Criticism: A Tradition and Its System* (Baltimore: The Johns Hopkins University Press, 1976), p. 6.
3. See Stanley E. Fish, "Normal Circumstances, Literal Language, Direct Speech Acts, the Ordinary, the Everyday, the Obvious, What Goes without Saying, and Other Special Cases," *Critical Inquiry* 4, no. 4 (Summer 1978): 627–28.

upon our previous reading. Radical breaks are tiring, demanding, uncomfortable, and sometimes wholly beyond our comprehension.

Though the argument is not usually couched in precisely these terms, a considerable segment of the most recent feminist rereadings of women writers allows the conclusion that, where those authors have dropped out of sight, the reason may be due not to any lack of merit in the work but, instead, to an incapacity of predominantly male readers to properly interpret and appreciate women's texts—due, in large part, to a lack of prior acquaintance. The fictions which women compose about the worlds they inhabit may owe a debt to prior, influential works by other women or, simply enough, to the daily experience of the writer herself or, more usually, to some combination of the two. The reader coming upon such fiction, with knowledge of neither its informing literary traditions nor its real-world contexts, will thereby find himself hard-pressed, though he may recognize the words on the page, to competently decipher its intended meanings. And this is what makes the recent studies by Spacks, Moers, Showalter, Gilbert and Gubar, and others so crucial. For, by attempting to delineate the connections and interrelations that make for a female literary tradition, they provide us invaluable aids for recognizing and understanding the unique literary traditions and sex-related contexts out of which women write.

The (usually male) reader who, both by experience and by reading, has never made acquaintance with those contexts—historically, the lying-in room, the parlor, the nursery, the kitchen, the laundry, and so on—will necessarily lack the capacity to fully interpret the dialogue or action embedded therein; for, as every good novelist knows, the meaning of any character's action or statement is inescapably a function of the specific situation in which it is embedded.[4] Virginia Woolf therefore quite properly anticipated the male reader's inclination to write off what he could not understand, abandoning women's writings as offering "not merely a difference of view, but a view that is weak, or trivial, or sentimental because it differs from his own." In her 1929 essay on "Women and Fiction," Woolf grappled most obviously with the ways in which male writers and male subject matter had already preempted the language of literature. Yet she was also tacitly commenting on the problem of (male) audience and conventional reading expectations when she speculated that the woman writer might well "find that she is perpetually wishing to alter the established values [in literature]—to make serious what appears insignificant to a man, and trivial what is to him important."[5] "The 'competence' necessary for understanding [a] literary message . . . depends upon a great number of codices," after all; as Cesare Segre has pointed out, to be competent, a reader must either share or at least be familiar with, "in addition to the code language . . . the codes of custom, of society, and of conceptions of the world"[6] (what Woolf meant by "values"). Males ignorant of women's "values" or conceptions of the world will necessarily, thereby, be poor readers of works that in any sense recapitulate their codes.

The problem is further exacerbated when the language of the literary text is largely dependent upon figuration. For it can be argued, as Ted Cohen has shown, that while "in general, and with some obvious qualifications . . . all literal use of language is accessible to all whose language it is . . . figurative use

4. Ibid., p. 643.
5. Virginia Woolf, "Women and Fiction," in her *Granite and Rainbow: Essays* (London: Hogarth, 1958), p. 81.

6. Cesare Segre, "Narrative Structures and Literary History," *Critical Inquiry* 3, no. 2 (Winter 1976): 272–73.

can be inaccessible to all but those who share information about one another's knowledge, beliefs, intentions, and attitudes."[7] There was nothing fortuitous, for example, in Charlotte Perkins Gilman's decision to situate the progressive mental breakdown and increasing incapacity of the protagonist of *The Yellow Wallpaper* in an upstairs room that had once served as a nursery (with barred windows, no less). But the reader unacquainted with the ways in which women traditionally inhabited a household might not have taken the initial description of the setting as semantically relevant; and the progressive infantilization of the adult protagonist would thereby lose some of its symbolic implications. Analogously, the contemporary poet who declares, along with Adrienne Rich, the need for "a whole new poetry beginning here" is acknowledging that the materials available for symbolization and figuration from women's contexts will necessarily differ from those that men have traditionally utilized:

> Vision begins to happen in such a life
> as if a woman quietly walked away
> from the argument and jargon in a room
> and sitting down in the kitchen, began turning in her lap
> bits of yarn, calico and velvet scraps,
> . . . .
> pulling the tenets of a life together
> with no mere will to mastery,
> only care for the many-lived, unending
> forms in which she finds herself.[8]

What, then, is the fate of the women writer whose competent reading community is composed only of members of her own sex? And what, then, the response of the male critic who, on first looking into Virginia Woolf or Doris Lessing, finds all of the interpretative strategies at his command inadequate to a full and pleasurable deciphering of their pages? Historically, the result has been the diminished status of women's products and their consequent absence from major canons. Nowadays, however, by pointing out that the act of "interpreting language is no more sexually neutral than language use or the language system itself," feminist students of language, like Nelly Furman, help us better understand the crucial linkage between our gender and our interpretive, or reading, strategies. Insisting upon "the contribution of the . . . reader [in] the active attribution of significance to formal signifiers,"[9] Furman and others promise to shake us all—female and male alike—out of our canonized and conventional aesthetic assumptions.

3. *Since the grounds upon which we assign aesthetic value to texts are never infallible, unchangeable, or universal, we must reexamine not only our aesthetics but, as well, the inherent biases and assumptions informing the critical methods which (in part) shape our aesthetic responses.* I am, on the one hand, arguing that men will be better readers, or appreciators, of women's books when they have read more of them (as women have always been taught to become astute readers of men's texts). On the other hand, it will be noted,

---

7. Ted Cohen, "Metaphor and the Cultivation of Intimacy," *Critical Inquiry* 5, no. 1 (Autumn 1978): 9.

8. From Adrienne Rich's "Transcendental Etude" in her *The Dream of a Common Language: Poems 1974–1977* (New York: W. W. Norton and Co., 1978), pp. 76–77.

9. Furman, "The Study of Women and Language," p. 184.

the emphasis of my remarks shifts the act of critical judgment from assigning aesthetic valuations to texts and directs it, instead, to ascertaining the adequacy of any interpretive paradigm to a full reading of both female and male writing. My third proposition—and, I admit, perhaps the most controversial—thus calls into question that recurrent tendency in criticism to establish norms for the evaluation of literary works when we might better serve the cause of literature by developing standards for evaluating the adequacy of our critical methods.[1] This does not mean that I wish to discard aesthetic valuation. The choice, as I see it, is not between retaining or discarding aesthetic values; rather, the choice is between having some awareness of what constitutes (at least in part) the bases of our aesthetic responses and going without such an awareness. For it is my view that insofar as aesthetic responsiveness continues to be an integral aspect of our human response system—in part spontaneous, in part learned and educated—we will inevitably develop theories to help explain, formalize, or even initiate those responses.

In challenging the adequacy of received critical opinion or the imputed excellence of established canons, feminist literary critics are essentially seeking to discover how aesthetic value is assigned in the first place, where it resides (in the text or in the reader), and, most importantly, what validity may really be claimed by our aesthetic "judgments." What ends do those judgments serve, the feminist asks; and what conceptions of the world or ideological stances do they (even if unwittingly) help to perpetuate? In so doing, she points out, among other things, that any response labeled "aesthetic" may as easily designate some immediately experienced moment or event as it may designate a species of nostalgia, a yearning for the components of a simpler past, when the world seemed known or at least understandable. Thus the value accorded an opera or a Shakespeare play may well reside in the viewer's immediate viewing pleasure, or it may reside in the play's nostalgic evocation of a once-comprehensible and ordered world. At the same time, the feminist confronts, for example, the reader who simply cannot entertain the possibility that women's worlds are symbolically rich, the reader who, like the male characters in Susan Glaspell's 1917 short story, "A Jury of Her Peers," has already assumed the innate "insignificance of kitchen things."[2] Such a reader, she knows, will prove himself unable to assign significance to fictions that attend to "kitchen things" and will, instead, judge such fictions as trivial and as aesthetically wanting. For her to take useful issue with such a reader, she must make clear that what appears to be a dispute about aesthetic merit is, in reality, a dispute about the *contexts of judgment*; and what is at issue, then, is the adequacy of the prior assumptions and reading habits brought to bear on the text. To put it bluntly: we have had enough pronouncements of aesthetic valuation for a time; it is now our task to evaluate the imputed norms and normative reading patterns that, in part, led to those pronouncements.

By and large, I think I've made my point. Only to clarify it do I add this coda: when feminists turn their attention to the works of male authors which have traditionally been accorded high aesthetic value and, where warranted,

1. "A recurrent tendency in criticism is the establishment of false norms for the evaluation of literary works," notes Robert Scholes in his *Structuralism in Literature: An Introduction* (New Haven: Yale University Press, 1974), p. 131.
2. For a full discussion of the Glaspell short story which takes this problem into account, please see my "A Map for Rereading: Or, Gender and the Interpretation of Literary Texts," forthcoming in a Special Issue on Narrative, *New Literary History* (1980) [published in vol. 11, pp. 451–67].

follow Olsen's advice that we assert our "right to say: this is surface, this fal-sifies reality, this degrades,"[3] such statements do not necessarily mean that we will end up with a diminished canon. To question the source of the aes-thetic pleasures we've gained from reading Spenser, Shakespeare, Milton, and so on, does not imply that we must deny those pleasures. It means only that aesthetic response is once more invested with epistemological, ethical, and moral concerns. It means, in other words, that readings of *Paradise Lost* which analyze its complex hierarchal structures but fail to note the implica-tions of gender within that hierarchy; or which insist upon the inherent (or even inspired) perfection of Milton's figurative language but fail to note the consequences, for Eve, of her specifically gender-marked weakness, which, like the flowers to which she attends, requires "propping up"; or which con-centrate on the poem's thematic reworking of classical notions of martial and epic prowess into Christian (moral) heroism but fail to note that Eve is sty-listically edited out of that process—all such readings, however useful, will no longer be deemed wholly adequate. The pleasures we had earlier learned to take in the poem will not be diminished thereby, but they will become part of an altered reading attentiveness.

These three propositions I believe to be at the theoretical core of most cur-rent feminist literary criticism, whether acknowledged as such or not. If I am correct in this, then that criticism represents more than a profoundly skepti-cal stance toward all other preexisting and contemporaneous schools and methods, and more than an impassioned demand that the variety and vari-ability of women's literary expression be taken into full account, rather than written off as caprice and exception, the irregularity in an otherwise regular design. It represents that locus in literary study where, in unceasing effort, female self-consciousness turns in upon itself, attempting to grasp the deep-est conditions of its own unique and multiplicitous realities, in the hope, eventually, of altering the very forms through which the culture perceives, expresses, and knows itself. For, if what the larger women's movement looks for in the future is a transformation of the structures of primarily male power which now order our society, then the feminist literary critic demands that we understand the ways in which those structures have been—and continue to be—reified by our literature and by our literary criticism. Thus, along with other "radical" critics and critical schools, though our focus remains the power of the word to both structure and mirror human experience, our over-riding commitment is to a radical alteration—an improvement, we hope—in the nature of that experience.

What distinguishes our work from those similarly oriented "social con-sciousness" critiques, it is said, is its lack of systematic coherence. Pitted against, for example, psychoanalytic or Marxist readings, which owe a deci-sive share of their persuasiveness to their apparent internal consistency as a system, the aggregate of feminist literary criticism appears woefully deficient in system, and painfully lacking in program. It is, in fact, from all quarters, the most telling defect alleged against us, the most explosive threat in the minefield. And my own earlier observation that, as of 1976, feminist literary criticism appeared "more like a set of interchangeable strategies than any

---

3. Olsen, *Silences*, p. 45.

coherent school or shared goal orientation," has been taken by some as an indictment, by others as a statement of impatience. Neither was intended. I felt then, as I do now, that this would "prove both its strength *and* its weakness,"[4] in the sense that the apparent disarray would leave us vulnerable to the kind of objection I've just alluded to; while the fact of our diversity would finally place us securely where, all along, we should have been: camped out, on the far side of the minefield, with the other pluralists and pluralisms.

In our heart of hearts, of course, most critics are really structuralists (whether or not they accept the label) because what we are seeking are patterns (or structures) that can order and explain the otherwise inchoate; thus, we invent, or believe we discover, relational patternings in the texts we read which promise transcendence from difficulty and perplexity to clarity and coherence. But, as I've tried to argue in these pages, to the imputed "truth" or "accuracy" of these findings, the feminist must oppose the painfully obvious truism that what is attended to in a literary work, and hence what is reported about it, is often determined not so much by the work itself as by the critical technique or aesthetic criteria through which it is filtered or, rather, read and decoded. All the feminist is asserting, then, is her own equivalent right to liberate new (and perhaps different) significances from these same texts; and, at the same time, her right to choose which features of a text she takes as relevant because she is, after all, asking new and different questions of it. In the process, she claims neither definitiveness nor structural completeness for her different readings and reading systems, but only their usefulness in recognizing the particular achievements of woman-as-author and their applicability in conscientiously decoding woman-as-sign.

That these alternate foci of critical attentiveness will render alternate readings or interpretations of the same text—even among feminists—should be no cause for alarm. Such developments illustrate only the pluralist contention that, "in approaching a text of any complexity . . . the reader must choose to emphasize certain aspects which seem to him crucial" and that, "in fact, the variety of readings which we have for many works is a function of the selection of crucial aspects made by the variety of readers." Robert Scholes, from whom I've been quoting, goes so far as to assert that "there is no single 'right' reading for any complex literary work," and, following the Russian formalist school, he observes that "we do not speak of readings that are simply true or false, but of readings that are more or less rich, strategies that are more or less appropriate."[5] Because those who share the term "feminist" nonetheless practice a diversity of critical strategies, leading, in some cases, to quite different readings, we must acknowledge among ourselves that sister critics, "having chosen to tell a different story, may in their interpretation identify different aspects of the meanings conveyed by the same passage."[6]

4. Annette Kolodny, "Literary Criticism," Review Essay in *Signs* 2, no. 2 (Winter 1976): 420.
5. Scholes, *Structuralism in Literature*, p. 144–45. These comments appear within his explication of Tzvetan Todorov's theory of reading.
6. I borrow this concise phrasing of pluralistic modesty from M. H. Abrams's "The Deconstructive Angel," *Critical Inquiry* 3, no. 3 (Spring 1977):

427. Indications of the pluralism that was to mark feminist inquiry were to be found in the diversity of essays collected by Susan Koppelman Cornillon for her early and ground-breaking anthology, *Images of Women in Fiction: Feminist Perspectives* (Bowling Green, Ohio: Bowling Green University Popular Press, 1972).

Adopting a "pluralist" label does not mean, however, that we cease to disagree; it means only that we entertain the possibility that different readings, even of the same text, may be differently useful, even illuminating, within different contexts of inquiry. It means, in effect, that we enter a dialectical process of examining, testing, even trying out the contexts—be they prior critical assumptions or explicitly stated ideological stances (or some combination of the two)—that led to the disparate readings. Not all will be equally acceptable to every one of us, of course, and even those prior assumptions or ideologies that are acceptable may call for further refinement and/or clarification. But, at the very least, because we will have grappled with the assumptions that led to it, we will be better able to articulate *why* we find a particular reading or interpretation adequate or inadequate. This kind of dialectical process, moreover, not only makes us more fully aware of what criticism is, and how it functions; it also gives us access to its future possibilities, making us conscious, as R. P. Blackmur put it, "of what we have done," "of what can be done next, or done again,"[7] or, I would add, of what can be done differently. To put it still another way: just because we will no longer tolerate the specifically sexist omissions and oversights of earlier critical schools and methods does not mean that, in their stead, we must establish our own "party line."

In my view, our purpose is not and should not be the formulation of any single reading method or potentially procrustean set of critical procedures nor, even less, the generation of prescriptive categories for some dreamed-of nonsexist literary canon.[8] Instead, as I see it, our task is to initiate nothing less than a playful pluralism, responsive to the possibilities of multiple critical schools and methods, but captive of none, recognizing that the many tools needed for our analysis will necessarily be largely inherited and only partly of our own making. Only by employing a plurality of methods will we protect ourselves from the temptation of so oversimplifying any text—and especially those particularly offensive to us—that we render ourselves unresponsive to what Scholes has called "its various systems of meaning and their interaction."[9] Any text we deem worthy of our critical attention is usually, after all, a locus of many and varied kinds of (personal, thematic, stylistic, structural, rhetorical, etc.) relationships. So, whether we tend to treat a text as a *mimesis*, in which words are taken to be recreating or representing viable worlds; or whether we prefer to treat a text as a kind of equation of communication, in which decipherable messages are passed from writers to readers; and whether we locate meaning as inherent in the text, the act of reading, or in some collaboration between reader and text—whatever our predilection, let us not generate from it a straitjacket that limits the scope of possible analysis. Rather, let us generate an ongoing dialogue of competing potential possibilities—among feminists and, as well, between feminist and nonfeminist critics.

---

7. R. P. Blackmur, "A Burden for Critics," *The Hudson Review* 1 (1948): 171. Blackmur, of course, was referring to the way in which criticism makes us unconscious of how art functions; I use his wording here because I am arguing that that same awareness must also be focused on the critical act itself. "Consciousness," he avers, "is the way

we feel the critic's burden."
8. I have earlier elaborated my objection to prescriptive categories for literature in "The Feminist as Literary Critic," Critical Response in *Critical Inquiry* 2, no. 4 (Summer 1976): 827–28.
9. Scholes, *Structuralism in Literature*, pp. 151–52.

The difficulty of what I describe does not escape me. The very idea of pluralism seems to threaten a kind of chaos for the future of literary inquiry while, at the same time, it seems to deny the hope of establishing some basic conceptual model which can organize all data—the hope which always begins any analytical exercise. My effort here, however, has been to demonstrate the essential delusions that inform such objections: If literary inquiry has historically escaped chaos by establishing canons, then it has only substituted one mode of arbitrary action for another—and, in this case, at the expense of half the population. And if feminists openly acknowledge ourselves as pluralists, then we do not give up the search for patterns of opposition and connection—probably the basis of thinking itself; what we give up is simply the arrogance of claiming that our work is either exhaustive or definitive. (It is, after all, the identical arrogance we are asking our nonfeminist colleagues to abandon.) If this kind of pluralism appears to threaten both the present coherence of and the inherited aesthetic criteria for a canon of "greats," then, as I have earlier argued, it is precisely that threat which, alone, can free us from the prejudices, the strictures, and the blind spots of the past. In feminist hands, I would add, it is less a threat than a promise.

What unites and repeatedly invigorates feminist literary criticism, then, is neither dogma nor method but, as I have indicated earlier, an acute and impassioned *attentiveness* to the ways in which primarily male structures of power are inscribed (or encoded) within our literary inheritance; the consequences of that encoding for women—as characters, as readers, and as writers; and, with that, a shared analytic *concern* for the implications of that encoding not only for a better understanding of the past, but also for an improved reordering of the present and future as well. If that *concern* identifies feminist literary criticism as one of the many academic arms of the larger women's movement, then that *attentiveness*, within the halls of academe, poses no less a challenge for change, generating, as it does, the three propositions explored here. The critical pluralism that inevitably follows upon those three propositions, however, bears little resemblance to what Robinson has called "the greatest bourgeois theme of all, the myth of pluralism, with its consequent rejection of ideological commitment as 'too simple' to embrace the (necessarily complex) truth."[1] Only ideological commitment could have gotten us to enter the minefield, putting in jeopardy our careers and our livelihood. Only the power of ideology to transform our conceptual worlds, and the inspiration of that ideology to liberate long-suppressed energies and emotions, can account for our willingness to take on critical tasks that, in an earlier decade, would have been "abandoned in despair or apathy."[2] The fact of differences among us proves only that, despite our shared commitments, we have nonetheless refused to shy away from complexity, preferring rather to openly disagree than to give up either intellectual honesty or hard-won insights.

---

1. Lillian Robinson, "Dwelling in Decencies: Radical Criticism and the Feminist Perspective," *College English* 32, no. 8 (May 1971); reprinted in *Sex, Class, and Culture*, p. 11.
2. "Ideology bridges the emotional gap between things as they are and as one would have them be, thus insuring the performance of roles that might otherwise be abandoned in despair or apathy," comments Geertz in "Ideology as a Cultural System," p. 205.

Finally, I would argue, pluralism informs feminist literary inquiry not simply as a description of what already exists but, more importantly, as the only critical stance consistent with the current status of the larger women's movement. Segmented and variously focused, the different women's organizations neither espouse any single system of analysis nor, as a result, express any wholly shared, consistently articulated ideology. The ensuing loss in effective organization and political clout is a serious one, but it has not been paralyzing; in spite of our differences, we have united to *act* in areas of clear mutual concern (the push for the Equal Rights Amendment is probably the most obvious example). The trade-off, as I see it, had made possible an ongoing and educative dialectic of analysis and preferred solutions, protecting us thereby from the inviting traps of reductionism and dogma. And so long as this dialogue remains active, both our politics and our criticism will be free of dogma—but never, I hope, of feminist ideology, in all its variety. For, "whatever else ideologies may be—projections of unacknowledged fears, disguises for ulterior motives, phatic expressions of group solidarity" (and the women's movement, to date, has certainly been all of these, and more)—whatever ideologies express, they are, as Geertz astutely observes, "most distinctively, maps of problematic social reality and matrices for the creation of collective conscience." And despite the fact that "ideological advocates . . . tend as much to obscure as to clarify the true nature of the problems involved," as Geertz notes, "they at least call attention to their existence and, by polarizing issues, make continued neglect more difficult. Without Marxist attack, there would have been no labor reform; without Black Nationalists, no deliberate speed."[3] Without Seneca Falls,[4] I would add, no enfranchisement of women, and without "consciousness raising," no feminist literary criticism nor, even less, women's studies.

Ideology, however, only truly manifests its power by ordering the *sum* of our actions.[5] If feminist criticism calls anything into question, it must be that dog-eared myth of intellectual neutrality. For, what I take to be the underlying spirit, or message, of any consciously ideologically premised criticism—that is, that ideas are important *because* they determine the ways we live, or want to live, in the world—is vitiated by confining those ideas to the study, the classroom, or the pages of our books. To write chapters decrying the sexual stereotyping of women in our literature, while closing our eyes to the sexual harassment of our women students and colleagues; to display Katharine Hepburn and Rosalind Russell in our courses on "The Image of the Independent Career Women in Film," while managing not to notice the paucity of female administrators on our own campus; to study the women who helped make universal enfranchisement a political reality, while keeping silent about our activist colleagues who are denied promotion or tenure; to include segments on "Women in the Labor Movement" in our American studies or women's studies courses, while remaining willfully ignorant of the department secretary fired for her efforts to organize a clerical workers' union; to glory in the delusions of "merit," "privilege," and "status" which accompany

---

3. Ibid., p. 220, 205.
4. Seneca Falls, N.Y., was the site of the first women's rights convention in the United States in July 1848 [editor's note].
5. I here follow Frederic Jameson's view in *The*

Prison-House of Language: A Critical Account of Structuralism and Russian Formalism (Princeton: Princeton University Press, 1974), p. 107, that: "Ideology would seem to be that grillwork of form, convention, and belief which orders our actions."

campus life in order to insulate ourselves from the millions of women who labor in poverty—all this is not merely hypocritical; it destroys both the spirit and the meaning of what we are about. It puts us, however unwittingly, in the service of those who laid the minefield in the first place. In my view, it is a fine thing for many of us, individually, to have traversed the minefield; but that happy circumstance will only prove of lasting importance if, together, we expose it for what it is (the male fear of sharing power and significance with women) and deactivate its components, so that others, after us, may literally dance through the minefield.

1980, 2007

MARGARET HOMANS
b. 1952

Active in the women's studies program at Yale University, Margaret Homans has taught courses exploring feminist perspectives on literature since 1978. In 1980, her *Women Writers and Poetic Identity: Dorothy Wordsworth, Emily Brontë, and Emily Dickinson* elaborated on the dynamics of inspiration that are usually associated with the (implicitly female) figure of the poet's muse. While in that book she went on to provide close readings of the verse of three women, many of her later essays deal with the fiction of George Eliot and Virginia Woolf. In *Bearing the Word: Language and the Female Experience in Nineteenth-Century Women's Writing* (1986) and *Royal Representations: Queen Victoria and British Culture, 1837–1876* (1998), Homans focuses on the impact of nineteenth-century British culture on women and images of women. The co-editor (with Adrienne Munich and Gillian Beer) of *Remaking Queen Victoria* (1997), Homans has recently published influential essays on African American women writers and on feminist theory.

From Woman Writers and Poetic Identity

From *Chapter 1. The Masculine Tradition*

In Romantic poetry the self and the imagination are primary. During and after the Romantic period it was difficult for women who aspired to become poets to share in this tradition, not for constitutional reasons but for reasons that women readers found within the literature itself.[1] Where the masculine self dominates and internalizes otherness, that other is frequently identified as feminine, whether she is nature, the representation of a human woman, or

---

1. For an illuminating reading of Romantic images of women, see Irene Taylor and Gina Luria, "Gender and Genre: Women in British Romantic Literature," in *What Manner of Woman: Essays on English and American Life and Literature*, ed. Marlene Springer (New York: New York University Press, 1977), pp. 98–123; for more general accounts of literature's part in perpetuating a patriarchal culture that is oppressive to women, see, for example, Simone de Beauvoir, *The Second Sex*, trans. and ed. H. M. Parshley (French edition 1949; New York: Knopf, 1953), or Kate Millett, *Sexual Politics* (New York: Doubleday, 1970). [Except as indicated, all notes are Homans's.]

some phantom of desire. Although this tradition culminates in Romantic poetry, it originates in the Bible, which directly and through Milton's transmission reinforces the Romantic reading of gender.[2] To be for so long the other and the object made it difficult for nineteenth-century women to have their own subjectivity. To become a poet, given these conditions, required nothing less than battling a valued and loved literary tradition to forge a self out of the materials of otherness. It is not surprising that so few women succeeded at this effort; very few even conceived of the possibility of trying.

This chapter will concentrate on two major ways in which women readers must have found woman's otherness reinforced: her association with nature and her exclusion from a traditional identification of the speaking subject as male. Although for the purposes of analysis these topics will be considered separately, here and in the chapters on the three individual authors, they are in fact complementary aspects of one larger problem.

William Wordsworth's feminization of nature is the most obvious example of sexual polarization in the literary tradition that would have shaped women poets' conception of poetry. When nature is Mother Nature for Wordsworth, she is valued because she is what the poet is not. She stands for a lost memory, hovering just at the edge of consciousness, of a time before the fall into self-consciousness and into subject-object relations with nature, whether that original unity took place in earliest infancy or, fictively, before birth.[3] As the object of the poet's love, Mother Nature is the necessary complement to his imaginative project, the grounding of an imagination so powerful that it risks abstraction without her. But he views her with a son's mixture of devoted love and resistance to the constraints she would place on his imaginative freedom. She is no more than what he allows her to be. It has become customary for feminist theorists and historians to invoke the idea of a matriarchal society that predated the dualistic patriarchies of Egypt, Greece, and western culture thereafter. This matriarchy is generally described as originating in the worship of fertility, in which the earth is a mother goddess and all nature, including humanity, is her creation and her domain. Whether this matriarchal society is mythic or historical, that the memory of it should be kept alive demonstrates that some portion of the human mind likes the notion that women could be as powerful as men. But there is an important distinction to be made between women and the "feminine principle," and the myth emphasizes the latter over the former. The powers of Wordsworth's maternal nature or of this prehistoric matriarchy have no necessary bearing on the powers of real women. Whether as a cultural or political memory, or as personal myth transmitted into poetry, Mother Nature is not a helpful model for women aspiring to be poets. She is prolific biologically, not linguistically, and she is as destructive as she is creative.

There are many other models of femininity in literature, but Nature is doubly imposing. She has a special status not just as a figure of the mother but also as a mother figure in that, as the most powerful feminine figure in Romantic poetry, she dominates the consciousness of women entering the

---

2. See Mary Daly, *The Church and the Second Sex* (1968; 2nd ed. New York: Harper & Row, 1975).
3. See also Northrop Frye's account of Wordsworthian Mother Nature in his *A Study of English*

Romanticism (New York: Random House, 1968), pp. 16–20, in which he argues that this figure is a revival of the ancient mother goddess.

tradition as newcomers. She was there before them, as the mother precedes the daughters. For the male poets of the Romantic period, the poets of the past and the figures of the poet represented in their works constitute a father figure against whom the younger poet, picturing himself as a son, must define himself.[4] If the figure of the powerful poet of the past is the father, in this family romance, then the mother is surely the Mother Nature represented as the object of that poet's love. Freud tells us that it is the father-son conflict that provokes growth and creativity in the son. His view of the mother-daughter relation is somewhat different, but for the women poets this is surely the major formative conflict. The women poets must cast off their image of themselves as objects, as the other, in the manner of daughters refusing to become what their mothers have been. The difficulty is that the image of Mother Nature is so appealing. The women poets do not want to dissociate themselves either from Nature or from nature even though they know they must.

None of the poets treated here became mothers themselves. Two lost their mothers early, Dorothy Wordsworth at the age of six and Emily Brontë when she was three, and Dickinson's remarks about her shy and traditional mother suggest what the other poets might have felt about theirs had they lived.[5] "I never had a mother" signifies for Dickinson, perhaps, her sense of distance from her mother's life and concerns. Dorothy especially suffered from being an orphan, and yet literature may have benefited from her and Brontë's not having had images of compliant femininity to love and emulate. Carroll Smith-Rosenberg has shown from diaries and letters written by relatively ordinary nineteenth-century women how intensely close and untroubled relations normally were between mothers and daughters.[6] But these daughters had no other ambition than to become what their mothers were: good wives and mothers. Contemporary women are startled at these revelations because dissonant relations between mothers and daughters are now the rule rather than the exception, if the mother is a "mother-woman" like Madame Ratignolle in Kate Chopin's *The Awakening*, and if the daughter aspires to be anything more than that. Nineteenth-century women poets are more appropriately grouped, in this respect, with twentieth-century women than with their contemporaries. To be writers they cannot foster, as Wordsworth does, intimate relations with maternal nature. They cannot be docile daughters of Nature because they know it is all too possible to pass from continuity to identification and thence to a loss of their own identity. Lynn Sukenick uses the term "matrophobia" to refer to Martha Quest's fear of becoming too like her own mother in Doris Lessing's *Children of Violence*, but the term applies as well to nineteenth-century women poets' relations with Mother Nature.[7]

4. Harold Bloom, *The Anxiety of Influence* (New York: Oxford University Press, 1973).

5. A note on names: although it is condescending to refer to an adult and a writer by her first name, it is not quite possible to refer to Dorothy Wordsworth as "Wordsworth," even where William Wordsworth is not included in the discussion, and it is clumsy to use the full name. Dorothy Wordsworth will be Dorothy from here on. Dickinson is certainly Dickinson, and Emily Brontë may

be able to claim Brontë, as least in the present context.

6. Carroll Smith-Rosenberg, "The Female World of Love and Ritual: Relations between Women in Nineteenth-Century America," *Signs*, 1, No. 1 (1975), 1–29.

7. Lynn Sukenick, "Feeling and Reason in Doris Lessing's Fiction," *Contemporary Literature*, 14 (1973), 519.

According to Freudian psychology, women both reject and then masochistically imitate their mothers. Seeing the world androcentrically, Freud insists that the oedipal theory apply to women as well as it does to men. Because girls must conform to the oedipal pattern they are obliged to reject the object of their first love, the mother, in order to redirect their love to masculine objects. They must take a circuitous route through pre-oedipal and oedipal stages whereas boys follow an undeviating path: "In the course of time . . . a girl has to change her erotogenic zone and her object—both of which a boy retains."[8] Freud's assertion that the girl not only redirects her love toward her father but also actively rejects her mother is based on his questionable definition of females as castrated males. The girl, discovering her "lack," holds her mother responsible. This theory of femininity may have been and may even still be descriptively accurate, but only because women have internalized their oppressors' negative view of femininity. If women reject maternal figures it is because they have been conditioned to do so by a masculine culture that held Freud's beliefs long before Freud articulated them.

Yet insofar as the mother has feelings of inferiority, or views herself as psychically castrated, the daughter has good reason for her matrophobia. Karen Horney examines cultural factors that may better account for what Freud took to be a biological matter.[9] Citing the "masculine character of our civilization," in which women are restricted to the narrowest of functions, Horney says that "a girl is exposed from birth onward to the suggestion—inevitable, whether conveyed brutally or delicately—of her inferiority, an experience that constantly stimulates her masculinity complex" (p. 69). The women held up as models of femininity to other women are those who, by their passivity and infantility, pose the least threat to the "superiority of the masculine principle." Clara Thompson interprets penis envy, the correlate in Freud's thinking to feminine "castration," as a symbol for women's quite rational envy of the power and privilege associated with being a man.[1] These interpretations make sense of the girl's rejection of her mother as herself "castrated" and as responsible for the daughter's cultural castration. It is the mother's cultural powerlessness that the daughter is rejecting, not the mother herself. She denies her love for and identification with her mother only insofar as the mother stands for a situation that the daughter wishes to rectify.

Mother Nature is hardly powerless, but, enormous as her powers are, they are not the ones that her daughters want if they are to become poets. A human mother's giving birth may be an extraordinarily active event, but as a model for the daughter's vocational ambitions it is simply not applicable, because it stems from what she is, not from what she does (Horney, p. 145). Milton's Mother Earth, giving birth to herself, is passive and requires the active agency of "Main Ocean" to complete the process, in the following passage from *Paradise Lost*:

8. [*New Introductory Lectures on Psycho-Analysis,* in] *The Standard Edition of the Complete Psychological Works of Sigmund Freud,* trans. and ed. James Strachey and Anna Freud (London: Hogarth Press and Institute of Psycho-Analysis, 1964), XXII, 119.
9. Karen Horney, "The Flight from Womanhood" (1926) and "The Dread of Woman" (1932), in *Feminine Psychology* (New York: Norton, 1967), pp. 54–70, 133–146.
1. Clara Thompson, "Penis Envy in Women," *Psychiatry,* 6 (1943), 123–125; rpt. in *Psychoanalysis and Women,* ed. Jean B. Miller (New York: Brunner, Mazel, 1973), pp. 43–47.

> The Earth was form'd, but in the Womb as yet
> Of Waters, Embryon immature involv'd,
> Appear'd not: over all the face of Earth
> Main Ocean flow'd, not idle, but with warm
> Prolific humor soft'ning all her Globe,
> Fermented the great Mother to conceive,
> Satiate with genial moisture, . . .
>   (VII, 276–282)[2]

Mother Nature is also traditionally associated with death as much as with life. Even Wordsworth, who attributes to nature an active and beneficent love, retains the tradition of her amorality in his portrayal of her mixed ministries of fear and love. She has no consciousness, only materiality and an elusive presence; no center, only diffuseness. Writing poetry would seem to require of the writer everything that Mother Nature is not, and the first project of any poet who is also a daughter must be to keep herself from becoming her mother.

One critic of Freud, Luce Irigaray, finds that this somewhat involuntary rejection of the mother may be responsible for depriving the daughter of a strong sense of identity and therefore of subjectivity.[3] Without subjectivity, women are incapable of self-representation, the fundamental of masculine creativity. Irigaray suggests that a new feminine creativity, and a renovation of culture, would result from women's recovering the maternal origins from which masculine culture separates them. Returning to her proper origins, a woman will acquire so strong a sense of identity that she will not need to search for self in everything she sees; creativity will begin with an acknowledgment that the rest of the world is not to be possessed. (Cixous also praises women's potentially greater respect for otherness.) This original creativity would be free from the masculine trait of domination by the central self. But Freud's theory of femininity describes almost the same position, if negatively, since Freud uses it to deny creativity to women: cut off from origins, a woman has no central self by means of which to subjugate the objective world. But although Irigaray's formula would seem the more positive, the feminine self in the Wordsworthian tradition finds herself in a peculiar dilemma. To identify with the mother in this case would be to identify with nature, and to identify with nature would be to put an end to writing about nature.

The traditions surrounding Mother Nature in Romantic poetry affect Dorothy and Brontë more than Dickinson, because the British writers are more concerned with nature than are the Americans. The literary tradition in which Dickinson finds herself, as defined largely by Emerson, transcends Wordsworth's respectful view of nature. Emerson is as much or more self-centered than the British Romantics, but his exaggeration of this mode is

---

2. All quotations from Milton's *Paradise Lost* are from *John Milton: Complete Poems and Major Prose*, ed. Merritt Y. Hughes (New York: Bobbs-Merrill, 1957), cited hereafter as *PL* followed by book and line numbers.
3. Luce Irigaray, *Speculum de l'autre femme* (Paris: Éditions de Minuit, 1974). The first section

of the book, "La Tache aveugle d'un vieux rêve de symétrie" (pp. 9–162), is devoted to a point-by-point critique of the path Freud charts for girls, particularly in the "Lecture on Femininity." If women are indeed not mirror images of men, then the Freudian scheme becomes groundless.

helpful to Dickinson, his female successor. Because his self is so inclusive, he cares less for the specific characteristics of the "NOT ME,"[4] so that Dickinson is not confronted with the same relentless myth of female nature and female objects of desire that Brontë and Dorothy Wordsworth face. Enormous as Emerson's egotism is, it is more easily adapted by a woman, because it has no sexually defined objects. Dickinson's sense of her femininity is more evident in reference to rhetoric than to maternal nature, and this chapter will return to questions of rhetoric later on. But the two matters are not entirely separable, and Dickinson does write about Mother Nature, just as Dorothy and Brontë also encounter rhetorical problems.

Wordsworth's major characterizations of nature as maternal occur in *The Prelude*, published in 1850, two years after Brontë's death. But several poems by Wordsworth available to all early nineteenth-century readers characterize nature as maternal or feminine, most notably two central formulations of poetic project, the verse Prospectus to *The Excursion* and "Ode: Intimations of Immortality."[5] In the Prospectus to *The Excursion* Wordsworth's "spousal verse" for the marriage between the intellect and nature assumes a masculine "Mind of Man" for the poetic psyche, and it assumes the traditional feminine characterization of nature for his counterpart.

> Paradise, and groves
> Elysian, Fortunate Fields—like those of old
> Sought in the Atlantic Main—why should they be
> A history only of departed things,
> Or a mere fiction of what never was?
> For the discerning intellect of Man,
> When wedded to this goodly universe
> In love and holy passion, shall find these
> A simple produce of the common day.
> —I, long before the blissful hour arrives,
> Would chant, in lonely peace, the spousal verse
> Of this great consummation.

By invoking the idea of pagan paradises in this context, the poet images the communion between the mind and nature in the manner of Plato's primordial androgyne, so that the fall is like the separation of the sexes. Through the reference to Milton, here and elsewhere in the Preface, the poet relates his bridal "external world" to Milton's maternal nature of Book VII of *Paradise Lost*. First the "great Mother" emerges from the womb of waters; later,

> the bare Earth, till then
> Desert and bare, unsightly, unadorn'd,

---

4. See Emerson's *Nature* (1836), introduction [editor's note].

5. All quotations from Wordsworth are from *The Poetical Works of William Wordsworth*, 5 vols., ed. E. de Selincourt and H. Darbishire (London: The Clarendon Press of Oxford University Press, 1940–1949), cited hereafter (where necessary) as *PW* followed by volume and page numbers; and from *The Prelude: Or Growth of a Poet's Mind*, ed. E. de Selincourt, 2nd ed. rev. H. Darbishire (London: The Clarendon Press of Oxford University Press, 1959). I quote from the 1805 version of *The Prelude*, rather than from the more familiar version of 1850 (except where otherwise noted), since most of my citations will pertain to Dorothy Wordsworth, and the 1805 version is the closer to the many versions she would have known.

> Brought forth the tender Grass, whose verdure clad
> Her Universal Face with pleasant green,
> Then Herbs of every leaf, that sudden flow'r'd
> Op'ning thir various colors, and made gay
> Her bosom smelling sweet.
>
> (VII, 313–319)

Wordsworth's image of the universal marriage is beautiful and convincing in itself and because it exalts as it typifies the rest of his project. But it depends on identifying matter and otherness as female and subjectivity as male.

Maternal nature in the Intimations Ode is less exalted than the bridal universe of the Prospectus to *The Excursion*. Man is here the child of heaven, but the foster-child of Earth, who is explicitly opposed to the memory of a primordial heaven.

> Earth fills her lap with pleasures of her own;
> Yearnings she hath in her own natural kind,
> And, even with something of a Mother's mind,
>   And no unworthy aim,
>   The homely Nurse doth all she can
> To make her Foster-child, her Inmate Man,
>   Forget the glories he hath known,
> And that imperial palace whence he came.

Self-involved, Mother Earth has no capacity for understanding her foster-child's infinite desires, and opposes transcendence. Only by transforming nature into a reminder of "What was so fugitive"—the infant's unconscious communion with heavenly things—does the poet cease to feel threatened by natural objects and find a renewed intimacy with them. Maternal nature is depersonalized into "ye Fountains, Meadows, Hills, and Groves," and the new relation that the poet prescribes means a shift from living "beneath your more habitual sway" to a less hierarchical love. The poet learns that he can still love nature without submitting to her control and without being like her. Similarly in "Tintern Abbey" the two stages of youth that the speaker has now passed are both characterized by a likeness between youth and nature. The "glad animal movements" "of my boyish days" give way only to the time "when like a roe / I bounded o'er the mountains." Growing up depends on being able to have a separate identity and to "look on nature" rather than seeing nature from within.

Although the poet values his own distance, most of the female figures depicted in his poetry are like nature or merged with nature. For some, like Dorothy in "Tintern Abbey" or in *The Prelude*, or his wife in "She was a Phantom of delight," being like nature is seen by the poet as felicitous. For others it is more sinister, because being like nature is a fatality. Lucy, Ruth, the Mad Mother, Martha Ray, several vagrant women, and Margaret in Book I of *The Excursion* undergo a dissolution of identity, either by literally dying or by entering a termless, semiconscious life-in-death as a part of natural process. Some of them are themselves mothers, inflicting on their hapless children what they themselves receive from nature. All are daughters of Nature. Young boys and old men are represented as sharing this experience of a vegetative or naturalized life. The Boy of Winander "Blew mimic hootings to the silent owls,"[6] and the old man of "Animal Tranquillity and Decay" "is insensibly subdued / To settled quiet." But the poet's own active subjectivity is almost the sole representative of adult man, and he assures us that his consciousness maintains a loving distance from nature. In these others, male and female, he represents a possibility for the self that he cannot consciously adopt for himself, a merging with nature that is at once desired and feared.

The Lucy poems image a feminine figure for whom there is no discontinuity between imaginative sympathy with nature and death, and a masculine speaker for whom Lucy's death is non-catastrophic, sanctifying nature as well as darkening it. In "Three years she grew in sun and shower" Lucy is most explicitly the daughter, or foster-daughter, of Mother Nature, who, self-involved as in the Intimations Ode, takes possession of Lucy in order to have a child of her own. The mother's purpose is to make her daughter be like herself. The Church Fathers interpreted Genesis to mean that only Adam was formed in God's image, leaving Eve open to interpretation. This new Eve is to be made in Nature's image, for Nature's beauty "shall pass into her face:"

> "She shall be sportive as the fawn
> That wild with glee across the lawn
> Or up the mountain springs;
> And her's shall be the breathing balm,
> And her's the silence and the calm
> Of mute insensate things.
>
> "The floating clouds their state shall lend
> To her; for her the willow bend;
> Nor shall she fail to see
> Even in the motions of the Storm
> Grace that shall mould the Maiden's form
> By silent sympathy."

Like God's creating Word, Nature's "shall" is immediately efficacious, although the reader is carefully kept from knowing whether Lucy's development into a natural creature preceded her death, or whether, more startlingly, her early death is the manner in which her naturalization is accomplished.

> Thus Nature spake—The work was done—
> How soon my Lucy's race was run!
> She died, . . .

Though Lucy leaves the speaker bereft, her legacy to him is synonymous with the natural world of which she herself has become a part:

> She died, and left to me
> This health, this calm, and quiet scene.

In "I travelled among unknown men" England draws the speaker back from his travels not to a particular spot but to a region diffusely consecrated by Lucy's lingering memory.

> And she I cherished turned her wheel
> Beside an English fire.

---

6. *Prelude* 5.398 (1850, 5.373) [editor's note].

> Thy mornings showed, thy nights concealed,
>   The bowers where Lucy played;
> And thine too is the last green field
>   That Lucy's eyes surveyed.

That wheel, though it seems to indicate a domestic image, is not quite specific enough to be representational, and projects instead Lucy's death in the last poem in the series, where she is "Rolled round in earth's diurnal course, / With rocks, and stones, and trees." Lucy, apparently complicitous in her own disappearance into nature, once turned the wheel that now turns her. Not only is she Mother Nature's daughter in appearance and bearing, her wheel-turning is the predecessor of nature's wheel-turning, so that the daughter is the mother of the mother in an ominous closed circling of their own.

Although from the point of view of the nineteenth-century woman reader the Lucy poems trace problematic distinctions between subject and object, to a modern reader they demonstrate Wordsworth's exceptionally tactful restraint about such distinctions. Frances Ferguson reads them as the poet's effort to school himself not to appropriate his poetic object, which he traces out of sight until in the last poem Lucy's having been at all is conjectural.[7] By repeating an experience of loss they curtail his usual tendency to dominate in subject-object relations. But these two readings are not irreconcilable. Although Lucy escapes his grasp as an object—it is nature instead that appropriates her—elusiveness is one of the qualities of otherness in a larger definition of appropriation, and Lucy's vanishing into nature contributes to nature's consistent otherness.

*   *   *

The women poets were under no obligation to take their self-images from Wordsworth's representations of femininity, but Wordsworth had behind him a range of models, from "the figure of the youth as virile poet" of the poets of sensibility, whom Shelley and Keats in turn adapt for their personae in their early romances of the self,[8] to the august intonations of Milton and his predecessors in epic voice. Dorothy, reading Byron and Shelley in her later years, and Brontë reading them as a child, would have found there feminine figures less fatal than Wordsworth's Mother Nature, but no more helpful. Shelley's Witch of Atlas is a feminine figure for creativity, but her creation is sterile and flawed, much as, when Coleridge pictures the mind as the passive and feminine Aeolian harp, its product is "idle flitting phantasies" rather than imagination. Both Byron and Shelley frequently create female figures of imaginative desire. Like Blake's emanations, they embody the object of the poet's quest, either narcissistically, as in Manfred's guilty love for his sister Astarte,[9] or as the perfect complement to the poet, as is the case with Asia in *Prometheus Unbound* or Emilia in "Epipsychidion." Either way, they mirror the poet or his protagonist, and bear no relation to real women, as Shelley himself knew well, to his loss. Though these ethereal females hardly seem

---

7. Frances Ferguson, *Wordsworth: Language as Counter-Spirit* (New Haven: Yale University Press, 1977), pp. 173–194.
8. Harold Bloom, *The Visionary Company: A Reading of English Romantic Poetry* (1961; rev. ed. Ithaca: Cornell University Press, 1971), pp. 217–218.
9. In Byron's *Manfred* (1817). "Emanations": in Blake's mythology, aspects of the object-world; in imaginative states they are female, emanating from and uniting with an integrated male being [editor's note].

classifiable as objects, in the manner of natural objects, they have no more subjectivity than rocks or stones or trees. Wordsworth's maternal nature or naturalized feminine figures like Lucy resemble emanations, in that they are generated by the need of the powerful central consciousness for a beloved object. But these feminine figures also provide an image of what the poet's mind is not. Lucy is an admonitory image of the vegetation of the poet's mind that would take place if the poet were himself to come under the domination of Mother Nature.

The literary images available to women all demonstrate to women their unfitness for poetry. Equally responsible for negative models of feminine poethood is the patriarchal tradition of Christianity, which, unlike as it is to Wordsworthian paganistic reverence for Mother Nature, fosters an analogous view of femininity. The Judaeo-Christian tradition is notoriously misogynistic. The Church Fathers and later interpreters did a great deal to augment the identification of woman with sin, thereby justifying her religious and secular oppression, but there is ample evidence of misogyny in both Old and New Testaments. Brontë and Dickinson, raised in intensely religious households, attended church seldom or never but nonetheless read their Bibles, so that even though they avoided listening to sermons on the abject nature of woman, they were exposed to the Bible's calumnies. Biblical misogyny was not easily disregarded, as it was so deeply ingrained in culture, and because it is often so beautifully expressed. The women poets also read *Paradise Lost*, which magnifies religious misogyny while conveying it into literary tradition.[1]

The creation story, both in Genesis and in Milton's retelling, makes physical creation the power of a masculine deity, depriving the feminine figure of her one remaining prerogative. The story about Adam's rib comes as close as possible to saying that man can now give birth, along with all the other priorities given to him by Jehovah.[2] Eve is made to appear inferior to Adam in a variety of ways. Blamed for the fall, she is morally weak. Although the first creation story, in the first book of Genesis, offers a myth of original equality, it is the second one (Genesis 2), written earlier, that has been emphasized by later readers, as if it were an interpretation or expansion, rather than a contradiction, of the first. Milton's account of the creation in Book VII of *Paradise Lost* follows Genesis 1, but for Adam's account of his own creation in Book VIII Milton turns to Genesis 2, so that Adam is created first and Eve as an afterthought, formed for Adam's use and delight. Although it is clear that Eve was part of God's plan from the beginning, the fact that we learn of her creation from Adam's point of view emphasizes that she is as if Adam had invented her. Only Adam is formed in God's image, and, in the King James Version if not in the original (the translation is what matters for the women poets of England and America), Eve is Adam's "help meet," or, according to Milton,

> Thy likeness, thy fit help, thy other self,
> Thy wish, exactly to thy heart's desire.
> (*PL* VIII, 450–451)

1. Sandra M. Gilbert discusses, from a slightly different point of view, this and other inhibiting effects of Milton on women writers, in "Patriarchal Poetry and Women Readers: Reflections on Milton's Bogey," *PMLA*, 93 (1978), 368–382.
2. See Elizabeth Gould Davis, *The First Sex* (1971; rpt. Harmondsworth, Middlesex: Penguin, 1976), pp. 143–144.

As Adam is created in God's image, Eve is created in Adam's. Even though both have "looks divine," "Hee for God only, shee for God in him" makes plain their hierarchical relationship.

In Genesis 2 and in *Paradise Lost*, the delay between Adam's creation and Eve's permits Adam one other substantial advantage over Eve: conversation with God. Adam receives directly from God the command not to eat from the tree of the knowledge of good and evil, and in Milton Adam is able to discuss with God his desire for a helpmate. Eve never hears God's voice directly, but only through Adam's transmission. The outstanding feature of the creation in Genesis 1 is that the masculine deity creates with language. God's Word is what supplants feminine fecundity, and when that Word is made flesh it takes a masculine form. The Logos is a masculine prerogative, handed down from Father to Son, and it is in words of approximately the same language that God addresses Adam and not Eve. God deprives Eve of her dignity by not speaking to her directly, with the result that Milton can say that she prefers to listen only to Adam, "not capable her ear / Of what was high" (*PL* VIII, 49–50). The first human language act, naming the animals, is likewise Adam's. Synonymous with the things they name, his words have a portion of the power of God's own verbal powers, whereby words create the things they name: "and whatsoever Adam called every living creature, that *was* the name thereof" (Genesis 2:19). Though God empowers this naming, the names are original with Adam, who thus shares, in a limited way, in the creation itself. Excluded from the community of conversation shared by God and Adam, and deprived of an equal share in inventing human language, it is quite reasonable for Eve to respond more readily than Adam to the verbal appeal of another outsider. The first being who speaks to her is the serpent, and her first speech is, in reply to him, a recitation of the command not to eat from the tree. Adam participates in the invention of language, but Eve only repeats something that she has been told and that she perhaps does not fully believe.

The men poets who wrote at a time when the Bible still provided culture with its dominant metaphorical framework inherited and relied on this language tradition, whether they knew it or not. Though in 1821 Wordsworth accuses himself of blasphemy when his imagination presumes "To act the God among external things," his mind, at its most free, knows its own powers of divinity. Coleridge defines imagination so that the poet is the direct inheritor of God's self-asserting "I AM."[3] The poet's creations are shadows of God's creation, because they ritually repeat the state of chaos that preceded the creation: the secondary imagination "dissolves, diffuses, dissipates, in order to recreate."[4] Emerson, even more powerfully than the British writers, makes the poet in the image of the Son, his speech Adamic, and poetry the inheritor of divinity:

> The poet is the sayer, the namer, and represents beauty. He is a sovereign, and stands on the center. For the world is not painted or adorned, but is from the beginning beautiful; and God has not made some beautiful things, but Beauty is the creator of the universe. Therefore the poet is not any permissive potentate, but is emperor in his own right.
>
> (*CW*, III, 7)[5]

---

3. See Exodus 3.14 [editor's note].
4. *Biographia Literaria*, Chapter 13; from the text edited by J. Shawcross (London: The Clarendon Press of Oxford University Press, 1907).

5. "The Poet," from the centenary edition, *The Complete Works of Ralph Waldo Emerson*, ed. Edward Waldo Emerson (Boston: Houghton Mifflin, 1903–1904), cited as *CW*.

It is typical of the Judaeo-Christian tradition of language that his thoughts should run from poetry to centrality and rule. When he says "Words are also actions, and actions are a kind of words" (CW, III, 8), he is reaffirming the linkage between the Logos and the human poet.

Eve, and women after her, have been dislocated from the ability to feel that they are speaking their own language. They could not speak, with a right to personal usage, of the godlike powers of the mind. That Brontë and Dickinson always refused to be believers in orthodox religion, though Dorothy became more devout as she grew older, correlates with the degree of their imaginative freedom and poetic power. It seems that it was necessary, or at least helpful, to break free from the belief that a masculine divinity was the first and best speaker. Brontë and Dickinson were fortunate that their minister fathers respected their daughters' independence of mind. This tolerance saved the daughters the effort of personal rebellion and allowed them to direct their energies against the tradition instead.

✻   ✻   ✻

1980

NINA BAYM
b. 1936

With *Woman's Fiction: A Guide to Novels by and about Women in America, 1820–1870* (1978), Nina Baym effected a transformation in scholarly assessment of the nineteenth-century novels produced by a group Nathaniel Hawthorne had denounced as a "damn'd mob of scribbling women." But "Melodramas of Beset Manhood" (1981), reprinted here, tackles the politics of canon formation in such a way as to make the American case exemplary of canonization in general. In addition to writing *American Women Writers and the Work of History, 1790–1860* (1995), Baym has edited reprints of Kate Chopin, Hawthorne, Maria Susanna Cummins, Judith Sargent Murray, and E. D. E. N. Southworth. Retired from teaching at the University of Illinois at Urbana-Champaign, she currently serves as general editor of *The Norton Anthology of American Literature*.

From Melodramas of Beset Manhood: How Theories of American Fiction Exclude Women Authors

This paper is about American literary criticism rather than American literature. It proceeds from the assumption that we never read American literature directly or freely, but always through the perspective allowed by theories. Theories account for the inclusion and exclusion of texts in anthologies, and theories account for the way we read them. My concern is with the fact that the theories controlling our reading of American literature have led to the exclusion of women authors from the canon.

Let me use my own practice as a case in point. In 1977 there was published a collection of essays on images of women in major British and American literature, to which I contributed.[1] The American field was divided chronologically among six critics, with four essays covering literature written prior to World War II. Taking seriously the charge that we were to focus only on the major figures, the four of us—working quite independently of each other—selected altogether only four women writers. Three of these were from the earliest period, a period which predates the novel: the poet Anne Bradstreet and the two diarists Mary Rowlandson and Sarah Kemble Knight. The fourth was Emily Dickinson. For the period between 1865 and 1940 no women were cited at all. The message that we—who were taking women as our subject—conveyed was clear: there have been almost no major women writers in America; the major novelists have all been men.

Now, when we wrote our essays we were not undertaking to reread all American literature and make our own decisions as to who the major authors were. That is the point: we accepted the going canon of major authors. As late as 1977, that canon did not include any women novelists. Yet, the critic who goes beyond what is accepted and tries to look at the totality of literary production in America quickly discovers that women authors have been active since the earliest days of settlement. Commercially and numerically they have probably dominated American literature since the middle of the nineteenth century. As long ago as 1854, Nathaniel Hawthorne complained to his publisher about the "damn'd mob of scribbling women" whose writings—he fondly imagined—were diverting the public from his own.

Names and figures help make this dominance clear. In the years between 1774 and 1799—from the calling of the First Continental Congress to the close of the eighteenth century—a total of thirty-eight original works of fiction were published in this country.[2] Nine of these, appearing pseudonymously or anonymously, have not yet been attributed to any author. The remaining twenty-nine are the work of eighteen individuals, of whom four are women. One of these women, Susannah Rowson, wrote six of them, or more than a fifth of the total. Her most popular work, *Charlotte* (also known as *Charlotte Temple*), was printed three times in the decade it was published, nineteen times between 1800 and 1810, and eighty times by the middle of the nineteenth century. A novel by a second of the four women, Hannah Foster, was called *The Coquette* and had thirty editions by mid-nineteenth century. *Uncle Tom's Cabin*, by a woman, is probably the all-time biggest seller in American history. A woman, Mrs. E.D.E.N. Southworth, was probably the most widely read novelist in the nineteenth century. How is it possible for a critic or historian of American literature to leave these books, and these authors, out of the picture?

I see three partial explanations for the critical invisibility of the many active women authors in America. The first is simple bias. The critic does not like the idea of women as writers, does not believe that women can be writers, and hence does not see them even when they are right before his eyes. His theory or his standards may well be nonsexist but his practice is not. Certainly,

---

1. Marlene Springer, ed., *What Manner of Woman: Essays on English and American Life and Literature* (New York: New York Univ. Press, 1977) [all notes are Baym's].

2. See Lyle Wright, *American Fiction 1774–1850* (San Marino, Calif.: Huntington Library Press, 1969).

an *a priori* resistance to recognizing women authors as serious writers has functioned powerfully in the mindset of a number of influential critics. One can amusingly demonstrate the inconsistencies between standard and practice in such critics, show how their minds slip out of gear when they are confronted with a woman author. But this is only a partial explanation.

A second possibility is that, in fact, women have not written the kind of work that we call "excellent," for reasons that are connected with their gender although separable from it. This is a serious possibility. For example, suppose we required a dense texture of classical allusion in all works that we called excellent. Then, the restriction of a formal classical education to men would have the effect of restricting authorship of excellent literature to men. Women would not have written excellent literature because social conditions hindered them. The reason, though gender-connected, would not be gender per se.

The point here is that the notion of the artist, or of excellence, has efficacy in a given time and reflects social realities. The idea of "good" literature is not only a personal preference, it is also a cultural preference. We can all think of species of women's literature that do not aim in any way to achieve literary excellence as society defines it: e.g., the "Harlequin Romances." Until recently, only a tiny proportion of literary women aspired to artistry and literary excellence in the terms defined by their own culture. There tended to be a sort of immediacy in the ambitions of literary women leading them to professionalism rather than artistry, by choice as well as by social pressure and opportunity. The gender-related restrictions were really operative, and the responsible critic cannot ignore them. But again, these restrictions are only partly explanatory.

There are, finally, I believe, gender-related restrictions that do not arise out of cultural realities contemporary with the writing woman, but out of later critical theories. These theories may follow naturally from cultural realities pertinent to their own time, but they impose their concerns anachronistically, after the fact, on an earlier period. If one accepts current theories of American literature, one accepts as a consequence—perhaps not deliberately but nevertheless inevitably—a literature that is essentially male. This is the partial explanation that I shall now develop.

Let us begin where the earliest theories of American literature begin, with the hypothesis that American literature is to be judged less by its form than its content. Traditionally, one ascertains literary excellence by comparing a writer's work with standards of performance that have been established by earlier authors, where formal mastery and innovation are paramount. But from its historical beginnings, American literary criticism has assumed that literature produced in this nation would have to be ground-breaking, equal to the challenge of the new nation, and completely original. Therefore, it could not be judged by referring it back to earlier achievements. The earliest American literary critics began to talk about the "most American" work rather than the "best" work because they knew no way to find out the best other than by comparing American to British writing. Such a criticism struck them as both unfair and unpatriotic. We had thrown off the political shackles of England; it would not do for us to be servile in our literature. Until a tradition of American literature developed its own inherent forms, the early critic looked for a standard of Americanness rather than a standard of excellence.

Inevitably, perhaps, it came to seem that the quality of "Americanness," whatever it might be, *constituted* literary excellence for American authors. Beginning as a nationalistic enterprise, American literary criticism and theory has retained a nationalist orientation to this day.

Of course, the idea of Americanness is even more vulnerable to subjectivity than the idea of the best. When they speak of "most American," critics seldom mean the statistically most representative or most typical, the most read or the most sold. They have some qualitative essence in mind, and frequently their work develops as an explanation of this idea of "American" rather than a description and evaluation of selected authors. The predictable recurrence of the term "America" or "American" in works of literary criticism treating a dozen or fewer authors indicates that the critic has chosen his authors on the basis of their conformity to his idea of what is truly American. For examples: *American Renaissance, The Romance in America, Symbolism and American Literature, Form and Fable in American Fiction, The American Adam, The American Novel and Its Tradition, The Place of Style in American Literature* (a subtitle), *The Poetics of American Fiction* (another subtitle). But an idea of what is American is no more than an idea, needing demonstration. The critic all too frequently ends up using his chosen authors as demonstrations of Americanness, arguing through them to his definition.

So Marius Bewley explains in *The Eccentric Design* that "for the American artist there was no social surface responsive to his touch. The scene was crude, even beyond successful satire," but later, in a concluding chapter titled "The Americanness of the American Novel," he agrees that "this 'tradition' as I have set it up here has no room for the so-called realists and naturalists."[3] F. O. Matthiessen, whose *American Renaissance* enshrines five authors, explains that "the one common denominator of my five writers, uniting even Hawthorne and Whitman, was their devotion to the possibilities of democracy."[4] The jointly written *Literary History of the United States* proclaims in its "address to the reader" that American literary history "will be a history of the books of the great and the near-great writers in a literature which is most revealing when studied as a by-product of American experience."[5] And Joel Porte announces confidently in *The Romance in America* that "students of American literature . . . have provided a solid theoretical basis for establishing that the rise and growth of fiction in this country is dominated by our authors' conscious adherence to a tradition of non-realistic romance sharply at variance with the broadly novelistic mainstream of English writing. When there has been disagreement among recent critics as to the contours of American fiction, it has usually disputed, not the existence *per se* of a romance tradition, but rather the question of which authors, themes, and stylistic strategies *deserve* to be placed with certainty at the heart of that tradition" (emphasis added).[6]

Before he is through, the critic has had to insist that some works in America are much more American than others, and he is as busy excluding certain writers as "un-American" as he is including others. Such a proceeding in the

3. Marius Bewley, *The Eccentric Design* (New York: Columbia Univ. Press, 1963), 15, 291.
4. F. O. Matthiessen, *American Renaissance* (New York: Oxford Univ. Press, 1941), ix.
5. Robert E. Spiller et al., eds., *Literary History of* the United States (New York: Macmillan, 1959), xix.
6. Joel Porte, *The Romance in America* (Middletown, Conn.: Wesleyan Univ. Press, 1969), ix.

political arena would be extremely suspect, but in criticism it has been the method of choice. Its final result goes far beyond the conclusion that only a handful of American works are very good. *That* statement is one we could agree with, since very good work is rare in any field. But it is odd indeed to argue that only a handful of American works are really American.[7]

Despite the theoretical room for an infinite number of definitions of Americanness, critics have generally agreed on it—although the shifting canon suggests that agreement may be a matter of fad rather than fixed objective qualities.[8] First, America as a nation must be the ultimate subject of the work. The author must be writing about aspects of experience and character that are American only, setting Americans off from other people and the country from other nations. The author must be writing his story specifically to display these aspects, to meditate on them, and to derive from them some generalizations and conclusions about "the" American experience. To Matthiessen the topic is the possibilities of democracy; Sacvan Bercovitch (in *The Puritan Origins of the American Self*) finds it in American identity. Such content excludes, at one extreme, stories about universals, aspects of experience common to people in a variety of times and places—mutability, mortality, love, childhood, family, betrayal, loss. Innocence versus experience is an admissable theme *only* if innocence is the essence of the American character, for example.

But at the other extreme, the call for an overview of America means that detailed, circumstantial portrayals of some aspect of American life are also, peculiarly, inappropriate: stories of wealthy New Yorkers, Yugoslavian immigrants, southern rustics. Jay B. Hubbell rather ingratiatingly admits as much when he writes, "in both my teaching and my research I had a special interest in literature as a reflection of American life and thought. This circumstance may explain in part why I found it difficult to appreciate the merits of the expatriates and why I was slow in doing justice to some of the New Critics. I was repelled by the sordid subject matter found in some of the novels written by Dreiser, Dos Passos, Faulkner, and some others."[9] Richard Poirier writes that "the books which in my view constitute a distinctive American tradition . . . resist within their pages forces of environment that otherwise dominate the world" and he distinguishes this kind from "the fiction of Mrs. Wharton, Dreiser, or Howells."[1] The *Literary History of the United States* explains that "historically, [Edith Wharton] is likely to survive as the memorialist of a dying aristocracy" (1211). And so on. These exclusions abound in all the works which form the stable core of American literary criticism at this time.

Along with Matthiessen, the most influential exponent of this exclusive Americanness is Lionel Trilling, and his work has particular applicability because it concentrates on the novel form. Here is a famous passage from his 1940 essay, "Reality in America," in which Trilling is criticizing Vernon Parrington's selection of authors in *Main Currents in American Thought*:

> A culture is not a flow, nor even a confluence; the form of its existence is struggle—or at least debate—it is nothing if not a dialectic. And in any

7. A good essay on this topic is William C. Spengemann's "What Is American Literature?" *Centennial Review*, 22 (1978), 119–38.
8. See Jay B. Hubbell, *Who Are the Major American Authors?* (Durham, N.C.: Duke Univ. Press,
1972).
9. Ibid., 335–36.
1. Richard Poirier, *A World Elsewhere: The Place of Style in American Literature* (New York: Oxford Univ. Press, 1966), 5.

culture there are likely to be certain artists who contain a large part of the dialectic within themselves, their meaning and power lying in their contradictions; they contain within themselves, it may be said, the very essence of the culture. To throw out Poe because he cannot be conveniently fitted into a theory of American culture . . . to find his gloom to be merely personal and eccentric . . . as Hawthorne's was . . . to judge Melville's response to American life to be less noble than that of Bryant or of Greeley, to speak of Henry James as an escapist . . . this is not merely to be mistaken in aesthetic judgment. Rather it is to examine without attention and from the point of view of a limited and essentially arrogant conception of reality the documents which are in some respects the most suggestive testimony to what America was and is, and of course to get no answer from them.[2]

Trilling's immediate purpose is to exclude Greeley and Bryant from the list of major authors and to include Poe, Melville, Hawthorne, and James. We probably share Trilling's aesthetic judgment. But note that he does not base his judgment on aesthetic grounds; indeed, he dismisses aesthetic judgment with the word "merely." He argues that Parrington has picked the wrong artists because he doesn't understand the culture. Culture is his real concern.

But what makes Trilling's notion of culture more valid than Parrington's? Trilling really has no argument; he resorts to such value-laden rhetoric as "a limited and essentially arrogant conception of reality" precisely because he cannot objectively establish his version of culture over Parrington's. For the moment, there are two significant conclusions to draw from this quotation. First, the disagreement is over the nature of our culture. Second, there is no disagreement over the value of literature—it is valued as a set of "documents" which provide "suggestive testimony to what America was and is."

One might think that an approach like this which is subjective, circular, and in some sense nonliterary or even antiliterary would not have had much effect. But clearly Trilling was simply carrying on a longstanding tradition of searching for cultural essence, and his essays gave the search a decided and influential direction toward the notion of cultural essence as some sort of tension. Trilling succeeded in getting rid of Bryant and Greeley, and his choice of authors is still dominant. They all turn out—and not by accident— to be white, middle-class, male, of Anglo-Saxon derivation or at least from an ancestry which had settled in this country before the big waves of immigration which began around the middle of the nineteenth century. In every case, however, the decision made by these men to become professional authors pushed them slightly to one side of the group to which they belonged. This slight alienation permitted them to belong, and yet not to belong, to the so-called "mainstream." These two aspects of their situation—their membership in the dominant middle-class white Anglo-Saxon group, and their modest alienation from it—defined their boundaries, enabling them to "contain within themselves" the "contradictions" that, in Trilling's view, constitute the "very essence of the culture." I will call the literature they produced, which Trilling assesses so highly, a "consensus criticism of the consensus."

This idea plainly excludes many groups but it might not seem necessarily to exclude women. In fact, nineteenth-century women authors were overwhelmingly white, middle-class, and Anglo-Saxon in origin. Something more

2. Lionel Trilling, *The Liberal Imagination* (New York: Anchor, 1950), 7–9.

than what is overtly stated by Trilling (and others cited below) is added to exclude them. What critics have done is to assume, for reasons shortly to be expounded, that the women writers invariably represented the consensus, rather than the criticism of it; to assume that their gender made them part of the consensus in a way that prevented them from partaking in the criticism. The presence of these women and their works is acknowledged in literary theory and history as an impediment and obstacle, that which the essential American literature had to criticize as its chief task.

So, in his lively and influential book of 1960, *Love and Death in the American Novel*, Leslie Fiedler describes women authors as creators of the "flagrantly bad best-seller" against which "our best fictionists"—all male—have had to struggle for "their integrity and their livelihoods."[3] And, in a 1978 reader's introduction to an edition of Charles Brockden Brown's *Wieland*, Sydney J. Krause and S. W. Reid write as follows:

> What it meant for Brown personally, and belles lettres in America historically, that he should have decided to write professionally is a story unto itself. Americans simply had no great appetite for serious literature in the early decades of the Republic—certainly nothing of the sort with which they devoured . . . the ubiquitous melodramas of beset womanhood, "tales of truth," like Susanna Rowson's *Charlotte Temple* and Hannah Foster's *The Coquette*.[4]

There you see what has happened to the woman writer. She has entered literary history as the enemy. The phrase "tales of truth" is put in quotes by the critics, as though to cast doubt on the very notion that a "melodrama of beset womanhood" could be either true or important. At the same time, ironically, they are proposing for our serious consideration, as a candidate for intellectually engaging literature, a highly melodramatic novel with an improbable plot, inconsistent characterizations, and excesses of style that have posed tremendous problems for all students of Charles Brockden Brown. But, by this strategy it becomes possible to begin major American fiction historically with male rather than female authors. The certainty here that stories about women could not contain the essence of American culture means that the matter of American experience is inherently male. And this makes it highly unlikely that American women would write fiction encompassing such experience. I would suggest that the theoretical model of a story which may become the vehicle of cultural essence is: "a melodrama of beset manhood." This melodrama is presented in a fiction which, as we'll later see, can be taken as representative of the author's literary experience, his struggle for integrity and livelihood against flagrantly bad best-sellers written by women. Personally beset in a way that epitomizes the tensions of our culture, the male author produces his melodramatic testimony to our culture's essence—so the theory goes.

Remember that the search for cultural essence demands a relatively uncircumstantial kind of fiction, one which concentrates on national universals (if I may be pardoned the paradox). This search has identified a sort of nonrealistic narrative, a romance, a story free to catch an essential, idealized Amer-

3. Leslie Fiedler, *Love and Death in the American Novel* (New York: Criterion Books, 1960), 93.
4. Charles Brockden Brown, *Wieland*, ed. Sydney J. Krause and S. W. Reid (Kent, Ohio: Kent State Univ. Press, 1978), xii.

ican character, to intensify his essence and convey his experience in a way that ignores details of an actual social milieu. This nonrealistic or antisocial aspect of American fiction is noted—as a fault—by Trilling in a 1947 essay, "Manners, Morals, and the Novel." Curiously, Trilling here attacks the same group of writers he had rescued from Parrington in "Reality in America." But, never doubting that his selection represents "the" American authors, he goes ahead with the task that really interests him—criticizing the culture through its representative authors. He writes:

> The novel in America diverges from its classic [i.e., British] intention which . . . is the investigation of the problem of reality beginning in the social field. The fact is that American writers of genius have not turned their minds to society. Poe and Melville were quite apart from it; the reality they sought was only tangential to society. Hawthorne was acute when he insisted that he did not write novels but romances—he thus expressed his awareness of the lack of social texture in his work. . . . In America in the nineteenth century, Henry James was alone in knowing that to scale the moral and aesthetic heights in the novel one had to use the ladder of social observation.[5]

Within a few years after publication of Trilling's essay, a group of Americanists took its rather disapproving description of American novelists and found in this nonrealism or romanticism the essentially American quality they had been seeking. The idea of essential Americanness then developed in such influential works of criticism as *Virgin Land* by Henry Nash Smith (1950), *Symbolism and American Literature* by Charles Feidelson (1953), *The American Adam* by R. W. B. Lewis (1955), *The American Novel and Its Tradition* by Richard Chase (1957), and *Form and Fable in American Fiction* by Daniel G. Hoffman (1961). These works, and others like them, were of sufficiently high critical quality, and sufficiently like each other, to compel assent to the picture of American literature that they presented. They used sophisticated New Critical close-reading techniques to identify a myth of America which had nothing to do with the classical fictionist's task of chronicling probable people in recognizable social situations.

The myth narrates a confrontation of the American individual, the pure American self divorced from specific social circumstances, with the promise offered by the idea of America. This promise is the deeply romantic one that in this new land, untrammeled by history and social accident, a person will be able to achieve complete self-definition. Behind this promise is the assurance that individuals come before society, that they exist in some meaningful sense prior to, and apart from, societies in which they happen to find themselves. The myth also holds that, as something artificial and secondary to human nature, society exerts an unmitigatedly destructive pressure on individuality. To depict it at any length would be a waste of artistic time; and there is only one way to relate it to the individual—as an adversary.

One may believe all this and yet look in vain for a way to tell a believable story that could free the protagonist from society or offer the promise of such freedom, because nowhere on earth do individuals live apart from social groups. But in America, given the original reality of large tracts of wilderness,

---

5. *The Liberal Imagination*, 206.

the idea seems less a fantasy, more possible in reality or at least more believable in literary treatment. Thus it is that the essential quality of America comes to reside in its unsettled wilderness and the opportunities that such a wilderness offers to the individual as the medium on which he may inscribe, unhindered, his own destiny and his own nature.

As the nineteenth century wore on, and settlements spread across the wilderness, the struggle of the individual against society became more and more central to the myth; where, let's say, Thoreau could leave in Chapter I of *Walden*, Huckleberry Finn has still not made his break by the end of Chapter XLII (the conclusion) of the book that bears his name. Yet, one finds a struggle against society as early as the earliest Leatherstocking tale (*The Pioneers*, 1823). In a sense, this supposed promise of America has always been known to be delusory. Certainly by the twentieth century the myth has been transmuted into an avowedly hopeless quest for unencumbered space (*On the Road*), or the evocation of flight for its own sake (*Rabbit, Run* and *Henderson the Rain King*), or as pathetic acknowledgment of loss—e.g., the close of *The Great Gatsby* where the narrator Nick Carraway summons up "the old island here that flowered once for Dutch sailors' eyes—a fresh, green breast of the new world . . . the last and greatest of all human dreams" where man is "face to face for the last time in history with something commensurate to his capacity for wonder."

We are all very familiar with this myth of America in its various fashionings and owing to the selective vision that has presented this myth to us as the whole story, many of us are unaware of how much besides it has been created by literary Americans. Keeping our eyes on this myth, we need to ask whether anything about it puts it outside women's reach. In one sense, and on one level, the answer is no. The subject of this myth is supposed to stand for human nature, and if men and women alike share a common human nature, then all can respond to its values, its promises, and its frustrations. And in fact as a teacher I find women students responsive to the myth insofar as its protagonist is concerned. It is true, of course, that in order to represent some kind of believable flight into the wilderness, one must select a protagonist with a certain believable mobility, and mobility has until recently been a male prerogative in our society. Nevertheless, relatively few men are actually mobile to the extent demanded by the story, and hence the story is really not much more vicarious, in this regard, for women than for men. The problem is thus not to be located in the protagonist or his gender per se; the problem is with the other participants in his story—the entrammelling society and the promising landscape. For both of these are depicted in unmistakably feminine terms, and this gives a sexual character to the protagonist's story which does, indeed, limit its applicability to women. And this sexual definition has melodramatic, misogynist implications.

In these stories, the encroaching, constricting, destroying society is represented with particular urgency in the figure of one or more women. There are several possible reasons why this might be so. It seems to be a fact of life that we all—women and men alike—experience social conventions and responsibilities and obligations first in the persons of women, since women are entrusted by society with the task of rearing young children. Not until he reaches mid-adolescence does the male connect up with other males whose primary task is socialization; but at about this time—if he is heterosexual—

his lovers and spouses become the agents of a permanent socialization and domestication. Thus, although women are not the source of social power, they are experienced as such. And although not all women are engaged in socializing the young, the young do not encounter women who are not. So from the point of view of the young man, the only kind of women who exist are entrappers and domesticators.

For heterosexual man, these socializing women are also the locus of powerful attraction. First, because everybody has social and conventional instincts; second, because his deepest emotional attachments are to women. This attraction gives urgency and depth to the protagonist's rejection of society. To do it, he must project onto the woman those attractions that he feels, and cast her in the melodramatic role of temptress, antagonist, obstacle—a character whose mission in life seems to be to ensnare him and deflect him from life's important purposes of self-discovery and self-assertion. (A Puritan would have said: from communion with Divinity.) As Richard Chase writes in *The American Novel and Its Tradition*, "The myth requires celibacy." It is partly against his own sexual urges that the male must struggle, and so he perceives the socializing and domesticating woman as a doubly powerful threat; for this reason, Chase goes on to state, neither Cooper nor "any other American novelist until the age of James and Edith Wharton" could imagine "a fully developed woman of sexual age."[6] Yet in making this statement, Chase is talking about his myth rather than Cooper's. (One should add that, for a homosexual male, the demands of society that he link himself for life to a woman make for a particularly misogynist version of this aspect of the American myth, for the hero is propelled not by a rejected attraction, but by true revulsion.) Both heterosexual and homosexual versions of the myth cooperate with the hero's perceptions and validate the notion of woman as threat.

Such a portrayal of women is likely to be uncongenial, if not basically incomprehensible, to a woman. It is not likely that women will write books in which women play this part; and it is by no means the case that most novels by American men reproduce such a scheme. Even major male authors prominent in the canon have other ways of depicting women; e.g., Cooper's *Pathfinder* and *The Pioneers*, Hemingway's *For Whom the Bell Tolls*, Fitzgerald's *The Beautiful and The Damned*. The novels of Henry James and William Dean Howells pose a continual challenge to the masculinist bias of American critical theory. And in one work—*The Scarlet Letter*—a "fully developed woman of sexual age" who is the novel's protagonist has been admitted into the canon, but only by virtue of strenuous critical revisions of the text that remove Hester Prynne from the center of the novel and make her subordinate to Arthur Dimmesdale.

※   ※   ※

[T]he role of entrapper and impediment in the melodrama of beset manhood is reserved for women. Also, the role of the beckoning wilderness, the attractive landscape, is given a deeply feminine quality. Landscape is deeply imbued with female qualities, as society is; but where society is menacing and destructive, landscape is compliant and supportive. It has the attributes

---

6. Richard Chase, *The American Novel and Its Tradition* (New York: Anchor, 1957), 55, 64.

simultaneously of a virginal bride and a nonthreatening mother; its female qualities are articulated with respect to a male angle of vision: what can nature do for me, asks the hero, what can it give me?

Of course, nature has been feminine and maternal from time immemorial, and Henry Nash Smith's *Virgin Land* picks up a timeless archetype in its title. The basic nature of the image leads one to forget about its potential for imbuing any story in which it is used with sexual meanings, and the gender implications of a female landscape have only recently begun to be studied. Recently, Annette Kolodny has studied the traditional canon from this approach.[7] She theorizes that the hero, fleeing a society that has been imagined as feminine, then imposes on nature some ideas of women which, no longer subject to the correcting influence of real-life experience, become more and more fantastic. The fantasies are infantile, concerned with power, mastery, and total gratification: the all-nurturing mother, the all-passive bride. Whether one accepts all the Freudian or Jungian implications of her argument, one cannot deny the way in which heroes of American myth turn to nature as sweetheart and nurture, anticipating the satisfaction of all desires through her and including among these the desires for mastery and power. A familiar passage that captures these ideas is one already quoted: Carraway's evocation of the "fresh green breast" of the new world. The fresh greenness is the virginity that offers itself to the sailors, but the breast promises maternal solace and delight. *The Great Gatsby* contains our two images of women: while Carraway evokes the impossible dream of a maternal landscape, he blames a nonmaternal woman, the socialite Daisy, for her failure to satisfy Gatsby's desires. The true adversary, of course, is Tom Buchanan, but he is hidden, as it were, behind Daisy's skirts.

I have said that women are not likely to cast themselves as antagonists in a man's story; they are even less likely, I suggest, to cast themselves as virgin land. The lack of fit between their own experience and the fictional role assigned to them is even greater in the second instance than in the first. If women portray themselves as brides or mothers it will not be in terms of the mythic landscape. If a woman puts a female construction on nature—as she certainly must from time to time, given the archetypal female resonance of the image—she is likely to write of it as more active, or to stress its destruction or violation. On the other hand, she might adjust the heroic myth to her own psyche by making nature out to be male—as, for example, Willa Cather seems to do in O *Pioneers!* But a violated landscape or a male nature does not fit the essential American pattern as critics have defined it, and hence these literary images occur in an obscurity that criticism cannot see. Thus, one has an almost classic example of the "double bind." When the woman writer creates a story that conforms to the expected myth, it is not recognized for what it is because of a superfluous sexual specialization in the myth as it is entertained in the critics' minds. (Needless to say, many male novelists also entertain this version of the myth, and do not find the masculinist bias with which they imbue it to be superfluous. It is possible that some of these novelists, especially those who write in an era in which literary criticism is a powerful influence, have formed their ideas from their reading in criticism.) But if she

---

7. Annette Kolodny, *The Lay of the Land* (Chapel Hill: Univ. of North Carolina Press, 1975).

does not conform to the myth, she is understood to be writing minor or trivial literature.

* * *

1981

JANE TOMPKINS
b. 1940

As an activist in higher education, Jane Tompkins has dedicated her energies to restoring wonder and excitement to learning. Especially in *A Life in School: What the Teacher Learned* (1996), she has criticized the anxiety and competitiveness fostered by traditional pedagogy in American colleges and universities, "the ways in which the conventions of classroom teaching stunt and warp students." Her holistic approach to education came after a career dedicated to critical writing that integrated the literary text with readers' responses to it or incorporated the formal issues of feminism with the personal perspectives of the feminist critic. Educated at Bryn Mawr College and Yale University, Tompkins taught in English departments at Temple University and Duke University before she moved into the College of Education at the University of Illinois at Chicago. In such books as *Reader-Response Criticism: From Formalism to Post-Structuralism* (editor and contributor, 1980), *Sensational Designs: The Cultural Work of American Fiction, 1790–1860* (1985), and *West of Everything: The Inner Life of Westerns* (1992), Tompkins often undermines traditional assumptions about so-called high and low genres, as she does in the following selection, her reassessment of sentimentality in *Uncle Tom's Cabin*.

From Sentimental Power: *Uncle Tom's Cabin* and the Politics of Literary History

* * *

The thesis I will argue in this essay is diametrically opposed to the one [Ann] Douglas advances.[1] It holds that the popular domestic novel of the nineteenth century represents a monumental effort to reorganize culture from the woman's point of view, that this body of work is remarkable for its intellectual complexity, ambition, and resourcefulness, and that, in certain cases, it offers a critique of American society far more devastating than any delivered by better-known critics such as Hawthorne and Melville. Finally, it suggests that the enormous popularity of these novels, which in Douglas's eyes is cause for suspicion bordering on disgust, is a reason for paying close attention to them. *Uncle Tom's Cabin* was, in almost any terms one can think of, the most important book of the century. It was the first American novel ever to sell over a million copies and its impact is generally thought to have been

---

1. In *The Feminization of American Culture* (New York: Alfred A. Knopf, 1977) [editor's note; except as indicated, all notes are Tompkins's].

incalculable. Expressive of and responsible for the values of its time, it also belongs to a genre, the sentimental novel, whose chief characteristic is that it is written by, for, and about women. In this respect, *Uncle Tom's Cabin* is not exceptional but representative. It is the *summa theologica*[2] of nineteenth-century America's religion of domesticity, a brilliant redaction of the culture's favorite story about itself—the story of salvation through motherly love. Out of the ideological materials they had at their disposal, the sentimental novelists elaborated a myth that gave women the central position of power and authority in the culture; and of these efforts *Uncle Tom's Cabin* is the most dazzling exemplar.

I have used words like "monumental" and "dazzling" to describe Stowe's novel and the tradition of which it is a part because they have for too long been the casualties of a set of critical attitudes which equate intellectual merit with a certain kind of argumentative discourse and certain kinds of subject matter. * * *

The inability of twentieth-century critics either to appreciate the complexity and scope of a novel like Stowe's, or to account for its enormous popular success, stems from their assumptions about the nature and function of literature. In modernist thinking, literature is by definition a form of discourse that has no designs on the world. It does not attempt to change things, but merely to represent them, and it does so in a specifically literary language whose claim to value lies in its uniqueness. Consequently, works whose stated purpose is to influence the course of history, and which therefore employ a language that is not only not unique but common and accessible to everyone, do not qualify as works of art. Literary texts, such as the sentimental novel, which make continual and obvious appeals to the reader's emotions and use technical devices that are distinguished by their utter conventionality, epitomize the opposite of everything that good literature is supposed to be. "For the literary critic," writes J. W. Ward, summing up the dilemma posed by *Uncle Tom's Cabin*, "the problem is how a book so seemingly artless, so lacking in apparent literary talent, was not only an immediate success but has endured."[3]

* * *

It is not my purpose, however, to drag Hawthorne and Melville from their pedestals, nor to claim that the novels of Harriet Beecher Stowe, Fanny Fern, and Elizabeth Stuart Phelps are good in the same way that *Moby-Dick* and *The Scarlet Letter* are; rather I will argue that the work of the sentimental writers is complex and significant in ways *other than* those which characterize the established masterpieces. I will ask the reader to set aside some familiar categories for evaluating fiction—stylistic intricacy, psychological subtlety, epistemological complexity—and to see the sentimental novel not as an artifice of eternity answerable to certain formal criteria and to certain psychological and philosophical concerns, but as a political enterprise, halfway between sermon and social theory, that both codifies and attempts to mold the values of its time.

---

2. I.e., summary of all theology (the shortened Latin form of the work by St. Thomas Aquinas of that title) [editor's note].

3. J. W. Ward, *Red, White, and Blue; Men, Books, and Ideas in American Culture* (New York: Oxford University Press, 1961), p. 75.

The power of a sentimental novel to move its audience depends upon the audience's being in possession of the conceptual categories that constitute character and event. That storehouse of assumptions includes attitudes towards the family and towards social institutions, a definition of power and its relation to individual human feeling, notions of political and social equality, and above all, a set of religious beliefs which organize and sustain the rest. Once in possession of the system of beliefs that undergirds the patterns of sentimental fiction, it is possible for modern readers to see how its tearful episodes and frequent violations of probability were invested with a structure of meanings that fixed these works, for nineteenth-century readers, not in the realm of fairy tale or escapist fantasy, but in the very bedrock of reality. I do not say that we can read sentimental fiction exactly as Stowe's audience did—that would be impossible—but that we can and should set aside the modernist prejudices which consign this fiction to oblivion, in order to see how and why it worked for its readers, in its time, with such unexampled effect.

Let us consider the episode in *Uncle Tom's Cabin* singled out by Douglas as the epitome of Victorian sentimentalism—the death of little Eva—because it is the kind of incident most offensive to the sensibilities of twentieth-century academic critics. It is on the belief that this incident is nothing more than a sob story that the whole case against sentimentalism rests. Little Eva's death, so the argument goes, like every other sentimental tale, is awash with emotion but does nothing to remedy the evils it deplores. According to Douglas, it is "essentially decorative," because it leaves the slave system and the other characters unchanged. This trivializing view of the episode is grounded in assumptions about power and reality so common that we are not even aware they have been invoked. For example, Douglas can say of little Eva with calculated irony that "her greatest act is dying" because she assumes, and expects us to assume also, that dying could not possibly be a great act.[4] But in the system of belief which undergirds Stowe's enterprise, dying is the supreme form of heroism. In *Uncle Tom's Cabin*, death is the equivalent not of defeat but of victory; it brings an access of power not a loss of it; it is not only the crowning achievement of life, it *is* life, and Stowe's entire presentation of little Eva is designed to dramatize this fact.

Stories like the death of little Eva are compelling for the same reason that the story of Christ's death is compelling; they enact a philosophy, as much political as religious, in which the pure and powerless die to save the powerful and corrupt, and thereby show themselves more powerful than those they save. They enact, in short, a *theory* of power in which the ordinary or "common sense" view of what is efficacious and what is not (a view to which Douglas and most modern critics are committed) is simply reversed, as the very possibility of social action is made dependent on the action taking place in individual hearts. Little Eva's death is not only not a "decorative" incident, it enacts the drama of which all the major episodes of the novel are transformations, the idea, central to Christian soteriology, that the highest human calling is to give one's life for another. It presents one version of the ethic of sacrifice on which the entire novel is based and contains in some form all of

---

4. Douglas, *Feminization of American Culture*, p. 2.

the motifs that, by their frequent recurrence, constitute the novel's ideological framework.

Little Eva's death, moreover, is also a transformation of stories circulating in the culture at large. It may be found, for example, in a dozen or more versions in the evangelical sermons of the Reverend Dwight Lyman Moody when he preached in Great Britain and Ireland in 1875. In one version it is called "The Child Angel" and it concerns a beautiful golden-haired girl of seven, her father's pride and joy, who dies and, by appearing to him in a dream in which she calls to him from heaven, brings him salvation.[5] The tale shows that by dying even a child can be the instrument of redemption for others, since in death she acquires a spiritual power over those who loved her beyond what she possessed in life.

The power of the dead or the dying to redeem the unregenerate is a major theme of nineteenth-century popular fiction and religious literature. Mothers and children are thought to be uniquely capable of this work. In a sketch entitled "Children" published the year after *Uncle Tom* came out Stowe writes: "Wouldst though know, o parent what is that faith which unlocks heaven? Go not to wrangling polemics, or creeds and forms of theology, but draw to thy bosom thy little one, and read in that clear trusting eye the lesson of eternal life."[6] If children because of their purity and innocence can lead adults to God while living, their spiritual power when they are dead is greater still. Death, Stowe argues in a pamphlet, entitled "Ministration of Departed Spirits," enables the Christian to begin his "real work." God takes people from us sometimes so that their "ministry can act upon us more powerfully from the unseen world."[7]

> The mother would fain electrify the heart of her child. She yearns and burns in vain to make her soul effective on its soul, and to inspire it with a spiritual and holy life; but all her own weaknesses, faults, and mortal cares, cramp and confine her till death breaks all fetters: and then, first truly alive, risen, purified, and at rest, she may do calmly, sweetly, and certainly, what, amid the tempest and tossings of her life, she labored for painfully and fitfully.[8]

When the spiritual power of death is combined with the natural sanctity of childhood, the child becomes an angel endowed with salvific force.

Most often, it is the moment of death that saves, when the dying child, glimpsing for a moment the glory of heaven, testifies to the reality of the life to come. Uncle Tom knows that this will happen when little Eva dies, and explains it to Miss Ophelia as follows:

> "You know it says in Scripture, 'At midnight there was a great cry made. Behold the bridegroom cometh.' That's what I'm spectin' now, every night, Miss Feely,—and I couldn't sleep out o' hearin' no ways."
> "Uncle Tom, what makes you think so?"
> "Miss Eva, she talks to me. The Lord, he sends his messenger in the soul. I must be thar, Miss Feely; for when that ar blessed child goes into

5. Reverend Dwight Lyman Moody, *Sermons and Addresses,* in *Narrative of Messrs. Moody and Sankey's Labors in Great Britain and Ireland with Eleven Addresses and Lectures in Full* (New York: Anson D. F. Randolph and Co., 1975).
6. "Children," in *Uncle Sam's Emancipation;*
Earthly Care, a Heavenly discipline; and other sketches (Philadelphia: W. P. Hazard, 1853), p. 83.
7. Harriet Beecher Stowe, *Ministration of Departed Spirits* (Boston: American Tract Society, n.d.), pp. 4, 3.
8. Ibid., p. 3.

the kingdom, they'll open the door so wide, we'll all get a look in at the glory, Miss Feely."[9]

Little Eva does not disappoint them. She exclaims at the moment when she passes "from death into life" "O, love!—joy!—peace!" And her exclamation echoes those of scores of children who die in Victorian fiction and sermon literature with heaven in their eyes. Dickens's Paul Dombey, seeing the face of his dead mother, dies with the words "The light about the head is shining on me as I go!" The fair, blue-eyed young girl in Lydia Sigourney's *Letters to Mothers*, "death's purple tinge upon her brow," when implored by her mother to utter one last word, whispers "Praise!"[1]

Of course, it could be argued by critics of sentimentalism that the prominence of stories about the deaths of children is precisely what is wrong with the literature of the period; rather than being cited as a source of strength, the presence of such stories in *Uncle Tom's Cabin* should be regarded as an unfortunate concession to the age's fondness for lachrymose scenes. But to dismiss such scenes as "all tears and flapdoodle" is to leave unexplained the popularity of the novels and sermons that are filled with them, unless we choose to believe that a generation of readers was unaccountably moved to tears by matters that are intrinsically silly and trivial. That popularity is better explained, I believe, by the relationship of these scenes to a pervasive cultural myth which invests the suffering and death of an innocent victim with just the kind of power that critics deny to Stowe's novel, the power to work in, and change, the world.

This is the kind of action which little Eva's death in fact performs. It proves its efficacy not through the sudden collapse of the slave system but through the conversion of Topsy, a motherless, godless black child who has up until that point successfully resisted all attempts to make her "good." Topsy will not be "good" because, never having had a mother's love, she believes that no one can love her. When Eva suggests that Miss Ophelia would love her if only she were good, Topsy cries out: "No, she can't bar[2] me, cause I'm a nigger!—she'd soon have a toad touch her! Ther can't nobody love niggers, and niggers can't do nothin'! *I* don't care."

> "O, Topsy, poor child, *I* love you!" said Eva, with a sudden burst of feeling, and laying her little thin, white hand on Topsy's shoulder; "I love you, because you haven't had any father, or mother, or friends;—because you've been a poor, abused child! I love you, and I want you to be good. I am very unwell, Topsy, and I think I shan't live a great while; and it really grieves me, to have you be so naughty. I wish you would try to be good, for my sake;—it's only a little while I shall be with you."
>
> The round, keen eyes of the black child were overcast with tears;—large, bright drops rolled heavily down one by one, and fell on the little white hand. Yes, in that moment, a ray of real belief, a ray of heavenly love, had penetrated the darkness of her heathen soul! She laid her head down between her knees, and wept and sobbed,—while the beautiful

9. Harriet Beecher Stowe, *Uncle Tom's Cabin; or, Life Among the Lowly* (New York: Harper & Row, 1965), pp. 295–96. This Harper Classic gives the text of the first edition originally published by John P. Jewett and Company of Boston and Cleveland in 1852. All future references to *Uncle Tom's Cabin* will be to this edition; page numbers are given in parentheses in the text.
1. Charles Dickens, *Dombey and Son* (Boston: Estes and Lauriat, 1882), p. 278; Lydia H. Sigourney, *Letters to Mothers* (Hartford: Hudson and Skinner, 1838).
2. I.e., bear [editor's note].

child, bending over her, looked like the picture of some bright angel stooping to reclaim a sinner. (283)

The rhetoric and imagery of this passage, its little white hand, its ray from heaven, bending angel, and plentiful tears suggest a literary version of the kind of polychrome religious picture that hangs on Sunday school walls. Words like "kitsch," "camp," and "corny" come to mind. But what is being dramatized here bears no relation to these designations. By giving Topsy her love, Eva initiates a process of redemption whose power, transmitted from heart to heart, can change the entire world. And indeed the process has begun. From that time on Topsy is "different from what she used to be" (eventually she will go to Africa and become a missionary to her entire race), and Miss Ophelia, who overhears the conversation, is different, too. When little Eva is dead and Topsy cries out "ther an't *nobody* left now," Miss Ophelia answers her in Eva's place:

> "Topsy, you poor, child," she said, as she led her into her room, "don't give up! *I* can love you, though I am not like that dear little child. I hope I've learnt something of the love of Christ from her. I can love you; I do, and I'll try to help you to grow up a good Christian girl."
>
> Miss Ophelia's voice was more than her words, and more than that were the honest tears that fell down her face. From that hour, she acquired an influence over the mind of the destitute child that she never lost. (300)

The tears of Topsy and of Miss Ophelia, which we find easy to ridicule, are the sign of redemption in *Uncle Tom's Cabin*; not words but the emotions of the heart bespeak a state of grace, and these are known by the sound of a voice, the touch of a hand, but chiefly, in moments of greatest importance, by tears. When Tom lies dying on the plantation on the Red River, the disciples to whom he has preached testify to their conversion by weeping.

> Tears had fallen on that honest, insensible face,—tears of late repentance in the poor, ignorant heathen, whom his dying love and patience had awakened to repentance. . . . (420)

Even the bitter and unregenerate Cassy, "moved by the sacrifice that had been made for her," breaks down; "moved by the few last words which the affectionate soul had yet strength to breathe, . . . the dark, despairing woman had wept and prayed" (420). When George Shelby, the son of Tom's old master, arrives too late to free him, "tears which did honor to his manly heart fell from the young man's eyes as he bent over his poor friend." And when Tom realizes who is there, "the whole face lighted up, the hard hands clasped, and tears ran down the cheeks" (420). The vocabulary of clasping hands and falling tears is one which we associate with emotional exhibitionism, with the overacting that kills true feeling off through exaggeration. But the tears and gestures of Stowe's characters are not in excess of what they feel; if anything they fall short of expressing the experiences they point to—salvation, communion, reconciliation.

* * *

Characters in the novel are linked to each other in exactly the same way that places are—with reference to a third term that is the source of their identity. The figure of Christ is the common term which unites all of the novel's good characters, who are good precisely in proportion as they are imitations of him. Eva and Tom head the list (she reenacts the Last Supper and he the crucifixion) but they are also linked to most of the slaves, women, and children in the novel by the characteristics they all share: piety, impressionability, spontaneous affection—and victimization.[3] In this scene, Eva is linked with the "spirits bright" (she later becomes a "bright immortal form") both because she can see them and is soon to join them, and because she, too, always wears white and is elsewhere several times referred to as an "angel." When Eva dies, she will join her father's mother, who was also named Evangeline, and who herself always wore white, and who, like Eva, is said to be " 'the direct and living embodiment of the New Testament.' " And this identification, in its turn, refers back to Uncle Tom who is " 'all the moral and Christian virtues bound in black morocco complete.' " The circularity of this train of association is typical of the way the narrative doubles back on itself: later on, Cassy, impersonating the ghost of Legree's saintly mother, will wrap herself in a white sheet.[4]

The scene I have been describing[5] is a node with a network of allusion in which every character and event in the novel has a place. The narrative's rhetorical strength derives in part from the impression it gives of taking every kind of detail in the world into account, from the preparation of breakfast to the orders of the angels, and investing those details with a purpose and a meaning which are both immediately apprehensible and finally significant. The novel reaches out into the reader's world and colonizes it for its own eschatology: that is, it not only incorporates the homely particulars of "Life among the Lowly" into its universal scheme, but it gives them a power and a centrality in that scheme which turns the socio-political order upside-down. The totalizing effect of the novel's iterative organization and its doctrine of spiritual redemption are inseparably bound to its political purpose—which is to bring in the day when the meek—which is to say, women—will inherit the earth.

The specifically political intent of the novel is apparent in its forms of address. Stowe addresses her readers not simply as individuals but as citizens of the United States: "to you, generous, noble-minded men and women of the South," "farmers of Massachusetts, of New Hampshire, of Vermont," "brave and generous men of New York," "and you, mothers of America." She speaks to her audience directly in the way the Old Testament prophets spoke to Israel, exhorting, praising, blaming, warning of the wrath to come. "This is

---

3. The associations that link slaves, women, and children are ubiquitous and operate on several levels. Besides being described in the same set of terms, these characters occupy parallel structural positions in the plot. They function chiefly as mediators between God and the unredeemed, so that, e.g., Mrs. Shelby intercedes for Mr. Shelby, Mrs. Bird for Senator Bird, Simon Legree's mother (unsuccessfully) for Simon Legree, Little Eva and St. Clare's mother for St. Clare, Tom Loker's mother for Tom Loker, Eliza for George Harris (spiritually, she is the agent of his conversion), and for Harry Harris (physically, she saves him from being sold down the river), and Tom for all the slaves on the Legree plantation (spiritually, he converts them) and for all the slaves of the Shelby plantation (physically, he is the cause of their being set free).

4. For a parallel example, see Alice Crozier's analysis of the way the lock of hair that little Eva gives Tom becomes transformed into the lock of hair that Simon Legree's mother sent to Simon Legree. *The Novels of Harriet Beecher Stowe* (New York: Oxford University Press, 1969), pp. 29–31.

5. Eva's conflation of Lake Ponchartrain with the "sea of glass" of the New Jerusalem (Revelation 4.6) as she sits with Tom (pp. 261–62) [editor's note].

an age of the world when nations are trembling and convulsed. Almighty influence is abroad, surging and heaving the world, as with an earthquake. And is America safe? . . . O, Church of Christ, read the signs of the times!" (451). Passages like these, descended from the revivalist rhetoric of "Sinners in the Hands of an Angry God,"[6] are intended, in the words of a noted scholar, "to direct an imperiled people toward the fulfillment of their destiny, to guide them individually towards salvation, and collectively toward the American city of God."[7]

These sentences are from Sacvan Bercovitch's *The American Jeremiad*, an influential work of modern scholarship which, although it completely ignores Stowe's novel, makes us aware that *Uncle Tom's Cabin* is a jeremiad in the fullest and truest sense. A jeremiad, in Bercovitch's definition, is "a mode of public exhortation . . . designed to join social criticism to spiritual renewal, public to private identity, the shifting 'signs of the times' to certain traditional metaphors, themes, and symbols."[8] (I must note here, parenthetically, that invaluable as Bercovitch's book is, it provides a striking instance of how totally academic criticism has foreclosed on sentimental fiction; since, even when a sentimental novel fulfills a man's theory to perfection, he cannot see it. For him the work doesn't even exist.) Despite the fact that his study takes no note of the most obvious and compelling instance of the jeremiad since the Great Awakening, Bercovitch's description in fact provides an excellent account of the combination of elements that made Stowe's novel work: among its characters, settings, situations, symbols, and doctrines, the novel establishes a set of correspondences which, as I have indicated, unite the disparate realms of experience Bercovitch names—social and spiritual, public and private, theological and political—*and*, through the vigor of its representations, attempts to move the nation as a whole toward the vision it proclaims.

The tradition of the jeremiad throws light on *Uncle Tom's Cabin* because Stowe's novel was political in exactly the same way the jeremiad was: both were forms of discourse in which "theology was wedded to politics and politics to the progress of the kingdom of God."[9] In her attack on sentimentalism, Ann Douglas argues that the sentimental writers were "profoundly disaffected from politics," "self-immersed and self-congratulatory," cut off from any "awareness of class and interest, of societal structure, which genuine political consciousness fosters." She contrasts their work unfavorably to that of the Puritan theologians and the American romantics, who "clearly [had] a genuinely political and historical sense."[1] This judgment, which stems from an inordinately narrow view of politics, misunderstands the relationship between discourse and power which the jeremiad presupposes. The jeremiad strives to persuade its listeners to a providential view of human history which serves, among other things, to maintain the Puritan theocracy in power. Its fusion of theology and politics is not only doctrinal, in that it ties the salvation of the individual to the community's historical enterprise, it is practical as well, for it reflects the interests of Puritan ministers in their bid to retain

---

6. A famous sermon delivered in 1741 by the New England Congregational minister Jonathan Edwards, whose fervid preaching started the Great Awakening—a series of religious revivals in the colonies [editor's note].
7. Sacvan Bercovitch, *The American Jeremiad* (Madison: University of Wisconsin Press, 1978), p. 9.
8. Ibid., p. xi.
9. Ibid., p. xiv.
1. Douglas, *Feminization of American Culture*, pp. 306–7.

spiritual and secular authority. The sentimental novel, too, is an act of persuasian aimed at defining social reality; the difference is that the jeremiad represents the interests of Puritan ministers, while the sentimental novel represents the interests of middle-class women. But the relationship between rhetoric and history in both cases is the same. In both cases it is not as if rhetoric and history stand opposed, with rhetoric made up of wish-fulfillment and history made up of recalcitrant facts that resist rhetoric's onslaught. Rhetoric *makes* history by shaping reality to the dictates of its political design; it makes history by convincing the people of the world that its description of the world is the true one. The sentimental novelists make their bid for power by positing the kingdom of heaven on earth as a world over which women exercise ultimate control. If history did not take the course these writers recommended, it is not because they were not political, but because they were insufficiently persuasive.

Uncle Tom's Cabin, however, unlike its counterparts in the sentimental tradition, was spectacularly persuasive in conventional political terms: it convinced a nation to go to war and to free its slaves. But in terms of its own conception of power, a conception it shares with other sentimental fiction, the novel was a political failure. Stowe conceived her book as an instrument for bringing about the day when the world would be ruled not by force but by Christian love. The novel's deepest political aspirations are expressed only secondarily in its devastating attack on the slave system; the true goal of Stowe's rhetorical undertaking is nothing less than the institution of the kingdom of heaven on earth. Embedded in the world of *Uncle Tom's Cabin*, which is the fallen world of slavery, there appears an idyllic picture, both utopian and Arcadian, of the form human life would assume if Stowe's readers were to heed her moral lesson. In this vision, described in the chapter entitled "The Quaker Settlement," Christian love fulfills itself not in war but in daily living, and the principle of sacrifice is revealed not in crucifixion but in motherhood. The form that society takes bears no resemblance to the current social order. Man-made institutions—the church, the courts of law, the legislatures, the economic system—are nowhere in sight. The home is the center of all meaningful activity, women perform the most important tasks, work is carried on in a spirit of mutual cooperation, and the whole is guided by a Christian woman who, through the influence of her "loving words," "gentle moralities," and "motherly loving kindness," rules the world.

Stowe locates her domestic Eden in the center of the American continent—Indiana—and in a rural environment, for not the commercial or industrial but the agricultural mode of life is her economic model. The Quaker community which surrounds and mirrors the home is specifically religious, pacifist, and egalitarian. As the home is the center of the community and the community of the nation, so the kitchen is the center of the home, and at *its* center Stowe locates the symbol of maternal comfort, the rocking chair, throne of the presiding deity. The rocking chair is "motherly and old," its "wide arms breathed hospitable invitation, seconded by the solicitation of its feather cushions,—a real comfortable, persuasive old chair, and worth, in the way of honest, homely enjoyment, a dozen of your plush or brochetelle drawing-room gentry" (135). The image is ideologically charged in a manner typical of Stowe's narrative. Metonymically, the rocking chair stands for the mother and therefore gathers to itself the cluster of associations which the novel has already established around the maternal figure. Ontologically, it represents the "real" thing, as opposed to gaudier versions of itself which, with their plush and brochetelle, exist for appearance's sake. By contrast with the drawing room "gentry," the rocking chair, "old" and "homely," is identified with the lower social orders, but despite this association (though in fact because of it) the rocking chair is morally superior because it affords "honest . . . enjoyment." It performs genuine service since its wide arms and feather cushions offer comfort and "hospitable invitation." And finally, towards the end of the description, the chair attains the status of a mystical object; its "creechy crawchy" sounds are "music":

> For why? for twenty years or more, nothing but loving words and gentle moralities, and motherly loving kindness, had come from that chair;— head-aches and heart-aches innumerable had been cured there,—difficulties spiritual and temporal solved there,—all by one good, loving woman, God bless her! (136)

The woman in question *is* God in human form. Seated in her kitchen at the head of her table, passing out coffee and cake for breakfast, Rachel Halliday, the millenarian counterpart of little Eva, enacts the redeemed form of the Last Supper. This is Holy Communion as it will be under the new dispensation: instead of the breaking of bones, the breaking of bread. The preparation of breakfast exemplifies the way people will work in the ideal society; there will be no competition, no exploitation, no commands. Motivated by self-sacrificing love, and joined to one another by its cohesive power, people will perform their duties willingly and with pleasure: moral suasion will take the place of force. "All moved obediently to Rachel's gentle 'Thee had better,' or more gentle 'Hadn't thee better?' in the work of getting breakfast. . . . Everything went on so sociably, so quietly, so harmoniously, in the great kitchen,—it seemed so pleasant to everyone to do just what they were doing, there was an atmosphere of mutual confidence and good fellowship everywhere" (141–42).

The new matriarchy which Isabella Beecher Hooker[2] had dreamed of leading, pictured here in the Indiana kitchen ("for a breakfast in the luxurious valleys of Indiana is . . . like picking up the rose-leaves and trimming the bushes in Paradise") constitutes the most politically subversive dimension of Stowe's novel, more disruptive and far-reaching in its potential consequences then even the starting of a war or the freeing of slaves. Nor is the ideal of matriarchy simply a daydream; Catherine Beecher, Stowe's elder sister, had offered a groundplan for the realization of such a vision in her *Treatise on Domestic Economy* (1841), which the two sisters republished in an enlarged version entitled *The American Woman's Home* in 1869.[3] Dedicated "To the Women

---

2. Harriet Beecher Stowe's half-sister; she is mentioned in the omitted introduction of this essay [editor's note].

3. For an excellent discussion of Beecher's *Treatise* and of the entire cult of domesticity, see Kathryn Kish Sklar, *Catherine Beecher, A Study in American Domesticity* (New York: W. W. Norton, 1976). Copyright, 1973, by Yale University. For other helpful discussions of the topic, see Barbara G. Berg, *The Remembered Gate: Origins of American Feminism, The Woman and the City, 1800–1860* (New York: Oxford University Press, 1978); Sandra Sizer, *Gospel Hymns and Social Religion* (Philadelphia: Temple University Press, 1979); Ronald G. Walters, *The Antislavery Appeal, American Abolitionism after 1830* (Baltimore: Johns Hopkins University Press, 1976); and Barbara Welter, "The Cult of True Womanhood, 1820–1860," *American Quarterly* 18 (1966): 151–74.

of America, in whose hands rest the real destinies of the republic," this is an instructional book on homemaking in which a wealth of scientific information and practical advice are pointed toward a millenarian goal. Centering on the home, for these women, is not a way of indulging in narcissistic fantasy, as Douglas has argued, or a turning away from the world into self-absorption and idle reverie, it is the prerequisite of world conquest—defined as the reformation of the human race through the proper care and nurturing of its young. Like *Uncle Tom's Cabin*, *The American Woman's Home* situates the minutiae of domestic life in relation to their soteriological function: "What, then is the end designed by the family state which Jesus Christ came into this world to secure? It is to provide for the training of our race . . . by means of the self-sacrificing labors of the wise and good . . . with chief reference to a future immortal existence."[4] "The family state," the authors announce at the beginning, "is the aptest earthly illustration of the heavenly kingdom, and . . . woman is its chief minister."[5] In the body of the text the authors provide women with everything they need to know for the proper establishment and maintenance of home and family, from the construction of furniture ("The bed frame is to be fourteen inches wide, and three inches in thickness. At the head, and at the foot, is to be screwed a notched two-inch board, three inches wide, as in Fig. 8"), to architectural plans, to chapters of instruction on heating, ventilation, lighting, healthful diet, the preparation of food, cleanliness, the making and mending of clothes, the care of the sick, the organization of routines, financial management, psychological health, the care of infants, the managing of young children, home amusement, the care of furniture, planting gardens, the care of domestic animals, the disposal of waste, the cultivation of fruit, and providing for "the helpless, the homeless, and the vicious." After each of these activities has been treated in detail, they conclude by describing the ultimate aim of the domestic enterprise. The founding of a "truly 'Christian family' " will lead to the gathering of a "Christian neighborhood." This "cheering example," they continue:

> would soon spread, and ere long colonies from these prosperous and Christian communities would go forth to shine as "lights of the world" in all the now darkened nations. Thus the "Christian family" and "Christian neighborhood" would become the grand ministry, as they were designed to be, in training our whole race for heaven.[6]

The imperialistic drive behind the encyclopedism and determined practicality of this household manual flatly contradicts Douglas's picture of the American cult of domesticity as a "mirror-phenomenon," "self-immersed" and "self-congratulatory." *The American Woman's Home* is a blueprint for colonizing the world in the name of the "family state" under the leadership of Christian women. What is more, people like Stowe and Catherine Beecher were speaking not simply for a set of moral and religious values. In speaking for the home, they speak for an economy—household economy—which had

4. Catherine Beecher and Harriet Beecher Stowe, *The American Woman's Home: or, Principles of Domestic Science; Being a Guide to the Formation and Maintenance of Economical, Healthful, Beau-* *tiful, and Christian Homes* (New York: J. B. Ford and Co., 1869), p. 18.
5. Ibid., p. 19.
6. Ibid., pp. 458–59.

supported New England life since its inception. The home, rather than representing a retreat or a refuge from a crass industrial-commercial world, offers an economic *alternative* to that world, one which calls into question the whole structure of American society that was growing up in response to the increase in trade and manufacturing.[7] Stowe's image of a Utopian community as presented in Rachel Halliday's kitchen is not simply a Christian dream of communitarian cooperation and harmony, it is a reflection of the real communitarian practices of village life, practices which had depended upon cooperation, trust, and a spirit of mutuality. In order to sustain themselves economically, rural communities had had not merely to dream but to practice the reciprocity and mutual supportiveness that characterize the Quaker community in Stowe's novel.

One could argue, then, that for all its revolutionary fervor *Uncle Tom's Cabin* is a conservative book, because it advocates a return to an older way of life—household economy—in the name of the nation's most cherished social and religious beliefs. Even the woman's centrality might be seen as harking back to the "age of homespun" when the essential goods were manufactured in the home and their production was carried out and guided by women. But Stowe's very conservatism—her reliance on established patterns of living and traditional beliefs—is precisely what gives her novel its revolutionary potential. By pushing those beliefs to an extreme and by insisting that they be applied universally, not just to one segregated corner of civil life but to the conduct of all human affairs, Stowe means to effect a radical transformation of her society. The brilliance of the strategy is that it puts the central affirmations of a culture into the service of a vision that would destroy the present economic and social institutions; by resting her case, absolutely, on the saving power of Christian love and on the sanctity of motherhood and the family, Stowe relocates the center of power in American life, placing it not in the government, nor in the courts of law, nor in the factories, nor in the marketplace, but in the kitchen. And that means that the new society will not be controlled by men but by women. The image of the home created by Stowe and Catherine Beecher in their treatise on domestic science is in no sense a shelter from the stormy blast of economic and political life, a haven from reality divorced from fact which allows the machinery of industrial capitalism to grind on; it is conceived as a dynamic center of activity, physical and spiritual, economic and moral, whose influence spreads out in everwidening circles. To this activity—and this is the crucial innovation—men are incidental. Although the Beecher sisters pay lip service on occasion to male supremacy, women's roles occupy virtually the whole of their attention and dominate the scene. Male provender is deemphasized in favor of female processing. Men provide the seed but women bear and raise the children. Men provide the flour but women bake the bread and get the breakfast. The removal of the male from the center to the periphery of the human sphere is the most radical component of this mil-

7. For a detailed discussion of the changes referred to here, see Christopher Clark, "Household Economy, Market Exchange and the Rise of Capitalism in the Connecticut Valley, 1800–1860," *Journal of Social History* 13, no. 2 (Winter 1979): 169–89, and Nancy F. Cott, *The Bonds of Womanhood: "Woman's Sphere" in New England, 1780–1835* (New Haven: Yale University Press, 1977).

lenarian scheme which is rooted so solidly in the most traditional values—religion, motherhood, home, and family. Exactly what position men will occupy in the millenium is specified by a detail inserted casually into Stowe's description of the Indiana kitchen. While the women and children are busy preparing breakfast, Simeon Halliday, the husband and father, stands "in his shirt-sleeves before a little looking-glass in the corner, engaged in the anti-patriarchal activity of shaving" (141–42).

With this detail, so innocently placed, Stowe reconceives the role of men in human history: while Negroes, children, mothers, and grandmothers do the world's primary work, men groom themselves contentedly in a corner. The scene, as Douglas notes is often the case in sentimental fiction, is "intimate," the backdrop is "domestic," the tone at times is even "chatty"; but the import, as Douglas does not recognize, is world-shaking. The enterprise of sentimental fiction, as Stowe's novel attests, is anything but domestic, in the sense of being limited to purely personal concerns; its mission, on the contrary, is global and its interests identical with the interests of the race. If the fiction written in the nineteenth century by women whose works sold in the hundreds of thousands has seemed narrow and parochial to the critics of the twentieth century, that narrowness and parochialism belong not to these works nor to the women who wrote them; they are the beholders' share.[8]

1981

8. In a recent article in *Signs*, "The Sentimentalists: Promise and Betrayal in the Home," Mary Kelley characterizes the main positions in the debate over the significance of sentimental fiction as follows: (1) the Cowie-Welter thesis, which holds that women's fiction expresses an "ethics of conformity" and accepts the stereotype of the woman as pious, pure, submissive, and dedicated to the home, and (2) the Papashvily-Garrison thesis, which sees sentimental fiction as profoundly subversive of traditional ideas of male authority and female subservience. Kelley locates herself somewhere in between, holding that sentimental novels convey a "contradictory message": "they tried to project an Edenic image," Kelley writes, but their own tales "subverted their intentions," by showing how often women were frustrated and defeated in the performance of their heroic roles. My own position is that the sentimental novelists are both conformist and subversive, but not, as Kelley believes, in a self-contradictory way. They used the central myth of their culture—the story of Christ's death for the sins of mankind—as the basis for a new myth which reflected their own interests. They regarded their vision of the Christian home as God's kingdom on earth as the fulfillment of the Gospel, "the end . . . which Jesus Christ came into this world to secure," in exactly the same way that the Puritans believed that their mission was to found the "American city of God," and that Christians believe the New Testament to be a fulfillment of the old. Revolutionary ideologies, typically, announce themselves as the fulfillment of old promises or as a return to a golden age. What I am suggesting here, in short, is that the argument over whether the sentimental novelists were radical or conservative is a false issue. The real problem is how we, in the light of everything that has happened since they wrote, can understand and appreciate their work. Mary Kelley, "The Sentimentalists: Promise and Betrayal in the Home," *Signs* 4, no. 3 (Spring 1979): 434–46; Alexander Cowie, "The Vogue of the Domestic Novel, 1850–1870," *South Atlantic Quarterly* 41 (October 1942): 420; Barbara Welter, "The Cult of True Womanhood: 1820–1860," *American Quarterly* 18 (Summer 1966): 151–74; Helen Waite Papashvily, *All the Happy Endings: A Study of the Domestic Novel in America, the Women Who Wrote It, the Women Who Read It, in the Nineteenth Century* (New York: Harper and Bros., 1956); Dee Garrison, "Immoral Fiction in the Late Victorian Library," *American Quarterly* 28 (Spring 1976): 71–80.

ELAINE SHOWALTER
b. 1941

Elaine Showalter's edited volume *Women's Liberation and Literature* (1971) has been credited as being the first textbook on women in literature. Currently retired from the English Department at Princeton University, she has played a central role in the establishment of the academic fields of women's literature and feminist criticism. In *A Literature of Their Own: British Women Novelists from Brontë to Lessing* (1977) and in a number of groundbreaking essays, she began to conceptualize not only the periods of women's literary history but also the stages in feminist literary criticism as well as their relationship to the stages in African American literary criticism. Particularly interested and trained in the history of medicine, Showalter has examined physical and mental diseases in such volumes as *The Female Malady: Women, Madness, and English Culture, 1830–1980* (1985) and the controversial *Hystories: Hysterical Epidemics and Modern Culture* (1997); however, she has also continued to publish extensively on women's literature (in *Sister's Choice: Tradition and Change in American Women's Writing,* 1991), on the sexual politics of late-nineteenth- and early-twentieth-century culture (in *Sexual Anarchy: Gender and Culture at the Fin-de-Siècle,* 1990), and on the history of feminism itself (in *Inventing Herself: Claiming a Feminist Intellectual Heritage,* 2001). In 2005–06, she was Avery Fellow at the Huntington Library, where she worked on the literary history of American women writers from 1650 to 2000 for an anthology to be published by Knopf.

From Feminist Criticism in the Wilderness

From *Pluralism and the Feminist Critique*

* * *

There are two distinct modes of feminist criticism, and to conflate them (as most commentators do) is to remain permanently bemused by their theoretical potentialities. The first mode is ideological; it is concerned with the feminist as *reader,* and it offers feminist readings of texts which consider the images and stereotypes of women in literature, the omissions and misconceptions about women in criticism, and woman-assign in semiotic systems. This is not all feminist reading can do; it can be a liberating intellectual act, as Adrienne Rich proposes:

> A radical critique of literature, feminist in its impulse, would take the work first of all as a clue to how we live, how we have been living, how we have been led to imagine ourselves, how our language has trapped as well as liberated us, how the very act of naming has been till now a male prerogative, and how we can begin to see and name—and therefore live—afresh.[1]

This invigorating encounter with literature, which I will call *feminist reading* or the *feminist critique,* is in essence a mode of interpretation, one of

1. Adrienne Rich, "When We Dead Awaken: Writing as Re-Vision," [except as indicated, all notes are Showalter] *On Lies Secrets, and Silence* (New York: W. W. Norton, 1979), p. 35.

many which any complex text will accommodate and permit. It is very difficult to propose theoretical coherence in an activity which by its nature is so eclectic and wide-ranging, although as a critical practice feminist reading has certainly been very influential. But in the free play of the interpretive field, the feminist critique can only compete with alternative readings, all of which have the built-in obsolescence of Buicks, cast away as newer readings take their place. As [Annette] Kolodny, the most sophisticated theorist of feminist interpretation, has conceded:

> All the feminist is asserting, then, is her own equivalent right to liberate new (and perhaps different) significances from these same texts; and, at the same time, her right to choose which features of a text she takes as relevant because she is, after all, asking new and different questions of it. In the process, she claims neither definitiveness nor structural completeness for her different readings and reading systems, but only their usefulness in recognizing the particular achievements of woman-as-author and their applicability in conscientiously decoding woman-as-sign.

Rather than being discouraged by these limited objectives, Kolodny found them the happy cause of the "playful pluralism" of feminist critical theory, a pluralism which she believes to be "the only critical stance consistent with the current status of the larger women's movement."[2] Her feminist critic dances adroitly through the theoretical minefield.

Keenly aware of the political issues involved and presenting brilliant arguments, Kolodny nonetheless fails to convince me that feminist criticism must altogether abandon its hope "of establishing some basic conceptual model." If we see our critical job as interpretation and reinterpretation, we must be content with pluralism as our critical stance. But if we wish to ask questions about the process and the contexts of writing, if we genuinely wish to define ourselves to the uninitiated, we cannot rule out the prospect of theoretical consensus at this early stage.

All feminist criticism is in some sense revisionist, questioning the adequacy of accepted conceptual structures, and indeed most contemporary American criticism claims to be revisionist too. The most exciting and comprehensive case for this "revisionary imperative" is made by Sandra Gilbert: at its most ambitious, she asserts, feminist criticism "wants to decode and demystify all the disguised questions and answers that have always shadowed the connections between textuality and sexuality, genre and gender, psychosexual identity and cultural authority."[3] But in practice, the revisionary feminist critique is redressing a grievance and is built upon exist

2. Annette Kolodny, "Dancing through the Minefield: Some Observations on the Theory, Practice, and Politics of a Feminist Literary Criticism," in *The New Feminist Criticism: Essays on Women, Literature, and* Theory, ed. Elaine Showalter (New York: anthem, 1985), p. 160. The complete theoretical case for a feminist hermeneutics is outlined in Kolodny's essays, including "Some Notes on Defining a 'Feminist Literary Criticism,'" *Critical Inquiry* 2 (Autumn 1975): 75–92; "A Map for Rereading; or, Gender and the Interpretation of Literary Texts," in *The New Feminist Critic* pp. 46–62; and "The Theory of Feminist Criticism" (paper delivered at the National Center for the Humanities Conference on Feminist Criticism, Research Triangle Park, N.C., March 1981).

3. Sandra M. Gilbert, "What Do Feminist Critics Want? A Postcard from the Volcano," in *The New Feminist Criticism* p. 36.

ing models. No one would deny that feminist criticism has affinities to other contemporary critical practices and methodologies and that the best work is also the most fully informed. Nonetheless, the feminist obsession with correcting, modifying, supplementing, revising, humanizing, or even attacking male critical theory keeps us dependent upon it and retards our progress in solving our own theoretical problems. What I mean here by "male critical theory" is a concept of creativity, literary history, or literary interpretation based entirely on male experience and put forward as universal. So long as we look to androcentric models for our most basic principles—even if we revise them by adding the feminist frame of reference—we are learning nothing new. And when the process is so one-sided, when male critics boast of their ignorance of feminist criticism, it is disheartening to find feminist critics still anxious for approval from the "white fathers" who will not listen or reply. Some feminist critics have taken upon themselves a revisionism which becomes a kind of homage; they have made Lacan the ladies' man of *Diacritics* and have forced Pierre Macherey into those dark alleys of the psyche where Engels feared to tread. According to Christiane Makward, the problem is even more serious in France than in the United States: "If neofeminist thought in France seems to have ground to a halt," she writes, "it is because it has continued to feed on the discourse of the masters."[4]

It is time for feminist criticism to decide whether between religion and revision we can claim any firm theoretical ground of our own. In calling for a feminist criticism that is genuinely women centered, independent, and intellectually coherent, I do not mean to endorse the separatist fantasies of radical feminist visionaries or to exclude from our critical practice a variety of intellectual tools. But we need to ask much more searchingly what we want to know and how we can find answers to the questions that come from *our* experience. I do not think that feminist criticism can find a usable past in the androcentric critical tradition. It has more to learn from women's studies than from English studies, more to learn from international feminist theory than from another seminar on the masters. It must find its own subject, its own system, its own theory, and its own voice. As Rich writes of Emily Dickinson, in her poem "I Am in Danger—Sir—," we must choose to have the argument out at last on our own premises.

Defining the Feminine: Gynocritics and the Woman's Text

> *A woman's writing is always feminine; it cannot help being feminine; at its best it is most feminine; the only difficulty lies in defining what we mean by feminine.*
>
> Virginia Woolf[5]

---

4. Christiane Makward, "To Be or Not to Be . . . A Feminist Speaker," in *The Future of Difference*, ed. Hester Eisenstein and Alice Jardine (Boston: G. K. Hall, 1980), p. 102. On Lacan, see Jane Gallop, "The Ladies' Man," *Diacritics* 6 (Winter 1976): 28–

34; on Macherey, see the Marxist-Feminist Literature Collective's "Women's Writing," *Ideology and Consciousness* 3 (Spring 1978): 27–48.
5. Woolf, "Women Novelists" (1918) [editor's note].

> *It is impossible to define a feminine practice of writing, and this is an impossibility that will remain, for this practice will never be theorized, enclosed, encoded—which doesn't mean that it doesn't exist.*
> Hélène Cixous, "The Laugh of the Medusa"

In the past decade, I believe, this process of defining the feminine has started to take place. Feminist criticism has gradually shifted its center from revisionary readings to a sustained investigation of literature by women. The second mode of feminist criticism engendered by this process is the study of women *as writers*, and its subjects are the history, styles, themes, genres, and structures of writing by women; the psychodynamics of female creativity; the trajectory of the individual or collective female career; and the evolution and laws of a female literary tradition. No English term exists for such a specialized critical discourse, and so I have invented the term "gynocritics." Unlike the feminist critique, gynocritics offers many theoretical opportunities. To see women's writing as our primary subject forces us to make the leap to a new conceptual vantage point and to redefine the nature of the theoretical problem before us. It is no longer the ideological dilemma of reconciling revisionary pluralisms but the essential question of difference. How can we constitute women as a distinct literary group? What is *the difference* of women's writing?

Patricia Meyer Spacks, I think, was the first academic critic to notice this shift from an androcentric to a gynocentric feminist criticism. In *The Female Imagination* (1975), she pointed out that few feminist theorists had concerned themselves with women's writing. Simone de Beauvoir's treatment of women writers in *The Second Sex* "always suggests an a priori tendency to take them less seriously than their masculine counterparts"; Mary Ellmann, in *Thinking about Women*, characterized women's literary success as escape from the categories of womanhood; and, according to Spacks, Kate Millett, in *Sexual Politics*, "has little interest in woman imaginative writers."[6] Spacks' wide-ranging study inaugurated a new period of feminist literary history and criticism which asked, again and again, how women's writing had been different, how womanhood itself shaped women's creative expression. In such books as Ellen Moers's *Literary Women* (1976), my *A Literature of Their Own* (1977), Nina Baym's *Woman's Fiction* (1978), Sandra Gilbert and Susan Gubar's *The Madwoman in the Attic* (1979), and Margaret Homans's *Women Writers and Poetic Identity* (1980), and in hundreds of essays and papers, women's writing asserted itself as the central project of feminist literary study.

This shift in emphasis has also taken place in European feminist criticism. To date, most commentary on French feminist critical discourse has stressed its fundamental dissimilarity from the empirical American orientation, its unfamiliar intellectual grounding in linguistics, Marxism, neo-Freudian and Lacanian psychoanalysis, and Derridean deconstruction. Despite these differences, however, the new French feminisms have much in common with radical American feminist theories in terms of intellectual affiliations and

---

6. Patricia Meyer Spacks, *The Female Imagination* (New York: Alfred A. Knopf, 1975), pp. 19, 32.

rhetorical energies. The concept of *écriture féminine,* the inscription of the female body and female difference in language and text, is a significant theoretical formulation in French feminist criticism, although it describes a Utopian possibility rather than a literary practice. Hélène Cixous, one of the leading advocates of *écriture féminine*, has admitted that, with only a few exceptions, "there has not yet been any writing that inscribes femininity," and Nancy Miller explains that *écriture féminine* "privileges a textuality of the avant-garde, a literary production of the late twentieth century, and it is therefore fundamentally a hope, if not a blueprint, for the future."[7] Nonetheless, the concept of *écriture féminine* provides a way of talking about women's writing which reasserts the *value* of the feminine and identifies the theoretical project of feminist criticism as the analysis of difference. In recent years, the translations of important work by Julia Kristeva, Cixous, and Luce Irigaray and the excellent collection *New French Feminisms* have made French criticism much more accessible to American feminist scholars.[8]

English feminist criticism, which incorporates French feminist and Marxist theory but is more traditionally oriented to textual interpretation, is also moving toward a focus on women's writing.[9] The emphasis in each country falls somewhat differently: English feminist criticism, essentially Marxist, stresses oppression; French feminist criticism, essentially psychoanalytic, stresses repression; American feminist criticism, essentially textual, stresses expression. All, however, have become gynocentric. All are struggling to find a terminology that can rescue the feminine from its stereotypical associations with inferiority.

Defining the unique difference of women's writing, as Woolf and Cixous have warned, must present a slippery and demanding task. Is difference a matter of style? Genre? Experience? Or is it produced by the reading process, as some textual critics would maintain? Spacks calls the difference of women's writing a "delicate divergency," testifying to the subtle and elusive nature of the feminine practice of writing. Yet the delicate divergency of the woman's text challenges us to respond with equal delicacy and precision to the small but crucial deviations, the cumulative weightings of experience and exclusion, that have marked the history of women's writing. Before we can chart this history, we must uncover it, patiently and scrupulously; our theories must be firmly grounded in reading and research. But we have the opportunity, through gynocritics, to learn something solid, enduring, and real about the relation of women to literary culture.

Theories of women's writing presently make use of four models of difference: biological, linguistic, psychoanalytic, and cultural. Each is an effort to

7. Hélène Cixous, "The Laugh of the Medusa," trans. Keith and Paula Cohen, *Signs* 1 (Summer 1976): 878. Nancy K. Miller, "Emphasis Added: Plots and Plausibilities in Women's Fiction," in *The New Feminist Criticism*, pp. 339–60.
8. For an overview, see Domna C. Stanton, "Language and Revolution: The Franco-American Disconnection," in Eisenstein and Jardine, *Future of Difference*, pp. 73–87, and Elaine Marks and Isabelle de Courtivron, eds., *New French Feminisms* (Amherst: University of Massachusetts Press, 1979); all further references to *New French Feminisms,* abbreviated *NFF,* will hereafter be included with translator's name parenthetically in the text.
9. Two major works are the manifesto of the Marxist-Feminist Literature Collective, "Women's Writing," and the papers from the Oxford University lectures on women and literature, Mary Jacobus, ed., *Women Writing and Writing about Women* (New York: Barnes & Noble Imports, 1979).

define and differentiate the qualities of the woman writer and the woman's text; each model also represents a school of gynocentric feminist criticism with its own favorite texts, styles, and methods. They overlap but are roughly sequential in that each incorporates the one before. I shall try now to sort out the various terminologies and assumptions of these four models of difference and evaluate their usefulness.

Women's Writing and Woman's Body

More body, hence more writing.
Cixous, "The Laugh of the Medusa"

Organic or biological criticism is the most extreme statement of gender difference, of a text indelibly marked by the body: anatomy is textuality. Biological criticism is also one of the most sibylline and perplexing theoretical formulations of feminist criticism. Simply to invoke anatomy risks a return to the crude essentialism, the phallic and ovarian theories of art, that oppressed women in the past. Victorian physicians believed that women's physiological functions diverted about twenty percent of their creative energy from brain activity. Victorian anthropologists believed that the frontal lobes of the male brain were heavier and more developed than female lobes and thus that women were inferior in intelligence.

While feminist criticism rejects the attribution of literal biological inferiority, some theorists seem to have accepted the *metaphorical* implications of female biological difference in writing. In *The Madwoman in the Attic*, for example, Gilbert and Gubar structure their analysis of women's writing around metaphors of literary paternity. "In patriarchal western culture," they maintain, ". . . the text's author is a father, a progenitor, a procreator, an aesthetic patriarch whose pen is an instrument of generative power like his penis." Lacking phallic authority, they go on to suggest, women's writing is profoundly marked by the anxieties of this difference: "If the pen is a metaphorical penis, from what organ can females generate texts?"[1]

To this rhetorical question Gilbert and Gubar offer no reply; but it is a serious question of much feminist theoretical discourse. Those critics who, like myself, would protest the fundamental analogy might reply that women generate texts from the brain or that the word-processor, with its compactly coded microchips, its inputs and outputs, is a metaphorical womb. The metaphor of literary paternity, as Auerbach has pointed out in her review of *The Madwoman*, ignores "an equally timeless and, for me, even more oppressive metaphorical equation between literary creativity and childbirth."[2] Certainly metaphors of literary *maternity* predominated in the eighteenth and nineteenth centuries; the process of literary creation is analogically much more similar to gestation, labor, and delivery than it is to insemination. Describing Thackeray's plan for *Henry Esmond*, for example, Douglas Jerrold jovially remarked, "You have heard, I suppose, that Thackeray is big with twenty parts, and unless he is wrong in his time, expects the first installment

1. Sandra M. Gilbert and Susan Gubar, *The Madwoman in the Attic: The Woman Writer and the Nineteenth-Century Literary Imagination* (New Haven, Conn.: Yale University Press, 1979), pp. 6, 7.
2. Nina Auerbach, review of *Madwoman, Victorian Studies* 23 (Summer 1980): 506.

at Christmas."[3] (If to write is metaphorically to give birth, from what organ can males generate texts?)

Some radical feminist critics, primarily in France but also in the United States, insist that we must read these metaphors as more than playful; that we must seriously rethink and redefine biological differentiation and its relation to women's writing. They argue that "women's writing proceeds from the body, that our sexual differentiation is also our source."[4] In *Of Woman Born*, Rich explains her belief that

> female biology . . . has far more radical implications than we have yet come to appreciate. Patriarchal thought has limited female biology to its own narrow specifications. The feminist vision has recoiled from female biology for these reasons; it will, I believe, come to view our physicality as a resource rather than a destiny. In order to live a fully human life, we require not only *control* of our bodies . . . we must touch the unity and resonance of our physicality, the corporeal ground of our intelligence.[5]

Feminist criticism written in the biological perspective generally stresses the importance of the body as a source of imagery. Alicia Ostriker, for example, argues that contemporary American women poets use a franker, more pervasive anatomical imagery than their male counterparts and that this insistent body language refuses the spurious transcendence that comes at the price of denying the flesh. In a fascinating essay on Whitman and Dickinson, Terence Diggory shows that physical nakedness, so potent a poetic symbol of authenticity for Whitman and other male poets, had very different connotations for Dickinson and her successors, who associated nakedness with the objectified or sexually exploited female nude and who chose instead protective images of the armored self.[6]

Feminist criticism which itself tries to be biological, to write from the critic's body, has been intimate, confessional, often innovative in style and form. Rachel Blau DuPlessis's "Washing Blood," the introduction to a special issue of *Feminist Studies* on the subject of motherhood, proceeds, in short lyrical paragraphs, to describe her own experience in adopting a child, to recount her dreams and nightmares, and to meditate upon the "healing unification of body and mind based not only on the lived experiences of motherhood as a social institution . . . but also on a biological power speaking through us."[7] Such criticism makes itself defiantly vulnerable, virtually bares its throat to the knife, since our professional taboos against self-revelation are

3. Douglas Jerrold, quoted in Kathleen Tillotson, *Novels of the Eighteen-Forties* (London: Oxford University Press, 1961), p. 39 n. James Joyce imagined the creator as female and literary creation as a process of gestation; see Richard Ellmann, *James Joyce: A Biography* (London: Oxford University Press, 1959), pp. 306–8.
4. Carolyn G. Burke, "Report from Paris: Women's Writing and the Women's Movement," *Signs* 3 (Summer 1978): 851.
5. Adrienne Rich, *Of Woman Born: Motherhood as Experience and Institution* (New York: W. W. Norton, 1976), p. 62. Biofeminist criticism has been influential in other disciplines as well: e.g., art critics, such as Judy Chicago and Lucy Lippard, have suggested that women artists are compelled to use a uterine or vaginal iconography of centralized focus, curved lines, and tactile or sensuous forms. See Lippard, *From the Center: Feminist Essays on Women's Art* (New York: E. P. Dutton, 1976).
6. See Alicia Ostriker, "Body Language: Imagery of the Body in Women's Poetry," in *The State of the Language*, ed. Leonard Michaels and Christopher Ricks (Berkeley: University of California Press, 1980), pp. 247–63, and Terence Diggory, "Armoured Women, Naked Men: Dickinson, Whitman, and Their Successors," in *Shakespeare's Sisters: Feminist Essays on Women Poets*, ed. Sandra M. Gilbert and Susan Gubar (Bloomington: Indiana University Press, 1979), pp. 135–50.
7. Rachel Blau DuPlessis, "Washing Blood," *Feminist Studies* 4 (June 1978): 10. The entire issue is an important document of feminist criticism.

so strong. When it succeeds, however, it achieves the power and the dignity of art. Its existence is an implicit rebuke to women critics who continue to write, according to Rich, "from somewhere outside their female bodies." In comparison to this flowing confessional criticism, the tight-lipped Olympian intelligence of such texts as Elizabeth Hardwick's *Seduction and Betrayal* or Susan Sontag's *Illness as Metaphor* can seem arid and strained.

Yet in its obsessions with the "corporeal ground of our intelligence," feminist biocriticism can also become cruelly prescriptive. There is a sense in which the exhibition of bloody wounds becomes an initiation ritual quite separate and disconnected from critical insight. And as the editors of the journal *Questions féministes* point out, "it is . . . dangerous to place the body at the center of a search for female identity. . . . The themes of otherness and of the Body merge together, because the most visible difference between men and women, and the only one we know for sure to be permanent . . . is indeed the difference in body. This difference has been used as a pretext to 'justify' full power of one sex over the other" (trans. Yvonne Rochette-Ozzello, *NFF*, p. 218). The study of biological imagery in women's writing is useful and important as long as we understand that factors other than anatomy are involved in it. Ideas about the body are fundamental to understanding how women conceptualize their situation in society; but there can be no expression of the body which is unmediated by linguistic, social, and literary structures. The difference of woman's literary practice, therefore, must be sought (in Miller's words) in "the body of her writing and not the writing of her body."[8]

Women's Writing and Women's Language

> *The women say, the language you speak poisons your glottis tongue palate lips. They say, the language you speak is made up of words that are killing you. They say, the language you speak is made up of signs that rightly speaking designate what men have appropriated.*
> Monique Wittig, *Les Guérillères*[9]

Linguistic and textual theories of women's writing ask whether men and women use language differently; whether sex differences in language use can be theorized in terms of biology, socialization, or culture; whether women can create new languages of their own; and whether speaking, reading, and writing are all gender marked. American, French, and British feminist critics have all drawn attention to the philosophical, linguistic, and practical problems of women's use of language, and the debate over language is one of the most exciting areas in gynocritics. Poets and writers have led the attack on what Rich calls "the oppressor's language," a language sometimes criticized as sexist, sometimes as abstract. But the problem goes well beyond reformist efforts to purge language of its sexist aspects. As Nelly Furman explains, "It is through the medium of language that we define and categorize areas of difference and similarity, which in turn allow us to comprehend the world around us. Male-centered categorizations predominate in American English

8. Nancy K. Miller, "Women's Autobiography in France: For a Dialectics of Identification," in *Women and Language in Literature and Society*, ed. Sally McConnell-Ginet, Ruth Borker, and Nelly Furman (New York: Praeger, 1980), p. 271.

9. The (female) guerrilla warriors (French, though *guérillères* is Wittig's coinage) [editor's note].

and subtly shape our understanding and perception of reality; this is why attention is increasingly directed to the inherently oppressive aspects for women of a male-constructed language system."[1] According to Carolyn Burke, the language system is at the center of French feminist theory:

> The central issue in much recent women's writing in France is to find and use an appropriate female language. Language is the place to begin: a *prise de conscience* must be followed by a *prise de la parole*. . . . In this view, the very forms of the dominant mode of discourse show the mark of the dominant masculine ideology. Hence, when a woman writes or speaks herself into existence, she is forced to speak in something like a foreign tongue, a language with which she may be personally uncomfortable.[2]

Many French feminists advocate a revolutionary linguism, an oral break from the dictatorship of patriarchal speech. Annie Leclerc, in *Parole de femme,* calls on women "to invent a language that is not oppressive, a language that does not leave speechless but that loosens the tongue" (trans. Courtivron, *NFF*, p. 179). Chantal Chawaf, in an essay on "La chair linguistique," connects biofeminism and linguism in the view that women's language and a genuinely feminine practice of writing will articulate the body:

> In order to reconnect the book with the body and with pleasure, we must disintellectualize writing. . . . And this language, as it develops, will not degenerate and dry up, will not go back to the fleshless academicism, the stereotypical and servile discourses that we reject.
> . . . Feminine language must, by its very nature, work on life passionately, scientifically, poetically, politically in order to make it invulnerable. [Trans. Rochette-Ozzello, *NFF*, pp. 177–78]

But scholars who want a women's language that *is* intellectual and theoretical, that works *inside* the academy, are faced with what seems like an impossible paradox, as Xavière Gauthier has lamented: "As long as women remain silent, they will be outside the historical process. But, if they begin to speak and write *as men do,* they will enter history subdued and alienated; it is a history that, logically speaking, their speech should disrupt" (trans. Marilyn A. August, *NFF*, pp. 162–63). What we need, Mary Jacobus has proposed, is a women's writing that works within "male" discourse but works "ceaselessly to deconstruct it: to write what cannot be written," and according to Shoshana Felman, "the challenge facing the woman today is nothing less than to 'reinvent' language, . . . to speak not only against, but outside of the specular phallogocentric structure, to establish a discourse the status of which would no longer be defined by the phallacy of masculine meaning."[3]

Beyond rhetoric, what can linguistic, historical, and anthropological research tell us about the prospects for a women's language? First of all, the concept of a women's language is not original with feminist criticism; it is very ancient and appears frequently in folklore and myth. In such myths, the

---

1. Nelly Furman, "The Study of Women and Language: Comment on Vol. 3, No. 3," *Signs* 4 (Autumn 1978): 182.
2. Burke, "Report from Paris," p. 844. ["*Prise de consciousness*": a hold on consciousness; "*prise de la parole*": a hold on speech (French)—[editor's note.]
3. Jacobus, "The Difference of View," in *Women Writing and Writing about Women,* pp. 12–13. Shoshana Felman, "Women and Madness: The Critical Phallacy," *Diacritics* 5 (Winter 1975): 10.

essence of women's language is its secrecy; what is really being described is the male fantasy of the enigmatic nature of the feminine. Herodotus, for example, reported that the Amazons were able linguists who easily mastered the languages of their male antagonists, although men could never learn the women's tongue. In *The White Goddess*, Robert Graves romantically argues that a women's language existed in a matriarchal stage of prehistory; after a great battle of the sexes, the matriarchy was overthrown and the women's language went underground, to survive in the mysterious cults of Eleusis and Corinth and the witch covens of Western Europe. Travelers and missionaries in the seventeenth and eighteenth centuries brought back accounts of "women's languages" among American Indians, Africans, and Asians (the differences in linguistic structure they reported were usually superficial). There is some ethnographic evidence that in certain cultures women have evolved a private form of communication out of their need to resist the silence imposed upon them in public life. In ecstatic religions, for example, women, more frequently than men, speak in tongues, a phenomenon attributed by anthropologists to their relative inarticulateness in formal religious discourse. But such ritualized and unintelligible female "languages" are scarcely cause for rejoicing; indeed, it was because witches were suspected of esoteric knowledge and possessed speech that they were burned.[4]

From a political perspective, there are interesting parallels between the feminist problem of a women's language and the recurring "language issue" in the general history of decolonization. After a revolution, a new state must decide which language to make official: the language that is "psychologically immediate," that allows "the kind of force that speaking one's mother tongue permits"; or the language that "is an avenue to the wider community of modern culture," a community to whose movements of thought only "foreign" languages can give access.[5] The language issue in feminist criticism has emerged, in a sense, after our revolution, and it reveals the tensions in the women's movement between those who would stay outside the academic establishments and the institutions of criticism and those who would enter and even conquer them.

The advocacy of a women's language is thus a political gesture that also carries tremendous emotional force. But despite its unifying appeal, the concept of a women's language is riddled with difficulties. Unlike Welsh, Breton, Swahili, or Amharic, that is, languages of minority or colonized groups, there is no mother tongue, no genderlect spoken by the female population in a society, which differs significantly from the dominant language. English and American linguists agree that "there is absolutely no evidence that would suggest the sexes are preprogrammed to develop structurally different linguistic systems." Furthermore, the many specific differences in male and female speech, intonation, and language use that have been identified cannot be explained in terms of "two separate sex-specific languages" but need to be considered instead in terms of styles, strategies, and contexts of linguistic performance.[6] Efforts at quantitative analysis of language in texts by men or

4. On women's language, see Sarah B. Pomeroy, *Goddesses, Whores, Wives, and Slaves: Women in Classical Antiquity* (New York: Schocken Books, 1976), p. 24; Sally McConnell-Ginet, "Linguistics and the Feminist Challenge," in *Women and Language*, p. 14; and Ioan M. Lewis, *Ecstatic Religion* (1971), cited in Shirley Ardener, ed., *Perceiving Women* (New York: Halsted Press, 1978), p. 50.
5. Clifford Geertz, *The Interpretation of Cultures* (New York: Basic Books, 1973), pp. 241–42.
6. McConnell-Ginet, "Linguistics and the Feminist Challenge," pp. 13, 16.

women, such as Mary Hiatt's computerized study of contemporary fiction, *The Way Women Write* (1977), can easily be attacked for treating words apart from their meanings and purposes. At a higher level, analyses which look for "feminine style" in the repetition of stylistic devices, image patterns, and syntax in women's writing tend to confuse innate forms with the overdetermined results of literary choice. Language and style are never raw and instinctual but are always the products of innumerable factors, of genre, tradition, memory, and context.

The appropriate task for feminist criticism, I believe, is to concentrate on women's access to language, on the available lexical range from which words can be selected, on the ideological and cultural determinants of expression. The problem is not that language is insufficient to express women's consciousness but that women have been denied the full resources of language and have been forced into silence, euphemism, or circumlocution. In a series of drafts for a lecture on women's writing (drafts which she discarded or suppressed), Woolf protested against the censorship which cut off female access to language. Comparing herself to Joyce, Woolf noted the differences between their verbal territories: "Now men are shocked if a woman says what she feels (as Joyce does). Yet literature which is always pulling down blinds is not literature. All that we have ought to be expressed—mind and body—a process of incredible difficulty and danger."[7]

"All that we have ought to be expressed—mind and body." Rather than wishing to limit women's linguistic range, we must fight to open and extend it. The holes in discourse, the blanks and gaps and silences, are not the spaces where female consciousness reveals itself but the blinds of a "prison-house of language." Women's literature is still haunted by the ghosts of repressed language, and until we have exorcised those ghosts, it ought not to be in language that we base our theory of difference.

*　　*　　*

Women's Writing and Women's Culture

> *I consider women's literature as a specific category, not because of biology, but because it is, in a sense, the literature of the colonized.*
> Christiane Rochefort,
> "The Privilege of Consciousness"

A theory based on a model of women's culture can provide, I believe, a more complete and satisfying way to talk about the specificity and difference of women's writing than theories based in biology, linguistics, or psychoanalysis. Indeed, a theory of culture incorporates ideas about women's body, language, and psyche but interprets them in relation to the social contexts in which they occur. The ways in which women conceptualize their bodies and their sexual and reproductive functions are intricately linked to their cultural environments. The female psyche can be studied as the product or construction of cultural forces. Language, too, comes back into the picture, as we consider the social dimensions and determinants of language use, the shaping of linguistic behavior by cultural ideals. A cultural theory acknowledges that there are important differences between women as writers: class,

---

7. Virginia Woolf, "Speech, Manuscript Notes," *The Pargiters: The Novel-Essay Portion of the Years 1882–1941,* ed. Mitchell A. Leaska (New York: New York Public Library, 1977), p. 164.

race, nationality, and history are literary determinants as significant as gender. Nonetheless, women's culture forms a collective experience within the cultural whole, an experience that binds women writers to each other over time and space. It is in the emphasis on the binding force of women's culture that this approach differs from Marxist theories of cultural hegemony.

Hypotheses of women's culture have been developed over the last decade primarily by anthropologists, sociologists, and social historians in order to get away from masculine systems, hierarchies, and values and to get at the primary and self-defined nature of female cultural experience. In the field of women's history, the concept of women's culture is still controversial, although there is agreement on its significance as a theoretical formulation. Gerda Lerner explains the importance of examining women's experience in its own terms:

> Women have been left out of history not because of the evil conspiracies of men in general or male historians in particular, but because we have considered history only in male-centered terms. We have missed women and their activities, because we have asked questions of history which are inappropriate to women. To rectify this, and to light up areas of historical darkness we must, for a time, focus on a *woman-centered* inquiry, considering the possibility of the existence of a female culture *within* the general culture shared by men and women. History must include an account of the female experience over time and should include the development of feminist consciousness as an essential aspect of women's past. This is the primary task of women's history. The central question it raises is: What would history be like if it were seen through the eyes of women and ordered by values they define?[8]

In defining female culture, historians distinguish between the roles, activities, tastes, and behaviors prescribed and considered appropriate for women and those activities, behaviors, and functions actually generated out of women's lives. In the late-eighteenth and nineteenth centuries, the term "woman's sphere" expressed the Victorian and Jacksonian vision of separate roles for men and women, with little or no overlap and with women subordinate. Woman's sphere was defined and maintained by men, but women frequently internalized its precepts in the American "cult of true womanhood" and the English "feminine ideal." Women's culture, however, redefines women's "activities and goals from a woman-centered point of view. . . . The term implies an assertion of equality and an awareness of sisterhood, the communality of women." Women's culture refers to "the broad-based communality of values, institutions, relationships, and methods of communication" unifying nineteenth-century female experience, a culture nonetheless with significant variants by class and ethnic group (*MFP*, pp. 52, 54).

Some feminist historians have accepted the model of separate spheres and have seen the movement from woman's sphere to women's culture to women's-rights activism as the consecutive stages of an evolutionary political process. Others see a more complex and perpetual negotiation taking

---

8. Gerda Lerner, "The Challenge of Women's History," in *The Majority Finds Its Past: Placing Women in History* (New York: Oxford University Press, 1979); all further references to this book, abbreviated *MFP*, will hereafter be included parenthetically in the text.

place between women's culture and the general culture. As Lerner has argued:

> It is important to understand that "woman's culture" is not and should not be seen as a subculture. It is hardly possible for the majority to live in a subculture. . . . Women live their social existence within the general culture and, whenever they are confined by patriarchal restraint or segregation into separateness (which always has subordination as its purpose), they transform this restraint into complementarity (asserting the importance of woman's function, even its "superiority") and redefine it. Thus, women live a duality—as members of the general culture and as partakers of women's culture. [*MFP*, p. 52]

Lerner's views are similar to those of some cultural anthropologists. A particularly stimulating analysis of female culture has been carried out by two Oxford anthropologists, Shirley and Edwin Ardener. The Ardeners have tried to outline a model of women's culture which is not historically limited and to provide a terminology for its characteristics. Two essays by Edwin Ardener, "Belief and the Problem of Women" (1972) and "The 'Problem' Revisited" (1975), suggest that women constitute a *muted group,* the boundaries of whose culture and reality overlap, but are not wholly contained by, the *dominant (male) group.* A model of the cultural situation of women is crucial to understanding both how they are perceived by the dominant group and how they perceive themselves and others. Both historians and anthropologists emphasize the incompleteness of androcentric models of history and culture and the inadequacy of such models for the analysis of female experience. In the past, female experience which could not be accommodated by androcentric models was treated as deviant or simply ignored. Observation from an exterior point of view could never be the same as comprehension from within. Ardener's model also has many connections to and implications for current feminist literary theory, since the concepts of perception, silence, and silencing are so central to discussions of women's participation in literary culture.[9]

By the term "muted," Ardener suggests problems both of language and of power. Both muted and dominant groups generate beliefs or ordering ideas of social reality at the unconscious level, but dominant groups control the forms or structures in which consciousness can be articulated. Thus muted groups must mediate their beliefs through the allowable forms of dominant structures. Another way of putting this would be to say that all language is the language of the dominant order, and women, if they speak at all, must speak through it. How then, Ardener asks, "does the symbolic weight of that other mass of persons express itself?" In his view, women's beliefs find expression through ritual and art, expressions which can be deciphered by the ethnographer, either female or male, who is willing to make the effort to perceive beyond the screens of the dominant structure.[1]

Let us now look at Ardener's diagram of the relationship of the dominant and the muted group:

9. See, e.g., Tillie Olsen, *Silences* (New York: Delacorte Press, 1978); Sheila Rowbotham, *Woman's Consciousness, Man's World* (New York: Penguin Books, 1974), pp. 31–37; and Marcia Landy, "The Silent Woman: Towards a Feminist Critique," in *The Authority of Experience,* ed. Arlyn Diamond and Lee R. Edwards (Amherst: University of Massachusetts Press, 1977), pp. 16–27.
1. Edwin Ardener, "Belief and the Problem of Women," in S. Ardener, *Perceiving Women,* p. 3.

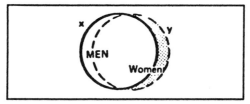

Unlike the Victorian model of complementary spheres, Ardener's groups are represented by intersecting circles. Much of muted circle Y falls within the boundaries of dominant circle X; there is also a crescent of Y which is outside the dominant boundary and therefore (in Ardener's terminology) "wild." We can think of the "wild zone" of women's culture spatially, experientially, or metaphysically. Spatially it stands for an area which is literally no-man's-land, a place forbidden to men, which corresponds to the zone in X which is off limits to women. Experientially it stands for the aspects of the female lifestyle which are outside of and unlike those of men; again, there is a corresponding zone of male experience alien to women. But if we think of the wild zone metaphysically, or in terms of consciousness, it has no corresponding male space since all of male consciousness is within the circle of the dominant structure and thus accessible to or structured by language. In this sense, the "wild" is always imaginary; from the male point of view, it may simply be the projection of the unconscious. In terms of cultural anthropology, women know what the male crescent is like, even if they have never seen it, because it becomes the subject of legend (like the wilderness). But men do not know what is in the wild.

For some feminist critics, the wild zone, or "female space," must be the address of a genuinely women-centered criticism, theory, and art, whose shared project is to bring into being the symbolic weight of female consciousness, to make the invisible visible, to make the silent speak. French feminist critics would like to make the wild zone the theoretical base of women's difference. In their texts, the wild zone becomes the place for the revolutionary women's language, the language of everything that is repressed, and for the revolutionary women's writing in "white ink." It is the Dark Continent in which Cixous's laughing Medusa and Wittig's *guérillères* reside. Through voluntary entry into the wild zone, other feminist critics tell us, a woman can write her way out of the "cramped confines of patriarchal space."[2] The images of this journey are now familiar in feminist quest fictions and in essays about them. The writer/heroine, often guided by another woman, travels to the "mother country" of liberated desire and female authenticity; crossing to the other side of the mirror, like Alice in Wonderland, is often a symbol of the passage.

Many forms of American radical feminism also romantically assert that women are closer to nature, to the environment, to a matriarchal principle at once biological and ecological. Mary Daly's *Gyn/Ecology* and Margaret Atwood's novel *Surfacing* are texts which create this feminist mythology. In English and American literature, women writers have often imagined Amazon Utopias, cities or countries situated in the wild zone or on its border: Elizabeth Gaskell's gentle *Cranford* is probably an Amazon Utopia; so is Charlotte

2. Mari McCarty, "Possessing Female Space: 'The Tender Shoot,' " *Women's Studies* 8 (1981): 368.

Perkins Gilman's *Herland* or, to take a recent example, Joanna Russ's *While-away*. A few years ago, the feminist publishing house Daughters, Inc. tried to create a business version of the Amazon Utopia; as Lois Gould reported in the *New York Times Magazine* (2 January 1977), "They believe they are building the working models for the critical next stage of feminism: full independence from the control and influence of 'male-dominated' institutions—the news media, the health, education, and legal systems, the art, theater, and literary worlds, the banks."

These fantasies of an idyllic enclave represent a phenomenon which feminist criticism must recognize in the history of women's writing. But we must also understand that there can be no writing or criticism totally outside of the dominant structure; no publication is fully independent from the economic and political pressures of the male-dominated society. The concept of a woman's text in the wild zone is a playful abstraction: in the reality to which we must address ourselves as critics, women's writing is a "double-voiced discourse" that always embodies the social, literary, and cultural heritages of both the muted and the dominant.[3] And insofar as most feminist critics are also women writing, this precarious heritage is one we share; every step that feminist criticism takes toward defining women's writing is a step toward self-understanding as well; every account of a female literary culture and a female literary tradition has parallel significance for our own place in critical history and critical tradition.

Women writing are not, then, *inside* and *outside* of the male tradition; they are inside two traditions simultaneously, "undercurrents," in Ellen Moers's metaphor, of the mainstream. To mix metaphors again, the literary estate of women, as Myra Jehlen says, "suggests . . . a more fluid imagery of interacting juxtapositions, the point of which would be to represent not so much the territory, as its defining borders. Indeed, the female territory might well be envisioned as one long border, and independence for women, not as a separate country, but as open access to the sea." As Jehlen goes on to explain, an aggressive feminist criticism must poise itself on this border and must see women's writing in its changing historical and cultural relation to that other body of texts identified by feminist criticism not simply as literature but as "men's writing."[4]

The difference of women's writing, then, can only be understood in terms of this complex and historically grounded cultural relation. An important aspect of Ardener's model is that there are muted groups other than women; a dominant structure may determine many muted structures. A black American woman poet, for example, would have her literary identity formed by the dominant (white male) tradition, by a muted women's culture, and by a muted black culture. She would be affected by both sexual and racial politics in a combination unique to her case; at the same time, as Barbara Smith points out, she shares an experience specific to her group: "Black women writers constitute an identifiable literary tradition . . . thematically, stylistically, aesthetically, and conceptually. Black women writers manifest common approaches to the act of creating literature as a direct result of the specific

3. Susan Lanser and Evelyn Torton Beck, "[Why] Are There No Great Women Critics? And What Difference Does It Make?" in *The Prism of Sex: Essays in the Sociology of Knowledge,* ed. Beck and Julia A. Sherman (Madison: University of Wisconsin Press, 1979), p. 86.
4. Myra Jehlen, "Archimedes and the Paradox of Feminist Criticism," *Signs* 6 (Fall 1981): 582.

political, social, and economic experience they have been obliged to share."[5] Thus the first task of a gynocentric criticism must be to plot the precise cultural locus of female literary identity and to describe the forces that intersect an individual woman writer's cultural field. A gynocentric criticism would also situate women writers with respect to the variables of literary culture, such as modes of production and distribution, relations of author and audience, relations of high to popular art, and hierarchies of genre.

Insofar as our concepts of literary periodization are based on men's writing, women's writing must be forcibly assimilated to an irrelevant grid; we discuss a Renaissance which is not a renaissance for women, a Romantic period in which women played very little part, a modernism with which women conflict. At the same time, the ongoing history of women's writing has been suppressed, leaving large and mysterious gaps in accounts of the development of genre. Gynocentric criticism is already well on the way to providing us with another perspective on literary history. Margaret Anne Doody, for example, suggests that "the period between the death of Richardson and the appearance of the novels of Scott and Austen" which has "been regarded as a dead period, a dull blank" is in fact the period in which late eighteenth-century women writers were developing "the paradigm for women's fiction of the nineteenth century—something hardly less than the paradigm of the nineteenth-century novel itself."[6] There has also been a feminist rehabilitation of the female gothic, a mutation of a popular genre once believed marginal but now seen as part of the great tradition of the novel.[7] In American literature, the pioneering work of Ann Douglas, Nina Baym, and Jane Tompkins, among others, has given us a new view of the power of women's fiction to feminize nineteenth-century American culture.[8] And feminist critics have made us aware that Woolf belonged to a tradition other than modernism and that this tradition surfaces in her work precisely in those places where criticism has hitherto found obscurities, evasions, implausibilities, and imperfections.[9]

Our current theories of literary influence also need to be tested in terms of women's writing. If a man's text, as Bloom and Edward Said have maintained, is fathered, then a woman's text is not only mothered but parented; it confronts both paternal and maternal precursors and must deal with the problems and advantages of both lines of inheritance. Woolf says in *A Room of One's Own* that "a woman writing thinks back through her mothers." But a woman writing unavoidably thinks back through her fathers as well; only male writers can forget or mute half of their parentage. The dominant culture need not consider the muted, except to rail against "the woman's part"

5. Barbara Smith, "Toward a Black Feminist Criticism," in *The New Feminist Criticism*, p. 174. See also Gloria T. Hull, "Afro-American Women Poets: A Bio-Critical Survey," in Gilbert and Gubar, *Shakespeare's Sisters*, pp. 165–82, and Elaine Marks, "Lesbian Intertextuality," in *Homosexualities and French Literature*, ed. Marks and George Stambolian (Ithaca, N.Y.: Cornell University Press, 1979).

6. Margaret Anne Doody, "George Eliot and the Eighteenth-Century Novel," *Nineteenth-Century Fiction* 35 (December 1980): 267–68.

7. See, e.g., Judith Wilt, *Ghosts of the Gothic: Austen, Eliot, and Lawrence* (Princeton, N.J.:

Princeton University Press, 1980).

8. See Ann Douglas, *The Feminization of American Culture* (New York: Alfred A. Knopf, 1977); Nina Baym, *Woman's Fiction: A Guide to Novels by and about Women in America, 1820–1870* (Ithaca, N.Y.: Cornell University Press, 1978); and Jane P. Tompkins, "Sentimental Power: *Uncle Tom's Cabin* and the Politics of Literary History," in *The New Feminist Criticism*, pp. 81–104.

9. See, e.g., the analysis of Woolf in Sandra M. Gilbert, "Costumes of the Mind: Transvestism as Metaphor in Modern Literature," *Critical Inquiry* 7 (Winter 1980): 391–417.

in itself. Thus we need more subtle and supple accounts of influence, not just to explain women's writing but also to understand how men's writing has resisted the acknowledgment of female precursors.

We must first go beyond the assumption that women writers either imitate their male predecessors or revise them and that this simple dualism is adequate to describe the influences on the woman's text. I. A. Richards once commented that the influence of G. E. Moore had had an enormous negative impact on his work: "I feel like an obverse of him. Where there's a hole in him, there's a bulge in me."[1] Too often women's place in literary tradition is translated into the crude topography of hole and bulge, with Milton, Byron, or Emerson the bulging bogeys on one side and women's literature from Aphra Behn to Adrienne Rich a pocked moon surface of revisionary lacunae on the other. One of the great advantages of the women's-culture model is that it shows how the female tradition can be a positive source of strength and solidarity as well as a negative source of powerlessness; it can generate its own experiences and symbols which are not simply the obverse of the male tradition.

How can a cultural model of women's writing help us to read a woman's text? One implication of this model is that women's fiction can be read as a double-voiced discourse, containing a "dominant" and a "muted" story, what Gilbert and Gubar call a "palimpsest." I have described it elsewhere as an object/field problem in which we must keep two alternative oscillating texts simultaneously in view: "In the purest feminist literary criticism we are . . . presented with a radical alteration of our vision, a demand that we see meaning in what has previously been empty space. The orthodox plot recedes, and another plot, hitherto submerged in the anonymity of the background, stands out in bold relief like a thumbprint." Miller too sees "another text" in women's fiction, "more or less muted from novel to novel" but "always there to be read."[2]

Another interpretative strategy for feminist criticism might be the contextual analysis that the cultural anthropologist Clifford Geertz calls "thick description." Geertz calls for descriptions that seek to understand the meaning of cultural phenomena and products by "sorting out the structures of signification . . . and determining their social ground and import."[3] A genuinely "thick" description of women's writing would insist upon gender and upon a female literary tradition among the multiple strata that make up the force of meaning in a text. No description, we must concede, could ever be thick

1. I. A. Richards, quoted in John Paul Russo, "A Study in Influence: The Moore-Richards Paradigm," *Critical Inquiry* 5 (Summer 1979): 687. 2. Showalter, "Literary Criticism," Review Essay, *Signs* 1 (Winter 1975): 435; Miller, "Emphasis Added," p. 357. To take one example, whereas *Jane Eyre* had always been read in relation to an implied "dominant" fictional and social mode and had thus been perceived as flawed, feminist readings foreground its muted symbolic strategies and explore its credibility and coherence in its own terms. Feminist critics revise views like those of Richard Chase, who describes Rochester as castrated, thus implying that Jane's neurosis is penis envy, and G. Armour Craig, who sees the novel as Jane's struggle for superiority, to see Jane instead as healthy within her own system, that is, a *women's* society. See Chase, "The Brontës; or, Myth Domesticated,"

in *Jane Eyre* (New York: W.W. Norton, 1971), pp. 462–71; Craig, "The Unpoetic Compromise: On the Relation between Private Vision and Social Order in Nineteenth-Century English Fiction," in *Society and Self in the Novel*, ed. Mark Schorer (New York: Columbia University Press, 1956), pp. 30–41; Nancy Pell, "Resistance, Rebellion, and Marriage: The Economics of *Jane Eyre*," *Nineteenth-Century Fiction* 31 (March 1977): 397–420; Helene Moglen, *Charlotte Brontë: The Self Conceived* (New York: W. W. Norton, 1977); Adrienne Rich, "*Jane Eyre*: The Temptations of a Motherless Woman," *MS*, October 1973; and Maurianne Adams, "*Jane Eyre*: Woman's Estate," in Diamond and Edwards, *Authority of Experience*, pp. 137–59. 3. Geertz, *Interpretation of Cultures*, p. 9.

enough to account for all the factors that go into the work of art. But we could work toward completeness, even as an unattainable ideal.

In suggesting that a cultural model of women's writing has considerable usefulness for the enterprise of feminist criticism, I don't mean to replace psychoanalysis with cultural anthropology as the answer to all our theoretical problems or to enthrone Ardener and Geertz as the new white fathers in place of Freud, Lacan, and Bloom. No theory, however suggestive, can be a substitute for the close and extensive knowledge of women's texts which constitutes our essential subject. Cultural anthropology and social history can perhaps offer us a terminology and a diagram of women's cultural situation. But feminist critics must use this concept in relation to what women actually write, not in relation to a theoretical, political, metaphoric, or visionary ideal of what women ought to write.

I began by recalling that a few years ago feminist critics thought we were on a pilgrimage to the promised land in which gender would lose its power, in which all texts would be sexless and equal, like angels. But the more precisely we understand the specificity of women's writing not as a transient byproduct of sexism but as a fundamental and continually determining reality, the more clearly we realize that we have misperceived our destination. We may never reach the promised land at all; for when feminist critics see our task as the study of women's writing, we realize that the land promised to us is not the serenely undifferentiated universality of texts but the tumultuous and intriguing wilderness of difference itself.

1981, 1985

MONIQUE WITTIG
1935–2003

Born in Alsace, France, Monique Wittig studied philosophy and literature at the Sorbonne before winning the Prix Medici for her first novel, *L'Opoponax* (1964; trans. 1966). But it was her second novel, *Les Guérillères* (1969; trans. 1971), that captured the attention of American feminists, with its depiction of Amazonian warriors attempting to establish a utopian society; the interest of American feminists grew with *Lesbian Peoples: Material for a Dictionary* (1976; trans. 1979), which she coauthored with Sande Zeig. During the mid-1970s, Wittig moved to the United States, where she taught at the University of California, Berkeley; the University of Southern California; Vassar College; Duke University; New York University; and the University of Arizona. "One Is Not Born a Woman" (1981) first appeared in *Feminist Issues,* a journal that published many of her other essays and on whose editorial board she served. Like Adrienne Rich, Wittig sought to uncover the social construction of heterosexuality. And like Simone de Beauvoir, whose words she quotes in her title, Wittig argued that although a consideration of material conditions is crucial to understanding the relationship between the sexes, a Marxist approach cannot fully account for an explanation of women's subordination. In two novels, *The Lesbian Body* (1973; trans. 1975) and *Across the Acheron* (1985; trans. 1987), and in her collection of essays, *The Straight Mind* (1992), Wittig stages her disagreements with Luce Irigaray, Hélène Cixous, and Julia Kristeva in a manner that makes clear why so-called French feminist theory cannot be reduced to a monolithic field.

One Is Not Born a Woman

A materialist feminist[1] approach to women's oppression destroys the idea that women are a "natural group": "a racial group of a special kind, a group perceived *as natural*, a group of men considered as materially specific in their bodies."[2] What the analysis accomplishes on the level of ideas, practice makes actual at the level of facts: by its very existence, lesbian society destroys the artificial (social) fact constituting women as a "natural group." A lesbian society[3] pragmatically reveals that the division from men of which women have been the object is a political one and shows how we have been ideologically rebuilt into a "natural group." In the case of women, ideology goes far since our bodies as well as our minds are the product of this manipulation. We have been compelled in our bodies and in our minds to correspond, feature by feature, with the *idea* of nature that has been established for us. Distorted to such an extent that our deformed body is what they call "natural," what is supposed to exist as such before oppression. Distorted to such an extent that in the end oppression seems to be a consequence of this "nature" within ourselves (a nature which is only an *idea*). What a materialist analysis does by reasoning, a lesbian society accomplishes practically: not only is there no natural group "women" (we lesbians are a living proof of it), but as individuals as well we question "woman," which for us, as for Simone de Beauvoir thirty years ago, is only a myth. She said: "One is not born, but becomes a woman. No biological, psychological, or economic fate determines the figure that the human female presents in society: it is civilization as a whole that produces this creature, intermediate between male and eunuch, which is described as feminine."[4]

However, most of the feminists and lesbian-feminists in America and elsewhere still believe that the basis of women's oppression *is biological as well as* historical. Some of them even claim to find their sources in Simone de Beauvoir.[5] The belief in mother right and in a "prehistory" when women created civilization (because of a biological predisposition) while the coarse and brutal men hunted (because of a biological predisposition), is symmetrical with the biologizing interpretation of history produced up to now by the class of men. It is still the same method of finding in women and men a biological explanation of their division, outside of social facts. For me this could never constitute a lesbian approach to women's oppression, since it assumes that the basis of society or the beginning of society lies in heterosexuality. Matriarchy is no less heterosexual than patriarchy: it is only the sex of the oppressor that changes. Furthermore, not only is this conception still imprisoned in the categories of sex (woman and man), but it holds onto the idea that the capacity to give birth (biology) is what defines a woman. Although practical facts and ways of living contradict this theory in lesbian society, there are lesbians who affirm that "women and men are different species or races (the

---

1. Christine Delphy, "For a Feminist Materialism," *Feminist Issues* 1, no. 2 (winter 1981) [except as indicated, all notes are Wittig's].

2. Colette Guillaumin, "Race et nature: Système des marques, idée de groupe naturel et rapport sociaux," *Pluriel* 11 (1977).

3. I use the word society with an extended anthropological meaning, since strictly speaking it does not refer to societies in the sense that lesbian societies do not exist completely autonomously from heterosexual social systems. Nevertheless, they are more than simply communities.

4. Simone de Beauvoir, *The Second Sex* [trans. H. M. Parshley] (New York: Bantam, 1952), p. 249.

5. Redstockings, *Feminist Revolution* (New York: Random House, 1978), p. 18.

words are used interchangeably): men are biologically inferior to women; male violence is a biological inevitability . . ."[6] By doing this, by admitting that there is a "natural" division between women and men, we naturalize history, we assume that men and women have always existed and will always exist. Not only do we naturalize history, but also consequently we naturalize the social phenomena which express our oppression, making change impossible. For example, instead of seeing giving birth as a forced production, we see it as a "natural," "biological" process, forgetting that in our societies births are planned (demography), forgetting that we ourselves are programmed to produce children, while this is the only social activity "short of war"[7] that presents such a great danger of death. Thus, as long as we will be "unable to abandon by will or impulse a lifelong and centuries-old commitment to childbearing as *the* female creative act,"[8] gaining control of the production of children will mean much more than the mere control of the material means of this production: women will have to abstract themselves from the definition "woman" which is imposed upon them.

A materialist feminist approach shows that what we take for the cause or origin of oppression is in fact only the *mark*[9] imposed by the oppressor: the "myth of woman,"[1] plus its material effects and manifestations in the appropriated consciousness and bodies of women. Thus, this mark does not preexist oppression: Colette Guillaumin has shown that before the socioeconomic reality of black slavery, the concept of race did not exist, at least not in its modern meaning, since it was applied to the lineage of families. However, now, race, exactly like sex, is taken as an "immediate given," a "sensible given," "physical features," belonging to a natural order. But what we believe to be a physical and direct perception is only a sophisticated and mythic construction, an "imaginary formation,"[2] which reinterprets physical features (in themselves as neutral as any others but marked by the social system) through the network of relationships in which they are perceived. (They are seen *black*, therefore they *are* black; they are seen as *women*, therefore, they *are* women. But before being *seen* that way, they first had to be *made* that way.) A lesbian consciousness should always remember and acknowledge how "unnatural," compelling, totally oppressive, and destructive being "woman" was for us in the old days before the women's liberation movement. It was a political constraint and those who resisted it were accused of not being "real" women. But then we were proud of it, since in the accusation there was already something like a shadow of victory: the avowal by the oppressor that "woman" is not something that goes without saying, since to be one, one has to be a "real" one. We were at the same time accused of wanting to be men. Today this double accusation has been taken up again with enthusiasm in the context of the women's liberation movement by some feminists and also, alas, by some lesbians whose political goal seems somehow to be becoming more and more "feminine." To refuse to be a woman, however, does not mean that one has to become a man. Besides, if we take as an example the perfect

6. Andrea Dworkin, "Biological superiority, the world's most dangerous and deadly idea," *Heresies* 6 (1989):46.
7. Ti-Grace Atkinson, *Amazon Odyssey* (New York: Links Books, 1974), p. 15.

8. Dworkin, op. cit., p. 55.
9. Guillaumin, op. cit.
1. Beauvoir, op. cit.
2. Guillaumin, op. cit.

"butch," the classic example which provokes the most horror, whom Proust would have called a woman/man, how is her alienation different from that of someone who wants to become a woman? Tweedledum and Tweedledee.[3] At least for a woman, wanting to become a man proves that she escapes her initial programming. But even if she would like to, with all her strength, she cannot become a man. For becoming a man would demand from a woman not only the external appearance of a man but his consciousness as well, that is, the consciousness of one who disposes by right of at least two "natural" slaves during his life span. This is impossible and one feature of lesbian oppression consists precisely of making women out of reach for us, since women belong to men. Thus a lesbian *has to* be something else, a not-woman, a not-man, a product of society, not a product of nature, for there is no nature in society.

The refusal to become (or to remain) heterosexual always meant to refuse to become a man or a woman, consciously or not. For a lesbian this goes further than the refusal of the *role* "woman." It is the refusal of the economic, ideological, and political power of a man. This, we lesbians, and nonlesbians as well, knew before the beginning of the lesbian and feminist movement. However, as Andrea Dworkin emphasizes, many lesbians recently "have increasingly tried to transform the very ideology that has enslaved us into a dynamic, religious, psychologically compelling celebration of female biological potential."[4] Thus, some avenues of the feminist and lesbian movement lead us back to the myth of woman which was created by men especially for us, and with it we sink back into a natural group. Thirty years ago we stood up to fight for a sexless society.[5] Now we find ourselves entrapped in the familiar deadlock of "woman is wonderful." Thirty years ago Simone de Beauvoir underlined particularly the false consciousness which consists of selecting among the features of the myth (that women are different from men) those which look good and using them as a definition for women. What the concept of "woman is wonderful" accomplishes is that it retains for defining women the best features (best according to whom?) which oppression has granted us, and it does not radically question the categories "man" and "woman," which are political categories and not natural givens. It puts us in a position of fighting within the class "women" not as the other classes do, for the disappearance of our class, but for the defense of "woman" and its reenforcement. It leads us to develop with complacency "new" theories about our specificity: thus, we call our passivity "nonviolence," when the main and emergent point for us is to fight our passivity (our fear, rather, a justified one). The ambiguity of the term "feminist" sums up the whole situation. What does "feminist" mean? Feminist is formed with the word "femme," "woman," and means: someone who fights for women. For many of us it means someone who fights for women as a class and for the disappearance of this class. For many others it means someone who fights for woman and her defense—for the myth, then, and its reenforcement. But why was the word "feminist" chosen if it retains the least ambiguity? We chose to call ourselves "feminists" ten years ago, not in order to support or reenforce the myth

---

3. I.e., two individuals or groups that are practically indistinguishable, personified as two brothers in Lewis Carroll's *Through the Looking-Glass* (1872).

4. Dworkin, op. cit.

5. Atkinson, op. cit., p. 6: "If feminism has any logic at all, it must be working for a sexless society."

of woman nor to identify ourselves with the oppressor's definition of us, but rather to affirm that our movement had a history and to emphasize the political link with the old feminist movement.

It is then this movement that we can put in question for the meaning that it gave to feminism. It so happens that feminism in the last century could never resolve its contradictions on the subject of nature/culture, woman/society. Women started to fight for themselves as a group and rightly considered that they shared common features of oppression. But for them these features were natural and biological rather than social. They went so far as to adopt the Darwinist theory of evolution. They did not believe like Darwin, however, "that women were less evolved than men, but they did believe that male and female natures had diverged in the course of evolutionary development and that society at large reflected this polarization."[6] "The failure of early feminism was that it only attacked the Darwinist charge of female inferiority, while accepting the foundations of this charge—namely, the view of woman as 'unique.' "[7] And finally it was women scholars—and not feminists—who scientifically destroyed this theory. But the early feminists had failed to regard history as a dynamic process which develops from conflicts of interests. Furthermore, they still believed as men do that the cause (origin) of their oppression lay within themselves. And therefore the feminists of this first front after some astonishing victories found themselves at an impasse out of a lack of reasons for fighting. They upheld the illogical principle of "equality in difference," an idea now being born again. They fell back into the trap which threatens us once again: the myth of woman.

Thus it is our historical task, and only ours, to define what we call oppression in materialist terms, to make it evident that women are a class, which is to say that the category "woman" as well as the category "man" are political and economic categories not eternal ones. Our fight aims to suppress men as a class, not through a genocidal, but a political struggle. Once the class "men" disappears, "women" as a class will disappear as well, for there are no slaves without masters. Our first task, it seems, is to always thoroughly dissociate "women" (the class within which we fight) and "woman," the myth. For "woman" does not exist for us: it is only an imaginary formation, while "women" is the product of a social relationship. We felt this strongly when everywhere we refused to be called a "*woman's* liberation movement." Furthermore, we have to destroy the myth inside and outside ourselves. "Woman" is not each one of us, but the political and ideological formation which negates "women" (the product of a relation of exploitation). "Woman" is there to confuse us, to hide the reality "women." In order to be aware of being a class and to become a class we have to first kill the myth of "woman" including its most seductive aspects (I think about Virginia Woolf when she said the first task of a woman writer is to kill "the angel in the house."[8]) But to become a class we do not have to suppress our individual selves, and since no individual can be reduced to her/his oppression we are also confronted with the historical necessity of constituting ourselves as the individual subjects of our history as well. I believe this is the reason why all these attempts at "new" def-

---

6. Rosalind Rosenberg, "In Search of Woman's Nature," *Feminist Studies* 3, no. 1/2 (1975): 144.
7. Ibid., p. 146.

8. I.e., the Victorian ideal of self-sacrificing womanhood; see Woolf's "Professions for Women" (1942) [editor's note].

initions of woman are blossoming now. What is at stake (and of course not only for women) is an individual definition as well as a class definition. For once one has acknowledged oppression, one needs to know and experience the fact that one can constitute oneself as a subject (as opposed to an object of oppression), that one can become *someone* in spite of oppression, that one has one's own identity. There is no possible fight for someone deprived of an identity, no internal motivation for fighting, since although I can fight only with others, first I fight for myself.

The question of the individual subject is historically a difficult one for everybody. Marxism, the last avatar of materialism, the science which has politically formed us, does not want to hear anything about a "subject." Marxism has rejected the transcendental subject, the subject as constitutive of knowledge, the "pure" consciousness. All that thinks per se, before all experience, has ended up in the garbage can of history, because it claimed to exist outside matter, prior to matter, and needed God, spirit, or soul to exist in such a way. This is what is called "idealism." As for individuals, they are only the product of social relations, therefore their consciousness can only be "alienated." (Marx, in *The German Ideology,* says precisely that individuals of the dominating class are also alienated although they are the direct producers of the ideas that alienate the classes oppressed by them. But since they draw visible advantages from their own alienation they can bear it, without too much suffering.) There exists such a thing as class consciousness, but a consciousness which does not refer to a particular subject, except as participating in general conditions of exploitation at the same time as the other subjects of their class, all sharing the same consciousness. As for the practical class problems—outside of the class problems as traditionally defined—that one could encounter (for example, sexual problems), they were considered as "bourgeois" problems that would disappear with the final victory of the class struggle. "Individualistic," "subjectivist," "petit bourgeois," these were the labels given to any person who had shown problems which could not be reduced to the "class struggle" itself.

Thus Marxism has refused the attribute of being a subject to the members of oppressed classes. In doing this, Marxism, because of the ideological and political power this "revolutionary science" immediately exercised upon the workers' movement and all other political groups, has prevented all categories of oppressed peoples from constituting themselves historically as subjects (subjects of their struggle, for example). This means that the "masses" did not fight for themselves but for *the* party or its organizations. And when an economic transformation took place (end of private property, constitution of the socialist state), no revolutionary change took place within the new society, because the people themselves did not change.

For women, Marxism had two results. It prevented them from being aware that they are a class and therefore from constituting themselves as a class for a very long time, by leaving the relation "women/men" outside of the social order, by turning it into a natural relation, doubtlessly for Marxists the only one along with the relation of mothers to children to be seen this way, and by hiding the class conflict between men and women behind a natural division of labor (*The German Ideology*). This concerns the theoretical (ideological) level. On the practical level, Lenin, *the* party, all the communist parties up to now, including all the most radical political groups, have always reacted to any attempt on the part of women to reflect and form groups based on their own class problem with an accusation of divisiveness. By uniting, we women, are dividing the strength of the people. This means that for the Marxists women *belong* either to the bourgeois class, or to the proletariat class, in other words, to the men of these classes. In addition, Marxist theory does not allow women any more than other classes of oppressed people to constitute themselves as historical subjects, because Marxism does not take into account the fact that a class also consists of individuals one by one. Class consciousness is not enough. We must try to understand philosophically (politically) these concepts of "subject" and "class consciousness" and how they work in relation to our history. When we discover that women are the objects of oppression and appropriation, at the very moment that we become able to perceive this, we become subjects in the sense of cognitive subjects, through an operation of abstraction. Consciousness of oppression is not only a reaction to (fight against) oppression. It is also the whole conceptual reevaluation of the social world, its whole reorganization with new concepts, from the point of view of oppression. It is what I would call the science of oppression created by the oppressed. This operation of understanding reality has to be undertaken by every one of us: call it a subjective, cognitive practice. The movement back and forth between the levels of reality (the conceptual reality and the material reality of oppression, which are both social realities) is accomplished through language.

It is we who historically must undertake the task of defining the individual subject in materialist terms. This certainly seems to be an impossibility since materialism and subjectivity have always been mutually exclusive. Nevertheless, and rather than despairing of ever understanding, we must recognize the *need* to reach subjectivity in the abandonment by many of us to the myth "woman" (the myth of woman being only a snare that holds us up). This real necessity for everyone to exist as an individual, as well as a member of a class, is perhaps the first condition for the accomplishment of a revolution, without which there can be no real fight or transformation. But the opposite is also true; without class and class consciousness there are no real subjects, only alienated individuals. For women to answer the question of the individual subject in materialist terms is first to show, as the lesbians and feminists did, that supposedly "subjective," "individual," "private" problems are in fact social problems, class problems; that sexuality is not for women an individual and subjective expression, but a social institution of violence. But once we have shown that all so-called personal problems are in fact class problems, we will still be left with the question of the subject of each singular woman—not the myth, but each one of us. At this point, let us say that a new personal and subjective definition for all humankind can only be found beyond the categories of sex (woman and man) and that the advent of individual subjects demands first destroying the categories of sex, ending the use of them, and rejecting all sciences which still use these categories as their fundamentals (practically all social sciences).

To destroy "woman," does not mean that we aim, short of physical destruction, to destroy lesbianism simultaneously with the categories of sex, because lesbianism provides for the moment the only social form in which we can live freely. Lesbian is the only concept I know of which is beyond the categories of sex (woman and man), because the designated subject (lesbian) is *not* a woman, either economically, or politically, or ideologically. For what makes a woman is a specific social relation to a man, a relation that we have previously called servitude,[9] a relation which implies personal and physical obligation as well as economic obligation ("forced residence,"[1] domestic corvée, conjugal duties, unlimited production of children, etc.), a relation which lesbians escape by refusing to become or to stay heterosexual. We are escapees from our class in the same way as the American runaway slaves were when escaping slavery and becoming free. For us this is an absolute necessity; our survival demands that we contribute all our strength to the destruction of the class of women within which men appropriate women. This can be accomplished only by the destruction of heterosexuality as a social system which is based on the oppression of women by men and which produces the doctrine of the difference between the sexes to justify this oppression.

1981

9. In an article published by *L'Idiot International* (mai 1970) whose original title was "Pour un mouvement de libération des femmes" [For a women's liberation movement].

1. Christiane Rochefort, *Les Stances à Sophie* (Paris: Grasset, 1963).

BONNIE ZIMMERMAN
b. 1947

In 1956, Jeannette Foster brought out her important book *Sex Variant Women in Literature,* which was reprinted in 1975 by Barbara Grier; however, lesbian literature did not receive serious academic attention until critics from Barbara Smith and Lillian Faderman to Catharine Stimpson, Martha Vicinus, and Biddy Martin filled in the intricacies of its evolution. Within this field of study, the 1981 publication of "What Has Never Been" (in *Feminist Studies*) established Bonnie Zimmerman as a pioneer in pointing out the implicitly heterosexual biases (or "heterosexism") of mainstream feminists' editorial and scholarly approach to literary and social history. Since 1978, Zimmerman has taught at San Diego State University, where she helped form, direct, and chair one of the earliest women's studies departments. In *The Safe Sea of Women: Lesbian Fiction, 1969–1989* (1990), she went on to map the fiction of the 1970s and '80s that qualified, from her perspective, as "lesbian fiction." Attempting to set the parameters of that term as well as those of lesbian criticism, Zimmerman negotiates between extratextual evidence about the avowed sexual orientation of authors and intertextual evidence of an absorption with the emotional and erotic attachments between women.

From What Has Never Been:
An Overview of Lesbian Feminist Criticism[1]

* * *

Unmasking heterosexist assumptions in feminist literary criticism has been an important but hardly primary task for lesbian critics. We are more con-

1. An earlier version of this paper was presented at the first annual convention of the National Women's Studies Association, Lawrence, Kansas, May 1979 [except as indicated, all notes are Zimmerman's].

cerned with the development of a unique lesbian feminist perspective or, at the very least, determining whether or not such a perspective is possible. In order to do so, lesbian critics have had to begin with a special question: "When is a text a 'lesbian text' or its writer a 'lesbian writer' "?[2] Lesbians are faced with this special problem of definition: presumably we know when a writer is a "Victorian writer" or a "Canadian writer." To answer this question, we have to determine how inclusively or exclusively we define "lesbian." Should we limit this appellation to those women for whom sexual experience with other women can be proven? This is an almost impossible historical task, as many have noted, for what constitutes proof? Women have not left obvious markers in their private writings. Furthermore, such a narrow definition "names" lesbianism as an exclusively sexual phenomenon which, many argue, may be an inadequate construction of lesbian experience, both today and in less sexually explicit eras. This sexual definition of lesbianism also leads to the identification of literature with life, and thus can be an overly defensive and suspect strategy.

Nevertheless, lesbian criticism continues to be plagued with the problem of definition. One perspective insists that

> desire must be there and at least somewhat embodied. . . . That carnality distinguishes it from gestures of political sympathy for homosexuals and from affectionate friendships in which women enjoy each other, support each other, and commingle their sense of identity and well-being.[3]

A second perspective, which might be called a school, claims, on the contrary, that "the very meaning of lesbianism is being expanded in literature, just as it is being redefined through politics."[4] An articulate spokeswoman for this "expanded meaning" school of criticism is Adrienne Rich, who offers a compelling inclusive definition of lesbianism:

> I mean the term *lesbian continuum* to include a range—through each woman's life and throughout history—of woman-identified experience; not simply the fact that a woman has had or consciously desired genital experience with another woman. If we expand it to embrace many more forms of primary intensity between and among women, including the sharing of a rich inner life, the bonding against male tyranny, the giving and receiving of practical and political support . . . we begin to grasp breadths of female history and psychology which have lain out of reach as a consequence of limited, mostly clinical, definitions of 'lesbianism.'[5]

This definition has the virtue of deemphasizing lesbianism as a static entity and of suggesting interconnections among the various ways in which women bond together. However, all inclusive definitions of lesbianism risk blurring the distinctions between lesbian relationships and non-lesbian female friendships, or between lesbian identity and female-centered identity. Some lesbian writers would deny that there are such distinctions, but this position is reduc-

2. Susan Sniader Lanser, "Speaking in Tongues: *Ladies Almanack* and the Language of Celebration," *Frontiers* 4, no. 3 (Fall 1979): 39.

3. Catharine R. Stimpson, "Zero Degree Deviancy: A Study of the Lesbian Novel," unpublished paper, p. 2 [published as "Zero Degree Deviancy: The Lesbian Novel in English," *Critical Inquiry* 8 (Winter 1981): 363–80].

4. Barbara Smith, "Toward a Black Feminist Criticism," *Conditions: Two* 1, no. 2 (October 1977): 39. It is sometimes overlooked that Smith's pathbreaking article on black feminist criticism is also a lesbian feminist analysis.

5. Adrienne Rich, "Compulsory Heterosexuality and Lesbian Existence," *Signs* 5, no. 4 (Summer 1980): 648–49.

tive and of mixed value to those who are developing lesbian criticism and theory and who may need limited and precise definitions. In fact, reductionism is a serious problem in lesbian ideology. Too often, we identify lesbian and woman, or feminist; we equate lesbianism with any close bonds between women or with political commitment to women. These identifications can be fuzzy and historically questionable, as, for example, in the claim that lesbians have a unique relationship with nature or (as Rich also has claimed) that all female creativity is lesbian. By so reducing the meaning of lesbian, we have in effect eliminated lesbianism as a meaningful category.

A similar problem arises when lesbian theorists redefine lesbianism politically, equating it with strength, independence, and resistance to patriarchy. This new political definition then influences the interpretation of literature: "If in a woman writer's work a sentence refuses to do what it is supposed to do, if there are strong images of women and if there is a refusal to be linear, the result is innately lesbian literature."[6] The concept of an "innately" lesbian perspective or aesthetic allows the critic to separate lesbianism from biographical content which is an essential development in lesbian critical theory. Literary interpretation will, of course, be supported by historical and biographical evidence, but perhaps lesbian critics should borrow a few insights from new criticism. If a text lends itself to a lesbian reading, then no amount of biographic "proof" ought to be necessary to establish it as a lesbian text.[7] Barbara Smith, for example, interprets Toni Morrison's *Sula* as a lesbian novel, regardless of the author's affectional preference. But we need to be cautious about what we call "innately" lesbian. Why is circularity or strength limited to lesbians, or, similarly, why is love of nature or creativity? It is certainly not evident that women, let alone lesbians, are "innately" anything. And, although it might require a lesbian perspective to stress the dominant relationship between Nel and Sula ("All that time, all that time, I thought I was missing Jude"), it is difficult to imagine a novel so imbued with heterosexuality as lesbian.

Almost midway between the inclusive and exclusive approaches to a definition of lesbianism lies that of Lillian Faderman in her extraordinary overview, *Surpassing the Love of Man: Romantic Friendship and Love Between Women From the Renaissance to the Present*. Faderman's precise definition of lesbianism provides a conceptual framework for the four hundred years of literary history explored by the text:

> "Lesbian" describes a relationship in which two women's strongest emotions and affections are directed toward each other. Sexual contact may be a part of the relationship to a greater or lesser degree, or it may be entirely absent. By preference the two women spend most of their time together and share most aspects of their lives with each other.[8]

6. Bertha Harris, quoted by Smith, "Toward a Black Feminist Criticism," p. 33.
7. Supportive historical and biographical information about women writers can be found in a number of recent articles, in addition to those cited elsewhere in this paper. See, for example, Judith Schwarz, "*Yellow Clover*: Katherine Lee Bates and Katherine Coman," pp. 59–67; Josephine Donovan, "The Unpublished Love Poems of Sarah Orne Jewett," pp. 26–31; and Margaret Cruikshank, "Geraldine Jewsbury and Jane Carlyle," pp. 60–64, all in Special Issue on Lesbian History, *Frontiers* 4, no. 3 (Fall 1979).
8. Lillian Faderman, *Surpassing the Love of Men: Romantic Friendship and Love Between Women From the Renaissance to the Present* (New York: William Morrow and Co., 1981), pp. 17–18.

Broader than the exclusive definition of lesbianism—for Faderman argues that not all lesbian relationships may be fully embodied—but narrower than Rich's "lesbian continuum," this definition is both specific and discriminating. The book is slightly marred by a defensive, overexplanatory tone, caused, no doubt, by her attempt to neutralize the "intense charge of the word *lesbian*"; note, for example, that this charged word is omitted from the title.[9] Furthermore, certain problems remain with her framework, as with any that a lesbian critic or historian might establish. The historical relationship between genital sexuality and lesbianism remains unclear, and we cannot identify easily lesbianism outside a monogamous relationship. Nevertheless, despite problems in definition that may be inherent in lesbian studies, the strength of *Surpassing the Love of Men* is partially the precision with which Faderman defines her topic and chooses her texts and subjects.

This problem of definition is exacerbated by the problem of silence. One of the most pervasive themes in lesbian criticism is that woman-identified writers, silenced by a homophobic and misogynistic society, have been forced to adopt coded and obscure language and internal censorship. Emily Dickinson counseled us to "tell all the truth/but tell it slant," and critics are now calculating what price we have paid for slanted truth. The silences of heterosexual women writers may become lies for lesbian writers, as Rich warns: "a life 'in the closet' . . . [may] spread into private life, so that lying (described as *discretion*)[1] becomes an easy way to avoid conflict or complication." Gloria T. Hull recounts the moving story of just such a victim of society, the black lesbian poet Angelina Weld Grimké, whose "convoluted life and thwarted sexuality" marked her slim output of poetry with images of self-abnegation, diminution, sadness, and the wish for death. The lesbian writer who is working class or a woman of color may be particularly isolated, shackled by conventions and, ultimately, silenced "with [her] real gifts stifled within."[2] What does a lesbian writer do when the words cannot be silenced? Critics are pointing to the codes and strategies for literary survival adopted by many women. For example, Willa Cather may have adopted her characteristic male persona in order to express safely her emotional and erotic feelings for other women.[3] Thus, a writer some critics call antifeminist or at least disappointing may be better appreciated when her lesbianism is taken into account. Similarly, many ask whether Gertrude Stein cultivated obscurity, encoding her lesbianism in order to express hidden feelings and evade potential enemies. Or, on the other hand, Stein may have been always a declared lesbian, but a victim of readers' (and scholars') unwillingness or inability to pay her the close and sympathetic attention she requires.[4]

9. Adrienne Rich, " 'It Is the Lesbian in Us . . . ,' " in *On Lies, Secrets, and Silence* (New York: W.W. Norton & Co., 1979), p. 202.
1. Rich, "Women and Honor: Some Notes on Lying (1975)," in *On Lies, Secrets, and Silence*, p. 190.
2. Gloria T. Hull, " 'Under the Days': The Buried Life and Poetry of Angelina Weld Grimké," The Black Women's Issue, *Conditions: Five* 2, no. 2 (Autumn 1979): 23, 20.
3. Joanna Russ, "To Write 'Like a Woman': Transformations of Identity in Willa Cather," paper presented at the MLA convention, in San Francisco, December 1979. On coding in other writers, see also, Ann Cothran and Diane Griffin Crowder, "An Optical Thirst for Invisible Water: Image Structure, Codes and Recoding in Colette's *The Pure*

and the Impure," paper presented at the MLA convention, New York, December 1978; and Annette Kolodny, "The Lady's Not For Spurning: Kate Millett and the Critics," *Contemporary Literature* 17, no. 4 (Fall 1976): 541–62.
4. Two male critics—Edmund Wilson and Robert Bridgman—first suggested the connection between Stein's obscurity and her lesbianism. Jane Rule in *Lesbian Images* and Dolores Klaich in *Woman Plus Woman* both follow their analysis. Cynthia Secor has argued that Stein did declare her lesbianism in her writing ("Can We Call Gertrude Stein a Non-Declared Lesbian Writer?") in a paper presented at the MLA convention, San Francisco, December 1979.

The silence of "Shakespeare's [lesbian] sister" has meant that modern writers have had little or no tradition with which to nurture themselves. Feminist critics such as Moers, Showalter, and Gilbert and Gubar have demonstrated the extent and significance of a female literary tradition, but the lesbian writer developed her craft alone (and perhaps this is the significance of the title of *the* lesbian novel about novel writing, *The Well of Loneliness*). Elly Bulkin's much-reprinted article on lesbian poetry points out that lesbian poets "have their work shaped by the simple fact of their having begun to write without knowledge of such history and with little or no hope of support from a woman's and/or lesbian writing community."[5] If white women can at least imagine a lesbian literature, the black lesbian writer, as Barbara Smith demonstrates, is even more hampered by the lack of tradition: "Black women are still in the position of having to 'imagine,' discover and verify Black lesbian literature because so little has been written from an avowedly lesbian perspective."[6] Blanche Wiesen Cook points out further that all lesbians are affected by this absence of tradition and role models, or the limiting of role models to Hall's Stephen Gordon.[7] She also reminds us that our lesbian foremothers and networks were not simply lost and forgotten; rather, our past has been "erased," obliterated by the actions of a hostile society.[8]

It would appear then that lesbian critics are faced with a set of problems that make our work particularly delicate and problematic, requiring caution, sensitivity, and flexibility as well as imagination and risk. Lesbian criticism begins with the establishment of the lesbian text: the creation of language out of silence. The critic must first define the term "lesbian" and then determine its applicability to both writer and text, sorting out the relation of literature to life. Her definition of lesbianism will influence the texts she identifies as lesbian, and, except for the growing body of literature written from an explicit lesbian perspective since the development of a lesbian political movement, it is likely that many will disagree with various identifications of lesbian texts. It is not only *Sula* that may provoke controversy, but even the "coded" works of lesbian writers like Gertrude Stein. The critic will need to consider whether a lesbian text is one written by a lesbian (and if so, how do we determine who is a lesbian?), one written about lesbians (which might be by a heterosexual woman or a man), or one that expresses a lesbian "vision" (which has yet to be satisfactorily outlined). But despite the problems raised by def-

---

5. Bulkin, " 'Kissing Against the Light": A Look at Lesbian Poetry," *Radical Teacher* 10 (December 1978): 8. This article was reprinted in *College English* and *Women's Studies Newsletter*.
6. Smith, "Toward a Black Feminist Criticism," p. 39.
7. The protagonist of Radclyffe Hall's *The Well of Loneliness* (1928) [editor's note].
8. Blanche Wiesen Cook, " 'Women Alone Stir My Imagination': Lesbianism and the Cultural Tradition," *Signs* 4, no. 4 (Summer 1979): 718–39. A curious example of contemporary denial of lesbianism—the obliteration of the lesbian tradition such as it is—is found in Judith Hallett, "Sappho and Her Social Context: Sense and Sensuality," *Signs* 4, no. 3 (Spring 1979): 447–64. Sappho, of course, personifies "lesbian existence," indeed lesbian *possibility*, as well as female poetic creativity. Hallett, however, essentially denies Sappho's love for women with her conclusion that "she did not represent herself in her verses as having expressed homosexual feelings physically." One might certainly argue that no other possible interpretation can exist for Sappho's "He is more than a hero" (Mary Barnard's translation). Eva Stigers, in "Romantic Sensuality, Poetic Sense: A Response to Hallett on Sappho" (same issue, pp. 464–71), contends that Sappho "chose female homosexual love as the vehicle because lesbian love offered the most receptive setting for romantic *eros*." This interpretation may more accurately reflect the perspective of the nineteenth-century romantic poets who rediscovered Sappho. However, Stiger's argument that Sappho used lesbian love to create an alternate world in which male values are not dominant and in which to explore the female experience provides a starting point for a feminist analysis of Sappho's influence on her modern lesbian followers. A fine exposition of this "Sappho model" in French lesbian literature is provided by Elaine Marks in her essay "Lesbian Intertextuality."

inition, silence and coding, and absence of tradition, lesbian critics have begun to develop a critical stance. Often this stance involves peering into shadows, into the spaces between words, into what has been unspoken and barely imagined. It is a perilous critical adventure with results that may violate accepted norms of traditional criticism, but which may also transform our notions of literary possibility.

One of the first tasks of this emerging lesbian criticism has been to provide lesbians with a tradition, even if a retrospective one. Jane Rule, whose *Lesbian Images* appeared about the same time as [Ellen Moers's] *Literary Women*, first attempted to establish this tradition.[9] Although her text is problematic, relying overly much on biographical evidence and derivative interpretations and including some questionable writers (such as Dorothy Baker) while omitting others, *Lesbian Images* was a milestone in lesbian criticism. Its importance is partially suggested by the fact that it took five years for another complete book—Faderman's—to appear on lesbian literature. In a review of *Lesbian Images*, I questioned the existence of a lesbian "great tradition" in literature, but now I think I was wrong.[1] Along with Rule, Dolores Klaich in *Woman Plus Woman* and Louise Bernikow in the introduction to *The World Split Open* have explored the possibility of a lesbian tradition,[2] and recent critics such as Faderman and Cook in particular have begun to define that tradition, who belongs to it, and what links the writers who can be identified as lesbians. Cook's review of lesbian literature and culture in the early twentieth century proposes "to analyze the literature and attitudes out of which the present lesbian feminist works have emerged, and to examine the continued denials and invalidation of the lesbian experience."[3] Focusing on the recognized lesbian networks in France and England that included Virginia Woolf, Vita Sackville-West, Ethel Smythe, Gertrude Stein, Radclyffe Hall, Natalie Barney, and Romaine Brooks, Cook provides an important outline of a lesbian cultural tradition and an insightful analysis of the distortions and denials of homophobic scholars, critics, and biographers.

Faderman's *Surpassing the Love of Men*, like her earlier critical articles, ranges more widely through a literary tradition of romantic love between women (whether or not one calls that "lesbian") from the sixteenth to the twentieth centuries. Her thesis is that passionate love between women was labeled neither abnormal nor undesirable—probably because women were perceived to be asexual—until the sexologists led by Krafft-Ebing and Havelock Ellis "morbidified" female friendship around 1900.

Although she does not always clarify the dialectic between idealization and condemnation that is suggested in her text, Faderman's basic theory is quite convincing. Most readers, like myself, will be amazed at the wealth of information about women's same-sex love that Faderman has uncovered. She rescues from heterosexual obscurity Mary Wollstonecraft, Mary Wortley Montagu, Anna Seward, Sarah Orne Jewett, Edith Somerville, "Michael Field," and many others, including the Scottish schoolmistresses whose les-

9. Jane Rule, *Lesbian Images* (Garden City, N.Y.; Doubleday & Co., 1975).

1. Bonnie Zimmerman, "The New Tradition," *Sinister Wisdom* 2 (Fall 1976): 34–41.

2. Dolores Klaich, *Woman Plus Woman: Attitudes Toward Lesbianism* (New York: William Morrow,

1974); Louise Bernikow, *The World Split Open: Four Centuries of Women Poets in England and America, 1552–1950* (New York: Vintage Books, 1974).

3. Cook, "Women Alone Stir My Imagination," p. 720.

bian libel suit inspired Lillian Hellman's *The Children's Hour.* Faderman has also written on the theme of same-sex love and romantic friendship in poems and letters of Emily Dickinson; in novels by Henry James, Oliver Wendell Holmes, and Henry Wadsworth Longfellow; and in popular magazine fiction of the early twentieth century.[4]

Faderman is preeminent among those critics who are attempting to establish a lesbian tradition by rereading writers of the past previously assumed to be heterosexual or "spinsters." As song-writer Holly Near expresses it: "Lady poet of great acclaim/ I have been misreading you/ I never knew your poems were meant for me."[5] It is in this area of lesbian scholarship that the most controversy—and some of the most exciting work—occurs. Was Mary Wollstonecraft's passionate love for Fanny Blood, recorded in *Mary, A Fiction,* lesbian? Does Henry James dissect a lesbian relationship in *The Bostonians?* Did Emily Dickinson address many of her love poems to a woman, not a man? How did Virginia Woolf's relationships with Vita Sackville-West and Ethel Smythe affect her literary vision? Not only are some lesbian critics increasingly naming such women and relationships "lesbian," they are also suggesting that criticism cannot fail to take into account the influence of sexual and emotional orientation on literary expression.

In the establishment of a self-conscious literary tradition, certain writers have become focal points both for critics and for lesbians in general, who affirm and celebrate their identity by "naming names," establishing a sense of historical continuity and community through the knowledge that incontrovertibly great women were also lesbians. Foremost among these heroes (or "heras") are the women who created the first self-identified lesbian feminist community in Paris during the early years of the twentieth century. With Natalie Barney at its hub, this circle included such notable writers as Colette, Djuna Barnes, Radclyffe Hall, Renée Vivien, and, peripherally, Gertrude Stein. Contemporary lesbians—literary critics, historians, and layreaders— have been drawn to their mythic and mythmaking presence, seeing in them a vision of lesbian society and culture that may have existed only once before—on the original island of Lesbos.[6] More interest, however, has been paid to their lives so far than to their art. Barnes's portraits of decadent, tormented lesbians and homosexuals in *Nightwood* and silly, salacious ones in *The Ladies Almanack* often prove troublesome to lesbian readers and critics.[7] However, Elaine Marks's perceptive study of French lesbian writers traces a tradition and how it has changed, modified by circumstance and by feminism, from the Sappho of Renée Vivien to the amazons of Monique Wittig.[8]

4. See Lillian Faderman's articles: "The Morbidification of Love Between Women by Nineteenth-Century Sexologists," *Journal of Homosexuality* 4, no. 1 (Fall 1978): 73–90; "Emily Dickinson's Letters to Sue Gilbert," *Massachusetts Review* 18, no. 2 (Summer 1977): 197–225; "Emily Dickinson's Homoerotic Poetry," *Higginson Journal* 18 (1978): 19–27; "Female Same-Sex Relationships in Novels by Longfellow, Holmes, and James," *New England Quarterly* 60, no. 3 (September 1978): 309–32; and "Lesbian Magazine Fiction in the Early Twentieth Century," *Journal of Popular Culture* 11, no. 4 (Spring 1978): 800–17.

5. Holly Near, "Imagine My Surprise," on *Imagine My Surprise!* (Redwood Records, 1978).

6. See Klaich, chap. 6. Also, see Bertha Harris, "The More Profound Nationality of their Lesbianism: Lesbian Society in Paris in the 1920's," *Amazon Expedition* (New York: Times Change Press, 1973), pp. 77–88; and Gayle Rubin's Introduction to Renée Vivien's *A Woman Appeared to Me,* trans. Jeanette Foster (Reno, Nev.: Naiad Press, 1976). [Lesbos was the home of the Greek poet Sappho (born ca. 600 B.C.E.)—editor's note.]

7. For example, see Lanser, "Speaking in Tongues."

8. Marks, "Lesbian Intertextuality," in *Homosexualities and French Literature,* ed. George Stambolian and Elaine Marks (Ithaca, N.Y.: Cornell University Press, 1979), pp. 353–77.

The problems inherent in reading lesbian literature primarily for role modeling is most evident with Hall—the most notorious of literary lesbians—whose archetypal "butch," Stephen Gordon, has bothered readers since the publication of *The Well of Loneliness*. Although one critic praises it as "the standard by which all subsequent similar works are measured," most contemporary lesbian feminists would, I believe, agree with Faderman's harsh condemnation that it "helped to wreak confusion in young women."[9] Such an extraliterary debate is not limited to lesbian novels and lesbian characters; I am reminded of the intense disappointment expressed by many feminists over George Eliot's disposal of Dorothea Brooke in *Middlemarch*. In both cases, the cry is the same: why haven't these writers provided us with appropriate role models? Cook may be justified in criticizing Hall for creating a narrow and debilitating image for lesbians who follow, but my reading of the novel (and that of Catharine Stimpson in an excellent study of the lesbian novel) convinces me that both Hall's hero and message are highly complex.[1] In looking to writers for a tradition, we need to recognize that the tradition may not always be a happy one. Women like Stephen Gordon exist alongside characters like Molly Bolt, in Rita Mae Brown's *Rubyfruit Jungle*, but lesbians may also question whether or not the incarnation of a "politically correct" but elusive and utopian mythology provides our only appropriate role model.

As with Hall, many readers and critics are strongly antipathetic to Stein, citing her reactionary and antifeminist politics and her role-playing relationship with Alice B. Toklas. However, other critics, by carefully analyzing Stein's actual words, establish, convincingly to my reading, that she did have a lesbian and feminist perspective, calling into question assumptions about coding and masculine role playing. Cynthia Secor, who is developing an exciting lesbian feminist interpretation of Stein, argues that her novel *Ida* attempts to discover what it means to be a female person, and that the author profited from her position on the boundaries of patriarchal society: "Stein's own experience as a lesbian gives her a critical distance that shapes her understanding of the struggle to be one's self. Her own identity is not shaped as she moves into relation with a man." Similarly, Elizabeth Fifer points out that Stein's situation encouraged her to experiment with parody, theatricality, role playing, and "the diversity of ways possible to look at homosexual love and at her love object." Dierdre Vanderlinde finds in *Three Lives* "one of the earliest attempts to find a new language in which to say, 'I, woman-loving woman, exist.' " Catharine Stimpson places more critical emphasis on Stein's use of masculine pronouns and conventional language, but despite what may have been her compromise, Stimpson feels that female bonding in Stein provides her with a private solution to woman's mind-body split.[2]

9. Lillian Faderman and Ann Williams, "Radclyffe Hall and the Lesbian Image," *Conditions: One* 1, no. 1 (April 1977): 40; and Sybil Korff Vincent, "Nothing Fails Like Success: Radclyffe Hall's *The Well of Loneliness*," unpublished paper.
1. Stimpson, "Zero Degree Deviancy," pp. 8–17.
2. Cynthia Secor, "*Ida*, A Great American Novel," *Twentieth Century Literature* 24, no. 1 (Spring 1978): 99; Elizabeth Fifer, "Is Flesh Advisable: The Interior Theater of Gertrude Stein," *Signs* 4, no. 3 (Spring 1979): 478; Dierdre Vanderlinde,

"Gertrude Stein: Three Lives," paper presented at MLA convention, San Francisco, December 1979, p. 10; and Catharine Stimpson, "The Mind, and Body and Gertrude Stein," *Critical Inquiry* 3, no. 3 (Spring 1977): 489–506. Like Stimpson on Stein, Lanser, in "Speaking in Tongues," suggests that Djuna Barnes in *Ladies Almanack* "writes through the lesbian body, celebrating not the abstraction of a sexual preference, but female sexuality and its lesbian expression."

Along with Stein, Dickinson's woman-identification has drawn the most attention from recent critics, and has generated considerable controversy between lesbian and other feminist critics. Faderman insists that Dickinson's love for women must be considered homosexual, and that critics must take into account her sexuality (or affectionality). Like most critics who accept this lesbian identification of Dickinson, she points to Susan Gilbert Dickinson as Emily's primary romantic and sexual passion. Both Faderman and Bernikow thus argue that Dickinson's "muse" was sometimes a female figure as well as a male.[3] Some of this work can be justifiably criticized for too closely identifying literature with life; however, by altering our awareness of what is *possible*—namely, that Dickinson's poetry was inspired by her love for a woman—we also can transform our response to the poetry. Paula Bennett daringly suggests that Dickinson's use of crumbs, jewels, pebbles, and similar objects was an attempt to create "clitoral imagery." In a controversial paper on the subject, Nadean Bishop argues forcefully that the poet's marriage poems must be reread in light of what she considers to have been Dickinson's consummated sexual relationship with her sister-in-law.[4]

The establishment of a lesbian literary tradition, a "canon," as my lengthy discussion suggests, has been the primary task of critics writing from a lesbian feminist perspective. But it is not the only focus to emerge. For example, lesbian critics, like feminist critics in the early seventies, have begun to analyze the images, stereotypes, and mythic presence of lesbians in fiction by or about lesbians. Bertha Harris, a major novelist as well as a provocative and trailblazing critic, considers the lesbian to be the prototype of the monster and "the quintessence of all that is female; and female enraged . . . . a lesbian is. . . . that which has been unspeakable about women."[5] Harris offers this monstrous lesbian as a female archetype who subverts traditional notions of female submissiveness, passivity, and virtue. Her "tooth-and-claw" image of the lesbian is ironically similar to that of Ellen Moers, although from a lesbian rather than heterosexual point of view. But the very fact that Moers presents the lesbian-as-monster in a derogatory context and Harris in a celebratory one suggests that there is an important dialectic between how the lesbian articulates herself and how she is articulated and objectified by others. Popular culture, in particular, exposes the objectifying purpose of the lesbian-as-monster image, such as the lesbian vampire first created by Joseph Sheridan LeFanu's 1871 ghost story, "Carmilla," and revived in early 1970s "B" films as a symbolic attack on women's struggle for self-identity.[6] Other

3. Lillian Faderman and Louise Bernikow, "Comment on Joanne Feit Diehl's '"Come Slowly—Eden,"'" *Signs* 4, no. 1 (Autumn 1978): 188–95. For another perspective on woman as muse, see my paper, "'The Dark Eye Beaming': George Eliot, Sara Hennell and the Female Muse" (presented at MLA convention, "George Eliot and the Female Tradition," 1980); and Arlene Raven and Ruth Iskin, "Through the Peephole: Toward a Lesbian Sensibility in Art," *Chrysalis* no. 4 (1977): 19–31. Contemporary lesbian interpretations of Dickinson were anticipated by Rebecca Patterson in *The Riddle of Emily Dickinson* (Boston: Houghton Mifflin, 1951).
4. Paula Bennett, "The Language of Love: Emily Dickinson's Homoerotic Poetry," *Gai Saber* 1, no.

1 (Spring 1977): 13–17; Bennett, "Emily Dickinson and the Value of Isolation," *Dickinson Studies* 36 (1979): 13–17; Bennett's paper presented at the MLA, 1979; and Nadean Bishop, "Renunciation in the Bridal Poems of Emily Dickinson," paper presented at the National Women's Studies Convention, Bloomington, Indiana, May 16–20, 1980.
5. Bertha Harris, "*What we mean to say*: Notes Toward Defining the Nature of Lesbian Literature," *Heresies* 3 (Fall 1977): 7–8. Also, Harris, "The Purification of Monstrosity: The Lesbian as Literature," paper presented at the MLA convention, New York, December 1974.
6. Bonnie Zimmerman, "'Daughters of Darkness': Lesbian Vampires," *Jump Cut* no. 24–25 (March

critics also have analyzed the negative symbolic appearance of the lesbian in literature. Ann Allen Shockley, reviewing black lesbian characters in American fiction, notes that "within these works exists an undercurrent of hostility, trepidation, subtlety, shadiness, and in some instances, ignorance culling forth homophobic stereotypes."[7] Homophobic sterotypes are also what Judith McDaniel and Maureen Brady find in abundance in recent commercial fiction (such as *Kinflicks*, *A Sea Change*, *Some Do* and *How to Save Your Own Life*) by avowedly feminist novelists. Although individuals might disagree with McDaniel and Brady's severe criticism of specific novels, their overall argument is unimpeachable. Contemporary feminist fiction, by perpetuating stereotyped characters and themes (such as the punishment theme so dear to pre-feminist lesbian literature), serves to "disempower the lesbian."[8] Lesbian, as well as heterosexual, writers present the lesbian as Other, as Julia Penelope Stanley discovered in prefeminist fiction: "the lesbian character creates for herself a mythology of darkness, a world in which she moves through dreams and shadows."[9] Lesbian critics may wish to avoid this analysis of the lesbian as Other because we no longer wish to dwell upon the cultural violence done against us. Yet this area must be explored until we strip these stereotypes of their inhibiting and dehumanizing presence in our popular culture and social mythology.

Lesbian critics have also delved into the area of stylistics and literary theory. If we have been silenced for centuries and speak an oppressor's tongue, then liberation for the lesbian must begin with language. Some writers may have reconciled their internal censor with their speech by writing in code, but many critics maintain that modern lesbian writers, because they are uniquely alienated from the patriarchy, experiment with its literary style and form. Julia Penelope Stanley and Susan Wolfe, considering such diverse writers as Virginia Woolf, Gertrude Stein, Kate Millett, and Elana Dykewoman, claim that "a feminist aesthetic, as it emerges out of women's evolution, grounds itself in female consciousness and in the unrelenting language of process and change."[1] In this article, the authors do not call their feminist aesthetic a lesbian feminist aesthetic, although all the writers they discuss are, in fact, lesbians. Susan Wolfe later confronted this fact: "Few women who continue to identify with men can risk the male censure of 'women's style,' and few escape the male perspective long enough to attempt it."[2] Through examples from Kate Millett, Jill Johnston, and Monique Wittig, she illustrates her contention that lesbian literature is characterized by the use of the continuous present, unconventional grammar and neologism; and that it breaks boundaries between art and the world, between events and our perceptions of them, and between past, present, and the dream world. It is, as even the proponents

1981): 23–24. See also, Jane Caputi, " 'Jaws': Fish Stories and Patriarchal Myth," *Sinister Wisdom* 7 (Fall 1978): 66–81.

7. Ann Allen Shockley, "The Black Lesbian in American Literature: An Overview," *Conditions: Five* 2, no. 2 (Autumn 1979): 136.

8. Maureen Brady and Judith McDaniel, "Lesbians in the Mainstream: Images of Lesbians in Recent Commercial Fiction," *Conditions: Six* 2, no. 3 (Summer 1980): 83.

9. Julia Penelope Stanley, "Uninhabited Angels: Metaphors for Love," *Margins* 23 (August 1975): 8.

1. Julia Penelope Stanley and Susan J. Wolfe, "Toward a Feminist Aesthetic," *Chrysalis*, no. 6 (1978): 66.

2. Susan J. Wolfe, "Stylistic Experimentation in Millett, Johnston, and Wittig," paper presented at the MLA convention, New York, December 1978, p. 3. On lesbian stylistics, see Lanser, "Speaking in Tongues"; and Martha Rosenfield, "Linguistic Experimentation in Monique Wittig's *Le Corps lesbien*," paper presented at the MLA convention, 1978.

of this theory admit, highly debatable that all lesbian writers are modernists, or that all modernists are lesbians. If Virginia Woolf wrote in non-linear, stream-of-consciousness style because she was a lesbian (or "woman-identified") how does one explain Dorothy Richardson whose *Pilgrimage,* despite one lesbian relationship, is primarily heterosexual? If both Woolf and Richardson can be called "feminist" stylists, then how does one explain the nonlinear experimentation of James Joyce or Alain Robbe-Grillet, for example? The holes that presently exist in this theory should not, however, detract from the highly suggestive overlap between experimental and lesbian writers. Nor should we ignore the clear evidence that many contemporary, self-conscious lesbian writers (such as Wittig, Johnston, Bertha Harris and June Arnold) are choosing an experimental style as well as content.

This development of a self-conscious lesbian literature and literary theory in recent years has led a number of critics to investigate the unifying themes and values of current literature. Such an attempt has been made by Elly Bulkin, who traces the various sources of contemporary lesbian poetry, analyzes "the range of lesbian voices," and advises feminist teachers how to teach lesbian poetry. Mary Carruthers, in asking why so much contemporary feminist poetry is also lesbian, observes that the "lesbian love celebrated in contemporary women's poetry requires an affirmation of the value of femaleness, women's bodies, women's sexuality—in women's language."[3] Jane Gurko and Sally Gearhart compare contemporary lesbian and gay male literature, attempting to discern to what extent one or the other transforms heterosexual ideology. They claim that, unlike gay male literature, lesbian literature "does express a revolutionary model of sexuality which in its structure, its content, and its practice defies the fundamental violent assumptions of patriarchal culture."[4] There is a danger in this attempt to establish a characteristic lesbian vision or literary value system, one that is well illustrated by this article. In an attempt to say *this* is what defines a lesbian literature, we are easily tempted to read selectively, omitting what is foreign to our theories. Most contemporary lesbian literature does embrace a rhetoric of nonviolence, but this is not universally true; for example, M. F. Beal's *Angel Dance* is a lesbian hard-boiled detective novel and Monique Wittig's *Le Corps lesbien*[5] is infused with a violent eroticism that is, nonetheless, intensely nonpatriarchal. Violence, role playing, disaffection, unhappiness, suicide, and self-hatred, to name a few "taboo" subjects, all exist within the lesbian culture, and a useful criticism will have to effectively analyze these as *lesbian* themes and issues, regardless of ideological purity.

Lesbian feminist criticism faces a number of concerns that must be addressed as it grows in force and clarity. Among these concerns is the fact that this criticism is dominated by the politics of lesbian separatism. This is exemplified by the following statement from *Sinister Wisdom,* a journal that has developed a consistent and articulate separatist politics,

3. Mary Carruthers, "Imagining Women: Notes Toward a Feminist Poetic," *Massachusetts Review* 20, no. 2 (Summer 1979): 301.
4. Jane Gurko and Sally Gearhart, "The Sword and the Vessel Versus the Lake on the Lake: A Lesbian Model of Nonviolent Rhetoric," paper presented at the MLA convention, 1979, p. 3.
5. *The Lesbian Body* (1973; trans. from French 1975) [editor's note].

'lesbian consciousness' is really a point of view, a view from the boundary. And in a sense every time a woman draws a circle around her psyche, saying 'this is a room of *my own*.' and then writes from within that 'room,' she's inhabiting lesbian consciousness.[6]

The value of separatism which, I believe, has always provided the most exciting theoretical developments in lesbian ideology, is precisely this marginality: lesbian existence "on the periphery of patriarchy."[7] Separatism provides criticism, as it did for lesbian politics, a cutting edge and radical energy that keeps us moving forward rather than backward either from fear or complacency. Those critics who maintain a consciously chosen position on the boundaries (and not one imposed by a hostile society) help to keep lesbian and feminist criticism radical and provocative, preventing both from becoming another arm of the established truth. At the same time, however, it is essential that separatist criticism does not itself become an orthodoxy, and thus repetitive, empty, and resistant to change. Lesbian criticism, as Kolodny has argued about feminist criticism, has more to gain from resisting dogma than from monotheism.[8] Understandably, those critics and scholars willing to identify themselves publicly as lesbians also have tended to hold radical politics of marginality. Exposing one's self to public scrutiny as a lesbian may in fact entail marginality through denial of tenure or loss of job, and those lesbians willing to risk these consequences usually have a political position that justifies their risk. However, to me it seems imperative that lesbian criticism develop diversity in theory and approach. Much as lesbians, even more than heterosexual feminists, may mistrust systems of thought developed by and associated with men and male values, we may, in fact, enrich our work through the insights of Marxist, structuralist, semiotic, or even psychoanalytic criticism. Perhaps "male" systems of thought are incompatible with a lesbian literary vision, but we will not know until we attempt to integrate these ideas into our work.[9]

Similarly, lesbian criticism and cultural theory in general can only gain by developing a greater specificity, historically and culturally. We have tended to write and act as if lesbian experience—which is perceived as that of a contemporary, white middle-class feminist—is universal and unchanging. Although most lesbians know that this is not the case, we too often forget to apply rigorous historical and cross-cultural tools to our scholarship. Much of this ahistoricity occurs around the shifting definitions of lesbianism from one era and one culture to another. To state simply that Wollstonecraft "was" a lesbian because she passionately loved Fanny Blood, or Susan B. Anthony was a lesbian because she wrote amorous letters to Anna Dickinson, without accounting for historical circumstances, may serve to distort or dislocate the actual meaning of these women's lives (just as it is distorting to *deny* their love for women). There are also notable differences among the institution of the *berdache* (the adoption by one sex of the opposite gender role) in Native American tribes; *faute de mieux* lesbian activity tolerated in France (as in

6. Harriet Desmoines, "Notes for a Magazine II," *Sinister Wisdom* 1, no. 1 (July 1976): 29.
7. Wolfe, "Stylistic Experimentation," p. 16.
8. Annette Kolodny, "Dancing Through the Minefield: Some Observations on the Theory, Practice and Politics of a Feminist Literary Criticism," *Fem-*

inist Studies 6, no. 1 (Spring 1980): 1–25.
9. For example, a panel at the 1980 MLA convention (Houston), "Literary History and the New Histories of Sexuality," presented gay and lesbian perspectives on contemporary French philosophies.

Colette's *Claudine* novels); idyllic romantic friendships (such as that of the famous Ladies of Llangollen[1]); and contemporary self-conscious lesbianism. I do believe that there is a common structure—a lesbian "essence"—that may be located in all these specific historical existences, just as we may speak of a widespread, perhaps universal, structure of marriage or the family. However, in each of these cases—lesbianism, marriage, the family—careful attention to history teaches us that differences are as significant as similarities, and vital information about female survival may be found in the different ways in which women have responded to their historical situation. This tendency toward simplistic universalism is accompanied by what I see as a dangerous development of biological determinism and a curious revival of the nineteenth-century feminist notion of female (now lesbian) moral superiority—that women are uniquely caring and superior to inherently violent males. Although only an undertone in some criticism and literature, any such sociobiological impulse should be questioned at every appearance.

The denial of meaningful differences among women is being challenged, particularly around the issue of racism. Bulkin has raised criticisms about the racism of white lesbian feminist theory. She has written that

> if I can put together—or think someone else can put together—a viable piece of feminist criticism or theory whose base is the thought and writing of white women/lesbians and expect that an analysis of racism can be tacked on or dealt with later as a useful addition, it is a measure of the extent to which I partake of that white privilege.[2]

Implicit in the criticism of Bulkin and other antiracist writers is the belief that lesbians, because of our experience of stigma and exclusion from the feminist mainstream, ought to be particularly sensitive to the dynamic between oppression and oppressing. White lesbians who are concerned about eradicating racism in criticism and theory have been greatly influenced as well by the work of several black lesbian feminist literary critics, such as Gloria T. Hull, Barbara Smith, and Lorraine Bethel.[3] Such concern is not yet present over the issue of class, although the historical association of lesbianism with upper-class values has often been used by left-wing political groups and governments to deny legitimacy to homosexual rights and needs. Lesbian critics studying the Barney circle, for example, might analyze the historical connections between lesbianism and class status. Lesbian critics might also develop comparisons among the literatures of various nationalities because the lesbian canon is of necessity cross-national. We have barely explored the differences between American, English, French, and German lesbian literature (although *Surpassing the Love of Men* draws some distinctions), let alone non-Western literature. The paucity of lesbian scholars trained in these lit-

1. Eleanor Butler and Sarah Posonby, who (at 39 and 23, respectively), after running away together against the wishes of their families, set up house in Wales in 1780; they became celebrated figures of the Romantic era, and had many famous visitors [editor's note].
2. Elly Bulkin, "Racism and Writing: Some Implications for White Lesbian Critics," *Sinister Wisdom* 13 (Spring 1980): 16.
3. A highly recommended resource on black les-

bians is *The Black Women's Issue, Conditions: Five* 2, no. 2, edited by Lorraine Bethel and Barbara Smith (Autumn 1979). Two additional publications have recently appeared: Cherríe Moraga and Gloria Anzaldúa, eds., *This Bridge Called My Back: Writings by Radical Women of Color* (Watertown, MA: Persephone Press, 1981), and J.R. Roberts, *Black Lesbians: An Annotated Bibliography* (Tallahassee: Naiad Press, 1981).

eratures has so far prevented the development of a truly international lesbian literary canon.

As lesbian criticism matures, we may anticipate the development of ongoing and compelling political and practical concerns. At this time, for example, lesbians are still defining and discovering texts. We are certainly not as badly off as we were in the early seventies when the only lesbian novels in print were *The Well of Loneliness*, *Rubyfruit Jungle*, and Isable Miller's *Patience and Sarah*. However, texts published prior to 1970 are still difficult to find, and even *The Well of Loneliness* is intermittently available at the whim of publishers.[4] Furthermore, the demise of Diana Press and the apparent slowdown of Daughters (two of the most active lesbian publishing houses) leaves many major works unavailable, possibly forever. As the boom in gay literature subsides, teachers of literature will find it very difficult to unearth teachable texts. Scholars have the excellent Arno Press series, *Homosexuality: Lesbians and Gay Men in Society, History, and Literature*, but, as Faderman's monumental scholarship reveals, far more lesbian literature exists than anyone has suspected. This literature needs to be unearthed, analyzed, explicated, perhaps translated, and made available to readers.

As lesbian critics, we also need to address the exclusion of lesbian literature from not merely the traditional, but also the feminist canon. Little lesbian literature has been integrated into the mainstream of feminist texts, as evidenced by what is criticized, collected, and taught. It is a matter of serious concern that lesbian literature is omitted from anthologies or included in mere token amounts, or that critical works and Modern Language Association panels still exclude lesbianism. It may as yet be possible for heterosexual feminists to claim ignorance about lesbian literature; however, lesbian critics should make it impossible for that claim to stand much longer. Lesbianism is still perceived as a minor and somewhat discomforting variation within the female life cycle, when it is mentioned at all. Just as we need to integrate lesbian material and perspectives into the traditional and feminist canons, we might also apply lesbian theory to traditional literature. Feminists have not only pointed out the sexism in many canonical works, but have also provided creative and influential rereadings of these works; similarly lesbians might contribute to the rereading of the classics. For example, *The Bostonians*, an obvious text, has been reread often from a lesbian perspective, and we could reinterpret D. H. Lawrence's antifeminism or Doris Lessing's compromised feminism (particularly in *The Golden Notebook*) by relating these attitudes to their fear of or discomfort with lesbianism. Other texts or selections of texts—such as Rossetti's "Goblin Market" or the relationship between Lucy Snowe and Ginevra Fanshawe in *Villette*[5]—might reveal a subtext that could be called lesbian. Just as few texts escape a feminist re-vision, few might invade a lesbian transformation.

This last point—that there is a way in which we might "review" literature as lesbians—brings me to my conclusion. In a brief period of a few years, crit-

---

4. In a response to my complaint about *The Well of Loneliness* being out of print, an editor at Washington Square Press remarked that "the existence in any mass-market form of a minor work of fiction is itself something of a wonder . . ." (personal correspondence, 29 January 1981). This attitude does not bode well for readers and teachers of lesbian literature.

5. By Charlotte Brontë (1853) [editor's note].

ics have begun to demonstrate the existence of a distinct lesbian aesthetic, just as feminists have outlined elements of a female aesthetic. Certain components of this aesthetic or critical perspective are clear:

> Perhaps lesbian feminist criticism [or literature, I would add] is a political or thematic perspective, a kind of imagination that can see beyond the barriers of heterosexuality, role stereotypes, patterns of language and culture that may be repressive to female sexuality and expression.[6]

A lesbian artist very likely would express herself differently about sexuality, the body, and relationships. But are there other—less obvious—unifying themes, ideas, and imagery that might define a lesbian text or subtext? How, for example, does the lesbian's sense of outlaw status affect her literary vision? Might lesbian writing, because of the lesbian's position on the boundaries, be characterized by a particular sense of freedom and flexibility or, rather, by images of violently imposed barriers, the closet? Or, in fact, is there a dialectic between freedom and imprisonment unique to lesbian writing? Do lesbians have a special perception of suffering and stigma, as so much prefeminist literature seems to suggest? What about the "muse," the female symbol of literary creativity: do women writers create a lesbian relationship with their muse as May Sarton asserts?[7] If so, do those writers who choose a female muse experience a freedom from inhibition because of that fact, or might there be a lack of creative tension in such a figurative same-sex relationship? I feel on solid ground in asserting that there are certain topics and themes that define lesbian culture, and that we are beginning to define a lesbian symbolism. Lesbian literature may present a unified tradition of thematic concerns such as that of unrequited longing, a longing of almost cosmic totality because the love object is denied not by circumstance or chance, but by necessity. The tension between romantic love and genital sexuality takes a particular form in woman-to-woman relationships, often articulated through musings on the difference between purity and impurity (culminating in Colette's study of variant sexuality, *The Pure and the Impure*). Lesbian literature approaches the theme of development or the quest in a manner different from that of men or heterosexual women.[8] Lesbian literature, as lesbian culture in general, is particularly flexible on issues of gender and role identification; even *The Well of Loneliness* hints at the tragedy of rigid gender roles. Because of this flexibility, lesbian artists and writers have always been fascinated with costuming, because dress is an external manifestation of gender roles lesbians often reject.[9] As we read and reread literature from a lesbian perspective, I am confident we will continue to expand our understanding of the lesbian literary tradition and a lesbian aesthetic.

This essay has suggested the vigor of lesbian criticism and its value to all feminists in raising awareness of entrenched heterosexism in existing texts,

6. Judith McDaniel, "Lesbians & Literature" *Sinister Wisdom* 2 (Fall 1976): 2.
7. This claim is made by the main character in *Mrs. Stevens Hears the Mermaids Singing* (1965), whom Sarton has described as autobiographical [editor's note].
8. See my essay, "Exiting from Patriarchy: The Lesbian Novel of Development," forthcoming in *Formation/Deformation/Transformation: The Female Novel of Development*, ed. Elizabeth Abel, Marianne Hirsch, and Elizabeth Langland [pub-

lished as *The Voyage In: Fictions of Female Development* (Hanover, N.H.: University Press of New England, 1983); see pp. 247–57]. Also see Jane Gurko, "The Shape of Sameness: Contemporary Lesbian Autobiographical Narratives," paper presented to the Gay Rhetoric Panel at the MLA Convention, Houston, December 1980.
9. This idea was suggested by Joan Biren (JEB) in her slide show, "Lesbian Images in Photography 1850–1980."

clarifying the lesbian traditions in literature through scholarship and reinterpretation, pointing out barriers that have stood in the way of free lesbian
expression, explicating the recurring themes and values of lesbian literature,
and exposing the dehumanizing stereotypes of lesbians in our culture. Many
of the issues that face lesbian critics—resisting dogma, expanding the canon,
creating a non-racist and non-classist critical vision, transforming our readings of traditional texts, and exploring new methodologies—are the interests
of all feminist critics. Because feminism concerns itself with the removal of
limitations and impediments in the way of female imagination, and lesbian
criticism helps to expand our notions of what is *possible* for women, then all
women would grow by adopting for themselves a lesbian vision. Disenfran-
chised groups have had to adopt a double-vision for survival; one of the political transformations of recent decades has been the realization that
enfranchised groups—men, whites, heterosexuals, the middle class—would
do well to adopt that double-vision for the survival of us all. Lesbian literary
criticism simply restates what feminists already know, that one group cannot
name itself "humanity" or even "woman": "We're not trying to become part of
the old order misnamed 'universal' which has tabooed us; we are transforming the meaning of 'universality.' "[1] Whether lesbian criticism will survive
depends as much upon the external social climate as it does upon the creativity and skill of its practitioners. If political attacks on gay rights and freedom grow; if the so-called Moral Majority wins its fight to eliminate gay
teachers and texts from the schools (it would be foolhardy to believe they will
exempt universities); and if the academy, including feminist teachers and
scholars, fails to support lesbian scholars, eradicate heterosexist values and
assumptions, and incorporate the insights of lesbian scholarship into the
mainstream; then current lesbian criticism will probably suffer the same fate
as did Jeanette Foster's *Sex Variant Women* in the fifties. Lesbian or heterosexual, we will all suffer from that loss.

1981

1. Elly Bulkin, "An Interview with Adrienne Rich: Part II," *Conditions: Two* 1, no. 2 (October 1977): 58.

CAROL GILLIGAN
b. 1936

Carol Gilligan, a social psychologist and educational theorist, began teaching at Harvard University in 1967; in 1970, she served as a research assistant for Lawrence
Kohlberg, noted for his research on moral development. In part because of her interviews with men thinking about enlisting for the Vietnam War and women contemplating abortions, she eventually criticized the male bias of Kohlberg's work; and her
book *In a Difference Voice: Psychological Theory and Women's Development* (1982)
suggests that women engage in unique processes of moral decision-making that are
undervalued by a thinker like Kohlberg. So-called difference feminists—those who
emphasize less the need for equality and more the capacities of each sex—embraced
Gilligan's view that women tend to behave in terms of an ethics of care, whereas men

tend to follow an ethics of justice. While teaching at Harvard, Gilligan was active in the Harvard Project on Women's Psychology and Girls' Development. Besides accepting subsequent positions at New York University and the University of Cambridge, she has published a number of books on psychotherapy and on gender and race relations, including (with Lyn Mikel Brown) *Meeting at the Crossroads: Women's Psychology and Girls' Development* (1992) and (with Jill McLean Taylor and Amy M. Sullivan) *Between Voice and Silence: Women and Girls, Race and Relationship* (1995). In *The Birth of Pleasure* (2002), Gilligan seeks to untangle pleasure and desire from the narratives of death and loss to which they have historically been harnassed.

From In a Different Voice: Psychological Theory and Women's Development

From *Chapter 1. Woman's Place in Man's Life Cycle*

* * *

The criticism that Freud makes of women's sense of justice,[1] seeing it as compromised in its refusal of blind impartiality, reappears not only in the work of Piaget but also in that of Kohlberg. While in Piaget's account (1932) of the moral judgment of the child, girls are an aside, a curiosity to whom he devotes four brief entries in an index that omits "boys" altogether because "the child" is assumed to be male, in the research from which Kohlberg derives his theory, females simply do not exist. Kohlberg's (1958, 1981) six stages that describe the development of moral judgment from childhood to adulthood are based empirically on a study of eighty-four boys whose development Kohlberg has followed for a period of over twenty years. Although Kohlberg claims universality for his stage sequence, those groups not included in his original sample rarely reach his higher stages (Edwards, 1975; Holstein, 1976; Simpson, 1974). Prominent among those who thus appear to be deficient in moral development when measured by Kohlberg's scale are women, whose judgments seem to exemplify the third stage of his six-stage sequence. At this stage morality is conceived in interpersonal terms and goodness is equated with helping and pleasing others. This conception of goodness is considered by Kohlberg and Kramer (1969) to be functional in the lives of mature women insofar as their lives take place in the home. Kohlberg and Kramer imply that only if women enter the traditional arena of male activity will they recognize the inadequacy of this moral perspective and progress like men toward higher stages where relationships are subordinated to rules (stage four) and rules to universal principles of justice (stages five and six).

Yet herein lies a paradox, for the very traits that traditionally have defined the "goodness" of women, their care for and sensitivity to the needs of others, are those that mark them as deficient in moral development. In this version of moral development, however, the conception of maturity is derived from the study of men's lives and reflects the importance of individuation in their development. Piaget (1970), challenging the common impression that a developmental theory is built like a pyramid from its base in infancy, points out that a conception of development instead hangs from its vertex of matu-

1. See Freud's "On Some Psychical Consequences of the Anatomical Distinction between the Sexes" (1925), cited earlier in the chapter.

rity, the point toward which progress is traced. Thus, a change in the definition of maturity does not simply alter the description of the highest stage but recasts the understanding of development, changing the entire account.

When one begins with the study of women and derives developmental constructs from their lives, the outline of a moral conception different from that described by Freud, Piaget, or Kohlberg begins to emerge and informs a different description of development. In this conception, the moral problem arises from conflicting responsibilities rather than from competing rights and requires for its resolution a mode of thinking that is contextual and narrative rather than formal and abstract. This conception of morality as concerned with the activity of care centers moral development around the understanding of responsibility and relationships, just as the conception of morality as fairness ties moral development to the understanding of rights and rules.

This different construction of the moral problem by women may be seen as the critical reason for their failure to develop within the constraints of Kohlberg's system. Regarding all constructions of responsibility as evidence of a conventional moral understanding, Kohlberg defines the highest stages of moral development as deriving from a reflective understanding of human rights. That the morality of rights differs from the morality of responsibility in its emphasis on separation rather than connection, in its consideration of the individual rather than the relationship as primary, is illustrated by two responses to interview questions about the nature of morality. The first comes from a twenty-five-year-old man, one of the participants in Kohlberg's study:

> [*What does the word morality mean to you?*] Nobody in the world knows the answer. I think it is recognizing the right of the individual, the rights of other individuals, not interfering with those rights. Act as fairly as you would have them treat you. I think it is basically to preserve the human being's right to existence. I think that is the most important. Secondly, the human being's right to do as he pleases, again without interfering with somebody else's rights.
>
> [*How have your views on morality changed since the last interview?*] I think I am more aware of an individual's rights now. I used to be looking at it strictly from my point of view, just for me. Now I think I am more aware of what the individual has a right to.

Kohlberg (1973) cites this man's response as illustrative of the principled conception of human rights that exemplifies his fifth and sixth stages. Commenting on the response, Kohlberg says: "Moving to a perspective outside of that of his society, he identifies morality with justice (fairness, rights, the Golden Rule), with recognition of the rights of others as these are defined naturally or intrinscially. The human being's right to do as he pleases without interfering with somebody else's rights is a formula defining rights prior to social legislation" (pp. 29–30).

The second response comes from a woman who participated in the rights and responsibilities study. She also was twenty-five and, at the time, third-year law student:

> [*Is there really some correct solution to moral problems, or is everybody's opinion equally right?*] No, I don't think everybody's opinion is equally right. I think that in some situations there may be opinions that are equally valid, and one could conscientiously adopt one of several courses

of action. But there are other situations in which I think there are right and wrong answers, that sort of inhere in the nature of existence, of all individuals here who need to live with each other to live. We need to depend on each other, and hopefully it is not only a physical need but a need of fulfillment in ourselves, that a person's life is enriched by cooperating with other people and striving to live in harmony with everybody else, and to that end, there are right and wrong, there are things which promote that end and that move away from it, and in that way it is possible to choose in certain cases among different courses of action that obviously promote or harm that goal.

[*Is there a time in the past when you would have thought about these things differently?*] Oh, yeah, I think that I went through a time when I thought that things were pretty relative, that I can't tell you what to do and you can't tell me what to do, because you've got your conscience and I've got mine.

[*When was that?*] When I was in high school. I guess that it just sort of dawned on me that my own ideas changed, and because my own judgment changed, I felt I couldn't judge another person's judgment. But now I think even when it is only the person himself who is going to be affected, I say it is wrong to the extent it doesn't cohere with what I know about human nature and what I know about you, and just from what I think is true about the operation of the universe, I could say I think you are making a mistake.

[*What led you to change, do you think?*] Just seeing more of life, just recognizing that there are an awful lot of things that are common among people. There are certain things that you come to learn promote a better life and better relationships and more personal fulfillment than other things that in general tend to do the opposite, and the things that promote these things, you would call morally right.

This response also represents a personal reconstruction of morality following a period of questioning and doubt, but the reconstruction of moral understanding is based not on the primacy and universality of individual rights, but rather on what she describes as a "very strong sense of being responsible to the world." Within this construction, the moral dilemma changes from how to exercise one's rights without interfering with the rights of others to how "to lead a moral life which includes obligations to myself and my family and people in general." The problem then becomes one of limiting responsibilities without abandoning moral concern. When asked to describe herself, this woman says that she values "having other people that I am tied to, and also having people that I am responsible to. I have a very strong sense of being responsible to the world, that I can't just live for my enjoyment, but just the fact of being in the world gives me an obligation to do what I can to make the world a better place to live in, no matter how small a scale that may be on." Thus while Kohlberg's subject worries about people interfering with each other's rights, this woman worries about "the possibility of omission, of your not helping others when you could help them."

The issue that this woman raises is addressed by Jane Loevinger's fifth "autonomous" stage of ego development, where autonomy, placed in a context of relationships, is defined as modulating an excessive sense of responsibility through the recognition that other people have responsibility for their own destiny. The autonomous stage in Loevinger's account (1970) witnesses a relinquishing of moral dichotomies and their replacement with "a feeling for the complexity and multifaceted character of real people and real situations" (p. 6). Whereas the rights conception of morality that informs Kohlberg's principled level (stages five and six) is geared to arriving at an objectively fair or just resolution to moral dilemmas upon which all rational persons could agree, the responsibility conception focuses instead on the limitations of any particular resolution and describes the conflicts that remain.

Thus it becomes clear why a morality of rights and noninterference may appear frightening to women in its potential justification of indifference and unconcern. At the same time, it becomes clear why, from a male perspective, a morality of responsibility appears inconclusive and diffuse, given its insistent contextual relativism. Women's moral judgments thus elucidate the pattern observed in the description of the developmental differences between the sexes, but they also provide an alternative conception of maturity by which these differences can be assessed and their implications traced. The psychology of women that has consistently been described as distinctive in its greater orientation toward relationships and interdependence implies a more contextual mode of judgment and a different moral understanding. Given the differences in women's conceptions of self and morality, women bring to the life cycle a different point of view and order human experience in terms of different priorities.

The myth of Demeter and Persephone, which McClelland (1975) cites as exemplifying the feminine attitude toward power, was associated with the Eleusinian Mysteries celebrated in ancient Greece for over two thousand years. As told in the Homeric *Hymn to Demeter*, the story of Persephone indicates the strengths of interdependence, building up resources and giving, that McClelland found in his research on power motivation to characterize the mature feminine style. Although, McClelland says, "it is fashionable to conclude that no one knows what went on in the Mysteries, it is known that they were probably the most important religious ceremonies, even partly on the historical record, which were organized by and for women, especially at the onset before men by means of the cult of Dionysos began to take them over." Thus McClelland regards the myth as "a special presentation of feminine psychology" (p. 96). It is, as well, a life-cycle story par excellence.

Persephone, the daughter of Demeter, while playing in a meadow with her girlfriends, sees a beautiful narcissus which she runs to pick. As she does so, the earth opens and she is snatched away by Hades, who takes her to his underworld kingdom. Demeter, goddess of the earth, so mourns the loss of her daughter that she refuses to allow anything to grow. The crops that sustain life on earth shrivel up, killing men and animals alike, until Zeus takes pity on man's suffering and persuades his brother to return Persephone to her mother. But before she leaves, Persephone eats some pomegranate seeds, which ensures that she will spend part of every year with Hades in the underworld.

The elusive mystery of women's development lies in its recognition of the continuing importance of attachment in the human life cycle. Woman's place in man's life cycle is to protect this recognition while the developmental litany intones the celebration of separation, autonomy, individuation, and natural rights. The myth of Persephone speaks directly to the distortion in this view by reminding us that narcissism leads to death, that the fertility of the earth is in some mysterious way tied to the continuation of the mother-daughter relationship, and that the life cycle itself arises from an alternation between the world of women and that of men. Only when life-cycle theorists divide their attention and begin to live with women as they have lived with men will their vision encompass the experience of both sexes and their theories become correspondingly more fertile.

WORKS CITED

Edwards, Carolyn P. 1975. "Societal Complexity and Moral Development: A Kenyan Study." *Ethos* 3: 505–27.

Holstein, Constance. 1976. "Development of Moral Judgment: A Longitudinal Study of Males and Females." *Child Development* 47: 51–61.

Kohlberg, Lawrence. 1958. "The Development of Modes of Thinking and Choices in Years 10 to 16." Ph.D. diss., University of Chicago.

———. 1973. "Continuities and Discontinuities in Childhood and Adult Moral Development Revisited." In *Collected Papers on Moral Development and Moral Education*. Cambridge, Mass.: Moral Education Research Foundation, Harvard University.

———. 1981. *The Philosophy of Moral Development*. San Francisco: Harper & Row.

Kohlberg, L., and R. Kramer. 1969. "Continuities and Discontinuities in Child and Adult Moral Development." *Human Development* 12: 93–120.

Loevinger, Jane, and Ruth Wessler. 1970. *Measuring Ego Development*. San Francisco: Jossey-Bass.

McClelland, David C. 1975. *Power: The Inner Experience*. New York: Irvington.

Piaget, Jean. 1932 [1965]. *The Moral Judgment of the Child*. Trans. Marjorie Gabain. New York: Free Press.

———. 1970. *Structuralism*. Trans. and ed. Chaninah Maschler. New York: Basic Books.

Simpson, Elizabeth L. 1974. "Moral Development Research: A Case Study of Scientific Cultural Bias." *Human Development* 17: 80–106.

1982

LILLIAN ROBINSON
1941–2006

In *Sex, Class, and Culture* (1978), *Monstrous Regiment: The Lady Knight in Sixteenth-Century Epic* (1985), *In the Canon's Mouth: Dispatches from the Culture Wars* (1977), and *Wonder Women: Feminism and Superheroes* (2004), and as a contributor to *Feminist Scholarship: Kindling in the Groves of Academe* (1985) as well as to *Revealing Lines: Autobiography, Biography and Gender* (1990), Lillian Robinson produced important scholarship on the gender and class biases implicit in canon formation; that is, on the material causes that shape what is deemed a great work or a masterpiece, what is considered trivial or minor. In recognition of the activist leadership role she played both inside and outside the academy, she was named principal of the Simone de Beauvoir Institute at Concordia University in Montreal before her untimely death.

Treason Our Text: Feminist Challenges to the Literary Canon

Successful plots have often had gunpowder in them. Feminist critics
have gone so far as to take treason to the canon as our text.[1]
— JANE MARCUS

The lofty seat of canonized bards (Pollok, 1827).

As with many other restrictive institutions, we are hardly aware of it until we
come into conflict with it; the elements of the literary canon are simply
absorbed by the apprentice scholar and critic in the normal course of graduate education, without anyone's ever seeming to inculcate or defend them.
Appeal, were any necessary, would be to the other meaning of "canon," that
is, to established standards of judgment and of taste. Not that either definition is presented as rigid and immutable—far from it, for lectures in literary
history are full of wry references to a benighted though hardly distant past
when, say, the metaphysical poets were insufficiently appreciated or Vachel
Lindsay was the most modern poet recognized in American literature.
Whence the acknowledgment of a subjective dimension, sometimes generalized as "sensibility," to the category of taste. Sweeping modifications in the
canon are said to occur because of changes in collective sensibility, but individual admissions and elevations from "minor" to "major" status tend to be
achieved by successful critical promotion, which is to say, demonstration that
a particular author does meet generally accepted criteria of excellence.

The results, moreover, are nowhere codified: they are neither set down in
a single place, nor are they absolutely uniform. In the visual arts and in
music, the cold realities of patronage, purchase, presentation in private and
public collections, or performance on concert programs create the conditions
for a work's canonical status or lack of it. No equivalent set of institutional
arrangements exists for literature, however. The fact of publication and even
the feat of remaining in print for generations, which are at least analogous to
the ways in which pictures and music are displayed, are not the same sort of
indicators; they represent less of an investment and hence less general
acceptance of their canonicity. In the circumstances, it may seem somewhat
of an exaggeration to speak of "the" literary canon, almost paranoid to call it
an institution, downright hysterical to characterize that institution as restrictive. The whole business is so much more informal, after all, than any of these
terms implies, the concomitant processes so much more gentlemanly. Surely,
it is more like a gentlemen's agreement than a repressive instrument—isn't
it?

But a gentleman is inescapably—that is, by definition—a member of a privileged class and of the male sex. From this perspective, it is probably quite
accurate to think of the canon as an entirely gentlemanly artifact, considering how few works by nonmembers of that class and sex make it into the
informal agglomeration of course syllabi, anthologies, and widely
commented-upon "standard authors" that constitutes the canon as it is gen-

---

1. Jane Marcus, "Gunpowder Treason and Plot,"
talk delivered at the School of Criticism and Theory, Northwestern University, colloquium "The
Challenge of Feminist Criticism," November 1981.
Seeking authority for the sort of creature a literary
canon might be, I turned, like many another, to the
Oxford English Dictionary. The tags that head up
the several sections of this essay are a by-product
of that effort rather than of any more exact and
laborious scholarship. [All notes are Robinson's.]

erally understood. For, beyond their availability on bookshelves, it is through the teaching and study—one might even say the habitual teaching and study—of certain works that they become institutionalized as canonical literature. Within that broad canon, moreover, those admitted but read only in advanced courses, commented upon only by more or less narrow specialists, are subjected to the further tyranny of "major" versus "minor."

For more than a decade now, feminist scholars have been protesting the apparently systematic neglect of women's experience in the literary canon, neglect that takes the form of distorting and misreading the few recognized female writers and excluding the others. Moreover, the argument runs, the predominantly male authors in the canon show us the female character and relations between the sexes in a way that both reflects and contributes to sexist ideology—an aspect of these classic works about which the critical tradition remained silent for generations. The feminist challenge, although intrinsically (and, to my mind, refreshingly) polemical, has not been simply a reiterated attack, but a series of suggested alternatives to the male-dominated membership and attitudes of the accepted canon. In this essay, I propose to examine these feminist alternatives, assess their impact on the standard canon, and propose some directions for further work. Although my emphasis in each section is on the substance of the challenge, the underlying polemic is, I believe, abundantly clear.

The presence of canonized forefathers (Burke, 1790).

Start with the Great Books, the traditional desert-island ones, the foundation of courses in the Western humanistic tradition. No women authors, of course, at all, but within the works thus canonized, certain monumental female images: Helen, Penelope, and Clytemnestra, Beatrice and the Dark Lady of the Sonnets, Bérénice, Cunégonde, and Margarete. The list of interesting female characters is enlarged if we shift to the Survey of English Literature and its classic texts; here, moreover, there is the possible inclusion of a female author or even several, at least as the course's implicit "historical background" ticks through and past the Industrial Revolution. It is a possibility that is not always honored in the observance. *"Beowulf"* to Virginia Woolf" is a pleasant enough joke, but though lots of surveys begin with the Anglo-Saxon epic, not all that many conclude with *Mrs. Dalloway*. Even in the nineteenth century, the pace and the necessity of mass omissions may mean leaving out Austen, one of the Brontës, or Eliot. The analogous overview of American literary masterpieces, despite the relative brevity and modernity of the period considered, is likely to yield a similarly all-male pantheon; Emily Dickinson may be admitted—but not necessarily—and no one else even comes close.[2] Here again, the male-authored canon contributes to

2. In a survey of 50 introductory courses in American literature offered at 25 U.S. colleges and universities, Emily Dickinson's name appeared more often than that of any other woman writer: 20 times. This frequency puts her in a fairly respectable twelfth place. Among the 61 most frequently taught authors, only 7 others are women; Edith Wharton and Kate Chopin are each mentioned 8 times, Sarah Orne Jewett and Anne Bradstreet 6 each, Flannery O'Connor 4 times, Willa Cather and Mary Wilkins Freeman each 3 times.

The same list includes 5 black authors, all of them male. Responses from other institutions received too late for compilation only confirmed these findings. See Paul Lauter, "A Small Survey of Introductory Courses in American Literature," *Women's Studies Quarterly* 9 (Winter 1981): 12. In another study, 99 professors of English responded to a survey asking which works of American literature published since 1941 they thought should be considered classics and which books should be taught to college students. The work mentioned by

the body of information, stereotype, inference, and surmise about the female sex that is generally in the culture.

Once this state of affairs has been exposed, there are two possible approaches for feminist criticism. It can emphasize alternative readings of the tradition, readings that reinterpret women's character, motivations, and actions and that identify and challenge sexist ideology. Or it can concentrate on gaining admission to the canon for literature by women writers. Both sorts of work are being pursued, although, to the extent that feminist criticism has defined itself as a subfield of literary studies—as distinguished from an approach or method—it has tended to concentrate on writing by women.

In fact, however, the current wave of feminist theory began as criticism of certain key texts, both literary and paraliterary, in the dominant culture. Kate Millett, Eva Figes, Elizabeth Janeway, Germaine Greer, and Carolyn Heilbrun all use the techniques of essentially literary analysis on the social forms and forces surrounding those texts.[3] The texts themselves may be regarded as "canonical" in the sense that all have had significant impact on the culture as a whole, although the target being addressed is not literature or its canon.

In criticism that is more strictly literary in its scope, much attention has been concentrated on male writers in the American tradition. Books like Annette Kolodny's *The Lay of the Land* and Judith Fetterley's *The Resisting Reader* have no systematic, comprehensive equivalent in the criticism of British or European literature.[4] Both of these studies identify masculine values and imagery in a wide range of writings, as well as the alienation that is their consequence for women, men, and society as a whole. In a similar vein, Mary Ellmann's *Thinking About Women* examines ramifications of the tradition of "phallic criticism" as applied to writers of both sexes.[5] These books have in common with one another and with overarching theoretical manifestos like *Sexual Politics* a sense of having been betrayed by a culture that was supposed to be elevating, liberating, and one's own.

By contrast, feminist work devoted to that part of the Western tradition which is neither American nor contemporary is likelier to be more evenhanded. "Feminist critics," declare Lenz, Greene, and Neely in introducing their collection of essays on Shakespeare, "recognize that the greatest artists do not necessarily duplicate in their art the orthodoxies of their culture; they may exploit them to create character or intensify conflict, they may struggle

---

the most respondents (59 citations) was Ralph Ellison's *Invisible Man*. No other work by a black appears among the top 20 that constitute the published list of results. Number 19, *The Complete Stories of Flannery O'Connor*, is the only work on this list by a woman. (*Chronicle of Higher Education*, September 29, 1982.) For British literature, the feminist claim is not that Austen, the Brontës, Eliot, and Woolf are habitually omitted, but rather that they are by no means always included in courses that, like the survey I taught at Columbia some years ago, had room for a single nineteenth-century novel. I know, however, of no systematic study of course offerings in this area more recent than Elaine Showalter's "Women in the Literary Curriculum," *College English* 32 (May 1971): 855–62.

3. Kate Millett, *Sexual Politics* (Garden City, N.Y.: Doubleday, 1970); Eva Figes, *Patriarchal Attitudes* (New York: Stein & Day, 1970); Elizabeth Janeway, *Man's World, Woman's Place: A Study in Social

Mythology (New York: William Morrow, 1971); Germaine Greer, *The Female Eunuch* (New York: McGraw-Hill, 1971); Carolyn G. Heilbrun, *Toward a Recognition of Androgyny* (New York: Harper & Row, 1974). The phenomenon these studies represent is discussed at greater length in a study of which I am a co-author; see Ellen Carol DuBois, Gail Paradise Kelly, Elizabeth Lapovsky Kennedy, Carolyn W. Korsmeyer, and Lillian S. Robinson, *Feminist Scholarship: Kindling in the Groves of Academe* (Urbana: University of Illinois Press, 1985).

4. Annette Kolodny, *The Lay of the Land: Metaphor as Experience and History in American Life and Letters* (Chapel Hill: University of North Carolina Press, 1975); Judith Fetterley, *The Resisting Reader: A Feminist Approach to American Fiction* (Bloomington: Indiana University Press, 1978).

5. Mary Ellmann, *Thinking About Women* (New York: Harcourt, Brace & World, 1968).

with, criticize, or transcend them."[6] From this perspective, Milton may come in for some censure, Shakespeare and Chaucer for both praise and blame, but the clear intention of a feminist approach to these classic authors is to enrich our understanding of what is going on in the texts, as well as how— for better, for worse, or for both—they have shaped our own literary and social ideas.[7] At its angriest, none of this reinterpretation offers a fundamental challenge to the canon *as canon*; although it posits new values, it never suggests that, in the light of those values, we ought to reconsider whether the great monuments are really so great, after all.

> *Such is all the worlde hathe confirmed and agreed upon, that it is authentique and canonical* (T. Wilson, 1553).

In an evolutionary model of feminist studies in literature, work on male authors is often characterized as "early," implicitly primitive, whereas scholarship on female authors is the later development, enabling us to see women—the writers themselves and the women they write about—as active agents rather than passive images or victims. This implicit characterization of studies addressed to male writers is as inaccurate as the notion of an inexorable evolution. In fact, as the very definition of feminist criticism has come increasingly to mean scholarship and criticism devoted to women writers, work on the male tradition has continued. By this point, there has been a study of the female characters or the views on the woman question of every major—perhaps every known—author in Anglo-American, French, Russian, Spanish, Italian, German, and Scandinavian literature.[8]

Nonetheless, it is an undeniable fact that most feminist criticism focuses on women writers, so that the feminist efforts to humanize the canon have usually meant bringing a woman's point of view to bear by incorporating works by women into the established canon. The least threatening way to do so is to follow the accustomed pattern of making the case for individual writers one by one. The case here consists in showing that an already recognized woman author has been denied her rightful place, presumably because of the general devaluation of female efforts and subjects. More often than not, such work involves showing that a woman already securely established in the canon belongs in the first rather than the second rank. The biographical and critical efforts of R.W.B. Lewis and Cynthia Griffin Wolff, for example, have attempted to enhance Edith Wharton's reputation in this way.[9] Obviously, no challenge is presented to the particular notions of literary quality, timeless-

6. Carolyn Ruth Swift Lenz, Gayle Greene, and Carol Thomas Neely, eds., *The Woman's Part: Feminist Criticism of Shakespeare* (Urbana: University of Illinois Press, 1980), p. 4. In this vein, see also Juliet Dusinberre, *Shakespeare and the Nature of Woman* (London: Macmillan, 1975); Irene G. Dash, *Wooing, Wedding, and Power: Women in Shakespeare's Plays* (New York: Columbia University Press, 1981).

7. Sandra M. Gilbert, "Patriarchal Poetics and the Woman Reader: Reflections on Milton's Bogey," *PMLA* 93 (May 1978): 368–82. The articles on Chaucer and Shakespeare in *The Authority of Experience: Essays in Feminist Criticism*, ed. Arlyn Diamond and Lee R. Edwards (Amherst: University of Massachusetts Press, 1977), reflect the complementary tendency.

8. As I learned when surveying fifteen years' worth of *Dissertation Abstracts* and MLA programs, much of this work has taken the form of theses or conference papers rather than books and journal articles.

9. See R. W. B. Lewis, *Edith Wharton: A Biography* (New York: Harper & Row, 1975); Cynthia Griffin Wolff, *A Feast of Words: The Triumph of Edith Wharton* (New York: Oxford University Press, 1977); see also Marlene Springer, *Edith Wharton and Kate Chopin: A Reference Guide* (Boston: G.K. Hall, 1976).

ness, universality, and other qualities that constitute the rationale for canon-icity. The underlying argument, rather, is that consistency, fidelity to those values, requires recognition of at least the few best and best-known women writers. Equally obviously, this approach does not call the notion of the canon itself into question.

> *We acknowledge it Canonlike, but not*
> *Canonicall* (Bishop Barlow, 1601).

Many feminist critics reject the method of case-by-case demonstration. The wholesale consignment of women's concerns and productions to a grim area bounded by triviality and obscurity cannot be compensated for by tokenism. True equity can be attained, they argue, only by opening up the canon to a much larger number of female voices. This is an endeavor that eventually brings basic aesthetic questions to the fore.

Initially, however, the demand for wider representation of female authors is substantiated by an extraordinary effort of intellectual reappropriation. The emergence of feminist literary study has been characterized, at the base, by scholarship devoted to the discovery, republication, and reappraisal of "lost" or undervalued writers and their work. From Rebecca Harding Davis and Kate Chopin through Zora Neale Hurston and Mina Loy to Meridel LeSueur and Rebecca West, reputations have been reborn or remade and a female counter-canon has come into being, out of components that were largely unavailable even a dozen years ago.[1]

In addition to constituting a feminist alternative to the male-dominated tradition, these authors also have a claim to representation in "the" canon. From this perspective, the work of recovery itself makes one sort of *prima facie* case, giving the lie to the assumption, where it has existed, that aside from a few names that are household words—differentially appreciated, but certainly well known—there simply has not been much serious literature by women. Before any aesthetic arguments have been advanced either for or against the admission of such works to the general canon, the new literary scholarship on women has demonstrated that the pool of potential applicants is far larger than anyone has hitherto suspected.

1. See, for instance, Rebecca Harding Davis, *Life in the Iron Mills* (Old Westbury, N.Y.: Feminist Press, 1972), with a biographical and critical Afterword by Tillie Olsen; Kate Chopin, *The Complete Works*, ed. Per Seyersted (Baton Rouge: Louisiana State University Press, 1969); Alice Walker, "In Search of Zora Neale Hurston," *Ms.*, March 1975, pp. 74–75; Robert Hemenway, *Zora Neale Hurston* (Urbana: University of Illinois Press, 1978): Zora Neale Hurston, *I Love Myself When I Am Laughing and Also When I Am Looking Mean and Impressive* (Old Westbury: Feminist Press, 1979), with introductory material by Alice Walker and Mary Helen Washington; Carolyn G. Burke, "Becoming Mina Loy," *Women's Studies* 7 (1979): 136–50; Meridel LeSueur, *Ripening* (Old Westbury: Feminist Press,

1981); on LeSueur, see also Mary McAnally, ed., *We Sing Our Struggle: A Tribute to Us All* (Tulsa, Okla.: Cardinal Press, 1982); *The Young Rebecca: Writings of Rebecca West, 1911–1917*, selected and introduced by Jane Marcus (New York: Viking Press, 1982).

The examples cited are all from the nineteenth and twentieth centuries. Valuable work has also been done on women writers before the Industrial Revolution. See Joan Goulianos, ed., By a Woman Writt: *Literature from Six Centuries by and about Women* (Indianapolis: Bobbs-Merrill, 1973); Mary R. Mahl and Helene Koon, eds., *The Female Spectator: English Women Writers before 1800* (Bloomington: Indiana University Press, 1977).

> *Would Augustine, if he held all the books to have an equal right to*
> *canonicity . . . have preferred some to others?*
> (W. Fitzgerald, trans. Whitaker, 1849).

But the aesthetic issues cannot be forestalled for very long. We need to understand whether the claim is being made that many of the newly recovered or validated texts by women meet existing criteria or, on the other hand, that those criteria themselves intrinsically exclude or tend to exclude women and hence should be modified or replaced. If this polarity is not, in fact, applicable to the process, what are the grounds for presenting a large number of new female candidates for (as it were) canonization?

The problem is epitomized in Nina Baym's introduction to her study of American women's fiction between 1820 and 1870:

> Reexamination of this fiction may well show it to lack the esthetic, intellectual and moral complexity and artistry that we demand of great literature. I confess frankly that, although I have found much to interest me in these books, I have not unearthed a forgotten Jane Austen or George Eliot or hit upon the one novel that I would propose to set alongside *The Scarlet Letter*. Yet I cannot avoid the belief that "purely" literary criteria, as they have been employed to identify the best American works, have inevitably had a bias in favor of things male—in favor of, say, a whaling ship, rather than a sewing circle as a symbol of the human community. . . . While not claiming any literary greatness for any of the novels . . . in this study, I would like at least to begin to correct such a bias by taking their content seriously. And it is time, perhaps—though this task lies outside my scope here—to reexamine the grounds upon which certain hallowed American classics have been called great.[2]

Now, if students of literature may be allowed to confess to one Great Unreadable among the Great Books, my own *bête noire* has always been the white whale; I have always felt I was missing something in *Moby Dick* that is clearly there for many readers and that is there for me when I read, say, Aeschylus or Austen. So I find Baym's strictures congenial, at first reading. Yet the contradictory nature of the position is also evident on the face of it. Am I or am I not being invited to construct a (feminist) aesthetic rationale for my impatience with *Moby Dick*? Do Baym and the current of thought she represents accept "esthetic, intellectual and moral complexity and artistry" as the grounds of greatness, or are they challenging those values as well?

As Myra Jehlen points out most lucidly, this attractive position will not bear close analysis: "[Baym] is having it both ways, admitting the artistic limitations of the women's fiction . . . and at the same time denying the validity of the rulers that measure these limitations, disdaining any ambition to reorder the literary canon and, on second thought, challenging the canon after all, or rather challenging not the canon itself but the grounds for its selection."[3] Jehlen understates the case, however, in calling the duality a paradox, which is, after all, an intentionally created and essentially rhetorical phenomenon.

2. Nina Baym, *Women's Fiction: A Guide to Novels by and about Women in America, 1820–70* (Ithaca: Cornell University Press, 1978), pp. 14–15.

3. Myra Jehlen, "Archimedes and the Paradox of Feminist Criticism," *Signs* 6 (Summer 1981): 592.

What is involved here is more like the *agony* of feminist criticism, for it is the champions of women's literature who are torn between defending the quality of their discoveries and radically redefining literary quality itself.

Those who are concerned with the canon as a pragmatic instrument rather than a powerful abstraction—the compilers of more equitable anthologies or course syllabi, for example—have opted for an uneasy compromise. The literature by women that they seek—as well as that by members of excluded racial and ethnic groups and by working people in general—conforms as closely as possible to the traditional canons of taste and judgment. Not that it reads like such literature as far as content and viewpoint are concerned, but the same words about artistic intent and achievement may be applied without absurdity. At the same time, the rationale for a new syllabus or anthology relies on a very different criterion: that of truth to the culture being represented, the *whole* culture and not the creation of an almost entirely male white elite. Again, no one seems to be proposing—aloud—the elimination of *Moby Dick* or *The Scarlet Letter,* just squeezing them over somewhat to make room for another literary reality, which, joined with the existing canon, will come closer to telling the (poetic) truth.

The effect is pluralist, at best, and the epistemological assumptions underlying the search for a more fully representative literature are strictly empiricist: by including the perspective of women (who are, after all, half-the-population), we will know more about the culture as it actually was. No one suggests that there might be something in this literature itself that challenges the values and even the validity of the previously all-male tradition. There is no reason why the canon need speak with one voice or as one man on the fundamental questions of human experience. Indeed, even as an elite white male voice, it can hardly be said to do so. Yet a commentator like Baym has only to say "it is time, perhaps . . . to reexamine the grounds," *while not proceeding to do so,* for feminists to be accused of wishing to throw out the entire received culture. The argument could be more usefully joined, perhaps, if there *were* a current within feminist criticism that went beyond insistence on representation to consideration of precisely how inclusion of women's writing alters our view of the tradition. Or even one that suggested some radical surgery on the list of male authors usually represented.

After all, when we turn from the construction of pantheons, which have no *prescribed* number of places, to the construction of course syllabi, then something does have to be eliminated each time something else is added, and here ideologies, aesthetic and extra-aesthetic, do necessarily come into play. Is the canon and hence the syllabus based on it to be regarded as the compendium of excellence or as the record of cultural history? For there comes a point when the proponent of making the canon recognize the achievement of both sexes has to put up or shut up; either a given woman writer is good enough to replace some male writer on the prescribed reading list or she is not. If she is not, then either she should replace him anyway, in the name of telling the truth about the culture, or she should not, in the (unexamined) name of excellence. This is the debate that will have to be engaged and that has so far been broached only in the most "inclusionary" of terms. It is ironic that in American literature, where attacks on the male tradition have been most bitter and the reclamation of women writers so spectacular, the appeal has still been only to pluralism, generosity, and guilt. It is populism without the politics of populism.

> *To canonize your owne writers* (Polimanteria, 1595).

Although I referred earlier to a feminist counter-canon, it is only in certain rather restricted contexts that literature by women has in fact been explicitly placed "counter" to the dominant canon. Generally speaking, feminist scholars have been more concerned with establishing the existence, power, and significance of a specifically female tradition. Such a possibility is adumbrated in the title of Patricia Meyer Spacks's *The Female Imagination;* however, this book's overview of selected themes and stages in the female life-cycle as treated by some women writers neither broaches nor (obviously) suggests an answer to the question whether there is a female imagination and what characterizes it.[4]

Somewhat earlier, in her anthology of British and American women poets, Louise Bernikow had made a more positive assertion of a continuity and connection subsisting among them.[5] She leaves it to the poems, however, to forge their own links, and, in a collection that boldly and incisively crosses boundaries between published and unpublished writing, literary and anonymous authorship, "high" art, folk art, and music, it is not easy for the reader to identify what the editor believes it is that makes women's poetry specifically *"women's."*

Ellen Moers centers her argument for a (transhistorical) female tradition upon the concept of "heroinism," a quality shared by women writers over time with the female characters they created.[6] Moers also points out another kind of continuity, documenting the way that women writers have read, commented on, and been influenced by the writings of other women who were their predecessors or contemporaries. There is also an unacknowledged continuity between the writer and her female reader. Elaine Showalter conceives the female tradition, embodied particularly in the domestic and sensational fiction of the nineteenth century, as being carried out through a kind of subversive conspiracy between author and audience.[7] Showalter is at her best in discussing this minor "women's fiction." Indeed, without ever making a case for popular genres as serious literature, she bases her arguments about a tradition more solidly on them than on acknowledged major figures like Virginia Woolf. By contrast, Sandra Gilbert and Susan Gubar focus almost exclusively on key literary figures, bringing women writers and their subjects together through the theme of perceived female aberration—in the act of literary creation itself, as well as in the behavior of the created persons or personae.[8]

Moers's vision of a continuity based on "heroinism" finds an echo in later feminist criticism that posits a discrete, perhaps even autonomous "women's culture." The idea of such a culture has been developed by social historians

4. Patricia Meyer Spacks, *The Female Imagination* (New York: Alfred A. Knopf, 1975).
5. *The World Split Open: Four Centuries of Women Poets in England and America, 1552–1950,* ed. and intro. Louise Bernikow (New York: Vintage Books, 1974).
6. Ellen Moers, *Literary Women: The Great Writers* (Garden City, N.Y.: Doubleday, 1976).

7. Elaine Showalter, *A Literature of Their Own: British Women Novelists from Brontë to Lessing* (Princeton, N.J.: Princeton University Press, 1977).
8. Sandra M. Gilbert and Susan Gubar, *The Madwoman in the Attic: The Woman Writer and the Nineteenth-Century Literary Imagination* (New Haven, Conn.: Yale University Press, 1979).

studying the "homosocial" world of nineteenth-century women.[9] It is a view that underlies, for example, Nina Auerbach's study of relationships among women in selected novels, where strong, supportive ties among mothers, daughters, sisters, and female friends not only constitute the real history in which certain women are conceived as living but function as a normative element as well.[1] That is, fiction in which positive relations subsist to nourish the heroine comes off much better, from Auerbach's point of view, than fiction in which such relations do not exist.

In contrast, Judith Lowder Newton sees the heroines of women's fiction as active, rather than passive, precisely because they do live in a man's world, not an autonomous female one.[2] Defining their power as "ability" rather than "control," she perceives "both a preoccupation with power and subtle power strategies" being exercised by the women in novels by Fanny Burney, Jane Austen, Charlotte Brontë, and George Eliot. Understood in this way, the female tradition, whether or not it in fact reflects and fosters a "culture" of its own, provides an alternative complex of possibilities for women, to be set beside the pits and pedestals offered by all too much of the Great Tradition.

Canonize such a multifarious Genealogie of Comments (Nashe, 1593).

Historians like Smith-Rosenberg and Cott are careful to specify that their generalizations extend only to white middle- and upper-class women of the nineteenth century. Although literary scholars are equally scrupulous about the national and temporal boundaries of their subject, they tend to use the gender term comprehensively. In this way, conclusions about "women's fiction" or "female consciousness" have been drawn or jumped to from considering a body of work whose authors are all white and comparatively privileged. Of the critical studies I have mentioned, only Bernikow's anthology, *The World Split Open*, brings labor songs, black women's blues lyrics, and anonymous ballads into conjunction with poems that were written for publication by professional writers, both black and white. The other books, which build an extensive case for a female tradition that Bernikow only suggests, delineate their subject in such a way as to exclude not only black and working-class authors but any notion that race and class might be relevant categories in the definition and apprehension of "women's literature." Similarly, even for discussions of writers who were known to be lesbians, this aspect of the female tradition often remains unacknowledged; worse yet, some of the books that develop the idea of a female tradition are openly homophobic, employing the word "lesbian" only pejoratively.[3]

9. Carroll Smith-Rosenberg, "The Female World of Love and Ritual: Relations Between Women in Nineteenth-Century America," Signs 1 (Fall 1975): 1–30; Nancy F. Cott, The Bonds of Womanhood: "Woman's Sphere" in New England, 1780–1830 (New. Haven, Conn.: Yale University Press, 1977).
1. Nina Auerbach, Communities of Women: An Idea in Fiction (Cambridge, Mass.: Harvard University Press, 1979). See also Janet M. Todd, Women's Friendship in Literature (New York: Columbia University Press, 1980); Louise Bernikow, Among Women (New York: Crown, 1980).
2. Judith Lowder Newton, Women, Power, and

Subversion: Social Strategies in British Fiction (Athens: University of Georgia Press, 1981).
3. On the failings of feminist criticism with respect to black and lesbian writers, see Barbara Smith, "Toward a Black Feminist Criticism," in The New Feminist Criticism: Essays on Women, Literature, and Theory, ed. Elaine Showalter (New York: Pantheon, 1985), pp. 168–85; Mary Helen Washington, "New Lives and New Letters: Black Women Writers at the End of the Seventies," College English 43 (January 1981): 1–11; Bonnie Zimmerman, "What Has Never Been: An Overview of Lesbian Feminist Literary Criticism," in The New Feminist Criticism, pp. 200–24.

Black and lesbian scholars, however, have directed much less energy to polemics against the feminist "mainstream" than to concrete, positive work on the literature itself. Recovery and reinterpretation of a wealth of unknown or undervalued texts has suggested the existence of both a black women's tradition and a lesbian tradition. In a clear parallel with the relationship between women's literature in general and the male-dominated tradition, both are by definition part of women's literature, but they are also distinct from and independent of it.

There are important differences, however, between these two traditions and the critical effort surrounding them. Black feminist criticism has the task of demonstrating that, in the face of all the obstacles a racist and sexist society has been able to erect, there is a continuity of black women who have written and written well. It is a matter of gaining recognition for the quality of the writing itself and respect for its principal subject, the lives and consciousness of black women. Black women's literature is also an element of black literature as a whole, where the recognized voices have usually been male. A triple imperative is therefore at work: establishing a discrete and significant black female tradition, then situating it within black literature and (along with the rest of that literature) within the common American literary heritage.[4] So far, unfortunately, each step toward integration has met with continuing exclusion. A black women's tradition has been recovered and revaluated chiefly through the efforts of black feminist scholars. Only some of that work has been accepted as part of either a racially mixed women's literature or a two-sex black literature. As for the gatekeepers of American literature in general, how many of them are willing to swing open the portals even for Zora Neale Hurston or Paule Marshall? How many have heard of them?

The issue of "inclusion," moreover, brings up questions that echo those raised by opening the male-dominated canon to women. How do generalizations about women's literature "as a whole" change when the work of black women is not merely added to but fully incorporated into that tradition? How does our sense of black literary history change? And what implications do these changes have for reconsideration of the American canon?

Whereas many white literary scholars continue to behave as if there were no major black woman writers, most are prepared to admit that certain well-known white writers were lesbians for all or part of their lives. The problem is getting beyond a position that says either "so *that's* what was wrong with her!" or, alternatively, "it doesn't matter who she slept with—we're talking about literature." Much lesbian feminist criticism has addressed theoretical questions about *which* literature is actually part of the lesbian tradition, all writing by lesbians, for example, or all writing by women about women's rela-

---

4. See, e.g., Smith, "Toward a Black Feminist Criticism"; Barbara Christian, *Black Women Novelists: The Development of a Tradition, 1892–1976* (Westport, Conn.: Greenwood Press, 1980); Erlene Stetson, ed., *Black Sister: Poetry by Black American Women, 1764–1980* (Bloomington: Indiana University Press, 1981) and its forthcoming sequel; Gloria Hull, "Black Women Poets from Wheatley to Walker," in *Sturdy Black Bridges: Visions of Black Women in Literature*, ed. Roseann P. Bell et al. (Garden City, N.Y.: Anchor Books, 1979); Mary Helen Washington, "Introduction: In Pursuit of Our Own History," *Midnight Birds: Stories of Contemporary Black Women Writers* (Garden City, N.Y.: Anchor Books, 1980); the essays and bibliographies in *But Some of Us Are Brave: Black Women's Studies*, ed. Gloria Hull, Patricia Bell Scott, and Barbara Smith (Old Westbury, N.Y.: Feminist Press, 1982).

tions with one another. Questions of class and race enter here as well, both in their own guise and in the by now familiar form of "aesthetic standards." Who speaks for the lesbian community: the highly educated experimentalist with an unearned income or the naturalistic working-class autobiographer? Or are both the *same kind* of foremother, reflecting the community's range of cultural identities and resistance?[5]

A cheaper way of Canon-making in a corner (Baxter, 1639).

It is not only members of included social groups, however, who have challenged the fundamentally elite nature of the existing canon. "Elite" is a literary as well as a social category. It is possible to argue for taking all texts seriously as texts without arguments based on social oppression or cultural exclusion, and popular genres have therefore been studied as part of the female literary tradition. Feminists are not in agreement as to whether domestic and sentimental fiction, the female Gothic, the women's sensational novel functioned as instruments of expression, repression, or subversion, but they have successfully revived interest in the question as a legitimate cultural issue.[6] It is no longer automatically assumed that literature addressed to the mass female audience is necessarily bad because it is sentimental, or for that matter, sentimental because it is addressed to that audience. Feminist criticism has examined without embarrassment an entire literature that was previously dismissed solely because it was popular with women and affirmed standards and values associated with femininity. And proponents of the "continuous tradition" and "women's culture" positions have insisted that this material be placed beside women's "high" art as part of the articulated and organic female tradition.

This point of view remains controversial within the orbit of women's studies, but the real problems start when it comes into contact with the universe of canon formation. Permission may have been given the contemporary critic to approach a wide range of texts, transcending and even ignoring the traditional canon. But in a context where the ground of struggle—highly contested, moreover—concerns Edith Wharton's advancement to somewhat more major status, fundamental assumptions have changed very little. Can Hawthorne's "d—d mob of scribbling women" *really* be invading the realms so long sanctified by Hawthorne himself and his brother geniuses? Is this what feminist criticism or even feminist cultural history means? Is it—to apply some outmoded and deceptively simple categories—a good development or a bad one? If these questions have not been raised, it is because women's literature and the female tradition tend to be evoked as an autonomous cultural experience, not impinging on the rest of literary history.

5. See Zimmerman, "What Has Never Been"; Adrienne Rich, "Jane Eyre: Trials of a Motherless Girl," *Lies, Secrets, and Silence: Selected Prose, 1966–1978* (New York: W. W. Norton, 1979); Lillian Faderman, *Surpassing the Love of Men: Romantic Friendship and Love Between Women from the Renaissance to the Present* (New York: William Morrow, 1981); the literary essays in *Lesbian Studies,* ed. Margaret Cruikshank (Old Westbury, N.Y.: Feminist Press, 1982).

6. Some examples on different sides of the question are: Ann Douglas, *The Feminization of American Culture* (New York: Alfred A. Knopf, 1976); Elaine Showalter, *A Literature of Their Own* and her article "Dinah Mulock Craik and the Tactics of Sentiment: A Case Study in Victorian Female Authorship," *Feminist Studies* 2 (May 1975): 5–23; Katherine Ellis, "Paradise Lost: The Limits of Domesticity in the Nineteenth-Century Novel," *Feminist Studies* 2 (May 1975): 55–65.

Wisdome under a ragged coate is seldome canonicall (Crosse, 1603).

Whether dealing with popular genres or high art, commentary on the female tradition usually has been based on work that was published at some time and was produced by professional writers. But feminist scholarship has also pushed back the boundaries of literature in other directions, considering a wide range of forms and styles in which women's writing—especially that of women who did not perceive themselves as writers—appears. In this way, women's letters, diaries, journals, autobiographies, oral histories, and private poetry have come under critical scrutiny as evidence of women's consciousness *and expression*.

Generally speaking, feminist criticism has been quite open to such material, recognizing that the very conditions that gave many women the impetus to write made it impossible for their culture to define them as writers. This acceptance has expanded our sense of possible forms and voices, but it has not challenged our received sense of appropriate style. What it amounts to is that if a woman writing in isolation and with no public audience in view nonetheless had "good"—that is, canonical—models, we are impressed with the strength of her text when she applies what she has assimilated about writing to her own experiences as a woman. If, however, her literary models were chosen from the same popular literature that some critics are now beginning to recognize as part of the female tradition, then she has not got hold of an expressive instrument that empowers her.

At the Modern Language Association meeting in 1976, I included in my paper the entire two-page autobiography of a participant in the Summer Schools for Women Workers held at Bryn Mawr in the first decades of the century. It is a circumstantial narrative in which events from the melancholy to the melodramatic are accumulated in a serviceable, somewhat hackneyed style. The anonymous "Seamer on Men's Underwear" had a unique sense of herself both as an individual and as a member of the working class. But was she a writer? Part of the audience was as moved as I was by the narrative, but the majority was outraged at the piece's failure to meet the criteria—particularly, the "complexity" criteria—of good art.

When I developed my remarks for publication, I wrote about the problems of dealing with an author who is trying too hard to write elegantly, and attempted to make the case that clichés or sentimentality need not be signals of meretricious prose and that ultimately it is honest writing for which criticism should be looking.[7] Nowadays, I would also address the question of the female tradition, the role of popular fiction within it, and the influence of that fiction on its audience. It seems to me that, if we accept the work of the professional "scribbling woman," we have also to accept its literary consequences, not drawing the line at the place where that literature may have been the force that enabled an otherwise inarticulate segment of the population to grasp a means of expression and communication.

Once again, the arena is the female tradition itself. If we are thinking in terms of canon formation, it is the alternative canon. Until the aesthetic argu-

---

7. Lillian S. Robinson, "Working/Women/Writing," *Sex, Class, and Culture* (Bloomington: Indiana University Press, 1978), p. 252.

ments can be fully worked out in the feminist context, it will be impossible to argue, in the general marketplace of literary ideas, that the novels of Henry James ought to give place—a *little* place, even—to the diaries of his sister Alice. At this point, I suspect most of our male colleagues would consider such a request, even in the name of Alice James, much less the Seamer on Men's Underwear, little more than a form of "reverse discrimination"—a concept to which some of them are already overly attached. It is up to feminist scholars, when we determine that this is indeed the right course to pursue, to demonstrate that such an inclusion would constitute a genuinely affirmative action for all of us.

The development of feminist literary criticism and scholarship has already proceeded through a number of identifiable stages. Its pace is more reminiscent of the survey course than of the slow processes of canon formation and revision, and it has been more successful in defining and sticking to its own intellectual turf, the female counter-canon, than in gaining general canonical recognition for Edith Wharton, Fanny Fern, or the female diarists of the Westward Expansion. In one sense, the more coherent our sense of the female tradition is, the stronger will be our eventual case. Yet the longer we wait, the more comfortable the women's literature ghetto—separate, apparently autonomous, and far from equal—may begin to feel.

At the same time, I believe the challenge cannot come only by means of the patent value of the work of women. We must pursue the questions certain of us have raised and retreated from as to the eternal verity of the received standards of greatness or even goodness. And, while not abandoning our newfound female tradition, we have to return to confrontation with "the" canon, examining it as a source of ideas, themes, motifs, and myths about the two sexes. The point in so doing is not to label and hence dismiss even the most sexist literary classics, but to enable all of us to apprehend them, finally, in all their human dimensions.

1983, 1985

DONNA HARAWAY
b. 1944

The last few words of "A Manifesto for Cyborgs" (1985)—"I would rather be a cyborg than a goddess"—set off a plethora of conversations among thinkers reconsidering the relationship between feminism and science even as they suggested to some readers a phenomenon known as the *posthuman*, which is based on human to machine and on human animal to nonhuman animal interconnections not only in the future of science fiction but also in the present we confront daily. Part organism and part machine, the cyborg represents an unstable hybridity. Liminality also characterizes Haraway's first two books, *Primate Visions: Gender, Race, and Nature in the World of Modern Science* (1989) and *Simians, Cyborgs, and Women: The Reinvention of Nature* (1991), which traverse the usual divide between the humanities and the sciences so as to clarify how technology has begun to change the nature of nature itself, altering human nature, nonhuman nature, and the permeable borders between these two fundamental categories of being. One of the first cyberfeminists, Donna Haraway received a Ph.D. in biology from Yale University in 1972 and has taught in the History of Consciousness Program at the University of California, Santa Cruz, and at the European Graduate School in Saas-Fee, Switzerland. *The Haraway Reader* (2004) collects many of her most influential essays.

From A Manifesto for Cyborgs: Science, Technology, and Socialist Feminism in the 1980s

An Ironic Dream of a Common Language[1] *for Women in the Integrated Circuit*

This essay is an effort to build an ironic political myth faithful to feminism, socialism, and materialism. Perhaps more faithful as blasphemy is faithful, than as reverent worship and identification. Blasphemy has always seemed to require taking things very seriously. I know no better stance to adopt from within the secular-religious, evangelical traditions of United States politics, including the politics of socialist-feminism. Blasphemy protects one from the moral majority within, while still insisting on the need for community. Blasphemy is not apostasy. Irony is about contradictions that do not resolve into larger wholes, even dialectically, about the tension of holding incompatible things together because both or all are necessary and true. Irony is about humor and serious play. It is also a rhetorical strategy and a political method, one I would like to see more honored within socialist feminism. At the center of my ironic faith, my blasphemy, is the image of the cyborg.

A cyborg is a cybernetic organism, a hybrid of machine and organism, a creature of social reality as well as a creature of fiction. Social reality is lived social relations, our most important political construction, a world-changing fiction. The international women's movements have constructed "women's experience," as well as uncovered or discovered this crucial collective object. This experience is a fiction and fact of the most crucial, political kind. Liberation rests on the construction of the consciousness, the imaginative apprehension, of oppression, and so of possibility. The cyborg is a matter of fiction and lived experience that changes what counts as women's experience in the late twentieth century. This is a struggle over life and death, but the boundary between science fiction and social reality is an optical illusion.

Contemporary science fiction is full of cyborgs—creatures simultaneously animal and machine, who populate worlds ambiguously natural and crafted. Modern medicine is also full of cyborgs, of couplings between organism and machine, each conceived as coded devices, in an intimacy and with a power that was not generated in the history of sexuality. Cyborg "sex" restores some of the lovely replicative baroque of ferns and invertebrates (such nice organic prophylactics against heterosexism). Cyborg replication is uncoupled from organic reproduction. Modern production seems like a dream of cyborg colonization of work, a dream that makes the nightmare of Taylorism seem idyllic. And modern war is a cyborg orgy, coded by C^3I, command-

---

1. A reference to the feminism of Adrienne Rich, author of a 1978 collection of poetry titled *The Dream of a Common Language* [editor's note; except as indicated, all notes are Haraway's; her original references are, where appropriate, updated in square brackets].

control-communication-intelligence, an $84 billion item in 1984's U.S. defense budget. I am making an argument for the cyborg as a fiction mapping our social and bodily reality and as an imaginative resource suggesting some very fruitful couplings. Foucault's biopolitics is a flaccid premonition of cyborg politics, a very open field.

By the late twentieth century, our time, a mythic time, we are all chimeras, theorized and fabricated hybrids of machine and organism; in short, we are cyborgs. The cyborg is our ontology, it gives us our politics. The cyborg is a condensed image of both imagination and material reality, the two joined centers structuring any possibility of historical transformation. In the traditions of "Western" science and politics—the tradition of racist, male-dominant capitalism; the tradition of progress; the tradition of the appropriation of nature as resource for the productions of culture; the tradition of reproduction of the self from the reflections of the other—the relation between organism and machine has been a border war. The stakes in the border war have been the territories of production, reproduction, and imagination. This essay is an argument for *pleasure* in the confusion of boundaries and for *responsibility* in their construction. It is also an effort to contribute to socialist-feminist culture and theory in a post-modernist, non-naturalist mode and in the utopian tradition of imagining a world without gender, which is perhaps a world without genesis, but maybe also a world without end. The cyborg incarnation is outside salvation history.

The cyborg is a creature in a post-gender world; it has no truck with bisexuality, pre-Oedipal symbiosis, unalienated labor, or other seductions to organic wholeness through a final appropriation of all the powers of the parts into a higher unity. In a sense, the cyborg has no origin story in the Western sense; a "final" irony since the cyborg is also the awful apocalyptic *telos* of the "West's" escalating dominations of abstract individuation, an ultimate self untied at last from all dependency, a man in space. An origin story in the "Western," humanist sense depends on the myth of original unity, fullness, bliss and terror, represented by the phallic mother from whom all humans must separate, the task of individual development and of history, the twin potent myths inscribed most powerfully for us in psychoanalysis and Marxism. Hilary Klein has argued[2] that both Marxism and psychoanalysis, in their concepts of labor and of individuation and gender formation, depend on the plot of original unity out of which difference must be produced and enlisted in a drama of escalating domination of woman/nature. The cyborg skips the step of original unity, of identification with nature in the Western sense. This is its illegitimate promise that might lead to subversion of its teleology as star wars.[3]

The cyborg is resolutely committed to partiality, irony, intimacy, and perversity. It is oppositional, utopian, and completely without innocence. No longer structured by the polarity of public and private, the cyborg defines a technological polis based partly on a revolution of social relations in the *oikos*, the household. Nature and culture are reworked; the one can no longer be

2. For example, see Klein's "Marxism, Psychoanalysis, and Mother Nature," *Feminist Studies* 15 (1989): 255–78 [editor's note].
3. I.e., the Strategic Defense Initiative announced by President Ronald Reagan in 1983; the program sought to develop a space-based system to defend the United States against incoming missiles [editor's note].

the resource for appropriation or incorporation by the other. The relationships for forming wholes from parts, including those of polarity and hierarchical domination, are at issue in the cyborg world. Unlike the hopes of Frankenstein's monster, the cyborg does not expect its father to save it through a restoration of the garden; i.e., through the fabrication of a heterosexual mate, through its completion in a finished whole, a city and cosmos. The cyborg does not dream of community on the model of the organic family, this time without the Oedipal project. The cyborg would not recognize the Garden of Eden; it is not made of mud and cannot dream of returning to dust. Perhaps that is why I want to see if cyborgs can subvert the apocalypse of returning to nuclear dust in the manic compulsion to name the Enemy. Cyborgs are not reverent; they do not re-member the cosmos. They are wary of holism, but needy for connection—they seem to have a natural feel for united front politics, but without the vanguard party. The main trouble with cyborgs, of course, is that they are the illegitimate offspring of militarism and patriarchal capitalism, not to mention state socialism. But illegitimate offspring are often exceedingly unfaithful to their origins. Their fathers, after all, are inessential.

I will return to the science fiction of cyborgs at the end of this essay, but now I want to signal three crucial boundary breakdowns that make the following political fictional (political scientific) analysis possible. By the late twentieth century in United States scientific culture, the boundary between human and animal is thoroughly breached. The last beachheads of uniqueness have been polluted if not turned into amusement parks—language, tool use, social behavior, mental events, nothing really convincingly settles the separation of human and animal. And many people no longer feel the need of such a separation; indeed, many branches of feminist culture affirm the pleasure of connection of human and other living creatures. Movements for animal rights are not irrational denials of human uniqueness; they are clear-sighted recognition of connection across the discredited breach of nature and culture. Biology and evolutionary theory over the last two centuries have simultaneously produced modern organisms as objects of knowledge and reduced the line between humans and animals to a faint trace re-etched in ideological struggle or professional disputes between life and social sciences. Within this framework, teaching modern Christian creationism should be fought as a form of child abuse.

Biological-determinist ideology is only one position opened up in scientific culture for arguing the meanings of human animality. There is much room for radical political people to contest for the meanings of the breached boundary.[4] The cyborg appears in myth precisely where the boundary

4. Useful references to left and/or feminist radical science movements and theory and to biological/biotechnological issues include: Ruth Bleier, *Science and Gender: A Critique of Biology and Its Themes on Women* (New York: Pergamon, 1984); Elizabeth Fee, "Critiques of Modern Science: The Relationship of Feminist and Other Radical Epistemologies," and Evelyn Hammonds, "Women of Color, Feminism, and Science," papers for Symposium on Feminist Perspectives on Science, University of Wisconsin, 11–13 April 1985 (proceedings to be published by Pergamon) [Ruth Bleier, ed., *Feminist Approaches to Science* (New York: Pergamon, 1986)]; Stephen J. Gould, *Mismeasure of Man* (New York: Norton, 1981); Ruth Hubbard, Mary Sue Henifin and Barbara Fried, eds., *Biological Woman, the Convenient Myth* (Cambridge, Mass.: Schenkman, 1982); Evelyn Fox Keller, *Reflections on Gender and Science* (New Haven: Yale University Press, 1985); R. C. Lewontin, Steve Rose, and Leon Kamin, *Not in Our Genes* (New York: Pantheon, 1984); *Radical Science Journal*, 26 Freegrove Road, London N7 9RQ; *Science for the People*, 897 Main St., Cambridge, MA 02139.

between human and animal is transgressed. Far from signaling a walling off of people from other living beings, cyborgs signal disturbingly and pleasurably tight coupling. Bestiality has a new status in this cycle of marriage exchange.

The second leaky distinction is between animal-human (organism) and machine. Pre-cybernetic machines could be haunted; there was always the specter of the ghost in the machine. This dualism structured the dialogue between materialism and idealism that was settled by a dialectical progeny, called spirit or history, according to taste. But basically machines were not self-moving, self-designing, autonomous. They could not achieve man's dream, only mock it. They were not man, an author to himself, but only a caricature of that masculinist reproductive dream. To think they were otherwise was paranoid. Now we are not so sure. Late-twentieth-century machines have made thoroughly ambiguous the difference between natural and artificial, mind and body, self-developing and externally-designed, and many other distinctions that used to apply to organisms and machines. Our machines are disturbingly lively, and we ourselves frighteningly inert.

Technological determinism is only one ideological space opened up by the reconceptions of machine and organism as coded texts through which we engage in the play of writing and reading the world.[5] "Textualization" of everything in post-structuralist, post-modernist theory has been damned by Marxists and socialist feminists for its utopian disregard for lived relations of domination that ground the "play" of arbitrary reading.[6] It is certainly true

5. Starting points for left and/or feminist approaches to technology and politics include: Ruth Schwartz Cowan, More Work for Mother: The Ironies of Household Technology from the Open Hearth to the Microwave (New York: Basic Books, 1983); Joan Rothschild, Machina ex Dea: Feminist Perspectives on Technology (New York: Pergamon, 1983); Sharon Traweek, [Beantimes and Lifetimes: The World of High Energy Physics (Cambridge, Mass.: Harvard University Press, 1988)]; R. M. Young and Les Levidov, eds., Science, Technology, and the Labour Process, vols. 1–2 (London: CSE Books, 1981–85); Joseph Weizenbaum, Computer Power and Human Reason (San Francisco: Freeman, 1976); Langdon Winner, Autonomous Technology: Technics out of Control as a Theme in Political Thought (Cambridge, Mass.: MIT Press, 1977; Langdon Winner, [The Whale and the Reactor (Chicago: University of Chicago Press, 1986)]; Jan Zimmerman, ed., The Technological Woman: Interfacing with Tomorrow (New York: Praeger, 1983); Global Electronics Newsletter, 867 West Dana St., #204, Mountain View, CA 94041; Processed World, 55 Sutter St., San Francisco, CA 94104; ISIS, Women's International Information and Communication Service. P.O. Box 50 (Cornavin), 1211 Geneva 2, Switzerland, and Via Santa Maria dell'Anima 30, 00186 Rome, Italy. Fundamental approaches to modern social studies of science that do not continue the liberal mystification that it all started with Thomas Kuhn, include: Karin Knorr-Cetina, The Manufacture of Knowledge (Oxford: Pergamon, 1981); K. D. Knorr-Cetina and Michael Mulkay, eds., Science Observed: Perspectives on the Social Study of Science (Beverly Hills, Calif.: Sage, 1983); Bruno Latour and Steve Woolgar, Laboratory Life: The Social Construction of Scientific Facts (Beverly Hills, Calif.: Sage, 1979); Robert M. Young, "Interpreting the Production of Science," New Scientist, vol. 29 (March 1979), pp. 1026–28. More is claimed than is known about room for contesting productions of science in the mythic/material space of "the laboratory": the 1984 Directory of the Network for the Ethnographic Study of Science, Technology, and Organizations lists a wide range of people and projects crucial to better radical analysis; available from NBSSTO, P.O. Box 11442, Stanford, CA 94305. [Kuhn's highly influential book is The Structure of Scientific Revolutions (Chicago: University of Chicago Press, 1962)—editor's note.]

6. Fredric Jameson, "Postmodernism, or, The Cultural Logic of Late Capitalism," New Left Review, July/August 1984, pp. 53–94. See Marjorie Perloff, " 'Dirty' Language and Scramble Systems," Sulfur 11 (1984), pp. 178–83; Kathleen Fraser, Something (Even Human Voices) in the Foreground, a Lake (Berkeley, Calif.: Kelsey St. Press, 1984).

A provocative, comprehensive argument about the policies and theories of "post-modernism" is made by Fredric Jameson, who argues that post-modernism is not an option, a style among others, but a cultural dominant requiring radical reinvention of left politics from within; there is no longer any place from without that gives meaning to the comforting fiction of critical distance. Jameson also makes clear why one cannot be for or against post-modernism, an essentially moralist move. My position is that feminists (and others) need continuous cultural reinvention, post-modernist critique, and historical materialism; only a cyborg would have a chance. The old dominations of white capitalist patriarchy seem nostalgically innocent now: they normalized heterogeneity, e.g., into man and woman, white and black. "Advanced capitalism" and post-modernism release heterogeneity without a norm, and we are flattened, without subjectivity, which requires depth, even unfriendly and drowning depths. It is time to write The Death of the Clinic. The clinic's methods required bodies

that post-modernist strategies, like my cyborg myth, subvert myriad organic wholes (e.g., the poem, the primitive culture, the biological organism). In short, the certainty of what counts as nature—a source of insight and a promise of innocence—is undermined, probably fatally. The transcendent authorization of interpretation is lost and with it the ontology grounding "Western" epistemology. But the alternative is not cynicism or faithlessness, i.e., some version of abstract existence, like the accounts of technological determinism destroying "man" by the "machine" or "meaningful political action" by the "text." Who cyborgs will be is a radical question; the answers are a matter of survival. Both chimpanzee and artifacts have politics, so why shouldn't we?[7]

The third distinction is a subset of the second: the boundary between physical and non-physical is very imprecise for us. Pop physics books on the consequences of quantum theory and the indeterminacy principle are a kind of popular scientific equivalent to the Harlequin romances as a marker of radical change in American white heterosexuality: they get it wrong, but they are on the right subject. Modern machines are quintessentially microelectronic devices: they are everywhere and they are invisible. Modern machinery is an irreverent upstart god, mocking the Father's ubiquity and spirituality. The silicon chip is a surface for writing; it is etched in molecular scales disturbed only by atomic noise, the ultimate interference for nuclear scores. Writing, power, and technology are old partners in Western stories of the origin of civilization, but miniaturization has changed our experience of mechanism. Miniaturization has turned out to be about power; small is not so much beautiful as pre-eminently dangerous, as in cruise missiles. Contrast the TV sets of the 1950s or the news cameras of the 1970s with the TV wrist bands or hand-sized video cameras now advertised. Our best machines are made of sunshine; they are all light and clean because they are nothing but signals, electromagnetic waves, a section of a spectrum. And these machines are eminently portable, mobile—a matter of immense human pain in Detroit and Singapore. People are nowhere near so fluid, being both material and opaque. Cyborgs are ether, quintessence.

The ubiquity and invisibility of cyborgs is precisely why these sunshine-belt machines are so deadly. They are as hard to see politically as materially. They are about consciousness—or its simulation.[8] They are floating signifiers moving in pickup trucks across Europe, blocked more effectively by the witch-weavings of the displaced and so unnatural Greenham women,[9] who read the cyborg webs of power very well, than by the militant labor of older

---

and works; we have texts and surfaces. Our dominations don't work by medicalization and normalization anymore; they work by networking, communications redesign, stress management. Normalization gives way to automation, utter redundancy. Michel Foucault's *Birth of the Clinic* [1963], *History of Sexuality* [1976], and *Discipline and Punish* [1975] name a form of power at its moment of implosion. The discourse of biopolitics gives way to technobabble, the language of the spliced substantive; no noun is left whole by the multinationals. These are their names, listed from one issue of *Science*: Tech-Knowledge, Genentech, Allergen, Hybritech, Compupro, Genen-cor, Syntex, Allelix, Agrigenetics Corp., Syntro, Codon, Repligen, Micro-Angelo from Scion Corp., Percom Data, Inter Systems, Cyborg Corp., Statcom Corp., Intertec. If we are imprisoned by language,

then escape from that prison house requires language poets, a kind of cultural restriction enzyme to cut the code; cyborg heteroglossia is one form of radical culture politics.

7. Frans de Waal, *Chimpanzee Politics: Power and Sex among the Apes* (New York: Harper & Row, 1982); Langdon Winner, "Do Artifacts Have Politics?" *Daedalus*, winter 1980.

8. Jean Baudrillard, *Simulations*, trans. P. Foss, P. Patton, P. Beitchman (New York: Semiotext(e), 1983). Jameson ("Postmodernism," p. 66) points out that Plato's definition of the simulacrum is the copy for which there is no original, i.e., the world of advanced capitalism; of pure exchange.

9. Protesters who fought for nearly twenty years (beginning in 1982) against nuclear cruise missiles being placed at the U.S. Air Force base at Greenham Common, England note].

masculinist politics, whose natural constituency needs defense jobs. Ultimately the "hardest" science is about the realm of greatest boundary confusion, the realm of pure number, pure spirit, C³I, cryptography, and the preservation of potent secrets. The new machines are so clean and light. Their engineers are sun-worshipers mediating a new scientific revolution associated with the night dream of post-industrial society. The diseases evoked by these clean machines are "no more" than the minuscule coding changes of an antigen in the immune system, "no more" than the experience of stress. The nimble little fingers of "Oriental" women, the old fascination of little Anglo-Saxon Victorian girls with doll houses, women's enforced attention to the small take on quite new dimensions in this world. There might be a cyborg Alice taking account of these new dimensions.[1] Ironically, it might be the unnatural cyborg women making chips in Asia and spiral dancing in Santa Rita whose constructed unities will guide effective oppositional strategies.

So my cyborg myth is about transgressed boundaries, potent fusions, and dangerous possibilities which progressive people might explore as one part of needed political work. One of my premises is that most American socialists and feminists see deepened dualisms of mind and body, animal and machine, idealism and materialism in the social practices, symbolic formulations, and physical artifacts associated with "high technology" and scientific culture. From *One-Dimensional Man* to *The Death of Nature*,[2] the analytic resources developed by progressives have insisted on the necessary domination of technics and recalled us to an imagined organic body to integrate our resistance. Another of my premises is that the need for unity of people trying to resist worldwide intensification of domination has never been more acute. But a slightly perverse shift of perspective might better enable us to contest for meanings, as well as for other forms of power and pleasure in technologically-mediated societies.

From one perspective, a cyborg world is about the final imposition of a grid of control on the planet, about the final abstraction embodied in a Star War apocalypse waged in the name of defense, about the final appropriation of women's bodies in a masculinist orgy of war.[3] From another perspective, a cyborg world might be about lived social and bodily realities in which people are not afraid of their joint kinship with animals and machines, not afraid of permanently partial identities and contradictory standpoints. The political struggle is to see from both perspectives at once because each reveals both dominations and possibilities unimaginable from the other vantage point. Single vision produces worse illusions than double vision or many-headed monsters. Cyborg unities are monstrous and illegitimate; in our present political circumstances, we could hardly hope for more potent myths for resistance and recoupling. I like to imagine LAG, the Livermore Action Group,[4] as a kind of cyborg society, dedicated to realistically converting the laboratories

1. I.e., like the heroine of Lewis Carroll's *Alice's Adventures in Wonderland* (1865), able to be[both very small and very large [editor's.

2. Herbert Marcuse, *One-Dimensional Man* (Boston: Beacon, 1964); Carolyn Merchant, *Death of Nature* (San Francisco: Harper & Row, 1980).

3. Zoe Sofia, "Exterminating Fetuses," *Diacritics*,

vol. 14, no. 2 (summer 1984), pp. 47–59, and "Jupiter Space" (Pomona, Calif.: American Studies Association, 1984).

4. A direct action protest group that sought to stop the development of nuclear weapons technology at Lawrence Livermore National Laboratory in Livermore, California [editor's note].

that most fiercely embody and spew out the tools of technological apocalypse, and committed to building a political form that actually manages to hold together witches, engineers, elders, perverts, Christians, mothers, and Leninists long enough to disarm the state. Fission Impossible is the name of the affinity group in my town. (Affinity: related not by blood but by choice, the appeal of one chemical nuclear group for another, avidity.)

Fractured Identities

It has become difficult to name one's feminism by a single adjective—or even to insist in every circumstance upon the noun. Consciousness of exclusion through naming is acute. Identities seem contradictory, partial, and strategic. With the hard-won recognition of their social and historical constitution, gender, race, and class cannot provide the basis for belief in "essential" unity. There is nothing about being "female" that naturally binds women. There is not even such a state as "being" female, itself a highly complex category constructed in contested sexual scientific discourses and other social practices. Gender, race, or class consciousness is an achievement forced on us by the terrible historical experience of the contradictory social realities of patriarchy, colonialism, and capitalism. And who counts as "us" in my own rhetoric? Which identities are available to ground such a potent political myth called "us," and what could motivate enlistment in this collectivity? Painful fragmentation among feminists (not to mention among women) along every possible fault line has made the concept of *woman* elusive, an excuse for the matrix of women's dominations of each other. For me—and for many who share a similar historical location in white, professional middle class, female, radical, North American, mid-adult bodies—the sources of a crisis in political identity are legion. The recent history for much of the U.S. left and U.S.. feminism has been a response to this kind of crisis by endless splitting and searches for a new essential unity. But there has also been a growing recognition of another response through coalition—affinity, not identity.[5]

*   *   *

In my taxonomy, which like any other taxonomy is a reinscription of history, radical feminism can accommodate all the activities of women named by socialist feminists as forms of labor only if the activity can somehow be sexualized. Reproduction had different tones of meanings for the two tendencies, one rooted in labor, one in sex, both calling the consequences of domination and ignorance of social and personal reality "false consciousness."

Beyond either the difficulties or the contributions in the argument of any one author, neither Marxist nor radical feminist points of view have tended to embrace the status of a partial explanation; both were regularly constituted as totalities. Western explanation has demanded as much; how else could the

---

5. Powerful developments of coalition politics emerge from "third world" speakers, speaking from nowhere, the displaced center of the universe, earth: "We live on the third planet from the sun"—*Sun Poem* by Jamaican writer Edward Kamau Braithwaite, review by Nathaniel Mackey, *Sulfur*, 11 (1984), pp. 200–205. *Home Girls*, ed. Barbara Smith (New York: Kitchen Table, Women of Color Press, 1983), ironically subverts naturalized identities precisely while constructing a place from which to speak called home. See esp. Bernice Reagan, "Coalition Politics, Turning the Century," pp. 356–68.

"Western" author incorporate its others? Each tried to annex other forms of domination by expanding its basic categories through analogy, simple listing, or addition. Embarrassed silence about race among white radical and socialist feminists was one major, devastating political consequence. History and polyvocality disappear into political taxonomies that try to establish genealogies. There was no structural room for race (or for much else) in theory claiming to reveal the construction of the category woman and social group women as a unified or totalizable whole. The structure of my caricature looks like this:

> Socialist Feminism—
>> structure of class//wage labor//alienation
>> labor, by analogy reproduction, by extension sex, by addition race
> Radical Feminism—
>> structure of gender//sexual appropriation//objectification
>> sex, by analogy labor, by extension reproduction, by addition race

In another context, the French theorist Julia Kristeva claimed women appeared as a historical group after World War II, along with groups like youth. Her dates are doubtful; but we are now accustomed to remembering that as objects of knowledge and as historical actors, "race" did not always exist, "class" has a historical genesis, and "homosexuals" are quite junior. It is no accident that the symbolic system of the family of man—and so the essence of woman—breaks up at the same moment that networks of connection among people on the planet are unprecedentedly multiple, pregnant, and complex. "Advanced capitalism" is inadequate to convey the structure of this historical moment. In the "Western" sense, the end of man is at stake. It is no accident that woman disintegrates into women in our time. Perhaps socialist feminists were not substantially guilty of producing essentialist theory that suppressed women's particularity and contradictory interests. I think we have been, at least through unreflective participation in the logics, languages, and practices of white humanism and through searching for a single ground of domination to secure our revolutionary voice. Now we have less excuse. But in the consciousness of our failures, we risk lapsing into boundless difference and giving up on the confusing task of making partial, real connection. Some differences are playful; some are poles of world historical systems of domination. "Epistemology" is about knowing the difference.

The Informatics of Domination

In this attempt at an epistemological and political position, I would like to sketch a picture of possible unity, a picture indebted to socialist and feminist principles of design. The frame for my sketch is set by the extent and importance of rearrangements in worldwide social relations tied to science and technology. I argue for a politics rooted in claims about fundamental changes in the nature of class, race, and gender in an emerging system of world order analogous in its novelty and scope to that created by industrial capitalism; we are living through a movement from an organic, industrial society to a polymorphous, information system—from all work to all play, a deadly game. Simultaneously material and ideological, the dichotomies may be expressed in the following chart of transitions from the comfortable old hierarchical dominations to the scary new networks I have called the informatics of domination:

Representation	Simulation
Bourgeois novel, realism	Science fiction, post-modernism
Organism	Biotic component
Depth, integrity	Surface, boundary
Heat	Noise
Biology as clinical practice	Biology as inscription
Physiology	Communications engineering
Small group	Subsystem
Perfection	Optimization
Eugenics	Population control
Decadence, *Magic Mountain*	Obsolescence, *Future Shock*
Hygiene	Stress Management
Microbiology, tuberculosis	Immunology, AIDS
Organic division of labor	Ergonomics/cybernetics of labor
Functional specialization	Modular construction
Reproduction	Replication
Organic sex role specialization	Optimal genetic strategies
Biological determinism	Evolutionary inertia, constraints
Community ecology	Ecosystem
Racial chain of being	Neo-imperialism, United Nations humanism
Scientific management in home/fractory	Global factory/Electronic cottage
Family/Market/Factory	Women in the Integrated Circuit
Family wage	Comparable worth
Public/Private	Cyborg citizenship
Nature/Culture	Fields of difference
Cooperation	Communications enhancement
Freud	Lacan
Sex	Genetic engineering
Labor	Robotics
Mind	Artificial Intelligence
World War II	Star Wars
White Capitalist Patriarchy	Informatics of Domination

This list suggests several interesting things.[6] First, the objects on the right-hand side cannot be coded as "natural," a realization that subverts naturalistic coding for the left-hand side as well. We cannot go back ideologically or materially. It's not just that "god" is dead; so is the "goddess." In relation to objects like biotic components, one must think not in terms of essential properties, but

---

6. My previous efforts to understand biology as a cybernetic command-control discourse and organisms as "natural-technical objects of knowledge" are: "The High Cost of Information in Post—World War II Evolutionary Biology," *Philosophical Forum*, vol. 13, nos. 2–3 (1979), pp. 206–37; "Signs of Dominance: From a Physiology to a Cybernetics of Primate Society," *Studies in History of Biology* 6 (1983), pp. 129–219; "Class, Race, Sex, Scientific Objects of Knowledge: A Socialist-Feminist Perspective on the Social Construction of Productive Knowledge and Some Political Consequences," in Violet Haas and Carolyn Perucci, eds., *Women in Scientific and Engineering Professions* (Ann Arbor: University of Michigan Press, 1984), pp. 212–29.

in terms of strategies of design, boundary constraints, rates of flows, systems logics, costs of lowering constraints. Sexual reproduction is one kind of reproductive strategy among many, with costs and benefits as a function of the system environment. Ideologies of sexual reproduction can no longer reasonably call on the notions of sex and sex role as organic aspects in natural objects like organisms and families. Such reasoning will be unmasked as irrational, and ironically corporate executives reading *Playboy* and anti-porn radical feminists will make strange bedfellows in jointly unmasking the irrationalism.

Likewise for race, ideologies about human diversity have to be formulated in terms of frequencies of parameters, like blood groups or intelligence scores. It is "irrational" to invoke concepts like primitive and civilized. For liberals and radicals, the search for integrated social systems gives way to a new practice called "experimental ethnography" in which an organic object dissipates in attention to the play of writing. At the level of ideology, we see translations of racism and colonialism into languages of development and underdevelopment, rates and constraints of modernization. Any objects or persons can be reasonably thought of in terms of disassembly and reassembly; no "natural" architectures constrain system design. The financial districts in all the world's cities, as well as the export-processing and free-trade zones, proclaim this elementary fact of "late capitalism." The entire universe of objects that can be known scientifically must be formulated as problems in communications engineering (for the managers) or theories of the text (for those who would resist). Both are cyborg semiologies.

One should expect control strategies to concentrate on boundary conditions and interfaces, on rates of flow across boundaries—and not on the integrity of natural objects. "Integrity" or "sincerity" of the Western self gives way to decision procedures and expert systems. For example, control strategies applied to women's capacities to give birth to new human beings will be developed in the languages of population control and maximization of goal achievement for individual decision-makers. Control strategies will be formulated in terms of rates, costs of constraints, degrees of freedom. Human beings, like any other component or subsystem, must be localized in a system architecture whose basic modes of operation are probabilistic, statistical. No objects, spaces, or bodies are sacred in themselves; any component can be interfaced with any other if the proper standard, the proper code, can be constructed for processing signals in a common language. Exchange in this world transcends the universal translation[7] effected by capitalist markets that Marx analyzed so well. The privileged pathology affecting all kinds of components in this universe is stress—communications breakdown.[8] The cyborg is not subject to Foucault's biopolitics; the cyborg simulates politics, a much more potent field of operations.

This kind of analysis of scientific and cultural objects of knowledge which have appeared historically since World War II prepares us to notice some important inadequacies in feminist analysis which has proceeded as if the organic, hierarchical dualisms ordering discourse in "the West" since Aristotle still ruled. They have been cannibalized, or as Zoe Sofia (Sofoulis) might put it, they have been "techno-digested." The dichotomies between mind and body, animal and

---

7. Of individual labor power into commodities [editor's note].

8. E. Rusten Hogness, "Why Stress? A Look at the Making of Stress, 1936–56," available from the author, 4437 Mill Creek Rd., Healdsburg, CA 95448.

human, organism and machine, public and private, nature and culture, men and women, primitive and civilized are all in question ideologically. The actual situation of women is their integration/exploitation into a world system of production/reproduction and communication called the informatics of domination. The home, workplace, market, public arena, the body itself—all can be dispersed and interfaced in nearly infinite, polymorphous ways, with large consequences for women and others—consequences that themselves are very different for different people and which make potent oppositional international movements difficult to imagine and essential for survival. One important route for reconstructing socialist-feminist politics is through theory and practice addressed to the social relations of science and technology, including crucially the systems of myth and meanings structuring our imaginations. The cyborg is a kind of disassembled and reassembled post-modern collective and personal self. This is the self feminists must code.

Communications technologies and biotechnologies are the crucial tools recrafting our bodies. These tools embody and enforce new social relations for women worldwide. Technologies and scientific discourses can be partially understood as formalizations, i.e., as frozen moments, of the fluid social interactions constituting them, but they should also be viewed as instruments for enforcing meanings. The boundary is permeable between tool and myth, instrument and concept, historical systems of social relations and historical anatomies of possible bodies, including objects of knowledge. Indeed, myth and tool mutually constitute each other.

Furthermore, communications sciences and modern biologies are constructed by a common move—*the translation of the world into a problem of coding*, a search for a common language in which all resistance to instrumental control disappears and all heterogeneity can be submitted to disassembly, reassembly, investment, and exchange.

In communications sciences, the translation of the world into a problem in coding can be illustrated by looking at cybernetic (feedback controlled) systems theories applied to telephone technology, computer design, weapons deployment, or data base construction and maintenance. In each case, solution to the key questions rests on a theory of language and control; the key operation is determining the rates, directions, and probabilities of flow of a quantity called information. The world is subdivided by boundaries differentially permeable to information. Information is just that kind of quantifiable element (unit, basis of unity) which allows universal translation, and so unhindered instrumental power (called effective communication). The biggest threat to such power is interruption of communication. Any system breakdown is a function of stress. The fundamentals of this technology can be condensed into the metaphor C^3I, command-control-communication-intelligence, the military's symbol for its operations theory.

In modern biologies, the translation of the world into a problem in coding can be illustrated by molecular genetics, ecology, socio-biological evolutionary theory, and immunobiology. The organism has been translated into problems of genetic coding and read-out. Biotechnology, a writing technology, informs research broadly.[9] In a sense, organisms have ceased to exist as

9. A left entry to the biotechnology debate: *GeneWatch*, a Bulletin of the Committee for Responsible Genetics, 5 Doane St. 4th floor, Boston, MA 02109; Susan Wright, ["Recombinant DNA Technology and Its Social Transformation, 1972–82," *Osiris*, 2d ser., vol. 2 (1996), pp. 303–

objects of knowledge, giving way to biotic components, i.e., special kinds of information processing devices. The analogous moves in ecology could be examined by probing the history and utility of the concept of the ecosystem. Immunobiology and associated medical practices are rich exemplars of the privilege of coding and recognition systems as objects of knowledge, as constructions of bodily reality for us. Biology is here a kind of cryptography. Research is necessarily a kind of intelligence activity. Ironies abound. A stressed system goes awry; its communication processes break down; it fails to recognize the difference between self and other. Human babies with baboon hearts evoke national ethical perplexity—for animal-rights activists at least as much as for guardians of human purity. Gay men, Haitian immigrants, and intravenous drug users[1] are the "privileged" victims of an awful immune-system disease that marks (inscribes on the body) confusion of boundaries and moral pollution.

But these excursions into communications sciences and biology have been at a rarefied level; there is a mundane, largely economic reality to support my claim that these sciences and technologies indicate fundamental transformations in the structure of the world for us. Communications technologies depend on electronics. Modern states, multinational corporations, military power, welfare-state apparatuses, satellite systems, political processes, fabrication of our imaginations, labor-control systems, medical constructions of our bodies, commercial pornography, the international division of labor, and religious evangelism depend intimately upon electronics. Microelectronics is the technical basis of simulacra, i.e., of copies without originals.

Microelectronics mediates the translations of *labor* into robotics and word processing; *sex* into genetic engineering and reproductive technologies; and *mind* into artificial intelligence and decision procedures. The new biotechnologies concern more than human reproduction. Biology as a powerful engineering science for redesigning materials and processes has revolutionary implications for industry, perhaps most obvious today in areas of fermentation, agriculture, and energy. Communications sciences and biology are constructions of natural-technical objects of knowledge in which the difference between machine and organism is thoroughly blurred; mind, body, and tool are on very intimate terms. The "multinational" material organization of the production and reproduction of daily life and the symbolic organization of the production and reproduction of culture and imagination seem equally implicated. The boundary-maintaining images of base and superstructure, public and private, or material and ideal never seemed more feeble.

*   *   *

Cyborgs: A Myth of Political Identity

*   *   *

Writing is pre-eminently the technology of cyborgs, etched surfaces of the late twentieth century. Cyborg politics is the struggle for language and the struggle against perfect communication, against the one code that translates

---

60] and "Recombinant DNA: The Status of Hazards and Controls," *Environment,* July/August 1982; Edward Yoxen, *The Gene Business* (New York: Harper & Row, 1983).

1. The three groups most closely associated with AIDS when it was first identified in the 1980s [editor's note].

all meaning perfectly, the central dogma of phallogocentrism. That is why cyborg politics insist on noise and advocate pollution, rejoicing in the illegitimate fusions of animal and machine. These are the couplings which make Man and Woman so problematic, subverting the structure of desire, the force imagined to generate language and gender, and so subverting the structure and modes of reproduction of "Western" identity, of nature and culture, of mirror and eye, slave and master, body and mind. "We" did not originally choose to be cyborgs, but choice grounds a liberal politics and epistemology that imagines the reproduction of individuals before the wider replications of "texts."

From the perspective of cyborgs, freed of the need to ground politics in "our" privileged position of the oppression that incorporates all other dominations, the innocence of the merely violated, the ground of those closer to nature, we can see powerful possibilities. Feminisms and Marxisms have run aground on Western epistemological imperatives to construct a revolutionary subject from the perspective of a hierarchy of oppressions and/or a latent position of moral superiority, innocence, and greater closeness to nature. With no available original dream of a common language or original symbiosis promising protection from hostile "masculine" separation, but written into the play of a text that has no finally privileged reading or salvation history, to recognize "oneself" as fully implicated in the world, frees us of the need to root politics in identification, vanguard parties, purity, and mothering. Stripped of identity, the bastard race teaches about the power of the margins and the importance of a mother like Malinche.[2] Women of color have transformed her from the evil mother of masculinist fear into the originally literate mother who teaches survival.

This is not just literary deconstruction, but liminal transformation. Every story that begins with original innocence and privileges the return to wholeness imagines the drama of life to be individuation, separation, the birth of the self, the tragedy of autonomy, the fall into writing, alienation; i.e., war, tempered by imaginary respite in the bosom of the Other. These plots are ruled by a reproductive politics—rebirth without flaw, perfection, abstraction. In this plot women are imagined either better or worse off, but all agree they have less selfhood, weaker individuation, more fusion to the oral, to Mother, less at stake in masculine autonomy. But there is another route to having less at stake in masculine autonomy, a route that does not pass through Woman, Primitive, Zero, the Mirror Stage[3] and its imaginary. It passes through women and other present-tense, illegitimate cyborgs, not of Woman born, who refuse the ideological resources of victimization so as to have a real life. These cyborgs are the people who refuse to disappear on cue, no matter how many times a "Western" commentator remarks on the sad passing of another primitive, another organic group done in by "Western" technology, by writing.[4]

2. In an earlier passage not included here, Haraway discusses Malinche—daughter of an Aztec chieftain, and the translator and mistress of the Spanish conquistador Cortés—as "mother of the mestizo 'bastard' race of the new world" [editor's note].

3. Part of Jacques Lacan's theory of identity formation, according to which a child passes from the "Imaginary" an infant into the "Symbolic" (the dimension of language, law, and the father) [editor's note].

4. James Clifford argues persuasively for recognition of continuous cultural reinvention, the stubborn non-disappearance of those "marked" by Western imperializing practices; see "On Ethnographic Allegory" [in James Clifford and George E. Marcus, eds., *Writing Culture: The Poetics and Politics of Ethnography* (Berkeley: University of California Press, 1986), pp. 98–121] and "On Ethnographic Authority," *Representations*, vol. 1, no. 2 (1983), pp. 118–46.

These real-life cyborgs, e.g., the Southeast Asian village women workers in Japanese and U.S. electronics firms described by Aihwa Ong, are actively rewriting the texts of their bodies and societies. Survival is the stakes in this play of readings.

To recapitulate, certain dualisms have been persistent in Western traditions; they have all been systemic to the logics and practices of domination of women, people of color, nature, workers, animals—in short, domination of all constituted as *others*, whose task is to mirror the self. Chief among these troubling dualisms are self/other, mind/body, culture/nature, male/female, civilized/primitive, reality/appearance, whole/part, agent/resource, maker/made, active/passive, right/wrong, truth/illusion, total/partial, God/man. The self is the One who is not dominated, who knows that by the service of the other; the other is the one who holds the future, who knows that by the experience of domination, which gives the lie to the autonomy of the self. To be One is to be autonomous, to be powerful, to be God; but to be One is to be an illusion, and so to be involved in a dialectic of apocalypse with the other. Yet to be other is to be multiple, without clear boundary, frayed, insubstantial. One is too few, but two are too many.

High-tech culture challenges these dualisms in intriguing ways. It is not clear who makes and who is made in the relation between human and machine. It is not clear what is mind and what body in machines that resolve into coding practices. Insofar as we know ourselves in both formal discourse (e.g., biology) and in daily practice (e.g., the homework economy in the integrated circuit), we find ourselves to be cyborgs, hybrids, mosaics, chimeras. Biological organisms have become biotic systems, communications devices like others. There is no fundamental, ontological separation in our formal knowledge of machine and organism, of technical and organic.

One consequence is that our sense of connection to our tools is heightened. The trance state experienced by many computer users has become a staple of science-fiction film and cultural jokes. Perhaps paraplegics and other severely handicapped people can (and sometimes do) have the most intense experiences of complex hybridization with other communication devices. Anne McCaffrey's *The Ship Who Sang* explored the consciousness of a cyborg, hybrid of girl's brain and complex machinery, formed after the birth of a severely handicapped child. Gender, sexuality, embodiment, skill all were reconstituted in the story. Why should our bodies end at the skin, or include at best other beings encapsulated by skin? From the seventeenth century till now, machines could be animated—given ghostly souls to make them speak or move or to account for their orderly development and mental capacities. Or organisms could be mechanized—reduced to body understood as resource of mind. These machine/organism relationships are obsolete, unnecessary. For us, in imagination and in other practice, machines can be prosthetic devices, intimate components, friendly selves. We don't need organic holism to give impermeable wholeness, the total woman and her feminist variants (mutants?). Let me conclude this point by a very partial reading of the logic of the cyborg monsters of my second group of texts, feminist science fiction.

The cyborgs populating feminist science fiction make very problematic the statuses of man or woman, human, artifact, member of a race, individual identity, or body. Katie King clarifies how pleasure in reading these fictions is not largely based on identification.[5] Students facing Joanna Russ for the first time, students who have learned to take modernist writers like James Joyce or Virginia Woolf without flinching, do not know what to make of *The Adventures of Alyx* or *The Female Man*, where characters refuse the reader's search for innocent wholeness while granting the wish for heroic quests, exuberant eroticism, and serious politics. *The Female Man* is the story of four versions of one genotype, all of whom meet, but even taken together do not make a whole, resolve the dilemmas of violent moral action, nor remove the growing scandal of gender. The feminist science fiction of Samuel Delany, especially *Tales of Neveryon*, mocks stories of origin by redoing the neolithic revolution, replaying the founding moves of Western civilization to subvert their plausibility. James Tiptree, Jr., an author whose fiction was regarded as particularly manly until her "true" gender was revealed, tells tales of reproduction based on non-mammalian technologies like alternation of generations or male brood pouches and male nurturing. John Varley constructs a supreme cyborg in his arch-feminist exploration of Gaea, a mad goddess—planet—trickster—old woman—technological device on whose surface an extraordinary array of post-cyborg symbioses are spawned. Octavia Butler writes of an African sorceress pitting her powers of transformation against the genetic manipulations of her rival (*Wild Seed*), of time warps that bring a modern U.S. black woman into slavery where her actions in relation to her white master-ancestor determine the possibility of her own birth (*Kindred*), and of the illegitimate insights into identity and community of an adopted cross-species child who came to know the enemy as self (*Survivor*).

Because it is particularly rich in boundary transgressions, Vonda McIntyre's *Superluminal* can close this truncated catalogue of promising monsters who help redefine the pleasures and politics of embodiment and feminist writing. In a fiction where no character is "simply" human, human status is highly problematic. Orca, a genetically altered diver, can speak with killer whales and survive deep ocean conditions, but she longs to explore space as a pilot, necessitating bionic implants jeopardizing her kinship with the divers and cetaceans. Transformations are effected by virus vectors carrying a new developmental code, by transplant surgery, by implants of microelectronic devices, by analogue doubles, and other means. Laenea becomes a pilot by accepting a heart implant and a host of other alterations allowing survival in transit at speeds exceeding that of light. Radu Dracul survives a virus-caused plague on his outerworld planet to find himself with a time sense that changes the boundaries of spatial perception for the whole species. All the characters explore the limits of language, the dream of communicating experience, and the necessity of limitation, partiality, and intimacy even in this world of protean transformation and connection.

---

5. See Haraway's note to an earlier passage not included here: "Katie, King, 'The Pleasure of Repetition and the Limits of Identification in Feminist Science Fiction: Reimaginations of the Body after the Cyborg,' California American Studies Association, Pomona, 1984. An abbreviated list of feminist science fiction underlying themes of this essay: Octavia Butler, *Wild Seed, Mind of My Mind, Kin-* *dred, Survivor*; Suzy McKee Charnas, *Motherlines*; Samuel Delany, *Tales of Neveryon*; Anne McCaffrey, *The Ship Who Sang, Dinosaur Planet*; Vonda McIntyre, *Superluminal, Dreamsnake*; Joanna Russ, *Adventures of Alix, The Female Man*; James Tiptree, Jr. [pseudonym of Alice Sheldon], *Star Songs of an Old Primate, Up the Walls of the World*; John Varley, *Titan, Wizard, Demon*" [editor's note].

Monsters have always defined the limits of community in Western imaginations. The Centaurs and Amazons of ancient Greece established the limits of the centered polis of the Greek male human by their disruption of marriage and boundary pollutions of the warrior with animality and woman. Unseparated twins and hermaphrodites were the confused human material in early modern France who grounded discourse on the natural and supernatural, medical and legal, portents and diseases—all crucial to establishing modern identity.[6] The evolutionary and behavioral sciences of monkeys and apes have marked the multiple boundaries of late-twentieth-century industrial identities. Cyborg monsters in feminist science fiction define quite different political possibilities and limits from those proposed by the mundane fiction of Man and Woman.

There are several consequences to taking seriously the imagery of cyborgs as other than our enemies. Our bodies, ourselves;[7] bodies are maps of power and identity. Cyborgs are no exceptions. A cyborg body is not innocent; it was not born in a garden; it does not seek unitary identity and so generate antagonistic dualisms without end (or until the world ends); it takes irony for granted. One is too few, and two is only one possibility. Intense pleasure in skill, machine skill, ceases to be a sin, but an aspect of embodiment. The machine is not an *it* to be animated, worshiped and dominated. The machine is us, our processes, an aspect of our embodiment. We can be responsible for machines; *they* do not dominate or threaten us. We are responsible for boundaries; we are they. Up till now (once upon a time), female embodiment seemed to be given, organic, necessary; and female embodiment seemed to mean skill in mothering and its metaphoric extensions. Only by being out of place could we take intense pleasure in machines, and then with excuses that this was organic activity after all, appropriate to females. Cyborgs might consider more seriously the partial, fluid, sometimes aspect of sex and sexual embodiment. Gender might not be global identity after all.

The ideologically charged question of what counts as daily activity, as experience, can be approached by exploiting the cyborg image. Feminists have recently claimed that women are given to dailiness, that women more than men somehow sustain daily life, and so have a privileged epistemological position potentially. There is a compelling aspect to this claim, one that makes visible unvalued female activity and names it as the ground of life. But *the* ground of life? What about all the ignorance of women, all the exclusions and failures of knowledge and skill? What about men's access to daily competence, to knowing how to build things, to take them apart, to play? What about other embodiments? Cyborg gender is a local possibility taking a global vengeance. Race, gender, and capital require a cyborg theory of wholes and parts. There is no drive in cyborgs to produce total theory, but there is an intimate experience of boundaries, their construction and deconstruction. There is a myth system waiting to become a political language to ground one way of looking at science and technology and challenging the informatics of domination.

6. Page DuBois, *Centaurs and Amazons* (Ann Arbor: University of Michigan Press, 1982); Lorraine Daston and Katharine Park, "Hermaphrodites in Renaissance France," ms., n.d. Katharine Park and Lorraine Daston, "Unnatural Conceptions: The Study of Monsters in 16th and 17th Century France and England," *Past and Present*, no. 92 (August 1981), pp. 20–54.

7. The title of a best-selling feminist book on women's health and sexuality (first published in 1973, it was in its 4th ed. by 1985) [editor's note].

One last image: organisms and organismic, holistic politics depend on metaphors of rebirth and invariably call on the resources of reproductive sex. I would suggest that cyborgs have more to do with regeneration and are suspicious of the reproductive matrix and of most birthing. For salamanders, regeneration after injury, such as the loss of a limb, involves regrowth of structure and restoration of function with the constant possibility of twinning or other odd topographical productions at the site of former injury. The regrown limb can be monstrous, duplicated, potent. We have all been injured, profoundly. We require regeneration, not rebirth, and the possibilities for our reconstitution include the utopian dream of the hope for a monstrous world without gender.

Cyborg imagery can help express two crucial arguments in this essay: (1) the production of universal, totalizing theory is a major mistake that misses most of reality, probably always, but certainly now; (2) taking responsibility for the social relations of science and technology means refusing an anti-science metaphysics, a demonology of technology, and so means embracing the skillful task of reconstructing the boundaries of daily life, in partial connection with others, in communication with all of our parts. It is not just that science and technology are possible means of great human satisfaction, as well as a matrix of complex dominations. Cyborg imagery can suggest a way out of the maze of dualisms in which we have explained our bodies and our tools to ourselves. This is a dream not of a common language, but of a powerful infidel heteroglossia. It is an imagination of a feminist speaking in tongues to strike fear into the circuits of the super-savers of the new right. It means both building and destroying machines, identities, categories, relationships, spaces, stories. Though both are bound in the spiral dance, I would rather be a cyborg than a goddess.

1985

BARBARA JOHNSON
b. 1947

Lucidity and lyricism characterize the elegant essays of Barbara Johnson. A translator of Jacques Derrida and student of Paul de Man, Johnson has published a number of books with the word "difference" in their titles: *The Critical Difference: Essays in the Contemporary Rhetoric of Reading* (1980), *A World of Difference* (1987), and *The Feminist Difference: Literature, Psychoanalysis, Race, and Gender* (1998). It stands for her attentiveness to the binary oppositions in languages and in genres deconstructed by Derrideans as well as to the tensions between deconstruction and feminism and the frictions between black and white, or between lesbian and heterosexual feminists. Whether interpreting the verse of Charles Baudelaire and Stéphane Mallarmé or the fiction of Edgar Allan Poe and Herman Melville, she refrains from simply applying theory to literature but instead explores the theoretical resonance of literature, as she does in her examinations of the work of Zora Neale Hurston. Like "Apostrophe, Ani-

mation, and Abortion," her essay on African American women poets, our selection typifies Johnson's ability to explore the political and psychological meanings of complex
rhetorical strategies. Her contributions to *The Norton Anthology of Theory and Criticism* have helped innumerable students appreciate the philosophical traditions that
shaped her own intellectual evolution. For many years a professor of English and comparative literature at Harvard University, Barbara Johnson produced *Mother Tongues:
Sexuality, Trials, Motherhood, Translation* in 2003, an evocative meditation on the linguistic, psychological, professional, and visionary struggles of a quite unlikely trinity:
Baudelaire, Walter Benjamin, and Sylvia Plath.

From Thresholds of Difference:
Structures of Address in Zora Neale Hurston

In preparing to write this paper, I found myself repeatedly stopped by conflicting conceptions of the structure of address into which I was inserting
myself. It was not clear to me what I, a white deconstructor, was doing talking about Zora Neale Hurston, a black novelist and anthropologist, or to
whom I was talking. Was I trying to convince white establishment scholars
who long for a return to Renaissance ideals that the study of the Harlem
Renaissance is not a trivialization of their humanistic pursuits? Was I trying
to contribute to the attempt to adapt the textual strategies of literary theory
to the analysis of Afro-American literature? Was I trying to rethink my own
previous work and to re-referentialize the notion of difference so as to move
the conceptual operations of deconstruction out of the realm of abstract linguistic universality? Was I talking to white critics, black critics, or myself?

Well, all of the above. What finally struck me was the fact that what I was
analyzing in Hurston's writings was precisely, again and again, her strategies
and structures of problematic address. It was as though I were asking her for
answers to questions I did not even know I was unable to formulate. I had a
lot to learn, then, from Hurston's way of dealing with multiple agendas and
heterogeneous implied readers. I will focus here on three texts that play interesting variations on questions of identity and address: two short essays, "How
It Feels to Be Colored Me"[1] and "What White Publishers Won't Print,"[2] and
a book-length collection of folktales, songs, and hoodoo practices entitled
Mules and Men.[3]

One of the presuppositions with which I began was that Hurston's work
was situated "outside" the mainstream literary canon and that I, by implication, was an institutional "insider." I soon came to see, however, not only that
the insider becomes an outsider the minute she steps out of the inside but
also that Hurston's work itself was constantly dramatizing and undercutting
just such inside/outside oppositions, transforming the plane geometry of

1. See Zora Neale Hurston, "How It Feels to Be
Colored Me," *World Tomorrow* 11 (May 1928):
215–16; rpt. in *I Love Myself When I Am Laughing
and Then Again When I Am Looking Mean and
Impressive: A Zora Neale Hurston Reader,* ed. Alice
Walker (Old Westbury, N.Y., 1979), pp. 152–155;
all further references to this work, abbreviated
"CM," will be to this edition and will be included
in the text [except as indicated, all notes are Johnson's].

2. See Hurston, "What White Publishers Won't
Print," *Negro Digest* 8 (Apr. 1950): 85–89; rpt. in *I
Love Myself When I Am Laughing,* pp. 169–73; all
further references to this work, abbreviated "WP,"
will be to this edition and will be included in the
text.
3. See Hurston, *Mules and Men* (1935; Bloomington, Ind., 1978); all further references to this
work, abbreviated *MM,* will be included in the
text.

physical space into the complex transactions of discursive exchange. In other words, Hurston could be read not just as an *example* of the "noncanonical" writer but as a commentator on the dynamics of any encounter between an inside and an outside, any attempt to make a statement about difference.

One of Hurston's most memorable figurations of the inside/outside structure is her depiction of herself as a threshold figure mediating between the all-black town of Eatonville, Florida, and the big road traveled by passing whites:

> The front porch might seem a daring place for the rest of the town, but it was a gallery seat for me. My favorite place was atop the gatepost. Proscenium box for a born first-nighter. Not only did I enjoy the show, but I didn't mind the actors knowing that I liked it. I usually spoke to them in passing. . . .
>
> They liked to hear me "speak pieces" and sing and wanted to see me dance the parse-me-la, and gave me generously of their small silver for doing these things. . . . The colored people gave no dimes. They deplored any joyful tendencies in me, but I was their Zora nevertheless. ["CM," pp. 152–53]

The inside/outside opposition here opens up a reversible theatrical space in which proscenium box becomes center stage and small silver passes to the boxholder-turned-actor.

Hurston's joyful and lucrative gatepost stance between black and white cultures was very much a part of her Harlem Renaissance persona and was indeed often deplored by fellow black artists. Langston Hughes, who for a time shared with Hurston the problematic patronage of the wealthy Charlotte Mason, wrote of Hurston:

> Of th[e] "niggerati," Zora Neale Hurston was certainly the most amusing. Only to reach a wider audience, need she ever write books—because she is a perfect book of entertainment in herself. In her youth she was always getting scholarships and things from wealthy white people, some of whom simply paid her just to sit around and represent the Negro race for them, she did it in such a racy fashion. . . . To many of her white friends, no doubt, she was a perfect "darkie."[4]

"Representing the Negro race for whites" was nevertheless in many ways the program of the Harlem Renaissance. While Hurston has often been read and judged on the basis of personality alone, her "racy" adoption of the "happy darkie" stance, which was a successful strategy for survival, does not by any means exhaust the representational strategies of her *writing*.

Questions of identity, difference, and race-representation are interestingly at issue in the 1928 essay entitled "How It Feels to Be Colored Me," in which the gatepost passage appears. Published in *World Tomorrow*, a white journal sympathetic to Harlem Renaissance writers, the essay is quite clearly a response to the unspoken question inevitably asked by whites of the black artist. Since any student of literature trained in the European tradition and interested in Hurston out of a concern for the noncanonical is implicitly asking her that same question, a close reading of that essay is likely to shed light on what is at stake in such an encounter.

---

4. Langston Hughes, *The Big Sea: An Autobiography* (New York, 1963), pp. 238–39.

The essay is divided into a series of vignettes, each of which responds to the question differently. The essay begins, "I am colored but I offer nothing in the way of extenuating circumstances except the fact that I am the only Negro in the United States whose grandfather on the mother's side was *not* an Indian chief" ("CM," p. 152). Collapsed into this sentence are two myths of black identity, the absurdity of whose juxtaposition sets the tone for the entire essay. On the one hand, it implies that being colored is a misdemeanor for which some extenuation must be sought. On the other hand, it implies that among the stories Negroes tell about themselves the story of Indian blood is a common extenuation, dilution, and hence effacement of the crime of being colored. By making *lack* of Indian blood into an extenuating circumstance and by making explicit the absurdity of seeking extenuating circumstances for something over which one has no control, Hurston is shedding an ironic light both on the question ("How does it feel to be colored you?") and on one possible answer ("I'm not 100 percent colored"). Hurston is saying in effect, "I am colored but I am different from other members of my race in that I am not different from my race."[5]

While the first paragraph thus begins, "I am colored," the second starts, "I remember the very day that I *became* colored" ("CM," p. 152; my emphasis). The presuppositions of the question are again undercut. If one can become colored, then one is not born colored, and the definition of "colored" shifts. Hurston goes on to describe her "pre-colored" childhood spent in the all-black town of Eatonville, Florida. "During this period," she writes, "white people differed from colored to me only in that they rode through town and never lived there" ("CM," p. 152). It was not that there was no difference, it was that difference needed no extenuation.

> But changes came in the family when I was thirteen, and I was sent to school in Jacksonville. I left Eatonville, the town of the oleanders, as Zora. When I disembarked from the river-boat at Jacksonville, she was no more. It seemed that I had suffered a sea change. I was not Zora of Orange County any more, I was now a little colored girl. I found it out in certain ways. In my heart as well as in the mirror, I became a fast brown—warranted not to rub nor run. ["CM," p. 153]

In this sea change, the acquisition of color is a *loss* of identity: the "I" is no longer Zora, and "Zora" becomes a "she." "Everybody's Zora" had been constituted not by *an* Other but by the system of otherness itself, the ability to role-play rather than the ability to play any particular role. Formerly an irrepressible speaker of pieces, she now becomes a speaker of withholdings: "I found it out in certain ways."

The acquisition of color, which is here a function of motion (from Eatonville to Jacksonville), ends up entailing the fixity of a correspondence between inside and outside: "In my heart as well as in the mirror, I became a fast brown—warranted not to rub nor run." But the speed hidden in the word "fast," which belies its claim to fixity, is later picked up to extend the "color = motion" equation and to transform the question of race into the image of a road race:

> The terrible struggle that made me an American out of a potential slave said "On the line!" The Reconstruction said "Get set!"; and the genera-

5. This formulation was suggested to me by a student, Lisa Cohen.

tion before said "Go!" I am off to a flying start and I must not halt in the stretch to look behind and weep. ["CM," p. 153]

Later, however, "I am a dark rock surged upon"—a stasis in the midst of motion ("CM," p. 154).

The remainder of the essay is dotted with sentences playing complex variations on the title words "feel," "color," and "me":

But I am not tragically colored.

I do not always feel colored.

I feel most colored when I am thrown against a sharp white background. At certain times I have no race, I am *me*.

I have no separate feelings about being an American citizen and colored. ["CM," pp. 153, 154, 155]

The feelings associated with being colored are, on the one hand, the denial of sorrow and anger ("There is no great sorrow dammed up in my soul"; "Sometimes I feel discriminated against, but it does not make me angry" ["CM," pp. 153, 155]) and, on the other, the affirmation of strength and excitement ("I have seen that the world is to the strong regardless of a little pigmentation more or less"; "It is quite exciting to hold the center of the national stage" ["CM," p. 153]). Each case involves a reversal of implicit white expectations: I am not pitiful but powerful; being colored is not a liability but an advantage. "No one on earth ever had a greater chance for glory. . . . The position of my white neighbor is much more difficult" ("CM," p. 153).

There is one point in the essay, however, when Hurston goes out of her way to conform to a stereotype very much in vogue in the 1920s. The passage bears citing in its entirety:

Sometimes it is the other way around. A white person is set down in our midst, but the contrast is just as sharp for me. For instance, when I sit in the drafty basement that is The New World Cabaret with a white person, my color comes. We enter chatting about any little nothing that we have in common and are seated by the jazz waiters. In the abrupt way that jazz orchestras have, this one plunges into a number. It loses no time in circumlocutions, but gets right down to business. It constricts the thorax and splits the heart with its tempo and narcotic harmonies. This orchestra grows rambunctious, rears on its hind legs and attacks the tonal veil with primitive fury, rending it, clawing it until it breaks through to the jungle beyond. I follow those heathen—follow them exultingly. I dance wildly inside myself; I yell within, I whoop; I shake my assegai above my head, I hurl it true to the mark *yeeeeoouw!* I am in the jungle and living in the jungle way. My face is painted red and yellow and my body is painted blue. My pulse is throbbing like a war drum. I want to slaughter something—give pain, give death to what, I do not know. But the piece ends. The men of the orchestra wipe their lips and rest their fingers. I creep back slowly to the veneer we call civilization with the last tone and find the white friend sitting motionless in his seat, smoking calmly.

"Good music they have here," he remarks, drumming the table with his fingertips.

Music. The great blobs of purple and red emotion have not touched him. He has only heard what I felt. He is far away and I see him but dimly across the ocean and the continent that have fallen between us. He is so pale with his whiteness then and I am *so* colored. ["CM," p. 154]

"Feeling" here, instead of being a category of which "colored" is one example, becomes instead a *property* of the category "colored" ("He has only heard what I felt"). While the passage as a whole dramatizes the image of the exotic primitive, its relation to expectations and presuppositions is not as simple as it first appears. Having just described herself as feeling "most colored when I am thrown against a sharp white background," Hurston's announcement of having it "the other way around" leads one to expect something other than a description of "feel[ing] most colored." Yet there is no other way around. The moment there is a juxtaposition of black and white, what "comes" is color. But the colors that come in the passage are skin *paint*, not skin complexion: red, yellow, blue, and purple. The "tonal veil" is rent indeed, on the level at once of color, of sound, and of literary style. The move into the jungle is a move into mask; the return to civilization is a return to veneer. Either way, what is at stake is an artificial, ornamental surface.

Hurston undercuts the absoluteness of the opposition between white and black in another way as well. In describing the white man as "drumming the table with his fingertips," Hurston places in his body a counterpart to the "war drum" central to the jungle. If the jungle represents the experience of the body as such, the surge of bodily life external to conscious knowledge ("give pain, give death to what, I do not know"), then the nervous gesture is an alienated synecdoche for such bodily release.

In an essay entitled "What White Publishers Won't Print" written for *Negro Digest* in 1950, twenty-two years after "How It Feels to Be Colored Me," Hurston again takes up this "jungle" stereotype, this time to disavow it. The contrast between the two essays is significant:

> This insistence on defeat in a story where upperclass Negroes are portrayed, perhaps says something from the subconscious of the majority. Involved in western culture, the hero or heroine, or both, must appear frustrated and go down to defeat, somehow. Our literature reeks with it. It is the same as saying, "You can translate Virgil, and fumble with the differential calculus, but can you really comprehend it? Can you cope with our subtleties?"
>
> That brings us to the folklore of "reversion to type." This curious doctrine has such wide acceptance that it is tragic. One has only to examine the huge literature on it to be convinced. No matter how high we may *seem* to climb, put us under strain and we revert to type, that is, to the bush. Under a superficial layer of western culture, the jungle drums throb in our veins. ["WP," p. 172]

There are many possible explanations for Hurston's changed use of this image. For one thing, the exotic primitive was in vogue in 1928, while this was no longer the case in 1950. For another, she was addressing a white readership in the earlier essay and a black readership here. But the most revealing difference lies in the way the image is embedded in a structure of address. In the first essay, Hurston describes the jungle feeling as an art, an *ability* to feel, not a reversion. In the second, the jungle appears as a result of "strain." In the first, Hurston can proclaim "I am this"; but when the image is repeated as "you are that," it changes completely. The content of the image may be the same, but its interpersonal use is different. The study of Afro-American literature as a whole poses a similar problem of address: any attempt to lift out of a text an image or essence of blackness is bound to violate the interlocutionary strategy of its formulation.

"What White Publishers Won't Print" is a complex meditation on the possibility of representing difference in order to erase it. Lamenting the fact that "the average, struggling, non-morbid Negro is the best-kept secret in America," Hurston explains the absence of a black *Main Street* by the majority's "indifference, not to say scepticism, to the internal life of educated minorities." The revelation to the public of the Negro who is "just like everybody else" is "the thing needed to do away with that feeling of difference which inspires fear and which ever expresses itself in dislike" ("WP," pp. 173, 170, 171, 173). The thing that prevents the publication of such representations of Negroes is thus said to be the public's *in*difference to finding out that there *is* no difference. Difference is a misreading of sameness, but it must be represented in order to be erased. The resistance to finding out that the Other is the same springs out of the reluctance to admit that the same is Other. If the average man could recognize that the Negro was "just like him," he would have to recognize that he was just like the Negro ("WP," p. 171). Difference disliked is identity affirmed. But the difficulty of pleading for a representation of difference *as* sameness is exemplified by the almost unintelligible distinction in the following sentence:

> As long as the majority cannot conceive of a Negro or a Jew feeling and reacting inside just as they do, the majority will keep right on believing that people who do not feel like them cannot possibly feel as they do. ["WP," p. 171]

The difference between difference and sameness can barely be said. It is as small and as vast as the difference between "like" and "as."

Hurston ends "How It Feels to Be Colored Me," too, with an attempt to erase difference. She describes herself as "a brown bag of miscellany" whose contents are as different from each other as they are similar to those of other bags, "white, red, and yellow" ("CM," p. 155). The outside is no guarantee of the nature of the inside. The last sentence of the article, which responds distantly to the title, is "Who knows?" ("CM," p. 155).

By the end of the essay, then, Hurston has conjugated a conflicting and ironic set of responses to her title. Far from answering the question of "how it feels to be colored me," she deconstructs the very grounds of an answer, replying "Compared to what? As of when? Who is asking? In what context? For what purpose? With what interests and presuppositions?" What Hurston rigorously shows is that questions of difference and identity are always a function of a specific interlocutionary situation—and the answers, matters of strategy rather than truth. In its rapid passage from image to image and from formula to formula, Hurston's *text* enacts the questions of identity as a process of *self*-difference that Hurston's *persona* often explicitly denies.

* * *

Despite Boas' prefatory claim[6] that Hurston has made "an unusual contribution to our knowledge of the true inner life of the Negro," the nature of such "knowledge" cannot be taken for granted (*MM*, p.x). Like Hurston's rep-

---

6. As Johnson mentions at the outset of her discussion of *Mules and Men*, not included here, the book begins with a preface by Franz Boas, Hurston's mentor in anthropology [editor's note].

resentation of "colored me," her collection of folktales forces us to ask not "Has an 'inside' been accurately represented?" but "What is the nature of the dialogic situation into which the representation has been called?" Since this is always specific, always a play of specific desires and expectations, it is impossible to conceive of a pure inside. There is no universalized Other, no homogeneous "us," for the self to reveal itself *to*. Inside the chemise is the other side of the chemise: the side on which the observer can read the nature of his or her own desire to see.

Mules and Men ends, unexpectedly, with one final tale. Hurston has just spent 150 pages talking not about folktales but about hoodoo practices. Suddenly, after a break but without preamble, comes the following tale:

> Once Sis Cat got hongry and caught herself a rat and set herself down to eat 'im. Rat tried and tried to git loose but Sis Cat was too fast and strong. So jus' as de cat started to eat 'im he says "Hol' on dere, Sis Cat! Ain't you got no manners atall? You going set up to de table and eat 'thout washing yo' face and hands?"
>
> Sis Cat was mighty hongry but she hate for de rat to think she ain't got no manners, so she went to de water and washed her face and hands and when she got back de rat was gone.
>
> So de cat caught herself a rat again and set down to eat. So de Rat said, "Where's yo' manners at, Sis Cat? You going to eat 'thout washing yo' face and hands?"
>
> "Oh, Ah got plenty manners," de cat told 'im. "But Ah eats mah dinner and washes mah face and uses mah manners afterwards." So she et right on 'im and washed her face and hands. And cat's been washin' after eatin' ever since.
>
> I'm sitting here like Sis Cat, washing my face and usin' my manners.
> [*MM*, pp. 251–52]

So ends the book. But what manners is she using? Upon reading this strange, unglossed final story, one cannot help wondering who, in the final analysis, has swallowed what. The reader? Mrs. Mason? Franz Boas? Hurston herself? As Nathan Huggins writes after an attempt to determine the sincerity of Hurston's poses and self-representations, "It is impossible to tell from reading Miss Hurston's autobiography who was being fooled."[7] If, as Hurston often implies, the essence of telling "lies" is the art of conforming a narrative to existing structures of address while gaining the upper hand, then Hurston's very ability to fool us—or to fool us into *thinking* we have been fooled—is itself the only effective way of conveying the rhetoric of the "lie." To turn one's own life into a trickster tale of which even the teller herself might be the dupe certainly goes far in deconstructing the possibility of representing the truth of identity.

If I initially approached Hurston out of a desire to re-referentialize difference, what Hurston gives me back seems to be difference as a suspension of reference. Yet the terms "black" and "white," "inside" and "outside," continue to matter. Hurston suspends the certainty of reference not by erasing these differences but by foregrounding the complex dynamism of their interaction.

1985

---

7. Nathan Irvin Huggins, *Harlem Renaissance* (London, 1971), p. 133.

PAULA GUNN ALLEN
b. 1939

Speaking back to her "white sisters" because of their exclusive emphasis on women's oppression, Paula Gunn Allen draws on the matrilineal and woman-centered perspectives of Native American cultures to diversify feminist conversations. Born in Cubero, New Mexico, to a Laguna Sioux mother and a Lebanese American father, Allen attended the University of Oregon as well as the University of New Mexico, where in 1975 she earned a Ph.D. in American Indian studies. In addition to her many volumes of verse, *The Sacred Hoop: Recovering the Feminine in American Indian Traditions* (1986; rev. ed., 1992) and two volumes she edited, *Studies in American Indian Literature: Critical Essays and Course Designs* (1983) and *Spider Woman's Granddaughters: Traditional Tales and Contemporary Writing by Native American Women* (1989), have been extensively used to educate students in Native American literature. Our selection, first published in *North Dakota Quarterly* and reprinted in *The Sacred Hoop*, is animated by an interest in oral storytelling and by a commitment to exploring the reading process. Cultural assumptions, Allen demonstrates, mark translations as well as interpretations of texts that might be produced in traditional tribal contexts and then marketed for and understood within Euro-American frameworks. What difference, she asks, does the gender of the author and the reader make in tribal or Euro-American interpretive communities?

From The Sacred Hoop: Recovering the Feminine in American Indian Traditions

From *Kochinnenako in Academe: Three Approaches to Interpreting a Keres Indian Tale*

❊   ❊   ❊

To demonstrate the interconnections between tribal and feminist approaches as I use them in my work, I have developed an analysis of a traditional "Yellow Woman" story of the Laguna-Acoma Keres, as re-cast by my mother's great uncle, John M. Gunn, in his book *Schat Chen*.[1] My analysis utilizes three possible approaches and demonstrates the relationship of context to meaning, illuminating three consciousness styles, and providing students with a traditionally tribal and non-racist, feminist understanding of traditional and contemporary American Indian life.

Some Theoretical Considerations

❊   ❊   ❊

John Gunn got the story I am using here from a Keres-speaking informant and did the translating himself. The story, which he titles "Sh-ah-cock and

---

1. John M. Gunn, *Schat-Chen: History, Traditions and Narratives of the Queres Indians of Laguna and Acoma* (1917; reprint, New York: AMS, 1980). Gunn, my mother's great uncle, lived among the Lagunas all of his adult life. He spoke Laguna (Keres) and gathered information in somewhat informal ways while sitting in the sun visiting with older people. He married Meta Atseye, my grandmother, years after her husband (John Gunn's brother) died, and may have taken much of his information from her stories or explanations of Laguna ceremonial events. She had a way of "translating" terms and concepts from Keres into English and from a Laguna conceptual framework into an American one—as she understood it. For example, she used to refer to the Navajo people as "gypsies," probably because they traveled in covered wagons. [Except as indicated, all notes are Allen's.]

Miochin or the Battle of the Seasons," is in reality a ritual, here cast in narrative form. The ritual brings about the change of season and of moiety[2]
among the Keres. Gunn doesn't mention this, perhaps because he was interested in stories and not in religion, or perhaps because his informant didn't
mention the connection to him.

What is interesting about his rendering is the interpolation of European,
classist, conflict-centered patriarchal assumptions which are used as plotting
devices. These interpolations have the effect of dislocating the significance
of the tale, and of subtly altering the ideational context of woman-centered,
largely pacifistic people whose ritual story this is. I have developed three critiques of the tale as it appears in his book, using feminist and tribal understandings to discuss the various meanings of the story when it is read from
three different perspectives.

In the first reading, I apply tribal understanding to the story. In the second, I apply the sort of feminist perspective I applied to traditional stories,
historical events, traditional culture, and contemporary literature when I
began developing a feminist perspective. The third reading applies what I
am calling a "feminist-tribal perspective." Each of these analyses is somewhat less detailed than it might be; but as I am interested in detailing modes
of perception, and their impact on our understanding of cultural artifacts
(and by extension our understanding of people who come from different cultural contexts than our own), rather than critiquing a story, they are adequate.

Yellow Woman Stories

The Keres of Laguna and Acoma Pueblos in New Mexico have stories that
are called "Yellow Woman" stories. The themes and to a large extent the
motifs of these stories are always female-centered, and they are always told
from Yellow Woman's point of view. Virtually any story that has a female protagonist can be a Yellow Woman story as long as its purpose is to clarify
aspects of women's lives in general. Some older recorded versions of Yellow
Woman tales (as in Gunn) make her the daughter of the *hocheni*. Gunn translates this to "ruler." But Keres notions of the *hocheni*'s function and position
as *cacique* or "mother chief" differ greatly from Anglo-European ideas of
rulership.

However, for Gunn to render *hocheni* as "ruler" is congruent with the
European folk tale tradition, and his use of the term may have been one
used by Gunn's informants, who were often Carlisle or Menaul Indian
School educated, in an attempt to find an equivalent term signifying the
deep respect and reverence the *hocheni tyi'a'muni* is granted and a term
that Gunn could comprehend. Or he might have selected the term because
he was writing a book for an anonymous Keres audience, one which
included himself. As he spoke Laguna Keres, I think he was doing the translations himself, and his renderings of words (and contexts) were likely influenced by the way Lagunas themselves rendered local terms into English,
but I doubt that he was conscious of the extent to which his renderings
reflected European traditions and simultaneously distorted Laguna-Acoma
ones.

---

2. One of the two principal political classes into which matrilineal and matrifocal Native American tribes
are divided [editor's note].

Gunn was deeply aware of the importance and intelligence of the Keresan tradition, but he was also unable to grant it independent existence. His major impulse was to link the Western Keres with the Sumerians, in some strange way, in order to demonstrate the justice of his assessment of their intelligence.[3]

However it may be, Kochinnenako, Yellow Woman, is in some sense a name that means Woman-Woman because among the Keres, yellow is the color for women (as pink and red are among Anglo-European Americans), and it is the color ascribed to the northwest. Keres women paint their faces yellow on certain ceremonial occasions, and are so painted at death so that the guardian at the gate of the spirit world, Naiya Iyatiku (Mother Corn Woman), will recognize that the newly arrived person is a woman. It is also the name of a particular Iriaku, corn mother (sacred corn-ear bundle), and Yellow Woman stories, in their original form, detail rituals in which the Iriaku figures prominently.

*   *   *

Many Yellow Woman tales highlight her alienation from the people—she lives with her grandmother at the edge of the village, for example, or she is in some way atypical, maybe a woman who refuses to marry, one who is known for some particular special talent, or one who is very quick-witted and resourceful. In many ways Kochinnenako is a role-model, though she models some behaviors that are not likely to occur in the lives of many who hear the stories about her. She is, one might say, the Spirit of Woman.

* * * Not that all the stories are graced with a happy ending. Some come to a tragic conclusion, and sometimes this conclusion is the result of someone's inability to follow the rules or perform a ritual in the proper way.

Other Kochinnenako stories are about her centrality to the harmony, balance, and prosperity of the group. "Sh-ah-cock and Miochin" is one of these. John Gunn prefaces the narrative with the comment that while this story is about a battle, war stories are rarely told by the Keres as they are not "a warlike people" and "very rarely refer to their exploits in war."

Sh-ah-cock and Miochin or the Battle of the Seasons

In the Kush-kut-ret-u-nah-tit (white village of the north) was once a ruler by the name of Hut-cha-mun Ki-uk (the broken prayer stick), one of whose daughters, Ko-chin-ne-nako, became the bride of Sh-ah-cock (the spirit of winter), a person of very violent temper. He always manifested his presence by blizzards of snow or sleet or by freezing cold, and on account of his alliance with the ruler's daughter, he was most of the time in the vicinity of Kush-kutret, and as these manifestations continued from month to month and year to year, the people of Kush-kutret found that their crops would not mature, and finally they were compelled to subsist on the leaves of the cactus.

On one occasion Ko-chin-ne-na-ko had wandered a long way from home in search of the cactus and had gathered quite a bundle and was preparing to carry home by singeing off the thorns, when on looking up she found herself confronted by a very bold but handsome young man.

3. An unpublished manuscript in my possession written by John Gunn after *Schat-Chen* is devoted to his researches and speculations into this idea.

His attire attracted her gaze at once. He wore a shirt of yellow woven from the silks of the corn, a belt made from the broad green blades of the same plant, a tall pointed hat made from the same kind of material and from the top of which waved a yellow corn tassel. He wore green leggings woven from kow-e-nuh, the green stringy moss that forms in springs and ponds. His moccasins were beautifully embroidered with flowers and butterflies. In his hand he carried an ear of green corn.

His whole appearance proclaimed him a stranger and as Ko-chin-ne-na-ko gazed in wonder, he spoke to her in a very pleasing voice asking her what she was doing. She told him that on account of the cold and drought, the people of Kush-kutret were forced to eat the leaves of the cactus to keep from starving.

"Here," said the young man, handing her the ear of green corn. "Eat this and I will go and bring more that you may take home with you."

He left her and soon disappeared going towards the south. In a short time he returned bringing with him a big load of green corn. Ko-chin-ne-na-ko asked him where he had gathered the corn and if it grew near by. "No," he replied, "it is from my home far away in the south, where the corn grows and the flowers bloom all the year round. Would you not like to accompany me back to my country?" Ko-chin-ne-na-ko replied that his home must be very beautiful, but that she could not go with him because she was the wife of Sh-ah-cock. And then she told him of her alliance with the Spirit of Winter, and admitted that her husband was very cold and disagreeable and that she did not love him. The strange young man urged her to go with him to the warm land of the south, saying that he did not fear Sh-ah-cock. But Ko-chin-ne-na-ko would not consent. So the stranger directed her to return to her home with the corn he had brought and cautioned her not to throw any of the husks out of the door. Upon leaving he said to her, "You must meet me at this place tomorrow. I will bring more corn for you."

Ko-chin-ne-na-ko had not proceeded far on her homeward way ere she met her sisters who, having become uneasy because of her long absence, had come in search of her. They were greatly surprised at seeing her with an armful of corn instead of cactus. Ko-chin-ne-na-ko told them the whole story of how she had obtained it, and thereby only added wonderment to their surprise. They helped her to carry the corn home; and there she had again to tell her story to her father and mother.

When she had described the stranger even from his peaked hat to his butterfly moccasins, and had told them that she was to meet him again on the day following, Hutchamun Kiuk, the father, exclaimed:

"It is Mi-o-chin!"

"It is Mi-o-chin! It is Mi-o-chin!" echoed the mother. "Tomorrow you must bring him home with you."

The next day Ko-chin-ne-na-ko went again to the spot where she had met Mi-o-chin, for it was indeed Mi-o-chin, the Spirit of Summer. He was already there, awaiting her coming. With him he had brought a huge bundle of corn.

Ko-chin-ne-na-ko pressed upon him the invitation of her parents to accompany her home, so together they carried the corn to Kush Kut-ret. When it had been distributed there was sufficient to feed all the people of the city. Amid great rejoicing and thanksgiving, Mi-o-chin was welcomed at the Hotchin's (ruler's) house.

In the evening, as was his custom, Sh-ah-cock, the Spirit of the Winter, returned to his home. He came in a blinding storm of snow and hail and sleet, for he was in boisterous mood. On approaching the city, he felt within his very bones that Mi-o-chin was there, so he called in a loud and blustering voice:

"Ha! Mi-o-chin, are you here?"

For answer, Mi-o-chin advanced to meet him.

Then Sh-ah-cock, beholding him, called again,

"Ha! Mi-o-chin, I will destroy you."

"Ha! Sh-ah-cock, I will destroy you," replied Mi-o-chin, still advancing.

Sh-ah-cock paused, irresolute. He was covered from head to foot with frost (skah). Icycles [sic] (ya-pet-tu-ne) draped him round. The fierce, cold wind proceeded from his nostrils.

As Mi-o-chin drew near, the wintry wind changed to a warm summer breeze. The frost and icycles melted and displayed beneath them, the dry, bleached bulrushes (ska-ra ska-ru-ka) in which Sh-ah-cock was clad.

Seeing that he was doomed to defeat, Sh-ah-cock cried out:

"I will not fight you now, for we cannot try our powers. We will make ready, and in four days from this time, we will meet here and fight for supremacy. The victor shall claim Ko-chin-ne-na-ko for his wife."

With this, Sh-ah-cock withdrew in a rage. The wind again roared and shook the very houses; but the people were warm within them, for Mi-o-chin was with them.

The next day Mi-o-chin left Kush Kutret for his home in the south. Arriving there, he began to make his preparations to meet Sh-ah-cock in battle.

First he sent an eagle as a messenger to his friend, Ya-chun-ne-ne-moot (kind of shaley rock that becomes very hot in the fire), who lived in the west, requesting him to come and help to battle with Sh-ah-cock. Then he called together the birds and the four legged animals—all those that live in sunny climes. For his advance guard and shield he selected the bat (pickikke), as its tough skin would best resist the sleet and hail that Sh-ah-cock would hurl at him.

Meantime Sh-ah-cock had gone to his home in the north to make his preparations for battle. To his aid he called all the winter birds and all of the four legged animals of the wintry climates. For his advance guard and shield he selected the Shro-ak-ah (a magpie).

When these formidable forces had been mustered by the rivals, they advanced, Mi-o-chin from the south and Sh-ah-cock from the north, in battle array.

Ya-chun-ne-ne-moot kindled his fires and piled great heaps of resinous fuel upon them until volumes of steam and smoke ascended, forming enormous clouds that hurried forward toward Kush Kut-ret and the battle ground. Upon these clouds rode Mi-o-chin, the Spirit of Summer, and his vast army. All the animals of the army, encountering the smoke from Ya-chun-ne-ne-moot's fires, were colored by the smoke so that, from that day, the animals from the south have been black or brown in color.

Sh-ah-cock and his army came out of the north in a howling blizzard and borne forward on black storm clouds driven by a freezing wintry wind. As he came on, the lakes and rivers over which he passed were frozen and the air was filled with blinding sleet.

When the combatants drew near to Kush Kut-ret, they advanced with fearful rapidity. Their arrival upon the field was marked by fierce and terrific strife.

Flashes of lightning darted from Mi-o-chin's clouds. Striking the animals of Sh-ah-cock, they singed the hair upon them, and turned it white, so that, from that day, the animals from the north have worn a covering of white or have white markings upon them.

From the south, the black clouds still rolled upward, the thunder spoke again and again. Clouds of smoke and vapor rushed onward, melting the snow and ice weapons of Sh-ah-cock and compelling him, at length, to retire from the field. Mi-o-chin, assured of victory, pursued him. To save himself from total defeat and destruction, Sh-ah-cock called for an armistice.

This being granted on the part of Mi-o-chin, the rivals met at Kush Kut-ret to arrange the terms of the treaty. Sh-ah-cock acknowledged himself defeated. He consented to give up Ko-chin-ne-na-ko to Mi-o-chin. This concession was received with rejoicing by Ko-chin-ne-na-ko and all the people of Kush Kut-ret.

It was then agreed between the late combatants that, for all time thereafter, Mi-o-chin was to rule at Kush Kut-ret during one-half of the year, and Sh-ah-cock was to rule during the remaining half, and that neither should molest the other.[4]

Or so John Gunn tells the tale, which I have quoted in its entirety because the way it is told lends itself to three kinds of analysis—that of an Indian literary commentator, that of a feminist, and that of an Indian feminist (or a feminist Indian).

John Gunn's version has a formal plot structure that makes the account seem to be a narrative. But had he translated it directly from the Keres, even in "narrative" form, as in a story-telling session, its ritual nature would have been more clearly in evidence.

How the account might go, if it were done that way, I can only surmise, based on renderings of Keres rituals in narrative forms I am acquainted with. But it would have sounded more like the following than like Gunn's rendition of it:

Long ago. Eh. There in the North. Yellow Woman. Up northward she went. Then she picked burrs and cactus. Then here went Summer. From the south he came. Above there he arrived. Thus spoke Summer. "Are you here? How is it going?" said Summer. "Did you come here?" thus said Yellow Woman. Then answered Yellow Woman. "I pick these poor things because I am hungry." "Why do you not eat corn and melons?" asked Summer. Then he gave her some corn and melons. "Take it!" Then thus spoke Yellow Woman, "It is good. Let us go. To my house I take you." "Is not your husband there?" "No. He went hunting deer. Today at night he will come back."

Then in the north they arrived. In the west they went down. Arrived then

---

4. Gunn, *Schat-Chen*, pp. 217–22.

they in the east. "Are you here?" Remembering Prayer Sticks said. "Yes," Summer said. "How is it going?" Summer said. Then he said, "Your daughter Yellow Woman, she brought me here." "Eh. That is good." Thus spoke Remembering Prayer Sticks. . . .

The story would continue, with many of the elements contained in Gunn's version, but organized along the axis of directions, movement of the participants, their maternal relationships to each other (daughter, mother, mother chief, etc.), and events sketched in only as they pertained to directions and the division of the year into its ritual/ceremonial segments, one of which belongs to the Kurena (summer supernaturals or powers who are connected to the Summer people or clans and the other which belongs to the Kashare, perhaps in conjunction with the Kopishtaya, the Spirits).

Summer, Mi-o-chin, is the Shiwana who lives on the south mountain, and Sh-ah-cock is the Shiwana who lives on the north mountain.[5] It is interesting to note that the Kurena wear three eagle feathers and *ctc'otika'* feathers (white striped) on their heads, bells, and woman's dress, and carry a reed flute, which, perhaps, is connected with Iyatiku's sister, Istoakoa, Reed Woman.

A Keres Interpretation

When a traditional Keres reads this tale, she listens with certain information about her people in mind: she knows, for example, that *Hutchamun Kiuk* (properly it means "Remembering Prayer Sticks" though Gunn translates this as "Broken Prayer Sticks"),[6] refers to the ritual (sacred) identity of the *cacique* and that the story is a narrative version of a ceremony related to the planting of corn. She knows that Lagunas and Acomas don't have rulers in the Anglo-European sense of monarchs, lords, and such (though they in recent times have elected governors, but that's another matter), and that a person's social status is determined by her mother's clan and position in it, rather than by her relationship to the *cacique* as his daughter. (Actually, in various accounts, the *cacique* refers to Yellow Woman as his mother, so the designation of her as his daughter is troublesome unless one is aware that relationships in the context of their ritual significance are being delineated here.)

In any case, our hypothetical Keresan reader also knows that the story is about a ritual that takes place every year, and that the battle imagery refers to events that take place during the ritual; she is also aware that Kochin-nenako's will, as expressed in her attraction to Miochin, is a central element of the ritual. She knows further that the ritual is partly about the coming of summer and partly about the ritual relationship and exchange of primacy between the two divisions of the tribe, and that the ritual described in the narrative is enacted by men, dressed as Miochin and Sh-ah-cock, and that Yellow Woman in her Corn Mother aspect is the center of this and other sacred rites of the Kurena, though in this ritual she may also be danced by a Kurena mask dancer.

---

5. In his *Keresan Texts* (vol. VIII, part I, Publications of the American Ethnological Society [New York: American Ethnological Society, 1928]), Franz Boas writes, "The second and the fourth of the shiwana appear in the tale of summer and winter. . . . Summer wears a shirt of buckskin with squash ornaments, shoes like moss to which parrot feathers are tied. His face is painted with red mica and flowers are tied on to it. . . . Winter wears a shirt of icicles and his shoes are like ice. His shirt is shiny and to its end are tied turkey feathers and eagle feathers" (p. 284).

6. Boas, p. 288. Boas says he made the same mistake at first, having misheard the word they used.

* * *

A traditional Keres, at least, is satisfied by the story because it reaffirms a Keres sense of rightness, of propriety. It is a tale that describes ritual events, and the Keres reader can visualize the ritual itself when reading Gunn's story. Such a reader is likely to be puzzled by the references to rulers and by the tone of heroic romance, but will be reasonably satisfied by the account because in spite of its Westernized changes, it still ends happily with the orderly transfer of focality between the moieties and seasons that has been accomplished in all its seasonal splendor as winter in New Mexico blusters and sleets its way north, and summer sings and warms its way home. In the end, the primary Keresan values of harmony, balance, and the centrality of woman in their maintenance have been validated, and the fundamental Keres principal of proper order is celebrated and affirmed once again.

A Modern Feminist Interpretation

A non-Keres feminist, reading this tale, is likely to suppose that this narrative is about the importance of men and the use of a passive female figure as a pawn in their bid for power.[7] And, given the way Gunn renders the story, she would have good reason to make such an inference. As Gunn recounts it, the story opens in classic patriarchal style and implies certain patriarchal complications: that Kochinnenako has married a man who is violent and destructive. She is the ruler's daughter, which might suggest that the traditional Keres are concerned with the abuses of power of the wealthy. This in turn suggests that the traditional Keres social system, like the traditional Anglo-European ones, suffered from oppressive class structures in which the rich and powerful bring misery to the people, who, in the tale, are reduced to bare subsistence seemingly as a result of her unfortunate alliance. A reader making the usual assumptions Western readers make when enjoying folk tales will think she is reading a sort of Robin Hood story, replete with a lovely maid Marian, an evil Sheriff, and a green-clad agent of social justice with the Indian name *Miochin*.

Given the usual assumptions that underly European folk tales, given the Western romantic view of the Indian that is generally America's only view, and given the usual anti-patriarchal bias that characterizes feminist analysis, a feminist reader might assume that Kochinnenako has been compelled to make an unhappy match by her father the ruler who must be gaining some power from the alliance. Besides, his name is given as "Broken Prayer Stick," which might be taken to mean that he is an unholy man, remiss in his religious duties and weak in spiritual accomplishment.

7. When my sister, Carol Lee Sanchez, spoke to her university Woman's Studies class about the position of centrality women hold in our Keres tradition, one young woman, a self-identified radical feminist, was outraged. She insisted that Ms. Sanchez, and other Laguna women, had been "brainwashed" into believing that we had power over our lives. After all, she knew that no women anywhere has even had that kind of power; her feminist studies had made that "fact" quite plain to her. The kind of cultural chauvinism that has been promulgated by well-intentioned but culturally entranced feminists can lead to serious misunderstandings such as this one, and in the process become a new racism based on what becomes the feminist canon. Not that feminists can be faulted entirely on this—they are, after all, reflecting the research and interpretation done in a patriarchal context, by male-biased researchers and scholars, most of whom would avidly support the young radical feminist's strenuous position. It's too bad, though, that feminists fall into the patriarchal trap.

Nor does Gunn's tale clarify these issues. Instead it proceeds in a way best calculated to confirm a feminist's interpretation of the tale as only another example of the low status women in tribal cultures hold. (Certainly an inordinate amount of effort on the part of students and recorders of traditional American Indian life has gone into creating the impression that the white woman's lot was glorious when and if compared to that of the savage squaw!) In accordance with his most sacred of American myths, Gunn makes it clear that Kochinnenako is not happy in her marriage; she thinks Sh-ah-cock is "cold and disagreeable, and she cannot love him." Certainly, contemporary American women will read that to mean that Sh-ah-cock is an emotionally uncaring, perhaps cruel husband, and that Kochinnenako is forced by her position in life to accept a life bereft of warmth and love. Our feminist reader might imagine that Kochinnenako, like many women, has been socialized into submission. So obedient is she, it seems, so lacking in spirit and independence, that she doesn't seize her chance to escape a bad situation, preferring instead to remain obedient to the patriarchal institution of marriage. As it turns out (in Gunn's tale), Yellow Woman is delivered from the clutches of her violent and unwanted mate by the timely intervention of a much more pleasant man, our hero.

A radical feminist is likely to read the story for its content vis-à-vis racism and resistance to oppression. From a radical perspective, it is politically significant that Sh-ah-cock is white. That is, winter is white. Snow is white. Blizzards are white. Clearly, while the story does not give much support to concepts of a people's struggles, it could be construed to mean that the oppressor is designated white in the story because the Keres are engaged in serious combat with white colonial power, and given the significance of storytelling in tribal cultures, are chronicling that struggle in this tale. Read this way, it would seem to acknowledge the right and duty of the people in overthrowing the hated white dictator who, by this account, possesses the power of life and death over them.

❖   ❖   ❖

When read as a battle narrative, the story as Gunn renders it makes clear that the superiority of Miochin rests as much in his commitment to the welfare of the people as in his military prowess, and that because his attempt to free the people is backed up by their active invitation to him to come and liberate them, he is successful. Because of his success he is entitled to the hand of the ruler's daughter, Kochinnenako, one of the traditional Old World spoils of victory. Similarly, Sh-ah-cock is defeated not only because he is violent and oppressive, but also because the people, like Kochinnenako, find that they cannot love him.

A radical lesbian separatist might find herself uncomfortable with the story even though it is so clearly correct in identifying the enemy as white and violent, though, because the overthrow of the tyrant is placed squarely in the hands of another male figure, Miochin. This rescue is likely to be viewed with a jaundiced eye by many feminists (though more romantic women might be satisfied with it, since it's a story about an Indian woman of long ago), as Kochinnenako has to await the coming of a handsome stranger for her salvation, and her fate is decided by her father and the more salutory suitor Miochin.* * *

Some readers (like me) might find themselves hoping that Miochin is really female, disguised by males as one of them in order to buttress their position of relative power. After all, this figure is dressed in yellow and green, colors associated with corn, a plant always associated with Woman.* * *

An Indian-Feminist Interpretation

The feminist interpretation I have sketched—which is a fair representation of an early reading of my own from what I took to be a feminist perspective—proceeds from two unspoken assumptions. These assumptions are that women are essentially powerless and that conflict is basic to human experience. The first is a fundamental feminist position, while the second is basic to Anglo-European thought; neither, however, is characteristic of Keres thought. To a modern feminist, marriage is an institution developed to establish and maintain male supremacy, and as the "ruler's" daughter, whom Kochinnenako marries determines which male will hold power over the people and who will inherit the throne.[8]

When Western assumptions are applied to tribal narratives, they become mildly confusing and moderately annoying from any perspective.[9] Western assumptions about the nature of human society (and thus of literature) when contextualizing a tribal story or ritual must necessarily leave certain elements unclear. For if the battle between Summer Spirit and Winter Spirit is about the triumph of warmth, generosity, and kindness over coldness, miserliness, and cruelty, supremacy of the good over the bad, why does the hero grant his protagonist rights over the village and Kochinnenako for half of each year?

* * *

Essentially what is happening is that Summer (a mask dancer dressed as Miochin) asks Kochinnenako permission, in a ritual manner, to enter the village. She (a mask dancer dressed as Yellow Woman or Iriaku—Yellow Corn) follows a specified ritual order of responses and events that enable Summer to enter. Some of these are acts she must perform and words she must say, and others are prohibitions. One of the latter is that she must not "throw any

---

8. For a detailed exposition of what this dynamic consists of, see Adrienne Rich, "Compulsory Heterosexuality and Lesbian Existence," *Signs: Journal of Women in Culture and Society*, vol. 4, no. 4 (Summer 1980): 630–61. Rpt. as a pamphlet with an updated foreword (Denver: Antelope Publications, 1982), 1612 St. Paul, Denver, Colorado, 80206.

9. Elaine Jahner, a specialist in Lakota language and oral literature, has suggested to me that the Western obsession with Western plot in narrative structure led early informant George Sword to construct narratives in the Western fashion and tell them as Lakota traditional stories. Research has shown that Sword's stories are not recognized as Lakota traditional stories by Lakotas themselves; but the tribal narratives that are so recognized are loosely structured and do not exhibit the reliance on central theme or character that is so dear to the hearts of Western collectors. As time has gone by, the Sword stories have become a sort of model for later Lakota storytellers who, out of a desire to convey the tribal tales to Western collectors, have changed the old structures to ones more pleasing to American and European ears.

Education in Western schools, exposure to mass media, and the need to function in a white-dominated world have subtly but perhaps permanently altered the narrative structures of the old tales and with them the tribal conceptual modes of tribespeople. The shift has been away from associative, synchronistic, event-centered narrative and thought to a linear, foreground-centered one. Concurrently, tribal social organization and interpersonal relations have taken a turn toward authoritarian, patriarchal, linear, and misogynist modes—hence the rise of violence against women, an unthinkable event in older, more circular and tribal times.

of the husks out of the door," a command that establishes both the identity of Miochin and constitutes his declaration of his ritual intention and his ritual relationship to her. It is also a directive to the people on the proper way to handle the corn.

Agency is Kochinnenako's ritual role here, and it is through her ritual agency that the orderly, harmonious transfer of primacy between the Summer and Winter people is accomplished. This transfer of course takes place at the time of the year that winter goes north and summer comes to the pueblo from the south, the time when the sun moves north, along the line the sun makes along the edge of the sun's house as ascertained by the Hotchin who is the calendar keeper and the official who determines the proper solar and astronomical times for various ceremonies. Thus, in the proper time, Kochinnenako empowers Summer to enter the village. Kochinnenako's careful observance of the ritual requirements of the situation, joined with the proper conduct of her sisters, her mother, the priests (symbolized by the title *Hutchamum Kiuk*, whom Gunn identifies as the ruler and Yellow Woman's father though he could as properly—more properly, actually—be called her mother), the animals and birds, the weather and the people at last bring summer to the village, ending the winter and the famine that accompanies winter's end.

A feminist who is conscious of tribal thought and practice will know that the real story of Sh-ah-cock and Miochin underscores the central role that woman plays in the orderly life of the people. Reading Gunn's version, she will be aware of the vast gulf between the Lagunas and John Gunn in their understanding of the role of women in a traditional gynecentric society such as that of the Western Keres. Knowing that the central role of woman is harmonizing spiritual relationships between the people and the rest of the universe, and empowering ritual activities, she will be able to read the story for its Western colonial content, aware that Gunn's version reveals more about American consciousness when it meets with tribal thought than it does about the tribe. When the story is analyzed from within the context to which it rightly belongs, its feminist content becomes clear, as do the various purposes to which a tribal story can be put by industrialized patriarchal people.

* * *

She will know that the story is about how the Mother Corn who is Iyatiku's "daughter"—that is, her essence in one of its aspects—comes to live as Remembering Prayer Stick's daughter first with the Winter people and then with the Summer people, and so on.

The net effect of Gunn's rendition of the story is the unhappy wedding of the woman-centered tradition of the western Keres to patriarchal Anglo-European tradition, and thus the dislocation of the central position of Keres women by their assumption under the rule of men. When one understands that the *Hotchin* is the person who tells the time and prays for all the people, even the white people, and that the *Hutchamun Kiuk* is the ruler only in the sense that the Constitution of the United States is the ruler of the citizens and government of the United States, the Keres organization of men, women, spirit folk, equinoxes, seasons, and clouds into a balanced and integral dynamic will be seen reflected in the narrative. Knowing this, she will also be able to see how the interpolations of patriarchal thinking distort all the relationships in the story, and, by extension, how such impositions of patriarchy upon gynocracy work to disorder harmonious social and spiritual relationships.

*   *   *

In the end, the tale I have analyzed is not about Kochinnenako or Sha-ahcock and Miochin. It is about the change of seasons, and it is about the centrality of woman as agent and empowerer of that change. It is about how a people engage themselves as a people within the spiritual cosmos of their lives and in an ordered and proper way that bestows the dignity of each upon all with careful respect, folkish humor, and ceremonial delight. It is about how everyone is part of the background that shapes the meaning and value of each one's life. It is about propriety, mutuality, and the dynamics of socio-environmental change.

1986

BARBARA CHRISTIAN
1943–2000

For almost thirty years, Barbara Christian taught English, African American studies, and women's studies at the University of California, Berkeley, where she was the first black woman to receive tenure. She arrived there from a Catholic mission school in her native St. Thomas, having completed her undergraduate education at Marquette University and having earned a doctorate from Columbia University. Three of her pioneering works established the parameters of African American feminist studies: *Black Women Novelists: The Development of a Tradition, 1892–1976* (1980), *Black Feminist Criticism: Perspectives on Black Women Writers* (1985), and *From the Inside Out: Afro-American Women's Literary Tradition and the State* (1987). With its punning title, "The Race for Theory," which has become a touchstone in many feminist classrooms, has sometimes been read as an outright attack on theory—especially the poststructuralist French theory associated with such male and female thinkers as Jacques Derrida and Julia Kristeva—and certainly Christian questions its pertinence for nonwhite and non-Western women. However, the essay also can be understood as an interrogation of the term *theory* itself: perhaps, Christian suggests, stories and poems, proverbs and songs theorize in a different key. Through her editorial work, Barbara Christian helped make race a crucially significant lens for comprehending how gender dynamics operate: especially in her casebook on Alice Walker's *Everyday Use* (1994), her section of *The Norton Anthology of African American Literature* (1997), and her contribution as co-editor to *Female Subjects in Black and White: Race, Psychoanalysis, Feminism* (1997).

The Race for Theory

I have seized this occasion to break the silence among those of us, critics, as we are now called, who have been intimidated, devalued by what I call the race for theory. I have become convinced that there has been a takeover in the literary world by Western philosophers from the old literary elite, the neutral humanists. Philosophers have been able to effect such a take-over because so much of the literature of the West has become pallid, laden with despair, self-indulgent, and disconnected. The New Philosophers, eager to understand a world that is today fast escaping their political control, have redefined literature so that the distinctions implied by that term, that is, the distinctions between everything written and those things written to evoke feeling as well as to express thought, have been blurred. They have changed literary critical language to suit their own purposes as philosophers, and they have re-invented the meaning of theory.

My first response to this realization was to ignore it. Perhaps, in spite of the egocentrism of this trend, some good might come of it. I had, I felt, more pressing and interesting things to do, such as reading and studying the history and literature of black women, a history that had been totally ignored, a contemporary literature bursting with originality, passion, insight, and beauty. But unfortunately it is difficult to ignore this new take-over, theory has become a commodity because that helps determine whether we are hired or promoted in academic institutions—worse, whether we are heard at all. Due to this new orientation, works (a word which evokes labor) have become texts. Critics are no longer concerned with literature, but with other critics' texts, for the critic yearning for attention has displaced the writer and has conceived of himself as the center. Interestingly in the first part of this century, at least in England and America, the critic was usually also a writer of poetry, plays, or novels. But today, as a new generation of professionals develops, he or she is increasingly an academic. Activities such as teaching or writing one's response to specific works of literature have, among this group, become subordinated to one primary thrust, that moment when one creates a theory, thus fixing a constellation of ideas for a time at least, a fixing which no doubt will be replaced in another month or so by somebody else's competing theory as the race accelerates. Perhaps because those who have effected the take-over have the power (although they deny it) first of all to be published, and thereby to determine the ideas which are deemed valuable, some of our most daring and potentially radical critics (and by *our* I mean black, women, Third World) have been influenced, even co-opted, into speaking a language and defining their discussion in terms alien to and opposed to our needs and orientation. At least so far, the creative writers I study have resisted this language.[1]

"For people of color have always theorized—but in forms quite different from the Western form of abstract logic. And I am inclined to say that our theorizing (and I intentionally use the verb rather than the noun) is often in narrative forms, in the stories we create, in riddles and proverbs, in the play with language, since dynamic rather than fixed ideas seem more to our liking. How else have we managed to survive with such spiritedness the assault on our bodies, social institutions, countries, our very humanity? And women, at least the women I grew up around, continuously speculated about the nature of life through pithy language that unmasked the power relations of their world. It is this language, and the grace and pleasure with which they played with

1. For another view of the debate this "privileged" approach to Afro-American texts has engendered, see Joyce A. Joyce, " 'Who the Cap Fit': Unconsciousness and Unconscionableness in the Criticism of Houston A. Baker, Jr., and Henry Louis Gates, Jr.," *New Literary History* 18 (1987): 371–84. I had not read Joyce's essay before I wrote my own. Clearly there are differences between Joyce's view and my own. [All notes are Christian's.]

it, that I find celebrated, refined, critiqued in the works of writers like Toni Morrison and Alice Walker. My folk, in other words, have always been a race of theory—though more in the form of the hieroglyph, a written figure which is both sensual and abstract, both beautiful and communicative. In my own work I try to illuminate and explain these hieroglyphs, which is, I think, an activity quite different from the creating of the hieroglyphs themselves. As the Buddhists would say, the finger pointing at the moon is not the moon.

In this discussion, however, I am more concerned with the issue raised by my first use of the term, *the race for theory*, in relation to its academic hegemony, and possibly of its inappropriateness to the energetic emerging literatures in the world today. The pervasiveness of this academic hegemony is an issue continually spoken about—but usually in hidden groups, lest we, who are disturbed by it, appear ignorant to the reigning academic elite. Among the folk who speak in muted tones are people of color, feminists, radical critics, creative writers, who have struggled for much longer than a decade to make their voices, their various voices, heard, and for whom literature is not an occasion for discourse among critics but is necessary nourishment for their people and one way by which they come to understand their lives better. Clichéd though this may be, it bears, I think, repeating here.

The race for theory, with its linguistic jargon, its emphasis on quoting its prophets, its tendency towards 'Biblical' exegesis, its refusal even to mention specific works of creative writers, far less contemporary ones, its preoccupations with mechanical analyses of language, graphs, algebraic equations, its gross generalizations about culture, has silenced many of us to the extent that some of us feel we can no longer discuss our own literature, while others have developed intense writing blocks and are puzzled by the incomprehensibility of the language set adrift in literary circles. There have been, in the last year, any number of occasions on which I had to convince literary critics who have pioneered entire new areas of critical inquiry that they did have something to say. Some of us are continually harassed to invent wholesale theories regardless of the complexity of the literature we study. I, for one, am tired of being asked to produce a black feminist literary theory as if I were a mechanical man. For I believe such theory is prescriptive—it ought to have some relationship to practice. Since I can count on one hand the number of people attempting to be black feminist literary critics in the world today, I consider it presumptuous of me to invent a theory of how we *ought* to read. Instead, I think we need to read the works of our writers in our various ways and remain open to the intricacies of the intersection of language, class, race, and gender in the literature. And it would help if we share our process, that is, our practice, as much as possible since, finally, our work *is* a collective endeavor.

The insidious quality of this race for theory is symbolized for me by a term like 'Minority Discourse'[2]—a label that is borrowed from the reigning theory of the day but which is untrue to the literatures being produced by our writers, for many of our literatures (certainly Afro-American literature) are central, not minor. I have used the passive voice in my last sentence construction, contrary to the rules of Black English, which like all languages has a particular value system, since I have not placed responsibility on any particular per-

2. This paper was originally written for a conference at the University of California at Berkeley entitled "Minority Discourse," and held on 29–31 May 1986.

son or group. But that is precisely because this new ideology has become so prevalent among us that it behaves like so many of the other ideologies with which we have had to contend. It appears to have neither head nor center. At the least, though, we can say that the terms 'minority' and 'discourse' are located firmly in a Western dualistic or 'binary' frame which sees the rest of the world as minor, and tries to convince the rest of the world that it *is* major, usually through force and then through language, even as it claims many of the ideas that we, its 'historical' other, have known and spoken about for so long. For many of us have never conceived of ourselves only as somebody's *other*.

Let me not give the impression that by objecting to the race for theory I ally myself with or agree with the neutral humanists who see literature as pure expression and will not admit to the obvious control of its production, value, and distribution by those who have power, who deny, in other words, that literature is, of necessity, political. I am studying an entire body of literature that has been denigrated for centuries by such terms as *political*. For an entire century Afro-American writers, from Charles Chestnutt in the nineteenth century through Richard Wright in the 1930s, Imamu Baraka in the 1960s, Alice Walker in the 1970s, have protested the literary hierarchy of dominance which declares when literature is literature, when literature is great, depending on what it thinks is to its advantage. The Black Arts Movement of the 1960s, out of which Black Studies, the Feminist Literary Movement of the 1970s, and Women's Studies grew, articulated precisely those issues, which came *not* from the declarations of the New Western Philosophers but from these groups' reflections on their own lives. That Western scholars have long believed their ideas to be universal has been strongly opposed by many such groups. Some of my colleagues do not see black critical writers of previous decades as eloquent enough. Clearly they have not read Wright's 'A blueprint for Negro Writing', Ellison's *Shadow and Act*, Chesnutt's resignation from being a writer, or Alice Walker's 'In search of Zora Neale Hurston'.[3] There are two reasons for this general ignorance of what our writer-critics have said. One is that black writing has been generally ignored in the USA. Since we, as Toni Morrison has put it, are seen as a discredited people, it is no surprise, then, that our creations are also discredited. But this is also due to the fact that until recently, dominant critics in the Western world have also been creative writers who have had access to the upper-middle-class institutions of education and, until recently, our writers have decidedly been excluded from these institutions and in fact have often been opposed to them. Because of the academic world's general ignorance about the literature of black people, and of women, whose work too has been discredited, it is not surprising that so many of our critics think that the position arguing that literature is political begins with these New Philosophers. Unfortunately, many of our young critics do not investigate the reasons *why* that statement—literature is political—is now acceptable when before it was not; nor do we look to our own

3. See Ralph Ellison, *Shadow and Act* (New York: Random House, 1964); Robert M. Fransworth, introduction to *The Marrow of Tradition*, by Charles Chesnutt (Ann Arbor, Mich.: Michigan Paperbacks, 1969), v–xvii; Addison Gayle Jr., ed., *The Black Aesthetic* (Garden City, N.Y.: Doubleday Anchor Press, 1971); LeRoi Jones, *Home: Social Essays* (New York: William Morrow, 1966); Larry Neal, "The Black Arts Movement," in Gayle, ed., *The Black Aesthetic*, 272–90; Alice Walker, "In Search of Zora Neale Hurston," *Ms.* 3, no. 9 (March 1975); 74+; Richard Wright, "A Blueprint for Negro Writing," *New Challenge* 11 (1937): 53–65.

antecedents for the sophisticated arguments upon which we can build in order to change the tendency of any established Western idea to become hegemonic.

For I feel that the new emphasis on literary critical theory is as hegemonic as the world which it attacks. I see the language it creates as one which mystifies rather than clarifies our condition, making it possible for a few people who know that particular language to control the critical scene—that language surfaced, interestingly enough, just when the literature of peoples of color, of black women, of Latin Americans, of Africans, began to move to 'the center'. Such words as *center* and *periphery* are themselves instructive. *Discourse, canon, texts*, words as Latinate as the tradition from which they come, are quite familiar to me. Because I went to a Catholic Mission school in the West Indies I must confess that I cannot hear the word 'canon' without smelling incense, that the word 'text' immediately brings back agonizing memories of Biblical exegesis, that 'discourse' reeks for me of metaphysics forced down my throat in those courses that traced *world* philosophy from Aristotle through Thomas Aquinas to Heidegger. 'Periphery' too is a word I heard throughout my childhood, for if anything was seen as being at the periphery, it was those small Caribbean islands which had neither land mass nor military power. Still I noted how intensely important this periphery was, for US troops were continually invading one island or another if any change in political control even seemed to be occurring. As I lived among folk for whom language was an absolutely necessary way of validating our existence, I was told that the minds of the world lived only in the small continent of Europe. The metaphysical language of the New Philosophy, then, I must admit, is repulsive to me and is one reason why I raced from philosophy to literature, since the latter seemed to me to have the possibilities of rendering the world as large and as complicated as I experienced it, as sensual as I knew it was. In literature I sensed the possibility of the integration of feeling/ knowledge, rather than the split between the abstract and the emotional in which Western philosophy inevitably indulged.

Now I am being told that philosophers are the ones who write literature, that authors are dead, irrelevant, mere vessels through which their narratives ooze, that they do not work nor have they the faintest idea what they are doing; rather, they produce texts as disembodied as the angels. I am frankly astonished that scholars who call themselves marxists or post-marxists could seriously use such metaphysical language even as they attempt to deconstruct the philosophical tradition from which their language comes. And as a student of literature, I am appalled by the sheer ugliness of the language, its lack of clarity, its unnecessarily complicated sentence constructions, its lack of pleasurableness, its alienating quality. It is the kind of writing for which composition teachers would give a freshman a resounding F.

Because I am a curious person, however, I postponed readings of black women writers I was working on and read some of the prophets of this new literary orientation. These writers did announce their dissatisfaction with some of the cornerstone ideas of their own tradition, a dissatisfaction with which I was born. But in their attempt to change the orientation of Western scholarship, they, as usual, concentrated on themselves and were not in the slightest interested in the worlds they had ignored or controlled. Again I was supposed to know *them*, while they were not at all interested in knowing *me*.

Instead they sought to 'deconstruct' the tradition to which they belonged even as they used the same forms, style, language of that tradition, forms that necessarily embody its values. And increasingly as I read them and saw their substitution of their philosophical writings for literary ones, I began to have the uneasy feeling that their folk were not producing any literature worth mentioning. For they always harkened back to the masterpieces of the past, again reifying the very texts they said they were deconstructing. Increasingly, as *their* way, *their* terms, *their* approaches remained central and became the means by which one defined literary critics, many of my own peers who had previously been concentrating on dealing with the other side of the equation, the reclamation and discussion of past and *present* Third World literatures, were diverted into continually discussing the new literary theory.

From my point of view as a critic of contemporary Afro-American women's writing, this orientation is extremely problematic. In attempting to find the deep structures in the literary tradition, a major preoccupation of the new New Criticism, many of us have become obsessed with the nature of reading itself to the extent that we have stopped writing about literature being written today. Since I am slightly paranoid, it has begun to occur to me that the literature being produced *is* precisely one of the reasons why this new philosophical-literary-critical theory of relativity is so prominent. In other words, the literature of blacks, women of South America and Africa, etc., as overtly 'political' literature, was being preempted by a new Western concept which proclaimed that reality does not exist, that everything is relative, and that every text is silent about something—which indeed it must necessarily be.

There is, of course, much to be learned from exploring how we know what we know, how we read what we read, an exploration which, of necessity, can have no end. But there also has to be a 'what', and that 'what', when it is even mentioned by the New Philosophers, are texts of the past, primarily Western male texts, whose norms are again being transferred onto Third World, female texts as theories of reading proliferate. Inevitably a hierarchy has now developed between what is called theoretical criticism and practical criticism, as mind is deemed superior to matter. I have no quarrel with those who wish to philosophize about how we know what we know. But I do resent the fact that this particular orientation is so privileged and has diverted so many of us from doing the first readings of the literature being written today as well as of past works about which nothing has been written. I note, for example, that there is little work done on Gloria Naylor, that most of Alice Walker's works have not been commented on—despite the rage around *The Color Purple*[4]— that there has yet to be an in-depth study of Frances Harper, the nineteenth-century abolitionist poet and novelist. If our emphasis on theoretical criticism continues, critics of the future may have to reclaim the writers we are now ignoring, that is, if they are even aware these artists exist.

I am particularly perturbed by the movement to exalt theory, as well, because of my own adult history. I was an active member of the Black Arts Movement of the 1960s and know how dangerous theory can become. Many today may not be aware of this, but the Black Arts Movement tried to create

4. Alice Walker, *The Color Purple* (New York: Harcourt Brace Jovanovich, 1982). The controversy surrounding the novel and the subsequent film are discussed in Calvin Hernton, *The Sexual Mountain and Black Women Writers* (New York: Doubleday, 1987), chaps. 1 and 2.

Black Literary Theory and in doing so became prescriptive. My fear is that when Theory is not rooted in practice, it becomes prescriptive, exclusive, elitist.

An example of this prescriptiveness is the approach the Black Arts Movement took towards language. For it, blackness resided in the use of black talk which they defined as hip urban language. So that when Nikki Giovanni reviewed Paule Marshall's *Chosen Place, Timeless People*, she criticized the novel on the grounds that it was not black, for the language was too elegant, too white.[5] Blacks, she said, did not speak that way. Having come from the West Indies where we do, some of the time, speak that way, I was amazed by the narrowness of her vision. The emphasis on *one way* to be black resulted in the works of Southern writers being seen as non-black since the black talk of Georgia does not sound like the black talk of Philadelphia. Because the ideologues, like Baraka, came from the urban centers, they tended to privilege their way of speaking, thinking, writing, and to condemn other kinds of writing as not being black enough. Whole areas of the canon were assessed according to the dictum of the Black Arts Nationalist point of view, as in Addison Gayle's *The Way of the New World*, while other works were ignored because they did not fit the scheme of cultural nationalism.[6] Older writers like Ralph Ellison and James Baldwin were condemned because they saw that the intersection of Western and African influences resulted in a new Afro-American culture, a position with which many of the Black Nationalist ideologues disagreed. Writers were told that writing love poems was not being black. Further examples abound.

It is true that the Black Arts Movement resulted in a necessary and important critique both of previous Afro-American literature and of the white-established literary world. But in attempting to take over power, it, as Ishmael Reed satirizes so well in *Mumbo Jumbo*, became much like its opponent, monolithic and downright repressive.[7]

It is this tendency towards the monolithic, monotheistic, and so on, that worries me about the race for theory. Constructs like the *center* and the *periphery* reveal that tendency to want to make the world less complex by organizing it according to one principle, to fix it through an idea which is really an ideal. Many of us are particularly sensitive to monolithism because one major element of ideologies of dominance, such as sexism and racism, is to dehumanize people by stereotyping them, by denying them their variousness and complexity. Inevitably, monolithism becomes a metasystem, in which there is a controlling ideal, especially in relation to pleasure. Language as one form of pleasure is immediately restricted, and becomes heavy, abstract, prescriptive, monotonous.

Variety, multiplicity, eroticism are difficult to control. And it may very well be that these are the reasons why writers are often seen as *persona non grata* by political states, whatever form they take, since writers/artists have a tendency to refuse to give up their way of seeing the world and of playing with possibilities; in fact, their very expression relies on that insistence. Perhaps that is why creative literature, even when written by politically reactionary

---

5. Nikki Giovanni, review of Paule Marshall, *Chosen Place, Timeless People*, in *Negro Digest* 19, no. 3 (January 1970): 51–52, 84.

6. Addison Gayle Jr., *The Way of the New World:*

The Black Novel in America (Garden City, N.Y.: Doubleday Anchor Press, 1975).

7. Ishmael Reed, *Mumbo Jumbo* (Garden City, N.Y.: Doubleday Anchor Press, 1972).

people, can be so freeing, for in having to embody ideas and recreate the world, writers cannot merely produce 'one way'.

The characteristics of the Black Arts Movement are, I am afraid, being repeated again today, certainly in the other area to which I am especially tuned. In the race for theory, feminists, eager to enter the halls of power, have attempted their own prescriptions. So often I have read books on feminist literary theory that restrict the definition of what *feminist* means and overgeneralize about so much of the world that most women as well as men are excluded. Seldom do feminist theorists take into account the complexity of life—that women are of many races and ethnic backgrounds with different histories and cultures and that as a rule women belong to different classes that have different concerns. Seldom do they note these distinctions, because if they did they could not articulate a theory. Often as a way of clearing themselves they do acknowledge that women of color, for example, do exist, then go on to do what they were going to do anyway, which is to invent a theory that has little relevance for us.

That tendency towards monolithism is precisely how I see the French feminist theorists. They concentrate on the female body as the means to creating a female language, since language, they say, is male and necessarily conceives of woman as other.[8] Clearly many of them have been irritated by the theories of Lacan for whom language is phallic. But suppose there are peoples in the world whose language was invented primarily in relation to women, who after all are the ones who relate to children and teach language. Some Native American languages, for example, use female pronouns when speaking about non-gender-specific activity. Who knows who, according to gender, created languages. Further, by positing the body as the source of everything French feminists return to the old myth that biology determines everything and ignore the fact that gender is a social rather than a biological construct.

I could go on critiquing the positions of French feminists who are themselves more various in their points of view than the label which is used to describe them, but that is not my point. What I am concerned about is the authority this school now has in feminist scholarship—the way it has become *authoritative discourse*, monologic, which occurs precisely because it does have access to the means of promulgating its ideas. The Black Arts Movement was able to do this for a time because of the political movements of the 1960s—so too with the French feminists who could not be inventing 'theory' if a space had not been created by the women's movement. In both cases, both groups posited a theory that excluded many of the people who made that space possible. Hence one of the reasons for the surge of Afro-American women's writing during the 1970s and its emphasis on sexism in the black community is precisely that when the ideologues of the 1960s said *black*, they meant *black male*.[9]

I and many of my sisters do not see the world as being so simple. And perhaps that is why we have not rushed to create abstract theories. For we know there are countless women of color, both in America and in the rest of the

8. See Ann Rosalind Jones, "Writing the Body: Toward an Understanding of *l'écriture féminine*," *Feminist Studies* 7, no. 2 (Summer 1981): 247–63.
9. See June Jordan, *Civil Wars* (Boston: Beacon Press, 1981); Audre Lorde, "The Master's Tools Will Never Dismantle the Master's House," in her *Sister Outsider* (Trumansburg, N.Y.: Crossing Press, 1984), 110–14.

world, to whom our singular ideas would be applied. There is, therefore, a caution we feel about pronouncing black feminist theory that might be seen as a decisive statement about Third World women. This is not to say we are not theorizing. Certainly our literature is an indication of the ways in which our theorizing, of necessity, is based on our multiplicity of experiences.

There is at least one other lesson I learned from the Black Arts Movement. One reason for its monolithic approach had to do with its desire to destroy the power which controlled black people, but it was a power which many of its ideologues wished to achieve. The nature of our context today is such that an approach which desires power singlemindedly must of necessity become like that which it wishes to destroy. Rather than wanting to change the whole model, many of us want to be at the center. It is this point of view that writers like June Jordan and Audre Lorde continually critique even as they call for empowerment, as they emphasize the fear of difference among us and our need for leaders rather than a reliance on ourselves.

For one must distinguish the desire for power from the need to become empowered—that is, seeing oneself as capable of and having the right to determine one's life. Such empowerment is partially derived from a knowledge of history. The Black Arts Movement did result in the creation of Afro-American Studies as a concept, thus giving it a place in the university where one might engage in the reclamation of Afro-American history and culture and pass it on to others. I am particularly concerned that institutions such as black studies and women's studies, fought for with such vigor and at some sacrifice, are not often seen as important by many of our black or women scholars precisely because the old hierarchy of traditional departments is seen as superior to these 'marginal' groups. Yet, it is in this context that many others of us are discovering the extent of our complexity, the interrelationships of different areas of knowledge in relation to a distinctly Afro-American or female experience. Rather than having to view our world as subordinate to others, or rather than having to work as if we were hybrids, we can pursue ourselves as subjects.

My major objection to the race for theory, as some readers have probably guessed by now, really hinges on the question, 'For whom are we doing what we are doing when we do literary criticism?' It is, I think, the central question today, especially for the few of us who have infiltrated academia enough to be wooed by it. The answer to that question determines what orientation we take in our work, the language we use, the purposes for which it is intended.

I can only speak for myself. But what I write and how I write is done in order to save my own life.[1] And I mean that literally. For me literature is a way of knowing that I am not hallucinating, that whatever I feel/know is. It is an affirmation that sensuality is intelligence, that sensual language is language that makes sense. My response, then, is directed to those who write what I read and to those who read what I read—put concretely—to Toni Morrison and to people who read Toni Morrison (among whom I would count few academics). That number is increasing, as is the readership of Walker and Mar-

---

1. This phrase is taken from the title of one of Alice Walker's essays, "Saving the Life That Is Your Own: The Importance of Models in the Artist's Life," in her *In Search of Our Mothers' Gardens: Womanist Prose* (New York: Harcourt Brace Jovanovich, 1983), 3–14.

shall. But in no way is the literature Morrison, Marshall, or Walker create supported by the academic world. Nor given the political context of our society, do I expect that to change soon. For there is no reason, given who controls these institutions, for them to be anything other than threatened by these writers.

My readings do presuppose a need, a desire among folk who like me also want to save their own lives. My concern, then, is a passionate one, for the literature of people who are not in power has always been in danger of extinction or of cooptation, not because we do not theorize, but because what we can even imagine, far less who we can reach, is constantly limited by societal structures. For me, literary criticism is promotion as well as understanding, a response to the writer to whom there is often no response, to folk who need the writing as much as they need anything. I know, from literary history, that writing disappears unless there is a response to it. Because I write about writers who are now writing, I hope to help ensure that their tradition has continuity and survives.

So my 'method', to use a new 'lit. crit.' word, is not fixed but relates to what I read and to the historical context of the writers I read *and* to the many critical activities in which I am engaged, which may or may not involve writing. It is a learning from the language of creative writers, which is one of surprise, so that I might discover what language I might use. For my language is very much based on what I read and how it affects me, that is, on the surprise that comes from reading something that compels you to read differently, as I believe literature does. I, therefore, have no set method, another prerequisite of the new theory, since for me every work suggests a new approach. As risky as that might seem, it is, I believe, what intelligence means—a tuned sensitivity to that which is alive and therefore cannot be known until it is known. Audre Lorde puts it in a far more succinct and sensual way in her essay 'Poetry is not a luxury':

> As they become known to and accepted by us, our feelings and the honest exploration of them become sanctuaries and spawning grounds for the most radical and daring of ideas. They become a safe-house for that difference so necessary to change and the conceptualization of any meaningful action. Right now, I could name at least ten ideas I would have found intolerable or incomprehensible and frightening, except as they came after dreams and poems. This is not idle fantasy, but a disciplined attention to the true meaning of 'it feels right to me.' We can train ourselves to respect our feelings and to transpose them into a language so they can be shared. And where that language does not yet exist, it is our poetry which helps to fashion it. Poetry is not only dream and vision; it is the skeleton architecture of our lives. It lays the foundations for a future of change, a bridge across our fears of what has never been before.[2]

1987, 1989

---

2. Audre Lorde, "Poetry Is Not a Luxury," in *Sister Outsider*, 37.

HORTENSE SPILLERS
b. 1942

Black, White, and in Color: Essays on American Literature and Culture (2003) collects the essays in which Hortense Spillers brought feminist, psychoanalytic, and post-structuralist theories into critical race studies. For some years the Frederick J. Whiton Professor of English at Cornell University and now the Gertrude Conaway Vanderbilt Professor at Vanderbilt University, Spillers addresses a host of authors from Zora Neale Hurston and Gwendolyn Brooks to William Faulkner, Ralph Ellison, and Toni Morrison, as she did in editing the collection *Comparative American Identities: Race, Sex, and Nationality in the Modern Text* (1990) and a section of *The Norton Anthology of African American Literature* (1997). In *Conjuring: Black Women, Fiction, and Literary Tradition* (co-edited with Marjorie Pryse, 1985), Spillers helped stimulate feminist scholarship on the spiritual and ethnographic conventions at work in black women's aesthetic achievements. Yet "Mama's Baby, Papa's Maybe: An American Grammar Book" (1987) remains her most frequently taught essay, in part because it foregrounds the ways in which contemporary black families are pathologized by sociologists and psychologists, and then links this dynamic to the history of the slave trade. In particular, Spillers asks, what traces remain from a history that bought and sold black men and women as ungendered or degendered commodities? How were maternity, paternity, and kinship systems shaped by slave laws and customs? A passionate protest against slavery, "Mama's Baby, Papa's Maybe" also provides insight into the long-term social as well as psychological effects of slavery on African American men and women.

From Mama's Baby, Papa's Maybe: An American Grammar Book

Let's face it. I am a marked woman, but not everybody knows my name. "Peaches" and "Brown Sugar," "Sapphire"[1] and "Earth Mother," "Aunty," "Granny," God's "Holy Fool," a "Miss Ebony First," or "Black Woman at the Podium": I describe a locus of confounded identities, a meeting ground of investments and privations in the national treasury of rhetorical wealth. My country needs me, and if I were not here, I would have to be invented.

W. E. B. DuBois predicted as early as 1903[2] that the twentieth century would be the century of the "color line." We could add to this spatiotemporal configuration another thematic of analogously terrible weight: if the "black woman" can be seen as a particular figuration of the split subject that psychoanalytic theory posits, then this century marks the site of "its" profoundest revelation. The problem before us is deceptively simple: the terms enclosed in quotation marks in the preceding paragraph isolate overdetermined nominative properties. Embedded in bizarre axiological ground, they demonstrate a sort of telegraphic coding; they are markers so loaded with mythical prepossession that there is no easy way for the agents buried beneath them to come clean. In that regard, the names by which I

1. Wife of the Kingfish on *Amos and Andy*, a popular early radio and television show featuring stereotyped black characters.
2. In *The Souls of Black Folk* (1903).

am called in the public place render an example of signifying property *plus*. In order for me to speak a truer word concerning myself, I must strip down through layers of attenuated meanings, made an excess in time, over time, assigned by a particular historical order, and there await whatever marvels of my own inventiveness. The personal pronouns are offered in the service of a collective function.

In certain human societies, a child's identity is determined through the line of the Mother, but the United States, from at least one author's point of view, is not one of them: "In essence, the Negro community has been forced into a matriarchal structure which, because it is so far out of line with the *rest of American society,* seriously retards the progress of the group as a whole, and imposes a crushing burden on the Negro male and, in consequence, on a great many Negro women as well" (Moynihan 75; emphasis mine).

The notorious bastard, from Vico's banished Roman mothers of such sons, to Caliban, to Heathcliff, and Joe Christmas,[3] has no official female equivalent. Because the traditional rites and laws of inheritance rarely pertain to the female child, bastard status signals to those who need to know which son of the Father's is the legitimate heir and which one the impostor. For that reason, property seems wholly the business of the male. A "she" cannot, therefore, qualify for bastard, or "natural son" status, and that she cannot provides further insight into the coils and recoils of patriarchal wealth and fortune. According to Daniel Patrick Moynihan's celebrated "Report" of the late sixties, the "Negro Family" has no Father to speak of—his Name, his Law, his Symbolic function[4] mark the impressive missing agencies in the essential life of the black community, the "Report" maintains, and it is, surprisingly, the fault of the Daughter, or the female line. This stunning reversal of the castration thematic, displacing the Name and the Law of the Father to the territory of the Mother and Daughter, becomes an aspect of the African-American female's misnaming. We attempt to undo this misnaming in order to reclaim the relationship between Fathers and Daughters within this social matrix for a quite different structure of cultural fictions. For Daughters and Fathers are here made to manifest the very same *rhetorical* symptoms of absence and denial, to embody the double and contrastive agencies of a *prescribed* internecine degradation. "Sapphire" enacts her "Old Man" in drag, just as her "Old Man" becomes "Sapphire" in outrageous caricature.

In other words, in the historic outline of dominance, the respective subject-positions of "female" and "male" adhere to no symbolic integrity. At a time when current critical discourses appear to compel us more and more decidedly toward gender "undecidability," it would appear reactionary, if not dumb, to insist on the integrity of female/male gender. But undressing these conflations of meaning, as they appear under the rule of dominance, would restore, as figurative possibility, not only Power to the Female (for Maternity), but also Power to the Male (for Paternity). We would gain, in short, the *potential* for gender differentiation as it might express itself along a range

3. Characters in Shakespeare's *The Tempest* (1611), Emily Brontë's *Wuthering Heights* (1847), and William Faulkner's *Light in August* (1932), respectively.
4. Terms associated with the psycholinguistic theories of Jacques Lacan, not with Moynihan; in those theories, "Name-of-the-Father" refers to the function of the father in the Symbolic dimension, the realm of law and language.

of stress points, including human biology in its intersection with the project of culture.

Though among the most readily available "whipping boys" of fairly recent public discourse concerning African-Americans and national policy, "The Moynihan Report" is by no means unprecedented in its conclusions; it belongs, rather, to a class of symbolic paradigms that 1) inscribe "ethnicity" as a scene of negation and 2) confirm the human body as a metonymic figure for an entire repertoire of human and social arrangements. In that regard, the "Report" pursues a behavioral rule of public documentary. Under the Moynihan rule, "ethnicity" itself identifies a total objectification of human and cultural motives—the "white" family, by implication, and the "Negro Family," by outright assertion, in a constant opposition of binary meanings. Apparently spontaneous, these "actants" are *wholly* generated, with neither past nor future, as tribal currents moving out of time. Moynihan's "Families" are pure present and always tense. "Ethnicity" in this case freezes in meaning, takes on constancy, assumes the look and the affects of the Eternal. We could say, then, that in its powerful stillness, "ethnicity," from the point of view of the "Report," embodies nothing more than a mode of memorial time, as Roland Barthes outlines the dynamics of myth (see "Myth Today" 109–59; esp. 122–23). As a signifier that has no movement in the field of signification, the use of "ethnicity" for the living becomes purely appreciative, although one would be unwise not to concede its dangerous and fatal effects.

"Ethnicity" perceived as mythical time enables a writer to perform a variety of conceptual moves all at once. Under its hegemony, the human body becomes a defenseless target for rape and veneration, and the body, in its material and abstract phase, a resource for metaphor. For example, Moynihan's "tangle of pathology" provides the descriptive strategy for the work's fourth chapter, which suggests that "underachievement" in black males of the lower classes is primarily the fault of black females, who achieve out of all proportion, both to their numbers in the community and to the paradigmatic example before the nation: "Ours is a society which presumes male leadership in private and public affairs. . . . A subculture, such as that of the Negro American, in which this is not the pattern, is placed at a distinct disadvantage" (75). Between charts and diagrams, we are asked to consider the impact of qualitative measure on the black male's performance on standardized examinations, matriculation in schools of higher and professional training, etc. Even though Moynihan sounds a critique on his own argument here, he quickly withdraws from its possibilities, suggesting that black males should reign because that is the way the majority culture carries things out: "It is clearly a disadvantage for a minority group to be operating under one principle, while the great majority of the population . . . is operating on another" (75). Those persons living according to the perceived "matriarchal" pattern are, therefore, caught in a state of social "pathology."

Even though Daughters have their own agenda with reference to this order of Fathers (imagining for the moment that Moynihan's fiction—and others like it—does not represent an adequate one and that there *is*, once we discover him, a Father here), my contention that these social and cultural subjects make doubles, unstable in their respective identities, in effect transports us to a common historical ground, the socio-political order of the New World. That order, with its human sequence written in blood, *represents* for its

African and indigenous peoples a scene of *actual* mutilation, dismember-ment, and exile. First of all, their New-World, diasporic plight marked a *theft of the body*—a willful and violent (and unimaginable from this distance) sev-ering of the captive body from its motive will, its active desire. Under these conditions, we lose at least *gender* difference *in the outcome,* and the female body and the male body become a territory of cultural and political maneu-ver, not at all gender-related, gender-specific. But this body, at least from the point of view of the captive community, focuses a private and particular space, at which point of convergence biological, sexual, social, cultural, lin-guistic, ritualistic, and psychological fortunes join. This profound intimacy of interlocking detail is disrupted, however, by externally imposed meanings and uses: 1) the captive body becomes the source of an irresistible, destructive sensuality; 2) at the same time—in stunning contradiction—the captive body reduces to a thing, becoming *being for* the captor; 3) in this absence *from* a subject position, the captured sexualities provide a physical and biological expression of "otherness"; 4) as a category of "otherness," the captive body translates into a potential for pornotroping and embodies sheer physical pow-erlessness that slides into a more general "powerlessness," resonating through various centers of human and social meaning.

But I would make a distinction in this case between "body" and "flesh" and impose that distinction as the central one between captive and liberated subject-positions. In that sense, before the "body" there is the "flesh," that zero degree of social conceptualization that does not escape concealment under the brush of discourse, or the reflexes of iconography. Even though the European hegemonies stole bodies—some of them female—out of West African communities in concert with the African "middleman," we regard this human and social irreparability as high crimes against the *flesh,* as the per-son of African females and African males registered the wounding. If we think of the "flesh" as a primary narrative, then we mean its seared, divided, ripped-apartness, riveted to the ship's hole, fallen, or "escaped" overboard.

One of the most poignant aspects of William Goodell's contemporaneous study of the North American slave codes gives precise expression to the tor-tures and instruments of captivity. Reporting an instance of Jonathan Edwards's observations on the tortures of enslavement, Goodell narrates: "The smack of the whip is all day long in the ears of those who are on the plantation, or in the vicinity; and it is used with such dexterity and severity as not only to lacerate the skin, but to tear out small portions of the flesh at almost every stake" (221). The anatomical specifications of rupture, of altered human tissue, take on the objective description of laboratory prose— eyes beaten out, arms, backs, skulls branded, a left jaw, a right ankle, punc-tured; teeth missing, as the calculated work of iron, whips, chains, knives, the canine patrol, the bullet.

These undecipherable markings on the captive body render a kind of hiero-glyphics of the flesh whose severe disjunctures come to be hidden to the cul-tural seeing by skin color. We might well ask if this phenomenon of marking and branding actually "transfers" from one generation to another, finding its various *symbolic substitutions* in an efficacy of meanings that repeat the ini-tiating moments? As Elaine Scarry describes the mechanisms of torture (Scarry 27–59), these lacerations, woundings, fissures, tears, scars, openings, ruptures, lesions, rendings, punctures of the flesh create the distance between what I would designate a cultural *vestibularity* and the *culture,* whose state apparatus, including judges, attorneys, "owners," "soul drivers," "overseers," and "men of God," apparently colludes with a protocol of "search and destroy." This body whose flesh carries the female and the male to the frontiers of survival bears in person the marks of a cultural text whose inside has been turned outside.

The flesh is the concentration of "ethnicity" that contemporary critical discourses neither acknowledge nor discourse away. It is this "flesh and blood" entity, in the vestibule (or "pre-view") of a colonized North America, that is essentially ejected from "The Female Body in Western Culture" (see Suleiman, ed.), but it makes good theory, or commemorative "herstory" to want to "forget," or to have failed to realize, that the African female subject, under these historic conditions, is not only the target of rape—in one sense, an interiorized violation of body and mind—but also the topic of specifically *externalized* acts of torture and prostration that we imagine as the peculiar province of *male* brutality and torture inflicted by other males. A female body strung from a tree limb, or bleeding from the breast on any given day of field work because the "overseer," standing the length of a whip, has popped her flesh open, adds a lexical and living dimension to the narratives of women in culture and society (Davis 9). This materialized scene of unprotected female flesh—of female flesh "ungendered"—offers a praxis and a theory, a text for living and for dying, and a method for reading both through their diverse mediations.

Among the myriad uses to which the enslaved community was put, Goodell identifies its value for medical research: "Assortments of diseased, *damaged,* and disabled Negroes, deemed incurable and otherwise worthless are *bought up,* it seems . . . by medical institutions, to be experimented and operated upon, for purposes of 'medical education' and the interest of medical science" (86–87; Goodell's emphasis). From the *Charleston Mercury* for October 12, 1838, Goodell notes this advertisement:

> 'To planters and others.—Wanted, fifty Negroes, any person, having sick Negroes, considered incurable by their respective physicians, and wishing to dispose of them, Dr. S. will pay cash for Negroes affected with scrofula, or king's evil, confirmed hypochondriasm, apoplexy, diseases of the liver, kidneys, spleen, stomach and intestines, bladder and its appendages, diarrhea, dysentery, etc. The highest cash price will be paid, on application as above.' at No. 110 Church Street, Charleston. (87; Goodell's emphasis)

This profitable "atomizing" of the captive body provides another angle on the divided flesh: we lose any hint or suggestion of a dimension of ethics, of relatedness between human personality and its anatomical features, between one human personality and another, between human personality and cultural institutions. To that extent, the procedures adopted for the captive flesh demarcate a total objectification, as the entire captive community becomes a living laboratory.

The captive body, then, brings into focus a gathering of social realities as well as a metaphor for *value* so thoroughly interwoven in their literal and figurative emphases that distinctions between them are virtually useless. Even though the captive flesh/body has been "liberated," and no one need pretend that even the quotation marks do not *matter*, dominant symbolic activity, the ruling episteme that releases the dynamics of naming and valuation, remains grounded in the originating metaphors of captivity and mutilation so that it is as if neither time nor history, nor historiography and its topics, shows movement, as the human subject is "murdered" over and over again by the passions of a bloodless and anonymous archaism, showing itself in endless disguise. Faulkner's young Chick Mallison in *The Mansion* calls "it" by other names— "the ancient subterrene atavistic fear . . ."(227). And I would call it the Great Long National Shame. But people do not talk like that anymore—it is "embarrassing," just as the retrieval of mutilated female bodies will likely be "backward" for some people. Neither the shameface of the embarrassed, nor the not-looking-back of the self-assured is of much interest to us, and will not help at all if rigor is our dream. We might concede, at the very least, that sticks and bricks *might* break our bones, but words will most certainly *kill* us.

The symbolic order that I wish to trace in this writing, calling it an "American grammar," begins at the "beginning," which is really a rupture and a radically different kind of cultural continuation. The massive demographic shifts, the violent formation of a modern African consciousness, that take place on the subsaharan Continent during the initiative strikes which open the Atlantic Slave Trade in the fifteenth century of our Christ, interrupted hundreds of years of black African culture. We write and think, then, about an outcome of aspects of African-American life in the United States under the pressure of those events. I might as well add that the familiarity of this narrative does nothing to appease the hunger of recorded memory, nor does the persistence of the repeated rob these well-known, oft-told events of their power, even now, to startle. In a very real sense, every writing as revision makes the "discovery" all over again.

2

The narratives by African peoples and their descendants, though not as numerous from those early centuries of the "execrable trade" as the researcher would wish, suggest, in their rare occurrence, that the visual shock waves touched off when African and European "met" reverberated on both sides of the encounter. The narrative of the "Life of Olaudah Equiano, or Gustavus Vassa, the African. Written by Himself," first published in London in 1789, makes it quite clear that the first Europeans Equiano observed on what is now Nigerian soil were as unreal for him as he and others must have been for the European captors. The cruelty of "these white men with horrible looks, red faces, and long hair," of these "spirits," as the narrator would have it, occupies several pages of Equiano's attention, alongside a first-hand account of Nigerian interior life (27 ff.). We are justified in regarding the outcome of Equiano's experience in the same light as he himself might have— as a "fall," as a veritable descent into the loss of communicative force.

If, as Todorov points out, the Mayan and Aztec peoples "lost control of communication" (61) in light of Spanish intervention, we could observe, similarly, that Vassa falls among men whose language is not only strange to him, but whose habits and practices strike him as "astonishing":

> [*The sea, the slave ship*] *filled me with astonishment, which was soon converted into terror, when I was carried on board. I was immediately handled, and tossed up to see if I were sound, by some of the crew; and I was now*

> *persuaded that I had gotten into a world of bad spirits, and that they were*
> *going to kill me. Their complexions, too, differing so much from ours, their*
> *long hair, and the language they spoke (which was different from any I had*
> *ever heard), united to confirm me in this belief.* (Equiano 27)

The captivating party does not only "earn" the right to dispose of the captive body as it sees fit, but gains, consequently, the right to name and "name" it: Equiano, for instance, identifies at least three different names that he is given in numerous passages between his Benin homeland and the Virginia colony, the latter and England—"Michael," "Jacob," "Gustavus Vassa" (35; 36).

The nicknames by which African-American women have been called, or regarded, or imagined on the New World scene—the opening lines of this essay provide examples—demonstrate the powers of distortion that the dominant community seizes as its unlawful prerogative. Moynihan's "Negro Family," then, borrows its narrative energies from the grid of associations, from the semantic and iconic folds buried deep in the collective past, that come to surround and signify the captive person. Though there is no absolute point of chronological initiation, we might repeat certain familiar impression points that lend shape to the business of dehumanized naming. Expecting to find direct and amplified reference to African women during the opening years of the Trade, the observer is disappointed time and again that this cultural subject is concealed beneath the mighty debris of the itemized account, between the lines of the massive logs of commercial enterprise that overrun the sense of clarity we believed we had gained concerning this collective humiliation. Elizabeth Donnan's enormous, four-volume documentation becomes a case in point.

✻   ✻   ✻

The conditions of "Middle Passage" are among the most incredible narratives available to the student, as it remains not easily imaginable. Late in the chronicles of the Atlantic Slave Trade, Britain's Parliament entertained discussions concerning possible "regulations" for slave vessels. A Captain Perry visited the Liverpool port, and among the ships that he inspected was "The Brookes," probably the most well-known image of the slave galley with its representative *personae* etched into the drawing like so many cartoon figures. Elizabeth Donnan's second volume carries the "Brookes Plan," along with an elaborate delineation of its dimensions from the investigative reporting of Perry himself: "Let it now be supposed . . . further, that every man slave is to be allowed six feet by one foot four inches for room, every woman five feet ten by one foot four, every boy five feet by one foot two, and every girl four feet six by one foot . . ." (2:592, n). The owner of "The Brookes," James Jones, had recommended that "five females be reckoned as four males, and three boys or girls as equal to two grown persons" (2:592).

These scaled inequalities complement the commanding terms of the dehumanizing, ungendering, and defacing project of African persons that De Azurara's narrator might have recognized.[5] It has been pointed out to me that these measurements do reveal the application of the gender rule to the material conditions of passage, but I would suggest that "gendering" takes place within the confines of the domestic, an essential metaphor that then spreads

---

5. Spillers discusses this narrative in the omitted portion of the essay.

its tentacles for male and female subject over a wider ground of human and social purposes. Domesticity appears to gain its power by way of a common origin of cultural fictions that are grounded in the specificity of proper names, more exactly, a patronymic, which, in turn, situates those persons it "covers" in a particular place. Contrarily, the cargo of a ship might not be regarded as elements of the domestic, even though the vessel that carries it is sometimes romantically (ironically?) personified as "she." The human cargo of a slave vessel—in the fundamental effacement and remission of African family and proper names—offers a *counter*-narrative to notions of the domestic.

Those African persons in "Middle Passage" were literally suspended in the "oceanic," if we think of the latter in its Freudian orientation as an analogy for undifferentiated identity: removed from the indigenous land and culture, and not-yet "American" either, these captive persons, without names that their captors would recognize, were in movement across the Atlantic, but they were also *nowhere* at all. Inasmuch as, on any given day, we might imagine, the captive personality did not know where s/he was, we could say that they were the culturally "unmade," thrown in the midst of a figurative darkness that "exposed" their destinies to an unknown course. Often enough for the captains of these galleys, navigational science of the day was not sufficient to guarantee the intended destination. We might say that the slave ship, its crew, and its human-as-cargo stand for a wild and unclaimed richness of *possibility* that is not interrupted, not "counted"/"accounted," or differentiated, until its movement gains the land thousands of miles away from the point of departure. Under these conditions, one is neither female, nor male, as both subjects are taken into "account" as *quantities*. The female in "Middle Passage," as the apparently smaller physical mass, occupies "less room" in a directly translatable money economy. But she is, nevertheless, quantifiable by the same rules of accounting as her male counterpart.

It is not only difficult for the student to find "female" in "Middle Passage," but also, as Herbert S. Klein observes, "African women did not enter the Atlantic slave trade in anything like the numbers of African men. At all ages, men outnumbered women on the slave ships bound for America from Africa" (Klein 29). Though this observation does not change the reality of African women's captivity and servitude in New World communities, it does provide a perspective from which to contemplate the *internal* African slave trade, which, according to Africanists, remained a predominantly *female* market. Klein nevertheless affirms that those females forced into the trade were segregated "from men for policing purposes" ("African Women" 35). He claims that both "were allotted the same space between decks . . . and both were fed the same food" (35). It is not altogether clear from Klein's observations *for whom* the "police" kept vigil. It is certainly known from evidence presented in Donnan's third volume ("New England and the Middle Colonies") that insurrection was both frequent and feared in passage, and we have not yet found a great deal of evidence to support a thesis that female captives participated in insurrectionary activity (see White 63–64). Because it was the rule, however—not the exception—that the African female, in both indigenous African cultures and in what becomes her "home," performed tasks of hard physical labor—so much so that the quintessential "slave" is *not* a male, but a female—we wonder at the seeming docility of the subject, granting her a "feminization" that enslavement kept at bay. Indeed, across the spate of discourse that I examined for this writing, the acts of enslavement and responses to it comprise a more or less agonistic engagement of confrontational hostilities among males. The visual and historical evidence betrays the dominant discourse on the matter as incomplete, but *counter*-evidence is inadequate as well: the sexual violation of captive females and their own express rage against their oppressors did not constitute events that captains and their crews rushed to record in letters to their sponsoring companies, or sons on board in letters home to their New England mamas.

One suspects that there are several ways to snare a mockingbird, so that insurrection might have involved, from time to time, rather more subtle means than mutiny on the "Felicity," for instance. At any rate, we get very little notion in the written record of the life of women, children, and infants in "Middle Passage," and no idea of the fate of the pregnant female captive and the unborn, which startling thematic Bell Hooks addresses in the opening chapter of her pathfinding work (see Hooks 15–49). From Hooks's lead, however, we might guess that the "reproduction of mothering" in this historic instance carries few of the benefits of a *patriarchilized* female gender, which, from one point of view, is the *only* female gender there is.

The relative silence of the record on this point constitutes a portion of the disquieting lacunae that feminist investigation seeks to fill. Such silence is the nickname of distortion, of the unknown human factor that a revised public discourse would both undo and reveal. This cultural subject is inscribed historically as anonymity/anomie in various public documents of European-American mal(e)venture, from Portuguese De Azurara in the middle of the fifteenth century, to South Carolina's Henry Laurens in the eighteenth.

What confuses and enriches the picture is precisely the sameness of anonymous portrayal that adheres tenaciously across the division of gender. In the vertical columns of accounts and ledgers that comprise Donnan's work, the terms "Negroes" and "Slaves" denote a common status. For instance, entries in one account, from September 1700 through September 1702, are specifically descriptive of the names of ships and the private traders in Barbados who will receive the stipulated goods, but "No. Negroes" and "Sum sold for per head" are so exactly arithmetical that it is as if these additions and multiplications belong to the other side of an equation (Donnan 2:25). One is struck by the detail and precision that characterize these accounts, as a narrative, or story, is always implied by a man or woman's *name*: "Wm. Webster," "John Dunn," "Thos. Brownbill," "Robt. Knowles." But the "other" side of the page, as it were, equally precise, throws no *face* in view. It seems that nothing breaks the uniformity in this guise. If in no other way, the destruction of the African name, of kin, of linguistic, and ritual connections is so obvious in the vital stats sheet that we tend to overlook it. Quite naturally, the trader is not interested, in any *semantic* sense, in this "baggage" that he must deliver, but that he is not is all the more reason to search out the metaphorical implications of *naming* as one of the key sources of a bitter Americanizing for African persons.

The loss of the indigenous name/land provides a metaphor of displacement for other human and cultural features and relations, including the displacement of the genitalia, the female's and the male's desire that engenders future. The fact that the enslaved person's access to the issue of his/her own body is not entirely clear in this historic period throws in crisis all aspects of the blood relations, as captors apparently felt no obligation to acknowledge them. Actually trying to understand how the confusions of consanguinity worked becomes the project, because the outcome goes far to explain the rule of gender and its application to the African female in captivity.

3

Even though the essays in Claire C. Robertson's and Martin A. Klein's *Women and Slavery in Africa* have specifically to do with aspects of the internal African slave trade, some of their observations shed light on the captivities of the Diaspora. At least these observations have the benefit of altering the kind of questions we might ask of these silent chapters. For example, Robertson's essay, which opens the volume, discusses the term "slavery" in a wide variety of relationships. The enslaved person as *property* identifies the most familiar element of a most startling proposition. But to overlap *kinlessness* on the requirements of property might enlarge our view of the conditions of enslavement. Looking specifically at documents from the West African societies of Songhay and Dahomey, Claude Meillassoux elaborates several features of the property/kinless constellation that are highly suggestive for our own quite different purposes.

Meillassoux argues that "slavery creates an economic and social agent whose virtue lies in being outside the kinship system" ("Female Slavery," Robertson and Klein 50). Because the Atlantic trade involved heterogeneous social and ethnic formations in an explicit power relationship, we certainly cannot mean "kinship system" in precisely the same way that Meillassoux observes at work within the intricate calculus of descent among West African societies. However, the idea becomes useful as a point of contemplation when we try to sharpen our own sense of the African female's reproductive uses within the diasporic enterprise of enslavement and the genetic reproduction of the enslaved. In effect, under conditions of captivity, the offspring of the female does not "belong" to the Mother, nor is s/he "related" to the "owner," though the latter "possesses" it, and in the African-American instance, often fathered it, *and,* as often, without whatever benefit of patrimony. In the social outline that Meillassoux is pursuing, the offspring of the enslaved, "being unrelated both to their begetters and to their owners . . . , find themselves in the situation of being orphans" (50).

In the context of the United States, we could not say that the enslaved offspring was "orphaned," but the child does become, under the press of a patronymic, patrifocal, patrilineal, and patriarchal order, the man/woman on the boundary, whose human and familial status, by the very nature of the case, had yet to be defined. I would call this enforced state of breach another instance of vestibular cultural formation where "kinship" loses meaning, *since it can be invaded at any given and arbitrary moment by the property relations.* I certainly do not mean to say that African peoples in the New World did not maintain the powerful ties of sympathy that bind blood-relations in a network of feeling, of continuity. It is precisely that relationship—not customarily recognized by the code of slavery—that historians have long identified as the inviolable "Black Family" and further suggest that this structure remains one of the supreme social achievements of African-Americans under conditions of enslavement (see John Blassingame 79 ff.).

Indeed, the *revised* "Black Family" of enslavement has engendered an older tradition of historiographical and sociological writings than we usually think. Ironically enough, E. Franklin Frazier's *Negro Family in the United States* likely provides the closest *contemporary* narrative of conceptualization for the "Moynihan Report." Originally published in 1939, Frazier's work underwent two redactions in 1948 and 1966. Even though Frazier's outlook on this familial configuration remains basically sanguine, I would support Angela Davis's skeptical reading of Frazier's "Black Matriarchate" (Davis 14). "*Except where the master's will was concerned,*" Frazier contends, this matriarchal figure "developed a spirit of independence and a keen sense of her personal rights" (47; emphasis mine). The "exception" in this instance tends to be overwhelming, as the African-American female's "dominance" and "strength" come to be interpreted by later generations—both black and white, oddly enough—as a "pathology," as an instrument of castration. Frazier's larger point, we might suppose, is that African-Americans developed such resourcefulness under conditions of captivity that "family" must be conceded as one of their redoubtable social attainments. This line of interpretation is pursued by Blassingame and Eugene Genovese (*Roll, Jordan, Roll* 70–75), among other U.S. historians, and indeed assumes a centrality of focus in our own thinking about the impact and outcome of captivity.

It seems clear, however, that "Family," as we practice and understand it "in the West"—the *vertical* transfer of a bloodline, of a patronymic, of titles and entitlements, of real estate and the prerogatives of "cold cash," from *fathers* to *sons* and in the supposedly free exchange of affectional ties between a male and a female of *his* choice—becomes the mythically revered privilege of a free and freed community. In that sense, African peoples in the historic Diaspora had nothing to prove, *if* the point had been that they were not capable of "family" (read "civilization"), since it is stunningly evident, in Equiano's narrative, for instance, that Africans were not only capable of the concept and the practice of "family," including "slaves," but in modes of elaboration and naming that were at least as complex as those of the "nuclear family" "in the West."

Whether or not we decide that the support systems that African-Americans derived under conditions of captivity should be called "family," or something else, strikes me as supremely impertinent. The point remains that captive persons were *forced* into patterns of dispersal, beginning with the Trade itself, into the *horizontal* relatedness of language groups, discourse formations, bloodlines, names, and properties by the legal arrangements of enslavement. It is true that the most "well-meaning" of "masters" (and there must have been some) *could not, did not* alter the *ideological* and hegemonic mandates of dominance. It must be conceded that African-Americans, under the press of a hostile and compulsory patriarchal order, bound and determined to destroy them, or to preserve them only in the service and at the behest of the "master" class, exercised a degree of courage and will to survive that startles the imagination even now. Although it makes good revisionist history to read this tale *liberally,* it is probably truer than we know at this distance (and truer than contemporary social practice in the community would suggest on occasion) that the captive person developed, time and again, certain ethical and sentimental features that tied her and him, *across* the landscape to others, often sold from hand to hand, of the same and different blood in a common fabric of memory and inspiration.

We might choose to call this connectedness "family," or "support structure," but that is a rather different case from the moves of a dominant symbolic order, pledged to maintain the supremacy of race. It is that order that forces "family" to modify itself when it does not mean family of the "master," or dominant enclave. It is this rhetorical and symbolic move that declares primacy over any other human and social claim, and in that political order of things, "kin," just as gender formation, has no decisive legal or social efficacy.

We return frequently to Frederick Douglass's careful elaborations of the arrangements of captivity, and we are astonished each reading by two dispersed, yet poignantly related, familial enactments that suggest a connection between "kinship" and "property." Douglass tells us early in the opening chapter of the 1845 *Narrative* that he was separated in infancy from his mother: "For what this separation is [sic] done, I do not know, unless it be to hinder the development of the child's affection toward its mother, and to blunt and destroy the natural affection of the mother for the child. This is the inevitable result" (22).

Perhaps one of the assertions that Meillassoux advances concerning indigenous African formations of enslavement might be turned as a question, against the perspective of Douglass's witness: is the genetic reproduction of the slave and the recognition of the rights of the slave to his or her offspring a check on the *profitability* of slavery? And how so, if so? We see vaguely the route to framing a response, especially to the question's second half and perhaps to the first: the enslaved must not be permitted to perceive that he or she has any human rights that matter. Certainly if "kinship" were possible, the property relations would be undermined, since the offspring would then "belong" to a mother and a father. In the system that Douglass articulates, genetic reproduction becomes, then, not an elaboration of the life-principle in its cultural overlap, but an extension of the boundaries of proliferating properties. Meillassoux goes so far as to argue that "slavery exists where the slave class is reproduced through institutional apparatus: war and market" (50). Since, in the United States, the market of slavery identified the chief institutional means for maintaining a class of enforced servile labor, it seems that the biological reproduction of the enslaved was not alone sufficient to reenforce the estate of slavery. If, as Meillassoux contends, "femininity loses its sacredness in slavery" (64), then so does "motherhood" as female blood-rite/right. To that extent, the captive female body locates precisely a moment of converging political and social vectors that mark the flesh as a prime commodity of exchange. While this proposition is open to further exploration, suffice it to say now that this open exchange of female bodies in the raw offers a kind of Ur-text[6] to the dynamics of signification and representation that the gendered female would unravel.

For Douglass, the loss of his mother eventuates in alienation from his brother and sisters, who live in the same house with him: "The early separation of us from our mother had well nigh blotted the fact of our relationship from our memories" (45). What could this mean? The *physical* proximity of

---

6. Source text, originating text.

the siblings survives the mother's death. They grasp their connection in the physical sense, but Douglass appears to mean a *psychological* bonding whose success mandates the *mother's* presence. Could we say, then, that the *feeling* of kinship is not inevitable? That it describes a relationship that appears "natural," but must be "cultivated" under actual material conditions? If the child's humanity is mirrored initially in the eyes of its mother, or the maternal function, then we might be able to guess that the social subject grasps the whole dynamic of resemblance and kinship by way of the same source.

There is an amazing thematic synonymity on this point between aspects of Douglass's *Narrative* and Malcolm El-Hajj Malik El Shabazz's *Autobiography of Malcolm X* (21 ff.). Through the loss of the mother, in the latter contemporary instance, to the institution of "insanity" and the state—a full century after Douglass's writing and under social conditions that might be designated a post-emancipation neo-enslavement—Malcolm and his siblings, robbed of their activist father in a kkk-like ambush, are not only widely dispersed across a makeshift social terrain, but also show symptoms of estrangement and "disremembering" that require many years to heal, and even then, only by way of Malcolm's prison ordeal turned, eventually, into a redemptive occurrence.

The destructive loss of the natural mother, whose biological/genetic relationship to the child remains unique and unambiguous, opens the enslaved young to social ambiguity and chaos: the ambiguity of his/her fatherhood and to a structure of other relational elements, now threatened, that would declare the young's connection to a genetic and historic future by way of their own siblings. That the father in Douglass's case was most likely the "master," not by any means special to Douglass, involves a hideous paradox. Fatherhood, at best a supreme cultural courtesy, attenuates here on the one hand into a monstrous accumulation of power on the other. One has been "made" and "bought" by disparate currencies, linking back to a common origin of exchange and domination. The denied genetic link becomes the chief strategy of an undenied ownership, as if the interrogation into the father's identity—the blank space where his proper name will fit—were answered by the fact, *de jure* of a material possession. "And this is done," Douglass asserts, "too obviously to administer to the [masters'] own lusts, and make a gratification of their wicked desires profitable as well as pleasurable" (23).

Whether or not the captive female and/or her sexual oppressor derived "pleasure" from their seductions and couplings is not a question we can politely ask. Whether or not "pleasure" is possible at all under conditions that I would aver as non-freedom for both or either of the parties has not been settled. Indeed, we could go so far as to entertain the very real possibility that "sexuality," as a term of implied relationship and desire, is dubiously appropriate, manageable, or accurate to *any* of the familial arrangements under a system of enslavement, from the master's family to the captive enclave. Under these arrangements, the customary lexis of sexuality, including "reproduction," "motherhood," "pleasure," and "desire" are thrown into unrelieved crisis.

If the testimony of Linda Brent/Harriet Jacobs is to be believed, the official mistresses of slavery's "masters" constitute a privileged class of the tormented, if such contradiction can be entertained (Brent 29–35). Linda Brent/Harriet Jacobs recounts in the course of her narrative scenes from a "psychodrama," opposing herself and "Mrs. Flint," in what we have come to consider the classic alignment between captive woman and free. Suspecting that her husband, Dr. Flint, has sexual designs on the young Linda (and the doctor is nearly humorously incompetent at it, according to the story line), Mrs. Flint assumes the role of a perambulatory nightmare who visits the captive woman in the spirit of a veiled seduction. Mrs. Flint imitates the incubus who "rides" its victim in order to exact confession, expiation, and anything else that the immaterial power might want. (Gayle Jones's *Corregidora* [1975] weaves a contemporary fictional situation around the historic motif of entangled female sexualities.) This narrative scene from Brent's work, dictated to Lydia Maria Child, provides an instance of a repeated sequence, purportedly based on "real" life. But the scene in question appears to so commingle its signals with the fictive, with casebook narratives from psychoanalysis, that we are certain that the narrator has her hands on an explosive moment of New-World/U.S. history that feminist investigation is beginning to unravel. The narrator recalls:

> *Sometimes I woke up, and found her bending over me. At other times she whispered in my ear, as though it were her husband who was speaking to me, and listened to hear what I would answer. If she startled me, on such occasion, she would glide stealthily away; and the next morning she would tell me I had been talking in my sleep, and ask who I was talking to. At last, I began to be fearful for my life. . . .* (Brent 33)

The "jealous mistress" here (but "jealous" for whom?) forms an analogy with the "master" to the extent that male dominative modes give the male the material means to fully act out what the female might only *wish*. The mistress in the case of Brent's narrative becomes a metaphor for *his* madness that arises in the ecstasy of unchecked power. Mrs. Flint enacts a male alibi and prosthetic motion that is mobilized at *night*, at the material place of the dream work. In both male and female instances, the subject attempts to *inculcate* his or her will into the vulnerable, supine body. Though this is barely hinted on the surface of the text, we might say that Brent, between the lines of her narrative, demarcates a sexuality that is neuter-bound, inasmuch as it represents an open vulnerability to a gigantic sexualized repertoire that may be alternately expressed as male/female. Since the gendered female *exists* for the male, we might suggest that the ungendered female—in an amazing stroke of pansexual potential—might be invaded/raided by another *woman* or man.

If *Incidents in the Life of a Slave Girl* were a novel, and not the memoirs of an escaped female captive, then we might say that "Mrs. Flint" is also the narrator's projection, her creation, so that for all her pious and correct umbrage toward the outrage of her captivity, some aspect of Linda Brent is released in a manifold repetition crisis that the doctor's wife comes to stand in for. In the case of both an imagined fiction and the narrative we have from Brent/Jacobs/Child, published only four years before the official proclamations of Freedom, we could say that African-American women's community and Anglo-American women's community, under certain shared cultural conditions, were the twin actants on a common psychic landscape, were subject to the same fabric of dread and humiliation. Neither could claim her body and its various productions—for quite different reasons, albeit—as her own, and in the case of the doctor's wife, *she* appears not to have wanted *her* body at all, but to desire to enter someone else's, specifically, Linda Brent's, in an apparently classic instance of sexual "jealousy" and appropriation. In fact, from one point of view, we cannot unravel one female's narrative from the other's, cannot decipher one without tripping over the other. In that sense, these "threads cable-strong" of an incestuous, interracial genealogy uncover slavery in the United States as one of the richest displays of the psychoanalytic dimensions of culture before the science of European psychoanalysis takes hold.

4

But just as we duly regard similarities between life conditions of American women—captive and free—we must observe those undeniable contrasts and differences so decisive that the African-American female's historic claim to the territory of womanhood and "femininity" still tends to rest too solidly on the subtle and shifting calibrations of a liberal ideology. Valerie Smith's reading of the tale of Linda Brent as a tale of "garreting" enables our notion that female gender for captive women's community is the tale writ between the lines and in the not-quite spaces of an American domesticity. It is this tale that we try to make clearer, or, keeping with the metaphor, "bring on line."

If the point is that the historic conditions of African-American women might be read as an unprecedented occasion in the national context, then gender and the arrangements of gender are both crucial and evasive. Holding, however, to a specialized reading of female gender as an *outcome* of a certain political, socio-cultural empowerment within the context of the United States, we would regard dispossession as the *loss* of gender, or one of the chief elements in an altered reading of gender: "Women are considered of no value, *unless* they continually increase their owner's stock. They were put on par with animals" (Brent 49; emphasis mine). Linda Brent's witness appears to contradict the point I would make, but I am suggesting that even though the enslaved female reproduced other enslaved persons, we do not read "birth" in this instance as a reproduction of mothering precisely because the female, like the male, has been robbed of the parental right, the parental function. One treads dangerous ground in suggesting an equation between female gender and mothering; in fact, feminist inquiry/praxis and the actual day-to-day living of numberless American women—black and white—have gone far to break the enthrallment of a female subject-position to the theoretical and actual situation of maternity. Our task here would be lightened considerably if we could simply slide over the powerful "No," the significant exception. In the historic formation to which I point, however, motherhood and female gendering/ungendering appear so intimately aligned that they *seem* to speak the same language. At least it is plausible to say that motherhood, while it does not exhaust the problematics of female gender, offers one prominent line of approach to it. I would go farther: Because African-American women experienced uncertainty regarding their infants' lives in the historic situation, gendering, in its coeval reference to African-American women, *insinuates* an implicit and unresolved puzzle both within current feminist discourse *and* within those discursive communities that investigate the entire problematics of culture. Are we mistaken to suspect that history—at least in this instance— repeats itself yet again?

Every feature of social and human differentiation disappears in public discourses regarding the African-American person, as we encounter, in the juridical codes of slavery, personality reified. William Goodell's study not only demonstrates the rhetorical and moral passions of the abolitionist project, but also lends insight into the corpus of law that underwrites enslavement. If "slave" is perceived as the essence of stillness (an early version of "ethnicity"), or of an undynamic human state, fixed in time and space, then the law articulates this impossibility as its inherent feature: "Slaves shall be deemed, sold, taken, reputed and adjudged in law to be *chattels personal,* in the hands of their owners and possessors, and their executors, administrators, and assigns, to all intents, constructions, and purposes whatsoever" (23; Goodell's emphasis).

Even though we tend to parody and simplify matters to behave as if the various civil codes of the slave-holding United States were monolithically informed, unified, and executed in their application, or that the "code" itself is spontaneously generated in an undivided historic moment, we read it nevertheless as exactly this—the *peak points,* the salient and characteristic features of a human and social procedure that evolves over a natural historical sequence and represents, consequently, the narrative *shorthand* of a transaction that is riddled, *in practice,* with contradictions, accident, and surprise. We could suppose that the legal encodations of enslavement stand for the statistically average case, that the legal code provides the *topics* of a project increasingly threatened and self-conscious. It is, perhaps, not by chance that the laws regarding slavery appear to crystallize in the precise moment when agitation against the arrangement becomes articulate in certain European and New-World communities. In that regard, the slave codes that Goodell describes are themselves an instance of the counter and isolated text that seeks to silence the contradictions and antitheses engendered by it. For example, aspects of Article 461 of the South Carolina Civil Code call attention to just the sort of uneasy oxymoronic character that the "peculiar institution" attempts to sustain in transforming *personality* into *property.*

1) The "slave" is movable by nature, but "immovable by the operation of law" (Goodell 24). As I read this, law itself is compelled to a point of saturation, or a reverse zero degree, beyond which it cannot move in the behalf of the enslaved *or* the free. We recall, too, that the "master," under these perversions of judicial power, is impelled to *treat* the enslaved as property, and not as person. These laws stand for the kind of social formulation that armed forces will help excise from a living context in the campaigns of civil war. They also embody the untenable human relationship that Henry David Thoreau believed occasioned acts of "civil disobedience," the moral philosophy to which Martin Luther King, Jr. would subscribe in the latter half of the twentieth century.

2) Slaves shall be *reputed* and *considered* real estate, "subject to be mortgaged, according to the rules prescribed by law" (Goodell 24). I emphasize "reputed" and "considered" as predicate adjectives that invite attention because they denote a *contrivance,* not an intransitive "is," or the transfer of nominative property from one syntactic point to another by way of a weakened copulative. The status of the "reputed" can change, as it will significantly before the nineteenth century closes. The mood here—the "shall be"—is pointedly subjunctive, or the situation devoutly to be wished. The

slave-holding class is forced, in time, to think and do something else is the narrative of violence that enslavement itself has been preparing for a couple of centuries.

Louisiana's and South Carolina's written codes offer a paradigm for praxis in those instances where a *written* text is missing. In that case, the "chattel principle has . . . been affirmed and maintained by the courts, and involved in legislative acts" (Goodell 25). In Maryland, a legislative enactment of 1798 shows so forceful a synonymity of motives between branches of comparable governance that a line between "judicial" and "legislative" functions is useless to draw: "In case the personal property of a ward shall consist of specific articles, such as slaves, working beasts, animals of any kind, stock, furniture, plates, books, and so forth, the *Court* if it shall deem it advantageous to the ward, may at any time, pass an order for the sale thereof" (56). This inanimate and corporate ownership—the voting district of a ward—is here spoken for, or might be, as a single slave-holding male in determinations concerning property.

The eye pauses, however, not so much at the provisions of this enactment as at the details of its delineation. Everywhere in the descriptive document, we are stunned by the simultaneity of disparate items in a grammatical series: "Slave" appears in the same context with beasts of burden, *all* and *any* animal(s), various livestock, and a virtually endless profusion of domestic content from the culinary item to the book. Unlike the taxonomy of Borges's "Certain Chinese encyclopedia," whose contemplation opens Foucault's *Order of Things*, these items from a certain American encyclopedia do not sustain discrete and localized "powers of contagion," nor has the ground of their concatenation been desiccated beneath them. That imposed uniformity comprises the shock, that somehow this mix of named things, live and inanimate, collapsed by contiguity to the same text of "realism," carries a disturbingly prominent item of misplacement. To that extent, the project of liberation for African-Americans has found urgency in two passionate motivations that are twinned—1) to break apart, to rupture violently the laws of American behavior that make such *syntax* possible; 2) to introduce a new *semantic* field/fold more appropriate to his/her own historic movement. I regard this twin compulsion as distinct, though related, moments of the very same narrative process that might appear as a concentration or a dispersal. The narratives of Linda Brent, Frederick Douglass, and Malcolm El-Hajj Malik El-Shabazz (aspects of which are examined in this essay) each represent both narrative ambitions as they occur under the auspices of "author."

Relatedly, we might interpret the whole career of African-Americans, a decisive factor in national political life since the mid-seventeenth century, in light of the *intervening, intruding* tale, or the tale—like Brent's "garret" space—"between the lines," which are already inscribed, as a *metaphor* of social and cultural management. According to this reading, gender, or sex-role assignation, or the clear differentiation of sexual stuff, sustained elsewhere in the culture, does not emerge for the African-American female in this historic instance, except indirectly, except as a way to reenforce through the process of birthing, "the reproduction of the relations of production" that involves "the reproduction of the values and behavior patterns necessary to maintain the system of hierarchy in its various aspects of gender, class, and race or ethnicity" (Margaret Strobel, "Slavery and Reproductive Labor in

Mombasa," Robertson and Klein 121). Following Strobel's lead, I would suggest that the foregoing identifies one of the three categories of reproductive labor that African-American females carry out under the regime of captivity. But this replication of ideology is never simple in the case of female subject-positions, and it appears to acquire a thickened layer of motives in the case of African-American females.

If we can account for an originary narrative and judicial principle that might have engendered a "Moynihan Report," many years into the twentieth century, we cannot do much better than look at Goodell's reading of the *partus sequitur ventrem*[7]: the condition of the slave mother is "forever entailed on all her remotest posterity." This maxim of civil law, in Goodell's view, the "genuine and degrading principle of slavery, inasmuch as it places the slave upon a level with brute animals, prevails universally in the slave-holding states" (Goodell 27). But what is the "condition" of the mother? Is it the "condition" of enslavement the writer means, or does he mean the "mark" and the "knowledge" of the *mother* upon the child that here translates into the culturally forbidden and impure? In an elision of terms, "mother" and "enslavement" are indistinct categories of the illegitimate inasmuch as each of these synonymous elements defines, in effect, a cultural situation that is *father-lacking*. Goodell, who does not only report this maxim of law as an aspect of his own factuality, but also regards it, as does Douglass, as a fundamental degradation, supposes descent and identity through the female line as comparable to a brute animality. Knowing already that there are human communities that align social reproductive procedure according to the line of the mother, and Goodell himself might have known it some years later, we can only conclude that the provisions of patriarchy, here exacerbated by the preponderant powers of an enslaving class, declare Mother Right, by definition, a negating feature of human community.

Even though we are not even talking about any of the matriarchal features of social production/reproduction—matrifocality, matrilinearity, matriarchy—when we speak of the enslaved person, we perceive that the dominant culture, in a fatal misunderstanding, assigns a matriarchist value where it does not belong; actually *misnames* the power of the female regarding the enslaved community. Such naming is false because the female could not, in fact, claim her child, and false, once again, because "motherhood" is not perceived in the prevailing social climate as a legitimate procedure of cultural inheritance.

The African-American male has been touched, therefore, by the *mother*, *handed* by her in ways that he cannot escape, and in ways that the white American male is allowed to temporize by a fatherly reprieve. This human and historic development—the text that has been inscribed on the benighted heart of the continent—takes us to the center of an inexorable difference in the depths of American women's community: the African-American woman, the mother, the daughter, becomes historically the powerful and shadowy evocation of a cultural synthesis long evaporated—the law of the Mother—only and precisely because legal enslavement removed the African-American male not so much from sight as from *mimetic* view as a partner in the prevailing social fiction of the Father's name, the Father's law.

7. Literally, "the offspring follows the womb" (Latin).

Therefore, the female, in this order of things, breaks in upon the imagination with a forcefulness that marks both a denial and an "illegitimacy." Because of this peculiar American denial, the black American male embodies the *only* American community of males which has had the specific occasion to learn *who* the female is within itself, the infant child who bears the life against the could-be fateful gamble, against the odds of pulverization and murder, including her own. It is the heritage of the *mother* that the African American male must regain as an aspect of his own personhood—the power of "yes" to the "female" within.

This different cultural text actually reconfigures, in historically ordained discourse, certain *representational* potentialities for African-Americans: 1) motherhood as female blood-rite is outraged, is denied, at the *very same time* that it becomes the founding term of a human and social enactment; 2) a dual fatherhood is set in motion, comprised of the African father's *banished* name and body and the captor father's mocking presence. In this play of paradox, only the female stands *in the flesh*, both mother and mother-dispossessed. This problematizing of gender places her, in my view, *out* of the traditional symbolics of female gender, and it is our task to make a place for this different social subject. In doing so, we are less interested in joining the ranks of gendered femaleness than gaining the *insurgent* ground as female social subject. Actually *claiming* the monstrosity (of a female with the potential to "name"), which her culture imposes in blindness, "Sapphire" might rewrite after all a radically different text for a female empowerment.

WORKS CITED

Barthes, Roland. *Mythologies*. Trans. Annette Lavers. New York: Hill and Wang, 1972.
Blassingame, John. *The Slave Community: Plantation Life in the Antebellum South*. New York: Oxford University Press, 1972.
Brent, Linda [pseud. of Harriet Jacobs]. *Incidents in the Life of a Slave Girl*. Ed. L. Maria Child. Introduced by Walter Teller. 1861. Reprint, New York: Harvest/HBJ Book, 1973.
Davis, Angela Y. *Women, Race, and Class*. New York: Random House, 1981.
De Azurara, Gomes Eannes. *The Chronicle of the Discovery and Conquest of Guinea*. Trans. C. Raymond Beazley and Edgar Prestage. London: Hakluyt Society, 1896, 1897. Reprinted in Donnan 1:18–41.
Donnan, Elizabeth. *Documents Illustrative of the History of the Slave Trade to America*. 4 vols. Washington, D.C.: Carnegie Institution of Washington, 1932.
Douglass, Frederick. *Narrative of the Life of Frederick Douglass An American Slave, Written by Himself*. 1845. Reprint, New York: Signet Books, 1968.
El-Shabazz, Malcolm El-Hajj Malik. *Autobiography of Malcolm X*. With Alex Haley. Introduced by M. S. Handler. New York: Grove Press, 1966.
Equiano, Olaudah. "The Life of Olaudah Equiano, or Gustavus Vassa, The African, Written by Himself." In *Great Slave Narratives*, introduced and selected by Arna Bontemps, 1–192. Boston: Beacon Press, 1969.
Faulkner, William. *The Mansion*. 1959. Reprint, New York: Vintage Books, 1965.
Frazier, E. Franklin. *The Negro Family in the United States*. Rev. with foreword by Nathan Glazer. Chicago: University of Chicago Press, 1966.
Genovese, Eugene. *Roll, Jordan, Roll: The World the Slaves Made*. New York: Pantheon Books, 1974.
Goodell, William. *The American Slave Code in Theory and Practice Shown by Its Statutes, Judicial Decisions, and Illustrative Facts*. 3rd ed. New York: American and Foreign Anti-Slavery Society, 1853.

Hooks, Bell. *Ain't I a Woman: Black Women and Feminism.* Boston: South End Press, 1981.

Klein, Herbert S. "African Women in the Atlantic Slave Trade." Robertson and Klein 29–39.

Meillassoux, Claude. "Female Slavery." Robertson and Klein 49–67.

Moynihan, Daniel P. "The Moynihan Report" [*The Negro Family: The Case for National Action.* Washington, D.C.: U.S. Department of Labor, 1965]. In *The Moynihan Report and the Politics of Controversy: A Transaction Social Science and Public Policy Report*, ed. Lee Rainwater and William L. Yancey, 47–94. Cambridge: MIT Press, 1967.

Robertson, Claire C., and Martin A. Klein, eds. *Women and Slavery in Africa.* Madison: University of Wisconsin Press, 1983.

Scarry, Elaine. *The Body in Pain: The Making and Unmaking of the World.* New York: Oxford University Press, 1985.

Smith, Valerie. "Loopholes of Retreat: Architecture and Ideology in Harriet Jacobs's *Incidents in the Life of a Slave Girl*." Paper presented at the 1985 American Studies Association Meeting, San Diego. Cited in Henry Louis Gates, Jr. "What's Love Got to Do With It?" *New Literary History* 18.2 (Winter 1987): 360.

Strobel, Margaret. "Slavery and Reproductive Labor in Mombasa." Robertson and Klein 111–30.

Suleiman, Susan Rubin, ed. *The Female Body in Western Culture.* Cambridge, Mass.: Harvard University Press, 1986.

Todorov, Tzvetan. *The Conquest of America: The Question of the Other.* Trans. Richard Howard. New York: Harper Colophon Books, 1984.

White, Deborah Grey. *Ar'n't I A Woman? Female Slaves in the Plantation South.* New York: Norton, 1985.

1987

CAROLYN HEILBRUN
1926–2003

Literary critic, biographer, memoirist, and writer of detective novels, Carolyn Heilbrun once described herself as "having been rescued, by feminism, from the rejection and heartbreak" that her life might have been, had she tried to follow in the path of the three men who served as her teachers. In *When Men Were the Only Models We Had: My Teachers Barzun, Fadiman, and Trilling* (2002), she recalled a time when male scholars could not conceive of mentoring their female students; however, Heilbrun herself mentored many younger colleagues and students during the thirty-three years she taught at Columbia University and then for the decade until her death. The author of more than a dozen best-selling novels featuring the detective Kate Fansler and composed under the pseudonym Amanda Cross, Heilbrun pioneered feminist approaches to literature with *Toward a Recognition of Androgyny: Aspects of Male and Female in Literature* (1973) and *Reinventing Womanhood* (1979). For many readers, Heilbrun's *The Last Gift of Time: Life beyond Sixty* (1997) also represented a breakthrough effort, in this case by confronting the challenges that older women experience during the aging process. Whether by establishing Columbia's Institute for Research on Women and Gender or writing the life of Gloria Steinem or co-editing (with Nancy K. Miller) Columbia University Press's Gender and Culture series, she dedicated herself to the institutionalization of feminist studies, as her biographer Susan Kress has demonstrated. Our selection comes from one her most popular books, *Writing a Woman's Life* (1988).

From Writing a Woman's Life

From *Introduction*

> *To justify an unorthodox life by writing about it is to* reinscribe *the original violation, to reviolate masculine turf.*
> —NANCY K. MILLER

There are four ways to write a woman's life: the woman herself may tell it, in what she chooses to call an autobiography; she may tell it in what she chooses to call fiction; a biographer, woman or man, may write the woman's life in what is called a biography; or the woman may write her own life in advance of living it, unconsciously, and without recognizing or naming the process. In this book, I shall discuss three of these four ways, omitting, for the most part, an analysis of the fictions in which many women have written their lives. For these stories in women's fiction, both the conventional and the subversive, have been examined in recent years with great brilliance and sophistication by a new generation of literary critics, and the work of these feminist critics has been so penetrating and persuasive that learning to read fictional representations of gender arrangements in our culture, whether of difference, oppression, or possibility, is an opportunity now available to anyone who will take the time to explore this vast and compelling body of criticism.

It has been otherwise with the lives of women. True, numberless biographies of women have appeared in recent years, many of them making use of new feminist theory developed by literary critics, psychologists, and historians. In 1984, I wrote in an article in the *New York Times Book Review*[1] that, since 1970, I had added seventy-three new biographies of women to my library. That number has certainly doubled by now, and yet there are countless biographies of women that I have not acquired. In 1984, I rather arbitrarily identified 1970 as the beginning of a new period in women's biography because *Zelda* by Nancy Milford had been published that year. Its significance lay above all in the way it revealed F. Scott Fitzgerald's assumption that he had a right to the life of his wife, Zelda, as an artistic property. She went mad, confined to what Mark Schorer has called her ultimate anonymity—to be storyless. Anonymity, we have long believed, is the proper condition of woman. Only in 1970 were we ready to read not that Zelda had destroyed Fitzgerald, but Fitzgerald her: he had usurped her narrative.

With equal arbitrariness, I would name 1973 as the turning point for modern women's autobiography. The transformation in question can be seen most clearly in the American poet, novelist, and memoirist May Sarton. Her *Plant Dreaming Deep*, an extraordinary and beautiful account of her adventure in buying a house and living alone, published in 1968, eventually dismayed her as she came to realize that none of the anger, passionate struggle, or despair of her life was revealed in the book. She had not intentionally concealed her pain: she had written in the old genre of female autobiography, which tends

---

1. Heilbrun, "Discovering the Lost Lives of Women," *New York Times Book Review,* June 24, 1984, p. 1+.

to find beauty even in pain and to transform rage into spiritual acceptance. Later, reading her idealized life in the hopeful eyes of those who saw her as exemplar, she realized that, in ignoring her rage and pain, she had unintentionally been less than honest. Changing times helped bring her to this realization. In her next book, *Journal of a Solitude*, she deliberately set out to recount the pain of the years covered by *Plant Dreaming Deep*. Thus the publication of *Journal of a Solitude* in 1973 may be acknowledged as the watershed in women's autobiography.

I call it the watershed not because honest autobiographies had not been written before that day but because Sarton deliberately retold the record of her anger. And, above all other prohibitions, what has been forbidden to women is anger, together with the open admission of the desire for power and control over one's life (which inevitably means accepting some degree of power and control over other lives). Nor have those born earlier than Sarton honored the watershed, or deigned to notice it. No memoir has been more admired and loved in recent years than Eudora Welty's *One Writer's Beginnings*. Yet I think there exists a real danger for women in books like Welty's in the nostalgia and romanticizing in which the author, and we in reading them, indulge. Virginia Woolf remarked that "very few women yet have written truthful autobiographies."

Let us look at what Eudora Welty wrote about Jane Austen:

> The felicity the novels have for us must partly lie in the confidence they take for granted between the author and her readers. We remember that the young Jane read her chapters aloud to her own lively, vocative family, upon whose shrewd intuition, practiced and eager estimation of conduct, and general rejoicing in character she relied almost as well as she could rely on her own. The novels still have the bloom of shared pleasure. The young author enjoyed from the first a warm confidence in an understanding reception. As all her work testifies, her time, her place, her location in society, are no more matters to be taken in question than the fact that she was a woman. She wrote from a perfectly solid and firm foundation, and her work is wholly affirmative. . . . Jane Austen was born knowing a great deal—for one thing, that the interesting situations of life can, and notably do, take place at home. In country parsonages the dangerous confrontations and the decisive skirmishes can very conveniently be arranged. [1969, 4–5]

The woman who wrote those words about Jane Austen in 1969 is the same woman who wrote *One Writer's Beginnings* in 1983. But the Jane Austen she describes is not the Jane Austen I or many others read today, nor do we believe in this account of the perfect family nourishing her happy talent. Similarly, I do not believe in the bittersweet quality of *One Writer's Beginnings*, nor do I suppose that the Eudora Welty there evoked could have written the stories and novels we have learned to celebrate. Welty, like Austen, has long been read for what she can offer of reassurance and the docile acceptance of what is given; she has been read as the avatar of a simpler world, with simpler values broadly accepted. In this both Austen and Welty have, of course, been betrayed. But only Welty, living in our own time, has camouflaged herself. Like Willa Cather, like T. S. Eliot's widow, she wishes to keep meddling hands off the life. To her, this is the only proper behavior for the Mississippi lady she so proudly is.

As her interviewer noted in the *Paris Review*, Welty is "extremely private and won't answer anything personal about herself or about friends" (273). Michael Kreyling reported that Welty prizes loyalty and gratitude and disapproves of critics who approach writers with "insufficient *tolerance* and *sympathy*" (414–15). There can be no question that to have written a truthful autobiography would have defied every one of her instincts for loyalty and privacy.

But why should I criticize Eudora Welty for having written the only autobiography possible to her? From what I know and have heard, she is the kindest, gentlest person imaginable. What then do I want from her? Would life not be preferable if we were all like Eudora Welty?

It would. Yet, since we are not, her genius as a writer of stories rescues her and us from her nostalgia. But it is that nostalgia, rendered with all the charm and grace of which she is capable, that has produced this autobiography, that same nostalgia that has for so many years imprisoned women without her genius or her rewards. Nostalgia, particularly for childhood, is likely to be a mask for unrecognized anger.

If one is not permitted to express anger or even to recognize it within oneself, one is, by simple extension, refused both power and control. Virginia Woolf's *Three Guineas* is an example of a feminist essay that was universally condemned at its publication because of its anger, its terrible "tone." Brenda Silver, writing of this reaction, asks: "What voice would be 'natural' or 'appropriate' for a woman writing a feminist complaint or critique of her culture?" (20). Mary Poovey has remarked on Caroline Norton's difficulty in finding a proper language or form in her mid-nineteenth-century battle to change the laws governing divorce and child custody (quoted in Silver, 20). Forbidden anger, women could find no voice in which publicly to complain; they took refuge in depression or madness. As Mary Ellmann has pointed out, "the most consistent critical standard applied to women is *shrillness:* blame something written by a woman as *shrill*, praise something as *not shrill*" (in Silver, 13). The other favorite term, of course, is *strident*.

These days the term may be "feminist" *tout court*. Michiko Kakutani, reviewing in the *New York Times* a biography of Margaret Bourke-White by Vicki Goldberg, writes that Bourke-White would, in her profession of photography, "be compelled to break all the conventional expectations for womanly conduct." But, Kakutani adds, "instead of simply trying to view her subject through the lens of feminist ideology, Ms. Goldberg judiciously examines the conflicts the photographer experienced herself." Apparently the phrase "feminist ideology" has here taken the place of "shrill" and "strident." I have long puzzled over this remark, and wanted to write Kakutani to ask her what she thought the "lens of feminist ideology" was. I had been trying to define it for years. One thing is clear: if it exists, Goldberg, in her excellent biography, was using it. "Feminist ideology" is another word for trying to understand, in the life of a woman, the life of the mind, which is, as Nancy Miller has noted, "not coldly cerebral but impassioned" (1980, 265).

To denounce women for shrillness and stridency is another way of denying them any right to power. Unfortunately, power is something that women abjure once they perceive the great difference between the lives possible to men and to women, and the violence necessary to men to maintain their position of authority. I have had students walk out of a class when I declared that power is a reasonable subject for discussion. But however unhappy the concept of power and control may make idealistic women, they delude themselves if they believe that the world and the condition of the oppressed can be changed without acknowledging it. Ironically, women who acquire power are more likely to be criticized for it than are the men who have always had it. As Deborah Cameron, an English linguistic theorist, has sardonically observed, male defense of its own power has decreed that nothing "is more ridiculous than a woman who imitates a male activity and is therefore no longer a woman. This can apply not only to speaking and writing, but also to the way a woman looks, the job she does, the way she behaves sexually, the leisure pursuits she engages in, the intellectual activities she prefers and so on *ad infinitum*. Sex differentiation must be rigidly upheld by whatever means are available, for men can be men only if women are unambiguously women" (155–156).

Women of accomplishment, in unconsciously writing their future lived lives, or, more recently, in trying honestly to deal in written form with lived past lives, have had to confront power and control. Because this has been declared unwomanly, and because many women would prefer (or think they would prefer) a world without evident power or control, women have been deprived of the narratives, or the texts, plots, or examples, by which they might assume power over—take control of—their own lives. The women's movement began, in fact, with discussions of power, powerlessness, and the question of sexual politics. But investigations into the qualities of womanliness have moved away from the point where male power must be analyzed and seen only in relation to female powerlessness. As Myra Jehlen has written, the danger of attempting to find, in this history of female powerlessness, a "female tradition" of autonomy is that, "in the effort to flesh out this vision," one finds that what is depicted is "not actual independence but action despite dependence—and not a self-defined female culture either, but a subculture born out of oppression and either stunted or victorious only at often-fatal cost" (581–82). The brutal truth, Jehlen knows, is that "all women must destroy in order to create" (583). "No woman can assume herself because she has yet to create herself, and this the sentimentalists, acceding to their society's definition [of women] did not do" (593). Jehlen understands the hardest fact of all for women to admit and defend: that woman's selfhood, the right to her own story, depends upon her "ability to act in the public domain" (596).

Although feminists early discovered that the private is the public, women's exercise of power and control, and the admission and expression of anger necessary to that exercise, has until recently been declared unacceptable. Yet many of the topics I propose to examine in this book—"unwomanly" ambition, marriage, friendships with women and love for women, aging, female childhood—can be seen accurately only in the light of movements toward *public* power and control. Women need to learn how publicly to declare their right to public power.

The true representation of power is not of a big man beating a smaller man or a woman. Power is the ability to take one's place in whatever discourse is essential to action and the right to have one's part matter. This is true in the Pentagon, in marriage, in friendship, and in politics.

In this book I want to examine how women's lives have been contrived, and how they may be written to make clear, evident, out in the open, those events, decisions, and relationships that have been invisible outside of women's fictions, where literary critics have revealed, in the words of Gilbert and Gubar, "the woman's quest for her own story" (1979, 22). I wish to suggest new ways of writing the lives of women, as biographers, autobiographers, or, in the anticipation of living new lives, as the women themselves.

This is a feminist undertaking. I define *feminist*, using Nancy Miller's words, as the wish "to articulate a self-consciousness about women's identity both as inherited cultural fact and as process of social construction" and to "protest against the available fiction of female becoming." Women's lives, like women's writing, have, in Miller's words, a particularly "vulnerable relation to the culture's central notions of plausibility." It is hard to suppose women can mean or want what we have always been assured they could not possibly mean or want. Miller has shown us how "the literal failure to read women's writing has other theoretical implications." The same may be said of reading women's lives. Unlike the reading of the classics—or of men's lives, or of women's lives as events in the destinies of men—which always include "the frame of *interpretations* that have been elaborated over generations of critical activity," reading women's lives needs to be considered in the absence of "a structure of critical" or biographical commonplace (1988, 129). It all needs to be invented, or discovered, or resaid.

My parents' generation grew up with the Rubáiyát of Omar Khayyám in the Edward FitzGerald version, and so, in time, did I. Its bittersweet flavor of inevitability and wisdom haunted my early years. A much-quoted verse (LXXI) reads:

> The Moving Finger writes; and, having writ,
> Moves on: nor all our Piety nor Wit
>   Shall lure it back to cancel half a Line,
> Nor all your Tears wash out a Word of it.

This used to seem evidently, obviously, true. But, at least insofar as women's lives are concerned, it is wrong. Lines can be canceled and washed out; and what the Moving Finger writ may, all along, have been misread. I suggest that it has indeed been misread, and that women have mistakenly supposed themselves deprived of the Piety and Wit certainly sufficient to lure it back.

Feminist criticism, scholarship, and theory have gone further in the last two decades than I, even in my most intense time of hope, could have envisioned. Yet I find myself today profoundly worried about the dissemination of these important new ideas to the general body of women, conscious or unconscious of the need to retell and reencounter their lives. I brood also on the dissensions that have grown among feminist scholars and theoreticians. These divisions, the arguments among scholars about theories, approaches, methodology, are not, of themselves, either dangerous or unexpected. Every new field of knowledge develops these differences. Indeed, they are essential to the progress of understanding. I am certainly not blaming female scholars for failing to maintain a unity men have never achieved, and which is not, in fact, conducive to the flowering of any discipline or to the reorganization of knowledge.

Yet there is a real danger that in rewriting the patriarchal text, scholars will get lost in the intellectual ramifications of their disciplines and fail to reach out to the women whose lives must be rewritten with the aid of the new intellectual constructs. I mean no anti-intellectual complaint here. Without intellectual and theoretical underpinnings, no movement can succeed; the failure of feminism to sustain itself in previous incarnations may well be attributable to its lack of underlying theoretical discourse. But we are in danger of refining the theory and scholarship at the expense of the lives of the women who need to experience the fruits of research.

For this reason, I have chosen to write of women's lives, rather than of the texts I have been trained to analyze and enjoy. I risk a great danger: that I shall bore the theorists and fail to engage the rest, thus losing both audiences. If this does, indeed, occur, I shall at least have failed as the result of a conscious choice, one made in knowledge, insofar as that is ever possible, of the dangers, the challenges, and the vitality whose price is risk.

Safety and closure, which have always been held out to women as the ideals of female destiny, are not places of adventure, or experience, or life. Safety and closure (and enclosure) are, rather, the mirror of the Lady of Shalott. They forbid life to be experienced directly. Lord Peter Wimsey once said that nine-tenths of the law of chivalry was a desire to have all the fun.[2] The same might well be said of patriarchy.

* * *

WORKS CITED

Cameron, Deborah. *Feminism and Linguistic Theory*. London: Macmillan, 1985.

Gilbert, Sandra M., and Susan Gubar. *The Madwoman in the Attic: The Woman Writer and the Nineteenth-Century Literary Imagination*. New Haven: Yale University Press, 1979.

Jehlen, Myra. "Archimedes and the Paradox of Feminist Criticism." *Signs* 6, no. 4 (1984): 575–601.

Kakutani, Michiko. "A Life in Pictures." *New York Times,* June 28, 1986.

Kreyling, Michael. "Words into Criticism: Eudora Welty's Essays and Reviews." In *Eudora Welty: Critical Essays*, ed. Peggy Whitman Prenshaw, pp. 411–22. Jackson: University Press of Mississippi, 1979.

Miller, Nancy K. *The Heroine's Text: Readings in the French and English Novel, 1722–1782*. New York: Columbia University Press, 1980.

———. *Subject to Change: Reading Feminist Writing*. New York: Columbia University Press, 1988.

Sarton, May. *Plant Dreaming Deep*. New York: Norton, 1968.

———. *Journal of a Solitude*. New York: Norton, 1973.

Silver, Brenda. "Anger, Authority, and Tones of Voice: The Case of *Three Guineas*" (unpublished MS). [See "The Authority of Anger: *Three Guineas* as Case Study," *Signs* 16, no. 2 [1991]: 340–70.]

Welty, Eudora. "A Note on Jane Austen." *Shenandoah* 20, no. 3 (1969): 3–7.

———. Interview. *Writers at Work: The Paris Review Interviews, Fourth Series*, ed. George Plimpton, pp. 273–92. New York: Penguin Books, 1977.

———. *One Writer's Beginnings*. Cambridge, Mass.: Harvard University Press, 1983.

1988

2. In Dorothy Sayers's *Gaudy Night* (1935), chap. 14. "The Lady of Shalott": the central figure in (and title of) an 1832 poem by Tennyson; looking at life directly, rather than in her mirror, leads to her death.

CAROLYN DINSHAW
b. 1956

As a background to her investigation of the engendering of Chaucer's poetics, the medievalist Carolyn Dinshaw offers here a fine analysis of the notion, widespread in the classical period and the Middle Ages, that books are metaphorically the "sons" of masculine minds and must therefore be protected with "paternal care." Focusing to begin with on the vision of "the masculine structure of literary tradition" that emerges in the writings of Richard of Bury, bishop of Durham in the mid–fourteenth century, Dinshaw develops her argument into a sophisticated discussion of the long-standing tendency in Western culture to metaphorize the textual surface—"the letter of the text, the *signifier*"—as a misleadingly pleasurable and disturbingly feminine veil that must be stripped away to reveal the pure truth of the male spirit.

A professor of social and cultural analysis as well as English at New York University, Dinshaw earned a Ph.D. from Princeton in 1982. In addition to *Chaucer's Sexual Poetics* (1989) and other work on Chaucer, she has published *Getting Medieval: Sexualities and Communities, Pre- and Postmodern* (1999) and co-edited (with David Wallace) *The Cambridge Companion to Medieval Women's Writing* (2003). She is also a founding co-editor of *GLQ: A Journal of Lesbian and Gay Studies.*

From Chaucer's Sexual Poetics

From *Introduction*

* * *

Richard of Bury, bishop of Durham in the mid-fourteenth century, makes the masculine structure of literary tradition exceptionally clear in his *Philobiblon* (completed in 1345), and hence this work makes an apt starting point for my investigation of the gender valence of medieval literary activity. Richard openly identifies the care and preservation of books with the care and preservation of the patriarchy.

The bishop of Durham wrote his treatise in defense of his vast and costly collection of books: his detractors had accused him of lavishing too much money and attention on them. (At the same time that he was defending his library, he was defending his embattled northern diocese against the Scots, and his king against the French.) Books, both ancient and modern, Richard argues, contain the treasure of wisdom and thus must be preserved. He urgently exhorts men not to be seduced (*subtrahit*) away from the "paternal care of books" (*paterna cultura librorum*) by the lures of "stomach, dress, or houses" (which are, we note, the Wife of Bath's concerns).[1] Paternal care is necessary to preserve the purity of the race of books against the loss of their ancient nobility, against defilement by impostors pretending to be authors: paternal care is necessary lest "the sons," as he puts it, be "robbed of the names of their true fathers."[2] Indeed, the handing down or

---

1. *The Philobiblon of Richard of Bury,* ed. and trans. Ernest C. Thomas (London: Kegan, Paul, Trench, and Co., 1887), ch. 6, sec. 87 [except as indicated, all notes are Dinshaw's; some of her notes have been edited].
2. Ibid., ch. 4, sec. 68.

transcribing of ancient books, Richard writes, "is, as it were, the begetting of fresh sons, on whom the office of the father may devolve, lest it suffer detriment."[3] The ideas of passing on old books and of old books' essential role in new learning were common enough in the Middle Ages. No one, however, discloses the patriarchal investment in this idea more forthrightly than Richard. In the act of preserving books, Richard argues, one protects against violations of property, territory, lineage, and family—against violations of the patriarchy.

Women's active participation in a literary culture characterized in this way was obviously extremely limited. To be sure, some women in the Middle Ages *did* own and compose texts—a few overcame institutional obstacles and obtained the necessary education and leisure to read and write.[4] And, by the late fourteenth century, they passed on their books to their daughters as well as to their son.[5] But women's disenfranchisement within the literary sphere was certain, and medieval attitudes about women's expression preserved strong classical and biblical prohibitions.[6] Juvenal writes, for example, in his *Sixth Satire*, that virulently antifeminist diatribe whose influence extended to Walter Map, Jean de Meun, and Boccaccio: "Wives shouldn't try to be public speakers; they shouldn't use rhetorical devices; they shouldn't read all the classics—there ought to be some things women don't understand."[7] Aristotle's theory of social class structure in his *Politics* is based on the prohibition of women's expression:

> All classes must be deemed to have their special attributes; as the poet [Sophocles] says of women, "Silence is a woman's glory"; but this is not equally the glory of man.[8]

3. Ibid., ch. 16, sec. 207.
4. These women are, of course, the exceptions; their own discourse and that of those around them make their exceptional status clear. Christine de Pizan's extended treatise on social obstacles to women's achievements, *Le Livre de la cité des dames* [The book of the city of ladies, 1405], may be taken as an epitome here. See Susan Schibanoff's recent analysis of Christine's attempt to read as a woman (to read, that is, according to her own experiences and knowledge), "Taking the Gold Out of Egypt: The Art of Reading as a Woman," in *Gender and Reading*, ed. Elizabeth A. Flynn and Patrocinio P. Schweikart (Baltimore: Johns Hopkins University Press, 1986), pp. 83–106. Among the many recent discussions of medieval women's literary achievements, see Kathleen Walkup's brief comments in "By Sovereign Maidens' Might: Notes on Women in Printing," *Fine Print* 11, no. 2 (April 1985): 100–104; Peter Dronke, *Women Writers of the Middle Ages: A Critical Study of Texts from Perpetua to Marguerite Porete* (Cambridge: Cambridge University Press, 1984); Katharina M. Wilson, ed., *Medieval Women Writers* (Athens: University of Georgia Press, 1984); and Joan M. Ferrante, "The Education of Women in the Middle Ages in Theory, Fact, and Fantasy," in *Beyond Their Sex: Learned Women of the European Past*, ed. Patricia H. Labalme (New York: New York University Press, 1980), pp. 9–42.
5. Lady Alice West, Hampshire, for example, in a will proved in 1395, leaves to her son "a peyre Matins bookis," among other items, but to his wife she leaves "a masse book, and alle the bokes that I

have of latyn, englisch, and frensch" (see *Fifty Earliest English Wills in the Court of Probate, London, A.D. 1387–1439*, ed. Frederick J. Furnivall, EETS o.s. 78 [London: Trübner, 1882], p. 5).
6. "Disenfranchisement" is R. Howard Bloch's term in his comments on woman's place in social history in "Medieval Misogyny," *Representations*, no. 20 (Fall 1987): 1–24. That social structure did not accommodate literary women is suggested by the thirteenth-century author of *Urbain le Courtois*, who advises "mon filz chier" [my dear son] against choosing a bride who can read (*Urbain le Courtois*, ed. Paul Meyer, *Romania* 32 [1903]: 72, ll. 57–64). I was pointed to this text by John F. Benton, "Clio and Venus: An Historical View of Medieval Love," in *The Meaning of Courtly Love*, ed. F. X. Newman (Albany: State University of New York Press, 1968), pp. 19–42.
7. Juvenal, *Satires* 6.448–51, ed. G. G. Ramsay, Loeb Classical Library (Cambridge, Mass.: Harvard University Press, 1940), p. 120; trans. Roger Killian et al., in Sarah Pomeroy, *Goddesses, Whores, Wives, and Slaves: Women in Classical Antiquity* (New York: Schocken, 1975), p. 172. This passage is quoted by Lee Patterson, in his " 'For the Wyves love of Bathe': Feminine Rhetoric and Poetic Resolution in the *Roman de la Rose* and the *Canterbury Tales*," *Speculum* 58 (1983): 656.
8. Aristotle, *Politics* 1260a28–31 (trans. Benjamin Jowett, in *The Complete Works of Aristotle*, ed. Jonathan Barnes [Princeton, N.J.: Princeton University Press, 1984], 2: 2000). Cited in Prudence Allen, R.S.M., *The Concept of Woman: The Aristotelian Revolution, 750 B.C. to A. D. 1250*

Aquinas, in his commentary on the *Politics*, repeats this formula—as does Averroës in his commentary on the Aristotelian text—and corroborates it with a biblical injunction, Saint Paul's prohibition (in 1 Cor. 14:34–35) of women's speaking in public: "Let women keep silence in the churches: for it is not permitted them to speak, but to be subject, as also the law saith. But if they would learn anything, let them ask their husbands at home" ("Mulieres in ecclesiis taceant, non enim permittitur eis loqui, sed subditas esse, sicut et lex dicit. Si quid autem volunt discere, domi viros suos interrogent"). Aquinas conflates the classical and biblical traditions and continues the discourse in his own works.[9] Significantly, Saint Paul's admonition to Timothy (in 1 Tim. 2:11–12) about women's speaking—"Let the women learn in silence, with all subjection. But I suffer not a woman to teach, nor to use authority over the man: but to be in silence" ("Mulier in silentio discat cum omni subiectione. Docere autem mulierem non permitto, neque dominari in virum: sed esse in silentio")—directly follows his admonitions (in 1 Tim. 2:9–10) about the adornment of women's bodies: such proscriptions as these on women's teaching, women's speaking, women's writing reflect intense and anxious responses to woman's physical being.[1]

A defining characteristic of the female, in both classical and Christian exegetical traditions, is her corporeality, her association with matter and the physical body as opposed to the male's association with form and soul.[2] Aristotle's political analysis of woman, mentioned above, is clearly related to his theory of the metaphysical female principle as *steresis*, the totally passive privation of the male principle, and is subtended by his association of her physical being with matter (as opposed to the male being, which is characterized by form, animation, and generation).[3] As Vern L. Bullough has suggested, assumptions about women's body common in the ancient world were power-

---

(Montreal: Eden Press, 1985), p. 110. This encyclopedic volume contains thorough examination and documentation of classical traditions of thinking about "woman" and their continuation into the Christian era.

9. For what is appropriate for the decorum of a woman or her integrity—that she be silent—comes from the modesty that is appropriate to women, but this does not pertain to the decorum of a man; rather, he should speak as is fitting. Therefore the Apostle warns, Let women keep silent in the churches and if they wish to learn anything, let them ask their husbands at home (I Cor. 14:34)

(Aquinas, *In octo libros Politicorum Aristotelis expositio* 1.10, ed. Raymundi M. Spiazzi [Taurini: Marietti, 1966], p. 50)

Cited in Allen, *The Concept of Woman*, p. 400; I have altered her translation here.

1. Cf. R. Howard Bloch, who argues in "Medieval Misogyny" that masculine proscriptions on adornment are directed at its "perverse secondariness" and are not proscriptions of the flesh per se. Such secondariness, he argues, is a condition of the female at the Creation, a condition of ornament, and indeed a condition of all figuration or representation. As I shall develop more fully below, it seems to me that the exegetical assimilation of literality and carnality to femininity is more thorough and profound than the assimilation of the loss of the literal to femininity

that Bloch suggests.

2. For the exegetical tradition, see below in this section. For the classical tradition, examples of the association of the female with matter abound: see Aristotle, *Generation of Animals* 738b20–25, trans. A. L. Peck, Loeb Classical Library (Cambridge, Mass.: Harvard University Press, 1953), p. 12; and Pliny the Elder, *Natural History* 7.15, ed. H. Rackham, Loeb Classical Library (Cambridge, Mass.: Harvard University Press, 1942), p. 549. This association was steadily carried through to the end of the Middle Ages by Averroës, *Colliget* 2.10, supp. 1 (*Aristotelis opera cum Averrois commentariis* [Frankfurt am Main: Minerva Verlag, 1962], p. 23); Albertus Magnus, *Quaestiones super De animalibus* 5.4, ed. Ephrem Filthaut, vol. 12, *Opera omnia* (Monasterii Westfalorum in Aedibus Aschendorff, 1955), pp. 155–56; and Aquinas, *Summa theologica* 1a.92.1 and 3a.32.4 (*Opera omnia* [Parma, 1852–73; rpt. New York: Musurgia, 1948]).

3. Aristotle rejected any idea of an active contribution of seed or formative matter by the mother. The seed was a male product only, and existed "by potentiality, and we know what is the relation of potentiality to actuality," he argues in *Parts of Animals* 641b25–642a2 (trans. A. L. Peck, Loeb Classical Library [Cambridge, Mass.: Harvard University Press, 1937], pp. 73–75). If the male seed is potentiality, therefore, the female matter is actuality. See Allen, *The Concept of Woman*, pp. 90–91, 95–103.

ful determinants of the development of medieval law and doctrine regarding women: woman was seen in various classical medical and scientific writings as defective, deformed, or mutilated man; man turned inside out; a creature whose anatomy wouldn't stay still; a creature who needed to be kept under control.[4] Medieval limitations of woman's expression seem, in the final analysis, inseparable from the regulation of woman's body. The history, established recently, of the gynecological treatises by Trotula (who is included in Jankyn's "book of wikked wyves") is itself a neat testimony to the correlation between the masculine silencing of women's writing (and appropriation of women's voices) and the masculine control of their bodies: as John F. Benton has demonstrated, three treatises commonly attributed in the Middle Ages to Trotula were in fact written by men, whose control of medical theory and gynecological literature in the Middle Ages was complete.[5] The intense emotion—simultaneous fascination and repulsion—behind the connection of woman's body and woman's speech is expressed in Jean Gerson's almost obsessive comment about Saint Bridget: he speaks of her "insatiable itch to see and to speak, not to mention . . . the itch to touch."[6]

But clearly, if we return to consider Richard of Bury's genealogical allegory of literary tradition, we can see that a female is necessary to perpetuate the lineage, however passive her participation may be.[7] And thus it is *her* purity

---

4. For discussion of the development of medieval ideas of women out of classical scientific and medical treatises, see Vern L. Bullough, "Medieval Medical and Scientific Views of Women," *Viator: Medieval and Renaissance Studies* 4 (1973): 485–501. For woman as defective man, see Aristotle, *Generation of Animals* 728a13–27 (Loeb ed., p. 103); and Galen, *On the Usefulness of the Parts of the Body* 14.5–6 (trans. Margaret Tallmadge May [Ithaca, N.Y.: Cornell University Press, 1968], 2:627–28. For woman as deformed man, see Aristotle, *Generation of Animals* 737a26–30, 775a12–16 (Loeb ed., pp. 175, 459–61). For woman as man turned inside out, see Galen, *Usefulness* 14.6 (trans. May, 2:628–30). Christian writers retained the classical notion of woman as imperfect; they adapted it to the notion that God's creation of male and female was flawless by distinguishing between *universal* nature and *particular* nature: the generation of men and women on the level of universal nature was willed by God, although the generation of individual women is a defect in the order of nature. See Allen, *The Concept of Woman*, p. 393. For the distinction between the individual and the species of humans, see Albertus Magnus, *Quaestiones super De animalibus* 15.2; and Aquinas, *Summa theologica* 1a.75.4. On the creation of the female, see Aquinas, *Summa theologica* 1a.92.1. For discussion of the synthesis of Aristotle, Genesis, and New Testament discourse on the female, see Patricia Parker, *Literary Fat Ladies* (London: Methuen, 1987), pp. 178–85.
5. John F. Benton, "Trotula, Women's Problems, and the Professionalization of Medicine in the Middle Ages," *Bulletin of the History of Medicine* 59 (1985): 30–53. For the distinctive roles of *medicus* (male doctor) and *obstetrix* (female midwife)—theory and practice—see the brief comments in Helen Rodnite Lemay, "William of Saliceto on Human Sexuality," *Viator* 12 (1981): 180–81.
6. Jean Gerson, *De probatione spirituum* 11 (1415), in *Oeuvres complètes*, ed. P. Glorieux

(Paris: Desclée, 1960–73), 9:184. The treatise, prompted by Bridget's canonization, concerns false inspiration and attempts to provide some criteria for detecting it. Clearly, gender is at issue in this treatise; Gerson warns theologians of religious fervor in young people and in women, claiming that more is at stake than mere waste of time. For brief discussion of Gerson's treatise, see Barbara Obrist, "The Swedish Visionary: Saint Bridget," in *Medieval Women Writers*, ed. Katharina M. Wilson (Athens: University of Georgia Press, 1984), pp. 227–39; the translation appears on p. 236.
7. Aristotle emphasizes the active role of the male in reproduction over the purely passive role of the female:

> Thus, if the male is the active partner, the one who originates the movement, and the female *qua* female is the passive one, surely what the female contributes to the semen of the male will not be semen but material [for the semen to work upon].
>
> (*Generation of Animals* 729a25–30 [Loeb ed., p. 103])

Aristotle's rejection of the female seed or any female formative material was a clear break with earlier writers on generation (Parmenides, Empedocles, Democritus, Anaxagoras, the Hippocratic writings) and was not followed by Galen or, later, Averroës or Albertus Magnus. All agreed, however, that passivity was the key to the female role in reproduction: Aquinas, for example, wrote that the female was necessary but passive in reproduction (see *Summa theologica* 3a.32.4, also 1a.98.2 and 1a.118.1; *De anima* 11.5 [*Opera omnia*, 8:500]; and *Summa contra gentiles* 4.11.1 [*Opera omnia*, 5:307–8]). The male seed was understood to have primary importance. See the summary discussion in John T. Noonan, Jr., *Contraception: A History of Its Treatment by the Catholic Theologians and Canonists* (Cambridge, Mass.: Harvard University Press, 1966), pp. 88–91, and Allen, *The Concept of Woman*, esp. p. 97.

upon which the purity of the race depends.[8] This necessary protection of woman's purity associates her, allegorically, with the wisdom that must be protected, the truth contained in the old books to be preserved by the *paterna cultura*. Writing a few years after Richard of Bury, Boccaccio suggests an association of the female with the truth contained within books when, in his *Genealogia deorum gentilium*, he declares that the truth must be protected from the "gaze of the irreverent," so that "they cheapen not by too common familiarity."[9] And in this connection he points elsewhere in the *Genealogia* to the opening of Macrobius' commentary on the *Somnium Scipionis* (c. 400). At the beginning of that commentary, Macrobius presents a fully sexualized image of truths that must not be prostituted, must not be made into whores. He writes that the secrets of Nature that the text contains are wrapped in mysteries, veiled in the mysterious representations of fabulous narratives, so that the vulgar may not see and profane them. In an exemplum, Macrobius cites the brash Numenius, who expounded the sacred Eleusinian mysteries and thereby made prostitutes of them: the Eleusinian goddesses appeared to Numenius in a dream, wearing the garments of courtesans and standing by an open brothel.[1] The body of Nature, as Macrobius argues—or *nuda veritas*,[2] as Richard of Bury refers to the hidden body—must be kept secret, clothed in the garments, veils, protective coverings of fiction, poetry, mystery.

This is, of course, the standard medieval analysis of the allegorical text: it contains truth veiled by obscurity. Augustine, Lactantius, Isidore of Seville, Vincent of Beauvais, Petrarch, Dante, Boccaccio use this figure of the veil to describe passages in both biblical and secular literature.[3] The figure is used in the service of quite different arguments, of course: Augustine identifies the veil of allegorical language in both biblical and pagan texts, delighting in the scriptural passages while condemning the pagan; Augustine's condemnation was mitigated through the period, as Lee Patterson remarks, until, at the end of the Middle Ages, Boccaccio argues for the licitness of the act of reading pagan fable.[4] Nonetheless, the structure of the allegorical text and the process of reading it remain the same from Augustine to Boccaccio: the spiritually healthy reader will discover the truth under the veil of fiction, under the covering of poetical words. As Boccaccio argues, fiction pleases even the unlearned by its surface blandishments, and it exercises the minds of the learned in the discovery of its beautiful, hidden truth (*Genealogia* 14.9).

8. See Aquinas' comments on monogamy in *Summa contra gentiles* 3.123: monogamy is natural to the human species because there is in men (*hominibus*) a certain natural solicitude to be certain of their offspring:

> So, whenever there are obstacles to the ascertaining of offspring they are opposed to the natural instinct of the human species. But, if a husband could put away his wife, or a wife her husband, and have sexual relations with another person, certitude as to offspring would be precluded, for the wife would be united first with one man and later with another. So, it is contrary to the natural instinct of the human species for a wife to be separated from her husband.
> (*Opera omnia* 5:260; trans. Vernon J. Bourke, *Summa contra gentiles* [Notre Dame; Ind.: University of Notre Dame Press, 1975], vol. 3, pt. 2, p. 148)

9. Boccaccio, *Genealogia deorum gentilium* 14.13, ed. Vincenzo Romano (Bari: Laterza, 1951), 2:715; trans. Charles G. Osgood, under the title *Boccaccio on Poetry* (Indianapolis: Bobbs-Merrill, 1956), pp. 59–60.
1. Macrobius, *Commentarii in Somnium Scipionis* 1.2.19, ed. J. Willis (Leipzig: Teubner, 1963), pp. 7–8; trans. William Harris Stahl, *Commentary on the Dream of Scipio* (New York: Columbia University Press, 1952), pp. 86–87.
2. Naked truth (Latin) [editor's note].
3. For a short bibliography of medieval uses of this figure of the veiled text, see *Boccaccio on Poetry*, p. 157 n. 8.
4. On the relation of Augustine and Boccaccio here, see Lee W. Patterson, "Ambiguity and Interpretation: A Fifteenth-Century Reading of *Troilus and Criseyde*," *Speculum* 54 (1979): 327–29.

So allegorical interpretation is, in this sense, undressing the text—unveiling the truth, revealing a body figuratively represented as female. This interpretive activity is only for initiates of the highest intelligence, Macrobius argues; only available to the learned, Boccaccio argues; and only for men, as the diction of heterosexual culture suggests. Richard of Bury, again, provides a clear example of this gendering of allegorical reading: in describing the difficult and tedious task of discovering the truth in a classical text, he uses the language of seduction: "The wisdom of the ancients devised a remedy by which to entice the wanton minds of men by a kind of pious fraud, the delicate Minerva secretly lurking beneath the image of pleasure."[5] The garments—that "image of pleasure"—seduce the reader to look further, to the body of Minerva. The image appeals to the "wanton minds of men" through the senses. It is the lying surface, the letter of the text, the *signifier*.

But according to Richard of Bury (and Augustine before him), the reader must pass beyond that pleasurable surface, the signifier, to the hidden truth beneath, the signified.[6] To stop at the image of pleasure is to succumb to the seductions directed at the reader's "wantonness." To stop at the signifier is to enjoy something that should be used, to put it in Augustine's terms in the *De doctrina christiana* (3.5.7). In Richard's statement, then, we have the suggestion of another discourse, one that *reverses* the valence of woman as truth of the text: it's the patristic association of the surface of the text (the letter) with carnality (the flesh, the body), and carnality with woman—an association I alluded to earlier in reference to "Adam Scriveyn."[7] Taking pleasure of the text is analogous to taking carnal pleasure of a woman: "letter" and "bele chose" are the site of that illicit bliss. Woman, in this Pauline model of reading, is not the "hidden truth" but is dangerous cupidity: she is what must be passed through, gone beyond, left, discarded, to get to the truth, the spirit of the text. When Dante, in *Inferno* 9, admonishes his reader to "mark the doctrine under the veil of strange verses," he links that veil with the threat of feminine beauty posed by Medusa.[8]

Saint Paul associated the letter of the text with death—with everything old, sinful; with things of the flesh. The text, as Claudius of Turin (c. 800) suggested of Scripture, has a body and a soul; to read literally is to read carnally (*litteraliter vel carnaliter*).[9] Earlier, Origen was concerned that the spiritual meaning of the Song of Songs could be missed by the carnal man; he warns not only that the carnally minded reader should not read this text but that youths should not even hold it in their hands—as though it is itself a dangerously seductive body.[1] The further association of the body, the carnal, with woman is commonplace in exegetes throughout the Middle Ages, from the

5. Richard of Bury, *Philobiblon*, ch. 13, sec. 180. I have altered Thomas' translation slightly.

6. This is where Boccaccio's project diverges from the strictly moral Augustinian one echoed by Richard of Bury: Boccaccio suggests a relaxation in regard to pleasure in the letter—if the reader himself is armed by faith, a certain delectation of the letter might be allowable (*Genealogia* 14.18). See Patterson, "Ambiguity and Interpretation," pp. 327–29.

7. I.e., "Adam Scrivener," from a brief poem by Chaucer [editor's note].

8. *Inferno* 9.62–63, in *The Divine Comedy: Inferno*, ed. and trans. Charles S. Singleton (Princeton, N.J.: Princeton University Press,

1970), 1:92–3. See John Freccero, "Medusa: The Letter and the Spirit," in his *Dante: The Poetics of Conversion*, ed. Rachel Jacoff (Cambridge, Mass.: Harvard University Press, 1986), pp. 119–35.

9. In *The Study of the Bible in the Middle Ages*, 3d ed., rev. (Oxford: Basil Blackwell, 1983), Beryl Smalley begins her chapter "The Fathers" by quoting Claudius, *In libros informationum litterae et spiritus super Leviticum praefatio*, and suggesting that he "sums up the patristic tradition as it had reached the scholars of Charlemagne's day" (p. 1).

1. Origen, *The Song of Songs: Commentary and Homilies*, trans. and ed. R. P. Lawson (Westminster, Md.: Newman Press, 1957), pp. 22–23.

church fathers to Chaucer's Parson: in tropological accounts of the Fall (by Philo of Alexandria, Augustine, John Scottus Eriugena, and the Parson, to name a few), Eve is associated with the carnal appetite, Adam with higher intellectual faculties. I've already alluded to the fallenness of language, in reference to "Adam Scriveyn"—the letter's fragmented, transitory nature, its association with the postlapsarian, newly mortal body and with Eve. Boccaccio associates the letter with "the fruit of sin," as seductive and enticing as the temptation used on the first woman and by her on the first man.[2]

To follow out this Pauline model of reading would mean to discard altogether the model of woman as central, naked truth of the text, to rigorously pass through the text's female body on the way to its spirit—its male spirit, as Ambrose and others suggest.[3] Augustine dismissed pagan fable as worthless precisely because he considered it to have only false or empty "spirit" below its enticing letter.[4] But Jerome addresses the problem of reading classical fable using a subtler model—Jerome, author of the notoriously antifeminist *Adversus Jovinianum* (a text the Wife of Bath knows and abhors), and a reader who was plagued by the seductions of classical style.[5] He likens the classical text to the beautiful captive woman in Deuteronomy 21:10–13.[6] The biblical passage reads:

> Si egressus fueris ad pugnam contra inimicos tuos, et tradiderit eos Dominus Deus tuus in manu tua, captivosque duxeris, et videris in

2. See Philo of Alexandria: "The serpent is a symbol of desire[,] . . . and woman is a symbol of sense, and man, of mind" (*Questions and Answers on Genesis* 1.47, trans. Ralph Marcus, Loeb Classical Library [Cambridge, Mass.: Harvard University Press, 1953], supp. 1, p. 27); Philo: "The mind in us—call it Adam—having met with outward sense, called Eve . . ." (*On the Cherubim* 17–19 [Loeb ed., p. 43]); Augustine, *De civitate Dei* 14.10–26, CC 47 (Turnhout: Brepols, 1955), pp. 430–50); Augustine, *De trinitate* 12.12, ed. W. J. Mountain, CC 50 (Turnhout: Brepols, 1968), pp. 371–73; Augustine, *De sermone Domini in monte* 1.12.36, ed. A. Mutzenbecher, CC 35 [Turnhout: Brepols, 1967], p. 39); and John Scottus Eriugena, *De divisione naturae* 4.16 (PL 122:814B–29B). For a discussion of this tradition of tropological analysis of the Fall, see D. W. Robertson, Jr., *A Preface to Chaucer* (Princeton, N.J.: Princeton University Press, 1962), pp. 69–75. See also Albertus Magnus: "Briefly, therefore, everyone is to be warned away from every woman as from a poisonous serpent or a horned devil" (*Quaestiones super De animalibus* 15.11). Boccaccio's association of the letter of the text with the fruit of sin (*mala frux*) appears in *Genealogia* 14.15.

3. It is tempting, in fact, to develop a theory of the transsexual text, based on the metaphor of transsexuality used by Ambrose and by Jerome. Bullough quotes and translates both church fathers: Ambrose writes

> She who does not believe is a woman and should be designated by the name of her bodily sex, whereas she who believes progresses to complete manhood, to the measure of the adulthood of Christ.
> (*Expositio evangeliis secundum Lucam* [PL 15: 1844]; quoted in Bullough, "Medieval Medical and Scientific Views of Women," p. 499)

And Jerome states:

> As long as woman is for birth and children, she is different from man as body is from soul. But if she wishes to serve Christ more than the world, then she will cease to be a woman and will be called man.
> (*Commentariorum in Epistolam ad Ephesios libri* 3 [PL 26:533]; quoted in Bullough, "Medieval Medical and Scientific Views," p. 499)

But in other—and more characteristic—places in the fathers, following Paul in 1 Timothy 2:15, woman's redeeming characteristic is her childbearing function, an idea that is carried into the metaphorics of discourse on the letter, as we shall see.

4. Augustine, *De doctrina christiana* 3.7 (ed. J. Martin, CC 32 [Turnhout: Brepols, 1962], pp. 84–85). Secular works, such as those of the Platonists, can be read, according to Augustine, if their occasional, useful precepts or truths are taken for better use by Christians. He likens these truths stolen from the pagan texts to gold taken from Egyptians by the Israelites (*De doctrina* 2.40 [pp. 73–75]).

5. Augustine is concerned with the truths of pagan philosophers—specifically, Neoplatonists—but Jerome, when discussing the virtues of classical texts, alludes more to Terence and Virgil than to Plato, as Henri de Lubac notes in "La belle captive," ch. 4, pt. 5, of *Exégèse médiévale* (Paris: Aubier, 1959), vol. 1, pt. 1, p. 293. [*Against Jovinian* praised virginity and attacked opposition to Christian asceticism—editor's note.]

6. Henri de Lubac points out that Jerome got this image from Origen (in a homily on Leviticus), who likens the captive woman to the pagan text but associates her beauties with the rational wisdom the Christian might find there—not, as does Jerome, with the elegances of classical rhetoric and language (*Exégèse médiévale*, vol. 1, pt. 1, pp. 291–92).

numero captivorum mulierem pulchram, et adamaveris eam, voluerisque habere uxorem, introduces eam in domum tuam: quae radet caesariem, et circumcidet ungues, et deponet vestem, in qua capta est: sedensque in domo tua, flebit patrem et matrem suam uno mense: et postea intrabis ad eam, dormiesque cum illa, et erit uxor tua.

[If thou go out to fight against thy enemies, and the Lord thy God deliver them into thy hand, and thou lead them away captives, And seest in the number of the captives a beautiful woman, and lovest her and wilt have her to wife, Thou shalt bring her into thy house: and she shall shave her hair, and pare her nails, And shall put off the raiment, wherein she was taken: and shall remain in thy house, and mourn for her father and mother one month: and after that thou shalt go in unto her, and shalt sleep with her, and she shall be thy wife.]

Jerome defends his reading of the pagan text on the basis of its carnal attractiveness, the elegance of classical style: "Is it surprising that I, too, admiring the fairness of her form and the grace of her eloquence, desire to make that secular wisdom which is my captive and handmaid, a matron of the true Israel?"[7] He is attracted by its beauty, but, finally, the way to read the pagan text properly is to *divest* it of its sinful seductions, its Pauline deadness: to strip it of its garments, shave its hair, and pare its nails.

Nevertheless, the text, though stripped, doesn't stop being a woman. The Pauline model *would* discard the female when the male spirit has been uncovered. But Jerome's captive woman is instead betrothed and married (indeed, this is an enactment of the paradigm of marriage as a trade of women between men at war that Lévi-Strauss outlines[8]); she begets servants for God, just like Richard of Bury's "sons." The truth of the text is itself feminine and fertile. The alien woman, of an enemy people, has been won by the triumphant warrior; her pagan seductions have been removed, but her essential beauties are nurtured by washing, shaving, and clothing and are now put to Christian use. The text's wisdom and truth are the key to the increase and multiplication of the faithful; the warrior takes the alien from her people, has her unclothed and reclothed in a ritual preparation for the nuptials, and transforms her from alien seductress to fecund wife.

Jerome thus represents the reading of the pagan text as a captive woman's passage between men, her marriage, and her domestication. The reader is drawn to the text by its attractive appearance; the text is then interpreted—stripped of its stylistic and fictional blandishments, revealing and preparing its wisdom for Christian use. Jerome stresses the harsh necessity of taking a sharp razor to the woman, of making her bald, of scrubbing her with niter, of getting rid of all her carnal attractions.[9] That harshness is an index of the urgency in early Christendom of putting behind the temptations of pagan literature. But the act of interpretation is itself pleasurable, as the metaphor of ritual

7. Jerome, *Epistulae*, letter 70 (to Magnus), ed. I. Hilberg, CSEL 54 (Vienna: F. Tempsky, 1910), 1:702; trans. W. H. Fremantle, *A Select Library of Nicene and Post-Nicene Fathers of the Christian Church* 1892; rpt. Grand Rapids, Mich.: Eerdmans, n.d., 6: 149.
8. In a note to an earlier passage not included here, Dinshaw cites Claude Lévi-Strauss's *Structural Anthropology* (trans. 1963) and *Elementary Structures of Kinship* (trans. 1969), as well as Gayle Rubin's "The Traffic in Women': Notes toward a 'Political Economy' of Sex" (1975).
9. See Jerome, *Epistulae*, letter 66 (to Pammachius) (1:658).

purification and arraying for the bridal suggests.[1] The tradition of later exegetes who use this figure of the beautiful captive confirms this sense that both harshness and pleasure are intimated here: the commentators fall into two camps, "les accueillants et les sévères," according to de Lubac.[2] Augustine acknowledges this pleasure of interpretation—with a certain amount of wonder—in relation to the figurative surface of some scriptural passages, in his *De doctrina*:

> No one doubts that things are perceived more readily through similitudes and that what is sought with difficulty is discovered with more pleasure.[3]

There is pleasure in the very act of interpretation—in the discovering and converting the truth of the text under the figures and ornaments of its letter. Boccaccio quotes both Augustine and Petrarch (*Invectives*, bk. 3) on this "delightful task" (*Genealogia* 14.12).

In Jerome's example of the captive woman, the pleasure is one-way: the woman's desires are not consulted or recognized. Indeed, as she is passed between men, from alien camp to Israelite household, masculine desire is the only motivating force. Guillaume de St.-Thierry calls attention (albeit inadvertently) to this ignoring of the female's desire (continued by all the others who follow Jerome's use of the figure) when he unprecedentedly adapts the captive image to represent the human soul longing for Christ, the victorious warrior.[4] In other uses of the image, by Peter Damian and Gregory IX, for example, the woman is to be "enslaved" by the warrior. Gregory IX reduces the image rather severely in an early twelfth-century letter: the captive woman should be obedient and subject to the warrior, just as man should dominate woman and spirit should dominate flesh.[5] Any subtle attractions and interactions of bride and warrior, text and interpreter are eliminated by Gregory here, and one point is clear: no independent desire of woman is vouchsafed. The value of the feminine (and the letter) is thus shifting and contradictory in exegetical tradition, ranging from Jerome's apparent nurturing of the feminine to Gregory's drastic reduction. But the hermeneutic paradigm itself remains resolutely patriarchal.

✳ ✳ ✳

1989

---

1. Jerome returns to this metaphor at two other important interpretive moments: letter 21 (to Damasus), and letter 66 (to Pammachius). As Laura Kendrick has recently suggested, interpretive pleasure lies not solely in the transformation of the carnal text into a spiritual one but also "in preserving, by such legitimization, the arousing, carnal images of the original text" (*Chaucerian Play: Comedy and Control in the "Canterbury Tales"* [Berkeley: University of California Press, 1988], p. 28). Her original and provocative argument concerns interpretation as more a veiling—a cover-up—than a stripping, but her comments on serious exegesis as "feed[ing] on the arousing aspects of the text" while taming and transforming them are appropriate to my discussion here.

2. Henri de Lubac, *Exégèse médiévale*, vol. 1, pt. 1, p. 300. ["*Les accueillants et les sévères*": the welcoming and the severe (French)—editor's note.]

3. Augustine, *De doctrina* 2.6.8; trans. Robertson, in *Preface to Chaucer*, p. 38. It is significant that both Augustine and Jerome quote the *Canticles* in this connection: that text is an intensely erotic one whose female object is transformed from secular bride to the Church, in a pleasurable application of the cloak of interpretation.

4. Guillaume de St.-Thierry, *Expositio super Cantica canticorum* 4 (PL 180:473–546; quoted in de Lubac, *Exégèse médiévale*, vol. 1, pt. 1, pp. 301–2). De Lubac also implicitly acknowledges this ignoring of female desire when he comments that Peter the Venerable could hardly use the image in his correspondence with Heloise and so uses Augustine's Egyptian gold image (p. 298).

5. Gregory IX to the masters of theology at Paris, 7 July 1228; cited by de Lubac, *Exégèse médiévale*, vol. 1, pt. 1, p. 300.

DIANA FUSS
b. 1960

Three of Diana Fuss's quite distinct scholarly inquiries and one important edited anthology demonstrate her ability to negotiate between different sorts of differences in nuanced critical reflections. *Essentially Speaking: Feminism, Nature and Difference* (1989), from which our selection is taken, examines the conflicts between so-called essentialists and so-called social constructionists in order to engage feminists on both sides of this debate in more productive dialogues. Framed by a psychoanalytic approach, *Identification Papers* (1995) takes on the dynamics of identification within homophobic and racist contexts that place social pressures on what or who particular human beings identify with or as. Informed by architectural theory, *The Sense of an Interior: Four Writers and the Rooms That Shaped Them* (2004) meditates on the ways in which creativity is fashioned by and in turn fashions the physical locations within which writing takes place. The winner of several awards, the anthology *Inside/Out: Lesbian Theories, Gay Theories* (1991) helped establish the field of queer theory through essays that addressed AIDS, pornography, pedagogy, activism, and popular as well as high cultural representations of sexuality. Since 1988, Diana Fuss has taught at Princeton University.

From Essentially Speaking

1. The "Risk" of Essence

One of the prime motivations behind the production of this book is the desire to break or in some way to weaken the hold which the essentialist/constructionist binarism has on feminist theory. It is my conviction that the deadlock created by the long-standing controversy over the issue of human essences (essential femininity, essential blackness, essential gayness . . .) has, on the one hand, encouraged more careful attention to cultural and historical specificities where perhaps we have hitherto been too quick to universalize but, on the other hand, foreclosed more ambitious investigations of specificity and difference by fostering a certain paranoia around the perceived threat of essentialism. It could be said that the tension produced by the essentialist/constructionist debate is responsible for some of feminist theory's greatest insights, that is, the very tension is constitutive of the field of feminist theory. But it can also be maintained that this same dispute has created the current impasse in feminism, an impasse predicated on the difficulty of theorizing the social in relation to the natural, or the theoretical in relation to the political. The very confusion over whether or not the essentialist/constructionist tension is beneficial or detrimental to the health of feminism is itself overdetermined and constrained by the terms of the opposition in question.

One needs, therefore, to tread cautiously when mapping the boundaries of this important structuring debate for feminism. This chapter will begin by identifying the two key positions which are largely responsible for the current deadlock, and it will discuss some of the strengths and weaknesses of each position. One of the main contentions of this book is that essentialism, when held most under suspicion by constructionists, is often effectively doing its work elsewhere, under other guises, and sometimes laying the groundwork for its own critique. The bulk of the chapter will therefore address the way in which essentialism is *essential* to social constructionism, a point that powerfully throws into question the stability and impermeability of the essentialist/constructionist binarism. To this end I will look closely at currently two of the most important and influential theories of anti-essentialism, Lacanian psychoanalysis and Derridean deconstruction. In both cases I intend to demonstrate the way in which the logic of essentialism can be shown to be irreducible even in those discourses most explicitly concerned with repudiating it.

ESSENTIALISM VS. CONSTRUCTIONISM

Essentialism is classically defined as a belief in true essence—that which is most irreducible, unchanging, and therefore constitutive of a given person or thing. This definition represents the traditional Aristotelian understanding of essence, the definition with the greatest amount of currency in the history of Western metaphysics.[1] In feminist theory, essentialism articulates itself in a variety of ways and subtends a number of related assumptions. Most obviously, essentialism can be located in appeals to a pure or original femininity, a female essence, outside the boundaries of the social and thereby untainted (though perhaps repressed) by a patriarchal order. It can also be read in the accounts of universal female oppression, the assumption of a totalizing symbolic system which subjugates all women everywhere, throughout history and across cultures. Further, essentialism underwrites claims for the autonomy of a female voice and the potentiality of a feminine language (notions which find their most sophisticated expression in the much discussed concept of *écriture féminine*).[2] Essentialism emerges perhaps most strongly within the very discourse of feminism, a discourse which presumes upon the unity of its object of inquiry (women) *even* when it is at pains to demonstrate the differences within this admittedly generalizing and imprecise category.

Constructionism, articulated in opposition to essentialism and concerned with its philosophical refutation, insists that essence is itself a historical construction. Constructionists take the refusal of essence as the inaugural moment of their own projects and proceed to demonstrate the way previously assumed self-evident kinds (like "man" or "woman") are in fact the effects of complicated discursive practices. Anti-essentialists are engaged in interrogating the intricate and interlacing processes which work together to produce all seemingly "natural" or "given" objects. What is at stake for a constructionist are systems of representations, social and material practices, laws of discourses, and ideological effects. In short, constructionists are concerned above all with the *production* and *organization* of differences, and they there-

1. A comprehensive discussion of the essence/accident distinction is elaborated in Book Z [7] of Aristotle's *Metaphysics*. For a history of the philosophical concept of essentialism, readers might wish to consult David H. DeGrood, *Philosophies of Essence: An Examination of the Category of Essence* (Amsterdam: B. R. Gruner Publishing, 1976), or Richard Rorty, *Philosophy and the Mirror of Nature* (Princeton: Princeton University Press, 1979). [Except as indicated, all notes are Fuss's.]
2. See, for example, Hélène Cixous's contribution to Cixous and Catherine Clément, *La jeune neé* (1975), trans. Betsy Wing as *The Newly Born Woman* (Minneapolis: University of Minnesota Press, 1986).

fore reject the idea that any essential or natural givens precede the processes of social determination.[3]

Essentialists and constructionists are most polarized around the issue of the relation between the social and the natural. For the essentialist, the natural provides the raw material and determinative starting point for the practices and laws of the social. For example, sexual difference (the division into "male" and "female") is taken as prior to social differences which are presumed to be mapped on to, *a posteriori*, the biological subject. For the constructionist, the natural is itself posited as a construction of the social. In this view, sexual difference is discursively produced, elaborated as an effect of the social rather than its *tabula rasa*, its prior object. Thus while the essentialist holds that the natural is *repressed* by the social, the constructionist maintains that the natural is *produced* by the social.[4] The difference in philosophical positions can be summed up by Ernest Jones's question: "Is woman born or made?" For an essentialist like Jones, woman is born not made; for an anti-essentialist like Simone de Beauvoir, woman is made not born.[5]

Each of these positions, essentialism and constructionism, has demonstrated in the range of its deployment certain analytical strengths and weaknesses. The problems with essentialism are perhaps better known. Essentialist arguments frequently make recourse to an ontology which stands outside the sphere of cultural influence and historical change. "Man" and "woman," to take one example, are assumed to be ontologically stable objects, coherent signs which derive their coherency from their unchangeability and predictability (there have *always* been men and women it is argued). No allowance is made for the historical production of these categories which would necessitate a recognition that what the classical Greeks understood by "man" and "woman" is radically different from what the Renaissance French understood them to signify or even what the contemporary postindustrial, postmodernist, poststructuralist theoretician is likely to understand by these terms. "Man" and "woman" are not stable or universal categories, nor do they have the explanatory power they are routinely invested with. Essentialist arguments are not necessarily ahistorical, but they frequently theorize history as an unbroken continuum that transports, across cultures and through time,

3. I want to emphasize here that most feminist theorists are, in fact, *both* essentialists and constructionists. E. Ann Kaplan, who often takes the essentialist/anti-essentialist distinction as a primary organizational frame in her discussions of film and television criticism, has identified four "types" of feminism: bourgeois feminism, Marxist feminism, radical feminism, and poststructuralist feminism ("Feminist Criticism and Television," in *Channels of Discourse: Television and Contemporary Criticism,* ed. Robert C. Allen [Chapel Hill: University of North Carolina Press, 1987], 216). The first three types—bourgeois, Marxist, and radical—Kaplan categorizes under the rubric "essentialist"; the fourth type—poststructuralist—she labels "anti-essentialist." I would submit that the division here is much too simplistic to be useful: it sees *all* poststructuralist feminists as anti-essentialists and *all other* feminists as essentialists. Such a schema cannot adequately account, for example, for the work of Luce Irigaray, a poststructuralist Derridean who many consider to be an essentialist; nor can it account for a theorist like

Monique Wittig who appears to fall into at least two of Kaplan's essentialist categories, Marxist feminism and radical feminism, and yet who identifies herself as a committed social constructionist. We must be extremely wary of using the constructionist/essentialist opposition as a taxonomic device for elaborating oversimplified and deceptive typologies (another powerful argument to be made in favor of working to subvert, rather than to reify, this particularly pervasive dualism).

4. I am reminded of that curious but common saying, "second nature." The qualifier "second" implies orders, gradations, types of "nature." It further implies that some "kinds" of nature may be closer to the ideal or prototype than others—indeed, that some may be more "natural" than others. Essentialism here crumbles under the weight of its own self-contradiction and opens the door to viewing essence as a social construct, a production of language.

5. Beauvoir famously made this claim in *The Second Sex* (1949; trans. 1952). Jones (1879–1958), Welsh psychoanalyst [editor's note].

categories such as "man" and "woman" without in any way (re)defining or indeed (re)constituting them. History itself is theorized as essential, and thus unchanging; its essence is to generate change but not itself to *be* changed.

Constructionists, too, though they might make recourse to historicity as a way to challenge essentialism, nonetheless often work with uncomplicated or essentializing notions of history. While a constructionist might recognize that "man" and "woman" are produced across a spectrum of discourses, the categories "man" and "woman" still remain constant. Some minimal point of commonality and continuity necessitates at least the linguistic retention of these particular terms. The same problem emerges with the sign "history" itself, for while a constructionist might insist that we can only speak of *histories* (just as we can only speak of feminisms or deconstructionisms) the question that remains unanswered is what motivates or dictates the continued semantic use of the term "histories"? This is just one of many instances which suggest that essentialism is more entrenched in constructionism than we previously thought. In my mind, it is difficult to see how constructionism can *be* constructionism without a fundamental dependency upon essentialism.

It is common practice in social constructionist argumentation to shift from the singular to the plural in order to privilege heterogeneity and to highlight important cultural and social differences. Thus, woman becomes women, history becomes histories, feminism becomes feminisms, and so on. While this maneuver does mark a break with unitary conceptual categories (eternal woman, totalizing history, monolithic feminism), the hasty attempts to pluralize do not operate as sufficient defenses or safeguards against essentialism. The plural category "women," for instance, though conceptually signaling heterogeneity nonetheless semantically marks a collectivity; constructed or not, "women" still occupies the space of a linguistic unity. It is for this reason that a statement like "American women are 'x' " is no less essentializing than its formulation in the singular, "*The* American woman is 'x.' " The essentialism at stake is not countered so much as *displaced*.

If essentialism is more entrenched in constructionist logic than we previously acknowledged, if indeed there is no sure way to bracket off and to contain essentialist maneuvers in anti-essentialist arguments, then we must also simultaneously acknowledge that there is no essence to essentialism, that essence *as* irreducible has been *constructed* to be irreducible. Furthermore, if we can never securely displace essentialism, then it becomes useful for analytical purposes to distinguish between *kinds* of essentialisms, as John Locke has done with his theory of "real" versus "nominal" essence. Real essence connotes the Aristotelian understanding of essence as that which is most irreducible and unchanging about a thing; nominal essence signifies for Locke a view of essence as merely a linguistic convenience, a classificatory fiction we need to categorize and to label. Real essences are discovered by close empirical observation; nominal essences are not "discovered" so much as assigned or produced—produced specifically by language.[6] This specific distinction

6. For example, the nominal essence of gold (Locke's favorite example) would be "that complex idea the word gold stands for, let it be, for instance, a body yellow, of a certain weight, malleable, fusible, and fixed"; its real essence would be "the constitution of the insensible parts of that body, on which those qualities, and all the other properties of gold depend" (John Locke, *An Essay Concerning Human Understanding* [London: Printed by Elizabeth Holt for Thomas Bassett, 1690], 13.6). Locke discusses real versus nominal essence in numerous passages of *An Essay Concerning Human Understanding*, the most important of which are 2.31; 3.3; 3.6; 3.10; 4.6; and 4.12.

between real and nominal essence corresponds roughly to the broader oppositional categories of essentialism and constructionism: an essentialist assumes that innate or given essences sort objects naturally into species or kinds, whereas a constructionist assumes that it is language, the names arbitrarily affixed to objects, which establishes their existence in the mind. To clarify, a rose by any other name would still be a rose—for an essentialist; for a constructionist, a rose by any other name would not be a rose, it would be something altogether rather different.

Certainly, Locke's distinction between real and nominal essence is a useful one for making a political wedge into the essentialist/constructionist debate. When feminists today argue for maintaining the notion of a *class* of women, usually for political purposes, they do so I would suggest on the basis of Locke's nominal essence. It is Locke's distinction between nominal and real essence which allows us to work with the category of "women" as a *linguistic* rather than a natural kind, and for this reason Locke's category of nominal essence is especially useful for anti-essentialist feminists who want to hold onto the notion of women as a group without submitting to the idea that it is "nature" which categorizes them as such. And yet, however useful the "real" versus "nominal" classification may be for clarifying the relation between essence and language (transposing essence as an effect of language), the distinction it proposes is far from an absolute one. Real essence is itself a nominal essence—that is, a linguistic kind, a product of naming. And nominal essence is still an essence, suggesting that despite the circulation of different kinds of essences, they still all share a common classification *as essence*. I introduce the Lockean theory of essence to suggest both that it is crucial to discriminate between the ontological and linguistic orders of essentialism and that it is equally important to investigate their complicities as types of essentialisms, members of the same semantic family.

My point here, and throughout this book, is that social constructionists do not definitively escape the pull of essentialism, that indeed essentialism subtends the very idea of constructionism. Let me take another example, one often cited as the exemplary problem which separates the essentialist from the constructionist: the question of "the body." For the essentialist, the body occupies a pure, pre-social, pre-discursive space. The body is "real," accessible, and transparent; it is always *there* and directly interpretable through the senses. For the constructionist, the body is never simply there, rather it is composed of a network of effects continually subject to sociopolitical determination. The body is "always already" culturally mapped; it never exists in a pure or uncoded state. Now the strength of the constructionist position is its rigorous insistence on the production of social categories like "the body" and its attention to systems of representation. But this strength is not built on the grounds of essentialism's demise, rather it works its power by strategically deferring the encounter with essence, displacing it, in this case, onto the concept of sociality.

To say that the body is always already deeply embedded in the social is not by any sure means to preclude essentialism. Essentialism is embedded in the idea of the social and lodged in the problem of social determination (and even, as I will later argue, directly implicated in the deconstructionist turn of phrase "always already"). Too often, constructionists presume that the category of the social automatically escapes essentialism, in contradistinction to the way the category of the natural is presupposed to be inevitably entrapped within it. But there is no compelling reason to assume that the natural is, in essence, essentialist and that the social is, in essence, constructionist. If we are to intervene effectively in the impasse created by the essentialist/constructionist divide, it might be necessary to begin questioning the *constructionist* assumption that nature and fixity go together (naturally) just as sociality and change go together (naturally). In other words, it may be time to ask whether essences can change and whether constructions can be normative.

LACANIAN PSYCHOANALYSIS

It has often been remarked that biological determinism and social determinism are simply two sides of the same coin: both posit an utterly passive subject subordinated to the shaping influence of either nature or culture, and both disregard the unsettling effects of the psyche.[7] There is a sense in which social constructionism can be unveiled as merely a form of sociological essentialism, a position predicated on the assumption that the subject is, in essence, a social construction. It may well be that at this particular historical moment it has become imperative to retrieve the subject from a total subordination to social determination. Perhaps that is why so many feminist theorists have turned to psychoanalysis as a more compelling, less essentializing account of the constructionist process. Psychoanalysis is in many ways the anti-essentialist discourse *par excellence* in that sexual difference is taken as something to be *explained* rather than assumed. But even psychoanalysis cannot do its work without making recourse to certain essentialist assumptions.

This is an important point since, next to deconstruction, psychoanalysis is generally the discourse most strongly identified as sufficiently able to repudiate metaphysical idealism and its reliance upon essentialism. Lacan refuses all treatments of the subject which take as self-evident an essential, pre-given identity; he is more concerned with displacing the classical humanist subject by demonstrating the production of the subject in language. I will have much more to say about Lacan's semiotic decentering of the subject in subsequent chapters, but for now I am interested in whether an account of the subject based on language can fully detach itself from the essentialist notions it claims so persistently to disinherit. I locate three main areas where Lacan leans heavily on essentialist underpinnings in order to advance an anti-essentialist argument: his emphasis on the speaking subject; his much heralded return to Freud; and, finally, his controversial theory of woman. Each of these points will be addressed in turn, but first it is imperative not to miss the point that constructionism is heavily indebted to Lacan for some of its greatest insights. Even a necessarily abbreviated account of Lacan's sophisticated and complex theory of the psyche will underscore the immense importance of his work for social constructionists.

Lacan's contribution to constructionism emerges out of his revision of some key Freudian concepts. For Freud, the Oedipus complex is the funda-

---

7. Currently, the subjects of agency, change, and determination are beginning to receive more careful consideration, especially from social constructionists. In my mind, one of the most impressive attempts to come to grips with this difficult series of problems is Paul Smith's *Discerning the Subject* (Minneapolis: University of Minnesota Press, 1988).

mental structure responsible for the formation of sexual identity in the child. But Lacan insists that while oedipal relations and the complicated processes of identification and desire they engender are crucial to the child's psychical development, the Oedipus complex is not a given but rather itself a problem to be elucidated through psychoanalytic inquiry. According to Lacan, Freud "falsifies the conception of the Oedipus complex from the start, by making it define as natural, rather than normative, the predominance of the paternal figure."[8] For Lacan the Oedipus complex is not biologically framed but symbolically cast; in fact, it is a product of that order which Lacan labels "the Symbolic." More specifically, the Symbolic represents the order of language which permits the child entry into subjectivity, into the realm of speech, law, and sociality. The Imaginary signifies the mother-child dyad which the Symbolic interrupts through the agency of the paternal function—the "Name-of-the-Father," rather than the biological father *per se*. Through this important shift from the father to the Name-of-the-Father, Lacan denaturalizes the Oedipal structure which Freud takes as universal, de-essentializes Freud's theory of subject constitution by opening it up to the play of language, symbol, and metaphor.

A second important point of revision which further positions Lacan as more "truly" anti-essentialist than Freud pertains to the role of the phallus in sexual differentiation. Here, too, Lacan faults his predecessor for failing to make the crucial distinction between anatomical organ (the penis) and representational symbol (the phallus). Freud repeatedly collapses the two, leaving himself vulnerable to charges of biologism and essentialism. Lacan is more careful to separate them, insisting that the phallus is not a fantasy, not an object, and most especially not an organ (the penis or the clitoris).[9] The phallus is instead a *signifier*, a privileged signifier of the Symbolic order which may point to the penis as the most visible mark of sexual difference but nevertheless cannot be reduced to it. This non-coincidence of phallus and penis is important because "the relation of the subject to the phallus is set up regardless of the anatomical difference between the sexes" ("The Meaning of the Phallus," 76). In a sense, the phallus is *prior* to the penis; it is the privileged mark through which both sexes accede to sexual identity by a recognition and acceptance of castration.

There are a number of problems with Lacan's penis/phallus distinction which will be discussed here and at greater length in Chapter Four. To the extent that the phallus risks continually conjuring up images of the penis, that is, to the extent that the bar between these two terms cannot be rigidly sustained, Lacan is never very far from the essentialism he so vigorously disclaims. It is true that the phallus is *not* the penis in any simple way; as a signifier it operates as a sign in a signifying chain, a symbolic metaphor and not a natural fact of difference. But it is also true that this metaphor derives its power from the very object it symbolizes; the phallus is pre-eminently a metaphor but it is also metonymically close to the penis and derives much of its signifying importance from this by no means arbitrary relation. It is precisely because a woman does not have a penis that her relation to the phallus, the signifying order, the order of language and the law, is so complicated

8. Jacques Lacan, "Intervention on Transference," in *Feminine Sexuality: Jacques Lacan and the école freudienne*, by Juliet Mitchell and Jacqueline Rose

(New York: Norton, 1982), 69.
9. Jacques Lacan, "The Meaning of the Phallus," in Mitchell and Rose, *Feminine Sexuality*, 79.

and fraught with difficulties. The privileging of the phallus as "transcendental signifier" (the signifier without a signified) has led to charges that Lacan is endorsing the phallocentrism he purports to critique. Luce Irigaray and Jacques Derrida have both detected in Lacan a perpetuation and strengthening of phallocentrism rather than its undoing.[1] This charge in turn has led to counter-charges that Lacan's detractors have confused the messenger with the message; at least two important defenders of Lacan, Juliet Flower Mac-Cannell and Ellie Ragland-Sullivan, insist that Lacan is merely *describing* the effects of a phallocentric logic and not *prescribing* or in any way deploying them himself.[2] But in my mind these defenses are ultimately unconvincing, since "description" is never a pure form and can never escape a certain complicity with its object. Derrida, one of the first to take Lacan to task for the "phallogocentric transcendentalism" of his thinking, observes that "description is a 'participant' when it induces a practice, an ethics, and an institution, and therefore a politics that insure the truth of the tradition."[3] Such is the case with Lacan I would argue. But I must also add that despite Derrida's disclaimers that he has produced anything resembling a practice, an ethics, an institution, or a politics, Derridean deconstruction is no less "free" than Lacanian psychoanalysis from a pervasive albeit hidden (all the more pervasive because it is hidden) reliance upon essentialism. Both discourses profess to inhabit a theoretical space free of the taint of essentialism, but as I now hope to show, the very staking out of a *pure* anti-essentialist position simply reinscribes an inescapable essentialist logic.

While Lacan strategically employs linguistics to clean Freud's house of biologism, essentialism quietly returns to poststructuralist psychoanalysis through the back door, carried on the soles of Lacan's theory of signification. Lacan is careful to specify that when he says the subject is constituted in language, language does *not* signify for him mere social discourse. Lacan is here following Ferdinand de Saussure's description of language as a system of relational signs, where meaning is a product of differences between signs and not an essential property of any fixed sign. Saussure makes a well-known distinction between "speech" and "language" in which speech (the individual communication act) is "accidental" and language (the communal system of rules and codes which govern speech) is "essential."[4] Lacan, recognizing the inseparability of one from the other, sees both language and speech as "essential" to the founding of the human subject. For Lacan is first and foremost concerned with "the speaking subject" and with "the subjection of the subject to the signifier."[5] In Lacanian psychoanalysis, speech is firmly inscribed as a discourse of truth; simply put, "speech connotes truth."[6] The case can

1. See Luce Irigaray, "Così Fan Tutti," in *Ce Sexe qui n'en est pas un* (1977), trans. Catherine Porter with Carolyn Burke as *This Sex Which Is Not One* (Ithaca, N.Y.: Cornell University Press, 1985), and Jacques Derrida, "Le Facteur de la Vérité," in *La carte postale* (1980), trans. Alan Bass as *The Post Card* (Chicago: University of Chicago Press, 1987).
2. See Juliet Flower MacCannell, *Figuring Lacan: Criticism and the Cultural Unconscious* (Lincoln: University of Nebraska Press, 1986), chap. 1, and Ellie Ragland-Sullivan, *Jacques Lacan and the Philosophy of Psychoanalysis* (Urbana: University of Illinois Press, 1986), chap. 5.

3. Derrida, "Le Facteur de la Vérité," in *The Post Card*, 481.
4. Ferdinand de Saussure, *Course in General Linguistics* (1915), trans. Wade Baskin (New York: Philosophical Library, 1959), 14.
5. Jacques Lacan, "The Subversion of the Subject and the Dialectic of Desire in the Freudian Unconscious," in *Écrits*, trans. Alan Sheridan (New York: Norton, 1977), 304.
6. Jacques Lacan, "The Function and Field of Speech and Language in Psychoanalysis," in *Écrits*, 43. As we might expect, Derrida criticizes Lacan's adherence to the metaphysical privilege accorded to speech over writing. Idealism, Derrida argues, is

be stated even more strongly. What is irreducible to the discourse of psycho-analysis ("the talking cure") is speech. And, within the terms of this discourse, what is universal to psychoanalysis is the production of the subject *in the Symbolic*. From its institutional beginnings, psychoanalysis has relied upon "the function and field of speech and language" as its essential de-essentializing mechanisms of subject constitution, and (in Lacan's own words) it has taken as "self-evident fact that it deals solely with words."[7]

This brings us to the essentialism within Lacan's overall aim to return the institution of psychoanalysis to its authentic Freudian roots. Lacan's mission is to restore psychoanalysis to its essential truths, to what is most radical and irreducible about it. I must disagree with those commentators on Lacan who interpret his notion of a "return to Freud" as "merely a slogan."[8] Lacan's goal is to reinstate the truth of psychoanalysis, to recapture "the Freudian experi-ence along authentic lines."[9] The "return to Freud" may be in part a slogan (a rallying cry to turn psychoanalysis away from the distorted humanist appro-priations of Freud by object-relations theorists and other post-Freudians) but it is also a symptom of Lacan's own complicity with an unacknowledged humanism (a sign of a certain susceptibility to the lure of meaning and Truth). In "The Freudian Thing, or the Meaning of the Return to Freud in Psychoanalysis," Lacan employs the logic of the chiasmus to argue that "the meaning of a return to Freud is a return to the meaning of Freud."[1] The "return to Freud" cannot be easily divorced from the notions of authenticity, recuperation, and truth-discourse which it repeatedly invokes. Perhaps it is this indissociability of the idea of return from the ideology of humanism which compels Lacan to acknowledge, at the end of the English selection of *Ecrits*, that it is humanism which marks the return of the repressed in his own work: "I must admit that I am partial to a certain form of humanism, a humanism that . . . has a certain quality of candour about it: 'When the miner comes home, his wife rubs him down . . . ' I am left defenceless against such things."[2]

The choice of a working-class couple (a wife attending to the material bod-ily needs of her miner-husband) to signal his "defencelessness" in the face of lived experience is an unusual example for Lacan, who generally makes few references in his work to class positions or material relations. This tendency points to an important vestige of essentialism in Lacan's theory of subjectiv-ity: the assumption that the subject is raceless and classless. The Lacanian subject is a sexed subject first and last; few allowances are made for the way in which other modes of difference might complicate or even facilitate the account of identity formation Lacan outlines along the axis of sex alone. Within the specific realm of sexual differentiation, essentialism emerges most strongly in Lacan's very attempts to displace the essence of "woman." Of real

lodged in Lacan's emphasis on *logos as phonē*, on the truth of the spoken word, on the privileging of voice and the vocalizable (see "Le Facteur de la Vérité," 413–96).

7. Lacan, "Intervention on Transference," 63.
8. Bice Benvenuto and Roger Kennedy, *The Works of Jacques Lacan* (New York: St. Martin's Press, 1986), 10. These writers are correct to point out that most if not all psychoanalysts presume to have access to the "real" Freud; however, in a project as

rigorously anti-essentialist as Lacan's, the reten-tion of this mythology of the true Freud cannot be so easily dismissed—it must be *explained*.
9. Lacan, "Agency of the Letter in the Uncon-scious or Reason Since Freud," in *Écrits*, 171.
1. Jacques Lacan, "The Freudian Thing," in *Écrits*, 117.
2. Jacques Lacan, "The Subversion of the Subject and the Dialectic of Desire in the Freudian Uncon-scious," in *Écrits*, 324.

material women, such as the miner's wife, Lacan has nothing to say, readily admits his knowing ignorance. But of "woman" as sign Lacan has everything to say (especially since women, as we shall see, cannot say "it" themselves).

In Seminar XX, devoted to the enigma of woman and the riddle of femininity, Lacan tells us that woman, as such, does not exist:

> when any speaking being whatever lines up under the banner of women it is by being constituted as not all that they are placed within the phallic function. It is this that defines the . . . the what?—the woman precisely, except that *The* woman can only be written with *The* crossed through. There is no such thing as *The* woman, where the definite article stands for the universal.[3]

On the surface, Lacan's erasure of the "The" in "The woman" is a calculated effort to de-essentialize woman. Eternal Woman, the myth of Woman, Transcendental Woman—all are false universals for Lacan, held in place only by the dubious efforts of the "signifier which cannot signify anything"—the definite article "the" ("God and the *Jouissance* of ~~The~~ Woman," 144). But is Lacan's mathematical "woman" (in "Seminar of 21 January 1975" he describes woman as an "empty set") any less universalizing than the metaphysical notion of woman he seeks to challenge? Essence quickly reappears as a "risk" Lacan cannot resist taking: "There is no such thing as *The* woman since of her essence—having already risked the term, why think twice about it?—of her essence, she is not all" ("God and the *Jouissance* of ~~The~~ Woman," 144). The project to de-essentialize "woman" is activated on the grounds of simultaneously re-essentializing her. The "risk" lies in the double gesture, the very process of transgressing the essentialist/constructionist divide.

In defining the essence of woman as "not all," the penis/phallus distinction once again comes into play, but this time as a way to keep essentialism in place. "It is through the phallic function that man takes up his inscription as all," Lacan explains in "A Love Letter."[4] All speaking beings are allowed to place themselves on the side of the not all, on the side of woman. Woman's supplementary *jouissance*, a *jouissance* "beyond the phallus," is "proper" to biological women but not exclusive to them. Men (specifically male mystics for Lacan) can also occupy the subject-position "woman"; in fact, "there are men who are just as good as women. It does happen" ("God and the *Jouissance* of ~~The~~ Woman," 147). But, importantly, the converse is not true for Lacan: not all speaking beings are allowed to inscribe themselves on the side of the all, since only men have penises which give them more direct access to "the phallic function." Exclusion from *total* access to the Symbolic's privileged transcendental signifier has certain implications for the already castrated woman, not the least of which is a highly problematized relation to speech and language. "There is woman only as excluded by the nature of things which is the nature of words" we are told ("God and the *Jouissance* of ~~The~~ Woman," 144). Speaking specifically of woman's *jouissance* beyond the phallus, Lacan can only conclude that it is "impossible to tell whether the woman can say anything about it—whether she can say what she knows of it" ("A Love Letter," 159).

---

3. Jacques Lacan, "God and the *Jouissance* of ~~The~~ Woman," in Mitchell and Rose, Feminine Sexuality, 144.

4. Jacques Lacan, "A Love Letter," in Mitchell and Rose, *Feminine Sexuality*, 150.

Derrida's attempts to speak (as) woman have provoked considerable controversy, but little has been said of Lacan's perhaps more veiled attempts to do the same. Desire *for* the Other often manifests itself as desire to speak as Other, from the place of the Other (some would even say, *instead* of the Other). I read Lacan's difficult and equivocal style not just as a strategic evocation of the laws of the Unconscious (which is how it is usually understood) but also, since woman is presumed to be closer to the Unconscious, as an attempt to approximate the speech-less, the not all, the elusive figure of Woman who personifies Truth. Through the device of the quotation marks, Lacan literally assumes the voice of Woman/Truth in "The Freudian Thing" (esp. 121–23). But in a more general way, through the evasive and elliptical style which is his trademark, Lacan attempts to bring woman to the point of speech by approximating the vanishing point in his own speech. In his theory of woman as "not all," Lacan posits the essence of woman as an enigmatic excess or remainder. In this regard, woman remains for Lacan the enigma she was for Freud. In fact, essence operates in Lacan as a leftover classical component which re-emerges in his theory of woman precisely because it is woman who escapes complete subjection to the Symbolic and its formative operations. In her inscription as not all (as Truth, lack, Other, *objet a*,[5] God) woman becomes for Lacan the very repository of essence.

DERRIDEAN DECONSTRUCTION

And what of Derrida's theory of essence? Does Derrida "transcend" essentialism more successfully than Lacan, and if not, where is it inscribed and what implications might it hold for the most rigorous anti-essentialist discourse of all: deconstruction? My position here is that the possibility of any radical constructionism can only be built on the foundations of a hidden essentialism. Derrida would, of course, be quick to agree that despite the dislocating effects of deconstruction's strategies of reversal/displacement we can never get beyond metaphysics, and therefore, since all of Western metaphysics is predicated upon Aristotle's essence/accident distinction, we can never truly get beyond essentialism. This is why we should not be surprised to see certain metaphysical holds operative in Derrida's own work, supporting even his relentless pursuit of binary oppositions and phenomenological essences. My interest in exploring what Derrida calls "fringes of irreducibility"[6] as they operate in deconstruction itself is motivated not by a desire to demonstrate that Derrida is a *failed* constructionist (this would be a pointless exercise, given the terms of my argument) but by an interest in uncovering the ways in which deconstruction deploys essentialism against itself, leans heavily on essence in its determination to displace essence. Derrida's theory of woman is one place to start, though as I hope to show, essentialism works its logic through a number of important "Derrideanisms," including the emphasis upon undecidability and the related notions of contradiction and heterogeneity.

---

5. The other as object (*a* stands for *autre*, "other"), the unattainable that is desired [editor's note].
6. Jacques Derrida, *Positions* (1972), trans. Alan Bass as *Positions* (Chicago: University of Chicago Press, 1981), 67.

Woman and undecidability are, in fact, rather closely linked in Derrida's work. This intimate association is most evident in *Spurs* (1978)[7] where Derrida attempts to come to grips with the question "What is woman?" through a sustained reading of the inscription of woman in Nietzsche's philosophy. Woman occupies for Nietzsche the site of a contradiction: she represents both truth and non-truth, distance and proximity, wisdom and deceit, authenticity and simulation. But Derrida points out that woman can be none of these things, in essence, since "there is no such thing as a woman, as a truth in itself of woman in itself" (101). Like Lacan, Derrida's project is to displace the essence of woman, but also like Lacan, Derrida is actively engaged in the redeployment of essentialism elsewhere. For Derrida, woman operates as the very figure of undecidability. It is woman as undecidable variable who displaces the rigid dualisms of Western metaphysics: "The question of the woman suspends the decidable opposition of true and non-true and inaugurates the epochal regime of quotation marks which is to be enforced for every concept belonging to the system of philosophical decidability" (107). Woman, in short, is yet another figure for *différance*, the mechanism which undoes and disables "ontological decidability" (111). But more than this, she is the non-place which centers deconstruction's own marginal status in philosophical discourse. When Gayatri Spivak identifies the phenomenon of woman's "double displacement" in deconstruction, she is referring to the tendency of deconstruction to announce its own displacement by situating woman as a figure of displacement.[8] While there may be nothing essentialistic about this maneuver *per se*, one at least has to recognize that positing woman as a figure of displacement risks, in its effects, continually displacing real material women.

"Choreographies" (1982)[9] extends Derrida's critique of the essence of woman by warning against the dangers of seeking to locate and to identify "woman's place": "in my view there is no one place for woman. It is without a doubt risky to say that there is no place for woman, but this idea is not antifeminist . . ." (68). There is an interesting slippage here from the claim that "there is no one place for woman" to the claim that "there is no place for woman"—two rather different statements indeed. But Derrida's point seems to be simply that a "woman's place," a single place, must necessarily be essentializing. This is doubtless true, but we need to ask whether positing multiple places for women is necessarily any *less* essentializing. Does "woman's *places*" effectively challenge the unitary, metaphysical notion of the subject/woman who presumably fills these particular places and not others? Derrida also makes the claim in "Choreographies" that there is no essence of woman, at least no "essence which is rigorously or properly identifiable" (72). Here one sees more clearly the opening for essentialism's re-entry onto the stage of deconstruction, for in the end Derrida does not so much challenge that woman has an essence as insist that we can never "rigorously" or "prop-

7. Jacques Derrida, *Éperons: Les styles de Nietzsche* (1978), trans. Barbara Harlow as *Spurs: Nietzsche's Styles* (Chicago: University of Chicago Press, 1979) [hereafter cited parenthetically in the text].
8. See Gayatri Chakravorty Spivak, "Displacement and the Discourse of Woman," in *Displacement: Derrida and After,* ed. Mark Krupnick (Bloomington: Indiana University Press, 1983), 169–95; and "Love Me, Love My Ombre, Elle," *Diacritics* 14, no. 4 (Winter 1984): 19–36.
9. Jacques Derrida, "Choreographies," interview with Christie V. McDonald, *Diacritics* 12, no. 2 (Summer 1982): 66–76 [hereafter cited parenthetically in the text].

erly" identify it. Woman's essence is simply "undecidable," a position which frequently inverts itself in deconstruction to the suggestion that it is the essence of woman to *be* the undecidable. To say that woman's essence is to be the undecidable is different from claiming that woman's essence is undecidable and different still from claiming that it is undecidable whether woman has an essence at all. Derrida's theory of essence moves between and among these contradictory positions, playing upon the undecidability and ambiguity which underwrites his own deconstructionist maneuvers.

Let me shift focus then to deconstruction itself and to its decisive encounter with Husserlian phenomenology. It is by no means insignificant that Derrida's earliest published pieces manifest a preoccupation with essentialism and especially with the place of essence in phenomenology. Phenomenology is defined in Husserl's *Logical Investigations* (1901)[1] as the study of the essence of human consciousness. Essence is not a question of empirical investigation but rather a matter of pure abstractions—the very foundation of logic and mathematics. A case is made by Husserl for "an *a priori* necessity of essence" (443); objects are seen to have "pure essences" which are self-evidently true—"non-empirical, universal, and unconditionally valid" (446). Husserl believed that by removing essence from the empirical realm of natural science and relocating it in the universal realm of pure logic he was achieving a radical break with metaphysics. Essence, in this early twentieth-century phenomenological view, is not something that lies behind a given thing, but rather essence is that which is most *self-evident* and *self-given* about that thing: a figure is, in essence, a triangle if the sum of its angles add up to 180 degrees. In Husserlian phenomenology, then, it is self-evidence which operates as the basis of epistemology, the validation of the truth of all knowledge.

Derrida explicitly takes on the project to displace phenomenological essence in several of his early works, including *Speech and Phenomena* (1967),[2] and his aim is what we have now come to see as characteristically Derridean: "to see the phenomenological critique of metaphysics betray itself as a moment within the history of metaphysical assurance."[3] Because transcendental phenomenology is rooted in the idea of *givenness*, Derrida's tactic is to apply enough analytical pressure to the concept of self-evidence to pry open phenomenology's deeply rooted investments with metaphysics. To the extent that Husserl's work aspires to be a science of essence, phenomenology emerges not as metaphysics' most radical subversion but as its most successful reinscription. Phenomenology, Derrida shows, seeks not only to preserve the central place of essence in metaphysics, it also seeks to return metaphysics to its own essence—its essence as "first philosophy." Derrida's critique of Husserl's epistemology of essences is a particularly persuasive one,

1. Edmund Husserl, *Logical Investigations,* trans. N. N. Findlay (London: Routledge and Kegan Paul, 1970), vol. 2 [hereafter cited parenthetically in the text].

2. Other early interrogations of phenomenology can be found in Derrida's introduction to Husserl's *L'Origine de la Géométrie* (1962), trans. John Leavey as *Edmund Husserl's "Origin of Geometry": An Introduction* (Pittsburgh: Duquesne University Press, 1978); "Form and Meaning: A Note on the Phenomenology of Language," in *Marges de la philosophie* (1972), trans. Alan Bass as *Margins of Philosophy* (Chicago: University of Chicago Press, 1982); and " 'Genesis and Structure' and Phenomenology," in *L'Écriture et la différence* (1967), trans. David Alan Bass as *Writing and Difference* (Chicago: University of Chicago Press, 1978).

3. Jacques Derrida, *La voix et le phénomène: Introduction au problème du signe dans la phénoménologie de Husserl* (1967), trans. David Allison as *Speech and Phenomena: And Other Essays on Husserl's Theory of Signs* (Evanston, Ill.: Northwestern University Press, 1973), 5.

for he convincingly demonstrates that essences, as Husserl understands them, are pre-cultural and atemporal and therefore inescapably ontological.[4]

In yet another twist of the metaphysical screw, deconstruction itself can only sustain its project to undo the normative operations of phenomenal essences by activating the "philosopheme" of essence under other, less obvious guises. Essence manifests itself in deconstruction in that most pervasive, most recognizable of Derridean phrases, "always already" (*toujours déjà*).[5] This phrase marks a phenomenological carryover in Derrida's work, a point of refuge for essentialism which otherwise, in deconstruction, comes so consistently under attack. It is my belief that "always already" frequently appears at those points where Derrida wishes to put the brakes on the analysis in progress and to make a turn in another direction. Occurrences of "always already" (or sometimes its abbreviated form "always") function as stop signs that alert us to some of Derrida's central assumptions—for example, his assumption in "Racism's Last Word" that the name "apartheid" is not merely the "last word" but also the first word of racism: "hasn't *apartheid* always been the archival record of the unnameable?"[6] Importantly, the controversy and debate which has surrounded Derrida's piece on apartheid rests heavily on this seemingly innocent and innocuous little word, "always." Consider Anne McClintock and Rob Nixon's much debated materialist response to Derrida's "Racism's Last Word":

> When Derrida asks, "Hasn't *apartheid* always been the archival record of the unnameable?" (p. 291), the answer is a straightforward no. Despite its notoriety and currency overseas, the term *apartheid* has not always been the "watchword" of the Nationalist regime (p. 291). It has its own history, and that history is closely entwined with a developing ideology of race.

What Nixon and McClintock are objecting to is the idealism in Derrida's work, the "severance of word from history."[7] Not only do I believe that there is some basis for such a claim, I would also maintain that it is the use of the term "always" which operates as the hidden trip wire which captures the word *apartheid* in the prison house of language. Yet Derrida himself objects strongly to the charge that he has failed to historicize properly the word *apartheid*, and he objects on the grounds that Nixon and McClintock have merely substituted *their* version of "always" for *his* version of "always"—in other words, that it is they, and not he, who have taken the contested word out of its proper context:

> Once again you mistake the most evident meaning of my question. It did not concern the use of the word *by* the Nationalist regime but its *use value* in the world, "its notoriety and currency overseas," as you so rightly

---

4. Derrida also provides a particularly incisive critique of Husserl's theory of signs. As a science, phenomenology is blind to its own medium, its own status as discourse; what is self-evident in Husserl's work, and therefore outside the realm of his phenomenological investigation, is precisely the materiality of language and the historicity of the sign.

5. Though we have come to associate this phrase with Derrida, it has, in fact, a more extended philosophical history. One can detect its recurrence in the works of such disparate theorists as Husserl,

Heidegger, Althusser, and Lacan. For Derrida's discussion of Heidegger's use of "always already," see "The Ends of Man," in *Margins of Philosophy*, 124–25.

6. Jacques Derrida, "Le Dernier Mot du Racism," trans. Peggy Kamuf as "Racism's Last Word," *Critical Inquiry* 12, no. 1 (Autumn 1985): 291.

7. Anne McClintock and Rob Nixon, "No Names Apart: The Separation of Word and History in Derrida's 'Le Dernier Mot du Racisme,'" *Critical Inquiry* 13, no. 1 (Autumn 1986): 141.

put it. The word "always" in my text referred to this notoriety and there is little matter here for disagreement. But I never said that *apartheid* has "always" been the *literal* "watchword" *within* the Nationalist regime. And I find the way you manage to slip the "always" out of *my* sentence ("but hasn't *apartheid* always been the archival record of the unnameable?") and into *yours* ("the term *apartheid* has not always been the 'watchword' of the Nationalist regime") to be less than honest. To be honest, you would have had to quote the whole sentence in which I myself speak of the "watchword" as such.[8]

No one can turn a criticism back upon his opponents more dexterously and more dramatically than Derrida, and yet I am compelled to wonder why Derrida thinks his use of the term "always" is *more* "self-evident" than Nixon and McClintock's; there is a not so subtle presumption here that Nixon and McClintock have bastardized the term "always" by reading it historically, temporally, "literally"—sullied its purer metaphorical, indeed *metaphysical*, connotations with less sophisticated materialist trappings.

A danger implicit in the ready application of the logic of *toujours déjà* is the temptation to rely upon the "always already" self-evident "nature" of "always already." The fact that "always already" is a phrase that has been so readily appropriated (and on occasion parodied) in academic circles immediately casts suspicion on its efficacy. At the present moment, "always already" has such wide currency amongst poststructuralists and non-poststructuralists alike that it has lost much of the rhetorical power and energy which characterizes its appearances in Derrida's work. Consider Houston Baker's otherwise suggestive discussion of the blues as "the multiplex enabling *script* in which Afro-American cultural discourse is inscribed."[9] In *Blues, Ideology, and Afro-American Literature: A Vernacular Theory* (1984), Baker identifies the blues as the central trope in Afro-American culture, but exactly why the blues have come to function as the *primary* "script" of Afro-American literature is by no means clear. Just when we expect an explanation from Baker on his choice of the blues, he tells us that "they are what Jacques Derrida might describe as the 'always already' of Afro-American culture" (4). But why the blues? Why not, as at least one other critic of Afro-American culture has wondered, "spirituals, jubilees, hollers, work songs . . . or jazz"?[1] Or why not, for that matter, an expressive cultural form *other* than music? Baker's invocation of "always already" is a surprising moment in a context which clearly demands historicization; while the specificity of the blues genre is rigorously historicized in Baker's text, the *choice* of the blues (as the very quintessence of Afro-American expressive culture) curiously is not. The danger (and the usefulness) of "always already" is that it *implies* essence, it hints at an irreducible core that requires no further investigation. In so doing, it frequently puts a stop to analysis, often at an argument's most critical point.

In Derrida's work "always already" operates as something of a contradiction: it arrests analysis at a crucial stage, but it also shifts analytical gears and

8. Jacques Derrida, "But, beyond . . . (Open Letter to Anne McClintock and Rob Nixon)," trans. Peggy Kamuf, *Critical Inquiry* 13, no. 1 (Autumn 1986): 160 [hereafter cited parenthetically in the text].

9. Houston A. Baker Jr., *Blues, Ideology, and Afro-American Literature: A Vernacular Theory* (Chicago: University of Chicago Press, 1984), 4 [hereafter cited parenthetically in the text].

1. Stephen Tracy, review of Houston Baker's *Blues, Ideology, and Afro-American Literature*, in *MELUS* 12, no. 2 (Summer 1985): 100.

moves us along in another direction, much like the "switch engines" of one of Baker's railway roundhouses. It is a technique which deliberately frustrates closure and keeps meaning in play; but it is also a technique that relies upon the self-evidence of contradiction and heterogeneity. In his response to Nixon and McClintock, we see that what gets fetishized in Derrida's work is precisely this notion of contradiction:

> Far from relying on "monoliths" or "bulky homogeneities," I constantly emphasize heterogeneity, contradictions, tensions, and uneven development. "Contradiction" is the most frequently occurring word in my text. (165)

By my count (since we seem to be engaged in a numbers game here), the most frequently occurring word (noun?) in Derrida's "Racism's Last Word" is not "contradiction" but "apartheid." Could we not say that, within the terms of Derrida's investigation, "apartheid" has been symptomatically erased by "contradiction," and is this not Nixon and McClintock's point in the end? "Contradiction" emerges as the "always already" of deconstruction, its irreducible inner core without which it could not do its work. It is *essential* to deconstruction, and as such it runs the risk of reification and solidification, a point that Derrida seems elsewhere to be fully aware of ("Différance," for example) and yet here he does not hesitate to summon contradiction's unassailable power to silence his critics. After citing the many instances in which he spoke of contradiction in "Racism's Last Word," Derrida writes, angrily: "Is that a sign of monolithic thinking and a preference for homogeneity? This will surely have been the first time I have met with such a reproach, and I fear you deserve it more than I do" (165). Derrida holds a mirror up to his detractors and reflects their charges of "monolithic thinking" and "homogeneity" back to them; unwilling to recognize any possible contradictions within his own discourse, willing only (in surprisingly unDerridean fashion) to treat contradiction on a thematic level and not on a deeper textual level.

"THE RISK OF ESSENCE MAY HAVE TO BE TAKEN"

Despite the uncertainty and confusion surrounding the sign "essence," more than one influential theorist has advocated that perhaps we cannot do without recourse to irreducibilities. One thinks of Stephen Heath's by now famous suggestion, "the risk of essence may have to be taken."[2] It is poststructuralist feminists who seem most intrigued by this call to risk essence. Alice Jardine, for example, finds Stephen Heath's proclamation (later echoed by Gayatri Spivak) to be "one of the most thought-provoking statements of recent date."[3] But not all poststructuralist feminists are as comfortable with the prospect of re-opening theory's Pandora's box of essentialism. Peggy Kamuf warns that calls to risk essentialism may in the end be no more than veiled defenses against the unsettling operations of deconstruction:

---

2. Stephen Heath, "Difference," *Screen* 19, no. 3 (Autumn 1978): 99.
3. Alice Jardine, "Men in Feminism: Odor di Uomo or Compagnons de Route?" in *Men in Feminism*, ed. Jardine and Paul Smith (New York: Methuen, 1987), 58.

How is one supposed to understand essence as a *risk* to be run when it is by definition the non-accidental and therefore hardly the apt term to represent danger or risk? Only over against and in impatient reaction to the deconstruction of the subject can "essence" be made to sound excitingly dangerous and the phrase "the risk of essence" can seem to offer such an appealing invitation. . . . "Go for it," the phrase incites. "If you fall into 'essence,' you can always say it was an accident."[4]

In Kamuf's mind, risking essence is really no risk at all; it is merely a clever way of preserving the metaphysical safety net should we lose our balance walking the perilous tightrope of deconstruction.

But the call to risk essence is not merely an "impatient reaction" to deconstruction (though it might indeed be this in certain specific instances); it can also operate as a deconstructionist strategy. "Is not strategy itself the real risk?" Derrida asks in his seminar on feminism.[5] To the deconstructionist, strategy of any kind is a risk because its effects, its outcome, are always unpredictable and undecidable. Depending on the historical moment and the cultural context, a strategy can be "radically revolutionary or deconstructive" or it can be "dangerously reactive" (193). What is risky is giving up the security—and the fantasy—of occupying a single subject-position and instead occupying two places at once. In a word, "we have to negotiate" (202). For an example of this particular notion of "risk" we can turn to Derrida's own attempts to dare to speak as woman. For a male subject to speak as woman can be radically de-essentializing; the transgression suggests that "woman" is a social space which any sexed subject can fill. But because Derrida never specifies *which* woman he speaks as (a French bourgeois woman, an Anglo-American lesbian, and so on), the strategy to speak as woman is simultaneously re-essentializing. The risk lies in the difficult negotiation between these apparently contradictory effects.

It must be pointed out here that the constructionist strategy of specifying more precisely these sub-categories of "woman" does not necessarily preclude essentialism. "French bourgeois woman" or "Anglo-American lesbian," while crucially emphasizing in their very specificity that "woman" is by no means a monolithic category, nonetheless reinscribe an essentialist logic at the very level of historicism. Historicism is not always an effective counter to essentialism if it succeeds only in fragmenting the subject into multiple identities, each with its own self-contained, self-referential essence. The constructionist impulse to specify, rather than definitively counteracting essentialism, often simply redeploys it through the very strategy of historicization, rerouting and dispersing it through a number of micropolitical units or sub-categorical classifications, each presupposing its own unique interior composition or metaphysical core.

There is an important distinction to be made, I would submit, between "deploying" or "activating" essentialism and "falling into" or "lapsing into"

4. Peggy Kamuf, "Femmeninism," in Jardine and Smith, eds., *Men in Feminism,* 96.
5. Jacques Derrida, "Women in the Beehive," in Jardine and Smith, eds., *Men in Feminism,* 192 [hereafter cited parenthetically in the text].
6. Toril Moi's *Sexual/Textual Politics: Feminist Lit-*

essentialism. "Falling into" or "lapsing into" implies that essentialism is inherently reactionary—inevitably and inescapably a problem or a mistake.[6] "Deploying" or "activating," on the other hand, implies that essentialism may have some strategic or interventionary value. What I am suggesting is that the political investments of the sign "essence" are predicated on the subject's complex positioning in a particular social field, and that the appraisal of this investment depends not on any interior values intrinsic to the sign itself but rather on the shifting and determinative discursive relations which produced it. As subsequent chapters will more forcefully suggest, the radicality or conservatism of essentialism depends, to a significant degree, on *who* is utilizing it, *how* it is deployed, and *where* its effects are concentrated.

It is important not to forget that essence is a sign, and as such historically contingent and constantly subject to change and to redefinition. Historically, we have never been very confident of the definition of essence, nor have we been very certain that the definition of essence is to *be* the definitional. Even the essence/accident distinction, the inaugural moment of Western metaphysics, is by no means a stable or secure binarism. The entire history of metaphysics can be read as an interminable pursuit of the essence of essence, motivated by the anxiety that essence may well be accidental, changing and unknowable. Essentialism is not, and has rarely been, monolithically coded. Certainly it is difficult to identify a single philosopher whose work does not attempt to account for the question of essentialism in some way; the repeated attempts by these philosophers to fix or to define essence suggest that essence is a slippery and elusive category, and that the sign itself does not remain stationary or uniform.

The deconstruction of essentialism, rather than putting essence to rest, simply raises the discussion to a more sophisticated level, leaps the analysis up to another higher register, above all, keeps the sign of essence in play, even if (indeed *because*) it is continually held under erasure. Constructionists, then, need to be wary of too quickly crying "essentialism." Perhaps the most dangerous problem for anti-essentialists is to see the category of essence as "always already" knowable, as immediately apparent and naturally transparent. Similarly, we need to beware of the tendency to "naturalize" the category of the natural, to see this category, too, as obvious and immediately perceptible *as such*. Essentialism may be at once more intractable and more irrecuperable than we thought; it may be essential to our thinking while at the same time there is nothing "quintessential" about it. To insist that essentialism is always and everywhere reactionary is, for the constructionist, to buy into essentialism in the very act of making the charge; *it is to act as if essentialism has an essence.*

1989

erary Theory (New York: Methuen, 1985) provides a particularly good example of how this locution can be used to dismiss entire schools of feminist thought—in Moi's case, to discredit "Anglo-American" feminism. Moi's sweeping criticism of writers as diverse as Elaine Showalter, Myra Jehlen, Annette Kolodny, Sandra Gilbert, and Susan Gubar consists mainly in mapping out in detail the points in which their analyses "slip into" essentialism and therefore "reinscribe patriarchal humanism." Such an ostensibly anti-essentialist critique can only be built on the grounds of the twin assumptions that essentialism is, in essence, "patriarchal" and that "patriarchal humanism" has an essence which is inherently, inevitably reactionary.

EVE KOSOFSKY SEDGWICK
b. 1950

Through two challenging and groundbreaking books, *Between Men: English Litera-ture and Male Homosocial Desire* (1985) and *Epistemology of the Closet* (1990), Eve Kosofsky Sedgwick helped pioneer the emergence of queer theory. What distin-guishes queer theory from the gay and lesbian scholarship of earlier thinkers is a rejection of identity politics; that is, a questioning of the very terms *gay* and *lesbian*. Factoring sexuality into the study of gender, Sedgwick emphasizes, on the one hand, the historical parameters of the divide between homo- and heterosexuality in nineteenth- and twentieth-century Western cultures and, on the other hand, the pro-liferation of complex attachments, orientations, and activities within decidedly diverse heterosexual and homosexual communities. In *Between Men,* for example, Sedgwick studies the ways in which men establish homo*social* bonds through their rivalry over a woman—a triangulation fueled by homophobia, a fear of homosexual-ity far more powerful among men in our culture than among women. In *Epistemol-ogy of the Closet,* Sedgwick examines not only the centrality of *the closet* as the notion illuminates issues of concealment and disclosure in literature and philosophy but also the complicated fissures and alliances between advocates of the pro-gay and feminist movements. A Distinguished Professor of English at the Graduate Center at the City University of New York, Sedgwick has produced a number of influential critical anthologies as well as a book of poetry, *Fat Art, Thin Art* (1994), and a mem-oir, *A Dialogue on Love* (1999). In *Touching Evil: Affect, Pedagogy, Performativity* (2003), she examines a range of emotional states to deepen our understanding of the habits and pratices of cognition.

From Epistemology of the Closet

> The lie, the perfect lie, about people we know, about the relations
> we have had with them, about our motive for some action, formu-
> lated in totally different terms, the lie as to what we are, whom we
> love, what we feel with regard to people who love us . . . —that lie
> is one of the few things in the world that can open windows for us
> on to what is new and unknown, that can awaken in us sleeping
> senses for the contemplation of universes that otherwise we should
> never have known.
>
> <div align="right">Proust, <i>The Captive</i></div>

The epistemology of the closet is not a dated subject or a superseded regime of knowing. While the events of June, 1969,[1] and later vitally reinvigorated many people's sense of the potency, magnetism, and promise of gay self-disclosure, nevertheless the reign of the telling secret was scarcely overturned with Stonewall. Quite the opposite, in some ways. To the fine antennae of public attention the freshness of every drama of (especially involuntary) gay uncovering seems if anything heightened in surprise and delectability, rather than staled, by the increasingly intense atmosphere of public articulations of and about the love that is famous for daring not speak its name. So resilient

---

1. The riots that broke out when police raided the Stonewall Inn, a gay bar in New York's Greenwich Village; this act of resistance is often seen as mark-ing the birth of the gay pride movement [editor's note; except as indicated, all notes are Sedgwick's].

and productive a structure of narrative will not readily surrender its hold on important forms of social meaning. As D. A. Miller points out in an aegis-creating essay, secrecy can function as

> the subjective practice in which the oppositions of private/public, inside/outside, subject/object are established, and the sanctity of their first term kept inviolate. And the phenomenon of the "open secret" does not, as one might think, bring about the collapse of those binarisms and their ideological effects, but rather attests to their fantasmatic recovery.[2]

Even at an individual level, there are remarkably few of even the most openly gay people who are not deliberately in the closet with someone personally or economically or institutionally important to them. Furthermore, the deadly elasticity of heterosexist presumption means that, like Wendy in *Peter Pan*, people find new walls springing up around them even as they drowse: every encounter with a new classful of students, to say nothing of a new boss, social worker, loan officer, landlord, doctor, erects new closets whose fraught and characteristic laws of optics and physics exact from at least gay people new surveys, new calculations, new draughts and requisitions of secrecy or disclosure. Even an out gay person deals daily with interlocutors about whom she doesn't know whether they know or not; it is equally difficult to guess for any given interlocutor whether, if they did know, the knowledge would seem very important. Nor—at the most basic level—is it unaccountable that someone who wanted a job, custody or visiting rights, insurance, protection from violence, from "therapy," from distorting stereotype, from insulting scrutiny, from simple insult, from forcible interpretation of their bodily product, could deliberately choose to remain in or to reenter the closet in some or all segments of their life. The gay closet is not a feature only of the lives of gay people. But for many gay people it is still the fundamental feature of social life; and there can be few gay people, however courageous and forthright by habit, however fortunate in the support of their immediate communities, in whose lives the closet is not still a shaping presence.

To say, as I will be saying here, that the epistemology of the closet has given an overarching consistency to gay culture and identity throughout this century is not to deny that crucial possibilities around and outside the closet have been subject to most consequential change, for gay people. There are risks in making salient the continuity and centrality of the closet, in a historical narrative that does not have as a fulcrum a saving vision—whether located in past or future—of its apocalyptic rupture. A meditation that lacks that particular utopian organization will risk glamorizing the closet itself, if only by default; will risk presenting as inevitable or somehow valuable its exactions, its deformations, its disempowerment and sheer pain. If these risks are worth running, it is partly because the nonutopian traditions of gay writing, thought, and culture have remained so inexhaustibly and gorgeously productive for later gay thinkers, in the absence of a rationalizing or often even of a forgiving reading of their politics. The epistemology of the closet has also been, however, on a far vaster scale and with a less honorific inflection, inexhaustibly productive of modern Western culture and history at large. While

---

2. D. A. Miller, "Secret Subjects, Open Secrets," in his *The Novel and the Police* (Berkeley: University of California Press, 1988), p. 207.

that may be reason enough for taking it as a subject of interrogation, it should not be reason enough for focusing scrutiny on those who inhabit the closet (however equivocally) to the exclusion of those in the ambient heterosexist culture who enjoin it and whose intimate representational needs it serves in a way less extortionate to themselves.

I scarcely know at this stage a consistent alternative proceeding, however; and it may well be that, for reasons to be discussed, no such consistency is possible. At least to enlarge the circumference of scrutiny and to vary by some new assays of saltation the angle of its address will be among the methodological projects of this discussion.

✳ ✳ ✳

In Montgomery County, Maryland, in 1973, an eighth-grade earth science teacher named Acanfora was transferred to a nonteaching position by the Board of Education when they learned he was gay. When Acanfora spoke to news media, such as "60 Minutes" and the Public Broadcasting System, about his situation, he was refused a new contract entirely. Acanfora sued. The federal district court that first heard his case supported the action and rationale of the Board of Education, holding that Acanfora's recourse to the media had brought undue attention to himself and his sexuality, to a degree that would be deleterious to the educational process. The Fourth Circuit Court of Appeals disagreed. They considered Acanfora's public disclosures to be protected speech under the First Amendment. Although they overruled the lower court's rationale, however, the appellate court affirmed its decision not to allow Acanfora to return to teaching. Indeed, they denied his standing to bring the suit in the first place, on the grounds that he had failed to note on his original employment application that he had been, in college, an officer of a student homophile organization—a notation that would, as school officials admitted in court, have prevented his ever being hired. The rationale for keeping Acanfora out of his classroom was thus no longer that he had disclosed too much about his homosexuality, but quite the opposite, that he had not disclosed enough.[3] The Supreme Court declined to entertain an appeal.

It is striking that each of the two rulings in *Acanfora* emphasized that the teacher's homosexuality "itself" would not have provided an acceptable ground for denying him employment. Each of the courts relied in its decision on an implicit distinction between the supposedly protected and bracketable fact of Acanfora's homosexuality proper, on the one hand, and on the other hand his highly vulnerable management of information about it. So very vulnerable does this latter exercise prove to be, however, and vulnerable to such a contradictory array of interdictions, that the space for simply existing as a gay person who is a teacher is in fact bayonetted through and through, from both sides, by the vectors of a disclosure at once compulsory and forbidden.

A related incoherence couched in the resonant terms of the distinction of *public* from *private* riddles the contemporary legal space of gay being. When

3. On this case see Michael W. La Morte, "Legal Rights and Responsibilities of Homosexuals in Public Education," *Journal of Law and Education* 4, no. 23 (July 1975): 449–67, esp. 450–53; and Jeanne La Borde Scholz, "Comment: Out of the Closet, Out of a Job: Due Process in Teacher Disqualification," *Hastings Law Quarterly* 6 (Winter 1979): 663–717, esp. 682–84.

it refused in 1985 to consider an appeal in *Rowland v. Mad River Local School District*, the U.S. Supreme Court let stand the firing of a bisexual guidance counselor for coming out to some of her colleagues; the act of coming out was judged not to be highly protected under the First Amendment because it does not constitute speech on a matter "of public concern." It was, of course, only eighteen months later that the same U.S. Supreme Court ruled, in response to Michael Hardwick's contention that it's nobody's business if he do, that it ain't:[4] if homosexuality is not, however densely adjudicated, to be considered a matter of *public* concern, neither in the Supreme Court's binding opinion does it subsist under the mantle of the *private*.[5]

The most obvious fact about this history of judicial formulations is that it codifies an excruciating system of double binds, systematically oppressing gay people, identities, and acts by undermining through contradictory constraints on discourse the grounds of their very being. That immediately political recognition may be supplemented, however, by a historical hypothesis that goes in the other direction. I want to argue that a lot of the energy of attention and demarcation that has swirled around issues of homosexuality since the end of the nineteenth century, in Europe and the United States, has been impelled by the distinctively indicative relation of homosexuality to wider mappings of secrecy and disclosure, and of the private and the public, that were and are critically problematical for the gender, sexual, and economic structures of the heterosexist culture at large, mappings whose enabling but dangerous incoherence has become oppressively, durably condensed in certain figures of homosexuality. "The closet" and "coming out," now verging on all-purpose phrases for the potent crossing and recrossing of almost any politically charged lines of representation, have been the gravest and most magnetic of those figures.

The closet is the defining structure for gay oppression in this century. The legal couching, by civil liberties lawyers, of *Bowers v. Hardwick* as an issue in the first place of a Constitutional right to privacy, and the liberal focus in the aftermath of that decision on the image of the *bedroom invaded by policemen*—"Letting the Cops Back into Michael Hardwick's Bedroom," the *Native* headlined[6]—as though political empowerment were a matter of getting the cops back on the street where they belong and sexuality back into the impermeable space where *it* belongs, are among other things extensions of, and testimony to the power of, the image of the closet. The durability of the image is perpetuated even as its intelligibility is challenged in antihomophobic responses like the following, to *Hardwick*, addressed to gay readers:

> What can you do—alone? The answer is obvious. You're *not* alone, and you can't afford to try to be. That closet door—never very secure as pro-

4. In *Bowers v. Hardwick* (1986), the Supreme Court upheld the constitutionality of a law that criminalized sodomy, defined as oral and anal sex, performed in private by consenting adults; it overturned this ruling in 2003 [editor's note].

5. Nan Hunter, director of the ACLU's Lesbian and Gay Rights Project, analyzed *Rowland* in "Homophobia and Academic Freedom," a talk at the 1986 Modern Language Association National Convention. There is an interesting analysis of the limitations, for gay-rights purposes, of both the right of privacy and the First Amendment guaran-

tee of free speech, whether considered separately or in tandem, in "Notes: The Constitutional Status of Sexual Orientation: Homosexuality as a Suspect Classification," *Harvard Law Review* 98 (April 1985): 1285–1307, esp. 1288–97. For a discussion of related legal issues that is strikingly apropos of, and useful for, the argument made in *Epistemology of the Closet*, see Janet E. Halley, "The Politics of the Closet: Towards Equal Protection for Gay, Lesbian, and Bisexual Identity," *UCLA Law Review* 36 (1989): 915–76.

6. *New York Native*, no. 169 (July 14, 1986): 11.

tection—is even more dangerous now. You must come out, for your own sake and for the sake of all of us.[7]

The image of coming out regularly interfaces the image of the closet, and its seemingly unambivalent public siting can be counterposed as a salvational epistemologic certainty against the very equivocal privacy afforded by the closet: "If every gay person came out to his or her family," the same article goes on, "a hundred million Americans could be brought to our side. Employers and straight friends could mean a hundred million more." And yet the Mad River School District's refusal to hear a woman's coming out as an authentically public speech act is echoed in the frigid response given many acts of coming out: "That's fine, but why did you think I'd want to know about it?"

Gay thinkers of this century have, as we'll see, never been blind to the damaging contradictions of this compromised metaphor of *in* and *out* of the closet of privacy. But its origins in European culture are, as the writings of Foucault have shown, so ramified—and its relation to the "larger," i.e., ostensibly nongay-related, topologies of privacy in the culture is, as the figure of Foucault dramatized, so critical, so enfolding, so representational—that the simple vesting of some alternative metaphor has never, either, been a true possibility.

I recently heard someone on National Public Radio refer to the sixties as the decade when Black people came out of the closet. For that matter, I recently gave an MLA talk purporting to explain how it's possible to come out of the closet as a fat woman. The apparent floating-free from its gay origins of that phrase "coming out of the closet" in recent usage might suggest that the trope of the closet is so close to the heart of some modern preoccupations that it could be, or has been, evacuated of its historical gay specificity. But I hypothesize that exactly the opposite is true. I think that a whole cluster of the most crucial sites for the contestation of meaning in twentieth-century Western culture are consequentially and quite indelibly marked with the historical specificity of homosocial/homosexual definition, notably but not exclusively male, from around the turn of the century.[8] Among those sites are, as I have indicated, the pairings secrecy/disclosure and private/public. Along with and sometimes through these epistemologically charged pairings, condensed in the figures of "the closet" and "coming out," this very specific crisis of definition has then ineffaceably marked other pairings as basic to modern cultural organization as masculine/feminine, majority/minority, innocence/initiation, natural/artificial, new/old, growth/decadence, urbane/provincial, health/illness, same/different, cognition/paranoia, art/kitsch, sincerity/sentimentality, and voluntarity/addiction. So permeative has the suffusing stain of homo/heterosexual crisis been that to discuss any of these indices in any context, in the absence of an antihomophobic analysis, must perhaps be to perpetuate unknowingly compulsions implicit in each.

7. Philip Bockman, "A Fine Day," *New York Native*, no. 175 (August 25, 1986): 13.
8. A reminder that "the closet" retains (at least the chronic potential of) its gay semantic specification: a media flap in June, 1989, when a Republican National Committee memo calling for House Majority Leader Thomas Foley to "come out of the liberal closet" and comparing his voting record with that of an openly gay Congressman, Barney Frank, was widely perceived (and condemned) as insinuating that Foley himself is gay. The committee's misjudgment about whether it could maintain deniability for the insinuation is an interesting index to how unpredictably full or empty of gay specificity this locution may be perceived to be.

For any modern question of sexuality, knowledge/ignorance is more than merely one in a metonymic chain of such binarisms. The process, narrowly bordered at first in European culture but sharply broadened and accelerated after the late eighteenth century, by which "knowledge" and "sex" become conceptually inseparable from one another—so that knowledge means in the first place sexual knowledge; ignorance, sexual ignorance; and epistemological pressure of any sort seems a force increasingly saturated with sexual impulsion—was sketched in Volume I of Foucault's *History of Sexuality*. In a sense, this was a process, protracted almost to retardation, of exfoliating the biblical genesis by which what we now know as sexuality is fruit—apparently the only fruit—to be plucked from the tree of knowledge. Cognition itself, sexuality itself, and transgression itself have always been ready in Western culture to be magnetized into an unyielding though not an unfissured alignment with one another, and the period initiated by Romanticism accomplished this disposition through a remarkably broad confluence of different languages and institutions.

In some texts, such as Diderot's *La Religieuse*, that were influential early in this process, the desire that represents sexuality per se, and hence sexual knowledge and knowledge per se, is a same-sex desire.[9] This possibility, however, was repressed with increasing energy, and hence increasing visibility, as the nineteenth-century culture of the individual proceeded to elaborate a version of knowledge/sexuality increasingly structured by its pointed cognitive *refusal* of sexuality between women, between men. The gradually reifying effect of this refusal[1] meant that by the end of the nineteenth century, when it had become fully current—as obvious to Queen Victoria as to Freud—that knowledge meant sexual knowledge, and secrets sexual secrets, there had in fact developed one particular sexuality that was distinctively constituted *as* secrecy: the perfect object for the by now insatiably exacerbated epistemological/sexual anxiety of the turn-of-the-century subject. Again, it was a long chain of originally scriptural identifications of a sexuality with a particular cognitive positioning (in this case, St. Paul's routinely reproduced and reworked denomination of sodomy as the crime whose name is not to be uttered, hence whose accessibility to knowledge is uniquely preterited) that culminated in Lord Alfred Douglas's epochal public utterance, in 1894, "*I am the Love that dare not speak its name.*"[2] In such texts as *Billy Budd* and *Dorian Gray* and through their influence, the subject—the thematics—of knowledge and ignorance themselves, of innocence and initiation, of secrecy and disclosure, became not contingently but integrally infused with one particular object of cognition: no longer sexuality as a whole but even more specifically, now, the homosexual topic. And the condensation of the world of possibilities surrounding same-sex sexuality—including, shall we say, both gay desires and the most rabid phobias against them—the condensation of this plurality to *the homosexual topic* that now formed the accusative case of modern processes of personal knowing, was not the least infliction of the turn-of-the-century crisis of sexual definition.

9. On this, see my "Privilege of Unknowing," *Genders*, no. 1 (Spring 1988): 102–24.
1. On this, see [my] *Between Men: English Literature and Male Homosocial Desire* (New York: Columbia University Press, 1985).

2. Lord Alfred Douglas, "Two Loves," *The Chameleon* 1 (1894): 28 (emphasis added). [Douglas was the lover of Oscar Wilde; their relationship led to Wilde's conviction and imprisonment on sodomy charges in 1895—editor's note.]

To explore the differences it makes when secrecy itself becomes manifest as *this* secret, let me begin by twining together in a short anachronistic braid a variety of exemplary narratives—literary, biographical, imaginary—that begin with the moment on July 1, 1986, when the decision in *Bowers v. Hardwick* was announced, a moment which, sandwiched between a weekend of Gay Pride parades nationwide, the announcement of a vengeful new AIDS policy by the Justice Department, and an upcoming media-riveting long weekend of hilarity or hysteria focused on the national fetishization in a huge hollow blind spike-headed female body of the abstraction Liberty, and occurring in an ambient medium for gay men and their families and friends of wave on wave of renewed loss, mourning, and refreshed personal fear, left many people feeling as if at any rate one's own particular car had finally let go forever of the tracks of the roller coaster.

In many discussions I heard or participated in immediately after the Supreme Court ruling in *Bowers v. Hardwick*, antihomophobic or gay women and men speculated—more or less empathetically or venomously—about the sexuality of the people most involved with the decision. The question kept coming up, in different tones, of what it could have felt like to be a closeted gay court assistant, or clerk, or justice, who might have had some degree, even a very high one, of instrumentality in conceiving or formulating or "refining" or logistically facilitating this ruling, these ignominious majority opinions, the assaultive sentences in which they were framed.

That train of painful imaginings was fraught with the epistemological distinctiveness of gay identity and gay situation in our culture. Vibrantly resonant as the image of the closet is for many modern oppressions, it is indicative for homophobia in a way it cannot be for other oppressions. Racism, for instance, is based on a stigma that is visible in all but exceptional cases (cases that are neither rare nor irrelevant, but that delineate the outlines rather than coloring the center of racial experience); so are the oppressions based on gender, age, size, physical handicap. Ethnic/cultural/religious oppressions such as anti-Semitism are more analogous in that the stigmatized individual has at least notionally some discretion—although, importantly, it is never to be taken for granted how much—over other people's knowledge of her or his membership in the group: one could "come out as" a Jew or Gypsy, in a heterogeneous urbanized society, much more intelligibly than one could typically "come out as," say, female, Black, old, a wheelchair user, or fat. A (for instance) Jewish or Gypsy identity, and hence a Jewish or Gypsy secrecy or closet, would nonetheless differ again from the distinctive gay versions of these things in its clear ancestral linearity and answerability, in the roots (however tortuous and ambivalent) of cultural identification through each individual's originary culture of (at a minimum) the family.

Proust, in fact, insistently suggests as a sort of limit-case of one kind of coming out precisely the drama of Jewish self-identification, embodied in the Book of Esther and in Racine's recasting of it that is quoted throughout the "Sodom and Gomorrah" books of *A la recherche*.[3] The story of Esther seems a model for a certain simplified but highly potent imagining of coming out and its transformative potential. In concealing her Judaism from her hus-

---

3. I.e., Proust's *Remembrance of Things Past*; these volumes were published between 1921 and 1923 [editor's note].

band, King Assuérus (Ahasuerus), Esther the Queen feels she is concealing, simply, her identity: "The King is to this day unaware who I am."[4] Esther's deception is made necessary by the powerful ideology that makes Assuérus categorize her people as unclean ("cette source impure" [1039]) and an abomination against nature ("Il nous croit en horreur à toute la nature" [174]). The sincere, relatively abstract Jew-hatred of this fuddled but omnipotent king undergoes constant stimulation from the grandiose cynicism of his advisor Aman (Haman), who dreams of an entire planet exemplarily cleansed of the perverse element.

> I want it said one day in awestruck centuries:
> "There once used to be Jews, there was an insolent race;
> widespread, they used to cover the whole face of the earth;
> a single one dared draw on himself the wrath of Aman,
> at once they disappeared, every one, from the earth."
> (476–80)

The king acquiesces in Aman's genocidal plot, and Esther is told by her cousin, guardian, and Jewish conscience Mardochée (Mordecai) that the time for her revelation has come; at this moment the particular operation of suspense around her would be recognizable to any gay person who has inched toward coming out to homophobic parents. "And if I perish, I perish," she says in the Bible (Esther 4:16). That the avowal of her secret identity will have an immense potency is clear, is the premise of the story. All that remains to be seen is whether under its explosive pressure the king's "political" animus against her kind will demolish his "personal" love for her, or vice versa: will he declare her as good as, or better, dead? Or will he soon be found at a neighborhood bookstore, hoping not to be recognized by the salesperson who is ringing up his copy of *Loving Someone Jewish*?

The biblical story and Racinian play, bearable to read in their balance of the holocaustal with the intimate only because one knows how the story will end,[5] are enactments of a particular dream or fantasy of coming out. Esther's eloquence, in the event, is resisted by only five lines of her husband's demurral or shock: essentially at the instant she names herself, both her ruler and Aman see that the anti-Semites are lost ("*AMAN, tout bas*: Je tremble"[6] [1033]). Revelation of identity in the space of intimate love effortlessly overturns an entire public systematics of the natural and the unnatural, the pure and the impure. The peculiar strike that the story makes to the heart is that Esther's small, individual ability to risk losing the love and countenance of her master has the power to save not only her own space in life but her people.

It would not be hard to imagine a version of *Esther* set in the Supreme Court in the days immediately before the decision in *Bowers v. Hardwick*. Cast as the ingenue in the title role a hypothetical closeted gay clerk, as Assuérus a hypothetical Justice of the same gender who is about to make a majority of five in support of the Georgia law. The Justice has grown fond of

---

4. Jean Racine, *Esther*, ed. H. R. Roach (London: George G. Harrap, 1949), line 89; my translation. Further citations of this play will be noted by line number in the text.
5. It is worth remembering, of course, that the biblical story still ends with mass slaughter: while Racine's king *revokes* his orders (1197), the bibli-

cal king *reverses* his (Esther 8:5), licensing the Jews' killing of "seventy and five thousand" (9:16) of their enemies, including children and women (8:11).
6. HAMAN, *under his breath*: I tremble (French) [editor's note].

the clerk, oddly fonder than s/he is used to being of clerks, and . . . In our compulsive recursions to the question of the sexualities of court personnel, such a scenario was close to the minds of my friends and me in many forms. In the passionate dissenting opinions, were there not the traces of others' comings-out already performed; could even the dissents themselves represent such performances, Justice coming out to Justice? With the blood-let tatters of what risky comings-out achieved and then overridden—friends', clerks', employees', children's—was the imperious prose of the majority opinions lined? More painful and frequent were thoughts of all the coming out that had not happened, of the women and men who had not in some more modern idiom said, with Esther,

> I dare to beg you, both for my own life
> and the sad days of an ill-fated people
> that you have condemned to perish with me.
>   (1029–31)

What was lost in the absence of such scenes was not, either, the opportunity to evoke with eloquence a perhaps demeaning pathos like Esther's. It was something much more precious: evocation, articulation, of the dumb Assuérus in all his imperial ineloquent bathos of unknowing: "A périr? Vous? Quel peuple?" ("To perish? You? What people?" [1032]). "What people?" indeed—why, as it oddly happens, the very people whose eradication he personally is just on the point of effecting. But only with the utterance of these blank syllables, making the weight of Assuérus's powerful ignorance suddenly audible—not least to him—in the same register as the weight of Esther's and Mardochée's private knowledge, can any open flow of power become possible. It is here that Aman begins to tremble.

Just so with coming out: it can bring about the revelation of a powerful unknowing *as* unknowing, not as a vacuum or as the blank it can pretend to be but as a weighty and occupied and consequential epistemological space. Esther's avowal allows Assuérus to make visible two such spaces at once: "You?" "What people?" He has been blindly presuming about herself,[7] and simply blind to the race to whose extinction he has pledged himself. What? *you're* one of *those*? Huh? *you're* a *what*? This frightening thunder can also, however, be the sound of manna falling.

✳   ✳   ✳

There is no question that to fixate, as I have done, on the scenario sketched here more than flirts with sentimentality. This is true for quite explicable reasons. First, we have too much cause to know how limited a leverage any individual revelation can exercise over collectively scaled and institutionally embodied oppressions. Acknowledgment of this disproportion does not mean that the consequences of such acts as coming out can be circumscribed within *predetermined* boundaries, as if between "personal" and "political" realms, nor does it require us to deny how disproportionately powerful and disruptive such acts can be. But the brute incommensurability has nonethe-

---

7. In Voltaire's words, "un roi insensé qui a passé six mois avec sa femme sans savoir, sans s'informer même qui elle est" (in Racine, *Esther*, pp. 83–84). [A senseless (or mad) king who has passed six months with his wife without knowing, without even inquiring who she is—editor's note.]

less to be acknowledged. In the theatrical display of an *already institutional-ized* ignorance no transformative potential is to be looked for.

There is another whole family of reasons why too long a lingering on moments of *Esther*-style avowal must misrepresent the truths of homophobic oppression; these go back to the important differences between Jewish (here I mean Racinian-Jewish) and gay identity and oppression. Even in the "Sodom and Gomorrah" books of Proust, after all, and especially in *La Prisonnière*,[8] where *Esther* is so insistently invoked, the play does not offer an efficacious model of transformative revelation. To the contrary: *La Prisonnière* is, notably, the book whose Racine-quoting hero has the most disastrous incapacity either to come out or *to be come out to.*

The suggested closeted Supreme Court clerk who struggled with the possibility of a self-revelation that *might* perceptibly strengthen gay sisters and brothers, but *would* radically endanger at least the foreseen course of her or his own life, would have an imagination filled with possibilities beyond those foreseen by Esther in her moment of risk. It is these possibilities that mark the distinctive structures of the epistemology of the closet. The clerk's authority to describe her or his own sexuality might well be impeached; the avowal might well only further perturb an already stirred-up current of the open secret; the avowal might well represent an aggression against someone with whom the clerk felt, after all, a real bond; the nongay-identified Justice might well feel too shaken in her or his own self-perception, or in the perception of the bond with the clerk, to respond with anything but an increased rigor; the clerk might well, through the avowal, be getting dangerously into the vicinity of the explosive-mined closet of a covertly gay Justice; the clerk might well fear being too isolated or self-doubting to be able to sustain the consequences of the avowal; the intersection of gay revelation with underlying gender expectations might well be too confusing or disorienting, for one or the other, to provide an intelligible basis for change.

To spell these risks and circumscriptions out more fully in the comparison with *Esther*:

1. Although neither the Bible nor Racine indicates in what, if any, religious behaviors or beliefs Esther's Jewish identity may be manifested, *there is no suggestion that that identity might be a debatable, a porous, a mutable fact about her.* "Esther, my lord, had a Jew for her father" (1033)—ergo, Esther is a Jew. Taken aback though he is by this announcement, Assuérus does not suggest that Esther is going through a phase, or is just angry at Gentiles, or could change if she only loved him enough to get counseling. Nor do such undermining possibilities occur to Esther. The Jewish identity in this play—whatever it may consist of in real life in a given historical context—has a solidity whose very unequivocalness grounds the story of Esther's equivocation and her subsequent self-disclosure. In the processes of gay self-disclosure, by contrast, in a twentieth-century context, questions of authority and evidence can be the first to arise. "How do you know you're really gay? Why be in such a hurry to jump to conclusions? After all, what you're saying is only based on a few feelings, not real actions [or *alternatively*: on a few actions, not necessarily your real feelings]; hadn't you better talk to a therapist and find out?" Such responses—and their occurrence in the people come

8. The third volume of "Sodom and Gomorrah," translated as *The Captive* [editor's note].

out to can seem a belated echo of their occurrence in the person coming out—reveal how problematical at present is the very concept of gay identity, as well as how intensely it is resisted and how far authority over its definition has been distanced from the gay subject her- or himself.

2. *Esther expects Assuérus to be altogether surprised by her self-disclosure; and he is.* Her confident sense of control over other people's knowledge about her is in contrast to the radical uncertainty closeted gay people are likely to feel about who is in control of information about their sexual identity. This has something to do with a realism about secrets that is greater in most people's lives than it is in Bible stories; but it has much more to do with complications in the notion of gay identity, so that no one person can take control over all the multiple, often contradictory codes by which information about sexual identity and activity can seem to be conveyed. In many, if not most, relationships, coming out is a matter of crystallizing intuitions or convictions that had been in the air for a while already and had already established their own power-circuits of silent contempt, silent blackmail, silent glamorization, silent complicity. After all, the position of those who think they *know something about one that one may not know oneself* is an excited and empowered one—whether what they think one doesn't know is that one somehow *is* homosexual, or merely that one's supposed secret is known to them. The glass closet can license insult ("I'd never have said those things if I'd *known* you were gay!"—yeah, sure); it can also license far warmer relations, but (and) relations whose potential for exploitiveness is built into the optics of the asymmetrical, the specularized, and the inexplicit.[9] There are sunny and apparently simplifying versions of coming out under these circumstances: a woman painfully decides to tell her mother that she's a lesbian, and her mother responds, "Yeah, I sort of thought you might be when you and Joan started sleeping together ten years ago." More often this fact makes the closet and its exits not more but less straightforward, however; not, often, more equable, but more volatile or even violent. Living in and hence coming out of the closet are never matters of the purely hermetic; the personal and political geographies to be surveyed here are instead the more imponderable and convulsive ones of the open secret.

3. *Esther worries that her revelation might destroy her or fail to help her people, but it does not seem to her likely to damage Assuérus, and it does not indeed damage him.* When gay people in a homophobic society come out, on the other hand, perhaps especially to parents or spouses, it is with the consciousness of a potential for serious injury that is likely to go in both directions. The pathogenic secret itself, even, can circulate contagiously *as* a secret: a mother says that her adult child's coming out of the closet with her has plunged her, in turn, into the closet in her conservative community. In fantasy, though not in fantasy only, against the fear of being killed or wished dead by (say) one's parents in such a revelation there is apt to recoil the often more intensely imagined possibility of its killing *them.* There is no guarantee that being under threat from a double-edged weapon is a more powerful position than getting the ordinary axe, but it is certain to be more destabilizing.

4. The inert substance of *Assuérus seems to have no definitional involvement with the religious/ethnic identity of Esther.* He sees neither himself nor their

9. On this, see "Privilege of Unknowing," esp. p. 120.

relationship differently when he sees that she is different from what he had thought her. The double-edged potential for injury in the scene of gay coming out, by contrast, results partly from the fact that the erotic identity of the person who receives the disclosure is apt also to be implicated in, hence perturbed by it. This is true first and generally because erotic identity, of all things, is never to be circumscribed simply as itself, can never not be relational, is never to be perceived or known by anyone outside of a structure of transference and countertransference. Second and specifically it is true because the incoherences and contradictions of homosexual identity in twentieth-century culture are responsive to and hence evocative of the incoherences and contradictions of compulsory heterosexuality.[1]

5. *There is no suggestion that Assuérus might himself be a Jew in disguise.* But it is entirely within the experience of gay people to find that a homophobic figure in power has, if anything, a disproportionate likelihood of being gay and closeted. Some examples and implications of this are discussed toward the end of Chapter 5; there is more to this story. Let it stand here merely to demonstrate again that gay identity is a convoluted and off-centering possession if it is a possession at all; even to come out does not end anyone's relation to the closet, including turbulently the closet of the other.

6. *Esther knows who her people are and has an immediate answerability to them.* Unlike gay people, who seldom grow up in gay families; who are exposed to their culture's, if not their parents', high ambient homophobia long before either they or those who care for them know that they are among those who most urgently need to define themselves against it; who have with difficulty and always belatedly to patch together from fragments a community, a usable heritage, a politics of survival or resistance; unlike these, Esther has intact and to hand the identity and history and commitments she was brought up in, personified and legitimated in a visible figure of authority, her guardian Mardochée.

7. Correspondingly, *Esther's avowal occurs within and perpetuates a coherent system of gender subordination.* Nothing is more explicit, in the Bible, about Esther's marriage than its origin in a crisis of patriarchy and its value as a preservative of female discipline. When the Gentile Vashti, her predecessor as Ahasuerus's queen, had refused to be put on exhibition to his drunk men friends, "the wise men, which knew the times," saw that

> Vashti the queen hath not done wrong to the king only, but also to all the princes, and to all the people that are in all the provinces of the king Ahasuerus. For this deed of the queen shall come abroad unto all women, so that they shall despise their husbands in their eyes, when it shall be reported.
>
> (Esther 1:13–17)

Esther the Jew is introduced onto this scene as a salvific ideal of female submissiveness, her single moment of risk with the king given point by her customary pliancy. (Even today, Jewish little girls are educated in gender roles—fondness for being looked at, fearlessness in defense of "their people," nonsolidarity with their sex—through masquerading as Queen Esther at Purim; I have a snapshot of myself at about five, barefoot in the pretty

---

1. This phrase evokes Adrienne Rich's essay "Compulsory Heterosexuality and Lesbian Existence" (1980).

"Queen Esther" dress my grandmother made [white satin, gold spangles], making a careful eyes-down toe-pointed curtsey at [presumably] my father, who is manifest in the picture only as the flashgun that hurls my shadow, pillaring up tall and black, over the dwarfed sofa onto the wall behind me.) Moreover, the literal patriarchism that makes coming out to *parents* the best emotional analogy to Esther's self-disclosure to her *husband* is shown with unusual clarity to function through the male traffic in women: Esther's real mission, as a wife, is to get her guardian Mardochée installed in place of Aman as the king's favorite and advisor. And the instability and danger that by contrast lurk in the Gentile Aman's relation to the king seem, Iago-like, to attach to the inadequate heterosexual buffering of the inexplicit intensities between them. If the story of Esther reflects a firm Jewish choice of a minority politics based on a conservative reinscription of gender roles, however, such a choice has never been able to be made intelligibly by gay people in a modern culture (although there have been repeated attempts at making it, especially by men). Instead, both within and outside of homosexual-rights movements, the contradictory understandings of same-sex bonding and desire and of male and female gay identity have crossed and recrossed the definitional lines of gender identity with such disruptive frequency that the concepts "minority" and "gender" themselves have lost a good deal of their categorizing (though certainly not of their performative) force.

Each of these complicating possibilities stems at least partly from the plurality and the cumulative incoherence of modern ways of conceptualizing same-sex desire and, hence, gay identity; an incoherence that answers, too, to the incoherence with which *hetero*sexual desire and identity are conceptualized. A long, populous theoretical project of interrogating and historicizing the self-evidence of the pseudo-symmetrical opposition homosexual/ heterosexual (or gay/straight) as categories of persons will be assumed rather than summarized here. Foucault among other historians locates in about the nineteenth century a shift in European thought from viewing same-sex sexuality as a matter of prohibited and isolated genital *acts* (acts to which, in that view, anyone might be liable who did not have their appetites in general under close control) to viewing it as a function of stable definitions of *identity* (so that one's personality structure might mark one as *a homosexual*, even, perhaps, in the absence of any genital activity at all). Thus, according to Alan Bray, "To talk of an individual [in the Renaissance] as being or not being 'a homosexual' is an anachronism and ruinously misleading,"[2] whereas the period stretching roughly between Wilde and Proust was prodigally productive of attempts to name, explain, and define this new kind of creature, the homosexual person—a project so urgent that it spawned in its rage of distinction an even newer category, that of the heterosexual person.[3]

To question the natural self-evidence of this opposition between gay and straight as distinct kinds of persons is not, however, as we saw in the Introduction, to dismantle it. Perhaps no one should wish it to do so; substantial groups of women and men under this representational regime have found

2. Alan Bray, *Homosexuality in Renaissance England* (London: Gay Men's Press, 1982), p. 16.
3. On this, see Jonathan Katz, *Gay/Lesbian Almanac: A New Documentary* (New York: Harper

and Row), pp. 147–50, and David M. Halperin, *One Hundred Years of Homosexuality* (New York: Routledge, 1989), p. 155n.1 and pp. 158–59n.17.

that the nominative category "homosexual," or its more recent near-synonyms, does have a real power to organize and describe their experience of their own sexuality and identity, enough at any rate to make their self-application of it (even when only tacit) worth the enormous accompanying costs. If only for this reason, the categorization commands respect. And even more at the level of groups than of individuals, the durability of any politics or ideology that would be so much as *permissive* of same-sex sexuality has seemed, in this century, to depend on a definition of homosexual persons as a distinct, minority population, however produced or labeled.[4] Far beyond any cognitively or politically enabling effects on the people whom it claims to describe, moreover, the nominative category of "the homosexual" has robustly failed to disintegrate under the pressure of decade after decade, battery after battery of deconstructive exposure—evidently not in the first place because of its meaningfulness to those whom it defines but because of its indispensableness to those who define themselves as against it.

For surely, if paradoxically, it is the paranoid insistence with which the definitional barriers between "the homosexual" (minority) and "the heterosexual" (majority) are fortified, in this century, by nonhomosexuals, and especially by men against men, that most saps one's ability to believe in "the homosexual" as an unproblematically discrete category of persons. Even the homophobic fifties folk wisdom of *Tea and Sympathy*[5] detects that the man who most electrifies those barriers is the one whose own current is at most intermittently direct. It was in the period of the so-called "invention of the 'homosexual' " that Freud gave psychological texture and credibility to a countervalent, universalizing mapping of this territory, based on the supposed protean mobility of sexual desire and on the potential bisexuality of every human creature; a mapping that implies no presumption that one's sexual penchant will always incline toward persons of a single gender, and that offers, additionally, a richly denaturalizing description of the psychological motives and mechanisms of male paranoid, projective homophobic definition and enforcement. Freud's antiminoritizing account only gained, moreover, in influence by being articulated through a developmental narrative in which heterosexist and masculinist ethical sanctions found ready camouflage. If the new common wisdom that hotly overt homophobes are men who are "insecure about their masculinity" supplements the implausible, necessary illusion that there could be a *secure* version of masculinity (known, presumably, by the coolness of its homophobic enforcement) and a stable, intelligible way for men to feel about other men in modern heterosexual capitalist patriarchy, what tighter turn could there be to the screw of an already off-center, always at fault, endlessly blackmailable male identity ready to be manipulated into any labor of channeled violence?[6]

It remained for work emerging from the later feminist and gay movements to begin to clarify why the male paranoid project had become so urgent in the maintenance of gender subordination; and it remained for a stunningly efficacious coup of feminist redefinition to transform lesbianism, in a predominant view, from a matter of female virilization to one of woman-

---

4. Conceivably, contemporary liberal/radical feminism, on the spectrum stretching from NOW to something short of radical separatism, could prove to be something of an exception to this rule—though, of course, already a much compromised one.

5. A Broadway play (1953–55) that was adapted into a movie (1956) [editor's note].

6. For a fuller discussion of this, see Chapter 4.

identification.[7] Although the post-Stonewall, predominantly male gay liberation movement has had a more distinct political presence than radical lesbianism and has presented potent new images of gay people and gay communities, along with a stirring new family of narrative structures attached to coming out, it has offered few new analytic facilities for the question of homo/heterosexual definition prior to the moment of individual coming out. That has not, indeed, been its project. In fact, except for a newly productive interest in historicizing gay definition itself, the array of analytic tools available today to anyone thinking about issues of homo/heterosexual definition is remarkably little enriched from that available to, say, Proust. Of the strange plethora of "explanatory" schemas newly available to Proust and his contemporaries, especially in support of minoritizing views, some have been superseded, forgotten, or rendered by history too unpalatable to be appealed to explicitly. (Many of the supposedly lost ones do survive, if not in sexological terminology, then in folk wisdom and "commonsense." One is never surprised, either, when they reemerge under new names on the Science page of the *Times*; the men-women of Sodom matriculate as the "sissy boys" of Yale University Press.)[8] But there are few new entries. Most moderately to well-educated Western people in this century seem to share a similar understanding of homosexual definition, independent of whether they themselves are gay or straight, homophobic or antihomophobic. That understanding is close to what Proust's probably was, what for that matter mine is and probably yours. That is to say, it is organized around a radical and irreducible incoherence. It holds the minoritizing view that there is a distinct population of persons who "really are" gay; at the same time, it holds the universalizing views that sexual desire is an unpredictably powerful solvent of stable identities; that apparently heterosexual persons and object choices are strongly marked by same-sex influences and desires, and vice versa for apparently homosexual ones; and that at least male heterosexual identity and modern masculinist culture may require for their maintenance the scapegoating crystallization of a same-sex male desire that is widespread and in the first place internal.[9]

It has been the project of many, many writers and thinkers of many different kinds to adjudicate between the minoritizing and universalizing views of sexual definition and to resolve this conceptual incoherence. With whatever success, on their own terms, they have accomplished the project, none of them has budged in one direction or other the absolute hold of this yoking of contradictory views on modern discourse. A higher *valuation* on the transformative and labile play of desire, a higher *valuation* on gay identity and gay community: neither of these, nor their opposite, often far more potent depre-

---

7. See, for example, Radicalesbians, "The Woman Identified Woman," reprinted in Anne Koedt, Ellen Levine, and Anita Rapone, eds., *Radical Feminism* (New York: Quadrangle, 1973), pp. 240–45; and Adrienne Rich, "Compulsory Heterosexuality and Lesbian Existence," *Signs* 5, no. 4 (1980): 631–660.

8. I'm referring here to the publicity given to Richard Green's *The "Sissy Boy Syndrome" and the Development of Homosexuality* on its 1987 publication. The intensely stereotypical, homophobic journalism that appeared on the occasion seemed to be legitimated by the book itself, which seemed, in turn, to be legitimated by the status of Yale University Press itself.

9. Anyone who imagines that this perception is confined to antihomophobes should listen, for instance, to the college football coach's ritualistic scapegoating and abjection of his team's "sissy" (or worse) personality traits. D. A. Miller's "*Cage aux folles*: Sensation and Gender in Wilkie Collins's *The Woman in White*" (in his *The Novel and the Police,* pp. 146–91, esp. pp. 186–90) makes especially forcefully the point (oughtn't it always to have been obvious?) that this whole family of perceptions is if anything less distinctively the property of cultural criticism than of cultural enforcement.

ciations, seems to get any purchase on the stranglehold of the available and ruling paradigm-clash. And this incoherence has prevailed for at least three-quarters of a century. Sometimes, but not always, it has taken the form of a confrontation or nonconfrontation between politics and theory. A perfect example of this potent incoherence was the anomalous legal situation of gay people and acts in this country after one recent legal ruling. The Supreme Court in *Bowers v. Hardwick* notoriously left the individual states free to prohibit any *acts* they wish to define as "sodomy," by whomsoever performed, with no fear at all of impinging on any rights, and particularly privacy rights, safeguarded by the Constitution; yet only shortly thereafter a panel of the Ninth Circuit Court of Appeals ruled (in *Sergeant Perry J. Watkins v. United States Army*) that homosexual *persons,* as a particular kind of person, *are* entitled to Constitutional protections under the Equal Protection clause.[1] To be gay in this system is to come under the radically overlapping aegises of a universalizing discourse of acts and a minoritizing discourse of persons. Just at the moment, at least within the discourse of law, the former of these prohibits what the latter of them protects; but in the concurrent public-health constructions related to AIDS, for instance, it is far from clear that a minoritizing discourse of persons ("risk groups") is not even more oppressive than the competing, universalizing discourse of acts ("safer sex"). In the double binds implicit in the space overlapped by the two, at any rate, every matter of definitional control is fraught with consequence.

The energy-expensive but apparently static clinch between minoritizing and universalizing views of *homo/heterosexual definition* is not, either, the only major conceptual siege under which modern homosexual and heterosexist fates are enacted. The second one, as important as the first and intimately entangled with it, has to do with defining the relation to gender of homosexual persons and same-sex desires. (It was in this conceptual register that the radical-feminist reframing of lesbianism as woman-identification was such a powerful move.) Enduringly since at least the turn of the century, there have presided two contradictory *tropes of gender* through which same-sex desire could be understood. On the one hand there was, and there persists, differently coded (in the homophobic folklore and science surrounding those "sissy boys" and their mannish sisters, but also in the heart and guts of much living gay and lesbian culture), the trope of inversion, *anima muliebris in corpore virili inclusa*—"a woman's soul trapped in a man's body"—and vice versa. As such writers as Christopher Craft have made clear, one vital impulse of this trope is the preservation of an essential *heterosexuality* within desire itself, through a particular reading of the homosexuality of persons: desire, in this view, by definition subsists in the current that runs between one male self and one female self, in whatever sex of bodies these selves may be manifested.[2] Proust was not the first to demonstrate—nor, for that matter, was the Shakespeare of the comedies—that while these attributions of "true" "inner" heterogender may be made to stick, in a haphazard way, so long as dyads of people are all that are in question, the broadening of view to include any larger circuit of desire must necessarily reduce the inversion or liminality

---

1. When Watkins's reinstatement in the army was supported by the full Ninth Circuit Court of Appeals in a 1989 ruling, however, it was on narrower grounds.

2. Christopher Craft, " 'Kiss Me with Those Red Lips': Gender and Inversion in Bram Stoker's *Dracula*," *Representations*, no. 8 (Fall 1984): 107–34, esp. 114.

trope to a choreography of breathless farce. Not a jot the less for that has the trope of inversion remained a fixture of modern discourse of same-sex desire; indeed, under the banners of androgyny or, more graphically, "genderfuck," the dizzying instability of this model has itself become a token of value.

Charged as it may be with value, the persistence of the inversion trope has been yoked, however, to that of its contradictory counterpart, the trope of gender separatism. Under this latter view, far from its being of the essence of desire to cross boundaries of gender, it is instead the most natural thing in the world that people of the same gender, people grouped together under the single most determinative diacritical mark of social organization, people whose economic, institutional, emotional, physical needs and knowledges may have so much in common, should bond together also on the axis of sexual desire. As the substitution of the phrase "woman-identified woman" for "lesbian" suggests, as indeed does the concept of the continuum of male or female homosocial desire, this trope tends to reassimilate to one another identification and desire, where inversion models, by contrast, depend on their distinctness. Gender-separatist models would thus place the woman-loving woman and the man-loving man each at the "natural" defining center of their own gender, again in contrast to inversion models that locate gay people—whether biologically or culturally—at the threshold between genders.

The immanence of each of these models throughout the history of modern gay definition is clear from the early split in the German homosexual rights movement between Magnus Hirschfeld, founder (in 1897) of the Scientific-Humanitarian Committee, a believer in the "third sex" who posited, in Don Mager's paraphrase, "an exact equation . . . between cross-gender behaviors and homosexual desire"; and Benedict Friedländer, co-founder (in 1902) of the Community of the Special, who concluded to the contrary "that homosexuality was the highest, most perfect evolutionary stage of gender differentiation."[3] As James Steakley explains, "the true *typus inversus*," according to this latter argument, "as distinct from the effeminate homosexual, was seen as the founder of patriarchal society and ranked above the heterosexual in terms of his capacity for leadership and heroism."[4]

Like the dynamic impasse between minoritizing and universalizing views of homosexual definition, that between transitive and separatist tropes of homosexual gender has its own complicated history, an especially crucial one for any understanding of modern gender asymmetry, oppression, and resistance. One thing that does emerge with clarity from this complex and contradictory map of sexual and gender definition is that the possible grounds to be found there for alliance and cross-identification among various groups will also be plural. To take the issue of gender definition alone: under a gender-separatist topos, lesbians have looked for identifications and alliances among women in general, including straight women (as in Adrienne Rich's "lesbian continuum" mode)[5]; and gay men, as in Friedländer's model—or more recent "male liberation" models—of masculinity, might look for them among men in

3. Don Mager, "Gay Theories of Gender Role Deviance," *SubStance* 46 (1985): 32–48; quoted from 35–36. His sources here are John Lauritsen and David Thorstad, *The Early Homosexual Rights Movement* (New York: Times Change Press, 1974), and James D. Steakley, *The Homosexual Emanci-*

pation Movement in Germany (New York: Arno Press, 1975).
4. Steakley, *The Homosexual Emancipation Movement in Germany*, p. 54.
5. See Rich, "Compulsory Heterosexuality" [editor's note].

	Separatist:	Integrative:
Homo/hetero *sexual* definition:	*Minoritizing*, e.g., gay identity, "essentialist," third-sex models, civil rights models	*Universalizing*, e.g., bisexual potential, "social constructionist," "sodomy" models, "lesbian continuum"
Gender definition:	*Gender separatist*, e.g., homosocial continuum, lesbian separatist, manhood-initiation models	*Inversion/liminality/ transitivity*, e.g., cross-sex, androgyny, gay/lesbian solidarity models

Models of Gay/Straight Definition
in Terms of Overlapping Sexuality and Gender

general, including straight men. "The erotic and social presumption of women is our enemy," Friedländer wrote in his "Seven Theses on Homosexuality" (1908).[6] Under a topos of gender inversion or liminality, in contrast, gay men have looked to identify with straight women (on the grounds that they are also "feminine" or also desire men), or with lesbians (on the grounds that they occupy a similarly liminal position); while lesbians have analogously looked to identify with gay men or, though this latter identification has not been strong since second-wave feminism, with straight men. (Of course, the political outcomes of all these trajectories of potential identification have been radically, often violently, shaped by differential historical forces, notably homophobia and sexism.) Note, however, that this schematization over "the issue of gender definition alone" also does impinge on the issue of homo/heterosexual definition, as well, and in an unexpectedly chiasmic way. Gender-*separatist* models like Rich's or Friedländer's seem to tend toward *universalizing* understandings of homo/heterosexual potential. To the degree that gender-*integrative* inversion or liminality models, such as Hirschfeld's "third-sex" model, suggest an alliance or identity between lesbians and gay men, on the other hand, they tend toward gay-*separatist*, minoritizing models of specifically gay identity and politics. Steakley makes a useful series of comparisons between Hirschfeld's Scientific-Humanitarian Committee and Friedländer's Community of the Special: "Within the homosexual emancipation movement there was a deep factionalization between the Committee and the Community. . . . [T]he Committee was an organization of men and women, whereas the Community was exclusively male. . . . The Committee called homosexuals a third sex in an effort to win the basic rights accorded the other two; the Community scorned this as a beggarly plea for mercy and touted the notion of supervirile bisexuality."[7] These crossings are quite contingent, however; Freud's universalizing understanding of sexual definition seems to go with an integrative, inversion model of gender definition, for instance. And, more broadly, the routes to be taken across this misleadingly

6. Steakley, *The Homosexual Emancipation Movement in Germany*, p. 68. ["*Typas Inversus*": inverted type (Latin); *invert* was another name for "homosexual"—editor's note.]
7. Steakley, *The Homosexual Emancipation Movement in Germany*, pp. 60–61.

symmetrical map are fractured in a particular historical situation by the profound asymmetries of gender oppression and heterosexist oppression.

Like the effect of the minoritizing/universalizing impasse, in short, that of the impasse of gender definition must be seen first of all in the creation of a field of intractable, highly structured discursive incoherence at a crucial node of social organization, in this case the node at which *any* gender is discriminated. I have no optimism at all about the availability of a standpoint of thought from which either question could be intelligibly, never mind efficaciously, adjudicated, given that the same yoking of contradictions has presided over all the thought on the subject, and all its violent and pregnant modern history, that has gone to form our own thought. Instead, the more promising project would seem to be a study of the incoherent dispensation itself, the indisseverable girdle of incongruities under whose discomfiting span, for most of a century, have unfolded both the most generative and the most murderous plots of our culture.

1990

BELL HOOKS
b. 1952

Born Gloria Jean Watkins, bell hooks took her pseudonym in order to honor a great-grandmother whose legacy of outspokenness she wished to carry on. From *Ain't I a Woman: Black Women and Feminism* (1981) on through such volumes as *Talking Back: Thinking Feminist, Thinking Black* (1989), *Black Looks: Race and Representation* (1992), *Teaching to Transgress: Education as the Practice of Freedom* (1994), *Art on My Mind: Visual Politics* (1995), and *The Will to Change: Men, Masculinity, and Love* (2004), she has forged links between the feminist and the civil rights movements. Gender analysis, without a consideration of racial and class issues, only perpetuates the erasure of most women's oppression, or so she argues in many essays and books that analyze popular film and music, religion and spirituality, pedagogy and black cultural history. A public intellectual who seeks to write to readers inside and outside the academy, bell hooks followed her first volume of memoir, *Bone Black: Memories of Girlhood* (1996), with a series of autobiographical publications. Exceptionally prolific, she honors a realistic and political investment in identity politics that makes it possible for African Americans to resist social injustices; however, she also examines how essentialist ideas about blackness can be exploited to curtail the freedom of black people.

Postmodern Blackness

Postmodernist discourses are often exclusionary even as they call attention to, appropriate even, the experience of "difference" and "Otherness" to provide oppositional political meaning, legitimacy, and immediacy when they are accused of lacking concrete relevance. Very few African-American intellectuals have talked or written about postmodernism. At a dinner party I talked about trying to grapple with the significance of postmodernism for contemporary black experience. It was one of those social gatherings where only one other black person was present. The setting quickly became a field of contestation. I was told by the other black person that I was wasting my time, that "this stuff does not relate in any way to what's happening with black people." Speaking in the presence of a group of white onlookers, staring at us as though this encounter were staged for their benefit, we engaged in a passionate discussion about black experience. Apparently, no one sympathized with my insistence that racism is perpetuated when blackness is associated solely with concrete gut level experience conceived as either opposing or having no connection to abstract thinking and the production of critical theory. The idea that there is no meaningful connection between black experience and critical thinking about aesthetics or culture must be continually interrogated.

My defense of postmodernism and its relevance to black folks sounded good, but I worried that I lacked conviction, largely because I approach the subject cautiously and with suspicion.

Disturbed not so much by the "sense" of postmodernism but by the conventional language used when it is written or talked about and by those who speak it, I find myself on the outside of the discourse looking in. As a discursive practice it is dominated primarily by the voices of white male intellectuals and/or academic elites who speak to and about one another with coded familiarity. Reading and studying their writing to understand postmodernism in its multiple manifestations, I appreciate it but feel little inclination to ally myself with the academic hierarchy and exclusivity pervasive in the movement today.

Critical of most writing on postmodernism, I perhaps am more conscious of the way in which the focus on "Otherness and difference" that is often alluded to in these works seems to have little concrete impact as an analysis or standpoint that might change the nature and direction of postmodernist theory. Since much of this theory has been constructed in reaction to and against high modernism, there is seldom any mention of black experience or writings by black people in this work, specifically black women (though in more recent work one may see a reference to Cornel West, the black male scholar who has most engaged postmodernist discourse). Even if an aspect of black culture is the subject of postmodern critical writing, the works cited will usually be those of black men. A work that comes immediately to mind is Andrew Ross's chapter "Hip, and the Long Front of Color" in *No Respect: Intellectuals and Popular Culture;* while it is an interesting reading, it constructs black culture as though black women have had no role in black cultural production. At the end of Meaghan Morris' discussion of postmodernism in her collection of essays *The Pirate's Fiancée: Feminism, Reading, Postmodernism,* she provides a bibliography of works by women, identifying them as important contributions to a discourse on postmodernism that offer new insight as well as challenging male theoretical hegemony. Even though many of the works do not directly address postmodernism, they address similar concerns. There are no references to works by black women.

The failure to recognize a critical black presence in the culture and in most scholarship and writing on postmodernism compels a black reader, particularly a black female reader, to interrogate her interest in a subject where those who discuss and write about it seem not to know black women exist or even to consider the possibility that we might be somewhere writing or saying something that should be listened to, or producing art that should be seen, heard, approached with intellectual seriousness. This is especially the case with works that go on and on about the way in which postmodernist discourse has opened up a theoretical terrain where "difference and Otherness" can be considered legitimate issues in the academy. Confronting both the absence of recognition of black female presence that much postmodernist theory re-inscribes and the resistance on the part of most black folks to hearing about real connection between postmodernism and black experience, I enter a discourse, a practice, where there may be no ready audience for my words, no clear listener, uncertain then, that my voice can or will be heard.

During the sixties, the black power movement was influenced by perspectives that could easily be labeled modernist. Certainly many of the ways black folks addressed issues of identity conformed to a modernist universalizing agenda. There was little critique of patriarchy as a master narrative among black militants. Despite the fact that black power ideology reflected a modernist sensibility, these elements were soon rendered irrelevant as militant protest was stifled by a powerful, repressive postmodern state. The period directly after the black power movement was a time when major news magazines carried articles with cocky headlines like "Whatever Happened to Black America?" This response was an ironic reply to the aggressive, unmet demand by decentered, marginalized black subjects who had at least momentarily successfully demanded a hearing, who had made it possible for black liberation to be on the national political agenda. In the wake of the black power movement, after so many rebels were slaughtered and lost, many of these voices were silenced by a repressive state; others became inarticulate. It has become necessary to find new avenues to transmit the messages of black liberation struggle, new ways to talk about racism and other politics of domination. Radical postmodernist practice, most powerfully conceptualized as a "politics of difference," should incorporate the voices of displaced, marginalized, exploited, and oppressed black people. It is sadly ironic that the contemporary discourse which talks the most about heterogeneity, the decentered subject, declaring breakthroughs that allow recognition of Otherness, still directs its critical voice primarily to a specialized audience that shares a common language rooted in the very master narratives it claims to challenge. If radical postmodernist thinking is to have a transformative impact, then a critical break with the notion of "authority" as "mastery over" must not simply be a rhetorical device. It must be reflected in habits of being, including styles of writing as well as chosen subject matter. Third world nationals, elites, and white critics who passively absorb white supremacist thinking, and therefore never notice or look at black people on the streets or at their jobs, who render us invisible with their gaze in all areas of daily life, are not likely to produce liberatory theory that will challenge racist domination, or promote a breakdown in traditional ways of seeing and thinking about reality, ways of constructing aesthetic theory and practice. From a different standpoint, Robert Storr makes a similar critique in the global issue of *Art in America* when he asserts:

> To be sure, much postmodernist critical inquiry has centered precisely on the issues of "difference" and "Otherness." On the purely theoretical plane the exploration of these concepts has produced some important results, but in the absence of any sustained research into what artists of

color and others outside the mainstream might be up to, such discussions become rootless instead of radical. Endless second guessing about the latent imperialism of intruding upon other cultures only compounded matters, preventing or excusing these theorists from investigating what black, Hispanic, Asian and Native American artists were actually doing.[1]

Without adequate concrete knowledge of and contact with the non-white "Other," white theorists may move in discursive theoretical directions that are threatening and potentially disruptive of that critical practice which would support radical liberation struggle.

The postmodern critique of "identity," though relevant for renewed black liberation struggle, is often posed in ways that are problematic. Given a pervasive politic of white supremacy which seeks to prevent the formation of radical black subjectivity, we cannot cavalierly dismiss a concern with identity politics. Any critic exploring the radical potential of postmodernism as it relates to racial difference and racial domination would need to consider the implications of a critique of identity for oppressed groups. Many of us are struggling to find new strategies of resistance. We must engage decolonization as a critical practice if we are to have meaningful chances of survival even as we must simultaneously cope with the loss of political grounding which made radical activism more possible. I am thinking here about the postmodernist critique of essentialism as it pertains to the construction of "identity" as one example.

Postmodern theory that is not seeking to simply appropriate the experience of "Otherness" to enhance the discourse or to be radically chic should not separate the "politics of difference" from the politics of racism. To take racism seriously one must consider the plight of underclass people of color, a vast majority of whom are black. For African-Americans our collective condition prior to the advent of postmodernism and perhaps more tragically expressed under current postmodern conditions has been and is characterized by continued displacement, profound alienation, and despair. Writing about blacks and postmodernism, Cornel West describes our collective plight:

> There is increasing class division and differentiation, creating on the one hand a significant black middle-class, highly anxiety-ridden, insecure, willing to be co-opted and incorporated into the powers that be, concerned with racism to the degree that it poses contraints on upward social mobility; and, on the other, a vast and growing black underclass, an underclass that embodies a kind of walking nihilism of pervasive drug addiction, pervasive alcoholism, pervasive homicide, and an exponential rise in suicide. Now because of the deindustrialization, we also have a devastated black industrial working class. We are talking here about tremendous hopelessness.[2]

This hopelessness creates longing for insight and strategies for change that can renew spirits and reconstruct grounds for collective black liberation struggle. The overall impact of postmodernism is that many other groups now share with black folks a sense of deep alienation, despair, uncertainty, loss of

1. Robert Storr, "The Global Issue: A Symposium," *Art in America* 77 (1989): 88.
2. Cornel West, "The Political Intellectual," inter-view with Anders Stephanson, *Flash Art* (1987); reprinted in *The Cornel West Reader* (New York: Basic Civitas Books, 1999), p. 284.

a sense of grounding even if it is not informed by shared circumstance. Radical postmodernism calls attention to those shared sensibilities which cross the boundaries of class, gender, race, etc., that could be fertile ground for the construction of empathy—ties that would promote recognition of common commitments, and serve as a base for solidarity and coalition.

Yearning is the word that best describes a common psychological state shared by many of us, cutting across boundaries of race, class, gender, and sexual practice. Specifically, in relation to the post-modernist deconstruction of "master" narratives, the yearning that wells in the hearts and minds of those whom such narratives have silenced is the longing for critical voice. It is no accident that "rap" has usurped the primary position of rhythm and blues music among young black folks as the most desired sound or that it began as a form of "testimony" for the underclass. It has enabled underclass black youth to develop a critical voice, as a group of young black men told me, a "common literacy." Rap projects a critical voice, explaining, demanding, urging. Working with this insight in his essay "Putting the Pop Back into Postmodernism," Lawrence Grossberg comments:

> The postmodern sensibility appropriates practices as boasts that announce their own—and consequently our own—existence, like a rap song boasting of the imaginary (or real—it makes no difference) accomplishments of the rapper. They offer forms of empowerment not only in the face of nihilism but precisely through the forms of nihilism itself: an empowering nihilism, a moment of positivity through the production and structuring of affective relations.[3]

Considering that it is as subject one comes to voice, then the postmodernist focus on the critique of identity appears at first glance to threaten and close down the possibility that this discourse and practice will allow those who have suffered the crippling effects of colonization and domination to gain or regain a hearing. Even if this sense of threat and the fear it evokes are based on a misunderstanding of the postmodernist political project, they nevertheless shape responses. It never surprises me when black folks respond to the critique of essentialism, especially when it denies the validity of identity politics by saying, "Yeah, it's easy to give up identity, when you got one." Should we not be suspicious of postmodern critiques of the "subject" when they surface at a historical moment when many subjugated people feel themselves coming to voice for the first time? Though an apt and oftentimes appropriate comeback, it does not really intervene in the discourse in a way that alters and transforms.

Criticisms of directions in postmodern thinking should not obscure insights it may offer that open up our understanding of African-American experience. The critique of essentialism encouraged by postmodernist thought is useful for African-Americans concerned with reformulating outmoded notions of identity. We have too long had imposed upon us from both the outside and the inside a narrow, constricting notion of blackness. Postmodern critiques of essentialism which challenge notions of universality and static over-determined identity within mass culture and mass consciousness can open up new possibilities for the construction of self and the assertion of agency.

3. Lawrence Grossberg, "Putting the Pop Back into Postmodernism," in *Universal Abandon: The Politics of Postmodernism*, ed. Andrew Ross (Minneapolis: University of Minnesota Press, 1988), p. 181.

Employing a critique of essentialism allows African-Americans to acknowledge the way in which class mobility has altered collective black experience so that racism does not necessarily have the same impact on our lives. Such a critique allows us to affirm multiple black identities, varied black experience. It also challenges colonial imperialist paradigms of black identity which represent blackness one-dimensionally in ways that reinforce and sustain white supremacy. This discourse created the idea of the "primitive" and promoted the notion of an "authentic" experience, seeing as "natural" those expressions of black life which conformed to a preexisting pattern or stereotype. Abandoning essentialist notions would be a serious challenge to racism. Contemporary African-American resistance struggle must be rooted in a process of decolonization that continually opposes re-inscribing notions of "authentic" black identity. This critique should not be made synonymous with a dismissal of the struggle of oppressed and exploited peoples to make ourselves subjects. Nor should it deny that in certain circumstances this experience affords us a privileged critical location from which to speak. This is not a re-inscription of modernist master narratives of authority which privilege some voices by denying voice to others. Part of our struggle for radical black subjectivity is the quest to find ways to construct self and identity that are oppositional and liberatory. The unwillingness to critique essentialism on the part of many African-Americans is rooted in the fear that it will cause folks to lose sight of the specific history and experience of African-Americans and the unique sensibilities and culture that arise from that experience. An adequate response to this concern is to critique essentialism while emphasizing the significance of "the authority of experience."[4] There is a radical difference between a repudiation of the idea that there is a black "essence" and recognition of the way black identity has been specifically constituted in the experience of exile and struggle.

When black folks critique essentialism, we are empowered to recognize multiple experiences of black identity that are the lived conditions which make diverse cultural productions possible. When this diversity is ignored, it is easy to see black folks as falling into two categories: nationalist or assimilationist, black-identified or white-identified. Coming to terms with the impact of postmodernism for black experience, particularly as it changes our sense of identity, means that we must and can rearticulate the basis for collective bonding. Given the various crises facing African-Americans (economic, spiritual, escalating racial violence, etc.), we are compelled by circumstance to reassess our relationship to popular culture and resistance struggle. Many of us are as reluctant to face this task as many non-black postmodern thinkers who focus theoretically on the issue of "difference" are to confront the issue of race and racism.

Music is the cultural product created by African-Americans that has most attracted postmodern theorists. It is rarely acknowledged that there is far greater censorship and restriction of other forms of cultural production by black folks—literary, critical writing, etc. Attempts on the part of editors and publishing houses to control and manipulate the representation of black culture, as well as the desire to promote the creation of products that will attract the widest audience, limit in a crippling and stifling way the kind of work

4. The title of a 1977 collection of essays of feminist criticism, edited by Arlyn Diamond and Lee R. Edwards.

many black folks feel we can do and still receive recognition. Using myself as an example, that creative writing I do which I consider to be most reflective of a postmodern oppositional sensibility, work that is abstract, fragmented, non-linear narrative, is constantly rejected by editors and publishers. It does not conform to the type of writing they think black women should be doing or the type of writing they believe will sell. Certainly I do not think I am the only black person engaged in forms of cultural production, especially experimental ones, who is constrained by the lack of an audience for certain kinds of work. It is important for postmodern thinkers and theorists to constitute themselves as an audience for such work. To do this they must assert power and privilege within the space of critical writing to open up the field so that it will be more inclusive. To change the exclusionary practice of postmodern critical discourse is to enact a postmodernism of resistance. Part of this intervention entails black intellectual participation in the discourse.

In his essay "Postmodernism and Black America," Cornel West suggests that black intellectuals "are marginal—usually languishing at the interface of Black and white cultures or thoroughly ensconced in Euro-American settings." He cannot see this group as potential producers of radical postmodernist thought. While I generally agree with this assessment, black intellectuals must proceed with the understanding that we are not condemned to the margins. The way we work and what we do can determine whether or not what we produce will be meaningful to a wider audience, one that includes all classes of black people. West suggests that black intellectuals lack "any organic link with most of Black life" and that this "diminishes their value to Black resistance." This statement bears traces of essentialism. Perhaps we need to focus more on those black intellectuals, however rare our presence, who do not feel this lack and whose work is primarily directed towards the enhancement of black critical consciousness and the strengthening of our collective capacity to engage in meaningful resistance struggle. Theoretical ideas and critical thinking need not be transmitted solely in written work or solely in the academy. While I work in a predominantly white institution, I remain intimately and passionately engaged with black community. It's not like I'm going to talk about writing and thinking about postmodernism with other academics and/or intellectuals and not discuss these ideas with underclass non-academic black folks who are family, friends, and comrades. Since I have not broken the ties that bind me to underclass poor black community, I have seen that knowledge, especially that which enhances daily life and strengthens our capacity to survive, can be shared. It means that critics, writers, and academics have to give the same critical attention to nurturing and cultivating our ties to black community that we give to writing articles, teaching, and lecturing. Here again I am really talking about cultivating habits of being that reinforce awareness that knowledge can be disseminated and shared on a number of fronts. The extent to which knowledge is made available, accessible, etc. depends on the nature of one's political commitments.

Postmodern culture with its decentered subject can be the space where ties are severed or it can provide the occasion for new and varied forms of bonding. To some extent, ruptures, surfaces, contextuality, and a host of other happenings create gaps that make space for oppositional practices which no longer require intellectuals to be confined by narrow separate spheres with no meaningful connection to the world of the everyday. Much postmodern engagement with culture emerges from the yearning to do intellectual work that connects with habits of being, forms of artistic expression, and aesthetics that inform the daily life of writers and scholars as a well as a mass population. On the terrain of culture, one can participate in critical dialogue with the uneducated poor, the black underclass who are thinking about aesthetics. One can talk about what we are seeing, thinking, or listening to; a space is there for critical exchange. It's exciting to think, write, talk about, and create art that reflects passionate engagement with popular culture, because this may very well be "the" central future location of resistance struggle, a meeting place where new and radical happenings can occur.

1990

JUDITH BUTLER
b. 1956

As an avowed feminist, Judith Butler set out to dismantle or destabilize the distinction between gender and sex that had animated so many earlier feminist thinkers from the 1960s on. In her highly influential *Gender Trouble: Feminism and the Subversion of Identity* (1990), she troubled the term usually associated with the natural, physical, anatomical difference between men and women by arguing that sex is no less socially constructed than gender. Butler's emphasis on the social production of sex and gender led to a conclusion in which the drag show epitomizes the "performativity" of a femininity or a masculinity that can be subverted through parody. It also led to her next book with its title speaking back to those critics who had faulted her for neglecting corporeal embodiment: *Bodies That Matter: On the Discursive Limits of "Sex"* (1993). Trained in philosophy at Yale University, Butler teaches at the University of California, Berkeley. What she brings to feminist discourse, in particular through her critique of identity politics, is the philosophic sophistication of a poststructuralism indebted to the thinking of Michel Foucault. *Excitable Speech: A Politics of the Performative* (1997), *The Psychic Life of Power: Theories in Subjection* (1997), *Antigone's Claim: Kinship between Life and Death* (2000), *Undoing Gender* (2004), and *Precarious Life: The Power of Mourning and Violence* (2004) extend Judith Butler's commitment to using poststructuralist feminism to deal with the key issues of social justice and peace facing men and women today.

Imitation and Gender Insubordination[1]

> So what is this divided being introduced into language through gender? It is an impossible being, it is a being that does not exist, an ontological joke.
>
> *Monique Wittig*[2]

---

1. Parts of this essay were given as a presentation at the Conference on Homosexuality at Yale University in October, 1989 [except as indicated, all notes are Butler's].

2. "The Mark of Gender," *Feminist Issues* 5, no. 2 (1985): 6.

Beyond physical repetition and the psychical or metaphysical repetition, is there an *ontological* repetition? . . . This ultimate repetition, this ultimate theatre, gathers everything in a certain way; and in another way, it destroys everything; and in yet another way, it selects from everything.

Gilles Deleuze[3]

To Theorize as a Lesbian?

At first I considered writing a different sort of essay, one with a philosophical tone: the "being" of being homosexual. The prospect of *being* anything, even for pay, has always produced in me a certain anxiety, for "to be" gay, "to be" lesbian seems to be more than a simple injunction to become who or what I already am. And in no way does it settle the anxiety for me to say that this is "part" of what I am. To write or speak *as a lesbian* appears a paradoxical appearance of this "I," one which feels neither true nor false. For it is a production, usually in response to a request, to come out or write in the name of an identity which, once produced, sometimes functions as a politically efficacious phantasm. I'm not at ease with "lesbian theories, gay theories," for as I've argued elsewhere,[4] identity categories tend to be instruments of regulatory regimes, whether as the normalizing categories of oppressive structures or as the rallying points for a liberatory contestation of that very oppression. This is not to say that I will not appear at political occasions under the sign of lesbian, but that I would like to have it permanently unclear what precisely that sign signifies. So it is unclear how it is that I can contribute to this book[5] and appear under its title, for it announces a set of terms that I propose to contest. One risk I take is to be recolonized by the sign under which I write, and so it is this risk that I seek to thematize. To propose that the invocation of identity is always a risk does not imply that resistance to it is always or only symptomatic of a self-inflicted homophobia. Indeed, a Foucaultian perspective might argue that the affirmation of "homosexuality" is itself an extension of a homophobic discourse. And yet "discourse," he writes on the same page, "can be both an instrument and an effect of power, but also a hindrance, a stumbling-block, a point of resistance and a starting point for an opposing strategy."[6]

So I am skeptical about how the "I" is determined as it operates under the title of the lesbian sign, and I am no more comfortable with its homophobic determination than with those normative definitions offered by other members of the "gay or lesbian community." I'm permanently troubled by identity categories, consider them to be invariable stumbling-blocks, and understand them, even promote them, as sites of necessary trouble. In fact, if the category were to offer no trouble, it would cease to be interesting to me: it is precisely the *pleasure* produced by the instability of those categories which sustains the various erotic practices that make me a candidate for the category to begin with. To install myself within the terms of an identity category would be to turn against the sexuality that the category purports to describe; and this might be true for any identity category which seeks to control the very eroticism that it claims to describe and authorize, much less "liberate."

3. *Différence et répétition* (Paris: PUF, 1968), 374; my translation.
4. *Gender Trouble: Feminism and the Subversion of Identity* (New York: Routledge, 1990).
5. *Inside/Out: Lesbian Theories, Gay Theories*, ed. Diana Fuss (New York: Routledge, 1991) [editor's note].
6. Michel Foucault, *The History of Sexuality, Vol. 1*, trans. John Hurley (New York: Random House, 1980), 101.

And what's worse, I do not understand the notion of "theory," and am hardly interested in being cast as its defender, much less in being signified as part of an elite gay/lesbian theory crowd that seeks to establish the legitimacy and domestication of gay/lesbian studies within the academy. Is there a pre-given distinction between theory, politics, culture, media? How do those divisions operate to quell a certain intertextual writing that might well generate wholly different epistemic maps? But I am writing here now: is it too late? Can this writing, can any writing, refuse the terms by which it is appropriated even as, to some extent, that very colonizing discourse enables or produces this stumbling block, this resistance? How do I relate the paradoxical situation of this dependency and refusal?

If the political task is to show that theory is never merely *theoria*, in the sense of disengaged contemplation, and to insist that it is fully political (*phronesis* or even *praxis*[7]), then why not simply call this operation *politics*, or some necessary permutation of it?

I have begun with confessions of trepidation and a series of disclaimers, but perhaps it will become clear that *disclaiming*, which is no simple activity, will be what I have to offer as a form of affirmative resistance to a certain regulatory operation of homophobia. The discourse of "coming out" has clearly served its purposes, but what are its risks? And here I am not speaking of unemployment or public attack or violence, which are quite clearly and widely on the increase against those who are perceived as "out" whether or not of their own design. Is the "subject" who is "out" free of its subjection and finally in the clear? Or could it be that the subjection that subjectivates the gay or lesbian subject in some ways continues to oppress, or oppresses most insidiously, once "outness" is claimed? What or who is it that is "out," made manifest and fully disclosed, when and if I reveal myself as lesbian? What is it that is now known, anything? What remains permanently concealed by the very linguistic act that offers up the promise of a transparent revelation of sexuality? Can sexuality even remain sexuality once it submits to a criterion of transparency and disclosure, or does it perhaps cease to be sexuality precisely when the semblance of full explicitness is achieved?[8] Is sexuality of any kind even possible without that opacity designated by the unconscious, which means simply that the conscious "I" who would reveal its sexuality is perhaps the last to know the meaning of what it says?

To claim that this is what I *am* is to suggest a provisional totalization of this "I." But if the I can so determine itself, then that which it excludes in order to make that determination remains constitutive of the determination itself. In other words, such a statement presupposes that the "I" exceeds its determination, and even produces that very excess in and by the act which seeks to exhaust the semantic field of that "I." In the act which would disclose the true and full content of that "I," a certain radical *concealment* is thereby produced. For it is always finally unclear what is meant by invoking the lesbian-signifier, since its signification is always to some degree out of one's control, but also because its *specificity* can only be demarcated by exclusions that return to disrupt its claim to coherence. What, if anything, can lesbians be said to share? And who will decide this question, and in the name of whom?

7. "Thought, will" and "practice, action": Greek terms, as is *theōria* [editor's note].
8. Here I would doubtless differ from the very fine analysis of Hitchcock's *Rope* offered by D. A. Miller in "Anal *Rope*," in Fuss, ed., *Inside/Out*.

If I claim to be a lesbian, I "come out" only to produce a new and different "closet." The "you" to whom I come out now has access to a different region of opacity. Indeed, the locus of opacity has simply shifted: before, you did not know whether I "am," but now you do not know what that means, which is to say that the copula is empty, that it cannot be substituted for with a set of descriptions.[9] And perhaps that is a situation to be valued. Conventionally, one comes out *of* the closet (and yet, how often is it the case that we are "outted" when we are young and without resources?); so we are out of the closet, but into what? what new unbounded spatiality? the room, the den, the attic, the basement, the house, the bar, the university, some new enclosure whose door, like Kafka's door,[1] produces the expectation of a fresh air and a light of illumination that never arrives? Curiously, it is the figure of the closet that produces this expectation, and which guarantees its dissatisfaction. For being "out" always depends to some extent on being "in"; it gains its meaning only within that polarity. Hence, being "out" must produce the closet again and again in order to maintain itself as "out." In this sense, *outness* can only produce a new opacity; and *the closet* produces the promise of a disclosure that can, by definition, never come. Is this infinite postponement of the disclosure of "gayness," produced by the very act of "coming out," to be lamented? Or is this very deferral of the signified *to be valued*, a site for the production of values, precisely because the term now takes on a life that cannot be, can never be, permanently controlled?

It is possible to argue that whereas no transparent or full revelation is afforded by "lesbian" and "gay," there remains a political imperative to use these necessary errors or category mistakes, as it were (what Gayatri Spivak might call "catachrestic" operations: to use a proper name improperly[2]), to rally and represent an oppressed political constituency. Clearly, I am not legislating against the use of the term. My question is simply: which use will be legislated, and what play will there be between legislation and use such that the instrumental uses of "identity" do not become regulatory imperatives? If it is already true that "lesbians" and "gay men" have been traditionally designated as impossible identities, errors of classification, unnatural disasters within juridico-medical discourses, or, what perhaps amounts to the same, the very paradigm of what calls to be classified, regulated, and controlled, then perhaps these sites of disruption, error, confusion, and trouble can be the very rallying points for a certain resistance to classification and to identity as such.

The question is not one of *avowing* or *disavowing* the category of lesbian or gay, but, rather, why it is that the category becomes the site of this "ethical" choice? What does it mean to *avow* a category that can only maintain its specificity and coherence by performing a prior set of *disavowals*? Does this make "coming out" into the avowal of disavowal, that is, a return to the closet under the guise of an escape? And it is not something like heterosexuality or bisexuality that is disavowed by the category, but a set of identificatory and practical crossings between these categories that renders the discreteness of

9. For an example of "coming out" that is strictly unconfessional and which, finally, offers no content for the category of lesbian, see Barbara Johnson's deftly constructed "Sula Passing: No Passing" presentation at UCLA, May 1990.
1. See Franz Kafka's parable "Before the Law" (from chapter 9 of *The Trial*, 1925; first published separately in 1916), in which a man spends his entire life waiting to receive permission to pass through the gate to the Law [editor's note].
2. Gayatri Chakravorty Spivak, "Displacement and the Discourse of Woman," in *Displacement: Derrida and After*, ed. Mark Krupnick (Bloomington: Indiana University Press, 1983).

each equally suspect. Is it not possible to maintain and pursue heterosexual identifications and aims within homosexual practice, and homosexual identifications and aims within heterosexual practices? If a sexuality is to be disclosed, what will be taken as the true determinant of its meaning: the phantasy structure, the act, the orifice, the gender, the anatomy? And if the practice engages a complex interplay of all of those, which one of this erotic dimensions will come to stand for the sexuality that requires them all? Is it the *specificity* of a lesbian experience or lesbian desire or lesbian sexuality that lesbian theory needs to elucidate? Those efforts have only and always produced a set of contests and refusals which should by now make it clear that there is no necessarily common element among lesbians, except perhaps that we all know something about how homophobia works against women— although, even then, the language and the analysis we use will differ.

To argue that there might be a *specificity* to lesbian sexuality has seemed a necessary counterpoint to the claim that lesbian sexuality is just heterosexuality once removed, or that it is derived, or that it does not exist. But perhaps the claim of specificity, on the one hand, and the claim of derivativeness or non-existence, on the other, are not as contradictory as they seem. Is it not possible that lesbian sexuality is a process that reinscribes the power domains that it resists, that it is constituted in part from the very heterosexual matrix that it seeks to displace, and that its specificity is to be established, not *outside* or *beyond* that reinscription or reiteration, but in the very modality and effects of that reinscription. In other words, the negative constructions of lesbianism as a fake or a bad copy can be occupied and reworked to call into question the claims of heterosexual priority. In a sense I hope to make clear in what follows, lesbian sexuality can be understood to redeploy its 'derivativeness' in the service of displacing hegemonic heterosexual norms. Understood in this way, the political problem is not to establish the specificity of lesbian sexuality over and against its derivativeness, but to turn the homophobic construction of the bad copy against the framework that privileges heterosexuality as origin, and so 'derive' the former from the latter. This description requires a reconsideration of imitation, drag, and other forms of sexual crossing that affirm the internal complexity of a lesbian sexuality constituted in part within the very matrix of power that it is compelled both to reiterate and to oppose.

On the Being of Gayness as Necessary Drag

The professionalization of gayness requires a certain performance and production of a "self" which is the *constituted effect* of a discourse that nevertheless claims to "represent" that self as a prior truth. When I spoke at the conference on homosexuality in 1989,[3] I found myself telling my friends

3. Let me take this occasion to apologize to the social worker at that conference who asked a question about how to deal with those clients with AIDS who turned to Bernie Segal and others for the purposes of psychic healing. At the time, I understood this questioner to be suggesting that such clients were full of self-hatred because they were trying to find the causes of AIDS in their own selves. The questioner and I appear to agree that any effort to locate the responsibility for AIDS in those who suffer from it is politically and ethically wrong. I thought the questioner, however, was prepared to tell his clients that they were self-hating, and I reacted too strongly (too strongly) to the paternalistic prospect that this person was going to pass judgment on someone who was clearly not only suffering, but already passing judgment on him or herself. To call another person self-hating is itself an act of power that calls for some kind of scrutiny, and I think in response to someone who is already dealing with AIDS, that is perhaps the last thing one needs to hear. I also happened to have a friend who sought out advice from Bernie Segal, not with the belief that there is an exclusive or even primary psychic

beforehand that I was off to Yale to be a lesbian, which of course didn't mean that I wasn't one before, but that somehow then, as I spoke in that context, I *was* one in some more thorough and totalizing way, at least for the time being. So I *am* one, and my qualifications are even fairly unambiguous. Since I was sixteen, being a lesbian is what I've been. So what's the anxiety, the discomfort? Well, it has something to do with that redoubling, the way I can say, I'm going to Yale to be a lesbian; a lesbian is what I've been being for so long. How is it that I can both "be" one, and yet endeavor to be one at the same time? When and where does my being a lesbian come into play, when and where does this playing a lesbian constitute something like what I am? To say that I "play" at being one is not to say that I am not one "really"; rather, how and where I play at being one is the way in which that "being" gets established, instituted, circulated, and confirmed. This is not a performance from which I can take radical distance, for this is deep-seated play, psychically entrenched play, *and this "I" does not play its lesbianism as a role*. Rather, it is through the repeated play of this sexuality that the "I" is insistently reconstituted as a lesbian "I"; paradoxically, it is precisely the *repetition* of that play that establishes as well the *instability* of the very category that it constitutes. For if the "I" is a site of repetition, that is, if the "I" only achieves the semblance of identity through a certain repetition of itself, then the I is always displaced by the very repetition that sustains it. In other words, does or can the "I" ever repeat itself, cite itself, faithfully, or is there always a displacement from its former moment that establishes the permanently non-self-identical status of that "I" or its "being lesbian"? What "performs" does not exhaust the "I"; it does not lay out in visible terms the comprehensive content of that "I," for if the performance is "repeated," there is always the question of what differentiates from each other the moments of identity that are repeated. And if the "I" is the effect of a certain repetition, one which produces the semblance of a continuity or coherence, then there is no "I" that precedes the gender that it is said to perform; the repetition, and the failure to repeat, produce a string of performances that constitute and contest the coherence of that "I."

But *politically*, we might argue, isn't it quite crucial to insist on lesbian and gay identities precisely because they are being threatened with erasure and obliteration from homophobic quarters? Isn't the above theory *complicitous* with those political forces that would obliterate the possibility of gay and lesbian identity? Isn't it "no accident" that such theoretical contestations of identity emerge within a political climate that is performing a set of similar obliterations of homosexual identities through legal and political means?

The question I want to raise in return is this: ought such threats of obliteration dictate the terms of the political resistance to them, and if they do,

---

cause or solution for AIDS, but that there might be a psychic contribution to be made to surviving with AIDS. Unfortunately, I reacted quickly to this questioner, and with some anger. And I regret now that I didn't have my wits about me to discuss the distinctions with him that I have just laid out.

Curiously, this incident was invoked at a CLAGS (Center for Lesbian and Gay Studies) meeting at CUNY sometime in December of 1989 and, according to those who told me about it, my angry denunciation of the social worker was taken to be symptomatic of the political insensitivity of a "theorist" in dealing with someone who is actively engaged in AIDS work. That attribution implies that I do not do AIDS work, that I am not politically engaged, and that the social worker in question does not read theory. Needless to say, I was reacting angrily on behalf of an absent friend with AIDS who sought out Bernie Segal and company. So as I offer this apology to the social worker, I wait expectantly that the CLAGS member who misunderstood me will offer me one in turn. [Segal is an American physician who advocates patients' empowerment and has written and spoken extensively on the healing potential of the individual—editor's note.]

do such homophobic efforts to that extent win the battle from the start? There is no question that gays and lesbians are threatened by the violence of public erasure, but the decision to counter that violence must be careful not to reinstall another in its place. Which version of lesbian or gay ought to be rendered visible, and which internal exclusions will that rendering visible institute? Can the visibility of identity *suffice* as a political strategy, or can it only be the starting point for a strategic intervention which calls for a transformation of policy? Is it not a sign of despair over public politics when identity becomes its own policy, bringing with it those who would 'police' it from various sides? And this is not a call to return to silence or invisibility, but, rather, to make use of a category that can be called into question, made to account for what it excludes. That any consolidation of identity requires some set of differentiations and exclusions seems clear. But which ones ought to be valorized? That the identity-sign I use now has its purposes seems right, but there is no way to predict or control the political uses to which that sign will be put in the future. And perhaps this is a kind of openness, regardless of its risks, that ought to be safeguarded for political reasons. If the rendering visible of lesbian/gay identity now presupposes a set of exclusions, then perhaps part of what is necessarily excluded is *the future uses of the sign.* There is a political necessity to use some sign now, and we do, but how to use it in such a way that its futural significations are not *foreclosed?* How to use the sign and avow its temporal contingency at once?

In avowing the sign's strategic provisionality (rather than its strategic essentialism), that identity can become a site of contest and revision, indeed, take on a future set of significations that those of us who use it now may not be able to foresee. It is in the safeguarding of the future of the political signifiers—preserving the signifier as a site of rearticulation—that Laclau and Mouffe discern its democratic promise.[4]

Within contemporary U.S. politics, there are a vast number of ways in which lesbianism in particular is understood as precisely that which cannot or dare not *be.* In a sense, Jesse Helms's attack on the NEA for sanctioning representations of "homoeroticism" focuses various homophobic fantasies of what gay men are and do on the work of Robert Mapplethorpe.[5] In a sense, for Helms, gay men exist as objects of prohibition; they are, in his twisted fantasy, sadomasochistic exploiters of children, the paradigmatic exemplars of "obscenity"; in a sense, the lesbian is not even produced within this discourse as a prohibited object. Here it becomes important to recognize that oppression works not merely through acts of overt prohibition, but covertly, through the constitution of viable subjects and through the corollary constitution of a domain of unviable (un)subjects—*abjects,*[6] we might call them—who are neither named nor prohibited within the economy of the law. Here oppression works through the production of a domain of unthinkability and unnameability. Lesbianism is not explicitly prohibited in part because it has

4. E.g., see Ernesto Laclau and Chantal Mouffe, *Hegemony and Socialist Strategy: Towards a Radical Democratic Politics,* trans. Winston Moore and Paul Cammack (London: Verso, 1985) [editor's note].

5. See my "The Force of Fantasy: Feminism, Mapplethorpe, and Discursive Excess," *differences* 2, no. 2 (Summer 1990). Since the writing of this essay, lesbian artists and representations have also come under attack. [Helms (b. 1921), conservative senator from North Carolina (1972–2002)—editor's note.]

6. The abject, according to the French cultural theorist and psychoanalyst Julia Kristeva, is what is still unconsciously desired—and thus is viewed as filthy and disgusting—after the subject's consciousness creates the proper separation between subject and object [editor's note].

not even made its way into the thinkable, the imaginable, that grid of cultural intelligibility that regulates the real and the nameable. How, then, to "be" a lesbian in a political context in which the lesbian does not exist? That is, in a political discourse that wages its violence against lesbianism in part by excluding lesbianism from discourse itself? To be prohibited explicitly is to occupy a discursive site from which something like a reverse-discourse can be articulated; to be implicitly proscribed is not even to qualify as an object of prohibition.[7] And though homosexualities of all kinds in this present climate are being erased, reduced, and (then) reconstituted as sites of radical homophobic fantasy, it is important to retrace the different routes by which the unthinkability of homosexuality is being constituted time and again.

It is one thing to be erased from discourse, and yet another to be present within discourse as an abiding falsehood. Hence, there is a political imperative to render lesbianism visible, but how is that to be done outside or through existing regulatory regimes? Can the exclusion from ontology itself become a rallying point for resistance?

Here is something like a confession which is meant merely to thematize the impossibility of confession: As a young person, I suffered for a long time, and I suspect many people have, from being told, explicitly or implicitly, that what I "am" is a copy, an imitation, a derivative example, a shadow of the real. Compulsory heterosexuality sets itself up as the original, the true, the authentic; the norm that determines the real implies that "being" lesbian is always a kind of miming, a vain effort to participate in the phantasmatic plenitude of naturalized heterosexuality which will always and only fail.[8] And yet, I remember quite distinctly when I first read in Esther Newton's *Mother Camp: Female Impersonators in America*[9] that drag is not an imitation or a copy of some prior and true gender; according to Newton, drag enacts the very structure of impersonation by which *any gender* is assumed. Drag is not the putting on of a gender that belongs properly to some other group, i.e. an act of *ex*propriation or *ap*propriation that assumes that gender is the rightful property of sex, that "masculine" belongs to "male" and "feminine" belongs to "female." There is no "proper" gender, a gender proper to one sex rather than

7. It is this particular ruse of erasure which Foucault for the most part fails to take account of in his analysis of power. He almost always presumes that power takes place through discourse as its instrument, and that oppression is linked with subjection and subjectivation, that is, that it is installed as the formative principle of the identity of subjects.

8. Although miming suggests that there is a prior model which is being copied, it can have the effect of exposing that prior model as purely phantasmatic. In Jacques Derrida's "The Double Session" in *Dissemination,* trans. Barbara Johnson (Chicago: University of Chicago Press, 1981), he considers the textual effect of the mime in Mallarmé's "Mimique." There Derrida argues that the mime does not imitate or copy some prior phenomenon, idea, or figure, but constitutes—some might say *performatively*—the phantasm of the original in and through the mime:

He represents nothing, imitates nothing, does not have to conform to any prior referent with the aim of achieving adequation or verisimilitude. One can here foresee an objection: since

the mime imitates nothing, reproduces nothing, opens up in its origin the very thing he is tracing out, presenting, or producing, he must be the very movement of truth. Not, of course, truth in the form of adequation between the representation and the present of the thing itself, or between the imitator and the imitated, but truth as the present unveiling of the present. . . . But this is not the case. . . . We are faced then with mimicry imitating nothing; faced, so to speak, with a double that couples no simple, a double that nothing anticipates, nothing at least that is not itself already double. There is no simple reference. . . . This speculum reflects no reality: it produces mere "reality-effects". . . . In this speculum with no reality, in this mirror of a mirror, a difference or dyad does exist, since there are mimes and phantoms. But it is a difference without reference, or rather reference without a referent, without any first or last unit, a ghost that is the phantom of no flesh . . . (206)

9. Esther Newton, *Mother Camp: Female Impersonators in America* (Chicago: University of Chicago Press, 1972).

another, which is in some sense that sex's cultural property. Where that notion of the "proper" operates, it is always and only *improperly* installed as the effect of a compulsory system. Drag constitutes the mundane way in which genders are appropriated, theatricalized, worn, and done; it implies that all gendering is a kind of impersonation and approximation. If this is true, it seems, there is no original or primary gender that drag imitates, but *gender is a kind of imitation for which there is no original;* in fact, it is a kind of imitation that produces the very notion of the original as an *effect* and consequence of the imitation itself. In other words, the naturalistic effects of heterosexualized genders are produced through imitative strategies; what they imitate is a phantasmatic ideal of heterosexual identity, one that is produced by the imitation as its effect. In this sense, the "reality" of heterosexual identities is performatively constituted through an imitation that sets itself up as the origin and the ground of all imitations. In other words, heterosexuality is always in the process of imitating and approximating its own phantasmatic idealization of itself—*and failing.* Precisely because it is bound to fail, and yet endeavors to succeed, the project of heterosexual identity is propelled into an endless repetition of itself. Indeed, in its efforts to naturalize itself as the original, heterosexuality must be understood as a compulsive and compulsory repetition that can only produce the *effect* of its own originality; in other words, compulsory heterosexual identities, those ontologically consolidated phantasms of "man" and "woman," are theatrically produced effects that posture as grounds, origins, the normative measure of the real.[1]

Reconsider then the homophobic charge that queens and butches and femmes are imitations of the heterosexual real. Here "imitation" carries the meaning of "derivative" or "secondary," a copy of an origin which is itself the ground of all copies, but which is itself a copy of nothing. Logically, this notion of an "origin" is suspect, for how can something operate as an origin if there are no secondary consequences which retrospectively confirm the originality of that origin? The origin requires its derivations in order to affirm itself as an origin, for origins only make sense to the extent that they are differentiated from that which they produce as derivatives. Hence, if it were not for the notion of the homosexual *as* copy, there would be no construct of heterosexuality *as* origin. Heterosexuality here presupposes homosexuality. And if the homosexual *as* copy *precedes* the heterosexual as *origin,* then it seems only fair to concede that the copy comes before the origin, and that homosexuality is thus the origin, and heterosexuality the copy.

But simple inversions are not really possible. For it is only *as* a copy that homosexuality can be argued to *precede* heterosexuality as the origin. In other words, the entire framework of copy and origin proves radically unstable as each position inverts into the other and confounds the possibility of any stable way to locate the temporal or logical priority of either term.

---

1. In a sense, one might offer a redescription of the above in Lacanian terms. The sexual "positions" of heterosexually differentiated "man" and "woman" are part of the *Symbolic,* that is, an ideal embodiment of the Law of sexual difference which constitutes the object of imaginary pursuits, but which is always thwarted by the "real." These symbolic positions for Lacan are by definition impossi- ble to occupy even as they are impossible to resist as the structuring telos of desire. I accept the former point, and reject the latter one. The imputation of universal necessity to such positions simply encodes compulsory heterosexuality at the level of the Symbolic, and the "failure" to achieve it is implicitly lamented as a source of heterosexual pathos.

But let us then consider this problematic inversion from a psychic/political perspective. If the structure of gender imitation is such that the imitat*ed* is to some degree produced—or, rather, *re*produced—by imitation (see again Derrida's inversion and displacement of mimesis in "The Double Session"), then to claim that gay and lesbian identities are implicated in heterosexual norms or in hegemonic culture generally is not to *derive* gayness from straightness. On the contrary, *imitation* does not copy that which is prior, but produces and *inverts* the very terms of priority and derivativeness. Hence, if gay identities are implicated in heterosexuality, that is not the same as claiming that they are determined or derived from heterosexuality, and it is not the same as claiming that that heterosexuality is the only cultural network in which they are implicated. These are, quite literally, *inverted* imitations, ones which invert the order of imitated and imitation, and which, in the process, expose the fundamental dependency of "the origin" on that which it claims to produce as its secondary effect.

What follows if we concede from the start that gay identities as derivative inversions are in part defined in terms of the very heterosexual identities from which they are differentiated? If heterosexuality is an impossible imitation of itself, an imitation that performatively constitutes itself as the original, then the imitative parody of "heterosexuality"—when and where it exists in gay cultures—is always and only an imitation of an imitation, a copy of a copy, for which there is no original. Put in yet a different way, the parodic or imitative effect of gay identities works neither to copy nor to emulate heterosexuality, but rather, to expose heterosexuality as an incessant and *panicked* imitation of its own naturalized idealization. That heterosexuality is always in the act of elaborating itself is evidence that it is perpetually at risk, that is, that it "knows" its own possibility of becoming undone: hence, its compulsion to repeat which is at once a foreclosure of that which threatens its coherence. That it can never eradicate that risk attests to its profound dependency upon the homosexuality that it seeks fully to eradicate and never can or that it seeks to make second, but which is always already there as a prior possibility.[2] Although this failure of naturalized heterosexuality might constitute a source of pathos for heterosexuality itself—what its theorists often refer to as its constitutive malaise—it can become an occasion for a subversive and proliferating parody of gender norms in which the very claim to originality and to the real is shown to be the effect of a certain kind of naturalized gender mime.

It is important to recognize the ways in which heterosexual norms reappear within gay identities, to affirm that gay and lesbian identities are not only structured in part by dominant heterosexual frames, but that they are *not* for that reason *determined* by them. They are running commentaries on those naturalized positions as well, parodic replays and resignifications of precisely those heterosexual structures that would consign gay life to discursive domains of unreality and unthinkability. But to be constituted or structured in part by the very heterosexual norms by which gay people are oppressed is not, I repeat, to be claimed or determined by those structures. And it is not necessary to think of such heterosexual constructs as the pernicious intrusion of "the straight mind," one that must be rooted out in its entirety. In a way,

2. Of course, it is Eve Kosofsky Sedgwick's *Epistemology of the Closet* (Berkeley: University of California Press, 1990) which traces the subleties of this kind of panic in Western heterosexual epistemes.

the presence of heterosexual constructs and positionalities in whatever form in gay and lesbian identities presupposes that there is a gay and lesbian repetition of straightness, a recapitulation of straightness—which is itself a repetition and recapitulation of its own ideality—within its own terms, a site in which all sorts of resignifying and parodic repetitions become possible. The parodic replication and resignification of heterosexual constructs within non-heterosexual frames brings into relief the utterly constructed status of the so-called original, but it shows that heterosexuality only constitutes itself as the original through a convincing act of repetition. The more that "act" is expropriated, the more the heterosexual claim to originality is exposed as illusory.

Although I have concentrated in the above on the reality-effects of gender practices, performances, repetitions, and mimes, I do not mean to suggest that drag is a "role" that can be taken on or taken off at will. There is no volitional subject behind the mime who decides, as it were, which gender it will be today. On the contrary, the very possibility of becoming a viable subject requires that a certain gender mime be already underway. The "being" of the subject is no more self-identical than the "being" of any gender; in fact, coherent gender, achieved through an apparent repetition of the same, produces as its *effect* the illusion of a prior and volitional subject. In this sense, gender is not a performance that a prior subject elects to do, but gender is *performative* in the sense that it constitutes as an effect the very subject it appears to express. It is a *compulsory* performance in the sense that acting out of line with heterosexual norms brings with it ostracism, punishment, and violence, not to mention the transgressive pleasures produced by those very prohibitions.

To claim that there is no performer prior to the performed, that the performance is performative, that the performance constitutes the appearance of a "subject" as its effect is difficult to accept. This difficulty is the result of a predisposition to think of sexuality and gender as "expressing" in some indirect or direct way a psychic reality that precedes it. The denial of the *priority* of the subject, however, is not the denial of the subject; in fact, the refusal to conflate the subject with the psyche marks the psychic as that which exceeds the domain of the conscious subject. This psychic excess is precisely what is being systematically denied by the notion of a volitional "subject" who elects at will which gender and/or sexuality to be at any given time and place. It is this excess which erupts within the intervals of those repeated gestures and acts that construct the apparent uniformity of heterosexual positionalities, indeed which compels the repetition itself, and which guarantees its perpetual failure. In this sense, it is this excess which, within the heterosexual economy, implicitly includes homosexuality, that perpetual threat of a disruption which is quelled through a reenforced repetition of the same. And yet, if repetition is the way in which power works to construct the illusion of a seamless heterosexual identity, if heterosexuality is compelled to *repeat itself* in order to establish the illusion of its own uniformity and identity, then this is an identity permanently at risk, for what if it fails to repeat, or if the very exercise of repetition is redeployed for a very different performative purpose? If there is, as it were, always a compulsion to repeat, repetition never fully accomplishes identity. That there is a need for a repetition at all is a sign that identity is not self-identical. It requires to be instituted again and again, which is to say that it runs the risk of becoming *de*-instituted at every interval.

So what is this psychic excess, and what will constitute a subversive or *de*-instituting repetition? First, it is necessary to consider that sexuality always exceeds any given performance, presentation, or narrative which is why it is not possible to derive or read off a sexuality from any given gender presentation. And sexuality may be said to exceed any definitive narrativization. Sexuality is never fully "expressed" in a performance or practice; there will be passive and butchy femmes, femmy and aggressive butches, and both of those, and more, will turn out to describe more or less anatomically stable "males" and "females." There are no direct expressive or causal lines between sex, gender, gender presentation, sexual practice, fantasy and sexuality. None of those terms captures or determines the rest. Part of what constitutes sexuality is precisely that which does not appear and that which, to some degree, can never appear. This is perhaps the most fundamental reason why sexuality is to some degree always closeted, especially to the one who would express it through acts of self-disclosure. That which is excluded for a given gender presentation to "succeed" may be precisely what is played out sexually, that is, an "inverted" relation, as it were, between gender and gender presentation, and gender presentation and sexuality. On the other hand, both gender presentation and sexual practices may corollate such that it appears that the former "expresses" the latter, and yet both are jointly constituted by the very sexual possibilities that they exclude.

This logic of inversion gets played out interestingly in versions of lesbian butch and femme gender stylization. For a butch can present herself as capable, forceful, and all-providing, and a stone butch may well seek to constitute her lover as the exclusive site of erotic attention and pleasure. And yet, this "providing" butch who seems *at first* to replicate a certain husband-like role, can find herself caught in a logic of inversion whereby that "providingness" turns to a self-sacrifice, which implicates her in the most ancient trap of feminine self-abnegation. She may well find herself in a situation of radical need, which is precisely what she sought to locate, find, and fulfill in her femme lover. In effect, the butch inverts into the femme or remains caught up in the specter of that inversion, or takes pleasure in it. On the other hand, the femme who, as Amber Hollibaugh has argued, "orchestrates" sexual exchange,[3] may well eroticize a certain dependency only to learn that the very power to orchestrate that dependency exposes her own incontrovertible power, at which point she inverts into a butch or becomes caught up in the specter of that inversion, or perhaps delights in it.

Psychic Mimesis

What stylizes or forms an erotic style and/or a gender presentation—and that which makes such categories inherently unstable—is a set of *psychic identifications* that are not simple to describe. Some psychoanalytic theories tend to construe identification and desire as two mutually exclusive relations to love objects that have been lost through prohibition and/or separation. Any

3. Amber Hollibaugh and Cherríe Moraga, "What We're Rollin Around in Bed With: Sexual Silences in Feminism," in *Powers of Desire: The Politics of Sexuality*, ed. Ann Snitow, Christine Stansell, and Sharon Thompson (New York: Monthly Review Press, 1983), 394–405.

intense emotional attachment thus divides into either wanting to have someone or wanting to be that someone, but never both at once. It is important to
consider that identification and desire can coexist, and that their formulation
in terms of mutually exclusive oppositions serves a heterosexual matrix. But
I would like to focus attention on yet a different construal of that scenario,
namely, that "wanting to be" and "wanting to have" can operate to differentiate mutually exclusive positionalities internal to lesbian erotic exchange.
Consider that identifications are always made in response to loss of some
kind, and that they involve a certain *mimetic practice* that seeks to incorporate the lost love within the very "identity" of the one who remains. This was
Freud's thesis in "Mourning and Melancholia" in 1917 and continues to
inform contemporary psychoanalytic discussions of identification.[4]

For psychoanalytic theorists Mikkel Borch-Jacobsen and Ruth Leys, however, identification and, in particular, identificatory mimetism, *precedes* "identity" and constitutes identity as that which is fundamentally "other to itself."
The notion of this Other *in* the self, as it were, implies that the self/Other distinction is *not* primarily external (a powerful critique of ego psychology follows
from this); the self is from the start radically implicated in the "Other." This theory of primary mimetism differs from Freud's account of melancholic incorporation. In Freud's view, which I continue to find useful, incorporation—a kind
of psychic miming—is a response to, and refusal of, *loss*. Gender as the site of
such psychic mimes is thus constituted by the variously gendered Others who
have been loved and lost, where the loss is suspended through a melancholic
and imaginary incorporation (and preservation) of those Others into the psyche. Over and against this account of psychic mimesis by way of incorporation
and melancholy, the theory of primary mimetism argues an even stronger position in favor of the non-self-identity of the psychic subject. Mimetism is not
motivated by a drama of loss and wishful recovery, but appears to precede and
constitute desire (and motivation) itself; in this sense, mimetism would be prior
to the possibility of loss and the disappointments of love.

Whether loss or mimetism is primary (perhaps an undecidable problem),
the psychic subject is nevertheless constituted internally by differentially
gendered Others and is, therefore, never, as a gender, self-identical.

In my view, the self only becomes a self on the condition that it has suffered a separation (grammar fails us here, for the "it" only becomes differentiated through that separation), a loss which is suspended and provisionally
resolved through a melancholic incorporation of some "Other." That "Other"
installed in the self thus establishes the permanent incapacity of that "self"
to achieve self-identity; it is as it were always already disrupted by that Other;
the disruption of the Other at the heart of the self is the very condition of that
self's possibility.[5]

---

4. Mikkel Borch-Jacobsen, *The Freudian Subject*
(Stanford: Stanford University Press, 1988); for
citations of Ruth Leys's work, see notes 5 and 7,
below.
5. For a very fine analysis of primary mimetism
with direct implications for gender formation, see
Ruth Leys, "The Real Miss Beauchamp: The History and Sexual Politics of the Multiple Personality
Concept," in *Feminists Theorize the Political,* eds.
Judith Butler and Joan W. Scott (New York: Routledge, forthcoming 1991 [published 1992]). For
Leys, a primary mimetism or suggestibility requires

that the "self" from the start is constituted by its
incorporations; the effort to differentiate oneself
from that by which one is constituted is, of course,
impossible, but it does entail a certain "incorpora-
tive violence," to use her term. The violence of
identification is in this way in the service of an
effort at differentiation, to take the place of the
Other who is, as it were, installed at the foundation
of the self. That this replacement, which seeks to
be a displacement, fails, and must repeat itself endlessly, becomes the trajectory of one's psychic
career.

Such a consideration of psychic identification would vitiate the possibility of any stable set of typologies that explain or describe something like gay or lesbian identities. And any effort to supply one—as evidenced in Kaja Silverman's recent inquiries into male homosexuality[6]—suffer from simplification, and conform, with alarming ease, to the regulatory requirements of diagnostic epistemic regimes. If incorporation in Freud's sense in 1914 is an effort to *preserve* a lost and loved object and to refuse or postpone the recognition of loss and, hence, of grief, then to become *like* one's mother or father or sibling or other early "lovers" may be an act of love and/or a hateful effort to replace or displace. How would we "typologize" the ambivalence at the heart of mimetic incorporations such as these?[7]

How does this consideration of psychic identification return us to the question, what constitutes a subversive repetition? How are troublesome identifications apparent in cultural practices? Well, consider the way in which heterosexuality naturalizes itself through setting up certain illusions of continuity between sex, gender, and desire. When Aretha Franklin sings, "you make me feel like a natural woman,"[8] she seems at first to suggest that some natural potential of her biological sex is actualized by her participation in the cultural position of "woman" as object of heterosexual recognition. Something in her "sex" is thus expressed by her "gender" which is then fully known and consecrated within the heterosexual scene. There is no breakage, no discontinuity between "sex" as biological facticity and essence, or between gender and sexuality. Although Aretha appears to be all too glad to have her naturalness confirmed, she also seems fully and paradoxically mindful that that confirmation is never guaranteed, that the effect of naturalness is only achieved as a consequence of that moment of heterosexual recognition. After all, Aretha sings, you make me feel *like* a natural woman, suggesting that this is a kind of metaphorical substitution, an act of imposture, a kind of sublime and momentary participation in an ontological illusion produced by the mundane operation of heterosexual drag.

But what if Aretha were singing to me? Or what if she were singing to a drag queen whose performance somehow confirmed her own?

How do we take account of these kinds of identifications? It's not that there is some kind of *sex* that exists in hazy biological form that is somehow *expressed* in the gait, the posture, the gesture; and that some sexuality then expresses both that apparent gender or that more or less magical sex. If gender is drag, and if it is an imitation that regularly produces the ideal it attempts to approximate, then gender is a performance that *produces* the illusion of an inner sex or essence or psychic gender core; it *produces* on the skin, through the gesture, the move, the gait (that array of corporeal theatrics understood as gender presentation), the illusion of an inner depth. In effect, one way that genders gets naturalized is through being constructed as an inner psychic or physical *necessity*. And yet, it is always a surface sign, a signification on and with the public body that produces this illusion of an inner depth, necessity or essence that is somehow magically, causally expressed.

6. See Silverman's *Male Subjectivity at the Margins* (New York: Routledge, 1992) [editor's note].
7. Here again, I think it is the work of Ruth Leys which will clarify some of the complex questions of gender constitution that emerge from a close psychoanalytic consideration of imitation and identi- fication. Her forthcoming book manuscript will doubtless galvanize this field: *The Subject of Imitation*.
8. "(You Make Me Feel Like) A Natural Woman," written by Carole King, was a hit single when recorded by Franklin in 1967 [editor's note].

To dispute the psyche as *inner depth*, however, is not to refuse the psyche altogether. On the contrary, the psyche calls to be rethought precisely as a compulsive repetition, as that which conditions and disables the repetitive performance of identity. If every performance repeats itself to institute the effect of identity, then every repetition requires an interval between the acts, as it were, in which risk and excess threaten to disrupt the identity being constituted. The unconscious is this excess that enables and contests every performance, and which never fully appears within the performance itself. The psyche is not "in" the body, but in the very signifying process through which that body comes to appear; it is the lapse in repetition as well as its compulsion, precisely what the performance seeks to deny, and that which compels it from the start.

To locate the psyche within this signifying chain as the instability of all iterability is not the same as claiming that it is inner core that is awaiting its full and liberatory expression. On the contrary, the psyche is the permanent failure of expression, a failure that has its values, for it impels repetition and so reinstates the possibility of disruption. What then does it mean to pursue disruptive repetition within compulsory heterosexuality?

Although compulsory heterosexuality often presumes that there is first a sex that is expressed through a gender and then through a sexuality, it may now be necessary fully to invert and displace that operation of thought. If a regime of sexuality mandates a compulsory performance of sex, then it may be only through that performance that the binary system of gender and the binary system of sex come to have intelligibility at all. It may be that the very categories of sex, of sexual identity, of gender are produced or maintained in the *effects* of this compulsory performance, effects which are disingenuously renamed as causes, origins, disingenuously lined up within a causal or expressive sequence that the heterosexual norm produces to legitimate itself as the origin of all sex. How then to expose the causal lines as retrospectively and performatively produced fabrications, and to engage gender itself as an inevitable fabrication, to fabricate gender in terms which reveal every claim to the origin, the inner, the true, and the real as nothing other than the effects of *drag*, whose subversive possibilities ought to be played and replayed to make the "sex" of gender into a site of insistent political play? Perhaps this will be a matter of working sexuality *against* identity, even against gender, and of letting that which cannot fully appear in any performance persist in its disruptive promise.

1991

ELIZABETH ABEL
b. 1945

From 1980 until 1982, the prestigious journal *Critical Inquiry* published a number of key feminist articles that Elizabeth Abel put together in *Writing and Sexual Difference* (1982), essays that put the lie to what she called "one litany of familiar accusations" leveled against feminist critics: "reductiveness, dogmatism, insensitivity to literary values." Her own writing also dispels such charges. Especially in *Virginia Woolf and the Fictions of Psychoanalysis* (1989) and in the volume she edited with Helene Moglen and Barbara Christian, *Female Subjectivity in Black and White: Race, Psychoanalysis, Feminism* (1997), Abel engages the complex theories of psychoanalysis through a perspective sensitive to the impact of gender and race on subjectivity. Our selection illuminates her interest in how readers interpret racial signs and what those interpretations tell us about the assumptions underpinning racial stereotypes as well as the communications between black and white women. Its analysis prepares the way for the work that currently engages Abel, a cultural studies investigation into the significance of photographs documenting the "separate but equal" policy governing access to bathrooms, drinking fountains, and restaurants throughout the South during the period directly before the civil rights movement.

From Black Writing, White Reading: Race and the Politics of Feminist Interpretation

1

> I realize that the set of feelings that I used to have about French men I now have about African-American women. Those are the people I feel inadequate in relation to and try to please in my writing. It strikes me that this is not just idiosyncratic.
> —Jane Gallop, "Criticizing Feminist Criticism"

Twyla opens the narrative of Toni Morrison's provocative story "Recitatif" (1982) by recalling her placement as an eight-year-old child in St. Bonaventure, a shelter for neglected children, and her reaction to Roberta Fisk, the roommate she is assigned: "The minute I walked in . . . I got sick to my stomach. It was one thing to be taken out of your own bed early in the morning— it was something else to be stuck in a strange place with a girl from a whole other race. And Mary, that's my mother, she was right. Every now and then she would stop dancing long enough to tell me something important and one of the things she said was that they never washed their hair and they smelled funny. Roberta sure did. Smell funny, I mean."[1] The racial ambiguity so deftly installed at the narrative's origin through codes that function symmetrically for black women and for white women ("they never washed their hair and

---

1. Toni Morrison, "Recitatif," in *Confirmation: An Anthology of African American Women*, ed. Amiri Baraka (LeRoi Jones) and Amina Baraka (New York: Morrow, 1983), p. 243; hereafter abbreviated "R." I am deeply indebted to Lula Fragd for bringing this story to my attention and to Toni Morrison for generously discussing it with me. I am also very grateful to Margaret Homans for sharing with me an early draft of " 'Racial Composition': Metaphor and Body in the Writing of Race," which became central to my thinking on writing and race; and to Janet Adelman, John Bishop, Mitchell Breitwieser, Carolyn Dinshaw, Catherine Gallagher, Anne Goldman, Crystal Gromer, Dori Hale, Saidiya Hartman, Marianne Hirsch, Tania Modleski, Helene Moglen, Michael Rogin, Dianne Sadoff, Susan Schweik, Valerie Smith, Hortense Spillers, and Jean Wyatt for their helpful comments on this essay. [All notes are Abel's.]

they smelled funny") intensifies as the story tracks the encounters of its two female protagonists over approximately thirty years. Unmediated by the sexual triangulations (the predations of white men on black women, the susceptibility of black men to white women) that have dominated black women's narrative representations of women's fraught connections across racial lines, the relationship of Twyla and Roberta discloses the operations of race in the feminine.[2] This is a story about a black woman and a white woman; but which is which?

I was introduced to "Recitatif" by a black feminist critic, Lula Fragd. Lula was certain that Twyla was black; I was equally convinced that she was white; most of the readers we summoned to resolve the dispute divided similarly along racial lines. By replacing the conventional signifiers of racial difference (such as skin color) with radically relativistic ones (such as who smells funny to whom) and by substituting for the racialized body a series of disaggregated cultural parts—pinks-scalloped socks, tight green slacks, large hoop earrings, expertise at playing jacks, a taste for Jimi Hendrix or for bottled water and asparagus—the story renders race a contested terrain variously mapped from diverse positions in the social landscape. By forcing us to construct racial categories from highly ambiguous social cues, "Recitatif" elicits and exposes the unarticulated racial codes that operate at the boundaries of consciousness. To underscore the cultural specificity of these codes, Morrison writes into the text a figure of racial undecidability: Maggie, the mute kitchen worker at St. Bonaventure, who occasions the text's only mention of skin color, an explicitly ambiguous sandy color, and who walks through the text with her little kid's hat and her bowed legs "like parentheses," her silent self a blank parenthesis, a floating signifier ("R," p. 245). For both girls a hated reminder of their unresponsive mothers, Maggie is not "raced" to Twyla (that is, she is by default white); to Roberta, she is black. The two girls' readings of Maggie become in turn clues for our readings of them, readings that emanate similarly from our own cultural locations.

My own reading derived in part from Roberta's perception of Maggie as black; Roberta's more finely discriminating gaze ("she wasn't pitch-black, I knew," is all Twyla can summon to defend her assumption that Maggie is white) seemed to me to testify to the firsthand knowledge of discrimination ("R," p. 259). Similarly, Roberta is sceptical about racial harmony. When she and Twyla retrospectively discuss their tense encounter at a Howard Johnson's where Twyla was a waitress in the early 1960s, they read the historical context differently: " 'Oh, Twyla, you know how it was in those days: black—white. You know how everything was.' But I didn't know. I thought it was just the opposite. Busloads of blacks and whites came into Howard Johnson's together. They roamed together then: students, musicians, lovers, protesters.

---

2. The intervention of white men in relationships between black and white women is repeatedly represented in slave narratives, best epitomized perhaps by Harriet Jacobs, *Incidents in the Life of a Slave Girl: Written by Herself* (1861); the intervention of white women in black heterosexual relationships is most fully explored in the civil rights fiction typified by Alice Walker, *Meridian* (1976). For a study of American literary representations of the relationships between black and white women in the nineteenth-century South, see Minrose C. Gwin, *Black and White Women of the Old South: The Peculiar Sisterhood in American Literature* (Knoxville: University of Tennessee Press, 1985); for an optimistic characterization of interracial female friendships in recent American women's fiction, see Elizabeth Schultz, "Out of the Woods and into the World: A Study of Interracial Friendships between Women in American Novels," in *Conjuring: Black Women, Fiction, and Literary Tradition*, ed. Marjorie Pryse and Hortense J. Spillers (Bloomington: Indiana University Press, 1985), pp. 67–85.

You got to see everything at Howard Johnson's and blacks were very friendly with whites in those days" ("R," p. 255). In the civil rights movement that Twyla sees as a common struggle against racial barriers, Roberta sees the distrust of white intervention and the impulse toward a separatist Black Power movement: she has the insider's perspective on power and race relations.

It was a more pervasive asymmetry in authority, however, that secured my construction of race in the text, a construction I recount with considerable embarrassment for its possible usefulness in fleshing out the impulse within contemporary white feminism signalled by the "not just idiosyncratic" confession that stands as this paper's epigraph. As Gallop both wittily acknowledges the force of African-American women's political critique of white academic feminism's seduction by "French men" and, by simply transferring the transference, reenacts the process of idealization that unwittingly obscures more complex social relations, I singled out the power relations of the girls from the broader network of cultural signs.[3] Roberta seemed to me consistently the more sophisticated reader of the social scene, the subject presumed by Twyla to know, the teller of the better (although not necessarily more truthful) stories, the adventurer whose casual mention of an appointment with Jimi Hendrix exposes the depths of Twyla's social ignorance (" 'Hendrix? Fantastic,' I said. 'Really fantastic. What's she doing now?' " ["R," p. 250]). From the girls' first meeting at St. Bonaventure, Twyla feels vulnerable to Roberta's judgment and perceives Roberta (despite her anxiety about their differences) as possessing something she lacks and craves: a more acceptably negligent mother (a sick one rather than a dancing one) and, partially as a consequence, a more compelling physical presence that fortifies her cultural authority. Twyla is chronically hungry; Roberta seems to her replete, a daughter who has been adequately fed and thus can disdain the institutional Spam and Jell-O that Twyla devours as a contrast to the popcorn and Yoo-Hoo that had been her customary fare. The difference in maternal stature, linked in the text with nurture, structures Twyla's account of visiting day at St. Bonaventure. Twyla's mother, smiling and waving "like she was the little girl," arrives wearing tight green buttocks-hugging slacks and a ratty fur jacket for the chapel service, and bringing no food for the lunch that Twyla consequently improvises out of fur-covered jelly beans from her Easter basket ("R," p. 246). "Bigger than any man," Roberta's mother arrives bearing a huge cross on her chest, a Bible in the crook of her arm, and a basket of chicken, ham, oranges, and chocolate-covered graham crackers ("R," p. 247). In the subsequent Howard Johnson scene that Twyla's retrospective analysis links with the frustrations of visiting day ("The wrong food is always with the wrong people. Maybe that's why I got into waitress work later—to match up the right people with the right food" ["R," p. 248]) the difference in stature is replayed between the two daughters. Roberta, sitting in a booth with "two guys smothered in head and facial hair," her own hair "so big and wild I could hardly see her face," wearing a "powder-blue halter and shorts

3. *Transference* is Gallop's own term for her relation to black feminist critics. In her *Around 1981: Academic Feminist Literary Theory* (New York: Routledge, 1992), esp. pp. 169–70, Gallop critiques the idealization and exoticization of black women, but she limits herself to making the transference conscious rather than positing alternatives to it. In "Transferences: Gender and Race: The Practice of Theory," delivered at the University of California, Berkeley, 3 Apr. 1992, Deborah E. McDowell, who had inadvertently occasioned Gallop's comments about transference, deliberately spoke back from, and thereby exploded, the position of the transferential object.

outfit and earrings the size of bracelets," rebuffs Twyla, clad in her waitress outfit, her knees rather than her midriff showing, her hair in a net, her legs in thick stockings and sturdy white shoes ("R," p. 249). Although the two bodies are never directly represented, the power of metonymy generates a contrast between the amplitude of the sexualized body and the skimpiness and pallor of the socially harnessed body. Twyla's sense of social and physical inadequacy vis-à-vis Roberta, like her representation of her mother's inferiority to Roberta's, signalled Twyla's whiteness to me by articulating a white woman's fantasy (my own) about black women's potency.[4] This fantasy's tenaciousness is indicated by its persistence in the face of contrary evidence. Roberta's mother, the story strongly implies, is mentally rather than physically ill, her capacity to nurture largely fictional; Roberta, who is never actually represented eating, is more lastingly damaged than Twyla by maternal neglect, more vulnerable as an adult to its memory, a weakness on which Twyla capitalizes during their political conflicts as adults; the tenuousness of the adult Roberta's own maternal status (she acquires stepchildren, rather than biological children, through her marriage to an older man) may also testify figuratively to a lack created by insufficient mothering.

Pivoting not on skin color, but on size, sexuality, and the imagined capacity to nurture and be nurtured, on the construction of embodiedness itself as a symptom and source of cultural authority, my reading installs the (racialized) body at the center of a text that deliberately withholds conventional racial iconography. Even in her reading of this first half of the story, Lula's interpretation differed from mine by emphasizing cultural practices more historically nuanced than my categorical distinctions in body types, degrees of social cool, or modes of mothering. Instead of reading Twyla's body psychologically as white, Lula read Twyla's name as culturally black; and she placed greater emphasis on Roberta's language in the Howard Johnson scene—her primary locution being a decidedly white hippie "Oh, wow"—than on the image of her body gleaned by reading envy in the narrative gaze and by assigning racial meaning to such cultural accessories as the Afro, hoop earrings, and a passion for Jimi Hendrix that actually circulated independently of race throughout the counterculture of the 1960s; as Lula knew and I did not, Jimi Hendrix appealed more to white than to black audiences.[5] Roberta's coldness in this scene—she barely acknowledges her childhood friend—becomes, in Lula's reading, a case of straightforward white racism, and Twyla's surprise at the rebuff reflects her naivete about the power of personal loyalties and social movements to undo racial hierarchies.

4. The "not just idiosyncratic" nature of this fantasy is suggested by Gallop's accounts in "Tongue Work" and "The Coloration of Academic Feminism" in *Around 1981*, pp. 143–76 and 67–74, and, by extension through the analogies she draws between constructions of race and class, in "Annie Leclerc Writing a Letter, with Vermeer," in *The Poetics of Gender*, ed. Nancy K. Miller (New York: Columbia University Press, 1986), pp. 137–56. In her analysis of the black woman's telling role in Joan Micklin Silver's film *Crossing Delancey*, Tania Modleski outlines an especially exploitative enactment of this fantasy; see Tania Modleski, *Feminism without Women: Culture and Criticism in a "Postfeminist" Age* (New York: Routledge, 1991), pp.

129–30. In Richard Dyer, "Paul Robeson: Crossing Over," in *Heavenly Bodies: Film Stars and Society* (London: British Film Institute, 1986), Dyer succinctly summarizes the most pervasive, nongendered version of this fantasy: "Black and white discourses on blackness seem to be valuing the same things—spontaneity, emotion, naturalness—yet giving them a different implication. Black discourses see them as contributions to the development of society, white as enviable qualities that only blacks have" (p. 79).

5. On the general phenomenon of black innovation and white imitation in postwar American culture, see Kobena Mercer, "Black Hair/Style Politics," *New Formations* 3 (Winter 1987): 33–54.

More importantly, however, this scene was not critical for Lula's reading. Instead of the historical locus that was salient for me—not coincidentally, I believe, since the particular aura of (some) black women for (some) white women during the civil rights movement is being recapitulated in contemporary feminism (as I will discuss later)—what was central to her were scenes from the less culturally exceptional 1970s, which disclosed the enduring systems of racism rather than the occasional moments of heightened black cultural prestige. In general, Lula focussed less on cultural than on economic status, and she was less concerned with daughters and their feelings toward their mothers than with these daughters' politics after they are mothers.

When Twyla and Roberta meet in a food emporium twelve years after the Howard Johnson scene, Twyla has married a fireman and has one child and limited income; Roberta has married an IBM executive and lives in luxury in the wealthy part of town with her husband, her four stepchildren, and her Chinese chauffeur. Twyla concludes in a voice of seemingly racial resentment: "Everything is so easy for them. They think they own the world" ("R," p. 252). A short time later the women find themelves on opposite sides of a school integration struggle in which both their children are faced with bussing: Twyla's to the school that Roberta's stepchildren now attend, and Roberta's to a school in a less affluent neighborhood. After Twyla challenges Roberta's opposition to the bussing, Roberta tries to defuse the conflict: " 'Well, it is a free country.' 'Not yet, but it will be,' " Twyla responds ("R," p. 256). Twyla's support of bussing, and of social change generally, and Roberta's self-interested resistance to them position the women along the bitter racial lines that split the fraying fabric of feminism in the late 1970s and early 1980s.[6]

Privileging psychology over politics, my reading disintegrates in the story's second half. Lula's reading succeeds more consistently, yet by constructing the black woman (in her account, Twyla) as the politically correct but politically naive and morally conventional foil to the more socially adventurous, if politically conservative, white woman (Roberta), it problematically racializes the moral (op)positions Morrison opens to revaluation in her extended (and in many ways parallel) narrative of female friendship, Sula.[7] Neither reading can account adequately for the text's contradictory linguistic evidence, for if Twyla's name is more characteristically black than white, it is perhaps best known as the name of a white dancer, Twyla Tharp, whereas Roberta shares her last name, Fisk, with a celebrated black (now integrated) university. The text's heterogeneous inscriptions of race resist a totalizing reading.

Propelled by this irresolution to suspend my commitment to the intentional fallacy, I wrote to Toni Morrison. Her response raised as many questions as it resolved. Morrison explained that her project in this story was to

6. For a particularly powerful statement of the disenchantment bred among women of color by white women's opposition to bussing, see Nikki Giovanni, "Why Weren't Our 'Sisters in Liberation' in Boston?" *Encore*, 6 Jan. 1975, p. 20.
7. By tracing the course of a friendship from girlhood through adulthood, "Recitatif" filters the narrative of *Sula* (1973) through the lens of race, replacing the novel's sexual triangulation with the tensions of racial difference. It is hard for me to imagine that the critical question that Sula, Roberta's knowing, transgressive counterpart, poses to Nel—"How do you know? . . . About who was good. How do you know it was you?"—could be translated, in "Recitatif," into a white woman's challenge to a woman of color (Morrison, *Sula* [New York: Knopf, 1973], p. 146).

substitute class for racial codes in order to drive a wedge between these typically elided categories.[8] Both eliciting and foiling our assumption that Roberta's middle-class marriage and politics, and Twyla's working-class perspective, are reliable racial clues, Morrison incorporated details about their husbands' occupations that encourage an alternative conclusion. If we are familiar (as I was not) with IBM's efforts to recruit black executives and with the racial exclusiveness of the firemen's union in upstate New York, where the story is set, we read Roberta as middle-class black and Twyla as working-class white. Roberta's resistance to bussing, then, is based on class rather than racial loyalties: she doesn't want her (middle-class black) stepchildren bussed to a school in a (white) working-class neighborhood; Twyla, conversely, wants her (white) working-class child bussed to a middle-class school (regardless of that school's racial composition). What we hear, from this perspective, in Twyla's envy of Roberta, "Everything is so easy for them," and in her challenge to the status quo—it's not a free country "but it will be"—is class rather than (or perhaps compounded by) racial resentment, the adult economic counterpart to Twyla's childhood fantasy of Roberta's plenitude.

By underscoring the class-based evidence for reading Twyla as white, Morrison confirms at once my own conclusion and its fantasmatic basis. Morrison's weighting of social detail, her insistence on the intersections, however constructed, between race and class, are more closely aligned with Lula's political perspective than with my psychological reading, fueled by racially specific investments that the text deliberately solicits and exposes. By both inviting and challenging racialized readings that are either "right" for the "wrong" reasons or "wrong" for the "right" ones, "Recitatif" focusses some questions to address to the massive, asymmetrical crossing of racial boundaries in recent feminist criticism. If white feminist readings of black women's texts disclose white critical fantasies, what (if any) value do these readings have—and for whom?[9] How do white women's readings of black women's biological bodies inform our readings of black women's textual bodies? How do different critical discourses both inflect and inscribe racial fantasies? What rhetorical strategies do these discourses produce, and (how) do these strategies bear on the value of the readings they ostensibly legitimate?

✳ ✳ ✳

8. In this exchange (November 1990), Morrison provided a more detailed account of her intentions than she does in her only (and very recently) published comment on the story, in the preface to her *Playing in the Dark: Whiteness and the Literary Imagination* (Cambridge, Mass.: Harvard University Press, 1992): "The kind of work I have always wanted to do requires me to learn how to maneuver ways to free up the language from its sometimes sinister, frequently lazy, almost always predictable employment of racially informed and determined chains. (The only short story I have ever written, 'Recitatif,' was an experiment in the removal of all racial codes from a narrative about two characters of different races for whom racial identity is crucial)" (p. xi).

9. Although I realize that by isolating white / black dynamics of reading from white feminist readings of texts by other women of color I am reinforcing the unfortunate collapse of "color" and "black,"

encompassing such a diverse textual field within a single analysis would blur important differences. In contrast, for example, to black feminist complaints about the white feminist misrecognition of the politics and language of black feminism, Norma Alarcón protests the Anglo-American feminist resistance to granting theoretical status to the multiple-voiced subjectivity of women of color; see Norma Alarcón, "The Theoretical Subject(s) of *This Bridge Called My Back* and Anglo-American Feminism," in *Making Face, Making Soul: Haciendo Caras*, ed. Gloria Anzaldúa (San Francisco: Aunt Lute Foundation Books, 1990), pp. 356–69. For a different perception of white feminism's response to the multiple voicing characterizing texts by women of color, see Teresa de Lauretis, "Eccentric Subjects: Feminist Theory and Historical Consciousness," *Feminist Studies* 16 (Spring 1990): 115–50.

To produce an allegory about reading and race, I omitted aspects of the story—most importantly, its own conclusion—that complicate the division between the characters and, consequently, between their readers. "Recitatif" ends with parallel recognitions by Twyla and Roberta that each perceived the mute Maggie as her own unresponsive, rejecting mother, and therefore hated and wanted to harm her. After dramatizing the differences produced by race and class, the story concludes with the shared experience of abandoned little girls who, in some strange twist of the oedipal story, discover that they killed (wanted to kill), as well as loved (wanted to love), their mothers (see "R," p. 261).[1] Sameness coexists with difference, psychology with politics. Race enforces no absolute distinctions between either characters or readers, all of whom occupy diverse subject positions, some shared, some antithetical.[2] By concluding with a psychological narrative that crosses differences (indeed, with a variant of *the* universalizing psychological narrative), "Recitatif" complicates, without cancelling, both its narrative of difference and the differences in reading that this narrative provokes.

Race enters complexly into feminist reading. Case studies . . . do indicate certain pervasive tendencies among white feminists, who have tended to read black women's texts through critical lenses that filter out the texts' embeddedness in black political and cultural traditions and that foreground instead their relation to the agendas of white feminism, which the texts alter, or prefigure, but ultimately reconfirm. For despite Jane Gallop's account of the displacement of French men by African-American women as figures of authority for white feminists, the discourses produced by French (and German and American) men continue to shape the reading habits of white feminists, who are usually better trained in literary theory than in African-American cultural studies. There has been little in white feminism comparable to the detailed reconstructions of black women's literary traditions produced by Barbara Christian, Mary Helen Washington, Deborah E. McDowell, Gloria T. Hull, Nellie Y. McKay, or Margaret B. Wilkerson; or to the mapping of this literature's social and discursive contexts produced by Hazel Carby, Barbara Smith, Valerie Smith, bell hooks, Michele Wallace, Audre Lorde, or June Jordan.[3]

1. I am borrowing, with thanks, Sue Schweik's insights and formulation.

2. For a powerful statement of a similar conclusion about race and reading, see Mary Helen Washington, "How Racial Differences Helped Us Discover Our Common Ground," in *Gendered Subjects: The Dynamics of Feminist Teaching*, ed. Margo Culley and Catherine Portuges (Boston: Routledge and Kegan Paul, 1985), pp. 221–29. Washington decides: "I will never again divide a course outline and curriculum along racial lines (as I did in 'Images of Women') so that the controlling purpose is to compare the responses of white women and black women, because I see how much the class imitates the syllabus. I do not want to see black women in opposition to white women as though that division is primary, universal, absolute, immutable, or even relevant" (pp. 227–28).

3. This is not an inclusive list of black feminist critical projects, practitioners, or texts; it merely calls attention to some influential examples of black feminist writing on, or collections of, black women writers, such as *Black Women Novelists: The Development of a Tradition, 1892–1976*, ed. Christian (Westport, Conn., 1980) and Christian, *Black*

Feminist Criticism: Perspectives on Black Women Writers (New York: Pergamon Press, 1985); Washington, *Black-Eyed Susans: Classic Stories by and about Black Women* (Garden City, N. Y.: Anchor Books, 1975), *Midnight Birds: Stories by Contemporary Black Women Writers* (Garden City, N.Y.: Anchor Books, 1980), and *Invented Lives: Narratives of Black Women 1860–1960* (Garden City, N.Y.: Doubleday, 1987); McDowell, "New Directions for Black Feminist Criticism," in *The New Feminist Criticism: Essays on Women, Literature, and Theory,* ed. Elaine Showalter (New York: Pantheon, 1985), pp. 186–99, and *Slavery and the Literary Imagination*, ed. McDowell and Arnold Rampersad (Baltimore: Johns Hopkins University Press, 1989); the series, Black Women Writers (Boston: Beacon, 1987—); Hull, *Color, Sex, and Poetry: Three Women Writers of the Harlem Renaissance* (Bloomington: Indiana University Press, 1987) and *Give Us Each Day: The Diary of Alice Dunbar-Nelson* (New York: Norton, 1984); *Critical Essays on Toni Morrison*, ed. Nellie Y. McKay (Boston: G. K. Hall, 1988); *Nine Plays by Black Women*, ed. Margaret B. Wilkerson (New York: New American Library, 1986); Carby, *Reconstructing Womanhood: The Emergence of the*

Instead, we have tended to focus our readings on the "celebrity" texts—pre-eminently those by Hurston, Walker, and Morrison—rather than on "thick" descriptions of discursive contexts, and have typically written articles or chapters (rather than books) representing black women's texts as literary and social paradigms for white readers and writers. In these texts we have found alternative family structures, narrative strategies, and constructions of subjectivity: alternative, that is, to the cultural practices of white patriarchy, with which literature by white women has come to seem uncomfortably complicit.[4] The implied audience for this critical venture has been white.

The critical picture is not, however, entirely black and white. As the work of Hortense J. Spillers demonstrates especially well, black feminists draw from, as well as criticize, a range of "high" theoretical discourses, including the psychoanalytic discourses that have functioned more prominently within white feminism.[5] As Deborah E. McDowell has powerfully argued, moreover, white feminist tendencies to construct black feminism as "high" theory's political "other" reinscribe, rather than rework, the theory/politics opposition.[6] White feminist criticism is itself fractured by class and generational differences that partially undo the racial divide. Some still-unpublished essays, particularly those by a new and differently educated generation of graduate students, and some essays that are published less visibly than those analyzed in this paper, more closely approximate the historical and political concerns of black feminist criticism. Yet however interwoven with and ruptured by other differences, race remains a salient source of the fantasies and allegiances that shape our ways of reading.

Difference, however, paradoxically increases the value of crossing racial boundaries in reading. Our inability to avoid inscribing racially inflected investments and agendas limits white feminism's capacity either to imper-

Afro-American Woman Novelist (New York: Oxford University Press, 1987); Barbara Smith, "Toward a Black Feminist Criticism," in *All the Women Are White, All the Blacks Are Men, But Some of Us Are Brave: Black Women's Studies*, ed. Gloria T. Bull, Patricia Bell Scott, and Smith (Old Westbury, N.Y.: Feminist Press, 1982), pp. 157–75; Valerie Smith, "Black Feminist Theory and the Representation of the 'Other,' " in *Changing Our Own Words: Essays on Criticism, Theory, and Writing by Black Women*, ed. Cheryl A. Wall (New Brunswick, N.J.: Rutgers University Press, 1989), and *Self-Discovery and Authority in Afro-American Narrative* (Cambridge, Mass.: Harvard University Press, 1987); hooks, *Ain't I a Woman: Black Women and Feminism* (Boston: South End Press, 1981), *Feminist Theory from Margin to Center* (Boston: South End Press, 1984), *Talking Back: Thinking Feminist, Thinking Black* (Boston: South End Press, 1989), and *Yearning: Race, Gender, and Cultural Politics* (Boston: South End Press, 1990); Michele Wallace, *Invisibility Blues: From Pop to Theory* (London: Verso, 1990); Audre Lorde, *Sister Outsider: Essays and Speeches* (Trumansburg, N.Y.: Crossing Press, 1984); and June Jordan, *Civil Wars* (Boston: Beacon Press, 1981).

4. For some recent white feminist accounts of the alternatives offered by black women's texts, see Elizabeth Abel, "Race, Class, and Psychoanalysis? Opening Questions," in *Conflicts in Feminism*, ed. Marianne Hirsch and Evelyn Fox Keller (New York: Routledge, 1990), pp. 184–204; Hirsch, *The Mother/Daughter Plot: Narrative, Psychoanalysis,* *Feminism* (Bloomington: Indiana University Press, 1989), esp. pp. 176–99; Molly Hite, *The Other Side of the Story: Structures and Strategies of Contemporary Feminist Narrative* (Ithaca: Cornell University Press, 1989), pp. 103–26; Elizabeth Meese, *(Ex)Tensions: Re-Figuring Feminist Criticism* (Urbana: University of Illinois Press, 1990), pp. 129–54 (and, for other women of color, chaps. 2 and 5); Roberta Rubenstein, *Boundaries of the Self: Gender, Culture, Fiction* (Urbana: University of Illinois Press, 1987), pp. 125–63 (and all of part 2 for other women of color); and Jean Wyatt, *Reconstructing Desire: The Role of the Unconscious in Women's Reading and Writing* (Chapel Hill: University of North Carolina Press, 1990), pp. 164–209.

5. For some examples of Spillers's revisionist use of psychoanalytic theory, see her "Interstices: A Small Drama of Words," in *Pleasure and Danger: Exploring Female Sexuality*, ed. Carol Vance (Boston: Routledge and K. Paul, 1984), pp. 73–100, and "Mama's Baby, Papa's Maybe: An American Grammar Book," *Diacritics* 17 (Summer 1987): 65–81. Spillers's work productively complicates the distinction Susan Thistlethwaite draws in her *Sex, Race, and God: Christian Feminism in Black and White* (New York: Crossroad, 1989) between the psychological focus of white feminism and the sociopolitical focus of black feminism.

6. McDowell made this argument in a paper entitled "Residues," delivered at the Wisconsin Conference on Afro-American Studies in the Twenty-First Century.

sonate black feminism, and potentially to render it expendable, or to counter its specific credibility. More important, white feminist readings contribute, however inadvertently, to a project many black feminists endorse: the racialization of whiteness.[7] As masculinity takes shape in part through its constructions of femininity, whiteness—that elusive color that seems not to be one—gains materiality through the desires and fantasies played out in its interpretations of blackness, interpretations that, by making the unconscious conscious, supplement articulated ideologies of whiteness with less accessible assumptions. Reading black women's texts, and reading our readings of them, is one (although certainly not the only) strategy for changing our habitual perception that "race is always an issue of Otherness that is not white: it is black, brown, yellow, red, purple even."[8]

Articulating the whiteness implied through the construction of blackness approaches, through a different route, the goal of Toni Morrison's recent critical project: "to avert the critical gaze from the racial object to the racial subject; from the described and imagined to the describers and imaginers; from the serving to the served."[9] There is a significant political difference, of course, between Morrison analyzing European-American texts and white feminist theorists staking critical claims to the African-American texts that constitute a privileged and endangered terrain of black feminist inquiry.[1] The risks of this intervention have been circumscribed, however, by the effectiveness of black feminists in establishing the authority of their own positions and by the failure of "high" theory to secure some unproblematic grounding for white feminists by either resolving or displacing the politics of reading and race. If we produce our readings cautiously and locate them in a self-conscious and self-critical relation to black feminist criticism, these risks, I hope, would be counterbalanced by the benefits of broadening the spectrum of interpretation, illuminating the social determinants of reading, and deepening our recognition of our racial selves and the "others" we fantasmatically construct—and thereby expanding the possibilities of dialogue across as well as about racial boundaries.

1993

7. Carby and hooks have both written pervasively and eloquently about this need; for some recent examples, see Carby, "The Politics of Difference," *Ms.,* Sept.–Oct. 1990, pp. 84–85, and hooks, "Critical Interrogation: Talking Race, Resisting Racism," *Inscriptions* 5 (1989): 159–62. On whiteness as "the metaphor for the metaphorical production of the Subject as one devoid of properties," see David Lloyd, "Race under Representation," *Oxford Literary Review,* nos. 1–2 (1991): 13. On the asymmetry of the system of racial marking, which "inscribes the system of domination on the body of the individual, assigning to the individual his/her place as a dominated person" while not

assigning "any place to the dominator," who remains unmarked, see Colette Guillaumin, "Race and Nature: The System of Marks," *Feminist Issues* 8 (Fall 1988): 41.
8. hooks, "Critical Interrogation," p. 162.
9. Morrison, *Playing in the Dark,* p. 90.
1. In "The Race for Theory," *Cultural Critique* 6 (Spring 1987): 51–63, Christian powerfully demonstrates the distorting effects of literary theory's intervention in the reading of black women's texts. Although she does not hold white *feminists* responsible for this intervention, her argument clearly applies to white feminist (as well as masculinist) theoretical discourses.

ISOBEL ARMSTRONG
b. 1937

"Formidable" and "epochal" are the words reviewers used to describe the historical scope of Isobel Armstrong's *Victorian Poetry: Poetry, Aesthetics, Politics* (1993). Because of this book and her co-editing (with Joseph Bristow and Cath Sharrock) of *Nineteenth-Century Women Poets: An Oxford Anthology* (1996), Armstrong is considered one of the foremost voices engaged in a critical conversation about the so-called poetess tradition. Like Stuart Curran and Susan Wolfson, Armstrong brings a keen sense of aesthetics to the cultural contexts that shaped the genres and the tonal registers of Romantic and Victorian women poets. A professor emerita of English and the humanities at the University of London, Armstrong has helped reconfigure our ideas about the political and social significance of sentiment, even as she has excavated many nineteenth-century British writers who, though popular in their own time, had been removed from anthologies and gone untaught for many decades.

From Victorian Poetry: Poetry, Poetics and Politics

From *12. 'A Music of Thine Own':*
Women's Poetry—An Expressive Tradition?

PRECURSORS

The altar, 'tis of death! for there are laid
The sacrifice of all youth's sweetest hopes.
It is a dreadful thing for woman's lip
To swear the heart away; yet know that heart
Annuls the vow while speaking, and shrinks back
From the dark future which it dares not face.
The service read above the open grave
Is far less terrible than that which seals
The vow that binds the victim, not the will:
For in the grave is rest.
     (Letitia Landon [L.E.L.])[1]

Swept into limbo is the host
 Of heavenly angels, row on row;
The Father, Son, and Holy Ghost,
 Pale and defeated, rise and go.
The great Jehovah is laid low,
 Vanished his burning bush and rod—
  Say, are we doomed to deeper woe?
  Shall marriage go the way of God?

Monogamous, still at our post,
 Reluctantly we undergo
Domestic round of boiled and roast,
 Yet deem the whole proceeding slow.
Daily the secret murmurs grow;
 We are no more content to plod
Along the beaten paths—and so
 Marriage must go the way of God.

---

1. "The Marriage Vow," in *Life and Literary Remains of L.E.L.*, ed. Laman Blanchard, 2 vols. (London, 1841), 2:277 [except as indicated, all notes are Armstrong's].

Soon, before all men, each shall toast
    The seven strings unto his bow,
Like beacon fires along the coast,
    The flames of love shall glance and glow.
Nor let nor hindrance man shall know,
    From natal bath to funeral sod;
Perennial shall his pleasures flow
    When marriage goes the way of God.

Grant, in a million years at most,
    Folk shall be neither pairs nor odd—
Alas! we shan't be there to boast
    'Marriage has gone the way of God.'
                    (Amy Levy, 1915)[2]

It is not difficult to find, from the beginning to the end of the nineteenth century, poems of protest such as those by Letitia Landon, writing early in the century, and Amy Levy, writing towards the end, in which an overt sexual politics addresses the institutions and customs which burden women, including, in Levy's case, the taboo against lesbianism. There is Elizabeth Barrett Browning's outburst against the trivial education which trains women for marriage in *Aurora Leigh* (1856), and which conditions them into acceptability 'As long as they keep quiet by the fire/And never say "no" when the world says "ay" ', a statement which perhaps adds another kind of complexity to Robert Browning's 'By the Fire-side' (1855).[3] There is Christina Rossetti's passionate wish to be a 'man',[4] and as one moves later into the century there are, if possible, fiercer expressions of protest in the work of poets such as Augusta Webster and Mathilde Blind. And yet the poems by Landon and Levy are as interesting for their differences as for their common theme. For Landon marriage is a terminal moment which requires the language of sacrifice and victim. For Levy, the end of marriage and the 'law' of God still leaves a patriarchy intact, for it is men who benefit from promiscuity, not women, and the narrow coercions of heterosexual pairing continue. Ironically, a world without marriage still goes 'The way of God' by perpetuating His patriarchal ways informally.

Yet it is too easy to describe the work of these very different women as a women's tradition based on a full frontal attack on oppression. Though such an attack undoubtedly often existed, a concentration on moments of overt protest can extract the content of a direct polemic about women's condition in a way which retrieves the protest, but not the poem. It is sometimes tempting to extrapolate such material from the poems (because they supply it in such abundance), personalising, psychologising or literalising by translating this material back into what is known or constructed as socioeconomic patriarchal history in a univocal way, so that all poems become poems about women's oppression. In this way the nature of the particular language and form of individual poems becomes obliterated by the concentration on a single theme.

Similarly, the same kind of difficulty attends the construction of a women's tradition according to a unique modality of feminine experience. For this

2. Amy Levy, *A Ballad of Religion and Marriage* (one of 12 privately printed pamphlets) 1915 (British Library catalogue).

3. Elizabeth Barrett Browning, *Aurora Leigh and*

Other Poems, ed. Cora Kaplan (London: Women's Press, 1978), 1:436–37.

4. Christina Rossetti, "I wish, and I wish I were a man" ("From the Antique," 1854).

would be to accept the distinction between two kinds of gender-based experience, male and female, and leaves uninvestigated a conventional, affective account of the feminine as a nature which occupies a distinct sphere of feeling, sensitivity and emotion quite apart from the sphere of thought and action occupied by men. This *was* a distinction frequently made by women poets themselves and by male critics in the nineteenth century, but it is necessary to be wary of it because, while it gave women's writing a very secure place in literary culture, it amounts to a kind of restrictive practice, confining the writing of women to a particular mode or genre. W. M. Rossetti, for instance, had this to say in his Preface to his edition of the poems of Felicia Hemans:

> Her sources of inspiration being genuine, and the tone of her mind being feminine in an intense degree, the product has no lack of sincerity: and yet it leaves a certain artificial impression, rather perhaps through a cloying flow of 'right-minded' perceptions of moral and material beauty than through any other defect. 'Balmy' it may be: but the atmosphere of her verse is by no means bracing. One might sum up the weak points in Mrs Hemans's poetry by saying that it is not only 'feminine' poetry (which under the circumstances can be no imputation, rather an encomium) but also 'female' poetry: besides exhibiting the fineness and charm of womanhood, it has the monotone of mere sex. Mrs Hemans has that love of good and horror of evil which characterize a scrupulous female mind; and which we may most rightly praise without concluding that they favour poetical robustness, or even perfection in literary form. She is a leader in that very modern phalanx of poets who persistently coordinate the impulse of sentiment with the guiding power of morals or religion. Everything must convey its 'lesson', and is indeed set forth for the sake of its lesson: but must at the same time have the emotional gush of a spontaneous sentiment.[5]

'Cloying', 'feminine', 'female', 'sentiment', 'lesson', 'emotional gush': not all this vocabulary is offered in a critical spirit, though it betrays uneasiness, but even the most cursory examination of the language here suggests the qualities attributed to women's poetry—conventional piety, didactic feeling, emotions, sentiment. Coventry Patmore parodies women's religious verse in *The Angel in the House* in a way which attributes the same qualities to their work. Honoria's pious sister entrusts a poem to the hero:

> Day after day, until today.
>   Imaged the others gone before,
> The same dull task, the weary way,
>   The weakness pardon'd o'er and o'er.
>
> The thwarted thirst, too faintly felt,
>   For joy's well nigh forgotten life,
> The restless heart, which, when I knelt,
>   Made of my worship barren strife.
>
> Ah, whence today's so sweet release,
>   This clearance light of all my care,

5. William Michael Rossetti, prefatory notice to *The Poetical Works of Felicia Hemans*, ed. Rossetti (London, 1873), p. xxvii.

This conscience free, this fertile peace,
  These softly folded wings of prayer,

This calm and more than conquering love,
  With which nought evil dares to cope,
This joy that lifts no glance above,
  For faith too sure, too sweet for hope?

O, happy time, too happy change,
  It will not live, though fondly nurst!
Full soon the sun will seem as strange
  As now the cloud which seems dispersed.[6]

Since the hero is courting one of three sisters, this is possibly a cruel parody of one of Anne Brontë's poems, but the conventions of women's writing were sufficiently established for it to be a parody of the work of Letitia Landon (in some moods), Adelaide Anne Procter or Christina Rossetti. What is interesting about it is that it suggests that there *were* recognised conventions established for women's verse by this time in the century (1854). Interestingly, Patmore's carefully regular quatrains pick up a *limited* assent to the sense of limit in neutrally simple religious and psychological language, a self-admonitory withdrawal from protest and a pious but none too easy recognition of the difficulties of transcending limit. His parody responds to pessimism rather than to piety, and even at the level of satire negotiates with more complex elements than the self-abnegation attributed to it by Patmore's hero.

It is probably no exaggeration to say that an account of women's writing as occupying a particular sphere of influence, and as working inside defined moral and religious conventions, helped to make women's poetry and the 'poetess' (as the Victorians termed the woman poet) respected in the nineteenth century as they never have been since. In a survey of poetry early in the century in *Blackwood's Magazine* John Wilson ('Christopher North') wrote enthusiastically of women poets, and a respectful study of British women poets appeared in 1848, *The Female Poets of Great Britain*, selected and edited by Frederic Rowton. At the end of the century Eric Robertson published his *English Poetesses* (1883). Though Robertson was less sympathetic than Rowton to women's poetry, believing that it would never equal the poetry of men, it is clear that the category of the 'poetess' was well established. Men assiduously edited women's work. Laman Blanchard edited Letitia Landon's *Life and Literary Remains* in 1841. W. M. Rossetti edited not only the work of his sister and Mrs Hemans but also Augusta Webster's *Mother and Daughter* sonnet sequence after her death (1895). Arthur Symons edited Mathilde Blind's works in 1900, with a memoir by Richard Garnett. It seems that men both enabled and controlled women's poetic production in a way that was often complex, and which requires more sustained discussion than can be given here. After a literary scandal about her association with a patron (probably William Maginn), Letitia Landon, in her early twenties, described her complete dependence on male help for the business of publication in moving terms.

6. *The Angel in the House* 1.2.2, in *The Poems of Coventry Patmore*, ed. Frederick Page (London: Oxford University Press, 1949), pp. 74–75.

Your own literary pursuits must have taught you how little, in them, a young woman can do without assistance. Place yourself in my situation. Could you have hunted London for a publisher, endured all the alternate hot and cold water thrown on your exertions; bargained for what sum they might be pleased to give; and, after all, canvassed, examined, nay quarrelled over accounts the most intricate in the world? And again, after success had procured money, what was I to do with it? Though ignorant of business I must know I could not lock it up in a box.[7]

Like Mrs Hemans, Letitia Landon relied on her earnings for the support of her family, and so her dependence on men to gain access to the publishing world was of great importance to her.

That middle-class women were hosted by men into the literary world through editions of their work may be one explanation for our lack of knowledge of working-class women poets, who were not edited in this way. Contrary to common understanding there were working-class women poets, and they are still being discovered.[8] Those we know of tend to have survived because they supported conventional morals, such as the anonymous millgirl who wrote eloquently on the Preston lockout in 1862 but connected working-class well-being with temperance. Bamford praised Ann Hawkshaw but she seems to have been an educated poet with strong working-class connections who produced orthodox-seeming work with unusual subtexts. Her *Dionysius the Areopagite* (1842), for instance, is ostensibly about Christian conversion. Quite apart from her vision of an egalitarian heaven, the story is primarily concerned with a relationship between two women. She was an impressively strong and independent writer who wrote a series of sonnets on British history with another subtext concerned with subjugation. Her shorter poems, 'Why am I a slave?' and 'The Mother to Her Starving Child', are impressive. The slave cannot understand his exclusion from 'the white man's home': 'Who had a right to bind these limbs/And make a slave of me?' The mother is forced to wish her child dead rather than see it starve—and then to go mad with grief. The pun on the 'relief' of madness is sombre, with the ironic social meaning of 'poor relief' shadowing the psychological term.[9] Her work is exceptional. The pastoral didacticism of Louisa Horsfield, a contemporary, contrasts with it. Horsfield retrieves the natural world from the social sins of drunkenness, truancy and immorality in a more conventional way.[1] Ellen Johnston, addressing occasional poems to local bodies and factory workers, moves from awkward heroic poetry to simple ballad and cheerful dialect verse (for instance, in 'The Working Man'). Some of her love poems, particularly 'The Maniac of the Green Wood', are moving, but her work discloses the difficulties of discovering a language in which to address both a total community and a 'literary' audience.[2] Poetry by working-class women could be as didactic as that of middle-class women, if not more so.

7. In Blanchard, ed., *Life and Literary Remains of L.E.L.*, 1:55.
8. See Julia Swindells, *Victorian Writing and Working Women: The Other Side of Silence* (Oxford: Polity Press, 1985). This study retrieves a number of unknown writers.
9. Ann Hawkshaw, *Dionysius the Areopagite* (London and Manchester, 1842); for the egalitarian heaven see *Dionysius*, pp. 97–99; "The Mother to Her Starving Child," pp. 170–72;
"Why am I a slave?" pp. 191–93. Subsequent volumes were *Poems for My Children* (London and Manchester, 1847); *Sonnets on Anglo-Saxon History* (London, 1854).
1. Louisa Horsfield, *The Cottage Lyre*, 2nd ed. (London and Leeds, 1862): "The Truant," pp. 44–47.
2. Ellen Johnston ("The Factory Girl"), *Autobiography, Poems and Songs* (Glasgow, 1862): "The Working Man," pp. 79–80; "The Maniac of the Green Wood," pp.15–19.

If, then, a middle-class women's tradition is constructed by reference to the Victorian notion of what was specifically feminine in poetry, it is likely to be formed not only out of what were predominantly male categories of the female but also out of categories which were regarded as self-evident and unproblematical. This does not enable one to take the analysis of women's poetry in the nineteenth century very far. On the other hand, it is undoubtedly the case that women wrote with a sense of belonging to a particular group defined by their sexuality, and that this sense comprehends political differences and very different kinds of poetic language. Letitia Landon recognised this when she wrote, in her 'Stanzas on the Death of Mrs Hemans', that the poet had made 'A music of thine own'.[3] So it is possible, in spite of the reservations and precautionary remarks expressed above, to consider women poets in terms of a 'music' of their own.

What was the 'music' of the Victorian woman poet? It can be listened to, first, by seeing what the poetry of Letitia Landon and Mrs Hemans could have meant to later writers, for these were the poets to which a number of them looked back as precursors. Even when there seems no direct link between these earlier and later writers it does seem as if they worked within a recognisable tradition understood by them to belong to women. Secondly, this music can be listened to through the dissonances women's poetry created by making problematical the affective conventions and feelings associated with a feminine modality of experience even when, and perhaps particularly when, poets worked within these conventions. Victorian expressive theory later in the century, one of the dominant aesthetic positions of the period, created a discourse which could accommodate a poetics of the feminine. But women poets relate to it in an ambiguous way and interrogate it even while they negotiate and assent to expressive theory. It was this assimilation of an aesthetic of the feminine which enabled the woman poet to revolutionise it from within, by using it to explore the way a female subject comes into being. The doubleness of women's poetry comes from its ostensible adoption of an affective mode, often simple, often pious, often conventional. But those conventions are subjected to investigation, questioned, or used for unexpected purposes. The simpler the surface of the poem, the more likely it is that a second and more difficult poem will exist beneath it.

Letitia Landon, already a prolifically successful poet publishing in periodicals and popular album books, published her first volume of poetry in 1824, *The Improvisatrice*. It was, she wrote,

> an attempt to illustrate that species of inspiration common in Italy, where the mind is warmed from earliest childhood by all that is beautiful in Nature and glorious in Art. The character depicted is entirely Italian, a young female with all the loveliness, vivid feeling, and genius of her own impassioned land. She is supposed to relate her own history; with which are intermixed the tales and episodes which various circumstances call forth.[4]

The Troubadour: Poetical Sketches of Modern Pictures; and Historical Sketches (1825) followed, and her last volume, reiterating the Italian theme,

---

3. In Blanchard, ed., *Life and Literary Remains of L.E.L.*, 2:245–48; 246.
4. Letitia Landon, preface to *The Improvisatrice*

(1824), in *Poetical Works*, 2 vols. (London, 1850), 1:xi.

was entitled *The Venetian Bracelet* (1829). The uncollected 'Subjects for Pictures' begins characteristically with a poem on Petrarch and Laura. The movement to Italy is taken up by Elizabeth Barrett Browning in *Aurora Leigh* (1856), and again by Christina Rossetti who in her extraordinary preface to *Monna Innominata*, as will be seen, considers the status of the Petrarchan tradition in relation to modern poetry by women. But perhaps the movement to Italy is less important in itself than the association of women's poetry with an 'impassioned land' or emotional space *outside* the definitions and circumscriptions of the poet's specific culture and nationality. As a child Letitia Landon invented a fantasy country located in Africa (it is the tragic irony of her career that she died there), very much as the Brontës were to do when they constructed Gondal and Angria (Angria was located in Africa), the imaginary lands from which so much of their poetry sprang. Adelaide Anne Procter's narrative poems move to Provence, Switzerland and Belgium. George Eliot's *The Spanish Gypsy* (1868) sends the heroine of the poem from the conflict between Moors and Spaniards to consolidate a Gipsy race in Africa. This need to move beyond cultural boundaries manifests itself in the work of the earlier poets as a form of historical and cultural syncretism which both juxtaposes different cultures and reshapes relationships between them. *The Improvisatrice* unfolds narratives within itself of Moorish and Christian conflict, and of Hindu suttee, for instance, which are juxtaposed. Felicia Hemans brings together British, French, Indian, German, American and Greek narratives from different historical periods in her *Records of Woman* (1828), which ends, in startling contrast to the historicised records, with an elegy on a recently dead poetess, Mary Tighe, taken as a point of reference by Landon in her elegy for Mrs Hemans. The dedication is made in a footnote, however, and the very possibility of a 'record' of woman is thus questioned.

This insistent figuring of movement across and between cultural boundaries, with its emphasis on travel, could be seen as a search for the exotic, an escape from restrictions into the 'other' of bourgeois society. Allied, as it so frequently is, with a metaphor of the prison, or of slavery, it could be seen as an attempt to transcend restrictions in fantasy, or an effort to discover a universal womanhood which transcends cultural differences. But it is rather to be associated with an attempt to discover ways of testing out the account of the feminine experienced in western culture by going outside its prescriptions. The flight across the boundary is often associated with the examination of extreme situations—of imprisonment, suffering, or captivity and slavery—and with an overdetermined emphasis on race and national culture, as if an enquiry is being conducted into the ways in which the feminine can be constituted. Mrs Hemans's elegy appears to emancipate its subject from cultural and historical determinations, but it suggests that we can only think of the poetess in this way when she is dead, and even that is problematical. The elegy has an uncanny aspect of contextlessness which makes it oddly surprising after the very specific 'records' which have preceded it.

The emphasis on the woman as traveller through the imagination can be associated with another aspect of Letitia Landon's account of the *Improvisatrice*. The poem is supposedly the utterance of a persona: it is a mask, a role-playing, a dramatic monologue; it is not to be identified with herself or her own feminine subjectivity. The simplest explanation for this is that, given the difficulties of acceptance experienced by women writers, the dramatic

form is used as a disguise, a protection against self-exposure and the exposure of feminine subjectivity. But, given the insistence on speaking in another
woman's voice, from Mrs Hemans to Augusta Webster and Amy Levy (these
last two wrote consciously as dramatic monologuists), it is worth considering
further as a phenomenon. The frequent adoption of a dramatised voice by
male poets in the Victorian period is, of course, to be connected with dramatic theories of poetry. But Landon's and Hemans's work predates these theories (though not, admittedly, the work of Walter Savage Landor, who might
be said to have initiated the dramatic monologue if we are content to think
of this as a tradition established by male writers), and it seems that such a
mask is peculiarly necessary for women writers. The adoption of the mask
appears to involve a displacement of feminine subjectivity, almost a travesty-
ing of femininity, in order that it can be made an object of investigation. It is
interesting, for instance, that one of Charlotte Brontë's earliest known poems
is a monologue by the wife of Pontius Pilate, and that Augusta Webster also
wrote a miniature drama between Pilate and his wife, in which the woman's
role and moral position is sharply distinguished from association with the
husband, as if both are testing out the extent to which it is the woman's function to identify unquestioningly with the husband (and, of course, with orthodox Christianity).[5] A number of poems by women testifying to a refusal to be
regarded as an object have been described by feminist critics, but by using a
mask a woman writer is in control of her objectification and at the same time
anticipates the strategy of objectifying women by being beforehand with it
and circumventing masculine representations.[6] This is the theme of
Christina Rossetti's poem about masking, 'Winter: My Secret'. It should come
as no surprise, then, that it was the women poets who 'invented' the dramatic
monologue.

The projection of self into roles is not, as will be seen, really opposed to the
axioms of expressive theory which assumes the projection of feeling and emotion onto or into an object, and thus it is not strange to find Letitia Landon
speaking of the search for an 'impassioned land', a space for the expression
of emotion. Brought up on Hume, she was fascinated by the nature of sensation (often isolating moments of sensation in a narrative), and with the pul-
sation of sympathy. She uses a metaphor of the responsively vibrating string
or chord of feeling which became so common that it could perhaps hardly be
said to originate with Hume, but she would certainly have found it in his
work, and it recurs in her poetry with an unusual intensity. Allowing as it does
of subliminal sexual meaning, it is a thoroughly feminised metaphor for her.
In her elegy on Mrs Hemans, for instance, she wrote, 'Wound to a pitch too
exquisite,/The soul's fine chords are wrung;/With misery and melody/They are
too highly strung'. Such intense vibrations, of course, can kill, as the 'chord'
becomes the result of a 'cord' or tightened string which ends sound or stran-
gles even while it produces it. This metaphor was to resonate in women's
poetry. Closely allied with it and partly deriving from it is another characteristic figure, the air. An air is a song and by association it is that which is

5. "Pilate's Wife's Dream," in *Poems of Charlotte Brontë*, ed. Tom Winnifrith (Oxford: Published for Shakespeare Head by Blackwell, 1984), p. 3.
6. For a description of objectification see Dolores Rosenblum, "Christina Rossetti: The Inward Pose," in *Shakespeare's Sisters: Feminist Essays on Women Poets*, ed. Sandra Gilbert and Susan Gubar (Bloomington: Indiana University Press, 1979), pp. 82–98.

breathed out, exhaled or expressed as breath, an expiration; and by further association it can be that which is breathed in, literally an 'influence', a flowing in, the air of the environment which sustains life; inspiration, a breathing in. All these meanings are present in the elegy, as perfume, breezes, breath or sighs, where they are figured as a responsive, finely organised feminine creativity, receptive to external influence, returning back to the world as music that has flowed in, an exhalation or breath of sound. It is the breath of the body and the breath as spirit. 'So pure, so sweet thy life has been,/So filling earth and air/with odours and with loveliness . . . And yet thy song is sorrowful,/Its beauty is not bloom;/The hopes of which it breathes, are hopes/That look beyond the tomb'.[7] Breath can dissipate, a fear peculiarly close to the Victorian woman poet. Expressive theory, as will be seen, tended to endorse and consolidate this figure. The body imprisons breath but involuntarily releases it: this is an apt figure for the release of feeling which cannot find external form.

Letitia Landon and Felicia Hemans each explore the multiplicity of roles and projections which they make available to themselves in different ways, and each takes the affective moment in different directions. A marked feature of Landon's work is the use of tenses in narrative, particularly the historic past, and the present tense used in a succession of discrete phrases to denote successive actions in the past. It is used in such a way that an action is registered, not *as* it happens but when it is either just over or just about to happen. Effects often precede causes. Seen in this way the agent is oddly detached from actions in the slight hiatus when actions are seen but not the agent's acting of them. Such a procedure makes uncertain how far the woman is in responsible control of cause and effect—she seems to *suffer* rather than to act. The woman herself seems to be displaced from action into the psychic experience existing in the gap between actions, and the whole weight of these lyrical narratives is thrown on the temporal space of the affective moment, the emotional space occurring just before or just after something has happened. In 'The Indian Bride', for instance, the girl's prenuptial journey alone on the Ganges is presented in moments which are either over or which precede their causes: 'She has lighted her lamp. . . . The maiden is weeping. Her lamp has decayed'.[8] The reunion with the lover follows the same syntactic pattern: 'Hark to the ring of the cymeter! . . . The warfare is over, the battle is won. . . . And Zaide hath forgotten in Azim's arms/All her so false lamp's falser alarms'. But the lamp is and is not 'false'. The bridegroom dies and she goes deterministically to her death: 'A prayer is muttered, a blessing said,—/Her torch is raised!—she is by the dead./She has fired the pile'.[9] The tenses both obliterate and sharply question, through this strategy of detachment, by whose agency the girl goes to her death, her own, or the mores of cultural ritual. Before this the narrator has analysed the moment of acute superstitious fear when the girl is on the Ganges without light in tenses which blur the distinction between what does happen and what will happen: 'How the pulses will beat, and the cheek will be dy'd'.[1] This becomes not only a description of the girl's immediate emotional present but also a *prediction* of the future. The

7. In Blanchard, ed., *Life and Literary Remains of L.E.L.*, 2:246, 245–46.
8. "The Indian Bride," in *The Improvisatrice*, in

Poetical Works, 1:28, 30.
9. Ibid., 1:31.
1. Ibid., 1:29.

affective moment is in the right and the wrong place, describing the girl's immediate fears, proleptically describing the emotions of her death. But the ambiguous status of the tenses proffering the moment of feeling suggests that the girl, or the lamp, was right after all. The irrational affective moment could be trusted, and retrospectively it expands to include her death. The tenses here foreground and investigate a world of intense sensation and emotion and implicitly ask what its place in experience is.

Landon wrote many poems which pictured pictures, freezing women in a static but intense moment just before or just after an event (usually an event of communal significance) has occurred. They become objects whose life is in suspension, waiting for a critical event to occur either through their own or someone else's agency, or else waiting choicelessly. But whether dependent or independent, it is as if emotion and sensation rush in to fill the vacuum of subjectivity. Whether feeling is precipitated by action or whether action is precipitated by feeling seems to be the question such poems raise. Whether consciousness is determined by feeling or action, and what it is when there is no action to be taken at all, and where choice is limited by cultural prescription, is at issue. 'Subjects for Pictures', for instance, considers the woman as subject, often subordinate to men, in innumerable variations on the theme of choice, alternating enclosed environments with open landscapes, moving from history to history, culture to culture, ritual to ritual, myth to myth, marriage, death, murder, revival. These are all studies in the dislocation between consciousness and action, where the subject is placed remorselessly in fixed locations, immobilised by ritual or vigil. In what way the moment of feeling relates to or is determined by the rituals of a culture is a problem which fascinates Landon.

Whether Letitia Landon's figures belong to cultural rituals or place themselves in a transgressive relation to them they are almost always at the mercy of passion. Accused of an excessive preoccupation with love, Landon defended herself by arguing for what is effectively a politics of the affective state: 'A highly cultivated state of society must ever have for concomitant evils, that selfishness, the result of indolent indulgence, and that heartlessness attendant on refinement, which too often hardens while it polishes'.[2] The choice of love as a theme can 'soften' and 'touch' and 'elevate'. 'I can only say, that for a woman, whose influence and whose sphere must be in the affections, what subject can be more fitting than one which it is her peculiar province to refine, to spiritualise, and exalt? . . . making an almost religion of its truth . . . woman, actuated by an attachment as intense as it is true, as pure as it is deep', is more 'admirable' as a heroine. For as she is in art, so she is 'in actual life'.[3] If Landon appears to be completely accepting the sentimental terms in which women were seen, she is turning them to moral and social account and arguing that women's discourse can soften what would now be called the phallocentric hardness and imaginative deficiencies of an overcivilised culture. It is as if she has taken over the melting softness of Burke's category of the 'beautiful', which he saw as an overrefined and 'feminine' principle in contradistinction to the strenuous labour of the 'sublime', and reappropriated it as a moral category which can dissolve overcivilised hardness. Burke associated

2. Preface to *The Venetian Bracelet* (1829), in *Poetical Works*, 1:xiv.   3. Ibid.

beauty with nostalgia for a condition which we have 'irretrievably lost'.[4] In particular its nature is questioned and explored when it hovers over that last situation occasioning the last rituals of a culture, death.

Her own early death, which seems to have been the result of an accidental overdose of poison, self-administered to cure a palsy, occasioning scandal and suspicion as her life had done, made her the Keats (or perhaps the Sylvia Plath) of women's poetry. Witty, exuberant and unconventional, and like Mrs Hemans a vigorous and energetic intellectual (just before she died she wrote to ask her brother to send to Africa ' "Thiers's History of the Revolution", in French, and all George Sand's works . . . send me also Lamb's works'),[5] she was seen as a seminal figure by later writers.

Rather than exploring what cultural ritual does to the feminine subject, Mrs Hemans figures the flight beyond it, and the condition of extremity and disintegration which occurs when constraints press upon consciousness. Her method is inward and psychological where Landon's is external and classical, but it is just as analytical, turning the expressive moment towards investigation and critique. The heroic rebel and the conformist stand in dialectical relationship to one another in her work, each in dialogue with the other as each is pushed to extremity. The archetypes of her work are represented in the first section of *Records of Woman*, 'Arabella Stuart', and 'Casabianca', a short poem about an episode occurring in the battle of the Nile. 'Arabella Stuart' is a monologue spoken in imprisonment by a woman whose disintegrating mind struggles, and fails, to make the past coherent. The meaning of her history collapses. It is this, as much as the endurance of immediate confinement, which dissolves her reason (though an implicit question here is what 'reason' means). Hers was a political imprisonment (she died in captivity), made at the instigation of James I after a secret marriage and an attempted flight to France. Arabella does not know what has happened to her husband, or whether he has deserted her. The monologue opens with a memory.

> 'Twas but a dream! I saw the stag leap free,
>   Under the boughs where early birds were singing;
> I stood o'ershadowed by the greenwood tree,
>   And heard, it seemed, a sudden bugle ringing
> Far through a royal forest. Then the fawn
> Shot, like a gleam of light, from grassy lawn
> To secret covert; and the smooth turf shook,
> And lilies quivered by the glade's lone brook,
> And young leaves trembled, as, in fleet career,
> A princely band, with horn, and hound, and spear,
> Like a rich masque swept forth. I saw the dance
> Of their white plumes, that bore a silvery glance
> Into the deep wood's heart; and all passed by
> Save one—I met the smile of *one* clear eye,
> Flashing out joy to mine. Yes, *thou* wert there,
> Seymour![6]

4. Edmund Burke, *A Philosophical Enquiry into the Origin of Our Ideas of the Sublime and the Beautiful* (1958; reprint, Notre Dame, Ind.: University of Notre Dame Press, 1968), p. 51.

5. In Blanchard, ed., *Life and Literary Remains of L.E.L.*, 1:205.

6. *Records of Women*, Section I, "Arabella Stuart," in Rossetti, ed., *Works of Hemans*, p. 144.

A superficial glance at this text will immediately register what appears to be a slightly mannered Keatsian diction followed by the faintly absurd address to Seymour. 'Yes, *thou* wert there'. But women's poetry deliberately risked absurdity, as Christina Rossetti was later to see. In the extremity of the memory it is precisely important that the lover was *there*, as he is *not* in the present moment of the voice speaking from prison. The diction is used to render the vestigial, uncertain and discontinuous retrieval by memory of an event which even then may have been a dream and 'seemed' (there is a double 'seeming', the event and the memory of it) like a masque. The movement of the eye and of light is uncertain, the gaze fleeting, as the mere insignia of the helmet plumes 'glance' into the wood, with a superficial lightness whose pun on glance/gaze casts doubt on the clear eye which gazes at the woman. And if Seymour was not 'there', it is not clear 'where' the woman is either, as her gaze is constantly displaced from stag to fawn to quivering lilies (aroused *and* fearful sexuality), to huntsmen, plumes and lover. Though stag and fawn stand as conventionalised proleptic figures of the hunted woman's condition later in her story (the syntax allows that both stag and woman are 'Under the boughs'), she is not quite identified with either, or symbolically split between both, as they escape to different hiding places. This split condition is a function of her imprisoned consciousness, but it appears to be just as much a condition of her freedom: she stood isolated, 'o'ershadowed' by the tree, subject and metaphorically imprisoned even when her isolation seemed to make possible the rebellious independence of the secret love affair and marriage. These are the bitter insights disclosed by a fracturing consciousness whose mind and history disintegrate simultaneously. The bitterness, indeed, rests precisely on an awareness that the rebellion was in fact in conformity with a romantic paradigm which failed to work.

Like the woman in 'Arabella Stuart' who 'stood' transfixed under the greenwood tree, the boy in 'Casabianca' 'stood' on the burning deck, and in both cases the word seems to denote positioning outside the control of the character. The boy is subject to commands, standing ground and withstanding the assault of battle in absolute obedience to the father's orders, responding unquestioningly to the law of the father. Ostensibly this is a tale of the heroism of simple obedience of son to father. But in the oedipal fiasco the heroism of absolute obedience is misplaced, for the dead father, beneath the deck, like the unconscious, is 'Unconscious of his son', and 'His voice no longer heard'.[7] Consummately, Hemans transposes the terror of a condition of not knowing and hearing to the father, marking the tragic irony of the son's situation, for it is he who rather 'no longer heard' his father's voice, but continues to obey that voice from the past when it no longer sounds in the present. But at a deeper level, the law of the father is founded on its imperviousness to the son's voice, begging for a relaxation of its commands. In the culminating destruction we are enjoined to 'Ask of the winds' (like the boy to his father) which 'strewed the sea' with 'fragments', what became of the son, who is burned and blown to pieces through the act of blind obedience. The voice of the 'natural' elements may, or may not, perhaps, operate with analogous laws as fierce as those of patriarchal imperatives (the voices of the father and the wind are set questioningly against one another), but the nat-

---

7. "Casabianca," in Rossetti, ed., *Works of Hemans*, pp. 373–74.

ural certainly wreaks as much havoc as the human law, whether they can be differentiated from one another or not. For a frightening moment the 'fragments' seem parts of the boy's body, resolve themselves into mast, helm and pennon 'That well had borne their part', in the final stanza, and then as frighteningly, with all the referential hazardousness of metaphor, become metonymic hints of fragmented phallic parts. The absoluteness of the patriarchal imperative is absolutely ravaging in its violence. There is a kind of exultation in this violent elegy about the way phallic law destroys itself: at the same time the boy's 'heart', both his courage and the centre of his being, the identity bound up with the patriarchal imperatives of heroism, has 'perished'. The remorselessness which separates out 'part' and 'heart' and rhymes them to suggest the way masculine identity is founded, also recognises that this is a law to the death, killing a child on a burning deck. The unmentioned element in this masculine tragedy is the mother, but, with its constant reminder that this is the death of a child (he was 13), victim of the crucial Napoleonic battle of the Nile, the voice of the poem is gendered as female and thus brings war and sexual politics together. It is at once a deeply affective lament and a strangely Medaean[8] lyric of castigation—and castration—which takes its revenge on war even as it sees that war takes revenge on itself.

1993

8. I.e., characteristic of Medea, the sorceress of Greek mythology who killed her own children to exact vengeance on their father [editor's note].

SUSAN BORDO
b. 1947

Women's bodies and the cultural forces that shape them are the subjects of Susan Bordo's most influential work, *Unbearable Weight: Feminism, Western Culture, and the Body* (1993). Although Bordo gains from Michel Foucault a keen awareness of the ways in which social discourses inscribe themselves on the engendering of human beings, she brings to the subject of anorexia and bulimia a politically activist perspective that emphasizes the salutary effects of feminism on women's daily lives. For her, the rise in eating disorders can be explained in terms of women's efforts to conform to prevailing cultural institutions even as they rebel against them. Like Elizabeth Grosz in *Volatile Bodies: Toward a Corporeal Feminism* (1994), Bordo thus seeks to use feminism to understand embodiment. A professor of English and gender studies at the University of Kentucky, Bordo has also authored *Twilight Zones: The Hidden Life of Cultural Images from Plato to O.J.* (1997) as well as *The Male Body: A New Look at Men in Public and in Private* (1999), and she has co-edited (with Alison Jaggar) *Gender/Body/Knowledge: Feminist Reconstructions of Being and Knowing* (1989) and edited *Feminist Interpretations of René Descartes* (1999). Our selection from *Unbearable Weight* was first published as an essay in 1989.

From Unbearable Weight: Feminism, Western Culture, and the Body

From *Chapter 5. The Body and the Reproduction of Femininity*

RECONSTRUCTING FEMINIST DISCOURSE ON THE BODY

The body—what we eat, how we dress, the daily rituals through which we attend to the body—is a medium of culture. The body, as anthropologist Mary Douglas has argued, is a powerful symbolic form, a surface on which the central rules, hierarchies, and even metaphysical commitments of a culture are inscribed and thus reinforced through the concrete language of the body.[1] The body may also operate as a metaphor for culture. From quarters as diverse as Plato and Hobbes to French feminist Luce Irigaray, an imagination of body morphology has provided a blueprint for diagnosis and / or vision of social and political life.

The body is not only a *text* of culture. It is also, as anthropologist Pierre Bourdieu and philosopher Michel Foucault (among others) have argued, a *practical*, direct locus of social control. Banally, through table manners and toilet habits, through seemingly trivial routines, rules, and practices, culture is "*made* body," as Bourdieu puts it—converted into automatic, habitual activity. As such it is put "beyond the grasp of consciousness . . . [untouchable] by voluntary, deliberate transformations."[2] Our conscious politics, social commitments, strivings for change may be undermined and betrayed by the life of our bodies—not the craving, instinctual body imagined by Plato, Augustine, and Freud, but what Foucault calls the "docile body," regulated by the norms of cultural life.[3]

Throughout his later "genealogical" works (*Discipline and Punish, The History of Sexuality*), Foucault constantly reminds us of the primacy of practice over belief. Not chiefly through ideology, but through the organization and regulation of the time, space, and movements of our daily lives, our bodies are trained, shaped, and impressed with the stamp of prevailing historical forms of selfhood, desire, masculinity, femininity. Such an emphasis casts a dark and disquieting shadow across the contemporary scene. For women, as study after study shows, are spending more time on the management and discipline of our bodies than we have in a long, long time. In a decade marked by a reopening of the public arena to women, the intensification of such regimens appears diversionary and subverting. Through the pursuit of an ever-changing, homogenizing, elusive ideal of femininity—a pursuit without a terminus, requiring that women constantly attend to minute and often whimsical changes in fashion—female bodies become docile bodies—bodies whose forces and energies are habituated to external regulation, subjection, transformation, "improvement." Through the exacting and normalizing disciplines of diet, makeup, and dress—central organizing principles of time and

1. Mary Douglas, *Natural Symbols* (New York: Pantheon, 1982) and *Purity and Danger* (London: Routledge and Kegan Paul, 1966) [except as indicated, all notes are Bordo's].
2. Pierre Bourdieu, *Outline of a Theory of Practice* (Cambridge: Cambridge University Press, 1977), p. 94 (emphasis in original).
3. On docility, see Michel Foucault, *Discipline*

and Punish (New York: Vintage, 1979), pp. 135–69. For a Foucauldian analysis of feminine practice, see Sandra Bartky, "Foucault, Femininity, and the Modernization of Patriarchal Power," in her *Femininity and Domination* (New York: Routledge, 1990); see also Susan Brownmiller, *Femininity* (New York: Ballantine, 1984).

space in the day of many women—we are rendered less socially oriented and more centripetally focused on self-modification. Through these disciplines, we continue to memorize on our bodies the feel and conviction of lack, of insufficiency, of never being good enough. At the farthest extremes, the practices of femininity may lead us to utter demoralization, debilitation, and death.

Viewed historically, the discipline and normalization of the female body—perhaps the only gender oppression that exercises itself, although to different degrees and in different forms, across age, race, class, and sexual orientation—has to be acknowledged as an amazingly durable and flexible strategy of social control. In our own era, it is difficult to avoid the recognition that the contemporary preoccupation with appearance, which still affects women far more powerfully than men, even in our narcissistic and visually oriented culture, may function as a backlash phenomenon, reasserting existing gender configurations against any attempts to shift or transform power relations.[4] Surely we are in the throes of this backlash today. In newspapers and magazines we daily encounter stories that promote traditional gender relations and prey on anxieties about change: stories about latch-key children, abuse in day-care centers, the "new woman's" troubles with men, her lack of marriageability, and so on. A dominant visual theme in teenage magazines involves women hiding in the shadows of men, seeking solace in their arms, willingly contracting the space they occupy. The last, of course, also describes our contemporary aesthetic ideal for women, an ideal whose obsessive pursuit has become the central torment of many women's lives. In such an era we desperately need an effective political discourse about the female body, a discourse adequate to an analysis of the insidious, and often paradoxical, pathways of modern social control.

Developing such a discourse requires reconstructing the feminist paradigm of the late 1960s and early 1970s, with its political categories of oppressors and oppressed, villains and victims. Here I believe that a feminist appropriation of some of Foucault's later concepts can prove useful. Following Foucault, we must first abandon the idea of power as something possessed by one group and leveled against another; we must instead think of the network of practices, institutions, and technologies that sustain positions of dominance and subordination in a particular domain.

Second, we need an analytics adequate to describe a power whose central mechanisms are not repressive, but *constitutive*: "a power bent on generating forces, making them grow, and ordering them, rather than one dedicated to

---

4. During the late 1970s and 1980s, male concern over appearance undeniably increased. Study after study confirms, however, that there is still a large gender gap in this area. Research conducted at the University of Pennsylvania in 1985 found men to be generally satisfied with their appearance, often, in fact, "distorting their perceptions [of themselves] in a positive, self-aggrandizing way" ("Dislike of Own Bodies Found Common among Women," *New York Times*, March 19, 1985, p. C1). Women, however, were found to exhibit extreme negative assessments and distortions of body perception. Other studies have suggested that women are judged more harshly than men when they deviate from dominant social standards of attractiveness. Thomas Cash et al., in "The Great American Shape-Up," *Psychology Today*, April 1986, p. 34, report that although the situation for men has changed, the situation for women has more than proportionally worsened. Citing results from 30,000 responses to a 1985 survey of perceptions of body image and comparing similar responses to a 1972 questionnaire, they report that the 1985 respondents were considerably more dissatisfied with their bodies than the 1972 respondents, and they note a marked intensification of concern among men. Among the 1985 group, the group most dissatisfied of all with their appearance, however, were teenage women. Women today constitute by far the largest number of consumers of diet products, attenders of spas and diet centers, and subjects of intestinal by-pass and other fat-reduction operations.

impeding them, making them submit, or destroying them." Particularly in the realm of femininity, where so much depends on the seemingly willing accept-ance of various norms and practices, we need an analysis of power "from below," as Foucault puts it; for example, of the mechanisms that shape and proliferate—rather than repress—desire, generate and focus our energies, construct our conceptions of normalcy and deviance.[5]

And, third, we need a discourse that will enable us to account for the sub-version of potential rebellion, a discourse that, while insisting on the neces-sity of objective analysis of power relation, social hierarchy, political backlash, and so forth, will nonetheless allow us to confront the mechanisms by which the subject at times becomes enmeshed in collusion with forces that sustain her own oppression.

This essay will not attempt to produce a general theory along these lines. Rather, my focus will be the analysis of one particular arena where the inter-play of these dynamics is striking and perhaps exemplary. It is a limited and unusual arena, that of a group of gender-related and historically localized dis-orders: hysteria, agoraphobia, and anorexia nervosa.[6] I recognize that these disorders have also historically been class- and race-biased, largely (although not exclusively) occurring among white middle- and upper-middle-class women. Nonetheless, anorexia, hysteria, and agoraphobia may provide a par-adigm of one way in which potential resistance is not merely undercut but *utilized* in the maintenance and reproduction of existing power relations.[7]

The central mechanism I will describe involves a transformation (or, if you wish, duality) of meaning, through which conditions that are objectively (and, on one level, experientially) constraining, enslaving, and even murderous, come to be experienced as liberating, transforming, and life-giving. I offer this analysis, although limited to a specific domain, as an example of how various contemporary critical discourses may be joined to yield an understanding of the subtle and often unwitting role played by our bodies in the symbolization and reproduction of gender.

THE BODY AS A TEXT OF FEMININITY

The continuum between female disorder and "normal" feminine practice is sharply revealed through a close reading of those disorders to which women have been particularly vulnerable. These, of course, have varied historically: neurasthenia and hysteria in the second half of the nineteenth century; ago-

---

5. Michel Foucault, *The History of Sexuality*, vol. 1, *An Introduction* (New York: Vintage, 1980), pp. 94, 136.

6. On the gendered and historical nature of these disorders: the number of female to male hysterics has been estimated at anywhere from 2:1 to 4:1, and as many as 80 percent of all agoraphobics are female (Annette Brodsky and Rachel Hare-Mustin, *Women and Psychotherapy* [New York: Guilford Press, 1980], pp. 116, 122). Although more cases of male eating disorders have been reported in the late eighties and early nineties, it is estimated that close to 90 percent of all anorectics are female (Paul Garfinkel and David Garner, *Anorexia Nervosa: A Multidimensional Perspective* [New York: Brunner/Mazel, 1982], pp. 112–13). For a sophis-ticated account of female psychopathology, with particular attention to nineteenth-century disor-

ders but, unfortunately, little mention of agora-phobia or eating disorders, see Elaine Showalter, *The Female Malady: Women, Madness and English Culture, 1830–1980* (New York: Pantheon, 1985). For a discussion of social and gender issues in ago-raphobia, see Robert Seidenberg and Karen DeCrow, *Women Who Marry Houses: Panic and Protest in Agoraphobia* (New York: McGraw-Hill, 1983). On the history of anorexia nervosa, see Joan Jacobs Brumberg, *Fasting Girls: The Emergence of Anorexia Nervosa as a Modern Disease* (Cambridge: Harvard University Press, 1988).

7. In constructing such a paradigm I do not pre-tend to do justice to any of these disorders in its individual complexity. My aim is to chart some points of intersection, to describe some similar pat-terns, as they emerge through a particular reading of the phenomenon—a political reading, if you will.

raphobia and, most dramatically, anorexia nervosa and bulimia in the second half of the twentieth century. This is not to say that anorectics did not exist in the nineteenth century—many cases were described, usually in the context of diagnoses of hysteria[8]—or that women no longer suffer from classical hysterical symptoms in the twentieth century. But the taking up of eating disorders on a mass scale is as unique to the culture of the 1980s as the epidemic of hysteria was to the Victorian era.[9]

The symptomatology of these disorders reveals itself as textuality. Loss of mobility, loss of voice, inability to leave the home, feeding others while starving oneself, taking up space, and whittling down the space one's body takes up—all have symbolic meaning, all have *political* meaning under the varying rules governing the historical construction of gender. Working within this framework, we see that whether we look at hysteria, agoraphobia, or anorexia, we find the body of the sufferer deeply inscribed with an ideological construction of femininity emblematic of the period in question. The construction, of course, is always homogenizing and normalizing, erasing racial, class, and other differences and insisting that all women aspire to a coercive, standardized ideal. Strikingly, in these disorders the construction of femininity is written in disturbingly concrete, hyperbolic terms: exaggerated, extremely literal, at times virtually caricatured presentations of the ruling feminine mystique. The bodies of disordered women in this way offer themselves as an aggressively graphic text for the interpreter—a text that insists, actually demands, that it be read as a cultural statement, a statement about gender.

Both nineteenth-century male physicians and twentieth-century feminist critics have seen, in the symptoms of neurasthenia and hysteria (syndromes that became increasingly less differentiated as the century wore on), an exaggeration of stereotypically feminine traits. The nineteenth-century "lady" was idealized in terms of delicacy and dreaminess, sexual passivity, and a charmingly labile and capricious emotionality.[1] Such notions were formalized and scientized in the work of male theorists from Acton and Krafft-Ebing[2] to Freud, who described "normal," mature femininity in such terms.[3] In this context, the dissociations, the drifting and fogging of perception, the nervous tremors and faints, the anesthesias,[4] and the extreme mutability of symptomatology associated with nineteenth-century female disorders can be seen to be concretizations of the feminine mystique of the period, produced accord-

8. Showalter, *The Female Malady*, pp. 128–29.
9. On the epidemic of hysteria and neurasthenia, see Showalter, *The Female Malady*; Carroll Smith-Rosenberg, "The Hysterical Woman: Sex Roles and Role Conflict in Nineteenth-Century America," in her *Disorderly Conduct: Visions of Gender in Victorian America* (Oxford: Oxford University Press, 1985).
1. Martha Vicinus, "Introduction: The Perfect Victorian Lady," in Martha Vicinus, ed., *Suffer and Be Still: Women in the Victorian Age* (Bloomington: Indiana University Press, 1972), pp. x–xi.
2. Richard von Kraft-Ebing (1840–1902), German physician best known for his *Psychopathia Sexualis* (1886). William Acton (1813–1875), English doctor and author of influential manuals on sexuality; he believed that "the majority of women . . . are not very much troubled with sexual feeling of any kind" [editor's note].
3. See Carol Nadelson and Malkah Notman, *The Female Patient* (New York: Plenum, 1982), p. 5;

E. M. Sigsworth and T. J. Wyke, "A Study of Victorian Prostitution and Venereal Disease," in Vicinus, *Suffer and Be Still*, p. 82. For more general discussions, see Peter Gay, *The Bourgeois Experience: Victoria to Freud*, vol. 1, *Education of the Senses* (New York: Oxford University Press, 1984), esp. pp. 109–68; Showalter, *The Female Malady*, esp. pp. 121–44. The delicate lady, an ideal that had very strong class connotations (as does slenderness today), is not the only conception of femininity to be found in Victorian cultures. But it was arguably the single most powerful ideological representation of femininity in that era, affecting women of all classes, including those without the material means to realize the ideal fully. See Helena Mitchie, *The Flesh Made Word* (New York: Oxford University Press, 1987), for discussions of the control of female appetite and Victorian constructions of femininity.
4. Losses of feeling in various parts of the body [editor's note].

ing to rules that governed the prevailing construction of femininity. Doctors described what came to be known as the hysterical personality as "impressionable, suggestible, and narcissistic; highly labile, their moods changing suddenly, dramatically, and seemingly for inconsequential reasons . . . egocentric in the extreme . . . essentially asexual and not uncommonly frigid"[5]—all characteristics normative of femininity in this era. As Elaine Showalter points out, the term *hysterical* itself became almost interchangeable with the term *feminine* in the literature of the period.[6]

The hysteric's embodiment of the feminine mystique of her era, however, seems subtle and ineffable compared to the ingenious literalism of agoraphobia and anorexia. In the context of our culture this literalism makes sense. With the advent of movies and television, the rules for femininity have come to be culturally transmitted more and more through standardized visual images. As a result, femininity itself has come to be largely a matter of constructing, in the manner described by Erving Goffman, the appropriate surface presentation of the self.[7] We are no longer given verbal descriptions or exemplars of what a lady is or of what femininity consists. Rather, we learn the rules directly through bodily discourse: through images that tell us what clothes, body shape, facial expression, movements, and behavior are required.

In agoraphobia and, even more dramatically, in anorexia, the disorder presents itself as a virtual, though tragic, parody of twentieth-century constructions of femininity. The 1950s and early 1960s, when agoraphobia first began to escalate among women, was a period of reassertion of domesticity and dependency as the feminine ideal. *Career woman* became a dirty word, much more so than it had been during the war, when the economy depended on women's willingness to do "men's work." The reigning ideology of femininity, so well described by Betty Friedan and perfectly captured in the movies and television shows of the era, was childlike, nonassertive, helpless without a man, "content in a world of bedroom and kitchen, sex, babies and home."[8] The housebound agoraphobic lives this construction of femininity literally. "You want me in this home? You'll have me in this home—with a vengeance!" The point, upon which many therapists have commented, does not need belaboring. Agoraphobia, as I. G. Fodor has put it, seems "the logical—albeit extreme—extension of the cultural sex-role stereotype for women" in this era.[9]

The emaciated body of the anorectic, of course, immediately presents itself as a caricature of the contemporary ideal of hyperslenderness for women, an ideal that, despite the game resistance of racial and ethnic difference, has become the norm for women today. But slenderness is only the tip of the iceberg, for slenderness itself requires interpretation. "C'est le sens qui fait vendre," said Barthes, speaking of clothing styles—it is meaning that makes the sale.[1] So, too, it is meaning that makes the body admirable. To the degree that

5. Smith-Rosenberg, *Disorderly Conduct*, p. 203.
6. Showalter, *The Female Malady*, p. 129.
7. Erving Goffman, *The Presentation of Self in Everyday Life* (Garden City, N.Y.: Anchor Doubleday, 1959).
8. Betty Friedan, *The Feminine Mystique* (New York: Dell, 1962), p. 36. The theme song of one such show ran, in part, "I married Joan . . . What a girl . . . what a whirl . . . what a life! I married Joan . . . What a mind . . . love is blind . . . what a wife!" [From *I Married Joan*, an NBC sitcom (1952–55)—editor's note.]

9. See I. G. Fodor, "The Phobic Syndrome in Women," in V. Franks and V. Burtle, eds., *Women in Therapy* (New York: Brunner/Mazel, 1974), p. 119; see also Kathleen Brehony, "Women and Agoraphobia," in Violet Franks and Esther Rothblum, eds., *The Stereotyping of Women* (New York: Springer, 1983).
1. In Jonathan Culler, *Roland Barthes* (New York: Oxford University Press, 1983), p. 74. [Roland Barthes (1915–1980), French literary critic—editor's note.]

anorexia may be said to be "about" slenderness, it is about slenderness as a citadel of contemporary and historical meaning, not as an empty fashion ideal. As such, the interpretation of slenderness yields multiple readings, some related to gender, some not. For the purposes of this essay I will offer an abbreviated, gender-focused reading. But I must stress that this reading illuminates only partially, and that many other currents not discussed here— economic, psychosocial, and historical, as well as ethnic and class dimensions—figure prominently.[2]

We begin with the painfully literal inscription, on the anorectic's body, of the rules governing the construction of contemporary femininity. That construction is a double bind that legislates contradictory ideals and directives. On the one hand, our culture still widely advertises domestic conceptions of femininity, the ideological moorings for a rigorously dualistic sexual division of labor that casts woman as chief emotional and physical nurturer. The rules for this construction of femininity (and I speak here in a language both symbolic and literal) require that women learn to feed others, not the self, and to construe any desires for self-nurturance and self-feeding as greedy and excessive.[3] Thus, women must develop a totally other-oriented emotional economy. In this economy, the control of female appetite for food is merely the most concrete expression of the general rule governing the construction of femininity: that female hunger—for public power, for independence, for sexual gratification—be contained, and the public space that women be allowed to take up be circumscribed, limited. * * * [S]lenderness, set off against the resurgent muscularity and bulk of the current male body-ideal, carries connotations of fragility and lack of power in the face of a decisive male occupation of social space. On the body of the anorexic woman such rules are grimly and deeply etched.

On the other hand, even as young women today continue to be taught traditionally "feminine" virtues, to the degree that the professional arena is open to them they must also learn to embody the "masculine" language and values of that arena—self-control, determination, cool, emotional discipline, mastery, and so on. Female bodies now speak symbolically of this necessity in their slender spare shape and the currently fashionable men's-wear look. * * * Our bodies, too, as we trudge to the gym every day and fiercely resist both our hungers and our desire to soothe ourselves, are becoming more and more practiced at the "male" virtues of control and self-mastery. * * * The anorectic pursues these virtues with single-minded, unswerving dedication. "Energy, discipline, my own power will keep me going," says ex-anorectic Aimee Liu, recreating her anorexic days. "I need nothing and no one else. . . . I will be master of my own body, if nothing else, I vow."[4]

The ideal of slenderness, then, and the diet and exercise regimens that have become inseparable from it offer the illusion of meeting, through the body, the contradictory demands of the contemporary ideology of femininity. Popular images reflect this dual demand. In a single issue of *Complete*

2. For other interpretive perspectives on the slenderness ideal, see "Reading the Slender Body" in *Unbearable Weight* (1993); Kim Chernin, *The Obsession: Reflections on the Tyranny of Slenderness* (New York: Harper and Row, 1981); Susie Orbach, *Hunger Strike: The Anorectic's Struggle as a Metaphor for Our Age* (New York: W. W. Norton, 1985).

3. See my "Hunger as Ideology" in *Unbearable Weight* for a discussion of how this construction of femininity is reproduced in contemporary commercials and advertisements concerning food, eating, and cooking.

4. Aimee Liu, *Solitaire* (New York: Harper and Row, 1979), p. 123.

Woman magazine, two articles appear, one on "Feminine Intuition," the other asking, "Are You the New Macho Woman?" In *Vision Quest*, the young male hero falls in love with the heroine, as he says, because "she has all the best things I like in girls and all the best things I like in guys," that is, she's tough and cool, but warm and alluring. In the enormously popular *Aliens*, the heroine's personality has been deliberately constructed, with near–comic book explicitness, to embody traditional nurturant femininity alongside breathtaking macho prowess and control; Sigourney Weaver, the actress who portrays her, has called the character "Rambolina."[5]

In the pursuit of slenderness and the denial of appetite the traditional construction of femininity intersects with the new requirement for women to embody the "masculine" values of the public arena. The anorectic, as I have argued, embodies this intersection, this double bind, in a particularly painful and graphic way.[6] I mean *double bind* quite literally here. "Masculinity" and "femininity," at least since the nineteenth century and arguably before, have been constructed through a process of mutual exclusion. One cannot simply add the historically feminine virtues to the historically masculine ones to yield a New Woman, a New Man, a new ethics, or a new culture. Even on the screen or on television, embodied in created characters like the *Aliens* heroine, the result is a parody. Unfortunately, in this image-bedazzled culture, we find it increasingly difficult to discriminate between parodies and possibilities for the self. Explored as a possibility for the self, the "androgynous" ideal ultimately exposes its internal contradiction and becomes a war that tears the subject in two—a war explicitly thematized, by many anorectics, as a battle between male and female sides of the self.[7]

PROTEST AND RETREAT IN THE SAME GESTURE

In hysteria, agoraphobia, and anorexia, then, the woman's body may be viewed as a surface on which conventional constructions of femininity are exposed starkly to view, through their inscription in extreme or hyperliteral form. They are written, of course, in languages of horrible suffering. It is as though these bodies are speaking to us of the pathology and violence that lurks just around the corner, waiting at the horizon of "normal" femininity. It is no wonder that a steady motif in the feminist literature on female disorder is that of pathology as embodied *protest*—unconscious, inchoate, and counterproductive protest without an effective language, voice, or politics, but protest nonetheless.

American and French feminists[8] alike have heard the hysteric speaking a language of protest, even or perhaps especially when she was mute. Dianne

5. I.e., a feminine version of Rambo, the hypermasculine hero played by Sylvester Stallone in three films (1982–88); *Aliens* was released in 1986, and *Vision Quest* in 1985 [editor's note].
6. Striking, in connection with this, is Catherine Steiner-Adair's 1984 study of high-school women, which reveals a dramatic association between problems with food and body image and emulation of the cool, professionally "together" and gorgeous superwoman. On the basis of a series of interviews, the high schoolers were classified into two groups: one expressed skepticism over the superwoman ideal, the other thoroughly aspired to it. Later administrations of diagnostic tests revealed that 94 percent of the pro-superwoman group fell into the eating-disordered range of the scale. Of the other group, 100 percent fell into the noneating-disordered range. Media images notwithstanding, young women today appear to sense, either consciously or through their bodies, the impossibility of simultaneously meeting the demands of two spheres whose values have been historically defined in utter opposition to each other.
7. See my "Anorexia Nervosa" in *Unbearable Weight*.
8. Shorthand for the primary orientation of feminists—sociological vs. psychoanalytic [editor's note].

Hunter interprets Anna O.'s[9] aphasia, which manifested itself in an inability to speak her native German, as a rebellion against the linguistic and cultural rules of the father and a return to the "mother-tongue": the semiotic babble of infancy, the language of the body. For Hunter, and for a number of other feminists working with Lacanian categories, the return to the semiotic level is both regressive and, as Hunter puts it, an "expressive" communication "addressed to patriarchal thought," "a self-repudiating form of feminine discourse in which the body signifies what social conditions make it impossible to state linguistically."[1] "The hysterics are accusing; they are pointing," writes Catherine Clément in *The Newly Born Woman*; they make a "mockery of culture."[2] In the same volume, Hélène Cixous speaks of "those wonderful hysterics, who subjected Freud to so many voluptuous moments too shameful to mention, bombarding his mosaic statute/law of Moses with their carnal, passionate body-words, haunting him with their inaudible thundering denunciations." For Cixous, Dora, who so frustrated Freud, is "the core example of the protesting force in women."[3]

The literature of protest includes functional as well as symbolic approaches. Robert Seidenberg and Karen DeCrow, for example, describe agoraphobia as a "strike" against "the renunciations usually demanded of women" and the expectations of housewifely functions such as shopping, driving the children to school, accompanying their husband to social events.[4] Carroll Smith-Rosenberg presents a similar analysis of hysteria, arguing that by preventing the woman from functioning in the wifely role of caretaker of others, of "ministering angel" to husband and children, hysteria "became one way in which conventional women could express—in most cases unconsciously—dissatisfaction with one or several aspects of their lives."[5] A number of feminist writers, among whom Susie Orbach is the most articulate and forceful, have interpreted anorexia as a species of unconscious feminist protest. The anorectic is engaged in a "hunger strike," as Orbach calls it, stressing that this is a political discourse, in which the action of food refusal and dramatic transformation of body size "expresses with [the] body what [the anorectic] is unable to tell us with words"—her indictment of a culture that disdains and suppresses female hunger, makes women ashamed of their appetites and needs, and demands that women constantly work on the transformation of their body.[6]

9. Bertha Pappenheim, the hysteric patient discussed in *Studies in Hysteria* (1895), by Freud and Josef Breuer [editor's note].

1. Dianne Hunter, "Hysteria, Psychoanalysis and Feminism," in Shirley Garner, Claire Kahane, and Madelon Sprengnether, eds., *The (M)Other Tongue* (Ithaca: Cornell University Press, 1986), p. 42. [Semiotic level: a mother-oriented use of language postulated by the French feminist Julia Kristeva—editor's note.]

2. Catherine Clément and Hélène Cixous, *The Newly Born Woman*, trans. Betsy Wing (Minneapolis: University of Minnesota Press, 1986), p. 42.

3. Clément and Cixous, *The Newly Born Woman*, p. 95. [Dora: the name Freud gave to his patient Ida Bauer in *Dora: An Analysis of a Case of Hysteria* (1904)—editor's note.]

4. Seidenberg and DeCrow, *Women Who Marry Houses*, p. 31.

5. Smith-Rosenberg, *Disorderly Conduct*, p. 208.

6. Orbach, *Hunger Strike*, p. 102. When we look into the many autobiographies and case studies of hysterics, anorectics, and agoraphobics, we find that these are indeed the sorts of women one might expect to be frustrated by the constraints of a specified female role. Sigmund Freud and Joseph Breuer, in *Studies on Hysteria* (New York: Avon, 1966), and Freud, in the later *Dora: An Analysis of a Case of Hysteria* (New York: Macmillan, 1963), constantly remark on the ambitiousness, independence, intellectual ability, and creative strivings of their patients. We know, moreover, that many women who later became leading social activists and feminists of the nineteenth century were among those who fell ill with hysteria and neurasthenia. It has become a virtual cliché that the typical anorectic is a perfectionist, driven to excel in all areas of her life. Though less prominently, a similar theme runs throughout the literature on agoraphobia.

One must keep in mind that in drawing on case studies, one is relying on the perceptions of other acculturated individuals. One suspects, for example, that the popular portrait of the anorectic as a

The anorectic, of course, is unaware that she is making a political statement. She may, indeed, be hostile to feminism and any other critical perspectives that she views as disputing her own autonomy and control or questioning the cultural ideals around which her life is organized. Through embodied rather than deliberate demonstration she exposes and indicts those ideals, precisely by pursuing them to the point at which their destructive potential is revealed for all to see.

The same gesture that expresses protest, moreover, can also signal retreat; this, indeed, may be part of the symptom's attraction. Kim Chernin, for example, argues that the debilitating anorexic fixation, by halting or mitigating personal development, assuages this generation's guilt and separation anxiety over the prospect of surpassing our mothers, of living less circumscribed, freer lives.[7] Agoraphobia, too, which often develops shortly after marriage, clearly functions in many cases as a way to cement dependency and attachment in the face of unacceptable stirrings of dissatisfaction and restlessness.

Although we may talk meaningfully of protest, then, I want to emphasize the counterproductive, tragically self-defeating (indeed, self-deconstructing) nature of that protest. Functionally, the symptoms of these disorders isolate, weaken, and undermine the sufferers; at the same time they turn the life of the body into an all-absorbing fetish, beside which all other objects of attention pale into unreality. On the symbolic level, too, the protest collapses into its opposite and proclaims the utter capitulation of the subject to the contracted female world. The muteness of hysterics and their return to the level of pure, primary bodily expressivity have been interpreted, as we have seen, as rejecting the symbolic order of the patriarchy and recovering a lost world of semiotic, maternal value. But *at the same time*, of course, muteness is the condition of the silent, uncomplaining woman—an ideal of patriarchal culture. Protesting the stifling of the female voice through one's own voicelessness—that is, employing the language of femininity to protest the conditions of the female world—will always involve ambiguities of this sort. Perhaps this is why symptoms crystallized from the language of femininity are so perfectly suited to express the dilemmas of middle-class and upper-middle-class women living in periods poised on the edge of gender change, women who have the social and material resources to carry the traditional construction of femininity to symbolic excess but who also confront the anxieties of new possibilities. The late nineteenth century, the post–World War II period, and the late twentieth century are all periods in which gender becomes an issue to be discussed and in which discourse proliferates about "the Woman Question," "the New Woman," "What Women Want," "What Femininity Is."

*   *   *

relentless overachiever may be colored by the lingering or perhaps resurgent Victorianism of our culture's attitudes toward ambitious women. One does not escape this hermeneutic problem by turning to autobiography. But in autobiography one is at least dealing with social constructions and attitudes that animate the subject's own psychic reality. In this regard the autobiographical literature on anorexia, drawn on in a variety of places in *Unbearable Weight*, is strikingly full of anxiety about the domestic world and other themes that suggest deep rebellion against traditional notions of femininity.

7. Kim Chernin, *The Hungry Self: Women, Eating, and Identity* (New York: Harper and Row, 1985), esp. pp. 41–93.

TEXTUALITY, PRAXIS, AND THE BODY

The "solutions" offered by anorexia, hysteria, and agoraphobia, I have suggested, develop out of the practice of femininity itself, the pursuit of which is still presented as the chief route to acceptance and success for women in our culture. Too aggressively pursued, that practice leads to its own undoing, in one sense. For if femininity is, as Susan Brownmiller has said, at its core a "tradition of imposed limitations,"[8] then an unwillingness to limit oneself, even in the pursuit of femininity, breaks the rules. But, of course, in another sense the rules remain fully in place. The sufferer becomes wedded to an obsessive practice, unable to make any effective change in her life. She remains, as Toril Moi has put it, "gagged and chained to [the] feminine role," a reproducer of the docile body of femininity.[9]

This tension between the psychological meaning of a disorder, which may enact fantasies of rebellion and embody a language of protest, and the practical life of the disordered body, which may utterly defeat rebellion and subvert protest, may be obscured by too exclusive a focus on the symbolic dimension and insufficient attention to praxis. As we have seen in the case of some Lacanian feminist readings of hysteria, the result of this can be a one-sided interpretation that romanticizes the hysteric's symbolic subversion of the phallocentric order while confined to her bed. This is not to say that confinement in bed has a transparent, univocal meaning—in powerlessness, debilitation, dependency, and so forth. The "practical" body is no brute biological or material entity. It, too, is a culturally mediated form; its activities are subject to interpretation and description. The shift to the practical dimension is not a turn to biology or nature, but to another "register," as Foucault puts it, of the cultural body, the register of the "useful body" rather than the "intelligible body."[1] The distinction can prove useful, I believe, to feminist discourse.

The intelligible body includes our scientific, philosophic, and aesthetic representations of the body—our cultural *conceptions* of the body, norms of beauty, models of health, and so forth. But the same representations may also be seen as forming a set of *practical* rules and regulations through which the living body is "trained, shaped, obeys, responds," becoming, in short, a socially adapted and "useful body."[2] Consider this particularly clear and appropriate example: the nineteenth-century hourglass figure, emphasizing breasts and hips against a wasp waist, was an intelligible *symbolic* form, representing a domestic, sexualized ideal of femininity. The sharp cultural contrast between the female and the male form, made possible by the use of corsets and bustles, reflected, in symbolic terms, the dualistic division of social and economic life into clearly defined male and female spheres. At the same time, to achieve the specified look, a particular feminine *praxis* was required—straitlacing, minimal eating, reduced mobility—rendering the female body unfit to perform activities outside its designated sphere. This, in Foucauldian terms, would be the "useful body" corresponding to the aesthetic norm.

8. Brownmiller, *Femininity*, p. 14.
9. Toril Moi, "Representations of Patriarchy: Sex and Epistemology in Freud's *Dora*," in Charles Bernheimer and Claire Kahane, eds., *In Dora's Case: Freud—Hysteria—Feminism* (New York: Columbia University Press, 1985), p. 192.
1. Foucault, *Discipline and Punish*, p. 136.
2. Foucault, *Discipline and Punish*, p. 136.

The intelligible body and the useful body are two arenas of the same discourse; they often mirror and support each other, as in the above illustration. Another example can be found in the seventeenth-century philosophic conception of the body as a machine, mirroring an increasingly more automated productive machinery of labor. But the two bodies may also contradict and mock each other. A range of contemporary representations and images, as noted earlier, have coded the transcendence of female appetite and its public display in the slenderness ideal in terms of power, will, mastery, the possibilities of success in the professional arena. These associations are carried visually by the slender superwomen of prime-time television and popular movies and promoted explicitly in advertisements and articles appearing routinely in women's fashion magazines, diet books, and weight-training publications. Yet the thousands of slender girls and women who strive to embody these images and who in that service suffer from eating disorders, exercise compulsions, and continual self-scrutiny and self-castigation are anything *but* the "masters" of their lives.

Exposure and productive cultural analysis of such contradictory and mystifying relations between image and practice are possible only if the analysis includes attention to and interpretation of the "useful" or, as I prefer to call it, the practical body. Such attention, although often in inchoate and theoretically unsophisticated form, was central to the beginnings of the contemporary feminist movement. In the late 1960s and early 1970s the objectification of the female body was a serious political issue. All the cultural paraphernalia of femininity, of learning to please visually and sexually through the practices of the body—media imagery, beauty pageants, high heels, girdles, makeup, simulated orgasm—were seen as crucial in maintaining gender domination.

Disquietingly, for the feminists of the present decade, such focus on the politics of feminine praxis, although still maintained in the work of individual feminists, is no longer a centerpiece of feminist cultural critique.[3] On the popular front, we find *Ms.* magazine presenting issues on fitness and "style," the rhetoric reconstructed for the 1980s to pitch "self-expression" and "power." Although feminist theory surely has the tools, it has not provided a critical discourse to dismantle and demystify this rhetoric. The work of French feminists has provided a powerful framework for understanding the inscription of phallocentric, dualistic culture on gendered bodies, but it has offered very little in the way of concrete analyses of the female body as a locus of practical cultural control. Among feminist theorists in this country, the study of cultural representations of the female body has flourished, and it has often been brilliantly illuminating and instrumental to a feminist rereading of culture.[4] But the study of cultural representations alone, divorced from consideration of their relation to the practical lives of bodies, can obscure and mislead.

3. A focus on the politics of sexualization and objectification remains central to the anti-pornography movement (e.g., in the work of Andrea Dworkin, Catharine MacKinnon). Feminists exploring the politics of appearance include Sandra Bartky, Susan Brownmiller, Wendy Chapkis, Kim Chernin, and Susie Orbach. And a developing feminist interest in the work of Michel Foucault has begun to produce a poststructuralist feminism oriented toward practice; see, for example, Irene Diamond and Lee Quinby, *Feminism and Foucault: Reflections on Resistance* (Boston: Northeastern University Press, 1988).

4. See, for example, Susan Suleiman, ed., *The Female Body in Western Culture* (Cambridge: Harvard University Press, 1986).

Here, Helena Mitchie's significantly titled *The Flesh Made Word* offers a striking example. Examining nineteenth-century representations of women, appetite, and eating, Mitchie draws fascinating and astute metaphorical connections between female eating and female sexuality. Female hunger, she argues, and I agree, "figures unspeakable desires for sexuality and power."[5] The Victorian novel's "representational taboo" against depicting women eating (an activity, apparently, that only "happens offstage," as Mitchie puts it) thus functions as a "code" for the suppression of female sexuality, as does the general cultural requirement, exhibited in etiquette and sex manuals of the day, that the well-bred woman eat little and delicately. The same coding is drawn on, Mitchie argues, in contemporary feminist "inversions" of Victorian values, inversions that celebrate female sexuality and power through images exulting in female eating and female hunger, depicting it explicitly, lushly, and joyfully.

Despite the fact that Mitchie's analysis centers on issues concerning women's hunger, food, and eating practices, she makes no mention of the grave eating disorders that surfaced in the late nineteenth century and that are ravaging the lives of young women today. The practical arena of women dieting, fasting, straitlacing, and so forth is, to a certain extent, implicit in her examination of Victorian gender ideology. But when Mitchie turns, at the end of her study, to consider contemporary feminist literature celebrating female eating and female hunger, the absence of even a passing glance at how women are *actually* managing their hungers today leaves her analysis adrift, lacking any concrete social moorings. Mitchie's sole focus is on the inevitable failure of feminist literature to escape "phallic representational codes."[6] But the feminist celebration of the female body did not merely deconstruct on the written page or canvas. Largely located in the feminist counterculture of the 1970s, it has been culturally displaced by a very different contemporary reality. Its celebration of female flesh now presents itself in jarring dissonance with the fact that women, feminists included, are starving themselves to death in our culture.

This is not to deny the benefits of diet, exercise, and other forms of body management. Rather, I view our bodies as a site of struggle, where we must *work* to keep our daily practices in the service of resistance to gender domination, not in the service of docility and gender normalization. This work requires, I believe, a determinedly skeptical attitude toward the routes of seeming liberation and pleasure offered by our culture. It also demands an awareness of the often contradictory relations between image and practice, between rhetoric and reality. Popular representations, as we have seen, may forcefully employ the rhetoric and symbolism of empowerment, personal freedom, "having it all." Yet female bodies, pursuing these ideals, may find themselves as distracted, depressed, and physically ill as female bodies in the nineteenth century were made when pursuing a feminine ideal of dependency, domesticity, and delicacy. The recognition and analysis of such contradictions, and of all the other collusions, subversions, and enticements through which culture enjoins the aid of our bodies in the reproduction of gender, require that we restore a concern for female praxis to its formerly central place in feminist politics.

1989, 1993

5. Mitchie, *The Flesh Made Word*, p. 13.   6. Mitchie, *The Flesh Made Word*, p. 149.

TERRY CASTLE
b. 1935

In a lively introduction to her massive anthology *The Literature of Lesbianism: A Historical Anthology from Ariosto to Stonewall* (2003), Terry Castle explains its "guiding presumption," namely "that love between women is a topic of serious and abiding human significance—bound up in as yet unfathomed ways with our deepest beliefs about nature and culture, sexuality and desire, femininity and masculinity, women and men." Such a belief animates her earlier scholarship on the eighteenth-century novel as well as the publications that followed her influential *The Apparitional Lesbian: Female Homosexuality and Modern Culture* (1993): *The Female Thermometer: Eighteenth Century Culture and the Invention of the Uncanny* (1995), *Noel Coward and Radclyffe Hall: Kindred Spirits* (1996), *Boss Ladies, Watch Out! Essays on Women, Sex, and Writing* (2002), and *Courage, Mon Amie* (2002). A professor of English at Stanford University, Terry Castle has written a number of award-winning essays and regularly contributes to the *London Review of Books* and *The New Republic*.

From The Apparitional Lesbian: Female Homosexuality and Modern Culture

From 3. *The Apparitional Lesbian*[1]

To try to write the literary history of lesbianism is to confront, from the start, something ghostly: an impalpability, a misting over, an evaporation, or "whiting out" of possibility. Take, for example, that first (and strangest) of lesbian love stories, Daniel Defoe's *The Apparition of Mrs. Veal* (1706). The heroine of this spectral yarn (which Defoe presents in typically hoaxing fashion as unvarnished "fact") is one Mrs. Bargrave, who lives in Canterbury with a cruel and unfeeling husband. While lamenting her sad state one morning, Mrs. Bargrave is amazed to see her oldest and dearest friend, Mrs. Veal, coming up the street to her door. The two friends have been estranged ever since Mrs. Veal, "a Maiden Gentlewoman of about 30 Years of Age," began keeping house for a brother in Dover. Overcome with joy, Mrs. Bargrave greets her long-lost companion and moves to kiss her. Just as the clock strikes noon, writes Defoe, "their Lips almost touched," but "*Mrs. Veal* drew her hand cross her own Eyes, and said, '*I am not very well*,' and so waved it."[1]

The touch of lips deferred, the two nonetheless converse lovingly. Mrs. Veal tells Mrs. Bargrave she is about to set off on a journey, and wished to see her again before doing so. She begs Mrs. Bargrave's forgiveness for the lapse in their friendship and reminds her of their former happy days, when they read "Drelincourt's Book of Death" together and comforted one another in affliction. Moved, Mrs. Bargrave fetches a devotional poem on Christian love, "Friendship in Perfection," and they read it aloud, musing on God's will and the happiness to come in the hereafter. "Dear Mrs. *Bargrave*," exclaims Mrs. Veal, "I shall love you forever." Then she draws her hand once again over her eyes. "*Don't you think I am mightily impaired by my Fits?*" she asks. (Mrs. Veal

---

1. Daniel Defoe, *A True Relation of the Apparition of one Mrs. Veal* (London, 1706; rpt., Los Angeles: William Andrews Clark Memorial Library, 1965), p. 3. Notations in parentheses refer to page numbers in this edition. [Except as indicated, all notes are Castle's.]

has suffered in the past from falling sickness.) "No," Mrs. Bargrave replies, "I think you look as well as I ever knew you" (4). Not long after, Mrs. Veal departs, as if in embarrassed haste.

It is not until the next day, when Mrs. Bargrave goes to look for Mrs. Veal at a nearby relative's, that the eerie truth is revealed: her friend has in fact been dead for two days, having succumbed to "fits" at exactly the stroke of noon on the day before Mrs. Bargrave saw her. The supposed "Mrs. Veal" was nothing less than an apparition. Suddenly it all makes sense. The spirit was undoubtedly heaven-sent, an excited Mrs. Bargrave now tells her friends, for all of its actions, including the mysterious "waving" off of her attempted kiss, displayed its "Wonderful Love to her, and Care of her, that she should not be affrighted." And Defoe himself, in his role of supposed reporter, concurs: the specter's great errand, he concludes, was "to comfort Mrs. *Bargrave* in her Affliction, and to ask her Forgiveness for her Breach of Friendship, and with a Pious Discourse to encourage her" (8). From this we learn "that there is a Life to come after this, and a Just God who will retribute to every one according to the Deeds done in the Body" (preface).

Why call this bizarre little fable a lesbian love story? One could, conceivably, read into its sparse and somewhat lugubrious detail a richer, more secular, and sensational narrative—cunningly secreted inside the uplifting homily on Christian doctrine. Mrs. Bargrave, the unhappy wife, and Mrs. Veal, the maiden gentlewoman—such a story might go—have in fact been clandestine lovers; they have been estranged by circumstances; Mrs. Veal dies; Mrs. Bargrave's vision is a kind of hysterical projection, in which the passion she feels for her dead friend is phantasmatically renewed. Defoe even gives a certain amount of evidence for this sort of fantasia. All the men mentioned in the story are either evil or unsympathetic: Mrs. Bargrave's husband is "barbarous"; Mrs. Veal's brother tries to stop Mrs. Bargrave from spreading the story of his sister's spectral visit. We are invited to imagine a male conspiracy against the lovers: they have been kept apart in life; they will be alienated (or so the brother hopes) in death. The fact that Defoe sometimes hints at erotic relationships between women elsewhere in his fiction—witness *Roxana*—might make such a "reading between the lines" seem even more enticing.[2]

And yet, this does not feel quite right: one is troubled by a certain crassness, anachronism, even narcissism in the reading. Is it not a peculiarly late twentieth-century moral and sexual infantilism that wishes to read into every story from the past some hidden scandal or provocation? And hasn't Defoe made it clear—more or less—that the relationship between Mrs. Bargrave and Mrs. Veal is strictly an incorporeal one? Mrs. Veal, after all, is an apparition—a mere collection of vapors—so much so that Mrs. Bargrave, as we are explicitly reminded, cannot even kiss her.

At the risk of dealing in paradoxes, I would like to argue that it is in fact the very ghostliness—the seeming ineffability—of the connection between Mrs. Bargrave and Mrs. Veal that makes *The Apparition of Mrs. Veal* an archetypally lesbian story. The kiss that doesn't happen, the kiss that *can't* happen, because one of the women involved has become a ghost (or else is direly haunted by ghosts) seems to me a crucial metaphor for the history of lesbian

---

2. On the hints of lesbianism in *Roxana* (1724), see my " 'Amy, who knew my Disease': A Psychosexual Pattern in Defoe's Roxana," *ELH* 46 (1979): 81–96.

literary representation since the early eighteenth century. Given the threat that sexual love between women inevitably poses to the workings of patriarchal arrangement, it has often been felt necessary to deny the carnal *bravada* of lesbian existence. The hoary misogynist challenge, "But what do lesbians do?" insinuates as much: *This cannot be. There is no place for this.* It is perhaps not so surprising that at least until around 1900 lesbianism manifests itself in the Western literary imagination primarily as an absence, as chimera or *amor impossibilia*[3]—a kind of love that, by definition, cannot exist. Even when "there" (like Stein's Oakland) it is "not there":[4] inhabiting only a recessive, indeterminate, misted-over space in the collective literary psyche. Like the kiss between Mrs. Bargrave and Mrs. Veal, it is reduced to a ghost effect: to ambiguity and taboo. It cannot be perceived, except apparitionally.

But how, one might object, to recognize (enough to remark) something as elusive as a ghost effect? By way of answer let us turn to another work, also from the eighteenth century, in which a similar apparitionality envelops—and ultimately obscures—the representational field. The work is Diderot's *La Religieuse* (1760), long recognized as a masterpiece of the erotic, though of what sort of eros its admirers (and detractors) have often been at a loss to specify.[5] We recall the story: Diderot's pathetic heroine, Suzanne Simonin, forced to become a nun by her selfish and obdurate family, is imprisoned within a series of corrupt convents, each worse than the last, where she is singled out for cruel and incessant persecution by her superiors. In letters smuggled out to various lawyers and secular officials, Suzanne recounts her sufferings and begs for release, though her cries for help go unheard. Diderot's first-person narrative itself masquerades as one of these letters, supposedly addressed to the Marquis de Croismare. Yet it also doubles as Diderot's own sensationalist assault on cloistered religious communities and the inhuman "wickedness" perpetrated within them.

As most of its modern commentators have remarked, a fear of sexual relations between women seems to suffuse—if not to rule—Diderot's story.[6] And yet how is this fear insinuated? Ineluctably, by shadow play—through a kind of linguistic necromancy, or calling up, of ghosts. Take Diderot's sleight-of-hand, for example, in the scene early in the novel in which the vicious mother superior at Long-champ, the first convent in which Suzanne is incarcerated, forces her to undergo a sadistic mock death as a punishment for disobedience. After being made to lie in a coffin, being drenched with freezing holy water, and trodden upon (as "a corpse") by her fellow nuns, the pitiful Suzanne is confined to her cell, without blankets, crucifix, or food. That

3. Impossible love (more properly, *impossibilis*; Latin) [editor's note].

4. Gertrude Stein famously said of Oakland, California, "There is no there there" (*Everybody's Autobiography*, 1937) [editor's note].

5. To sample some of the critical controversy see, for example, Vivienne Mylne, "What Suzanne Knew: Lesbianism and *La Religieuse*," *Studies on Voltaire and the Eighteenth Century* 208 (1982): 167–73; Jack Undank, "An Ethics of Discourse," in *Diderot: Digression and Dispersion*, ed. Undank and Herbert Josephs (Lexington, Ky.: French Forum, 1984); Rita Goldberg, *Sex and Enlightenment: Women in Richardson and Diderot* (Cambridge: Cambridge University Press, 1984), pp.

169–204; Walter E. Rex, "Secrets from Suzanne: The Tangled Motives of *La Religieuse*," in *The Attraction of the Contrary: Essays on the Literature of the French Enlightenment* (Cambridge: Cambridge University Press, 1987), pp. 125–35; and Eve Kosofsky Sedgwick, "Privilege of Unknowing," *Genders* 1 (Spring 1988): 102–24.

6. Cf. Goldberg, in *Sex and Enlightenment*, on Diderot's distaste for the lesbian mother superior: "Her sexual desire is so easily stimulated that we are meant to think of it as a kind of disease. . . . She is, in fact, an example of the dreaded *bomme-femme*, with the desires of a man and the body and supposed emotional weakness of a woman" (197–98).

night, at the behest of the superior, other nuns break into her room, shrieking and overturning objects, so that

> those who were not in the conspiracy alleged that strange things were going on in my cell, that they had heard mournful voices, shoutings and the rattlings of chains, and that I held communion with ghosts and evil spirits, that I must have made a pact with the devil and that my corridor should be vacated at once.[7]

A young nun, infected by the atmosphere of collective paranoia, sees Suzanne wandering in the corridor, becomes hysterical with terror, and flings herself into the bewildered Suzanne's arms. At this point, Suzanne tells the marquis, "the most criminal-sounding story was made out of it." Namely,

> that the demon of impurity had possessed me, and I was credited with intentions I dare not mention, and unnatural desires to which they attributed the obvious disarray of the young nun. Of course I am not a man, and I don't know what can be imagined about one woman and another, still less about one woman alone, but as my bed had no curtains and people came in and out of my room at all hours, what can I say, Sir? For all their circumspect behaviour, their modest eyes and the chastity of their talk, these women must be very corrupt at heart—anyway they know that you can commit indecent acts alone, which I don't know, and so I have never quite understood what they accused me of, and they expressed themselves in such veiled terms that I never knew how to answer them. (85–86)

An irrational yet potent symbolic logic is at work here: to be taken for a ghost is to be "credited" with unnatural desires. No other incriminating acts need be represented, no fleeting palpitation recorded—it is enough to become phantomlike in the sight of others, to change oneself (or be changed) from mortified flesh to baffled apparition. To "be a ghost" is to long, unspeakably, after one's own sex. At the same time—Diderot slyly suggests—the demonic opposite is also true: to love another woman is to lose one's solidity in the world, to evanesce, and fade into the spectral.

The notorious final section of *La Religieuse*—in which Suzanne is moved to a new convent and falls under the erotic sway of its depraved superior, "Madame * * * "—shows this last uncanny transformation most powerfully. Suzanne, we recollect, after being half-seduced by Madame * * * (who visits her nightly in her cell and excites her with ambiguous caresses), becomes afraid for her soul and begins to avoid her, on the advice of her confessor. Maddened by the young nun's rebuffs, Madame * * * pursues her like a specter, day and night. "If I went downstairs," writes Suzanne, "I would find her at the bottom, and she would be waiting for me at the top when I went up again" (169). Surprised by her on one occasion in the convent chapel, Suzanne actually mistakes the superior for an apparition, owing to what she calls a "strange effect" of the imagination, complicated by an optical illusion: "her position in relation to the church lamp had been such that only her face and the tips of her fingers had been lit up, the rest was in shadow, and that had given her a weird appearance" (165).

---

7. Diderot, *The Nun*, trans, Leonard Tancock (Harmondsworth, Middlesex: Penguin, 1974), p. 85. All references are to this edition.

As the superior's sexual obsession finally lapses into outright dementia—following upon a church inquiry instigated by Suzanne into abuses at the convent—her ghostly status is confirmed. As she passes "from melancholy to piety and from piety to frenzy," she becomes a nightwalker in the convent, raving, subject to terrible hallucinations, surrounded by imaginary phantasms. Sometimes, Suzanne tells the marquis, when she would come upon Madame * * *—barefoot, veiled, and in white—in the convent corridors, or being bled in the convent infirmary, the madwoman would cover her eyes and turn away, as though possessed. "I dare not describe all the indecent things she did and said in her delirium," says Suzanne; "She kept on putting her hand to her forehead as though trying to drive away unwanted thoughts or visions—what visions I don't know. She buried her head in the bed and covered her face with her sheets. 'It is the tempter!' she cried, 'it is he! What a strange shape he has put on! Get some holy water and sprinkle it over me. . . . Stop, stop, he's gone now' " (182). Exiled to a world of diabolical spirits, surrounded by horrific shapes she tries feebly to "fend off" with a crucifix, the naked and emaciated Madame * * * finally expires in an exhalation of curses—a ghost indeed of her former sensual and worldly self.

How are we to read such scenes? One is struck at once by the curious repetition of gesture: like the ghostly Mrs. Veal, putting hand to eyes and "waving" off the kiss of Mrs. Bargrave, Madame * * * raises her hand repeatedly to her face to obliterate those visions—the ghosts of her former love—that haunt and torment her. As if in closeup in some lost avant-garde film, the isolated hand over the eyes, caught forever in Manichaean black and white, makes the gesture of blockage, as though to cede into the void the memory (or hope) of a fleshly passion. But somewhat more insistently than in *The Apparition of Mrs. Veal,* the blocking motion is visible here as an authorial gesture as well—as the displaced representation, or symbolic show, of Diderovian motive. What better way to exorcize the threat of female homosexuality than by treating it as ghostly? By "waving" off, so to speak, the lesbian dimension of his own story, even as his heroine Suzanne exculpates herself from any complicity in the superior's erotic mania, Diderot establishes his credentials as law-abiding, slightly flirtatious, homophobic man of letters—the same man who could jealously complain to his lover Sophie Volland about the unnaturally "voluptuous and loving way" in which her own sister often embraced her.[8]

The literary history of lesbianism, I would like to argue, is first of all a history of derealization. Diderot's blocking gesture is symptomatic: in nearly all of the art of the eighteenth and nineteenth centuries, lesbianism, or its possibility, can only be represented to the degree that it is simultaneously "derealized," through a blanching authorial infusion of spectral metaphors. (I speak here of so-called polite or mainstream writing; the shadow discourse of pornography is of course another matter, and demands a separate analy-

---

8. See, for example, Diderot's letter to Volland of September 17, 1760 (in *Diderot's Letters to Sophie Volland,* trans. Peter France [London: Oxford University Press, 1972]), in which he animadverts on her sister's "curiously" erotic way with her (60). In a letter written August 3, 1759, Diderot coped with his imagined rival by transforming her, through simile, into airy nothingness. "It does not make me unhappy to be her successor," he wrote, "indeed it rather pleases me. It is as if I were pressing her soul between yours and mine. She is like a snowflake which will perhaps melt away between two coals of fire" (21). And later, after warning Sophie not to kiss her sister's portrait too often lest he find out, he says: "I put my lips to yours and kiss them, even if your sister's kisses are still there. But no, there's nothing there; hers are so light and airy" (24).

sis.[9]) One woman or the other must be a ghost, or on the way to becoming one. Passion is excited, only to be obscured, disembodied, decarnalized. The vision is inevitably waved off. Panic seems to underwrite these obsessional spectralizing gestures: a panic over love, female pleasure, and the possibility of women breaking free—together—from their male sexual overseers. Homophobia is the order of the day, entertains itself (wryly or gothically) with phantoms, then exorcizes them.

One might easily compile an anthology of spectralizing moments from the eighteenth-, nineteenth-, and even early twentieth-century literature of lesbianism. After the melodramatics of *La Religieuse*, one might turn, for example, to Théophile Gautier's *Mademoiselle de Maupin*, a novel that, despite its different tone and sensibility (comical-fantastic rather than morbid-sublime), also presents the sexual love of woman for woman as an essentially phantasmatic enterprise. Rosette, the lover of the narrator D'Albert, has fallen in love with Théodore, a mysterious young visitor to her country estate. What she does not know (nor any of the other characters) is that Théodore is in reality a woman in disguise, the handsome adventurer Madeleine de Maupin. Clad only in the most apparitional of night-gowns ("so clinging and so diaphanous that it showed her nipples, like those statues of bathing women covered with wet drapery"), Rosette comes to Théodore/Madeleine's room one moonlit evening and pleads with her to make love to her. When "Théodore" (assuming that Rosette is deluded about her sex) is reluctant, Rosette takes matters into her own hands. Although, she explains, "you find it wearisome to see me following your steps like this, like a loving ghost which can only follow you and would like to merge with your body . . . I cannot help doing it."[1] Then she pulls Théodore/Madeleine toward her and their lips meet in a ghostly, "almost imperceptible kiss" (306).

Aroused by Rosette to the point that she can no longer tell whether she is "in heaven or on earth, here or elsewhere, dead or living," "Théodore" now wonders for a fleeting instant what it would be like to give some "semblance of reality to this shadow of pleasure which my lovely mistress embraced with such ardour" (307). But how to turn shadow into substance? Her question goes unanswered, for just as Rosette slips naked into her bed, Rosette's brother, Alcibiades, bursts farcically into the room, sword in hand, to prevent the rape he imagines to be taking place. His mocking accusations underline the already free-floating spectral metaphorics of the scene: "It appears, then, my very dear and very virtuous sister, that having judged in your wisdom that my lord Théodore's bed was softer than yours, you came

---

9. The pornographic representation of lesbianism may nonetheless have influenced so-called mainstream representation more often—and more profoundly—than is commonly acknowledged. In a subsequent essay in *The Apparitional Lesbian*, pp. 107–49, I argue that various pornographic works written at the time of French Revolution depicting the supposed lesbian relationships of the French queen, Marie Antoinette, contributed directly—albeit covertly—to her incarnation in the nineteenth century as an icon of romantic female-female love. The distinction I make in the present essay between polite discourse and its pornographic "shadow," is in one sense an artificial one: from Diderot and Gautier to Zola and Djuna Barnes, mainstream writers taking up the theme of lesbianism have often, in fact, drawn upon the motifs and stock situations of pornographic discourse.

1. Gautier, *Mademoiselle de Maupin*, trans. Joanna Richardson (Harmondsworth, Middlesex: Penguin, 1981), p. 304. All further references are to this edition. Richardson's assertion in her introduction to the novel, that "the story is the least important part of the book," is characteristic, alas, of the way in which the majority of commentators have dealt with Gautier's cryptolesbian plot line. For a somewhat less repressive view, see Janet Sadoff, *Ambivalence, Ambiguity, and Androgyny in Théophile Gautier's "Mademoiselle de Maupin"* (Cambridge, Mass.: Harvard University Press, 1990).

to sleep here? Or perhaps there are ghosts in your room, and you thought that you would be safer in this one, under his protection?" (308). After wounding Alcibiades in an impromptu duel and fleeing on horseback into the woods around Rosette's house, Théodore/Madeleine is herself pursued by seeming phantoms:

> The branches of the trees, all heavy with dew, struck against my face and made it wet; one would have said that the old trees were stretching out their arms to hold me back and keep me for the love of their chatelaine. If I had been in another frame of mind, or a little superstitious, I could easily have believed that they were so many ghosts who wanted to seize me and that they were showing me their fists. (312)

Though carefully designed to maximize readerly titillation, Gautier's stagey scene of lesbian coitus interruptus is also a paradoxical statement on sexual ontology. Such spectral coupling as that between Rosette and Madeleine de Maupin must needs be interrupted, because otherwise *it might prove itself to exist*. What would happen, Gautier seems to ask, were Rosette to realize the true sex of her lover? The anxiety that pursues the novelist—or so his compulsive slippage into the language of the apparitional here suggests—is not so much that the ethereal Rosette might start back in blank dismay, but that the discovery of absence instead of presence (a haunting vacuity where the phallus should be) might bring with it its own perverse and unexpected joy. Yet Gautier can no more tolerate eros without a phallus than the dripping branches of the trees can hold back Madeleine de Maupin on behalf of their infatuated "chatelaine." Indeed, lest Rosette or her would-be lover bring into being some giddying new embodiment of love, the *amor impossibilia* must remain just that—a phantom or shadow in the comic narrative of desire.[2]

✷ ✷ ✷

Up to this point I have focused exclusively on the insubstantiality of the apparitional lesbian—her weightlessness, her sterility, her annoyingly diffident response to the imperatives of physical desire. She epitomizes "not-thereness": now you see her, but mostly you don't. Or do you? For the supernatural metaphor itself, obviously, suggests a different and perhaps more subtle way of thinking about the matter. A ghost, according to *Webster's Ninth,* is a spirit believed to appear in a "bodily likeness." To haunt, we find, is "to visit often," "to recur constantly and spontaneously," "to stay around or persist," or "to reappear continually." The ghost, in other words, is a paradox. Though nonexistent, it nonetheless *appears*. Indeed, so vividly does it appear—if only in the "mind's eye"—one feels unable to get away from it. It is surely in the latter, colloquial, and uncanny sense that Renée Vivien invokes the ghostly metaphor in her ecstatic sapphic reverie, *Une Femme*

---

2. The trees brushing Madeleine de Maupin's face bring to mind, of course, that waving gesture which I am suggesting often subverts the literary representation of lesbian desire. Yet here the gesture is displaced—with its meaning seemingly inverted—onto those anthropomorphic trees, which, like ghosts, want to *preserve* the possibility of a sexual union between Madeleine and Rosette. How to deal with the apparent contradiction? One way, it seems to me, would be to read "into" the narrative a second, unmentioned gesture: that of the rider, who finding her eyes momentarily blinded with dew, reflexively brushes back the very branches that brush her. In this second, hypothetical waving—so automatic as to preclude mention—will be found that motion of avoidance so often accompanying the literary threat of female homosexuality.

m'apparut (*A Woman Appeared to Me*; 1903). To be haunted by a woman—in the magical speech of desire—is ineluctably to see her.[3]

What of the spectral metaphor and the lesbian writer? For her, one suspects, "seeing ghosts" may be a matter—not so much of derealization—but of rhapsodical embodiment: a ritual calling up, or *apophrades*, in the old mystical sense. The dead are indeed brought back to life; the absent loved one returns. For the spectral vernacular, it turns out, contains its own powerful and perverse magic. Used imaginatively—repossessed, so to speak—the very trope that evaporates can also solidify. In the strangest turn of all, perhaps, the lesbian body itself returns: and the feeble, elegiac waving off—the gesture of would-be exorcism—becomes instead a new and passionate beckoning.

The intimate writings of women, not surprisingly, hint at such transvaluation. Violet Trefusis, writing to Vita Sackville-West from Cornwall at the height of their turbulent love affair in the summer of 1919, speaks of being possessed by her, as though she were present:

> Now it's Clovelly, I separated from you, but nevertheless haunted by you day and night. . . . The nights of music and ineffable longing for you—I used to stand by the open window, between the music and the garden. And in the garden were irises which cast very black shadows, and sometimes I would catch my breath: *surely* that was a figure in a leopard-skin that darted out into the dappled moonlight . . . [4]

"O mercy," she exclaims (as if incanting) "the things I want to write!"—

> You remember the caresses. . . .
> It seems I have never wanted you as I do now—
> When I think of your mouth. . . .
> When I think of . . . other things, all the blood rushes to my head,
> and I can almost imagine. . . . (150)

And again: "the house is haunted by your presence, and the sound of your voice calling me" (164).

Virginia Woolf, writing to the same Sackville-West in 1927, toward the end of their own love affair, playfully invites her to come with her to Hampton Court: "We'll dine; we'll haunt the terrace."[5] Later on she asks "dear Mrs. Nicholson," "Ain't it romantic—this visionary and aetherial presence brooding diaphanous over Gordon Square, like a silver spangled cloud? What are we to call her?"[6]

And in *For Sylvia*, the autobiographical memoir she composed for her lover, Sylvia Townsend Warner, in 1949, the poet Valentine Ackland uses the imagery of the spectral to conjure up a poignant vision of their emotional and physical bond. Thinking back to the cottage in Norfolk she and Townsend Warner shared in the 1930s, Ackland writes,

---

3. Witness the narrator's exclamation, after falling in love with the mysterious Vally, "I saw you today for the first time and already I am the shadow of your shadow." Later she refers to her as "the pale friend of my dreamless past," an "adored image [rising] against the darkness." See Vivien, *A Woman Appeared to Me*, trans., Jeannette H. Foster (Tallahassee, Fla.: Naiad, 1976), pp. 2–3 and 23–24.

4. Trefusis, Violet to Vita: *The Letters of Violet Trefusis to Vita Sackville-West*, ed. Mitchell A. Leaska and John Phillips (London: Methuen, 1989), p. 151. All further references are to this edition.

5. Woolf, *The Letters of Virginia Woolf*, ed. Nigel Nicolson and Joanne Trautmann, 6 vols. (New York: Harcourt Brace Jovanovich, 1980), 3:396.

6. Woolf, *Letters*, 3:428.

I dream of it now, too often, and when I am dead for sure my ghost will haunt there, loving and grieving—there, and along the Drove at Chaldon, where my Love stood beside the thorn tree and vowed her troth to me. Because of that vow and because of our life together I do not think that she will leave me alone, even when I am a ghost; and if she will walk with me, we will be happy—as we have always been, even in despair, together.[7]

But we need not confine ourselves to private invocations. The ghost metaphor also reappears, strikingly metamorphosed, in twentieth-century lesbian fiction. Perhaps inevitably Radclyffe Hall's *The Well of Loneliness* (1928) provides the paradigm. True, the story of Stephen Gordon's discovery of her sexual identity is composed in a powerfully dysphoric register, and in the novel's early chapters especially, a number of spectral metaphors, deployed in the traditional negative manner, help to advance this melancholy effect. In her maladroit and unhappy youth, Stephen is both a specter in the sight of others and a victim herself of tormenting erotic ghosts. Witness the passage in which Stephen's parents, Sir Philip and Anna, first suspect the truth about their daughter's frighteningly alien sexual nature:

He knew already, and she knew that he knew. Yet neither of them spoke it, this most unhappy thing, and their silence spread round them like a poisonous miasma. The spectre that was Stephen would seem to be watching, and Sir Philip would gently release himself from Anna, while she, looking up, would see his tired eyes, not angry any more, only very unhappy.[8]

Later, when Stephen falls miserably in love with Angela Crossby—the married woman who first flirts with, then spurns her—it is Angela who becomes a cruel and teasing ghost: "Pacing restlessly up and down her bedroom, Stephen would be thinking of Angela Crossby—haunted, tormented by

7. Ackland, *For Sylvia: An Honest Account* (New York: Norton, 1986), p. 132. The spectral metaphor crops up interestingly in lesbian slang of the 1930s. Witness the following scene in the pseudonymous *Diana: A Strange Autobiography* (1939), when the author enters a lesbian bar for the first time and strikes up a conversation with one of the regulars:

"Do you mind telling me," she said, "if you are one of us or a spook?"

I was embarrassed to be ignorant of lesbian jargon. Elizabeth had to explain what she meant by "spook":

"A woman who for some reason or other strays into lesbianism as second best. And stays because she likes it better."

"Once a woman is a spook she almost never prefers a man again," she went on like a teacher. "She may marry if she wants a home and children, but chances are she has a lesbian lover."

See Diana Frederics, *Diana: A Strange Autobiography* (New York: Citadel, 1948), pp. 123–24. The term *shadow* seems to have had a similar denotation. As Robert A. Schanke points out in a recent biography of the lesbian actress Eva Le Gallienne, when the husband of Le Galliene's lover, the starlet Josie Hutchinson, filed for divorce from Hutchinson in 1930, naming Le Gallienne as corespondent, "headlines in the *New York Daily News*

read 'Le Gallienne Shadow Actress is divorced,' 'shadow' being the common euphemism at the time for women who loved other women." "Some people will regard this as a new angle in the old love triangle," wrote a columnist in the *New York Daily Mirror*, "but the affinity of one girl for another is as old as the pyramids." See Schanke, *Shattered Applause: The Lives of Eva Le Gallienne* (Carbondale: Southern Illinois University Press, 1992), p. 88.

8. Hall, *The Well of Loneliness* (New York: Anchor, 1990), p. 81; all further references are to this edition. Clinicians writing about female homosexuality in the 1940s and 1950s sometimes took passages such as these as evidence of the morbid nature of lesbian desire. In *Female Homosexuality: A Psychodynamic Study of Lesbianism* (New York: Citadel, 1954), the American psychiatrist Frank S. Caprio observed that "lesbians are basically unhappy people. Many admit their unhappiness but others are deceived by their pseudoadjustment to life. They regard themselves as being 'different,' and as pointed out in *The Well of Loneliness*, that they were born that way. In general their attitude toward themselves is a negative one." Among Caprio's gloom-and-doom case histories, interestingly enough, is one involving a suicidal young woman—"Jessie"—who typically "covered her eyes with her arm when she began to talk of her problem." See Caprio, *Female Homosexuality*, pp. 176–80.

Angela's words that day in the garden: 'Could you marry me, Stephen?' and then by those other pitiless words: 'Can I help it if you're—what you obviously are?' " (152). After Angela takes a male lover, Stephen finds herself haunting the rose garden outside Angela's house, like some wretched "earth-bound spirit" (184).

In later chapters, however, ghosts of a different sort begin to haunt Stephen. It is worth recollecting, I think, that Radclyffe Hall herself was for most of her life an ardent spiritualist—a participant in seances and table rappings in the teens and twenties, a believer in apparitions, and a contributor on several occasions (with her lover Una Troubridge) to the *Journal of the Society for Psychical Research*. For almost twenty years, much in the manner of patients consulting a psychoanalyst, she and Troubridge communicated regularly with Hall's deceased lover "Ladye" (Mabel Batten) through a spirit medium, Mrs. Leonard. In Batten's words from beyond the grave Hall and Troubridge seem to have found not only day-to-day solace but a kind of mystic sanction for their own sexual relationship. The very dedication of *The Well of Loneliness*—"TO OUR THREE SELVES"—is an acknowledgment of the occult yet inspiring erotic triangle out of which Radclyffe Hall's novel itself was born.[9]

Yet Stephen, too, is a necromancer, and experiences her own ultimately liberating communion with spirits. We get a hint of what is to come in the famous "recognition" scene, midway through the novel. Here, like the heroine in some sapphic *Mysteries of Udolpho*, Stephen opens a locked bookcase in her dead father's study and discovers the works of the sexologist Krafft-Ebing, heavily annotated—with her own name—in her father's handwriting. While the room grows dusky with shadows, Stephen (who until now has felt nothing but bewilderment over her erotic longings) begins to read with increasing excitement. "Then suddenly," writes Radclyffe Hall, "she had got to her feet and was talking aloud—she was talking to her father: 'You knew! All the time you knew this thing, but because of your pity you wouldn't tell me' " (204). Confronting the phantasm of Sir Philip, whose tender understanding of her nature she now recognizes, Stephen also, as it were, confronts herself. For as his spectral presence instructs her, she is indeed one of those "thousands" marked out by God as different from the sexual norm. To be haunted thus, one might say, is to encounter one's own palpably lesbian self.

But the theme of spectral communion is realized even more starkly in *The Well*'s climactic final scenes. Tormented by self-hatred, Stephen has become convinced that her young lover Mary should live a more "normal" life—by marrying a man—and so deceives her into thinking she has been unfaithful. Falling for the ruse, Mary sorrowfully departs for Canada with Martin Hal-

---

9. On Radclyffe Hall's spiritualism and its relation to the *The Well of Loneliness*, see Michael Baker, *Our Three Selves: The Life of Radclyffe Hall* (New York: William Morrow, 1985), pp. 83–98. The intriguing relationship between spiritualism and lesbian proclivities—especially among Englishwomen at the turn of the century—has yet to be explored. The two women who wrote together in the 1890s under the names "Somerville and Ross" are a case in point. After the death in 1915 of Violet Martin ("Martin Ross"), her lifelong companion and erstwhile collaborator, Edith Somerville not only communicated with her through a spirit medium, but claimed to have written subsequent books with her dead friend's aid. "She is gone," wrote Somerville many years later, "but our collaboration has not ended." Edith Lees Ellis, the wife of Havelock Ellis and "Case History XXXVI" in Ellis's *Sexual Inversion* (1897) was another believer: she became addicted to spiritualism after the death of her lover, Lily, in 1903, and "spoke" with her repeatedly during numerous seances. See Maurice Collis, *Somerville and Ross* (London: Faber and Faber, 1968), pp. 176–84, and Phyllis Grosskurth, *Havelock Ellis* (New York: Knopf, 1980), pp. 211–12.

lam, who is in love with her. A despondent Stephen then returns alone to their flat on the Rue Jacob, only to find herself surrounded by "terrible" shapes—the hallucinatory images of those who have died, or suffered unspeakable anguish, over their lesbianism:

> The room seemed to be thronging with people. Who were they, these strangers with the miserable eyes? And yet, were they all strangers? Surely that was Wanda? And someone with a neat little hole in her side—Jamie clasping Barbara by the hand; Barbara with the white flowers of death on her bosom. Oh, but they were many, these unbidden guests, and they called very softly at first and then louder. They were calling her by name, saying: "Stephen Stephen!" The quick, the dead, and the yet unborn—all calling her, softly at first and then louder. (436)

Among these haunting Baudelairean shades there are some, Stephen sees, with "shaking, white-skinned, effeminate fingers"—male denizens of the homosexual underworld she has frequented with Mary—who reproach her bitterly for abandoning them: " 'You and your kind have stolen our birthright; you have taken our strength and have given us your weakness!' " The female spirits then join in, while moving ever closer: " 'We are coming, Stephen—we are still coming on, and our name is legion—you dare not disown us!' " (436–37). Reeling back in guilty horror, Stephen raises her arms as if "to ward them off," but the phantoms close "in and in" like a vividly pursuing horde. Then, writes Hall,

> They possessed her. Her barren womb became fruitful—it ached with its fearful and sterile burden. It ached with the fierce yet helpless children who would clamour in vain for their right to salvation. They would turn first to God, and then to the world, and then to her. . . .
> And now there was only voice, one demand; her own voice into which those millions had entered. A voice like the awful, deep rolling of thunder; a demand like the gathering together of great waters. A terrifying voice that made her ears throb, that made her brain throb, that shook her very entrails, until she must stagger and all but fall beneath this appalling burden of sound that strangled her in its will to be uttered. (437)

The novel ends with Stephen—shuddering like one in orgasm or labor—gasping out a dire collective plea for acceptance: "Acknowledge us, oh God, before the whole world. Give us also the right to our existence!" (437).

The less-than-pious reader may well have to suppress a laugh here; the style is pure Radclyffe Hall—hieratic, overwrought, full of melodramatic, dismal pomp. But infelicities of tone and taste should not distract us from the startling transformation the novelist also works on the conventional spectral figure. The blocking movement is there of course: by raising her arms as if to "ward off" the oncoming phantoms, Radclyffe Hall's self-loathing heroine somewhat oafishly pantomimes the repressive theatrics we have seen before in Defoe, Diderot, Mackenzie, and Strachey. But it's a useless move now—in fact seems to draw in, rather than repel, the encroaching host. It's as if—to mar Stevie Smith—Stephen were not drowning but waving.[1] And what ensues, despite the maundering mock religiosity of Hall's presentation, is a

---

1. An allusion to Stevie Smith's poem "Not Waving But Drowning" (1957) [editor's note].

loopy, delirious, untrammeled consummation: a kind of sex scene with ghosts. Overlaid and penetrated by the apparitional, Stephen is "possessed" in a fantastic convulsion indistinguishable in the end from sexual gratification. And while she labors and pants, struggling to give birth to a new erotic truth, all the pale and rejected revenants of the lesbian literary tradition seem to pervade her, to find embodiment within her—engrossing their voices within hers in a plangent affirmation of existence.

Radclyffe Hall's rewriting of tradition, it is true, might be considered incomplete: we do not get to gaze into Stephen's future or see what changes to her character will result from such wild intercourse with spirits. Whether Stephen will now evolve into an emphatically carnal being of the sort that Radclyffe Hall was herself remains to be seen. (The novelist in a letter to one of her lovers: "You must come here at once as you promised . . . I must have you—I *must*—I *must*—I *must*.")[2] Radclyffe Hall wrote, alas, no sequel to *The Well of Loneliness*. But what we do have is in its own way perhaps enough: a spectacular first breakout from the coils of homophobic repetition. By embracing the apparitional, by realizing its potential, so to speak, within her own body, Stephen Gordon also acts out a fierce and liberating movement from denial to acceptance. In place of the pristine half-truths of repression, she finds passionate congruence; in place of morbid evasion, the creative ferment of a desire encompassed and acknowledged.

And Radclyffe Hall's successors, one could argue, in fact write the sequel. Virtually every English or American lesbian novel composed since 1928 has been in one sense or another a response to, or trespass upon, *The Well of Loneliness*; one can sense its lingering emotional aftershocks even in such disaffected and ultimately retrograde works as *The Friendly Young Ladies* and *Olivia*.[3] (In some cases, as in Elizabeth Jolley's surreal *The Well* from 1986, the appropriation of Radclyffe Hall is at once brazen and mysterious.)[4] But the way in which Radclyffe Hall's followers have emulated her most interestingly, perhaps, has been precisely in restaging this uncanny transvaluation of the apparitional—by returning again and again to the ghostly metaphor and conjuring from it a multifarious imagery of erotic possibility.

✳   ✳   ✳

Why, since the eighteenth century, this phantasmagorical association between ghosts and lesbians? And why the seductive permutation of the

2. Cited in Baker, *Our Three Selves*, p. 311. The lover in question was Evguenia Souline, with whom Radclyffe Hall became infatuated in the 1930s. On another occasion, Radclyffe Hall warned her that "if you were in my flat at this moment, I would not protect you at all—I'd kill you with love—I'd kiss you until you asked for mercy. I'd kiss you all over that dear body of yours—I'd make that body of yours desire me until your desire of me was as pain" (Baker, *Our Three Selves*, p. 308).
3. Consider the following passage from *Olivia*, with its Radclyffe Hall-like resonances and uncanny play on the crucial word "loneliness": "Greatness and loneliness. 'Puissant et solitaire.' To live above the crowd in loneliness. To be condemned to loneliness by the greatness of one's qualities. To be condemned to live apart, however much one wanted the contact of warm human companionship. To be the Lord's anointed! Strange and dreadful fate! I forgot where I was as I thought of it" (Dorothy Strachey, *Olivia* [London: Virago, 1987], p. 60). The narrator is glossing De Vigny's *Moise*, which she and Mademoiselle Julie have just read aloud, but her words also eerily recall another "anointed" one: Stephen Gordon, likewise "condemned to live apart" in perpetual loneliness.
4. In Jolley's haunting fiction, two women—the older in love with the younger—accidentally hit a man in the darkness with their car. In a panic they throw his body down a well on their property. When they hear a voice emanating from the well they realize that he is still alive. Kathy, the younger woman, becomes fascinated by his voice and wishes to marry him. In the Poe-like penultimate scene, her jealous friend—for whom the idea of "that man, touching or handling [Kathy's] perfectly made and childlike body was repulsive"—has the well permanently sealed.

metaphor in the twentieth century? The answer, it seems to me, is not far to seek. The spectral figure is a perfect vehicle for conveying what must be called—though without a doubt paradoxically—that "recognition through negation" which has taken place with regard to female homosexuality in Western culture since the Enlightenment. Over the past three hundred years, I would like to suggest, the metaphor has functioned as the necessary psychological and rhetorical means for objectifying—and ultimately embracing—that which otherwise could not be acknowledged.

Psychoanalytic theory offers an interesting analogy. Freud, in his famous essay on negation (published three years before *The Well of Loneliness*) argued that the most important way in which repressed thoughts entered into individual consciousness, paradoxically, was through disavowal. To seek to negate an idea—as when one says of an unknown person in a dream, "it was *not* my mother"—was in fact, according to Freud, to affirm the truth of the idea on another level:

> We emend this: so it *was* his mother. In our interpretation we take the liberty of disregarding the negation and of simply picking out the subject-matter of the association. It is just as though the patient had said: "It is true that I thought of my mother in connection with this person, but I don't feel at all inclined to allow the association to count."[5]

Precisely "by the help of the symbol of negation," Freud concluded, "the thinking-process frees itself from the limitations of repression and enriches itself with the subject-matter without which it could not work efficiently."[6]

One might think of lesbianism as the "repressed idea" at the heart of patriarchal culture. By its very nature (and in this respect it differs significantly from male homosexuality) lesbianism poses an ineluctable challenge to the political, economic, and sexual authority of men over women. It implies a whole new social order, characterized—at the very least—by a profound feminine indifference to masculine charisma. (In its militant or "Amazonian" transformation lesbianism may also, of course, be associated with outright hostility toward men.) One might go so far as to argue—along with Adrienne Rich, Gayle Rubin, and others—that patriarchal ideology necessarily depends on the "compulsory" suppression of love between women.[7] As Henry Fielding put it in *The Female Husband*, the vehemently antilesbian pamphlet he published anonymously in 1746, once women gave way to "unnatural lusts," there was no civil "excess and disorder" they were not liable to commit.[8]

Beginning in Western Europe in the eighteenth century, with the gradual attenuation of moral and religious orthodoxies, the weakening of traditional

5. Freud, "Negation" (1925), in *The Standard Edition of the Complete Psychological Works of Sigmund Freud*, ed. James Strachey, 24 vols. (London: Hogarth, 1953–75), 19: 235.
6. Freud, "Negation," p. 236.
7. See Rich, "Compulsory Heterosexuality and Lesbian Existence," *Signs* 5, no. 4 (1980): 631–60, and Rubin, "The Traffic in Women: Notes on the 'Political Economy' of Sex," in *Toward an Anthropology of Women*, ed. Rayna R. Reiter (New York: Monthly Review Press, 1975), pp. 157–210. Society demands the suppression of same-sex love, argues Rubin, because such love destroys the distinction between "genders" on which patriarchal authority depends:

Gender is not only an identification with one sex; it also entails that sexual desire be directed towards the other sex. The sexual division of labor is implicated in both aspects of gender—male and female it creates them, and it creates them heterosexual. The suppression of the homosexual component of human sexuality, and by corollary, the oppression of homosexuals, is therefore a product of the same system whose rules and relations oppress women.

See Rubin, "Traffic in Women," p. 180.
8. Fielding, *The Female Husband*, in *The Female Husband and other Writings*, ed. Claude E. Jones (Liverpool: Liverpool University Press, 1960), p. 29.

family structures, urbanization, and the growing mobility and economic independence of women, male authority found itself increasingly under assault. And not surprisingly, with such far-reaching social changes in the offing, the "repressed idea" of love between women—one can speculate—began to manifest itself more threateningly in the collective psyche. Eighteenth- and nineteenth-century ideologues were at once fascinated and repelled by the possibility of women without sexual allegiance toward men.[9] And ultimately a backlash set in—characterized as we have seen in the writings of Diderot, Gautier, James,[1] and others, by an effort to derealize the threat of lesbianism by associating it with the apparitional.

From one angle this act of negation made a sort of morbid sense; for how better, one might ask, to exorcize the threat of lesbianism than by turning it into a phantom? The spectral metaphor had useful theological associations: witches, after all, dealt in spirits, and the witchcraft connection could be counted on to add an invidious aura of diabolism to any scene of female-female desire. ("Oh we wouldn't have stood a chance in that time," says Matt in Duffy's *Microcosm*, thinking of the Middle Ages; "sure sign of a witch to love your own sex."[2]) But more important by far was the way the apparitional figure seemed to obliterate, through a single vaporizing gesture, the disturbing carnality of lesbian love. It made of such love—literally—a phantasm: an ineffable anticoupling between "women" who weren't there.

—Or did it? As I have tried to intimate, the case could be made that the metaphor meant to derealize lesbian desire in fact did just the opposite. Indeed, strictly for repressive purposes, one could hardly think of a *worse* metaphor. For embedded in the ghostly figure, as even its first proponents seemed at times to realize, was inevitably a notion of reembodiment: of uncanny return to the flesh. "This image obsesses me, and follows me everywhere," says the narrator in Gautier's *Mademoiselle de Maupin*, "and I never see it more than when it isn't there" (180). To become an apparition was also to become endlessly capable of "appearing." And once there, the specter, like a living being, was not so easily gotten rid of. It demanded a response. It is precisely the demanding, importuning aspect of the apparitional that Radclyffe Hall depicted to such striking allegorical effect in the last pages of *The Well of Loneliness*.

Though in the course of this essay I have, for rhetorical purposes, implied a break between older "homophobic" invocations of the apparitional lesbian and later revisionist ones, it is perhaps more useful in the end to stress the continuity between them. If it is true that the first stage of recognition is denial, then the denial of lesbianism—through its fateful association with the spectral—was also the first stage of its cultural recognition. In the same way that the act of negation, in Freud's words, "frees the thinking process from repression," so the spectral metaphor provided the very imagery, paradoxi-

---

9. On the paradoxical male attitude toward lesbianism in the eighteenth century, see my " 'Matters Not Fit to Be Mentioned': Fielding's *The Female Husband*," *ELH* 49 (1982): 602–22. On nineteenth-century responses, see Lillian Faderman, *Surpassing the Love of Men: Romantic Friendship and the Love between Women from the Renaissance to the Present* (New York: William Morrow, 1981), especially pp. 277–94, and

Jonathan Katz, *Gay American History and Gay/Lesbian Almanac: A New Documentary* (New York: Harper and Row, 1983), passim.
1. In an omitted section of this chapter, Castle discusses Henry James's *The Bostonians* (1886) [editor's note].
2. Maureen Duffy, *The Microcosm* (1966; reprint, London: Virago, 1989), p. 271.

cally, through which the carnal truth of lesbianism might be rediscovered and reclaimed by lesbian writers.

This process of "recognition through negation" may have something to do, finally, with one of the most intriguing features of modern lesbian-themed literature—its tendency to hark back, by way of embedded intertextual references, to earlier works on the same subject. I mentioned in passing Stephen Gordon's "haunted" reading of Krafft-Ebing in *The Well of Loneliness* and Maureen Duffy's lengthy citation from Charlotte Charke's 1755 *Life*[3] in *The Microcosm*, but other examples abound. In both Colette's *Claudine à l'école* and Lillian Hellman's *The Children's Hour*, the characters are reading Gautier's *Mademoiselle de Maupin*; in Brigid Brophy's *The Finishing Touch*, the main character not only invokes Gautier but also Renée Vivien's *Une Femme m'apparut* and Proust's *Sodom et Gomorrhe*. In Christine Crow's *Miss X*, the narrator quotes (with irony) from Baudelaire's "Femmes damnées" and jokes compulsively about Radclyffe Hall's *Well of Loneliness*. In Sarah Schulman's *After Delores*, one of the narrator's friends is reading—and rewriting—Renault's *The Friendly Young Ladies*. For the reader attempting to proceed logically, as it were, through the canon of lesbian writing, such rampant intertextuality can bring with it an unsettling sense of déjà vu—if not a feeling of outright "possession" by the ghosts of the lesbian literary past.[4]

Yet the haunted nature of modern lesbian writing attests directly, I think, to the process by which lesbianism itself has entered into the imaginative life of the West over the past two centuries. It is a curious fact that for most readers of lesbian literature, at least until very recently, it has seldom mattered very much whether a given work of literature depicted love between women in a positive or negative light: so few in number have such representations been over the years, and so intense the cultural taboo against them, that virtually any novel or story dealing with the subject has automatically been granted a place in lesbian literary tradition. (Thus even such negative-seeming works as Diderot's *La Religieuse*, James's *The Bostonians*, or Renault's *The Friendly Young Ladies* continue to hold an acknowledged, if not exactly esteemed, place in the underground lesbian literary canon.[5]) Like the analyst, who, in Freud's words, "takes the liberty of disregarding [any] negation," interested readers have tended simply to "pick out the subject-matter" of lesbianism, regardless of surrounding context, in order to retrieve it for their own subversive imaginative ends.

In the case of the apparitional lesbian, twentieth-century lesbian writers have been able for the most part to ignore the negative backdrop against which she has traditionally (de)materialized. By calling her back to pas-

3. The autobiography of a transvestite actress, which Duffy paraphrases for almost 30 pages [editor's note].

4. The passage in Schulman's *After Delores* (New York: Dutton, 1988) is exemplary in this respect. Beatriz is describing a screenplay she is writing based on *The Friendly Young Ladies*. In Beatriz's new version, Leo and Helen are lesbians but do not acknowledge the fact to one another until an American woman seduces one of them. Then they are forced to confront the truth of their lives. As Beatriz says to the narrator, "You see, it forces them to confront the lie in their relationship and their com-

plicity in that lie, a lie that has consumed ten years of their lives" (54). The effect of this embedded invocation, even with Beatriz's critical reenvisioning of the plot, is to break down boundaries between Renault's novel and Schulman's own—to make the reader feel suspended, as it were, within a single lesbian Ur-text, replete with plots and counterplots, conjurings and reconjurings.

5. All three of these novels are featured prominently, for example, in Jeannette Foster's classic bibliographic study, *Sex Variant Women in Literature*, 3rd ed. (Tallahassee, Fla.: Naiad, 1985).

sionate, imbricated life—by invoking her both as lover and beloved—they have succeeded in transforming her from a negating to an affirming presence. But they have altered our understanding of the homophobic literature of the past as well. For once apprised of the apparitional lesbian's insinuating sensualism—and her scandalous bent for return—we can no longer read, say, the novels of Diderot or James without sensing something of her surreptitious erotic power. Indeed, like Mrs. Veal, she may haunt us most when she pretends to demur. For even at her most ethereal and dissembling, as when seeming to "wave off" the intrusive pleasures of the flesh, she cannot help but also signal—as if by secret benediction—that fall into flesh which is to come.

1993

CAROLYN DEVER
b. 1966

Carolyn Dever, who began her publishing career with *Death and the Mother from Dickens to Freud* (1998), is a professor of English at Vanderbilt University, where she directed the women's studies program and is now associate dean of the College of Arts and Sciences. Transnationalism, feminism, and queer theory have been the subjects in her more recent work. In *The Literary Channel: The Inter-national Invention of the Novel* (2001), co-edited with Margaret Cohen, Dever has collected essays on the international invention of the novel, for instance. And in *Skeptical Feminism: Activist Theory, Activist Practice* (2004), she explores the theory-practice debate among feminist thinkers. Whereas Annamarie Jagose maps the emergence of male and female queer theorists out of gay liberation in her useful survey titled *Queer Theory: An Introduction* (1996), our selection by Dever historicizes the evolution of lesbian studies up to the present time.

From Obstructive Behavior: Dykes in the Mainstream of Feminist Theory[1]

> A person or animal . . . that leaps over fences; . . . a transgressor of the laws of morality.
> —*Oxford English Dictionary*[2]

The "obstructive behavior" I hope to analyze in this chapter involves the consideration of "dykes," by which I mean obstructions that impede or redirect a current or flow. I want to argue that feminist theory has come into

---

1. With thanks to Kathryn Schwarz, Sarah Black, David A. Hedrich Hirsch, and Marvin J. Taylor [except as indicated, all notes are Dever's].
2. "Dike, dyke," *Oxford English Dictionary*, 2nd ed.

(Oxford: Clarendon Press, 1989), 4:659–60. All epigraphs that follow are excerpted from *OED* definitions of *dyke*, as cited here.

being in relation to a set of "dykes," through contact with critical obstructions that shape, divert, and otherwise help to define the mainstream. The function of these dykes is an ambiguous one; they are at once necessary and problematic, central yet diversionary. Dykes are not *of* the mainstream, but the mainstream necessarily shapes itself in response to the presence of dykes.

At its most literal level, my title should signify a concern with the tendentious shape-shifting that has characterized feminist theory, producing new and innovative theoretical concerns and applications. At another level, however, it should signify its concern with the discourse of "obstruction," with impudent behaviors and political impediments that have confronted, ideally to challenge and to change, academic feminism. At still another level, I am concerned with the discourses of sexuality in feminism, and the sense in which the issue of sexuality itself operates as a "dyke," as a shaping impediment. For colloquially, *dyke* itself signifies, sometimes rudely sometimes not, a way of being named or self-identifying as lesbian.[3] And the question of lesbians in the mainstream of feminist criticism has been the single most powerful "dyke" in the evolution of this critical discourse.

The *Oxford English Dictionary* definition of *dyke* or *dike* (the latter is the "more conventional" spelling), depends on an interestingly redoubled sense of ambiguity. The *OED* traces the etymology of *dyke* through a series of exchanges of masculine and feminine cases, evolving, perhaps ironically, from versions of the word *dick* in the masculine to versions of the word *dyke* in the feminine, pausing only in Icelandic at the neuter. Its history of etymological indeterminacy notwithstanding, *dyke* consistently signifies a form of diversionary obstruction, whether ditch, trench, mound, embankment, or dam, though the obstruction is conceived alternately as *either* a trench or a wall: "The application thus varies between 'ditch, dug out place,' and 'mound formed by throwing up the earth,' and may include both." Under its first definition, a dyke is "an excavation narrow in proportion to its length, a long and narrow hollow dug out of the ground; a DITCH, trench, or fosse," "such a hollow dug out to hold or conduct water." Under its second, it is "an embankment, wall, causeway," and still more specifically," ' a bank formed by throwing the earth out of the ditch' (Bosworth)," or "a wall or fence. . . . The wall of a city, a fortification."

Dyke is a word that presupposes the complication, conflation, even the collapse of binary categories. Confounding notions of masculinity and femininity in the case of etymology, of structure in the architectural significance of a barrier, conflicting definitions of *dyke* exploit an ambiguity at the heart of the concept itself. In its first definition, a "narrow hollow dug out of the ground," the function of the dyke is to enable another activity, such as the holding or the conducting of water, but is essentially passive: it exists primarily not as a presence but as an absence, as negative space, sculpted from the positive surface of the earth. Yet in its alternate definition, the dyke exceeds that positive surface, existing as the highly visible *surplus* of earth in fortifying relation to the populace whose existence it protects and enables; whether as a canal permitting transport from one place to another or as a protective wall impeding that transport, the well-being of its architects depends on the

3. For a discussion of theoretical appropriations of such disparaging terms as *queer*, see Judith Butler, "Critically Queer," in *Bodies That Matter: On the* *Discursive Limits of "Sex"* (New York: Routledge, 1993), esp. 226–30.

dyke's structural integrity. In either incarnation, the transformative capacity of the dyke remains its most powerful capital: articulating a space that is, by definition, both marginal and central, the dyke demarcates difference, transition, liminality, and vulnerability. That vulnerability inheres in the status of the dyke as a protective structure: without the need to guard against difference, against the threat of difference to destroy, the dyke would be completely unnecessary.

A slang definition, listed below and separated from the nearly three columns of dykes in the *OED*, reads as follows: "dike, dyke . . . [Of obscure origin.] A lesbian; a masculine woman."[4] Citing as its earliest usage a 1942 entry in the *American Thesaurus of Slang*, this dyke, of obscure origin, remains distinct from the *OED*'s other dykes, yet shares with them certain implications of liminality. Not only a lesbian but also a "masculine woman," the dyke, in this definition, blurs the borderline between masculinity and femininity. In her appearance, presumably in her affective alliances, she, like her fellow dykes, marks, embodies, and deconstructs that borderline by disrupting conventional practices of self-presentation and desire. Like the other dykes, this dyke offers a limit case and a liminal space, enabling definitions of inside and outside, enabling, through her location of and as a border, binary systems of logic which exploit fixed notions of identity and identifiability.

Mainstream feminism, I want to argue, has been defined by and against its relationship to dykes, depending precisely on the dyke's function as a borderline to mark the parameters of feminist theory and practice. For twenty-five years, feminists have displayed dramatic, symptomatic forms of ambivalence to lesbians in the mainstream. At once needing and abhorring the dykes that exist at and as the shaping margins of its discourse, feminist theory has struggled to accommodate competing desires for mainstream acceptance and individual sexual diversity. Catalyzing questions about sex, sexuality, eroticism, pleasure, identity, politics, and power, the dyke in the mainstream has always been the site of contention, the source of troubling questions, both for and within feminism.

Feminist Theory in the 1970s

> A ridge, embankment, long mound, or dam, thrown up to resist the encroachments of the sea, or to prevent low-lying lands from being flooded by seas, rivers, or streams.
> —*Oxford English Dictionary*

From the vocabulary of lesbian separatism in the 1970s through queer theory today, feminists have always engaged questions of sexuality. But although the vantage point of history often associates the early women's movement with the political enthusiasms of the Sexual Revolution, in fact, the very personal politics of sexual difference have historically marked the most dramatic fault lines among feminists. As early as 1970, at the Second Congress to Unite Women, twenty women stormed the meeting's plenary session with the words "Lavender Menace" emblazoned on their chests. Prompted to act by Betty Friedan's notorious, and perhaps apocryphal, remark that lesbians in

4. *OED*, 4:660.

the women's movement were a "lavender menace" who would ultimately impede cultural acceptance of feminist sympathies, the women calling themselves the "Lavender Menace" challenged conference members to confront discrimination against lesbians in the women's movement. Later renaming themselves "Radicalesbians," this group soon produced an essay titled "The Woman-Identified Woman," which argued that all sexualities exist in the service of patriarchy and that a challenge to rigid notions of sexuality must accompany feminist critiques of patriarchy. Women who fail to consider the erotic potential of other women are trapped in a patriarchal web, living their lives, setting their expectations, only in terms of their relationships to men; thus feminists fail to confront their full investment in patriarchal power until they confront the personal politics of their bedrooms. "Real" women, "feminine" women, the Radicalesbians suggest,

> are authentic, legitimate, real to the extent that we are the property of some man whose name we bear. To be a woman who belongs to no man is to be invisible, pathetic, inauthentic, unreal. He confirms his image of us—of what we have to be in order to be acceptable by him—but not our real selves; he confirms our womanhood—as he defines it, in relation to him—but cannot confirm our personhood, our own selves as absolutes. As long as we are dependent on the male culture for this definition, for this approval, we cannot be free.[5]

The Radicalesbians identify female homosexuality as a political choice. Lesbianism, within their rubric, is a political mandate more than an erotic one; the utopic vision of a lesbian-separatist community, often figured as the return of the Amazons, is frequently represented as the only plausible alternative within a radical and thoroughgoing critique of patriarchy. And indeed, this is a notion that looms large over the culture of feminist discourse to this day, for, as lesbian separatists throughout the early days of the Women's Movement insist, separatism remains a logical extreme of feminist critiques of patriarchy, a logical solution to often painfully paradoxical attempts to live a "feminist life." As Catharine MacKinnon writes, "Feminism is the epistemology of which lesbianism is an ontology."[6]

Lesbian separatism was one of the greatest challenges to and the greatest anxieties of early feminists. Ti-Grace Atkinson presents a summary of the theory informing political lesbianism in the collection *Amazon Odyssey*: "It is the commitment of individuals to common goals, and to the death if necessary, that determines the strength of the army. . . . Lesbianism is to feminism what the Communist Party was to the trade-union movement. Tactically, any feminist should fight to the death for lesbianism because of its strategic importance."[7] Invoking metaphors ranging from the martial to the economic, Atkinson emphasizes the importance of linking feminist theory and feminist practice: "I'm enormously less interested in whom you sleep with than I am

5. Radicalesbians, "The Woman-Identified Woman," in *Feminism in Our Time: The Essential Writings, World War II to the Present*, ed. Miriam Schneir (New York: Vintage, 1994), 166. Authorship of this essay has been attributed to Rita Mae Brown.
6. Catharine A. MacKinnon, "Feminism, Marxism, Method, and the State: An Agenda for Theory," in *The Signs Reader: Women, Gender, and Scholarship*, ed. Elizabeth Abel and Emily K. Abel (Chicago: University of Chicago Press, 1983), 247n46.
7. Ti-Grace Atkinson, "Lesbianism and Feminism: Justice for Women as 'Unnatural,' " in *Amazon Odyssey: The First Collection of Writings by the Political Pioneer of the Women's Movement* (New York: Links Books, 1974), 132, 134.

in with whom you're prepared to die."[8] Atkinson interrogates the inherently "political" nature of lesbianism, suggesting that affectional and erotic object choices themselves do not necessarily make a politics, but that lesbianism has occupied a politically significant structural position within feminism.

> Because of their particularly unique attempt at revolt, the lesbian role within the male / female class system becomes critical. Lesbianism is the "criminal" zone, what I call the "buffer" zone, between the two major classes comprising the sex class system. The "buffer" has both a unique nature and function within the system. And it is crucial that both lesbians and feminists understand the strategical significance of lesbianism to feminism. (136–37)

In Atkinson's analysis, the liminal lesbian position, the "buffer," becomes strategic turf: it is the battlefield of actual feminist practice, the space intervening between "oppressor" and "oppressed," men and women. Semantically, however, within the discursive structure of Atkinson's vision, lesbians are not women, nor are they men, feminists, oppressors, or oppressed; they exist, as dykes so often have, as the means of defining the difference between feminists and their oppressors; significantly, though, lesbians themselves manage to elude definition, categorization, political importance, even inclusion in this framework. That both "lesbians" and "feminists" must understand the crucial significance of lesbianism to feminism sacrifices lesbian interests to a larger feminist cause; nowhere are lesbians supposed to consider the significance of feminists, they are simply assumed to *be* feminists. Despite Atkinson's comment that "feminists should fight to the death for lesbians," she more frequently assumes the opposite logic: she sees lesbians as the front lines of the feminist army. Mainstream feminism for Atkinson, regardless of its radical politics, is a heterosexual movement; dykes exist merely to facilitate, protect, and maintain that mainstream. Unlike the Radicalesbians, for whom lesbianism is feminist theory in its purest form, for Atkinson, lesbianism is a means to an end, a strategic position on a much larger battleground.

Atkinson's interest in the concept of lesbianism originates in the persistence of homophobic invective against feminists: "from the outset of the Movement, most men automatically called all feminists 'lesbians.' This connection was so widespread and consistent that I began to wonder myself if maybe men didn't perceive some connection the Movement was overlooking" (135–36). Atkinson, like the Radicalesbians, wonders why feminism engenders this response: "Generally speaking, the Movement has reacted defensively to the charge of lesbianism: 'No, I'm not!' 'Yes, you are!' 'No, I'm not!' 'Prove it.' For myself I was so puzzled about the connection that I became curious. . . . Whenever the enemy keeps lobbing bombs into some area you consider unrelated to your defense, it's always worth investigating."[9] As Miriam Schneir points out in a recent discussion of the Radicalesbians, "The lesbian issue continued to generate personal and ideological splits among feminists—including among radical feminists—that sisterhood could not always surmount. Lesbians and straights both played a part in this unfortunate turn of events: Some straight feminists were afraid of being labeled dykes and wished to dissociate both the movement and themselves from

---

8. Ti-Grace Atkinson, "Strategy and Tactics: A Presentation of Political Lesbianism," in *Amazon*   *Odyssey,* 138.
9. Atkinson, "Lesbianism and Feminism," 131.

lesbianism, while some lesbians claimed that lesbianism was an example of feminism in action and preached that the only true feminists were those who renounced relations with the opposite sex entirely."[1] Rather than disavow the label "dyke," Atkinson attempts to appropriate it as "buffer": within her theoretical paradigm, lesbians exist on the front line of the gender wars. The logic here is that of a speech act: the men lobbing the explosive word *dyke* succeed in labeling all practicing feminists as dykes. Atkinson assumes that those who are called dykes necessarily become dykes, whether in theory or in practice. And within her vision of feminist activism, these dykes will be sacrificed, in theory or in practice, for a mainstream feminist utopic vision.

Feminist Theory in the Early 1980s

> The application thus varies between 'ditch, dug out place,' and 'mound formed by throwing up the earth,' and may include both.
> —*Oxford English Dictionary.*

Split between defensive responses to internalized homophobia and the political logic of separatism, feminist definitions of *lesbian* during the early 1980s are marked by a noteworthy ambivalence toward questions of sexual practice and erotic pleasure: lesbianism, when it enters into definitions of *feminism* at all, enters almost exclusively as a political ideal, undistinguished by any real erotic significance. Adrienne Rich's landmark essay "Compulsory Heterosexuality and Lesbian Existence" appeared in *Signs* in 1980. Rich's articulation of a "lesbian continuum" indicates a significant development in popular feminist attempts at self-definition. Interrogating heterosexuality as a vestigal structure of patriarchal power, Rich argues in the tradition of early political lesbians that "the denial of reality and visibility to women's passion for women, women's choice of women as allies, life companions, and community, the forcing of such relationships into dissimulation and their disintegration under intense pressure have meant an incalculable loss to the power of all women *to change the social relations of the sexes, to liberate ourselves and each other.*"[2] In the terms of Rich's argument, feminists historically have been their own worst enemies, thwarting their own political agendas through their failure to truly challenge "the social relations of the sexes." Rich suggests that homophobia informs feminists' unwillingness to ally themselves fully—politically, personally, or intellectually—with lesbians, duplicating the oppression of women more generally under patriarchal power structures and undermining the viability of all feminist theory. Recalling the Radicalesbians' argument about the need to theorize heterosexuality rigorously, not as a "natural" category but as a complex and problematic construct, Rich modifies their concluding exhortation of lesbianism as the feminist political ideal through the development of two strategic arguments.

The first, which encompasses the mission statement of Rich's essay, calls for a more comprehensive and rigorous feminist theory that takes into consideration all forms of erotic, political, and intellectual individuality; extending a critique of Dorothy Dinnerstein[3] to feminist theory as a whole,

---

1. Miriam Schneir, introduction to Radicalesbians, "The Woman-Identified Woman," 161.
2. Adrienne Rich, "Compulsory Heterosexuality and Lesbian Existence," in *The Lesbian and Gay Studies Reader*, ed. Henry Abelove, Michèle Aina Barale, and David M. Halperin (New York: Routledge, 1993), 244; italics in original.
3. Rich criticizes Dinnerstein's *The Mermaid and the Minotaur: Sexual Arrangements and the Human Malaise* (1978) [editor's note].

Rich writes: "[Dinnerstein] ignores, specifically, the history of women who—as witches, *femmes seules*, marriage resisters, spinsters, autonomous widows, and/or lesbians—have managed on various levels *not* to collaborate. It is this history, precisely, from which feminists have so much to learn and on which there is overall such blanketing silence" (230). Rich's form of feminist theory would have at its center the interrogation of "compulsory heterosexuality":

> The assumption that "most women are innately heterosexual" stands as a theoretical and political stumbling block for feminism. It remains a tenable assumption partly because lesbian existence has been written out of history or catalogued under disease, partly because is has been treated as exceptional rather than intrinsic, partly because to acknowledge that for women heterosexuality may not be a "preference" at all but something that has had to be imposed, managed, organized, propagandized, and maintained by force is an immense step to take if you consider yourself freely and "innately" heterosexual. Yet the failure to examine heterosexuality as an institution is like failing to admit that the economic system called capitalism or the caste system of racism is maintained by a variety of forces, including both physical violence and false consciousness. (238–39)

Calling for a rigorous analysis of the power dynamics at stake in "compulsory heterosexuality," Rich is sharply critical of feminist unwillingness to consider the full range of sexual diversity. Her suggestion that this analysis would be anxiety-producing because feminists themselves have something at stake in the institution of heterosexuality recalls the Radicalesbians' arguments about the political inconsistencies in most attempts to combine feminist theory with a bourgeois, heterosexual life. But Rich stops short of calling for political lesbianism, insisting instead on a feminist theoretical analysis of issues previously hidden by assumptions of normative heterosexuality.

In fact, Rich's second argument represents a neat appropriation of the anxieties that inevitably seem to accompany discussions of political lesbianism. She argues, through the radical expansion of the term *lesbian,* that all feminists, in fact, all women, are already lesbians; feminist thus becomes a subset of lesbian, rather than the other way around. She explains:

> I mean the term *lesbian continuum* to include a range—through each woman's life and throughout history—of woman-identified experience, not simply the fact that a woman has had or consciously desired genital sexual experience with another woman. If we expand it to embrace many more forms of primary intensity between and among women, including the sharing of a rich inner life, the bonding against male tyranny, the giving and receiving of practical and political support, if we can also hear it in such associations as *marriage resistance* and the "haggard" behavior identified by Mary Daly (obsolete meanings: "intractable," "willful," "wanton", and "unchaste," "a woman reluctant to yield to wooing"),[4] we begin to grasp breadths of female history and psychology which have lain

---

4. See Daly, *Gyn/Ecology: The Metaethics of Radical Feminism* (Boston: Beacon, 1978), 15 [editor's note].

out of reach as a consequence of limited, mostly clinical, definitions of *lesbianism*.[5]

Rich's identification of the "lesbian continuum" is the logical yield of her interrogation of compulsory heterosexuality. She emphasizes that the deconstruction of the assumptions and dynamics informing compulsory heterosexuality will bring into view many forms of profound interconnections among women, connections that have always existed but have been obscured from view by assumptions of normative heterosexuality. In naming these relationships "lesbian," Rich accommodates and thus begins to value women's relationships with one another across a wide range of behaviors that presumably includes, but is not limited to, the erotic: "As the term lesbian has been held to limiting, clinical associations in its patriarchal definition, female friendship and comradeship have been set apart from the erotic, thus limiting the erotic itself" (240).

In addition to the notion of the "lesbian continuum" and the critique of compulsory heterosexuality, the other significant innovation of Rich's argument is its shift in the locus of activism. Identifying her task as a primarily critical one, Rich targets an audience composed principally of feminist academics. She identifies literary criticism, as well as related modes of historical and social scientific research, as central to feminist praxis and instrumental in the process of locating the lesbian continuum; literary critics and other academics possess the ability to produce a more accurate version of women's history. Significantly, however, even as Rich empowers academics within feminist activism, academics also occupy the center of her target of critique: she condemns "the virtual or total neglect of lesbian existence in a wide range of writings, including feminist scholarship" (229). By the early 1980s, literary criticism is at ground zero in what was previously a grassroots political movement, as academic work is increasingly valorized as a primary form of feminist activist intervention. Rich's focus on literary criticism constructs feminist politics as a battleground of metacriticism; the issues at stake concern not only the practicalities of feminist critique in the world at large, but also the novels of Colette, Charlotte Brontë, and Toni Morrison, and the theoretical paradigms of Mary Daly, Catharine MacKinnon, and Nancy Chodorow. Focusing on the historical period from which Rich's essay emerged, Jane Gallop, in *Around 1981: Academic Feminist Literary Theory*, argues that in the early 1980s, feminism "entered the heart of a contradiction": "It became secure and prospered in the academy while feminism as a social movement was encountering major setbacks in a climate of new conservatism. The Reagan-Bush years began; the ERA was defeated. In the American academy feminism gets more and more respect while in the larger society women cannot call themselves feminist."[6]

Underscoring Gallop's argument regarding the yawning divide between academic feminism and the lives of women "in the larger society," bell hooks, writing in 1984, sees academic discourse as part of the problem, alienating mainstream women from feminist activism. "The ability to 'translate' ideas to an audience that varies in age, sex, ethnicity, degree of literacy is a skill fem-

---

5. Rich, "Compulsory Heterosexuality," 239; italics in original.

6. Jane Gallop, *Around 1981: Academic Feminist Literary Theory* (New York: Routledge, 1992), 10.

inist educators need to develop. Concentration of feminist educators in universities encourages habitual use of an academic style that may make it impossible for teachers to communicate effectively with individuals who are not familiar with either academic style or jargon."[7] hook's critique of self-conscious academic language extends from the same metacritical impulse as Rich's critical rereading of feminist texts for their prescriptions of compulsory heterosexuality. But hooks's target audience is somewhat different from Rich's; hooks sees the exclusionary language of academic feminism as part of a problematic system of oppressive power relationships relating to race, class, and gender. Far from escaping the pernicious implications of these power relations, hooks argues that feminists consistently *duplicate* them in their blindness to and exclusion of women of color and poor women. While Rich's critique focuses on assumptions of normative white middle-class status:

> White women who dominate feminist discourse today rarely question whether or not their perspective on women's reality is true to the lived experiences of women as a collective group. Nor are they aware of the extent to which their perspectives reflect race and class biases, although there has been a greater awareness of biases in recent years. Racism abounds in the writings of white feminists, reinforcing white supremacy and negating the possibility that women will bond politically across ethnic and racial boundaries. Past feminist refusal to draw attention to and attack racial hierarchies suppressed the link between race and class. (3)

Given hooks's useful insistence on sex, race, and class discrimination as symptoms of larger systemic problems, it is noteworthy that discrimination based on sexuality drops out of her larger structure of critique. hooks is deeply concerned that feminist theory address issues across lines of race and class, but to do so, she argues, feminism must begin to disassociate itself from its image as a movement consisting primarily of lesbians; she sees feminism as a movement dominated by dykes at the expense of diversity. hooks is sharply critical of what she perceives as the facile equation in mainstream feminism of lesbian sexuality with political correctness: "women who are not lesbians, who may or may not be in relationships with men feel that they are not 'real' feminists. This is especially true of women who may support feminism but who do not publiclly [sic] support lesbian rights" (151).

Unwilling to apply the same critique to homophobia that she does to racism, hooks exhorts feminists to "diversify" the public face of feminism by making clear that feminists are not necessarily lesbians or man-haters. In hooks's view, the failure of feminism to become a truly massive social movement inheres in its anxiety-producing association with nonhetero sexualities:

> My point is that feminism will never appeal to a mass-based group of women in our society who are heterosexual if they think that they will be looked down upon or seen as doing something wrong. . . . Just as feminist movement to end sexual oppression should create a social climate in which lesbians and gay men are no longer oppressed, a climate in which their sexual choices are affirmed, it should also create a climate in which

7. bell hooks, *Feminist Theory from Margin to Center* (Boston: South End Press, 1984), 111.

> heterosexual practice is freed from the constraints of heterosexism and can also be affirmed. One of the practical reasons for doing this is the recognition that the advancement of feminism as a political movement depends on the involvement of masses of women, a vast majority of whom are heterosexual. As long as feminist women (be they celibate, lesbian, heterosexual, etc.) condemn male sexuality, and by extension women who are involved sexually with men, feminist movement is undermined. (153)

The rhetoric of comprehensive, systemic analysis of power relations has shifted by this point to a more coercive rhetoric of marketing: "feminism will never appeal to a mass-based group of women in our society who are heterosexual *if* . . ." While hooks claims concern here for the discriminatory assumptions of heterosexism, nowhere else does she suggest that feminist theory pander to the comfort of the "vast majority" in exchange for a rigorous consideration of the rights and the existence of an endangered minority.

My critique of hooks's position is not a new one; in fact, the quote above is part of hooks's response to "lesbian feminist" Cheryl Clarke, who wrote an essay titled "The Failure to Transform: Homophobia in the Black Community," in which she remarks: " 'Hooks delivers a backhanded slap at lesbian feminists, a considerable number of whom are black. Hooks would have done well to attack the institution of heterosexuality as it is a prime cause of black women's oppression in America.' "[8] hooks replies, "Clearly Clarke misunderstands and misinterprets my point. I made no reference to heterosexism and it is the equation of heterosexual practice with heterosexism that makes it appear that Clarke is attacking the practice itself and not only heterosexism." Clarke's point, reminiscent of Rich, that hooks should examine "the institution of heterosexuality," is revealingly translated by hooks directly into "heterosexism": it is not Clarke but hooks who makes the equation of heterosexual practice and heterosexism.[9] The question of the problematic institutional dynamics of heterosexuality is neatly subsumed under this equation; hooks's discussion continues on into a critique of feminist heterophobic impulses, in defense of "the choice women make to be heterosexual" (154). Heterosexuality, not normally seen as an endangered category, makes a strange bedfellow with the other forms of oppression and exclusion hooks treats in this text, including racial and class prejudice. hooks's heterosexuality is vulnerable, defensive, embattled, but ironically, her need to defend heterosexual practice duplicates a function of the dyke: she is eager to set up protective walls around heterosexuality, thus liberating women everywhere into the radical freedom of heterosexual object choice. In another twist of irony, hooks begins to set up dykes to defend against dykes.

8. Quoted in hooks, *Feminist Theory,* 153. hooks responds again to the emotional, if not the intellectual, implications of this issue in the essay "Censorship from Left and Right," in *Outlaw Culture: Resisting Representations* (New York: Routledge, 1994), 71.
9. Interestingly, hooks herself later criticizes Madonna's book *Sex* for *its* conflation of the heterosexual and the heterosexist: "Even in the realm of male homoeroticism/homosexuality, Madonna's image usurps, takes over, subordinates. Coded always in *Sex* as heterosexual, her image is the dominant expression of heterosexism. . . . In the context of *Sex,* gay culture remains irrevocably linked to a system of patriarchal control framed by a heterosexist pornographic gaze" ("Power to the Pussy," in *Outlaw Culture,* 16–17).

hooks's logic at this point is complicated, for several reasons. In her larger argument, her desire to ensure that feminists are consistent in their critique of *any* form of compulsory sexuality, whether gay or straight, is a direct extension of powerful early feminist critiques of limiting patriarchal roles for women. However, in a book critiquing feminist marginalizations of women of color, it is strange that hooks's analysis of phobic exclusionary practices should fail to extend to her discussion of sexuality. The apparent suggestion that feminists should disassociate themselves—at least publicly—from the issue of lesbian sexuality seems linked to another paradigm of the 1970s, the antifeminist rhetoric which labeled feminists, often arbitrarily, as dykes, intimidating through the invocation of internalized homophobia. Instead of reading "mass-based" anxiety about lesbianism as a need for "mass-based" education about forms of prejudice as pernicious in the case of sexuality as in the case of race, hooks seems to suggest that feminists need only change the window dressing in order to appeal to a wider range of women; her feminist paradigm seems to sacrifice sexual diversity in the cause of racial diversity, while she bars altogether the possibility that lesbians of color might exist. This platform clearly—and perhaps ironically—returns to the scene of the "lavender menace," and backlash against the suggestion that the marketing of the feminist movement must occur under the aegis of "normative" sexuality.

While Barbara Smith echoes hooks's sharp criticism of white, middle-class feminist narcissism, she does not see the interests of black women and lesbians as mutually exclusive or even in competition, insisting on the importance of a feminist discourse that considers race and sexuality together: "Long before I tried to write this I realized that I was attempting something unprecedented, something dangerous, merely by writing about Black women writers from a feminist perspective and about Black lesbian writers from any perspective at all. . . . All segments of the literary world—whether establishment, progressive, Black, female, or lesbian—do not know, or at least act as if they do not know, that Black women writers and Black lesbian writers exist."[1] Jane Gallop claims, in a discussion of *The New Feminist Criticism* (the anthology in which Smith's essay is reprinted), that feminist criticism of the early and mid-1980s struggled explicitly with problems of self-definition and with issues of inclusion and exclusion.[2] Judith Roof argues that "the myriad differences among women are often reduced to the formula 'black and lesbian.' . . . I suspect that this . . . critical reliance upon black and lesbian is symptomatic of some underlying critical difficulty with multiplicity."[3] I would concur that within the discourses of feminist theory and criticism of the mid-1980s, the categories "black" and "lesbian" demarcate similar modes of "difference," both existing, in most cases, as "other than" a norm. The white, middle-class, heterosexual assumptions of that norm are made visible only through the tension produced by the defining presence of the other.

1. Barbara Smith, "Toward a Black Feminist Criticism," in *The New Feminist Criticism: Essays on Women, Literature, and Theory*, ed. Elaine Showalter (New York: Pantheon, 1985), 168.
2. See esp. Gallop's chap. 2, "The Problem of Definition," in *Around 1981*.
3. Judith Roof, *A Lure of Knowledge: Lesbian Sexuality and Theory* (New York: Columbia University Press, 1991), 217.

Feminist Theory in the Late 1980s

A mass of mineral matter, usually igneous rock, filling up a fissure
in the original strata, and sometimes rising from these like a mound
or wall, when they have been worn down by denudation.
—*Oxford English Dictionary*

Feminist theorists became increasingly preoccupied with the discursive
politics of "difference" in the years that followed these publications, to the
extent that race and sexuality are equated less often. But the contentious and
persistent question of dykes in the mainstream continued throughout this
period to serve a uniquely definitional function for feminist theory. In the
early 1980s, feminism was faced with a central division: some critics argued
that feminism was all about, too much about, lesbianism and lesbian sexuality; others argued that the heterosexist bias in feminist discourse betrayed
itself constantly in the marginalization and the silencing of lesbians and lesbian writers. This particular "dyke" shaped the peculiar path of feminist discourse in the second half of the 1980s.

Literary theory more generally was reinfused with the politics of activism
in the mid-1980s; as the AIDS epidemic ravaged the gay male community,
many critics turned to the complexities of male homoeroticism, discourses,
and representation with a sense of political urgency unseen since the early
days of the women's movement. Using the tools of feminist theory, literary
theorists began to focus on homosexuality through the newly repoliticized
discourses of masculinity. Interestingly and ironically, this development created yet another "dyke" in the world of literary criticism: while lesbians
belonged to the gay rights movement and the feminist movement, suddenly
they were *centrally* implicated in neither. Although questions of homosexuality were central to both feminist and gay male discourses, they were primarily about male homosexuality. Lesbians themselves existed at the
discursive margins, in and as the space between these two newly prominent
theoretical positions.

Through the middle years of the 1980s, the central terms of feminist literary theory underwent a significant paradigm shift, refocusing from a concern with the politics of female sex and sexuality to a theoretically broader
concern with the notion of gender. As Elaine Showalter points out in the
introduction to the anthology *Speaking of Gender,* which first appeared in
1989, "talking about gender means talking about both women and men."
"The introduction of gender into the field of literary studies marks a new
phase in feminist criticism, an investigation of the ways that all reading and
writing, by men as well as by women, is marked by gender. Talking about gender, moreover, is a constant reminder of the other categories of difference,
such as race and class, that structure our lives and texts, just as theorizing
gender emphasizes the parallels between feminist criticism, and other forms
of minority discourse."[4] The rise of gender studies over the course of the
1980s served practical as well as theoretical functions. Among other things,
it opened the doors of feminist theory unambiguously to male practitioners,
and as Showalter points out, presented a much more sophisticated notion of

4. Elaine Showalter, "Introduction: The Rise of Gender," in *Speaking of Gender,* ed. Showalter (New York:
Routledge, 1989), 2–3.

the ways in which language and power converge to shape a speaking subject, whether "male" or "female." The focus on gender served to further dismantle monolithic notions of "maleness" and "femaleness" per se, in exchange for a theory of gender as cultural construct, symptomatically reflecting larger cultural investments.

＊　＊　＊

[Terry] Castle's discomfort with the feminist absorption of lesbian concerns is also reflected, somewhat differently, however, in the initial theoretical[5] formulation of "queer theory," which occurred in a 1991 special issue of the journal *differences* dedicated to "Lesbian and Gay Sexualities." Again, the voice behind this formulation is that of a prominent feminist, Teresa de Lauretis. In her introduction to this issue, de Lauretis notes that while gay male and lesbian discourses have evolved along basically separate paths in the past, recent critical tendencies to see them as versions of one phenomenon, "lesbian and gay" (ladies first, of course), threaten to erase the specificity of that history. She writes, "our 'differences,' such as they may be, are less represented by the discursive coupling of those two terms in the politically correct phrase 'lesbian and gay,' than they are elided by most of the contexts in which the phrase is used; that is to say, differences are implied in it but then simply taken for granted or even covered over by the word 'and.' "[6] Thus occurs the birth of "queer theory," a metacritical praxis which is "intended to mark a certain critical distance" from the formulaic and reductive phrase "lesbian and gay." "Queer theory," writes de Lauretis, "conveys a double emphasis—on the conceptual and speculative work involved in discourse production, and on the necessary critical work of deconstructing our own discourses and their constructed silences" (iv). By definition a self-interrogating methodology, conditioned by a tradition of oppression, erasure, and silence to constantly examine its own "constructed silences," queer theory is, in theory, a school of thought that is always going back to school.

De Lauretis's logic is both provocative and problematic. To replace a phrase like "lesbian and gay" with a phrase like "queer theory" is quite literally to cover over any notion of lesbian and gay difference, to subsume male and female homosexuality within the single, potentially monolithic category "queer," to depend on the self-policing integrity of queer theorists themselves to "deconstruct . . . our own discourses and their constructed silences." In its ideal form, queer theory would be a constantly self-interrogating practice, and through that self-interrogation would succeed in retaining the specificity of lesbian and gay histories while also exploring the theoretical complexity of lesbian and gay difference. However, the replacement of a tripartite term— "lesbian and gay"—with a bipartite term—"queer theory"—appears to counteract de Lauretis's desire for increased specificity. And as queer theory begins to articulate itself as a practice distinct from feminist theory, the question of women, and particularly the question of lesbians, is persistently sidelined.

In the introduction to *Epistemology of the Closet*, Sedgwick addresses the question of a specifically lesbian-centered theoretical practice: "It seems

---

5. In Terry Castle, *The Apparitional Lesbian: Female Homosexuality and Modern Culture* (New York: Columbia University Press, 1993) [editor's note].

6. Teresa de Lauretis, "Queer Theory: Lesbian and Gay Sexualities, an Introduction," *differences* 3, no. 2 (Summer 1991): v–vi.

inevitable to me that the work of defining the circumferential boundaries, vis-à-vis lesbian experience and identity, of any gay male-centered theoretical articulation can be done only from the point of view of an alternative, feminocentric theoretical space, not from the heart of the male-centered project itself."[7] Within the context of a book that is quite explicitly at "the heart of the male-centered project itself," Sedgwick's discussion of a lesbian implication to gay male theory demonstrates great ambivalence. While this introduction, like the introduction to *Between Men*,[8] gives a nod to the urgent necessity for "feminocentric theoretical space," the place of lesbians in *Epistemology* is at best marginal. Acknowledging lesbian activists' work in the AIDS epidemic, Sedgwick writes, "The newly virulent homophobia of the 1980s, directed alike against women and men even though its medical pretext ought, if anything, logically to give a relative exemptive privilege to lesbians, reminds urgently that it is more to friends than to enemies that gay women and gay men are perceptible as distinct groups." Noting that lesbians, too, are vulnerable to AIDS, Sedgwick sees gay and AIDS activism as deeply indebted to lesbian practitioners and feminist theories:

> The contributions of lesbians to current gay and AIDS activism are weighty, not despite, but because of the intervening lessons of feminism. Feminist perspectives on medicine and health-care issues, on civil disobedience, and on the politics of class and race as well as of sexuality have been centrally enabling for the recent waves of AIDS activism. What this activism returns to the lesbians involved in it may include a more richly pluralized range of imaginings of lines of gender and sexual identification. (38-39)

Sedgwick is significantly vague about the yield of lesbian investment; that activism "*may* include a more richly pluralized range of imaginings" seems tepid consolation within a context of "virulent homophobia." Sedgwick is cautionary about the tendency of gay male discourse to "subsume" lesbian "experience and definition":

> The 'gay theory' I have been comparing with feminist theory doesn't mean exclusively gay male theory, but for the purpose of this comparison it includes lesbian theory insofar as that (a) isn't simply coextensive with feminist theory (i.e., doesn't subsume sexuality fully under gender) and (b) doesn't a priori deny all theoretical continuity between male homosexuality and lesbianism. But, again, the extent, construction, and meaning, and especially the history of any such theoretical continuity—not to mention its consequences for practical politics—must be open to every interrogation. (39)

Sedgwick, like de Lauretis, is always careful to argue that male and female homosexuality are very different phenomena, a useful and critical point. In fact, in this passage, as she tries to articulate a sufficiently specific and differentiated theoretical agenda for her text, Sedgwick recurs to an implicit structure of triangulation: gay male theoretical concerns, lesbian theoretical concerns, and feminist theoretical concerns are all related yet distinct enti-

7. Eve Kosofsky Sedgwick, *Epistemology of the Closet* (Berkeley: University of California Press, 1990), 39.

8. An earlier book by Sedgwick [editor's note].

ties. Once again, the "dyke" operates as the border, the literal site of connection and distinction between feminist and "gay" concerns in general. But as with all triangulated structures, as Sedgwick has demonstrated, one term is inevitably subordinated in favor of a dynamic connection between the other two. In Sedgwick's *Epistemology*, as in *Between Men*, the coincidence of feminist methodology and gay male subject matter consistently produces lesbian concerns as that third term, emerging occasionally, marginally, and principally in introductory matter. This is one example of a larger critical phenomenon in which, once again, the dyke demarcates the border of internal and external, offering a frame of reference but not a *mise en abîme*.[9]

At the risk of the inevitable pun, I would argue that while feminist theory engendered queer theory, the two remain distinct. By now the dualism that so profoundly shaped feminist discourse at the end of the 1970s and into the early 1980s is literalized in the separate entities of feminist and queer scholarship. But what has been factored out here, oddly enough, is the specificity of lesbian discourse: caught between the feminist and the queer, the lesbian, again, occupies the problematic third position in the triangle of contemporary critical discourse. And as with the triangular structure posited in Sedgwick's early analysis, the third term is not the one that counts; the animate connection here is the one between feminists and queers, while the third, the site of literal connection and disjunction, marks the space between without signifying itself. Lesbians occupy the subordinated place of the woman in the structure of triangular desire, in which the desiring relationship is constituted between feminists and queers.

Back in 1980, in "Compulsory Heterosexuality and Lesbian Existence," Rich produced what seems today a startlingly prescient commentary. She writes, "Lesbians have historically been deprived of a political existence through 'inclusion' as female versions of male homosexuality. To equate lesbian existence with male homosexuality because each is stigmatized is to erase female reality once again."[1] Equated not only with male homosexuals but with feminism in its most generalized form, lesbians remain consistently—and paradoxically—marginalized. And as a marginalized population, dykes serve a useful function within the context of feminist and queer theories alike, acting as the border against which the mainstream can define itself. The specific location of that margin, of that "dyke," is revealing of particular, often-shifting engagements within theoretical discourses as they struggle to define themselves, their constituencies, their politics, and their activism. The dyke in the mainstream marks the space of margin and connection, offering at once a point of view that is and is not of the central flow.

Within the metaphorical structure I have explored throughout this essay, I have argued that feminist theory has consistently seen the "dyke" as marginal, protective, and contingent, as facilitating the existence of a larger whole rather than independently significant. Yet the specificity of lesbian discourses and desires has independently significant value, not only as a metacritical instrument for the analysis of a broader feminist theory, but also as an historically complex cultural phenomenon in its own right. Behind the metaphorical, architectural dyke is another dyke, a figure too often margin-

9. Literally, "placing into the abyss" (French); generally, in art and literature, a frame-within-a-frame technique associated with infinite regress or self-reflexivity [editor's note].

1. Rich, "Compulsory Heterosexuality," 239.

alized, too frequently and too vaguely appropriated within larger theoretical paradigms of sexuality and politics. For let us recall that listed below and separated from the nearly three columns of *dykes* in the OED is the slang definition: "dike, dyke . . . *slang*. [Of obscure origin.] A lesbian; a masculine woman."

1997

PAULA M. L. MOYA
b. 1962

A graduate of the University of Houston and Cornell University, Paula M. L. Moya was born in New Mexico and currently teaches at Stanford University, where she directs the undergraduate program of the Center for Comparative Studies in Race and Ethnicity. A specialist in Chicana/o cultural studies and feminist theory, she has authored *Learning from Experience: Minority Identities, Multicultural Struggles* (2002) and coedited (with Michael Hames-Garcia) *Reclaiming Identity: Realist Theory and the Predicament of Postmodernism* (2000). Attuned to the sophisticated claims of poststructuralism and postmodernism, Moya nevertheless seeks to retain those identity claims that make marginalized or subordinated groups visible and empowered in their everyday lives. Along with such thinkers as Norma Alarcón, Teresa McKenna, and Sonia Saldívar-Hull, Moya has helped highlight the importance of Chicana studies.

From Postmodernism, "Realism," and the Politics of Identity: Cherríe Moraga and Chicana Feminism[1]

*   *   *

The problem posed by postmodernism is particularly acute for U.S. feminist scholars and activists of color, for whom "experience" and "identity" continue to be primary organizing principles around which they theorize and mobilize. Even women of color who readily acknowledge the nonessential nature of their political or theoretical commitments persist in referring to themselves as, for instance, "Chicana" or "Black" feminists, and continue to join organizations, such as *Mujeres Activas en Letras y Cambio Social* (MALCS), which are organized around principles of identity. For example, [Cherríe] Moraga acknowledges that women of color are not a " 'natural' affinity group" even as she works to build a movement around and for people who identify as women of color. She can do this, without contradiction, because her understanding of the identity "women of color" reconceptualizes the notion of

1. I want to thank Jacqui Alexander and Chandra Talpade Mohanty for pushing me to develop my ideas and giving me the opportunity, in this volume [*Feminist Genealogies, Colonial Legacies, Democratic Futures*], to express them. Many thanks as well to Linda Alcoff, Bernadette Andrea, Martin Bernal, Junot Díaz, Michael Hames-García, Ben Olguín, and Bill Wilkerson, whose careful readings of the manuscript helped me to think through what are some difficult and politically sensitive issues. I owe a debt of gratitude to Satya Mohanty for his intellectual guidance and scholarly example, and to Tim Young for nourishing me both intellectually and emotionally. Finally, I want to thank my daughters, Halina and Eva Martinez, for their inexhaustible (if not entirely voluntary) patience. It is for their sake I persevere. [All notes are Moya's.]

"identity" itself. Unlike postmodernist feminists who understand the concept of "identity" as inherently and perniciously "foundational," Moraga understands "identities" as relational and grounded in the historically produced social facts which constitute social locations.

Ironically, Moraga and other women of color are often called upon in postmodernist feminist accounts of identity to delegitimize any theoretical project that attends to the linkages between identity (with its experiential and cognitive components) and social location (the particular nexus of gender, race, class, and sexuality in which a given individual exists in the world). Such projects are derided by postmodernist feminists as theoretically mistaken and dangerously "exclusionary"—particularly in relation to women of color themselves.[2] Accordingly, I devote the first section of this article, "Postmodernist 'Cyborgs' and the Denial of Social Location," to an examination of the theoretical misappropriation of women of color—specifically Chicana activist and theorist Cherríe Moraga—by the influential postmodernist theorists Judith Butler and Donna Haraway. I criticize these two theorists not only because they appropriate Moraga's words without attending to her theoretical insights, but more importantly because they employ her work at key moments in their arguments to legitimate their respective theoretical projects. In the second section, "Toward a Realist Theory of Chicana Identity," I draw upon the work of Satya Mohanty to articulate a "realist" account of Chicana identity that goes beyond essentialism by theorizing the connections between social location, experience, cultural identity, and knowledge.[3] By demonstrating the cognitive component of cultural identity, I underscore the possibility that some identities can be more politically progressive than others *not* because they are "transgressive" or "indeterminate" but because they provide us with a critical perspective from which we can disclose the complicated workings of ideology and oppression. Finally, in " 'Theory in the Flesh': Moraga's Realist Feminism," I provide my own realist reading of Moraga, and show—by resituating Moraga's work within the cultural and historical conditions from which it emerged—that her elaboration of a "theory in the flesh"

2. In their introduction to *Feminists Theorize the Political*, Scott and Butler ask the following questions: "What are the points of convergence between a) poststructuralist criticisms of identity and b) recent theory by women of color that critically exposes the unified or coherent subject as a prerogative of white theory?"; "To what extent do the terms used to defend the universal subject encode fears about those cultural minorities excluded in, and by, the construction of that subject; to what extent is the outcry against the 'postmodern' a defense of culturally privileged epistemic positions that leave unexamined the excluded domains of homosexuality, race, and class?"; "What is the significance of the poststructuralist critique of binary logic for the theorization of the subaltern?"; and "How do universal theories of 'patriarchy' or phallogocentrism need to be rethought in order to avoid the consequences of a white-feminist epistemological/cultural imperialism?" My point is that such questions enact an unself-critical enlistment of the "woman of color," the "subaltern," and the "cultural minority" to serve as legitimators of the project entailed in "postmodern" or poststructuralist criticisms of identity.

3. When I use the term "realism" in this essay, I am *not* referring to the literary mode in which the details of the plot or characters are "true to life." I refer, instead, to a philosophical (and in particular, epistemological) position. Broadly speaking, a realist epistemology implies a belief in a "reality" that exists independently of our mental constructions of it. Thus, while our (better or worse) understandings of our world may provide our only access to "reality," our mental constructions of the world do not constitute the totality of what can be considered "real." It ought to be made clear that when the realist says that something is "real," she does not mean to say that it is *not* socially constructed; rather, her point is that is not *only* socially constructed. In the case of identity, for instance, the realist claim is that there is a nonarbitrary limit to the range of identities we can "construct" or "choose" for any person in a given social formation. It is that nonarbitrary limit that forms the boundary between (objective) "reality" and our (subjective) construction—or understanding—of it. For more on the implications of "realism" within the context of literary studies, see Satya Mohanty's "Colonial Legacies, Multicultural Futures: Relativism, Objectivity, and the Challenge of Otherness" esp. pp. 111–15.

gestures toward a realist theory of identity. A realist reading of Moraga's work presents a strong case for how and why the theoretical insights of women of color are necessary for understanding fundamental aspects of U.S. society.

Postmodernist "Cyborgs" and the Denial of Social Location

In her influential essay "A Manifesto for Cyborgs: Science, Technology and Socialist Feminism in the 1980s," Donna Haraway figures Chicanas as exemplary cyborgs and, as such, prototypical postmodern subjects.

✻   ✻   ✻

Haraway claims that "women of color" can be understood as a "cyborg identity, a potent subjectivity synthesized from fusions of outsider identities" (217). She bases her claim, in part, on her appropriation and misreading of the Mexicano/Chicano myth of Malinche—a misreading which allows Haraway to celebrate the symbolic birth of a new "bastard" race and the death of the founding myth of original wholeness:

> For example, retellings of the story of the indigenous woman Malinche, mother of the mestizo "bastard" race of the new world, master of languages, and mistress of Cortés, carry special meaning for Chicana constructions of identity. . . . Sister Outsider hints at the possibility of world survival not because of her innocence, but because of her ability to live on the boundaries, to write without the founding myth of original wholeness, . . . Malinche was mother here, not Eve before eating the forbidden fruit. Writing affirms Sister Outsider, not the Woman-before-the-Fall-into-Writing needed by the phallogocentric Family of Man. (217–18)[4]

✻   ✻   ✻

Haraway's reading of the Malinche myth ignores the complexity of the situation. She concludes her discussion of Malinche by claiming that, "Stripped of identity, the bastard race teaches about the power of the margins and the importance of a mother like Malinche. Women of color have transformed her from the evil mother of masculinist fear into the originally literate mother who teaches survival" (218–19). With this statement, Haraway conceals the painful legacy of the Malinche myth and overinvests the figure of Malinche with a questionable agency. Moreover, Haraway uncritically affirms a positionality (the margins) and a mode of existence (survival) that real live Chicanas have found to be rather less (instead of more) affirming. I do not mean to suggest that marginality and survival are not, in themselves, important and valuable. Certainly survival is valuable wherever the alternative is extinction. And, as I will argue, the experience and the theorizing of marginalized or oppressed people is important for arriving at a more objective understanding of the world. But I would suggest that neither marginality nor survival are sufficient goals for a feminist project, and that no theoretical account of feminist identity can be based exclusively on such goals.

4. The name "Sister Outsider" derives from Audre Lorde's book of the same name. Haraway's easy substitution of the name "Sister Outsider" for that of "Malinche," and her conflation of Chicana with Malinche with Sister Outsider signals her inattention to the differences (temporal, historical, and material) that exist between the three distinct categories of identity.

My point is that Haraway's conflation of cyborgs with women of color raises serious theoretical and political issues because she conceives the social identities of women of color in overly idealized terms. As previously noted, Haraway's conception of a cyborg is that of a creature who transcends or destroys boundaries. It is "the illegitimate offspring of militarism and patriarchal capitalism," "a kind of disassembled and reassembled, postmodern collective and personal self," a being "committed to partiality, irony, intimacy and perversity," who is "not afraid of permanently partial identities and contradictory standpoints," and who is "related [to other cyborgs] not by blood but by *choice*" (193, 205, 192, 196 emphasis added). The porosity and polysemy of the category "cyborg," in effect, leaves no criteria to determine who might *not* be a cyborg. Furthermore, since Haraway sees a lack of any essential criterion for determining who is a woman of color, anyone can be a woman of color. Thus, all cyborgs can be women of color and all women of color can be cyborgs. By sheer force of will (by "choice" as Haraway puts it) and by committing oneself (or refusing to commit oneself) to "permanently partial identities and contradictory standpoints," *anyone* can be either one or the other—or neither.[5]

*   *   *

Although far more cursory, Judith Butler's treatment of Moraga's writings is also a highly questionable attempt to enlist women of color for a postmodernist agenda. In her oft-cited work *Gender Trouble*, Butler extracts one sentence from Moraga, buries it in a footnote, and then misreads it in order to justify her own inability to account for the complex interrelations that structure various forms of human identity (see p. 153, n. 24). She reads Moraga's statement that "the danger lies in ranking the oppressions" to mean that we have no way of adjudicating among different kinds of oppressions—that any attempt to causally relate or hierarchize the varieties of oppressions people suffer constitutes an imperializing, colonizing, or totalizing gesture that renders the effort invalid. This misreading of Moraga follows on the heels of Butler's dismissal of Irigaray's notion of phallogocentrism (as globalizing and exclusionary) and clears the way for her to do away with the category of "women" altogether. Thus, although Butler at first appears to have understood the critiques of women (primarily of color) who have been historically precluded from occupying the position of the "subject" of feminism, it becomes clear that their voices have been merely instrumental to her. She writes,

> The opening discussion in this chapter argues that this globalizing gesture [to find universally shared structures of oppression along an axis of sexual difference] has spawned a number of criticisms from women who claim that the category of "women" is normative and exclusionary and is invoked with the unmarked dimensions of class and racial privilege

5. Linda Alcoff has suggested to me that Haraway might not intend to imply that "all cyborgs can be women of color"—that she meant only that "women of color" is one particular *kind* of cyborg identity. If so, we are left with "women of color cyborgs" and "white women cyborgs" (and perhaps other *kinds* of male cyborgs, as well). In that case, of what use is a cyborg identity? Unless a cyborg identity can effectively dismantle "difference" (and the effect "difference" has on our experiences of the world), it is at best innocuous, and at worst quite dangerous. We must acknowledge that a cyborg identity has the potential to become simply another veil to hide behind in order not to have to examine the differences that both constitute and challenge our self-conceptions.

intact. In other words, the insistence upon the coherence and unity of the category of women has effectively refused the multiplicity of cultural, social and political intersections in which the concrete array of 'women' are constructed. (14)

Butler's response to this critique is not to rethink her understanding of the category "women" but rather to throw it out altogether. Underlying her logic are the assumptions that because the varieties of oppressions cannot be "summarily" ranked, they cannot be ranked at all; because epistemological projects have been totalizing and imperializing, they are always and necessarily so; and unless a given category (such as "women") is transhistorical, transcultural, stable, and uncontestable, it is not an analytical and political category at all.

*   *   *

Common to both Haraway's and Butler's accounts of identity is the assumption of a postmodern "subject" of feminism whose identity is unstable, shifting, and contradictory: "she" can claim no grounded tie to any aspect of "her" identit(ies) because "her" anti-imperialist, shifting, and contradictory politics have no cognitive basis in *experience*. Ironically, although both Haraway and Butler lay claim to an anti-imperialist project, their strategies of resistance to oppression lack efficacy in a material world. Their attempts to disrupt gender categories (Butler), or to conjure away identity politics (Haraway), make it difficult to figure out who is "us" and who is "them," who is the "oppressed" and who is the "oppressor," who shares our interests and whose interests are opposed to ours.[6] Distinctions dissolve as all beings (human, plant, animal, and machine) are granted citizenship in the radically fragmented, unstable society of the postmodern world. "Difference" is magically subverted, and we find out that we really are all the same after all!

The key theoretical issue turns on Haraway and Butler's disavowal of the link between identity (with its experiential and cognitive components) and social location (the particular nexus of gender, race, class, and sexuality in which a given individual exists in the world). Haraway and Butler err in the assumption that because there is no *one-to-one* correspondence between social location and identity or knowledge, there is simply *no* connection between social location and identity or knowledge. I agree that in theory boundaries are infinitely permeable and power may be amorphous. The difficulty is that people do not live in an entirely abstract or discursive realm. They live as biologically and temporally limited, as well as socially situated, human beings. Furthermore, while the "postmodern" moment does represent a time of rapid social, political, economic, and discursive shifts, it does not represent a radical break with systems, structures, and meanings of the past. Power is not amorphous because oppression is systematic and structural. A politics of discourse that does not provide for some sort of bodily or concrete action outside the realm of the academic text will forever be inadequate to change the difficult "reality" of our lives. Only by acknowledging the specificity and "simultaneity of oppression," and the fact that some people are

6. As long as our world is hierarchically organized along relations of domination, categories such as "us" and "them," or "oppressed" and "oppressor" will retain their explanatory function. This is not because any one group belongs, in an essential way, to a particular category, but rather because the terms describe positions within prevailing social and economic relations.

more oppressed than others, can we begin to understand the systems and structures that perpetuate oppression in order to place ourselves in a position to contest and change them (Moraga, *Loving* 128).

Until we do so, Cherríe Moraga, together with other women of color, will find herself leaving from Guatemala only to arrive at Guatepeor.[7] She will find herself caught in the dilemma of being reduced to her Chicana lesbian body, or having to deny her social location (for which her body is a compelling metaphor) as the principal place from which she derives her insights. Moraga's dilemma appears as a contradiction to the theorist who recognizes a choice only between essentialist and postmodernist accounts of identity and knowledge. On the one hand, Moraga is articulating a "theory in the flesh," derived from "the physical realities of [women of colors'] lives—[their] skin color, the land or concrete [they] grew up on, [their] sexual longings"; on the other hand, she reminds us that "sex and race do not define a person's politics" (*Loving* 23, 149). How can a theory be derived from the "physical realities of [women of color's] lives" if "sex and race do not define a person's politics"? When we examine this paradox from what I will be calling a "realist" perspective, the contradiction will be dissolved. Theory, knowledge, and understanding can be linked to "our skin color, the land or concrete we grew up on, our sexual longings" without being uniformly determined by them. Rather, those "physical realities of our lives" will profoundly *inform* the contours and the context of both our theories and our knowledge.[8] The effects that the "physical realities of our lives" have on us, then, are what need to be addressed—not dismissed or dispersed—by theorists of social identity.

Toward a Realist Theory of Chicana Identity

In the following section I will draw upon Satya Mohanty's essay "The Epistemic Status of Cultural Identity: On *Beloved* and the Postcolonial Condition," to articulate a realist account of Chicana identity that theorizes the linkages between social location, experience, epistemic privilege, and cultural identity. I must emphasize that this project is not an attempt to rehabilitate an essentialist view of identity. The critiques of essentialism are numerous; the aporias of an essentialist notion of identity have been well documented.[9] The mistake lies in assuming that our options for theorizing identities are inscribed within the postmodernism/essentialism binary—that we are either

---

7. The Spanish-language proverb "Salir de Guatemala para entrar en Guatepeor" plays with the word fragment "mala" in "Guatemala" to suggest the dilemma of a person caught between a bad (mala) and a worse (peor) situation. The proverb roughly approximates the English-language proverb "To go from the frying pan into the fire."
8. At the risk of stating what should be obvious, this is as true for the white heterosexual politically conservative antifeminist as it is for the radical feminist lesbian of color. And yet, it is primarily women who address gender issues, and primarily people of color who address racial issues (both inside the academy and out). The unspoken assumption is that only women have gender and only people of color are racialized beings. This assumption reflects itself in the work of many male academics who only talk about gender when they are referring to women, and in the work of many white academics who only talk about race when

they are referring to people of color. A manifestation of this phenomenon can be found in Judith Butler's book *Bodies That Matter*, where she only theorizes race in the two chapters in which she discusses artistic productions by or about people of color.
9. When I refer to essentialism, I am referring to the notion that individuals or groups have an immutable and discoverable "essence"—a basic, unvariable, and presocial nature. As a theoretical concept, essentialism expresses itself through the tendency to see *one* social fact (class, gender, race, sexuality, etc.) as determinate in the last instance for the cultural identity of the individual or group in question. As a political strategy, essentialism has had both liberatory and reactionary effects. For one poststructuralist critique of essentialism that does not quite escape the postmodernist tendency I am critiquing in this essay, see Diana Fuss's book *Essentially Speaking*.

completely fixed and unitary or unstable and fragmented selves. The advantage of a realist theory of identity is that it allows for an acknowledgement of how the social facts of race, class, gender, and sexuality function in individual lives without *reducing* individuals to those social determinants.

I will begin by clarifying my claims and defining some terms. "Epistemic privilege," as I will use it in this essay, refers to a special advantage with respect to possessing or acquiring knowledge about how fundamental aspects of our society (such as race, class, gender, and sexuality) operate to sustain matrices of power. Although I will claim that oppressed groups may have epistemic privilege, I am not implying that social locations have epistemic or political meanings in a self-evident way. The simple fact of having been born a person of color in the United States or of having suffered the effects of heterosexism or of economic deprivation does not, in and of itself, give someone a better understanding or knowledge of the structure of our society. The key to claiming epistemic privilege for people who have been oppressed in a particular way stems from an acknowledgment that they have experiences—experiences that people who are not oppressed in that same way usually lack—that *can* provide them with information we all need to understand how hierarchies of race, class, gender, and sexuality operate to uphold existing regimes of power in our society. Thus, what is being claimed is not any *a priori* link between social location or identity and knowledge, but a link that is historically variable and mediated through the interpretation of experience.

"Experience," in this essay, refers to the fact of personally observing, encountering, or undergoing a particular event or situation. By this definition, experience is admittedly subjective. Experiences are not wholly external events; they do not just happen. Experiences happen to us, and it is our theoretically mediated interpretation of an event that makes it an "experience." The meanings we give our experiences are inescapably conditioned by the ideologies and "theories" through which we view the world. But what is at stake in my argument is not that experience is theoretically mediated, but rather that experience *in its mediated form* contains a "cognitive component" through which we can gain access to knowledge of the world (Mohanty, "Epistemic Status" 45). It is this contention, that it is "precisely in this *mediated* way that [personal experience] yields knowledge," that signals a theoretical departure from the opposed camps of essentialism and postmodernism (Mohanty, "Epistemic Status" 45).

The first claim of a realist theory of identity is that the different social facts (such as gender, race, class, and sexuality) that mutually constitute an individual's social location are casually relevant for the experiences she will have. Thus, a person who is racially coded as "white" in our society will usually face situations and have experiences that are significantly different from those of a person who is racially coded as "black."[1] Similarly, a person who is racially coded as "black" and who has ample financial resources at her disposal will usually face situations and have experiences that are significantly different from those of a person who is racially coded as "black" and lacks those

---

1. This can happen even if both individuals in the example are born into an African-American community and consider themselves "black." It should be clear that I am not talking about race as a biological category. I am talking about people who, for one reason or another, appear to others as "white" or "black." As I will demonstrate in my discussion of Moraga's work, this is an important distinction for theorizing the link between experience and cultural identity for people with real, but not visible, biological or cultural connections to minority communities.

resources. The examples can proliferate and become increasingly complex, but the basic point is this: the experiences a person is likely to have will be largely determined by her social location in a given society.[2] In order to appreciate the structural causality of the experiences of any given individual, we must take into account the mutual interaction of *all* the different social facts which constitute her social location, and situate them within the particular social, cultural, and historical matrix in which she exists.

The second basic claim of a realist theory of identity is that an individual's experiences will influence, but not entirely determine, the formation of her cultural identity. Thus, while I am suggesting that members of a group may share experiences as a result of their (voluntary or involuntary) membership in that group, I am not suggesting that they all come to the same conclusions about those experiences.[3] Because the theories through which humans interpret their experiences vary from individual to individual, from time to time, and from situation to situation, it follows that different people's interpretations of the same kind of experience will differ. For example, one woman may interpret her jealous husband's monitoring of her interactions with other men as a sign that "he really loves her," while another may interpret it in terms of the social relations of gender domination, in which a man may be socialized to see himself as both responsible for and in control of his wife's behavior. The kinds of identities these women construct for themselves will both condition and be conditioned by the kinds of interpretations they give to the experiences they have. (The first woman may see herself as a treasured wife, while the second sees herself as the victim in a hierarchically organized society in which, by virtue of her gender, she exists in a subordinate position.)

The third claim of a realist theory of identity is that there is a cognitive component to identity which allows for the possibility of error and of accuracy in interpreting experience. It is a feature of theoretically mediated experience that one person's understanding of the same situation may undergo revision over the course of time, thus rendering her subsequent interpretations of that situation more or less accurate. I have as an example my own experience of the fact that the other women in my freshman dorm at Yale treated me differently than they treated each other. My initial interpretation of the situation led me to conclude that they just did not like me—the individual, the particular package of hopes, dreams, habits, and mannerisms that I was. Never having had much trouble making friends, this experience was both troubling and humbling to me. As a "Spanish" girl from New Mexico, neither race nor racism were social realities that I considered as being relevant to me. I might have wondered (but I did not) why I ended up spending my first semester at Yale with the other brown-skinned, Spanish-surnamed woman in my residential college. It was only after I moved to Texas, where prejudice against Mexicans is much more overt, that I realized that regardless of how I saw myself, other people saw me as "Mexican." Reflecting back, I came to understand that while I had not seen the other women in my dorm

2. For an illuminating discussion of the way in which the social fact of gender has structured the experiences of at least one woman, and has profoundly informed the formation of her cultural identity, see Mohanty's "Epistemic Status," esp. pp. 46–51.
3. It is not even necessary that they recognize

themselves as members of that group. For example, a dark-skinned immigrant from Puerto Rico who refuses identification with African-Americans may nevertheless suffer racist experiences arising from the history of black/white race relations within the U.S. due to mainland U.S. citizens' inability to distinguish between the two distinct cultural groups.

as being particularly different from me, the reverse was not the case. Simultaneous with that understanding came the suspicion that my claim to a Spanish identity might be both factually and ideologically suspect. A little digging proved my suspicion correct.[4] In Texas, then, I became belatedly and unceremoniously Mexican-American. All this to illustrate the point that identities both condition and are conditioned by the kinds of interpretations people give to the experiences they have. As Mohanty says, "identities are ways of making sense of our experiences." They are "theoretical constructions that enable us to read the world in specific ways" (55).

The fourth claim of a realist theory of identity is that some identities, because they can more adequately account for the social facts constituting an individual's social location, have greater epistemic value than some others that same individual might claim. If, as in the case of my Spanish identity, I am forced to ignore certain salient facts of my social location in order to maintain my self-conception, we can fairly conclude that my identity is epistemically distorted. While my Spanish identity may have a measure of epistemic validity (mine is a Spanish surname; I undoubtedly have some "Spanish blood"), we can consider it less valid than an alternative identity which takes into consideration the ignored social facts (my "Indian blood," my Mexican cultural heritage) together with all the other social facts that are causally relevant for the experiences I might have. Identities have more or less epistemic validity to the extent that they "refer" outward to the world, that they accurately describe and explain the complex interactions between the multiple determinants of an individual's social location.[5] According to the realist theory of identity, identities are neither self-evident, unchanging, and uncontestable, nor are they absolutely fragmented, contradictory, and unstable. Rather, identities are subject to multiple determinations and to a continual process of verification which takes place over the course of an individual's life through her interaction with the society she lives in. It is in this process of verification that identities can be (and often are) contested, and that they can (and often do) change.

I want to consider now the possibility that my identity as a "Chicana" can grant me a knowledge about the world that is "truer," and more "objective," than an alternative identity I might claim as either a "Mexican-American," a "Hispanic," or an "American" (who happens to be of Mexican descent). When I refer to a Mexican-American, I am referring to a person of Mexican heritage born and/or raised in the United States whose nationality is U.S. American. The term for me is descriptive, rather than political. The term "Hispanic" is generally used to refer to a person of Spanish, Mexican, Puerto Rican, Dominican, Cuban, Chilean, Peruvian, etc. heritage who may or may not have a Spanish-surname, who may or may not speak Spanish, who can be of any racial extraction, and who resides in the U.S. As it is currently deployed, the term is so general as to be virtually useless as a descriptive or analytical

---

4. For an explanation of the historical origins of the myth that Spanish-surnamed residents of New Mexico are direct descendants of Spanish *conquistadores*, see Roldofo Acuña, *Occupied America*, 55–60; Nancie González, *The Spanish-Americans of New Mexico*, 78–83; and John Chavez, *The Lost Land*, 85–106.

5. Identities can be evaluated, according to

Mohanty, "using the same complex epistemological criteria we use to evaluate 'theories.'" He explains: "Since different experiences and identities refer to different aspects of *one* world, one complex causal structure that we call 'social reality,' the realist theory of identity implies that we can evaluate them comparatively by considering how adequately they explain this structure" ("Epistemic Status," 70–71).

tool. Moreover, the term has been shunned by progressive intellectuals for its overt privileging of the "Spanish" part of what, for many of the people it claims to describe, is a racially and culturally mixed heritage. A Chicana, according to the usage of women who identify that way, is a politically aware woman of Mexican heritage who is at least partially descended from the indigenous people of Mesoamerica and who was born and/or raised in the United States. What distinguishes a Chicana from a Mexican-American, a Hispanic, or an American of Mexican descent is her political awareness; her recognition of her disadvantaged position in a hierarchically organized society arranged according to categories of class, race, gender, and sexuality; and her propensity to engage in political struggle aimed at subverting and changing those structures.[6]

The fifth claim of a realist theory of identity is that our ability to understand fundamental aspects of our world will depend on our ability to acknowledge and understand the social, political, economic, and epistemic consequences of our own social location. If we can agree that our *one* social world is, as Mohanty asserts, "constitutively defined by relations of domination" (72), then we can begin to see how my cultural identity as a Chicana, which takes into account an acknowledgment and understanding of those relations, may be more epistemically valid than an alternative identity I might claim as a Mexican-American, a Hispanic, or an American. While a description of myself as a Mexican-American is not technically incorrect, the description implies a structural equivalence with other hyphenated Americans (Italian-Americans, German-Americans, African-Americans, etc.) that erases the differential social, political, and economic relations that obtain for different groups. This erasure is even more marked in the cultural identity of the Hispanic or American (of Mexican descent), whose self-conception often depends upon the idea that she is a member of one more assimilable ethnic group in what is simply a nation of immigrants.[7] Factors of race, gender, and class get obscured in these identities, while a normative heterosexuality is simply presumed. We find that in order to maintain her identity, the Hispanic or American (of Mexican descent) may have to repress or misinterpret her own or others' experiences of oppression. Moreover, she will most likely view her material situation (her "success" or "failure") as entirely a result of her individual merit, and dismiss structural relations of domination as irrelevant to her personal situation. Thus, my claim that social locations have epistemic consequences is not the same as claiming that a particular kind of knowledge

---

6. Historically, the term "Chicano" was a pejorative name applied to lower-class Mexican-Americans. Like the term "Black," it was consciously appropriated and revalued by (primarily) students during the Chicano Movement of the 1960s. According to the *Plan de Santa Barbara* the term specifically implies a politics of resistance to Anglo-American domination. The *Plan de Santa Barbara*, written in the Spring of 1969 at a California statewide conference in Santa Barbara, California, founded MEChA (*Movimiento Estudiantil Chicano de Aztlán*), and is probably the definitive position paper of the Chicano Student Youth Movement. The Plan is published as an appendix in Carlos Muñoz, *Youth, Identity, Power*, 191–202.
7. An example of the assimilationist "Hispanic" is

Linda Chavez, whose book *Out of the Barrio: Toward a New Politics of Hispanic Assimilation* suggests that Hispanics, like "previous" white ethnic groups, are rapidly assimilating into the mainstream of U.S. culture and society (2). Not only does Chavez play fast and loose with sociological and historical evidence, but her thesis cannot account for the social fact of race. She does not mention race as being casually relevant for the experiences of Hispanics, and she repeatedly refers to "non-Hispanic whites," a grammatical formulation which assumes that all Hispanics are white. She accounts for Puerto Ricans and Dominicans by considering them as "dysfunctional" "exceptions" to the white-Hispanic rule (139–59).

inheres in a particular social location. An individual's understanding of herself and the world will be mediated, more or less accurately, through her cultural identity.

The sixth and final claim of a realist theory of identity is that oppositional struggle is fundamental to our ability to understand the world more accurately. Mohanty, drawing upon the work of Sandra Harding and Richard Boyd, explains this Marxian idea in this way:

> In the case of social phenomena like sexism and racism, whose distorted representation benefits the powerful and the established groups and institutions, an attempt at an objective explanation is necessarily continuous with oppositional political struggles. Objective knowledge of such social phenomena is in fact often dependent on the theoretical knowledge that activism creates. For without these alternative constructions and accounts, our capacity to interpret and understand the dominant ideologies and institutions is limited to those created or sanctioned by these very ideologies and institutions. (51–52)

The "alternative constructions and accounts" generated through oppositional struggle provide new ways of looking at our world that always complicate and often challenge dominant conceptions of what is "right," "true," and "beautiful." They call to account the distorted representations of peoples, ideas, and practices whose subjugation is fundamental to the colonial, neo-colonial, imperialist, or capitalist project. Furthermore, because the well-being (and sometimes even survival) of the groups or individuals who engage in oppositional struggle depends on their ability to refute or dismantle dominant ideologies and institutions, their vision is usually more critical, their efforts more diligent, and their arguments more comprehensive than those of individuals or groups whose well-being is predicated on the maintenance of the status quo. Oppressed groups and individuals have a stake in knowing *"what it would take* to change [our world], on . . . identifying the central relations of power and privilege that sustain it and make the world what it is" (Mohanty, "Epistemic Status" 53). This is why "granting the possibility of epistemological privilege to the oppressed might be more than a sentimental gesture; in many cases in fact it is the only way to push us toward greater social objectivity" (Mohanty, "Epistemic Status" 72). Thus, a realist theory of identity demands oppositional struggle as a necessary (although not sufficient) step toward the achievement of an epistemically privileged position.

*   *   *

WORKS CITED

Acuña, Rodolfo. *Occupied America: A History of Chicanos.* 3rd ed. New York: Harper-Collins, 1988.
Butler, Judith. *Bodies That Matter: On the Discursive Limits of "Sex."* New York: Routledge, 1993.
———. *Gender Trouble.* New York: Routledge, 1990.

Butler, Judith, and Joan Scott, eds. *Feminists Theorize the Political*. New York: Routledge, 1992.

Chávez, John R. *The Lost Land: The Chicano Image of the Southwest*. Albuquerque: University of New Mexico Press, 1984.

Chavez, Linda. *Out of the Barrio: Toward a New Politics of Hispanic Assimilation*. New York: Basic Books, 1991.

Fuss, Diana. *Essentially Speaking: Feminism, Nature & Difference*. New York: Routledge, 1989.

González, Nancie L. *The Spanish-Americans of New Mexico: A Heritage of Pride*. Albuquerque: University of New Mexico Press, 1967.

Haraway, Donna. "A Manifesto for Cyborgs: Science, Technology, and Socialist Feminism in the 1980s." In *Feminism/Postmodernism*, ed. Linda J. Nicholson, 190–233. New York: Routledge, 1990.

Lorde, Audre. *Sister Outsider*. Trumansburg, N.Y.: Crossing Press, 1984.

Mohanty, Satya P. "Colonial Legacies, Multicultural Futures: Relativism, Objectivity, and the Challenge of Otherness." *PMLA* 110, no. 1 (1995): 108–18.

———. "The Epistemic Status of Cultural Identity: On *Beloved* and the Postcolonial Condition." *Cultural Critique*, no. 24 (Spring 1993): 41–80.

Moraga, Cherríe. *Loving in the War Years: Lo que nunca pasó por sus labios*. Boston: South End Press, 1983.

Muñoz, Carlos, Jr. *Youth, Identity, Power: The Chicano Movement*. London: Verso, 1989.

1997

GAYATRI CHAKRAVORTY SPIVAK
b. 1942

Feminist methodologies are explored within postcolonial frameworks in the highly influential writings of Gayatri Chakravorty Spivak, who was born in Calcutta, India, and came to the United States to do her graduate work at Cornell University. As a professor of comparative literature at the University of Iowa, the University of Texas, the University of Pittsburgh, and currently at Columbia University, Spivak has evolved her unique mix of deconstruction (she was the translator of Jacques Derrida's *Of Grammatology*, 1977), literary analysis (her first book was *Myself I Must Remake: The Life and Poetry of W. B. Yeats*, 1974), and multicultural as well as transnational politics (see her essays collected in *Other Worlds: Essays in Cultural Politics*, 1987, as well as *Outside the Teaching Machine*, 1993). All her writings are shaped by a deep commitment to first and third world dialogues (apparent in *A Critique of Postcolonial Reason: Toward a History of the Vanishing Present*, 1999). The violence not just of colonialism's past but also of postcolonialism's present and future engages her in the activist teaching she undertakes both in her native land and within the American academy: *Death of a Discipline* (2003), in particular, calls for a new comparative literature that will be responsive to linguistic, religious, and geopolitical diversity. What colonial and postcolonial violence means in terms of the silencing of women's voices and how or, indeed, whether intellectuals can refrain from further subordinating less privileged women: these are the subjects of her landmark 1988 essay "Can the Subaltern Speak?" (reproduced here in the version incorporated into *A Critique of Postcolonial Reason*).

From A Critique of Postcolonial Reason:
Toward a History of the Vanishing Present

From *Chapter 3. History*

[CAN THE SUBALTERN SPEAK?]

* * *

In the face of the possibility that the intellectual is complicit in the persistent constitution of the Other as the Self's shadow, a possibility of political practice for the intellectual would be to put the economic "under erasure," to see the economic factor as irreducible as it reinscribes the social text, even as it is erased, however imperfectly, when it claims to be the final determinant or the transcendental signified.[1]

Until very recently, the clearest available example of such epistemic violence was the remotely orchestrated, far-flung, and heterogeneous project to constitute the colonial subject as Other. This project is also the asymmetrical obliteration of the trace of that Other in its precarious Subject-ivity. It is well known that Foucault locates one case of epistemic violence, a complete overhaul of the episteme, in the redefinition of madness at the end of the European eighteenth century.[2] But what if that particular redefinition was only a part of the narrative of history in Europe as well as in the colonies? What if the two projects of epistemic overhaul worked as dislocated and unacknowledged parts of a vast two-handed engine? Perhaps it is no more than to ask that the subtext of the palimpsestic narrative of imperialism be recognized as "subjugated knowledge," "a whole set of knowledges that have been disqualified as inadequate to their task or insufficiently elaborated: naive knowledges, located low down on the hierarchy, beneath the required level of cognition or scientificity."[3]

This is not to describe "the way things really were" or to privilege the narrative of history as imperialism as the best version of history. It is, rather, to continue the account of how *one* explanation and narrative of reality was established as the normative one. A comparable account in the case(s) of Central and Eastern Europe is soon to be launched. To elaborate on this, let us consider for the moment and briefly the underpinnings of the British codification of Hindu Law.

Once again, I am not a South Asianist. I turn to Indian material because I have some accident-of-birth facility there.

Here, then, is a schematic summary of the epistemic violence of the codi-

1. This argument is developed further in Spivak, "Scattered Speculations on the Question of Value," in *In Other Worlds: Essays in Cultural Politics* (New York: Methuen, 1987), pp. 154–75. Once again, the *Anti-Oedipus* did not ignore the economic text, although the treatment was perhaps too allegorical. In this respect, the move from schizo- to rhyzo-analysis in *A Thousand Plateaus* was not, perhaps, salutary [Spivak's note]. Some of the author's notes have been edited, and some omitted. In *A Thousand Plateaus* (1980), Gilles Deleuze and Felix Guattari argue for a model of knowledge patterned on fungal rhizomes, which lack centralized control or structure; their earlier *Anti-Oedipus: Capitalism and Schizophrenia* (1972) criticizes both orthodox Marxism and institutional Freudianism.
2. See Foucault, *Madness and Civilization: A History of Insanity in the Age of Reason*, trans. Richard Howard (New York: Pantheon, 1965), pp. 251, 262, 269 [Spivak's note].
3. Foucault, *Power/Knowledge: Selected Interviews and Other Writings, 1972–1977*, ed. Colin Gordon (New York: Pantheon, 1980), p. 82 [Spivak's note].

fication of Hindu Law. If it clarifies the notion of epistemic violence, my final discussion of widow-sacrifice may gain added significance.

At the end of the eighteenth century, Hindu Law, insofar as it can be described as a unitary system, operated in terms of four texts that "staged" a four-part episteme defined by the subject's use of memory: *sruti* (the heard), *smriti* (the remembered), *sāstra* (the calculus), and *vyavahāra* (the performance). The origins of what have been heard and what was remembered were not necessarily continuous or identical. Every invocation of sruti technically recited (or reopened) the event of originary "hearing" or revelation. The second two texts—the learned and the performed—were seen as dialectically continuous. Legal theorists and practitioners were not in any given case certain if this structure described the body of law or four ways of settling a dispute. The legitimation, through a binary vision, of the polymorphous structure of legal performance, "internally" noncoherent and open at both ends, is the narrative of codification I offer as an example of epistemic violence.

Consider the often-quoted programmatic lines from Macaulay's infamous "Minute on Indian Education" (1835):

> We must at present do our best to form a class who may be interpreters between us and the millions whom we govern; a class of persons, Indian in blood and colour, but English in taste, in opinions, in morals, and in intellect. To that class we may leave it to refine the vernacular dialects of the country, to enrich those dialects with terms of science borrowed from the Western nomenclature, and to render them by degrees fit vehicles for conveying knowledge to the great mass of the population.[4]

The education of colonial subjects complements their production in law. One effect of establishing a version of the British system was the development of an uneasy separation between disciplinary formation in Sanskrit studies and the native, now alternative, tradition of Sanskirt "high culture." In the first section, I have suggested that within the former, the cultural explanations generated by authoritative scholars matched the epistemic violence of the legal project.

Those authorities would be *the very best* of the sources for the nonspecialist French intellectual's entry into the civilization of the Other.[5] I am, however, not referring to intellectuals and scholars of colonial production, like Shastri,[6] when I say that the Other as Subject is inaccessible to Foucault and Deleuze. I am thinking of the general nonspecialist, nonacademic population across the class spectrum, for whom the episteme operates its silent programming function. Without considering the map of exploitation, on what grid of "oppression" would they place this motley crew?

Let us now move to consider the margins (one can just as well say the silent, silenced center) of the circuit marked out by this epistemic violence, men and women among the illiterate peasantry, Aboriginals, and the lowest strata of

4. Thomas Babington Macaulay, "Minute on Indian Education," in *Selected Writings*, ed. John Clive and Thomas Pinney (Chicago: University of Chicago Press, 1972), p. 249 [Spivak's note].
5. I have discussed this issue in greater detail with reference to Julia Kristeva's *About Chinese Women*, trans. Anita Barrows (New York: Urizen, 1977), in

"French Feminism in an International Frame," in *In Other Worlds*, pp. 136–41 [Spivak's note].
6. Haraprasad Shastri (1853–1931), a Sanskrit scholar) described by Spivak earlier in the chapter as a "learned Indianist, [and] brilliant representative of the indigenous elite within colonial production."

the urban subproletariat. According to Foucault and Deleuze (in the First World, under the standardization and regimentation of socialized capital, though they do not seem to recognize this) and mutatis mutandis the metropolitan[7] "third world feminist" only interested in resistance within capital logic, the oppressed, if given the chance (the problem of representation cannot be bypassed here), and on the way to solidarity through alliance politics (a Marxist thematic is at work here) *can speak and know their conditions*. We must now confront the following question: On the other side of the international division of labor from socialized capital, inside *and* outside the circuit of the epistemic violence of imperialist law and education supplementing an earlier economic text, *can the subaltern speak?*

We have already considered the possibility that, given the exigencies of the inauguration of colonial records, the instrumental woman (the Rani of Sirmur) is not fully written.[8]

Antonio Gramsci's[9] work on the "subaltern classes" extends the class-position / class-consciousness argument isolated in *The Eighteenth Brumaire*.[1] Perhaps because Gramsci criticizes the vanguardistic position of the Leninist intellectual,[2] he is concerned with the intellectual's rôle in the subaltern's cultural and political movement into the hegemony. This movement must be made to determine the production of history as narrative (of truth). In texts such as *The Southern Question*, Gramsci considers the movement of historical-political economy in Italy within what can be seen as an allegory of reading taken from or prefiguring an international division of labor.[3] Yet an account of the phased development of the subaltern is thrown out of joint when his cultural macrology[4] is operated, however remotely, by the epistemic interference with legal and disciplinary definitions accompanying the imperialist project. When I move, at the end of this essay, to the question of woman as subaltern, I will suggest that the possibility of collectivity itself is persistently foreclosed through the manipulation of female agency.

The first part of my proposition—that the phased development of the subaltern is complicated by the imperialist project—is confronted by the "Subaltern Studies" group.[5] They *must* ask, Can the subaltern speak? Here we are within Foucault's own discipline of history and with people who acknowledge his influence. Their project is to rethink Indian colonial historiography from the perspective of the discontinuous chain of peasant insurgencies during the colonial occupation. This is indeed the problem of "the permission to narrate" discussed by Said.[6] As Ranajit Guha, the founding editor of the collective, argues,

---

7. Of or pertaining to the "mother country," as distinguished from its colony.

8. In an earlier chapter, Spivak discusses the British intervention in 1915 to prevent the widow-suicide of the widow of the deposed leader of the province of Sirmur, which completely obscured the Rani's motives and wishes.

9. In his *Prison Notebooks* (published 1948–51), Gramsci applies the word *subaltern* to the proletariat.

1. *The Eighteenth Brumaire of Louis Napoleon* (1852), Marx's analysis of the dictatorship (later emperorship) declared by President Louis Bonaparte of France in 1851. Spivak has already argued that Marx explores the "gap" between "class-position" (a group's location in the economic relations of production) and "class-consciousness" (a group's ability to represent to itself the interests that stem from its class position).

2. I.e., the belief held by Lenin (but not Marx) that the proletarian revolution must be led by a vanguard.

3. Antonio Gramsci, *The Southern Question*, trans. Pasquale Verdicchio (West Lafayette, Ind.: Bordighera, 1995) [Spivak's note].

4. Prolonged discourse.

5. A group of radical historians in India associated with the annual publication *Subaltern Studies* (founded in 1982).

6. Edward W. Said, "Permission to Narrate," *London Review of Books*, February 16, 1984 [Spivak's note].

> The historiography of Indian nationalism has for a long time been dom-
> inated by elitism—colonialist elitism and bourgeois-nationalist elit-
> ism . . . shar[ing] the prejudice that the making of the Indian nation and
> the development of the consciousness—nationalism—which confirmed
> this process were exclusively or predominantly elite achievements. In the
> colonialist and neo-colonialist historiographies these achievements are
> credited to British colonial rulers, administrators, policies, institutions,
> and culture; in the nationalist and neo-nationalist writings—to Indian
> elite personalities, institutions, activities and ideas.[7]

Certain members of the Indian elite are of course native informants for first-
world intellectuals interested in the voice of the Other. But one must nevertheless insist that the colonized subaltern *subject* is irretrievably
heterogeneous.

Against the indigenous elite we may set what Guha calls "the *politics* of the
people," both outside ("this was an *autonomous* domain, for it neither originated from elite politics nor did its existence depend on the latter") and inside
("it continued to operate vigorously in spite of [colonialism], adjusting itself
to the conditions prevailing under the Raj and in many respects developing
entirely new strains in both form and content") the circuit of colonial production. I cannot entirely endorse this insistence of determinate vigor and
full autonomy, for practical historiographic exigencies will not allow such
endorsements to privilege subaltern consciousness. Against the possible
charge that his approach is essentialist, Guha constructs a definition of the
people (the place of that essence) that can be only an identity-in-differential.
He proposes a dynamic stratification grid describing colonial social production at large. Even the third group on the list, the buffer group, as it were,
between the people and the great macro-structural dominant groups, is itself
defined as a place of in-betweenness. The classification falls into: "dominant
foreign groups," and "dominant indigenous groups at the all-India and at the
regional and local levels" representing the elite; and "[t]he social groups and
elements included in [the terms "people" and "subaltern classes"] represent[ing] *the demographic difference between the total Indian population and
all those whom we have described as the "elite."*[8]

"The task of research" projected here is "to investigate, identify and measure the *specific* nature and degree of the *deviation* of [the] elements [consti-
tuting item 3] from the ideal and situate it historically." "Investigate, identify,
and measure the specific": a program could hardly be more essentialist and
taxonomic. Yet a curious methodological imperative is at work. I have argued
that, in the Foucault-Deleuze conversation, a post-representationalist vocabulary[9] hides an essentialist agenda. In subaltern studies, because of the violence of imperialist epistemic, social, and disciplinary inscription, a project
understood in essentialist terms must traffic in a radical textual practice of
differences. The object of the group's investigation, in this case not even of
the people as such but of the floating buffer zone of the regional elite—is a
deviation from an *ideal*—the people or subaltern—which is itself defined as
a difference from the elite. It is toward this structure that the research is ori-

7. Ranajit Guha, *Subaltern Studies* I (1982): 1
[Spivak's note].
8. Guha, pp. 4, 8 [Spivak's note].

9. That is, a vocabulary that champions difference
and the undecidable.

ented, a predicament rather different from the self-diagnosed transparency of the first-world radical intellectual. What taxonomy can fix such a space? Whether or not they themselves perceive it—in fact Guha sees his definition of "the people" within the master-slave dialectic[1]—their text articulates the difficult task of rewriting its own conditions of impossibility as the conditions of its possibility. "At the regional and local levels [the dominant indigenous groups] . . . if belonging to social strata hierarchically inferior to those of the dominant all-Indian groups *acted in the interests of the latter and not in conformity to interests corresponding truly to their own social being.*"[2] When these writers speak, in their essentializing language, of a gap between interest and action in the intermediate group, their conclusions are closer to Marx than to the self-conscious naivete of Deleuze's pronouncement on the issue. Guha, like Marx, speaks of interest in terms of the social rather than the libidinal being. The Name-of-the-Father imagery in *The Eighteenth Brumaire* can help to emphasize that, on the level of class or group action, "true correspondence to own being" is as artificial or social as the patronymic.[3]

It is to this intermediate group that the second woman in this chapter belongs.[4] The pattern of domination is here determined mainly by gender rather than class. The subordinated gender following the dominant within the challenge of nationalism while remaining caught within gender oppression is not an unknown story.

For the (gender-unspecified) "true" subaltern group, whose identity is its difference, there is no unrepresentable subaltern subject that can know and speak itself; the intellectual's solution is not to abstain from representation. The problem is that the subject's itinerary has not been left traced so as to offer an object of seduction to the representing intellectual. In the slightly dated language of the Indian group, the question becomes, How can we touch the consciousness of the people, even as we investigate their politics? With what voice-consciousness can the subaltern speak?

My question about how to earn the "secret encounter" with the contemporary hill women of Sirmur is a practical version of this. The woman of whom I will speak in this section was not a "true" subaltern, but a metropolitan middle-class girl. Further, the effort she made to write or speak her body was in the accents of accountable reason, the instrument of self-conscious responsibility. Still her Speech Act[5] was refused. She was made to unspeak herself posthumously, by other women. In an earlier version of this chapter, I had summarized this historical indifference and its results as: the subaltern cannot speak.

The critique by Ajit K. Chaudhury, a West Bengali Marxist, of Guha's search for the subaltern consciousness can be taken as representative of a moment of the production process that includes the subaltern.[6] Chaudhury's perception that the Marxist view of the transformation of consciousness

---

1. The process of recognition and identification described by Georg Wilhelm Friedrich Hegel in *Phenomenology of Spirit* (1807).
2. Guha, p. 1 [Spivak's note].
3. I.e., the Name-of-the-Father, a term used by Jacques Lacan in describing the child's entrance into the realm of language, law, and the father.
4. Bhubaneswari Bhaduri (see below).
5. An allusion to the speech act theory of the English philosopher J. L. Austin (1911–1960), who examined how words can do things.
6. Since then, in the disciplinary fallout after the serious electoral and terrorist augmentation of Hindu nationalism in India, more alarming charges have been leveled at the group. See Aijaz Ahmad, *In Theory: Classes, Nations, Literature* (London: Verso, 1992), pp. 68, 194, 207–11; and Sumit Sarkar, "The Fascism of the Sangh Parivar," *Economic and Political Weekly,* January 30, 1993, pp. 163–67 [Spivak's note].

involves the knowledge of social relations seems, in principle, astute. Yet the heritage of the positivist ideology that has appropriated orthodox Marxism obliges him to add this rider: "This is not to belittle the importance of understanding peasants' consciousness or workers' consciousness *in its pure form.* This enriches our knowledge of the peasant and the worker and, possibly, throws light on how a particular mode takes on different forms in different regions, *which is considered a problem of second order importance in classical Marxism.*[7]

This variety of "internationalist Marxism," which believes in a pure, retrievable form of consciousness only to dismiss it, thus closing off what in Marx remain moments of productive bafflement, can at once be the occasion for Foucault's and Deleuze's rejection of Marxism *and* the source of the critical motivation of the subaltern studies groups. All three are united in the assumption that there *is* a pure form of consciousness. On the French scene, there is a shuffling of signifiers: "the unconscious" or "the subject-in-oppression" clandestinely fills the space of "the pure form of consciousness." In orthodox "internationalist" intellectual Marxism, whether in the First World or the Third, the pure form of consciousness remains, paradoxically, a material effect, and therefore a second-order problem. This often earns it the reputation of racism and sexism. In the subaltern studies group it needs development according to the unacknowledged terms of its own articulation.

Within the effaced itinerary of the subaltern subject, the track of sexual difference is doubly effaced.[8] The question is not of female participation in insurgency, or the ground rules of the sexual division of labor, for both of which there is "evidence." It is, rather, that, both as object of colonialist historiography and as subject of insurgency, the ideological construction of gender keeps the male dominant. If, in the contest of colonial production, the subaltern has no history and cannot speak, the subaltern as female is even more deeply in shadow.

In the first part of this chapter we meditate upon an elusive female figure called into the service of colonialism. In the last part we will look at a comparable figure in anti-colonialist nationalism. The regulative psychobiography of widow self-immolation will be pertinent in both cases. In the interest of the invaginated spaces[9] of this book, let us remind ourselves of the gradual emergence of the new subaltern in the New World Order.[1]

* * *

I am generally sympathetic with the call to make U.S. feminism more "theoretical." It seems, however, that the problem of the muted subject of the subaltern woman, though not solved by an "essentialist" search for lost origins, cannot be served by the call for more theory in Anglo-America either.

That call is often given in the name of a critique of "positivism," which is seen here as identical with "essentialism." Yet Hegel, the modern inaugurator of "the work of the negative," was not a stranger to the notion of essences.

---

7. Ajit K. Chaudhury, "New Wave Social Science," *Frontier* 16.24 (January 28, 1984), p. 10. Emphasis mine [Spivak's note].
8. I do not believe that the recent trend of romanticizing anything written by the Aboriginal or outcaste intellectual has lifted the effacement [Spivak's note].
9. An allusion to the *écriture féminine* (feminine

writing) championed by the French feminist Helène Cixous (b. 1937) as well as a description of Spivak's method of folding together various arguments.
1. A phrase coined by President George H. W. Bush to describe what was needed to replace East-West cold war rivalries after communism collapsed in Eastern Europe.

For Marx, the curious persistence of essentialism within the dialectic was a profound and productive problem. Thus, the stringent binary opposition between positivism/essentialism (read, U.S.) and "theory" (read, French or Franco-German via Anglo-American) may be spurious. Apart from repressing the ambiguous complicity between essentialism and critiques of positivism (acknowledged by Derrida in "Of Grammatology as a Positive Science"[2]), it also errs by implying that positivism is not a theory. This move allows the emergence of a proper name, a positive essence, Theory. And once again, the position of the investigator remains unquestioned. If and when this territorial debate turns toward the Third World, no change in the question of method is to be discerned. This debate cannot take into account that, in the case of the woman as subaltern, rather few ingredients for the constitution of the itinerary of the trace of a sexed subject (rather than an anthropological object) can be gathered to locate the possibility of dissemination.[3]

Yet I remain generally sympathetic to aligning feminism with the critique of positivism and the defetishization of the concrete. I am also far from averse to learning from the work of Western theorists, though I have learned to insist on marking their positionality as investigating subjects. Given these conditions, and as a literary critic, I tactically confronted the immense problem of the consciousness of the woman as subaltern. I reinvented the problem in a sentence and transformed it into the object of a simple semiosis.[4] What can such a transformation mean?

This gesture of transformation marks the fact that knowledge of the other subject is theoretically impossible. Empirical work in the discipline constantly performs this transformation tacitly. It is a transformation from a first-second person performance to the constatation in the third person.[5] It is, in other words, at once a gesture of control and an acknowledgement of limits. Freud provides a homology[6] for such positional hazards.

Sarah Kofman has suggested that the deep ambiguity of Freud's use of women as a scapegoat may be read as a reaction-formation to an initial and continuing desire to give the hysteric a voice, to transform her into the *subject* of hysteria.[7] The masculine-imperialist ideological formation that shaped that desire into "the daughter's seduction"[8] is part of the same formation that constructs the monolithic "third-world woman." No contemporary metropolitan investigator is not influenced by that formation. Part of our "unlearning" project is to articulate our participation in that formation—by *measuring* silences, if necessary—into the *object* of investigation. Thus, when confronted with the questions, Can the subaltern speak?" and Can the subaltern (as woman) speak? our efforts to give the subaltern a voice in history will be doubly open to the dangers run by Freud's discourse. It is in acknowledgment of these dangers rather than as solution to a problem that I put together the sentence "White men are saving brown women from brown men," a sentence

2. A section of Jacques Derrida's *Of Grammatology* (1967; trans. 1977 by Spivak).

3. An allusion to Derrida, one of whose important works is titled *Dissemination* (1972).

4. The process of producing signs (and thereby making meaning).

5. In speech act theory, an utterance that describes a condition, fact, or state of affairs.

6. An example of similarity in structure due to similar development.

7. Sarah Kofman, *The Enigma of Woman: Woman in Freud's Writings*, trans. Catherine Porter (Ithaca, N.Y.: Cornell University Press, 1985) [Spivak's note].

8. A reference both to Freud's work on female hysteria (viewed as a symptom of frustrated sexual desire for a male authority figure) and to *The Daughter's Seduction* (1982), a book by Jane Gallop that describes feminist appropriations of Freud.

that runs like a red thread through today's "gender and development." My impulse is not unlike the one to be encountered in Freud's investigation of the sentence "A child is being beaten."[9]

The use of Freud here does not imply an isomorphic analogy between subject-formation and the behavior of social collectives, a frequent practice, often accompanied by a reference to Reich,[1] in the conversation between Deleuze and Foucault. I am, in other words, not suggesting that "White men are saving brown women from brown men" is a sentence indicating a *collective* fantasy symptomatic of a *collective* itinerary of sadomasochistic repression in a *collective* imperialist enterprise. There is a satisfying symmetry in such an allegory, but I would rather invite the reader to consider it a problem in "wild psychoanalysis" than a clinching solution.[2] Just as Freud's insistence on making the woman the scapegoat in "A child is being beaten" and elsewhere discloses his political interests, however imperfectly, so my insistence on imperialist subject-production as the occasion for this sentence discloses a politics that I cannot step around.

*　　*　　*

A young woman of sixteen or seventeen, Bhubaneswari Bhaduri, hanged herself in her father's modest apartment in North Calcutta in 1926. The suicide was a puzzle since, as Bhubaneswari was menstruating at the time, it was clearly not a case of illicit pregnancy. Nearly a decade later, it was discovered, in a letter she had left for her elder sister, that she was a member of one of the many groups involved in the armed struggle for Indian independence. She had been entrusted with a political assassination. Unable to confront the task and yet aware of the practical need for trust, she killed herself.

Bhubaneswari had known that her death would be diagnosed as the outcome of illegitimate passion. She had therefore waited for the onset of menstruation. While waiting, Bhubaneswari, the *brahmacārini*[3] who was no doubt looking forward to good wifehood, perhaps rewrote the social text of sati-suicide in an interventionist way. (One tentative explanation of her inexplicable act had been a possible melancholia brought on by her father's death and her brother-in-law's repeated taunts that she was too old to be not-yet-a-wife.) She generalized the sanctioned motive for female suicide by taking immense trouble to displace (not merely deny), in the physiological inscription of her body, its imprisonment within legitimate passion by a single male. In the immediate context, her act became absurd, a case of delirium rather than sanity. The displacing gesture—waiting for menstruation—is at first a reversal of the interdict against a menstruating widow's right to immolate herself; the unclean widow must wait, publicly, until the cleansing bath of the

9. Freud, " 'A Child Is Being Beaten': A Contribution to the Study of the Origin of Sexual Perversion," in *The Standard Edition of the Complete Psychological Works of Sigmund Freud*, ed. James Strachey, 24 vols. (London: Hogarth, 1953–74), 17:175–204. For a list of ways in which Western criticism constructs "third world women," see Chandra Talpade Mohanty, "Under Western Eyes: Feminist Scholarship and Colonial Discourses," in *Third World Women and the Politics of Feminism*, ed. Mohanty et al. (Bloomington: Indiana University Press, 1991), pp. 51–80 [Spivak's note].

1. Wilhelm Reich, who attempted in *Mass Psychology of Fascism* (1933) to psychoanalyze a whole society.

2. Freud, " 'Wild' Psycho-Analysis," in *Standard Edition*, 11:221–27. A good deal of psychoanalytic social critique would fit this description [Spivak's note]. "Wild" psychoanalysis jumps too quickly to conclusions.

3. Female member of the Brahmin (upper) caste (Hindi).

fourth day, when she is no longer menstruating, in order to claim her dubious privilege.

In this reading, Bhubaneswari Bhaduri's suicide is an unemphatic, ad hoc, subaltern rewriting of the social text of *sati*-suicide as much as the hegemonic account of the blazing, fighting, familial Durga.[4] The emergent dissenting possibilities of that hegemonic account of the fighting mother are well documented and popularly well remembered through the discourse of the male leaders and participants in the Independence movement. The subaltern as female cannot be heard or read.

I know of Bhubaneswari's life and death through family connections. Before investigating them more thoroughly, I asked a Bengali woman, a philosopher and Sanskritist whose early intellectual production is almost identical to mine, to start the process. Two responses: (a) Why, when her two sisters, Saileswari and Raseswari, led such full and wonderful lives, are you interested in the hapless Bhubaneswari? (b) I asked her nieces. It appears that it was a case of illicit love.

I was so unnerved by this failure of communication that, in the first version of this text, I wrote, in the accents of passionate lament: the subaltern cannot speak! It was an inadvisable remark.

In the intervening years between the publication of the second part of this chapter in essay form and this revision, I have profited greatly from the many published responses to it. I will refer to two of them here: "Can the Subaltern Vote?" and "Silencing Sycorax."[5]

As I have been insisting, Bhubaneswari Bhaduri was not a "true" subaltern. She was a woman of the middle class, with access, however clandestine, to the bourgeois movement for Independence. Indeed the Rani of Sirmur, with her claim to elevated birth, was not a subaltern at all. Part of what I seem to have argued in this chapter is that woman's interception of the claim to subalternity can be staked out across strict lines of definition by virtue of their muting by heterogeneous circumstances. Gulari[6] cannot speak to us because indigenous patriarchal "history" would only keep a record of her funeral and colonial history only needed her as an incidental instrument. Bhubaneswari attempted to "speak" by turning her body into a text of woman / writing. The immediate passion of my declaration "the subaltern cannot speak," came from the despair that, in her own family, among women, in no more than fifty years, her attempt had failed. I am not laying the blame for the muting on the *colonial* authorities here, as Busia seems to think: "Gayatri Spivak's 'Can the Subaltern Speak?'—section 4 of which is a compelling explication of this role of disappearing in the case of Indian women in British legal history."[7]

I am pointing, rather, at her silencing by her own more emancipated granddaughters: a new mainstream. To this can be added two newer groups; one,

---

4. In Hindu mythology and religion, the warrior form of Devi (the divine mother goddess).
5. Lecrom Medovoi et al., "Can the Subaltern Vote?" *Socialist Review* 20.3 (July–September 1990): 133–49; and Abena Busia, "Silencing Sycorax: On African Colonial Discourse and the Unvoiced Female," *Cultural Critique*, no. 14 (Winter 1989–90): 81–104 [Spivak's note]. Spivak's

original essay was "Can the Subaltern Speak?" in *Marxism and the Interpretation of Culture*, ed. Cary Nelson and Lawrence Grossberg (Urbana: University of Illinois Press, 1988), pp. 271–313.
6. The family name of the Rani of Sirmur.
7. Busia, "Silencing Sycorax," p. 102 [Spivak's note].

the liberal multiculturalist metropolitan academy, Susan Barton's[8] great-granddaughters; as follows:

As I have been saying all along, I think it is important to acknowledge our complicity in the muting, in order precisely to be more effective in the long run. Our work cannot succeed if we always have a scapegoat. The post-colonial migrant investigator is touched by the colonial social formations. Busia strikes a positive note for further work when she points out that, after all, I am able to read Bhubaneswari's case, and therefore she *has* spoken in some way. Busia is right, of course. All speaking, even seemingly the most immediate, entails a distanced decipherment by another, which is, at best, an interception. That is what speaking is.

I acknowledge this theoretical point, and also acknowledge the practical importance, for oneself and others, of being upbeat about future work. Yet the moot decipherment by another in an academic institution (willy-nilly a knowledge-production factory) many years later must not be too quickly identified with the "speaking" of the subaltern. It is not a mere tautology to say that the colonial or postcolonial subaltern is defined as the being on the other side of difference, or an epistemic fracture, even from other groupings among the colonized. What is at stake when we insist that the subaltern speaks?

In "Can the Subaltern Vote?" the three authors apply the question of stakes to "political speaking." This seems to me to be a fruitful way of extending my reading of subaltern speech into a collective arena. Access to "citizenship" (civil society) by becoming a voter (in the nation) is indeed the symbolic circuit of the mobilizing of subalternity into hegemony. This terrain, ever negotiating between national liberation and globalization, allows for examining the casting of the vote itself as a performative convention given as constative "speech" of the subaltern subject. It is part of my current concerns to see how this set is manipulated to legitimize globalization; but it is beyond the scope of this book. Here let us remain confined to the field of academic prose, and advance three points:

1. Simply by being postcolonial or the member of an ethnic minority, we are not "subaltern." That word is reserved for the sheer heterogeneity of decolonized space.

2. When a line of communication is established between a member of sub-altern groups and the circuits of citizenship or institutionality, the subaltern has been inserted into the long road to hegemony. Unless we want to be romantic purists or primitivists about "preserving subalternity"—a contradiction in terms—this is absolutely to be desired. (It goes without saying that museumized or curricularized access to ethnic origin—another battle that must be fought—is not identical with preserving subalternity.) Remembering this allows us to take pride in our work without making missionary claims.

3. This trace-structure (effacement in disclosure) surfaces as the tragic emotions of the political activist, springing not out of superficial utopianism, but out of the depths of what Bimal Krishna Matilal has called "moral

8. The daughter whose mother refuses to acknowledge her as her own in Daniel Defoe's novel *Roxana: The Fortunate Mistress* (1724). The South African writer J. M. Coetzee uses Susan Barton as the narrator for much (but not all) of his retelling of the Robinson Crusoe story in his novel *Foe* (1987), a retelling that Spivak discusses at length in chapter 2 of *A Critique of Postcolonial Reason*.

love." Mahasweta Devi,[9] herself an indefatigable activist, documents this emotion with exquisite care in "Pterodactyl, Puran Sahay, and Pirtha."

And finally, the third group: Bhubaneswari's elder sister's eldest daughter's eldest daughter's eldest daughter is a new U.S. immigrant and was recently promoted to an executive position in a U.S.-based transnational. She will be helpful in the emerging South Asian market precisely because she is a well-placed Southern diasporic.

> For Europe, the time when the new capitalism *definitely* superseded the old can be established with fair precision: it was the beginning of the twentieth century . . . [With t]he boom at the end of the nineteenth century and the crisis of 1900–03 . . . [c]artels become one of the foundations of the whole of economic life. Capitalism has been transformed into imperialism.[1]

Today's program of global financialization carries on that relay. Bhubaneswari had fought for national liberation. Her great-grandniece works for the New Empire. This too is a historical silencing of the subaltern. When the news of this young woman's promotion was broadcast in the family amidst general jubilation I could not help remarking to the eldest surviving female member: "Bhubaneswari"—her nickname had been Talu—"hanged herself in vain," but not too loudly. Is it any wonder that this young woman is a staunch multiculturalist, believes in natural childbirth, and wears only cotton?

1999

9. Indian author (b. 1925), who writes in Bengali; some of her work has been translated into English by Spivak. Matilal (1935–1991), Indian philosopher who taught at Oxford University for many years.

1. V. I. Lenin, *Imperialism: The Highest Stage of Capitalism: A Popular Outline* [1916] (London: Junius; Chicago: Pluto, 1996), pp. 15, 17 [Spivak's note].

SHIRLEY GEOK-LIN LIM
b. 1944

Poet, novelist, memoirist, literary critic, and anthologist, Shirley Geok-lin Lim was born in Malacca, Malaysia. In 1980, she was the first woman and the first Asian to receive the Commonwealth Poetry Prize for her first book of verse, *Crossing the Peninsula and Other Poems*. Teaching at both the University of Hong Kong and the University of California, Santa Barbara, Lim has played a pioneering role in the emergence of Asian American literary and cultural studies. She has published numerous essays on postcolonial literature, Asian American fiction, and feminist theory in leading American journals, while her memoir, *Among the White Moon Faces: An Asian-American Memoir of Homelands* (1996), received the 1997 American Book Award. Along with the meditations of such critics as Elaine Kim, Sau-ling Wong, and King-Kok Cheung, Shirley Geok-lin Lim's work co-editing *The Forbidden Stitch: An Asian American Women's Anthology* (1989), as well as numerous critical anthologies, has helped make possible the mapping of Asian American literature produced by women from many different ethnic and geographical backgrounds.

From Complications of Feminist and Ethnic Literary Theories in Asian American Literature[1]

* * *

The asymmetrical goals of feminist and ethnic scholars within the same institutional structures have given rise to conflict and hostility.[2] The gender/ethnic split is mirrored, moreover, in *both* communities, among white feminists who, according to some women of color, have been defining feminism in narrow terms privileged by their positions as whites, and among men of color who, "desiring to maintain power over 'their women' at all costs, have been among the most willing reinforcers of the fears and myths about the women's movement, attempting to scare us away from figuring things out for ourselves."[3]

Nevertheless, feminist and ethnic literary discourses, although demonstrating this asymmetry, are often inextricably intertwined. Both practices have led to personally charged readings whose impetus and power relate critically suspect notions such as experience, the subjective, and the local to ideologies undergirding literary evaluation. Feminist and ethnic literary criticisms resist and interrogate the claim that aesthetic criteria form a dominant, autonomous, objective, privileged position.[4] Both are said to lack a specifying theory. Although feminist literary criticism is seen as more sociopolitically driven than literary by critics such as Ellen Messer-Davidow,[5] other critics such as Hazel V. Carby have questioned the value of an essentially black theory and practice of criticism, noting of Henry Louis Gates's ethnic-based theory that "the exposition of uniquely black literary strategies is accomplished as much through the work of Geoffrey Hartman, Harold Bloom, Jacques Lacan and others as it is through the insights of a wide range of African American critics, including Houston Baker, Amiri Imamu Baraka and Sterling Brown."[6] Generally, feminist and ethnic critics oppose hegemonic disciplines. Many have presented themselves as cultural pluralists and

1. This essay is a revised and expanded version of an article originally published in *Feminist Studies* 19 (Fall 1993): 571–96, by permission of the publisher, Feminist Studies, Inc. [all notes are Lim's].
2. Many women of color scholars have written of what Barbara Christian has called the "conflict of choice and possibility" caused by divergent ethnic and feminist lines of inquiry. See her article, "But Who Do You Really Belong to—Black Studies or Women's Studies?" In *Across Cultures: The Spectrum of Women's Lives*, ed. Emily K. Abel and Marjorie L. Pearson (New York: Gordon and Breach, 1989), 18. Patricia Zavella indicts "the early feminist criticisms of the nuclear family" and asserts that for some Chicanas "the white, middle-class focus of American feminism" implied a form of racism ("The Problematic Relationship of Feminism and Chicana Studies," ibid., 26).
3. Barbara Smith, introduction to *Home Girls: A Black Feminist Anthology* (New York: Kitchen Table, Women of Color Press, 1983), xxv.
4. See Donna Perry, "Procne's Song: The Task of Feminist Literary Criticism," in *Gender/Body/ Knowledge: Feminist Reconstructions of Being and Knowing*, ed. Alison M. Jaggar and Susan R. Bordo (New Brunswick: Rutgers University Press, 1989).

Perry nicely summarizes feminist literary criticism's political agenda, pointing out that "it originates in the critic's recognition that women, whatever their race or color, experience the world differently from men, that their status outside the dominant white male middle-class culture allows (or even compels) them to critique it. . . . The feminist literary critic is committed to changing the world by challenging patriarchal assumptions, judgments, and values, particularly as they affect women" (293).
5. Messer-Davidow argues that the "subject of feminist literary criticisms appears to be not literature but the feminist study of ideas about sex and gender that people express in literary and critical media" and from that premise concludes for a position of "perspectivity" which assumes that "we as diverse knowers must insert ourselves and our perspectives into the domain of the study and become, self-reflexively, part of the investigation." See "The Philosophical Bases of Feminist Literary Criticisms," *New Literary History* 19 (Autumn 1987): 11, 88.
6. Hazel V. Carby, "Telling Fruit from Roots," *Times Literary Supplement*, December 29, 1989–January 4, 1990, 1446.

revisionists calling attention to, among other things, neglected or omitted texts that, even by established standards, should be admitted into the canon.[7] They operate as interventionists disrupting the totalizing naturalization of white male culture.

These common purposes, however, do not imply that feminist and ethnic criticisms share inherently sympathetic identities or areas of overlap that allow them to synthesize critical orientations. Even when, bound together in a common cause of revising the canon, both feminist and ethnic critics select similar ethnic texts, one cannot assume that they share integral or identical traditions. My essay attempts to unpack textual instances in which ethnic and feminist issues have intersected to analyze how their diverging emphases necessitate an ethnic cultural nuancing of conventional Euro-American feminist positions on gender/power relations and a feminist critique of ethnic-specific identity. In the analysis of ethnic identity, politics, and feminist ideological conjunctions, I argue, first, that much of Asian American literature has been an active site of masculinist views and feminist resistance; and second, that these women's texts are symptomatic of the struggle to refigure the subject between the often oppositional demands of ethnic and gender identity. In addition, I argue that the increased presence of Filipino Americans and the entry of immigrants from recently decolonized Asian countries to the United States after the 1965 revision of the immigration laws, together with the introduction of postcolonial studies into the university, point to a further complication of periodization for Asian American women's writing. Thus postcolonial Asian American women's writing, foregrounding a globalized rather than U.S. domestic historical context, has made provisional earlier attempts at periodizing an Asian American women's literary tradition. The tension, to my mind, is not merely or wholly over the question of who should be read—male or female writers, whose canon is it, anyway?—but over how representation of the subject is negotiated between ethnic and feminist thematics and how a consideration of gender and of other categories such as nation and postcolonialism, in addition to ethnicity, problematizes issues of canon formation and periodization.

The polarities between masculinist and feminist assertions of identity were already in place in the traditional East Asian patriarchal constructions of society.[8] They were further exacerbated by a history of racism (similar histories

7. For a critique of the problematics of pluralism raised by feminist literary inquiry, see Annette Kolodny, "Dancing through the Minefield: Some Observations on the Theory, Practice, and Politics of a Feminist Literary Criticism," in *The New Feminist Criticism*, ed. Elaine Showalter (New York: Pantheon Books, 1985), 144–67. While Kolodny acknowledges that pluralism "seems to threaten a kind of chaos for the future of literary inquiry," she asserts that the task for feminist critics is "to initiate nothing less than a playful pluralism, responsive to the possibilities of multiple critical schools and methods" (161).

8. For discussions of women's positions in traditional Asian patriarchal social structures, see Kay Ann Johnson, *Women, the Family, and Peasant Revolution in China* (Chicago: University of Chicago Press, 1983); Marilyn Blatt Young, ed., *Women in China: Studies in Social Change and Feminism* (Ann Arbor: Center for Chinese Studies, University of Michigan, 1973); Judith Stacey, *Patriarchy and*

Socialist Revolution in China (Berkeley: University of California Press, 1983); Sharon L. Sievers, *Flowers in Salt: The Beginnings of Feminist Consciousness in Modern Japan* (Stanford: Stanford University Press, 1983); Susan Pharr, ed., *Political Women in Japan* (Berkeley: University of California Press, 1981); Takie Sugiyama Lebra, *Japanese Women: Constraint and Fulfillment* (Honolulu: University of Hawaii Press, 1984); Alice Chai, "Korean Women in Hawaii," in *Women in New Worlds*, 1903–1945, ed. Hilah F. Thomas and Rosemary Skinner Keller (Nashville: Abingdon Press, 1981), 77–87; Sheila Rowbotham, *Women, Resistance and Revolution* (New York: Vintage, 1972), especially the chapter "When the Sand-Grouse Flies to Heaven," 170–99; Sylvia A. Chipp and Justin J. Green, eds., *Asian Women in Transition* (University Park: Pennsylvania State University Press, 1980); Judy Chu, "Southeast Asian Women in Transition," paper presented at the Immigrant Women Project, Long Beach, Califor-

apply to Chinese, Japanese, South Asian, and Filipino male immigration and delayed or difficult entry for women) that disempowered Asian males and separated them for long periods from women and families, and by the entry of Asian social norms into a differently restrictive American culture.[9] These polarities can be seen as still operative in the debates over Asian American women marrying out and in the debates that occasionally flare up to illuminate the problems of power relations between Asian American men and women.[1]

It was only in the 1970s that the notion of a body of Asian American literature recognizable as a separate canon became common. This literature can be said to represent that paradoxical phenomenon known as a "new tradition." Even as the texts are self-conscious expressions of "a new political consciousness and identity," their commentaries locate them in a "recovered" ethnic history. Texts like Maxine Hong Kingston's *Woman Warrior* and *China Men* are like a slow development of photographs taken years ago; even as their textuality appears for the first time before our eyes, we are reminded that the images were posed in a time already past, that history and textuality form one subject.[2] The commentator observes the coloration of the text as it appears for the first time with a postmodern consciousness of the text's belatedness, an awareness that the images are to be understood in the contexts of a lapidary of discourses on and from the past: memoir, myth, family and community history, folktales, talk-story.[3] This insistence on past narratives, whether as Old World culture and values, immigrant history, race suffering, communal traditions, or earlier other language traces, is a marked feature of much Asian American literature and criticism, just as the recovery of a

---

nia, September 1984; Beverley Lindsay, ed., *Comparative Perspectives of Third World Women* (New York: Praeger, 1980); and Perdita Huston, *Third World Women Speak Out: Interviews in Six Countries on Change, Development and Basic Needs* (New York: Praeger, 1979). Recent studies of the role of international corporate capital and development in further eroding Asian women's human rights include Rachel Grossman, "Women's Place in the Integrated Circuit," *Southeast Asia Chronicle–Pacific Research* 66 (January–February 1979): 2–17; Marlyn, "The Sale of Sexual Labor in the Philippines: Marlyn's Story," introduced and translated by Brenda Stoltzfus, *Bulletin of Concerned Asian Scholars* 22 (1990): 13–19.

9. Sexual dysfunction and misogyny among Chinese immigrants, resulting from long separations from their womenfolk, a social phenomenon created by the various Asian Exclusion Acts between 1882 to 1943, are documented, for example, in Paul C. P. Siu's *The Chinese Laundryman: A Study of Social Isolation*, ed. John Kuo Wei Tchen (New York: New York University Press, 1987), esp. 250–71. Sucheta Mazumdar points out that "for immigrant women arrival in America can be liberating. Societal norms of the majority community frequently provide greater personal freedom than permitted in Asian societies" (p.15). See "General Introduction: A Woman-Centered Perspective on Asian American History," in *Making Waves*, ed. Asian Women United of California (Boston: Beacon Press, 1989), 1–22. Psychological studies have posited that "conflicts between traditional Chinese roles and feminist orientations may exist for many Chinese American females" (Stanley Sue and James K. Morishima, "Personality, Sex-Role Conflict, and Ethnic Identity," in *The Mental Health of*

Asian Americans [San Francisco: Jossey-Bass, 1982], 93–125).

1. The hostility roused in Asian American men at Asian American women who date or marry outside their ethnic community has not yet been documented, but various personal writings testify to its existence. See, for example, Tommy S. Kim's "Asian Goils Are Easy," in *Tealeaves* (University of California Berkeley, Fall 1989), 24:

> Oriental sluts with attitudes:
> I'm so, special so unique—no
> boy Chinee
> understand me—no
> satisfy need. . . .
> A race of Wong—
> wanna-be's: Suzie
> feeling sick
> 'cause she needs white dick
> to fix an itch
> in her too-tight twat.

2. See Carol Neubauer, "Developing Ties to the Past: Photography and Other Sources of Information on Maxine Hong Kingston's *China Men*," *MELUS* 10 (1983): 17–36, for a discussion of how Kingston uses photographs to help develop her strategy of memory in her memoirs.

3. For discussions of Kingston's postmodernist genre collages, see Linda Ching Sledge, "Maxine Hong Kingston's China Men: The Family Historian as Epic Poet," *MELUS* 7 (1980): 3–22, and Marilyn Yalom's "The Woman Warrior as Postmodern Autobiography," in *Approaches to Teaching Kingston's The Woman Warrior*, ed. Shirley Geoklin Lim (New York: Modern Language Association Press, 1991).

woman's culture, woman's language, and neglected women's texts and traditions forms a major feature of feminist criticism.[4]

Defining the Field

Three publication events mark the increasing acceptance of an Asian American canon: the appearance of three anthologies (*Asian American Authors,* 1972; *Asian-American Heritage: An Anthology of Prose and Poetry,* 1974; *Aiiieeeee!: An Anthology of Asian American Writers,* 1974) in the early 1970s; the first book-length study of the literature, Elaine H. Kim's *Asian American Literature: An Introduction to the Writings and Their Social Context,* in 1982; and the 1988 *Asian American Literature: An Annotated Bibliography* edited by King-Kok Cheung and Stan Yogi, which conferred academic legitimacy to the field through its publication by the Modern Language Association Press.[5] These publications relate coherent historiographies of an Asian American literary tradition and of the contesting of that tradition. In doing so, they also provide a grounding for the culture and affect its identity formation for the future.

Like feminist critics, these ethnic-identified critics share the task of identifying and countering stereotypes. Their criticism in the 1970s, exemplified by the influential introduction of *Aiiieeeee!,* was restricted to a critique of stereotypes of the emasculated Asian American male. These critics modeled their thinking on the militant African American antiacademic rhetoric manifested in Ishmael Reed's work.[6] Unfortunately, they also adopted Reed's sexist stance. Ironically, the attack on male stereotypes reiterated and reinforced stereotypes of females. In the *Aiiieeeee!* introduction, the animus against stereotypes appears specially reserved for women writers of Chinese American descent who were accused of collaborating with white supremacists in propagating the stereotypes of the submissive, patriotic, model and "dual-personality" (a psychological term used by sociologists of the 1950s to explain the consequences of biculturality on Japanese Americans) Asian American.[7]

Chinese American women writers were conspicuous for their absence from these anthologies. In the issue of the *Yardbird Reader* (1974), guest-edited by Frank Chin and Shawn Wong, only four women writers are represented: two

4. For examples of historical and archival recoveries, see Marlon K. Hom, *Songs of Gold Mountain: Cantonese Rhymes from San Francisco Chinatown* (Berkeley: University of California Press, 1987); Him Mark Lai, *A History Reclaimed: An Annotated Bibliography of Chinese Language Materials on the Chinese of America,* ed. Russell Leong and Jean Pang Yip (Los Angeles: Resource Development and Publications, Asian American Studies Center, University of California, 1986); Mark Him Lai, Genny Lim, and Judy Yung, eds. and trans., *Island: Poetry and History of Chinese Immigrants on Angel Island,* 1910–1940 (San Francisco: HOCDOI, 1980); and Sau-ling Wong, "Tales of Postwar Chinatown: Short Stories of the Bud, 1947–1948," *Amerasia* 14 (1988): 61–79.

5. Kai-yu Hsu and Helen Palubinskas, eds., *Asian-American Authors* (1972; rpt. Boston: Houghton Mifflin, 1976); David Hsin-Fu Wand, ed., *Asian-American Heritage: An Anthology of Prose and Poetry* (New York: Washington Square Press, 1974); Frank Chin et al., eds., *Aiiieeeee! An*

Anthology of Asian-American Writers (1974; rpt. Washington, D.C.: Howard University Press, 1983); Elaine H. Kim, *Asian American Literature: An Introduction to the Writings and Their Social Context* (Philadelphia: Temple University Press, 1982); King-Kok Cheung and Stan Yogi, *Asian American Literature: An Annotated Bibliography* (New York: MLA Press, 1988).

6. Ishmael Reed encouraged Frank Chin and Shawn Wong; Chin appeared in *Yardbird Reader* 2 (1973): 21–46; and *Yardbird Reader* 3, vi–x. Chin and Wong guest-edited a special Asian American issue of *Yardbird Reader* 3 (1974). Reed's invective against African American women writers for their feminist critiques of African American male abuse, which he claims is a form of scapegoating that plays to racist sentiments, is manifest in his polemical satire, *Reckless Eyeballing* (London: Allison & Busby, 1989).

7. See Chin et al., eds., *Aiiieeeee!,* 14–15, for a criticism of the stereotype of the demasculinized male in Asian American culture.

Japanese American short story writers, Hisaye Yamamoto and Wakako Yamauchi, a Filipina poet, Cyn. Zarco, and a Chinese-German American poet, Mei Berssenbrugge, against eleven men, of whom eight are Chinese Americans. In *Aiiieeeee!*, again only four women writers are included against ten men, and only one of the women was Chinese American, as opposed to five Chinese American male writers. One may be led to conclude from these selections that this ethnic literature up to the 1970s was full of talented male writers and most deficient in women writers. The 1991 *Big Aiiieeeee!*, which despite the title is a completely different anthology from the 1974 work, fails to include any Chinese American women writers.[8] That the 1974 selection is distorted is evident from the editors' introduction, which is replete with references to Chinese American women scholars and writers whose works are critiqued and denigrated. The 1974 anthology can be said to be superseded by the 1991 work, but its editorial arguments are still significant today because they helped form a generation of opinion on Asian American cultural identity.

Aiiieeeee! set out to be more than a collection of works by writers of Asian descent. The editors asserted an authority as culture makers and namers, authorizing their version of Asian American sensibility. In their introduction, they assailed the assumption of continuity between Asian American culture and Asian culture. The positive valuation of Asian culture undergirding the American perception of the Asian American, they argued, was "a work of racist art" to keep the Asian American estranged from America. This reified representation insists on an identity as Old World Asian, preventing the perception of dynamism, hybridity, New World vitality, and other more interactive qualities that characterize a burgeoning ethnic culture in the United States. Offering black American culture as their model, the editors argued that Asian Americans should "invent" their culture, not passively accept the distortions of high Asian cultural elements that white Americans foist on them. Consequently, they certified as authentic only those writers who exhibited "Asian American," rather than an Asian or Euro-American, sensibility. This sensibility, the editors concluded, was specifically constructed through male-centered language and culture: "Language is the medium of culture and the people's sensibility, including the style of manhood. . . . On the simplest level, a man in any culture speaks for himself. Without a language of his own, he is no longer a man."[9] The assumption, therefore, is that Asian American men who assert "manhood" decide, possess, and exhibit the legitimate cultural national sensibility.

Elaine H. Kim's chapter "Chinatown Cowboys and Warrior Women" in her study *Asian American Literature: An Introduction to the Writings and Their Social Context* provides an early critique of the masculinism evident in the *Aiiieeeee!* introduction. Analyzing Frank Chin's essays and dramas, Kim concludes that his "sexism, cynicism, and sense of alienation (among other factors) have prevented him from creating protagonists who can overcome the devastating effects of racism on Chinese American men."[1] In a later essay, Kim revises her critique to render a more harmonious, less oppositional read-

8. *The Big Aiiieeeee!*, ed. Jeffery Paul Chan, Frank Chin, Lawson Fusao Inada, and Shawn Wong (New York: Meridan, 1991).
9. Chin et al., eds., *Aiiieeeee!*, 35.

1. Elaine H. Kim, *Asian American Literature: An Introduction to the Writings and Their Social Context* (Philadelphia: Temple University Press, 1982), 189.

ing of Asian American writing. Agreeing in part with the *Aiiieeeee!* editors, Kim argues that U.S. race and gender hierarchies have objectified Asian Americans as permanent outsiders and sexual deviants: "Asian men have been coded as having no sexuality, while Asian women have nothing else." While such social realities have resulted in differences between nationalist and feminist concerns, the woman's voice in works such as Kingston's *Tripmaster Monkey*, she asserts, "dissolves binary oppositions of ethnicity and gender."[2]

My own reading of Asian American literature demonstrates less a solution than a continuous negotiation between often conflicting cultural constructions of ethnicity and gender. To my mind, in the years after publication of Kingston's *Woman Warrior* in 1976, Asian American literature has often been the site of conscious and explicit conflict, between women's ideas of culture and cultural nationalism as claimed by some males, preeminently presented in the *Aiiieeeee!* introduction and more curiously elaborated as neo-Confucianist ideology in Frank Chin's essay in *The Big Aiiieeeee!*[3] This gender split was explicitly caused by the intervention of feminist issues and is marked historically in the publication of two anthologies of women's writing in 1989, *The Forbidden Stitch: An Asian American Women's Anthology* and *Making Waves: An Anthology of Writings by and About Asian American Women*. These anthologies, though not directly addressing the masculinist ideology that undergirded the 1970s literary movement, exhibit a difference from the earlier anthologies in their constituting of ethnic subject and culture. Primarily, they are a stage for women who claim, not the minor representation given in the 1970s anthologies, but all of the attention. Men are present in the work, but they often appear as aggressors or ignorant of women's needs: "He beat me with the hem of a kimono"; "Father's belt"; "Men know nothing of sex."[4] Moreover, the works counter stereotypes of Asian American women in Asian and white cultures. *Making Waves* features sociological and historical essays that analyze images of Asian women in the media ("Lotus Blossoms Don't Bleed: Images of Asian Women") and express the dilemma of living biculturally in societies that insist on a hegemonic identity ("Growing up Asian in America").[5]

More significantly, in contrast to the 1970s male critique of the concept of "dual personality," the anthologies foreground the instabilities of identity and represent the oscillating and crisscrossing of national, racial, and subjective borders that characterize the experience of biculturalism: "How is one to know and define oneself? From the inside—within a context that is self defined, from a grounding in community and a connection with culture and history that are comfortably accepted? Or from the outside—in terms of messages received from the media and people who are often ignorant?"[6] Kesaya E. Noda's essay, for example, beginning in "confusions and distortions," resolves itself in its construction of "I am racially Japanese," "I am a Japan-

2. Elaine H. Kim, " 'Such Opposite Creatures': Men and Women in Asian American Literature," *Michigan Quarterly Review* 29 (Winter 1990): 69, 71.
3. Maxine Hong Kingston, *The Woman Warrior: Memoirs of a Girlhood among Ghosts* (New York: Knopf, 1976); Frank Chin, "Come All Ye Asian American Writers of the Real and the Fake," in *The Big Aiiieeeee!*, 1–92.
4. Shirley Geok-lin Lim and Mayumi Tsutakawa, eds., *The Forbidden Stitch: An Asian American Women's Anthology* (Corvallis, Ore.: Calyx, 1989), 85, 91. 79.
5. *Making Waves*, ed. Asian Women United of California, 308, 243.
6. Kesaya E. Noda, "Growing Up Asian in America," ibid., 244.

ese American," "I am a Japanese American woman." This tripartite construction of Asian American identity, affirmatively propositional, counters the
1970s syllogistic construction: "I am not Asian," "I am not white American,"
"I am Asian American (male)." The feminist intervention in the evolving tradition of this writing has led to a reclamation of mother/other origin, an affirmation of continuity or relation between origin and present tense, and a new
foregrounding of gender identity. Paradoxically, the absence of an attempt to
illuminate an Asian American sensibility has resulted in the affirmation of
sensibilities marked by softened categories, elastic cultural spaces, and a
more global antihegemonic construction of identity.

In contrast to the *Aiiieeeee!* anthology, neither women's anthology attempts
to explicate an exclusive boundary of ethnic sensibility. In fact, the selection
of works that manifest emotional and physical bonds to a non-American
homeland indicates an elastic sense of identity to encompass the past of Asian
national identity as well as an American writing in the present. Moreover, no
attempt is made to separate the selections into ethnic groups; work by South
Asian, Korean, Filipino, Japanese, Chinese, and other Asian American
women appear side by side organized thematically or sequentially. Thus,
together with an increased diversity of Asian national representations is a
decreased emphasis on categorical national difference. The very multiplicity
appears to result in a blurring of national boundaries and an assertion of organizational principles through commonalities of experience rather than differences of attributes.

The 1980s selections of Asian American women's writing share with the
1970s anthologies general themes of immigrant concerns and first-
generation conflicts, acknowledgment of cultural sources and roots in Asian
societies, and thematics of family bond and conflicts. *The Forbidden Stitch*
foregrounds new writing that manifests "subjectivity as gendered," inclusive
of a "contemporary Asian American culture [that] is not dictated from a central committee."[7] The editors of the 1980s anthologies worked in collectives,
as communities of women. The ethnic culture of these anthologies is nonau-
thoritative, decentered, nondogmatic, unprogrammatic, uncategorizing,
inclusive, qualities that some feminist theoreticians such as Carol Gilligan
argue characterize female sensibilities.[8]

The editors avoided propositions that constructed universalist notions of
Asian American women's experiences. In the introductory essay to *Making
Waves*, for example, Sucheta Mazumdar argues that for Asian Americans
whose histories of exclusion, isolation, discrimination, exploitation, and
internment result in "severe trauma," "ethnic identity supersedes gender and
class. For women of color, concerns arising out of racial identity are an integral aspect of their overall identity." Yet many exceptions exist to this general
observation. As Mazumdar elaborates: "The impact of gender on Asian
women in America varies enormously even within the same class and ethnic
group. While the idea that female children are of less value than male children permeates all Asian cultures . . . the effect of this value-system on an
American-born woman is quite different than on an immigrant one."

---

7. Lim and Tsutakawa, *Forbidden Stitch*, 14.
8. Carol Gilligan, *In a Different Voice: Psychologi-* *cal Theory and Women's Development* (Cambridge, Mass.: Harvard University Press, 1982).

For the Asian-born woman, moving away from a relatively closed patriarchal world into a relatively democratized, egalitarian, interrogative America, immigration can be a liberalizing and freeing experience. Mazumdar cites a national survey of college-educated women from India living in the United States that showed 33.3 percent of the women working in the technical fields and 50 percent in the academic fields describing themselves as feminists.[9] Traditional Asian valuation of authoritarian husbands is frequently subverted by the working woman's growing economic independence and interaction in larger social relations that reflect different, more positive values of the female.

✳ ✳ ✳

The Intervention of Postcoloniality

The pioneering work done by the two 1980s anthologies, *The Forbidden Stitch* and *Making Waves*, was carried forward by other women-centered anthologies in the 1990s, many of them more explicitly bounded by regional and more strictly defined identities.[1] Despite the complaint that South Asian American communities have been usually neglected in Asian American Studies, South Asian American women's anthologies now lead in numbers of publications.[2] These and other more recent publications, especially of Filipino American and Southeast Asian American works,[3] point to a further complication with the intersection of three, rather than two, emergent fields: not simply Women's Studies with its emphasis on the saliency of gender in constructing knowledge overlapping with Asian American literature, usually read within the interpretative practices of literary scholarship, most recently within a deconstructive unpacking of identity thematics, but also postcolonial writing, which foregrounds a global historical context, testifying to "the problem of oppression, of one nation or people constructing a discourse of violence to dominate others." The three overlapping contextual concerns, shared thematic resonances, and common theoretical terms are sutured in these texts—for example, Theresa Hak-Kyung Cha's *Dictee* and Jessica Hagedorn's *Dogeaters*—even as Trinh T. Minh-ha and other critics have attempted an integrated theory that will take into account feminist epistemology and postcolonial theory.[4]

Indeed, in addressing the overlaps, commonalities, and signal resonances among these tripartite fields, I note, for example, that each "field" shares an

9. Sucheta Mazumdar, "General Introduction: A Woman-Centered Perspective on Asian American History," in *Making Waves,* 15, 16.
1. See, for example, the sequel, *Making More Waves,* edited by Elaine H. Kim et al. (Boston: Beacon Press, 1997).
2. *Home to Stay: Asian American Women's Fiction,* ed. Carol Bruchac and Sylvia Watanabe (New York: Greenfield Press, 1990); *Our Feet Walk the Sky: Women of the South Asian Diaspora,* ed. Women of South Asian Descent Collective (San Francisco: Aunt Lute, 1993); *A Lotus of Another Color: An Unfolding of the South Asian Gay and Lesbian Experience,* ed. Rakesh Ratti (Boston: Alyson, 1993); *The Very Inside: An Anthology of Writing by Asian and Pacific Islander Lesbian and Bisexual Women* (Toronto: Sister Vision, 1994); *Living in America: Poetry and Fiction by South Asian Ameri-*can Writers, ed. Roshni Rustomji-Kerns (Boulder: Westview, 1995).
3. See the works of the Filipino American authors such as Jessica Hagedorn, especially *Dogeaters* (New York: Penguin, 1990) and M. Evelina Galang, *Her Wild American Self* (Minneapolis: Coffee House, 1996); also Malaysian American Shirley Geok-lin Lim, *Among the White Moon Faces: An Asian-American Memoir of Homelands* (New York: Feminist Press, 1996).
4. Theresa Hak-Kyung Cha, *Dictee* (1982; rpt., Berkeley: Third Woman Press, 1995); Trinh T. Minh-ha, *Woman, Native, Other: Writing Postcoloniality and Feminism* (Bloomington: Indiana University Press, 1989); and Minh-ha, *When the Moon Waxes Red: Representation, Gender, and Cultural Politics* (New York: Routledge, 1991).

interdisciplinary approach that is enlivened by the different methodologies associated with the humanities and social sciences: history, literary criticism, sociology, anthropology, art history, film studies, and so forth. Scholars also have noted the tendency in all three fields not only to blur disciplinary boundaries or to be pluri-disciplinary but to engage in antidisciplinary work. And more and more, paradigms drawn from cultural studies have moved into feminist, postcolonial, and Asian American literary inquiry.

The attempt at integrating interpretative practices specific to these fields goes against a deeply installed criticism of "unity" as an intellectually suspect concept, a criticism that may also appear to come out of paradoxically hegemonizing, reductive, and conservative impulses that seek to reify particularism as another form of totalizing principle. Indeed, the overlapping concerns have little to do with articulating a principle of unity as they are asking how we can effect a praxis of coalitional interpretative practices among feminist, postcolonial, and Asian American critical studies.

The analytical categories of imperialism, colonialism, and globalism raised, for example, in the chapters on Filipino American and South Asian literature, in *Reading the Literatures of Asian America*, one of the first edited volumes to focus on Asian American writing, resist the institutional erasure of feminist Asian American productions as also part of a postcolonial literature.[5] In the last fifteen years at least, feminist theory has grown in complexity and reach, including, most recently, a "cultural studies' broadening of feminist scholarship [and] intellectual currents that transcend national boundaries." According to Deborah A. Gordon, "the transnationalizing of North American feminism has changed its subject matter, methodology and sense of political purpose. Feminism's object is no longer only patriarchy or male dominance but also society, consumption, interpretation, nature, and culture. . . . Its subjects are most often modern, industrial states including the shifts of a global economy, ethnic hostilities, gender struggle, right-wing populism, and the demise of socialist governments," so setting into question "the ascendancy of a bourgeois feminism that seeks to win citizens' hearts and minds through free-market ideology."[6] Chandra Mohanty et al.'s edited volume, *Third World Women and the Politics of Feminism*, is one of the few texts to address what Cheryl Johnson-Odim conceptualizes as "common themes, different contexts" that interlink postcolonial matrixes of race, class, and imperialism in the U.S. First World territory.[7] Mohanty's introduction argues ably for a "focus on dynamic oppositional agency that clarifies the intricate connections between systemic relationships and the directionality of power" to demonstrate that "systems of racial, class, and gender domination do not have identical effects on women in the third world."[8] The feminist argument that simply adding the category of woman or of race to criticism as usual is "inadequate to address their lives . . . [and] yields inadequate accounts of *everyone else's* relationships to issues"[9] can be similarly extended to the interpretation

5. Shirley Geok-lin Lim and Amy Ling, *Reading the Literatures of Asian America* (Philadelphia: Temple University Press, 1992).
6. Deborah A. Gordon, "Feminism and Cultural Studies," *Feminist Studies* 12 (Summer 1995): 364, 367.
7. Chandra Mohanty et al., eds., *Third World Women and the Politics of Feminism* (Bloomington:

Indiana University Press, 1990).
8. Ibid., 13.
9. Sandra Harding, ". . . and Race"? Toward the Science Question," in Sandra Harding, *Whose Science? Whose Knowledge?: Thinking from Women's Lives* (Ithaca: Cornell University Press, 1991), 194.

of South, Southeast, and East Asian American texts in which the category of nation is a crucial analytical and thematic feature. As I have argued elsewhere, feminist literary praxis, from Nina Baym's criticism of male-centered U.S. traditions and themes to Sandra Gilbert and Susan Gubar's *Norton Anthology of Literature by Women*,[1] can be said to reproduce uncritically a Eurocentric-biased canon that also encodes, to paraphrase Sandra Harding, racial and national messages "in the very definition of their most abstract projects."[2] Decoding their messages, we can see how white U.S. feminist literary epistemology frequently takes "American" national identity as an unproblematized, unmarked center that functions as the condition for inclusion and so excludes consciousness of differently marked relations to a hegemonic imagination of U.S. national identity. Thus, even when race is admitted as an intersecting category for inquiry, with the admission of the work of women of color into the feminist canon, the category of nation often still remains unacknowledged.[3]

Transnationalism and Asian American Women's Writing

From its first inception in the student protest movements of 1968, Asian American Studies was posited as part of a Third World movement drawing its intellectual base from the anti-imperial struggles of colonized people. Gary Okihiro testifies to this tradition in his introduction to the 1988 collection *Reflections on Shattered Windows* that Asian American Studies, originating in and symbolized by the "demand of Third World strikers at San Francisco State [that] education . . . must be 'decolonized' . . . arose out of struggle, out of a critique of American society and the educational system that buttresses it, and out of a profound commitment to community."[4] Other Asian American scholars such as Michael Omi, together with sociologists like Robert Blauner, took a Marxist model in their analysis of Asian American history and communities. Asian Americans, identified with other ethnic Americans, belong historically to a proletariat class, internally colonized by a ruling class that owns the means of production.[5] "Assimilation" thus becomes theorized as a coercive process by which institutionalized racism deprives these communities of civil rights, economic advancement, and cultural integrity.

This colonial reading is still powerful in effecting a resistant reading of Ori-

1. *The Norton Anthology of Literature by Women*, compiled by Sandra M. Gilbert and Susan Gubar, 2d ed. (New York: Norton, 1996).
2. Harding, ". . . and Race," 199.
3. Chicana literary critics were among the first to include a problematizing of national identity in their critical consciousness, seen especially in the popularization of their tropes of the borderland and the mestiza identity. In Gloria Anzaldúa's work, for example, the borderlands and the mixed-race/cosmic-race metaphors are also literal, and sexual production, genre hybridity, bilingual stylistics, multiplying linguistic registers, and lesbian/bisexual addresses are ruptures of and into political consciousness. Arguably, in the centrality of the contested category of nation and the differently nuanced articulations of a colonized/diasporic/borderlands/mixed or hybrid

ethnic subject, Asian American literary tradition has as much in common with Chicana literature as it does with African American and Euro-American writing. See Gloria Anzaldúa, *Borderlands / La Frontera: The New Mestiza* (San Francisco: Aunt Lute, 1987); Anzaldúa, ed., *Making Face, Making Soul* (San Francisco: Aunt Lute, 1990).
4. Gary Okihiro, introduction to *Reflections on Shattered Windows* (Pullman: Washington State University Press, 1988), xvii, xviii.
5. Robert Blauner, in *From Different Shores: Perspectives on Race and Ethnicity in America* (New York: Oxford University Press, 1987); Michael Omi and Howard Winant, *Racial Formation in the United States from the 1960s to the 1990s* (New York: Routledge, 1994).

entalist representations and in instating an oppositional identity politics that has invigorated the work of authors such as Frank Chin and Jeffrey Paul Chan. But it is inadequate to explain the contemporary writing coming out of new Asian American immigrant writers (e.g., Jessica Hagedorn, Shirley Geok-lin Lim, Chitra Divakaruni),[6] who, paradoxically, have come from newly independent former colonies; nor the work of a younger group (such as Cynthia Kadohata)[7] that rejects the reified essentializing cultural nationalist separatism of the 1970s. Contemporary Asian American writing such as Kingston's *Tripmaster Monkey* or David Hwang's *M. Butterfly*[8] operates in a postmodern or postcolonial space where gendered subjectivity is playfully performed or critically constructed rather than naturalized and where postmodern strategies of narrative destabilize and disavow fixed categories of race, class, and gender identity. American feminists have tended to read the works of Maxine Hong Kingston, Bharati Mukherjee, and Gish Jen[9] in the frame of Western feminism and so miss the colonial / postcolonial locations from which these writers speak. These authors, for example, repeatedly narrativize, even if they do not equally problematize, a U.S. national identity. Although the reiterative strategies and constructions of the American nation in their works raise questions as to their purpose, their deconstructive elements, erased referents, rhetorical address, the relations between imagined nation and female subject suggested, and so forth, in the main, Euro-American feminists have read such fictive American-nation-enunciation moments as unproblematically transparent statements mimetic of social realities.

Intersections of ethnic and feminist theories that are not inflected by other complicating categories, such as nation and diaspora, are inadequate fully to illuminate the relations between and among such Asian American texts, that is, to account for the complexities of their diverse literary traditions. We see these complex traditions at work when we place Kingston's *Woman Warrior*, for example, in relation to Diana Chang's 1956 novel *The Frontiers of Love*.[1] Like Kingston's text, Chang's novel narrates the coming of age of a young Chinese American girl. But Chang's protagonist is a Eurasian, Sylvia Chen, who arrives at sexual and political consciousness at a historical moment of Japanese and European imperialism in China. The novel narrativizes the identity crises of race, sex, class, and nation that are so au courant today. But, although published almost twenty years before *The Woman Warrior* and set in World War II Shanghai, Chang's fiction hardly notes those Chinese patriarchal evils and attitudes that *The Woman Warrior*, despite its setting in a chiefly post–World War II U.S. space, continuously narrates. Clearly, instead of a chronological progression in the development of feminist-identified themes, we find discontinuities in the characterization of patriarchal Chinese

6. Chitra Divakaruni, *Arranged Marriage: Stories* (New York: Anchor, 1995); *The Mistress of Spices* (New York: Anchor, 1997).
7. Cynthia Kadohata, *The Floating World* (New York: Ballantine, 1989); also *In the Heart of the Valley of Love* (New York: Penguin, 1992).
8. Maxine Hong Kingston, *Tripmaster Monkey* (New York: Knopf, 1989); David Henry Hwang, *M. Butterfly* (New York: New American Library, 1988).

9. Bharati Mukherjee, *Wife* (New York: Penguin, 1987); Mukherjee, *The Middleman and Other Stories* (New York: Viking Penguin, 1988); Mukherjee, *Jasmine* (New York: Viking Penguin, 1989); also Gish Jen, *Typical American* (New York: Penguin, 1993); Jen, *Mona in the Promised Land* (New York: Knopf, 1996).
1. Diana Chang, *The Frontiers of Love* (1956; rpt. Seattle: University of Washington Press, 1994).

and Chinese American society in these two narratives. Do we conclude that Shanghai in the early 1940s was a less patriarchal world than Stockton's Chinatown in the 1950s and 1960s? What accounts for the apparent anomalies and discontinuities between these two imagined Chinese/Chinese American communities? Can acts of contextualization help us understand the differentiating social consequences of class on women's bodies? On the one hand, when we contextualize Chang's novel in a cosmopolitan, transnational, mixed-race, elite social history, we can better understand the operations of colonial racism in undermining any emergent national self and the densely woven reiterative third-person interiorized monologues that star the fiction. Kingston's putative memoir, on the other hand, must be contextualized in the working-class, segregated history of Chinese American communities during the era of the Exclusion Acts. The widely different contexts of these two books, when both are read within a canon of Chinese American women's writing, suggest that there are other continuities than those offered by feminist theory that link them as sister texts. That is, although an Asian American literary tradition is discernible in reading these women's narratives side by side, as the most recent Asian American publications increasingly demonstrate, feminist and ethnic identity theorization cannot account fully for the astonishing diversity and divergences contained in this tradition.

When we ask, What are the important texts that have formed the attitudes and approaches of those who are now writing Asian American fiction and critical studies, and how can we periodize this canon?—we are merely asking from a contingent and provisional base, for Asian American writing is being produced at an amazing pace, perhaps even more amazing in reference to the entire previous history of Asian Americans.[2] More significantly, while the opening salvo in the 1970s on the absence of Asian American writing was derived from an exclusionary criterion constructing an authentic ethnic identity, the interrogation and dismantling of this authentic essential ethnic subject has been the project and the catalyst for much of the efflorescence of Asian American writing in the 1980s and 1990s. The project is complicitously related to the contingent presence of postcolonial subjects and theory in U.S. cultural discourses, including the migrancy of South Asians geographically and intellectually into Asian American cultural sites, and so is directly linked to the production of a new and different literary tradition for Asian American writing. Contemporary Asian American literary tradition, marked by a fluidity or open-endedness in which the "national" origin/U.S. natal identity of the author is blurred or left undetermined or at least not pivotally signified as totalizing correspondence between text and social reality, opens up a space where the aesthetics or textual production can be submitted for appropriate scrutiny as signifying form.

One clear collection of texts in which postcolonial theory bears a relevant weight is that produced by diasporic and émigré or newly immigrant authors who are claiming or have been identified with an Asian American location. Among these I include the plethora of writing by South Asian immigrant women, beginning with Bharati Mukherjee and now including authors such

---

2. See "Asian American Literature, January 1992–June 1996: An Annotated Bibliography," compiled by Shirley Geok-lin Lim and Noelle Williams, *ADE Bulletin*, no. 116 (Spring 1997): 53–58.

as Sara Suleri, Bhapsi Sidhwa, Ginu Kamani, and a throng of women writers represented in the numerous South Asian women's anthologies that have appeared in the last five years.[3] Because South Asian American writing is produced within different cultural boundaries from U.S.-born authored texts, they inscribe different reconstitutions of memory and give rise to different fabrications of tradition, deploying in some instances transgressive, appropriative, and disavowing strategies. The narratives of the Burmese-born Wendy Law-Yone and the Vietnamese refugee Le Ly Hayslip[4] suggest that any survey of Asian American writing now must wrestle with the destabilizing notions of Asian American ethnic, national, and gender identities and the congruent problematizing of traditional authorial voicing, genre boundaries, and narrative stylistics that these new Asian American immigrant (and émigré/green card) literatures introduce.

The new horizon of postcolonial and feminist expectations illuminates older texts and permits a different reception of them. The recovery of diasporic identification complicates and inflects the master narrative of becoming American, suggests a postmodern, post-1960s tradition that brings into a different relief the older tradition of English-language memoirs and novels written by Asians in the United States in the period of transition between 1945 and 1969. This postcolonial reading, however, needs to take into greater account the category of gender, which is an especially vexed subset of inquiry in the postcolonial world. Incorporating a feminist epistemological dimension will allow us to revise simple reductions of social relations in these texts to Asian patriarchal structures. A critical feminist inquiry will subvert the unidirectional, univocal structuring of sexism as something that is done to women by men; instead, deessentializing gender attributes will permit us to note that sexism is also something that is done to Asian American men by U.S. society, sometimes with Asian American women as duplicitous agents. Kingston powerfully retells the story of white men turning Asian American male subjects into disempowered, that is, feminized, sex objects in the opening fable of Tang Ao in *China Men,* and David Hwang critically scrutinizes the overlapping of colonialist, imperialist, racist ideologies in the overdetermined gendering of female subjectivity in *M. Butterfly.* Similar demasculinization themes are sounded in narratives as historically apart as Jeanne Wakatsuki's *Farewell to Manzanar* and Law-Yone's *Coffin Tree.* Gender renegotiations, specifically in more feminist militant forms, have thus been interpreted not simply as social in character but as denoting a teleological shift in the de/structuring of Asian "manhood."

In Asian American women's texts, such as Chuang Hua's *Crossings* and Hua Ling Nieh's *Mulberry and Peach,*[5] of coming to the United States and staying; coming, returning, then re-returning; coming and returning repeatedly; born in the United States; traveling, traversing, in transition, unsettling

3. Sara Suleri, *Meatless Days* (Chicago: University of Chicago Press, 1989); Meena Alexander, *Fault Lines: A Memoir* (New York: Feminist Press, 1993); Bhapsi Sidhwa, *An American Brat* (Minneapolis: Milkweed, 1993); Ginu Kamani, *Junglee Girl* (San Francisco: Aunt Lute, 1995).
4. Wendy Law-Yone, *Irrawaddy Tango* (New York:

Knopf, 1993); Le Ly Hayslip with Jay Wurts, *When Heaven and Earth Changed Places* (New York: Plume, 1989).
5. Chuang Hua, *Crossings* (1968; rpt. Boston: Northeastern University Press, 1986); Hua Ling Nieh, *Mulberry and Peach* (1981; rpt. New York: Feminist Press, 1998).

rather than settling into a prescribed U.S. national identity, working out a schizophrenic epistemology rather than the paranoid rigid surveillance of the ideological nation, the impatience with the question of an authentic and authenticating Asian American identity in works points to what is emergent and different about recent Asian American literature. These works articulate a postcolonial, global consciousness—not simply cosmopolitan or binational or diasporic or immigrant—but all these strands bound together, imbricated within U.S.-based ideologies of society and the individual, within the English language, and within the genres of prose narratives.

The transition of the tradition from a cultural national to postcolonial consciousness has been elided by its contingent side-by-sideness with postmodern theorization. Asian American critical and literary consciousness seems to have moved from the national to the postmodern moment with hardly a glance at the contents of modernity in the cultural forms. Perhaps illustrating the collapse of temporal sense in the face of the spatially urgent globalization of Asian American identity formations, young Asian American critics have appropriated postmodern theories for Asian American studies, as seen in the 1995 volume *Privileging Positions: The Sites of Asian American Studies*. As the editor, Gary Okihiro, notes, four of the chapters "consider the intersections and divergencies of Asian American Studies and postmodernism and feminism."[6] The authors of these chapters look for an "affirmative postmodernism" that will "work toward alternative futures" and that will have "an integrative impact upon the disciplines across the academy," and they argue that the centrality of Asia puts Asian Americanists "in an excellent position to make powerful interventions in the dominant understanding of postmodernism and late capitalism." This intervention by young Asian American acadamics impatient with standing "at the edge of theoretical debates rather than sit[ting] in their midst"[7] resituates and redraws identity/subject formation but to my mind spectacularly elides any notion of the postcolonial, a lapse that has perhaps everything to do with the privileging of the East Asian over the South Asian in the volume, as Okihiro himself noted in his introduction. In the focus on late capitalism's penetration of the Pacific Rim sphere, class rather than nation forms the pivotal discursive category, with commodification taking the place of oppression under this paradigm of postmodernism.

To repeat, in Asian American literary studies, the entry of feminist epistemology has been particularly enlivening and productive in constructing standpoint knowledge of Asian American women's experiences and in the foregrounding of women's issues and examination of gender representations, as seen in the critical studies by Amy Ling and King-Kok Cheung, the first being a study of women writers of Chinese descent and the latter interpreting notions of silence and articulations in Asian American women's fictions.[8] But the absence of postcolonial critiques in these 1980s studies, like the absence of feminist critiques in the colonial readings of Asian American lit-

6. *Privileging Positions: The Sites of Asian American Studies*, ed. Gary Okihiro, Marilyn Alquizola, Dorothy Fujita Rony, and K. Scott Wong (Pullman: Washington State University Press, 1995), 4.
7. Ibid., 41.

8. Amy Ling, *Between Worlds: Women Writers of Chinese Ancestry* (Elmsford, N.Y.: Pergamon Press, 1990); King-Kok Cheung, *Articulate Silences: Hisaye Yamamoto, Maxine Hong Kingston, Joy Kogawa* (Ithaca: Cornell University Press, 1993).

erature in the 1970s, have tended to a reification of specific binaries, for example, of assimilation versus cultural nationalism, immigrant versus diasporic models, or masculinist versus feminist ideological representations, binaries that reflect the sameness versus difference camps that dominated feminist discourse in the 1980s, Feminist, postcolonial, and postmodern theorization breaks open these binaries, leading to further transformations of a once culturally nationalist Asian American literary tradition. Antihegemonic and antiauthoritarian, Asian American women's writing cannot be periodized or uniformly classified. The challenge of pluralism, of an ideology that seeks to include divergent, even conflictual, cultural components, is acutely articulated in such texts, situated in the intersections of ethnic and feminist identities.

2000

CHANDRA TALPADE MOHANTY
b. 1955

What does it mean to speak or write as a "first world" woman about "third world" women? Chandra Talpade Mohanty has posed this cautionary query while serving as a vigorous advocate for bringing postcolonial studies into feminism. Melding transnationalism with cultural studies, she argues against the proclivity of Western feminists to generalize about or caricature non-Western women. Frequently anthologized, "Under Western Eyes" (1988) first appeared in *Feminist Review* and was integrated into *Feminism without Borders: Decolonizing Theory, Practicing Solidarity* (2003), from which we have taken our selection. In the anthologies she has helped create—*Third World Women and the Politics of Feminism* (1991) and *Feminist Genealogies, Colonial Legacies, Democratic Futures* (1996)—Mohanty multiplies the differences among and between women so as to question ethnocentric or elitist assumptions about a universal, monolithic, or reductive feminism.

From Feminism without Borders: Decolonizing Theory, Practicing Solidarity

From *Under Western Eyes:*
Feminist Scholarship and Colonial Discourses

Any discussion of the intellectual and political construction of "Third World feminisms" must address itself to two simultaneous projects: the internal critique of hegemonic "Western" feminisms and the formulation of autonomous feminist concerns and strategies that are geographically, historically, and culturally grounded. The first project is one of deconstructing and dismantling; the second is one of building and constructing. While these projects appear to be contradictory, the one working negatively and the other positively, unless these two tasks are addressed simultaneously, Third World feminisms run the risk of marginalization or ghettoization from both mainstream (right and left) and Western feminist discourses.

It is to the first project that I address myself here. What I wish to analyze is specifically the production of the "Third World woman" as a singular, monolithic subject in some (Western) feminist texts. The definition of colonization I wish to invoke here is a predominantly discursive one, focusing on a certain mode of appropriation and codification of scholarship and knowledge about women in the Third World through the use of particular analytic categories employed in specific writings on the subject that take as their referent feminist interests as they have been articulated in the United States and Western Europe. If one of the tasks of formulating and understanding the locus of Third World feminisms is delineating the way in which they resist and work against what I am referring to as "Western feminist discourse," then an analysis of the discursive construction of Third World women in Western feminism is an important first step.

Clearly, neither Western feminist discourse nor Western feminist political practice is singular or homogeneous in its goals, interests, or analyses. However, it is possible to trace a coherence of effects resulting from the implicit assumption of "the West" (in all its complexities and contradictions) as the primary referent in theory and praxis. My reference to "Western feminism" is by no means intended to imply that it is a monolith. Rather, I am attempting to draw attention to the similar effects of various textual strategies used by writers that codify others as non-Western and hence themselves as (implicitly) Western. It is in this sense that I use the term "Western feminist." Similar arguments can be made about middle-class, urban African or Asian scholars who write about their rural or working-class sisters and assume their own middle-class cultures at the norm and codify working class histories and cultures as other. Thus, while this chapter focuses specifically on what I refer to as "Western feminist" discourse on women in the Third World, the critiques I offer also pertain to Third World scholars who write about their own cultures and employ identical strategies.

It ought to be of some political significance that the term "colonization" has come to denote a variety of phenomena in recent feminist and left writings in general. From its analytic value as a category of exploitative economic exchange in both traditional and contemporary Marxisms (see, in particular, Amin 1977, Baran 1962, and Frank 1967) to its use by feminist women of color in the United States to describe the appropriation of their experiences and struggles by hegemonic white women's movements (see especially Joseph and Lewis 1981, Moraga 1984, Moraga and Anzaldúa 1983, and Smith 1983), colonization has been used to characterize everything from the most evident economic and political hierarchies to the production of a particular cultural discourse about what is called the Third World.[1] However sophisticated or problematical its use as an explanatory construct, colonization almost invariably implies a relation of structural domination and a suppression—often violent—of the heterogeneity of the subject(s) in question.

1. Terms such as "Third World" and "First World" are very problematic, both in suggesting oversimplified similarities between and among countries labeled thus and in implicitly reinforcing existing economic, cultural, and ideological hierarchies that are conjured up in using such terminology. I use the term "Third World" with full awareness of its problems, only because this is the terminology available to us at the moment. Throughout this book, then, I use the term critically. [Except as indicated, all notes are Mohanty's.]

My concern about such writings derives from my own implication and investment in contemporary debates in feminist theory and the urgent political necessity of forming strategic coalitions across class, race, and national boundaries. The analytic principles discussed below serve to distort Western feminist political practices and limit the possibility of coalitions among (usually white) Western feminists, working-class feminists, and feminists of color around the world. These limitations are evident in the construction of the (implicitly consensual) priority of issues around which apparently all women are expected to organize. The necessary and integral connection between feminist scholarship and feminist political practice and organizing determines the significance and status of western feminist writings on women in the Third World, for feminist scholarship, like most other kinds of scholarship, is not the mere production of knowledge about a certain subject. It is a directly political and discursive practice in that it is purposeful and ideological. It is best seen as a mode of intervention into particular hegemonic discourses (e.g., traditional anthropology, sociology, and literary criticism); it is a political praxis that counters and resists the totalizing imperative of age-old "legitimate" and "scientific" bodies of knowledge. Thus, feminist scholarly practices (reading, writing, critiquing, etc.) are inscribed in relations of power—relations that they counter, resist, or even perhaps implicitly support. There can, of course, be no apolitical scholarship.

The relationship between "Woman" (a cultural and ideological composite other constructed through diverse representational discourses—scientific, literary, juridical, linguistic, cinematic, etc.) and "women" (real, material subjects of their collective histories) is one of the central questions the practice of feminist scholarship seeks to address. This connection between women as historical subjects and the representation of Woman produced by hegemonic discourses is not a relation of direct identity or a relation of correspondence or simple implication.[2] It is an arbitrary relation set up by particular cultures. I would like to suggest that the feminist writings I analyze here discursively colonize the material and historical heterogeneities of the lives of women in the Third World, thereby producing/representing a composite, singular "Third World woman"—an image that appears arbitrarily constructed but nevertheless carries with it the authorizing signature of Western humanist discourse.[3]

I argue that assumptions of privilege and ethnocentric universality, on the one hand, and inadequate self-consciousness about the effect of Western scholarship on the Third World in the context of a world system dominated by the West, on the other, characterize a sizable extent of Western feminist work on women in the Third World. An analysis of "sexual difference" in the form of a cross-culturally singular, monolithic notion of patriarchy or male dominance leads to the construction of a similarly reductive and homoge-

2. I am indebted to Teresa de Lauretis for this particular formulation of the project of feminist theorizing. See especially her introduction to her book *Alice Doesn't* (1984).

3. This argument is similar to Homi Bhabha's definition of colonial discourse as strategically creating a space for a subject people through the production of knowledge and the exercise of power: "[C]olonial discourse is an apparatus of power, an apparatus that turns on the recognition and disavowal of racial/cultural/historical differences. Its predominant strategic function is the creation of a space for a subject people through the production of knowledge in terms of which surveillance is exercised and a complex form of pleasure/unpleasure is incited. It (i.e., colonial discourse) seeks authorization for its strategies by the production of knowledge by coloniser and colonised which are stereotypical but antithetically evaluated" (Bhabha 1983, 23).

neous notion of what I call the "Third World difference"—that stable, ahistorical something that apparently oppresses most if not all the women in these countries. And it is in the production of this Third World difference that Western feminisms appropriate and colonize the constitutive complexities that characterize the lives of women in these countries. It is in this process of discursive World that power is exercised in much of recent Western feminist discourse, and this power needs to be defined and named.

* * *

WOMEN AS A CATEGORY OF ANALYSIS; OR, WE ARE ALL SISTERS IN STRUGGLE

The phrase "women as a category of analysis" refers to the crucial assumption that all women, across classes and cultures, are somehow socially constituted as a homogeneous group identified prior to the process of analysis. This is an assumption that characterizes much feminist discourse. The homogeneity of women as a group is produced not on the basis of biological essentials but rather on the basis of secondary sociological and anthropological universals. Thus, for instance, in any given piece of feminist analysis, women are characterized as a singular group on the basis of a shared oppression. What binds women together is a sociological notion of the "sameness" of their oppression. It is at this point that an elision takes place between "women" as a discursively constructed group and "women" as material subjects of their own history. Thus, the discursively consensual homogeneity of women as a group is mistaken for the historically specific material reality of groups of women. This results in an assumption of women as an always already constituted group, one that has been labeled powerless, exploited, sexually harassed, and so on, by feminist scientific, economic, legal, and sociological discourses. (Notice that this is quite similar to sexist discourse labeling women as weak, emotional, having math anxiety, etc.) This focus is not on uncovering the material and ideological specificities that constitute a particular group of women as "powerless" in a particular context. It is, rather, on finding a variety of cases of powerless groups of women to prove the general point that women as a group are powerless.

In this section I focus on six specific ways in which "women" as a category of analysis is used in Western feminist discourse on women in the Third World. Each of these examples illustrates the construction of "Third World women" as a homogeneous "powerless" group often located as implicit victims of particular socioeconomic systems. I have chosen to deal with a variety of writers—from Fran Hosken, who writes primarily about female genital mutilation, to writers from the Women in International Development (WID) school, who write about the effect of development policies on Third World women for both Western and Third World audiences. The similarity of assumptions about Third World women in all these texts forms the basis of my discussion. This is not to equate all the texts that I analyze, nor is it to equalize their strengths and weaknesses. The authors I deal with write with varying degrees of care and complexity; however, the effect of their representation of Third World women is a coherent one. In these texts women are defined as victims of male violence (Fran Hosken); as universal dependents (Beverly Lindsay and Maria Cutrufelli); victims of the colonial process (Maria Cutrufelli); victims of the Arab familial system (Juliette Minces); victims of the Islamic code (Patricia Jeffery); and, finally, victims of the economic development process (Beverly Lindsay and the [liberal] WID school). This mode of defining women primarily in terms of their object status (the way in which they are affected or not affected by certain institutions and systems) is what characterizes this particular form of the use of "women" as a category of analysis. In the context of Western women writing/studying women in the Third World, such objectification (however benevolently motivated) needs to be both named and challenged. As Valerie Amos and Pratibha Parmar argue quite eloquently, "Feminist theories which examine our cultural practices as 'feudal residues' or label us 'traditional,' also portray us as politically immature women who need to be versed and schooled in the ethos of Western feminism. They need to be continually challenged" (1984, 7).[4]

*　*　*

METHODOLOGICAL UNIVERSALISMS;
OR, WOMEN'S OPPRESSION AS A GLOBAL PHENOMENON

Western feminist writings on women in the Third World subscribe to a variety of methodologies to demonstrate the universal cross-cultural operation of male dominance and female exploitation. I summarize and critique three such methods below, moving from the simplest to the most complex.

First, proof of universalism is provided through the use of an arithmetic method. The argument goes like this: the greater the number of women who wear the veil, the more universal is the sexual segregation and control of women (Dearden 1975, 4–5). Similarly, a large number of different, fragmented examples from a variety of countries also apparently add up to a universal fact. For instance, Muslim women in Saudi Arabia, Iran, Pakistan, India, and Egypt all wear some sort of a veil. Hence, the argument goes, sexual control of women is a universal fact in those countries (Dearden 1975, 7, 10). Fran Hosken writes, "Rape, forced prostitution, polygamy, genital mutilation, pornography, the beating of girls and women, purdah (segregation of women) are all violations of basic human rights" (1981, 15). By equating purdah with rape, domestic violence, and forced prostitution, Hosken asserts that purdah's "sexual control" function is the primary explanation for its existence, whatever the context. Institutions of purdah are thus denied any cultural and historical specificity and contradictions, and potentially subversive aspects are totally ruled out.

In both these examples, the problem is not in asserting that the practice of wearing a veil is widespread. This assertion can be made on the basis of numbers. It is a descriptive generalization. However, it is the analytic leap from the practice of veiling to an assertion of its general significance in controlling women that must be questioned. While there may be a physical similarity in the veils worn by women in Saudi Arabia and Iran, the specific meaning attached to this practice varies according to the cultural and ideological context. In addition, the symbolic space occupied by the practice of purdah may be similar in certain contexts, but this does not automatically indicate that the practices themselves have identical significance in the social realm. For example, as is well known, Iranian middle-class women veiled themselves

---

4. I have discussed this particular point in detail in a critique of Robin Morgan's construction of "women's herstory" in her introduction to *Sister-* *hood Is Global* (1984); (see Mohanty 1987, esp. 35–37).

during the 1979 revolution[5] to indicate solidarity with their veiled, working-class sisters, while in contemporary Iran, mandatory Islamic laws dictate that all Iranian women wear veils. While in both these instances, similar reasons might be offered for the veil (opposition to the Shah and Western cultural colonization in the first case and the true Islamization of Iran in the second), the concrete meanings attached to Iranian women wearing the veil are clearly different in both historical contexts. In the first case, wearing the veil is both an oppositional and a revolutionary gesture on the part of Iranian middle-class women; in the second case, it is a coercive, institutional mandate (see Tabari 1980 for detailed discussion). It is on the basis of such context specific differentiated analysis that effective political strategies can be generated. To assume that the mere practice of veiling women in a number of Muslim countries indicates the universal oppression of women through sexual segregation not only is analytically reductive but also proves quite useless when it comes to the elaboration of oppositional political strategy.

Second, concepts such as reproduction, the sexual division of labor, the family, marriage, household, patriarchy, and so on are often used without their specification in local cultural and historical contexts. Feminists use these concepts in providing explanations for women's subordination, apparently assuming their universal applicability. For instance, how is it possible to refer to "the" sexual division of labor when the content of this division changes radically from one environment to the next and from one historical juncture to another? At its most abstract level, it is the fact of the differential assignation of tasks according to sex that is significant; however, this is quite different from the meaning or value that the content of this sexual division of labor assumes in different contexts. In most cases the assigning of tasks on the basis of sex has an ideological origin. There is no question that a claim such as "Women are concentrated in service-oriented occupations in a large number of countries around the world" is descriptively valid. Descriptively, then, perhaps the existence of a similar sexual division of labor (where women work in service occupations such as nursing, social work, etc., and men in other kinds of occupations) in a variety of different countries can be asserted. However, the concept of the "sexual division of labor" is more than just a descriptive category. It indicates the differential value placed on men's work versus women's work.

Often the mere existence of a sexual division of labor is taken to be proof of the oppression of women in various societies. This results from a confusion between and collapsing together of the descriptive and explanatory potential of the concept of the sexual division of labor. Superficially similar situations may have radically different, historically specific explanations and cannot be treated as identical. For instance, the rise of female-headed house-holds in middle-class America might be construed as a sign of great independence and feminist progress, the assumption being that this increase has to do with women choosing to be single parents, with an increasing number of lesbian mothers, and so on. However, the recent increase in female-headed households in Latin America,[6] which might at first be seen as indicating that women are acquiring more decision-making power, is concentrated among the poorest strata, where life choices are the most constrained economically. A similar argument can be

5. The Islamic revolution, led by Ayatollah Ruhollah Khomeini, which overthrew the shah of Iran, Muhammed Reza Shah Pahlevi [editor's note].

6. Harris 1983. Other MRG [Minority Rights Group] reports include Dearden 1975 and Jahan and Cho 1980.

made for the rise of female-headed families among black and Chicana women in the United States. The positive correlation between this and the level of poverty among women of color and white working-class women in the United States has now even acquired a name: the feminization of poverty. Thus, while it is possible to state that there is a rise in female-headed households in the United States and in Latin America, this rise cannot be discussed as a universal indicator of women's independence, nor can it be discussed as a universal indicator of women's impoverishment. The meaning of and explanations for the rise obviously vary according to the sociohistorical context.

Similarly, the existence of a sexual division of labor in most contexts cannot be sufficient explanation for the universal subjugation of women in the workforce. That the sexual division of labor does indicate a devaluation of women's work must be shown through analysis of particular local contexts. In addition, devaluation of women must also be shown through careful analysis. In other words, the "sexual division of labor" and "women" are not commensurate analytical categories. Concepts such as the sexual division of labor can be useful only if they are generated through local, contextual analyses (see Eldhom, Harris, and Young 1977). If such concepts are assumed to be universally applicable, the resultant homogenization of class, race, religion, and daily material practices of women in the Third World can create a false sense of the commonality of oppressions, interests, and struggles between and among women globally. Beyond sisterhood there are still racism, colonialism, and imperialism.

Finally, some writers confuse the use of gender as a superordinate category of analysis with the universalistic proof and instantiation of this category. In other words, empirical studies of gender differences are confused with the analytical organization of cross-cultural work. Beverly Brown's (1983) review of the book *Nature, Culture and Gender* (Strathern and McCormack 1980) best illustrates this point. Brown suggests that nature:culture and female:male are superordinate categories that organize and locate lesser categories (such as wild:domestic and biology:technology) within their logic. These categories are universal in the sense that they organize the universe of a system of representations. This relation is totally independent of the universal substantiation of any particular category. Brown's critique hinges on the fact that rather than clarify the generalizability of nature:culture :: female:male as superordinate organization categories, Nature, Culture and Gender construes the universality of this equation to lie at the level of empirical truth, which can be investigated through fieldwork. Thus, the usefulness of the nature:culture :: female:male paradigm as a universal mode of the organization of representation within any particular sociohistorical system is lost. Here, methodological universalism is assumed on the basis of the reduction of the nature:culture :: female:male analytic categories to a demand for empirical proof of its existence in different cultures. Discourses of representation are confused with material realities, and the distinction made earlier between "Woman" and "women" is lost. Feminist work that blurs this distinction (which is, interestingly enough, often present in certain Western feminists' self-representation) eventually ends up constructing monolithic images of "Third World women" by ignoring the complex and mobile relationships between their historical materiality on the level of specific oppressions and political choices, on the one hand, and their general discursive representations, on the other.

To summarize: I have discussed three methodological moves identifiable in feminist (and other academic) cross-cultural work that seeks to uncover a universality in women's subordinate position in society. The next and final section pulls together the previous ones, attempting to outline the political effects of the analytical strategies in the context of Western feminist writing on women in the Third World. These arguments are not against generalization as much as they are for careful, historically specific generalizations responsive to complex realities. Nor do these arguments deny the necessity of forming strategic political identities and affinities. Thus, while Indian women of different religions, castes, and classes might forge a political unity on the basis of organizing against police brutality toward women (see Kishwar and Vanita 1984), any analysis of police brutality must be contextual. Strategic coalitions that construct oppositional political identities for themselves are based on generalization and provisional unities, but the analysis of these group identities cannot be based on universalistic, ahistorical categories.

THE SUBJECT(S) OF POWER

✳   ✳   ✳

When the category of "sexually oppressed women" is located within particular systems in the Third World that are defined on a scale that is normed through Eurocentric assumptions, not only are Third World women defined in a particular way prior to their entry into social relations, but, since no connections are made between First and Third World power shifts, the assumption is reinforced that the Third World just has not evolved to the extent that the West has. This mode of feminist analysis, by homogenizing and systematizing the experiences of different groups of women in these countries, erases all marginal and resistant modes and experiences.[7] It is significant that none of the texts I reviewed in the Zed Press series[8] focuses on lesbian politics or the politics of ethnic and religious marginal organizations in Third World women's groups. Resistance can thus be defined only as cumulatively reactive, not as something inherent in the operation of power. If power, as Michel Foucault has argued, can be understood only in the context of resistance,[9] this mis-conceptualization is both analytically and strategically problematical. It limits theoretical analysis as well as reinforces Western cultural imperialism. For in the context of a First/Third World balance of power, feminist analyses that perpetrate and sustain the hegemony of the idea of the superiority of the West produce a corresponding set of universal images of the Third World woman, images such as the veiled woman, the powerful mother, the chaste virgin, the obedient wife, and so on. These images exist in universal, ahistorical splendor, setting in motion a colonialist discourse that exercises a very specific power in defining, coding, and maintaining existing First/Third World connections.

To conclude, let me suggest some disconcerting similarities between the typically authorizing signature of such Western feminist writings on women in the Third World and the authorizing signature of the project of humanism

7. I discuss the question of theorizing experience in Mohanty 1987 and Mohanty and Martin 1986.
8. A series titled "Women in the Third World," most of Mohanty's discussion of it is not included here [editor's note].
9. This is one of Foucault's (1978, 1980) central points in his reconceptualization of the strategies and workings of power networks.

in general—humanism as a Western ideological and political project that involves the necessary recuperation of the "East" and "Woman" as others. Many contemporary thinkers, including Michel Foucault (1978, 1980), Jacques Derrida (1974), Julia Kristeva (1980), Gilles Deleuze and Félix Guattari (1977), and Edward Said (1978), have written at length about the underlying anthropomorphism and ethnocentrism that constitute a hegemonic humanistic problematic that repeatedly confirms and legitimates (Western) man's centrality. Feminist theorists such as Luce Irigaray (1981), Sarah Kofman (see Berg 1982), and Hélène Cixous (1981) have also written about the recuperation and absence of woman/women within Western humanism. The focus of the work of all these thinkers can be stated simply as an uncovering of the political interests that underlie the binary logic of humanistic discourse and ideology, whereby, as a valuable essay puts it, "the first (majority) term (Identity, Universality, Culture, Disinterestedness, Truth, Sanity, Justice, etc.), which is, in fact, secondary and derivative (a construction), is privileged over and colonizes the second (minority) term (difference, temporality, anarchy, error, interestedness, insanity, deviance, etc.), which is, in fact, primary and originative" (Spanos 1984). In other words, it is only insofar as "woman/women" and "the East" are defined as others, or as peripheral, that (Western) man/humanism can represent him/itself as the center. It is not the center that determines the periphery, but the periphery that, in its boundedness, determines the center. Just as feminists such as Kristeva and Cixous deconstruct the latent anthropomorphism in Western discourse, I have suggested a parallel strategy in this in uncovering a latent ethnocentrism in particular feminist writings on women in the Third World.[1]

As discussed earlier, a comparison between Western feminist self-presentation and Western feminist representation of women in the Third World yields significant results. Universal images of the Third World woman (the veiled woman, chaste virgin, etc.), images constructed from adding the "Third World difference" to "sexual difference," are predicated upon (and hence obviously bring into sharper focus) assumptions about Western women as secular, liberated, and having control over their own lives. This is not to suggest that Western women are secular, liberated, and in control of their own lives. I am referring to a discursive self-presentation, not necessarily to material reality. If this were material reality, there would be no need for political movements in the West. Similarly, only from the vantage point of the

---

1. For an argument that demands a new conception of humanism in work on Third World women, see Lazreg 1988. While Lazreg's position might appear to be diametrically opposed to mine, I see it as a provocative and potentially positive extension of some of the implications that follow from my arguments. In criticizing the feminist rejection of humanism in the name of "essential Man," Lazreg points to what she calls an "essentialism of difference" within these very feminist projects. She asks: "To what extent can Western feminism dispense with an ethics of responsibility when writing about different women? The point is neither to subsume other women under one's own experience nor to uphold a separate truth for them. Rather, it is to allow them to be while recognizing that what they are is just as meaningful, valid, and comprehensible as what we are. . . . Indeed, when feminists essentially deny other women the humanity they claim for themselves, they dispense with any ethical constraint. They engage in the act of splitting the social universe into us and them, subject and objects" (99–100). This essay by Lazreg and an essay by Satya P. Mohanty (1989) suggest positive directions for self-conscious cross-cultural analyses, analyses that move beyond the deconstructive to a fundamentally productive mode in designating overlapping areas for cross-cultural comparison. The latter essay calls not for a "humanism" but for a reconsideration of the question of the "human" in a posthumanist context. It argues that there is no necessary incompatibility between the deconstruction of Western humanism and such a positive elaboration of the human, and that such an elaboration is essential if contemporary political-critical discourse is to avoid the incoherencies and weaknesses of a relativist position.

West is it possible to define the Third World as underdeveloped and economically dependent. Without the overdetermined discourse that creates the Third World, there would be no (singular and privileged) First World. Without the "Third World woman," the particular self-presentation of Western women mentioned above would be problematical. I am suggesting, then, that the one enables and sustains the other. This is not to say that the signature of Western feminist writings on the Third World has the same authority as the project of Western humanism. However, in the context of the hegemony of the Western scholarly establishment in the production and dissemination of texts, and in the context of the legitimating imperative of humanistic and scientific discourse, the definition of "the Third World woman" as a monolith might well tie into the larger economic and ideological praxis of "disinterested" scientific inquiry and pluralism that are the surface manifestations of a latent economic and cultural colonization of the "non-Western" world. It is time to move beyond the Marx who found it possible to say: they cannot represent themselves; they must be represented.

WORKS CITED

Amin, Samir. 1977. *Imperialism and Unequal Development.* New York: Monthly Review Press.

Amos, Valerie, and Pratibha Parmar. 1984. "Challenging Imperial Feminism." *Feminist Review,* no. 17: 3–19.

Baran, Paul A. 1962. *The Political Economy of Growth.* New York: Monthly Review Press.

Berg, Elizabeth. 1982. "The Third Woman." *Diacritics* 12, no. 2 (Summer): 11–20.

Bhabha, Homi. 1983. "The Other Question—The Stereotype and Colonial Discourse." *Screen* 24, no. 6 (November—December): 18–36.

Brown, Beverly. 1983. "Displacing the Difference—Review, Nature, Culture and Gender." *m/f,* no. 8: 79–89.

Cixous, Hélène. 1981. "The Laugh of the Medusa." Trans. Keith Cohen and Paula Cohen. In Marks and de Courtivron 1981: 245–64.

Cutrufelli, Maria Rosa. 1983. *Women of Africa: Roots of Oppression.* London: Zed Press.

De Lauretis, Teresa. 1984. *Alice Doesn't: Feminism, Semiotics, Cinema.* Bloomington: Indiana University Press.

Dearden, Ann, ed. 1975. *Arab Women.* Report no. 27. London: Minority Rights Group.

Deleuze, Giles, and Félix Guattari. 1977. *Anti-Oedipus: Capitalism and Schizophrenia.* Trans. Robert Hurley, Mark Seem, and Helen R. Lane. New York: Viking.

Derrida, Jacques. 1974. *Of Grammatology.* Trans. Gayatri Chakravorty Spivak. Baltimore: Johns Hopkins University Press.

Eldhom, Felicity, Olivia Harris, and Kate Young. 1977. "Conceptualizing Women." *Critique of Anthropology* 3, nos. 9–10: 101–30.

Foucault, Michel. 1978. *History of Sexuality.* Vol. 1, *An Introduction.* Trans. Robert Hurley. New York: Random House.

———. 1980. *Power/Knowledge: Selected Interviews and Other Writings, 1972–1977.* Ed. Colin Gordon; trans. Colin Gordon et al. New York: Pantheon.

Frank, Andre Gunder. 1967. *Capitalism and Underdevelopment in Latin America: Historical Studies of Chile and Brazil.* New York: Monthly Review Press.

Harris, Olivia, ed. 1983. *Latin American Women.* Report no. 57. London: Minority Rights Group.

Hosken, Fran. 1981. "Female Genital Mutilation and Human Rights." *Feminist Issues* 1, no. 3: 3–23.

Irigaray, Luce. 1981. "This Sex Which Is Not One" and "When the Goods Get Together." Trans. Claudia Reeder. In Marks and de Courtivron, 1981: 99–106, 107–10.

Jahan, Rounaq, and Hyoung Cho, eds. 1980. *Women in Asia.* Report no. 45. London: Minority Rights Group.

Jeffery, Patricia. 1979. *Frogs in a Well: Indian Women in Purdah.* London: Zed Press.

Joseph, Gloria, and Jill Lewis. 1981. *Common Differences: Conflicts in Black and White Feminist Perspectives.* Boston: Beacon Press.

Kishwar, Madhu, and Ruth Vanita. 1984. *In Search of Answers: Indian Women's Voices from Manushi.* London: Zed Press.

Kristeva, Julia. 1980. *Desire in Language: A Semiotic Approach to Literature and Art.* Ed. Leon S. Roudiez; trans. Thomas Gora, Alice Jardine, and Leon S. Roudiez. New York: Columbia University Press.

Lazreg, Marnia. 1988. "Feminism and Difference: The Perils of Writing as a Woman on Women in Algeria." *Feminist Issues* 14, no. 1: 81–107.

Lindsay, Beverly, ed. 1983. *Comparative Perspectives of Third World Women: The Impact of Race, Sex and Class.* New York: Praeger.

Marks, Elaine, and Isobel de Courtivron, eds. 1981. *New French Feminisms.* New York: Schocken Books.

Minces, Juliette. 1980. *The House of Obedience: Women in Arab Society.* London: Zed Press.

Mohanty, Chandra. 1987. "Feminist Encounters: Locating the Politics of Experience." *Copyright* 1 (Fall): 30–44.

Mohanty, Chandra, and Biddy Martin. 1986. "Feminist Politics: What's Home Got to Do with It?" In *Feminist Studies/Critical Studies,* ed. Teresa de Lauretis, 191–212. Bloomington: Indiana University Press.

Mohanty, Satya P. 1989. "Us and Them: On the Philosophical Bases of Political Criticism." *Yale Journal of Criticism* 2, no. 2 (Spring): 1–31.

Moraga, Cherríe. 1984. *Loving in the War Years: Lo Que Nunca Pasó por Sus Labios.* Boston: South End Press.

Moraga, Cherríe, and Gloria Anzaldúa, eds. 1983. *This Bridge Called My Back: Writings by Radical Women of Color.* 2nd ed. New York: Kitchen Table Press.

Morgan, Robin, ed. 1984. *Sisterhood Is Global: The International Women's Movement Anthology.* New York: Anchor Press/Doubleday; Harmondsworth: Penguin.

Said, Edward. 1978. *Orientalism.* New York: Random House.

Smith, Barbara, ed. 1983. *Home Girls: A Black Feminist Anthology.* New York: Kitchen Table Press.

Spanos, William V. 1984. "*Boundary 2* and the Polity of Interest: Humanism, the 'Center Elsewhere,' and Power." *Boundary 2* 12, no. 3–13, no. 1 (Spring–Fall): 173–214.

Strathern, Marilyn, and Carol McCormack, eds. 1980. *Nature, Culture and Gender.* Cambridge: Cambridge University Press.

Tabari, Azar. 1980. "The Enigma of the Veiled Iranian Women." *Feminist Review,* no. 5: 19–32.

1988, 2003

Part 3
Practice: Representative Readings and Analyses

On Medieval Women

After Marie de France composed her Breton lays, English gained ground in the fourteenth and fifteenth centuries, a period when a number of religious meditations were produced by women. Their work has received extensive attention from contemporary feminist critics. A number of these critics have also explored the role of women as readers of Early Middle English saints' lives or instruction manuals as well as examining images of femininity and sexuality in sermons, stories, and plays composed by men. Contemporary reassessments of the twelfth-century poet Marie de France; the anchoress Julian of Norwich, who recorded her mystical visions in *A Book of Showings* (1390); and the deeply spiritual laywoman Margery Kempe, who dictated the first autobiography in the English language (1436–38), clarify both the spiritual and psychological states and the aesthetic strategies of the first literary women in English literary history, while recent critiques of male-authored traditions address the cultural situation faced by literary women in the medieval period. In various ways, Marie, Julian, and Margery Kempe had to contend with male-dominated institutions that often castigated or sought to impede in women the self-articulation that artistry generally entails.

In the first of our selections, Caroline Walker Bynum illuminates the mystical tradition of Julian of Norwich, who described the "showings" of the maternal God she perceived in 1373. Bynum is professor of Western European Middle Ages at Princeton's Institute for Advanced Study; she has studied medieval piety and the roles Christianity assigned men and women not only in *Jesus as Mother: Studies in the Spirituality of the High Middle Ages*, from which our selection is drawn, but also in such award-winning books as *Holy Feast and Holy Fast: The Religious Significance of Food to Medieval Women* (1987), *Resurrection of the Body in Western Christianity, 200–1336* (1995), and *Last Things: Death and the Apocalypse in the Middle Ages* (2000). Next, Karma Lochrie explains how Margery Kempe managed to assert her right to teach against church authorities who approved and sometimes sought to enforce the silence of women. Kempe, who was often regarded during her life as a heretical eccentric, found strength not just in the endorsement of Julian of Norwich but also in a number of the popular debates and Latin texts about spirituality upon which she could draw. Karma Lochrie, a professor of English at Indiana University, is the author of *Margery Kempe and Translations of the Flesh* (1991), from which our selection comes, as well as *Covert Operations: The Medieval Uses of Secrecy* (1999) and *Heterosyncrasies: Female Sexuality When Normal Wasn't* (2005). In addition, she has co-edited *Constructing Medieval Sexuality* (1997).

Enlarging the scope from a single tradition or author to the issues clustered around how one should conceptualize the period of centuries now called medieval, Margaret Ezell summarizes the growth of scholarship on the early years of women's authorship in *Writing Women's Literary History* (1993). In doing so, she expresses a broader claim made by a number of feminist medievalists: namely, that critics need to resist any tendency to recount a teleological story about a progressively empowered literary history, for such an approach marginalizes the contributions of early women writers, readers, subjects, translators, and patrons of the arts. The John Paul Abbott Professor of Liberal Arts at Texas A&M University, Margaret Ezell more recently has examined the competition between print and manuscript productions in *Social Authorship and the Advent of Print* (1999). Our concluding selection takes up one character in the work of Marie de France—the *malmariée* (the unhappily married lady)—and in particular such women's expressions of discontent in both acts and words. According to Jennifer Willging, Marie's female characters exhibit exceptional independence of mind, despite the confining societal circumstances they face. An associate professor of French at Ohio State University, Jennifer Willging has published *Telling Anxiety* (2007), a book about contemporary women's writings in French.

CAROLINE WALKER BYNUM

From Jesus as Mother and Abbot as Mother[1]

From *Biblical and Patristic Background*

Any explanation of the medieval theme of God as mother must begin by noting that it is not an invention of twelfth-century devotional writers. In the Old Testament, God frequently speaks of himself as mother, bearing the Israelites in his bosom, conceiving them in his womb (e.g., Isa. 49:1, 49:15, and 66:11–13).[2] The wisdom of God is a feminine principle; in Ecclesiasticus she says: "I am the mother of fair love, and of fear, and of knowledge, and of holy hope. . . . Come over to me, all ye that desire me: and be filled with my fruits" (Eccles. 24:24–26).[3] In the New Testament such imagery is nonexistent. The gospel of John does apply to Christ some of the titles of the Old Testament wisdom literature (e.g., John 14:6),[4] but it uses no feminine language. Christ is, however, described as a hen gathering her chicks under her wings in Matt. 23:37.[5] And the contrast drawn in the Epistles between milk and meat as symbols of types of instruction (1 Cor. 3:1–2; Heb. 5:12; 1 Pet. 2:2) seems to have suggested to later writers that the apostles responsible for the Epistles, Peter and Paul, themselves provided the milk for beginners and should therefore be seen as mothers. The possibly gnostic *Odes* of Solomon, the apocryphal third-century Acts of Peter, and the writings of Clement, Origen, Irenacus, John Chrysostom, Ambrose, and Augustine all describe Christ as mother.[6] In general the Greek fathers, particularly those influenced by gnos-

1. Excerpted from chapter 4 of *Jesus as Mother: Studies in the Spirituality of the High Middle Ages* (1982) [editor's note].

2. See Phyllis Trible, "God, Nature of, in the Old Testament," *Interpreter's Dictionary of the Bible,* supplementary vol. (Nashville, 1976), pp. 368–69, and André Cabassut, "Une Dévotion médiévale pue connue: la dévotion à 'Jésus Notre Mère,'" *Mélanges Marcel Viller,* RAM 25 (1949): 237–37.

3. Edmund Colledge and James Walsh, eds., *A Book of Showings to the Anchoress Julian of Norwich,* 2 vols. (Toronto, 1978), 1:154.

4. Ibid.

5. Mark 3:35, where Christ refers to any faithful follower as his mother or brother, is a very different use of mother as symbol, although one on which twelfth-century Cistercians probably draw; cf. William of St. Thierry, *Meditative Orationes,* chap. 6, PL 180: cols. 225D–26A; Guerric of Igny, third Christmas sermon, chaps. 4–5, *Sermons,* 2 vols., ed. J. Morson and H. Costello, SC 166 and 202, Sér. mon. 31 and 43 (Paris, 1970–73), 1:196–200; first Epiphany sermon, chap. 6, *Sermons* 1:250; second sermon for Lent, chap. 2, *Sermons* 2:30; fourth sermon for Palm Sunday, chap. 5, *Sermons* 2:210–14; second sermon of SS. Peter

and Paul, chaps. 1–6, *Sermons* 2:380–94; second sermon for the Nativity of Mary, chaps. 35, *Sermons* 2:490–96; Adam of Perseigne, letter 4, *Correspondance,* ed. J. Bouvet, *Archives historiques du Maine* 12 (1952): 30; Gilbert of Hoyland, *Sermones in Canticum Solomonis,* sermon 5, PL 184: col. 32C; Francis of Assisi, *Epistola 1, Opuscula* (Quaracchi, 1904), p. 93.

6. See Cabussut, "Une dévotion peu connue"; Eleanor C. McLaughlin, " 'Christ My Mother': Feminine Naming and Metaphor in Medieval Spirituality," *Nashotah Review* 15 (1975): 228–48; Ritamary Bradley, "The Motherhood Theme in Julian of Norwich," *Fourteenth-Century English Mystics Newsletter* 2.4 (1976): 25–30; Elaine Pagels, "What Became of God the Mother? Conflicting Images of God in Early Christianity," *Signs* 2 (1976): 293–303; Pagels, *The Gnostic Gospels* (New York, 1979), pp. 48–69; Eleanor McLaughlin, "God's Body and Ours: Possibilities for Reformation in Medieval Spirituality," unpublished lecture, Vanderbilt Theological School, October 1976; Colledge and Walsh, *A Book of Showings.* To their references, I add: Irenaeus, *Adversus haereses,* bk. 3, chap. 24, par. 1, *Patrologia graeca,* ed. J.-P. Migne, 7: cols. 966–67; and Augustine, *In Iohan-*

ticism, seem to have been more at home with maternal metaphors.[7] The Latin translator of the Acts of Peter suppressed "mother" in his list of titles for Christ,[8] and the passing references to Christ's maternal love in Augustine and Ambrose in no way compare to the elaborate and lengthy passages that Clement of Alexandria devotes to the nursing Christ.[9] With the exception of Bede's references to God's wisdom as feminine,[1] the theme is unimportant in the early Middle Ages.

*　　*　　*

From *The Theme of "Mother Jesus" as a Reflection of Affective Spirituality*

Several of the scholars who have noticed the use of maternal imagery in medieval authors from Anselm of Canterbury to Julian of Norwich have associated this particular image with the rise, from the eleventh century on, of a lyrical, emotional piety that focuses increasingly on the humanity of Christ.[2] Descriptions of God as a woman nursing the soul at her breasts, drying its tears, punishing its petty mischief-making, giving birth to it in agony and travail, are part of a growing tendency to speak of the divine in homey images and to emphasize its approachability. If Christ presents himself to us as a child playing in a carpenter's shop or a young man stopping, dusty and tired, for a meal with friends, what can possibly be wrong with earthy metaphors that associate his love with that of female as well as male parents, his sustenance with milk as well as meat? Seeing Christ or God or the Holy Spirit as female is thus part of a later medieval devotional tradition that is characterized by increasing preference for analogies taken from human relationships,[3] a growing sense of God as loving and accessible, a general tendency toward fulsome language, and a more accepting reaction to all natural things, including the physical human body.[4] But the idea of mother Jesus is not merely an aspect of increasing attention to the human Christ. It also expresses quite specifically certain of the emphases that underlay the affective spirituality of the twelfth to the fourteenth centuries.[5]

The affective piety of the high Middle Ages is based on an increasing sense of, first, humankind's creation "in the image and likeness" of God and, sec-

nis Evangelium Tractatus CXXIV, chap. 15, par. 7, chap. 16, par. 2, chap. 18, par. 1, and chap. 21, par. 1, Corpus christianorum 36 (Turnhout, 1954), pp. 153, 165, 179, and 212.

7. Pagels, "God the Mother," and *Gnostic Gospels.*
8. Cabassut, "Une dévotion peu connue," p. 237.
9. Compare, for example, Ambrose, *De virginibus,* bk. 1, chap. 5, PL 16: col. 205, with Clement of Alexandria, *Paedagogus,* bk. 1, chap. 6, *Clement Alexandrinus,* 2 vols., ed. Otto Stählin, Die griechischen christlichen Schriftsteller der ersten drei Jahrhunderte 12 and 15 (Leipzig, 1936–39) 1:104–21.
1. Colledge and Walsh, *A Book of Showings* 1:154.
2. Cabassut, "Une dévotion peu connue"; Giles Constable, "Twelfth-Century Spirituality and the Late Middle Ages," *Medieval and Renaissance Studies* 5 (1971): 45–47; E. McLaughlin, " 'Christ My Mother' "; Eleanor C. McLaughlin, "Women, Power and the Pursuit of Holiness in Medieval Christianity," in *Women of Spirit: Female Leadership in the Jewish and Christian Traditions,* ed. Rosemary Ruether and Eleanor C. McLaughlin (New York, 1979), pp. 122–27.
3. This has been pointed out by R. Javelet, *Image*

et ressemblance au douzième siècle de saint Anselme à Alain de Lille, 2 vols. (Paris, 1967).
4. This latter point is stressed by E. McLaughlin, " 'Christ My Mother'," and "Women, Power. . . ." It should not, however, be misunderstood. From the twelfth century on, negative attitudes toward sexuality, at least among the religious, probably increased; see John Boswell, *Christianity, Social Tolerance, and Homosexuality: Gay People in Western Europe from the Beginning of the Christian Era to the Fourteenth Century* (Chicago, 1980).
5. Of those scholars who have written on maternal imagery, Bradley ("Motherhood Theme" and "Patristic Background of Motherhood Similitude in Julian of Norwich," *Christian Scholar's Review* 8 [1978]: 101–13), Kari Elizabeth Børresen ("Christ notre mère, la théologie de Julianne de Norwich," *Mitteilungen und Forschungsbeiträge der Cusanus-Gesellschaft* 13 [Mainz, 1978]: 320–29), and Colledge and Walsh (*A Book of Showings*) have been concerned with the theological tradition more than the devotional; all three treat this through a search for the sources of Julian of Norwich's trinitarian theology, which is expressed through the motherhood metaphor.

ond, the humanity of Christ as guarantee that what we are is inextricably joined with divinity. Creation and incarnation are stressed more than atonement and judgment. Christ is seen as the mediator who joins our substance to divinity and as the object of a profound experiential union; God is emphasized as creating and creative; the cooperation of the Trinity in the work of creation is stressed. The dominant note of piety is optimism and a sense of momentum toward a loving God. Concentration on the eucharist and on Christ's suffering in the Passion, which increases in thirteenth- and fourteenth-century devotions, is not primarily a stress on the sacrifice needed to bridge the enormous gap between us in our sin and God in his glory; it is rather an identification with the fact that Christ is what we are. Moreover, both the imaginative identification with Christ's humanity, which is so stressed by late medieval preachers and devotional writers, and the increased theological emphasis on creation and incarnation are answers to the major heresies of the twelfth to fourteenth centuries. Affirmation of God's creation of all things and of the joining of physicality to divinity countered Cathar dualism; affirmation of the centrality of the eucharist countered the neglect or abandonment of the church's rituals that was implicit in various antisacerdotal movements and in Free Spirit antinomianism. In addition to expressing and evoking the emotional response so highly valued in the twelfth and thirteenth centuries, the devotion to mother Jesus conveyed the specific emphases of this piety on mystical union and the eucharist.

In spiritual writers from Anselm to Julian, we find three basic stereotypes of the female or the mother: the female is generative (the foetus is made of her very matter) and sacrificial in her generation (birth pangs);[6] the female is loving and tender (a mother cannot help loving her own child);[7] the female is nurturing (she feeds the child with her own bodily fluid).[8] This threefold concept of the female parent seems to have been particularly appropriate to

6. Anselm, prayer 10, *Opera omnia*, ed. F. S. Schmitt, 6 vols. (Edinburgh, 1940–61), 3:33 and 39–41; Marguerite of Oingt, *Pagina meditationum*, chaps. 30, 32–33, 36–37 and 39, *Les oeuvres de Marguerite d'Oingt*, ed. and trans. Antonin Duraffour, P. Gardette and P. Durdilly, Publications de l'Institut de Linguistique Romane de Lyon 21 (Paris, 1965), pp. 77–79; and Julian of Norwich, *A Book of Showings*, the long text, passim and especially chaps. 58–60, 2:582–600. On the complex problems of the text of Julian's revelations, see also E. Colledge and J. Walsh, "Editing Julian of Norwich's Revelations: A Progress Report," *Mediaeval Studies* 38 (1976): 404–27. The theme of God as mother is developed in the later, longer version.
7. *Ancrene Riwle: The English Text of the Cotton Nero A. XIV*, ed. Mabel Day, Early English Text Society 225 (London 1952), p. 103 (and see also p. 180); Hugh Lacerta, *Liber de doctrina vel liber sententiarum seu rationum beati viri Stephani primi patris religionis Grandmontis*, chap. 10, CCCM 8 (Turnhout, 1968), p. 14; Bernard of Clairvaux, sermon 12, par. 4, OB 1:62–63; sermon 23, par. 2, 1:139–40; sermon 26, par. 6, 1:173; letter 258, PL 182: cols. 466A–67A; and *De diligendo Deo*, chap. 7, par. 17, OB 3:134; Julian, *A Book of Showings*, the long text, especially chaps. 61 and 63, 2:601–9 and 614–18; Gertrude the Great, *Revelationes Gertrudianae ac Mechtildianae* 1: *Sanctae Gertrudis magnae virginis ordinis sancti Benedicti Legatus divinae pietatis . . .* , ed. the monks of Solesmes [Dom Paquelin] (Paris, 1875), bk. 4, chap. 5, p. 314; and bk. 5, chap. 28, p. 546; Mechtild of Hackeborn, *Revelationes Gertrudianae ac Mechtildianae* 2: *Sanctae Mechtildis virginis ordinis sancti Benedicti Liber specialis gratiae*, ed. the monks of Solesmes (Paris, 1877), bk. 2, chap. 16, pp. 149–50; bk 3, chap. 9, p. 208; bk. 4, chap. 7, p. 264; and bk. 4, chap. 59, p. 311.
8. See Bernard of Clairvaux, letter 1, PL 182: cols. 72 and 76A–C; Bernard, sermon 10, par. 3, OB 1:45–50; sermon 23, par. 2, OB 1:139–40; Guerric, second sermon for SS. Peter and Paul, chap. 2, *Sermons* 2:384–86; Aelred, *De institutione*, chap. 31, in *Opera omnia*, 1, ed. A. Hoste and C. H. Talbot, CCCM 1 (Turnhout, 1971), p. 671; Thomas of Cantimpré, *Vita S. Lutgardis*, AASS: June, vol. 4 (Paris, 1867): 189–210, esp. bk. 1, chap. 1, sec. 2, pp. 191F–92A, and bk. 1, chap. 1, sec. 13, pp. 193C–E; the monk of Farne, chaps. 40 and 50–51, "The Meditations of the Monk of Farne," ed. Hugh Farmer, *Studia Anselmiana* 41–42, *Analecta monastica* 4 (1957): 182–83 and 189–90; Gertrude the Great, *Oeuvres spirituelles*, vols. 2 and 3: *Le Héraut*, SC 139 and 143, Sér. mon. 25 and 27 (Paris, 1968), bk. 3, chap. 4, 3:24; Richard Rolle, "Richard Rolle's Comment on the Canticles, Edited From MS Trinity College, Dublin, 153," ed. Elizabeth M. Murray (Ph.D. diss. Fordham, 1958), pp. 29–30 and 33; and Julian, *A Book of Showings*, the long text, chap. 60, 2:596–97.

convey the new theological concerns, more appropriate in fact than the image of the male parent if we understand certain details of medieval theories of physiology.

People in the high Middle Ages argued that the ideal child-rearing pattern was for the mother to nurse her own child; in medieval medical theory breast milk is processed blood.[9] According to medieval understanding of physiology, the loving mother, like the pelican who is also a symbol for Christ, feeds her child with her own blood. Thus, the connection of blood and milk in many medieval texts is based on more than merely the parallelism of two bodily fluids. Clement of Alexandria as early as the second century makes explicit the connection between breast milk and the blood supplied to the foetus in order to use the nursing Christ as an image of the eucharist.[1] In medieval legends like the lactation of St. Bernard[2] and in medieval devotions like the sacred heart,[3] milk and blood are often interchangeable, as are Christ's breasts and the wound in his side.[4] What writers in the high Middle Ages wished to say about Christ the savior who feeds the individual soul with his own blood was precisely and concisely said in the image of the nursing mother whose milk *is* her blood, offered to the child.

Medieval images of the maternal also stressed mother-love as instinctive and fundamental: the mother is tender and loving, sometimes dying to give the child life; she tempts or disciplines only with the welfare of the child in mind. Such imagery could, of course, be highly sentimental and was apt to bring affective response. It was peculiarly appropriate to a theological emphasis on an accessible and tender God, a God who bleeds and suffers less as a sacrifice or restoration of cosmic order than as a stimulus to human love.

Moreover, in medieval physiological theories—however confused they may be on the subject—the female in some sense provides the matter of the foetus, the male the life or spirit.[5] Medieval theologians sometimes stressed that, as Eve came from the matter of Adam, so Christ came from the matter of

9. Mary M. McLaughlin, "Survivors and Surrogates: Children and Parents from the Ninth to the Thirteenth Centuries," in *The History of Childhood,* ed. L. DeMause (New York, 1974), pp. 115–18; Michael Goodich, "Bartholomaeus Anglicus on Child-rearing," *History of Childhood Quarterly: The Journal of Psychohistory* 3 (1975): 80.
1. Clement, *Paedagogus,* bk. 1, chap. 6, *Clemens Alexandrinus* 1:104–21.
2. See Léon Dewez and Albert van Iterson, "La lactation de saint Bernard: Legende et iconographic," *Cîteaux in de Nederlanden* 7 (1956): 165–89. We should also note in this connection the legend, found in a work attributed to John Chrysostom and repeated by Guerric, that the apostle Paul bled milk rather than blood when he was beheaded (see Guerric of Igny, *Liturgical Sermons,* 2 vols., Cistercian Fathers Series 8 and 32 [Spencer, Mass., 1970–71], 2:154, n. 7). St. Catherine of Alexandria is also supposed to have bled milk when decapitated: see G. Bardy, "Catherine d'Alexandrie," DHGE 11 (Paris, 1949): cols. 1503–5. Moreover lactation as an act of filial piety (an adult female offering the breast to a parent or an adult in a desperate situation) was a solemn theme in the literature and religion of pagan antiquity; Adolphe de Ceulencer, "La Charité romaine dans la littérature et dans l'art," *Annales de l'Académie Royale d'archéologie de Belgique* 67

(Antwerp, 1919): 175–206. On medieval devotion to the Virgin's milk, see P. V. Bétérous, "A propos d'une des légends mariales les plus répandues: le 'lait de la Vierge,' " *Bullétin de l'association Guillaume Budé* 4 (1975): 403–11.
3. See Jean Leclercq, "Le sacré-coeur dans la tradition bénédictine au moyen âge," *Cor Jesu: Commentationes in litteras encyclicas Pii PP. XII 'Haurietis aquas',* 2 vols. (Rome, 1959), 2:3–28; see also Cyprien Vagaggini, "La dévotion au sacré-coeur chez sainte Mechtilde et sainte Gertrude," ibid., pp. 31–48.
4. For examples of this interchangeability, see Guerric of Igny, second sermon for SS. Peter and Paul, chap. 2, *Sermons* 2:384–86; Aelred, *De institutione,* chap. 31, *Opera omnia* 1:671; the monk of Farne, *Meditations,* chap. 40, "The Meditations of the Monk of Farne," ed. Farmer, pp. 182–83.
5. Vern L. Bullough, "Medieval Medical and Scientific Views of Women," *Viator* 4 (1973): 487–93. See also John F. Benton, "Clio and Venus: An Historical View of Medieval Love," *The Meaning of Courtly Love,* ed. F. X. Newman (Albany, 1969), p. 32, and Charles T. Wood, "Menstruation in the Middle Ages," *Speculum,* to appear [published as "The Doctor's Dilemma: Sin, Salvation, and the Menstrual Cycle in Medieval Thought," *Speculum* 56 (1981): 710–27].

Mary.[6] Thus, the mother was, to medieval people, especially associated with the procreation of the physicality, the flesh, of the child. Here again, the emphases of physiological theory were particularly useful, given the devotional concerns of the later Middle Ages. For a theology that stressed the humanity of Christ as a taking up into divinity of humankind's fleshliness, female generativity could be an important symbol. For a theology that maintained—over against Cathar dualism—the goodness of creation in all its physicality, a God who is mother and womb as well as father and animator could be a more sweeping and convincing image of creation than a father God alone. (It could also, of course, be dangerous, with implications of pantheism or antinomianism.) Thus, the growth of maternal names for God in the later Middle Ages reflects the general tendency to see God as "accessible" and "like man," to apply to him homey metaphors and anthropomorphic analogies; it also reflects the fact that what medieval authors assume the female to be coincided with what they increasingly wished to emphasize about God the creator and about the Incarnation.

* * *

1982

6. M.-T. d'Alverny, "Comment les théologiens . . . voient la femme?" *Cahiers de civilisation médiévale* 20 (1977): 115–24. See also Basile Studer, "Consubstantialis Patri, consubstantialis Matri: Une antithèse christologique chez Léon le Grand," *Revue des études Augustiniennes* 18 (1972): 87–115; and Karl F. Morrison, " 'Unum ex multis': Hincmar of Rheims' Medical and Aesthetic Rationales for Unification," in *Nascità dell'Europa ed Europa carolingia: un'equazione da verificare*, Settimane di Studio del Centro Italiano di Studi sull'Alto Medioevo 27 (Spoleto, 1980), forthcoming [published in 1981, pp. 583–712].

KARMA LOCHRIE

From From Utterance to Text[1]

* * *

The most significant endorsement of Kempe's visions comes from Julian of Norwich. Kempe shows Julian "very many holy speeches and dalliance that our Lord spoke to her soul" to determine whether there is any deceit in these spiritual locutions. Julian instructs Kempe to measure these experiences according to the worship they accrue to God and the profit to her fellow Christians. She also justifies Kempe's tears as tokens of the Holy Spirit in her soul. Finally, Julian encourages Kempe, "Set all your trust in God and fear not the language of the world."[2] Kempe's "holy dalyawns" and "comownyng" in the love of God with Julian last several days, providing a kind of oral testimony to the dalliance of God in Kempe's soul. Julian's advice that Kempe not

1. Excerpted from chapter 3 of *Margery Kempe and Translations of the Flesh* (1991) [editor's note].
2. *The Book of Margery Kempe*, ed. Sanford B. Meech and Hope Emily Allen, EETS, o.s. 212 (London: Oxford University Press, 1940), 43. All quotations from this text will hereafter be cited in the text. Translations are my own unless otherwise noted. For a modern English translation, see Barry A. Windeatt, *The Book of Margery Kempe* (New York: Penguin, 1985).

fear the language of the world is a significant one, for it advocates the divine locutions in the soul—dalliance—over and against all those speeches and writings which threaten to silence her.

Kempe's assertion of her own right to speak and teach directly challenges the "language of the world," including the writing of the Church Fathers and the clerical prerogative of speech. This challenge is complicated by the fact that it runs dangerously close to the boundaries of the Lollard heresy[3] in fifteenth-century England. The prescriptions against woman's speech in scriptural and patristic writing are invoked to protect the clerical prerogative to preach.

The most famous scriptural text used to support women's silence is that of St. Paul: "But I suffer not a woman to teach, nor to use authority over the man: but to be in silence. For Adam was first formed; then Eve. And Adam was not seduced, but woman being seduced, was in the transgression" (I Tim. 2:12–14). Various treatises on preaching further reinforce Paul's prohibition of women's assuming the pulpit, signifying as it does, a reversal in the natural hierarchy which leads to the downfall of humanity. In a later elaboration of St. Paul's doctrine by the Dominican Humbert de Romans (d. 1277), Eve herself becomes a sort of false priest who, being corrupted in her own soul, provokes immorality in the souls of others. " 'She spoke but once,' " he quotes Bernard, " 'and threw the whole world into disorder.' "[4]

Lollard activity in England during the fourteenth and fifteenth centuries circulated the antifeminist fears of woman's speech. One English preacher in Kempe's time, outraged over the growing number of laymen and -women who were usurping the clerical prerogative to read, interpret, and spread the Gospel, exclaimed: "Behold now we see so great a scattering of the Gospel, that simple men & women and those accounted ignorant laymen [*laici ydiote*] in the reputation of men, write and study the Gospel, as far as they can & know how, teach and scatter the Word of God."[5] Not only were these laywomen and men reading and scattering the gospel, but they were being so presumptuous as to dispute clerks in public.[6]

Records from the diocese of Norwich indicate that women Lollards were in fact "scattering the Gospel" in English translation.[7] While Lollards did not explicitly advocate that women should become preachers, they believed that any lay person could preach and teach the gospel and that all good people, even the *laisi ydiote*, were priests.[8] * * * Kempe's own preaching and teach-

3. An anticlerical movement for religious reform, led by followers of John Wycliffe in the late 14th and 15th centuries; it emphasized that supreme authority lay in the Bible, which laypeople could read and interpret for themselves [editor's note].
4. Humbert of Romans, *Treatise on Preaching*, ed. Walter M. Conlon, trans. The Dominican Students, Province of St. Joseph (Westminster, MD: Newman Press, 1951), 48. G. R. Owst discusses Humbert's remark in the context of the medieval sermon, *Preaching in Medieval England* (New York: Russell and Russell, 1965), 5.
5. Quoted in Owst, *Preaching in Medieval England*, 136. He notes that Robert Rypon, sub-prior of the monastery of Durham and prior of Finchale, also comments on the activities of Lollard lay preachers, 135n. Claire Cross documents the participation of women in the Lollard movement, " 'Great Reasoners in Scripture': The Activities of

Women Lollards 1380–1530," in *Medieval Women*, ed. Derek Baker (Oxford: Basil Blackwell, 1978), 359–80.
6. Margaret Aston, *Lollards and Reformers: Images and Literary in Late Medieval Religion* (London: Hambledon Press, 1984), 130. Reginald Pecock, bishop of Chicester, complained especially of the arrogance of women Lollards who "make themselves so wise by the Bible, that they "are most haughty of speech regarding clerks" (quoted in Aston, *Lollards and Reformers*, 51).
7. See Norman C. Tanner, ed., *Heresy Trials in the Diocese of Norwich, 1428–31* (London, 1977).
8. See Archbishop Courtney's examination of the Lollards of Leicester, including women, in Cross, " 'Great Reasoners in Scripture,' " 362. As Cross points out, Lollard activity in East Anglia where Kempe lived has been especially well documented.

ing raise the specter of Lollardy, causing townspeople to curse her and clerics to accuse her of Lollard beliefs.[9] * * * Her own trembling, quaking, and standing stock still indicate that she, at least, believes their threats and is very much afraid of them.

Kempe's efforts to authorize her own voice are thus very politicized and dangerous. She must assert her own orthodoxy as a Christian at the same time that she argues for her right to speak. Obviously, this is a contradiction which continually threatens to brand her as a Lollard. She has few *auctores*[1] whose writings she can bring to her own defense. If she tries to quote Scriptures, she again incriminates herself, for Lollards were said to have been able to read English translations of the Bible.[2] In fact, when Kempe does quote Luke to justify her speech to the Archbishop of York and his ministers, the clerics respond in unison: "Ah, sir, . . . we know well that she has a devil within her, for she speaks of the Gospel" (126). Access to vernacular translations of the gospels was tantamount to possession by the devil. Clearly, Kempe's access to the written word, like her bold speech, is both controversial and dangerous.

At issue in Kempe's first arraignment before Henry Bowet, Archbishop of York, is her publicity and her speech. * * * [Kempe] makes a case for her right to speak which is key to her authorization of herself as a mystic and her book as a whole. She defends her speech by citing a passage from Luke 9:27–28:

> And also þe Gospel makyth mencyon þat, whan þe woman had herd owr Lord prechyd, sche cam be-forn hym wyth a lowde voys & seyd, 'Blyssed be þe wombe þat þe bar & þe tetys þat ʒaf þe sowkyn.' Þan owr Lord seyd a-ʒen to hir, 'Forsoþe so ar þei blissed þat heryn þe word of God and kepyn it.' And þerfor, sir, me thynkyth þat be Gospel ʒeuyth me leue to spekyn of God (126).

> (And also the Gospel makes mention that, when the woman had heard our Lord preach, she came before him with a loud voice and said, 'Blessed be the womb which bore you and the teats which gave you suck.' Then our Lord responded to her, 'In truth so are they blessed who hear the word of God and keep it.' And therefore, sir, it seems to me that the Gospel gives me leave to speak of God.)

What is curious is that the Gospel passage does not explicitly endorse woman's speech, but rather her "hearing and keeping" of the word of God. Kempe's gloss of Luke seems rather forced and self-serving. However, there is an interesting precedent for Kempe's interpretation of Luke from a contemporary of hers. The self-confessed Lollard William Brute cites precisely the same passage in his argument for women's right to preach. His extensive gloss of the passage provides us with evidence of the Lollard argument for

9. For more on Kempe in the context of the Lollard movement, see Clarissa W. Atkinson, *Mystic and Pilgrim: The Book and World of Margery Kempe* (Ithaca, NY: Cornell University Press, 1983), 103–12; 151–54. David Aers also sees Kempe's resistance to authority as identifying her with the Lollard movement; see *Community, Gender, and Individual Identity: English Writing 1360–1430* (London: Routledge, 1988), 84.

1. Authors, teachers; authorities (Latin) [editor's note].

2. Women Lollards often knew Scriptures from having them read to them. In addition, however, they seem to have taught others including their own children passages from the Bible. See Cross, " 'Great Reasoners in Scripture,' " 370. Some of these Lollard women boasted of their learning. Margery Baxter claimed to have deceived a Carmelite, while another woman Lollard publicly declared that "she was as well learned as was the parish priest, in all things, except only in saying mass." See Meech and Allen's commentary in *The Book of Margery Kempe*, 315n, and Cross, 371.

women preachers, and perhaps, of the subtext of Kempe's gloss. While acknowledging Paul's virtual command that women be silent listeners rather than teachers of the World, Brute nevertheless makes a clever argument for women preachers:

Teaching and preaching the Word of God belongs to the priests and moreover, they are ordained in the Church as much by Christ as by his apostles. Paul teaches that women learn in silence with all subjection and that it is not permitted to woman to teach nor to have mastery over a man. Because, nevertheless, Paul does not say they are not able to teach nor to dominate a man, neither do I venture to affirm it, since women, holy virgins, have constantly preached the word of God and converted many to the faith at times when priests were too faint-hearted to speak the word.* * *[3]

A two-fold strategy emerges from Brute's defense of women's preaching. Brute negotiates the Pauline prohibition of women's speech by distinguishing between what women are capable of and what they are permitted, between what Paul explicitly forbids and what he fails to affirm. The example of teaching virgins contradicts Paul's prohibition, allowing Brute to insert exceptions to Paul's rule. His second strategy is to conflate the teaching that "it is more blessed to give than to receive" with the Christ's answer to the woman, rendering preaching the word more blessed than hearing and keeping it. In this way, Brute circumvents Paul's prohibition of women preachers.

Brute's defense helps to elucidate Kempe's own argument for her right to speak. Her "reading" of Luke and her assertion of her own teachings could be labeled Lollard. They are, in fact, Lollard arguments. She further threatens to speak of God "until the Pope and Holy Church ordain that no man shall be so bold as to speak of God." However, she does make a distinction between teaching and preaching which Lollards do not make. When a cleric produces the inevitable passage from St. Paul that "no woman should preach," she answers, "I preach not, sir, I come into no pulpit. I use but communication and good words, and that will I do while I live" (126).

*   *   *

Kempe's argument for woman's speech makes use of a popular debate of her time. But she is not the last to use the Lucan passage to authorize her own speech. In her *Book of the City of Ladies*, Christine de Pizan in the fifteenth century searches likewise for an argument for woman's speech which would refute the cultural idioms identifying it as "blameworthy and of such small authority." The allegorical figure of Reason, who appears to the despairing Christine, points to Christ's favoring of woman's speech by having his resurrection announced by a woman, Mary Magdalene, as well as to other examples from the Gospels. She concludes her testimony to woman's blessed speech with the same passage from Luke cited by Kempe. Interestingly, Christine does not include Christ's response, which is so crucial to Brute's exegesis of the passage. Instead she considers the woman's speech itself as a model of wisdom, boldness, and "great force of will." From this and her other examples she infers, "Thus you can understand, fair sweet friend, God has

3. William W. Capes, *The Register of John Trefnant, Bishop of Hereford* (Hereford, 1914), 345. The translation is my own. Meech and Allen cite Brute's feminism in connection with Lollard advocacy of women preachers, but they do not mention the parallel between Kempe's argument and Brute's, 315n. Margaret Aston summarizes Brute's defense of women's preaching, *Lollards and Reformers*, 52.

demonstrated that He has truly placed language in women's mouths so that He might be thereby served."[4]

This, too, is the lesson of Kempe's disputation with the clerics of York. Christ confers authority on women's speech when he blesses those "who hear the word and keep it." This authority, in turn, privileges the spoken word over the written word. Her defense of her own "bold speech" provides Kempe a means of interdicting the written tradition of *auctoritas*[5] which prohibits that speech. Both in her exchanges with Church authorities and in her mystical locutions, Kempe's voice "speaks between" the written antifeminist tradition and the written text of her own life, locating divine locution, and hence, true authority, in the place where she—and not the written text—is. True authority is always displaced elsewhere than the written text or textual tradition. Dalliance replaces *auctoritas* as the foundation of authorship and textual authority.

Dalliance also intercedes in the written traditions in Kempe's *Book*, as is the case with Kempe's vision of St. Paul, the primary scriptural *auctoritas* against woman's speech. In one of Christ's colloquies of reassurance, He thanks Kempe for her suffering and particularly for her weeping. As consolation for the hostility she endures, Christ reminds her, he once sent St. Paul to her:

> Daughter, I once sent Saint Paul to you to strengthen you and comfort you in order that you should boldly speak in my name from that day forward. And Saint Paul said to you that you had suffered much tribulation because of his writing, and he promised you that you should have as much grace in return for his love as ever you had shame or reproof for his love.

We do not learn which writings of St. Paul's have caused Kempe so much tribulation, but his encouragement of Kempe to "boldly speak in my name from that day forward" points to the passage from 1 Timothy quoted earlier. Paul's endorsement of Kempe's bold speech undermines those very writings which have caused her suffering. In effect, he interdicts his own writings in order to authorize Kempe's speech. Ironically, the same Pauline texts so often cited as authorities against woman's speech become for Kempe the source of her grace. She places the textual harassment experienced by all women writers at her own disposal as evidence of her grace, and hence her authority. While Julian had urged her not to fear the language of this world, Paul assures her that she need not heed the writings of this world that would silence her bold speech.

Interdiction is the practice by which Kempe establishes and justifies her own voice within the text. Her locutions with St. Paul and Christ occur in between the written texts of her life and the experience, just as her own dictation intercedes between the acts of reading and writing. Interdiction performs that "dispersing gesture" which Cixous attributes to women's writing—one which "breaks with explanation, interpretation, and all the authorities pinpointing localization." Kempe dislocates herself as author by

---

4. Christine de Pizan, *The Book of the City of Ladies*, trans. Earl Jeffrey Richards (New York: Persea Books, 1982), 30. I have discussed this passage in connection with Kempe's search for authority elsewhere, "*The Book of Margery Kempe*: A Marginal Woman's Quest for Literary Authority," *Journal of Medieval and Renaissance Studies* 16 (1986): 33–56.

5. Authority (Latin) [editor's note].

breaking with written authority. In the place of textual authority she substitutes the *volo* [I wish] of mystical desire which gives habitation to her speech.

This does not mean, however, that Kempe makes no reference to textual authorities; in fact, her *Book* does draw upon spiritual texts, and oddly enough, she clearly views it in the context of a Latin tradition.

*　*　*

Though we cannot know how much Latin Kempe knew, neither can we ignore the Latinity of her book. We need to be aware of the fact that the priest who read to her probably read from Latin texts of Hilton, Rolle, and Bridget even if he then translated or paraphrased his readings. Kempe's own spirituality seems to be most markedly influenced by the writings of Richard Rolle, particularly the Incendium Amoris. This is one of the works which Kempe had read to her before the Latin text was translated into Middle English by Richard Misyn in 1435–35.[6] In fact, traces of Rolle's Latin work survive in Kempe's book, not only in her images and mystical concepts but in her mystical idioms.

Kempe's text frequently makes reference to the "fire of love," a very common mystical idea attributed to Rolle in the *Incendium Amoris*.[7] Early in her book, she describes how her heart was consumed by the "ardowr of lofe." Since most other references are made to the fire, rather than the ardor, of love, Hope Emily Allen speculates that maybe Kempe is making a distinction between two types of fires (271n). Yet a reading of the Latin text of Rolle's treatise reveals that the Latin *ardor* was often used as a synonym for *ignis* (fire) and *amor* (love). Rolle explains in his prologue that he uses *ignis* metaphorically to describe *ardor*, the flame or heat of love.[8] It is interesting to note that Misyn translates the *ardor* of the Latin text as "here," "lufe," and "flaume," but not the English derivative, "ardor." Clearly, more than one translation of the Latin text is possible in Middle English. Kempe's use of the word "ardowr" follows the Latin more closely than Misyn's does, even though the word in Middle English does not have the same meaning as the Latin word. This could be the result of a literal translation of the Latin, either the priest's or her own. Whichever is the case, this is just one example of the Latin residues in Kempe's text.

Other borrowings from Rolle likewise recall the Latin text of the *Incendium Amoris*. Kempe's description of the first visitation of the fire of love, for example, is very close to Rolle's description of the same in his prologue. Kempe experiences the fire she feels in her breast and heart as truly "as a man would feel the material fire if he put his hand or his finger in it" (88). This material analogy is provided by Rolle as well in his prologue and in his English work, *The Form of Living*.[9] In this case, Kempe's use of Rolle could have come from either his Latin or his English writings.

6. She mentions having this book read to her after she returns from her visit to the Holy Land, which was at least fifteen years before Misyn's translation (153).
7. While this work is the main source for the "fire of love," other Latin and English writings by Rolle elaborate on this mystical experience, including the *Melos Amoris, Emendatio Vitae, The Form of Living, The Commandment*, and the lyrics [*Melos Amoris* and *Emendatio Vitae*: The *Song* or *Melody* of *Love* and *The Mending of Life*—author's note].
8. *The Incendium Amoris of Richard Rolle of Hampole*, ed. Margaret Deanesly, Publications of the University of Manchester, Historical Series, 26 (London, 1915), p. 146. Rolle also calls this warmth or love a "spiritual ardor" (147).
9. *English Writings of Richard Rolle, Hermit of Hampole*, ed. Hope Emily Allen (Oxford: Clarendon Press, 1931), 105.

She also renders the Rollean experience of the fire of love in her use of the verb "languryn." Rolle's fullest explication of the mystical lover's languor appears again in the *Incendium Amoris*. His explication of languishing comes from the declaration from the Song of Songs 5:8: "I adjure you, O daughters of Jerusalem, if you find my beloved, that you tell him that I languish for love." Rolle attributes this languishing to the lover's abundant love, which lacks the object of his love. More importantly, this languishing accompanies the fire of love, according to Rolle:

> Amoris ergo diuini incendii est mentem quam capit uulnerare: ut dicat, 'Uulnerata sum ego caritate,' et eciam languidam facere pro amore, (unde dicitur *Amore langueo,*) et inebriare: ut sic tendat ad dilectum, quod sui ipsius et omnium rerum obliuiscatur preter Christum.[1]

> (Therefore it is the mind which is wounded by the fire of divine love that is meant by, "I am wounded with love." Also when one is made languid and intoxicated for love, it is said, "I languish for love." For this is how one strives towards the beloved to the extent that he forgets himself and all things apart from Christ.)

Elsewhere in his Latin works, Rolle likewise attributes this "languor" to the wounding of the heart and the unsatisfied longing of the lover for his beloved.[2] Kempe's understanding of mystical languor closely approaches Rolle's, for she reserves the English verb *languren* only for her experience of the terrible lack of the object of her love. When she desires to be rid of the world, Christ instructs her that she must remain and "languren in lofe" (20). Her "languor" is often triggered by the "gret sowndys & gret melodijs" reminding her of Heaven and her own impatience for it (185). She needs only to hear the words uttered in a sermon, "Owr Lord Ihesu langurith for lofe" to be reduced to boisterous weeping (185). Her choice of words again invokes the Latin works of Rolle to her text. It is interesting to note that Kempe uses the verb "languryn" where the Middle English translation of the *Incendium Amoris* consistently translates *langueo* into "longyn."[3] Her choice of the English cognate for the Latin words *languor* and *ardor* echoes Rolle more directly than does the Middle English translation by Misyn.

Kempe's clearest echoes of Rolle occur in her metaphorical renderings of mystical union in terms of song or melody and smell. Rolle's three-fold distinction among the stages of mystical ascent—*calor*, *dulcor*, and *canor*, fire, sweetness, and song—is made in his *Incendium Amoris*, although it appears in his Middle English works as well.[4] Kempe experiences the heavenly melody described by Rolle in his Latin work when she awakens in the middle of the night to "a sound of melody so sweet and delectable, she thought, as though

---

1. *Incendium Amoris*, 195. The subject of languishing also comes up in the English work, *The Form of Living*, but it is more fully elaborated in the Latin works, see *English Writings*, ed. H. E. Allen, 103–4.
2. See Rolle, *Emendatio Vitae* in *The Fire of Love and the Mending of Life*, trans. M. L. Del Mastro (Garden City, NY: Image Books, 1981); and *Melos Amoris*, ch. 55, in *The Melos Amoris of Richard Rolle of Hampole*, ed. E. J. F. Arnould (Oxford: Basil Blackwell, 1957).
3. For a comparison with the Latin passage

quoted, see ch. 18, 40, where even *Amore langueo* is translated "for lufe I longe." For another example, compare Deanesly's edition of *Incendium Amoris*, 216–19, with Richard Misyn's Middle English translation, *The Fire of Love and the Mending of Life, or the Rule of Living*, ed. Ralph Harvey, EETS, o.s. 106 (London, 1896; rpt. 1973), 56–58.
4. See Rolle, *Incendium Amoris*, 182–91; also *The Form of Living* in *Richard Rolle, the English Writings*, ed. and trans. Rosamund S. Allen (New York: Paulist Press, 1988), 170–80.

she were in Paradise" (11). She later speaks of the "sowndys & melodijs" which she heard over a period of twenty-five years and which were so loud as to interfere with her conversations with people (87–88). These mystical references compare with Rolle's account of his own experience while he is reading the Psalms of a "suavitatem inuisibilis melodie" (sweet invisible melody) which overwhelms him. Not only does the divine voice become transformed into this invisible music, but the human response is also converted into song.[5]

More significant is Kempe's reference to the heavenly smells, because she could have been familiar with this mystical sensation in Rolle only through his Latin works.[6] The mystical comfort Kempe receives comes in the form of "sweet smells" which exceed all earthly odors and the power of speech to describe (87). Christ also offers Kempe the comfort of knowing that at her death he will remove body from soul "with great mirth and melody, with sweet smells and good odors" (51). The mysterious odors of divine visitation infuse Rolle's *Melos Amoris* as they do few of his other Latin or English works.[7] While these heavenly scents may be found in continental mysticism, in England they are almost exclusively characteristic of Rolle and Kempe.

This brief overview suggests that Kempe draws upon the Latin writings of Richard Rolle to characterize her mystical experiences.

        ✻   ✻   ✻

The Latin traces of Rolle's works are not the result of scribal mediation, nor do they reflect the efforts of Kempe to authorize her own discourse. Rather, they represent Kempe's own inscription of the Latin culture which excludes her into her text by way of translation. At the same time that her own text echoes Rolle, it rejects Latinity and authorization of written discourse altogether.

        ✻   ✻   ✻

1991

---

5. See Wolfgang Riehle's discussion of Rolle's musical imagery, *The Middle English Mystics*, trans. Bernard Standring (London: Routledge and Kegan Paul, 1981), 119–22. The *Melos Amoris* as well as the *Incendium Amoris* uses the related notions of song and melody to convey mystical dalliance; see Arnould, *Melos Amoris*, 20, 138–40.
6. In fact, Riehle claims that this particular mystical sensation is limited in English mysticism to the Latin works of Rolle, except for the negative experience of the devil's stench in Julian of Norwich's *Showings: Middle English Mystics*, 115–16.
7. *Melos Amoris*, ed. Arnould, 49, 83, 99, 119. Riehle also finds reference to smells in conjunction with the fire of love in *Emendatio Vitae: Middle English Mystics*, 116. The Misyn translation of this work describes the mystic's love as "swete smelland" and a "plesand odur," *The Mending of Life*, 125, 126.

MARGARET J. M. EZELL

From Writing Women's Literary History[1]

From *Introduction: Patterns of Inquiry*

> But what I find deplorable . . . looking about the bookshelves again, is that nothing is known about women before the eighteenth century. I have no model in my mind to turn about this way and that.
> —Virginia Woolf, *A Room of One's Own*

> Re-vision—the act of looking back, of seeing with fresh eyes, of entering an old text from a new critical direction—is for women more than a chapter in cultural history: it is an act of survival. Until we can understand the assumptions in which we are drenched we cannot know ourselves.
> —Adrienne Rich, "When We Dead Awaken: Writing as Re-Vision"

British and American feminist scholars from Virginia Woolf to the present traditionally have been concerned with historical issues in women's writings, in recovering lost texts and traditions. Such efforts have resulted in what is being hailed as the new feminist literary history: Elaine Showalter opens her 1985 anthology of current feminist literary theory by announcing that since the 1979 publication of Sandra Gilbert and Susan Gubar's *Madwoman in the Attic*, their basic insights into women's literary lives in the past have been "tested, supplemented, and extended," resulting in a "coherent, if still incomplete, narrative of female literary history, which describes the evolutionary stages of women's writings during the last 250 years."[2]

In making such statements, critics such as Showalter are asserting the coming of age of a new academic discipline, one that presents itself as different from and oppositional to the traditional patriarchal institution of literary criticism. However, as feminist theorists on both sides of the Atlantic have long pointed out, having institutional status brings the risk of losing that difference of perspective which being outside the institution offers. The question has already been raised to what extent feminist literary theory has benefited from its growing institutional reputation, from its appropriation and redirection of traditional literary criticism, and to what extent it has itself been appropriated and "domesticated" to fit within existing modes of patriarchal, institutional academic thought.

The question thus arises, how different is this evolutionary narrative of women's literary past from the traditional perception of literary history? For example, if the current model of women's literary history now offers a coherent narrative of women's literary lives for the last two hundred and fifty years, what was happening before 1700 and why is it not part of this narrative? Do the existing literary histories of women's writing, which first enabled the serious study of women's literature, paradoxically exclude or obscure significant blocks of early texts through the choice of certain models of historical progress?

In order to create a coherent narrative, any type of history must necessarily be selective in its choice of materials and in its presentation. This is as true for

---

1. Excerpted from the introduction to *Writing Women's Literary History* (1993) [editor's note].
2. Elaine Showalter, "Introduction: The Feminist Critical Revolution," in *The New Feminist Criticism: Essays on Women, Literature and Theory*, ed. Showalter (New York: Pantheon, 1985), p. 6.

literary history as for social, for women's literary history as well as for accounts of the traditional canon—it is as true for this study as for those it analyzes. The question about the writing of women's literary history then becomes, what are the principles of selection and exclusion in the current women's literary history and to what extent are they manifestations of unquestioned assumptions about women's texts, about historical periods, and about the nature of authorship? In short, is it possible to uncover and recognize the assumptions under which we as feminist literary critics have labored in producing our analyses of the past?

My call for a reconsideration of the direction of feminist literary history by those interested in "early" (that is, written before 1700) women's texts may seem unnecessary, given the increasing numbers of critical studies and editions of medieval and Renaissance women writers in the last five years. Those who study early women's texts can point with pride to the growing number of studies devoted to the analysis and presentation of pre-1700 women's writings. For example, recent critical studies of early women's texts, such as Elaine Beilin's *Redeeming Eve: Women Writers of the English Renaissance* and Elaine Hobby's *Virtue of Necessity: English Women's Writing 1649–88,* collections of essays such as Mary Beth Rose's *Women in the Middle Ages and the Renaissance: Literary and Historical Perspectives* and Margaret P. Hannay's *Silent but for the Word: Tudor Women as Patrons, Translators, and Writers of Religious Works* have joined anthologies of early women's writings such as Katharina Wilson's *Women Writers of the Renaissance and Reformation,* Betty Travitsky's *Paradise of Women: Writings by Englishwomen of the Renaissance*, and Elizabeth Alvilda Petroff's *Medieval Women's Visionary Literature* to mark clearly the emergence of a new area of critical endeavor. Works such as Patricia Crawford's checklist of women's publications between 1600 and 1700 in Mary Prior's *Women in English Society 1500–1800,* Dale Spender's *Mothers of the Novel: 100 Good Writers before Jane Austen,* and Janet Todd's *Dictionary of British and American Women Writers, 1660–1800* provide the essential archival data for future studies as they document bibliographically and biographically the existence and the activities of a large number of early women writers so recently rediscovered. Important scholarly editions of the works of Lady Mary Wroth, the Countess of Pembroke, and Lady Elizabeth Carew, to name only a sample, are in production even as this is being written; in addition, we are now witnessing the creation of electronic data bases of women's texts, bibliographies, and critical studies by groups such as the NEH-Brown University Women Writers Project, the Women Writers Bibliography Project at the University of Oklahoma, and the Arizona Center for Medieval and Renaissance Studies at Arizona State University, which is creating a data base of secondary source materials.

With this growing body of critical materials suggesting the increasing scholarly interest and institutional support for study in the area, there is certainly occasion for celebration among those interested in women writing before 1700. Lack of serious, scholarly attention to this subject is no longer the issue. And yet, despite such activities, when one turns to the accounts of feminist literary history and discussions of feminist theory analyzing "the tradition" of women's writing in English, to a striking degree women writing before 1700 are still not part of the "tradition" as it is currently formulated. That is to say, although we have increasing numbers of excellent studies of individual figures, the theoretical model of women's literary history and the construction of women's literary studies as a field rest upon the assumption that women before 1700 either were effectively silenced or constituted in an evolutionary model of "female literature" an early "imitative" phase, contained and co-opted in patriarchal discourse.

As I discuss in subsequent chapters, the marginalization of early women writers in the Anglo-American tradition is in part the result of the early emphasis in feminist studies on nineteenth-century texts. But, as I hope to demonstrate, it is also the result of certain models of historiography which have been imported into women's studies, without a careful scrutiny of the assumptions they contain about the nature of authorship and about the generation of literary history. In general, the main focus of attention by feminist scholars studying pre-1700 writers has been on the essential task of the recovery of these lost texts, asserting their existence and making available a body of women's writings. The emphasis, thus, has not been on questioning whether one can, for example, as is commonly found now, use the same critical framework and vocabulary to describe and analyze women's texts produced for the commercial nineteenth-century market and those written within a seventeenth-century coterie circle, whether the rhetoric created to depict nineteenth-century literary practices is indeed suitable to analyze the literary productions of earlier periods. For example, we frequently find the label "private" or "closet" writings used to describe female authorship; yet the question is typically not asked whether "private" writing or "closet" authorship is really the same phenomenon in the seventeenth and nineteenth centuries, given the historical condition of two very different modes of literary production. While studies and anthologies of medieval and Renaissance women writers clearly and definitely refute the premise that the tradition of women's writing must begin some two hundred and fifty years ago because before then women did not write in sufficient numbers or produce works of sufficient merit or interest, they typically do not engage either the categories or vocabulary provided by the model of women's literary history put forward by Virginia Woolf and her twentieth-century theoretical elaborators, Gilbert, Gubar, and Showalter.

*　　*　　*

1993

JENNIFER WILLGING

From The Power of Feminine Anger in Marie de France's "Yonec" and "Guigemar"[1]

Feminine anger is a frequent and intriguing element in Marie de France's *Lais.* While some of this anger is of a stereotypical nature, such as that of the rebuffed queen in "Lanval" ("Hell hath no fury like a woman scorned"), in other cases it is the more justifiable anger of the *malmariée*, as presented by Marie from a unique, that is, feminine, perspective. As the unhappy lady in "Yonec" rants passionately about her husband:

1. From *Florilegium* 14 (1995–96) [editor's note].

Quant il dit estre baptiziez,
Si fu al flum d'enfern plungiez:
Dur sunt li nerf, dures les veines,
Que de vif sanc sunt tutes pleines.

[When he was supposed to be baptized,
He was plunged into the river of hell:
His nerves are hard, his veins are hard,
All filled with living blood.] (vv. 87–90)[2]

The lady's lamentation in "Guigemar" is equally vitriolic, but aimed interestingly (as I shall develop later) not at her husband but rather at the old priest who guards her: "Ceo doins[e] Deus que mal feu l'arde!" ["May God grant that he burn in hell!"] (v. 348), she cries. The potency of the outbursts of Marie's characters and her apparent approval of them is surprising when set against the background of twelfth-century life, in which, Penny Gold maintains, "the hierarchical vision was a mental habit deeply ingrained in medieval minds" (151). This vision, according to Gold, which is both gender and class related, is what assured medieval women's (and men's) general acceptance of an oppressive social structure. Marie's representation of these two women's anger as justifiable seems doubly surprising when we consider her position as a writer for the court, dedicating her *Lais* as she did to a *nobles reis* (prologue, v. 43). Nonetheless, she was apparently unafraid to suggest that the hierarchical vision was not so deeply ingrained that it could suppress the *malmariée*'s (her version, at least) expression of the loneliness, frustration, boredom, and, above all, injustice she felt as a function of her inferior place in that hierarchy.

But perhaps even more surprising than Marie's *malmariées'* expression of their dissatisfaction is their remedy for it; that is, their adultery. Marie is openly approving of the adulterous affairs of her *malmariées*, women abused and oppressed by the odious men they are forced to marry, and therefore apparently skeptical of the religious and cultural precepts of her day concerning sexuality and marriage.[3] Jaques De Caluwé concludes that in the *Lais* the more reference there is to God, the greater the immorality (114; qtd. by Brumlik 14). Marie frequently juxtaposes human love (often illicit) with divine love, and in doing so, I will argue, not only authors but also authorizes conduct that deviates from and is critical of Church and state sanctioned morality.

The figure of the *malmariée* is, of course, not original to Marie, but is found in the same period both in more popular works such as the *fabliaux* and in courtly lyric and romances such as those of Chrétien de Troyes. * * * [But] Marie's representation is much more radical in that the solutions she offers are counter-conventional, subversive to, rather than supportive of, standard morality. While Chrétien's interest presumably lies in the maintenance of patriarchal authority and the legitimacy of heirs, Marie's lies without a doubt in the restoration of her *malmariées'* happiness and well being. Marie's role

2. All such references to Marie's work are from Ewert. The English translations are mine, but I have used the Hanning and Ferrante translation as a reference.
3. In Marie's *Lais*, justice generally prevails with punishment duly accorded to the wicked and compensation or revenge to the good. In the two *Lais*

already mentioned, as well as in "Laustic," "Chevrefoil," and "Milun," the moral of the story turns in favour of the married lady who loves another man, indicating that Marie's definitions of "good" and "wicked" are not necessarily dictated by conventional morality.

for the *malmariée* in resolving her own dilemma is active (self-fulfilling) rather than passive (self-denying), her action positive (accepting illicit love) rather than negative (rejecting marital consummation). In this way Marie's representation of the *malmariée* stands apart from those of her male contemporaries and descendants (even the most "enlightened").

I will focus for the most part on the two *malmariées* in the *Lais* of "Yonec" and "Guigemar," referring more often to passages in "Yonec" where the *malmariée* holds a more central place in the story. Both have been married off by their families against their wills to old, rich (and unattractive, one can surmise) men, presumably for the financial and social benefits with which such marriages would provide these families (see Flori 195–97). Laments the lady in "Yonec":

> Malëeit seient mi parent
> E li autre communalment
> Ki a cest gelus me donerent
> E a sun cors me marïerent!
>
> [A curse on my parents
> And all the others
> Who gave me to this jealous man
> And married me to his body!] (vv. 81–84)

She makes it clear that she has entered into this marriage against her will, and that it is strictly a union of bodies, not of minds or hearts. The motive of the husband, the instigator of the match, in marrying the lady is depicted as shallow and carnal, for it is *pur sa beauté* that the old man "loved" and married her, even though, as Marie points out, she is also *sage et curteise* (v. 22). Both she and the lady in "Guigemar" have been locked up in towers because of their husbands' irrational jealousy, which has filled them with the fear of being cuckolded and incited them to tyrannize their wives.

Both women as well have guards who act as eunuch figures, an old castrated priest in "Guigemar" and the widowed sister of the husband in "Yonec." The sister presumably is meant to serve as a sort of companion to the lady, but she turns out to be not much of an accomplice in the lady's capers, as it is she who reveals the presence of the lover, a magical bird that turns into a handsome knight, to the husband. The priest and the widow are also analogous in that they are both sexually powerless, the priest concretely so in that he "Les plus bas membres out perduz" ["has lost his nether members"] (v. 257), and the woman figuratively so in that she is both a widow and old, epithets which evoke the idea of sexual dormancy and frustration. Both figures could be seen as likely interested in thwarting any opportunities the young, beautiful ladies might have to fulfill their own desires. It is interesting to note that through these two characters, along with the old husbands (the husband in "Yonec" is assigned the adjectives "viel," "antis," and "Mut . . . trepassez en eage" all in the space of five lines [vv. 12–17]). Marie presents old age as a foil to youthful happiness, as a noxious agent that saps the youth and beauty from those who, like the ladies, are too long exposed to it. And so Marie sets up from the very beginning plots that will concern themselves with rebellion against the austerity and prudishness of old age and the conventions and oppressive religion that its leagues advocate.

It is important here, however, to point out the distinction that Marie makes between human codes of morality or religion (which these two undesirables represent) and what she presents as a more authentic spirituality, with which many of her *Lais* (in particular "Yonec" and "Eliduc") are saturated. She confines her critique to the former and offers the latter as a more deeply meaningful and fulfilling alternative. When the lady in "Yonec" laments her doleful situation, that of being locked up alone in her tower, she lists as her first grievance the fact that her husband will not allow her to go to church (v. 75). In making her wish for a handsome and brave knight to come and be her *ami*, despite the fact that she is a married woman, it is to God himself that she prays: "Deu, ki de tut ad poësté, / Il en face ma volenté!" ["God, who has power over everything, / Grant me my wish!"] (vv. 103–04). She apparently sees no conflict between her wish for a lover and her relationship with God. She throws in the stipulation, however, that this knight be so "Beaus e curteis, [pruz] e vaillanz, / Si que blamees n'en esteient" ["Handsome and courtly, brave and valiant, / That they [the ladies who fall in love with such knights] could not be blamed"] (vv. 98–99). And if he is *invisible* ("Ne nul fors eles nes veeient" ["No one would see them except their ladies"] v. 100), all the better, as then the world would not be able to see, and so condemn, her transgression.

When the bird-knight flies in and gives his economical avowal of his love for the lady (this economy is standard in the *Lais*) and demands hers in return, she asks him, with seemingly odd timing, if he believes in God. He replies smoothly:

> "Dame," dit il, "vus dites bien.
> Ne vodreie pur nule rien
> Que de mei i ait acheisun,
> Mescreauncë u suspesçun.
> Jeo crei mut bien al Creatur
> Que nus geta de la tristur,
> U Adam nus mist, nostre pere,
> Par le mors de la pumme amere.

> ["Lady," he said, "you speak wisely.
> I would not want for anything
> That there be accusation because of me,
> Or mistrust or suspicion.
> I believe strongly in the Creator,
> Who delivered us from the grief
> Into which Adam, our father, placed us
> Through the bite of the bitter apple.] (vv. 145–52)[4]

The knight assures the lady of his love for God, which calms her and wins her over, again economically. His striking *beauté*, to which Marie refers four times, does not seem to impede the rapidity of the lady's decision-making much either. In the lady's appreciation of the knight's physique, Marie perhaps allows her to play the role of the objectifying husband who loves her "pur sa beauté." But only briefly, for in the end it is the knight's catechism-like recitation of his belief in God, and his oath that despite his rather sinister arrival he comes from the side of the divine rather than the diabolical, that convince the lady he is capable of loving her in a spiritual as well as a sexual manner. It is this profession of faith,

---

4. Here it is interesting to note that if we were not already quite sure that the writer of these *lais* was a woman, this acquittal of Eve at the expense of her husband might serve to convince us!

given before both the literal and figurative "communion" of the lovers (assuming the lady's body, the knight takes the host, immediately after which the couple consummate their *coup de foudre*) that will distinguish their union from common adulterous affairs and make it truly "blameless."

But, interestingly, the lady's distinction and subsequent justification of her adultery, the elaboration of which takes over one hundred lines, finds no sanction in twelfth-century theology. John Baldwin gives us the theological context of Marie's stories by reminding us that in 1200 church doors throughout France were closed by papal interdict for nine months while King Philip dawdled in ending an adulterous affair (798).[5] Aside from the political power-play that this debate to some extent represents, it also serves to demonstrate the seriousness with which the Church took adultery, for with interdict the Pope claimed to hold in peril the fate of hundreds of thousands of souls.

Placing us squarely in this seemingly despotic theological atmosphere, Baldwin goes on to summarize and compare five discourses in sexual desire from five very different cross-sections of society, beginning at the top of the severity scale with a group of sober theologians in the Augustinian tradition, and finishing at the bottom with an irreverent writer of *fabliaux*. Focussing first on the theologians, Baldwin gives their formulation of the four principal causes or rationale for marriage: 1) for the sake of offspring, 2) rendering the marital debt between spouses, 3) avoiding fornication, and 4) fulfilling one's desires (803). The last two, it is well to remark, are sins, for wedding expressly and exclusively in order either to avoid extramarital or to enjoy intra-marital sexual relations does not pass marriage muster. Nowhere mentioned here is love; love is a justification neither for marriage nor for sexual intercourse, which, having just barely justification within marriage, has no excuse whatsoever outside of it. According to Augustine and his twelfth-century disciples, concupiscence, whether based on love or not, "recapitulated the primal disobedience and became the primordial venereal disease. Just as the first parents refused to obey God, so their genitals began to disobey rational and volitional commands" (801). The theologians regarded sexual intercourse as fundamentally sinful and so theoretically never truly blameless.

But one can easily question, and Baldwin does, the practical authority that the theologians held over the activities of the lay people, for at the same time that they are busy splitting hairs over whether sexual intercourse *within* a marriage is a mortal or just a venial sin, the characters in the *fabliaux* (and apparently the king himself) are guiltlessly and abundantly engaging in, and consummating, non-marital love affairs. In no way was Marie alone in her portrayal of unsanctioned love, although the writers of the *fabliaux* were much more brash and detail-oriented in their depiction of concupiscence, marital and otherwise. Baldwin demonstrates, as does Steven Nichols, that the twelfth century was not an Augustinian monologue and that while the Church was very present in the lives of lay people, its prescriptions on love and sex were not necessarily heeded, as demonstrated particularly through the *fabliaux* and in courtly romance.

Yet while Marie is not alone in her representation of illicit love, she is nevertheless exceptional in that she presents many of her stories as moral directives, contrary to the designs (or lack thereof) of the writers of the *fabliaux* in

---

5. The issue of the king's infidelities is obviously more complicated than suggested here, but only the above points serve the present argument.

their happy disregard for Church-sanctioned morality (Baldwin 806). In the prologue to her *Lais*, Marie says that such work as hers is an aid in the avoidance of vice, for the writer as well as the reader:

> Ki de vice se volt defendre
> Estudïer deit e entendre
> E grevos' ovre comencier:
> Par [ceo] se puet plus esloignier
> E de grant dolur delivrer.

> [He who wants to defend himself from vice
> Must study and understand
> And begin a weighty work:
> Through this he can better distance himself from vice
> And deliver himself from great sorrow.] (vv. 23–27)

She puts conventional morality into juxtaposition with the "morality" demonstrated in her *Lais*, and tries to reveal, particularly through the *malmariées*, the debilitating injustice of the former and the healing justice of the latter. In both stories, the ladies are married against their wills to husbands who represent the antithesis of the worthy knight-lover, "beaus e curteis, pruz e vaillanz." These marriages are not based in love but rather upon the need to produce heirs and to make profitable mergers of territories (interestingly the first two and only sinless causes of marriage according to the theologians). There can be no mistaking where Marie's sentiments lie and which side she wishes her readers to take. Her depiction of adultery in her *Lais* is not in the interest of irreverence, as it is for the writers of the *fabliaux*, not in doing away with morality itself; rather, it is in the interest of correcting that morality and making it more harmonious with human nature, desires and emotions. Marie offers a new morality that nourishes rather than represses human nature, making it less a state to be reviled and repressed, as theologians see it, than one to be embraced and nurtured.

It should be noted, however, that the approval of adultery that Marie demonstrates in these two *Lais* does not necessarily extend to the others. In "Bisclavret," the unfaithful wife has her nose bitten off by her offended werewolf-husband.[6] And in "Equitan" she is boiled alive (along with her lover, it is well to remember) for her transgression. The difference between the infidelities of these ladies and those of the *malmariées* lies in that those of the former are not incited by any mistreatment on the part of the husbands, but rather by the treachery of the wives themselves (although the husband in "Bisclavret" does neglect to tell her before she takes her vows that he is a werewolf). Adultery is only permitted to those (such as the *malmariées*) who have suffered injustice and to those (such as the bird-knight) whose characters demonstrate them worthy of love. * * * Morality, Marie demonstrates, is not fixed but depends on the situations and on the individual; the same act that is justifiable for the ladies in "Guigemar" and "Yonec" is not so for the wives in "Bisclavret" and "Equitan." In this way, Marie introduces in her *Lais* a notion of relativity and individuality that is rather uncharacteristic of her time and that calls into question some of its rigid universals.

---

6. According to Shulamith Shahar, under Frederick II of Sicily (1194–1250), the penalty for adultery for a woman (and not a man) was having her nose cut off (18).

＊　　＊　　＊

Marie's refusal in "Yonec" and "Guigemar" to accept separate moralities for reality and fantasy, this world and the next, indicates also a refusal to accept the separation of mind and body that twelfth-century theology espoused. This mind/body separation served as a basis for another most important distinction, that between man and woman (Bloch 23–24). Mind, the superior of the two elements, equalled other-worldly, spiritual, rational, man; while body equalled this worldly, carnal, irrational, woman. But Marie constantly confounds the real and the fantastic, the body and the imagination (the mind), both in her *Lais* and within the souls of her characters. The lady in "Yonec" is human and yet able to use the power of her imagination to summon the bird-knight; the bird-knight is divine yet human enough to impregnate the lady. The lady in "Guigemar" is fantastic yet human enough to be integrated into courtly life; Guigemar is human yet finds solutions to his troubles in the fantastic. Many of Marie's characters, whether male or female, contain both worldly and other-worldly elements, and it is exactly this internal duality in each that allows the union of each couple and the fulfillment of the love within it. Marie thus merges human, sexual love with divine, spiritual love, and, in doing so, renders the body/mind dichotomy inoperative. In representing human love as a form of or precursor to divine love, Marie refutes the theologians' precept that that which is corporeal, sensual, concupiscent (i.e., woman) is inherently evil.

＊ ＊ ＊ Through her portraits of the *malmariée*, Marie states her case for the profundity of women's emotional and spiritual capacities, capacities that had always been denied or reduced to predictable categories. In religious matters, her women demonstrate surprising independence of mind, in that by looking inward (rather than exclusively outward toward society) they design a "morality" that is conducive rather than destructive to their natures and their happiness and that is consequently often at odds with the morality of their societies. These ladies' anger is portrayed as a natural, human reaction to injustice and not the predictable ranting of the universal woman described in theological and other discourses of the time.[7] They are three- rather than two-dimensional, neither angels nor devils, virgins (God knows) nor whores. Marie's *malmariées* cannot be submitted to that process of appraisal that Howard Bloch says has "reduced women to the status of a category . . . [and] whose function was . . . the division of women from history by the annihilation of the identity of the individual." (196–97). But ultimately it is for men as well as for women, for all individuals, that Marie renders personal feelings such as loneliness, alienation, frustration, and injustice significant and so legitimizes discontent and action taken to allay these feelings. In a highly authoritarian and depersonalized society, Marie proposes that personal happiness and well-being matter. She unlocks the doors to the ebony towers and lets the *malmariées*, both the literal and the figurative, escape and run down to the sea.

---

7. Marie illustrates this conception of "woman" as a two-dimensional entity by giving Guigemar trouble in recognizing the love of his life when she appears in Meriaduc's court. Can't be her, he shrugs, "Femmes se resemblent asez" ["Women all look quite alike"] (v. 779). Intelligence never does appear on Marie's list of knightly virtues.

WORKS CITED

Baldwin, John W. "Five Discourses on Desire: Sexuality and Gender in Northern France around 1200." *Speculum* 66 (1991): 797–819.

Bloch, R. Howard. *Medieval Misogyny and the Invention of Western Romantic Love.* Chicago: U of Chicago P, 1991.

Brucker, Charles, ed. *Les fables.* By Marie de France. Louvain: Peeters, 1991.

Brumlik, Joan. "Thematic Irony in Marie de France's 'Guigemar' " *French Forum* 13 (1988): 5–16.

Caluwé, Jacques De. "L'élément chrétien dans les *Lais* de Marie de France." *Mélanges de littérature du moyen âge au XXe siècle offerts à Jeanne Lods.* Collection de l'École Normale Supérieure de Jeunes Filles 10 Paris: 1978.

Chrétien de Troyes. *Cligés.* Ed. A. Micha. Paris, 1957.

Despres, Denise L. "Redeeming the Flesh: Spiritual Transformation in Marie de France's 'Yonec.' " *Studia Mystica* 10.3 (1987): 26–39.

Evans, Dafydd. "Marie de France, Chrétien de Troyes and the *Malmariées.*" *Chrétien de Troyes and the Troubadours.* Ed. Peter S. Noble and Linda M. Paterson. Cambridge: St. Catherine's College, 1984. 159–71.

Flori, Jean. "Seigneurie, noblesse et chevalerie dans les *Lais* de Marie de France." *Romania* 108 (1987): 183–206.

Gold, Penny Schine. *The Lady and the Virgin: Image, Attitude, and Experience in Twelfth-Century France.* Chicago: U of Chicago P, 1985.

Hanning, Robert and Joan Ferrante, trans. *The Lais of Marie de France.* Durham: Labyrinth, 1982.

Lods, Jeanne, ed. *Les lais de Marie de France.* Paris: Librairie Honoré Champion, 1959.

Marie de France. *Lais.* Ed. Alfred Ewert. Oxford: Blackwell, 1960.

Nichols, Steven G. "An Intellectual Anthropology of Marriage in the Middle Ages." *The New Medievalism.* Ed. Marina S. Brownlee, Kevin Brownlee, and Stephen G. Nichols. Baltimore: Johns Hopkins UP, 1991. 70–98.

Shahar, Shulamith. *The Fourth Estate: A history of women in the Middle Ages.* Trans. Chaya Galai. New York: Methuen, 1983.

Smith, Jacqueline. "Robert of Abrissel: *Procurator Mulierum.*" *Medieval Women.* Ed. Derek Baker. Oxford: Blackwell, 1978. 175–84. Vol. 1 of *Studies in Church History.* 8 vols. 1978–91.

1993

On Aphra Behn and *Oroonoko*

Published in 1688, Aphra Behn's frequently taught novella—which may have been based on her journey to the sugar colony of Surinam in 1664—quickly morphed into numerous popular translations, dramatizations, and other spin-offs. Interpreted by some as a memoir, by others as a travelogue, and by still others as an imaginary voyage, *Oroonoko* deploys a female narrator focusing on a heroic "royal slave," and this juxtaposition has earned it recent attention as a pivotal document exemplifying late-seventeenth- and early-eighteenth-century attitudes toward gender and race. Both Laura Brown and Margaret Ferguson are attentive to the sexual dynamics of imperialism and the slave trade; however, they provide divergent perspectives on what Behn's approach to gender and empire signifies. Brown emphasizes the historical allusions Behn constructs around her African hero, whereas Ferguson, in a direct response to Brown (whose essay first appeared in 1987), considers the narrative allusions Behn constructs around that hero's African wife.

Laura Brown, who is John Wendell Anderson Professor of English at Cornell University, has composed *English Dramatic Form, 1660–1760: An Essay in Generic History* (1981), *Ends of Empire: Women and Ideology in Early Eighteenth-Century English Literature* (1993), and *Fables of Modernity: Literature and Culture in the English Eighteenth Century* (2001), and co-edited *The New Eighteenth Century: Theory, Politics, English Literature* (1987). Margaret Ferguson, a professor of English at the University of California, Davis, has authored *Trials of Desire: Renaissance Defenses of Poetry* (1984) as well as *Dido's Daughters: Literacy, Gender, and Empire in Early Modern England and France* (2003), and co-edited *Rewriting the Renaissance: The Discourses of Sexual Difference in Early Modern Europe* (1986) and *Postmodernism and Feminism* (1994).

Our last selection widens the framework of the discussion by dealing with Aphra Behn as a paradigm of the female author in the late seventeenth and early eighteenth centuries. Although Catherine Gallagher includes a nuanced reading of *Oroonoko* in her book *Nobody's Story: The Vanishing Acts of Women Writers in the Marketplace, 1670–1820* (1994), we reprint part of her opening chapter on the ways in which and the reasons why Aphra Behn staged a fabricated authorial identity. Gallagher's analysis illuminates the careers of a number of Behn's successors—Charlotte Lennox, Frances Burney, and Maria Edgeworth, for instance—all of whom engendered a rhetoric of authorship to stake out their roles in an expanding literary marketplace. Catherine Gallagher, the Eggers Professor of English Literature at the University of California, Berkeley, has also published *The Industrial Reformation of English Fiction: Social Discourse and Narrative Form, 1832–1867* (1985). She has co-edited *The Making of the Modern Body: Sexuality and Society in the Nineteenth Century* (with Thomas Laqueur, 1987) and *Practicing New Historicism* (with Stephen Greenblatt, 2000). In 2005, she published *The Body Economic: Life, Death, and Sensation in Political Economy and the Victorian Novel*.

LAURA BROWN

From The Romance of Empire:
Oroonoko and the Trade in Slaves[1]

> Our victims know us by their scars and by their chains, and it is this
> that makes their evidence irrefutable. It is enough that they show
> us what we have made of them for us to realize what we have made
> of ourselves.
>
> —Jean-Paul Sartre, Preface to
> Frantz Fanon's *The Wretched of the Earth*[2]

* * *

Although *Oroonoko* can serve as a theoretical test case for the necessary connection of race and gender—a model for the mutual interaction of the positions of the oppressed in the literary discourse of its own age, and a mirror
for modern criticism in which one political reading can be seen to reflect
another, one revisionist school a plurality of revisions. Sartre's juxtaposition
in the epigraph to this essay—"what we have made of them" and "what we
have made of ourselves"—suggests the reciprocal movement necessary for
such a political revisionism, both within the treatment of specific texts and
in the discipline of literary studies at large. In Sartre's reading of Fanon, that
reciprocity is the prerequisite for a relationship of mutual knowledge between
the colonizer and the colonized. In this reading of *Oroonoko*, the figure of the
woman in the imperialist narrative—a sign of "what we have made of ourselves"—provides the point of contact through which the violence of colonial
history—"what we have made of them"—can be represented.

* * *

The aim of this critical project, then, is to demonstrate the contemporaneity of issues of race and gender in a particular stage in the history of
British capitalism associated broadly with commodity exchange and colonialist exploitation. Their conjunction in this particular text is sufficient to
demonstrate the value of a pragmatic dialectical criticism, and indeed the
political importance of refusing to posit any opposition as absolute.

II

As a test case for "radical contemporaneity," *Oroonoko* may seem at first to
provide a rather recalcitrant model: the novella lends itself with great readi-
ness to the argument from alterity. Indeed, Behn's opening description of
"royal slave," Oroonoko, is a *locus classicus* of the trope of sentimental identification, by which the native "other" is naturalized as a European aristocrat.
In physical appearance, the narrator can barely distinguish her native prince
from those of England:

1. Excerpted from chapter 2 of *The New Eighteenth Century* (1987) [editor's note]. I would like
to thank Walter Cohen, Judy Frank, Jeff
Nunokawa, Felicity Nussbaum, and Mark Seltzer

for their help with early versions of this article.
2. Jean-Paul Sartre, Preface to *The Wretched of
the Earth*, by Frantz Fanon, trans. Constance Farrington (New York: Grove Press, 1968), p. 13.

* * *The most famous Statuary cou'd not form the Figure of a Man more admirably turn'd from head to foot . . . His Nose was rising and *Roman*, instead of *African* and flat. His mouth the finest shaped that could be seen[.] * * * The whole Proportion and Air of his Face was so nobly and exactly form'd, that bating his Colour, there could be nothing in Nature more beautiful, agreeable and Handsome.[3] (8).

If this account of Oroonoko's classical European beauty makes it possible to forget his face, the narrator's description of his character and accomplishments further elaborates the act of absolute identity through which he is initially represented:

Nor did the Perfections of his Mind come short of those of his Person; and whoever had heard him speak, wou'd have been convinced of their Errors, that all fine Wit is confined to the white Men, especially to those of Christendom . . . * * * He had heard of and admired the *Romans*: He had heard of the late Civil Wars in *England*, and the deplorable Death of our great Monarch; and wow'd discourse of it with all the Sense and Abhorrence of the Injustice imaginable. He had an extreme good and graceful Mien, and all the Civility of a well-bred great Man. He had nothing of Barbarity in his Nature, but in all Points address'd himself as if his Education had been in some *European* Court. (8, 7)

Oroonoko is thus not only a natural European and aristocrat, but a natural neoclassicist and Royalist as well, an absurdity generated by the desire for an intimate identification with the "royal slave." Like Columbus in Todorov's account,[4] Behn's narrator seems to have only two choices: to imagine the "other" either as absolutely different and hence inferior, or as identical and hence equal. The obvious mystification involved in Behn's depiction of Oroonoko as a European aristocrat in blackface does not necessarily damage the novella's emancipationist reputation; precisely this kind of sentimental identification was in fact the staple component of antislavery narratives for the next century and a half, in England and America. But the failure of Behn's novella to see beyond the mirror of its own culture here raises the question of Behn's relationship with the African slave.

For not only is the novella's protagonist an aristocratic hero, but his story is largely constructed in the tradition of heroic romance. * * * Oroonoko's exploits follow closely the pattern outlined by Eugene Waith for the "Herculean hero," the superhuman epic protagonist who plays a major role in heroic form from the classical period through the Renaissance.[5] Oroonoko is invincible in battle, doing singlehandedly "such things as will not be believed that Human Strength could perform" (30). He is also a man of wit and address, governed absolutely by his allegiance to the conventional aristocratic code of love and honor. When he declares his love to Imoinda, for instance, it is voiced entirely in the familiar terms of heroic romance: "Most happily, some new, and, till then, unknown Power instructed his Heart and Tongue in

3. *Oroonoko; or, The Royal Slave*, introduction by Lore Metzger (New York: Norton, 1973). Subsequent references to *Oroonoko* will be to this edition; page numbers are inserted parenthetically in the text.
4. In a passage omitted here, Brown has discussed Tzvetan Todorov, *The Conquest of America: The*

Question of the Other (*La conquête de l'Amérique: La question de l'autre*, Seuil 1982), trans. Richard Howard (New York: Harper and Row, 1984) [editor's note].
5. Eugene M. Waith, *The Herculean Hero in Marlowe, Chapman, Shakespeare and Dryden* (New York: Columbia University Press, 1962).

the Language of Love. . . . his Flame aim'd at nothing but Honour, if such a distinction may be made in Love" (10).

* * *

Emerging directly from this mystification is the persistent presence of the figure of the woman in *Oroonoko*. In heroic romance, of course, the desirable woman serves invariably as the motive and ultimate prize for male adventures. As this ideology evolved in the seventeenth-century French prose tradition, dominated by women writers like Madeleine de Scudéry and Madame de LaFayette, women became increasingly central to the romantic action. Behn's novellas, like other English prose works of the Restoration and early eighteenth century, draw extensively upon this French material, and the foregrounding of female authorship in *Oroonoko* through the explicit interventions of the female narrator signals the prevalent feminization of the genre.

This narrative must have women: it generates female figures at every turn. Not only is the protagonist represented as especially fond of the company of women (46), but female figures—either Imoinda or the narrator and her surrogates—appear as incentives or witnesses for almost all of Oroonoko's exploits. He fights a monstrous, purportedly immortal tiger for the romantic approval of his female admirers: "*What Trophies and Garlands, Ladies, will you make me, if I bring you home the Heart of this ravenous Beast* . . . We all promis'd he should be rewarded at all our hands" (51). * * * On the trip to the Indian tribes over which Oroonoko presides as expedition leader, the female figure is again the center of attention. Along with the narrator and her "Woman, a Maid of good Courage" (54), only one man agrees to accompany Oroonoko to the Indian town, and once there, the "*White* people," surrounded by the naked natives, stage a scene of cultural difference in which the fully clothed woman is the central spectacle:

> They were all naked; and we were dress'd . . . very glittering and rich; so that we appear'd extremely fine: my own Hair was cut short, and I had a taffety Cap, with black Feathers on my Head. . . . from gazing upon us round, they touch'd us, laying their Hands upon all the Features of our Faces, feeling our Breasts and Arms, taking up one Petticoat, then wondering to see another; admiring our Shoes and Stockings, but more our Garters, which we gave 'em, and they ty'd about their Legs. (55)

Even at the scene of Oroonoko's death, the narrator informs us, though she herself was absent, "my Mother and Sister were by him" (77).

The narrator herself makes it still more evident that the romantic hero is the production and expression of a female sensibility, of "only a Female Pen" (40). The narrator's act of modest self-effacement here, and again on the last page of the novella, signals the special relevance she claims for the female figure, in contrast to the "sublime" masculine wit that would have omitted the crucial naturalness and simplicity (1) of the tale for which the female pen has an innate affinity[.]

* * *

III

But the "normalizing" model of heroic romance does not account for all the material in Behn's representation of West Indian slavery. In fact, neither the theme of slavery nor the romantic action would seem to explain the extended account of the Caribs, the native Americans of Guiana, with which Behn begins. This opening description deploys another set of discursive conventions than those of romance: the natives are the novella's noble savages. The notion of natural innocence, which civilization and laws can only destroy, is obviously incompatible with the hierarchical aristocratic ideology of heroic form; Oroonoko, educated by a Frenchman, is admirable for his connection with—not his distance from   European civilization. The account of the Indians belongs partly to the tradition of travel narrative, by Behn's period a popular mode describing voyages and colonial expeditions to the new world and including detailed reports of marvels ranging from accurate botanical and ethnographic records to pure invention.[6]

Behn's opening description of the Indians establishes her credibility in this context, but in its almost exclusive emphasis on trade with the natives, it also indicates the economic backdrop of the history of the "royal slave":

> trading with them for * * * little Rarities; as *Marmosets* . . . *Cousheries*. . . . Then for little *Paraketoes*, great *Parrots*, *Muckaws*, and a thousand other Birds and Beasts of wonderful and surprizing Forms and Colours. For Skins of prodigious Snakes . . . also some rare Flies, of amazing Forms and Colours . . . Then we trade for Feathers, which they order into all Shapes[.] * * * Besides these, a thousand little Knacks, and Rarities in Nature; and some of Art, as their Baskets, Weapons, Aprons. (2)

The marvels here are all movable objects, readily transportable to a European setting, where they implicitly appear as exotic and desirable acquisitions. Behn's enumeration of these goods is typical of the age's economic and literary language, where the mere act of listing, the evocation of brilliant colors, and the sense of an incalculable numerousness express the period's fascination with imperialist accumulation.[7] But the Indians' goods are at best a small factor in the real economic connection between England and the West Indies; they serve primarily as a synecdoche for imperialist exploitation.

This opening context is centered upon the feathered habit which the narrator acquires, and which, she claims, became upon her return to England the dress of the Indian Queen in Dryden's heroic play of the same name (1664), an artifact of imperialism displayed in the most spectacular manner possible—adorning the female figure of a contemporary actress on the real stage of the Theatre Royal in Bridges Street. The foregrounding of female dress parallels the scene of the expedition to the Indian village, where the spectacle of the narrator's clothing is similarly privileged. And in general, the items in the opening account of imperialist trade reflect the acquisitive instincts of a specifically female sensibility—dress, skins, and exotic pets. Pets, indeed, in particular birds, were both sign and product of the expansion and commercialization of English society in the eighteenth century.[8] Even more important, the association of women with the products of mercantile

6. In the earlier period, Richard Hakluyt's *Principall Navigations* (1589) and Samuel Purchas's *Purchas his Pilgrimes* (1625); in the later period Sir Hans Sloane, *A Voyage To the Islands Madera, Barbados, Nieves, S. Christophers and Jamaica . . .* , 2 vols. (London, 1707); Churchill's *A Collection of Voyages and Travels* (London, 1732).

7. See my *Alexander Pope* (Oxford: Basil Black-

well, 1985), Chapter 1.

8. J. H. Plumb, "The Acceptance of Modernity," in *The Birth of a Consumer Society: The Commercialization of Eighteenth-Century England*, ed. Neil McKendrick, John Brewer, and Plumb (Bloomington: Indiana University Press, 1982), pp. 316–34; the reference to exotic birds is on pp. 321–22.

capitalism, and particularly the obsession with female adornment, is a strong cultural motif in this period of England's first major imperial expansion.[9] * * *

And of course the substantial trade and real profit was not in the Indians' buffalo skins, *Paraketoes*, or feathers, but in sugar and slaves. Behn's description of the slave trade, highly accurate in many of its details, is the shaping economic and historical context of *Oroonoko*. A letter written in 1663 to Sir Robert Harley—at whose house at St. John's Hill (49) the narrator claims to have resided—from one William Yearworth, his steward, may describe the arrival of the slave ship which Behn would have witnessed during her visit to the colony.[1]

> Theare is A genney man [a slave ship from the Guinea Coast] Ariued heare in This riuer of ye 24th of [January] This Instant att Sande poynt. Shee hase 130 nigroes one Borde; ye Comanders name [is] Joseph John Woode; shee has lost 54 negroes in ye viage. The Ladeyes that are heare lieu att St Johnes hill.[2]

Behn recounts the participation of African tribal leaders in collecting and selling slaves to European traders, the prearranged agreements for lots in the colonies, the deliberate dispersal of members of the same tribe around the plantations, the situation of the Negro towns, the imminence of rebellion, and the aggressive character of the Koromantyn (in Behn, Coramantien) slaves— the name given to the Gold Coast tribes from which Oroonoko comes.[3]

Behn's account of the black uprising—an obvious consequence of the slave trade—has no specific historical confirmation, but the situation is typical. Revolts and runaways, or marronage, were commonplace in the West Indies and Guiana throughout this period. In Jamaica rebellions and guerrilla warfare, predominantly led by Koromantyn ex-slaves, were virtually continuous from 1665 to 1740.[4] Marronage was common in Guiana as well during the period when *Oroonoko* is set: while Behn was in Suriname a group of escaped slaves led by a Koromantyn known as Jermes had an established base in the region of Para, from which they attacked local plantations.[5] * * *

The powerful act of "reductive normalizing" performed by the romantic narrative is somewhat countered, then, by a similarly powerful historical contextualization in Behn's account of trade. * * * We cannot read Behn's colonialist history uncritically, any more than we can her heroic romance. But we can read them together, because they are oriented around the same governing point of reference—the figure of the woman. In the paradigm of heroic romance, women are the objects and arbiters of male adventurism, just as, in the ideology of imperialist accumulation, women are the emblems and proxies of the whole male enterprise of colonialism. The female narrator and her proliferative surrogates connect romance and trade in *Oroonoko*, motivating

9. Neil McKendrick, "The Commercialization of Fashion," in *The Birth of a Consumer Society*, pp. 34–99, esp. p. 51.

1. See Angeline Goreau, *Reconstructing Aphra: A Social Biography of Aphra Behn* (New York: Dial Press, 1980), p. 56.

2. "Letters to Sir Robert Harley from the Stewards of His Plantations in Surinam. (1663–4)," reprinted in *Colonising Expeditions to the West Indies and Guiana, 1623–1667*, ed. V. T. Harlow (London: Hakluyt Society, 1925), p. 90.

3. Koromantyn or Coromantijn is a name derived from the Dutch fort at Koromantyn on the Gold Coast; in Suriname it designated slaves from the Fanti, Ashanti, and other interior Gold Coast tribes. For background and statistics on the tribal origins of the Bush Negroes of Guiana, see Richard Price, *The Guiana Maroons: A Historical and Bibliographical Introduction* (Baltimore: Johns Hopkins University Press, 1976), pp. 12–16.

4. Orlando Patterson, "Slavery and Slave Revolts: A Sociohistorical Analysis of the First Maroon War, 1665–1740," in *Maroon Societies: Rebel Slave Communities in the Americas*, ed. Richard Price, 1973; 2nd ed. (Baltimore: Johns Hopkins University Press, 1979), pp. 246–92, esp. pp. 256–70.

5. Price, *Guiana Maroons*, p. 23.

the hero's exploits, validating his romantic appeal, and witnessing his tragic fate. * * *

These two paradigms intersect in Oroonoko's antislavery speech:

> And why (said he) my dear Friends and Fellow-sufferers, should we be Slaves to an unknown People? Have they vanquished us nobly in Fight? Have they won us in Honourable Battle? And are we by the Chance of War become their Slaves? This wou'd not anger a noble Heart; this would not animate a Soldier's Soul: no, but we are bought and sold like Apes or Monkeys, to be the sport of Women, Fools and Cowards. (61)

The attack on slavery is voiced in part through the codes of heroic romance: the trade in slaves is unjust only if and when slaves are not honorably conquered in battle. But these lines also allude to the other ideology of Oroonoko, the feminization of trade that we have associated primarily with the Indians. Oroonoko's resentment at being "bought and sold like Apes or Monkeys . . . the sport of women" is plausible given the prominent opening description of the animals and birds traded by the Indians, in particular of the little "Marmosets, a sort of Monkey, as big as a Rat or Weasel, but of a marvellous and delicate shape, having Face and Hands like a Human Creature" (2). In conjunction with the image of the pet monkey, Oroonoko's critique of slavery reveals the critique of colonialist ideology in one of its most powerful redactions—the representation of female consumption, of monkeys and men.

In grounding the parallel systems of romance and trade, the female figure in Behn's novella plays a role like that outlined by Myra Jehlen, the role of "Archimedes' lever"—the famous paradoxical machine that could move the earth, if only it could have a place to stand.[6] Though they are marginal and subordinate to men, women have no extrinsic perspective, no objective status, in this narrative, either as the arbiters of romance or as the beneficiaries of colonialism. But though they have no independent place to stand, in their mediatory role between heroic romance and mercantile imperialism, they anchor the interaction of these two otherwise incompatible discourses. They make possible the superimposition of aristocratic and bourgeois systems—the ideological contradiction that dominates the novella. And in that contradiction we can locate a site beyond alterity, a point of critique and sympathy produced by the radical contemporaneity of issues of gender with those of romance and race.

IV

On the face of it, the treatment of slavery in Oroonoko is neither coherent nor fully critical. The romance motifs, with their elitist focus on the fate of African "princes," entail an ambiguous attack on the institution of slavery, and adumbrate the sentimental antislavery position of the eighteenth century. But the representation of trade and consumption, readily extended to the trade in slaves and the consumption of Oroonoko himself, and specifically imagined through a female sensibility, renders colonialism unambiguously attractive. This incoherence could be explored in further detail: in the narrative's confusion about the enslavement of Indians and the contradictory reasons given for their freedom; in the narrator's vacillation between friend-

6. Myra Jehlen, "Archimedes and the Paradox of Feminist Criticism," in The "Signs" Reader: Women, Gender and Scholarship, ed. Elizabeth Abel and Emily K. Abel (Chicago: University of Chicago Press, 1983), pp. 69–95.

ship with and fear of the "royal slave"; in the dubious role she plays in "diverting" Oroonoko with romantic tales so as to maintain his belief that he will be returned to Africa, her collusion in the assignment of spies to attend him in his meetings with the other slaves, and the quite explicit threat she uses to keep him from fomenting rebellion; and even in the fascination with dismemberment that pervades the novella's relation with the native "other"— both Indian and African—and that suggests a perverse connection between the female narrator and Oroonoko's brutal executioners.

A deeper critique of slavery emerges at the climactic moment in the ideological contradiction that dominates the novella. This insight originates in the hidden contemporary political referent of the narrative: the party quarrels in the West Indies and Guiana at the time of Behn's visit. Though the novella's account is sketchy, Behn names historical persons and evokes animosities traceable to the political tensions that emigrated to the colonies during the revolution and after the Restoration.[7] The relative political neutrality of the West Indies and Guiana attracted Royalists during the revolution and Parliamentarians and radicals after the Restoration. The rendering of the colonists' council (69), and the account of the contests for jurisdiction over Oroonoko reflect the reigning atmosphere of political tension in Suriname during the time of Behn's visit in 1663 and 1664, though without assigning political labels to the disputants. In fact, the Lord Governor of Suriname to whom the novella refers is Francis, Lord Willoughby of Parham, intimate of the royal family and of Lord Clarendon and constant conspirator against the Protectorate, who had received his commission for settlements in Guiana and elsewhere in the Caribbean from Charles II, at his court in exile. Willoughby is absent during Behn's narrative, but the current governor of the colony, William Byam, who orders Oroonoko's execution, was a key figure in the Royalist struggle for control of Barbados in the previous decade, and likewise in Suriname engaged in a continuous battle with the contingent of Parliamentarians in the colony. In 1662, immediately before Behn's arrival, Byam had accused a group of Independents, led by Robert Sandford, of conspiracy, summarily trying and ejecting them from the colony. Sandford was the owner of the plantation neighboring Sir Robert Harley's, St. John's Hill, the narrator's residence. Harley also was a Royalist and had been a friend of Willoughby, though a quarrel between the two during Harley's chancellorship of Barbados resulted in Willoughby's expulsion from that colony in 1664. There were few firm friendships beyond the Line in this tumultuous period of colonial adventurism. Indeed in 1665, shortly after Behn left Suriname, Willoughby himself, in a visit to Guiana meant to restore orderly government to the colony, was nearly assassinated by John Allen, who resented his recent prosecution for blasphemy and duelling.

Behn herself may have been engaged with these volatile politics through an alliance with a radical named William Scot, who went to the colony to escape prosecution for high treason in England, and whose father Thomas figured prominently on the Parliamentary side during the revolution and Commonwealth.[8] The radical connection makes some sense in that Byam, the notori-

7. See the documents under "Guiana" in the Hakluyt Society's *Colonizing Expeditions to the West Indies and Guiana, 1623–1667*, esp. "The Discription of Guyana," "To ye Right Honourable ye Lords of His Majesties most Honorable Privy Councel, The Case of ye Proscripts from Surinam with all Humility is briefely but most truely stated. 1662," and "Letters to Sir Robert Harley from the Stewards of his Plantations in Surinam. 1663–1664"; V. T. Harlow's detailed introduction to this reprint collection, esp. pp. xxvii–lv and lxvi–xcv; Goreau, *Reconstructing Aphra*, pp. 66–69; and Cyril Hamshere, *The British in the Caribbean* (Cambridge: Harvard University Press, 1972), pp. 64–65.

8. Goreau, *Reconstructing Aphra*, pp. 66–69.

ously ardent and high handed Royalist, is clearly the villain of the piece, and Colonel George Martin, Parliamentarian and brother to "*Harry Martin* the great *Oliverian*" (50), deplores the inhumanity of Oroonoko's execution. * * *

But there is no simple political allegory in Behn's novella. Though the Royalist Byam is Oroonoko's enemy, Behn describes Trefry, Oroonoko's friend, as Willoughby's overseer in Suriname; although he has not been historically identified, Trefry must have been a Royalist. His open struggle with Byam over Oroonoko's fate might allude to divisions within the Royalist camp, divisions which were frequent and intense in Barbados, for instance, when Willoughby came to power in that colony. More important than direct political correspondences, however, is the tenor of political experience in the West Indies and Guiana in this period. For Behn and others, the colonies stage an historical anachronism, the repetition of the English revolution, and the political endpoint of Behn's narrative is the reenactment of the most traumatic event of the revolution, the execution of Charles I.

From almost the instant of his beheading, the King's last days, and the climactic drama of his death, were memorialized by Royalist writers in a language that established the discourse of Charles's suffering as heroic tragedy. *The Life of Charles I*, written just after the Restoration and close to the year in which Oroonoko's story is set, suggests the tenor of this discourse:

> He entred this ignominious and gastly Theatre with the same mind as He used to carry His Throne, shewing no fear of death . . . [Bloody trophies from the execution were distributed among the King's murderers at the execution and immediately thereafter] . . . some out of a brutish malice would have them as spoiles and trophees of their hatred to their Lawfull Sovereign . . . He that had nothing Common in His Life and Fortune is almost profaned by a Vulgar pen. The attempt, I confess, admits no Apology but this, That it was fit that Posterity, when they read His Works . . . should also be told that His Actions were as Heroick as His Writings . . . Which not being undertaken by some Noble hand . . . I was by Importunity prevailed upon to imitate those affectionate Slaves, who would gather up the scattered limbs of some great Person that had been their Lord, yet fell at the pleasure of his Enemies.[9]

Related images appear in a version published in 1681, shortly before the writing of *Oroonoko*:

> * * *he suffered as an Heroick Champion . . . by his patient enduring the many insolent affronts of this subtile, false, cruel, and most implacable Generation, in their Barbarous manner of conventing, and Condemning him to Death; and to see his most bloodthirsty Enemies then Triumph over him. . . . they have made him *Glorious* in his Memory, throughout the World, by a Great, Universal and most durable Fame.[1]

Charles I was a powerful presence for Behn at the writing of *Oroonoko*, even though the story was composed only shortly before its publication in 1688, long after Charles's death, the Restoration, and even the intervening death of Charles II—the monarch with whom Behn's acquaintance was much more personal. Oroonoko's heroism is attached to that of Charles I not

9. Richard Perrinchiefe, *The Life of Charles 1* in *The Workes of King Charles The Martyr* (London, 1662), pp. 92–93, 118.

1. William Dugdale, *A Short View of the Late Troubles in England* (Oxford, 1681), pp. 371–75.

just generically—in the affinity of "Great Men" of "mighty Actions" and "large Souls" (7, 47)—but directly. Behn's slave name for Oroonoko—Caesar—is the same she repeatedly used for the Stuart monarchs: Charles II is Caesar in her poem "A Farewell to Celladon on His Going Into Ireland" (1684), as is James II and her "Poem to Her Sacred Majesty Queen Mary" (1689).[2] Oroonoko, as we have seen, is defined by his sympathy for Charles's "deplorable Death" (7). Sentenced, like Charles in these Royalist accounts, by the decree of a Council of "notorious Villains" (69) and irreverent swearers, and murdered by Banister, a "Fellow of absolute Barbarity, and fit to execute any Villainy" (76), "this great Man" (78), another royal martyr, endures his death patiently, "without a Groan, or a Reproach" (77). Even the narrator's final apology—though it refers specifically to female authorship—reproduces the conventional humble stance of the chroniclers of the King's death: "Thus died this great Man, worthy of a better Fate, and a more sublime Wit than mine to write his Praise; Yet, I hope, the Reputation of my pen is considerable enough to make his glorious Name to survive to all Ages" (78). "The Spectacle . . . of a mangled King" (77), at the close of the narrative,[3] when Oroonoko is quartered and his remains distributed around the colony, evokes with surprising vividness the tragic drama of Charles Stuart's violent death. The sense of momentous loss generated on behalf of the "royal slave" is the product of the hidden figuration in Oroonoko's death of the culminating moment of the English revolution.

But the tragedy is double in a larger sense. Abstractly speaking, both Charles I and Oroonoko are victims of the same historical phenomenon—those new forces in English society loosely associated with an antiabsolutist mercantile imperialism. The rapid rise of colonization and trade coincided with the defeat of absolutism in the seventeenth century. In a mediated sense the death of Charles I makes that of Oroonoko possible, and Oroonoko's death stands as a reminder of the massive historical shift that destroyed Charles Stuart and made England a modern imperialist power. Ironically, in this context, both King Charles and the African slave in the New World are victims of the same historical force.

We might imagine that the account of Oroonoko's death represents the moment of greatest mystification in the narrative, the proof of an absolute alterity in the confrontation between the colonialist and the native "other." What could be more divergent than the fate of Charles Stuart and that of an African slave? But the violent yoking of these two figures provides the occasion for the most brutally visceral contact that Behn's narrative makes with the historical experience of slavery in the West Indies and Guiana. Merely the information that Oroonoko is a Koromantyn (5) connects his story to eighteenth-century testimony on slavery and rebellion in the colonies. Bryan Edwards describes the character of slaves from this area:

> The circumstances which distinguish the Koromantyn, or Gold Coast, Negroes, from all others, are firmness both of body and mind; a ferociousness of disposition; but withal, activity, courage, and a stubbornness, or what an ancient Roman would have deemed an elevation, of soul, which prompts them to enterprizes of difficulty and danger; and enables them to meet death, in its most horrible shape, with fortitude or

2. William Spengemann, "The Earliest American Novel: Aphra Behn's *Oroonoko*," *Nineteenth-Century Fiction* 38 (1984): 401.

3. I am indebted to Adela Pinch (Department of English, Cornell University) for my reading of these lines.

indifference. . . . It is not wonderful that such men should endeavour, even by means the most desperate, to regain the freedom of which they have been deprived; nor do I conceive that any further circumstances are necessary to prompt them to action, than that of being sold into captivity in a distant country.[4]

Edwards is obviously drawn to epic romanticization, but his historical account suggests the experience behind the romance in Behn's narrative. So common was rebellion among the Koromantyns, that Gold Coast slave imports were cut off by the late eighteenth century to reduce the risk of insurrection.

Edwards recounts one such rebellion in Jamaica in 1760, which "arose at the instigation of a Koromantyn Negro of the name of Tacky, who had been a chief in Guiney" (II, 59–60). He details the execution of the rebel leaders * * *:

> The wretch that was burned was made to sit on the ground, and his body being chained to an iron stake, the fire was applied to his feet. He uttered not a groan, and saw his legs reduced to ashes with the utmost firmness and composure; after which one of his arms by some means getting loose, he snatched a brand from the fire that was consuming him, and flung it in the face of the executioner. (II, 61)

* * * And John Stedman, the period's most detailed reporter of the executions of rebel maroons, recounts the request of a man who had been broken on the rack: "I imagined him dead, and felt happy; till the magistrates stirring to depart, he writhed himself from the cross . . . rested his head on part of the timber, and asked the by-standers for a pipe of tobacco."[5]

In this context, Oroonoko's death takes on a significance entirely different from that conferred upon it through the paradigm of heroic romance or the figuration of Charles's death:

> [he] assur'd them, they need not tie him, for he would stand fix'd like a Rock, and endure Death so as should encourage them to die . . . He had learn'd to take Tobacco; and when he was assur'd he should die, he desir'd they should give him a Pipe in his Mouth, ready lighted; which they did: And the executioner came, and first cut off his Members, and threw them into the Fire; after that, with an ill-favour'd Knife, they cut off his Ears and his Nose, and burn'd them; he still smoak'd on, as if nothing had touch'd him; then they hack'd off one of his Arms, and still he bore up, and held

---

4. Bryan Edwards, The History, Civil and Commercial, of the British Colonies in the West Indies, 2 vols. (Dublin, 1793), rpt. (New York: Arno Press, 1972), II.59. Most of the detailed accounts of slavery in the West Indies and Guiana date from the later eighteenth century. But there is ample evidence of marronage, rebellion, and judicial torture throughout the West Indies and including Suriname from Behn's period on. Suriname passed out of British hands in 1667, and thus the fullest documentation of the treatment of rebel slaves in that country describes conditions under the Dutch. There is every reason to believe, however, in a continuity from British to Dutch practices historically in Suriname, just as there is every evidence of the same continuity throughout the West Indies and Guiana—British or Dutch—at any given moment in the long century and a half of active slave trade. For further documentation, in addition to the works cited in subsequent notes, see George Warren, An Impartial Description of Surinam upon the Continent of Guiana in America (London, 1667); Historical Essay on the Colony of Surinam, 1788, trans. Simon Cohen, ed. Jacob R. Marcus and Stanley F. Chyet (New York: Ktav Publishing House, 1974); Price, Guiana Maroons; Price, ed., Maroon Societies.

5. John Stedman, Narrative of a Five Years' Expedition Against the Revolted Negroes of Surinam (1796; rpt. Amherst: University of Massachusetts Press, 1972), p. 382. Stedman's book contains the fullest account available in this period of the punishments for maroons in the West Indies and Guiana. Price finds Stedman's descriptions "to have a solid grounding in fact," and he also shows that Suriname was the most brutal of the major plantation colonies of the New World (Guiana Maroons, pp. 25, 9).

his Pipe; but at the cutting off the other Arm, his Head sunk, and his Pipe dropt and he gave up the Ghost, without a Groan, or a Reproach. (77)

As far as this horrible fictional scene takes us from the image of Dryden's Antony or that of Charles Stuart, those radically irrelevant figures are the means by which this narrative finds its way to the historical experience of the Koromantyn slave—the means by which this passage offers not merely a fascination with the brutality depicted here and in the other historical materials I have cited, but a sympathetic memorialization of those human beings whose sufferings these words recall.

V

* * *

In Charles Stuart and Oroonoko we have seen two creatures who could never meet in this world joined as historical contemporaries through the contradictory logic of Behn's imperialist romance. We have used a feminist reading of colonialist ideology, which places women at the center of the structures of rationalization that justify mercantile expansion, to ground the account of the contradictions surrounding the representation of race in this work. And we have juxtaposed the figure of the woman—ideological implement of a colonialist culture—with the figure of the slave—economic implement of the same system. Though Behn never clearly sees herself in the place of the African slave, the mediation of the figure of the woman between the two contradictory paradigms upon which her narrative depends uncovers a mutuality beyond her conscious control.

These relationships of contemporaneity spring from the failures of discursive coherence in *Oroonoko,* from the interaction of the contradictory aristocratic and bourgeois paradigms that shape the novella. This interaction is the dialectical process that my reading of *Oroonoko* has aimed to define, the process by which we may "meet the Other on the same ground, in the same Time." By this means, we can position the African slave in Behn's novella not as a projection of colonialist discourse, contained or incorporated by a dominant power, but as an historical force in his own right and his own body. * * *

1987, 1993

MARGARET W. FERGUSON

From Juggling the Categories of Race, Class, and Gender: Aphra Behn's *Oroonoko*[1]

* * *

Let us look * * * at some of the ways in which the categories of race, class, and gender, understood as historically contingent and relational rather than

1. From *Women's Studies* 19 (1991) [editor's note]. Many colleagues and students have helped me with this essay; I owe special thanks to Judy Berman, Ann R. Jones, Mary Poovey, David Simpson, Valerie Smith, and Liz Wiesen.

foundational concepts, work in a mutually determining fashion in Behn's *Oroonoko* and in what we can reconstruct of the various historical discourses and shifting configurations of material life from which her book derives and to which it contributed substantially—most obviously by limning an image of the "Noble Negro" in ways that made it, as Laura Brown observes, "a crucial early text in the sentimental, antislavery tradition that grew steadily through-out the eighteenth century."[2]

Whatever the "facts" of Aphra Behn's birth (conflicting theories construct her as the illegitimate daughter of an aristocrat, male or female, or as the child of a barber or a wetnurse), the single most important determinant of her multiple class positions was arguably her access to, and later, her deployment of, the skills of literacy.[3] Her lack of a classical education meant that she was not "fully" literate in her culture's terms, but her ability to read and write English and several other European languages nonetheless allowed her to earn her living by her pen, first as a spy for Charles II and later as the author of plays, poems, novellas, and translations. Though classic Marxist theory does not consider intellectual work "direct production," the writer in the early modern era, as a member of an emergent class or caste of secular intellectuals ambiguously placed between their sometimes relatively humble origins and the nobility whom they frequently served and with whom they often imaginatively identified, was in many cases a producer of commodities for the market. Indeed the energy with which many humanist writers sought to distinguish their labor from "merely" clerkly or artisanal work suggests how fraught with anxiety (then as now) was the self-definition of persons who occupied the ambiguous class position of intellectual worker.[4] * * * At this point, I will insist only on foregrounding the fact that she *did* participate, as a producer of verbal commodities who explicitly if intermittently defined herself as oppressed by and financially dependent on wealthy men, but also as a member of an English "family" of slave owners (as it were) and as such, one who directly and "naturally" profited from others' labor.

2. Laura Brown, "The Romance of Empire: *Oroonoko* and the Trade in Slaves," in *The New Eighteenth Century*, ed. L. Brown and Felicity Nussbaum (New York: Methuen, 1987), p. 42.

3. According to Behn's first biographer, identified only as "One of the Fair Sex" and since identified both as Charles Gildon (by Montague Summers) and as Behn herself (by R.A. Day, "Aphra Behn's First Biographer," *Studies in Bibliography* 22 [1969], 227–40), she was a "gentlewoman by birth, of a good family in the City of Canterbury in Kent" (*History of the Life and Memoirs of Mrs. Behn*, London, 1696; quoted from Angeline Goreau, *Reconstructing Aphra: A Social Biography of Aphra Behn* [New York: The Dial Press, 1980], p. 8). Not until the late nineteenth century did anyone seek publicly to refashion Behn's biography; Sir Edward Gosse then lowered her social status on the evidence of a scribbled note, "Mrs Behn was daughter to a barber," in the margin of a recently discovered ms. by Anne Finch, the Countess of Winchelsea. Goreau provides an account of Gosse's "discovery" (given authority in his *Dictionary of National Biography* article on her) and subsequent biographical arguments on pp. 8–10 of *Reconstructing Aphra*. For further discussions of the "mystery" of Behn's birth and the manifold speculations it has engendered, see Goreau, pp. 11–13, 42–43; Sara Mendelson, *The Mental World*

of *Stuart Women: Three Studies* (Brighton: Harvester, 1987), pp. 116–120; and Maureen Duffey, *The Passionate Shepherdess: Aphra Behn, 1640–89* (London: Cape, 1977), chap. 1. See Goreau, pp. 12–13, for a discussion of the importance of Behn's (anomalous) education for her social status.

4. See Wlad Godzich, "The Culture of Illiteracy," *Enclitic* 8 (Fall 1984), 27–35, on humanist intellectuals as servants of the emerging nation states and the expanding international market of the early modern era. In *Trials of Desire: Renaissance Defenses of Poetry* (New Haven: Yale University Press, 1983), I analyzed some of the anxieties about social class articulated by writers such as Joachim du Bellay and Philip Sidney. For a subtle discussion of problems in defining the modern intellectual's work either according to a classic Marxist notion of "productive" labor (that is, labor that yields *surplus* value) or according to popular conceptions of what constitutes valuable work in a post-industrial society, see Evan Watkins, *Work Time: English Departments and the Circulation of Cultural Value* (Stanford: Stanford University Press, 1989). Watkins builds on Antonio Gramsci's "The Formation of The Intellectuals," in *Selections from the Prison Notebooks*, ed. and trans. Quintin Hoare and Geoffrey Nowell Smith (New York: International, 1971), pp. 5–23.

* * * In *Oroonoko*, set in the early 1660's, before Behn's rather mysterious marriage to a Dutch merchant, but written in 1688, long after she had ceased to be a wife, she defines her status as formed in crucial ways by her gender; she refers explicitly to her "female pen," and frequently presents herself as a heroine with features drawn from literary codes of romance and Petrarchan lyric.[5] Lurking behind her portrait of the author as a young, unmarried lady with great verbal facility is a complex body of cultural discourse on Woman and the forms of behavior she should eschew (talking and writing in public, which behavior is often equated with prostitution) and embrace (obedience to fathers and husbands being a prime command).[6] An emerging cultural discourse about women who went to the colonies—often, allegedly, to acquire the husbands they'd not found in England, or worse, to satisfy their "natural" lusts with men of color—also lurks behind Behn's self-portrait.[7] This cultural subtext, made into an explicit subplot of Thomas Southerne's 1696 stage version of *Oronooko*, seems particularly germane to Behn since, as Angeline Goreau has argued, her (adoptive?) father left her without a dowry when he died en route to Surinam.[8] Her novella at once partly reproduces the negative cultural subtext(s) of female gender and seeks to refute them.

Her social status is also defined as a function of her race, or, more precisely and provisionally, of her membership in a group of colonizing English white people who owned black slaves imported from Africa and who uneasily shared Surinam with another group of non-white persons, the native Carib Indians. We can conveniently trace some of the contradictions in the narrator's social identity, with its multiple "subject positions" created in part by competing allegiances according to race, class, and gender, if we examine the narrative "I" in relation to the text's different uses of the pronoun "we." With whom does the "I" align itself?[9]

The first stage of an answer is to say that the "I" aligns itself sometimes with a "we" composed of women: in these cases the "I" is definitely a "she." At other times, however, the "I" aligns—or in political terms, allies—itself with a "we" composed of property-owning English colonialists defending themselves against an Other (a "them") composed of African slaves or of native Indians, and sometimes of both. In these cases, the gender of the "I" is evidently less salient than are nationality, membership in a surplus-extracting

5. For a discussion of the date of *Oroonoko's* composition see George Guffey, "Aphra Behn's *Oroonoko*: Occasion and Accomplishment," in *Two English Novelists: Aphra Behn and Anthony Trollope*, co-authored with Andrew White (Los Angeles: William Andrews Clark Memorial Library, UCLA, 1975), pp. 15–16. All quotations from *Oroonoko* are from the text edited by Lore Metzger (New York: W.W. Norton & Co., 1973). The reference to the female pen is from p. 46. See Laura Brown, "The Romance of Empire," esp. 48–51, for a discussion of the story's debt to the traditions of heroic romance and, in particular, coterie aristocratic drama. Brown analyzes how Behn uses romance conventions to perform what Mary Louise Pratt has called a "reductive normalization" of the hero's alterity; in this "mystificatory" process, Brown argues, the figure of the woman, both as narrative "producer" and as consumer (audience-reader), is crucial.

6. For an excellent account and bibliography of the Renaissance ideology of normative femininity, see Ann Rosalind Jones, *The Currency of Eros:* *Women's Love Lyric in Europe, 1540–1620* (Bloomington: University of Indiana Press, 1990), chap. 1.

7. For examples of this gendered "colonial" cultural discourse see David Brion Davis, *The Problem of Slavery in Western Culture* (Ithaca: Cornell University Press, 1966), p. 277; Edward Long, *Candid Reflections upon the Judgement Lately Awarded by the Court of the King's Bench . . . on What is Commonly Called the Negro Cause* (London, 1772), cited by Davis in ibid.; and Goreau, pp. 48–49 (on the fears of "sodomy" that kept one lady living in Antigua housebound, and on the repercussions of the fact that men in the colonies greatly outnumbered women).

8. On Behn's situation after her father died, impoverished but also freer of paternal constraint than was thought proper, see Goreau, p. 42.

9. My account of the multiple alignments of the "I" is indebted to questions prepared by Judy Berman for a graduate seminar at the University of California, Berkeley, in the spring of 1988.

group, and color. Within these two basically contradictory subject positions, however, other configurations appear and disappear. "We" women, for instance, are sometimes opposed to cruel and powerful white men, and this opposition clearly participates in the interrogation of the institution of marriage which many of Behn's plays mount and which texts by other seventeenth-century English women pursue as well: Lady Mary Chudleigh, for instance, in a poem "To the Ladies," of 1703, wrote that "Wife and servant are the same, / But only differ in the name."[1] An opposition drawn along lines of gender within the British community allows—in the peculiar circumstances of colonialism—for an unusual alliance to flourish between white females, notably the narrator and her mother and sister, and the black slave Oroonoko: a community of the unjustly oppressed is thus formed, and indeed unjust oppression comes to be associated with a state of effeminacy figured, interestingly, as male impotence.[2]

The analogy between white women and Oroonoko, and particularly the alliance between the narrator and her hero, is, however, extremely volatile, partly because it poses an obvious double-pronged threat to the colonial social hierarchy in which white men occupied the top place. The narrator, as the unmarried daughter (so she claims) of the man who was supposed to govern the colony had he not died en route to his post, threatens the ideologies of patriarchy in some of the ways that Queen Elizabeth had a hundred years before Behn wrote her book. To claim, as Behn does in her prefatory letter to an aristocratic patron, that there was "none above me in that Country," and to depict herself as living in "the best house" in the colony (p. 49), is to engage in imaginative competition with the man who actually stood in for Behn's father, one Colonel William Byam, who is painted as a brutal tyrant in the text and who cordially despised Aphra Behn, according to the historical record.[3] Wielding an instrument of writing which she and her society saw as belonging to masculine prerogative, the narrator courts notoriety by representing herself as the sympathetic confidante of a black male slave who had, in his native land, been a prince engaged in erotic and by implication political rivalry with his grandfather and king.[4] The narrator and Caesar are allied in a multifaceted league of potential subversion.

1. Chudleigh's text, from her *Poems on Several Occasions* (London, 1703), is quoted from *First Feminists: British Women Writers 1578–1799*, ed. Moira Ferguson (Bloomington and Old Westbury: Indiana University Press and The Feminist Press, 1985), p. 237. Cf. the statement in a famous pamphlet entitled *The Levellers*, also from 1703, that "Matrimony is indeed become a meer Trade [.] They carry their daughters to *Smithfield* as they do Horses, and sell to the highest bidder." Quoted in Maximillian E. Novak and David Stuart Rodes's edition of Thomas Southerne's *Oroonoko* (Lincoln: University of Nebraska Press, 1976), p. xxiv. For an example of this analogy from later in the century, see Margaret Cavendish's equation of marriage with slavery in *CCXI Sociable Letters* (1664; facsimile ed., Menston, England: Scolar Press, 1969), p. 427.

2. Behn offers a more literal and comic representation of impotence in the first part of the novella, where Imoinda is taken from Oroonoko by his tyrannical but impotent grandfather; she also represents male impotence in many of her plays and in the poem "The Disappointment," a brilliantly revisionary instance of the Restoration subgenre of

"imperfect enjoyment" poems. On her deviation from male-authored poetic representations of impotence see Judith Kegan Gardiner, "Aphra Behn: Sexuality and Self-Respect," *Women's Studies* 7 (1980), 67–78, esp. 74–7; and also Margaret W. Ferguson, "A Room Not Their Own: Renaissance Women as Readers and Writers," in *The Comparative Perspective on Literature*, ed. Clayton Koelb and Susan Noakes (Ithaca: Cornell University Press, 1988), 112–4.

3. The quotation is from the "Epistle Dedicatory" to Lord Maitland, included in the edition of *Oroonoko* by Adelaide P. Amore (Washington, D.C.: University Press of America, 1987), p. 3, but not in the Norton edition. See Goreau, *Reconstructing Aphra*, pp. 68–9, for Byam's reasons for disliking Behn and his snide reference to her as "Astrea" in a letter to a friend in England.

4. See her preface to *The Lucky Chance*, where she requests "the Priviledge for my Masculine Part the Poet in me (if any such you will allow me) to tread in those successful Paths my Predecessors have so long thriv'd in," *The Works of Aphra Behn*, ed. Montague Summers, 6 vols. (1915; rpt. New York: Benjamin Blom, 1967), 3: 187.

As if to defuse that threat, the narrative counters the "we" composed of white women and Oroonoko with a stereotypical configuration, familiar from the Renaissance drama, which pits sexually vulnerable (and valuable) English women against a black man imagined as a villainous rapist.[5] One can see the "we" shifting in a striking fashion between these two poles in a passage that occurs near the end of the tale immediately after a description of how Caesar—as the narrator announces she is compelled to call Oroonoko after he assumes his slave identity in Surinam (p. 40)—leads a slave rebellion, is deserted by all but one of the other slaves, and is recaptured and brutally punished by white male property-owners. The narrator interrupts the plot's temporal progression to return to a point in the just-recounted story when the outcome of Oroonoko's rebellion was still uncertain. That uncertainty is oddly preserved for Behn's readers by her shift from the simple past tense to a subjunctive formulation that mixes past, present, and the possibility of a different future:

> You must know, that when the News was brought . . . that Caesar had betaken himself to the Woods, and carry'd with him all the Negroes, we were possess'd with extreme Fear, which no Persuasions could dissipate, that he would secure himself till night and then, that he would come down and cut all our throats. This Apprehension made all the Females of us fly down the River to be secured; and while we were away, they acted this Cruelty; for I suppose I had Authority and Interest enough there, had I suspected any such thing, to have prevented it: but we had not gone many Leagues, but the News overtook us, that Caesar was taken and whipped like a common Slave (pp. 67–8).

In this passage, the authorial "I" seems at once extraordinarily lucid and disturbingly blind about her own complicitly in her hero's capture and humiliating punishment. Had she been present, she "supposes" she could have prevented the cruelty which "they"—white men—wrought upon the black male slave.[6] Her claim to possess some singular social authority, however, is belied by her representation of herself as part of a group of weak females, a passive group possessed—and the play on that word is rich—not by men, black or white, but rather by an agent named Fear and quickly renamed Apprehension. That oddly abstract agent, however, turns out, if we look closely, to be a product of something the passage twice calls NEWS—a mode of verbal production that is often defined as unreliable in this text, and which belongs, significantly, to a semantic complex that names crucial features of Behn's own discourse in *Oroonoko*. The novella's opening pages announce that this is a "true" "eye-witness" account of things that happened in the "new Colonies,"

5. For a fine discussion of this stereotypical confrontation across color and gender lines, see Anthony Barthelemy, *Black Face Maligned Race: The Representation of Blacks in English Drama from Shakespeare to Southerne* (Baton Rouge: Louisiana State University Press, 1987), esp. Chap. 4, which explores numerous plays in which "failure by the [white] community to limit Moors sexually leads to their exercise of power and terror" (especially in the form of the property crime of rape), p. 123. Behn herself, in *Abdelazar; Or the Moor's Revenge* (1677), her adaptation for the Restoration stage of Dekker's *Lusis Dominion*, exploits the conventional image of the threateningly sexual black man; that play offers numerous

intriguing parallels to *Oroonoko*, among them the scene of Abdelazar's brutal execution, in which all the white men participate as if it were, in Barthelemy's phrase, "a communal activity" necessary for restoring the social order (p. 115).

6. Note that the most logical syntactic antecedent of "they" would be a group of *black* men composed of Oroonoko and his band, perpetrating the rape which one might easily construe as the referent for "this cruelty." The grammatical ambiguity arguably points to the struggle between the narrator's original perception of danger and her "corrected" but guiltily impotent retroactive perception that the white men, not the black ones, were her true enemies.

and the author advertising her wares, along with the lands her words represent, is well aware that she must offer "Novelty" to pique her English reader's interest, for "where there is no Novelty, there can be no Curiousity" (p. 3).[7] The author herself, it would seem, is both a producer and a consumer of "news," and in the passage about her roles in Oroonoko's aborted rebellion she represents her identity—and her agency—as an ambiguous function of the *circulation* of information.

Here, as in many other parts of the book, the narrative oscillates between criticizing and profiting from a "system" of circulation which includes not only words, among them the lies characteristic of male Christian slave traders, but bodies as well. In this disturbing oscillation, which has obviously contributed to the utter lack of critical consensus about whether Behn's book supports or attacks the institution of slavery, we can see the lineaments, I believe, of a more complex model of European colonization than Tzvetan Todorov posits in his book on *The Conquest of America*.[8] In contrast to Todorov's book and most instances of Renaissance travel literature I've read, Behn's novella construes the relation between Old World and New not only in terms of a binary opposition between self and other but also in terms of a highly unstable triangular model which, in its simplest version, draws relations of sameness and difference among a black African slave, a white English woman, and a group of native Americans who are described, in the book's opening pages, as innocents "so unadorned" and beautiful that they resemble "our first parents before the fall" (p. 3). Neither the white English woman nor the black African man share the Indians' (imputed) quality of primeval innocence. The narrator and Oroonoko-Caesar have both received European educations, albeit less good, we may suppose, than those accorded to privileged white men; and both are at once victims and beneficiaries of socioeconomic systems that discriminate kings from commoners and support the privileges of the nobility with the profits of the slave trade. Oroonoko is described as having captured and sold black slaves in African wars before he was himself enslaved by a dastardly lying Christian; and the narrator not only belongs to a slave-owning class but clearly supports the nationalistic colonizing enterprise which fueled and depended on the African slave trade.[9] She laments the loss of Surinam to the Dutch a few years after the events of the novella take place (interestingly, the English traded that colony for New Amsterdam, in "our" America, in 1667) and even uses a lush description of a gold-prospecting river trip to suggest the desirability—in 1688, on the eve of

---

7. Cf. the passage where the white male character Trefry is said to be "infinitely well pleased" with the "novel" of Oroonoko's and Imoinda's reunion (p. 44).

8. See, for instance, the diametrically opposed interpretations of George Guffey and Angeline Goreau on the issue of Behn's representation of black slaves. For Guffey, who reads confidently "through" the sign of Oroonoko's blackness to an English political subtext, the novella's ideological argument is not anti-slavery but against the enslavement of *kings*, specifically the Stuart king tenuously on England's throne in 1688: "through a series of parallels between James and the mistreated royal slave Oroonoko, [Behn] attempts to gain the sympathy of her reader for James, who . . . was in great danger of imminent deposition or worse" ("Aphra Behn's *Oroonoko*: Occasion and

Accomplishment," pp. 16–7). Goreau, in contrast (and equally confidently), sees Behn's "impassioned attack on the condition of slavery and defense of human rights" as "perhaps the first important abolitionist statement in the history of English literature" (*Reconstructing Aphra*, p. 289). See Tzvetan Todorov. *The Conquest of America: The Question of the Other* (New York: Harper, 1984).

9. The text is, however, significantly ambiguous about whether Behn could or did own slaves in her own right, as an unfathered, unmarried woman. In her prefatory letter to Maitland, she refers to Oroonoko as "my Slave," but she suggests, in the course of the story, that she lacked the power to dispose of her chattel property; she relates that she "assured" him, falsely, as it turns out, that he would be freed when the Governor arrived (p. 45).

William of Orange's accession to the British throne—of retaking the lost colony and its lost profits: "And 'tis to be bemoaned what his majesty lost by losing that part of America", she adds (p. 59).[1] By thus presenting a narrator and a hero who are both victims and beneficiaries of the international system of the slave trade, and by contrasting and comparing both characters, at different moments, to the exotic and "innocent" Indians, Behn provides a perspective on "the Conquest of America" that complicates, among other binary oppositions, the ethical one, infinitely labile in the literature of the imperial venture, between "we" as "good" and "them" as "evil"—or vice versa.

What even this account of the complexity of Behn's novella leaves out, however, is the ideological force of the "other" black slave in the story— Imoinda, Oroonoko's beloved, whom the English rename Clemene. Imoinda is doubly enslaved—to the whites, male and female, who have bought her and also, as the narrative insists, to her black husband. In striking contrast to the unmarried narrator, who stands, in relation to Oroonoko, as a queen or Petrarchan lady—lord to a vassal—a "Great Mistress" (p. 46)—Imoinda is an uncanny amalgam of European ideals of wifely subservience and European fantasies about wives of Oriental despots. She is thus the perfect embodiment, with the exception of her dark hue, of an image of the ideal English wife as the property, body and soul, of her husband. Wives like Imoinda—that is, *African* wives, as refracted in the mirror a white female English author holds up to this example of the Other—"have a respect for their Husbands equal to what other People pay a Deity; and when a Man finds any occasion to quit his Wife, if he love her, she dies by his hand; if not he sells her, or suffers some other to kill her" (p. 72).

This passage occurs late in the tale, immediately after Oroonoko has resolved to kill his pregnant wife for reasons that show him to be no less obsessed than Othello by a sexual jealousy intricately bound up with ideologies of property possession: "his great heart," the narrator approvingly explains, "could not endure the Thought" that Imoinda might, after his death, "become a Slave to the enraged Multitude," that is, be "ravished by every Brute" (p. 71). So, with Imoinda's joyful consent (she's considerably more compliant in her fate than Desdemona), he "sever[s] her yet smiling Face from that delicate Body, pregnant as it was with the fruits of tenderest Love" (p. 72).

Even this brief glance at Imoinda's death scene should suggest how odd it is that Imoinda's specificity as a *black wife* should be effaced not only from most critical narratives on Behn but also from the cover of the only inexpensive modern edition of the text, the Norton paperback edited by Lore Metzger.

*　*　*

Behn's text offers an ambiguous reflection on the role of intellectual producers and consumers in an expanding international market which included in the seventeenth century, as it still does in ours, books and bodies among

1. Cf. p. 48, where the narrator laments that "certainly had his late Majesty [Charles II], of sacred Memory, but seen and known what a vast and charming World he had been Master of in that Continent, he would never have parted so easily with it to the Dutch"; the passage goes on to adver- tise the natural riches of the (once and future) colony. On the British loss of Surinam (later Guiana) in exchange for New York, see Eric Williams, *From Columbus to Castro: The History of the Caribbean* (1970; rpt. New York: Vintage, 1984), p. 81.

its prime commodities. Behn's reflection on (and of) this market has many facets, one of which, uncannily but I think instructively, seems to anticipate the titillating representation of differently gendered and colored bodies that would advertise her story (but the possessive pronoun points to problems in the very conception of authorial "ownership") in the eighteenth century and again in the late twentieth.

The facet of Behn's "market representation" to which I'm referring is her textual staging of an implicit *competition* between the white English female author and the black African female slave-wife-mother-to-be. The competition is for Oroonoko's body and its power to engender something in the future, something that will outlive it. That power remains latent—impotent, one might say—without a female counterpart for which Behn offers two opposing images: Imoinda's pregnant body, holding a potential slave-laborer ("for," as the text reminds us, "all the Breed is theirs to whom the Parents belong"); and, alternatively, the author's "female pen," which she deploys to describe, with an unnerving blend of relish and horror, the scenes of Oroonoko's bodily dismemberment and eventual death following his leading of a slave revolt. She uses that pen also, as she tells the reader in the final paragraph, in hopes of making Oroonoko's "glorious Name to survive all Ages" (p. 78).

The narrator of course wins the competition. Through her pen flow at least some of the prerogatives of the English empire and its language, a language she has shown herself using, in one remarkable scene, as a potent instrument of sexual and political domination. In this scene, which explicitly pits an image of politically "dangerous" biological reproduction against an image of "safe" verbal production, the author presents herself most paradoxically as both a servant and a beneficiary of the eroticized socio-economic *system* of domination she describes. When some unnamed English authority figures perceive that Oroonoko is growing sullen because of the "Thought" that his child will belong not to him but to his owners, the narrator is "obliged," she tells us, to use her fiction-making powers to "divert" Oroonoko (and Imoinda too) from thoughts of "Mutiny." Mutiny is specifically tied to a problem in population management, a problem about which Behn's text—like much colonialist discourse, including chilling debates on whether it is better to "buy or breed" one's slaves—is fundamentally, and necessarily, ambivalent.[2] Mutiny, the narrator observes, "is very fatal sometimes in those Colonies that abound so with Slave, that they exceed the Whites in vast numbers" (p. 46). It is to abort the potential mutiny that the narrator is "obliged" to "discourse with Caesar, and to give him all the Satisfaction I possibly could"—which she does, entertaining him with stories about "the Loves of the Romans and great Men, which charmed him to my company." In an interestingly gendered division of narrative goods, she tells Imoinda stories about nuns.[3]

2. On the "buy or breed" debates, see Daniel P. Mannix in collaboration with Malcolm Cowley, *Black Cargoes: A History of the Atlantic Slave Trade 1518–1865* (New York: Viking. 1962), p. 23.
3. See Amore, "Introduction" to *Oroonoko*, for the hypothesis that this detail testifies to Behn's piety and possible Catholicism. Accepting the likelihood that she was indeed a Catholic, I wouldn't assume that the stories designed for Imoinda by the narrator are any more pious than Behn's own racy stories about nuns; indeed there may well be a bit of authorial self-reference (or even witty self-advertisement) here. See Behn's *History of the Nun, or, The Fair Vow Breaker* and *The Nun; or The Perjured Beauty*, both in *The Works of Aphra Behn*, ed. Montague Summers, vol. 5.

Playing a version of Othello to both her slaves, and thus dramatizing a complex mode of authorial "ownership" of characters cast in the role of enthralled audience, Behn represents herself creating a paradoxical *facsimile* of freedom, for herself, her immediate audience, and by implication, her largely female English readers as well, in which servitude is rendered tolerable by being eroticized, fantasized, "diverted" from activities, either sexual or military, that might work to dislodge the English from their precarious lordship of this new world land. Just how precarious their possession was the narrative acknowledges by repeatedly lamenting their loss of the land to the Dutch; but the deeper problems of the logic of colonialism are also signalled, albeit confusedly, by the contrast between the description of slave mutiny quoted above and the explanation offered early in the story for why the British do *not* enslave the native Indians, a group which, like the Africans, are essential to the colonialists' welfare; "they being on all occasions very useful to us," the narrator says, "we find it absolutely necessary to caress 'em as Friends, and not to treat 'em as Slaves, nor dare we do other, their numbers so far surpassing ours in that Continent" (p. 5).[4] This passage sheds an ironic light on the later moment when the narrator uses stories to divert Oroonoko from thoughts of mutiny, for we see that one logical solution to the mutiny problem, a solution that her stories to Oroonoko suppress but which her larger narrative only partially represses, is the possibility of *not* enslaving a group of "others" who outnumber you. Such a solution, with respect both to Africans and to Indians, had been recommended by a few early critics of the colonial enterprise; but Behn is far from joining the tiny group who voiced criticisms of the whole system of international trade based on forced labor by persons of many skin colors including freckled Irish white.[5]

In its characteristically disturbing way, Behn's novel shows us just enough about the author's competition with Imoinda, and the enmeshment of that competition within a larger socio-sexual-economic system, to make us uneasy when we hold the book *Oroonoko* in our hands and realize that the text itself

4. Since the blacks also greatly outnumbered the whites in the colony, Behn's explanation for the distinction in the English treatment of the two non-white groups is clearly problematic. The matter continues to be a site of debate in modern histories of slavery in the New World, for even though Indians *were* frequently enslaved, all of the colonial powers came, eventually, to *prefer* African to Amerindian slaves for reasons that confusingly blended economic, theological, and cultural explanations. Some modern historians, for instance Winthrop Jordan, in *White Over Black: American Attitudes Toward the Negro, 1550–1812* (Chapel Hill: University of North Carolina Press, 1968), invoke color difference as an explanation for why Africans came (eventually) to be seen as better (more "natural") slaves than Indians, but this view, cited and refuted by Barbara Fields, "Ideology and Race in American History," in *Region, Race and Reconstruction*, ed. J. Morgan Kousser and James M. McPherson (New York: Oxford University Press, 1982), seems anachronistic and reductive. More satisfactory discussions are given by Davis, *The Problem of Slavery*, who sees the distinction as an "outgrowth of the practical demands of trade and diplomacy" (p. 178) bolstered by ideological fictions about blackness (the biblical color of evil) and "noble savages"; and by William D. Phillips, Jr., *Slavery from Roman Times to the Early Transatlantic Trade* (Minneapolis: University of Minnesota Press, 1985), who, in discussing the commonly cited adage that "one Negro is worth four Indians" in terms of labor power, suggests that the difference between the Africans' experience in agricultural societies and the Amerindians in mainly hunting-gathering cultures helps account for this sobering ideological distinction (p. 184)—a distinction that makes a person's *economic* value stand in antithetical relation to his or her *moral* value (in European eyes, at least, which equated freedom with "natural" nobility).

5. For discussions of early critics of slavery such as Las Casas (who came only late in life to decry the enslavement of blacks as well as Indians) and Albornoz, see Davis. *The Problem of Slavery*, p. 189 and passim; Eric Williams, *From Columbus to Castro*, pp. 43–4; and Goreau, *Reconstructing Aphra*, p. 289 (on the Quaker George Fox's opposition to the system of slavery). On the legal and ideological distinctions very unevenly and gradually introduced between white and black slaves, see Phillips, p. 183.

invites us to see the book as a safe-sex substitute for the potentially mutinous but also economically valuable black slave child Oroonoko might have had with Imoinda. In a bizarre twisting of the old trope of book as child, Behn offers her contemporary English readers, and us too, a representation of an economy in which the white woman's book is born, quite starkly, from the death and silencing of black persons, one of them pregnant. Behind the scene of Oroonoko's final torture, which gruesomely anticipates Alice Walker's description, in her story of a cross-race rape during the U.S. Civil Rights struggle, of "white folks standing in a circle roasting something that had talked to them in their own language before they tore out its tongue," is the murder-sacrifice of the black woman and her unborn child.[6] And the threat represented by the black woman, I would suggest, is obscurely acknowledged to be even greater than the threat represented by the black man, so that the text finally has to enlist him, through enticements of European codes of masculine honor and Petrarchan romance, to suppress the one character who actually uses physical force rather than words to attack the highest legal representative of the colonial system, namely the male Lieutenant Governor. Reversing the Renaissance commonplace that defined deeds as masculine, words as feminine, Imoinda wounds Byam, the narrator tells us, with a poisoned arrow; he is saved, however—though the narrator clearly regrets this— by his Indian mistress, who sucks the venom from his wound. The white female narrator's own ambivalent relation to male English authority is figured here by the device of splitting "other" women into two roles: one rebellious and one erotically complicitous.

Imoinda's rebellious power—and the need to destroy it—are figured most strikingly, I think, in the two juxtaposed episodes where Oroonoko first kills a mother tiger and lays the whelp at the author's feet (p. 51) and then kills a property-destroying tiger—again female—and extracts her bullet-ridden heart to give to the English audience. At this moment Oroonoko is most transparently shown as a figure for the author of *Oroonoko*, a repository of novel curiosities which Behn offers to her readers as he offers the tiger's cub, and then its heart, to his owner-admirers:

> This heart the conqueror brought up to us, and 'twas a very great curiosity, which all the country came to see, and which gave Caesar occasion of making many fine Discourses, of Accidents in War, and strange Escapes. (p. 53)

Here Behn deliberately constructs her hero from echoes of Shakespeare; Oroonoko woos her and other British ladies as Othello wooed Desdemona with his eloquent story of his "most disastrous chances . . . moving accidents . . . hair breadth-scapes i' th' imminent deadly breach" (1.3.134–36).[7] With respect to the power relation between a narrator and an audience, this scene offers a mirror reversal of the one in which the narrator entertains her sullen, potentially mutinous hero with *her* culture's stories of "great [Roman] men." We can now see even more clearly that the "ground" of both scenes, the "material," as it were, from which the production and reception of exotic

6. Alice Walker, "Advancing Luna—and Ida B. Wells," in *You Can't Keep a Good Woman Down* (New York: Harcourt Brace Jovanovich, 1981), p. 93.

7. Quoted from the Signet *Othello*, ed. Alvin Kernan (New York: New American Library, 1963), p. 55.

stories derives, is the silent figure of the black woman—silent but by no means safe, as is suggested by the image of the female tiger and the narrative device of duplicating it.

* * *

1991

CATHERINE GALLAGHER

From Who Was That Masked Woman? The Prostitute and the Playwright in the Works of Aphra Behn[1]

Musing in 1821 on the vagaries of literary fashion, Walter Scott tells a story about his great aunt, who at the age of eighty wanted to reread a work of Aphra Behn's that she remembered finding delightful in her youth.

> One day she asked me, when we happened to be alone together, whether I had ever seen Mrs. Behn's novels—I confessed the charge.—Whether I could get her a sight of them?—I said, with some hesitation, I believed I could; but that I did not think she would like either the manners, or the language, which approached too near that of Charles II's time to be quite proper reading.

But the "good old lady" insisted.

> So I sent Mrs. Aphra Behn, curiously sealed up, with "private and confidential" on the packet, to my gay old grand-aunt. The next time I saw her afterwards, she gave me back Aphra, properly wrapped up, with nearly these words: "Take back your bonny Mrs. Behn; and, if you will take my advice, put her in the fire, for I found it impossible to get through the very first novel. But is it not," she said, "a very odd thing that I, an old woman of eighty and upwards, sitting alone, feel myself ashamed to read a book which, sixty years ago, I have heard read aloud for the amusement of large circles, consisting of the first and most creditable society in London?"[2]

Behn's book occasions the old woman's astonishment at her younger self and the society that bred her; her question reverberates with the shock of personal and cultural discontinuity, suddenly perceived. We can easily imagine her fragile sense of identity as she recalls herself publicly applauding what any proper lady, by the standards of the late eighteenth century, should instinctively have recognized as depraved. Such a "change of taste," Scott explains in his commentary on this story, "takes place insensibly without the

1. Excerpted from chapter 1 of *Nobody's Story: The Vanishing Acts of Women Writers in the Market-place, 1670–1820* (1994) [editor's note].
2. From a letter to Lady Louisa Stuart quoted in John Gibson Lockhart, *Memoirs of the Life of* Sir *Walter Scott*, rpt. in 5 vols. (New York, 1910), vol. 3, pp. 596–97.

parties being aware of it." The cultural revolution that Scott's great aunt "insensibly" lived is registered only retrospectively, as a deeply private, self-revelatory sense of shame. The story itself, by giving us three moments in the "life" of Aphra Behn's book, plots the development of this shamed self-consciousness as a shift from the public to the private consumption and eventual suppression of certain kinds of literature. His great aunt remembers public readings, probably in the 1730s,[3] whereas Scott himself, born in 1760, was no doubt introduced to Behn as a semipornographic writer whose works, though still in circulation, needed to be labeled "private and confidential" and had to be "curiously sealed" (a phrase that nicely catches the stimulating effect of the book's slide into contraband). Finally, the old lady returns the book, this time truly under wraps ("properly wrapped"), and advises that it circulate no more. Her uncanny private experience leads to the resolve that this book never be shared, that the intense sense of shame, which she recognizes as inappropriate to her privacy, remain utterly her own.[4]

For Scott himself the incident seems not to have such complex personal resonances. He recounts it mainly as an instance of the secret, "insensible" nature of any "change of taste." In most cases, Scott explains, such changes are arbitrary, mere matters of fashion, unpredictable and unaccountable; in the specific case of Aphra Behn, the change reflects progress. The increasingly private and shamefaced reading of Behn represents for Scott "the gradual improvement of the national taste and delicacy." Nevertheless, he concludes enigmatically, "The change that brings into and throws out of fashion particular styles of composition, is something of the same kind." The instability of Behn's reputation, its peculiar vulnerability to fluctuations in the social mores governing sexual propriety, shows the close link between feminine works and ephemeral ones. It is not surprising, then, that Scott's tone in telling the story of his great aunt's embarrassment is one of detached amusement.

Walter Scott and his great aunt were not the last commentators to reflect on the phenomenon of Aphra Behn in just these ways. Her works have been objects of both outrage and urbane antiquarian curiosity, and we are still pondering the mystery and significance of her career. If her success later seemed inexplicable to Walter Scott's great aunt, who actually experienced it, how much more mysterious must it seem to us, who must reconcile it with both the disappearance of her works from the canon and our belief in a strong prejudice against women writers in the seventeenth century. Hence, we still marvel at her incredible early acclaim; it strains our historical imagination and our sense of cultural continuity to realize that, after Dryden, Behn was the most prolific and probably the most popular writer of her time, with at least eighteen plays, several volumes of poetry, and numerous works of fiction that were in vogue for decades after her death. She was second only to Dryden also in the number of her plays (four) that were produced at court.[5]

---

3. Behn's *Love-Letters between a Nobleman and His Sister*, for example, was issued in book form in 1735.
4. On the categorization of Behn's work as pornographic, see Naomi Jacobs, "The Seduction of Aphra Behn," *Women's Studies* 18 (1991): 395–403.
5. Fidelis Morgan, ed., *The Female Wits: Women Playwrights of the Restoration* (London: Virago, 1981), p. 12. For a brief comparison of the careers of Dryden and Behn, see Deborah C. Payne, " 'And Poets Shall by Patron-Princes Live': Aphra Behn and Patronage," in *Curtain Calls: British and American Women and the Theater, 1660–1820*, ed. Mary Anne Schofield and Cecilia Macheski (Athens: Ohio Univ. Press, 1991), p. 107.

Moreover, the other Restoration playwrights to whom we might compare her, the men whose works were regularly produced by one of the two playhouses, had advantages of education and family that Behn lacked. According to her biographer Maureen Duffy, "Most were of the gentry or nobility, and almost all had university or Inns of Court education."[6] In contrast, Aphra Behn's origins are obscure, and we are hard-pressed to explain how such a sociological anomaly achieved such cultural prominence.[7]

If Scott's story only increases our wonder at Behn's success by assuring us that even one who had experienced it could not make sense of it half a century later, his letter nevertheless wraps the odd facts in a more familiar narrative. By linking Behn's decline to "improvements" in "delicacy," Scott gives us a succinct index of the pace of cultural change in the mid-eighteenth century and suggests the impact of that change on standards of decency for women writers in particular. Indeed, stories like Scott's have made Behn into a symbol for those vicissitudes of female literary reputation that are caused by changes in ideas of sexual propriety. Many students who cannot name a single work by Aphra Behn are quick to identify her as the excessively risqué "first Englishwoman to earn her living by her pen." No other author has the very fact of her initial market success so prominently in the forefront of her reputation that it often obscures everything else about her works. Everything, that is, except the infamous "bawdiness" that accounts, it seems, for both their contemporary success and their unacceptability to readers in the prudish centuries that followed. The history of Behn's reception, in short, is better known than her works, and it would be no exaggeration to say that she has become *the* figure for the volatility of the marketplace in women's literature.[8]

6. *The Passionate Shepherdess: Aphra Behn, 1640–1689* (London: Cape, 1977), p. 104. ["Inns of Court education": i.e., training as a lawyer—editor's note.]

7. There are competing early accounts of Behn's birth and social status. Her two most recent biographers draw very different conclusions from the evidence. Assuming that her maiden name was Johnson and that she was born around 1640 in Kent, Maureen Duffy thinks she was the daughter of Bartholomew Johnson, yeoman, and Elizabeth, née Denham, daughter of a "gentleman." Angeline Goreau makes the same initial assumptions but suggests that Behn was the illegitimate daughter of Lady Willoughby, whose husband was founder and governor of the English colony of Surinam. See *Reconstructing Aphra: A Social Biography of Aphra Behn* (New York: Dial, 1980), p. 13. This account would explain Behn's superior education and her trip to that colony. Both versions of her birth are highly speculative, and we simply do not know how she received her education or her introduction to literary and theatrical circles. Sara Heller Mendelson places her date of birth in the late 1640s; see *The Mental World of Stuart Women: Three Studies* (Brighton: Harvester, 1967), pp. 116–17. Earlier biographies of Behn include George Woodcock, *The Incomparable Aphra* (1948; rpt. as *The English Sappho* [Montreal: Black Rose, 1989]); and Frederick M. Link, *Aphra Behn* (New York: Twayne, 1968).

8. For a concise overview of Behn's career, see Janet Todd's introduction to *The Works of Aphra Behn*, ed. Todd, vol. 1 (Columbus: Ohio State Univ. Press, 1992), pp. ix–xxxv. Mary Ann O'Donnell surveys Behn's career and includes a selection

of her work in "Tory Wit and Unconventional Woman: Aphra Behn," in *Women Writers of the Seventeenth Century*, ed. Katharina M. Wilson and Frank J. Warnke (Athens: Univ. of Georgia Press, 1989), pp. 349–72. For a variety of recent critical approaches to Behn's writing, see Ros Ballaster, *Seductive Forms: Women's Amatory Fiction, 1684–1740* (Oxford: Clarendon Press, 1992), pp. 69–113; Bernard Duyfhuizen, " 'That Which I Dare Not Name': Aphra Behn's 'The Willing Mistress,' " *ELH* 58 (1991): 63–82; Judith Kegan Gardiner, "The First English Novel: Aphra Behn's *Love Letters*, the Canon, and Women's Tastes," *Tulsa Studies in Women's Literature* 8 (1989): 201–22; Dorothy Mermin, "Women Becoming Poets: Katherine Philips, Aphra Behn, Anne Finch," *ELH* 57 (1990): 335–55; Jacqueline Pearson, "Gender and Narrative in the Fiction of Aphra Behn," parts 1 and 2, *Review of English Studies* 42 (1991): 40–56 and 179–90; Jane Spencer, *The Rise of the Woman Novelist: From Aphra Behn to Jane Austen* (Oxford: Basil Blackwell, 1986), pp. 42–52; Dale Spender, *Mothers of the Novel: 100 Good Women Writers before Jane Austen* (London: Pandora, 1986), pp. 47–66; George Starr, "Aphra Behn and the Genealogy of the Man of Feeling," *Modern Philology* 87 (1990): 362–72; Janet Todd, *The Sign of Angellica: Women, Writing and Fiction, 1660–1800* (London: Virago, 1989), pp. 69–83; Donald R. Wehrs, "Eros, Ethics, Identity: Royalist Feminism and the Politics of Identity in Aphra Behn's *Love Letters*," *Studies in English Literature, 1500–1900* 32 (1992): 461–78; and the anthologies *Curtain Calls*, esp. essays by Frances Kavenik, Jessica Munns, Deborah C. Payne, and Rose Zimbardo; and *Fetter'd or Free? British Women Novelists,*

Aphra Behn herself initiated this emphasis on her struggles in the marketplace. In the very midst of her success she complained about a double standard in judging plays. For example, an oft quoted passage from the epistle to *Sir Patient Fancy* (1678) claims she had been censured for using language that any male playwright might use with impunity.[9] Following Behn's lead, and citing numerous contemporary attacks on both her character and works, her biographers have concluded that Behn's popularity was gained despite a heavy handicap imposed by her sex.[1]

However, the double standard Behn complains of did not seem to discourage attendance at her plays, nor is there much evidence that it forced her to change her style or to leave off writing plays in order to take up the less "public" genre of romance. There is a gap in her production of new plays between 1682 and 1685 during which she seems to have written a great many tales, but when she opened a new play in 1686, *The Lucky Chance*, it turned out to be as full of cuckolding and witty double entendre as anything she ever wrote. Behn was rewarded for this play with both a successful run and a predictable return of criticism, which she immediately used as the occasion for her finest self-defense, a fiery, defiant "epistle to the reader." Granted, the last play produced during her lifetime, her commedia dell'arte farce *The Emperor of the Moon*, might have been taken as evidence of moral reformation; it offended no one. The bawdy, satirical Behn, though, was resurrected in the posthumous production of *The Widow Ranter*; this play, however, received a relatively lukewarm reception because, a contemporary commentator suggested, "our Author" was dead and unable to supervise or cast the production.[2]

Even in the next century, although there was certainly a gradual insistence on sexual propriety in the theater, it developed slowly and applied to male as well as female playwrights. As Scott's great aunt testifies, Behn was a highly respected author until the middle of the eighteenth century, and her plays received the same posthumous treatment as her "nouvelles." Curiously, throughout the first half of the eighteenth century audiences seem to have accepted in old plays what they condemned in new ones. Hence, *The Rover*, certainly one of Behn's bawdiest plays, was a staple of the repertory until the 1760s. *The London Stage* records productions for almost every year between

1670–1815, ed. Mary Anne Schofield and Cecilia Macheski (Athens: Ohio Univ. Press, 1986), esp. essays by Jerry C. Beasley and Robert Adams Day. For a detailed bibliography of scholarship on Behn, see Mary Ann O'Donnell, *Aphra Behn: An Annotated Bibliography of Primary and Secondary Sources* (New York: Garland, 1986).

9. "I printed this play with all the impatient haste one ought to do, who would be vindicated from the most unjust and silly aspersion . . . ; *That it was Bawdy*, the least and most excusable fault in the men writers to whose plays they all crowd, as if they came to no other end than to hear what they condemn in this." To accept this complaint at face value, as Goreau does on pp. 233–34, one must ignore other evidence. First, in 1678 Behn was not singled out for chastisement because she was a woman; other playwrights were as heavily criticized that year. See Arthur H. Scouten and Robert D. Hume, "Restoration Comedy and Its Audiences, 1660–1776," in *The Rakish Stage: Studies in English Drama, 1660–1800*, ed. Robert D. Hume

(Carbondale: Southern Illinois Univ. Press, 1983), pp. 56–64. Second, in concentrating on Behn's complaint about her play's reception, we overlook both its good run and its remaining in the repertory until 1692.

1. See especially Goreau's chapter 11, "Success and Attack," pp. 207–35.

2. The dedication to the 1690 edition of the play complains that "the Play had not that Success which it deserv'd. . . . The main fault ought to lye on those who had the management of it. Had our Author been alive she would have Committed it to the Flames rather than suffer'd it to have been Acted with such Omissions as was made. . . . And Lastly, many of the Parts being false Cast, and given to those whose Tallants and Genius's Suited not our Authors Intention." *The Works of Aphra Behn*, ed. Montague Summers (London, 1915), vol. 4, pp. 221–22. Unless otherwise noted, subsequent quotations from Behn's works are from this edition, hereafter cited as *Works*.

1703 and 1743, when the productions began tapering off over two decades before disappearing altogether.[3] But the same pattern applies to a "classic" like Ben Jonson's *Epicoene*. Apparently, when standards of propriety became stricter, old plays were at first exempt and were then condemned in a heap, without distinguishing between Jacobean and Restoration, male and female authors.[4]

Since the evidence does not support the contention that Behn's career was hindered by general prejudices against either women playwrights or bawdy women playwrights, one might justifiably suspect that the author's complaints and her adversaries' insults were pieces of an elaborate rhetorical interaction that dictated the very terms in which she was conceived. As we will shortly see, Behn's prologues and prefaces were often artfully constructed in a rhetorical tradition that required her defamation. This is not to say that the defamation never took place, that it was a mere trope; it is only to say that Behn depended and capitalized on it. She especially depended on getting a barrage of abuse from wits of a rival political stripe, for, as we will see in Chapter 2, such harassment vouched for her effectiveness as a Tory writer. For the most part, men of her own party supported Behn staunchly, and if we simply count contemporary male judgments of her in print, we find that instances of praise outnumber those of blame by at least ten to one.[5] To understand this first female authorial success, we must enumerate the many cultural desires she satisfied.

I will be arguing that Behn's career was both enabled and shaped by a certain conjunction of Restoration theatrical, rhetorical, sexual, political, and economic exigencies. Laments about the obnoxious material necessities of one's career or the utter prostitution of one's rivals' careers were the normal language of the Restoration author's self-representations. These, in turn, can best be understood as instances of complicated arguments about the relationship between property and selfhood. Behn often feminized these concerns and created a novel authorial identity in doing so, but she was no more *impeded* by them than was Dryden or Wycherley. They formed the discourse that called her authorship into being and made her the great success she was.

In examining Behn's use of her gender to present herself as an author in the marketplace, we will encounter a set of Restoration paradoxes pertaining to authorship and self-ownership generally. These paradoxes are not unique in Behn's self-representations, but her gender gave them unusual depth and resonance. This chapter concerns itself primarily with the theatrical representation of the author; it shows why and how she staged her simultaneous presence and absence in the theater, audaciously using the metaphor of the author as prostitute to create distinctions between the obliging playwright and the withholding private person, the woman's body and her self, the stage and real life. She fabricated the impression of a continuous but mysterious authorial identity—never actually embodied on the stage but persisting and transforming itself from play to play—and aligned this idea of authorship with the "no thing" of female sex. The next chapter considers the representation

3. *Index to the London Stage, 1660–1800*, ed. William Van Lennep, Emmett L. Avery, Arthur H. Scouten, George Winchester Stone, Jr., and Charles Beecher Hogan, compiled by Ben Ross Schneider, Jr. (Carbondale: Southern Illinois Univ. Press, 1979), p. 61.

4. See Scouten and Hume, "Restoration Comedy and Its Audiences, 1660–1776," pp. 64–81.

5. For an itemized list of contemporary references (1677–1700), see O'Donnell, *Aphra Behn: An Annotated Bibliography of Primary and Secondary Sources*, pp. 327–43.

of the author in print; it probes the mystique of a bodiless medium that holds out promises of sovereignty and anonymity in the midst of commodification. Behn typically encapsulates these themes in the figure of the author-monarch, and hence her romance of the sovereign in the marketplace, *Oroonoko*, is interpreted here as an absolutist fantasy of disembodiment through representation and exchange.

Together the chapters contend that Behn created a complex authorial identity by drawing on seemingly irreconcilable metaphors—the author as prostitute and the author as monarch—that, despite their apparent incompatibility, lead into surprisingly similar explorations of the anomalies of Restoration authorship. Each metaphor rendered that authorship problematic in a different way, but from both Behn emerges as the heroine-victim of the marketplace, utterly sold yet pristinely unsoiled because able to separate herself from her physical being. This paradoxical effect, I will argue, is her ultimate and most compelling achievement as well as her most enduring commodity.[6]

* * *

When we speak of Behn making her living by her pen, * * * we do not mean she made a living primarily from having books published. Like most of the age's "professional writers"—by which most historians seem to mean people who had no means of livelihood other than writing—Behn was a playwright partly because the structure and financing of drama allowed for the support of writers. The theater as an institution changed abruptly when, after a twenty-year hiatus, it was restored along with the monarchy. The changes made playwriting a more independent, lucrative, and chancy activity than it had been. * * *

Playwriting had through this process also become a better differentiated activity, for which the writer seemed to receive money almost directly from a grateful audience. This "professionalization" produced a more personal relationship between playwright and audience than had previously existed. The author's benefit night provided an opportunity for rewarding or punishing playwrights quite specifically.[7]

* * *

Words like "professionalization" and "marketplace," while not altogether inaccurate in this case, can therefore be rather misleading unless we understand the jointly theatrical and personal nature of the third night. Moreover, it is only as part of this specialized financial arrangement that we can fully appreciate Aphra Behn's construction of her various authorial personae. Like other Restoration playwrights, Behn presents herself as a person to whom something is owed individually; she tries to engender a relationship of mutual obligation that will bring in an audience on the third night. Also like her fellow playwrights, she insists on her struggle against the staleness of theatrical effect that might arise from the very continuity of personality she stresses.

6. For different interpretations of Behn's self-presentation as commodity, see Elin Diamond, "*Gestus* and Signature in Aphra Behn's *The Rover*," *ELH* 56 (1989): 519–41; and Todd, *The Sign of Angellica*, pp. 69–83.

7. The highest income recorded for a third night is Shadwell's £130 for *The Squire of Alsatia* in 1668.

Perhaps we can estimate that Behn took in around £50 on successful benefit nights and also received handsome gifts from the nobles to whom she dedicated the printed books of the plays. See Duffy, p. 204, and the introduction to *The London Stage. Part I: 1660–1700*.

She presents herself as a playwright whose credit is based on a personal appeal, the appeal of the familiar author to whom the theatrical habitué is obliged, but who consequently must work to keep herself interesting, to dispel the boredom of familiarity. But unlike other Restoration playwrights, in constructing the first of her personae to be analyzed here, she uses explicitly and shockingly feminine tropes.

Conscious of her historical role, Aphra Behn introduced to the world of English letters the professional woman playwright as a newfangled whore. This persona has many functions in Behn's work: it titillates, scandalizes, arouses pity, and indicates the perils of public identity and the poignancy of authorship in general. The author-whore persona is the central figure in a dark comedy Behn played throughout her career, a comedy in which she exposes the bond between the liberty the stage offered women and their confinement behind both literal and metaphorical vizards. I will begin exploring the development of this persona in several short pieces: the epistles to *The Dutch Lover* (1673) and *Sir Patient Fancy* and the prologue to her first play, *The Forced Marriage* (1670). I will then describe the theatrical and larger cultural contexts informing the author-whore persona; and, finally, I will discuss one of her later plays, *The Lucky Chance*.

Introductory epistles to the printed plays, whether addressed to the general reader or a patron, created authorial effects very different from those produced by the plays' spoken prologues and epilogues. Normally appearing after the author's benefit night, the printed introductions cannot be seen as part of the immediate solicitation of the audience for support. Nevertheless, they were crucial to creating a sense of a "real" person behind the play and thus contribute importantly to the development of a long-term relationship between public and playwright, a sense of obligation that carried over from play to play. Behn's first such self-presentation, the epistle to *The Dutch Lover*, was continuous with the portrayals of the playwright in the early prologues and epilogues; this Aphra Behn, in a sustained tone of comic raillery, insists on her feminine seductiveness and the levity of her enterprise:

> Good, Sweet, Honey, Sugar-Candied Reader,
>   Which I think is more than anyone has called you yet, I must have a word or two with you before you advance into the Treatise; but 'tis not to beg your pardon for diverting you from your affairs, by such an idle Pamphlet as this is, for I presume you have not much to do and therefore are to be obliged to me for keeping you from worse employment.[8]

The comic feminine persona in this discourse is an adaptation of one that harks back at least to Chaucer's Wife of Bath; it is ribald, debunking, racy, digressive, and slightly madcap. Perhaps because it employs such obvious comic conventions and emphasizes its own inauthenticity, however, it proved less powerful than the rhetoric that emerged five years later, in the epistle to *Sir Patient Fancy*. This is the first of the epistles to be taken by commentators as an expression of Behn's actual sentiments. It is not a comic seduction but a complaint against what Behn presents as her ill-treatment at the hands

8. *Works*, vol. 1, p. 221.

of some female critics. She addresses her female readers here, claiming that the ladies should have been *particularly* forgiving of the play's bawdiness, for

> they ought to have had good Nature and justice enough to have attributed all its faults to the Authors unhappiness, who is forced to write for Bread and not ashamed to owne it, and consequently ought to write to please (if she can) an Age which has given severall proofs it was by this way of writing to be obliged, though it is a way too cheap for men of wit to pursue who write for Glory, and a way which even I despise as much below me.[9]

In addressing the ladies, Behn invokes the anomaly of her economic situation, its pathetic inappropriateness to an implied womanly norm. That very anomaly, however, is founded on the condition Behn shares with the ladies she addresses: a lack of independent property that obliges all women to earn their livelihood by pleasing men. Behn appeals to ladies for understanding because her very deviation from their pattern reveals a common female condition: she "ought . . . to please (if she can)." In the author's case, this shared condition enforces impropriety; it is only proper that she be improper, for what she "ownes" is only her lack of property. This is the unhappy situation of the prostitute, but Behn insists it is not a blamable one. Indeed, she describes it to prove her innocence; by selling bawdiness and then complaining of the necessity to do so, she assures her female readers that there is an innocent self above the exchange. Authorship for the marketplace and selfhood are here dissevered, for the author that can be inferred from the work is merely a "way of writing" dictated by the age, an alienable thing outside and beneath the true self. But it is precisely this severing, this inauthenticity, that is supposed to *oblige* the audience, to make them feel an obligation to the compromised author.

The effect of an authentic female self that Aphra Behn produces in such passages is based on the very need to sell her constructed authorial self. By making her authorial self an emanation of the marketplace, then, she saves this putative authentic self from contamination. The implied author of the plays is fashioned in the service of the male audience's fancy; but the implied author of the epistle claims to be Aphra Behn's unexchangeable, but also largely unrepresentable, self. Each of these authors is, in essence, an effect of the other, although the illusion created is that of the ontological priority of the woman who regrets her misrepresentations. All we know of this woman, however, are those misrepresentations, for in the case of the female author, as in the case of the prostitute, self-sale creates the illusion of an unknowable authenticity by never giving anything away, both in the sense of refusing to give free gratification and in the sense of refusing self-revelation. The epistle stresses that the professional woman author as prostitute is internally divided: what can be seen of her is never what she is, but the theatrical inauthenticity of what can be seen implies the existence of some hidden woman directing the drama of her self-sale.[1]

---

9. *Works*, vol. 4, p. 7.

1. For a contrasting interpretation, one that offers a sanitized version of Behn's authorial personae in the prologues, epistles dedicatory, and epilogues, see Cheri Davis Langdell, "Aphra Behn and Sexual Politics: A Dramatist's Discourse with Her Audience," in *Drama, Sex and Politics*, ed. James Redmond (Cambridge: Cambridge Univ. Press, 1985), pp. 109–28.

＊   ＊   ＊

Behn's femaleness gave her unique opportunities for self-presentation in her prologues and epilogues. The first prologue of her career incorporates standard conventions and carries them a step further by inviting the audience, through the metaphor of prostitution, to reflect on the self-alienation, and hence theatricality, of exchange in general. This prologue to *The Forced Marriage* (1670) is staged not only as a novel presentation of a playwright, but also as a *staged* novelty in which the author wittily allows her strategies to be laid bare so ostentatiously that the revelation of the strategy itself seems strategic. The prologue presents Aphra Behn's playwriting as an extension of her erotic play. In it, a male actor pretends to have temporarily escaped the control of the intriguing female playwright; he comes onstage to warn the gallants in the audience of their danger. This prologue added a sexual dimension to the Restoration convention of betraying the playwright: the comic antagonism between playwright and audience also becomes a battle in the war between the sexes. Playwriting, the actor warns, is a new weapon in woman's amorous arsenal. She will no longer wound only through the eyes, through her beauty, but will also use wit to gain a more permanent ascendancy.

> Women those charming victors, in whose eyes
> Lie all their arts, and their artilleries,
> Not being contented with the wounds they made,
> Would by new stratagems our lives invade.
> Beauty alone goes now at too cheap rates
> And therefore they, like wise and politic states,
> Court a new power that may the old supply,
> To *keep* as well as gain the victory:
> They'll join the force of wit to beauty now,
> And so *maintain* the right they have in you.

Here, woman's playwriting is wholly assimilated to the poetic conventions of amorous battle that normally informed lyric poetry. If the male poet had long depicted the conquering woman as necessarily chaste, debarring (and consequently debarred from) the act of sex itself, then his own poetry of lyric complaint and pleas for kindness could only be understood as attempts to overthrow the conqueror. Poetry in this lyric tradition is a weapon in a struggle that takes as its ground rule a woman's inability to conquer through sexual consummation: for the doing of the deed would be the undoing of her power.

Aphra Behn's first prologue stretches this lyric tradition to incorporate theater. Just as in lyric poetry, writing becomes part of a larger erotic contest. The woman's poetry, however, cannot have the same *end* as the man's. Indeed, according to the prologue, ends, in the sense of terminations, are precisely what a woman's wit is directed against. Writing is certainly on a continuum here with sex, but instead of leading to the act in which the woman's conquest is overturned, playwriting extends the woman's erotic power beyond the moment of sexual encounter. The prologue thus situates the drama inside the conventions of male lyric love poetry but then reverses the chronological relationship between sex and writing; the male poet writes before the sexual encounter, the woman between encounters. She thereby actually creates the possibility of a woman's version of sexual conquest. The woman now can have a "right" in the man that is not automatically self-canceling. She will not be immediately conquered and discarded because she will maintain her right through her writing. The woman's play of wit is the opposite of foreplay; it is a kind of afterplay specifically designed to resuscitate desire and keep a woman who has given herself sexually from being traded in for another woman. If the woman is successful in her poetic exchange, the actor warns the gallants, then they will no longer have the freedom of briskly exchanging mistresses:

> You'll never know the bliss of change; this art
> Retrieves (when beauty fades) the wandring heart.

Thus writing retroactively enables sex by ensuring its continuance, a point emphasized by the fusion of military and commercial metaphors. That is, war in the prologue is not a contest ending in a mere moment of conquest; rather, it resembles a battle for commercial advantage. Motivated in the first place by an unfavorable balance of trade ("Beauty alone goes now at too cheap rates"), it is designed not to destroy the enemy but to establish a monopoly, another sense of "right," on a growing number of sexual exchanges.

Aphra Behn, then, inaugurated her career by taking up the role of the seductive lyric poet. The drama the audience is about to see is framed by the larger drama of erotic exchange between a woman writer and a male audience. This prologue does what so many Restoration prologues do, makes of the play a drama within a drama, a series of conventional interactions inside another series of conventional interactions. But the very elaborateness of this staging, combined with the novelty of its metaphor, makes the love battle itself (the thing supposedly revealed) seem a strategic pose in a somewhat different drama. What kind of woman would stage her sexual desire as her primary motivation? The answer is a woman who might be suspected of not having any real affection, a woman for whom professions of amorousness and theatrical inauthenticity are the same thing: a prostitute.

Finally, just in case anyone in the audience might have missed this analogy, a dramatic interruption occurs, and the prologue becomes a debate about the motivation behind all this talk of strategy. The actor calls attention to the prostitutes in the audience, who were generally identified by their masks, and characterizes them as allies of the playwright, jokingly using their masks to expose them as spies in the amorous war:

> The poetess too, they say, has spies abroad,
> Which have dispers'd themselves in every road,
> I' th' upper box, pit, galleries; every face
> You find disguis'd in a black velvet case,
> My life on't; is her spy on purpose sent,
> To hold you in a wanton compliment;
> That so you may not censure what she's writ,
> Which done they face you down 'twas full of wit.

At this point, an actress comes onstage to refute the suggestion that the poetess's spies and supporters are prostitutes. Returning to the conceits linking money and warfare, her speech thus enacts the denial of prostitution that was all along implicit in the trope of amorous combat. She claims that the legion of the playwright's supporters, unlike prostitutes,

> scorns the petty spoils, and do prefer
> The glory not the interest of war.

> But yet our forces shall obliging prove,
> Imposing naught but constancy in love:
> That's all our aim, and when we have it too,
> We'll sacrifice it all to pleasure you.

What the last two lines make abundantly clear, in ironically justifying female promiscuity by the pleasure it gives to men, is that the prologue has given us the spectacle of a prostitute dramatically denying mercenary motivations.

The poetess, like the prostitute, is she who "stands out," as the etymology of the word "prostitute"[2] implies, but it is also she who is masked. Indeed, as the prologue emphasizes, the prostitute is she who stands out by virtue of her mask. The dramatic masking of the prostitute and the stagy masking of the playwright's interest in money are parallel cases of theatrical unmasking in which what is revealed is the parallel itself: the playwright is a whore.

When we put the spoken prologue to *The Forced Marriage* together with the printed epistle to *Sir Patient Fancy*, we notice that they both imply a woman hidden behind her own representations. In the prologue and the epistle the explanations for Aphra Behn's authorship are the two usual excuses for prostitution: addressing herself to the women, she claims the motive of want; addressing herself to the men, she claims the motive of love, but in a way that makes the claim seem merely strategic. The two motivations can be arranged into a narrative. Driven by financial necessity, the mistress pretends to take an amorous interest in her lover, to be desirous, like the lyric poet, simply of erotic intercourse. At the same time she might, as she implies in the epistle, despise the entire interaction. What all this amounts to is the dramatization of her lack of self-representation, which then implies that her true self is the sold self's seller. She thus implies the existence of an unseeable selfhood through the flamboyant alienation of her language.

*   *   *

Far from denying these assumptions, Aphra Behn's early authorial persona and much of her comedy are based on them. Like her contemporaries, she presented her writing as part of her sexual property, not just because it was bawdy, but because it was hers. All her properties, like those of other women, were the *potential* property of another; she could either reserve them and give herself whole in marriage, or she could barter them piecemeal, accepting self-division to achieve self-ownership and forfeiting the possibility of marriage.

*   *   *

Given the general delight of the Restoration in equating mental, sexual, and theatrical "parts" and its frequent likening of writing to prostitution and playwrights to bawds, one might argue that if Aphra Behn had not existed, the male playwrights would have had to invent her in order to increase the witty pointedness of their cynical self-reflections. For example, in the prologue written to Behn's posthumously produced *Widow Ranter*, the actor chides the self-proclaimed wits for contesting the originality of one another's productions and squabbling over literary property. Drawing on the metaphor of literary paternity, he concludes:

> But when you see these Pictures, let none dare
> To own beyond a Limb or single share;

---

2. From *pro*, meaning "before," and *statuere*, meaning "to set up or place." To prostitute is thus to set something, oneself perhaps, before someone else to offer it for sale.

> For where the Punk is common, he's a Sot,
> Who needs will father what the Parish got.[3]

These lines would lose half their mordancy if the playwright were not Aphra Behn, the poetess-punk, whose offspring cannot seem fully her own but whose right to them cannot be successfully challenged, since her promiscuous literary intercourse would make disputes about fatherhood unresolvable. By literalizing and embracing the playwright-prostitute metaphor, therefore, Aphra Behn was distinguished from other authors, but only as their prototypical representative. She became almost an allegorical figure of authorship for the Restoration, the writer and the strumpet muse combined. Even those who wished to keep the relationship between women and authorship strictly metaphorical were fond of the image: "What a pox have the women to do with the muses?" asks a character in a play attributed to Charles Gildon. "I grant you the poets call the nine muses by the names of women, but why so? . . . because in that sex they're much fitter for prostitution."[4] Given the ubiquity of the metaphor, it seems almost inevitable that Behn should have obliged the age by "owning" it.

Aphra Behn, therefore, created a persona that skillfully intertwined the age's available discourses concerning women, property, selfhood, and authorship. She found advantageous openings where other women found repulsive insults; she turned self-division into identity and impropriety into property. To understand her plays, we first have to understand these paradoxical relationships she helped construct between the female self and her written representations. However, we also have to remind ourselves once again that the primary nexus of exchange constituting these plays was not publication but theatrical production.

*　　*　　*

1988, 1994

---

3. *Works*, vol. 4, p. 224.
4. The lines are spoken by Critick, the comically negative wit in *A Comparison between the Two Stages* (London, 1702). The other characters in the play defend the writers under discussion, who are Mary Pix and Delarivier Manley.

On Charlotte Brontë's *Jane Eyre*

The "most alarming revolution of modern times has followed the invasion of *Jane Eyre*," declared the Victorian journalist Margaret Oliphant in 1855, remembering the storm that surrounded the publication of Charlotte Brontë's first novel to reach print—a storm that transformed the book's author from an obscure parson's daughter scribbling romances in Yorkshire to a sensational literary celebrity. Jane's impassioned and often rebellious narrative voice, Brontë's compellingly dramatic plot, Rochester's broodingly romantic yet problematic presence—all have been invoked to account for the novel's continuing charisma, a magnetism it exerts to this day not only among general readers and moviegoers (there have been numerous cinematic and video versions) but also among feminist critics and theoreticians, for whom it remains, as Gayatri Spivak puts it in a well-known essay we have excerpted here, "a cult text."

As the divergent analyses of Brontë's classic offered in our four selections indicate, however, contemporary feminist readers focus on notably different aspects of the book in attempting to explain its aesthetic power and cultural purpose. Sandra M. Gilbert's "A Dialogue of Self and Soul: Plain Jane's Progress," drawn from our coauthored *The Madwoman in the Attic* (1979), stresses the "anger, rebellion and rage" that link Brontë's apparently decorous heroine to her mad double, Bertha Mason Rochester, while Gayatri Chakravorty Spivak's "Three Women's Texts and a Critique of Imperialism," included in her *In Other Worlds: Essays in Cultural Politics* (1987), meditates on the Jamaican-born Creole, Bertha Mason, as "a figure produced by the axiomatics of imperialism" through whom "Brontë renders the human/animal frontier as acceptably indeterminate."

Both building on and differing with these two essays, Laura E. Donaldson's "The Miranda Complex," a chapter in her *Decolonizing Feminisms: Race, Gender, and Empire-Building* (1992), analyzes "the interweaving of oppressions" in an effort to incorporate "sexual, racial, cultural, national, and economic considerations" into a "politics of reading." Finally, Susan Fraiman's "Jane Eyre's Fall from Grace," a discussion drawn from her *Unbecoming Women: British Women Writers and the Novel of Development* (1993), foregrounds, instead of the raging figure of Bertha, the "underglossed Grace Poole," a working woman (like Jane) "whose lousy job has driven her to drink." Taken together, these readings—by turns psychoanalytic, cultural, "womanist," and sociological—dramatize the enduring richness and complexity of Brontë's novel even while they also reveal the range of hermeneutics that feminist critics have at their command.

In addition to *The Madwoman in the Attic*, Gilbert, Distinguished Professor Emerita at the University of California, Davis, has coauthored *No Man's Land: The Place of the Woman Writer in the Twentieth Century* (3 vols., 1988, 1989, 1994) with Susan Gubar, as well as eight volumes of poetry and numerous other critical works. Among the many influential texts produced by Spivak, Avalon Foundation Professor in the Humanities at Columbia University, are *Outside in the Teaching Machine* (1993), *A Critique of Post-Colonial Reason: Toward a History of the Vanishing Present* (1999), and *Death of a Discipline* (2003). Besides *Decolonizing Feminisms*, Laura E. Donaldson, an associate professor of English at Cornell University, has coauthored *Postcolonialism, Feminism and Religious Discourse* (2001) with Kwok Pui Lan. In addition to *Unbecoming Women*, Susan Fraiman, a professor of English at the University of Virginia, has published *Cool Men and the Second Sex* (2003) and a Norton Critical Edition of Jane Austen's *Northanger Abbey* (2003).

SANDRA M. GILBERT

From A Dialogue of Self and Soul: Plain Jane's Progress[1]

* * * We tend today to think of *Jane Eyre* as moral gothic, "myth domesticated," *Pamela's* daughter and *Rebecca's* aunt, the archetypal scenario for all those mildly thrilling romantic encounters between a scowling Byronic hero (who owns a gloomy mansion) and a trembling heroine (who can't quite figure out the mansion's floor plan). Or, if we're more sophisticated, we give Charlotte Brontë her due, concede her strategic as well as her mythic abilities, study the patterns of her imagery, and count the number of times she addresses the reader. But still we overlook the "alarming revolution" * * * which "followed the invasion of Jane Eyre." "Well, obviously *Jane Eyre* is a feminist tract, an argument for the social betterment of governesses and equal rights for women," Richard Chase somewhat grudgingly admitted in 1948. But like most other modern critics, he believed that the novel's power arose from its mythologizing of Jane's confrontation with masculine sexuality.[2]

Yet, curiously enough, it seems not to have been primarily the coarseness and sexuality of *Jane Eyre* which shocked the Victorian reviewers (though they disliked those elements in the book), but * * * its "anti-Christian" refusal to accept the forms, customs, and standards of society—in short, its rebellious feminism. They were disturbed not so much by the proud Byronic sexual energy of Rochester as by the Byronic pride and passion of Jane herself, not so much by the asocial sexual vibrations between hero and heroine as by the heroine's refusal to submit to her social destiny: "She has inherited in fullest measure the worst sin of our fallen nature—the sin of pride," declared Miss Rigby.[3] * * *

[But Jane's] story, providing a pattern for countless others, is * * * a story of enclosure and escape, a distinctively female *Bildungsroman* in which the problems encountered by the protagonist as she struggles from the imprisonment of her childhood toward an almost unthinkable goal of mature freedom are symptomatic of difficulties Everywoman in a patriarchal society must meet and overcome: oppression (at Gateshead), starvation (at Lowood), madness (at Thornfield), and coldness (at Marsh End).[4] Most important, her confrontation, not with Rochester but with Rochester's mad wife Bertha, is the book's central confrontation, an encounter * * * not with her own sexuality but with her own imprisoned "hunger, rebellion, and rage," a secret dialogue of self and soul on whose outcome * * * the novel's plot, Rochester's fate, and Jane's coming-of-age all depend. * * *

The third story is the most obviously emblematic quarter of Thornfield. Here, amid the furniture of the past, down a narrow passage with "two rows of small black doors, all shut, like a corridor in some Bluebeard's castle" (chap. 11), Jane first hears the "distinct formal mirthless laugh" of mad Bertha, Rochester's secret wife and in a sense her own secret self.[5] And just above this sinister corridor, leaning against the picturesque battlements and

1. Excerpted from chapter 10 of *The Madwoman in the Attic: The Woman Writer and the Nineteenth-Century Literary Imagination* (1979) [editor's note].
2. Richard Chase, "The Brontës, or Myth Domesticated," in *Jane Eyre*, ed. Richard J. Dunn (New York: Norton, 1971), pp. 464, 468.
3. *Quarterly Review* 84 (December 1848): 173–74.

4. These are, respectively, the house of Jane's aunt, where she lived after being orphaned; the school she attended between the ages of 10 and 18; the house where she served as governess in Edward Rochester's employ; and the house where she found refuge after she fled Thornfield [editor's note].
5. All references to *Jane Eyre* are to the Norton Critical Edition, ed. Richard J. Dunn (New York: Norton, 1971).

looking out over the world like Bluebeard's bride's sister Anne, Jane is to long again for freedom, for "all of incident, life, fire, feeling that I . . . had not in my actual existence" (chap. 12). These upper regions, in other words, symbolically miniaturize one crucial aspect of the world in which she finds herself. Heavily enigmatic, ancestral relics wall her in; inexplicable locked rooms guard a secret which may have something to do with *her*; distant vistas promise an inaccessible but enviable life.

Even more importantly, Thornfield's attic soon becomes a complex focal point where Jane's own rationality (what she has learned from Miss Temple) and her irrationality (her "hunger, rebellion, and rage") intersect. She never, for instance, articulates her rational desire for liberty so well as when she stands on the battlements of Thornfield, looking out over the world. However offensive these thoughts may have been to Miss Rigby—and both Jane and her creator obviously suspected they would be—the sequence of ideas expressed in the famous passage beginning "Anybody may blame me who likes" is as logical as anything in an essay by Wollstonecraft or Mill. What is somewhat irrational, though, is the restlessness and passion which, as it were, italicize her little meditation on freedom. "I could not help it," she explains,

> the restlessness was in my nature, it agitated me to pain sometimes. Then my sole relief was to walk along the corridor of the third story, backwards and forwards, safe in the silence and solitude of the spot, and allow my mind's eye to dwell on whatever bright visions rose before it.

And even more irrational is the experience which accompanies Jane's pacing:

> When thus alone, I not unfrequently heard Grace Poole's laugh: the same peal, the same low, slow ha! ha! which, when first heard, had thrilled me: I heard, too, her eccentric murmurs: stranger than her laugh.

Eccentric murmurs that uncannily echo the murmurs of Jane's imagination, and a low, slow ha! ha! which forms a bitter refrain to the tale Jane's imagination creates. Despite Miss Temple's training, the "bad animal" who was first locked up in the red-room is, we sense, still lurking somewhere, behind a dark door, waiting for a chance to get free. That early consciousness of "something near me" has not yet been exorcised. Rather, it has intensified. * * *

Grace Poole, the most enigmatic of the women Jane meets at Thornfield— "that mystery of mysteries, as I considered her"—is obviously associated with Bertha, almost as if, with her pint of porter, her "staid and taciturn" demeanor, she were the madwoman's public representative. "Only one hour in the twenty four did she pass with her fellow servants below," Jane notes, attempting to fathom the dark "pool" of the woman's behavior; "all the rest of her time was spent in some low-ceiled, oaken chamber of the third story; there she sat and sewed . . . as companionless as a prisoner in her dungeon" (chap. 17). And that Grace is as companionless as Bertha or Jane herself is undeniably true. Women in Jane's world, acting as agents for men, may be the keepers of other women. But both keepers and prisoners are bound by the same chains. In a sense, then, the mystery of mysteries which Grace Poole suggests to Jane is the mystery of her own life, so that to question Grace's position at Thornfield is to question her own.

Interestingly, in trying to puzzle out the secret of Grace Poole, Jane at one point speculates that Mr. Rochester may once have entertained "tender feelings" for the woman, and when thoughts of Grace's "uncomeliness" seem to refute this possibility, she cements her bond with Bertha's keeper by reminding herself that, after all "*You* are not beautiful either, and perhaps Mr. Rochester approves you" (chap. 16). Can appearances be trusted? Who is the slave, the master or the servant, the prince or Cinderella? What in other words, are the real relationships between the master of Thornfield and all these women whose lives revolve around his? None of these questions can, of course, be answered without reference to the central character of the Thornfield episode, Edward Fairfax Rochester.

* * * Why, Jane herself wonders, does Rochester have to trick people, especially women? What secrets are concealed behind the charades he enacts? One answer is surely that he himself senses his trickery is a source of power, and therefore, in Jane's case at least, an evasion of that equality in which he claims to believe. Beyond this, however, it is clear that the secrets Rochester is concealing or disguising throughout much of the book are themselves in Jane's—and Charlotte Brontë's—view secrets of inequality.

The first of these is suggested both by his name, apparently an allusion to the dissolute Earl of Rochester, and by Jane's own reference to the Bluebeard's corridor of the third story; it is the secret of masculine potency, the secret of male sexual guilt. For, like those pre-Byron heroes the real Restoration Rochester and the mythic Bluebeard (indeed, in relation to Jane, like any experienced adult male), Rochester has specific and "guilty" sexual knowledge which makes him in some sense her "superior." * * * Rochester's apparently improper recounting of his sexual adventures is a kind of acknowledgement of Jane's equality with him. His possession of the hidden details of sexuality, however—his knowledge, that is, of the *secret* of sex, symbolized both by his doll-like daughter Adèle and by the locked doors of the third story behind which mad Bertha crouches like an animal—qualifies and undermines that equality. And though his puzzling transvestism, his attempt to impersonate a *female* gypsy, may be seen as a semi-conscious effort to reduce this sexual advantage his masculinity gives him (by putting on a woman's clothes he puts on a woman's weakness), both he and Jane obviously recognize the hollowness of such a ruse. The prince is inevitably Cinderella's superior, Charlotte Brontë saw, not because his rank is higher than hers, but because it is *he* who will initiate *her* into the mysteries of the flesh.

That both Jane and Rochester are in some part of themselves conscious of the barrier which Rochester's sexual knowledge poses to their equality is further indicated by the tensions that develop in their relationship after their betrothal. Rochester, having secured Jane's love, almost reflexively begins to treat her as an inferior, a plaything, a virginal possession—for she has now become his initiate, his "mustard-seed," his "little sunny-faced . . . girl-bride." "It is your time now, little tyrant," he declares, "but it will be mine presently: and when once I have fairly seized you, to have and to hold, I'll just—figuratively speaking—attach you to a chain like this" (chap. 24). She, sensing his new sense of power, resolves to keep him "in reasonable check": "I never can bear being dressed like a doll by Mr. Rochester," she remarks, and, more significantly "I'll not stand you an inch in the stead of a seraglio. . . . I'll [prepare myself] to go out as a missionary to preach liberty to them that are enslaved" (chap. 24). While such assertions have seemed to some critics merely the consequences of Jane's (and Charlotte Brontë's) sexual panic, it should be clear from their context that, as is usual with Jane, they are political rather than sexual statements, attempts at finding emotional strength rather than expressions of weakness.

Finally, Rochester's ultimate secret, the secret that is revealed together with the existence of Bertha, the literal impediment to his marriage with Jane, is another and perhaps most surprising secret of inequality: but this time the hidden facts suggest the master's inferiority rather than his superiority. Rochester, Jane learns, after the aborted wedding ceremony, had married Bertha Mason for status, for sex, for money, for everything but love and equality. "Oh, I have no respect for myself when I think of that act!" he confesses. "An agony of inward contempt masters me. I never loved, I never esteemed, I did not even know her" (chap. 27). And his statement reminds us of Jane's earlier assertion of her own superiority: "I would scorn such a union [as the loveless one he hints he will enter into with Blanche]: therefore I am better than you" (chap. 23). In a sense, then, the most serious crime Rochester has to expiate is not even the crime of exploiting others but the sin of self-exploitation, the sin of Céline[6] and Blanche, to which he, at least, had seemed completely immune.

That Rochester's character and life pose in themselves such substantial impediments to his marriage with Jane does not mean, however, that Jane herself generates none. For one thing, "akin" as she is to Rochester, she suspects him of harboring all the secrets we know he does harbor, and raises defenses against them, manipulating her "master" so as to keep him "in reasonable check." In a larger way, moreover, all the charades and masquerades—the secret messages—of patriarchy have had their effect upon her. Though she loves Rochester the man, Jane has doubts about Rochester the husband even before she learns about Bertha. In her world, she senses, even the equality of love between true minds leads to the inequalities and minor despotisms of marriage. "For a little while," she says cynically to Rochester, "you will perhaps be as you are now, [but] . . . I suppose your love will effervesce in six months, or less. I have observed in books written by men, that period assigned as the farthest to which a husband's ardor extends" (chap. 24). He, of course, vigorously repudiates this prediction, but his argument— "Jane: you please me, and you master me [because] you seem to submit"— implies a kind of Lawrentian sexual tension and only make things worse. For when he asks "Why do you smile [at this], Jane? What does that inexplicable . . . turn of countenance mean?" her peculiar, ironic smile, reminiscent of Bertha's mirthless laugh, signals an "involuntary" and subtly hostile thought "of Hercules and Samson with their charmers." And that hostility becomes overt at the silk warehouse, where Jane notes that "the more he bought me, the more my cheek burned with a sense of annoyance and degradation. . . . I thought his smile was such as a sultan might, in a blissful and fond moment, bestow on a slave his gold and gems had enriched" (chap. 24).

Jane's whole life-pilgrimage, has, of course, prepared her to be angry in this way at Rochester's, and society's, concept of marriage. Rochester's loving tyranny recalls John Reed's unloving despotism, and the erratic nature of Rochester's favors ("in my secret soul I knew that his great kindness to me was balanced by unjust severity to many others" [chap. 15]) recalls Brocklehurst's[7] hypocrisy. * * *

[At this same time, throughout all this] Bertha * * * is Jane's truest and darkest double: she is the angry aspect of the orphan child, the ferocious secret self Jane has been trying to repress ever since her days at Gateshead. * * * Specifically, every one of Bertha's appearances—or, more accurately, her manifesta-

---

6. Adèle's dead mother, a French dancer [editor's note].
7. The unctuous clergyman who initially oversees Lowood [editor's note].

tions—has been associated with an experience (or repression) of anger on Jane's part. Jane's feeling of "hunger, rebellion, and rage" on the battlements, for instance, were accompanied by Bertha's "low, slow ha! ha!" and "eccentric murmurs." Jane's apparently secure response to Rochester's apparently egalitarian sexual confidences was followed by Bertha's attempt to incinerate the master in his bed. Jane's unexpressed resentment at Rochester's manipulative gypsy-masquerade found expression in Bertha's terrible shriek and her even more terrible attack on Richard Mason. Jane's anxieties about her marriage, and in particular her fears of her own alien "robed and veiled" bridal image, were objectified by the image of Bertha in a "white and straight" dress, "whether gown, sheet, or shroud I cannot tell." Jane's profound desire to destroy Thornfield, the symbol of Rochester's mastery and of her own servitude, will be acted out by Bertha, who burns down the house and destroys *herself* in the process as if she were an agent of Jane's desire as well as her own. And finally, Jane's disguised hostility to Rochester, summarized in her terrifying prediction to herself that "you shall, yourself, pluck out your right eve; yourself cut off your right hand" (chap. 27) comes strangely true through the intervention of Bertha, whose melodramatic death causes Rochester to lose both eye and hand.

These parallels between Jane and Bertha may at first seem somewhat strained. Jane, after all, is poor, plain, little, pale, neat, and quiet, while Bertha is rich, large, florid, sensual, and extravagant; indeed, she was once even beautiful, somewhat, Rochester notes, "in the style of Blanche Ingram." Is she not, then, as many critics have suggested, a monitory image rather than a double for Jane? . . . "Just as [Jane's] instinct for self-preservation saves her from earlier temptations," Adrienne Rich remarks, "so it must save her from becoming this woman by curbing her imagination at the limits of what is bearable for a powerless woman in the England of the 1840s."[8] Even Rochester himself provides a similar critical appraisal of the relationship between the two. "That is *my wife*," he says, pointing to mad Bertha,

> "And *this* is what I wished to have . . . this young girl who stands so grave and quiet at the mouth of hell, looking collectedly at the gambols of a demon. I wanted her just as a change after that fierce ragout. . . . Compare these clear eyes with the red balls yonder—this face with that mask—this form with that bulk. . . ." (chap. 26)

And of course, in one sense, the relationship between Jane and Bertha is a monitory one: while acting out Jane's secret fantasies, Bertha does (to say the least) provide the governess with an example of how not to act, teaching her a lesson more salutary than any Miss Temple ever taught.

Nevertheless, it is disturbingly clear from recurrent images in the novel that Bertha not only acts *for* Jane, she also acts *like* Jane. The imprisoned Bertha, running "backwards and forwards" on all fours in the attic, for instance, recalls not only Jane the governess, whose only relief from mental pain was to pace "backwards and forwards" in the third story, but also that "bad animal" who was ten-year-old Jane, imprisoned in the red-room, howling and mad. Bertha's "goblin appearance"—"half dream, half reality," says Rochester—recalls the lover's epithets for Jane: "malicious elf," "sprite," "changeling," as well as his playful accusation that she had magically downed

---

8. Adrienne Rich, "Jane Eyre: The Temptations of a Motherless Woman," *Ms.* 2, no 4 (October 1973): 72.

his horse at their first meeting. Rochester's description of Bertha as a "monster" ("a fearful voyage I had with such a monster in the vessel" [chap. 27]) ironically echoes Jane's own fear of being a monster ("Am I a monster? * * * is it impossible that Mr. Rochester should have a sincere affection for me?" [chap. 24]). * * * And most dramatic of all, Bertha's incendiary tendencies recall Jane's early flaming rages, at Lowood and at Gateshead, as well as that "ridge of lighted heath" [chap. 4] which she herself saw as emblematic of her mind in its rebellion against society. It is only fitting, therefore, that, as if to balance the child Jane's terrifying vision of herself as an alien figure in the "visionary hollow" of the red-room looking glass, the adult Jane first clearly perceives her terrible double when Bertha puts on the wedding veil intended for the second Mrs. Rochester, and turns to the mirror. At that moment, Jane sees "the reflection of the visage and features quite distinctly in the dark oblong glass," sees them as if they were her own (chap. 25). * * *

Jane's return to Thornfield, her discovery of Bertha's death and of the ruin her dream had predicted, her reunion at Ferndean with the maimed and blinded Rochester, and their subsequent marriage form an essential epilogue to that pilgrimage toward selfhood which had in other ways concluded at Marsh End, with Jane's realization that she could not marry St. John.[9] At that moment, "the wondrous shock of feeling had come like the earthquake which shook the foundations of Paul and Silas' prison; it had opened the doors of the soul's cell, and loosed its bands—it had wakened it out of its sleep" (chap. 36). For at that moment she had been irrevocably freed from the burden of her past, freed both from the raging specter of Bertha (which had already fallen in fact from the ruined wall of Thornfield) and from the self-pitying specter of the orphan child (which had symbolically, as in her dream, rolled from her knee), and at that moment, again as in her dream, she had *wakened* to her own self, her own needs. Similarly, Rochester, "caged eagle" that he seems (chap. 37), has been freed from what was for him the burden of Thornfield, though at the same time he appears to have been fettered by the injuries he received in attempting to rescue Jane's mad double from the flames devouring his house. That his "fetters" pose no impediment to a new marriage, that he and Jane are now, in reality, equals, is the thesis of the Ferndean section. * * *

Does Brontë's rebellious feminism—that "irreligious" dissatisfaction with the social order noted by Miss Rigby and *Jane Eyre's* other Victorian critics—compromise itself in this withdrawal? Has Jane exorcised the rage of her orphanhood only to retreat from the responsibilities her own principles implied? Tentative answers to these questions can be derived more easily from *The Professor, Shirley,* and *Villette* than from *Jane Eyre,* for the qualified and even (as in *Villette*) indecisive endings of Brontë's other novels suggest that she herself was unable clearly to envision viable solutions to the problem of patriarchal oppression. In all her books, writing * * * in a sort of trance, she was able to act out that passionate drive toward freedom which offended agents of the status quo, but in none was she able consciously to define the full meaning of achieved freedom—perhaps because no one of her contemporaries, not even a Wollstonecraft or a Mill, could adequately describe a society so drastically altered that the matured Jane and Rochester could really live in it.

9. The young clergyman whose family home is Marsh End; he wishes Jane to marry him because he seeks her help in his missionary work in India, not because he loves her. "Ferndean": a secluded house owned by Rochester; he retires there after the destruction of Thornfield [editor's note].

What Brontë could not logically define, however, she could embody in ten-uous but suggestive imagery, and in her last, perhaps most significant redef-initions of Bunyan. Nature in the largest sense seems now to be on the side of Jane and Rochester. *Ferndean*, as its name implies, is without artifice—"no flowers, no garden-beds"—but it is green as Jane tells Rochester he will be, green and ferny and fertilized by soft rains. Here isolated from society but flourishing in a natural order of their own making, Jane and Rochester will become physically "bone of [each other's] bone, flesh of [each other's] flesh" (chap. 38), and here the healing powers of nature will eventually restore the sight of one of Rochester's eyes. Here, in other words, nature, unleashed from social restrictions, will do "no miracle—but her best" (chap. 35). For not the Celestial City but a natural paradise, the country of Beulah "upon the bor-ders of heaven," where "the contact between bride and bridegroom [is] renewed," has all along been, we now realize, the goal of Jane's pilgrimage.

As for the Celestial City itself, Charlotte Brontë implies here (though she will later have second thoughts) that such a goal is the dream of those who accept inequities on earth, one of the many tools used by patriarchal society to keep, say, governesses in their "place." Because she believes this so deeply, she quite consciously concludes *Jane Eyre* with an allusion to *Pilgrim's Progress* and with a half-ironic apostrophe to that apostle of celestial transcendence, that shadow of "the warrior Greatheart," St. John Rivers. "His," she tells us, "is the exaction of the apostle, who speaks but for Christ when he says— 'Whosoever will come after me, let him deny himself and take up his cross and follow me' " (chap. 38). For it was, finally, to repudiate such a crucifying denial of the self that Brontë's "hunger, rebellion, and rage" led her to write *Jane Eyre* in the first place and to make it an "irreligious" redefinition, almost a parody, of John Bunyan's vision. And the astounding progress toward equality of plain Jane Eyre, whom Miss Rigby correctly saw as "the personification of an unre-generate and undisciplined spirit," answers by its outcome the bitter question Emily Dickinson was to ask fifteen years later: " 'My husband'—women say— / Stroking the Melody— / 'Is *this*—the way?' " No, Jane declares in her flight from Thornfield, *that* is not the way. *This*, she says—this marriage of true minds at Ferndean—this is the way. Qualified and isolated as her way may be, it is at least an emblem of hope. Certainly Charlotte Brontë was never again to indulge in quite such an optimistic imagining.

1979

GAYATRI CHAKRAVORTY SPIVAK

From Three Women's Texts and a Critique of Imperialism[1]

It should not be possible to read nineteenth-century British literature with-out remembering that imperialism, understood as England's social mission, was a crucial part of the cultural representation of England to the English. The role of literature in the production of cultural representation should not

---

1. From *Critical Inquiry* 12 (1985) [editor's note].

be ignored. These two obvious "facts" continue to be disregarded in the reading of nineteenth-century British literature. This itself attests to the continuing success of the imperialist project, displaced and dispersed into more modern forms.

If these "facts" were remembered, not only in the study of British literature but in the study of the literatures of the European colonizing cultures of the great age of imperialism, we would produce a narrative, in literary history, of the "worlding" of what is now called "the Third World." To consider the Third World as distant cultures, exploited but with rich intact literary heritages waiting to be recovered, interpreted, and curricularized in English translation fosters the emergence of "the Third World" as a signifier that allows us to forget that "worlding," even as it expands the empire of the literary discipline.[2]

It seems particularly unfortunate when the emergent perspective of feminist criticism reproduces the axioms of imperialism. A basically isolationist admiration for the literature of the female subject in Europe and Anglo-America establishes the high feminist norm. It is supported and operated by an information-retrieval approach to "Third World" literature which often employs a deliberately "nontheoretical" methodology with self-conscious rectitude.

In this essay, I will attempt to examine the operation of the "worlding" of what is today "the Third World" by what has become a cult text of feminism: *Jane Eyre*.[3] I plot the novel's reach and grasp, and locate its structural motors. I read *Wide Sargasso Sea* as *Jane Eyre*'s reinscription and *Frankenstein* as an analysis—even a deconstruction—of a "worlding" such as *Jane Eyre*'s.[4]

* * *

Before following the track of this unique imagination, let us consider the suggestion that the progress of *Jane Eyre* can be charted through a sequential arrangement of the family/counter-family dyad. In the novel, we encounter, first, the Reeds as the legal family and Jane, the late Mr. Reed's sister's daughter, as the representative of a near incestuous counter-family; second, the Brocklehursts, who run the school Jane is sent to, as the legal family and Jane, Miss Temple, and Helen Burns as a counter-family that falls short because it is only a community of women; third, Rochester and the mad Mrs. Rochester as the legal family and Jane and Rochester as the illicit counter-family. Other items may be added to the thematic chain in this sequence: Rochester and Céline Varens as structurally functional counter-family; Rochester and Blanche Ingram[5] as dissimulation of legality—and so on. It is during this sequence that Jane is moved from the counter-family to the family-in-law. In the next sequence, it is Jane who restores full family status to the as-yet-incomplete community of siblings, the Riverses. The final sequence of the book is a *community of families*, with Jane, Rochester, and their children at the center.

2. My notion of the "worlding of a world" upon what must be assumed to be uninscribed earth is a vulgarization of Martin Heidegger's idea; see "The Origin of the Work of Art," *Poetry, Language, Thought*, trans. Albert Hofstadter (New York, 1977), pp, 17–87.
3. See Charlotte Brontë, *Jane Eyre* (New York, 1960); all further references to this work, abbreviated *JE*, will be included in the text.

4. See Jean Rhys, *Wide Sargasso Sea* (Harmondsworth, 1966); all further references to this work, abbreviated WSS, will be included in the text. And see Mary Shelley, *Frankenstein; or, The Modern Prometheus* (New York, 1965).
5. The beautiful young woman whom Rochester is apparently courting. Céline Varens, the French dancer with whom he had an affair, is the dead mother of Jane's pupil, Adèle [editor's note].

In terms of the narrative energy of the novel, how is Jane moved from the place of the counter-family to the family-in-law? It is the active ideology of imperialism that provides the discursive field.

*   *   *

Let us consider the figure of Bertha Mason, a figure produced by the axiomatics of imperialism. Through Bertha Mason, the white Jamaican Creole, Brontë renders the human/animal frontier as acceptably indeterminate, so that a good greater than the letter of the Law can be broached. Here is the celebrated passage, given in the voice of Jane:

> In the deep shade, at the further end of the room, a figure ran backwards and forwards. What it was, whether beast or human being, one could not . . . tell: it grovelled, seemingly, on all fours; it snatched and growled like some strange wild animal: but it was covered with clothing, and a quantity of dark, grizzled hair, wild as a mane, hid its head and face. [*JE*, p. 295]

In a matching passage, given in the voice of Rochester speaking *to* Jane, Brontë presents the imperative for a shift beyond the Law as divine injunction rather than human motive. In the terms of my essay, we might say that this is the register not of mere marriage or sexual reproduction but of Europe and its not-yet-human Other, of soul making. The field of imperial conquest is here inscribed as Hell:

> "One night I had been awakened by her yells . . . it was a fiery West Indian night. . . .
>
> " 'This life,' said I at last, 'is hell!—this is the air—those are the sounds of the bottomless pit! *I have a right* to deliver myself from it if I can. . . . Let me break away, and go home to God!' . . .
>
> "A wind fresh from Europe blew over the ocean and rushed through the open casement: the storm broke, streamed, thundered, blazed, and the air grew pure. . . . It was true Wisdom that consoled me in that hour, and showed me the right path. . . .
>
> "The sweet wind from Europe was still whispering in the refreshed leaves, and the Atlantic was thundering in glorious liberty. . . .
>
> " 'Go,' said Hope, 'and live again in Europe. . . . You have done all that God and Humanity require of you.' " [*JE*, pp. 310–11; my emphasis]

It is the unquestioned ideology of imperialist axiomatics, then, that conditions Jane's move from the counter-family set to the set of the family-in-law. Marxist critics such as Terry Eagleton have seen this only in terms of the ambiguous *class* position of the governess.[6] Sandra Gilbert and Susan Gubar, on the other hand, have seen Bertha Mason only in psychological terms, as Jane's dark double.[7]

I will not enter the critical debates that offer themselves here. Instead, I will develop the suggestion that nineteenth-century feminist individualism could conceive of a "greater" project than access to the closed circle of the

---

6. See Terry Eagleton, *Myths of Power: A Marxist Study of the Brontës* (London, 1975); this is one of the general presuppositions of his book.

7. See Sandra M. Gilbert and Susan Gubar, *The Madwoman in the Attic: The Woman Writer and the Nineteenth-Century Literary Imagination* (New Haven, Conn., 1979), pp. 360–62.

nuclear family. This is the project of soul making beyond "mere" sexual reproduction. Here the native "subject" is not almost an animal but rather the object of what might be termed the terrorism of the categorical imperative.

I am using "Kant" in this essay as a metonym for the most flexible ethical moment in the European eighteenth century. Kant words the categorical imperative, conceived as the universal moral law given by pure reason, in this way: "In all creation every thing one chooses and over which one has any power, may be used *merely as means;* man alone, and with him every rational creature, is an *end in himself.*" It is thus a moving displacement of Christian ethics from religion to philosophy. As Kant writes: "With this agrees very well the possibility of such a command as: *Love God above everything, and thy neighbor as thyself.* For as a command it requires respect for a law which *commands love* and does not leave it to our own arbitrary choice to make this our principle."[8]

The "categorical" in Kant cannot be adequately represented in determinately grounded action. The dangerous transformative power of philosophy, however, is that its formal subtlety can be travestied in the service of the state. Such a travesty in the case of the categorical imperative can justify the imperialist project by producing the following formula: *make* the heathen into a human so that he can be treated as an end in himself.[9] This project is presented as a sort of tangent in *Jane Eyre,* a tangent that escapes the closed circle of the *narrative* conclusion. The tangent narrative is the story of St. John Rivers, who is granted the important task of concluding the *text.*

At the novel's end, the *allegorical* language of Christian psychobiography— rather than the textually constituted and seemingly *private* grammar of the creative imagination which we noted in the novel's opening—marks the inaccessibility of the imperialist project as such to the nascent "feminist" scenario. The concluding passage of *Jane Eyre* places St. John Rivers within the fold of *Pilgrim's Progress.* Eagleton pays no attention to this but accepts the novel's ideological lexicon, which establishes St. John Rivers' heroism by identifying a life in Calcutta[1] with an unquestioning choice of death. Gilbert and Gubar, by calling *Jane Eyre* "Plain Jane's progress," see the novel as simply replacing the male protagonist with the female. They do not notice the distance between sexual reproduction and soul making, both actualized by the unquestioned idiom of imperialist presuppositions evident in the last part of *Jane Eyre:*

> Firm, faithful, and devoted, full of energy, and zeal, and truth, [St. John Rivers] labours for his race. . . . His is the sternness of the warrior Greatheart, who guards his pilgrim convoy from the onslaught of Apollyon. . . . His is the ambition of the high master-spirit[s] . . . who stand without

---

8. Immanuel Kant, *Critique of Practical Reason, The "Critique of Pure Reason," the "Critique of Practical Reason" and Other Ethical Treatises, the "Critique of Judgement,"* trans. J. M. D. Meiklejohn et al. (Chicago, 1952), pp. 328, 326.

9. I have tried to justify the reduction of sociohistorical problems to formulas or propositions in my essay "Can the Subaltern Speak?" in *Marxist Interpretations of Culture,* ed. Cary Nelson (Urbana, Ill., forthcoming) [published as *Marxism and the Interpretation of Culture,* 1988]. The "travesty" I speak

of does not befall the Kantian ethic in its purity as an accident but rather exists within its lineaments as a possible supplement. On the register of the human being as child rather than heathen, my formula can be found, for example, in "What Is Enlightenment?" in Kant, *"Foundations of the Metaphysics of Morals," "What Is Enlightenment?" and a Passage from "The Metaphysics of Morals,"* trans. and ed. Lewis White Beck (Chicago, 1950). I have profited from discussing Kant with Jonathan Rée.

1. As a missionary [editor's note].

fault before the throne of God; who share the last mighty victories of the Lamb; who are called, and chosen, and faithful. [*JE*, p. 455]

Earlier in the novel, St. John Rivers himself justifies the project: "My vocation? My great work? . . . My hopes of being numbered in the band who have merged all ambitions in the glorious one of bettering their race—of carrying knowledge into the realms of ignorance—of substituting peace for war—freedom for bondage—religion for superstition—the hope of heaven for the fear of hell?" (*JE*, p. 376). Imperialism and its territorial and subject-constituting project are a violent deconstruction of these oppositions.

*   *   *

I have suggested that Bertha's function in *Jane Eyre* is to render indeterminate the boundary between human and animal and thereby to weaken her entitlement under the spirit if not the letter of the Law. When Rhys rewrites the scene in *Jane Eyre* where Jane hears "a snarling, snatching sound, almost like a dog quarrelling" and then encounters a bleeding Richard Mason (*JE*, p. 210), she keeps Bertha's humanity, indeed her sanity as critic of imperialism, intact. Grace Poole, another character originally in *Jane Eyre*, describes the incident to Bertha in *Wide Sargasso Sea*: "So you don't remember that you attacked this gentleman with a knife? . . . I didn't hear all he said except 'I cannot interfere legally between yourself and your husband'. It was when he said 'legally' that you flew at him' " (*WSS*, p. 150). In Rhys' retelling, it is the dissimulation that Bertha discerns in the word "legally"—not an innate bestiality—that prompts her violent *re*action.

*   *   *

1985

LAURA E. DONALDSON

From The Miranda Complex: Colonialism and the Question of Feminist Reading[1]

*   *   *

Frantz Fanon observed in *Black Skin, White Masks* that "the only means of breaking this vicious circle that throws me back on myself is to restore to the other, through mediation and recognition, his human reality. . . . The other has to perform the same operation. 'Action from one side only would be useless, because what is to happen can only be brought about by means of both.' "[2] Fanon's statement foregrounds the weakness in the position not only

---

1. Excerpted from chapter 1 of *Decolonizing Feminisms: Race, Gender & Empire Building* (1992), the revised version of an essay originally published in 1988. The "Miranda complex," a term coined by Donaldson, refers to the relationship between Miranda and Caliban as fellow victims of colonization in Shakespeare's *The Tempest* [editor's note].
2. Frantz Fanon, *Black Skin, White Masks*, trans. Charles Lam Markmann (New York: Grove Press, 1967), 217.

of [Sandra] Gilbert and [Susan] Gubar but also of [Gayatri] Spivak in "Three Women's Texts."[3] Spivak's failure to see how the white woman, as well as the "native" subject, suffers the ravages of colonialism not only calls her problematic of "feminist individualism in the age of imperialism" into question but also raises grave questions about any politics of reading that privileges one oppression over another. Barbara Smith drives this point "home" in *Home Girls: A Black Feminist Anthology* when she declares that "we [women of color] examined our lives and found that everything out there was kicking our behinds—race, class, sex, and homophobia. We saw no reason to rank oppressions, or, as many forces in the Black community would have us do, to pretend that sexism, among all the isms, was not happening to us."[4] This description of "womanism" affirms the interweaving of oppressions and incorporates sexual, racial, cultural, national, and economic considerations into any politics of reading.[5]

If the critical practice of *Madwoman* precludes a womanist ethic by its domestication and dissimulation of the "native" Other, then the practice of "Three Women's Texts" seems equally problematic in its presupposition that *Jane Eyre* perpetuates the individualist subject through the subjectivity of Jane herself (TWT 224). According to Louis Althusser in "Ideology and Ideological State Apparatuses," the classic realist text interpellates or constructs the relationship between narrative and reader so that the reading subject willingly accepts her status as the individual and noncontradictory locus of meaning. Spivak uses Althusser's formulation to argue that Jane's "privatization" in the opening of Brontë's text (exemplified by Jane's withdrawal from the dining room peopled by the Reed family into a subsidiary and isolated breakfast room) implies a "self-marginalized uniqueness" fertile with the ideology of bourgeois individualism. In Spivak's analysis, *Jane Eyre* as a feminist tract bears the offspring "militant female subject" (TWT 244–45), a woman who achieves her identity at the expense of the "native," not quite human, female Other.

This conclusion points to a weakness within Althusser's theory: because interpellation ignores the fissures that the violent and subterranean pressures of patriarchal society open between men and women, its uncritical adoption can lead one into false assumptions. Indeed, a false conflation of masculine and feminine subject positions certainly underlies Spivak's statement that "Gilbert and Gubar, by calling *Jane Eyre* 'Plain Jane's progress,' see the novel as simply replacing the male protagonist [of *Pilgrim's Progress*] with the female" (TWT 249). For Gilbert and Gubar, however, *Jane Eyre* parodies, rather than reproduces, the structure of the masculine quest plot and consequently narrates a distinctively feminine story of enclosure and escape (*MA* 314).

By contending that Jane's establishment of spatial and psychological boundaries connotes an "individualist" differentiation and autonomy, Spivak endows Jane with qualities usually ascribed to masculine development within

3. Gayatri Chakravorty Spivak, "Three Women's Texts and a Critique of Imperialism," *Critical Inquiry* 12 (1985): 243–61, cited in the text as TWT; see also Sandra M. Gilbert and Susan Gubar, *The Madwoman in the Attic: The Woman Writer and the Nineteenth-Century Literary Imagination* (New Haven: Yale University Press, 1979), cited in the text as *MA* [editor's note].

4. Barbara Smith, introduction to *Home Girls: A Black Feminist Anthology*, ed. Barbara Smith (New York: Kitchen Table, Women of Color Press, 1983), xxxii.

5. Chikwenye Okonjo Ogunyemi, "Womanism: The Dynamics of the Contemporary Black Female Novel in English," *Signs* 11 (1985): 64.

the capitalist patriarchal family. Nancy Chodorow notes in *The Reproduction of Mothering: Psychoanalysis and the Sociology of Gender* that the separation of the postoedipal boy from the mother requires him to engage in a more emphatic individuation and a more defensive firming of experienced ego boundaries than the postoedipal girl.[6] However, Jane's internalized practices of oppression—a "habitual mood of humiliation, self-doubt, forlorn depression"—place her in a subject(ed) position starkly contrasted to the masculine one iterated by Chodorow and assigned to her by Spivak. As her last name suggests, Jane is invisible as air and the heir to nothing (*MA* 342).

However, if we traverse the textual surface of *Jane Eyre*, a surface whose filmic qualities are much more pronounced than is usually realized, another interpretation of the relationship between Jane and Bertha emerges. Through the processes of cinematic suture, we glimpse a critical strategy more promising than Althusserian interpellation—not only for reading Brontë's very complex woman's text but also for developing a womanist politics of reading. Unlike interpellation, suture articulates itself in relation to culturally imposed differences between the positions of men and women: "As a process, a practice of signification, suture is an ideological operation with a particular function in relation to paternal ideology in that out of a system of differences it establishes a position in relation to the phallus. In so doing it places the spectator in relation to that position. . . . It is the imaginary unity, the sutured coherence, the imaginary sense of identity set up by the classic film which must be challenged by a feminist film practice to achieve a different constitution of the subject in relation to ideology."[7] If we imagine that Jane's "I" has become the "eye" of a camera, Spivak's characterization of her as a whitemale individualist Self becomes much more questionable:

> I now stood in the empty hall; before me was the breakfast-room door, and I stopped, intimidated and trembling. What a miserable little poltroon had fear, engendered of unjust punishment, made of me in those days! I feared to return to the nursery, and feared to go forward to the parlour; ten minutes I stood in agitated hesitation; the vehement ringing of the breakfast-room bell decided me; I *must* enter.
>
> "Who could want me?" I asked inwardly, as with both hands I turned the stiff door-handle which, for a second or two, resisted my efforts. "What should I see besides Aunt Reed in the apartment?—a man or a woman?" The handle turned, the door unclosed, and passing through and curtseying low, I looked up at—a black pillar!—such, at least, appeared to me, at first sight, the straight, narrow, sable-clad shape standing erect on the rug; the grim face at the top was like a carved mask, placed above the shaft by way of capital. . . .
>
> "Your name, little girl?"
>
> "Jane Eyre, sir."
>
> In uttering these words I looked up: he seemed to me a tall gentleman, but then I was very little; his features were large, and they and all the lines of his frame were equally harsh and prim.[8]

6. Nancy Chodorow, *The Reproduction of Mothering: Psychoanalysis and the Sociology of Gender* (Berkeley: University of California Press, 1978), 166–67.
7. Claire Johnston, "Towards a Feminist Film Practice: Some Theses," in *Movies and Methods:*

An Anthology, ed. Bill Nichols (Berkeley: University of California Press, 1985), 2:323.
8. Charlotte Brontë, *Jane Eyre*, ed. Margaret Smith (London: Oxford University Press, 1971), 31–32.

That Jane does *not* function as the individualist locus of her own meaning and activity emerges from her indeterminate stance in this passage. She is afraid to return to the nursery, yet also afraid to enter the parlor; her only action is an "agitated hesitation" that in many ways recalls the interpretive ambiguity of Pomba Gira.[9] In fact, what "decided me," that is, what provided the resolution to Jane's hesitation, originates externally rather than internally in the ringing of the breakfast-room bell. In contrast to the patriarchal I/eye who sees events as if in control of them, Jane's I/eye is powerless, passive, and stripped of its own self-determination.

At this point, the text makes a telling "cut" to the next paragraph, whose most extraordinary aspect is its framing of Brocklehurst in explicitly phallic terms: the black pillar standing erect (tumid penile shaft), whose grim face (glans) ejaculates the words (sperm) that engender "legitimate" meaning (biological and ideological patronymy). The significance of this context is underscored by the patriarchal conception of the phallus as whole, unitary, and simple and its corresponding perception of the vagina as chaotic and fragmented, or in filmic terms, the negative inverse of the masculine frame. The shot angle of Jane's—and consequently of the reader's—eye in this sequence is extremely revealing, for in contrast to high-angle shots that diminish the importance of the subject, low-angle shots emphasize the subject's power.[1] Jane's low-angle focus on Brocklehurst ("in uttering these words I looked up") articulates his power as both the subject of her discourse and the masculine Subject whose phallic presence implies her own castrated absence. Jane herself corroborates this pejorative positioning of women by describing how Brocklehurst, "bending from the perpendicular [flaccid after orgasm] . . . installed his person in the arm-chair." Just as Brocklehurst installs his person in Mrs. Reed's armchair, he textually installs a phallic Personhood over the castrated womanhood of Jane.

Jane Eyre's narrative cuts perform much the same role as the cuts of cinematic suture. Suture proceeds in the cinematic text through the joining of one shot to the next and comprises one of the most basic processes of that "compulsory and deliberate guidance of the thoughts and associations of the spectator" known as film editing.[2] Since the cut from one shot to the next guarantees that both preceding and subsequent shots will function as absences framing the meaning of the present, it also allows the cinematic text to be read as a signifying ensemble that converts one shot into both a signifier of the subsequent shot and the signified of the preceding one.[3] The cut described above "edits" the thoughts and associations of the reader into a similar signifying ensemble in which Jane's undecidability becomes a signifier of Brocklehurst as Phallus, and Brocklehurst as Phallus becomes the signified of Jane's undecidability. The ideological power of suture lies precisely in this editorial ability to reveal the absence of the castrated female in order to stitch over even more closely her temptation "to skid off-course, out-of-control, to

9. In an earlier section of the chapter not included here, Donaldson discusses Pomba Gira, a figure in Yoruba mythology (the cunning wife of the trickster figure Eshu) as emblematic of a richer signifying practice than that represented by the "madwoman in the attic," Bertha Mason, whom she describes as a "univocal" feminine Other [editor's note].
1. James Monaco, *How to Read a Film: The Art,*

Technology, Language, History, and Theory of Film and Media, rev. ed. (Oxford: Oxford University Press, 1981), 164.
2. Vsevolod Pudovkin, "On Editing," in *Film Theory and Criticism: Introductory Readings,* ed. Gerald Mast and Marshall Cohen, 3rd ed. (Oxford: Oxford University Press, 1985), 87.
3. Kaja Silverman, *The Subject of Semiotics* (Oxford: Oxford University Press, 1983), 205.

prefer castration to false plenitude."[4] As a strategy of reading, it belies Spivak's description of Jane as the feminist individualist—an autonomous and fixed entity—and foregrounds her position as a "subject"—the product of signifying activities that are both culturally specific and generally unconscious.[5]

* * *

1988, 1992

4. Ibid., 232.   5. Ibid., 130.

SUSAN FRAIMAN

From Jane Eyre's Fall from Grace[1]

* * *

There have been * * * readers since [Elizabeth] Rigby[2] aware that *Jane Eyre* is a dangerous book. Its feminism has been discussed at length. Virginia Woolf, oddly and famously, both criticized and incorporated it into *A Room of One's Own*; more than one contributor to the *Brontë Society Transactions* has, since Woolf, remarked it; and Carol Ohmann agreed with Margaret Blom in the early 1970s about its limitations.[3] But the book that has weighed most heavily in recent discussions of *Jane Eyre* is undoubtedly *The Madwoman in the Attic: The Woman Writer and the Nineteenth-Century Literary Imagination* (1979), whose foregrounding of the eponymous Bertha Mason (and the rise of feminist criticism in general) has attuned a host of critics to strains of feminism in Brontë. Gilbert and Gubar's dazzling discussion of female confinement, claustrophobia, rage, and rebellion ignores, however, the way issues of gender in *Jane Eyre* are crucially bound up with those of class. Terry Eagleton has, on the other hand, usefully investigated class tensions in *Jane Eyre* between the landed and industrial sectors of the ruling class, yet without more than passing attention to the categories of sexual difference that inform these tensions (*Myths*).

My project, like Rigby's and Eagleton's, is to stress the "Chartism" of *Jane Eyre*—the way it interrogates (though it may not finally threaten) the structures of class, the way it is part of a moment when coherence about class was failing—and to see this as inseparable from its feminism. What is at issue for me in this text, what is rattling in its attic and recurrently at large, is a woman who is also a worker. I want to take for the book's emblematic figure not the debauched, highborn Bertha Mason, suffering from sensual extravagance

1. Excerpted from chapter 4 of *Unbecoming Women: British Women Writers and the Novel of Development* (1993) [editor's note].
2. Author of an often-cited 1848 hostile review of *Jane Eyre*, discussed in detail in the omitted text [editor's note].
3. See Woolf, *A Room of One's Own* (1929); Linton Andrews, "Charlotte Brontë: The Woman and the Feminist" (1955); P. P. Sharma, "Charlotte Brontë: Champion of Woman's Economic Independence" (1965); Carol Ohmann, *Charlotte*

Brontë: The Limits of Her Feminism (1972); Margaret Blom, "Charlotte Brontë, Feminist *Manquée*" (1973). Also notable are Adrienne Rich's fine piece of early feminist criticism, "Jane Eyre: The Temptations of a Motherless Woman" (1973) and Elaine Showalter's chapter in *A Literature of Their Own* (1977). Since Gilbert and Gubar there have been many other significant feminist readings of Charlotte Brontë; later footnotes indicate those with whom this chapter is particularly in dialogue.

and inherited insanity but her plebeian caretaker: the under-glossed Grace Poole, whose lousy job has driven her to drink. To recuperate a fiction of development that ties Jane less to Bertha than to the working-class Grace is not to elide what some feminist critics have rightly insisted is the making of a bourgeois and imperialist as well as female subject.[4] I would argue, however, that the formation of Mrs. Rochester, like that of Lady Orville and Mrs. Darcy,[5] is continually interrupted and essentially destabilized by a second, subversive narrative, one that in this case involves the heroine's identification with other working women. Though written over by subsequent chapters, this radical narrative originates in the very first, Gateshead section of *Jane Eyre*—in what might tentatively be called its "primal scene"—and persists, submerged and contested, throughout the novel.[6]

✻   ✻   ✻

As if to emphasize Jane's still transient status, the curtain rises not on Rochester's manor house, but on "a room in the 'George Inn' at Millcote" (81). Once at Thornfield, she is welcomed by the housekeeper, Mrs. Fairfax, who immediately sets herself off from the rest of Rochester's staff. However lonely the winter, the kindly old lady explains, one dare not fraternize with Leah, John, or his wife, Mary. "They are only servants," she tells Jane, "and one can't converse with them on terms of equality: one must keep them at due distance, for fear of losing one's authority" (84). The motherly manager is no less observant of lines drawn above. Though related by marriage to Rochester's mother, she would "never presume on the connection" (87). Mrs. Fairfax cannot tell Jane about Rochester's personal qualities because to her his social ones suffice: he is a gentleman and a landowner, period. Consequently, as it turns out, she is willing to help guard his violent secrets. Mrs. Fairfax thus delimits for herself and models for Jane a position of extreme class conservatism, of scrupulous regard for the semiotics of station, a position referring as much to residual notions of birthright as to the bourgeois ideology of self-making. ✻ ✻ ✻

4. See especially Jina Politi's "*Jane Eyre* Classified" (1982), Gayatri Spivak's "Three Women's Texts and a Critique of Imperialism" (1985), and Penny Boumelha's " 'And What Do the Women Do?': Jane Eyre, Jamaica, and the Gentleman's House" (1988). Boumelha's excellent essay does close by stressing—in spite of what she sees as a highly conservative ending—the "range of narrative possibilities intimated in the course of the text" (119). But Boumelha describes these as "explorations . . . of the kinds and limits of power available to a middle-class white woman" (119), demonstrating Jane's ability to choose among several possible options, almost as if she were the male hero of a *Bildungsroman* (119). My own reading, by contrast, will emphasize a narrative possibility whose defiance of gender norms is coextensive with its defiance of class norms and, for that matter, the generic norms of the *Bildungsroman*. Susan Meyer's "Colonialism and the Figurative Strategy of *Jane Eyre*" (1990) and Cora Kaplan's forthcoming article on *Jane Eyre* and British nationalism also address the conservative class and racial implications of Brontë's novel.

5. I.e., the heroines married in the course of Frances Burney's *Evelina* (1778) and Jane Austen's *Pride and Prejudice* (1813), novels discussed in earlier chapters of Fraiman's book [editor's note].

6. I want both to invoke and, in some sense, to distance myself from Peter Brooks's narratological notion of the "primal scene." His appropriation of this term to characterize narrative material whose semantic urgency is tied to its temporal priority, and whose repression proceeds from its illicitness, helps me to suggest the weight I would give to *Jane Eyre*'s first chapters. In fact, my reading of Brontë's novel is in many ways congruent with Brooks's of *Great Expectations* (113–42). Like Brooks, I privilege a child's early communion with a marginal figure (the convict/the servant); trace the binding of this "criminal" plot by a more decorous "official" one (apprenticeship/courtship); and point to the uncanny return of the prohibited material. I differ from Brooks, however, in my attention to female instead of male development, female rather than male "deviance." (See chapter 5, note 11 for more on the gender specificity of *Great Expectations*, in contrast to *The Mill on the Floss*.) In addition, if Brooks's "master-plot" is psychoanalytic, mine is essentially political and Marxist-feminist; if his repressive force is ultimately the local, internalized superego, mine is the material coercion of ideology as well as juridical, social, and economic relations.

The new appeal of this mode for Jane is evident as she revises the Gateshead pattern of eavesdropping and spying on servants, so that now what is glamorous and desirable coincides with wealth. With the arrival of Rochester's aristocratic guests, Jane and Adèle, her bastard charge, position themselves to overhear the sound of beautiful ladies settling and arraying themselves. As the narrator recounts:

> Then light steps ascended the stairs; and there was a tripping through the gallery, and soft cheerful laughs, and opening and closing doors, and for a time, a hush.
> 'Elles changent de toilettes,'[7] said Adèle; who, listening attentively, had followed every movement. (146)

Later, as the ladies emerge from their rooms and flock through the gallery, Jane hovers in the shadows admiring their dresses, "lustrous through the dark," and listening to their "sweet subdued vivacity." The report continues:

> They then descended the staircase almost as noiselessly as a bright mist rolls down a hill. Their collective appearance had left on me an impression of high-born elegance such as I had never before received.
> I found Adèle peeping through the schoolroom-door, which she held ajar. 'What beautiful ladies!' cried she in English. (147)

In each of these cases, caught listening and looking, admiring and yearning, the guilty Jane quickly projects her feelings and actions onto Adèle, much as Lucy Snowe does onto little Polly Home.[8] But by the time Adèle expostulates "in English," Jane has begun to acknowledge and accept this newly reverent relation to "high-born elegance," and soon she openly joins the poor Parisian child in wishing after the fashionable guests. Banished alike from the drawing room, they eavesdrop together from the top of the stairs. * * *

This self-abasement before monied beauty appears, at first, to define Jane's sense of herself in relation to her raven-haired rival, Blanche. Using her paints, Jane reproduces Mrs. Fairfax's view of Blanche's noble proportions, then sketches her own meager form (141). The juxtaposed portraits—contrasting paint to crayon, ivory to paper, the well-wrought to the carelessly made—seem to argue the inferiority of poor governess to lady of rank at a fundamental, physical level. Blanche, in her mistreatment of Jane and her diatribe against governesses as a "class" (155), reinforces this view. * * * Surprisingly, however, here too the heroine manages defiantly to claim her lower social status as a morally superior one, for Jane no sooner insists on being undeserving because plebeian than she rephrases this with considerable class pride:

> Not that I humbled myself by a slavish notion of inferiority: on the contrary, I just said—"You have nothing to do with the master of Thornfield, further than to receive the salary he gives you. . . . He is not of your order: keep to your caste, and be too self-respecting to lavish the love of the whole heart, soul, and strength, where such a gift is not wanted and would be despised." (142)

---

7. They [i.e., the women] are changing clothes (French) [editor's note].

8. In Charlotte Brontë's *Villette* (1853) [editor's note].

With the angry recurrence of "slavish," the early narrative of rebellion and self-respect as a working woman reemerges, so that while Rochester pays Jane's wages, he cannot be said to own her soul; indeed, it is she, not he who has riches to "lavish."

In fact, Jane at Thornfield remains an unstable, ambiguous figure, still oscillating between two stories of growing up, both of which are represented by her pupil and double, Adèle Varens. Of mixed and stigmatized parentage, Adèle makes explicit the illegitimacy so often associated with Jane. The irregular mating of Adèle's mother and father was, as with Jane's, short lived, leaving its issue alone; as Jane starved and shivered at Lowood before finding a home at Thornfield, so Adèle was "destitute" before Rochester plucked her dispassionately from "the slime and mud of Paris" (127). Jane describes her student as "a lively child, who had been spoilt and indulged, and therefore was sometimes wayward." Under Jane's tutelage, however, "she soon forgot her little freaks, and became obedient and teachable" (95). Insofar as Jane's role as Adèle's governess involves the regulation of gender and class "waywardness"—the Brocklehurstian[9] chastisement of a poor girl's "little freaks"—the domesticated child dramatizes Jane's own capitulation to Lowood's educational process. At the same time, however, by keeping an eye on Adèle, Jane keeps before her a faded but provoking image of her own vulnerable and intractable pre-Lowood self. There is, indeed, a notable occasion—en route to Millcote, where Rochester would dress and bejewel Jane as a sultan would his favorite slave—on which Adèle resumes Jane's old role of caviller or questioner. Giddy with his conquest, the gentleman spins out a fantasy of complete possession: he will take Jane to the moon and bury her in a cave for his pleasure alone. "You will starve her," accuses Adèle. "I shall gather manna for her morning and night," replies Rochester, a man who has never known hunger. "What will she do for a fire?" Adèle demands. "Fire rises out of the lunar mountains," the poet explains dreamily. "I'll carry her up to a peak and lay her down on the edge of a crater." "Peu confortable!" retorts the little materialist. "She is far better as she is" (234), the girl concludes, and dismisses her guardian as "un vrai menteur"[1] (235). No wonder Rochester wanted to leave such a child at home, whose blunt observations needle him much as Jane once needled Mrs. Reed. And no wonder Jane sues to keep this little critic, who expresses (subsequent pages show) her very own thoughts.

Adèle's essential argument here—that Rochester's sexual pleasure may be Jane's deception and discomfort—is implicit in her very history as the daughter of Céline, a Parisian "opera-girl" and one of Rochester's several discarded mistresses. The first song Adèle lisps for Jane is about an abandoned woman (89). The first poem she recites is La Fontaine's "La Ligue des Rats," in which the collective efforts of mice fail to save a particular mouse from a ravenous cat (90). Through the pathetic character of Adèle and her refiguration of Céline, Brontë hints at what seems to me a recurrent fear in this book—the working woman's fear of the predatory gentleman. Feminist critics have tended to see the "bigamy" issue in *Jane Eyre* as merely a red herring. According to this view, Jane doesn't really want to be Rochester's child-bride any

---

9. By Mr. Brockhurst, who oversaw Lowood, Jane's school [editor's note].

1. A true liar. "Peu confortable!": uncomfortable! (French) [editor's note].

more than she wants to be his mistress; the revelation of Bertha's existence only encourages Jane to act on apprehensions she has had all along. But this reading for gender neglects the class aspect of Jane's female predicament. Marriage is [a] middle-class story, one that, however confining, offers at least a degree of social status and protection. It is not, at this juncture, the plot that imperils Brontë's heroine. For though Jane's accomplishments resemble Miss Temple's, her dependent, sexually vulnerable condition is closer to Adèle's/Céline's. As Mrs. Fairfax reminds her, "Gentlemen in [Mr. Rochester's] station are not accustomed to marry their governesses" (233). I would point out that a "mad" wife gives Rochester an excuse to do what men of his station *are* accustomed to do: to have not two wives but, rather, one wife and a mistress whose defamed status leaves her wholly at his mercy. It must, in short, be recognized that the governess's fate as mistress is even more socially disabling and personally degrading than that as wife; that the "marriage" and "mistress" plots are complementary versions of the same story; and that it is the second—what might be called, à la Steven Marcus, the "*other*" Victorian" plot—by which Jane is threatened here.

If the figures of Adèle and Céline help to bring out Jane's particular sexual vulnerability as a working woman, the figure of Grace Poole—also, Jane imagines, an abandoned mistress—invokes the earlier radical narrative by defining Jane's response to this vulnerability as an enraged and insurrectionary one. Jane hears the woman she calls "Grace Poole" laugh crazily at the close of her celebrated feminist-on-the-roof speech, which Virginia Woolf cited and many others have admired for its angry eloquence. Jane's proposal in this polemic of a story for women beyond puddings and stockings has earned it a distinguished place in the annals of "high feminist criticism."[2] Yet often as this scene has been discussed, Cora Kaplan has only recently called attention to what is perhaps its most revolutionary moment:

> It is in vain to say that human beings ought to be satisfied with tranquillity; they must have action; and they will make it if they cannot find it. Millions are condemned to a stiller doom than mine, and millions are in silent revolt against their lot. Nobody knows how many rebellions besides political rebellions ferment in the masses of life which people earth. Women are supposed to be very calm generally: but women feel just as men feel. (96)

Underlining the words *human beings, millions,* and *masses,* Kaplan argues that here Brontë begins to reinvent the generic "men," daring to make it genuinely democratic. Further, in its association of "masses" and "women," this passage represents "a significant moment of incoherence, where the congruence between the subordination of women and the radical view of class oppression becomes, for a few sentences, irresistible" ("Pandora's" 173).

2. The term *high feminist criticism* is Gayatri Spivak's, reproving the tendency to celebrate white female subjectivity at the expense of Third World subjects: "A basically isolationist admiration for the literature of the female subject in Europe and Anglo-America establishes the high feminist norm" (262). In her influential critique of *Jane Eyre,* Spivak sees Bertha as the "native female," whose death is the price of Jane's constitution as a female "individualist" in an age of imperialism (262–263). I am suggesting, however, that Jane's formation as individualist is interrogated by another suppressed but nonetheless dissenting developmental story; the text itself may share some of Spivak's qualms. Further, without disputing Spivak's characterization of Bertha as "native," I have chosen to focus on Grace Poole, the madwoman as working-class. As I will argue, Grace is both continuous with Bertha and, insofar as the Creole is aristocratic, opposed to her. Hardly a self-consistent signifier, the madwoman can, I think, sustain the weight of these plural meanings.

While agreeing with Kaplan that *Jane Eyre* keeps the masses but inconsistently in sight, I am asserting that Brontë links Jane's situation as a woman to her plight as a worker for more than a few sentences. My reading would bear out but extend Kaplan's sense that Brontë's class politics are "incoherent," straining against even as they reproduce dominant ideologies. For the insane laughter that closes this scene serves not, I think, to warn that "the association of feminism and class struggle leads to madness" ("Pandora's," 173). On the contrary, I would argue that it combines and concretely manifests these struggles in the figure of the serving woman, Grace Poole, who will be a continually disruptive presence at Thornfield. I take as axiomatic the coincidence, so thoroughly demonstrated by Gilbert and Gubar, of Jane's own fury with the "madwoman's" many acts of violence. I want to put special stress, however, on the fact that, for most of her residence at Thornfield, Jane thinks of this woman not as "Bertha" but as "Grace." Though Grace is in many ways continuous with Bertha (they are both in some sense Other), in class terms the mistress and her caretaker are, instead, opposed. Mrs. Rochester, for example, is feared by the servants for "her violent and unreasonable temper . . . absurd, contradictory, exacting orders" (269), and in this she is more her husband's double than Jane's. The abused wife is, at once, the abusive employer. The relation between the phlegmatic servant and raging arsonist may be thought of in another way as well. The image of the worker whose bland, obliging front conceals a desire to burn down the house seems a fairly transparent expression of middle-class fears and, for that matter, working-class hopes; Grace represents both of these affectional options for Jane.[3] I would offer, then, the madwoman "Grace Poole" as a figure capable of gathering into her all the unseen or scarcely seen lower-class women in this book and acting out their collective revenge. In her role as nurse she refers to Bessie; in her hypothetical past as Rochester's mistress she refers to Céline; and in her riotous outbreaks she refers to the young, disinherited Jane. I want, moreover, by emphasizing Grace over Bertha to link her incendiary recurrence not * * * to contemporary mass movements on behalf of women and of workers. * * *

I would like to look more closely at one such eruption: when "Grace" stabs the effete Mason, and Rochester enlists Jane's service in nursing him. Earlier in the day Jane had inauspiciously sworn, "I'd give my life to serve you" (179). Now in the dead of night Rochester has her fetch a sponge and salts, clean clothes, a cloak, a phial and glass—running up and down the stairs each time until (like the poor servant, Sam) her "calves must have ached with the exercise" (171). Jane sounds plaintive when she tells us her "untiring master" had still another errand for her (187). But all of this pales beside Jane's most grueling duty: the vigil she keeps with Mason, two hours of nursing that seem like a week.

> I must keep to my post, however. I must watch this ghastly countenance. . . . I must dip my hand again and again in the basin of blood and water, and wipe away the trickling gore. I must see the light of the unsnuffed candle wane on my employment. (184)

---

3. Here I would note that arson, as Robbins credits E. P. Thompson with remarking, was a crime typically associated with servants (191).

When his guests were alarmed by the midnight commotion, Mr. Rochester told them not to worry—it was only a servant having a nightmare. Unwittingly, Jane's master told the truth, for the distasteful and repetitious labor that ensues is, precisely, a servant's nightmare. The scene represents with some exactitude the social relationship central to my reading of Brontë's novel: between the ruling classes, one of whose prerogatives is to have their bodies tended in sickness and in health, and the serving women on whom the greatest burden of this care falls. What does it mean to discover this relationship at the heart of what turns out to be Jane's and Rochester's first night together, complete with pastoral aubade? Jane shudders to think that, throughout her ordeal, the woman she still calls Grace Poole is in the very next room. I would say, rather, that Grace is in the *same* room, or that for this interval Jane *is* Grace, while the servant's wild rage, though hidden, snarls and groans only a wall away. The night that identifies Jane with Grace is thus both monitory and exemplary: its thankless labor reveals to Jane the substructure of her class as well as gender relation to Rochester, even as the madwoman's proximity of violence urges her to resist this relation.

*   *   *

Whether they basically approve (Rich, Gilbert and Gubar) or disapprove (Spivak, Boumelha), feminist critics have usually seen Jane's [ultimate] development into a middle-class female subject as a success, the end of *Jane Eyre* as a cautiously "comic" one, and certainly it reaches a less ambiguous conclusion than any of Brontë's other novels. Yet Gilbert and Gubar, while calling "Jane's progress" an "emblem of hope" (371), agree with Robert Martin that Ferndean[4] is marked by an "autumnal quality" (369), and I would like * * * to elaborate on those aspects of the text that press against the happy ending. Some (male) commentators have linked their discomfort with the end to Rochester's symbolic castration, but I wonder—might some (female) readers' lingering unease spring less from their regret that Rochester is now less of a man than from their fear that he may, like Uncle Reed, remain too much of one? In making this case, I mean to distinguish between the heroine's own unprotesting happiness (or is it that she protests her happiness too loudly?) and those textual details that darkly suggest Ferndean may be nothing more than a still newer servitude. This is not, however, to see the conclusion as a simply defeatist one. For if the final pages are subdued, by naming (as Jane once did) a degraded condition, they may continue nevertheless to argue on behalf of the secretly rebellious masses.

In terms of gender, I am tempted, first of all, to see even the fallen Rochester as far more continuous with the trampling St. John Rivers[5] than Jane's passion for her master might suggest. We recall that she hears his voice in the middle of a frenzy wrought up by Rivers. Jane herself invokes the parallel, noting that "I was almost as hard beset by [St. John] now as I had been once before, in a different way, by another. I was a fool both times" (368). Rochester calls his lover to Ferndean, almost Bertha's prison-house, except that its damp walls would soon have killed her, and Rochester denies "a tendency to indirect assassination" (264). Is this deadly site an improvement over St. John's India, where Jane knows she would not last three months?

---

4. The house to which Rochester retires after he is crippled in the destruction of Thornfield [editor's note].

5. The cousin who wishes to marry Jane so that she may aid in his missionary work in India [editor's note].

Other similarities connect the two suitors. Both men play shepherd to Jane's little lost sheep—Rochester is fond of this metaphor, and Rivers invokes it vocationally; both men play professor to Jane's naive student, the unequal dyad that carries so much erotic weight in Brontë.[6] I suggest, in short, that if *Shirley* expresses ambivalence about marriage by splitting the heroine into an eager and a balking bride (Caroline versus Shirley), *Jane Eyre* may express a similar ambivalence by splitting the hero into a loving and a murderous husband. (Jane to St. John: "If I were to marry you, you would kill me. You are killing me now" [363].) * * *

It is sobering, moreover, to look at Rochester's crippling in terms of its effect not on him, but on Jane. True, it gives her the physical advantage and the importance of being relied upon. "I was then his vision, as I am still his right hand" (397), the bride of ten years boasts. But as Eagleton notes, becoming Rochester's "prop and guide" is an ambiguous achievement (*Myths*, 30). In fact, this role as interminable caretaker bears an uncanny resemblance to the maternal role women conventionally play in relation to men, and servants in relation to masters. It binds Jane in service to Rochester just as she feared being bound by Rivers—"as a useful tool" (366). As her husband's very eyes and hand, she is indeed "chained for life to a man," just as she was briefly chained to Mason, and Grace to the man-sized Bertha. There is also additional evidence of Jane's domestication in the fate of that littlest double, Adèle. Jane gets permission from Rochester to visit her stepdaughter at boarding school:

> She looked pale and thin: she said she was not happy. I found the rules of the establishment were too strict, its course of study too severe, for a child of her age: I took her home with me. I meant to become her governess once more: but I soon found this impracticable; my time and cares were now required by another—my husband needed them all. (396)

Adèle is placed in a "more indulgent" school where in time she becomes "docile, good-tempered, and well-principled." The reader hears nothing of her marriage and can only guess what this means for the daughter of Céline. Insofar as Adèle stands for Jane's oppositional child-self, it is ominous that she is banished from Ferndean, returned to a punitive Lowood, and at last reduced to grateful docility.[7]

In terms of class, the end of *Jane Eyre* finds Jane with all the privileges of an upper-bourgeois wife; now she is Miss Temple indeed. It is possible to read this, as Boumelha and Spivak do, as *Jane Eyre*'s greatest and only good: *Bildung* defined as social mobility, bourgeois female subjectivity gained at the working-class and native woman's expense. Certainly there is much, as we have seen, to support this narrative, which is increasingly predominant in the novel's final two sections. Jane's first act after her wedding, for example, is to hand the servant, John, a five-pound note saying, "Mr. Rochester told me to

6. Brontë first represents the eroticized student-teacher relationship in her tormented letters to Monsieur Heger, the married professor she fell in love with while studying in Belgium (1842–43). (See Linda Kauffman on this epistolary discourse of desire later transposed, she suggests, into *Jane Eyre*.) The dyad reappears in *The Professor* (written in 1846, published in 1857), a kind of pre-text for *Villette* (1853) told, however, from the professor's masculine perspective. The relationship takes what is probably its mildest form in *Jane Eyre* and its fiercest in *Shirley*. There the classroom becomes a charged erotic space in which class differences between a poor tutor and his aristocratic pupil are finally suspended as gender differences take over.
7. It is disturbing, too, to be told that Jane has no time for anyone but Rochester, not even for Adèle—not even, by implication, for herself. As Karen Chase pointedly remarks, "When [Jane] tells us in these last pages that 'I know no weariness of my Edward's society,' that, 'We talk, I believe, all day long' (ch. 38), then we must wonder when she has time to write" (75).

give you and Mary this" (395). It is a gesture that serves to crystallize the eco-
nomic/power relations present at the book's close. As with the beggar-
woman,[8] Jane demonstrates here that she has the power to bestow whereas
John and Mary can only thankfully receive, that she has access to capital
whereas they have only their own labor. Class is not, moreover, this transaction's sole category. Regardless of Jane's inheritance, it is Rochester who originates this donation; Mrs. Rochester—like a lunatic or idiot, without property
or any other legal rights of her own—only carries out his order. And
Rochester's male privilege is repeated at the working-class level as well, where
John controls the money that accrues to Mary. Yet Brontë does not, arguably,
put the rebel slave entirely to rest. If class servitude were figured by John and
Mary alone, one might guess that the story had simply naturalized their labor
as intrinsic to the Rochesters' status. Jane, however, reintroduces herself to
Rochester at Ferndean by assuming Mary's place and bringing her master
some water. "I stretched out to take a glass of water from a hireling, and it
was given me by you" (385), he says, marveling at her return. Might this imply
that a residual bit of the heroic remains with the hireling, requiring us still
to see and resent her subordination? Might it suggest that Jane, or at least
Jane Eyre, has not completely fallen from Grace?[9]

✵ ✵ ✵

WORKS CITED

Andrews, Linton. "Charlotte Brontë: The Woman and the Feminist." *Brontë Society
    Transactions* 12, no. 5 (1955): 351–60.
Blom, Margaret. "Charlotte Brontë, Feminist *Manquée*." *Bucknell Review* 21, no. 1
    (1973): 87–102.
Boumelha, Penny. " 'And What Do the Women Do?': Jane Eyre, Jamaica, and the Gen-
    tleman's House." *Southern Review* 21, no. 2 (1988): 111–22.
Brontë, Charlotte. *Jane Eyre.* 1847. Ed. Richard J. Dunn. New York: Norton, 1971.
Brooks, Peter. "Repetition, Repression, and Return: The Plotting of *Great Expecta-
    tions*." In *Reading for the Plot: Design and Intention in Narrative*, pp. 113–42.
    New York: Knopf, 1984.
Chase, Karen. *Eros and Style: The Representation of Personality in Charlotte Brontë,
    Charles Dickens, George Eliot.* New York: Methuen, 1984.
Eagleton, Terry. *Myths of Power: A Marxist Study of the Brontës.* New York: Knopf,
    1975.
Gilbert, Sandra M., and Susan Gubar. *The Madwoman in the Attic: The Woman Writer
    and the Nineteenth-Century Literary Imagination.* New Haven: Yale University
    Press, 1979.
Kaplan, Cora. "Pandora's Box: Subjectivity, Class and Sexuality in Socialist Feminist
    Criticism." In *Sea Changes: Culture and Feminism*, pp. 147–76. London:
    Verso, 1986.
———. " 'White Skin': *Jane Eyre* and the Making of British Nationality, 1840–1850."
    New Literary History (forthcoming).
Kauffman, Linda S. "*Jane Eyre:* The Ties That Blind." In *Discourses of Desire: Gender,
    Genre, and Epistolary Fiction*, pp. 159–201. Ithaca: Cornell University Press,
    1986.

8. The recipient of the several shillings in Jane's
purse in the morning after Rochester proposes to her
[editor's note].
9. See Robbins on "the servant in the ending" of
both *Jane Eyre* and *Shirley*, a trope he associates with
a vague utopianism, irresolute longings in the direction of a broader community (190–91; 128–29).

Marcus, Steven. *The Other Victorians: A Study of Sexuality and Pornography in Mid-Nineteenth-Century England*. 1964. New York: Norton, 1985.

Martin, Robert Bernard. *The Accents of Persuasion: Charlotte Brontë's Novels*. New York: Norton, 1966.

Meyer, Susan L. "Colonialism and the Figurative Strategy of *Jane Eyre*." *Victorian Studies* 33, no. 2 (1990): 247–68.

Ohmann, Carol. *Charlotte Brontë: The Limits of Her Feminism*. Old Westbury, N.Y.: Feminist Press, 1972.

Politi, Jina. "*Jane Eyre* Class-ified." *Literature and History* 8, no. 1 (1982): 55–66.

Rich, Adrienne. "Jane Eyre: The Temptations of a Motherless Woman." *Ms.* 2, no. 4 (October 1973). Reprinted in *On Lies, Secrets, and Silence: Selected Prose 1966–1978*, pp. 89–106. New York: Norton, 1979.

Rigby, Elizabeth. Review of *Jane Eyre*. *Quarterly Review* 15 (April 1848): 396–409. Reprinted in *Jane Eyre*, edited by Richard J. Dunn, pp. 449–53. New York: Norton, 1971.

Robbins, Bruce. *The Servant's Hand: English Fiction from Below*. New York: Columbia University Press, 1986.

Sharma, P. P. "Charlotte Brontë: Champion of Women's Economic Independence." *Brontë Society Transactions* 14 (1965): 38–40.

Showalter, Elaine. *A Literature of Their Own: British Women Novelists from Brontë to Lessing*. Princeton: Princeton University Press, 1977.

Spivak, Gayatri Chakrovorty. "Three Women's Texts and a Critique of Imperialism." *Critical Inquiry* 12, no. 1 (1985). Reprinted in *"Race," Writing, and Difference*, ed. Henry Louis Gates Jr., pp. 262–80. Chicago: University of Chicago Press, 1986.

Woolf, Virginia. *A Room of One's Own*. 1929. New York: Harcourt, 1957.

1993

ON EMILY DICKINSON

Mysteriously absent from her community, self-sequestered in her "father's house" for nearly three decades and yet mysteriously present to passersby who discerned her at her window or in her garden, dressed entirely in white and known as the "Myth of Amherst," Emily Dickinson as both a person and a poet constituted one of the major literary puzzles of the American nineteenth century. Was she a devoutly Christian poet, a spinster passionately disappointed in love, a sardonic agnostic, a sort of ethereal nun of art? To this day, such questions remain open, along with countless others that have been raised by feminist critics and theoreticians, who comb through Dickinson's letters, linguistic structures, prosodic experiments, and all the other relics of a poetic life that she lived, as she put it, "at the 'White Heat.' " Their combined effort is to decipher her texts, themes, and tones along with the contexts that shaped them. Our selections here—drawn from four exemplary feminist analyses of Dickinson's brilliant career as a female, perhaps (so these writers imply) proto-feminist artist—examine the ways in which her culturally defined gender inflected her deployment of the aesthetic genre in which she so superbly worked.

In " 'Come Slowly—Eden': An Exploration of Women Poets and Their Muse"—published first in *Signs* and then in *Dickinson and the Romantic Imagination* (1981)—Joanne Feit Diehl draws on Harold Bloom's theories of poetic influence to chart Dickinson's engagement with what this critic defines as a "Composite Precursor" who is identical with a simultaneously empowering and debilitating muse, noting that "wrestling as a metaphor for poetic creativity is related" to the poet's sense of "struggle when confronting the combined power of muse and male Precursor." Analyzing Dickinson's art from a different perspective, Cristanne Miller writes in "The Consent of Language and the Woman Poet"—a chapter of her *Emily Dickinson: A Poet's Grammar* (1987)—that this writer's linguistic structures prize "various strategies of disjunction, multiplicity of meaning, and indirection" that are "gender-linked and feminine"; for although the "Myth of Amherst" is not "a feminist poet in the political or social sense of that word," she is "conscious of gender as a defining feature of her life and conscious that gender affects ways of speaking."

Our excerpt from Mary Loeffelholz's *Dickinson and the Boundaries of Feminist Theory* (1991) draws on her chapter titled "Violence and the Other(s) of Identity" in a discussion of Dickinson's perennially puzzling and powerful "My Life had stood—a Loaded Gun." She engages with Diehl's work while also offering a sophisticated, intertextual reading of this crucial Dickinson poem in relation to the writings of Emily and Charlotte Brontë. Finally, approaching Dickinson from a more generalized biographical perspective while examining not just her intertextual but also her interpersonal female ties, Martha Nell Smith attempts to reconstruct the literary meaning of the poet's passion for the beloved friend and sister-in-law of whom she once wrote "When my hands are cut, her fingers will be found inside." Our selection is taken from the chapter titled "With the Exception of Shakespeare: Reconstructing Dickinson's Relationship with Susan Huntington Gilbert Dickinson" in Smith's *Rowing in Eden: Rereading Emily Dickinson* (1992).

Following her investigations of gender and genre in Dickinson, Joanne Feit Diehl, a professor of English at the University of California, Davis, has published a number of books on related topics, including *Women Poets and the American Sublime* (1990), *Elizabeth Bishop and Marianne Moore: The Psychodynamics of Creativity* (1993), and, most recently, an anthology titled *On Louise Glück: Change What You See* (2005). Cristanne Miller, professor and chair of English at SUNY-Buffalo, has published, besides her study of Dickinson, *Marianne Moore: Questions of Authority* (1995) and *Cultures of Modernism: Marianne Moore, Mina Loy, Else Lasker-Schüler: Gender and Literary Community in New York and Berlin* (2005). An associate professor of English at Northeastern University, Mary Loeffelholz followed her publication of *Dickinson and the Boundaries of Feminist Theory* with *Experimental Lives: Women and Literature, 1900–1945* (1992); she is presently the editor of *Studies in American Fiction*. In addition to *Rowing in Eden*, Martha Nell Smith, a professor of English at the University of Maryland, has joined with Suzanne Juhasz and Cristanne Miller to coauthor *Comic Power in Emily Dickinson* (1993); with Ellen Louise Hart she is co-editor of *Open Me Carefully: Emily Dickinson's Intimate Letters to Susan Huntington Dickinson* (1998), and she is also the founder and executive editor of the Dickinson Electronic Archives <emilydickinson.org>.

JOANNE FEIT DIEHL

From "Come Slowly—Eden": An Exploration of Women Poets and Their Muse[1]

> Swedenborg has written that we are each in the midst of a group of associated spirits who sleep when we sleep and become the *dramatis personae* of our dreams, and are always the other will that wrestles with our thought, shaping it to our despite.[2]

In his recent journeys along the "hidden roads that go from poem to poem," Harold Bloom explores the dilemma of a poet wrestling with his precursors.[3] Bloom has turned to the rhetorical systems of Vico, Nietzsche, Freud, and the Kabbalah to illuminate his own vision. His use of these systems assumes the poet to be male, for the tropes these models offer convey a specific sexual identity. The oedipal struggle, the son's war with the father, the desire for and resentment of the seductive female muse echo throughout these philosophies of origins.[4] Although Bloom keeps alluding to the sexual aspects of the poet's dilemma, he repeatedly avoids the question raised by his own speculations, "What if the poet be a woman?" But how might the process of influence differ for women poets, and how do women poets perceive their relation to a male-dominated tradition?[5]

---

1. From *Signs* 3.3 (1978) [editor's note].
2. William Butler Yeats, "Swedenborg, Mediums and the Desolate Places (1914)," in *Explorations* (New York: Macmillan Co., 1962), 1:56.
3. Harold Bloom, *The Anxiety of Influence: A Theory of Poetry* (New York: Oxford University Press, 1973), p. 96.
4. Because Freud's paradigm for the male has been so thoroughly explored elsewhere, I mention it here only in terms of Bloom's revision of Freudian theory. Of course Bloom defends himself against charges that his criticism is a reductive Freudian gesture. He has recently argued that "imagination, as Vico understood and Freud did not, is the faculty of self-preservation, and so the proper use of Freud, for the literary critic, is not so to apply Freud (or even revise Freud) as to arrive at an Oedipal interpretation of poetic history. I find such to be the usual misunderstanding that my own work provokes. In studying poetry we are not studying the mind, nor the Unconscious, even if there is an unconscious. We are studying a kind of labor that has its own latent principles, principles that can be uncovered and then taught systematically" ("Poetry, Revisionism, Repression," *Critical Inquiry* 2, no. 2 [Winter 1975]: 250). My aim is to avoid such a reductive misreading of Bloom's thought and, instead, to examine briefly the assumptions behind the rhetorical forms of his theory in order to arrive at a revised theory of poetic influence for women poets. Such an attempt must be careful to distinguish between the descriptive and prescriptive aspects of any theory that seeks to come to terms with a preexisting tradition. But once the argument is lifted out of a particular context and stands as a paradigm for "how poets make poems," it becomes open to analysis as a poetic construct in its own right; its rhetorical implications deserve close scrutiny. What the theory evades will come back to haunt it.
5. In *A Map of Misreading* (New York: Oxford University Press, 1975), Bloom writes, "Nor are there Muses, nymphs who *know*, still available to tell us the secrets of continuity, for the nymphs certainly are now departing. I prophesy though that the first true break with literary continuity will be brought about in generations to come, if the burgeoning religion of Liberated Woman spreads from its clusters of enthusiasts to dominate the West. Homer will cease to be the inevitable precursor, and the rhetoric and forms of our literature then may break at last from tradition" (p. 33). The ambivalence behind Bloom's assertion is clear. In the face of a loss of the muses, the male poet is denied his inspiration, the primitive fear of desiccation Ferenczi postulates will be fulfilled, the end of the poetic tradition Bloom has so celebrated will dry up. Such loss breeds a renewed fear and anxiety that manifest themselves in rhetorical defensiveness. Yet in between his defenses Bloom admits that women may now be inheriting power and making it their own. Only women can create the necessary discontinuities to break effectively from the past.

To address these questions, I have chosen to explore some women poets' perceptions of influence in the nineteenth century. Emily Dickinson, Elizabeth Barrett Browning, and Christina Rossetti not only show an awareness of the burdens of tradition but also present distinctly similar psychological patterns in dealing with tradition they face.[6] Indeed they offer an alternative line to the dominant male canon, the beginning of a countertradition of postromantic women poets.[7] Because Dickinson is central to this revision, she will be my primary subject here. I shall argue that her perception of influence leads us to a provisional formulation of a paradigm that applies more generally to nineteenth-century women poets as they seek independence from powerful male precursors. For Rossetti and Browning as well as Dickinson, the precursor becomes a composite male figure; finding themselves heirs to a long succession of fathers, these women share the vision of a father/lover that surpasses individuals. And so for them the composite father is the main adversary.[8]

Any discussion of influence should be informed by a more general sense of how the poet confronts basic existential events: life, death, the sources of his or her art. As a poet, Dickinson knew no innocence. Her poems attest to frustrated experience—crucial moments lost or anticipated possibilities rejected. Earlier events narrow her sphere of future action. Examining her past and her childhood, Dickinson recalls no privileged sanctuary. Taught to perceive children as lost souls who must find grace before they can be freed from guilt, she feels exiled, banished by a Calvinist consciousness from the "prenatal" possibility of grace. Unlike the romantics, she does not recall the "visionary gleam"[9] lost in the process of growth, for it has never been hers. When Dickinson invokes an Edenic garden, anxiety and shame mark her perception. In a letter written toward the end of her life, she states, "In all the circumference of Expression, those guileless words of Adam and Eve never were surpassed, 'I was afraid and hid Myself.' "[1] Critics have compared Dickinson's poems with Blake's *Songs of Innocence and of Experience*, but the comparison must concede an overriding difference—Dickinson writes only songs of experience. Those poems which adopt a vision of the young innocent are often her most searing comments. Noting her dark ironies, Clark Griffith remarks that those

6. For a discussion of these women's interrelationships, see Ellen Moers's *Literary Women* (New York: Doubleday & Co., 1976).
7. Dickinson first discovered E. B. Browning when she was a young girl. Of the experience she writes, "I think I was enchanted / When first a sombre Girl— / I read that Foreign Lady— / The Dark—felt beautiful— / And whether it was noon at night— / Or only Heaven—at Noon— / For very Lunacy of Light / I had not power to tell—" (*The Poems of Emily Dickinson*, ed. Thomas H. Johnson [Cambridge, Mass.: Harvard University Press, Belknap Press, 1968], no. 593; all subsequent references to Dickinson's poems are to this edition and will be cited in the text by number). Although Browning did not know Dickinson's work, Christina Rossetti did. Sent a copy of Dickinson's poems, Rossetti remarked, "She *had* (for she is dead) a wonderfully Blakean gift, but therewithal a startling recklessness of poetic ways and means" (*Family Letters of Christina Georgina Rossetti*, pp. 176–77, quoted in Eleanor Walter Thomas, *Christina Georgina Rossetti* [New York: Columbia University Press, 1931]). Thomas also draws a number of comparisons between Rossetti and Dickinson.
8. However, the serious possibility remains that another, less overt pattern can be discovered in

Dickinson's image of the origins of her creativity, one in which the other is identified as a woman. The female serves Dickinson most often not as direct inspiration but as audience and comforter. Susan Gilbert Dickinson, her sister-in-law, shared more of Dickinson's poems than anyone else during the poet's lifetime. And Dickinson listened to Sue's opinions, although she did not always follow her suggestions. Active women authors provided her with encouraging examples; she was especially interested in their work and seems to have identified them as members of a kind of literary sisterhood in whose triumphs she shared and from whom she gained strength. But the dominating "lover," the desired yet threatening master who retains the power to destroy or give life to the poet is, throughout Dickinson's poems and letters, male.
9. A famous phrase from William Wordsworth's "Ode: Intimations of Immortality from Recollections of Early Childhood" (1807).
1. No. 946, to Mr. and Mrs. E. J. Loomis, Autumn 1884, in *The Letters of Emily Dickinson*, ed. Thomas H. Johnson and Theodora Ward (Cambridge, Mass: Harvard University Press, Belknap Press, 1958), 3:846. All subsequent references to Dickinson's letters will be to this edition. [The quotation is from Genesis 3.10—editor's note.]

poems which assume the guise of innocence actually adopt it as a mask; through such irony and paradox, childlike trust is subverted.[2]

Resentment and anxiety are the mirror emotions which reflect Dickinson's vision of reality. The fear she experiences when contemplating the advent of any possible happiness arises from an already present knowledge, a foreboding which could only appear in one who had experienced, if subliminally, the anguished sum of life's promise. Her distrust of nature and her isolation from mother and God stem from this self-conscious absence of innocence; it depends upon an educated awareness of the experience's potential for destruction and injury. For example, in an early valentine sent to Elbridge G. Bowdoin, Dickinson's vision of erotic bliss is shadowed by her awareness of the other side of life. Within this highly conventional romantic frame, death and the swift punishment of God's law reside.

> The life doth prove the precept, who obey shall happy be,
> Who will not serve the sovereign, be hanged on fatal tree.

The reality principle overwhelms this paean to romance, and the prevailing consciousness creating the poem cannot free itself from death's imminence:

> The *worm* doth woo the *mortal*, death claims a living bride,
> Night unto day is married, morn unto eventide. . . .
>
> [1]

A Darwinian relentlessness invades even this instance of coquettish flirtation. Rather than attempt to subsume her anxiety by a posture of feigned innocence, Dickinson may attest to her own wariness. She confronts the apprehension which forces her to pause before accepting experiences of possible pleasure as well as pain.

> Come slowly—Eden!
> Lips unused to Thee—
> Bashful—sip thy Jessamines—
> As the fainting Bee—
>
> Reaching late his flower,
> Round her chamber hums—
> Counts his nectars—
> Enters—and is lost in Balms.
>
> [211]

According to Dickinson, the power of someone outside the self first awakens her from passivity. She depends upon an "other" to answer her call and heed her song. Without a responsive voice, supportive and alluring, she fears that she might lose the impetus to continue to write. Yet this awakening is associated with both the world of books and death. This coupling is hardly coincidental, for words themselves at once "enchant" and "infect" her. They carry a lethal potency akin to the attraction of death, which offers a solution to life's mysteries and the erotic satisfaction of sacrifice, giving one's self to an inscrutable lover. But death renders the soul silent, and communication between the dead and the living proves impossible. The temptation of death arises from her need to obviate the frustrations of experience, the fear of death from the defeating silence it imposes.

Dickinson's relation to this muse, the inspiriting force she invokes, adds to her perception of the Master Poet, a symbolic figure who subsumes the indi-

---

2. Clark Griffith, *The Long Shadow: Emily Dickinson's Tragic Poetry* (Princeton, N.J.: Princeton University Press, 1964), pp. 17–73, passim.

vidual poets that comprise his identity, and the Composite Precursor, who represents the collective force of the major influences upon her writing. Yet her sense of her muse differs fundamentally from that of the male romantics—Wordsworth, Keats, Shelley. For them the traditional vision of the feminine goddess, the image of the fecund if idealized or distant muse, lingers. The male poets retain the ability to separate their poetic fathers—mythic progenitors—from the muse. The relation between the male poet and his muse is a private courtship upon which the presence of the father impinges but in which the younger poet, depending upon his strength, may win his muse from the father to invoke the aura of inspiration he desires. The ritual of invocation itself serves as a propitiating gesture, a positive strategy to make one's obeisance to the forces of creativity. But not for Dickinson. Her dilemma of influence is at once complicated and radically simplified by her perception that the Composite Precursor and her muse are the same. The muse gains stature and his or her power increases through this identification. When Dickinson envisions her muse as male, she fears his priapic power and wards him off with intense anxiety as she simultaneously seeks to woo him.

> We shun it ere it comes,
> Afraid of Joy,
> Then sue it to delay
> And lest it fly,
> Beguile it more and more—
> May not this be
> Old Suitor Heaven,
> Like our dismay at thee?
> [1580]

Although Dickinson does not say here that she is explicitly describing her response to the advent of the muse, she has outlined what for her becomes a typical drama, whether the "it" refers to a season, a lover, or poetic inspiration.

For the male poet, the birth of a poem fulfills his maieutic impulse; he becomes both midwife and mother of his art. But Dickinson acknowledges a potential shift in psychic responsibility when the poet is a woman, from the self to the doubly potent muse. With this shift comes a heightened anxiety, a fear that the passivity a women poet had banished may return if the "ephebe" must prostrate herself before a masculine muse. This fear partially accounts for Dickinson's distrust of the visitor, her ambivalent responses toward the figure of the stranger in her poems. So great is the pressure the poet faces that she is tempted to relinquish her poetic ambitions and the power of action. Yet out of her struggle with passivity and retreat comes the triumph of a poem which records the terms of the confrontation:

* * *

> Nor would I be a Poet—
> It's finer—own the Ear—
> Enamored—impotent—content—
> The License to revere,
> A privilege so awful
> What would the Dower be,
> Had I the Art to stun myself
> With Bolts of Melody!
> [505]

Note that Dickinson speaks of "dower," the wealth one brings to marriage. If she brought what she has been saving to a wedding of the powers within herself, she would be stunned, struck by bolts (which recall the threatened phallic power of lightning); yet these bolts are made of melody, the music of the poem. Here language reflects the pull of attraction and terror that informs Dickinson's view of independence as a poet and the dangers attendant on creative self-sufficiency.

Dickinson's plea for independence signals another breakdown in the conventional romantic relationship of poet and muse. For implicit in the romantic view of the poet as quester is a self that pursues the dangerous, seductive female. Masculinity, associated with the active self, the literary voice of authority from the Bible onward, continues its dominance. Most immediately Milton's abiding presence confirms and deepens the masculine tenor of post-Enlightenment poetry. If the romantics assumed the poet to be a mental "hero," transferring the metaphor of the quest to the vocation of the poet, then the role of the woman was to wait, to taunt the poet with visions of bliss and, if he were lucky, possibly to lead him beyond the confines of the human into a realm of spiritual awakening accompanied by the punishment of death. Yet for the postromantic woman poet the roles of muse and poet have shifted. Because of this transference, Dickinson wavers between feeling that she must wait to receive her Master/muse and radical rejection of his presence. Threat of dependence foments rebellion; by casting off her Precursor, she fears that she may be relinquishing her muse as well. In the process of exorcising her Precursor, she may banish the source of her art. In her late poems, Dickinson asserts her independence of any master, yet she remains haunted by the possibility that she may have been robbed of his potency and power. Her poems vacillate between these two poles—the conflict remains unresolved and so must be reenacted in poem after poem.

* * *

The physicality of wrestling as a metaphor for poetic creativity is related to Dickinson's sense of struggle when confronting the combined power of muse and male Precursor. This double identity of stranger and preceptor is a source of the continuing ambivalence which pervades the poems. Her anxiety also reflects an ambivalence toward her own powers and the simultaneous need to banish all authorities outside the self. Yet she is frequently abashed by the power of the Precursor, the lover, God. This combined male figure fills her with what she calls "awe," an awareness and fear of the sublimity of her confrontations with the other. In order to accommodate her ambivalence, Dickinson seizes upon moments of gain and loss, of annunciation and departure. Each poem serves as a buffer, a momentary stopping of experience which embodies the control she longs to assert over existence. Writing to her cousins Louise and Frances Norcross, Dickinson explains how she reacts to the deaths which crowded her last years: "Each that we lose takes part of us; A cresent still abides, . . . I work to drive the awe away, yet awe impels the work."[3]

* * *

1978

---

3. No. 891, to Louise and Frances Norcross, late March 1884 (2:817).

CRISTANNE MILLER

From The Consent of Language and the Woman Poet[1]

* * *

In strategy and in its combination of stylistic elements, Dickinson's poetry more closely resembles theories of what feminist writing, or a woman's writing, an *écriture féminine*, would be than it resembles the actual work of other—even women—writers. One may go further. In several characteristics and in dominant strategies, Dickinson's language could almost have been designed as a model for several twentieth-century theories of what a woman's language might be.

I refer here to feminist theories of language and gender inclusively, even though it has become standard to regard feminist theory as fundamentally divided between Anglo-American and French perspectives and to acknowledge the many differences of theory within those broad groupings. These are useful and necessary distinctions in most contexts. When it comes to stylistic descriptions of what happens (or will happen) in a woman's (or feminine) text, however, there is remarkably little contradiction in the various theorists' claims.[2] Luce Irigaray's positing of feminine multiplicity from the basis of the plurality of female genitalia (lips of the labia) and erogenous zones; Julia Kristeva's theory that an *écriture féminine* is essentially negative (the construct *woman or feminine* has meaning only as Other or different from the masculine, which alone is positively asserted to exist); and Sandra Gilbert and Susan Gubar's, or Alicia Ostriker's, argument that women's writing has long existed but that it has been subversive (due to historically determined cultural and psychological constraints on the individual woman)—all lead to basically complementary descriptions of writing. Multiplicity, a negative stance, indirection, and subversion may easily be integrated within a single conception of style, and all aptly characterize Dickinson's poetry.[3]

Again, to clarify: I am arguing that Dickinson's reasons for choosing the language strategies she does and several of the primary characteristics of her language themselves can best be explained by feminist analysis of the stimulus for, and qualities of, women's writing. Furthermore, and as Dickinson herself suggests in several poems, the psychology or aesthetic that prizes the various strategies of disjunction, multiplicity of meaning, and indirection examined in Chapter 2 may itself be gender-linked and feminine. Dickinson does not write as she does because she is a woman; this is not an argument for biological determinism. Nor is she a feminist poet in the political or social sense of that word, as I explain later in this chapter. She is, however, con-

1. Excerpted from chapter 5 of *Emily Dickinson, A Poet's Grammer* (1987) [editor's note].
2. To simplify my text, from here on in the chapter when speaking of feminist theory or theories in general, I will use the phrase "women's writing" to cover the various territories delineated by the terms "feminine writing," or "feminist writing," or "women's writing," or *écriture féminine*. When referring to work of individual theorists, I will use their terminology without further explanation.
3. For primary statements of these positions, see Luce Irigaray's *This Sex Which Is Not One*, trans. Catherine Porter with Carolyn Burke (Ithaca, N.Y.: Cornell University Press, 1985), originally pub-

lished in 1977; Julia Kristeva's *Desire in Language: A Semiotic Approach to Literature and Art*, trans. Leon S. Roudiez, Alice Jardine, and Thomas Gora (New York: Columbia University Press, 1982) or excerpts from her work in *New French Feminisms: An Anthology*, ed. Elaine Marks and Isabelle de Courtivron (Amherst, Mass.: University of Massachusetts Press, 1980), 137–44; Sandra Gilbert and Susan Gubar's *Madwoman in the Attic: The Woman Writer and the Nineteenth-Century Literary Imagination* (New Haven: Yale University Press, 1979); and Alicia Ostriker's "The Thieves of Language: Women Poets and Revisionist Mythmaking," *Signs* 8 (1982): 69.

scious of gender as a defining feature of her life and conscious that gender affects ways of speaking, thus also the construction of her poems.

In 1924 Martha Dickinson Bianchi remembers her aunt as having been "feminist" in "latent tendency." From an early age, the poet appeared indignant "at being counted as *non compos* in a man's world of reality."[4] Certainly her letters and life provide considerable evidence that this is true. Dickinson was quick to assert herself if a correspondent slighted her—whether or not intentionally, and whether or not the form of her rejoinder was direct. She identified strongly with the major women writers of her day, particularly those Englishwomen of the generation preceding her own: pictures of George Eliot and Elizabeth Barrett Browning (along with Thomas Carlyle) hung on her bedroom wall. Dickinson read all she could find on the Brontës, including Mrs. Gaskell's *Life of Charlotte Brontë* and A. Mary F. Robinson's *Emily Brontë*. In a letter, she referred to Eliot as Mrs. Lewes—a name revealing her knowledge and implicit approval of the novelist's long-standing affair with George Henry Lewes, not just familiarity with the works of the public (masculine) author. She offered to give Higginson her copy of Eliot's poems, and read two biographies of Eliot as soon as they appeared (*Life*[5] II, 570, 585). When Samuel Bowles left for Italy, Dickinson asked him to "put one hand on the Head" of Barrett Browning's grave for her; another friend brought her a picture of the grave on his return—a gift he knew she would prize. Dickinson's admiration for Barrett Browning was known widely enough for three separate friends to send her copies of the English poet's portrait (one of which she offered to Higginson, L[6] 271).

In letters, Dickinson frequently refers to or quotes women writers, especially the Brontës, Eliot, and Barrett Browning. Of Barrett Browning and George Sand, who were discouraged by unsympathetic relatives, she writes: "That Mrs. Browning fainted, we need not read *Aurora Leigh* to know, when she lived with her English aunt; and George Sand 'must make no noise in her grandmother's bedroom.' Poor children! Women, now, queens, now!" (L 234). "What do I think of *Middlemarch*?" she responds to her Norcross cousins; "What do I think of glory—" (L 389). At Eliot's death, the poet claims the novelist as her own: "Now, *my* George Eliot" (L 710). Years earlier (in 1854), on reading Barrett Browning's poems for the first time, Dickinson summarizes her response to the poems with the same possessive pronoun: "My crown, indeed! I do not fear the king, attired in this grandeur" (L 171).[7] Walsh claims that Dickinson borrows ideas and phrases in great number from Barrett Browning's *Aurora Leigh,* finding that "at least sixty of Emily's poems can be related to distinct passages in Mrs. Browning's book, with echoes of at least an additional fifty hovering just out of reach."[8]

The strongest specific evidence for a feminine influence on Dickinson's life

---

4. Martha Dickinson Bianchi, *The Life and Letters of Emily Dickinson* (Boston and New York: Houghton Mifflin, 1924), 26, 27.

5. Miller's abbreviation for Richard B. Sewall's *The Life of Emily Dickinson* (New York: Farrar, Straus and Giroux, 1974) [editor's note].

6. Miller's abbreviation for Thomas H. Johnson's *The Letters of Emily Dickinson* (Cambridge, Mass.: Harvard University Press, 1958) [editor's note].

7. Vivian R. Pollak identifies the volume of poems that Henry Emmons gave the poet as Barrett Browning's (they were previously thought to be Poe's) in "Dickinson, Poe, and Barrett Browning: A Clarification," *New England Quarterly* 54 (March 1981): 121–24.

8. John Evangelist Walsh, *The Hidden Life of Emily Dickinson* (New York: Simon and Schuster, 1971), 108. I am skeptical of Walsh's claim that Dickinson borrowed so heavily but have no doubt that *Aurora Leigh* was an important poem to her. It is also clear that the two women shared a vocabulary and, to some extent, a common sensibility, as reflected in the passages Walsh designates.

and art comes in her cumulative responses to Elizabeth Barrett Browning's death. In the year following the English poet's death, Dickinson wrote three tributes to Barrett Browning—her only verse tributes to a contemporary writer. The first follows the posthumous publication of *Last Poems* in 1862: "Her - 'last poems' - / Poets - ended - / Silver - perished - with her Tongue - " (312).[9] This poem is remarkable for the extremity of its claim ("Poets - ended"), but also because Dickinson twice calls attention to the writer's gender, both times as a form of personal identification with the older woman. The poem identifies Barrett Browning metaphorically with music, once by calling her a "Flute" (that is, both an instrument of music and, by metonymy, player of the instrument) and once by comparing her favorably with robins (she has twice their "Tune"). Between these two metaphors, and as an aside in the middle of the sentence, Dickinson becomes curiously literal in her reference to the poet:

> Not on Record - bubbled other,
> Flute - or Woman -
> So divine -

In the context of the metaphors of poet as flute and robin, "Woman" should logically represent a category naturally or essentially poetic: like a flute, woman, or robin, she creates poetry out of herself. Clearly, however, women are neither natural instruments nor musicians, as the skilled pianist Dickinson must have known. The interjection instead seems to be an outbreak of pride, manifest in the speaker's impulsive, and in the immediate context inappropriate, labeling of her subject. The speaker reminds her audience that this great poet is a "Woman" and (unlike Eliot and the Brontës) "on Record" as such. The poem then ends with a question: Dickinson competitively meditates on what it would have been like if she had been the "Bridegroom" to honor the dead poet at her grave: "What, and if, Ourself a Bridegroom - / Put Her down - in Italy?" Preparing the dead, in Dickinson's poetry, is a rite to be guarded jealously and most often a right that the speaker claims of a lover. As husband of the poet, Dickinson would have a special privilege of contact. Significantly, the poem's poet remains a woman: rather than change Barrett Browning's sex and make herself bride to the older poet, Dickinson alters the sex of her speaker.

A second poem commemorates Barrett Browning's death and Dickinson's debt, recalling her request that Bowles touch the Englishwoman's grave for her: "I went to thank Her - / But She Slept - " (363). The third poem recalls the poet's first acquaintance with Barrett Browning:

> I think I was enchanted
> When first a sombre Girl -
> I read that Foreign Lady -

This poem attributes Dickinson's whole poetic calling or "Conversion" to the older woman's poetry. It ends:

> I could not have defined the change -
> Conversion of the Mind
> Like Sanctifying in the Soul -
> Is witnessed—not explained -

---

9. All poems are quoted from and follow the numbering of Thomas H. Johnson, *The Poems of Emily Dickinson* (Cambridge, Mass.: Harvard University Press, 1958) [editor's note].

'Twas a Divine Insanity -
The Danger to be Sane
Should I again experience -
'Tis Antidote to turn -

To Tomes of solid Witchcraft -
Magicians be asleep -
But Magic - hath an Element
Like Deity - to keep -   (593)

The use of the word "Conversion" and the repeated religious references mark with particular emphasis Barrett Browning's importance in the life of a woman who strenuously and successfully resisted all religious "Conversion," even when under severe pressure from her family, teachers, and peers to believe. According to this poem's language, Dickinson's great religious transformation, her "Sanctifying," is of the "Mind" rather than of the spirit, and it is like "Magic." Although the speaker realizes that choosing enchantment over the expected Christian salvation appears insane to her world, she calls the insanity "Divine" and sees the real "Danger" or sickness in being conventionally "Sane." Should she ever fall into those unhealthy ways again, poetry—particularly the poetry of this divinely insane female predecessor—will save her, will be her "Antidote" against the world's views of her proper activities and role.

Dickinson's description of the "Magic" that saves her as "Witchcraft" underlines the gender identification in the poem. "Sombre Girl" and "Foreign Lady" alike, and unlike their male counterparts, become witches, a specifically female vocation and a subversive one. Witches are feared and punished, not revered, for their craft. Yet they are unmistakably powerful. The contrast between feminine and masculine magic implied by Dickinson's use of "Witchcraft" may be articulated in the following line: "Magicians be asleep" can mean that any poet's "Magic" will last after its maker's death, but it may also contrast the sleepy ignorance of "Magicians" (a word usually masculine in connotation) with the alert "Witchcraft" of this woman.

Barrett Browning provided no major stylistic model for Dickinson, but she did provide proof that a woman could become a poet of international reputation. The Brontës and Barrett Browning were widely known before Dickinson began her serious writing. George Eliot (eleven years the poet's senior) published her fiction from 1858 to 1876, throughout Dickinson's most productive years. With these extraordinary models and with the several American women novelists and poets whose work she enjoyed, Dickinson could imagine herself to be both a serious and a woman writer.

Although Dickinson identified with these writers and cared about their lives, she did not actively support the political campaign for women's rights or, apparently, sympathize with women generally. In her letters, the poet never articulates an interest in the nineteenth-century women's movement; she mentions neither the widely publicized "Woman's Rights" conventions held in Massachusetts between the years 1850 and 1860 (when the poet was between 20 and 30 years old), nor Fuller's 1845 publication of *Woman in the Nineteenth Century,* nor the writings of any other contemporary feminist. And yet she must have been aware of the women's movement through her daily newspaper reading and her father's political career. The Seneca Falls, New York, Convention of 1848 received widespread coverage in the press—albeit mostly negative. Massachusetts hosted the First National Convention of Woman's Rights in Worcester, October 23–24, 1850, and other national or local women's rights conventions in 1851, 1854, 1855, and 1859.[1] In March of 1857, the "petition of Lucy Stone and others for equal rights for 'females' in the administration of government, for the right of suffrage, etc." was brought before the Massachusetts legislature, an event that again received considerable publicity.[2] All these conventions were crowded, and prominent people whom Dickinson respected, in particular Ralph Waldo Emerson (occasionally) and Thomas Wentworth Higginson (consistently), supported their demands—although her father at one point attacked "the women's Suffrage people."[3]

Dickinson's poetry suggests that she is ambivalent about identifying with women. She allies herself with archetypal or mythical women—Eve in several poems and letters, the "Strong Madonnas" of "Sweet Mountains - Ye tell Me no lie" (722), "Madonna" of "Only a Shrine, but Mine" (918) - but she also identifies with archetypal men (Moses, Jacob) and describes the conventional lady as "A Horror" (in "What Soft - Cherubic Creatures," 401).[4] Dickinson repeatedly notes the restrictions of a woman's life ("Born - Bridalled - Shrouded - / In a Day - ", 1072), yet she considers herself to be singular, not a member of an oppressed class.[5] The poet makes abundant use of vocabulary and analogies drawn from a woman's daily life and chores, but she does not use the rhetoric of the women's movement (or of any reform movement) in her poems.[6] Social reform is not Dickinson's concern. The breadth of circumstances in her life in which she sees an unfair differential of power and her association of conventional power and powerlessness with gender reveal the clarity of her vision, not a desire to revolutionize the world. One might speculate that Dickinson shows no interest in class and racial distinctions because these are categories in which she enjoys

1. There was a second National Convention on October 15–16, 1851 (again in Worcester), The New England Woman's Rights Convention in Boston on June 2, 1854, and other women's rights conventions in Boston on September 19–20, 1855, and on May 27, 1859.

2. The quotation marks around "females" evidently demarcate the language of the legislature. This quotation and the information on women's rights conventions are taken from *History of Woman Suffrage* by Elizabeth Cady Stanton, Susan B. Anthony, and Matilda Joslyn Gage (New York: Charles Mann, 1887), I, 215–62; and Angela Y. Davis, *Women, Race, and Class* (New York: Random House, 1981), 52.

3. Jay Leyda, *The Years and Hours of Emily Dickinson* (New Haven, Conn.: Yale University Press, 1960), II, 218. The period from 1850 to 1860 coincides with Edward Dickinson's most active political involvement in state affairs, making it almost inevitable that his daughter would have heard of or participated in discussion of the "woman question" at home. Furthermore, there was sufficient coming and going between Worcester, Boston, and Amherst in the Dickinson family for the poet to have received personal word about the women's rights campaign.

4. In *Women Writers and Poetic Identity: Dorothy Wordsworth, Emily Brontë, and Emily Dickinson* (Princeton: Princeton University Press, 1980), Margaret Homans discusses Dickinson's use of Eve in poems and letters (169–76, 194), as do Gilbert and Gubar in *Madwoman in the Attic* (648–50) and Barbara Mossberg in *Emily Dickinson:*

When a Writer Is a Daughter (Bloomington: Indiana University Press, 1983), 150–56. Sandra Gilbert uses the metaphor of poem 722 for the title and as the central metaphor of her essay "The Wayward Nun Beneath the Hill," in *Feminist Critics Read Emily Dickinson*, ed. Suzanne Juhasz (Bloomington: Indiana University Press, 183), 22–44.

5. Dickinson is no exception to her times in taking this position. Judith Fetterley writes that "on the subject of women's oppression, the collective voice of mid-nineteenth-century American women writers is essentially muted and indirect." Josephine Donovan's history of feminist thought characterizes most early nineteenth-century feminism as "liberal Enlightenment" thought, more interested in the natural doctrine of equal rights than in the radical notion of gender as class. In *Provisions: A Reader from Nineteenth-Century American Women* (Bloomington: Indiana University Press, 1985), 12; and *Feminist Theory: The Intellectual Traditions of American Feminism* (New York: Frederick Ungar, 1985), especially chap. 1.

6. "Slavery," for example, was the favorite nineteenth-century metaphor for social ills. The temperance people used it to describe drunkards (slaves to the bottle), evangelists used it for sinners, and labor reformers used it for the proletariat or lower class as well as the women's movement using it for women and, of course, abolitionists' talking about actual slaves before the war. Dickinson uses the word "slave" in only one poem ("The Lamp burns sure—within," 233), and "slavery" not at all.

social privilege. Like most of us, she recognizes power by noting the ways in which it is kept from her. Because she was protected by her father's financial stability and her parents' eagerness to support her at home, several of the political concerns of the women's movement may have seemed irrelevant to her immediate life. Her privilege in the areas of race, class, and social standing, however, may have sharpened her response to the irrational restrictions on behavior that she did see in her life and at home. Dickinson's relative security may have allowed her to note the discriminations of gender hierarchy without the confusion of simultaneous discrimination based on other stigmatized differences.

Without being interested in political feminism, then, Dickinson was extremely interested in the power relations between the sexes. The frequent lack of distinction in her poems between woman and child, and her occasional expression of envy of the child's lot over the woman's, contribute significantly to the evidence that Dickinson associated femininity with powerlessness and therefore with her need to create independent, disguised sources of power for herself.[7] Because power does not inhere in womanhood, its discovery, expression, and survival for a woman must be subversive and oblique. One of Dickinson's primary disguises in the bid for power is the exaggeratedly feminine mask of perpetual childhood. The *Ur*-plot of Dickinson's poems presents its speaker as apparently small, weak, uncertain or apologetic, irrational (to the extent that she relies on contradiction and conundrums), and naively wise—all traditional characteristics of childhood as well as stereotypes of femininity. Mossberg argues that Dickinson's pose of smallness and obedience will protect her from being punished for her cultural "heresies."[8] Nina Baym writes that "the child persona in Dickinson can be read both as the child within human beings generally or more specifically as the child within the *woman*, the child that woman is alleged to be and, crucially in Dickinson's case, the child that the woman is felt to be." Baym notes that Dickinson uses this persona almost exclusively for "the relation of the speaker to masculine figures"; the pose provides room for the needed tension between open resistance and complete acquiescence to the opposed male.[9]

Whether or not they are specifically gendered in the narrative of the poem, Dickinson's speakers assume the culturally feminine role of weakness and self-doubt while in fact powerfully undermining or rebelling against the figure of opposition in the poem's plot. The strategies of the poems, then—their obliquity, oppositional contrast, disruptiveness—are implicitly gender-linked. The speaker may play supplicant to God, child to father, abandoned or neglected love to absent lover, human being to (masculine) death, and so on, but she is always "small" relative to the power she objects to or rebels against, or seeks a closer exchange with.

        ☆   ☆   ☆

1987

7. Gilbert and Gubar (*The Madwoman in the Attic*, 587-94) and Mossberg (*When a Writer Is a Daughter*) note that the child pose bears direct relation to Dickinson's ambivalence about adult femininity and female sexuality. As a child, the poet/speaker does not have to take on the responsibilities and demureness of a woman; at least part of her wildness and unorthodoxy is excused (although Gilbert and Gubar and Mossberg also argue that the child pose becomes a crippling habit for the poet). As a boy, Dickinson is freest of all: there she finds the double advantages of childhood and maleness.

8. Mossberg, "Emily Dickinson's Nursery Rhymes," in *Feminist Critics Read Emily Dickinson*, 45; and *When a Writer Is a Daughter*, 90–91.

9. Nina Baym, "God, Father, and Lover in Dickinson's Poetry," in *Puritan Influences in American Literature*, ed. Emory Elliott (Urbana: University of Illinois Press, 1977), 207, 208. Like Gilbert and Gubar, Baym sees the child pose as more of a dilemma for Dickinson than a strategy for successful coping.

MARY LOEFFELHOLZ

From Violence and the Other(s) of Identity[1]

* * *

The Dickinson poem that Adrienne Rich so presciently invoked in 1965, "My Life had stood—a Loaded Gun" (poem 754),[2] has since then attracted diverse interpretations, especially feminist interpretations. It has become the locus of discussion for feminist critics concerned about accounting in some way for the aggression of Dickinson's poetry, beginning with Rich herself. In her 1975 essay "Vesuvius at Home," Rich names "My Life had stood—a Loaded Gun—" as the " 'onlie begetter' " of her vision of Dickinson, the poem Rich had "taken into myself over many years."[3] The language of Rich's critical essay suggestively echoes the issues of the poems Dickinson had already haunted and would later haunt for Rich. While not explicitly violent in the way of Dickinson's loaded gun, Rich's metaphor of incorporating, *eating* Dickinson's poem establishes, but only to transgress, the boundary between inside and outside. Invoking the dedication to the "onlie begetter" of Shakespeare's sonnets identifies Dickinson's poem with a male literary tradition (although the overriding aim of Rich's essay is to link Dickinson to other women writers) and identifies Dickinson herself with a phallic power (the loaded gun's power) of inseminating Rich's thoughts. It is hardly necessary to add that Rich's language is intimately, evocatively complicit in these respects with the language of Dickinson's poem itself. What it means to be inside or outside another identity; what it means to "take in" or possess; the very meaning of a boundary—are put into question by "My Life had stood—a Loaded Gun—." In this and other poems, Dickinson's often violent transactions with what is "outside" her reflect a situation for women poets of the dominant Anglo-American tradition in which, according to Joanne Feit Diehl, "the 'Other' is particularly dangerous . . . because he recognizes no boundaries, extending his presence into and through herself, where the self's physical processes, such as breath and pain, may assume a male identity."[4] The male Other who occasions her speech may also commandeer her very bodily identity, leaving no refuge of interiority that is her own. Adrienne Rich's reading of "My Life had stood—" internalizes Dickinson's struggle with the problem of boundary and violence,

---

1. Excerpted from chapter 3 of *Dickinson and the Boundaries of Feminist Theory* (1991) [editor's note].
2. The numbering of the poems follows that of *The Poems of Emily Dickinson*, ed. Thomas H. Johnson (Cambridge, Mass.: Harvard University Press, Belknap Press, 1955). Rich invokes Dickinson in her own poem "Face to Face" (1965) [editor's note].
3. Adrienne Rich, "Vesuvius at Home: The Power of Emily Dickinson" (1975), repr. in *On Lies, Secrets, and Silence: Selected Prose 1966–1978* (New York: W. W. Norton, 1979), 172. Albert J. Gelpi's essay "Emily Dickinson and the Deerslayer," in Sandra M. Gilbert and Susan Gubar, eds., *Shakespeare's Sisters: Feminist Essays on*

Women Poets (Bloomington: Indiana University Press, 1979), 122–34, drew on Rich's insights. Joanne Feit Diehl notes some of the more recent feminist interpretations in "Murderous Poetics: Dickinson, the Father, and the Text," in Lynda E. Boose and Betty S. Flowers, eds., *Daughters and Fathers* (Baltimore: Johns Hopkins University Press, 1989), 326–43. Important, although not explicitly feminist, readings have been advanced by Robert Weisbuch, in *Emily Dickinson's Poetry* (Chicago: University of Chicago: Press, 1975), 27–35, and Sharon Cameron, in *Lyric Time: Dickinson and the Limits of Genre* (Baltimore: Johns Hopkins University Press, 1979), 65–74.
4. Feit Diehl, "Murderous Poetics," 329.

rendering Dickinson both as the Other male ravisher and as an aspect of Rich's own interior.

Following the traces of Dickinson's insistence in Rich's poetry and criticism, in this chapter I will explore instances of violence as it is linked to boundaries between inside and out in Dickinson's poetry, and I will look at how this violence connects Dickinson's poetry to recurrent themes in other nineteenth-century poetry by women. The connection between violence and problems of boundary often operates, in these poems, through a specific rhetorical figure: chiasmus, a rhetorical crossing or inversion of elements. As in "My Life had stood—a Loaded Gun," or "Proud of my broken heart, since thou didst break it" (poem 1736), the assignment of passivity to one member of a pair and activity to the other may invert itself over the course of a poem. The loaded gun gains in power, autonomy, and consciousness while its Master falls asleep; the speaker of poem 1736 reneges on her initial vow *not* to partake of her Christ/lover's passion and usurps both their crucifixes by the poem's end. Aggression turned inwards, as masochism, becomes aggression turned outwards (and vice versa), in a crossing that Dickinson figures as the piercing of a boundary: "Thou canst not pierce tradition with the peerless puncture" (poem 1736). Self and other exchange places around this rhetorical violence of the chiasmus, Dickinson's linguistic Way of the Cross.

As Jacqueline Rose's and Jean Laplanche's psychoanalytic speculations suggest,[5] the rhetorical violence of Dickinson's poetry may participate in some intrinsic (for all we know to the contrary) violence of identity (always already divided, in Freudian and Lacanian thought) and sexual difference (always assumed under a psychic threat, castration). Feminist readings of Dickinson's violence, however, point also to the specificity of women writers' experience within the "tradition" that Dickinson's speaker so strangely offers to "pierce," a tradition that historically has done violence to women's literary productivity. Within this tradition, Joanne Feit Diehl suggests, it may be necessary for Dickinson to kill in order to live—to be killed in such a way that "she becomes agent rather than victim, even if the end be the same."[6] Aggression is not a matter solely of Dickinson's isolated psyche or even her biographical family; to think so would be to fall into the very trap of reifying an inside/outside opposition that, as Rose argues, psychoanalysis and feminism rightly collaborate to subvert.

Among the Others of tradition for Dickinson's aggressive poems are the writings of other women, especially Emily and Charlotte Brontë, and to a lesser extent, Elizabeth Barrett Browning.[7] Instances of violence, imprisonment, and bodily violation in the Brontës' and Barrett Browning's poetry and fiction bear comparison, at the very least, to Dickinson's poems. To put it more strongly still, the Brontës' writing may have served as a kind of collective female muse to Dickinson's poetry, in something of the way that Dickinson's "My Life had stood—a Loaded Gun—" has been a muse to Adrienne

---

5. See Jacqueline Rose, *Sexuality in the Field of Vision* (London: Verso, 1986), and Jean LaPlanche, *Life and Death in Psychoanalysis*, trans. Jeffrey Mehlman (Baltimore: Johns Hopkins University Press, 1976), cited earlier by Loeffelholz [editor's note].

6. Feit Diehl, "Murderous Poetics," 326.

7. See Rich's brief remarks in "Vesuvius at Home," 161, 174–75, which, along with Ellen Moers's *Literary Women* (Garden City, N.Y.: Doubleday, 1976), helped inaugurate serious consideration of Dickinson's relations to the Brontës as well as Barrett Browning and George Eliot.

Rich's poetry and critical writing. The complexity of Rich's relationship to Dickinson's poem, however, suggests that matters of boundary and identification are not automatically simplified or idealized when influence and inspiration become properties of relations between women writers. "Taking in" (as she put it) Dickinson's "My Life had stood—," Rich became host to a haunting guest who was not a self-identical, coherent, unified mother-image but part of a fierce contest over the boundaries of power and identity.

Dickinson's relation to the Brontës and other women writers may be no less complicated. Her "literary daughteronomy," in Sandra Gilbert's telling pun,[8] is not so much the "empty pack" (poem 650) of an utterly absent mother, as it is the inheritance of a painful internal/external division in the women writers with whom she most identified, writers who themselves had painfully difficult transactions with male literary tradition. Rather than the ideally untroubled mother-mirror of object-relations psychoanalysis, a female literary tradition—the Imaginary ego ideal of so much recent feminist criticism—may be fractured or inverted, a chiasmatic upside-down reflection, in its very conditions of possibility.[9] In Jane Gallop's words, " 'the other' is already inscribed *in* 'the mother tongue.' "[1] Dickinson's poems of captivity, of writing as a burial alive, of identification with a male child, of imagination experienced through the power of a male visitant, and of imagination experienced as torture or as love for a corpse partly rework and revise themes and images out of the prose and poetry of Emily and Charlotte Brontë, along with Elizabeth Barrett Browning. But these poems about the violence of boundaries may also be read for what they suggest about the relationship itself between Dickinson and her literary (m)Others and about the difficulties of conceiving a bounded and unified "women's literary tradition." These poems forge poetic identity out of dangerous relations between self and (m)Other, relations whose difficulties stand at the heart of disputes over the province of psychoanalysis in feminist literary theory.

* * *

1991

8. Sandra M. Gilbert, "Notes toward a Literary Daughteronomy," in Boose and Flowers, *Daughters and Fathers*, 256–77.
9. To take perhaps the most influential example, Elaine Showalter's "Feminist Criticism in the Wilderness" called in 1981 for the displacement of "feminist critique," based upon "the feminist as *reader*," with a new "gynocritics," based on "the study of women *as writers*"; gynocritics would yield a description of "the evolution and laws of a female literary tradition." "Feminist Criticism in the Wilderness," repr. in Elizabeth Abel, ed., *Writing and Sexual Difference* (Chicago: University of Chicago Press, 1982), 12, 14–15, emphasis in the original. Showalter's separation of women as readers from women as writers seems to me wholly untenable, and, indeed, it does not survive the conclusion of her own essay, in which women's cultural productions are seen (in the context of women's situation as a "muted" group) "as a double-voiced discourse," inevitably bearing the traces of women's reading of the dominant culture.

There have since been too many reexaminations of the ideal of "women's literary tradition" from too many critical angles to survey here. Nina Auerbach, writing on the Brontë sisters in the context of Romanticism, registers her own difficulties with "the female tradition" in thematic and psychological terms very close to my concerns in this chapter: "Female traditions are often celebrated as a nurturing, even a swaddling, ambience for a woman writer supposedly unheard in patriarchy. I want to free these traditions from their potential for constricting cant and self-flattery, their hypocritical protestations of womanly feeling. Like violence, self-deception is a human, not a male, instinct." *Romantic Imprisonment: Women and Other Glorified Outcasts* (New York: Columbia University Press, 1986), xxi.
1. Jane Gallop, "Reading the Mother Tongue: Psychoanalytic Feminist Criticism," in Françoise Meltzer, ed., *The Trial(s) of Psychoanalysis* (Chicago: University of Chicago Press, 1988), 130.

MARTHA NELL SMITH

From Reconstructing Dickinson's Relationship with Susan Huntington Gilbert Dickinson[1]

Unlike those to "Master," which force readers to wonder and question whether their addressee can ever be identified as other than imaginary, the letters and poems to Susan Huntington Gilbert Dickinson were sent to a real flesh-and-blood respondent.[2] Almost no one would dispute that one of the powerful facts of Emily Dickinson's life is that she was in love with Sue. But, as we have seen from examining the tradition of excisions initiated by the early editing of her poems and letters and by surveying the half-century of studies preoccupied with the "Master" letters as biographical documents, the extent to which this emotional and intellectual entanglement with a woman exerted influence over Dickinson's poetry remains insufficiently explored and examined. With Cheryl Walker I concur that, "for Emily," Susan "became the embodiment of female power" and "that Emily Dickinson's poetry was inspirited in important ways by women." Walker also recognizes that "so much has been made over the identity of the 'Master,' Emily's supposed male lover, that this fact" of women empowering Dickinson "has . . . been overlooked." In 1979 Dorothy Oberhaus lucidly described how hearsay, the testimony of the other woman Mabel Loomis Todd about the wife "dear Sue," has been treated as fact and has worked "to obscure Sue's close relationship with Dickinson."[3] And we have also observed that, because of its longevity and intensity, Dickinson's nearly forty-year involvement with Sue makes a good standard of comparison for all of Dickinson's other relationships. The most important characteristic about this powerfully sensual relationship was its very literary nature and the direct impact it had on Dickinson's poetic compositions. Emily Dickinson was not only in love with Sue, but, as is evinced by their voluminous correspondence, the two participated in a literary dialogue that lasted for decades, and the better part of Dickinson's life.

* * *

To Own a Susan of My Own

In the last ten years of their correspondence, Dickinson makes some of her most extravagant statements to Susan:

---

1. Excerpted from chapters 4 and 5 of *Rowing in Eden: Rereading Emily Dickinson* (1992) [editor's note].
2. When referring to Susan Gilbert, I try to use the name she seems to have preferred at the time about which I am writing, though in referring to her as a correspondent of Dickinson's (and not at a particular time), I often use Sue, the name she used throughout most of her adult years, to emphasize her intimacy with Emily. To conjecture Susan's preference, I have observed how she signs her name to letters and in the front of books. A late December 1890 letter to Higginson, for example, is signed "S. H. Dickinson" (see Millicent Todd Bingham, *Ancestors' Brocades: The Lit-*

erary Debut of Emily Dickinson [New York: Harper and Brothers, 1945], p. 86); I conclude, therefore, that at the time she preferred to be addressed with Huntington as her middle name. Similarly, in late letters to her, Dickinson begins to use "Susan" more frequently. A few paragraphs below I discuss the significance of Sue's struggles with naming.
3. See Cheryl Walker, *The Nightingale's Burden: Women Poets and American Culture* before 1900 (Bloomington: Indiana University Press, 1982), esp. pp. 105, 107; and Dorothy Huff Oberhaus, "In Defense of Sue," *Dickinson Studies* 48 (1983): 1–25, esp. 4.

> Susan knows
> she is a Siren -
> and that at a
> word from her,
> Emily would
> forfeit Righteousness -

> (H B II; L 554, 1878)[4]

These late "letters" not only are arranged on the page like poems, but the calligraphy is often striking, with the words and letters spaced far apart. These eye-catching physical embodiments underscore the astonishing content of many of this last decade's letter-poems. In the letter-poem urging her to cherish power before the kingdom and the glory, because it is "wilder" than either of them, Dickinson places Susan on a par with heavenly blessing:

> Susan -
> Whoever blesses -
> you always
> bless - the last -
> and often made
> the Heaven of
> Heavens - a sterile
> stimulus -

> (H B 37; L 583)

About three years before her death, Dickinson extolled Susan to the highest, setting her above any muse:

> To be Susan
> is Imagination,
> To have been
> Susan, a Dream -
> What depths
> of Domingo
> in that torrid
> Spirit!
> Emily'

> (H B 51; L 855, ABOUT 1883)

Like Manzanilla, Domingo is, in the Dickinson lexicon, fervent with activity, an exotic place of poetic inspiration (P 214).[5] A place of dimension, it is not superficial, a façade, but offers depths to plumb. As John the Apostle finds divine revelation on Patmos, so Dickinson the poet discovers "Gibraltar" or an island strong with language in her relationship with "Siren" Susan:

> It was like
> a breath from
> Gibraltar to hear

4. Manuscripts in the Dickinson Collection at the Houghton Library, Harvard University, Cambridge, Mass., are indicated by the initial H and the library catalogue letter and/or number; L refers to Thomas H. Johnson and Theodora Wards, eds., *The Letters of Emily Dickinson* (Cambridge, Mass.: Harvard University Press, Belknap Press, 1958), and uses the letter number assigned by Johnson.
5. P represents Thomas H. Johnson, ed., *The Poems of Emily Dickinson* (Cambridge, Mass.: Harvard University Press, Belknap Press, 1955), and uses the poem number assigned by Johnson.

> your voice again,
> Sue - Your impregnable
> syllables need
> no prop, to stand -
>
> (H B 89, L 722, LATE SUMMER 1881)

Though Higginson would have no way of comprehending her statement's full meaning, Dickinson told him of Susan's profound influence almost immediately. About two months after her correspondence with the *Atlantic Monthly* editor began, Dickinson wrote him: "Your letter gave no Drunkenness, because I tasted Rum before - Domingo comes but once - " (L 265, June 7, 1862). From the facts of her having just labored over various second stanzas trying to please Sue and of Dickinson's declarations throughout their relationship, especially the late one explicitly equating Susan with imagination itself, one can see that it is with the spirit and fact of Susan's creative thought that the poet finds herself intoxicated. By providing her with an encouraging audience who was not labeling her poetic performances "Dark" or "uncontrolled," Sue offered Dickinson a relationship that functioned as an Edenic isle in the sea of experience.

To Sue, Emily sends not only poems interrogating immortality or women's circumstance in conventional marriage, but also nature poems, poems about language and poetry-making, love poems, and cartoonlike layouts and drawings like the early depiction of "Music of the Spheres." With pink woods (H 255; P 6) and yellow lanes (H ST 25b; P 1650), a purple-flowered crocus, pungent and aromatic saffron exciting the nose and the palate as well as the eye (H ST 20c; P 1676), comic personifications with the sunset leaping like leopards or juggling her bonnet (P 228), Dickinson's poems to Sue sometimes seem like vignettes from the Sunday comics to today's reader. In sunsets, evenings, stars, moonrises, and the hills on the horizon she sees "cartoons," or exaggerated semblances, of the genteel life. "Hills erect their Purple Heads" and "Rivers lean" (H ST 18e; P 1688); "like Men and Women" out for a sidewalk or boardwalk stroll, with "a mighty Bow / Or trailing Courtesy," "Shadows walk / Upon the Hills . . ." as if they are players in a picture show (H 285; P 1105). A speaker proclaims the power of a magnificent dawn by "Musket" and precious, sparkling jewels, then settles in "The Parlor - of the Day - " (H 326; P 304). The sun's spectacle is "The guest . . . gold and crimson" (H 387; P 15); in autumn "The Maple wears a gayer scarf - / The field a scarlet gown - " (H 344; P 12). Comparing snowfall to sifting (H 278; P 311), the winds of an approaching storm to kneading (H 356; P 824), and Mother Nature's spring and summer ripening to baking (H B 147; P 1143), Dickinson makes their mutual experience in households an active principle of her verse. Apparently relishing the almost grotesque, often absurd images they form, the details of woman's experience govern her terms in these poems, dictating her choice of primary and delighting metaphors: a "Housewife in the Evening West," the setting sun, "sweeps with / many-colored Brooms - " (H 312; P 219); and "The Snow and Wind" sweep winter streets "Like Brooms of Steel" (H 283; P 1252). "Autumn begins to be inferred / By millinery . . . / Or . . . shawl . . ." (H ST 3; P 1682). If nature were a "mortal lady / Who had so little time," she would be at the mercy of others' "exigencies," would have to make herself constantly available to others, always allowing her business to be interruptible. Unlike Susan, who was, as wife and mother, called upon to entertain the desires and needs of others before her own, nature is one woman who determines the spending of her own time, even "To make some trifle fairer / That was too fair before—" (P 1762).

That ruminations on language are integral to their relationship is apparent from the many poems to Sue that take wordplay as their subject " 'Morning' - means 'Milking' / To the Farmer" relates morning's different connotations— of "Dawn," "Dice" (sewing in waved patterns), opportunity, breakfast, battle, and flood—to the farmer, maid, lover, epicure, hero, and miller (H 288; P 300). The astronomer sees "Arcturus," not a "Star," "*Zenith*," not "Heaven"; the botanist "stamens," not flowers; the zoologist species, instead of a butterfly at play among "Clover bells" (H 236; P 70).

Not surprisingly, then, in October 1883 when the two women face the devastating death of Susan and Austin's youngest son—formally named Gilbert in honor of his mother's maiden name, affectionately nicknamed "Gib" by his adoring family—Dickinson's letter-poems to Susan simultaneously acknowledge both the necessity to address the unfathomable senselessness of a dear joyous life so quickly cut short and language's lack when attempting to articulate the measure of the loss. Knowing that words alone will not suffice, Dickinson muses that perhaps one of nature's tokens will offer Susan at least momentary respite from pain:

> Perhaps the
> dear, grieved
> Heart would
> open to a
> flower, which
> blesses unre-
> quested, and
> serves without
> a Sound.
>
> (H L 50; L 869)

The constant memories that serve to remind Dickinson of the unrelenting absence of her little coconspirator who "rejoiced in Secrets - " (H B 79; L 868) are like heavy cargo which must be carried with no relief of a clear destination in sight. In other words, the havoc and despair wrought by Gib's succumbing to typhoid fever are the woes of sorrow unbound:

> Moving on in
> the Dark like
> Loaded Boats
> at Night, though
> there is no
> Course, there is
> Boundlessness -
>
> (H B 91; L 871)

Johnson's description of one of Dickinson's five writings to Susan in memory of little Gilbert (L 868, L 869, L 870, L 871, L 938) is an appropriate characterization of them all: "the form it takes is that of a letter, but in a truer sense it is a poem, an elegy of surpassing eloquence."[6] A year after Gib's decease, neither the miseries of missing the little boy nor a poignant sense of language's failure in the face of such family tragedies had ceased. On the verso of a draft of a letter-poem sent to Susan in October 1884 on the first anniversary of their most terrifying loss (L 938; H B 145), Dickinson inscribed the prose fragment: " 'Tis a dangerous moment for any one when the meaning goes out of things and Life stands straight - and punctual - and yet no content(s) (signal) come(s)" (PF 49).[7] However strong the will to comfort through language, meaning that will content the sufferers eludes the poet.

Though language fails to relieve Emily and Susan's agonies, Dickinson unequivocally declares that it nevertheless serves as their most reliable source for ecstasy. As her life drew to a close Dickinson continued to reiterate that Susan's command of language enticed her like no one else's:

> No Words
> ripple like
> Sister's -
> Their Silver
> genealogy is
> very sweet
> to trace -
>   Amalgams
> are abundant,
> but the lone
> student of
> the Mines
> adores Alloyless
> things -
>
> (H B 134; L 913, ABOUT 1884)

Though Johnson recognizes that at least one of these late letter-poems is "in a truer sense . . . a poem," he classifies that document and all its eloquent, sometimes elegiac, always poetic, peers to Susan as letters. In one of the most recent studies of the Emily-Sue relationship, Ellen Louise Hart discusses the genre-confounding editorial practices of Johnson and Bianchi as she analyzes the letter-poem beginning "Morning / might come / by Accident - / Sister - " (H B 90; L 912, 1884) by asserting that it has been "mistakenly presented by Dickinson's editors solely as a letter and not also as a poem." I will add that all of these late letter-poems have been erroneously reproduced simply as letters and that these textual misrepresentations occlude not only Susan's literary importance to Dickinson as primary audience but also limit our ability to analyze the poet's literary project. Furthering an argument similar to one made by Bennett—that Dickinson "had seen in death the one sure path to the fulfillment of her love"—Hart maintains that Emily hopes to join Sue "in the 'Costumeless Consciousness' (H 358; P 1454) of immortality, the mind without the body, limitless, free of artifice and the restrictions of gender."[8] Yet

6. Thomas H. Johnson, *Emily Dickinson: An Interpretive Biography* (Cambridge, Mass: Harvard University Press, Belknap Press, 1966), p. 43.
7. PF refers to the Prose Fragments printed in Johnson and Ward, *Letters*, 3:911–29.
8. Ellen Louise Hart, "The Encoding of Homo-erotic Desire: Emily Dickinson's Letters and Poems to Susan Dickinson, 1850–1886," *Tulsa Studies in Women's Literature* 9, no. 2 (Fall 1990): 252, 264. Paula Bennett's argument is in *My Life, a Loaded Gun: Female Creativity and Feminist Poetics* (Boston: Beacon, 1986), pp. 90–91. Dickinson's

whether Dickinson believed in an afterlife or immortality will ever be open to question.

As Johnson and other editors have reformulated Dickinson's writings to conform to foreordained genres, so readers can select poems and letters and construct compelling arguments to confirm their own desires and thus demonstrate that she did or did not believe in an afterlife or God. For every letter or poem evincing belief, there is one like the early letter to Sue stating, "Sermons on unbelief ever did attract me" (H L 9; L 176, 1854) or the late one to Mrs. Henry Hills declaring, "When Jesus tells us about his Father, we distrust him. When he shows us his Home, we turn away" (L 932, 1884). About such matters, it appears that Dickinson equivocated until the very end. About one matter readers can rest assured that she never equivocated. Through all the anger, disappointments, exultations, emotional distance, and intense spiritual, intellectual, and erotic unions that inevitably accompany a deep and lasting love relationship, Dickinson equated Sue with Eden, the land of imagination:

> Sue - to be
> lovely as you
> is a touching
> Contest, though
> like the Siege
> of Eden, impracticable,
> Eden never
> capitulates -
>   Emily'
>
> (H B 50; L 584, ABOUT 1878)

1992

---

mingling of genres is discussed [in *Rowing in Eden*] in chapters 2 and 3. Examples abound showing that editors have arbitrarily made poems; see "Silence is all we dread," a poem extrapolated by Johnson which, "arranged as prose, conclude[s] a letter" (H B 123; P 1251n; L 397, autumn 1873).

ON THE HARLEM RENAISSANCE

The *Harlem Renaissance* is something of a misnomer, for the phenomenon it labels neither occurred exclusively in Harlem nor constituted a rebirth. At the end of the nineteenth century and beginning of the twentieth century, many neighborhoods in a number of cities in the United States housed communities of black intellectuals and artists who—for the first time in American history—took as their collective mission the attempt to forge self-consciously African American traditions in philosophy, politics, fiction, poetry, painting, journalism, and music. When the Harlem Renaissance was originally mapped by mostly male scholars as an unprecedented cultural flowering of African American activism and art, the accomplishments of W. E. B. Du Bois, Langston Hughes, Jean Toomer, James Weldon Johnson, Alain Locke, Claude McKay, George Schuyler, and Paul Robeson crowded out the formidable achievements of women writers and artists from Anna Julia Cooper, Pauline Hopkins, Ida B. Wells-Barnett, and Alice Dunbar Nelson to Anne Spencer, Jessie Redmon Fauset, Georgia Douglas Johnson, Zora Neale Hurston, Nella Larsen, Marita Bonner, and Josephine Baker. In recent years, the pioneering efforts of innumerable feminist scholars and artists have redressed this imbalance.

In "On the Threshold of Woman's Era," which first appeared in a 1985 special issue of *Critical Inquiry* titled " 'Race,' Writing, and Difference," Hazel V. Carby questions conventional periodization by looking at the polemical work of previously neglected black women of letters during the last decade of the nineteenth century. Carby, the Charles C. and Dorothea S. Dilley Professor of African American Studies at Yale University, has published *Reconstructing Womanhood: The Emergence of the Afro-American Women Novelist* (1987), *Race Men* (1998), and *Cultures in Babylon: Black Britain and African America* (1999). Barbara Johnson's "The Quicksands of the Self" (1992) stands out among many excellent articles on the fiction of Nella Larsen. Johnson deftly summarizes early and influential approaches to Larsen's *Quicksand*, even as she broods on a coupling of women with narcissism that has shaped the history of psychoanalysis. For many years a professor of English and comparative literature at Harvard University, Barbara Johnson—whose work also appears in part 2 of the *Reader*—has published important essays on gender issues at work in African American poetry, fiction, and intellectual history. In 1990, she served as interim chair of Harvard's Department of Afro-American Studies.

The last two selections contextualize women's achievements by addressing influential discourses circulating during and then deployed about the Harlem Renaissance: narratives about primitivism and passing. With respect to primitivism, Ann duCille questions the efficacy of defining an essential black identity by conflating it with African or blues, rural or vernacular conventions. Does such a valuation of primitivism, she asks, devalue the work of important women writers? Judith Butler considers the resonance of passing in terms of homosexuals impersonating heterosexuals and black people posing as white people. How do narratives about sexual and racial passing, she asks, clarify taboos against homosexuality and miscegenation? Ann duCille was the chair and director of the Center for African American Studies at Wesleyan, and is now chair of the English Department. In *Skin Trade* (1996), she wrote about racial issues in popular American culture and within feminist discourse, while in *The Coupling Convention: Sex, Text, and Tradition in Black Women's Fiction* (1993), she considered how the illegality of marriage instituted under slavery influenced the history of black women's attitudes toward courtship, romance, and monogamy. An eminent philosopher in the Rhetoric Department at the University of California, Berkeley, Judith Butler—whose work appears in part 2 of the *Reader*—has collaborated with Ernesto Laclau and Slavoj Žižek on *Hegemony, Contingency, Universality: Contemporary Dialogues on the Left* (2000) and has most recently published *Giving an Account of Oneself* (2005), a consideration of what she calls "the partial opacity of the subject." In 2004, many of her essays were collected in *The Judith Butler Reader*, edited by Sara Salih.

HAZEL V. CARBY

From "On the Threshold of Woman's Era": Lynching, Empire, and Sexuality in Black Feminist Theory[1]

> If the fifteenth century discovered America to the Old World, the nineteenth is discovering woman to herself. . . .
> Not the opportunity of discovering new worlds, but that of filling this old world with fairer and higher aims than the greed of gold and the lust of power, is hers. Through weary, wasting years men have destroyed, dashed in pieces, and overthrown, but to-day we stand on the threshold of woman's era, and woman's work is grandly constructive. In her hand are possibilities whose use or abuse must tell upon the political life of the nation, and send their influence for good or evil across the track of unborn ages.
> —Frances E. W. Harper, "Woman's Political Future"

> The world of thought under the predominant man-influence, unmollified and unrestrained by its complementary force, would become like Daniel's fourth beast: "dreadful and terrible, and *strong* exceedingly;" "it had great iron teeth; it devoured and brake in pieces, and stamped the residue with the feet of it;" and the most independent of us find ourselves ready at times to fall down and worship this incarnation of power.
> —Anna Julia Cooper, *A Voice from the South*

My purpose in this essay is to describe and define the ways in which Afro-American women intellectuals, in the last decade of the nineteenth century, theorized about the possibilities and limits of patriarchal power through its manipulation of racialized and gendered social categories and practices. The essay is especially directed toward two academic constituencies: the practitioners of Afro-American cultural analysis and of feminist historiography and theory. The dialogue with each has its own peculiar form, characterized by its own specific history; yet both groups are addressed in an assertion of difference, of alterity, and in a voice characterized by an anger dangerously self-restrained. For it is not in the nature of Caliban to curse; rather, like Caliban, the black woman has learned from the behaviour of her master and mistress that if accommodation results in a patronizing loosening of her bonds, liberation will be more painful.

On the one hand, Afro-American cultural analysis and criticism have traditionally characterized the turn of the century as the age of Booker T. Washington and W. E. B. Du Bois. Afro-American studies frame our response to that period within a conceptual apparatus limiting historical interpretation to theories of exceptional male intellectual genius as exemplified in the texts *Up from Slavery* and *The Souls of Black Folk*. I wish to reconsider the decade of the 1890s as the "woman's era" not merely in order to insert women into the gaps in our cultural history (to compete for intellectual dominance with men) but to shift the object of interpretation from examples of individual intellectual genius to the collective production and interrelation of forms of knowledge among black women intellectuals. The intellectual discourse of black women during the 1890s includes a wide variety of cultural practices. This

---

1. From *Critical Inquiry* 12 (Autumn 1985).

essay, however, will concentrate on the theoretical analyses of race, gender, and patriarchal power found in the essays of Anna Julia Cooper, the journalism of Ida B. Wells, and the first novel of Pauline Hopkins.

On the other hand, feminist theory and its academic practice, "women's studies," appear if not content with, then at least consistent in, their limited concern with a small minority of the women of the planet: those white, middle-class inhabitants of the metropoles. Although feminist scholarship has made the histories of these women visible, it has done so by reconstituting patriarchal power on another terrain rather than by promising a strategy for its abolition. This leaves us with the same complaint as our nineteenth-century black foremothers: feminist theory supports and reproduces a racist hierarchy. Feminist investigations of nineteenth-century women writers actively ignore nonwhite women; some of the most recent, exciting, and innovative thinking on sexuality relegates black women to a paragraph and secondary sources. * * * I hope that a discussion of Cooper, Wells, and Hopkins in the context of the black women's movement will direct readers to consider more seriously how black feminists conceptualized the possibilities for resisting sexual oppression than the dismissal implied in "prudery" allows.

The decade of the 1890s was a time of intense activity and productivity for Afro-American women intellectuals. It opened with the publication of Frances Harper's *Iola Leroy,* Cooper's *Voice from the South,* and Wells' *Southern Horrors: Lynch Law in All Its Phases.*[1] In 1893, as part of the World's Columbian Exposition, the World's Congress of Representative Women met in Chicago. Among others, Hallie Q. Brown, Anna Julia Cooper, Fannie Jackson Coppin, Sarah J. Early, Frances Harper, Fannie Barrier Williams, and Frederick Douglass—six black women and one black man—addressed the gathering. Harper told her audience that she felt they were standing "on the threshold of woman's era"; in 1894, *Woman's Era* was the name chosen for the journal run by the Woman's Era Club in Boston.[2] The club movement grew rapidly among Afro-American women and culminated in the first Congress of Colored Women of the United States, which convened in Boston in 1895. In 1896, the National Federation of Colored Women and the National League of Colored Women united in Washington, D.C., to form the National Association of Colored Women (NACW). For the first time, black women were nationally organized to confront the various modes of their oppression.[3]

The decade opened and closed with the publication of novels by black women: Harper's *Iola* and the first of Hopkins' four novels, *Contending Forces* (1900). Both authors intended that their texts contribute to the struggle for social change in a period of crisis for the Afro-American community. Their novels were meant to be read as actively attempting to change the structure

---

1. See Frances E. W. Harper, *Iola Leroy; or, Shadows Uplifted* (Philadelphia, 1892), and Anna Julia Cooper, *A Voice from the South; By a Black Woman of the South* (Xenia, Ohio, 1892); all further references to this work, abbreviated *V*, will be included in the text. See also Ida B. Wells-Barnett, *On Lynchings: Southern Horrors; A Red Record, Mob Rule in New Orleans* (New York, 1969); all further references to *Southern Horrors* and *A Red Record,* respectively abbreviated *SH* and *RR*, are to this collection and will be included in the text. These were preceded by a novel by Emma Dunham Kelley ("Forget-me-not" [Emma Dunham Kelley], *Megda* [Boston, 1891]) and followed by the publication of a short story by Victoria Earle (Victoria Earle Matthews, *Aunt Lindy: A Story Founded on Real Life* [New York, 1893]) and a survey by Gertrude Mossel (Mrs. N. F. [Gertrude] Mossell, *The Work of the Afro-American Woman* [Philadelphia, 1894]).

2. Harper, "Woman's Political Future," in *World's Congress of Representative Women,* ed. May Wright Sewell, 2 vols. (Chicago, 1894), 1:433–34.

3. This paragraph draws upon material from my forthcoming book, *Uplifting as They Write: The Emergence of the Afro-American Woman Novelist* [published in 1987 with the title *Reconstructing Womanhood*].

of the Afro-American culture of which they were a part. As an integral part of a wider movement among black women intellectuals, these books both shaped and were shaped by strategies for resisting and defeating oppression. Organizing to fight included writing to organize. The novels do not merely reflect constituencies but attempt to structure Afro-American struggles in particular directions; both are loci of political and social interests that try to form, not just reveal, their constituencies. Afro-American women were attempting to define the political parameters of gender, race, and patriarchal authority and were constantly engaged with these issues in both fiction and nonfiction. The formation of the NACW provided a forum for the exchange of ideas among Afro-American women intellectuals, within a structure that disseminated information nationally. Black women's clubs provided a support for, but were also influenced by, the work of their individual members. Hopkins, for example, read from the manuscript of *Contending Forces* to the members of the Woman's Era Club in Boston; in turn, those members were part of the constituency that Hopkins tried to mobilize to agitate against Jim Crow segregation and the terrorizing practices of lynching and rape.

As intellectuals, these women organized around issues that addressed all aspects of the social organization of oppression. Arrival at the threshold of woman's era did not lead to concentration on what could be narrowly construed as women's issues—whether domestic concerns or female suffrage. Cooper characterized the opportunity this way: "To be a woman of the Negro race in America, and to be able to grasp the deep significance of the possibilities of the crisis, is to have a heritage . . . unique in the ages" (V, p. 144). Cooper saw the responsibility of the black woman to be the reshaping of society: "Such is the colored woman's office. She must stamp weal or woe on the coming history of this people" (V, p. 145). To illustrate the process of exchange of ideas within the discourse of the woman's era, I will concentrate on one object of analysis: a theory of internal and external colonization developed in the works of Cooper and Wells and finally figured in the fiction of Hopkins.

As indicated in the epigraphs to this essay, both Harper and Cooper associated imperialism with unrestrained patriarchal power. Prefiguring Hopkins, Harper and Cooper reassessed the mythology of the founding fathers in terms of rampant lust, greed, and destruction: they portray white male rule as bestial in its actual and potential power to devour lands and peoples. Cooper developed a complex analysis of social, political, and economic forces as being either distinctly masculine or feminine in their orientation and consequences. She saw an intimate link between internal and external colonization, between domestic racial oppression and imperialism. While her critique of imperialism and institutionalized domestic racism is a particularly good example of her larger theories of masculine and feminine practices and spheres of influence, it is important to stress that her categories were not dependent on biological distinction. Cooper made it clear in her application of such analyses that women could conform to masculinist attitudes and practices and men could display womanly virtues.

Cooper saw the imperialist or expansionist impulse, with its ideology of racial categorization, as a supreme manifestation of patriarchal power. She argued that the source of such flagrant abuse had to be questioned, challenged, and opposed:

Whence came this apotheosis of greed and cruelty? Whence this sneaking admiration we all have for bullies and prize-fighters? Whence the self-congratulation of "dominant" races, as if "dominant" meant "righteous" and carried with it a title to inherit the earth? Whence the scorn of so-called weak or unwarlike races and individuals, and the very comfortable assurance that it is their manifest destiny to be wiped out as vermin before this advancing civilization? [V, p. 51]

Cooper refers to Lowell's *Soul of the Far East,* an imperialist treatise which predicted the death of all Asian peoples and cultures " 'before the advancing nations of the West.' " She indicts the author as a "scion of an upstart race" who felt confident that, with the stroke of a pen, he could consign "to annihilation one-third the inhabitants of the globe—a people whose civilization was hoary headed before the parent elements that begot his race had advanced beyond nebulosity" (*V,* p. 52). The world under a dominant male influence is compared to the beast from the Book of Daniel, devouring all before it and demanding that it be worshiped as an incarnation of power. The complementary force, the female influence, is unable to restrain "the beast"; the rampant will to dominate and despise the weak is also present in the racist attitudes of white women. Cooper saw patriarchal power revealed in the imperialist impulse, but she also saw that that power was nurtured and sustained at home by an elite of white women preoccupied with maintaining their caste status (see *V,* pp. 86–87).

Cooper felt strongly that the only effective counter to patriarchal abuse of power—the feminine—had to be developed through the education of women. Education held possibilities for the empowerment of women, who could then shape the course of a future society which would exercise sensitivity and sympathy toward all who were poor and oppressed. White women, however, rarely exercised their power in sympathy with their black sisters. Cooper was well aware of this, and some of her most vituperative work attacks the exclusionary practices and discourse of white women's organizations which presumed to exist for and address the experiences of "women." Cooper challenged white women, as would-be leaders of reform, to revolutionize their thinking and practices. She challenged them to transform their provincial determination to secure gender and class interests at the expense of the rights of the oppressed (see *V,* pp. 123–24).

These gender and class interests were disguised when the issue of justice began to be displaced by debates about the dangers of social equality— debates that concerned the possible status of subject peoples abroad as well as the position of blacks in the United States. Cooper recognized—and condemned as fallacious—the concept of social equality with its implications of forced association between the races. This was not the social justice which blacks demanded. On the contrary, Cooper asserted, forced association was the manacled black male and the raped black woman, both internally colonized. Social equality masked the real issue: autonomy and the right to self-determination.

Cooper understood that the smoke screen of social equality obscured questions of heritage and inheritance which appeared in the figure of "blood" and gained consensual dominance both North and South (see *V,* pp. 103–4). She became convinced that the key to understanding the unwritten history of the

United States was the dominance of southern "influence, ideals, and ideas" over the whole nation. Cooper saw that the manipulative power of the South was embodied in the southern patriarch, but she describes its concern with "blood," inheritance, and heritage in entirely female terms and as a preoccupation that was transmitted from the South to the North and perpetuated by white women. The South represented not red blood but blue:

> If your own father was a pirate, a robber, a murderer, his hands are dyed in red blood, and you don't say very much about it. But if your great great great grandfather's grandfather stole and pillaged and slew, and you can prove it, your blood has become blue and you are at great pains to establish the relationship. . . . [The South] had blood; and she paraded it with so much gusto that the substantial little Puritan maidens of the North, who had been making bread and canning currants and not thinking of blood the least bit, began to hunt up the records of the *Mayflower* to see if some of the passengers thereon could not claim the honor of having been one of William the Conqueror's brigands, when he killed the last of the Saxon Kings and, red-handed, stole his crown and his lands. [V, pp. 103–4]

Ridicule effectively belittles and undermines the search for an aristocratic heritage and proof of biological racial superiority; it also masks a very serious critique of these ideologies that Hopkins was to develop in her fiction. The juxtaposition of "red" with "blue" blood reveals the hidden history of national and nationalist heritage to be based on the principles of murder and theft— piracy. Hopkins drew from this analysis of the methods of expansionism, as it applied to the colonization of the Americas and to the imperialist ventures of the United States, as she demystified the mythological pretensions of the American story of origins in her fiction.

By linking imperialism to internal colonization, Cooper thus provided black women intellectuals with the basis for an analysis of how patriarchal power establishes and sustains gendered and racialized social formations. White women were implicated in the maintenance of this wider system of oppression because they challenged only the parameters of their domestic confinement; by failing to reconstitute their class and caste interests, they reinforced the provincialism of their movement. Ultimately, however, Cooper placed her hopes for change on the possibility of a transformed woman's movement. She wanted to expand the rubric defining the concerns of women to encompass an ideal and practice that could inspire a movement for the liberation of all oppressed peoples, not just a movement for the defence of parochial and sectional interests in the name of "woman" (see V, p. 125).

* * *

For Cooper, imperialism linked all those oppressed under the domination of the United States. Patriarchy, for her, was embodied in these acts of violence; therefore she ultimately placed her focus and hopes for the future on a transformed woman's movement. [Ida B.] Wells, in her analysis of lynching,[4]

---

4. In a passage not included here, Carby discusses Wells's pamphlet *Southern Horrors: Lynch Law in All Its Phases*, published in 1892, and *A Red Record: Tabulated Statistics and Alleged Causes of Lynchings in the United States, 1892–1893–1894*, published in 1895 [editor's note].

provided for a more detailed dissection of patriarchal power, showing how it could manipulate sexual ideologies to justify political and economic subordination. Cooper had failed to address what proved central to the thesis of Wells—that white men used their ownership of the body of the white female as a terrain on which to lynch the black male. White women felt that their caste was their protection and that their interests lay with the power that ultimately confined them. Although Cooper identified the relation between patriarchal power and white women's practice of racial exclusion, she did not examine and analyse what forged that relation. She preferred to believe that what men taught women could be unlearned if women's education was expanded. Wells was able to demonstrate how a patriarchal system, which had lost its total ownership over black male bodies, used its control over women to attempt to completely circumscribe the actions of black males. As black women positioned outside the "protection" of the ideology of womanhood, both Cooper and Wells felt that they could see clearly the compromised role of white women in the maintenance of a system of oppression.

Black women listened, organized, and acted on the theses of both Wells and Cooper, but very few white women responded to their social critiques. Cooper was right to argue that a transformed woman's movement, purged of racism, would have provided a liberating experience for white women themselves. But racism led to concession, to segregated organizations, and, outside the antilynching movement, to a resounding silence about—and therefore complicity in—the attempt to eliminate black people politically, economically, and, indeed, physically.

Pauline Hopkins shared this very real fear that black people were threatened with annihilation. She addressed her plea to "all Negroes, whether Frenchmen, Spaniards, Americans or Africans to rediscover their history as one weapon in the struggle against oppression."[5] Hopkins challenged the readers of her work to bear witness to her testimony concerning the international dimensions of the crisis.

> The dawn of the Twentieth century finds the Black race fighting for existence in every quarter of the globe. From over the sea Africa stretches her hands to the American Negro and cries aloud for sympathy in her hour of trial. . . . In America, caste prejudice has received fresh impetus as the "Southern brother" of the Anglo-Saxon family has arisen from the ashes of secession, and like the prodigal of old, has been gorged with fatted calf and "fixin's."[6]

As a black intellectual, Hopkins conceived of her writing as an inspiration to political action, a pattern for encouraging forms of resistance and agitation, and an integral part of the politics of oppression.

Hopkins regarded fiction in particular as a cultural form of great historical and political significance. In the preface to her first novel, *Contending Forces* (1900), she asserted its "religious, political and social" value and urged other black writers to "*faithfully portray the inmost thoughts and feelings of the Negro*

---

5. Pauline Hopkins, "Toussaint L'Overture," *Colored American Magazine* 2 (Nov. 1900): 10, 24.

6. Hopkins, "Heroes and Heroines in Black," *Colored American Magazine* 3 (Jan. 1903): 211.

with all the fire and romance which lie dormant in our history."[7] History is the crucial element in Hopkins' fiction: current oppressive forces, she argued, must be understood in the context of past oppression. "Mob-law is nothing new. . . . The atrocity of the acts committed one hundred years ago are duplicated today, when slavery is supposed no longer to exist" (*CF*, pp. 14, 15). This thesis is a cornerstone of *Contending Forces*. Drawing upon the theoretical perspectives of women like Cooper and Wells as well as the central concerns of the black woman's movement as a whole, Hopkins figures lynching and rape as the two political weapons of terror wielded by the powers behind internal colonization.

* * *

At the heart of the text are two tales told at a public gathering by Luke Sawyer, who is black. In the first, a lynching is the central focus of concern; in the second, a rape. Both tales confirm the privileging of these two acts in Hopkins' thesis of "contending forces." The first history that Luke tells is of his father, whose success in trade resulted in competition with white traders, threats on his life, and, ultimately, a mob attack on his home and family. His act of self-defence—firing into the mob—is punished by lynching; the women are whipped and raped to death, the two babies slaughtered.

The second tale follows from the first. Luke escapes into the woods and is found by a black planter, Beaubean, who rescues him and takes him into his home to raise as a son. Beaubean has a wealthy and politically influential white half brother, who assumes a stance of friendship toward the whole family but particularly toward Beaubean's daughter, Mabelle. At the age of fourteen, Mabelle is kidnapped by this uncle, raped, and left a prisoner in a brothel. After weeks of searching, Beaubean finds Mabelle and confronts his brother with the crime—only to be asked "What does a woman of mixed blood, or any Negress, for that matter, know of virtue?" (*CF*, p. 261). Beaubean is offered a thousand dollars by his brother which he rejects with a threat to seek justice in a federal court. Beaubean's threat is promptly met with mob action: his house is set on fire and its occupants shot. Luke escapes with Mabelle and places her in a convent.

Hopkins concentrates on the practices of oppression—the consequences of white supremacy—in reconstructing the history of her characters. The predominance of mulattoes and octoroons in the novel is not intended to glorify the possibilities of the black race if only it would integrate with (and eventually lose itself within) the white.[8] On the contrary, Hopkins states categorically in this novel and throughout her work that "miscegenation, either *lawful* or *unlawful*, we *do not want*" (*CF*, p. 264). The presence of racially mixed characters throughout the text emphasizes particular social relations and practices and must be understood historically. Such characters are often the physical consequences of a social system that exercised white supremacy

---

7. Hopkins, *Contending Forces: A Romance Illustrative of Negro Life North and South* (1900; Carbondale, Ill., 1978), pp. 13, 14; all further references to this work, abbreviated *CF,*, will be included in the text.
8. Gwendolyn Brooks misunderstands Hopkins to be arguing for integration; see Brooks, afterword to Hopkins, *Contending Forces*, pp. 403–9.

through rape. Use of the mulatto figure, as a literary device, has two primary functions: it enables an exploration of the relation between the races while, at the same time, it expresses the relation between the races. It is a narrative mechanism of mediation frequently used in a period when social convention dictated an increased and more absolute distance between black and white. The figure of the mulatto allows for a fictional representation and reconstruction of the socially proscribed. Hopkins' particular use of such figuration is intended, in part, to demythologize concepts of "pure blood" and "pure race." More important, however, it is an attempt to demonstrate the crucial role of social, political, and economic interests in determining human behaviour by negating any proposition of degeneracy through amalgamation. Hopkins transposes contemporary accusations that miscegenation is the inmost desire of the nonwhite peoples of the earth by reconstructing miscegenation as the result of white rape.

Hopkins saw clearly that the threat to white supremacy was not black sexuality but the potential of the black vote. Rape, she argued, should be totally separated from the issue of violated white womanhood and then recast as part of the social, political, and economic oppression of blacks:

> "Lynching was instituted to crush the manhood of the enfranchised black. Rape is the crime which appeals most strongly to the heart of the home life. . . . *The men who created the mulatto race, who recruit its ranks year after year by the very means which they invoked lynch law to suppress,* bewailing the sorrows of violated womanhood!
>
> No; it is not rape. If the Negro votes, he is shot; if he marries a white woman, he is shot . . . or lynched—he is a pariah whom the National Government cannot defend. But if he defends himself and his home, then is heard the tread of marching feet as the Federal troops move southward to quell a 'race riot.' " [*CF,* pp. 270–71]

The analysis of rape and its links to lynching as a weapon of political terror is, obviously, shaped by the arguments and indictments of Wells. In Hopkins' fictional reconstruction of the social relations between white and black, the two parts of the text move across generations and thus, through historical knowledge, invalidate the understanding of cause and effect then being reasserted through white patriarchal supremacy. Hopkins offers her readers an alternative story of origins where the characters are not holistic creations but the terrain on which the consequences of the authorial assertion of history are worked through. This can be clearly seen in the creation of Sappho Clark, the dominant female figure in the text, who has two identities.

The disguise—that which hides true history—is Sappho, the poet of Lesbos, who was admired and loved by both men and women, though her erotic poetry was addressed to women. The Sappho of *Contending Forces* embodies the potential for utopian relationships between women and between women and men; she represents a challenge to a patriarchal order. To Dora, whose duties running the boarding house confine her to a domestic existence, Sappho is the independent woman who, in their intimate moments together, talks of the need for suffrage and the political activity of women (see *CF,* p. 125). Sappho disrupts Dora's complacency—Dora will "generally accept whatever the men tell me as right"—and leads her to reassess the importance of friend-ships with women. But Sappho as an ideal of womanhood does not exist except as a set of fictional possibilities. In order to function, to work and sur-vive, Sappho's younger self, Mabelle Beaubean, a product of miscegenation and the subject of rape, has had to bury her violated womanhood and deny her progeny. Like Sappho of Lesbos, Sappho Clark has a child, "whose form is like / gold flowers."[9] But unlike Sappho of Lesbos, Mabelle exists in a patri-archal order, her body is colonized, her child the fruit of rape. Sappho Clark journeys toward the retrieval of a whole identity, one which will encompass a combination of the elements of Sappho and Mabelle. Such an identity leads to an acceptance of a motherhood which, like that of Sappho of Lesbos, does not require that a male occupy the space of father.

The most significant absence in the network of social forces is the black father. In narrative, the father is a figure that mediates patriarchal control over women; in most texts by nineteenth-century black women, this control is exercised by white men who politically, socially, and economically attempt to deny patriarchal power to black men. The absent space in fiction by black women confirms this denial of patriarchal power to black men, but Hopkins uses that space to explore the possibilities of alternative black male figures. Black men are depicted in peer relations, as brothers, or as potential part-ners/lovers. Women are not seen as the subject of exchange between father and husband; neither are their journeys limited to the distance between daughter and wife. As partners, sexual or nonsexual, the narrative impulse is toward utopian relations between black men and black women.

Nineteenth-century black feminists cannot be dismissed simply as "spokes-people for prudery in their communities." Their legacy to us is theories that expose the colonization of the black female body by white male power and the destruction of black males who attempted to exercise any oppositional patri-archal control. When accused of threatening the white female body, the repository of heirs to property and power, the black male, and his economic, political, and social advancement, is lynched out of existence. Cooper, Wells, and Hopkins assert the necessity of seeing the relation between histories: the rape of black women in the nineties is directly linked to the rape of the female slave. Their analyses are dynamic and not limited to a parochial understand-ing of "women's issues"; they have firmly established the dialectical relation between economic/political power and economic/sexual power in the battle for control of women's bodies.

A desire for the possibilities of the uncolonized black female body occupies a utopian space; it is the false hope of Sappho Clark's pretend history. Black feminists understood that the struggle would have to take place on the ter-rain of the previously colonized: the struggle was to be characterized by redemption, retrieval, and reclamation—not, ultimately, by an unrestrained utopian vision. Sappho could not deny the existence of the raped Mabelle but, instead, had to reunite with the colonized self. Thus, these black femi-nists expanded the limits of conventional ideologies of womanhood to con-

9. Sappho, fragment 132, quoted in Sarah B. Pomeroy, *Goddesses, Whores, Wives, and Slaves: Women in Classical Antiquity* (New York, 1975), p. 54.

sider subversive relationships between women, motherhood without wife-hood, wifehood as a partnership outside of an economic exchange between men, and men as partners and not patriarchal fathers. As [Ellen] DuBois and [Linda] Gordon have argued so cogently, we have "150 years of feminist the-ory and praxis in the area of sexuality. This is a resource too precious to squander by not learning it, in all its complexity."[1] But let us learn *all* of it, not only in its complexity but also in its difference, and so stand again on the "threshold of woman's era"—an era that can encompass all women.

1985

1. Ellen Carol DuBois and Linda Gordon, "Seek-ing Ecstasy on the Battlefield: Danger and Plea-sure in Nineteenth-Century Feminist Sexual Thought," in *Pleasure and Danger: Exploring Female Sexuality*, ed. Carole S. Vance (Boston, 1984), p. 43.

BARBARA JOHNSON

From The Quicksands of the Self: Nella Larsen and Heinz Kohut[1]

Nella Larsen's first novel, *Quicksand,* was published in 1928, at the height of that period of black migration from the rural south to the urban north which led to an explosion in cultural and artistic creativity known as the Harlem Renaissance. The novel was immediately greeted with enthusiasm: it won second prize in literature from the Harmon Foundation, and W. E. B. Du Bois called it "the best piece of fiction that Negro America has produced since the heyday of Chesnutt."[2] Readers then and now have indeed read the novel as a dramatization of racial double consciousness,[3] in the form of the all-too-familiar topos of the tragic mulatto. * * *

* * * Critics like Barbara Christian, Hazel Carby, and Hortense Spillers have analyzed the ways in which the mulatto represents both a taboo and a synthesis, both the product of a sexual union that miscegenation laws tried to rule out of existence and an allegory for the racially divided society as a whole, both un-American and an image of America as such. * * *

1. Excerpted from chapter 2 of *The Feminist Dif-ference: Literature, Psychoanalysis, Race, and Gen-der* (1998); originally published in *Telling Facts* (1992) [editor's note].

2. Quoted in Deborah McDowell's introduction to Nella Larsen, *Quicksand and Passing* (New Brunswick, N.J.: Rutgers University Press, 1986), p. ix. All references to *Quicksand* are to this edi-tion.

3. Cf. Du Bois's famous formulation from *The Souls of Black Folk:* "It is a peculiar sensation, this double-consciousness, this sense of always looking at one's self through the eyes of others, of measur-ing one's soul by the tape of a world that looks on in amused contempt and pity. One ever feels his twoness,—an American, a Negro; two souls, two thoughts, two unreconciled strivings; two warring ideals in one dark body, whose dogged strength alone keeps it from being torn asunder" (*Three Negro Classics* [New York: Avon, 1965], p. 215).

Nella Larsen herself suggests that her novel should be read through the grid of the mulatto figure by choosing as her epigraph a stanza from a Langston Hughes poem entitled "Cross":

> My old man died in a fine big house.
> My ma died in a shack.
> I wonder where I'm gonna die,
> Being neither white nor black?[4]

Where one might expect a both/and, we find, as Spillers[5] and Hughes suggest, a neither/nor. Nella Larsen's project in *Quicksand* is to tell the story of the neither/nor self from within.

The question of that neither/nor of racial designation is tied, both in the epigraph and in the novel, to the question of *place:* shack or big house, North or South, Europe or America. In the Hughes poem, the father is white; the mother black. This corresponds to the historical realities of the sexual abuse of slave women by white slaveholders. Nella Larsen's protagonist's parentage, however, is reversed: her mother is a Danish immigrant and her father is a black American. This, I think, further complicates the question of race and place, both socially and geographically. The first sentence of the novel, "Helga Crane sat alone in her room," echoes not only the "in's" of the epigraph but even its very rhythm. The last clause of the opening paragraph of the novel continues that rhythm: "Helga Crane never opened her door." It is as though the novel originates within the "stanza" (which etymologically means "room") of its epigraph. The question of place thus intersects with a question of space, of personal space, of the inside/outside boundaries of the self. Helga Crane's closed door circumscribes a space filled with small luxuries: a Chinese carpet, a brass bowl, nasturtiums, oriental silk. Her room symbolizes the issue of the self as container (of value, positive or negative). And the title, *Quicksand,* extends the metaphor of space in a nightmarish direction: the self is utterly engulfed by the outside because there is nothing outside the engulfing outside to save it.

What, then, is the nature of the quicksand into which Helga Crane sinks in Nella Larsen's novel? Critics have offered various answers. Hiroko Sato writes: "The title, *Quicksand,* signifies the heroine Helga Crane's sexual desire, which was hidden beneath her beautiful and intelligent surface and came up at an unexpected moment and trapped her."[6] For Deborah McDowell, Hortense Thornton, and Cheryl Wall, on the other hand, it is not Helga's sexuality that has trapped her but rather her attempts to disavow it—her own and society's contradictory responses to it. To be respectable as a "lady" is to have no sexuality; to have sexuality is to be a jungle creature, an exotic primitive, or an oppressed wife and mother. These readings which focus on the centrality of black female sexuality are responses to earlier readings (mostly by male critics) which focused on the

4. Epigraph to Nella Larsen, *Quicksand,* in *Quicksand and Passing,* ed. Deborah McDowell (New Brunswick, N.J.: Rutgers University Press, 1986). All references to *Quicksand* are to this edition.
5. Hortense Spillers, "Notes on an Alternative Model—Neither/Nor," in *The Difference Within,* ed. Elizabeth Meese and Alice Parker (Amsterdam:

John Benjamins, 1989), pp. 165–88 [cited by Johnson in a passage omitted here—editor's note].
6. Hiroko Sato, "Under the Harlem Shadow: A Study of Jessie Fauset and Nella Larsen," in *The Harlem Renaissance Remembered,* ed. Arna Bontemps (New York: Dodd, Mead & Company, 1972), p. 84.

problems of the biracial self. * * * *Quicksand* is a complex analysis of the intersections of gender, sexuality, race, and class. It seems, therefore, somehow regressive and discordant to ask what use a "self-psychological" psychoanalytic perspective might be in understanding the novel. How can any insight be gained into all these structures by focussing on intra-psychic processes? Yet the inside/outside opposition on which such scruples are based is one that the novel constantly forces us to reexamine. It will also, I hope, force us to reexamine that opposition in the assumptions and interpretive frames of psychoanalysis.

* * * How, for example, can one account for the self-defeating or self-exhausting nature of Helga Crane's choices? At several points, Helga achieves economic autonomy—when teaching in a Southern black college or when working for an insurance company in New York—but she seems each time all too ready to flee to dependency. Economic autonomy does not provide something which economic dependency seems to promise. Then, too, Helga repeatedly reaches states of relative contentment—in Harlem, in Denmark, in Alabama—only to fall into depression again for no obvious reason. Chapter breaks often occur where psychological causation is missing. It is the *lack* of explicit precipitating cause that calls for explanation. And it is the difficulty of defining the causes of Helga's suffering that leads to irritation in many readers. * * *

[T]he description of Helga Crane's problems as "esoteric," "arrogant," and "spoiled"[7] suggests to me a parallel with the vague, ill-defined complaints of the middle-class patients treated by Heinz Kohut under the category of "narcissistic personality disorders." I will therefore turn to the work of Kohut as a framework for understanding what Larsen understood about the psychological effects of social conflicts, and then I will take Nella Larsen as a framework for questioning the limits of Kohut's description of the phenomenon he calls narcissism.

*   *   *

Heinz Kohut is known for having developed a psychoanalytic theory of what he called "Self Psychology." This theory has been seen by Lacanians as itself an example of entrapment in the fictions of the autonomous self as generated by the mirror stage. While such a critique may be justified, I would prefer to see Kohut's work as a parallel and much richer exploration of structures of mirroring of which the mirror stage is one example.

What does Kohut mean by a self? The self, he writes, should not be confused with the ego. The self is not a subject. The self is an image, a representation. Indeed, there may exist simultaneous contradictory self-representations in the same person. "The self, then, quite analogous to the representations of objects, is a *content* of the mental apparatus but is not . . . one of the *agencies* of the mind."[8] How is the self formed? Kohut answers: through empathic mirroring. The self is the internalization of the gaze of the other, generally the mother in Kohut's account. Instead of Lacan's statuelike visual self-representation in the

7. Described by Mary Helen Washington, *Invented Lives* (Garden City, N.J.: Anchor, 1987), pp. 159–60, in a passage omitted here [editor's note].

8. Heinz Kohut, *The Analysis of the Self* (New York: International Universities Press, 1971), p. xv.

mirror, for which the mother serves only as a baby stand, Kohut's self-representation derives from the approval-conveying "gleam in the mother's eye." In the early stages of the formation of the self, therefore, other people are not perceived as separate, true objects, but as parts of the self, as selfobjects. The function of selfobject can continue to be played by other people throughout an individual's life, including sexual partners, and especially, for Kohut, psychoanalysts.

The psychological structures appropriate to the earliest phase in the development of the self, according to Kohut, are the grandiose exhibitionistic self ("I am perfect") and the idealized omnipotent selfobject based on the parent ("you are perfect but I am part of you"). "The need of the budding self for the joyful response of the mirroring selfobject, the need of the budding self for the omnipotent selfobject's pleased acceptance of its merger needs, are primary considerations." If the child is not appropriately mirrored, is not given the message "what you are is valuable" at this stage, then the grandiose self and the desire to merge with the idealized selfobject do not fade away but become split off and retain their archaic demands. Rather than being progressively reality-tested and integrated, they keep the unfilled hunger for validation intact as an open wound. This, I think, is what Helga refers to as "a lack somewhere." Like Helga, the patients Kohut analyzes often have considerable talent and strong aesthetic investments. And, like Helga, they have a tendency to "react to sources of narcissistic disturbance by mixtures of wholesale withdrawal and unforgiving rage" (p. 65). Periods of heightened vitality and contentment are followed by a renewed sense of depletion, often brought about either by the anxiety that arises from an uncomfortable degree of excitement or by a rebuff or merely a lack of attention from the environment. Kohut's theory is, among other things, a revaluation of the moral valence of the term "narcissism," which is based not on self-satisfaction but on hollowness. Helga's apparent selfishness is based not on an excess of self but on a lack of self.

What does the novel tell us about the origins of Helga's narcissistic deficit? What kind of early mirroring does the novel describe? Her father, a black man she refers to as a gambler and a "gay suave scoundrel," deserted her mother, a Danish immigrant, before Helga could form any definite relation to him. The mother, "sad, cold, and remote," remarried, this time to a white man who treated Helga with malicious and jealous hatred. Helga thus has no early relations with black people except the image of her father as both desirable and unreliable, and she has increasingly negative relations with the white people that are her only family. But instead of becoming enraged at their lack of empathy for her, she actually learns to empathize with their view of her as a problem *for them*. "She saw herself for an obscene sore in all their lives, at all costs to be hidden. She understood, even while she resented. It would have been easier if she had not" (p. 29). In other words, she learns to identify with the rejecting other, to desire her own disappearance. Intimacy equals rejection; the price of intimacy is to satisfy the other's desire that she disappear. To be is not to be. It is no wonder that Helga's mode is flight, and that her first spoken words in the novel are "No, forever." The culminating scene of orgasmic conversion in the church is a stark acting out of the logic of self-erasure in a merger with the omnipotent other. As the church service begins, a hymn is being sung:

> Oh, the bitter shame and sorrow
> That a time could ever be,
> When I let the Savior's pity
> Plead in vain, and proudly answered:
> All of self and none of Thee,
> All of self and none of Thee . . .

As the hymn continues, the refrain changes:

> Some of self and some of Thee,
> Some of self and some of Thee . . .

Then:

> Less of self and more of Thee,
> Less of self and more of Thee . . .

Then, at the moment Helga surrenders to the conversion, the moment the text says "she was lost—or saved," the hymn's final refrain is acted out, but not stated:

> None of self and all of Thee,
> None of self and all of Thee.

The religious conversion, the merger with the omnipotent selfobject, momentarily overcomes the self's isolation but at the cost of the self's disappearance. The narcissistic plot here merges with the Oedipal plot: Helga's life, like her mother's, is drastically transformed by a moment of blind surrender.

This ecstatic disappearance is only the culmination of a series of encounters in the novel which present the narcissistic logic in other, less drastic, terms. Each time, Helga's vulnerable and defensively haughty self approaches a potential mirror and is, or perceives herself to be, mis-mirrored. I will analyze two of these moments, the opening encounter with Robert Anderson and the encounter with the Danish painter Axel Olsen.

Robert Anderson is the principal of the black school in which Helga is teaching at the start of the novel. She has become enraged at the school for its compliance with the low and self-denying expectations it has placed on its educational mission—complying with the image of blacks as hewers of wood and drawers of water, which has just been repeated to the assembled school by a white preacher. Helga has decided to leave the school immediately, and must tell Anderson her reasons. As she waits for him to receive her, she thinks about the school's disapproval of her love for bright colors and beautiful clothes. Upon entering his office, she sees "the figure of a man, at first blurred slightly in outline in that dimmer light." She feels confusion, "something very like hysteria," then a mysterious ease. She begins to explain her resignation to Dr. Anderson in an exchange that very much resembles an initial psychoanalytic session—he remains detached, prompting her to elaborate on her remarks, probing for her thoughts. She explains that she hates hypocrisy and the suppression of individuality and beauty. He then begins a discourse of wisdom, telling her that lies, hypocrisy, injustice are part of life that dedicated people put up with when the goals are so high. The text describes Helga's reactions to his words as follows:

> Helga Crane was silent, feeling a mystifying yearning which sang and throbbed in her. She felt again that urge for service, not now for her peo-

ple, but for this man who was talking so earnestly of his work, his plans, his hopes. An insistent need to be a part of them sprang up in her. With compunction tweaking at her heart for ever having entertained the notion of deserting him, she resolved not only to remain until June, but to return next year. (p. 20)

In this scene, then, Helga enters with a sense of her embattled grandiose self (her aesthetic difference, her individuality and creativity) but is drawn toward the appeal of the omnipotent selfobject, the merger with the idealized other. That merger can only exist, however, on the basis of perfect empathy. Anderson inadvertently breaks that empathy in the very words he uses to solidify it:

> "What we need is more people like you, people with a sense of values, and proportion, an appreciation of the rarer things of life. You have something to give which we badly need here in Naxos. You mustn't desert us, Miss Crane."
>
> She nodded, silent. He had won her. She knew that she would stay. "It's an elusive something," he went on. "Perhaps I can best explain it by the use of that trite phrase, 'You're a lady.' You have dignity and breeding."
>
> At these words turmoil rose again in Helga Crane. The intricate pattern of the rug which she had been studying escaped her. The shamed feeling which had been her penance evaporated. Only a lacerated pride remained. She took firm hold of the chair arms to still the trembling of her fingers.
>
> "If you're speaking of family, Dr. Anderson, why, I haven't any. I was born in a Chicago slum."
>
> The man chose his words, carefully he thought. "That doesn't at all matter, Miss Crane. Financial, economic circumstances can't destroy tendencies inherited from good stock. You yourself prove that!"
>
> Concerned with her own angry thoughts, which scurried here and there like trapped rats, Helga missed the import of his words. Her own words, her answer, fell like drops of hail.
>
> "The joke is on you, Dr. Anderson. My father was a gambler who deserted my mother, a white immigrant. It is even uncertain that they were married. As I said at first, I don't belong here. I shall be leaving at once. This afternoon. Goodmorning." (pp. 20–21)

In his act of delivering a compliment, Anderson puts his finger on a wound. By juxtaposing the words "lady" (which at Naxos signifies the denial of sexuality) and the word "breeding" (which for Helga is the name both for forbidden sexuality and for lack of family), he shows not only that he is not omnipotent (since he does not really know anything about her) but that what he wants to value in her is something she thinks she does not and cannot possess. The mirror breaks, the pattern in the rug loses its design, Helga fragments into chaotically scattering pieces, and she departs in a narcissistic rage.

In Denmark, Helga is drawn to the symmetrically opposite kind of narcissistic satisfaction. There, it is her grandiose exhibitionism that is initially mirrored, rather than her desire to merge with the idealized other. Whereas Helga's difference and fine clothes have been met with hostility and disapproval in the United States, the Danes are fascinated. They urge her to become more exhibitionistic, more exotic, more sensuous. Yet they are at the same time cold and detached. Instead of being repressed, Helga's exhibitionism is instead being expropriated, objectified, commodified, alienated.

This process comes to a head in her relation to Axel Olsen, the portrait painter. When she looks at the portrait he has painted of her, she says to herself: "It wasn't herself at all, but some disgusting sensual creature with her features. Bosh! pure artistic bosh and conceit! Nothing else." This has often been read as her refusal to acknowledge her own sexuality. But I think that, far from constituting a mirror designed to confirm her sexuality, this mirror gives her only someone else's narcissistic appropriation of it. She refuses the painter's offer of marriage out of a refusal to be owned by a white man. It is in Denmark that she first feels homesick for Negroes and identifies with, and forgives, her father for the first time. She returns to Harlem.

Several times in the novel, the potential mirror is not a person but a race, a "world." When Helga first arrives in Harlem, she feels keenly a "joy at seeming at last to belong somewhere." When she first arrives in Denmark, too, she says to herself, "This, then was where she belonged." Yet each time the surrounding mirror is incapable of sustaining the role of selfobject which she asks of it. The promise of belonging flips over into a pressure to conform. Each mirror limits even as it embraces. But instead of seeing that therefore she herself is composite, a mixture, a process rather than a product, that wholeness itself is a fiction—the problem and not the solution—she goes on believing that both she and the environment can be perfected, whole, nonself-different. For Helga, there is no middle, no compromise, no gray area—the only satisfaction must be total, pure, and therefore unreal, short-lived. She seeks to fill her narcissistic deficit with the environment, not for its own properties but in the attempt to substitute for a missing part of the self. The line between remedy and poison is a thin one—the magical selfobject must inevitably oppress and disappoint. What is different about Nella Larsen's treatment of these dynamics is that she shows race itself to be a kind of selfobject from which a self can derive both positive and negative mirroring. Kohut occasionally suggests as much, as when, in a footnote, he writes: "It may be helpful to say that the grandiose self . . . has such analogues in adult experience as, e.g., national and racial pride and prejudice (everything good is 'Inside,' everything bad and evil is assigned to the 'outsider'), while the relationship to the idealized parent imago may have its parallel in the relationship (including mystical mergers) of the true believer to his God" (p. 27). As an analysis of the narcissistic roots of racism and race pride, this is quite convincing. But it fails to account for the fact that what is a narcissistic structure for the individual is also a social, economic, and political structure in the world. Racial pride and prejudice are not merely interpersonal phenomena, but institutionalized structures in history and culture. In dealing with individual patients, Kohut generally neglects or subsumes the *social* mirroring environment in favor of the dynamics of the nuclear family.

* * * What Nella Larsen does is to articulate the relation between the mirroring environment of the nuclear family and the social messages from the environment which *also* affect the construction of the self. It is as though, for Kohut, the child has no independent experience of history, no relation to the world that is not filtered through the parental imagos. Yet the social world can indeed set up an artificially inflated or deflated narcissistic climate for the child. Racial privilege would offer an unearned archaic narcissistic bonus which, when threatened, would lead to the characteristic narcissistic rages of racism just as surely as the undeserved narcissistic injury resulting from the insertion of a black child into a hostile white environment would lead to the kinds of precarious self-consolidation Larsen documents in the absence of a strong black mirroring environment.

No matter how empathic a mother or father might be, he or she cannot always offset the formative mirroring of the environment. Indeed, in Kohut, the burden of good mirroring falls, again and again, on the mother. His case histories sound like accusations against the mother whose own context or needs are not analyzed. What Nella Larsen does is to locate the failures of empathy not in the mother but in the impossible ways in which the mother finds herself inscribed in the social order. Neither for Helga's mother nor for Helga herself as mother at the end of the novel is the social order nourishing, or even viable. And the split between fathers—the absent black father and the rejecting white father—cannot be understood apart from the stereotypical overdeterminations of such a split in American society as a whole.

The therapeutic desire to effect change in the self alone amputates the energies of change from their connections with the larger social and economic world. * * *

To see Helga purely from the inside or purely from the outside is to miss the genius of the text. It is the inside/outside opposition itself that needs to be questioned.

In addition to questioning the inside/outside opposition as an adequate model for the relation between the self and society, Larsen's novel also provides material for a critique of the conception of the self as a locus of value. Throughout this paper, I have echoed and extended Kohut's economic vocabulary of narcissistic investments, deficits, and assets, emphasizing the ways in which Helga Crane alternates between surplus value and lack, grandiosity and worthlessness, between an image of herself as a luxury item and an image of herself as garbage. What luxury and garbage have in common is that each is a form of excess with respect to an economy of use or need. Thus, for instance, after humiliating rejections by Uncle Peter's new wife and by the library personnel, Helga spends what little money she has on a book and a tapestry purse, "which she wanted but did not need," and resolves to go without dinner, attempting to fulfill a narcissistic hunger in preference to a physical one. As long as need is ignored, however, the narcissistic imbalance cannot be rectified. This emphasis on the isolated self as a locus of value (positive or negative) risks duplicating, in the psychological realm, the structures Marx identified as "the fetishism of the commodity"—the belief that the commodity, abstracted from both labor and use, "contains" value in and of itself. Both Larsen and Kohut indeed analyze a self that is very much structured like a commodity. This returns us to the perceived middle-classness of both Larsen and Kohut: it may well be that both the concept of the self and the analytical framework through which we have been discussing it can themselves be analyzed as artifacts of class.

* * *

1992, 1998

ANN duCILLE

From Blue Notes on Black Sexuality: Sex and the Texts of the Twenties and Thirties[1]

* * *

Ideology as the Mother of Invention

While black blues queens such as Bessie Smith and Ma Rainey sang of sex and sexuality—heterosexuality, homosexuality, bisexuality—with startling explicitness, black women writers of the 1920s and 1930s such as Jessie Fauset and Nella Larsen were in most instances considerably more reticent in their attentions to the black female body. Literary history and feminist criticism have often judged these writers harshly for what black scholar Gloria Hull calls "their restrained treatment of sex," which she says "helped to place them outside the sensational mainstream" of their era.[2] Black feminist critics such as Cheryl Wall and Barbara Christian reflect a widely held critical opinion when they argue that (like their nineteenth-century counterparts) Larsen and Fauset, along with most black women poets of the period, tried to rebut racist imaging of black women as morally loose by presenting a class of black women as prim, proper, and bourgeois as middle-class white ladies. In inventing sophisticated, light-skinned, middle-class heroines, the argument goes, these writers adhered to traditional notions of womanhood and made themselves and their characters slaves to the conventions of an "alien tradition." The "genuine," "more honest" poetry of the period, these critics insist, was the lyrics of blues singers such as Bessie Smith and Ma Rainey, whose artistic integrity and racial authenticity are confirmed by their displays of what Hull calls a "raunchy woman-proud sexuality that echoed the explicitness of this licentious era."[3]

While these readings of Fauset's and Larsen's work seem to me to miss the finer points of their social critiques, what I want to challenge here is the implicit definition of what "genuine," "authentic" African American art is. I want to point out some of the problems that arise when African American expressive culture is viewed through the lens of vernacular theories of cultural production and the master narrative of the blues as sexual signifier.

First, such evaluations often erase the contexts and complexities of a wide range of African American historical experiences and replace them with a single, monolithic, if valorized, construction: "authentic" blacks are southern, rural, and sexually uninhibited. "Middle-class," when applied to black artists and their subjects, becomes pejorative, a sign of having mortgaged one's black

---

1. Excerpted from chapter 4 of *The Coupling Convention: Sex, Text, and Tradition in Black Women's Fiction* (1993) [editor's note].
2. While Hull's remark is somewhat ambiguous, by "sensational mainstream" she appears to mean what she sees as the dominant (licentious) discourse of the black Harlem moment, rather than the cultural production of the period in general. See Gloria T. Hull, *Color, Sex, and Poetry: Three Women Writers of the Harlem Renaissance* (Bloomington: Indiana University Press, 1987), 25.

3. Barbara Christian, "Afro-American Women Poets: A Historical Introduction," in *Black Feminist Criticism: Perspectives on Black Women Writers* (New York: Pergamon, 1985), 122; Cheryl A. Wall, "Poets and Versifiers, Singers and Signifiers: Women of the Harlem Renaissance," in *Women, the Arts, and the 1920s in Paris and New York*, ed. Kenneth W. Wheeler and Virginia Lee Lussier (New Brunswick, NJ: Transaction, 1982), 75. Hull quotes essentially the same passages from Christian and Wall.

aesthetic to the alien conventions of the dominant culture. An era marked by the divergent value systems and colliding imperatives of such internally stratified constituencies as the black bourgeoisie, black bohemia, the working masses, black nationalists, the Harlem-centered literati, and the so-called Talented Tenth is narrowly characterized as "licentious" and sexually "sensational."

A second irony lies in the implication that Fauset's and Larsen's novels are somehow less than authentically black, where *black* is taken to mean sensational, licentious, raunchy. It is, as I argued in chapter 2, an internally dysfunctional reading of the racial subject and the semiotics of the black body that categorizes moral value by color and by class and defines "authentic blackness" as the absence thereof. Such evaluations, in effect, make class, culture, and morality linear concepts in which the genuine, honest, authentic black experience is that of a unilaterally permissive rural peasantry or a homogeneously uninhibited urban proletariat.

Third, such folk-rooted, hierarchical readings of Bessie's blues and Jessie's fiction ironically privilege what is ultimately a narrow representation of women's experiences. As a black feminist discourse or as a narrative theory of the black female subject, the fiction of Fauset and Larsen might actually be said to attend to a much wider array of "genuine" women's issues than the woman-proud lyrics of their blues-singing sisters. Cultural critic Sandra Lieb notes, for example, that such feminized subjects as motherhood, reproduction, children, and family relations are missing thematically from the repertoires of blues artists like Ma Rainey.[4] The omission of this "typically female" subject matter can, and I think should, be read as part of the particular, counterconventional politics of the classic blues, which necessarily transcends the image of archetypal earth mother. What is of interest to me here, however, is not the thematic silences of the classic blues but the fact that these silences have gone largely unnoted by the same feminist critics who chide Fauset and Larsen for *their* sins of omission—for their alleged inattention to the actual human conditions of the masses of black women of their era.

Addressing the limited view of women's lives offered by what she calls the "daughters of the Black middle class," Cheryl Wall argues that to "discover the broader dimensions of Black women's reality, one must turn to an art born from folk culture and perfected by women who had liberated their creative powers": the blues. This "folk art equals real life" equation is as problematic for the blues as expressive realism is for the novel. There is little evidence to support the assumption that the majority of or even many black women— even poor, southern, rural black women—lived the kind of sexually liberated lives or held the kind of freewheeling values refracted in the blues. Like other expressive media, the blues invoke the fantastic. They, too, create an unreal estate, a surreal realm, which even theorists who argue against expressive realism still claim as the authentic. Such readings of literary and social history place blues women outside ideology and bourgeois women in the midst of it. Fauset and Larsen are identified as daughters of the black middle class, manipulated by the moral and aesthetic dictates of white patriarchal order and governed by white standards of womanhood, beauty, femininity, and the

---

4. Sandra Lieb, *Mother of the Blues: A Study of Ma Rainey* (Amherst: University of Massachusetts Press, 1981), 81.

like. Bessie Smith, Ma Rainey, and Zora Neale Hurston, on the other hand, are invented by their audiences as signifying sisters, sexually and artistically liberated and unapologetically black, beyond the pale of white social influences. What does it mean, then, that Ma Rainey reportedly used lightening creams and heavy greasepaint to whiten her dark skin? One of her biographers suggests it means that Rainey, too, was not unaffected by ideology and "conform[ed] to the prejudice against dark skin (shared at the time by many blacks as well as whites)" (Lieb, 8). Perhaps it merely means, however, that Rainey had a fondness for the smell of the greasepaint as well as for the roar of the crowd. That is to say, whether written by Hurston or sung by Rainey, what Wall calls black women's reality is still *representation*, textual invention that the audience generates as *real*. Realism, in other words, is as much a code as romance, as much artifice as lightening creams and greasepaint.

The final irony I want to address lies in the choice of the classic blues of Bessie Smith as the privileged signifier of the genuine, authentic, pure black experience. This particular manifestation of the blues is, arguably, an appropriative art form that blends the material and techniques of traditional African American music with the presentational modes of popular *white* American musical theater, most specifically minstrelsy and vaudeville.[5] Some cultural historians maintain, in fact, that the music popularly called classic blues would be more appropriately labeled vaudeville blues, to reflect the degree to which the form was influenced by the American music hall and the vaudeville stage.[6]

As Ralph Ellison has argued, classic blues were both public entertainment and private ritual,[7] but the fact that what was once local lore could be packaged and distributed, I would argue, altered and institutionalized the form irrevocably, as video technology and mass production have altered reggae and rap. The classic blues, the variety of blues sung and recorded by professional performers such as Bessie Smith and Ma Rainey, are so called both because they standardized and universalized particular, recurrent lyrics, themes, and techniques, and because they re-formed the ritualistic elements of a once private or communal African American folk modality into public entertainment available for mass consumption. Although blues originally were recorded only by white women performers such as Sophie Tucker, black women stage and recording artists became the principal instruments through which the sexually explicit lyrics of the classic blues began to reach the ears of white Amer-

5. Originally, white minstrel shows and blackface vaudeville acts, which gained almost phenomenal popularity in the 1840s, were attempts on the part of white entertainers to represent what they viewed as authentic black plantation life, to imitate blacks in their "natural habitat," as it were. Black minstrels began to appear a decade later, and a number of black troupes toured the South in the 1860s. Many of the more successful groups, however, were eventually forced out of the business or taken over by significantly more successful and resourceful white companies. A number of blues stars, including Ma Rainey and Bessie Smith, began their careers touring in minstrel shows and tent performances that followed black migrant workers from harvest to harvest. See, for example, Lieb, *Mother of the Blues*, 4–5; LeRoi Jones [Amiri Baraka], *Blues People: The Negro Experience in White America and the Music That Developed from*

It (New York: Morrow, 1963), 81–94.

6. Lawrence W. Levine, *Black Culture and Black Consciousness: Afro-American Folk thought from Slavery to Freedom* (New York: Oxford University Press, 1977), 225.

7. Ralph Ellison, "Blues People," in *Shadow and Act* (New York: Vintage, 1972), 256–57. There are many differing opinions on the nature of both traditional and classic blues. In *Blues People*, for example, LeRoi Jones distinguishes between classic blues as public entertainment and traditional, or "primitive," blues as folklore. Ralph Ellison argues, however, that Jones's distinction is a false one: classic blues were both entertainment *and* folklore. "When they were sung professionally in theatres, they were entertainment," Ellison writes; "when danced to in the form of recordings or used as a means of transmitting the traditional verses and their wisdom, they were folklore."

ica as well as black in the early 1920s.[8] But the "whys" of the commercialization and the feminization of the blues—that is to say, how mass production mass-produced the black female as sexual subject—is a complex question that is often eclipsed by the stellar proportions of the phenomenon's "whos."

At least part of the "why" of the popularization and feminization of the blues must be located in the primitivist proclivities of the historical moment. Primitivism, as a prevalent ideology of the early twentieth century, is characterized by an exuberance for the simple, the at-once innocent and sexually uninhibited—qualities the primitivist ascribes to the racially othered, whose alterity is fetishized. Almost by definition, primitivism thrives on icons. In the early twentieth century, no single icon combined the erotic, the exotic, and the innocent to the extent that the new Negro seemed to; for the newly discovered African American was not new at all but ancient, primal, and primitive—a panacea for an overindustrialized society dying from an acute case of modernity. Such notions were fostered by the work of Sigmund Freud, who endowed "races at a low level of civilization" with an untrammeled sexuality, which he claimed both shielded them from neuroses and inhibited their cultural development. Civilization, Freud argued, advances at the expense of human sexuality. His "dark continent" metaphor for female sexuality was, as Mary Ann Doane has argued brilliantly, a deliberate attempt to link the unknowable female sexual self with the unknown, dark-skinned, "infantile" inhabitants of the African continent.[9]

Such linkages were not new with Freud, however. For centuries the black body had functioned as a sign of both the assumed excessive sexuality and the racial primitivism of the African. According to Sander Gilman, by the eighteenth century the sexuality of the black male and female had become an icon for deviant sexuality in general.[1] In the nineteenth century the fascination with the black female body, in particular, and the primitive sexual anatomy and appetite attributed to the African woman increased the degree to which the black female functioned as an erotic icon in the racial and sexual ideology of Western civilization. It is this iconography that Nella Larsen critiques in *Quicksand* (1928), for example, where a white Danish painter named Axel Olsen propositions the novel's mulatta heroine, Helga Crane, assuming that "the warm impulsive nature of the women of Africa" will make her eager to become his mistress.[2] It is this iconography that helped make a bare-breasted Josephine Baker the rage in Paris in the twenties. And it is this same iconog-

---

8. "Race records," as recordings of jazz, blues, ragtime, spirituals, gospel, and sermons were called, were marketed almost exclusively in black neighborhoods.
9. See Mary Ann Doane's chapter "Dark Continents: Epistemologies of Racial and Sexual Difference in Psychoanalysis and the Cinema" in her *Femmes Fatales: Feminism, Film Theory, Psychoanalysis* (New York: Routledge, 1991), 209–48.
1. Sander L. Gilman, "Black Bodies, White Bodies: Toward an Iconography of Female Sexuality in Late Nineteenth-Century Art, Medicine, and Literature," in *"Race," Writing, and Difference*, ed. Henry Louis Gates, Jr. (Chicago: University of Chicago Press, 1986), 223, 228, 232. This essay first appeared in *Critical Inquiry* (August 1985).

2. Nella Larsen, *Quicksand*, edited and with an introduction by Deborah McDowell (New Brunswick, NJ: Rutgers University Press, 1986), 87. Of the racial mythology that propels Olsen, Cheryl Wall writes: "Olsen knows nothing of African women, but that does not shake his belief in their exotic primitivism. Black women, he feels, are completely sentient, sexual beings. Helga Crane should confirm that belief. When she does not, it proves she has been contaminated by the West, has suffered the primordial female corruption." See Cheryl Wall, "Passing for What? Aspects of Identity in Nella Larsen's Novels," *Black American Literature Forum* 20 (Spring–Summer 1986): 104.

raphy that accounts, at least in part, for the hegemony of black women in the record industry throughout the decade.[3]

Under what might be called the cult of true primitivism, sex—the quintessential subject matter of the blues—was precisely what hot-blooded African women were assumed to have always in mind and body. Blues such as Mary Dixon's "All Around Mama" complemented that already established image:

> I've had men of all sizes, had 'em tall and lean
> Had 'em short, had 'em flabby, had 'em in between,
> I'm an all around mama, I'm an all around mama,
> I'm an all around mama, with an all around mind.[4]

Out of the mouths of black women such lyrics spoke boldly to sexual freedom and personal choice, but they also spoke to the racial and sexual iconography that cast the African woman as a hypersexual primitive. In singing the "Copulating Blues," the "Courting Blues," the "Empty Bed Blues," black women artists seemed to claim that image as their own, chew it up, and spit it out in the faces of their accusers. Whether self-affirming or self-deprecating (and many in the black community argued that it was the latter), the move fit the primitivism and exoticism of the thoroughly modern moment.

With such songs as "I'm a Mighty Tight Woman" and "Put a Little Sugar in *My Bowl*," red-hot mamas punned, parodied, and played with black female desire.[5] They in effect plumbed and inverted their positions as long-exploited, fetishized commodities. But identifying women blues artists as the site of a struggle for black female subjectivity necessarily raises complex questions about agency and interpellation, self and subject, person and persona. Problematizing Hazel Carby's observation that these blues women invented themselves as sexual subjects,[6] I want to suggest that the many colliding ideologies, colluding imperatives, and conflicting agendas of the era make it difficult to determine definitively who constructed whom in the cultural kaleidoscope of the 1920s and 1930s. If black women blues singers claimed their sexual subjectivity through their songs, did they also on some level objectify, exoticize, and eroticize the female body in the process? Did these infinitely inventive blues women create the moment through their songs and exploit that moment? Or did the moment create and exploit them? It was, after all, their ability to sell records that made black women so essential to the race record industry in the 1920s. They were abandoned by the industry as quickly as

3. It is interesting to note that black men sang raunchy, man-proud folk and traditional blues long before black women began to record what came to be called classic blues for such major production companies as Columbia, Paramount, and Okeh. In the early 1920s black composer Perry Bradford finally succeeded in convincing General Phonograph to permit black vocalist Mamie Smith, a veteran of the minstrel circuit, to record his "Crazy Blues" on the Okeh label. The commercial success of "Crazy Blues" spawned other recordings and the signing of other blues women throughout the music industry. By 1922 both race records and the race for records were on; the blues was big business, and blues women quickly became a prized commodity over which phonograph companies fought, at times bitterly, while bluesmen remained

largely unrecorded, perhaps because sex, the quintessential theme of the blues, was a subject more safely sung by black women than by black men.
4. Paul Oliver, *Screening the Blues: Aspects of the Blues Tradition* (London: Cassell, 1968); quoted in Daphne Duval Harrison, *Black Pearls: Blues Queens of the 1920s* (New Brunswick, NJ: Rutgers University Press, 1988), 105.
5. "I'm a Mighty Tight Woman" was recorded and made popular by Sippie Wallace; "Put a Little Sugar in My Bowl" was popularized by Bessie Smith.
6. Hazel Carby, "'It Just Be's Dat Way Sometime': The Sexual Politics of Black Women's Blues," in *Unequal Sisters: A Multicultural Reader in U.S. Women's History*, ed. Ellen Carol DuBois and Vicki L. Ruiz (New York: Routledge, 1990), 239 [editor's note].

they had been taken up when the increasing popularity of dance bands in the late twenties and early thirties created a new market and a new source of profit.[7] Perhaps the answer to the question of agency and interpellation lies somewhere between the two possibilities—in exploring the reflexive nature of ideology and invention, in examining critically the ideological aspects of the epoch that made possible the invention of both the explicitly sexual black female subjects sung in the songs of blues women like Bessie Smith and Ma Rainey and the often more covertly sexual subjects written in the fiction of Jessie Fauset, Nella Larsen, and Zora Neale Hurston.

Interestingly, despite their dismissal as "vapidly genteel lace-curtain romances,"[8] several of Fauset's and Larsen's novels, in particular, seem to me to lay the groundwork for such an ideologically charged analysis. Their fiction tackles some of the most significant social contradictions of the emerging modern era, including the questions of black female agency, cultural authenticity, and racial and sexual iconography.

*   *   *

*   *   * Fauset's and Larsen's fictions are important to literary and cultural theory not just because of what they tell us about the sexual, social, aesthetic, and intellectual codes of their time but because of what our responses to them can tell us about our own. Our moment echoes theirs in its romanticization of the folk and its preoccupation with cultural authenticity. That Fauset and Larsen are often left out or pushed to the margins—the "rear guard"—in contemporary mappings of African American expressive geographies suggests that we have learned little about the elusive (if not the illusive) nature of "the real colored thing" from the battles fought over the bodies of black female sexual icons such as Bessie Smith and Josephine Baker in the 1920s.

While I do not mean to diminish the significance of these artists or their accomplishments, I am left wondering what it is about *our* moment that has made us turn to theirs. What, for example, accounts for the current resurgence of interest in Josephine Baker's life and art, which has once again made of her a spectacle?[9] Are we, in our attempts at cultural criticism, modern-day primitivists? Are our Afrocentric interests and our vernacular theories and our feminist concerns for female agency colluding with primitivist proclivities like those that helped to bring the black "other" into vogue in the 1920s? Are we, like the moments in which they lived and worked, inventing these artists as icons? Insisting on this question—debating who (or what) invented whom— invokes an argument as eternally reflexive as which came first, chicken or egg, acorn or oak, flower or fruit? Perhaps what is most important is our own awareness of just how complex and ideologically charged are both the question and our attempts at answers.

1993

7. Harrison, *Black Pearls*, 8.
8. David Littlejohn, *Black on White: A Critical Survey of Writing by American Negroes* (New York: Grossman, 1966), 50–51.
9. I am thinking in particular of recent film representations of Baker's life, which include a 1987 British documentary, *Chasing a Rainbow*; a 1991 made-for-cable television movie, *The Josephine Baker Story*; and a second television movie and a feature film, both in the planning stage. In addition, two of Baker's French films from the 1930s, *Princess Tam-Tam* and *Zou-Zou*, have been rereleased with subtitles and shown to capacity crowds in theaters throughout the United States, as well as marketed on videocassette. See Phyllis Rose, "Exactly What Is It about Josephine Baker?" *New York Times*, March 10, 1991, H31.

JUDITH BUTLER

From Passing, Queering:
Nella Larsen's Psychoanalytic Challenge[1]

* * *

What would it mean * * * to consider the assumption of sexual positions, the disjunctive ordering of the human as "masculine" or "feminine" as taking place not only through a heterosexualizing symbolic with its taboo on homosexuality, but through a complex set of racial injunctions which operate in part through the taboo on miscegenation. Further, how might we understand homosexuality and miscegenation to converge at and as the constitutive outside of a normative heterosexuality that is at once the regulation of a racially pure reproduction? * * * Is there a way, then, to read Nella Larsen's text as engaging psychoanalytic assumptions not to affirm the primacy of sexual difference, but to articulate the convergent modalities of power by which sexual difference is articulated and assumed?

Consider, if you will, the following scene from Nella Larsen's *Passing*[2] in which Irene descends the stairs of her home to find Clare, in her desirable way, standing in the living room. At the moment Irene lights upon Clare, Brian, Irene's husband, appears to have found Clare as well. Irene thus finds Clare, finds her beautiful, but at the same time finds Brian finding Clare beautiful as well. The doubling will prove to be important. The narrative voice is sympathetic to Irene, but exceeds her perspective on those occasions on which Irene finds speaking to be impossible.

> She remembered her own little choked exclamation of admiration, when, on coming downstairs a few minutes later than she had intended, she had rushed into the living room where Brian was waiting and had found Clare there too. Clare, exquisite, golden, fragrant, flaunting, in a stately gown of shining black taffeta, whose long, full skirt lay in graceful folds about her slim golden feet; her glistening hair drawn smoothly back into a small twist at the nape of her neck; her eyes sparkling like dark jewels. (233)

Irene's exclamation of admiration is never voiced, choked back it seems, retained, preserved as a kind of seeing that does not make its way into speech. She would have spoken, but the choking appears to stifle her voice; what she finds is Brian waiting, Brian finding Clare as well, and Clare herself. The grammar of the description fails to settle the question of who desires whom: "she had rushed into the living room where Brian was waiting and had found Clare there too": is it Irene who finds Clare, or Brian, or do they find her together? And what is it that they find in her, such that they no longer find each other, but mirror each other's desire as each turns toward Clare. Irene will stifle the words which would convey her admiration. Indeed, the excla-

1. The following is a revised version of a lecture given at the University of Santa Cruz in October 1992 as part of a conference on "Psychoanalysis in African-American Contexts: Feminist Reconfigurations" sponsored by Elizabeth Abel, Barbara Christian, and Helene Moglen. [Excerpted from chapter 6 of *Bodies That Matter: On the Discursive Limits of "Sex"* (1993)—editor's note.]
2. *Passing*, in *An Intimation of Things Distant: The Collected Fiction of Nella Larsen*, Charles Larson, ed., foreword by Marita Golden (New York: Anchor Books, 1992), pp. 163–276.

mation is choked, deprived of air; the exclamation fills the throat and thwarts her speaking. The narrator emerges to speak the words Irene might have spoken: "exquisite, golden, fragrant, flaunting." The narrator thus states what remains caught in Irene's throat, which suggests that Larsen's narrator serves the function of exposing more than Irene herself can risk. In most cases where Irene finds herself unable to speak, the narrator supplies the words. But when it comes to explaining exactly how Clare dies at the end of the novel, the narrator proves as speechless as Irene.

The question of what can and cannot be spoken, what can and cannot be publicly exposed, is raised throughout the text, and it is linked with the larger question of the dangers of public exposure of both color and desire. Significantly, it is precisely what Irene describes as Clare's flaunting that Irene admires, even as Irene knows that Clare, who passes as white, not only flaunts but hides—indeed, is always hiding *in* that very flaunting. Clare's disavowal of her color compels Irene to take her distance from Clare, to refuse to respond to her letters, to try to close her out of her life. And though Irene voices a moral objection to Clare's passing as white, it is clear that Irene engages many of the same social conventions of passing as Clare. Indeed, when they both meet after a long separation, they are both in a rooftop cafe passing as white. And yet, according to Irene, Clare goes too far, passes as white not merely on occasion, but in her life, and in her marriage. Clare embodies a certain kind of sexual daring that Irene defends herself against, for the marriage cannot hold Clare, and Irene finds herself drawn by Clare, wanting to be her, but also wanting her. It is this risk-taking, articulated at once as a racial crossing and sexual infidelity, that alternately entrances Irene and fuels her moral condemnation of Clare with renewed ferocity.

After Irene convinces herself that Brian and Clare are having an affair, Irene watches Clare work her seduction and betrayal on an otherwise unremarkable Dave Freeland at a party. The seduction works through putting into question both the sanctity of marriage and the clarity of racial demarcations:

> Scraps of their conversation, in Clare's husky voice, floated over to her: ". . . always admired you . . . so much about you long ago . . . everybody says so . . . no one but you . . ." And more of the same. The man hung rapt on her words, though he was the husband of Felise Freeland, and the author of novels that revealed a man of perception and a devastating irony. And he fell for such pishposh! And all because Clare had a trick of sliding down ivory lids over astonishing black eyes and then lifting them suddenly and turning on a caressing smile. (254)

Here it is the trick of passing itself that appears to eroticize Clare, the covering over of astonishing black by ivory, the sudden concession of the secret, the magical transformation of a smile into a caress. It is the changeability itself, the dream of a metamorphosis, where that changeableness signifies a certain freedom, a class mobility afforded by whiteness that constitutes the power of that seduction. This time Irene's own vision of Clare is followed not only by a choking of speech, but by a rage that leads to the shattering of her tea cup, and the interruption of chatter. The tea spreads on the carpet like rage, like blood, figured as dark color itself suddenly uncontained by the strictures of whiteness: "Rage boiled up in her./There was a slight crash. On the floor at her feet lay the shattered cup. Dark stains dotted the bright rug. Spread. The chatter stopped. Went on. Before her. Zulena gathered up the white fragments" (254).

This shattering prefigures the violence that ends the story, in which Clare is discovered by Bellew, her white racist husband, in the company of African-Americans, her color "outed," which initiates her swift and quite literal demise: with Irene ambiguously positioned next to Clare with a hand on her arm, Clare falls from the window, and dies on the street below. Whether she jumped or was pushed remains ambiguous: "What happened next, Irene Redfield never afterwards allowed herself to remember. Never clearly. One moment Clare had been there, a vital glowing thing, like a flame of red and gold. The next she was gone" (271).

Prior to this moment, Bellew climbs the stairs to the Harlem apartment where the salon is taking place, and discovers Clare there; her being there is sufficient to convince him that she is black. Blackness is not primarily a visual mark in Larsen's story, not only because Irene and Clare are both light-skinned, but because what can be seen, what qualifies as a visible marking, is a matter of being able to read a marked body in relation to unmarked bodies, where unmarked bodies constitute the currency of normative whiteness. Clare passes not only because she is light-skinned, but because she refuses to introduce her blackness into conversation, and so withholds the conversational marker which would counter the hegemonic presumption that she is white. Irene herself appears to "pass" insofar as she enters conversations which presume whiteness as the norm without contesting that assumption. This dissociation from blackness that she performs through silence is reversed at the end of the story in which she is exposed to Bellew's white gaze in clear association with African-Americans. It is only on the condition of an association that conditions a naming that her color becomes legible. He cannot "see" her as black before that association, and he claims to her face with unrestrained racism that he would never associate with blacks. If he associates with her, she cannot be black. But if she associates with blacks, she becomes black, where the sign of blackness is contracted, as it were, through proximity, where "race" itself is figured as a contagion transmissable through proximity. The added presumption is that if he were to associate with blacks, the boundaries of his own whiteness, and surely that of his children, would no longer be easily fixed. Paradoxically, his own racist passion *requires* that association; he cannot be white without blacks and without the constant disavowal of his relation to them. It is only through that disavowal that his whiteness is constituted, and through the institutionalization of that disavowal that his whiteness is perpetually—but anxiously—reconstituted.[3]

Bellew's speech is overdetermined by this anxiety over racial boundaries. Before he knows that Clare is black, he regularly calls her "Nig," and it seems that this term of degradation and disavowal is passed between them as a kind of love toy. She allows herself to be eroticized by it, takes it on, acting as if it were the most impossible appellation for her. That he calls her "Nig" suggests

---

3. This suggests one sense in which "race" might be construed as performative. Bellew produces his whiteness through a ritualized production of its sexual barriers. This anxious repetition accumulates the force of the material effect of a circum-scribed whiteness, but its boundary concedes its tenuous status precisely because it requires the "blackness" that it excludes. In this sense, a dominant "race" is constructed (in the sense of *materialized*) through reiteration and exclusion.

that he knows or that there is a kind of knowingness in the language he speaks. And yet, if he can call her that and remain her husband, he cannot know. In this sense, she defines the fetish, an object of desire about which one says, "I know very well that this cannot be, but I desire this all the same," a formulation which implies its equivalence: "Precisely because this cannot be, I desire it all the more." And yet Clare is a fetish that holds in place both the rendering of Clare's blackness as an exotic source of excitation and the denial of her blackness altogether. Here the "naming" is riddled with the knowledge that he claims not to have; he notes that she is becoming darker all the time; the term of degradation permits him to see and not to see at the same time. The term sustains his desire as a kind of disavowal, one which structures not only the ambivalence in his desire for Clare, but the erotic ambivalence by which he constitutes the fragile boundaries of his own racial identity. To reformulate an earlier claim, then: although he claims that he would never associate with African-Americans, he requires the association and its disavowal for an erotic satisfaction that is indistinguishable from his desire to display his own racial purity.

In fact, it appears that the uncertain border between black and white is precisely what he eroticizes, what he needs in order to make Clare into the exotic object to be dominated.[4] His name, Bellew, like bellow, is itself a howl, the long howl of white male anxiety in the face of the racially ambiguous woman whom he idealizes and loathes. She represents the spectre of a racial ambiguity that must be conquered. But "Bellew" is also the instrument that fans the flame, the illumination that Clare, literally "light," in some sense *is*. Her luminescence is dependent on the life he breathes into her; her evanescence is equally a function of that power. "One moment Clare had been there, a vital glowing thing, like a flame of red and gold. The next she was gone./ There was a gasp of horror, and above it a sound not quite human, like a beast in agony. 'Nig! My God! Nig!' " Bellew bellows, and at that moment Clare vanishes from the window (271). His speech vacillates between degradation and deification, but opens and closes on a note of degradation. The force of that vacillation illuminates, inflames Clare, but also works to extinguish her, to blow her out. Clare exploits Bellew's need to see only what he wants to see, working not so much the appearance of whiteness, but the vacillation between black and white as a kind of erotic lure. His final naming closes down that vacillation, but functions also as a fatal condemnation—or so it seems.

For it is, after all, Irene's hand which is last seen on Clare's arm, and the narrator, who is usually able to say what Irene cannot, appears drawn into Irene's nonnarrativizable trauma, blanking out, withdrawing at the crucial moment when we expect to learn whose agency it was that catapulted Clare from the window and to her death below. That Irene feels guilt over Clare's death is not quite reason enough to believe that Irene pushed her, since one can easily feel guilty about a death one merely wished would happen, even when one knows that one's wish could not be the proximate cause of the death. The gap in the narrative leaves open whether Clare jumped, Irene

4. This is like the colonized subject who must resemble the colonizer to a certain degree, but who is prohibited from resembling the colonizer too well. For a fuller description of this dynamic, see Homi Bhabha, "Of Mimicry and Man: The Ambivalence of Colonial Discourse," *October*, no. 28 (Spring 1984): 126.

pushed, or the force of Bellew's words literally bellowed her out the window. It is, I would suggest, this consequential gap, and the triangulation that surrounds it, that occasions a rethinking of psychoanalysis, in particular, of the social and psychic status of "killing judgments." How are we to explain the chain that leads from judgment to exposure to death, as it operates through the interwoven vectors of sexuality and race?

Clare's fall: is this joint effort, or is it at least an action whose causes must remain not fully knowable, not fully traceable? This is an action ambiguously executed, in which the agency of Irene and Clare is significantly confused, and this confusion of agency takes place in relation to the violating speech of the white man. We can read this "finale," as Larsen calls it, as rage boiling up, shattering, leaving shards of whiteness, shattering the veneer of whiteness. Even as it appears that Clare's veneer of whiteness is shattered, it is Bellew's as well; indeed, it is the veneer by which the white project of racial purity is sustained. For Bellew thinks that he would never associate with blacks, but he cannot be white without his "Nig," without the lure of an association that he must resist, without the spectre of a racial ambiguity that he must subordinate and deny. Indeed, he reproduces that racial line by which he seeks to secure his whiteness through producing black women as the necessary and impossible object of desire, as the fetish in relation to which his own whiteness is anxiously and persistently secured.

※　※　※

I would agree with both [Deborah] McDowell and [Hazel] Carby[5] not only that is it unnecessary to choose whether this novella is "about" race or "about" sexuality and sexual conflict, but that the two domains are inextricably linked, such that the text offers a way to read the racialization of sexual conflict.

※　※　※

In a sense, the conflict of lesbian desire in the story can be read in what is almost spoken, in what is withheld from speech, but which always threatens to stop or disrupt speech. And in this sense the muteness of homosexuality converges in the story with the illegibility of Clare's blackness.

To specify this convergence let me turn first to the periodic use of the term "queering" in the story itself, where queering is linked to the eruption of anger into speech such that speech is stifled and broken, and then to the scene in which Clare and Irene first exchange their glances, a reciprocal seeing that verges on threatening absorption. Conversations in *Passing* appear to constitute the painful, if not repressive, surface of social relations. It is what Clare withholds in conversation that permits her to "pass"; and when Irene's conversation falters, the narrator refers to the sudden gap in the surface of language as "queer" or as "queering." At the time, it seems, "queer" did not yet mean homosexual, but it did encompass an array of meanings associated with the deviation from normalcy which might well include the sexual. Its meanings include: of obscure origin, the state of feeling ill or bad, not straight,

5. See Deborah E. McDowell, Introduction to *Quicksand and Passing*, by Nella Larsen (New Brunswick, N.J.: Rutgers University Press, 1986), and Hazel Carby, *Reconstructing Womanhood: The Emergence of the Afro-American* Woman Novelist (London: Oxford University Press, 1987) [editor's note].

obscure, perverse, eccentric. As a verb-form, "to queer" has a history of meaning: to quiz or ridicule, to puzzle, but also, to swindle and to cheat. In Larsen's text, the aunts who raise Clare as white forbid her to mention her race; they are described as "queer" (189). When Gertrude, another passing black woman, hears a racial slur against blacks, Larsen writes, "from Gertrude's direction came a queer little suppressed sound, a snort or a giggle" (202)— something queer, something short of proper conversation, passable prose. Brian's longing to travel to Brazil is described as an "old, queer, unhappy restlessness" (208), suggesting a longing to be freed of propriety.

That Larsen links queerness with a potentially problematic eruption of sexuality seems clear: Irene worries about her sons picking up ideas about sex at school; Junior, she remarks, " 'picked up some queer ideas about things— some things—from the older boys.' 'Queer ideas?' [Brian] repeated. 'D'you mean ideas about sex, Irene?' 'Ye-es. Not quite nice ones, dreadful jokes, and things like that' " (219-220). Sometimes conversation becomes "queer" when anger interrupts the social surface of conversation. Upon becoming convinced that Brian and Clare are having an affair, Irene is described by Larsen this way: "Irene cried out: 'But Brian, I —' and stopped, amazed at the fierce anger that had blazed up in her./ Brian's head came round with a jerk. His brows lifted in an odd surprise./ Her voice, she realized *had* gone queer" (249). As a term for betraying what ought to remain concealed, "queering" works as the exposure within language—an exposure that disrupts the repressive surface of language—of both sexuality and race. After meeting Clare's husband on the street with her black friend Felise, Irene confesses that she has previously "passed" in front of him. Larsen writes, "Felise drawled: 'Aha! Been 'passing' have you? Well, I've queered that' " (259).

In the last instance, queering is what upsets and exposes passing; it is the act by which the racially and sexually repressive surface of conversation is exploded, by rage, by sexuality, by the insistence on color.

Irene and Clare first meet up after years apart in a café where they are both passing as white. And the process by which each comes to recognize the other, and recognize her as black is at once the process of their erotic absorption each into the other's eyes. The narrator reports that Irene found Clare to be "an attractive-looking woman . . . with those dark, almost black, eyes and that wide mouth like a scarlet flower against the ivory of her skin . . . a shade too provocative" (177). Irene feels herself stared at by Clare, and clearly stares back, for she notes that Clare "showed [not] the slightest trace of disconcertment at having been detected in her steady scrutiny." Irene then "feel(s) her color heighten under the continued inspection, [and] slid her eyes down. What she wondered could be the reason for such persistent attention? Had she, in her haste in the taxi, put her hat on backwards?" From the start, then, Irene takes Clare's stare to be a kind of inspection, a threat of exposure which she returns first as scrutiny and distrust only then to find herself thoroughly seduced: "She stole another glance. Still looking. What strange languorous eyes she had!" Irene resists being watched, but then falls into the gaze, averts the recognition at the same time that she "surrenders" to the charm of the smile.

The ambivalence wracks the motion of the narrative. Irene subsequently tries to move Clare out of her life, refuses to answer her letters, vows not to invite her anywhere, but finds herself caught up by Clare's seduction. Is it that Irene cannot bear the identification with Clare, or is it that she cannot bear her desire for Clare; is it that she identifies with Clare's passing but needs to disavow it not only because she seeks to uphold the "race" that Clare betrays but because her desire for Clare will betray the family that works as the bulwark for that uplifted race? Indeed, this is a moral version of the family which opposes any sign of passion even within the marriage, even any passionate attachment to the children. Irene comes to hate Clare not only because Clare lies, passes, and betrays her race, but because Clare's lying secures a tentative sexual freedom for Clare, and reflects back to Irene the passion that Irene denies herself. She hates Clare not only because Clare has such passion, but because Clare awakens such passion in Irene, indeed, a passion *for* Clare: "In the look Clare gave Irene, there was something groping, and hopeless, and yet so absolutely determined that it was like an image of the futile searching and firm resolution in Irene's own soul, and increased the feeling of doubt and compunction that had been growing within her about Clare Kendry." She distrusts Clare as she distrusts herself, but this groping is also what draws her in. The next line reads: "She gave in" (231).

When Irene can resist Clare, she does it in the name of "race," where "race" is tied to the DuBoisian notion of uplift[6] and denotes an idea of "progress" that is not only masculinist but which, in Larsen's story, becomes construed as upward class mobility. This moral notion of "race" which, by the way, is often contested by the celebratory rhetoric of "color" in the text, also requires the idealization of bourgeois family life in which women retain their place in the family. The institution of the family also protects black women from a public exposure of sexuality that would be rendered vulnerable to a racist construction and exploitation. The sexuality that might queer the family becomes a kind of danger: Brian's desire to travel, the boys' jokes, all must be unilaterally subdued, kept out of public speech, not merely in the name of race, but in the name of a notion of racial progress that has become linked with class mobility, masculine uplift, and the bourgeois family. * * *

What becomes psychically repressed in *Passing* is linked to the specificity of the social constraints on black women's sexuality that inform Larsen's text. If, as Carby insists, the prospect of black women's sexual freedom at the time of Larsen's writing rendered them vulnerable to public violations, including rape, because their bodies continued to be sites of conquest within white racism, then the psychic resistance to homosexuality and to a sexual life outside the parameters of the family must be read in part as a resistance to an endangering public exposure.

To the extent that Irene desires Clare, she desires the trespass that Clare performs, and hates her for the disloyalty that that trespass entails. To the extent that Irene herself eroticizes Clare's racial trespass and Clare's clear lack of loyalty for family and its institutions of monogamy, Irene herself is in a double bind: caught between the prospect of becoming free from an ideology of "race" uncritical in its own masculinism and classism, on the one hand, and the violations of white racism that attend the deprivatization of black women's sexuality, on the other. Irene's psychic ambivalence toward Clare,

---

6. I.e., attributed to W. E. B. Du Bois (1868–1963) [editor's note].

then, needs to be situated in this historical double-bind.[7] At the same time, we can see mapped within Larsen's text the incipient possibility of a solidarity among black women. The identification between Clare and Irene might be read as the unlived political promise of a solidarity yet to come.

*   *   *

Freud writes of a certain kind of "jealousy" which appears at first to be the desire to have the heterosexual partner whose attention has wandered, but is motivated by a desire to occupy the place of that wandering partner in order to consummate a foreclosed homosexuality. He calls this a "delusional jealousy . . . what is left of a homosexuality that has run its course, and it rightly takes its position among the classical forms of paranoia. As an attempt at defence against an unduly strong homosexual impulse it may, in a man, be described in the formula: 'I do not love him, *she* loves him!' "[8] And, in a woman and in *Passing*, the following formula might apply: "I, Irene, do not love her, Clare: he, Brian, does!"

*   *   *

At the close of Larsen's *Passing*, it is Bellew who climbs the stairs and "sees" Clare, takes the measure of her blackness against the ideal of whiteness and finds her wanting. Although Clare has said that she longs for the exposure in order to become free of him, she is also attached to him and his norm for her economic well-being, and it is no accident—even if it is figured as one—that the exposure of her color leads straightway to her death, the literalization of a "social death." Irene, as well, does not want Clare free, not only because Irene might lose Brian, but because she must halt Clare's sexual freedom to halt her own. Claudia Tate argues that the final action is importantly ambiguous, that it constitutes a "psychological death" for Irene just as it literalizes death for Clare. Irene appears to offer a helping hand to Clare who somehow passes out the window to her death. Here, as Henry Louis Gates, Jr., suggests, passing carries the double meaning of crossing the color line and crossing over into death: passing as a kind of passing on.[9]

If Irene turns on Clare to contain Clare's sexuality, as she has turned on and extinguished her own passion, she does this under the eyes of the bellowing white man; his speech, his exposure, his watching divides them against each other. In this sense, Bellew speaks the force of the regulatory norm of whiteness, but Irene identifies with that condemnatory judgment. Clare is the promise of freedom at too high a price, both to Irene and to herself. It is not precisely Clare's race that is "exposed," but blackness itself is produced as marked and marred, a public sign of particularity in the service of the dissimulated universality of whiteness. If Clare betrays Bellew, it is in part because she turns the power of dissimulation against her white husband,

7. For an effort to reconcile psychoanalytic conflict and the problematic of incest and the specific history of the African-American family post-slavery, see Hortense J. Spillers, " 'The Permanent Obliquity of the In(pha)llibly Straight': In the Time of the Daughters and the Fathers," in Cheryl Wall, ed., *Changing Our Own Words* (New Brunswick, N.J.: Rutgers University Press, 1989), pp. 127–49.

8. Sigmund Freud, "Some Neurotic Mechanisms in Jealousy, Paranoia and Homosexuality" (1922), in *The Standard Edition of the Complete Works of Sigmund Freud*, ed. James Strachey, vol. 18 (London: Hogarth, 1955), p. 225.
9. Henry Louis Gates, Jr., *Figures in Black: Words, Signs, and the "Racial" Self* (New York: Oxford University Press, 1987), p. 202.

and her betrayal of him, at once a sexual betrayal, undermines the reproductive aspirations of white racial purity, exposing the tenuous borders that that purity requires. If Bellew anxiously reproduces white racial purity, he produces the prohibition against miscegenation by which that purity is guaranteed, a prohibition that requires strictures of heterosexuality, sexual fidelity, and monogamy. And if Irene seeks to sustain the black family at the expense of passion and in the name of uplift, she does it in part to avert the position for black women outside the family, that of being sexually degraded and endangered by the very terms of white masculinism that Bellew represents (for instance, she tells Clare not to come to the dance for the Negro Welfare Fund alone, that she'll be taken as a prostitute). Bellew's watching, the power of exposure that he wields, is a historically entrenched social power of the white male gaze, but one whose masculinity is enacted and guaranteed through heterosexuality as a ritual of racial purification. His masculinity cannot be secured except through a consecration of his whiteness. And whereas Bellew requires the spectre of the black woman as an object of desire, he must destroy this spectre to avoid the kind of association that might destabilize the territorial boundaries of his own whiteness. This ritualistic expulsion is dramatized quite clearly at the end of *Passing* when Bellew's exposing and endangering gaze and Clare's fall to death are simultaneous with Irene's offer of an apparently helping hand. Fearing the loss of her husband and fearing her own desire, Irene is positioned at the social site of contradiction: both options threaten to jettison her into a public sphere in which she might become subject, as it were, to the same bad winds. But Irene fails to realize that Clare is as constrained as she is, that Clare's freedom could not be acquired at the expense of Irene, that they do not ultimately enslave each other, but that they are both caught in the vacillating breath of that symbolic bellowing: "Nig! My God! Nig!"

If Bellew's bellowing can be read as a symbolic racialization, a way in which both Irene and Clare are interpellated by a set of symbolic norms governing black female sexuality, then the symbolic is not merely organized by "phallic power," but by a "phallicism" that is centrally sustained by racial anxiety and sexualized rituals of racial purification. Irene's self-sacrifice might be understood then as an effort to avoid becoming the object of that kind of sexual violence, as one that makes her cling to an arid family life and destroy whatever emergence of passion might call that safety into question. Her jealousy must then be read as a psychic event orchestrated within and by this social map of power. Her passion for Clare had to be destroyed only because she could not find a viable place for her own sexuality to live. Trapped by a promise of safety through class mobility, Irene accepted the terms of power which threatened her, becoming its instrument in the end. More troubling than a scene in which the white man finds and scorns his "Other" in the black women, this drama displays in all its painfulness the ways in which the interpellation of the white norm is reiterated and executed by those whom it would—and does—vanquish. This is a performative enactment of "race" that mobilizes every character in its sweep.

* * *

1993

ON SYLVIA PLATH

Much as *Jane Eyre* has long functioned as—in Gayatri Spivak's words—a "cult text" for feminist critics and theoreticians, so Sylvia Plath has held a similar (and perhaps similarly vexed) place of honor as a cult figure whose life and words have been tirelessly debated ever since her suicide in February 1963. Arguably, indeed, the psychoanalyst Jacqueline Rose is astute in her view that at least metaphorically speaking, Sylvia Plath "haunts" our culture, blurring the lines between myth and biography, the public and the private, just as the poet melds Holocaust imagery with domestic metaphor and family history in explosive verse that has both enthralled and confused countless readers. Our selections here reveal the range of ways in which contemporary feminist thinkers have sought to analyze such confluent (and sometimes conflicting) forces in discussions of some of Plath's most powerful texts.

In her essay on Plath's major "Bee Sequence," Susan Van Dyne—the author of *Revising Life: Sylvia Plath's Ariel Poems* (1993)—meditates on the literal as well as figurative dialogue that the poet established between her own earlier work (most notably *The Bell Jar*, written mainly in 1961) and some of her husband's texts when she recycled Ted Hughes's old manuscripts by typing new poems on the unused sides of the pages. Focusing more specifically on Plath's notorious "Daddy" in our extract from *The Haunting of Sylvia Plath* (1991), Jacqueline Rose seeks to identify the cultural and individual "psychic stakes" shaping this "poem of the murder of the father." Further investigating Plath's marital dilemmas, in a reading of "Daddy" drawn from *Her Husband: Hughes and Plath—A Marriage* (2003), her literary and biographical study of Plath and Hughes, Diane Middlebrook offers yet another view of this crucial text, noting that among other things, the poem is "a virtuoso —*performance*" that left Plath and a friend "rolling about the floor hooting with laughter" when the poet read it aloud on one occasion. Finally, in "Lessons from the Archive: Sylvia Plath and the Politics of Memory," an overview of recent work on Plath's career, Anita Helle argues that studies of this writer's art now call for a "politics of knowledge that considers wider definitions of archival value and archive formation."

In addition to writing *Revising Life*, Susan Van Dyne, a professor of English at Smith College, has co-edited *Women's Place in the Academy: Transforming the Liberal Arts Curriculum* (1985) with Marilyn Schuster. Among numerous other works, Jacqueline Rose, a psychoanalyst and professor at Queen Mary College of the University of London, has published a novel, *Albertine* (2001), as well as *On Not Being Able to Sleep: Psychoanalysis and the Modern World* (2003), and *The Question of Zion* (2005). A professor emerita of English at Stanford University, Diane Middlebrook preceded her book on Plath and Hughes with two other biographies, *Anne Sexton: A Biography* (1991) and *Suits Me: The Double Life of Billy Tipton* (1998), a study of a female jazz musician who lived and worked as a man for fifty years. An associate professor of English at Oregon State University, Anita Helle has edited *The Unraveling Archive: Essays on Sylvia Plath* (2006) and published critical essays on a range of modern and contemporary writers, including Mina Loy, Kay Boyle, Louise Glück, William Stafford, Sylvia Plath, and Audre Lorde.

SUSAN VAN DYNE

From "More Terrible Than Ever She Was":
The Manuscripts of Sylvia Plath's Bee Poems[1]

* * *

What prompted Plath to compose [the Bee Sequence] on the back of *The Bell Jar*? The novel itself was typed on the reverse of Smith College memorandum paper. During her year of teaching, she'd appropriated enough of the high-quality pink bond memo pads for several drafts of her anticipated novel. It could be that she still hoarded her stock of good paper. I'm prone to believe the gesture is also tinged with a desire for sympathetic magic. The novel was safely in the hands of the printer in October; it would be published the next January. Nothing gave Plath such a sense of security and conviction of her own generativity as the tangible evidence of past success. The impressive stack of novel manuscript was at once satisfying proof of her productivity and a familiar stimulus to feelings of creativity. The determination with which Plath apparently used each page in sequence may indicate too that she felt a challenge to match her earlier prose output with her current poetic creativity. I'm inclined to think her choice was more likely emotionally over-determined than accidental. As much as Plath pretended to dismiss her novel as a potboiler, she's chosen to re-use in composing the bee poems some of its most memorable sections: Esther Greenwood's near fatal attack of food poisoning while at *Ladies' Day*, her horrified witnessing of a baby being born and cadavers being dissected on a visit to her medical student boyfriend, and finally her accidental discovery of Buddy Willard's sexual history that foils his attempted seduction of Esther.

It seems too neat to be coincidence that Plath should begin drafting these poems that respond so immediately to the break-up of her marriage with Hughes on the reverse of the chapter that marks Esther Greenwood's discovery of Buddy Willard's deception. I think Plath knew these chapters contained some of her best material. It also seems likely she was re-reading the novel while she was composing the poems, whether to reassure herself of her proven talent or because this earlier narrative touched similar feelings of vulnerability, revulsion, and betrayal. Chapter 6 contains Esther's devastating comment that Buddy's proud display of male flesh reminded her of a "turkey neck and turkey gizzards." In drafting "The Bee Meeting" on the reverse of Chapter 6, Plath's indelible image seems to have penetrated the paper to reappear again in the speaker's sense of her exposure in the second stanza: "I am nude as a chicken neck, does nobody love me?"[2]

Although the three *Bell Jar* chapters make up the bulk of the material Plath composed on during this week, she drafts smaller sections on equally significant scraps borrowed from other sources. The Collection includes an earlier

1. Excerpted from *Stings: Original Drafts of the Dreams of the Poem Facsimile, Reproduced from the Sylvia Plath Collection at Smith College* (1982) [editor's note].
2. Quotations from the poetry in this essay will be from the manuscripts in the Sylvia Plath Collection of Smith College. [ ] brackets in these quotations enclose material deleted by the poet during her revision of a particular draft. Citations of published poems will be identified within the text as they appear in *The Collected Poems of Sylvia Plath*, edited by Ted Hughes (New York: Harper & Row, 1981), hereafter, *CP*.

aborted attempt at "Stings" begun two months earlier. The four versions of the fragment each appear on the reverse of several poems Hughes wrote marking Frieda's birth. At the very end of this cycle of composition, on October 9, Plath types the final poem on another Hughes manuscript, this time a handwritten scene from his play *The Calm*. Both Hughes manuscripts date from the spring of 1960. These remnants of Hughes' work, which Plath had often typed for him, must have recalled the significant event of that spring two years before, when their personal and professional lives seemed symbiotically and auspiciously fused in the birth of their first child, the acceptance of Plath's first book, *The Colossus*, and excellent reviews of Hughes' second book, *Lupercal*. Again, the themes of these pages may have prompted Plath's re-use of the manuscript.

Among her present needs in these poems was to re-examine her authority in producing babies and in producing poems. She also needed to sever her identification with Hughes as her alter ego and to will herself to survive the rupture. The summer after her marriage to Hughes and completing her study at Cambridge, she was inspired by reading Virginia Woolf to vow *"No children until I have done it. My health is making stories, poems, novels, of experience."* She hoped maternity and poetry were productively related: "I will write until I begin to speak my deep self, and then have children, and speak still deeper. The life of the creative mind first, then the creative body. For the latter is nothing to me without the first, and the first thrives on the rich earth roots of the latter."[3]

Would her faith in this optimistic analogy hold up under the test of her adult experience? Pragmatically, she questioned daily whether the birth of her babies would mean the death of her career as a writer without Ted to share the work and without sufficient income from her own publications to hire a nanny. Metaphorically, Plath attempts through these poems to deliver a reborn self who is defined independent of relationships. My guess is that by the time she typed the concluding poem in the sequence, she felt she'd done so. "Wintering" now overlies *The Calm*. The scene Plath borrows from Ted's play for scrap is, significantly, a deadly quarrel in which a wife accuses a husband of fraudulent artistic ambitions. Hughes' greater fame and financial promise as a writer, which had always caused Plath anxiety even while she pretended to admire her husband's successful headstart, must have deeply rankled the poet now alone with her infants far from the literary London scene. Material included in the worksheets of the bee poems suggests that anger rather than nostalgia led her to inscribe her own poetic autobiography on the leftovers of Hughes' literary past.

My point in describing the underside of Plath's worksheets in such detail is to restore an awareness the poet must have had during the process of composition: the story she tells about the experience of the summer and fall of 1962 is inscribed over earlier stories, her own and Hughes' past literary histories that she carefully preserved and now consciously returned to, whether for inspiration, reassurance, or vengeance. Plath's layered worksheets provide a literal realization of what Gilbert and Gubar have taught us to recognize as the palimpsestic nature of women's writing.[4] Reading the published version of the bee poems against the

---

3. Plath's journal entry was made in July, 1957, during a writing vacation on Cape Cod before her year of teaching at Smith. *The Journals of Sylvia Plath, 1950–1962*, edited by Frances McCullough and Ted Hughes (New York: Dial Press, 1982), pp. 164–65, hereafter cited in the text as *Journals*. The original journals are at Smith College. For convenience, page references are given to the published texts.

4. As if their stories were written on old parchment over earlier inscriptions, women writers produce "works whose surface designs conceal or obscure deeper, less accessible (and less socially acceptable) levels of meaning." Sandra M. Gilbert and Susan Gubar, *The Madwoman in the Attic: The Woman Writer and the Nineteenth-Century Literary Imagination* (New Haven: Yale University Press, 1979), p. 73.

worksheets brings to light a covert text, vital in arriving at the later meanings but intentionally suppressed because the poet could not allow herself or, what I believe was more frequently the case for Plath, because she no longer needed to say it. From Plath's habit of beginning new work on used paper, we recover a densely figured backdrop for the poems. Even more striking, Plath's deletions from early drafts emerge in a revealing pattern.

The manuscript of "Stings," the third poem and the stunning centerpiece of the sequence, shows the most dramatic signs of revision. In August she began and abandoned an early fragment about an incident in June. Writing her mother on June 15, Sylvia describes the bees getting into Ted's hair because he neglected to wear a hat while they were setting up a hive and moving a queen.[5] Most of the afternoon's events are transmuted into the first poem in the sequence, "The Bee Meeting." However, the fragment contains several lines that survive into the final version of "Stings," most notably, "They think death is worth it." Most of the speaker's attention in the fragment is focused on the folly of the bees' suicidal attack; their end is an inglorious military defeat: "Gelded and wingless. Not heroes. Not heroes."

When Plath returned to the poem in October she used the incident to tell another story: the wounding of the male figure by the bees takes second place to the speaker's recovery of the queen. The final text is clearly an empowering fiction in which the speaker identifies with the queen who makes her mark indelibly on the heavens. Plath would rejoice in a letter to her mother just ten days later: "To make a new life. I am a writer . . . I am a genius of a writer; I have it in me. I am writing the best poems of my life; they will make my name." (*Letters*, p. 468) As in each of the other poems in the series, the speaker of "Stings" broods about her ability to control or order generation, the bees' as well as her own.

Her choice of the queen as alter ego is profoundly ambivalent. The queen's special status is uncontested inside and outside the hive. Without her, the hive dies, production ceases. Yet her distinguishing characteristic is her excessive generativity: her queenly estate is, in fact, perpetual confinement. In lines edged with self-irony, Plath admits in "Stings" that her own recent history already resembles the queen's biological destiny: "Here is my honey-machine, / It will work without thinking." On the other hand, to own the queen, to think for the honey-machine means to control vicariously her life force. And of course, her hive's honey devolves to the bee-keeper.

To take up bee-keeping and even more to write about it, was deeply resonant for Plath. She was self-consciously imitating her father's authority, a mastery she both desires and disdains in the earlier poem "The Beekeeper's Daughter." Keeping bees also served apparently to validate and extend her sense of her own reproductive health. Plath enjoyed the neat parallel that the same woman who taught her bee-keeping served as midwife at the birth of Nicholas. Written out of the matrix of this layered experience, the bee poems represent not only an implied meditation on the roles of daughter, wife, and mother, but a simultaneous search for an adequate shape in which to conceive of herself as a generative and powerful poet.

Just as the keeper manipulates the queen's productivity, the poet sought to

---

5. *Letters Home*, edited by Aurelia Plath (New York: Harper & Row, 1975), p. 457, hereafter cited in the text as *Letters*.

exploit the queen as metaphor for her troubled questions about authorship. Repeatedly in the sequence, the powers of creation represented by the bees threaten to become agents of destruction. The speaker's conscious control over this transformation is alternately asserted and denied. Could identification with the queen confirm her self-image as naturally fertile and yet command for her the authority and liberty of independent self-expression? Could keeping the queen be consonant with releasing her from within? Remarkably, although the poet's correspondence with the queen is felt in the entire sequence, in all but one poem the queen's power is exercised obliquely. She governs the action but, except for "Stings," never appears.

In "Stings" the question of ownership, and of access to power, is initially posed with deceptive tranquility. The poem opens with a delicate and dangerous image of barter as the bare-handed speaker and an unnamed male transfer the honeycombs. The male and female figures appear innocently exposed ("Our cheesecloth gauntlets neat and sweet. / The throats of our wrists brave lilies"); the man smiles at the transaction. Yet the clean domesticity of setting up the hive and the honeyed sweetness of these images barely hint at the antagonism that is acknowledged in the drafts.

The anger Plath allows herself to express in the drafts clarifies the tension of "Stings." The earlier versions show the speaker engaged in a definition of herself that is primarily vengeful. She is the wronged wife and deserted mother whose verbal assault disfigures, emasculates, and finally destroys a male opponent. During the process of revision, Plath redirects her energy toward imagining an autonomous creative self in the queen. The scapegoat, who mysteriously appears in the eighth stanza and vanishes punished by the avenging bees in the ninth, has troubled many critics. He troubled Plath even more. In the first handwritten draft, he looms larger and much uglier. He also enters the poem a stanza earlier:

> It is almost over
> I am in control, I am in control.
> [Who is this third, this extra
> Who watches & helps not at all?]

The speaker's questions are meant to be rhetorical; she's identified him as an expendable, hindering force. Yet his appearance here threatens the control the speaker attempts, rather unconvincingly, to assert in her nervous, repetitive phrases. The amount of space and the intensity of affective response devoted to the scapegoat in the drafts is an unmistakable clue to the power this figure held for Plath. The scapegoat is aptly named; he's undoubtedly a composite of male authority figures whose role in the poet's generativity she would like, at this moment, to deny. "The sweat of his efforts a rain / Tugging the world to fruit" recalls father Otto Plath, the "maestro of the bees" (*CP*, p. 118), as much as Hughes, who fathered her children and, not incidentally, sometimes fathered her poems by suggesting subjects. That the speaker now feels the scapegoat is a jealous spy on her creative process is evident in his extended description which follows and which would remain in the poem until the penultimate version:

> Now he peers through a warped silver rain drop;
> Seven lumps on his head
> And a [great] big boss on his forehead.
>
> Black as the devil, & vengeful.

The name-calling and grotesque caricature in these lines make explicit the emotional projection that is underway throughout the poem. Feeling vengeful about her unexpected lack of control over her destiny, the poet sees the male figure as an evil spirit, a deformed troll who would block her rightful control of the queen bee's fertility. Her anger at the burdens of mothering, which Plath never expressed in her letters home, explodes in this burst of verbal vindictiveness; this devilish portrait of the male antagonist is one of the woman poet's monstrous offspring.

Plath labored even longer in the worksheets to give birth to a satisfying image of the terrible queen bee. She recognized in the first handwritten draft the authority of her claim "I / Have a self to recover, a queen." Nonetheless, she struggled through many variants in the next two drafts before bringing her into full view. She began this section over four separate times in her handwritten draft; she rewrites the concluding vision, beginning "more terrible than she ever was," another four times in the first typed draft. Having dispatched the male antagonist, the poet still had to envision an independent creativity for herself. Her first attempts remain largely reactive. The power Hughes has already exercised, Plath would restore in the poem to the queen. She is imagined "Rising this time, on wings of clear glass, / Over the deserted nurseries," or again. "Leaving the stiff wax, / The dead men at the lintel." She enacts the poet's unspeakable wishes to desert the nursery and to abandon "the stingless dead men." With each successive revision, the men are literally done to death: they are "stingless," then "rejected," then "old dead men," then simply, flatly "dead men." In the same line, the "deserted nurseries" remains constant and continues to appear as part of the closure in every draft until the last. Plath's instinctive first priority may have been to free her alter ego from the constraining definitions of wife and mother. Her process of recasting this vision, however, demonstrates vividly that the recovered self longs to leave her mark elsewhere than in the faces of her children. The queen's "more terrible" need is to inscribe her identity on the heavens.

* * *

The lion-red queen who scars the sky in her flight is clearly a blood relative of the lioness in "Ariel" who flies like an arrow into the "red / Eye, the cauldron of morning" and the red-haired Lady Lazarus who devours and, I'd assume, incorporates men in her own resurrection. Plath was preoccupied with imagining a psychic rebirth for herself as she approached her thirtieth birthday. "Lady Lazarus" came two weeks after she completed the bee sequence; "Ariel" was composed on her birthday, October 27. In the endings of each of these poems, the speaker experiences her new beginning as access to power that was violent, wounding, potentially consuming. Like so many women writers before her, Plath felt her poetic authority was destructive of personal relationships; similarly, the imagery of these conclusions confesses a familiar female ambivalence about whether the self can survive once these relational bonds have been burnt, peeled off, or abandoned.

And yet the end of this power in "Stings," I believe, is distinct from the other two poems. * * * I read the entire bee sequence as Plath's struggle to bring forth an articulate, intelligible self from the death-box of the hive.

* * *

Plath intended "Wintering," the last poem in the bee sequence, to close her second collection of poems. Like "The Arrival of the Bee Box," this poem is an attempt to give verbal shape to her inner resources. This poem lacks the manic metaphor-making wit used by the earlier speaker to defend her control over the dangerous contents of the bee box. Here, the speaker dares to descend herself to the interior. This time, rather than inchoate life clamoring for expression, she confronts a death-like stupor. Remembering that this poem was typed on the reverse of one of Hughes' plays (their shared earlier hopes for wealth) gives poignance to the speaker's hoarded reserves:

> I have whirled the midwife's extractor, I have my honey,
> [Half a dozen] Six jars of it,
> Six [gold, clear] corn nubs, six gold teeth,
> Six cat's eyes in [my] the wine cellar.

What did she have to show for this summer? This, her thirtieth year? These six years of marriage? Her stores are counted and recounted in the draft as a charm against "the black bunched in there like a bat." On the eighth of October, the distillation of experience into vision, her "six cat's eyes" that see in the dark, seemed uncertain protection against a winter alone. Whatever authority she claimed in the earlier poems as owner of the hive or as its ascending queen, she surrenders in this final identification with the bees' minimal, wordless survival:

> Now they ball in a mass.
> [Black ball]
> Black mind against all that white—
>
> . . . .
> [It is for] The woman still at her knitting,
> At the cradle of Spanish walnut,
> Her body a bulb in the cold and too dumb to think.

What the poet's interior promised or threatened changes throughout the sequence, the bee box delivers noisy, unruly maniacs who demand from their owner adequate translation. The wormy mahogany of "Stings" divulges a self-anointed queen. Finally, from the black hole of the cellar, the speaker utters a desperate prayer. Her difficulty with the conclusion of "Wintering" suggests her persistent uncertainty about the subject of her poetry, whether she must digest and express, in the terms of this poem, corpses or spring. The final questions are far from rhetorical in the first handwritten draft.

> Will the hive survive, will the gladiolas
> Succeed in banking their fires
> to enter another year?
> What will they taste [like] of the Christmas roses?
> Snow water? Corpses? [Thin, sweet Spring.]
>   [A sweet Spring?] Spring?
>   [Impossible spring?]
>   [What sort of spring?]
>   [O God, let them taste of spring.]

Later, in the typed draft, the poet appears more certain of "Snow water" and "Corpses" than of "Spring," which is crossed out and replaced by a tentative echo of the queen's ascent, "A glass wing?" Even through the third full draft of the poem, when all her other choices of image and phrase had been conclusively established, Plath had trouble believing in the certainty of spring as the end of her wintering. Her final revision, when it comes, moves in the opposite direction from her changes in "The Bee Meeting." Rather than introducing more questions, she wills herself to assert a compelling prophecy, continuing to hope, as she has throughout the rest of the sequence, that saying it would make it so: "The bees are flying. They taste the spring."

*   *   *

1982

JACQUELINE ROSE

From "Daddy"[1]

*   *   *

'Daddy' is a much more difficult poem to write about.[2] It is of course the poem of the murder of the father which at the very least raises the psychic stakes. It is, quite simply, the more aggressive poem. Hence, no doubt, its founding status in the mythology of Sylvia Plath. Reviewing the American publication of *Ariel* in 1966, *Time* magazine wrote:

> Within a week of her death, intellectual London was hunched over copies of a strange and terrible poem she had written during her last sick slide toward suicide. 'Daddy' was its title; its subject was her morbid love-hatred of her father; its style was as brutal as a truncheon. What is more, 'Daddy' was merely the first jet of flame from a literary dragon who in the last months of her life breathed a burning river of bale across the literary landscape.[3]

Writing on the Holocaust, Jean-François Lyotard suggests that two motifs tend to operate in tension, or to the mutual exclusion of each other—the preservation of memory against forgetfulness and the accomplishment of vengeance.[4] Do 'Little Fugue' and 'Daddy' take up the two motifs one after the other, or do they present something of their mutual relation, the psychic economy that ties them even as it forces them apart? There is a much clearer narrative in 'Daddy'—from victimisation to revenge. In this case it is the form of that sequence which has allowed the poem to be read purely personally as Plath's vindictive assault on Otto Plath and Ted Hughes (the transition from

---

1. Excerpted from chapter 6 of *The Haunting of Sylvia Plath* (1991) [editor's note].
2. Sylvia Plath, *Collected Poems*, ed. Ted Hughes (London: Faber and Faber, 1981), 12 October 1962, pp. 222–4 (strangely, the poem is omitted from the index), first published in *Encounter*, 21 October 1963, and in *Ariel* (London: Faber and Faber, 1965).
3. "The Blood Jet Is Poetry," review of *Ariel, Time*, 10 June 1966, pp. 118–20 (p. 118). The review is copiously illustrated with photographs from Aurelia Plath's personal collection. A letter from her to Ted Hughes suggests that she felt she had been tricked by the reviewer and that this, plus the cover of the issue of *The Atlantic* which published

"Johnny Panic and the Bible of Dreams" ("Sylvia Plath on Going Mad"), had contributed to her reluctance to see *The Bell Jar* published in the United States. Letter from Aurelia Plath to Ted Hughes, 11 April 1970, Correspondence, Sylvia Plath Collection, The Lilly Library, Indiana University, Bloomington, Indiana.
4. Jean-François Lyotard, *The Differend: Phrases in Dispute*, trans. Georges Van Den Abbeele (Manchester: Manchester University Press, 1988), p. 27. Lyotard is discussing the issue of Holocaust denial or the Faurisson debate, see p. 3 ff. See also Gill Seidel, *The Holocaust Denial: Antisemitism, Racism and the New Right* (Brighton: Beyond the Pale Collective, 1986).

the first to the second mirroring the biographical pattern of her life). Once again, however, it is only that preliminary privileging of the personal which allows the reproach for her evocation of history—more strongly this time, because this is the poem in which Plath identifies with the Jew.

The first thing to notice is the trouble in the time sequence of this poem in relation to the father, the technically impossible temporality which lies at the centre of the story it tells, which echoes that earlier impossibility of language in 'Little Fugue':

DADDY

You do not do, you do not do
Any more, black shoe
In which I have lived like a foot
For thirty years, poor and white,
Barely daring to breathe, or Achoo.

Daddy, I have had to kill you.
You died before I had time—
Marble-heavy, a bag full of God,
Ghastly statue, with one gray toe
Big as a Frisco seal

And a head in the freakish Atlantic
Where it pours bean green over blue
In the waters off beautiful Nauset.
I used to pray to recover you.
Ach, du.

What is the time sequence of these verses? On the one hand, a time of unequivocal resolution, the end of the line, a story that once and for all will be brought to a close: 'You do not do, you do not do/ Any more'. This story is legendary. It is the great emancipatory narrative of liberation which brings, some would argue, all history to an end. In this case, it assimilates, combines into one entity, more than one form of oppression—daughter and father, poor and rich—licensing a reading which makes of the first the meta-narrative of all forms of inequality (patriarchy the cause of all other types of oppression, which it then subordinates to itself). The poem thus presents itself as protest and emancipation from a condition which reduces the one oppressed to the barest minimum of human, but inarticulate, life: 'Barely daring to breathe or Achoo' (it is hard not to read here a reference to Plath's sinusitis). Blocked, hardly daring to breathe or to sneeze, this body suffers because the father has for too long oppressed.

If the poem stopped here then it could fairly be read, as it has often been read, in triumphalist terms—instead of which it suggests that such an ending is only a beginning, or repetition, which immediately finds itself up against a wholly other order of time: 'Daddy, I have had to kill you./ You died before I had time.' In Freudian terms, this is the time of 'Nachtraglichkeit' or after-effect: a murder which has taken place, but after the fact, because the father who is killed is already dead; a father who was once mourned ('I used to pray to recover you') but whose recovery has already been signalled, by what precedes it in the poem, as the precondition for his death to be repeated. Narrative as repetition—it is a familiar drama in which the father must be killed in so far as he is already dead. This at the very least suggests that, if this is the personal father, it is also what psychoanalysis terms the father of individual prehistory, the father who establishes the very possibility (or impossibility) of history as such.[5] It is through this father that the subject discovers—or fails to discover—her own history, as at once personal and part of a wider symbolic place. The time of historical emancipation immediately finds itself up against the problem of a no less historical, but less certain, psychic time.

This is the father as godhead, as origin of the nation and the word—graphically figured in the image of the paternal body in bits and pieces spreading across the American nation state: bag full of God, head in the Atlantic, big as a Frisco seal. Julia Kristeva terms this father 'Père imaginaire', which she then abbreviates 'PI'.[6] Say those initials out loud in French and what you get is 'pays' (country or nation)—the concept of the exile. Much has been made of Plath as an exile, as she goes back and forth between England and the United States. But there is another history of migration, another prehistory, which this one overlays— of her father, born in Grabow, the Polish Corridor, and her mother's Austrian descent: 'you are talking to me as a general American. In particular, my background is, may I say, German and Austrian.'[7]

If this poem is in some sense about the death of the father, a death both willed and premature, it is no less about the death of language. Returning to the roots of language, it discovers a personal and political history (the one as indistinguishable from the other) which once again fails to enter into words:

> In the German tongue, in the Polish town
> Scraped flat by the roller
> Of wars, wars, wars.
> But the name of the town is common.
> My Polack friend
>
> Says there are a dozen or two.
> So I never could tell where you
> Put your foot, your root,
> I never could talk to you.
> The tongue stuck in my jaw.
>
> It stuck in a barb wire snare.
> Ich, ich, ich, ich,
> I could hardly speak.
> I thought every German was you.
> And the language obscene

5. The concept comes from Freud, *The Ego and the Id*, 1923, in James Strachey, ed., *The Standard Edition of the Complete Psychological Works of Sigmund Freud*, 24 vols. (London: Hogarth, 1953–73), vol. XIX, pp. 31–2; Pelican Freud, 11, pp. 370–71, and *Group Psychology and the Analysis of the Ego*, 1921, *Standard Edition*, vol. XVIII, pp. 105–6; Pelican Freud, 12, pp. 134–5. It has been most fully theorised recently by Julia Kristeva in *Tales of Love*, trans. Leon S. Rudiez (New York: Columbia University Press, 1987), pp. 24–9.
6. For Kristeva this father founds the possibility of

identification for the subject and is critically linked to—enables the subject to symbolise—the orality, and hence the abjection, which was the focus of discussion of "Poem for a Birthday," in chapter 2. ["*Père imaginaire*": imaginary father (French). "Abjection": the forceful rendering of an aspect of oneself as "other" and thus despised (part of the process of constructing the subject)—editor's note.]
7. Peter Orr, "Sylvia Plath," in Peter Orr, ed., *The Poet Speaks* (London: Routledge & Kegan Paul, 1966), pp. 167–72 (p. 169).

Twice over, the origins of the father, physically and in language, are lost—through the wars which scrape flat German tongue and Polish town, and then through the name of the town itself, which is so common that it fails in its function to identify, fails in fact to name. Compare Claude Lanzmann, the film-maker of *Shoah*, on the Holocaust as 'a crime to forget the name', or Lyotard: 'the destruction of whole worlds of names'.[8] Wars wipe out names, the father cannot be spoken to, and the child cannot talk, except to repeat endlessly, in a destroyed obscene language, the most basic or minimal unit of self-identity in speech: 'ich, ich, ich, ich' (the first draft has 'incestuous' for 'obscene'). The notorious difficulty of the first-person pronoun in relation to identity—its status as shifter, the division or splitting of the subject which it both carries and denies—is merely compounded by its repetition here. In a passage taken out of her journals, Plath comments on this 'I':

> I wouldn't be I. But I am I now; and so many other millions are so irretrievably their own special variety of 'I' that I can hardly bear to think of it. I: how firm a letter; how reassuring the three strokes: one vertical, proud and assertive, and then the two short horizontal lines in quick, smug, succession. The pen scratches on the paper I . . . I . . . I . . . I . . . I . . . I.[9]

The effect, of course, if you read it aloud, is not one of assertion but, as with 'ich, ich, ich, ich', of the word sticking in the throat. Pass from that trauma of the 'I' back to the father as a 'bag full of God', and 'Daddy' becomes strikingly resonant of the case of a woman patient described at Hamburg, suspended between two utterances: 'I am God's daughter' and 'I do not know what I am' (she was the daughter of a member of Himmler's SS).[1]

In the poem, the 'I' moves backwards and forwards between German and English, as does the 'you' ('Ach, du'). The dispersal of identity in language follows the lines of a division or confusion between nations and tongues. In fact language in this part of the poem moves in two directions at once. It appears in the form of translation, and as a series of repetitions and overlappings—'ich', 'Ach', 'Achoo'—which dissolve the pronoun back into infantile patterns of sound. Note too how the rhyming pattern of the poem sends us back to the first line. 'You do not do, you do not do', and allows us to read it as both English and German: 'You du not du', 'You you not you'—'you' as 'not you' because 'you' do not exist inside a space where linguistic address would be possible.

I am not suggesting, however, that we apply to Plath's poem the idea of poetry as *écriture* (women's writing as essentially multiple, the other side of normal discourse, fragmented by the passage of the unconscious and the body into words). Instead the poem seems to be outlining the conditions under which that celebrated loss of the symbolic function takes place. Iden-

8. Claude Lanzmann in discussion of the film *Shoah*, Channel 4 Television, 27 October 1987; see also Lanzmann, *Shoah, An Oral History of the Holocaust: The Complete Text of the Film* (New York: Pantheon, 1985); Lyotard, "Judiciousness in Dispute, or Kant after Marx," in Murray Krieger, ed., *The Aims of Representation: Subject, Text, History* (New York: Columbia University Press, 1987), pp. 24–67 (p. 64).
9. Journals, July 1950–July 1953, The Sylvia Plath Collection, Smith College Library, Rare Book Room, Smith College, Northampton, Massachusetts, September 1950, p. 60 (*The Journals of Sylvia Plath*, ed. Frances McCullogh, consulting ed. Ted Hughes [New York: Random House, 1982], p. 20 [hereafter cited as *J*]).
1. F.-W. Eickhoff, "Identification and Its Vicissitudes in the Context of the Nazi Phenomenon," *International Journal of Psycho-Analysis* 67 (1986): 38.

tity and language lose themselves in the place of the father whose absence gives him unlimited powers. Far from presenting this as a form of liberation—language into pure body and play—Plath's poem lays out the high price, at the level of fantasy, that such a psychic process entails. Irruption of the semiotic (Kristeva's term for that other side of normal language), which immediately transposes itself into an alien, paternal tongue.

Plath's passionate desire to learn German and her constant failure to do so, is one of the refrains of both her journals and her letters home: 'Wickedly didn't do German for the last two days, in a spell of perversity and paralysis' . . . 'do German (that I *can* do)' . . . 'German and French would give me self-respect, why don't I act on this?' . . . 'Am very painstakingly studying German two hours a day' . . . 'At least I have begun my German. Painful, as if "part were cut out of my brain" ' . . . 'Worked on German for two days, then let up' . . . 'Take hold. Study German today.'[2] In *The Bell Jar*, Esther Greenwood says: 'every time I picked up a German dictionary or a German book, the very sight of those dense, black, barbed wire letters made my mind shut like a clam'.[3]

If we go back to the poem, then I think it becomes clear that it is this crisis of representation in the place of the father which is presented by Plath as engendering—forcing, even—her identification with the Jew. Looking for the father, failing to find him anywhere, the speaker finds him everywhere instead. Above all, she finds him everywhere in the language which she can neither address to him nor barely speak. It is this hallucinatory transference which turns every German into the image of the father, makes for the obscenity of the German tongue, and leads directly to the first reference to the Holocaust:

> And the language obscene
>
> An engine, an engine
> Chuffing me off like a Jew.
> A Jew to Dachau, Auschwitz, Belsen.
> I began to talk like a Jew.
> I think I may well be a Jew.
>
> The snows of the Tyrol, the clear beer of Vienna
> Are not very pure or true.
> With my gypsy ancestress and my weird luck
> And my Taroc pack and my Taroc pack
> I may be a bit of a Jew.

The only metaphor here is that first one that cuts across the stanza break—'the language obscene//An engine, an engine'—one of whose halves is language. The metaphor therefore turns on itself, becomes a comment on the (obscene) language which generates the metaphor as such. More important still, metaphor is by no means the dominant trope when the speaker starts to allude to herself as a Jew:

2. 4 July 1958, 7 July 1958, 11 October 1959, *J*, pp. 244, 246, 319; 13 October 1959, *Letters Home: Correspondence 1950–1963*, ed. Aurelia Schober Plath (London: Faber & Faber, 1975), p. 356; 13 October 1959, 19 October 1959, *J*, pp. 319, 321; Journals, 12 December 1958–15 November 1959, Smith, 7 November 1959, p. 94 (*J*, p. 327).
3. Sylvia Plath, *The Bell Jar* (London: Heinemann, 1963; Faber & Faber, 1966), p. 35.

> Chuffing me off *like* a Jew.
> I began to talk *like* a Jew.
> I *think* I may well be a Jew.
> I may be a *bit* of a Jew.

Plath's use of simile and metonymy keeps her at a distance, opening up the space of what is clearly presented as a partial, hesitant, and speculative identification between herself and the Jew. The trope of identification is not substitution but displacement, with all that it implies by way of instability in any identity thereby produced. Only in metaphor proper does the second, substituting term wholly oust the first; in simile, the two terms are co-present, with something more like a slide from one to the next; while metonymy is, in its very definition, only ever partial (the part stands in for the whole).

If the speaker claims to be a Jew, then, this is clearly not a simple claim ('claim' is probably wrong here). For this speaker, Jewishness is the position of the one without history or roots: 'So I never could tell where you/Put your foot, your root'. Above all, it is for her a question, each time suspended or tentatively put, of her participation and implication in the event. What the poem presents us with, therefore, is precisely the problem of trying to claim a relationship to an event in which—the poem makes it quite clear—the speaker did not participate. Given the way Plath stages this as a problem in the poem, presenting it as part of a crisis of language and identity, the argument that she simply uses the Holocaust to aggrandise her personal difficulties seems completely beside the point. Who can say that these were not difficulties which she experienced in her very person?[4]

If this claim is not metaphorical, then, we should perhaps also add that neither is it literal. The point is surely not to try and establish whether Plath was part Jewish or not. The fact of her being Jewish could not *legitimate* the identification—it is, after all, precisely offered as an identification—any more than the image of her father as a Nazi which now follows can be *invalidated* by reference to Otto Plath. One old friend wrote to Plath's mother on publication of the poem in the review of *Ariel* in *Time* in 1966 to insist that Plath's father had been nothing like the image in the poem (the famous accusation of distortion constantly brought to bear on Plath).[5]

Once again these forms of identification are not exclusive to Plath. Something of the same structure appears at the heart of Jean Stafford's most famous novel, *A Boston Adventure*, published in 1946.[6] The novel's heroine, Sonie Marburg, is the daughter of immigrants, a Russian mother and a German father who eventually abandons his wife and child. As a young woman, Sonie finds herself adopted by Boston society in the 1930s. Standing in a drawing-room, listening to the expressions of anti-Semitism, she speculates:

> I did not share Miss Pride's prejudice and while neither did I feel strongly partisan towards Jews, the subject always embarrassed me because, not being able to detect Hebraic blood at once except in a most obvious face, I was afraid that someone's toes were being trod on.[7]

4. "On one side I am a first generation American, on one side I'm a second generation American, and so my concern with concentration camps and so on is uniquely intense," Orr, "Sylvia Plath," p. 169.
5. Letter from Thomas J. Clohesy to Aurelia Plath, 4 September 1966, Smith, Section 5, Biography.
6. Jean Stafford, *A Boston Adventure* (1964; reprint, London: Hogarth, 1986).
7. Ibid., p. 335.

It is only one step from this uncertainty, this ubiquity and invisibility of the Jew, to the idea that she too might be Jewish: 'And even here in Miss Pride's sitting-room where there was no one to be offended (unless I myself were partly Jewish, a not unlikely possibility) . . . '.[8] Parenthetically and partially, therefore, Sonie Marburg sees herself as a Jew. Like Plath, the obverse of this is to see the lost father as a Nazi: 'what occurred to me as [Mrs. Hornblower] was swallowed up by a crowd of people in the doorway was that perhaps my father, if he had gone back to Würzburg, had become a Nazi'[9]—a more concrete possibility in Stafford's novel, but one which turns on the same binary, father/daughter, Nazi/Jew, that we see in Plath.

In Plath's poem, it is clear that these identities are fantasies, not for the banal and obvious reason that they occur inside a text, but because the poem addresses the production of fantasy as such. In this sense, I read 'Daddy' as a poem about its own conditions of linguistic and phantasmic production. Rather than casually produce an identification, it asks a question about identification, laying out one set of intolerable psychic conditions under which such an identification with the Jew might take place.

Furthermore—and this is crucial to the next stage of the poem—these intolerable psychic conditions are also somewhere the condition, or grounding, of paternal law. For there is a trauma or paradox internal to identification in relation to the father, one which is particularly focused by the Holocaust itself. At the Congress, David Rosenfeld described the 'logical-pragmatic paradox' facing the children of survivors: 'to be like me you must go away and not be like me; to be like your father, you must not be like your father'.[1] Lyotard puts the dilemma of the witness in very similar terms: 'if death is there [at Auschwitz], you are not there; if you are there, death is not there'[2] (compare Levi on the failure of witness). For Freud, such a paradox is structural, Oedipal, an inseparable part of that identification with the father of individual pre-history which is required of the child: '[The relation of the superego] to the ego is not exhausted by the precept: "You *ought to be* like this (like your father)." It also comprises the prohibition: "You *may not be* like this (like your father)".'[3] Paternal law is therefore grounded on an injunction which it is impossible to obey. Its cruelty, and its force, reside in the form of the enunciation itself.

'You stand at the blackboard, Daddy/In the picture I have of you'—it is not the character of Otto Plath, but his symbolic position which is at stake. In her story 'Among the Bumblebees', Plath writes of the father: 'Alice's father feared nothing. Power was good because it was power.'[4] Commenting on what he calls the '*père*-version' of the father, the French psychoanalyst Jacques Lacan writes: 'nothing worse than a father who proffers the law on every-

8. Ibid.
9. Ibid., p. 482.
1. David Rosenfeld, "Identification and Its Vicissitudes in Relation to the Nazi Phenomenon," *International Journal of Psycho-Analysis* 67 (1986): 62.
2. Lyotard, "Judiciousness in Dispute," p. 59. In a reply to Lyotard, Stephen Greenblatt takes issue with him on this specific question: Greenblatt,

"Capitalist Culture and the Circulatory System," in Krieger, ed., *The Aims of Representation*, pp. 257–73 (pp. 260–61).
3. Freud, *The Ego and the Id, Standard Edition*, p. 34; Pelican Freud, p. 374.
4. "Among the Bumblebees" (early 1950s), *Johnny Panic and the Bible of Dreams and Other Prose Writings* (London: Faber & Faber, 1977; rev. ed., 1979), pp. 259–66 (p. 263).

thing. Above all, spare us any father educators, rather let them be in retreat on any position as master.'[5] The reference is to the father of Schreber, eminent educationalist in pre-Nazi Germany, whose gymnasia have been seen as part of the institutional and ideological prehistory of what was to come.[6] It might then be worth quoting the following lines from Otto Plath's 'Insect Societies' (he was a professor of entomology, famous for his work *Bumblebees and their Ways*).[7] Whether or not they tell us anything about what he was like as a person, they can be cited as one version of such paternal 'perversion', of such an impossible paternal ideal: 'When we see these intelligent insects dwelling together in orderly communities of many thousands of individuals, their social instincts developed to a high degree of perfection, making their marches with the regularity of disciplined troops . . . ', or this citation from another professor, with which he concludes:

> Social instincts need no machinery of control over antisocial instincts. They simply have no antisocial tendencies. These were thoroughly eliminated many millions of years ago and the insects have progressed along a path of perfect social coordination. They have no need for policemen, lawyers, government officials, preachers or teachers because they are innately social. They have no need of learning the correct social responses. These are predetermined by their social constitution at the time of birth.[8]

Loss or absence of the father, but equally symbolic overpresence of the father (only the first is normally emphasised in relation to Plath)—it is the father as master who encapsulates the paradox at the heart of the paternal function, who most forcefully demands an identification which he also has to withhold or refuse. On more than one occasion, Plath relates the celebrated violence of her writing to the violence of that function. In 'Among the Bumblebees', the father sits marking scripts: 'the vicious little red marks he made on the papers were the color of the blood that oozed out in a thin line the day she cut her finger with the bread knife'.[9] And if we go back for a moment to 'Little Fugue', the same image can be traced out underneath the repeated 'blackness' of that text. On the back of the first draft is the passage from *The Bell Jar* in which Esther Greenwood is almost raped. The typescript has this line— 'In that light, the blood looked black'—crossed out and replaced with this one written by hand: 'Blackness, like ink, spread over the handkerchief'.[1] Underneath the poem to the father, a violence of writing—the poem's writing (the ink on the page), but equally his own. For those who would insist that what mattered most for Plath was the loss of her father, we might add that the only

5. Lacan, "Seminar of 21 January 1975," in Juliet Mitchell and Jacqueline Rose, eds., *Feminine Sexuality: Jacques Lacan and the école freudienne* (London: Macmillan, 1982), pp. 162–71 (p. 167).
6. Freud, "Psycho-Analytic Notes on an Autobiographical Account of a Case of Paranoia (Schreber)," 1911, *Standard Edition*, vol. XII, pp. 3–82; Pelican Freud, 9; see also Samuel Weber, introduction to Daniel Paul Schreber, *Memoirs of My Nervous Illness*, ed. Ida Macalpine and Richard Hunter (1955; new edition, Cambridge, Mass.: Harvard University Press, 1988), pp. vii–liv.
7. Otto Plath, *Bumblebees and Their Ways* (New York: Macmillan, 1934).

8. Otto E. Plath, "Insect Societies," in Carl Murchison, ed., *A Handbook of Social Psychology* (Worcester, Mass.: Clark University Press; London: Oxford University Press, 1935), pp. 83–141 (p. 83, 136–7). The first quote comes from the epigraph to the chapter and is part of a quotation from Thomas Belt, *The Naturalist in Nicaragua*, 1874; its account of the perfect regiment belongs to a more generally utopian image of community which ends with a quotation from Thomas More.
9. "Among the Bumblebees," p. 262.
1. "Little Fugue," Draft 1, page 2, verso, Smith, Ariel Poems.

other father who can stand in for this overmastery of the paternal function is the father who is dead.

One could then argue that it is this paradox of paternal identification that Nazism most visibly inflates and exploits. For doesn't Nazism itself also turn on the image of the father, a father enshrined in the place of the symbolic, all-powerful to the extent that he is so utterly out of reach? (and not only Nazism—Ceaușescu preferred orphans to make up his secret police). By rooting the speaker's identification with the Jew in the issue of paternity, Plath's poem enters into one of the key phantasmic scenarios of Nazism itself. As the poem progresses, the father becomes more and more of a Nazi (note precisely that this identity is not given, but is something which emerges). Instead of being found in every German, what is most frighteningly German is discovered retrospectively in him:

> I have always been scared of *you*
> With your Luftwaffe, your gobbledygoo.
> And your neat moustache,
> And your Aryan eye, bright blue.
> Panzer-man, panzer-man, O You—
>
> Not God but a swastika
> So black no sky could squeak through.

The father turns into the image of the Nazi, a string of clichés and childish nonsense ('your gobbledygoo'), of attributes and symbols (again the dominant trope is metonymy) which accumulate and cover the sky. This is of course a parody—the Nazi as a set of empty signs. The image could be compared with Virginia Woolf's account of the trappings of fascism in *Three Guineas*.[2]

Not that this makes him any the less effective, any the less frightening, any the less desired. In its most notorious statement, the poem suggests that victimisation by this feared and desired father is one of the fantasies at the heart of fascism, one of the universal attractions for women of fascism itself. As much as predicament, victimisation is also *pull*:

> Every woman adores a fascist,
> The boot in the face, the brute
> Brute heart of a brute like you.

For feminism, these are the most problematic lines of the poem—the mark of a desire that should not speak its name, or the shameful insignia of a new licence for women in the field of sexuality which has precisely gone too far: 'In acknowledging that the politically correct positions of the Seventies were oversimplified, we are in danger of simply saying once more that sex is a dark mystery, over which we have no control. "Take me—I'm yours", or "Every woman adores a fascist".'[3] The problem is only compounded by the ambiguity of the lines which follow that general declaration. Who is putting the boot in the face? The fascist certainly (woman as the recipient of a sexual violence

2. Virginia Woolf, *Three Guineas* (London: Hogarth, 1938; Harmondsworth: Penguin, 1977), p. 162.
3. Elizabeth Wilson, "Coming out for a brand new age," *Guardian*, 14 March 1989. The same line has also been taken as a slogan to explain German women's involvement in Nazism; see Murray Sayle,

"Adolf and the Women," *The Independent Magazine*, 9 November 1988: " 'Every woman adores a Fascist,' wrote Sylvia Plath. Is this why so many German women voted for Hitler, despite the male emphasis of the Nazi regime?" (caption under title).

she desires). But, since the agency of these lines is not specified, don't they also allow that it might be the woman herself (identification *with* the fascist being what every woman desires)?

There is no question, therefore, of denying the problem of these lines. Indeed, if you allow that second reading, they pose the question of women's implication in the ideology of Nazism more fundamentally than has normally been supposed.[4] But notice how easy it is to start dividing up and sharing out the psychic space of the text. Either Plath's identification with the Jew is the problem, or her desire for/identification with the fascist. Either her total innocence or her total guilt. But if we put these two objections or difficulties together? Then what we can read in the poem is a set of reversals which have meaning only in relation to each other: reversals not unlike those discovered in the fantasies of the patients described at Hamburg, survivors, children of survivors, children of Nazis—disjunct and sacrilegious parallelism which Plath's poem anticipates and repeats.

If the rest of the poem then appears to give a narrative of resolution to this drama, it does so in terms which are no less ambiguous than what has gone before. The more obviously personal narrative of the next stanzas—death of the father, attempted suicide at twenty, recovery of the father in the image of the husband—is represented as return or repetition: 'At twenty I tried to die/ And get back, back, back to you' . . . 'I made a model of you', followed by emancipation: 'So Daddy I'm finally through', and finally 'Daddy, daddy, you bastard, I'm through'. They thus seem to turn into a final, triumphant sequence the two forms of temporality which were offered at the beginning of the poem. Plath only added the last stanza—'There's a stake in your fat black heart', etc.—in the second draft to drive the point home, as it were (although even 'stake' can be read as signalling a continuing investment).

But for all that triumphalism, the end of the poem is ambiguous. For that 'through' on which the poem ends is given only two stanzas previously as meaning both ending: 'So daddy, I'm finally through' and the condition, even if failed in this instance, for communication to be possible: 'The voices just can't worm through'. How then should we read that last line—'Daddy, daddy, you bastard, I'm through'? Communication *as* ending, or dialogue *without end*? Note too how the final vengeance in itself turns on an identification— 'you bastard'—that is, 'you father without father', 'you, whose father, like my own, is in the wrong place'.[5]

                              *   *   *

Finally, I would suggest that 'Daddy' does allow us to ask whether the woman might not have a special relationship to fantasy—the only generalisation in the poem regarding women is, after all, that most awkward of lines: 'Every woman adores a fascist.' It is invariably taken out of context, taken out of the ghastly drama which shows where such a proposition might come from—what, for the woman who makes it, and in the worse sense, it might *mean*. Turning the criticism of Plath around once more, could we not read in that line a suggestion, or even a demonstration, that it is a woman who is most likely to articulate the power—perverse, recalcitrant, persistent—of fantasy as such? Nor would such

---

4. For a study of this difficult question, see Claudia Koonz, *Mothers in the Fatherland: Women, the Family and Nazi Politics* (London;

Jonathan Cape, 1987).
5. Thanks to Natasha Korda for pointing this out to me.

an insight be in any way incompatible with women's legitimate protest against a patriarchal world. This is for me, finally, the wager of Plath's work.

* * *

1991

DIANE MIDDLEBROOK

"Daddy"[1]

If we had to choose only one poem by Sylvia Plath on which to stake a claim to her importance, it would have to be "Daddy," Plath's brilliantly, playfully savage nursery-eye view of the domestic life of a few of Western culture's male authority figures: the father, the professor, and the military officer. The poem is poised between a daughter's tender nostalgia for a father loved, feared, and lost early in life, and that daughter's enraged recognition, at thirty, of the cost of her emotional collaboration with domination by a strong man. A first encounter with this angry poem—it endorses parricide—often knocks readers to the floor, and once they get up and dust off, such readers often turn their backs on Plath for good.

But Plath wasn't addressing these urgent words to her actual father, Otto Plath, though the poem is charged with feelings about him. And though she wrote the poem the day after Ted Hughes moved out of Court Green, apparently abandoning his own role as father, she wasn't writing about him, or only about him, either. No, she was saying good riddance to the attitude behind all those poems she had written in which fathers appear larger than life: as a sea god in "Full Fathom Five," as the hero Agamemnon in "Electra on Azalea Path," as the broken monumental sculpture of "The Colossus." In all of these, a daughter devotes herself abjectly to the service of memorializing an idealized father.

This, exactly, was the psychological program that had shaped not only Plath's poems about fathers, but her search for a husband, as she well knew. In fact, at Cambridge, after Richard Sassoon disappointed her marriage plans, Plath wrote in her journal about her "lust" for a father substitute, her longing "to live with the rich, chastened, wise mind of an older man. . . . I must beware, beware, of marrying for that."[2] As if on cue, Ted Hughes had entered her life: a man she considered older and wiser, whose violent language and rough behavior had really turned her on, and with whom she could act infantile—it was love at first sight. In "Daddy," Plath rebukes herself for not following the good advice she had given herself in her journal: "beware, beware." No, she had fallen for a father figure:

> I made a model of you,
> A man in black with a Meinkampf look
> . . . And I said I do, I do[3]

1. Excerpted from chapter 7 of *Her Husband: Hughes and Plath—A Marriage* (2003) [editor's note].
2. *The Journals of Sylvia Plath, 1950–1962*, ed. Karen V. Kukil (London: Faber and Faber, 2000), March 8, 1956, p. 230.
3. "Daddy," in Sylvia Plath, *Collected Poems*, ed. Ted Hughes (London: Faber and Faber, 1981), p. 224 [this work is hereafter cited as *CP*].

Plath expected her audience to recognize the Freudian principle behind these lines, that the woman's choice of marriage partner was scripted by the girl's emotional bond with her dad; and fathers were supposed to be disciplinarians. Her poem assumes that other women were going to find in the nursery rhymes of "Daddy" an explanation of their own love-hate relationships with strong men. The "I" in the poem gives the reader a place to stand to get a good angle on the mirror. Plath's powerful fantasies about her father provide some high-octane fuel in the poem, but "Daddy" is about more than that. It's about a girl's collusion with a man's sense of entitlement to be in charge of her; and it's a ferocious work of art that— riffing on a single vowel sound and offending left and right—has a lot in common with rap lyrics. How many things can you find to end in "ooo"? Plath starts out slow, with "do," "shoe," "blue." But the higher the ground of the trespass, the better the poem—that's the principle of satire. So: how about *"du,"* the pronoun reserved for intimacy, for children, and for animals in the German language? Come to think of it, how about "Jew"? Rhyming has its own wicked logic, and once it gets going—well, here's where it leads:

> [Since] I thought every German was you . . .
> I think I may well be a Jew[4]

"Daddy" is a virtuoso *performance.* When Plath read it to her friend Clarissa Roche during her visit to Court Green in November, Plath got the two of them rolling about the floor hooting with laughter.[5]

Another battlefront in Plath's artistic maturation during those months was separation from her mother. At some point before leaving Court Green to move to London that December, Plath got rid of *all* of Aurelia's letters, hundreds and hundreds of them.[6] And shortly after writing "Daddy"—possibly as a consequence of writing it—Plath wrote an ugly, muddled poem titled "Medusa,"[7] that puns on her mother's name. "Medusa" is the name for the immature stage of the *Aurelia* genus of jellyfish, and Plath draws symbolisms out of the resemblance of the body of a jellyfish to a placenta, its tentacles to the umbilical cord. Plath was attempting to divest herself of traits in Aurelia that had earned Hughes's derisive label "sentimental." How could she be motherly without extruding hearts and flowers? Most of Plath's women friends at that time were mothers, and she was actively seeking common ground with them. Notably, on the night Plath discovered Hughes's adultery, she had fled from Aurelia and had sought help from another mother, Elizabeth Compton, a woman her own age. Once Aurelia had returned to Wellesley, Plath again turned to her for moral support. But writing "Medusa," splitting off and silencing this aspect of Aurelia, seems to have cleared some psychological space for the positive images of mothering that infuse other poems of *Ariel.*

4. Ibid., p. 223.
5. Anne Stevenson, *Bitter Fame: A Life of Sylvia Plath* (1989; reprint, Boston: Houghton Mifflin/A Peter Davison Book, 1998), p. 277.
6. Aurelia Plath, interview with Richard Larschan, "Sylvia Plath and the Muth of the Monstrous Mother," episode 108, *Poets of New England* (video, produced by the University of Massachusetts, 2001). In his biography of Sylvia Plath, Paul Alexander claims that Aurelia saw Plath burn them, but Aurelia does not mention this in the interview with Larschan. See *Rough Magic,* 2nd ed. (New York: Da Capo, 1999), p. 286.
7. "Medusa," *CP,* pp. 224–26.

Indeed, it seems to have been childbearing that triggered Plath's imaginative metamorphosis during 1962, anchoring her imagination in her womanhood. Plath had always drawn her notions of how to live from literature. Virginia Woolf's published diaries had been a uniquely important resource to Plath in this regard, unique because Woolf was the only female writer whose name appeared along with that of Eliot, Joyce, Lawrence, and Proust on the reading lists from which college students drew their understanding of literary Modernism. But during the months of autumn and winter 1962–1963, while Plath was absorbing the truth that her separation from Hughes was irremediable, inescapable, and opportune, she began reading the work of other women writers. In August, Plath received from her American friend Anne Sexton a copy of *All My Pretty Ones*, the book of poems on which Sexton had been working while they both attended Robert Lowell's writing seminar at Boston University in 1959. Plath thanked Sexton in a warm letter of appreciation. "I was absolutely stunned and delighted" with the book, she wrote. "It is womanly in the greatest sense."[8] A couple of months later in an interview recorded for the BBC, Plath elaborated: Plath admired Sexton's "wonderfully craftsmanlike poems" because they explored "private and taboo subjects" such as being "a mother," and "a mother who has had a nervous breakdown," at that.[9]

In her own poetry about her children, Plath picked up where Sexton left off. Plath's poem on the taboo subject of motherhood take various forms, but all of them are a variety of custody battle. An aggressive example can be found in one of the poems Plath read on the occasion of that interview in London, "Nick and the Candlestick." It explores what was happening inside the family circle minus Hughes, as Plath sat alone with her baby son at the breast, in a chilly room lit by a candle. In the version Plath read for the BBC, the candlestick is described as a kneeling brass Atlas wearing a panther hide, and "Under the gold bowl of his navel where his phallus and balls should be, a panther claw . . ."[1] The phallic animal Plath associated with Hughes in "Pursuit" has shrunk to the scale of a table ornament, while the infant's presence swells to fill the firmament emptied by Hughes's departure.

> You are the one
> Solid the spaces lean on, envious.
> You are the baby in the barn[2]

Plath's importation of a Christ-child icon in the very last line changes the poem's gears. Unto us a child is born, unto us a son is given:[3] the empty space around the shabby little brass god has been enlivened by the warmth and weight of the living male child in her arms.

The poems in which Plath grappled with Hughes over their daughter are emotionally more complex. They focus on taking Frieda back from Ted, by usurping images from his poem "Full Moon and Little Frieda." Hughes's poem, written during early spring 1962, dramatizes the spontaneous artistry

8. Sylvia Plath to Anne Sexton, August 21, 1962. Quoted in Diane Middlebrook, *Anne Sexton: A Biography* (Boston: Houghton Mifflin/A Peter Davison Book, 1991), p. 174.
9. Peter Orr, "Sylvia Plath," in *The Poet Speaks*, ed. Peter Orr (London: Routledge and Kegan Paul, 1969), p. 168.

1. These lines were dropped in the version published in Plath's collected poems, but are printed in Stephen Tabor, *Sylvia Plath: An Analytical Bibliography* (London: Mansell Publishing, 1987), p. 143.
2. *CP*, p. 242.
3. Isaiah 9.6 (a phrase familiar from its setting in the chorus of Handel's *Messiah*) [editor's note].

of a young child who is just learning words. It is a quiet evening in the poem, the moment of moonrise, and the child is depicted as taut all over with her attentiveness, like

> A spider's web, tense for the dew's touch.
> A pail lifted, still and brimming—mirror
> To tempt a first star to a tremor[4]

The water in the lifted pail mirrors the sky, and is thus a metaphor for the child's uplifted face; the precision of "brimming" conveys that the rapt passivity of the child's watchfulness is a moment charged with creative possibility. When the child connects thing with word, she does so in an explosive, joyous repetition of a syllable: Moon! Moon! Moon! Moreover, "Full Moon and Little Frieda" is one of those works that reflect Hughes's artistic collusion with Plath. It advances from the point in Frieda's development where Plath's "Morning Song" left off: in Plath's poem, the infant's reach into language is configured in the image of rising balloons ("now you try / Your handful of notes; / The clear vowels rise . . ."); in Hughes, the round moon rising elicits the enclosure of vowels within consonants, notes morphing into words.

Plath, of course, was aware of this genealogy. In the call-and-response manner of their productive collusion, they had established this core vocabulary during 1960 in the poems they addressed to Frieda shortly after her birth. In poems written after their separation, Plath returned obsessively to two of Hughes's images in "Full Moon"—the mirror-pool and the star trembling on the water's surface. These mutate in Plath's poems to convey profound, aching abandonment.

> Intolerable vowels enter my heart.
>
> The child in the white crib revolves and sighs, . . .
> Then there are the stars—ineradicable, hard.
>
> > ("Event")
>
> The dew makes a star
>
> > ("Death & Co.")
>
> > this dark
> Ceiling without a star
>
> > ("Child")
>
> From the bottom of the pool, fixed stars
> Govern a life
>
> > ("Words")
>
> The mirrors are sheeted
>
> > ("Contusion")[5]

Submerged in these images is Plath's recognition that all her own separation issues had been revived by Hughes's desertion. According to Hughes, a typescript of "Full Moon and Little Frieda" was lying on Plath's desk at the

---

4. Ted Hughes, "Full Moon and Little Frieda," *Wodwo* (London: Faber and Faber, 1967), p. 182.
5. Excerpts from *CP*—"Event," p. 194; "Death & Co.," p. 255; "Child," p. 265; "Words," p. 270; "Contusion," p. 271.

time of her suicide.[6] Little Frieda herself was inconsolably sad, as Plath's stricken letters show; and Plath identified with that infantile, daughterly grief—these were the poems in which Plath mourned for Hughes.

But Plath had also found a poetic voice for everything that was positive in her single state, in "Ariel," the celebratory work she made on the day she turned thirty, October 27, 1962. Ariel was the name of the horse Plath was learning to ride that fall. Riding lessons were a very agreeable distraction from the difficulties of managing Court Green, "having to take on all a man's responsibilities as well as a woman's," she wrote to her aunt.[7] Plath's morning hours out on Dartmoor also gave her welcome relief from child care, and deepened her friendship with another woman in the protective network she was weaving, the riding mistress. Though Plath's English friends later expressed condescending amusement toward Plath's grandiose references to this workaday horse, Ariel,[8] it is evident from Plath's letters that her developing confidence in riding was a source of genuine pride, and that she felt a powerful bond with the animal.[9]

This raw material underwent miraculous condensation, refinement, and elevation to produce the poem. "Ariel" is the monument in Plath's poetry to the adrenaline rapture of the militant emotions seeking expression in her art. In "Ariel" Plath reclaims freedom for the female artist's body, detached from the child; and she alludes to herself in archaic language: "God's lioness," "the arrow." The female warrior on horseback. As the horse's pace accelerates, the wail of the child she has left behind fades to inaudibility. Someone else will mother the baby this morning. Stripped of all distractions, rapturous in the flow of thought and movement, she loses herself in the momentum of her purpose, reaching the instant of sunrise in the mind:

> at one with the drive
> Into the red
>
> Eye, the cauldron of morning.[1]

Riding, writing. She had written twenty poems that month alone, a dozen of them since Hughes's departure—"Terrific stuff," she reported to her mother, "as if domesticity had choked me."[2] But this was the poem from which Plath finally selected the title for the book she assembled in November 1962 out of the work that burst from her motherhood and her desertion by illusions about Hughes. The volume *Ariel* is the sublime scrapbook of Plath's integration of the duties of her domestic life with the requirements of her art. For about six weeks, Sylvia Plath's actual world was a realization of the aim she had set herself in a journal entry a year after she married Ted Hughes. She had been reading Virginia Woolf's *The Waves*, admiring Woolf's

6. Ted Hughes to Keith Sagar, June 18, 1998, Department of Manuscripts, The British Library, London.
7. Sylvia Plath to Dot, December 14, 1962, Sylvia Plath Collection, The Lilly Library, Indiana University, Bloomington, Indiana.
8. Ronald Hayman, *The Death and Life of Sylvia Plath* (New York: Birch Lane Press, 1991), p. 177.
9. According to Kate Moses, who interviewed the riding mistress, "starting in November 62, SP took her horseback riding lessons 2x a week . . . she was, according to her Dec. letters, off the leading rein by the end (meaning she was riding free, pre-

sumably with instructor nearby, but not with the two horses attached by a leading rein). But that doesn't change the fact that by her birthday, she couldn't have been proficient enough to gallop and probably wasn't even at the canter (unless on the leading rein, in a ring)." Kate Moses, e-mail to Diane Middlebrook, May 14, 2001.
1. "Ariel," *CP*, p. 240.
2. Sylvia Plath to Aurelia Plath, October 12, 1962, *Letters Home: Correspondence 1950–1963*, ed. Aurelia Schober Plath (London: Plath and Plath, 1975), p. 466.

skill at putting commonplace experience into unforgettable images. "I shall go better than she," Plath vowed. "I will be stronger: I will write until I begin to speak my deep self, and then have children, and speak still deeper."[3] Writing the poems of *Ariel* was the way Plath kept that promise.

2003

3. *Journals of Sylvia Plath,* July 17, 1957, p. 286.

ANITA HELLE

From Lessons from the Archive:
Sylvia Plath and the Politics of Memory[1]

*   *   *

"Otherbodies" and the Politics of the Fragment

Amid the explosion of books and articles on Plath since the millennium, the narrative in which the emergence of feminism coincides with Plath's mythologization as a universal symbol of pathos and triumph has broken down along a number of lines. A figure of great interest to Second Wave feminism and to histories of American womanhood at mid-century, Plath and her identities still do not conform to any monocular feminist lens. But the new archival research is also presenting us with a Plath who is more historically located and multiple by teaching us to be interested in Plath for her contradictory selves, accepting the disintegration we have to work with, both in the history of her reception and the materials themselves. The textual bodies of interest to contemporary Plath scholars are fragmentary in several senses: Plath's "haunting" of culture is an effect of the breakdown of emphasis on singular authorship to a focus on history and reception. Scholars can now read fragments of her multiple drafts, bits and pieces that have not yet found their place in broader narratives of interpretation, from Plath's visual collages to the enigmatic lists of topics for poems that played a role in Plath's habits of composition.

In one sense, the art work any writer leaves behind might be seen as a ghostly presence, a spectral "other body" of some kind, because the writer is no longer around to speak for it. The cultural obsessions that attach to Plath derive their phantasmagorical power from traumas that have been, at least in part, internalized for the readers and speakers of her poems; yet the historical process of reclamation and reinterpretation also draws us outward, to material relations. The issue of how to value and interpret the differing forms of fragmentary evidence and spectral "other bodies" that constitute Plath's legacy suggests the need for broader debate and definition of what is meant by archival "remains." Elizabeth Grosz's definition of "text" as a writer's partial or incomplete body of work, scattered but not incoherent, is relevant for its suggestion that archival memory is a multilayered process, dependent on

1. From *Feminist Studies* 31.3 (Fall 2005) [editor's note].

institutional forms of storage, access, and retrieval, and, more likely than not, subject to operations beyond individual control.

> A text is not the repository of knowledge or truths, the site for storage of information (and thus in danger of imminent obsolescence from the "revolution" in storage and retrieval that information technology has provided) . . . so much as a process of scattering thought, scrambling terms, concepts, and practices, forming linkages, becoming a form of action. A text is not merely a tool or instrument . . . rather, it is explosive, dangerously labile, with unpredictable consequences.[2]

At issue in reading Plath now is whether and how a new openness toward multiple social and literary responses to "explosive and dangerously labile" texts and materials can be sustained. * * * Plath studies, in part through their association with the confessional, have until recently been tied to private constructions of literary identity, to ideas of authority, authorship, and intellectual property. Now that * * * a new generation of scholars and readers is encountering Plath's writing, the effects of an era of criticism dominated by historiography, ethnography, geopolitics, and studies of popular culture are beginning to be felt.[3] Building on recent approaches, Plath studies calls for a politics of knowledge that considers wider definitions of archival value and archive formation.

In the meantime, the perimeter of the Plath archive is widening in important ways. More and different resources and narratives have developed from the "under life" of what has been thought worthy of archival preservation (including, in Plath's case, photographs, scrapbooks, journals, the "waste" from multiple drafts and discarded lines in addition to the published poems, novels, and stories). There are growing questions about how the politics of form (especially the complex registers of poetic form) interact with the ephemeral and the nonliterary. The much-debated question of what to make of Plath's practice of back-to-back writing, "recycling" drafts as Susan Van Dyne describes it, is partly self-reflexive, but it also has implications for other kinds of speculative economies, among them the uses of the fragment to construct more disjunctive and transgressive meanings.[4] Robin Peel in *Writing Back: Sylvia Plath and Cold War Politics* has brilliantly tracked the sources of references to global and international events in Plath's collage compositions, arguing that this work represents a reappropriation of a more experimental and socially critical modernism. Although Plath was not a poet who saw art as the equivalent of newspaper headlines, Peel claims that she understood and exploited these fragmentary references through her own practices of collaging the news. Plath, I would contend, similar to Marianne Moore, understood the usefulness of collections for her art: she collected not only paper scraps, but also cutouts of advertising art, "lucky purple stones" from the beaches of eastern Massachusetts, poems from anthologies (including poems by Adrienne Rich, which she also backshadows), maps, and rug scraps for the braided rugs she refers to in her journals. These are not all collections of the same order, but they are relevant to reading Plath in the contexts of material

2. Elizabeth Grosz, *Space, Time, and Perversion* (New York: Routledge, 1995), 126.
3. Janet Malcolm, *The Silent Woman: Sylvia Plath and Ted Hughes* (New York: Alfred A. Knopf, 1994).

4. Susan R. Van Dyne, *Revising Life: Sylvia Plath's Ariel Poems* (Chapel Hill: University of North Carolina Press, 1993).

culture in the postwar years of "Victory Culture," when terrors about the threat of extinction of the self were concealed and deferred through amassing lost objects.

The materiality of the archive stubbornly asserts itself in a handful of books in which the "other bodies" appear explicitly in the title or implicitly between the covers: Lynda K. Bundtzen's *The Other Ariel*, Tracy Brain's *The Other Sylvia Plath*, and Kate Moses's *Wintering: A Novel of Sylvia Plath*. Different "other bodies" and histories are being studied here, but each depends on a kind of archival research Plath scholars were unable to do a decade ago, research that distances itself from conventional biography and yet goes beyond the image of Plath's remains as merely phantasmagorical effects of her cultural "haunting." Bundtzen's *The Other Ariel*, a close reading of the *Ariel* Plath intended to be published, is an important guide to the "restored" *Ariel*, now that *Ariel: The Restored Edition* (foreword by Frieda Hughes) has been made available to the public. What I admire and find courageous about *The Other Ariel* is its willingness to complicate a familiar narrative—the narrative of Plath's own ordering of poems in *Ariel*—with a far grubbier narrative about Plath's artistic life that scholars have generally not been willing to touch. For anyone who sits down for five minutes to read the *Letters Home* manuscript, the collection of letters edited by Plath's mother, Aurelia (an "unabridged" edition of these letters and the full text of Aurelia Plath's intended introduction has not been published), it quickly becomes apparent that economics were part of the context of Plath's letters. Plath's habit was to give a regular accounting of what was earned and saved, as if money and writing were interwoven facets of the cultural capital she and Hughes were accumulating. Bundtzen writes: "[I] want to give priority . . . to Plath's pecuniary motives, if only to complicate or perhaps ironize the critical narratives that have elevated her writing ecstasy in the final months to something like aesthetic sainthood" (11). * * *

Plath appears as a more politically radical and experimental mid-century modernist than her confessional peers in Brain's *The Other Sylvia Plath*, especially in relation to issues that are close to our own time, such as environmentalism and cultural hybridity. "Other" here evokes that which is missing, marginal, or shunted aside as the "waste" or "errata" of the archive, compared to the pure, aesthetic product. The "marketing" of Plath through the ephemera of dust jackets, the material residues of Plath's British and American accents, vocabularies, and inflections on voice recordings, and the voluminous cuttings of Plath's art notebooks and kitchen collages, all count as "evidence," not of the biographical subject, but of the subject-in-history who writes poetry and prose.

*   *   *

Last in this trio of books that evoke missing or fragmented textual bodies, Moses's *Wintering: A Novel of Sylvia Plath* may not ostensibly appear to be derived from what scholars are finding in the new Plath archive. But this would be wrong. Although Moses has made up many details and episodes, she also draws from Plath's daily household calendar, a spiral bound "Letts" notebook in which grocery lists and recipes sit side-by-side with notes on BBC programs and beekeeping supplies. If anything has contributed toward the momentum to publish Plath's version of *Ariel*, it has been the spilling over into the public domain of so many scholarly projects attentive to Plath's version of that manuscript and the blurring of what is public and private in attachment to things Plathian.

* * *

Recent criticism and scholarship on Plath has produced an expanded and more flexible definition of the archive that Jacqueline Rose described a decade ago as, in essence, "the body of her writing."[5] Yet to apply the standard expectation that Plath's writing might be fully restored, as if the abundance of new material does not in every instance alter the history of exchanges over her meanings, is to sweep away the mediations that have also sustained such wide interest in Plath over four decades. Reading Plath may still be described as a call to wrestle with the terrors of our own time despite the temptation to discipline or curtail. But because Plath has grown multitudinous, it may be time to urge that citizen critics online and academic scholars and writers collaborate more often and more actively in reshaping the legacy. If Plath scholars have sometimes labored under the burden of the cultural obsession with Plath the high-voltage, sensational female spectacle, there is also much to learn from the desires and discourses that mediate attachment to the myth. The shifting zones of privacy have something to do with the various ways Plath's image might be reproduced. The first figure for the Plath archive was Lowell's representation of Plath's poems as bullets loaded into a cartridge through which the poet played a bloody game of "Russian roulette"—and lost.[6] Now, however, we can also read the image of Russian roulette as a commonplace of cold war rhetoric, a belligerent taunt at ballistic missile development. Even as we remember Plath's fatal rushes into destruction amid all the apocalyptic props of the cold war era, the file of archival knowledge expands. In the meantime, it appears nothing Plath left behind is going to waste.

2005

---

5. Jacqueline Rose, *The Haunting of Sylvia Plath* (Cambridge: Harvard University Press, 1991), 29.

6. Robert Lowell, foreword to *Ariel* (New York: Harper & Row, 1966), x.

Alternative Tables of Contents

Selections are listed chronologically within categories.

Historical Periods

Medieval

Early Modern

Eighteenth Century and Romanticism (British)

Victorian (British)

Eighteenth- and Nineteenth-Century American

Genres (selections from and about)

Epic, Folktale, Fable, Myth, Romance

Science Fiction and Fantasy

Topics

Selves/Subjects

Images of Women, Stereotypes of Femininity

Nation, Race, Ethnicity, Class

Sexualities

Permissions Acknowledgments

Elizabeth Abel: "Black Writing, White Reading: Race and Politics of Feminist Interpretation" from *Critical Inquiry* 19.3 (1993): 470–98. Reprinted by permission of the University of Chicago Press.

Paula G. Allen: "Kochinnenako in Academe: Three Approaches to Interpreting a Keres Indian Tale" by Paula G. Allen from *North Dakota Quarterly* 53.2, pp. 84–106. Copyright © 1985 by the North Dakota Quarterly, University of North Dakota.

Gloria Anzaldúa: From *Borderlands*/La Frontera: *The New Mestiza*, © 1987 by Gloria Anzaldúa. Reprinted by permission of Aunt Lute Books.

Isobel Armstrong: "A Music of Thine Own" from *Victorian Poetry, Poetics, Politics* by Isobel Armstrong. Copyright © 1996 by Routledge. Reproduced by permission of Taylor and Francis Books.

Margaret Atwood: "Paradoxes and Dilemmas" by Margaret Atwood. Copyright © 1976 by O.W. Toad Ltd., first appeared in *Women in the Canadian Mosaic*. Reprinted by permission of the author.

Jane Austen: "Letter to Jane Anna Elizabeth Austen" and "Plan of a Novel" by Jane Austen from *Jane Austen's Letters*, edited by Deidre Le Faye. Reprinted by permission of Oxford University Press.

Nina Baym: "Melodramas of Beset Manhood: How Theories of American Fiction Exclude Women Authors," *American Quarterly* 33.2 (1981): 129–39. Copyright © The American Studies Association. Reprinted with permission of The Johns Hopkins University Press.

Paula Bennett: "Introduction," from *My Life a Loaded Gun* by Paula Bennett. Copyright © 1986 by Paula Bennett. Reprinted by permission of Beacon Press.

Eavan Boland: "Letter to a Young Woman Poet" by Eavan Boland. Reprinted by permission of Carcanet Press Limited.

Susan Bordo: "The Body and the Reproduction of Femininity" from *Unbearable Weight* by Susan Bordo. Reprinted by permission of the University of California Press.

Laura Brown: "The Romance of Empire: *Oroonoko* and the Trade in Slaves" from *The New Eighteenth Century* by Felicity Nussbaum and Laura Brown, editors. Copyright © 1987 by Taylor and Francis Group. Reproduced by permission of Taylor and Francis Group, LLC.

Judith Butler: "Imitation and Gender Insubordination" by Judith Butler from *Inside/Out*, edited by Diana Fuss. Copyright © 1991 by Routledge. Reproduced by permission of Routledge/Taylor and Francis Group, LLC. "Passing Queer: Nella Larsen's Psycho-Analytic Challenge" from *Bodies That Matter: On the Discursive Limits of Sex* by Judith Butler. Copyright © 1993 by Routledge. Reproduced by permission of Routledge/Taylor and Francis Group, LLC.

Caroline Walker Bynum: Excerpts from *Jesus as Mother: Studies in the Spirituality of the High Middle Ages* by Caroline Walker Bynum. Reprinted by permission of the University of California Press.

Hazel Carby: "On the Threshold of Woman's Era: Lynching, Empire and Sexuality in Black Feminist Theory" from *Critical Inquiry* 12 (1985): 262–77. Reprinted by permission of the author and the University of Chicago Press.

Terry Castle: Excerpts from *The Apparitional Lesbian* by Terry Castle. Copyright © 1995 by Columbia University Press. Reprinted with permission of the publisher.

Nancy Chodorow: "Family Structure and Feminine Personality" from *Woman, Culture, and Society*, edited by Michelle Zimbalist Rosaldo and Louise Lamphere. Copyright © 1974 by the Board of Trustees of the Leland Stanford Junior University. All Rights Reserved. Used with permission of Stanford University Press.

Barbara Christian: "The Race for Theory" from *Cultural Critique* (Spring 1987). Copyright © 1987 by The University of Minnesota Press. Reprinted by permission.

Hélenè Cixous: "The Laugh of Medusa" by Hélenè Cixous, translated by K. Cohen and P. Cohen, from *The Signs Reader*, edited by Hélenè Cixous, pp. 279–97. Reprinted by permission of the University of Chicago Press.

Simone De Beauvoir: "Myths: Dreams, Fears, Idols" from *The Second Sex* by Simone De Beauvoir, translated by H. M. Parshley, copyright 1952 and renewed 1980 by Alfred A. Knopf, a division of Random House, Inc. Used by permission of Alfred A. Knopf, a division of Random House, Inc.

Germaine De Staël: "On Women Writers" from *An Extraordinary Woman: Selected Writing of Germaine De Staël*, ed. Vivian Folkenflick. Copyright © 1987 by Columbia University Press. Reprinted with permission of the publisher.

Carolyn Dever: "Obstructive Behavior: Dykes in the Mainstream of Feminist Theory" from *Cross-Purposes*, edited by Dana Heller. Reprinted by permission of the Indiana University Press.

Emily Dickinson: [Say If My Verse Is Alive], [My "Companions"], and [Fame] reprinted by permission of the publishers from *The Letters of Emily Dickinson*, edited by Thomas H. Johnson, Cambridge, Mass.: The Belknap Press of Harvard University Press, copyright © 1958, 1986 by the President and Fellows of Harvard College; 1914, 1924, 1932, 1942 by Martha Dickinson Bianchi; 1952 by Alfred Leete Hampson; 1960 by Mary L. Hampson.

Joanne F. Diehl: "Come Slowly Eden" by Joanne F. Diehl from *Signs* 3.3 (1978): 572–80. Reprinted by permission of the University of Chicago Press.

Carolyn Dinshaw: "Introduction" from *Chaucer's Sexual Poetics* by Carolyn Dinshaw. Reprinted by permission of the University of Wisconsin Press.

Laura E. Donaldson: Excerpts from *Decolonizing Feminisms: Race, Gender and Empire-Building* by Laura E. Donaldson. Copyright © 1992 by the University of North Carolina Press. Used by permission of the publisher.

A15

Ann duCille: "Blue Notes on Black Sexuality" from *The Coupling Convention* by Ann duCille. Reprinted by permission of Oxford University Press.

H.D. (Hilda Dolittle): Excerpts from *Notes on Thought and Vision* by H.D. Copyright © 1982 by the Estate of Hilda Doolittle. Reprinted by permission of City Lights Books.

Mary Ellmann: "Phallic Criticism" from *Thinking about Women*, copyright © 1968 by Mary Ellmann, reprinted by permission of Harcourt, Inc.

Margaret Ezell: *Writing Women's Literary History*, pp. 1–13. Copyright © 1992 by Margaret Ezell. Reprinted by permission of the Johns Hopkins University Press.

Jessie Fauset: Notes on "Letter to Alain Locke." Reprinted with permission from *Kindred Hands* by Jennifer Cognard-Black and Elizabeth MacLeod Walls. Published by the University of Iowa Press.

Margaret Ferguson: "Juggling the Categories of Race, Class & Gender" by Margaret Ferguson. Originally published in *Women's Studies*, volume 19. Copyright © 1991 by Taylor and Francis Group. Reproduced by permission of Taylor and Francis Group, LLC.

Judith Fetterley: "Introduction" from *The Resisting Reader* by Judith Fetterley. Reprinted by permission of the Indiana University Press.

Susan Fraiman: "Jane Eyre's Fall from Grace" from *Unbecoming Women* by Susan Fraiman. Copyright © 1993 by Columbia University Press. Reprinted with permission of the publisher.

Diana Fuss: "The Risk of Essence" from *Essentially Speaking* by Diana Fuss. Copyright © 1989 by Routledge/Taylor and Francis Group, LLC. Reproduced by permission of Routledge/Taylor and Francis Group, LLC.

Catherine Gallagher: "Who Was That Masked Woman?: The Prostitute and the Playwright in the Works of Aphra Behn" from *Nobody's Story: The Vanishing Acts of Women Writers in the Marketplace*. Copyright © 1994 by University of California Press. Used by permission of the publisher.

Sandra Gilbert: "A Dialogue of Self and Soul: Plain Jane's Progress" from *Madwoman in the Attic* by Sandra Gilbert and Susan Gubar. Used by permission of the Yale University Press.

Sandra Gilbert and Susan Gubar: "Infection in the Sentence" from *Madwoman in the Attic* by Sandra Gilbert and Susan Gubar. Used by permission of the Yale University Press.

Carol Gilligan: "Women's Place in Man's Life Cycle" reprinted by permission of the publisher of *In a Different Voice: Psychological Theory and Women's Development* by Carol Gilligan, pp. 18–23, Cambridge, Mass.: Harvard University Press, copyright © 1982, 1993 by Carol Gilligan.

Donna Haraway: "Manifesto for Cyborgs: Science, Technology, and Socialist Feminism in the 1980s," *Socialist Review* 80 (1985): 65–108. Reprinted by permission of the author.

Carolyn G. Heilbrun: Excerpts from *Writing a Woman's Life* by Carolyn G. Heilbrun. Copyright © 1988 by Carolyn G. Heilbrun. Used by permission of W. W. Norton and Company, Inc.

Lyn Hejinian: Excerpts from "The Rejection of Closure" from *The Language of Inquiry* by Lyn Hejinian. Reprinted by permission of the University of California Press.

Anita Helle: "Lessons from the Archive: Sylvia Plath and the Politics of Memory" from *Feminist Studies* 31.3 (Fall 2005). Reprinted by permission of the author.

Margaret Homans: Excerpts from *Women Writers and Poetic Identity*. © 1980 Princeton University Press. Reprinted by permission of Princeton University Press.

bell hooks: "Postmodern Blackness" from *Yearning = Race, Gender and Cultural Politics* by bell hooks. Reprinted by permission of Between the Lines and South End Press.

Luce Irigaray: Excerpt from *This Sex Which Is Not One* by Luce Irigaray from *New French Feminisms*, edited by Elaine Marks and Isabelle de Courtivron. Copyright © 1980 by University of Massachusetts Press. Used by permission. Translated by Catherine Porter and Carolyn Burke. Translation copyright © 1985 by Cornell University. Used by permission of the publisher, Cornell University Press.

Barbara Johnson: "The Quicksands of the Self: Nella Larsen and Heinz Kohut" by Barbara Johnson from *Telling Facts: History and Narration in Psycholanalysis*, pp. 184–99, edited by Joseph H. Smith and Humphrey Morris. Copyright © 1992. Reprinted by permission of the Johns Hopkins University Press. "Thresholds of Difference: Structures of Address in Zora Neale Hurston" from *Critical Inquiry* 12.1 (1985): 278–89. Reprinted by permission of the University of Chicago Press.

June Jordan: "The Difficult Miracle of Black Poetry in America" by June Jordan. Reprinted by permission from *The Massachusetts Review*, Volume 27, Number 2.

Joan Kelly-Gadol: "The Social Relation of the Sexes: Methodological Implication of Women's History" from *Signs* 1.4 (1976): 809–23. Reprinted by permission of the University of Chicago Press.

Annette Kolodny: "Dancing Through the Minefield" by Annette Kolodny. Copyright © 1979 by Annette Kolodny; all rights reserved. First published in *Feminist Studies* 6.1 (Spring 1980): 1–25.

Julia Kristeva: "Women's Time" by Julia Kristeva and translated by A. Jardine and H. Blake, from *Signs* 7.1 (1981): 13–35. Reprinted by permission of the University of Chicago Press.

Ursula K. Le Guin: "Is Gender Necessary? Redux" from *Dancing at the Edge of the World* by Ursula K. Le Guin, copyright © 1989 by Ursula K. Le Guin. Reprinted by permission of Grove/Atlantic, Inc.

Shirley Geok-lin Lim: "Feminist and Ethnic Literary Theories in Asian American Literature" was originally published in *Feminist Studies* 19.3 (Fall 1993): 571–95, by permission of the publisher, *Feminist Studies*, Inc.

Karma Lochrie: Excerpts from *Margery Kempe and Translations of the Flesh* by Karma Lochrie. Used by permission of the University of Pennsylvania Press.

Mary K. Loeffelholz: Excerpts from "Violence and the Other(s) of Identity: Dickinson and the Imaginary of Women's Literary Tradition" from *Dickinson and the Boundaries of Feminist Theory* by Mary Loeffelholz. Copyright © 1991 by the Board of Trustees of the University of Illinois. Used with permission of the University of Illinois Press.

Audre Lorde: "Poetry Is Not a Luxury" and "The Transformations of Silence into Language and Action" reprinted with permission from *Sister Outsider* by Audre Lorde. Copyright © 1984 by Audre Lorde, The Crossing Press, a division of Ten Speed Press.

Diane Middlebrook: "Daddy," from *Her Husband* by Diane Middlebrook, copyright © 2003 by Diane Middlebrook. Used by permission of Viking Penguin, a division of Penguin Group (USA) Inc.

Christanne Miller: Reprinted by permission of the publisher from *Emily Dickinson: A Poet's Grammar* by Christanne Miller, pp. 161–68. Cambridge, Mass.: Harvard University Press, copyright © 1987 by the President and Fellows of Harvard College.

Kate Millett: Excerpt from *Theory of Sexual Politics* by Kate Millett. Copyright © 1969, 1970, 1990, 2000 by Kate Millett (University of Illinois Press). Reprinted by permission of Georges Borchardt, Inc., for Kate Millett.

Juliet Mitchell: "Introduction" from *Psychoanalysis and Feminism* by Juliet Mitchell. Copyright © 2000 by Juliet Mitchell. Reprinted by permission of Basic Books, a member of Perseus Books.

Chandra Talpade Mohanty: From "Under Western Eyes: Feminist Scholarship and Colonial Discourse," in *boundary 2*, 12.3: 333–58. Copyright © 1986 by Duke University Press. All rights reserved. Used by permission of the publisher.

Marianne Moore: "Foreword to *A Marianne Moore Reader*," from *The Complete Prose of Marianne Moore* by Marianne Moore, edited by Patricia C. Willis. Copyright © 1986 by Clive E. Driver, Literary Executor of the Estate of Marianne Moore. Used by permission of Viking Penguin, a division of Penguin Group (USA), Inc.

Toni Morrison: "Unspeakable Things Unspoken" by Toni Morrison. Reprinted by permission of International Creative Management, Inc. Copyright © 1998 by Toni Morrison.

Paula Moya: Excerpts from "Post-Modernism, Realism, and the Politics of Identity" by Paula Moya from *Feminist Genealogies, Colonial Legacies, Democratic Futures*, edited by M. Jacqui Alexander. Copyright © 1996 by Routledge. Reproduced by permission of Taylor and Francis Books UK.

Anaïs Nin: Excerpt from *The Diary of Anaïs Nin, Volume II, 1934–1939*, Copyright © 1967 by Anaïs Nin and renewed 1995 by Rupert Pole and Gunther Stuhlmann. Reprinted by permission of Harcourt, Inc.

Tillie Olsen: "One Out of Twelve" from *Silences* by Tillie Olsen. Reprinted by permission of the Feminist Press.

Sherry Ortner: "Is Female to Male as Nature Is to Culture?" by Sherry Ortner from *Woman, Culture, and Society*, edited by Michelle Zimbalist Rosaldo and Louise Lamphere. Copyright © 1974 by the Board of Trustees of the Leland Stanford Junior University. All Rights Reserved. Used with permission of Stanford University Press.

Cynthia Ozick: "VI: Ambition" from *We Are the Crazy Lady, and Other Feisty Feminist Fables* by Cynthia Ozick. Copyright © 1972 by Cynthia Ozick. Originally appeared in *Ms.* Magazine. Reprinted with permission of the Melanie Jackson Agency, LLC.

Sylvia Plath: "Context" from *Johnny Panic and the Bible of Dreams* by Sylvia Plath. Copyright © 1952, 1953, 1954, 1955, 1956, 1957, 1960, 1961, 1962, 1963 by Sylvia Plath. Copyright © 1977, 1979 by Ted Hughes. Reprinted by permission of HarperCollins Publishers and Faber & Faber Ltd.

Adrienne Rich: "When We Awaken Dead: Writing as Re-Vision," from *On Lies, Secrets, and Silence: Selected Prose 1966–1978* by Adrienne Rich. Copyright © 1979 by W. W. Norton and Company, Inc. Used with permission of the author and W. W. Norton and Company, Inc. "The Loser," Copyright © 1993, 167, 1963 by Adrienne Rich, from *Collected Early Poems: 1950–1970* by Adrienne Rich. Used with permission of the author and W. W. Norton and Company, Inc. "Notes toward a Politics of Location," from *Arts of the Possible: Essays and Conversations* by Adrienne Rich. Copyright © 2001 by Adrienne Rich. Used with permission of the author and W. W. Norton and Company, Inc. "Aunt Jennifer's Tigers," "Orion," "Planetarium," the lines from "Snapshots of a Daughter-in-Law," from *The Fact of a Doorframe: Selected Poems 1950–2001* by Adrienne Rich. Copyright © 2002 by Adrienne Rich. Copyright © 2001, 1999, 1995, 1989, 1986, 1984, 1981, 1967, 1963, 1962, 1961, 1960, 1959, 1958, 1957, 1956, 1955, 1954, 1953, 1952, 1951 by Adrienne Rich. Used with permission of the author and W. W. Norton and Company, Inc.

Dorothy Richardson: "Foreword" from *Pilgrimage* by Dorothy Richardson (New York: Alfred A. Knopf, 1938).

Lillian Robinson: "Treason Our Text: Feminist Challenges to the Literary Canon," *Tulsa Studies in Women's Literature* 2.1. Copyright © 1983 by the University of Tulsa. Reprinted by permission of the publisher and the author.

Jacqueline Rose: Reprinted by permission of the publisher from "Daddy" in *The Haunting of Sylvia Plath* by Jacqueline Rose, pp. 222–38, Cambridge, Mass.: Harvard University Press, copyright © 1991 by Jacqueline Rose.

Gayle Rubin: Excerpts from *The Traffic in Women: Notes on the 'Political Economy'* by Gayle Rubin. All rights reserved. Used by permission of Duke University Press on behalf of the author.

Joanna Russ: "What Can a Heroine Do?" from *To Write Like a Woman: Essays in Feminism and Science Fiction* by Joanna Russ. Reprinted by permission of Diana Fitch Literary Agency.

Eve Sedgwick: Excerpts from *Epistemology of the Closet* by Eve Sedgwick. Reprinted by permission of the University of California Press.

Elaine Showalter: Excerpts from "Feminist Criticism in the Wilderness" by Elaine Showalter. Reprinted by permission of the Elaine Markson Literary Agency.

Martha Nell Smith: "To Be Susan Is Imagination: Dickinson's Poetry Workshop" from *Rowing in Eden: Rereading Emily Dickinson* by Martha Nell Smith, copyright © 1992. By permission of the University of Texas Press.

Hortense J. Spillers: "Mama's Baby, Papa's Maybe: An American Grammar Book," from *Diacritics* 17.2 (1987): 65–81, copyright © 1987 by the Johns Hopkins University Press.

Gayatri Chakravorty Spivak: Reprinted by permission of the publisher from *A Critique of Post-Colonial Reason: Toward A History of the Vanishing Present* by Gayatri Chakravorty Spivak, pp. 266–74, 282–84, 306–11, Cambridge, Mass.: Harvard University Press, copyright © 1999 by the President and Fellows of Harvard College. "Three Women's Texts and a Critique of Imperialism" by Gayatri Chakravorty Spivak from *Critical Inquiry* 12 (Autumn 1985). Reprinted by permission of the author.

Harriet Beecher Stowe: Notes to the letters reprinted with permission from *Kindred Hands* by Jennifer Cognard-Black and Elizabeth MacLeod Walls. Published by the University of Iowa Press.

Jane Tompkins: "Sentimental Power: *Uncle Tom's Cabin* and the Politics of Literary History." Copyright © 1978 by Jane Tompkins. Reprinted by permission of The Johns Hopkins University Press.

Susan Van Dyne: " 'More Terrible Than Ever She Was': The Manuscripts of Sylvia Plath's Bee Poems" from *Stings: Original Drafts of the Dreams of the Poem Facsimile, Reproduced from the Sylvia Plath Collection at Smith College*. Copyright © 1982 by Smith College and the Estate of Sylvia Plath. Used by permission of Smith College and Faber and Faber on behalf of the Estate of Sylvia Plath.

Alice Walker: "In Search of Our Mothers' Gardens" from *In Search of Our Mothers' Gardens: Womanist Prose*, copyright © 1974 by Alice Walker, reprinted by permission of Harcourt, Inc. "Women" from *Revolutionary Petunias and Other Poems*, copyright © 1970 and renewed 1998 by Alice Walker, reprinted by permission of Harcourt, Inc.

Index